ON A SUNBEAM

ON A SUNBEAM

TILLIE WALDEN

:01
First Second
NEW YORK

First Second

Published by First Second
First Second is an imprint of Roaring Brook Press, a division of
Holtzbrinck Publishing Holdings Limited Partnership
175 Fifth Avenue, New York, NY 10010
fiercereads.com

Library of Congress Control Number: 2017957414

Paperback ISBN: 978-1-250-17813-8
Hardback ISBN: 978-1-250-17814-5

Our books may be purchased in bulk for promotional, educational, or business use.
Please contact your local bookseller or the Macmillan Corporate and Premium Sales Department
at (800) 221-7945 ext. 5442 or by e-mail at MacmillanSpecialMarkets@macmillan.com.

First edition, 2018
Book design by Andrew Arnold and Molly Johanson

Printed in China

Paperback: 10 9 8
Hardcover: 10 9 8 7 6 5 4

Drawn on 9x12 Canson Bristol board with a ragtag collection of Faber Castell pens, Uni Pens, and
some pens I got in Japan that I don't know the name of. The coloring and cleaning up was done in
Photoshop CC with a very tiny bamboo tablet that, despite all odds, continues to survive.

CHAPTER 1

3

Jules, show Mia to your room. It's late and she must be tired.

um, Charlotte didn't introduce herself.

She heard my name already. She can figure it out.

Play nice, you two.

whatever

hi

You should be in bed now too, Jules.

It's 8:30, Alma, Jesus...

Alma's a bit of a freak about us getting enough sleep. Try not to argue.

oh, ok

Oh, and Ell doesn't talk. No one told me that when I got here and I felt like an idiot. And they're non-binary.

No one told you?

I mean, they didn't do it on purpose.

Alma, Ell, and Char have been together for ages. They didn't think about it.

6

7

GET UP, MIA!

Hurry up! Or we'll miss breakfast!

hup, hup, hup

Ahh, it looks GREAT!

eat up

Pass the cream.

What's the deal with the new job?

Jules, don't take all the bacon!

Where you going?

We're close to landing and I'd rather not crash.

It's an old religious site that's gonna be a museum.

Is it fucked?

Very. Everything is falling apart. We have a lot of work to do.

I WANT TO SEE IT FIRST.

did we crash?

Just a rough landing.

FIRST ONE OUT WINS AT ALL THINGS EVER!

11

5 years earlier

Mia

We're going.

12

13

14

15

17

21

Hey

Hello

You wanna come eat with us?

No, thanks.

Seriously, they don't care. You can come.

I'd prefer to eat alone.

Could you please leave now?

I was just trying to be nice, you freak.

It's almost lights-out.

I'll be right back.

23

Apply the sealant while I attach this.

Slow down. Yep, just like that.

Perfect.

Go help Jules with the tile. And bring down the extra stone while you're at it.

What am I doing?

You surviving?

maybe

Let's take lunch. I'll text Alma.

But Char said...

Don't worry. I'll tell 'er.

Meet me by the creepy prison thing.

Mia!

GAH

I got us, like, thirty sandwiches. And some coffee to pep you up.

I think I'm dying.

Dude, you're doing GREAT.

Took me months before I could get through a whole day without turning into jelly.

29

31

It wasn't just old, it was **forgotten**. Almost all records of this place have been lost or destroyed.

I learned about a bunch of the new-wave space religions in school. I had a whole class on it.

Seriously? What kind of school did you go to?

Boarding School.

What School?

Uh...Cleary's School for Girls...

Wow, ritzy.

It's nothing. What's the deal with this place, anyway?

I don't know a lot. All I could figure out is basic facts. It was a small religion, only about 200 followers. They all lived here, supposedly. Each person had about ten rooms to themselves.

The central belief was all about finding this one object. They thought that holiness was tangible, and that the founder had hidden it somewhere in this complex.

That's why this whole place is full of tricks. Hidden rooms, stairs that lead nowhere.

They couldn't just... ask the founder where the thing was?

She died. And the rest of the group went crazy looking. Some thought the founder returned to The Staircase, where she was from, and never actually died.

Apparently a group went to The Staircase looking for her. And of **course** they were all never seen again...

What?

What...

...The Staircase. They really went there?

32

33

34

You CHEATER!

How did you get such a good hand??

Don't give me that look. I can still win.

Hey.

Hey, dude. Come to watch me destroy Ell?

Is...everything good?

I'm golden.

You gonna sleep? We can play downstairs.

No, no. Just gonna lie down for a second.

HAH! Take this—LASER BEAM.

It's... a lot more complicated than I thought. I knew I would be, you know, doing construction. But this feels like a lot more...

It is a lot more. We wear a lot of hats. Sometimes we're fixing walls, other times we're restoring art. Every job is a little different.

It can be frustrating, though. Every now and then we're hired to turn a place full of history into some shitty office space. That always breaks my heart.

But it also means we're often the last ones to see a place before it's gone. And Char keeps records of everywhere we go. So even if it's gone, we won't forget.

I was sorta expecting to just do... hard labor... Like, mindless stuff.

Well, it is just labor when you get down to it. But if you want to find meaning, it's there.

Is there something else you want to ask me?

Are you and Jules okay?

Char told me you were worried.

Do we have all the pieces?

I'm making more popcorn.

How exactly do you play this?

We'll teach you as we go.

Wizard totally beats Cat.

Not ALL cats.

Yeah, scottish folds are powerful.

GAH! What a lucky roll!

You're not winning this time, Jules. My platoon is headed straight for the flying castle.

You're really competitive, Jules...

Former figure skater. It's in her blood.

Good lord.

SHHHUTUP

Ohhh

CHAPTER 3

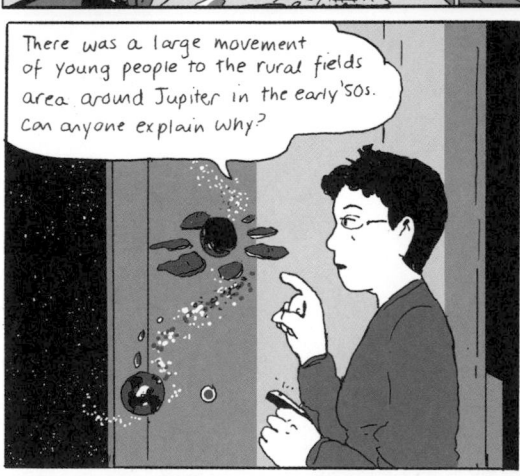

There was a large movement of young people to the rural fields area around Jupiter in the early '50s. Can anyone explain why?

Living was affordable and they were harvesting a resource in great demand!

Well PUT, Alex.

I want everyone to take out their edu-sets and watch the migration, taking notes on any patterns you notice!

Ughhh

Dude, mine is broken.

Did you hear Crissy got kicked out?

No way.

Focus, please!

43

44

That's all for today, girls.

Yessss

Mia, a word.

Noooo

You should really be using this time to catch up on your schoolwork. I've noticed a dip in your grades.

I'm trying.

Then try harder. I want to see you show some effort.

Okay, okay

I've known you for more than three years, and you've always been a great student. Is anything going on?

NO

Well, I'm here if you need me.

Were you listening?!

Yes.

Ugh, GRACE. You do not have a future in espionage.

Come on, we've got like twenty minutes of free hour left!

Slow down, Mia!

45

46

48

So that's the soccer team. They suck. Those side rooms are for yoga and stuff. And through the windows—do you see that tower?

Yeah, I see it.

That's where they play LUX.

Uh...LUX?

It's a Cleary original. You haven't heard of it?

Not at all.

Oh, MAN, you've been living under a rock...

It's our school sport. Basically it's a big treasure hunt for these colored orbs called planets. But you search for them in these crazy dark tunnels in ships that you get to build yourself! And every semester there's a HUGE tournament!

You sound like a big fan.

It's literally the coolest thing in this whole school.

Snuck in...right... well, um

Well, YES, yes of COURSE she snuck in! She couldn't contain her passion! How could you turn away someone with such dedication!

No. Fish.

She'll do ANYTHING. Any task and she'll devote herself.

I guess I could use some help with cleaning and running supplies. It's not very glamorous.

Be here at five am tomorrow.

Five am

THANK YOU FOR THIS OPPORTUNITY

MIA WILL WORK HARD AND—

Come ON, let's go!

55

CHAPTER 4

You comin' to bed?

mhmm

Are Char's journals really that interesting?

mhmm

You're not listening to me, are you?

What?

Don't stay up too late, you Scholar.

Aktis is already FULL, we...we...

Mia?

MIA!

Jules??

Take it slow. The boards are not toys.

Have you seen Grace? I couldn't find her at lunch.

Maybe try the library?

Grace! I need to talk to you!

I have to get to drama club. Can't it wait till free hour?

This is important.

Fine. Talk fast.

Ok, so like, um, well, you have your writing and you're so good and I, like, wait—

MIA.

Sneak into Lux tower with me at night so I can practice flying and catching planets.

That doesn't sound like a good idea.

No, it is! It is!

The only way for me to get good at Lux is if I practice. Then when I've gotten super good I can prove to Coach Miller that I should have a spot on the team!

hmm.

Say yes.

Why do you need me? Can't you do this dangerous escapade on your own?

I...I dunno. I just thought, whatever. It was dumb.

No, wait. Let's do it. I've read that life experience helps with the authenticity of your prose.

Uh, what?

um, I never do anything crazy. So... maybe I should try it out.

68

71

We're ok, Ell.
Just an...
accident.

I'm so
sorry, Jules.

Ah, man, it's
ok, it's ok.

C'mere

Mia...

CHAPTER 5

I could tell the teachers and you'd get expelled.

Go for it.

Today we'll be talking about Deep Space.

It's a region in the southwestern corner of our galaxy. Who can tell me the three main regions? Susie?

Willows, Bat Wings, and The Staircase.

Very good.

Now who can talk to me about why these districts are so dangerous?

No one?

Mia, could you come with me?

I don't know what you're talking about.

Mia, be serious. What happened last night?

Uh... I slept? Exciting stuff.

Coach Miller has told us she's caught you sneaking into the tower before. What do you have to say for yourself?

Wow, really?

The door was unlocked so I just walked in. And Coach Miller freaked.

86

Have a seat, Grace.

Miaaa

Hey, shithead.

hahaa

Your girlfriend started bawling during study hall.

It was GROSS.

Guess you haven't figured out how to treat your women yet...

93

Do you understand what happens next? What this could mean?

no

What was that?

No. I don't know.

If we decide to report the incident, which we are required to do, it puts Char's whole career on the line.

She's a liability, Char. What if something like this happens again?

Come ON, she's no more reckless than Jules. Don't exaggerate.

She **destroye**—

Why didn't you tell me where she went to school?

What?

All you told me when she came was that she went to boarding school. You didn't tell me **which** school.

Char, why are we **talking** about this?!

It's the school from that... job... isn't it?

I didn't want to bring it up. I know you didn't like that job...

That's an understatement. It was an insane risk.

But we didn't get caught.

It left Elliot shattered. You always forget that part.

Come onnn.
You have to eat,
Mia. You'll just
be more miserable
if you're hungry.

Jules...

It's been two
weeks. No more
sulking is allowed.

OK, WHAT'S
THE DEAL?

Jules—

Jules, inside
voice.

Mia said that YOU
said that she's leaving.
And I said that my
tía isn't a soulless
monster. So, WHAT'S THE
DEAL?

It's ok,
Jules...

Alma, we should
talk to them.

You want to explain, or should I?

mmm, you. Now there's too much pressure.

ALL RIGHT, everyone sit down and listen UP.

First things first, Mia. You won't be leaving us.

But your job will be changing. We'll have a chat about that later.

and...

What?

Char is going to file a report. With Mia staying, it's too risky not to.

No... Char...

you can't...

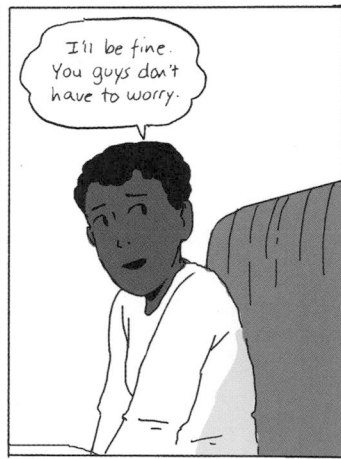

I'll be fine. You guys don't have to worry.

OKAY, enough of this. Jules, Mia, get plates. Eli, help me with the chili.

I set the table LAST NIGHT. Why me??

Let's use paper plates so we don't have to do dishes...

Alma, can I have a beer?

NO PAPER PLATES.

Let's go, you two!

God, I'm starving.

105

111

128

130

Claire... you're being crazy. You should listen to Mom—

BZZZ

Shit

Ahh

CHAR, TURN YOUR PHONE OFF ohmygod

Mom... you're dating the HAIRDRESSER?!

136

137

CHAPTER 8

140

142

Let's not talk about finals, ok?

Thank you.

Aaaah!

Hurry up!

Everyone is giddy.

Probably 'cause of the dance.

Dance?

Oh, right. I always forget you're still kind of new.

Dance?

Whenever there's a big test, the seniors throw a dance in the gym. It's tradition.

I just... I guess I just assumed you didn't want to go 'cause you didn't say anything...

Well you didn't say anything, either!

I mean it's just a dance, it's not a big deal...

Well... when does it start?

Eight... at the gym.

145

Hey.

Hey.

I stole a flower from a girl and got dressed really fast so I don't look good and you look so nice and I still can't believe you're my girlfriend and I shoulda ordered you flowers and made you a card and—

Mia—

And I stole a hoverboard from the gym, cause I've always wanted to pick you up in my very own ship but I don't HAVE a ship I only have a stolen hoverboard—

MIA!

Let's go to the dance.

148

I mean...you never wondered? The crash? The fight? I got you out of ALL of that.

But **HOW**? How?!

I can't tell you..

I ...

And...I wish I could, but I can't.

And I'm sure you think I'm making this up and you probably hate me now.

161

I'm not sure what *this is*. Why won't she speak to me? Her file didn't mention any—

THEY. Not "she."

Elliot isn't the chatty type.

You are all on **very** thin ice. Your insubordination will be reported and there **will** be consequences.

NOW. Jules. Tell me about your work today.

Hmm. You know, it's really **tough** to remember, Jo.

But I'm sure **you** get that. You can't remember one person's pronouns.

Was that helpful, Jo?

164

165

What do we do now?

Drink?

Absolutely.

Ugh, this tastes terrible. I love it.

I didn't know Alma would get like this without Char...

Man, I didn't, either... But I guess they've never really been apart for long, so they don't know how to deal.

Plus she's not used to being so powerless.

How long have they... you know...

Dated? Ages. They met when they were teenagers, back when Alma was doing all that illegal flying shit.

Illegal flying?

Haha, Alma hates that I know about it. She's embarrassed now. So, remember those years when everyone was super into moving to all the unexplored areas of space? Everyone wanted to be a god-damn trailblazer...

167

Oh. Is that how they met Elliot? They all worked for the same group?

Elliot... No... not exactly.

Elliot... Elliot was one of their jobs. A flag went up somewhere in Deep Space...

There was Elliot. Waiting for them.

169

Yep. I don't really know what happened next. All I know is that Ell stayed with them after that.

I used to ask Alma all the time about those years. About what they did together... but she wouldn't tell me.

Deep Space... You don't know where, exactly?

Nope. Ell doesn't talk about their past.

It still makes me angry sometimes.

Why?

It's just like... Sometimes it doesn't feel fair. I'll never have what they have...

No matter how much I try... I can't get in. It's...

Exclusive.

YES. Exactly.

I feel that sometimes.

170

Why are adults so stupid?

hmn.?

It's like the older you get the more you forget that you can **change** things.

Which is stupid because adults have money. Which means you can afford to buy a sledgehammer and break down the room you're stuck in.

Kids don't have sledge-hammer money...

Jules... where are we going?

Gotta check on Alma. She keeps going to sleep at her desk or the floor or something.

Gotta get her into her bed...

173

174

175

CHAPTER 10

All right, team! It's the big day! The tournament is in **five hours**!

yes! It works!

Where is the damn drill?

We're gonna need an extra Scale here.

The wing is too weak!

agh

Kelsey, come ON.

Mia— who is this?

I got this.

This is Abigail. She's here to help.

You didn't run this by me.

Come on, Coach! Every ship needs to be polished for the game tonight. It'll take forever on my own!

Just for today.

You got it!

OK. We're even now.

hmm

Come ON. It was ONE flower.

True. Okay, we're even.

...

Hey! Mia and... Mia's friend—we need your help.

Polish the eyes and wings. Use this stuff.

Did you get your results?

oh yeah.

Totally bombed. Failed every section of the test except for biology... Gotta do summer school now.

Oh SHIT! Do your moms know?

Not yet.

Mia! You're late!

Sorry! Lux ran over!

You gotta change.

Faster!

Ahh

We'll go in for thirty minutes. No chatting. This is supposed to be exercise.

183

189

190

The clock has started and the players now have two minutes to prepare their ships!

Soo Kim will be flying the three-wing, two-cylinder ship Neptune.

WE CLEANED THAT SHIP!

Thirty more seconds!

Grace! I cleaned—

Grace?

195

201

Take this route exactly and you should get out with no problems.

And don't delay. Within a few hours the mountains will move and the path will be blocked.

Time to go, Gracie.

208

Thanks.

You can keep my cat, Paul. I don't think he's really allowed here.

That's the most she's said to us this whole month.

What're they thinking? The Hills sending their youngest to school *outside* The Staircase?

I'm just glad we got her here. If anything had gone wrong... well, Eil wouldn't be the only fugitive anymore.

Welcome to Cleary's, Grace.

CHAPTER 11

221

222

Is this because you got in trouble for me?!

NO.

Then... can you tell me now?

Tell you What?

Everything.

ok.

I'm...I'm from The Staircase.

hah!

what?

no

It's more than that, really.

The Staircase... it's ours. My family sort of runs it. Or Owns it, I guess.

H-how...

We have since the beginning. We founded it.

And I was the first to ever leave.

The principal Knows. That's why I can't ever get in **real** trouble. She's...scared of me. Of my family.

224

225

227

228

229

231

236

242

244

247

CHAPTER 12

I'm Mia. You must be...

Well, obviously, we got the wrong room.

You're joking.

SERIOUSLY, Mattie?

This is ALL Grace's stuff.

hmm

Her blanket.

Her posters.

Yeah, I guess you're right. This looks like her writing on the floor.

AHH HER STORY

She'll get upset if she sees the pages out of order!

We KNOW that! PICK IT UP!

This tore...

HURRY!

Just to confirm—
this is Grace's room?

yes

And where
is Grace?

I'm not
telling.

Why?

You're
going to
take her
away.

Where'd you
get that necklace,
Mia?

Uhh, Janey?

The doorknob
is moving.

It's been a year since I last saw you.

Can I at least get a hug?

Helen's right. You did get taller.

What's happened? Why are you here?

I'll explain everything.

LITTLE SHIT

RRRRRK

Little help over here?!

Let Mia GO! Helen, Mattie! Get OFF HER!

She HIT ME!

I don't CARE!

Grace

Are you okay?

Not really.

Are you okay?

Not at all.

ohhhh

Okay, Grace

What?

You two are a THING!

Grace!! Your first girlfriend! Why didn't you tell us?

Grace!

What a great pair.

We are so proud of you.

I'm glad Grace has someone strong looking out for her.

ohmyGOD stop you are so embarrassing.

The situation at home has changed. The house... well, we had to leave it.

We've moved underground.

Mom got hurt during the move. We were attacked and she fell off her horse.

She can't walk anymore, but she's fine. Still running the whole show.

But...the fighting is bad and the borders are a mess. And we realized... well, **Mom** realized...

It's only getting worse. The land... everything is starting to deteriorate. It could make the edges of the staircase impossible to cross.

Basically...

...if you don't come home now... you might never be able to make it back.

258

265

266

270

CHAPTER 13

I tried to get in touch with her, stupidly.

I still didn't really understand where she had gone. I tried sending her things, bugged the principal for info. But nothing would ever reach her. Where she lives... well, it's totally closed off.

I just want to talk to her!

I want to ask her if she's ok. If she isn't, I want to give her a way out.

And if she is, if she's happy... I just want to say good-bye.

So, let me just see if I've got this right.

You want us to infiltrate one of the most deadly and secluded areas of space...

..to talk to this girl?

I get it.

Quiet, Jules.

What? You mean it?

Absolutely.

Jules, get the ship in the dock. We need to pack up—quietly.

Yessir!

You mean, we're going NOW?

But our jobs... YOUR job, Alma...

If Char were here she'd say we're all being impulsive...

But doing the "safe" thing... the "right" thing... that got us all screwed.

I'm done with that. We'll do this.

And we'll do it because we WANT to.

All right, bring it in. Mia, you look like you could use a hug.

I COULD USE A HUG.

OK. Let's get ready to go.

We have a stop to make before we start our next can job.

There it is.

Where in God's name have you all BEEN?!

You know, I'd recommend starting a convo with "hi" or "howdy."

This place needs to be finished in **TWO WEEKS**.

Or, and I know this is probably a reach for you, a "how are you?"

That's IT. You are all done. I'm getting a new crew out here.

Hey, Alma, looks like we just got fired.

This sure is a pickle.

Oops

I really don't fucking understand this.

What?

THIS

All of you have been rude, insubordinate, and just plain shits since I got here. I don't deserve this!

Jo, Jo.

I think you're forgetting a key part of this puzzle.

I'll admit that I have, at times, been slightly jerkish to you. But only for excellent reasons.

This is ridiculous.

No way, you stay RIGHT here and listen to me. Do you remember the night you showed up here?

Yes. So?

We were pissed when you showed up. Char was gone and we were **broken**. And we could've just taken that out on you.

But we didn't. You showed up and Alma made you dinner. We made you a bed, even played cards together.

And we TOLD you, we told you that Ell didn't talk, we told you their pronouns.

And you IGNORED us.

I don't need to know that stuff! This is a job, none of that is important.

No. No way. You don't get to decide that.

You don't get to decide what's important for us. You can choose for yourself, but no one else.

Fuck yeah, Jules.

286

287

291

I mean, right after she left I was a mess. I Completely fell apart.

But I came back. Misery seemed so useless. And the next school year I roomed with some good friends, joined more sports.

I played on our Lux team. My friend Abby joined, too. We lost every game and it was so much fun.

Oh, and that girl, the bully? Cristine? We got to be pretty tight, if you can believe it. We hung out a lot in senior year.

301

304

CHAPTER 14

Slow down, Jules...

Alma, should we...?

Right. Listen up, team.

We've had a few days to rest but it's time to get organized. The Second Winter hits The Staircase in two months and we do **not** want to deal with that.

If we can make it happen, I'd like to push off in two weeks.

Ell and I have just about finished the plan to get in and our routes when we're there.

What's the gist?

Start with the surface. Do a sweep of the Hill lands and see if we can find anything.

But that's really just to be thorough. Most likely she's underground because of the weather. And our intel says Helen was seen down below, too.

That's gotta be a massive area to cover. What's the timeline?

One month, max. We'll cover as much as we can in that time...

310

We meeting in here?

Yep, come on in.

Get settled, everyone.

I'm settled.

haha

AHHH

FOCUS! We have a lot to go through and NOT a lot of time.

That's better. Now. Who needs a refresher on TS? Or do we all know the basic history?

I don't know anything!

But the Hills would have none of that. TS's extreme weather was eroding their environment, but they'd persevered and stayed to protect the land. For its beauty, the animals, and, well...

It was their home. They wouldn't just let people come in and trample over it.

When the Hills turned down all the offers to join treaties or sell out, everyone shunned them.

This entire galaxy wrote a joint law making TS illegal. No one could go near it.

TS responded by doing the same. They closed their doors to every other world.

The relationship between TS and outside is tense, to say the least. Planets send assassins to take out the Hills, thinking without them they'll finally get access to TS and all its resources.

But that would never work. The people who live in TS, about 100,000, are just as dedicated as the Hills are when it comes to protecting this environment.

All right. Beautifully told, babe. My turn. The ship needs to be cleaned out and we have to lose any excess weight. Clear out all books, games, and statues.

Char—can you search the attic for our winter gear? We're going to need it. Hats, jackets, boots, the works.

yep.

And you two—you need some training. We're going into **hostile** territory. Char and Ell could just about win any fight, but you two need to get ready.

Come at me, Mia.

322

Cute.

Don't get discouraged.
You're making progress
so let's keep it up.

What ARE
you?!

Wow. It's so CLEAN.

We've had a floor this whole time?

That's the last of the junk.

It's not JUNK.

328

We were only with her a few weeks. Almost got killed trying to get her out...

But we got her to school.

To you.

We got to her once, Mia. We can get to her again.

Please fix your jacket. It's driving me crazy.

Can one of you do me a favor?

Name it.

Do you know how to cut hair?

332

Closed up?

CHAPTER 15

You need more layers. We're landing soon.

You're kidding. I'm already wearing a ton.

The air is going to be freezing and the dust that blows around is sharp.

FINE.

338

The ship is in camouflage mode so we're good to go.

Jules, you're with me. Ell, you lead Alma and Mia.

Take these maps and mark the areas you cover. Add anything else you think we should know. Patrols, animals, loose rock, things like that.

We need to find out if people are still living on the surface. Ell said there used to be small towns between these cliffs. If they're still around, we'll find them.

Back at the cave in four hours. This is just the first sweep. Don't take any unnecessary risks.

Be safe.

There's the old Hill compound. Let's see if it's really abandoned.

Lead the way, Ell.

351

354

We've been looking
out here for days.
She's not here, Char.
No one is.

She's right. No
way Grace is on
the surface.

Everyone has
moved underground.
The towns that used
to be here are gone.

360

362

Ell first. Then Mia, Jules, Alma, and I'll be at the back. Stay quiet, everyone.

Ell, whenever you're ready.

Ell! Behind us!

They're coming at us from both sides!

Ell! No—

Hey—

Who's over there?!

Shit! Here they come!

377

382

383

384

391

397

398

CHAPTER 17

Let's go, Elliot.

Is the ink packed?

I think so.

Check

It's all here.

411

412

413

414

415

418

420

421

424

427

428

430

434

437

What's wrong with her?

She was with a Tessian Fox, our oldest creature.

She must have gotten past our barrier. The air past that point is toxic. By the look of her, she's breathed far too much of it. She's quite sick.

Tell me how to make her better.

442

444

445

451

454

Knock

Go away, Jane. I'm BUSY.

CHAPTER 19

471

472

Because I **did** know you.

I knew you and I—

I didn't get to say good-bye.

475

476

477

487

491

492

494

Are you guys really ok?

I found this lollipop so I'm doing way better.

GODDAMMIT, MIA, I WAS SO SCARED!

I was, too.

Hello, there.

Um, everyone. There's someone you should meet.

506

510

Rewiring everything was so annoying...

But at least we have our own rooms. No more of Jules' snoring.

I heard that.

Is it time?

It's time.

Alma's totally gonna cry.

Did you check your list? You have everything?

We're all set.

Are you guys gonna be ok? Won't you get, like, bored?

Do you remember...

...crashing that ship at school? In the middle of the night?

I'll never forget.

You don't have a great track record with flying machinery.

I think you'll find I'm a little better than when I was fourteen.

Call me if a red light turns on. I need to go help Jules and Ell!

525

A huge thank you to Ricky Miller for working with me while **On a Sunbeam** originally came out as a slightly sporadic webcomic. And a big thanks to all you folks who read and supported this story in its early form.

As always, thank you to Connie Hsu for sticking by my side and helping me turn wild drawings into a real goddamn book. Thank you to everyone at First Second for all your support and hard work.

Thank you, Seth. Always and forever.

And thanks to my parents for continuing to cheer me on through all this.

♡

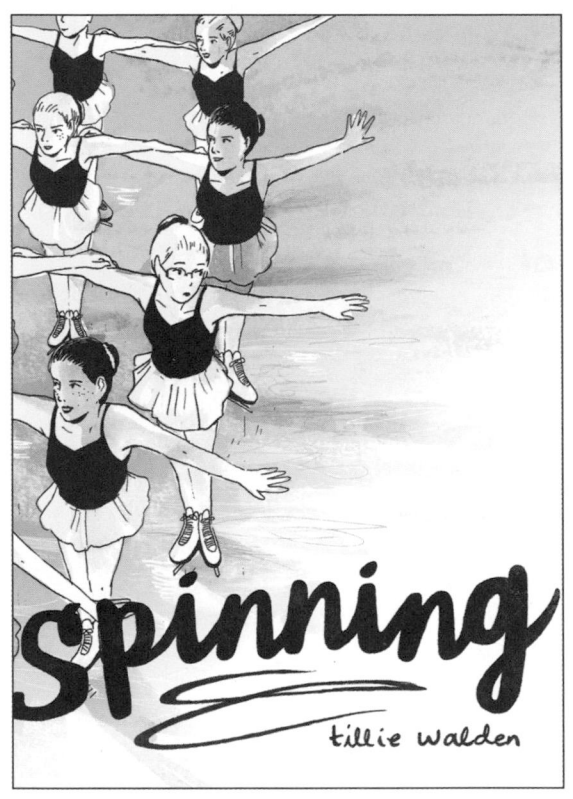

A.V. Club Best Book of the Year
Paste Best Book of the Year
Wired Best Comic of the Year

"This beautiful story about sorrow, growth, and triumph
will resonate in every reader's heart."

—Laurie Halse Anderson,
New York Times–bestselling author and two-time National Book Award finalist

Tillie Walden is a cartoonist and illustrator from Austin, TX. She is the creator of the graphic memoir Spinning from First Second Books. She is also the creator of the Ignatz Award winning book The End of Summer and the Eisner nominated story I Love This Part. Tillie is a graduate of The Center for Cartoon Studies, a comics MFA program in Vermont.

For more information on Tillie and her work, please go to tilliewalden.com.

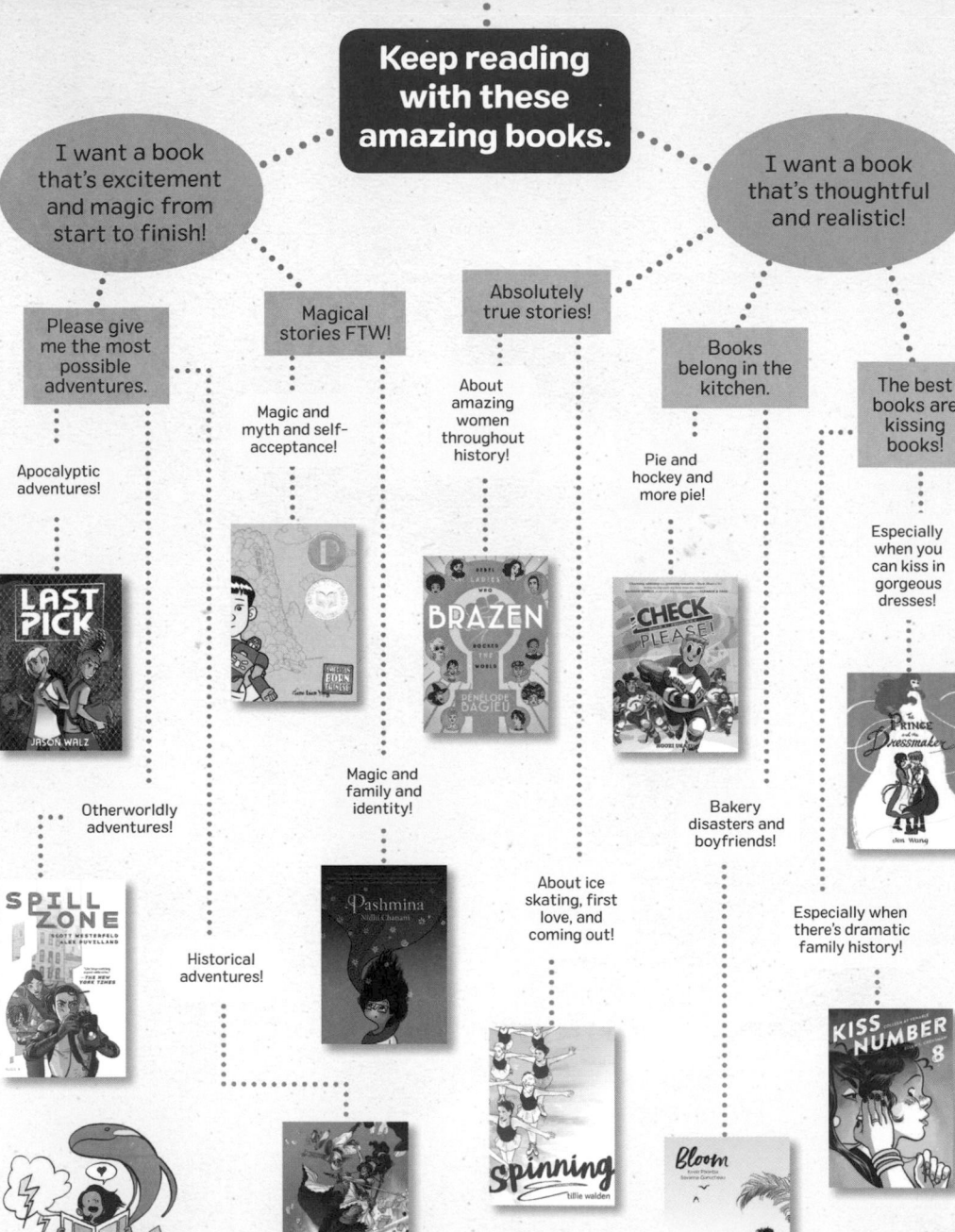

I LOVE GRAPHIC NOVELS!

Keep reading with these amazing books.

I want a book that's excitement and magic from start to finish!

Please give me the most possible adventures.

Apocalyptic adventures!

LAST PICK — JASON WALZ

Otherworldly adventures!

SPILL ZONE — SCOTT WESTERFELD, ALEX PUVILLAND

Historical adventures!

Delilah Dirk — Tony Cliff

Magical stories FTW!

Magic and myth and self-acceptance!

Magic and family and identity!

Pashmina — Nidhi Chanani

I want a book that's thoughtful and realistic!

Absolutely true stories!

About amazing women throughout history!

BRAZEN — BÉNÉDICTE DAGIEU

About ice skating, first love, and coming out!

Spinning — Tillie Walden

Books belong in the kitchen.

Pie and hockey and more pie!

CHECK PLEASE!

Bakery disasters and boyfriends!

Bloom

The best books are kissing books!

Especially when you can kiss in gorgeous dresses!

The Prince and the Dressmaker — Jen Wang

Especially when there's dramatic family history!

KISS NUMBER 8

:01
First Second
firstsecondbooks.com

THE
SEVEN
MINUTES

———

a novel by
IRVING WALLACE

SIMON AND SCHUSTER • NEW YORK

To
Fanny, Constance, Molly
who made it possible
&
To
Sylvia, David, Amy
who approved

Mrs. Digby told me that when she lived in London with her sister Mrs. Brooke, they were every now and then honoured by the visits of Dr. Johnson. He called on them one day soon after the publication of his immortal dictionary. The two ladies paid him due compliments on the occasion. Amongst other topics of praise they very much commended the omission of all *naughty* words. "What, my dears! then you have been looking for them?" said the moralist.

—H. D. BEST, *Personal and Literary Memorials*
(London, 1829)

THE SEVEN MINUTES

I

By ELEVEN O'CLOCK in the morning the sun had come out, and now the women of Oakwood, most of them housewives in summer attire and most of them at the wheels of their own cars, were converging on the business district to do their shopping.

In the suddenly thickening traffic, the green two-door Ford coupe with a nasty dent in its front fender was at last forced to slow down.

Slumped in the seat beside the driver, Otto Kellog grunted his displeasure, then sat up impatiently to get his bearings. He resented delays at a time like this, when he was anxious about what he must soon do. He wanted to get it over with as quickly as possible.

There was a jarring screech as Iverson, who was driving the car, slammed on the brake, muttering, "Goddam women drivers."

"Yeah," said Kellog. "Wish they'd get moving."

In the rear, the third occupant of the coupe, Eubank, older, more tolerant, less often exposed to the outside world than his companions, seemed to be enjoying the interval. He had brought himself forward from the back seat to peer over Iverson's shoulder through the windshield. "So this is Oakwood," he said. "Attractive. I don't know how many times I've been out this way, but I guess I never paid much attention before."

"Nothing so different," said Iverson, easing his foot off the brake. "It's still Los Angeles County."

"Well, it just looks more prosperous and settled down," said Eubank.

"Maybe not for long," said Iverson. "We're going to shake them

11

up a little today." He glanced at Kellog, and grinned. "What do you say, Otto? Ready for action?"

"Yeah," said Kellog, "providing we ever get there." He squinted through his sunglasses. "Third Street's the next corner. You turn right the next corner."

"I know," said Iverson.

The traffic was moving again, loosening, and the green coupe moved with it along Center Boulevard, and then swung sharply onto Third Street.

The vehicle and foot traffic was thinner here on the side street. The man at the wheel showed relief. "There it is, middle of the block," he said. "You can see the sign just after the Acme Jewelers. See it? Fremont's Book Emporium. How do you like that for a name? Emporium."

"Looks like there's plenty of parking," said Eubank. "I was worried there might not be any parking close by."

"There's always enough room once you get off Center Boulevard," said Iverson. He spun the wheels of the car toward the curb, and expertly brought it to a halt before the jewelry shop. As he reached to turn off the ignition, he spotted a young blonde, in tight sweater and shorts, stepping out in front of the car, preparing to cross the street. Iverson emitted a low whistle. "Hey now, lookit those tits." He watched the blonde as she hurried to the other side. "Not bad all over, I'd say, but me, I'm strictly a tit man. I like them big and bouncing." He sought agreement from his front-seat partner. "What do you say, Otto?"

At the moment, Kellog had no interest in his friend's preoccupation with women. He had a one-track mind, and the track was already occupied. His right hand fidgeted inside his plaid sport jacket, working beneath his left armpit. At last, satisfied, he looked up, his long face serious and tight. "Am I all right?" he asked Iverson as he secured the middle button of his jacket and fixed the collar of his open sport shirt. "Does it show?"

"Nothing shows," said Iverson. "You look like a regular anyone-for-tennis type. Naw, I'm kidding. You look okay, Otto—like an insurance salesman or accountant who's taken the morning off to shop for his wife."

"I hope so."

"Don't worry."

"What time is it?"

"It's eleven—eleven-fourteen."

"I'd better get going." He twisted around in his seat. "You set back there, Tony?"

Eubank patted the open lid of the suitcase on the rear seat. "All systems in go position."

Kellog returned his attention to the driver. "You'll stay right here?"

"I'm not moving an inch till you need me."

"Okay," said Kellog. "I won't be more than ten minutes."

He opened the door on his side, lifted himself out of the car stiffly, closed the door, and stood a moment on the sidewalk straightening his jacket. Then, casually, he walked past the jewelry shop, approached the bookstore, moved past its recessed entrance and planted himself before the main display window. On the lower right-hand corner of the window was a painted representation of Pegasus and beneath it, in Spencerian lettering, "Ben Fremont's Book Emporium, Established 1947." In the other corner of the main window, Scotch-taped inside and at eye level, was a full-page newspaper advertisement for a new novel.

Kellog edged toward the advertisement. He studied the bold-faced heading:

A WEEK FROM TOMORROW
PUBLISHING HISTORY
WILL BE MADE!

Kellog's eyes ran swiftly down the rest of the advertisement.

After 35 Years of Suppression, the Most Reviled and Praised Novel in History—Written by an Expatriate American—Will Be Available to the Public at Last

You must read—
"The most widely and completely banned book of all time."

Osservatore Romano, Rome

You must read—
"The most obscene piece of pornography written since

13

Gutenberg invented movable type. . . . Brilliant as a private revelation, but unforgivable as a public confession."

Le Figaro, Paris

You must read—
"One of the most honest, sensitive, and distinguished works of art created in modern Western literature."

Sir Esmond Ingram, London Times

WITH GENUINE PRIDE,
SANFORD HOUSE, PUBLISHERS,
OFFERS AMERICA AND THE WORLD
THE UNEXPURGATED ORIGINAL VERSION
OF THE UNDERGROUND MODERN CLASSIC

THE SEVEN MINUTES

BY

J J JADWAY

There was more, Kellog could see, but he did not bother to read it. He had read it all in last Sunday's newspaper.

Briefly, Kellog's gaze shifted to the contents of the display window. The window contained many books, three soaring pyramids of books, but all the volumes were one book, bearing one and the same title. Each copy featured a white dust jacket, and on the front cover was delicately etched the faint outline of a nude young woman lying on her back with her bent legs up high and wide apart. Imprinted over this, in artistically simulated longhand, color red, was the title *The Seven Minutes*, and below it "by J J Jadway."

J, no period, J, no period, Jadway.

Yeah.

Kellog slipped his right hand inside his sport jacket, groped beneath his armpit, touched the cold metal, and then he was ready.

Quickly he entered the store. It was a bright, cheerful, cluttered store. Down the middle of the floor area were rectangular tables piled high with recent publications. Standing by the nearest table, which was stacked with copies of *The Seven Minutes*, Kellog searched the interior. In the rear there were two people, appar-

14

ently customers, one an elderly gentleman poking about the shelves beneath the placard reading PAPERBACKS, the other a small woman, probably somebody's mother, browsing near the sign reading JUVENILES. A short distance from the customers, an overweight lady wearing a smock was removing books from a carton and setting them on a table.

Then Kellog became aware of one more person on the premises. To his left, fifteen feet from him, bookcases jutted out from the wall to form an alcove. This was barricaded on the open side by a counter on which rested a cash register and another column of copies of *The Seven Minutes*, and propped on a stool behind the counter, leafing through invoices, was a slightly built man of perhaps forty years. Offsetting the sparse hair on top of his head were thick brown sideburns. He also wore heavy-lensed, metal-rimmed spectacles, and they distorted his eyes. He had a hook of a nose, an undershot jaw, and a pallid pink complexion. His brown sweater was erratically buttoned down the front.

Kellog had never seen the man before, but Iverson had, and Iverson had described him.

Kellog held his breath, went woodenly to the cash register, and exhaled. "Hi," he said, the insurance salesman taking the morning off to shop for his wife.

The wispy, myopic man looked up, immediately offered a customer-tailored smile, and said courteously, "Good morning, sir." He slid off his stool, putting aside the invoices. "Anything I can do for you this morning, or would you prefer just to browse about?"

"Is Mr. Fremont, Ben Fremont—is he here?"

"I'm Ben Fremont."

"Oh, good to meet you. I'm trying to remember if I've ever been in here before. Very nice. I should make more time for books, but I guess I'm too busy, what with being on the road half the time. It's my wife who's the reader in the family. She's one of your customers. I mean, from time to time she comes in."

"That's fine," said Ben Fremont. "I'm sure I'd recognize her name—"

"No. She just drops in from time to time. Yeah. And I won't let her have no charge. You know women."

"Sure, sure."

"Anyway, I'm here as a proxy. Seems like she got herself a kidney-stone attack. It's out now, she's doing okay, but she's still over at Saint John's Hospital and she wants some reading. You can get awfully tired of television."

"More people are reading books than ever, thanks to television," agreed Fremont seriously. "There is nothing like the experience of a good book, as your wife obviously knows."

"A good book," repeated Kellog. "Yeah, that's what I want to get her."

"Well, now, we've got something to satisfy every taste. If you could give me an idea . . ."

Kellog stepped closer to the bookstore proprietor. "The old girl reads everything. Even history. But mostly I guess it's fiction, novels. Anyway, for the hospital, I don't think it should be anything too deep or sad-like. Maybe something kind of fast and easy to read through, something with a little snap to it. And new, it should be real new, so's I won't be getting anything she's already got from her friends. I asked her to give me some help last night—what does she want?—but she just said, 'Otto, you go and surprise me. And if you get real stuck, you go over to Ben Fremont's and ask what he suggests.' So here I am."

"Well, now, I'm sure we can find—"

"Of course," Kellog interrupted, leaning over the counter, lowering his voice, "I don't think she'd mind if the book had a little realistic life to it. You know, something with a bit of—well . . ."

"Oh, sure, sure, I understand."

"Don't get me wrong. She goes for the heavy intellectual stuff too, but she sure got a kick out of that *Lady Chatterley*. Now, that was a kick, a real kick, if you know what I mean. Still, it was a classic, but at least it wasn't boring. Well, there she is in the hospital, and if you've got anything half as good and brand new . . ."

"Half as good?" Fremont had come to life. "The minute you described your wife, I was going to suggest something. Listen, I've got a brand-new book in, spanking new, not even officially published yet, and this book, it's ten times as good as *Chatterley* or any similar classic, maybe a hundred times better. I'm telling that to every woman who comes in the shop, and I don't recommend everything. In a couple weeks, I'll bet you, the eyes of every woman reader in Oakwood, in all of Los Angeles, will be glued to this book." Fremont snatched a volume from the pile beside the cash register. "Here it is. She's in the hospital? Here's just what the doctor ordered."

Kellog began to lift his sunglasses. "What's that cover say?"

Fremont's forefinger pointed at the title on the front jacket. *"The Seven Minutes*, by J J Jadway. This is something no woman'll ever forget. Your wife, it'll excite her, absolutely excite her—and yet it's literature."

"Oh, it's literature. Well. I'm not sure, maybe that's not exactly—"

"Forgive me. I misled you with that word. I just meant it's nothing to be ashamed to read if you are a reader, a sophisticated reader like your wife. Most people, not being sophisticated, being clods or puritans, they might take offense at the whole thing. But if you know what life's all about, you can appreciate the frankness of a novel like this. As far as I'm concerned, you can take them all, the books by Cleland, D. H. Lawrence, Frank Harris, Henry Miller, and they're like reading the Bobbsey Twins compared to reading Jadway. They don't know a thing about sex, and nobody ever did, until Jadway came along. He invented it. He invented it for *The Seven Minutes*, except his is real, realer than anything I ever read."

"You read the book?"

"Twice. First time in Paris. The Étoile edition. The French wouldn't allow publication in French, and the United States and Great Britain wouldn't allow publication in English, so there was only that little special Paris edition for tourists. Then I read this first public edition, the very first for the general public. Didn't you see the big ad in the Sunday paper? The most banned book ever."

"Why was *The Seven Minutes* banned like that?" Kellog wanted to know. "Is it obscene? Is that why?"

Fremont frowned. "This book was banned because—yes, I guess you might say it was banned in every country in the world because it was considered obscene. Until one big publisher in New York finally had the courage to say, Maybe the world's grown up a little, at least some people, and maybe now's the time to bring

17

it out—because, whatever this book has been called, obscene or whatever, it is still a masterpiece."

"How can a book be obscene and still be a masterpiece?"

"This one is. It's both."

"Do *you* think the book obscene, Mr. Fremont?"

"Who am I to say? That's only another word. There's a four-letter word some people think is dirty and other people think is beautiful. So there we are. Some people, maybe most people, will say this is dirty, but there'll be plenty of people who'll say it's worthwhile."

"Sophisticated readers, you mean."

"That's right. They don't give a damn about obscenity if in the end they have some great reading that gives them new insights and understanding into human nature."

"And this book does that?" asked Kellog.

"It sure does."

"Despite those bannings? What's there about it? I mean, what's it about?"

"Simple, very simple, like all great art," said Fremont. "A girl, young woman, is lying in bed thinking about love, that's the essence."

"And that's what the fuss is about?" said Kellog. "You almost had me interested, but when you put it that way—that sounds pretty dull."

"Dull? Wait a minute, listen to me. I said she's lying in bed, sure, but while she's lying there she's getting laid, I mean really laid. And all the while she's thinking, on her back thinking, and Jadway shows us what's in her mind about what's happening to her down below, and what's in her mind about other men she's had or ones she wished she'd had. The way it's done—it's enough to drive you crazy."

Kellog grinned. "Sounds a little better now. That's more like it. And you think this is the sort of thing my wife would enjoy?"

Fremont grinned back. "It'll sure take her mind off her kidney stone."

"How much is it?"

"Six dollars and ninety-five cents."

"That's a helluva lot of money for such a little book."

"Dynamite comes in small packages," said Fremont. "This is

18

dynamite, guaranteed. The book's not even out yet, officially, until next week. We get our shipments here on the Coast early, and so we had to unpack and put our copies right out because there was such a big demand since the advance advertising. Already Jadway's our biggest seller."

"Wrap it up. You've sold me." Kellog had his wallet out. "Here's a ten. Can you change a ten?"

"Sure thing."

Kellog waited as Ben Fremont rang up the sale, made change, then placed the receipt and the copy of *The Seven Minutes* in a striped paper bag.

"I'm sorry I was such a tough customer," Kellog said apologetically.

Fremont smiled as he handed the striped bag across the counter. "I like a discerning customer. I don't mind being challenged. Keeps me on my toes. And don't worry about the book. It'll help your wife get on her feet fast, believe me. Good day."

The second that he was out in the sunlight once again, Kellog slid his hand inside his sport jacket and flipped the lever on the box beneath his armpit. Hastily he headed in the direction of the waiting Ford coupe, and as he did so he hoisted the striped paper bag above his head. Immediately Ike Iverson stepped out of the car, carrying a similar bag, and strode over to join him in front of the jewelry shop.

As they met, Kellog asked, "How did Eubank do in the back seat?"

"Came in loud and clear," said Iverson. "Sa-ay, you were in there long enough."

"Those literary conversations take a little doing," said Kellog with a wink. He shook his purchase. "But it's in the bag. Duncan'll be happy. Well, we'd better start comparing."

Kellog removed his copy of *The Seven Minutes* from the striped bag. He opened the book, found the loose end paper at the front of the book, located his pen, and carefully signed it with his initials and the date. When he finished, Iverson was beside him, also holding a copy of *The Seven Minutes*.

"Ready? Let's get it over with," said Iverson. "Same jacket and title, right?"

"Check."

19

"Same publisher, publication date, copyright, correct?"

"Check."

"Same number of printed pages, right?"

"Exactly, check."

"Let's compare the marked passages in my book with the same pages in the book you just bought."

"Okay," said Kellog.

Working quickly, the two men compared a half-dozen pages.

"The same," concluded Iverson. "Well, Otto, the books are identical, agreed?"

"Agreed."

"Guess we'd better pay Mr. Fremont another visit."

"Yeah," said Kellog, returning his book to the bag.

"Otto, don't forget your Fargo unit."

Kellog reached into his sport jacket, found the switch beside the microphone of his portable Fargo F-600 intelligence unit. He pushed the lever. "It's on."

Briskly, striding in step, the two returned to Fremont's Book Emporium and entered it.

Once inside, Kellog saw that Ben Fremont was still behind the counter next to the cash register, busy pouring a Coke into a large paper cup. Kellog led the way, with Iverson right behind him.

Fremont had just brought the soft drink to his lips when he recognized Kellog. "Why, hello again—"

"Mr. Fremont," said Kellog, "—you *are* Ben Fremont, proprietor of Fremont's Book Emporium, aren't you?"

"What do you mean? Of course I am. You know that."

"Mr. Fremont, we'll have to introduce ourselves officially. I am Sergeant Kellog, assigned to the Vice Bureau of the Los Angeles County Sheriff's Office." He held out his badge, then returned it to his pocket. "My partner here is Officer Iverson, also of the Sheriff's Vice Bureau."

The bookseller appeared bewildered. "I—I don't get it," he said, setting his Coke down hard and spilling it. "What's going on with—?"

"Ben Fremont," said Kellog, "we are placing you under arrest for violation of Section 311.2 of the California Penal Code. The Code states that every person who knowingly offers to distribute any obscene matter is guilty of a misdemeanor. Under Section

20

311a, 'obscenity' means that to the average person, applying contemporary community standards, the predominant appeal of the work in question, taken as a whole, is to prurient interest. That's to say, the work goes beyond customary limits of candor in its descriptions, and is utterly without redeeming social importance. The District Attorney believes that the book *The Seven Minutes*, by J J Jadway, would be found obscene if taken to court, and therefore you are to be put under arrest for selling that book."

Ben Fremont, mouth agape, face ashen, gripped the counter's edge, trying to find words. "Wait a minute, wait, now, you can't arrest me. I'm just a guy who sells books. There are thousands of us. You can't."

"Mr. Fremont," said Kellog, "you are under arrest, absolutely. Now, for your own sake, don't cause any trouble. We want all your invoices from Sanford House for purchased copies of this book. We've got to confiscate every copy of *The Seven Minutes* on the premises, and take them into our custody. We'll also have to take that advertisement from the window, and any other promotional materials concerning the book."

"What about me?"

"I thought you remembered the procedure. Never mind. We have a police vehicle outside. You will have to accompany us to the Sheriff's Office on West Temple Street for booking."

"Sheriff's Office? For what—for what, dammit, I'm no criminal!"

Kellog became suddenly impatient. "For selling an obscene work. Didn't you yourself tell me ten or fifteen minutes ago—"

Iverson hastily came forward, placing a restraining hand on Kellog's shoulder. "One minute, Otto. Let me tell the gentleman his rights." He addressed himself to the bookseller. "Mr. Fremont, everything you said before your arrest and everything you are saying now is being recorded by a wireless transmitter attached to Sergeant Kellog's person and relayed to a magnetic tape recorder in our police vehicle outside. You did not have to be apprised of your rights before your arrest. Now that you are under arrest, it is my duty to warn you that you need answer no questions, that you have the right to remain silent, that you have the right to the presence of an attorney. Now you've been fully informed. If you want to ask questions, answer questions, that's up to you."

"I'm not saying another word to either one of you, goddammit!"

21

Fremont shouted. "I'm not saying anything until I have an attorney!"

"You can make a call," said Kellog, controlled. "You can call your attorney and have him meet you at the Sheriff's head-quarters."

Instantly Fremont's anger vanished, and what was left was fear. "I—I don't have an attorney. I mean, I don't even know one. I've only got an accountant. I'm just a—"

"Well, you can have the court appoint—" Kellog began.

"No, no, wait," Fremont interrupted. "I just remembered. The publisher's salesman, the Sanford House salesman out here, when he sold me the books he said—he said if there was ever any kind of trouble, to call him right away, because they were standing behind their book, and young Sanford, he's the publisher, he'd pitch in, he'd get any one of us an attorney. I'm going to call their salesman. Can I call him?"

"Make any call you want," said Kellog. "Only make it fast."

Fremont grabbed for the telephone. But before dialing he stared at the officers. It was as if some new thought had crossed his mind and he was considering whether to speak what was on his mind. He spoke. "Listen, do you guys have any idea what you're doing?" he said, voice trembling. "You think it's nothing. You think you're just arresting some poor little nobody bookseller and that's the end of it. Well, maybe you're not. You know what you're really doing? You're arresting a dead author and his book—you're ar-resting a *book*, something a man had to say. You're arresting and fingerprinting a freedom, one of our democratic freedoms, and if you think that's nothing, you wait and see what can happen. . . ."

IT WAS WHEN he was driving along Wilshire Boulevard, halfway between the law office in Beverly Hills that he had just left forever and his three-room apartment in Brentwood, that the complete realization of what had happened to him struck Mike Barrett with its fullest impact.

After all the years of struggle, he was liberated.

He was one of the emancipated ones. He had made it.

From the corner of his eye, he could see the carton on the seat next to him. An hour ago he had filled it with the personal papers and effects that had accumulated in the firm's walnut desk, the desk which had been his desk as an employee, for two years. The contents of the carton, in a way, represented the corpus of one frustrating, unfulfilled, second-rate legal career spanning a decade of his thirty-six years. The carton itself, the act of its removal, symbolized a victory that (on the blackest of the sleepless and self-hating nights) he had nearly given up hope of ever achieving.

It wanted a celebration, a triumphal parade, an arch, at least a garland. Well, they were all present in his head and his heart. But still, some outer celebration of independence won and success attained was required. Firmly holding the wheel of the car with one hand, he undid the knot of his tie with his free hand, and yanked the tie off. Next the shirt collar. He unbuttoned it and spread it open. Tieless at high noon of a working day. *Lèse-majesté* in the kingdom of the American Bar Association, unless you are *majesté* himself. Then the Latin phrase came to him. *Rex non potest peccare*. The king can do no wrong.

God, what a lovely day. The sun, beautiful. The City of the Angels, beautiful. The people in the streets, his subjects, beautiful. Osborn Enterprises, Inc., beautiful. Faye Osborn, beautiful. All friends, beaut— No, maybe not all—not Abe Zelkin. Abe, beautiful, yes their friendship, yes, that too, except that it might not exist a few hours from now, and he felt guilty, and a blemish suddenly marred the face of joy.

He became aware of Westwood passing outside his top-down Pontiac convertible, and there were people, the sidewalks were crowded with people, and they were not his subjects applauding him on this great day. They were Abe Zelkin admonishing him for selling out.

Honest Abe. Who the hell needs a conscience for a nag when he has a friend like Honest Abe?

Yet, curiously, and in truth, it had been Abe Zelkin who had planted the seed that had borne this day, the undoing of Zelkin and Barrett, the doing of Osborn and Barrett. His mind sought the beginnings, bit by bit revived them, to give him his brief before he pleaded his case to Zelkin at lunch.

Where had it begun? Harvard University? No. That had been his friendship with Phil Sanford, when they had roomed together. No, not Harvard, but sometime later, in New York City. Not at that big factory of a law firm he had started with, because he had not liked that firm, had still been interested in defending human rights, not property rights, in retrospect immaturely idealistic, a stupid legal hick with a cowlick for a brain. It was that next place, that hothouse for the flower children of the law, the Good Government Institute on Park Avenue, where your salary consisted of elbow patches for your threadbare coats and quotations from Cardozo and Holmes on the high purpose of the law. The Good Government Institute, a foundation supported by twenty big-business corporations as a sop to their own bad consciences, where every case was derived from the overflow of the American Civil Liberties Union and where every client was the ever-present underdog. Six years of that, of living off peanuts because you felt that you were upending a few evils and many wrongs, deluded into thinking that they were the real enemies, until you learned that they were only prop windmills to keep you busy putting on a public-relations show for the Institute's founders. Six years to learn the identities of the real enemies, to learn that your work was a fraud, that the do-gooding was a fake. Six years to learn the truth of how you'd been manipulated by the power people. When he and Abe Zelkin had learned, they had both got out.

They had quit within a month of each other. Barrett had been the first to quit. His disillusionment with the Institute had become complete due to his mother's death. He had obtained some hints of evidence that the newly marketed drug which had been administered to keep his mother alive had actually hastened her death. And, since he could scent like a pointer, he had soon learned of other untimely deaths from aplastic anemia, a side effect induced by this same drug. Shocked, Barrett had built up his sketchy outline of a legal case, found an eligible complainant, and finally presented his memorandum to the managing director of the Institute. The memorandum was an indictment of one of America's most renowned pharmaceutical companies. Barrett requested funds for a thorough investigation, and urged, if the findings substantiated his suspicions, a legal prosecution of the drug company or a hearing before the federal Food and Drug Administration. He was positive that he would be encouraged to go ahead.

Eventually, the managing director of the Institute had summoned Barrett to a private meeting. The director spoke, and Barrett listened, stunned. Barrett's request to proceed with an

24

investigation, to be followed by a lawsuit or a hearing, had been turned down by the governing board. His evidence had been regarded as too flimsy, and, besides—oh, besides, it just wasn't the kind of clear-cut case in which the Institute wished to become involved. Barrett's disbelief and bewilderment lasted only forty-eight hours. At the end of that time, after discreet inquiries, he had learned the truth. One of the Institute's chief backers and major contributors was the very pharmaceutical company that Barrett had attempted to indict.

The following day, Mike Barrett had resigned from the staff of the Good Government Institute.

Abe Zelkin, after a similar disappointment, had resigned a short time after Barrett.

And then each of them had had to make his choice. How well Barrett remembered. Zelkin had made his choice first: He had moved to California, been admitted to the bar, and taken a post with the Los Angeles office of the American Civil Liberties Union.

But Barrett had been made too cynical by the realities to emulate Zelkin's choice. So he made his own choice. If you can't fight them, join them. He had joined the world of power, of big business, of big government. If he was to remain a do-gooder, he would concentrate on doing good for one person, himself. The name of the grownups' game was—money. He would be a grownup, too. It was goodbye to all salaries of eight thousand a year and bonuses of to-thine-own-self-be-true. It was hello to a new life of eighteen thousand a year and a new goal, which was: to become, by whatever means—by osmosis, by training, by association—one of Them, one of the powerful ones.

The new life began with a position as a minor associate of a huge law firm on Madison Avenue—a beehive of forty attorneys—that specialized in corporate law. It had been a dreary two years. The work had been technical, grinding, monotonous. He had rarely had an opportunity to see a client and he had not once seen a courtroom, an arena he had so much enjoyed in his Institute days. He had been expected to employ his spare time participating in New York civic and cultural affairs, as prescribed by the firm's elders. Opportunities for meaningful financial advancement had been few. Since he had been unhappy, restless and moody, his limited social life had been unhappy. There had been two love affairs, one with an attractive brunette divorcee, the other with a bright redheaded fashion model, and, while both had been physically satisfying, they had not satisfied him otherwise. Because he had been bored with himself, he had become bored with others.

His situation was becoming clearer. He had tried to go to the other side—to stop fighting them, to join them—and become one of them. Oh, they welcomed every Faust with open arms, enlisted each with glowing promises, let each and every one eat cake instead of bread—and then assigned each to hard labor in the dungeon of corporate law, mergers, taxation; and then they threw away the key. Yes, it was clearer. You could serve the powerful, but not easily join them—because there wasn't enough room at the top, because *somebody* had to serve them, and because their magic really never rubbed off. Or so it seemed to Barrett, in his worst despair, at the time.

A drastic change was wanted, and one day the possibility of a change was offered. In one of his monthly letters, Abe Zelkin had written of the many big-paying positions open for able and experienced attorneys in Los Angeles. Zelkin himself had been offered several, and resisted them, although admittedly one or two had been magnificent and even glamorous. From this the lure of California had grown in Barrett's mind, and, shortly after, he had made his decision and made the change.

He had passed the California bar examination, and a few months later he had found himself installed in a small but beautifully decorated office as one of fourteen attorneys working for the successful business-management firm of Thayer and Turner on Rodeo Drive in Beverly Hills. All of the clients were either celebrated or wealthy, or both, and the proximity to success had once more given Barrett hope that he might strike it rich. Yet, after almost two years—hard, demanding years in his office, in the firm's law library, in courtrooms, and in the offices of affluent clients—during which he had gradually specialized in tax law, Barrett had slowly begun to come to the conclusion that he was not one of those fated to make it big.

His assets were many, and he could be coolly objective about them. He wasn't classically handsome, true, but he had a rugged, weatherbeaten face. Part Polish, part Irish-Welsh, he had a craggy face marked only by scowl lines, the faint remnants of contracting brows and puckering eyes that grew out of skepticism and disappointment (like those of a quick, slightly aging light-heavyweight boxer who was beginning to be hit more often and was still in the semi-windups). He possessed a shag of matted black hair, restless, roving eyes, a short, straight nose, hollow cheeks, square jaw. He was just below six feet in height, with supple, sloping shoulders, a sinewy swimmer's body. His outer demeanor was loose, casual, ambling, slouching, careless, but, like every man, he knew that he owned another man inside, and this one was alert, tense, crouching, a sprinter waiting for the gun. Only there was no gun.

At work, Barrett was serious, dedicated, quiet, steady. On his own time he could be personable (when not moody), since he had a fair sense of the ridiculous and a strong strain of sardonic humor, along with an accurate instinct for perceiving how other people felt and an understanding of why they behaved as they did. He was an easy and arresting talker when he cared, which was no longer often. He was well read beyond Sir William Blackstone. He had meant to major in English literature, but he had also wanted to be practical, and law offered a broader horizon. Also, he possessed two unique qualities marvelously useful in the practice of law. The first quality was that of an almost freakish memory. Like his more illustrious predecessors, Rabbi Elijah of Lithuania, who had memorized the entire contents of twenty-five hundred scholarly volumes, including the Talmud and the Bible, and like Cardinal Mezzofanti, nineteenth-century curator of the Vatican Library, who had learned 186 languages and seventy-two dialects, Barrett's eye was a camera obscura, forever capturing the sacred and the profane, the momentous and the trivial, and imprinting these on his brain, there stored for instant reference and recall. He could, on demand, recite most of the Code of Hammurabi, the Dred Scott decision, Shakespeare's will, and Sir John Strange's epitaph ("Here lies an honest lawyer and that is Strange"). The second quality was that of a questing, trapping mind, one that enjoyed mysteries, riddles, games, all the unsolved phenomena of Charles Fort. He knew that he was suited for the profession of law, and he was stimulated by its promise of fresh challenges. Next to law, literature was merely a self-indulgence, a defrosting of the past.

Yet, though the surface assets were there, the hidden defects, or certain lacks, were there also, no question, no doubt about it, especially when you thought about it at three in the morning. He had skill in his work, but he lacked financial and social aggressiveness. While creative, he was not sufficiently self-promoting to claim credit where credit was due. He was too thoughtful and intelligent, perhaps too self-deprecating, to define himself or his role publicly. He was neither extrovert nor introvert, but ambivert, at once intrepid and outgoing, uncertain and withdrawn. When he had fallen from the family tree, he guessed, his ego had been flawed in the accident.

Barrett doubted that his seniors, Thayer and Turner, had ever thought of him as a unique personality, an indispensable individual. And the worst of it—yes, the very worst of it, his secret—was that he did not believe in what he was doing. He did not believe that it was important (beyond the comfortable sustenance it afforded him), and, secret or no secret, this absence of commitment may have shown up on his employers' built-in radars. It was as if— well, hell, as if Henry David Thoreau had finally taken a job as a tax attorney. That was it. It was like that.

He had reached dead end, he had decided, some months ago. The job had become as tiresome and routine as waking every morning, and Los Angeles was, as some kindred soul had once put it, just one goddam beautiful day after another. In desperation, he had even spent four successive fifty-minute sessions with a psychoanalyst, but his sense of futility had not been dispelled. He had not wanted to discuss his departed mother and father, or really to go into his Id and flawed Ego, and he had canceled the fifth appointment.

Then, overnight, as if the smog had cleared to reveal a pot of hope at the end of the rainbow, a small miracle had happened. And, a few weeks after that, there had been a greater revelation, a bigger miracle, and the pot of hope had become a pot of gold.

The first, the hope, had come from Abe Zelkin. By now, Zelkin was a fixture in the community, with respectable connections, and he had decided to quit the American Civil Liberties Union and open his own office in Los Angeles. There was a definite promise of clients, the kind of Scopes-Vanzetti clients he and Barrett had once dreamed about, and cases that would enrich their lives if not their pocketbooks, important and never-ending opportunities to challenge injustice and inhumanity and bigotry. To open his own office, Zelkin wanted a partner. He wanted Barrett.

The offer to be young again, to do good works, invest each day with meaning, had excited Barrett. He would be independent. He would be alive. He would help others. He would have everything —except what he had so long thought he had wanted the most, and that was riches, which also translated as power.

Barrett was interested, very interested, but still hesitant. He wanted to think about it. He wanted the next move to be right, and he had to be certain. But yes, it was a good idea, the idea of Zelkin and Barrett, Counselors at Law, Specialists in Idealism, and he thought he would go for it. Zelkin had said to him that there was no hurry, because Zelkin still had to clean up a number of cases. When they were under control he would ask Barrett again, and if Barrett was ready they'd put up their shingle.

That was the Zelkin pot of hope. And four weeks later, like a vision out of the blue, there was the Osborn pot of gold. And then it was that Barrett had known he had made it, finally made it.

With surprise, he emerged from his reliving of the recent past, to find that he had automatically turned off Wilshire Boulevard onto San Vicente Boulevard and that he was almost home. On Barrington Avenue he headed the convertible toward The Torcello (the owner had never quite forgotten that honeymoon in Italy), the six-story building constructed around a patio and a swimming pool where he had leased a three-room apartment after his first year in Los Angeles.

Reaching the building, Barrett swung his car into the cavernous opening beside the entrance walk, and drove into the subterranean garage. Getting out of the car, he checked his watch. There was still an hour before his appointment with Abe Zelkin. Plenty of time to shower again, change into a lighter suit, and rehearse what he would tell Zelkin.

He came around the convertible, bent down and removed the carton heavy with his past, and then jauntily made his way to the elevator. It carried him smoothly to the third floor of The Torcello. He went down the corridor, opened his door, deposited the carton in a dark recess of the guest closet, and then went to dial the switchboard.

The living-room shutters were closed against the sun, and his apartment was cool. The room seemed less his own, and less comfortable, than it used to be, although admittedly it was smarter. This was Faye's doing. Like so many wealthy women with time on their hands, she carried a decorator's card. When she had first laid eyes upon his furnished apartment, she had shuddered. "The taste these landlords have. What's the period they've done it in? Early San Fernando Valley?" Soon the landlord's sloppy, cushiony sofa had been replaced by an expensive reproduction of an austere Chippendale camel-back sofa. Soon, too, the walls had been covered with hemp-cloth, the lighting had become recessed, and a late-Victorian roll-top desk and a French country-style chair of walnut and cane had dominated one corner. After the first beachhead, the invasion of good taste had continued. He had submitted to a glass-and-steel coffee table, too low to have any use whatsoever except as an object upon which to nick his shins and fully awaken him in the morning. Most recently, the telephone had been inconveniently tucked out of sight inside a carved wooden cabinet that had found its way to Decorators' Row on Robertson Boulevard from the Swiss Village in Paris. On the cabinet stood a lamp and two fragile pieces of Limoges. Whenever he was alone, as he was now, Barrett would reverse the position of the Limoges and the telephone.

Removing the telephone from the cabinet, Barrett placed the Limoges inside, set the telephone down next to the curved arm of the sofa, and dialed the switchboard operator in the lobby.

"Mike Barrett here. Any calls?"

"Oh, I'm glad you're back, Mr. Barrett. Two long-distance calls, urgent, in the last half hour. They were both from the same party. A Mr. Philip Sanford in New York. He wants you to call him the minute you get in. He left his business and home numbers."

"Let's see. It's only twenty after three in New York. Try his office."

Rising from the sofa, stripping off his shirt and tossing it aside, he went into the kitchenette for a soft drink. As he prepared it, his mind went to Phil Sanford. There were two things odd about Sanford's successive calls. He telephoned at long intervals, but

30

when he did, a few times each year, it was always in the evening. Furthermore, the calls were always casual, unhurried, the reaching out of a lonely friend for a reaffirmation of friendship. Poor Sanford got little warmth from his wife and none at all from his tyrannical father. But this morning's calls apparently had not been social. They had been urgent. And now Barrett wondered why.

Sipping his root beer, Barrett thought of his old friend and of their friendship, a friendship that was older although less easy than the one with Abe Zelkin. After Harvard, when he and Philip Sanford had both gone to New York, he to become a disenchanted do-gooder, Sanford to start out as an editor in his father's famous publishing house, he saw his college roommate frequently. Not only did he like Phil, but he owed him much after all that Phil had done during Barrett's year of crisis with his mother. Even after Phil Sanford married, Barrett continued to meet his friend for their weekly lunch at the Baroque Restaurant and to go occasionally with him to some sports event at Madison Square Garden. Since moving to California, Barrett had seen Sanford only a half-dozen times. These occasions had afforded Barrett no pleasure. Phil Sanford had always sounded gloomy when talking about his wife and two children, and he had been as miserable as ever over his helpless serfdom in Sanford House, which his father ran as a one-man operation.

But the last time Barrett had seen Phil Sanford, only three months ago or less, when Barrett had flown into New York on some overnight business and they had dined together in the Oak Room of The Plaza, it had been a happier meeting than usual. Sanford's life had changed short months before this reunion with Barrett. For the first time, he had been given an opportunity to prove himself. While he was filled with anxieties, he was also filled with enthusiasm.

That giant of publishing, Wesley R. Sanford, Phil's father, had been felled by a sudden stroke. While it had not been a massive stroke, it had been a warning one, severe enough to force him into retirement. In the eyes of the stricken gray giant, Sanford House, so long the discoverer and sponsor of authors who had been knighted with the Nobel Prize in literature, the Pulitzer Prize, the Prix Goncourt, was now a house without a head. Phil Sanford, the only heir, had always been regarded with condescension, even disdain, by his mighty father. It was as if the self-made giant had always known that he could not sire another in his image. He had regarded his son as a pygmy, a weakling, an incompetent, a total disappointment. This had been Phil's Cross, and the fact that he had suffered such treatment for so long without going off on his own had infected Phil's wife, who had also come to see him as weak and gutless.

The word that Wesley R. Sanford had left a flourishing publishing business without a satisfactory heir had passed rapidly from Publishers' Row to Wall Street. Great communications complexes, conglomerates seeking diversification of their holdings, were eager to buy up the firm, with its valuable back list and prestigious name. Only partially recovering from his stroke, Wesley R. Sanford, it had appeared, would decide to sell. And then his only son had gone to his bedside and, for the first time, pleaded for a chance. Whether illness had deprived the convalescing giant of resolution or whether he had been waiting for such an appeal from his heir and been impressed by it, Wesley R. Sanford had gruffly told his son that he would have his chance.

Philip Sanford had been given two years to prove himself as a capable independent publisher. If in that period he kept the firm in the black, maintained and expanded its prestige, the firm would remain in the family, with Philip as its president and eventual owner. However, if Philip's guidance proved faulty in that period, he would be removed from the head office, and the publishing house would be sold off lock, stock, and back list to one of the communications industries vying for it.

Unused to decision-making and authority, Philip Sanford had got off to a poor start. Of the first twenty books published under his direction in his first year, the majority had been failures, and the rest had either barely broken even or made only minor profits. Not one could be called distinguished or had become a best seller. Not one had made a major subsidiary-sales strike to book clubs or paperback reprinters. At last, with the courage born of sheer desperation, Philip Sanford had made an effort to escape his father's shadow and become his own man. He had determined to publish what he wanted to publish and not what he thought his father might have published. He had acquired a novel that he had read and admired during a sea crossing from Le Havre to New York, a book that had never been permitted to be published openly in any English-speaking nation in the world. It was a work called *The Seven Minutes*, and on the publication and success of this novel Philip Sanford had staked his entire future.

When Barrett had dined with Sanford in New York that last time, Sanford had been manic about the book's possibilities. For the first time in modern literary history, the climate was right for the appearance of such a book, Sanford had insisted. A Western world that had finally accepted *Lady Chatterley's Lover* and *Fanny Hill* would be mature enough to accept *The Seven Minutes*. The book was already on the presses. Interest within the trade was mounting. It promised to be a smash hit. And then Sanford would have his publishing house, his haven, his future, and he would finally be his own man. Discussion of Phil's survival had occupied most of their evening together. Only in the last ten minutes had Barrett been asked about himself. He had complained about his own crawling career at Thayer and Turner. He had cited as the only bright spots Abe Zelkin's offer and his own fondness for Willard Osborn's daughter.

And now, suddenly, Philip Sanford wanted to speak to Barrett about something urgent. Considering what he knew of Sanford's life, what could possibly be urgent that might concern him?

The telephone at his elbow was ringing.

He snatched up the receiver. "Hello?"

"Mike?" It was Sanford's voice. No secretary had preceded him. That underlined urgency. "Is that you, Mike?"

"None other. How've you been, Phil? Sorry to have missed your calls. I just got in. How's everything?"

"As usual, as usual, if you mean the family. This is something else. It's a business matter. Mike, I'm certainly relieved you called this soon."

Barrett was immediately aware of the tone of Sanford's voice. It was nervous, harried. "You sound as if there's something important on your mind. If it's anything I can—"

"You can, you can help me."

"Shoot."

"Mike, remember when you were here last, I told you that I was having a rough go of it with my first list, *my* books, not the carry-overs from Wesley R.?"

Barrett remembered that Sanford had always referred to his father, Wesley R. Sanford, as Wesley R. He had never been able to call him Father. "Yes, but you were optimistic—"

"Exactly. Because of one book I had in the works. *The Seven Minutes*, by J J Jadway. I was putting all my chips on that one. All or nothing. Remember?"

Barrett nodded at the telephone. "That's right. The novel no one had dared publish in thirty-five years. I saw your opening ad last Sunday. Tremendous."

Sanford's voice had become anxious. "You've seen the book, haven't you? I had an advance copy airmailed to you."

Guiltily, Barrett's eyes flicked toward his bedroom door. He *had* received the advance complimentary copy about three weeks ago, and the book had been resting unopened on the lamp table beside his double bed ever since. He had intended to read it so that he could write his friend an encouraging thank-you note, but there had been so much happening to him since that he had been unable to get to it. Goddam good intentions. "Yes, I received it, Phil. It's next to my bed. Every day I've resolved to write and thank you, wish you well, but I've just been up to my ass in a million things. I skimmed the whole thing, and I'd say the book is everything you've been saying, a winner, a real winner."

"It is," Sanford affirmed excitedly. "It's shaping up to be the blockbuster of the year, maybe the biggest seller in a decade. You've no idea what's been going on with the wholesalers and the stores. We're still days from official publication, and we've had a second printing. We've got two hundred thousand in print, and we've already shipped a hundred thirty thousand. Do you realize what that means, Mike? Hell, you know plenty about the book business from listening to me over the years. Take your average novel. If it's a first book, and Jadway's is a first book, his only book, well, maybe you print four thousand copies for openers, and maybe your salesmen pick up two thousand advance orders and you ship these on consignment—any of them can be returned if they don't sell—and maybe a half year or year later we wind up having sold seven hundred fifty copies. That's the part of the book business, behind the hullabaloo of reviews and advertising, that the public knows nothing about. But once every few years, if you're lucky, you get hold of a blockbuster, a first novel that just takes off like a jet. And that's *The Seven Minutes*. Of course, it had built-in propulsion. All the bannings. The talk about its being dirty, which it isn't. Now, for the first time in thirty-five years, people can see what it's really about. So we have orders for a hundred thirty thousand copies, and we'll have had the whole two hundred thousand ordered a week after it's out. That's only the beginning, Mike. Once it's on display everywhere, and selling, and people are talking about it, arguing about it, word of mouth will keep it soaring. We could go to three hundred thousand or four hundred thousand copies in a few months. And that's the least of it. We'll put it up for bidding with the paperback reprinters. Once we've made it respectable, shown it's been accepted, they'll be outbidding one another for the reprint rights. That can be a million dollars as a start, not counting future sales and royalties, and don't forget that Sanford House, the publisher, keeps fifty per cent of the paperback income. You see what I mean, Mike? No limit. Do you know what *Lady Chatterley's Lover* had sold at the last report? In hardcover and paperback it had sold over six million copies, and it is probably closer to seven million copies by now. Well, that's what we've got here, maybe bigger, much bigger, with *The Seven Minutes*. And you know my situation, Mike, that'll make Wesley R. sit up, sick as he is, and that'll put me in business on my own for keeps. You know what that means to me, Mike, nobody but you outside the family knows what that means."

The almost hysterical torrent of words abruptly stopped. There was only heavy breathing to be heard over the transcontinental telephone.

Barrett said, "Yes, I know." Then he wondered. "It sounds to me as if you've got your winner."

"I *have* my winner, Mike—*if* nothing goes wrong."

Not thinking, almost automatically, Barrett started to say, "But what could go—"

"Censorship," Sanford interrupted. "I've got nothing if the police won't let the stores sell the book and won't let people buy it. If that happens, I not only won't have a success, I'll have an utter disaster. Wesley R. will boot me out of here in nothing flat, and so will my sweet Betty girl. I'll lose the business and my kids. I won't have anything except the trust fund from my mother, and that's

35

not enough to keep the insides of a man alive, believe me, Mike, it's not."

Barrett was becoming mildly irritated with his friend's forebodings. "Phil, you've got a good thing going, so why anticipate a disaster when there's no likelihood of one? Censorship? Little chance. We're living in a different age now. Everything's open and on the table. Everyone knows the Queen has legs. In fact, they know she's got a damn sight more. You can get *Fanny Hill* on any drugstore rack. Remember when we used to rent mimeograph copies at school? Remember reading about 'that delicious cleft of flesh, into which the pleasing hairgrown mount over it, parted and presented a most inviting entrance'? And *Lady Chatterley*, remember Connie 'putting her arms round his white slender loins, and drawing him to her so that her hanging, swinging breasts touched the top of the stirring, erect phallos'? And that sold—what did you say?—six to seven million copies. That's the way it is now and will be for some years, maybe forever, unless people get tired of truth and we slide back to the age of the asterisk again. But not now. People are less afraid of sex, especially when it's presented artfully—"

"Jadway's book hasn't been repressed just for sex alone," Sanford interrupted. "It's because some of the sex is sacrilegious."

"I don't give a damn what it is," said Barrett. "Plenty of experts who've read it secretly have proclaimed publicly that it is a work of art. You have no problems. Don't anticipate problems that don't exist."

"Mike, wait, I've been leading up to it. That's why I've been trying to get hold of you. You see—"

A sudden suspicion hit Barrett. His friend was used to living in the future, picturing future success, future trouble, maybe this, maybe that, just as some people lived in the past. This was one of Sanford's most exasperating shortcomings, since it kept him from speaking honestly of the present.

"One moment, Phil," Barrett cut in. "You've been saying over and over you've got it made if nothing goes wrong." He paused. "*Has* something gone wrong?"

There was the briefest silence. "Yes," said Sanford.

"Why didn't you say so in the first place?"

"I was trying to explain how important all this is to me."

"What's happened?" Barrett demanded to know.

"A bookstore owner in your city got arrested a couple of hours ago for selling *The Seven Minutes*. Maybe I'm overreacting, making too much of it, because I'm on edge. It's probably just a little matter. Still, I want to make sure that's all it is and nothing more."

"Okay, tell me."

"Our Coast salesman got a desperate call from a bookstore owner—let me see, I have everything written down—a Ben Fremont, he owns Fremont's Book Emporium in Oakwood, wherever that is."

"Oakwood's an upper-middle-class community, fair-sized, in West Los Angeles, between the Westwood and Brentwood areas and the city of Santa Monica, about ten minutes from where I am. It's unincorporated, not part of the city of Los Angeles, but in the county of Los Angeles. All right, what happened next?"

"Fremont's a good account, but he's not big, and he doesn't have an attorney. So he phoned our salesman for help, for protection, and of course we've got to give it. The salesman called me and I called you. Apparently there's a group out there in Oakwood called the STDL, the Strength Through Decency League—those self-righteous names—and their president, a Mrs. St. Clair, read the book and registered an immediate protest with the District Attorney of Los Angeles. I guess this comes under his jurisdiction—"

"That's right. The D.A.'s Office and the Los Angeles County Sheriff's Office are in charge of the unincorporated areas."

"Well, the District Attorney got Mrs. St. Clair's protest, and he in turn sent a letter to the Sheriff asking for an immediate investigation, and once the District Attorney had his full report he prepared a criminal complaint, and he had two deputies of the County Sheriff's Vice Bureau go in and arrest Ben Fremont this morning. They confiscated all copies of *The Seven Minutes* Fremont still had on hand. About eighty copies."

"Go on. Was there anything else?"

Sanford quickly recounted the few fragmentary facts about the arrest that Fremont had relayed to the company salesman. "Fremont's been in jail several hours now, waiting to be bailed out," Sanford went on. "I want him bailed out at once. We'll stand good for that, and for any other costs. I'd send one of our own

37

attorneys out, but that takes time and, besides, our attorneys don't know California law. I need someone in Los Angeles who can act immediately and who knows his way around out there. And someone who understands what I've got at stake. Mike, I can't have this little matter blown up out of proportion. I want it settled quietly and at once. Then the book trade will know we are standing behind every bookseller and behind the book. Then everyone will go ahead and sell it without being worried. There may be one or two other small arrests like this. We'll have to back them up just like this. What we have to do is give the book a chance to start selling in the big stores and chains in the largest cities. After a few weeks or months, once it has had its wide public acceptance, no law-enforcement agency will bother to get in our way. We'll be safe. That's why I want to quash the little nuisance arrests at the outset, before the big stores panic. I want this settled right away, quietly, as little as possible in the newspapers. Of course I thought of you, Mike. I know you have a job, but if you could . . ."

"I left Thayer and Turner this morning, Phil. I have something much bigger coming up. I'll catch you up on it another time. But it just happens I am free. I'll be glad to pitch in."

"Great! That's great, Mike. I needed someone I could trust, someone who knows what this means to me. I'm sure you can wrap this up overnight."

Barrett had found his pen and a pad of scratch paper. "You say this Ben Fremont's down at the central jail? We'll have to put up bond, bail him out today. How do you want to plead?"

"Do you mean guilty or not guilty?"

"Yes. If he pleads not guilty, that means a trial."

"God, no. I want to get him out of this fast and quietly, to assure other bookmen they don't have to worry, yet get him out with a minimum of publicity."

"Then we'd plead guilty. Now, as far as I can remember, if you're convicted for purveying pornography in California, and it's a first offense, that's a misdemeanor. You can be fined a thousand dollars plus five dollars for each unit of obscene material on hand. Fremont had eighty books, so that's four hundred more—fourteen hundred dollars. And you can go to jail for six months. A second offense means a felony—two thousand dollars fine, plus the four hundred, and into the clink for one year. This is Fremont's first offense?"

"It's his second, Mike, his second. He was arrested once before —I don't know how many years ago, even he's forgotten—when he had a smaller shop in downtown Los Angeles. I believe it was a magazine thing then. If this is a felony, that means a full year in jail? I can't let a bookseller selling our book go to jail for that long."

"Well, it's that or a not-guilty plea and a public trial," said Barrett.

Sanford groaned. "That's just as bad."

"There is one more possibility," said Barrett. "If this arrest doesn't get too much publicity—"

"I don't think it will."

"Well, if it doesn't, I might be able to get the whole thing over with quickly and quietly. Enter a guilty plea, pay the fine, and arrange for the sentence to be suspended."

"That would be perfect!"

"I think I can swing it. We have a District Attorney here now— his name is Elmo Duncan—who's a very decent, straight sort of person. But he's a realist. He knows where to give and where to get, and so I'd guess he's the kind of man you can talk to. I know him socially. I've met him two or three times at parties at the Willard Osborns'. If I went to him, he'd remember. He'd also remember I'm going out with Osborn's daughter. I think I can persuade him to be reasonable."

"Mike, you don't know how much I appreciate this favor—"

Barrett wanted to interrupt and tell Sanford that this was no favor, merely the smallest down payment on a debt that he had long owed Sanford, and which he had not forgotten. But he said nothing. He allowed Sanford to go on.

"—because I was really worried about this, but now I feel better, much better. Mike, you're a miracle man."

"Not yet," said Barrett wryly. "Not until I get cooperation from our District Attorney. I think I can manage it. Tell you what. I'll phone Elmo Duncan and try to make an appointment for this afternoon. Then I'll get hold of a bail bondsman I know down on Hill Street, and I'll see that he springs your bookseller. Then I'll look in on your bookseller—" he was making notes on his scratch pad now—"Ben Fremont in Oakwood, right?—and I'll find out exactly what happened and learn what he said and calm him down. Then, hopefully, I'll be seeing the District Attorney. As soon as I have something definite from him, I'll telephone you. It might not be until tomorrow."

"Whatever you say, Mike. Just as long as I know you've taken over."

"I've taken over. In forty-eight hours we'll be able to talk about other things."

"Thanks, Mike."

"I'll be in touch," said Barrett.

After hanging up, he thoughtfully finished his root beer. Putting the empty glass aside, he realized that he was hungry. Then he remembered his lunch date with Abe Zelkin. They had agreed to meet at the Brown Derby in Beverly Hills, a convenience to both of them since it was twenty minutes from Barrett's apartment and only fifteen minutes from Zelkin's new office, a suite in a recently opened high-rise building on the east side of Beverly Hills.

Before making his calls to the bondsman and to the District Attorney, Barrett decided to telephone Zelkin's secretary. He would request that she have Zelkin make the lunch date a half hour later, and that Zelkin bring along a photocopy of the section of the California Penal Code that dealt with the purveying of obscene matter. At least that would give him something else to talk to Zelkin about before he faced the moment of truth. It was going to be tough, this meeting. He wished that he could simply explain the facts of life to Zelkin: Abe, listen, honest and poor is good, very good, but believe me, Abe, honest and rich is better, far better.

He wondered whether Zelkin would understand—or, at least, would forgive him.

THEY WERE SITTING in a comfortable semicircular booth, beneath the framed caricatures of show-business personalities, finishing their drinks, and had not talked very much at this point. The Brown Derby was crowded and noisy, and they were among the silent few.

Mike Barrett, pretending to reread the photocopy of the cen-

40

sorship section of the California Penal Code, could see Abe Zelkin across from him, sipping a martini, absorbed in the large menu. He looked relaxed and cheerful, which increased Barrett's guilt. Of course, as Barrett knew, Zelkin always looked relaxed and cheerful, and like an innocent—deceptively so, for nature's face masked a tiger, especially when he was tracking evidence for a case in which he believed. Barrett had once thought, and was now reminded, that Abe Zelkin's head had the appearance of a small, happy pumpkin, if the pumpkin were adorned with an unruly sprout of black hair and a tiny egg of a nose upon which were perched oversized black-rimmed bifocal spectacles. He was short, potbellied, and there was always a trace of cigar ash on his lapels. Big men wanted to protect him, and big women wanted to mother him, unaware that this lovable toy-sized human had a brain one part missile detector, one part rocket launcher.

Zelkin had two eccentricities and one obsession. His eccentricities were: absolute honesty—toward others, toward himself—no matter what the consequences and total purity of language; rarely did he employ swear words (when well shaken, he inclined toward the stilted curses of penny-dreadful literature). His primary obsession was the United States Constitution's Bill of Rights, and the encroachments being made upon it. He liked to echo the sentiments of Chief Justice Warren, who had once remarked that if the Bill of Rights were introduced as a new piece of legislation today, there were strong doubts that Congress would pass it into law.

A waiter had approached. "Are you ready to order yet, gentlemen?"

Zelkin lowered his menu. "What about you, Mike? Want another drink?"

Barrett cupped a hand over his glass of Scotch and water. "I'm standing pat. Let's eat. What are you having?"

"If I had my way, I know what I'd want." Ruefully, Zelkin considered his protruding stomach. "But last night my youngest crawled up on my lap, and she poked at my belly and she said, 'Papa, are you pregnant?' Where in the devil she learned that word—progressive nurseries or television, of course—but I got the message." He shrugged at the waiter. "Broiled hamburger steak, medium, no potatoes, no nothing. And some black coffee."

41

"Make it two coffees," said Barrett. "And a chef's salad for me. French dressing."

The waiter had gone. They were alone. And Barrett wasn't yet ready for truth. He had mentioned Philip Sanford's call and the Ben Fremont arrest briefly when they had met. The Fremont matter was still a welcome diversion. He held up Zelkin's photocopies. "This statutory definition of obscenity really makes the head swim. There's no clear-cut guideline."

Zelkin grinned. "Richard Kuh—he used to be assistant district attorney in New York—once remarked that trying to define obscenity is as frustratingly impossible as trying to nail custard pie to trees. And Judge Curtis Bok said it was like trying to come to grips with a greased pig. But I'll go along with Justice Stewart. He once said something to the effect that maybe he couldn't define obscenity, but, by golly, he knew obscenity when he saw it."

"Well, maybe," said Barrett doubtfully. "I'd prefer to go along with Havelock Ellis—how can you define a notion so nebulous that it resides not in the thing contemplated, but in the mind of the contemplating person? You show one man a picture of a nude woman and he says Art, and you show the same to the next fellow and he says Dirty Postcard."

"My dear Michael, a nude woman is *always* Art."

Barrett laughed. "You've solved that one. I wish it were as simple with a book. Here we've got Sanford, who, despite his commercial interest, really believes this Jadway book is the essence of purity, and there we've got Elmo Duncan, guardian of public safety, who by his very act this morning is saying the same book is filthy. On the one hand, Sanford insisting the book has social importance, and on the other Duncan insisting its appeal is solely to a—where's that definition?—yes, to a 'shameful and morbid interest' in nudity and sex and is 'utterly without redeeming social importance.' And with that poor bookseller caught helplessly in between."

Zelkin finished his martini. "Well, sometimes a good trial—and the appeals that might follow it—can be a long step toward working out a more satisfactory definition."

"Not this time," said Barrett. "I know Sanford doesn't want a trial, but he doesn't relish a guilty plea either. He just wants the whole thing quietly quashed. I guess he's right. Anyway, I have an

42

appointment with our District Attorney at three-thirty." He paused. "I hope he's as agreeable behind his desk as he is at a dinner party."

"How well do you know him?" asked Zelkin.

"We're not on a first-name basis, nothing like that. He's been a guest at the Osborns' several times when I was there with Faye."

"That won't hurt you."

"No—no, I suppose not." Barrett stared across the table. "How well do *you* know him?"

"Duncan? Oh, fairly well. We're not exactly bosom friends, but after he was elected, when I was still with the Civil Liberties Union, I had many occasions to meet him in and out of court." Zelkin unfurled his napkin and draped it across his lap. "I like him. I don't know if I can tell you anything useful. You want to know his assets? A Vietnam hero with two Purple Hearts. Thirty-two years old. Big family man. Four children. An able attorney, honest, decent, square. A dynamic public speaker, marvelous television personality, not flamboyant but direct and forceful. But a political creature, by instinct. He knows he's a winner. When he was elected district attorney it was by the biggest landslide in our local elective history. Elmo Duncan knows he's bigger than his present job. Now the word is out that someone else, someone who counts, knows it, too. Ever hear of Luther Yerkes?"

"The Global Industries fellow? Aircraft and electronics. Of course. I once read about him in *Fortune* magazine. There wasn't much in it about him, only about his holdings and his worth—millions, billions, something like that. I didn't know he lived out here."

"He sure does," said Zelkin. "Luther Yerkes has a place in Malibu, a thirty-room cottage in Bel-Air, and a pad in Palm Springs. You don't know all this because Yerkes doesn't like publicity. He likes money. He likes power. He doesn't care about fame. Makes sense. Anyway, according to well-founded rumor, Yerkes wants his own senator in Washington—not a senator from California, but a senator from Yerkes. As you know, our incumbent, Senator Walter Nickels, is up for re-election come soon. Our Senator Nickels is in the doghouse with Moneybags Yerkes. Seems that Senator Nickels has been pressing in Congress to head up an investigation of aircraft industries who've allegedly conspired to overcharge and otherwise gouge Uncle Sam in cost-plus government contracts. And Luther Yerkes has more government contracts than anyone. And he doesn't like any snotty legislator giving him trouble. So how to stop such an investigation from getting under way? Cut down its leader, of course. Get rid of him, and serve warning on his cohorts of what can happen to them if they get out of line. So how to get rid of the leader within due process? Simply find someone more attractive, and build that someone up, and have that someone run against Nickels and crush him at the polls. Who's the someone? You guessed it. Elmo Duncan, boy D.A. of L.A. on the rise. I haven't got photographs to prove it. I do hear the whispering. And note that our District Attorney has suddenly blossomed as an authority on everything from A to Zygo. These last months, whenever you hear someone making a public speech you can be sure it is Elmo Duncan. In short, Mike, our Elmo Duncan is presently in the business of wanting to be loved by everybody, especially by everybody who is somebody. Your Willard Osborn II is somebody. And Faye Osborn is his daughter. And you are Faye's fiancé. Now you want a small favor from Elmo Duncan. My guess is you'll get it, so relax."

"I feel better already," said Barrett.

Zelkin had removed his spectacles and was wiping them with his napkin. "In one way it's too bad," he muttered, "your having to sweep the arrest of Ben Fremont under the rug. If it could only be brought to trial, it would be the perfect case for Barrett and Zelkin to start their partnership with. It's our meat, Mike, a good cause, a challenge, a publicity natural, everything. But what the heck, we'll have plenty of other cases coming up." Zelkin pulled on his spectacles again, and squinted at Barrett. "You *are* going to quit Thayer and Turner, aren't you?"

Barrett felt the lump in his throat. He swallowed. "I've already quit them, Abe. I quit them this morning."

Zelkin slapped his hands together. "Great!" he exclaimed. "My gosh, why did you keep me in suspense? Why didn't you tell me right away?"

Barrett's forehead felt warm. He tried not to squirm. "Well, Abe, first let me tell you, let me explain—"

"Excuse me, gentlemen." It was the waiter, rolling the cart with their lunch plates up to their booth. "Sorry to be so long.

44

The hamburger steak takes time. It's all here hot, maybe even the chef's salad's hot."

Zelkin had tossed aside his napkin and was sliding out of the booth. "Hold still, Mike," he said exuberantly. "Before you tell me about it, let me go to the little boys' room. Be right back. I want to know everything that happened."

Unhappily, Barrett watched him go bouncing off toward the bar in the rear.

Miserable, ignoring the waiter, who was setting down the plates, Barrett sat back against the padded booth, closed his eyes, and tried to review what had happened and assess how it would sound to his friend—or ex-friend.

It had begun with the Osborn account.

Willard Osborn II, president of Osborn Enterprises, Inc., owned or controlled the majority stock in fourteen television and radio stations in Los Angeles, Phoenix, Las Vegas, San Francisco, Seattle, Denver, and elsewhere in the West. His interests in these stations alone, not including additional investments in motion-picture companies, tape-manufacturing firms, amusement centers, hotels, amounted to forty-two million dollars. While Osborn was no Luther Yerkes, no super-tycoon, he was, as the saving goes, comfortable. He was also ambitious. Persisting in his quest for empire, Osborn had become involved in an intricate negotiation over an immense new possible acquisition. His bargaining had been stalemated because the new business presented a compli-cated tax problem. In an effort to learn whether the problem could be resolved, he had taken on the management company of Thayer and Turner. And Thayer and Turner, as was their cus-tom, had fragmented various aspects of the difficult taxation ob-stacle, and farmed these parts out to their junior members. To how many, Mike Barrett did not know, except that he was one of those assigned full-time on a crash program to create a tax struc-ture that would make Osborn's negotiation feasible.

The work had been almost crushingly difficult, days without hours, weekends without rest, a project both back-breaking and mind-splitting. As much as he had come to detest tax law, Barrett had enjoyed the Osborn project. He had enjoyed it because it brought him close to dissecting the anatomy of power. For once, he could see it up close—so that legal precedents and business

45

figures became translated into stately mansions and royal gardens —and it intrigued him and spurred his creativity. He had been reluctant to give up his papers, his findings, researches, suggestions, and to live among lesser people and problems again, but at last he had turned in his part of the job.

He had not heard another word about the Osborn project until several months later, about four months ago, when old Thayer had announced at a staff meeting that their report had enabled Osborn Enterprises to conclude successfully a history-making multimillion-dollar deal in communications. Now Thayer, on behalf of himself and Turner, wanted to thank every person in the firm who had participated in this dedicated team effort.

Three days after that meeting, old Thayer had summoned Mike Barrett to his office alone. He had offered Barrett a sherry. Unusual. Then he had said that Willard Osborn wished to meet Barrett briefly that very afternoon. No, not at the Osborn Tower Building, but at Osborn's residence north of Sunset Boulevard in Holmby Hills. When Barrett had wondered what it was all about, Thayer had hesitated, then replied that Osborn merely wished to meet him. "I think you will find it interesting," Thayer had added with a pinched smile.

After lunch, Barrett had driven to the Osborn hillside residence. Even though he had been prepared for grandeur, from the reports of colleagues who had been fortunate enough to be invited to the residence, the Spanish hacienda exceeded his expectations. Osborn had remodeled his mansion, Barrett had heard, after the Palacio Liria, the Alba town house near the Plaza de España in Madrid. Barrett had seen photographs of the original, and the smaller replica was equally impressive. There were the colorful gardens guarding the rolling driveway, and beneath tile roofing there were adobe façades with Doric columns in front of imposing pilasters.

Awed, Barrett had allowed himself to be led by an immaculately uniformed maid through the vast entrance hall, down a long, wide passage, and into the high-ceilinged library. There, surrounded by Flemish paintings, and with a magnificent Goya oil as his backdrop, waited Willard Osborn II. He was lounging on a sofa near his ornate desk, teasing a friendly wolfhound, when Barrett appeared. Osborn rose immediately—a tall, droopy, aris-

46

tocratic man with whitish hair, heavy-lidded eyes, angular features—and he shook Barrett's hand. He signaled Barrett to the sofa, and then sat beside him.

Slowly he turned toward Barrett and studied him. "Well, Mr. Barrett," he said after a pause, "you may wonder why I had Thayer send you around. For one thing, I wanted to thank you personally. For another, I wanted to have a look at a young man responsible for making me, in tax savings, two million dollars."

Barrett's eyebrows shot upward when he heard the figure. Osborn did not hide his amusement. "It's true, Mr. Barrett," he went on. "Oh, it wasn't easy to ascertain to whom the credit belonged. Thayer and Turner would have liked to take the credit themselves, or prattle about teamwork, but I wouldn't have that nonsense. I pinned them down. It turned out that, of the many ideas submitted, it was yours that was both the most novel and the most practicable, and it was yours around which they built their proposal." He paused. "A clever legal device—gimmick, as my television colleagues like to put it—and most imaginative. In a time of mediocrity, it is not often that I have the good fortune to meet a young man like yourself. I would be fascinated to know precisely how you conceived the whole tax structure. But first, will you have a cup of coffee with me?"

During coffee they were joined by a third person. Faye Osborn, the host's daughter and only offspring, fresh from the tennis court, had put her head into the library to remind her father of some social engagement. She had been introduced to Barrett. Meeting him, being told of his accomplishment, she had asked if she might have coffee with them.

For the next half hour, it had become increasingly difficult for Barrett to keep his mind on tax matters. Faye's eyes never left him. She seemed to be examining him with the cool objectivity of a horsewoman studying a derby winner soon to be auctioned off for stud. As for Barrett, he found his attention constantly diverted by the glacial beauty of Faye's face and the perfection of her figure. Her sun-blanched blond hair was drawn tightly backward and caught up by a red ribbon. Her features were fine, flawless, Grecian. Her open-throated white blouse offered glimpses of the slopes of her full breasts. Her gracefully crossed legs were long and shapely. Perhaps twenty-eight years old, Barrett guessed. Fin-

47

ishing school in Switzerland, he guessed. And spoiled, he was sure.

When the coffee and conversation had ended, it was Fay Osborn who saw him to the door. At the door she said, "I'm having some interesting people in Saturday night for a buffet dinner. I'd love to have you come."

"I'd be delighted."

"I'm pleased." She stared at him. "Is there someone you want to bring?"

"Not especially."

"Then bring yourself alone. I'll cancel my date. Do you mind being my partner?"

"I was hoping that was it."

And that was it. In the next two months, Mike Barrett had become a regular at the Osborn mansion, always Faye's partner. One evening, as they were returning to Holmby Hills from the Philharmonic Auditorium, Faye asked to see his apartment. After two drinks, curled up against him, she said that she loved him. He admitted that he loved her.

"Why haven't you shown it?" she whispered.

"What do you mean?"

"You've never invited me up here before. And I still haven't seen the bedroom."

"I've been afraid to. You have too much money. It puts me down."

"What if I were a shopgirl or somebody's secretary?"

"I'd have undressed you on the first date."

Her hand caressed his thigh. "Mike, you inverted snob, please undress me."

After that evening, he had begun seeing Faye four and five times a week. Sometimes Willard Osborn II was present, and Barrett often felt that the elder Osborn was taking his measure. Frequently, in the monotony of his legal work, Barrett caught himself daydreaming about what might be possible. It was this daydreaming, alone, that made him hesitate when Abe Zelkin had called him a month ago. Zelkin had wanted to know whether he had made up his mind yet about their partnership. Earlier Barrett had made up his mind to quit the rat race and join up with Zelkin. Now he had hesitated. Perhaps he was merely another one of Faye's indulgences, and perhaps he misread the elder Osborn's interest in him. Yet the daydreams continued. He had told Zelkin that he was overloaded at the office. Also, there was some prospect of a raise, and he wasn't certain yet whether he should leave. Could Abe give him a little more time? Zelkin had said, "A little more, but not too much, Mike. For myself, I can't wait. I've given my notice to the ACLU. I'm quitting and setting up my own office. I can't carry it by myself. I've got several good guys who want to go in with me, but none of them is you, Mike. Look, I'll carry the load alone for a month and keep your desk ready and waiting. I'm expecting you to say yes by then. I'll wait for you to call."

Barrett had continued putting off that call. But three days ago he had almost decided that, while his relationship with Faye was the real thing, his hope about her father was something else and quite unreal, and that he should telephone Zelkin and agree to their partnership. Then, two days ago, Faye had telephoned. Her father wanted to see him that evening, after dinner, on business.

On business. His hope danced, until he grabbed it and locked it out of sight.

There they were, that evening, in the library once more, he and Willard Osborn II.

"Michael," Osborn had said, "I think you're shrewd enough to know I've been keeping an eye on you. I've been waiting for the right moment to bring this up. Now the timing is right, and I've made up my mind. I'm sure you've heard me discuss that Midwest television network that was coming on the market. I can have it, if certain tax details can be worked out. I need the right man to negotiate this. I've had the choice of promoting one of my older men or taking on someone new. I've decided on someone new. There's only one condition. The new man would have to be available to take over by early next week. Michael, how would you like to be a vice-president of Osborn Enterprises starting at seventy-five thousand a year?"

The jackpot, at long last.

There had been an excited sleepless night. His mind had been a happy Mardi Gras, except for one very real demon. He was on a project that might take weeks to resolve, and he had an understanding with his employers that he would not abandon a project

49

without their consent. Yesterday morning he had been in the office early, awaiting Thayer's arrival. He had gone in to see Thayer, and he had blurted out Osborn's fantastic proposal. Sniffing, Thayer had listened. As he finished, Barrett felt that he could expect resistance. But old Thayer had merely sat up and said, "I'll send Magill in to see you. Brief him on your project, and he'll take over. You can terminate tomorrow morning. Good luck. It's our policy never to stand in anyone's way." By the emphasis Thayer put on "anyone's way" Barrett knew that the old man did not mean Barrett's way, but Osborn's way. And this morning he was free.

He had wanted to telephone Faye immediately, and then her father, and make his acceptance formal. Instead, he had called Abe Zelkin to make a lunch date, not having the courage to tell him on the phone what had happened. He still wanted to telephone the Osborns, but his sense of order, of chronology, of first things first, would not permit him to do it. He must see Zelkin first, get that unhappy task over with, clear the decks, and then he would be truly free.

And here he was with Abe Zelkin.

Barrett slowly opened his eyes to the present, and to his surprise there was Zelkin, in the booth across from him, grinning at him.

"I was wondering when you'd come out of the trance," said Zelkin. "For a guy with only good news, you sure looked stricken. Or were you in yoga meditation, and was that the face of ecstasy? Well, I tell you, I feel good, Mike." He picked up his knife and fork and dug into the hamburger steak. "It's sure taken us long enough to get together."

"Abe, let me—"

"Okay, I'm sorry. You were going to tell me how it happened."

"Yes, let me tell you the whole thing." He picked at his salad without eating it. "It goes back to that day when I first met Faye Osborn. You remember, I told you about that."

"Great girl, Faye."

"Yes, but that's not the story. The story is her old man. Now, don't bust in, Abe. Let me tell it all, because that's why I'm here."

Carefully, sorting and rearranging the events that he had just reviewed in his memory, Barrett began to relate the growth of his relationship with Willard Osborn II. Eventually he came to the point where Faye had told him that her father wanted to see him privately. Then he began to recount the meeting with Osborn in his library the night before last, and he tried not to watch Zelkin when he quoted Willard Osborn's offer of seventy-five thousand a year and a vice-presidency.

He tried not to watch, but he could not help seeing Zelkin's pumpkin face come up from the hamburger and go taut beneath the fat. Zelkin ceased eating.

It was no use avoiding the hurt eyes. Barrett looked up. "I'm seeing Osborn tomorrow night. I'm going to accept his job. I'm sorry, Abe, but I have to. I don't feel there's any choice. Much as I have wanted to go with you, something like this Osborn thing comes up once in a lifetime. I can't let the brass ring pass. I've got to grab. I—I hope you'll try to understand."

Absently Zelkin touched the napkin to his mouth. "Well, what the devil, what can I say? I can't say what I offered you is better as far as material things go. I mean, our law office could give you only crumbs compared to this. You could work thirty years and still never see seventy-five thousand dollars in three years, let alone one. And, while I got us some nice attractive offices, they'd be like storage rooms compared to what Osborn can give you. And clients—well, you know, we'd have the helpless and the dregs alongside the big shots you're going to be meeting with now. The question is . . . what you're after."

Barrett would not allow himself to weaken. "I know what I'm after, Abe."

"Do you? I never felt you were certain, even after you threw over the Good Government Institute to play Get Rich Quick. After all, you *were* considering going in with me."

"I was. That was sincere. But that was before this Osborn position came up. That's the one I've spent years waiting for."

Zelkin shook his head. "I'm still not convinced that's what you want. Forget the do-good part of you. Technically, you can do good for the rich, too. Like A. J. Liebling once put it about the columnist Westbrook Pegler. He said, 'Pegler is a courageous defender of minorities—for example, the people who pay large income taxes.' Forgive me, Mike. I didn't mean to say it to shiv you. I meant it as a funny. Only it came out bitter. Let me put it this way, Mike. You are an attorney, and what you're going into isn't law, it's business. You're going to become a businessman. Granted that in the eyes of the world you'll be a big success. But in your own eyes, Mike, you've got to see sooner or later that the challenges won't be the same as in our kind of law. The people won't be the same as real people, and they won't need the kind of help only you could give the clients who'd come to us. What's there in it for you?"

"Money," said Barrett bluntly. Nobody, not even Zelkin, was going to cast him as some goddam Benedict Arnold. "Honest money, honestly earned. As Milton put it, 'Money brings honor, friends, conquest, and realms.' Aptly from *Paradise Regained.*"

"Well, as Thackeray put it," said Zelkin softly, " 'We often buy money very much too dear.' "

Barrett was suddenly exasperated. "Abe, to quote nobody but myself, please don't give me any more of that crap. Let me tell you something, something that I've never told you about completely. My mother scrimped and pinched pennies and deprived herself to put me through Harvard, through law school. She and the old man came over on immigration boats, steerage, when they were kids, and grew up scared and alone, and were pushed around because they were poor. After they met up and got married in Chicago, my father worked twenty-five hours a day to keep his head above water and set aside a few bucks for a rainy day. And when he keeled over, there was that sum in the bank, a pitiful sum by our lights, to keep my mother and me alive."

"Mike, I know about such things," said Zelkin. "It wasn't so different with my parents."

"All right, then it should be easier for you to comprehend the rest. Because when I got out of high school, my mother wouldn't play it safe with her little loot. She knew what it was all about in little golden America. It was money talks, and if you want to learn the language you'd better go to school, and it better be the best school around. And then if you make it, you'll be somebody and you can be independent and nobody can push you around. So she shot what was left on her son, so he could go to Harvard and make it. So far, so good, and some of that you already know."

"Of course I know, and I can appreciate—"

"You can't fully appreciate what I'm saying, Abe, because

there's something you don't know. And after you hear it, Abe, don't give me any of that Freudian twaddle about mothers and sons and why my mother did it and what that's done to me and that crap. Look, I'm as grown-up as you and I'm a big Freud man, but I'm sick and tired of a whole smart-ass generation that makes you some kind of neurotic nut if you say something good about your mother, or defend her, or say you owe her something. Well, dammit, I say the way Confucius say that I owed her plenty. She did nothing for me in order to get paid back. She did it for the pleasure of knowing I might be more than she and my father had been by society's standards. But I owed her plenty, and when it was time to pay back, when she was in need, I couldn't pay her, because I didn't have the legal tender of the realm. I had only the counterfeit scrip of idealism."

"Mike, I didn't mean—"

"Let me finish," Barrett went on, harshly. "I'll make it short and sour. After school, I passed up some good opportunities to take that job with the Institute and make the world more humane for humanity. It was just about the time I met you. My mother came down with a serious illness, serious. I'll spare you the medical details. To stay alive, she needed the best surgeons, the best care, the best of everything. She needed money. Where was the money? I'm talking about life-and-death money now, not luxury money. Where was it? No more rainy-day fund. That had been invested in me. And me, I was too busy doing good to save a dime."

"You were busy doing what you had to do, making your way. You were only beginning—"

"Abe, don't give me any prefab apologies for my guilts. What I was doing was copping out, turning my back on realities and responsibilities, indulging myself in my little anarchy and pretending there wasn't a great big real world out there that had to be dealt with. Look, Abe, the facts. I needed fast money, and I didn't have it. I had praise and merit badges, but they weren't legal tender. Money was legal tender, and I determined to get it. Do you know where I went scratching for it?"

"I have no idea, Mike," said Zelkin quietly.

"I had only one hookup with the world of affluence. Phil Sanford. I went to him. Long before this, he had once begged me to come into his family's publishing house with him and make some real dough, and I'd treated his invitation like I'd been invited to work in a house of sin. I was an attorney and I belonged outside, busily attorneying. Now here I was, hat in hand, saying I had changed my mind and I wouldn't mind taking a better-paying job with Sanford House. Well, I'll always give credit to Phil for this. He may be a lightweight and insensitive in some areas, but that day I went to him his third ear was on my wave length and his perceptions were keen. He sensed trouble and he insisted on knowing why this drastic change of heart about my choice of career. At first I wouldn't tell him, but after we went out and belted a few drinks I spilled my guts, told him the whole thing. Well, he wouldn't have me diverted from my profession by my need for money. 'Why, if it's only money,' he said—*only* money— and he pressed the money I needed on me. A loan. With it I bought the best surgeons, and they saved my mother, and with it I was able to give her the best care possible in her remaining days. That should have been my lesson. Money talks. Money saves. Money shall make you free. But one lesson is not enough when you're young. It wasn't until my mother had another crisis—and this part you know about—and they began treating her with that drug which, we found out later, should have been banned, that I learned my second lesson. After the drug killed her, I learned the do-gooders wouldn't do good if they had to fight one of the sources of their income. No, not until then did I get lesson number two and the full message. That's when I made my vow. I'm a slave, I told myself, and only money can set me free, and if the Main Chance ever comes, I vow to take advantage of it. That's why I have to go with Osborn Enterprises."

Zelkin had been very still, staring down at his empty coffee cup. Finally he nodded. "I see," he said. "I mean, I can understand."

"Just to be sure you do," said Barrett, "let me add one last thing. I've met some of the Hollywood entertainment crowd, and they have a popular saying, one that is crude but tells it all in a single sentence. The saying is, 'You've got it made when you've got "fuck-you" money.' That's it in a nutshell. When you've got enough money to say, 'Fuck you, buster,' to any bastard on earth, then and only then are you your own man. I intend to be my own man."

Zelkin smiled weakly. "I read you loud and clear, Mike, only— only there are many ways of being your own man."

"Fair enough." Barrett extracted his credit card from his wallet and placed it on the restaurant check. "Let me pay, Abe. After all, I'm going to be a vice-president."

"Okay. I'll get it next time."

Barrett suddenly felt better. "I'm glad you said 'next time.' I was hoping you would. I didn't want this to hurt our friendship."

"Don't worry," said Zelkin. "I like rich friends, too."

Barrett signed the credit-card charge slip, put down a tip, and consulted his wristwatch. "I'd better hustle. I've got less than a half hour to get downtown to the Hall of Justice and our Mr. Duncan. You don't mind if I rush off, Abe? Remember, it is my farewell performance as a do-gooder—a do-gooder who also wants to clean up his last debt."

IT WAS THREE MINUTES before his scheduled appointment when Mike Barrett strode toward the half-century-old building where District Attorney Elmo Duncan had his headquarters and exerted control over 260 lawyers in his department. Above the high arched entrance, chiseled into stone, were the intimidating words HALL OF JUSTICE.

Pushing through one of the doors, Barrett hastened down the short flight of steps, went past the familiar lobby arcade with its numerous food-and-drink-vending machines, and caught the elevator. On the sixth floor, he found the curved modernistic reception desk, and he was directed straight ahead through another doorway into another broad corridor. Across from the press room he came upon the door with lettering painted on its glass panel that said "Elmo Duncan, District Attorney."

Inside, there was a medium-sized room with two desks. On the one to his left was a name marker for "Lt. Hogan," whom Barrett knew to be the District Attorney's driver and bodyguard. The chair at this desk was unoccupied. Across the room, past the grouping of extra chairs and beside a copying machine, was the other desk, a busier-looking one, and this one was occupied. Not until Barrett had reached the clacking typewriter did the receptionist become aware of him. She looked up apologetically as he introduced himself. Quickly consulting her appointment sheet, she nodded and told Barrett that District Attorney Duncan was expecting him in the office of Mr. Victor Rodriguez, his special assistant and chief of the Appellate Division. Mr. Rodriguez' office was at the opposite end of the corridor. She would buzz the District Attorney and alert him that Mr. Barrett was on his way.

Retracing his route, Barrett continued up the corridor until he came to the Appellate Division. As he entered, the lone occupant of the room, a pretty, brown-haired girl, ceased typing and stood up. "Mr. Barrett? Right this way. The District Attorney can see you now."

She held open a door to an inner office, and Barrett thanked her and walked past her. Two men were standing beside a table that was backed up against a desk, and they were deep in conversation. Barrett recognized Elmo Duncan at once. He was the taller of the pair, at least six feet tall. He had slick blond hair, narrow blue eyes, a thin nose and a cleft chin. His complexion was light and faintly freckled. He was tastefully dressed in a tailored blue alpaca suit and a blue-and-white-striped shirt. His companion, stockier, had jet-black curly hair and a swarthy face with a conspicuous nose over a neatly trimmed but full moustache.

The moment that the door had closed behind Barrett, Duncan looked up, broke off his conversation, and came forward with a broad smile and an extended hand. Shaking hands, he said, "Good to see you, Mr. Barrett. Sorry to give you all that legwork. I can only get things done when I slip out of my office. Victor and I— Oh, perhaps you two haven't met. This is Victor Rodriguez, my assistant. Victor, meet Mike Barrett, one of our more successful attorneys."

Barrett shook Rodriguez' hand as Duncan stood beside them.

"Mr. Rodriguez will be leaving us—he has an outside meeting —unless you need him here," said Duncan. "You said you wanted to discuss the—the— What was that fellow's name?"

"Ben Fremont," said Rodriguez.

"Yes, Fremont," said Duncan. "Well, Victor Rodriguez is the man in charge of our pornography cases. Of course, like everything else, I review them, but if you'd prefer to have Mr. Rodriguez sit in . . ."

"That won't be necessary," said Barrett.

Quickly Rodriguez took leave of them. Duncan gestured toward two leather chairs facing the desk. "Sit down. Make yourself comfortable."

Barrett went to one of the leather chairs and pulled it away from the shelves of law books and closer to the desk. Duncan had gone behind the glass-topped desk and lowered himself into the leather swivel chair. He indicated a pitcher of water, but Barrett shook his head. Duncan offered a pack of cigarettes. "I'll stay with my pipe, if you don't mind," said Barrett.

Duncan lit his cigarette, while Barrett busied himself filling his English shell briar and then applying a match to the tobacco.

"I guess this is the first time I've seen you outside Willard Osborn's little palace," Duncan said. "How is Willard these days? I don't have time for television, but everyone else seems to watch it, so I suppose he's doing tolerably well."

Barrett smiled. "I'd say he has no problems beyond Internal Revenue."

"I wish that were my only problem," said Duncan cheerfully. "You know, Willard Osborn's one of the few wealthy men I've met whom I'd like even if he were poor. He's very clever and entertaining."

Barrett agreed. He was tempted to let the District Attorney know that he would shortly be a vice-president in the Osborn Enterprises, to impress him even more. But, as Duncan went on, Barrett saw that it was not necessary to identify himself further with Osborn. Elmo Duncan was doing it for him. The District Attorney was recalling several of the Osborn dinner parties at which Barrett had been present, and he was saying complimentary things about Faye, and then he was digressing into a long anecdote about a lawsuit in which Osborn had been involved and which was a perfect example of Osborn's shrewdness.

Time was passing, and abruptly Elmo Duncan stopped, lit a fresh cigarette off the stub of the old one, rolled his swivel chair in tight to the desk, and said, "Enough of that. I'm sure you want to get down to business. What can I do for you, Mr. Barrett?"

Barrett took the pipe from his mouth, emptied it into the ashtray on the desk. "You can do me a favor," he said.

"You name it. Anything—within reason."

"I'm not here for Willard Osborn. I'm here representing another client, an old friend of mine in New York. Philip Sanford, the head of Sanford House, publisher of *The Seven Minutes*, that book—"

"I know. The Ben Fremont matter."

"Exactly." Barrett studied the handsome blond behind the desk. "Mr. Duncan, may I ask, have you read the book?"

"To be quite frank about it—no."

"Neither have I," said Barrett. "But a number of important critics and professors have read it and had written about it long before its first publication in the United States, and they have found considerable merit in it. This is not some piece of hard-core pornography created for commercial profit and dumped into drugstores and bookshops by some sleazy printer of filth out in Reseda or Van Nuys. This is the life's work of a legendary figure of the thirties, and it is being published by one of the most renowned and prestigious firms in the book trade. This little action by the police this morning has caused my client some embarrassment and may cause him considerable financial hardship. So I thought it made sense to come up here and—"

"Let me see," said Elmo Duncan as he lifted a pile of manila folders from the edge of the desk. "Let me see what this is all about." He was checking the folder tabs. "Here it is. 'Fremont, Ben. Section 311.'"

He extracted the folder and set the others aside. Before opening it he said, "Of course, I'm sure you understand, we don't make these arrests casually. They are always preceded by a careful investigation. I do know that after the complaint was received, Rodriguez and his aide—that's Pete Lucas, who's a specialist in pornography and a capable trial attorney to boot—both read the book in question with care. Well, let me see." He opened the folder and began scanning and turning the pages inside.

Barrett remained silent and busied himself with refilling and lighting his pipe. Puffing steadily, he waited.

When Duncan was through with the folder, he placed it on the desk, and rubbed his chin. "Well, now, what I'm going to tell you is off the record, but what I think it comes down to is this. Mrs. Olivia St. Clair, president of the STDL in Oakwood, filed the complaint. Pete Lucas, and then Victor Rodriguez, as I said, read the novel. There was no question in their minds but that it was pornographic. The question was whether it was legally obscene by contemporary community standards."

"Since the book has been seized, I wanted to make that point," said Barrett quickly. "Once, in Flaubert's time, *Madame Bovary* was considered obscene. Today it's merely a mild and sad story about an unfaithful wife. Why, recently I read a respectably published memoir of an anonymous Victorian gentleman—it was called *My Secret Life*—in which the author explicitly recounts how he 'fucked'—his word—twelve hundred women of twenty-seven countries and eighty nationalities. The only one he missed, I think, was a Laplander."

Duncan had been squirming uneasily, but now he forced a laugh.

"That's right," Barrett went on. "When that Victorian wrote his book, he couldn't get it published. In our time it has been a best seller, and I don't think it made any reader's hair turn white. Why? Because times have changed. It's a new ball game. As one professor pointed out, sexual activity is no longer contrary to the prevailing ethos. So why not write about sex as openly as it is being performed? I think it was Anatole France who said—of all sexual aberrations, chastity is the strangest."

Duncan gave the slightest smile, but did not speak. He waited.

Since he still had the floor, Barrett decided to take advantage of it. "Nor do I think this openness about sex has hurt any of us in our country. Dr. Steven Marcus once wrote about this new permissiveness. 'It does not indicate to me moral laxness, or fatigue, or deterioration on the part of society. It suggests rather that pornography has lost its old danger, its old power.' I fully concur."

The District Attorney stirred. "Well, there is a good deal of truth in much of what you say, but I can't agree with it entirely. Perhaps some pornography has lost its old danger, but not all of it, I'm afraid. We could spend a day, a week maybe, arguing this highly complicated problem."

"Forgive me," said Barrett. "I didn't intend to go on the way I did. We all get carried away sometime. I meant to confine myself to the Jadway book. I'll admit that in the thirties, forties, fifties, *The Seven Minutes* might have been regarded as obscene, but today—? Mr. Duncan, have you been to the movies lately? Have you seen for yourself, on the screen, acted out, not only copulation, but female masturbation, homosexuality, well, you name it? I only contend that today, to the average person, by contemporary community standards, by modern standards, the Jadway book is no more or less explicit than other works of far less artistic merit. So why the arrest?"

"Yes, well, yes, that was the debatable point. But our people finally came to the decision they did for two reasons. A large group of average and community-minded women had made the complaint, thereby reflecting that this book had exceeded what is acceptable by contemporary standards—"

"Do you consider the kind of women who form a decency club as average?" said Barrett acidly.

"Of course I do," said Duncan with surprise. "They're no different from any other women. They marry, have children, do housework, cook, entertain, read books. Certainly they're as average as can be."

Barrett wanted to challenge the District Attorney on this, but he realized that Duncan was sincere—hadn't Abe Zelkin called him "honest" and "square"?—and nothing would be gained by antagonizing him. Barrett kept his peace.

"And if ladies like that, a big organization, a very big one—" Duncan went on.

A big organization translated into a lot of voters, Barrett thought, remembering that Zelkin had also called the District Attorney "political."

"—if they feel disturbed by this book, it tells us that maybe there are more people in Oakwood with high standards of decency than may be evident in the numbers who attend some of the films you mentioned. That was first in our minds. Second, and more important, was that we felt this whole outpouring of shock literature, disgusting sadomasochistic slime, was increasing and must be stopped, especially must be stopped so that it is not available to the young and impressionable. Perhaps, as you stated it, times have changed, moral boundaries have expanded, allowing for more candor and tolerance. Yet there are limits, there must be boundaries somewhere. Perhaps, as one Congregationalist clergyman so aptly put it, this country is suffering from an orgy of open-mindedness. I remember attending a speech delivered in the East by Pennsylvania Supreme Court Justice Michael Musmanno. In that address he said, 'A wide river of filth is sweeping across the nation, befouling its shores and spreading over the land its nauseating stench. But what is most disturbing of all is that persons whose noses should be particularly sensitive to this olfactory assault do not smell it at all. I refer to District Attorneys and prosecuting officers throughout the nation.' Well, Mr. Barrett, I've never forgotten those words. I intend to be one of the District Attorneys who does smell the stench."

"Certainly," said Barrett. "Everyone wants to do away with the smell of commercialized hard-core pornography—"

Duncan held up his hand. "No. The sleazy back-street peddlers of hard-core pornography are not the ones we worry about. We worry that this same kind of obscene matter will be given respectability by notable imprints like Sanford House and become available in every bookstore. It is precisely because of Sanford's reputation that we selected this Jadway book, to serve notice on the powerful publishers that this thing has reached its outer limit and must come to an end. Now, this was the basis for the arrest this morning. But actually, Mr. Barrett, I don't want to overstate our case or my feelings. I mean, specifically in the matter of Ben Fremont I don't feel that strongly. I do feel strongly about the whole trend in literature and motion pictures in this country, but I had no intention of making the People versus Ben Fremont our *cause célèbre*. No. We have more important crimes on our investigative agenda and court calendar. This is a relatively small thing."

"Well, then . . ."

"It's those women in Oakwood. They were pressuring our office, with some justification, and we had to satisfy them. I'm sure you can understand that."

"And with Fremont's arrest you've satisfied them," said Barrett.

"Right," said Duncan. "We've done our duty. But now, also, you have a client and you have a duty. I'm willing to be cooperative, within the limitations of what has already happened. The arrest has been made. The accused has been booked. You've got him out on bail. What's the next step you have in mind?"

Barrett drew on his pipe, and watched the smoke billow upward. At last he leaned against the desk. "I want to be reasonable, too, Mr. Duncan. I think this would satisfy my client. I would like to see Ben Fremont plead guilty and have him pay a fine of twenty-four hundred dollars, but in return his one-year jail sentence might be suspended. If that trade could be arranged, that would satisfy us."

"Mmm, well, if that could be arranged, you do understand that entering a plea of guilty would be tantamount to a banning of *The Seven Minutes* throughout Oakwood. All the other bookstores in Oakwood would be afraid of the STDL and of our proceeding against them also."

"We don't give a damn about Oakwood," said Barrett. "Let it be unavailable there. In that way, you've satisfied the STDL in that community. Since Oakwood is an unincorporated part of Los Angeles County, a separate area even though it comes under your jurisdiction, it means the book could be suppressed there but would still be sold elsewhere in Los Angeles County."

"That's right."

"Very well. My client is interested in the rest of Los Angeles County, and the effect of any action in Los Angeles on booksellers in other large cities around the country. If the book can remain on sale in most of Los Angeles County, that's all that counts. As for Oakwood, no one in that community will any longer be offended by seeing the book there. And those who want the book can drive a few blocks farther, to Brentwood or Westwood or some other nearby section of Los Angeles, and buy it. That's what it comes to. And in a week or two the book will be on sale in the large cities throughout the nation, and it will have its acceptance. The shock of it will be mitigated by this acceptance, and there won't be any further trouble over it. There you have it, Mr. Duncan."

Barrett waited.

Elmo Duncan stubbed out his cigarette, came to his feet thoughtfully, thrust his hands into his trouser pockets, and walked slowly around the area between the swivel chair and the shelves of massive legal tomes lining the wall.

Abruptly he stopped his pacing.

"Mr. Barrett, what you've suggested sounds reasonable enough to me."

"Good."

"We'll satisfy those ladies. As for Lucas and Rodriguez, they're so immersed in this sort of thing, I'm sometimes inclined to think they're oversensitive to every word they read. Of course, it's understandable. They have to field complaints almost daily. They must answer the complainants, like the group in Oakwood. But I know I can contain my assistants. In fact, I could come to an agreement with you right here and now about reducing the charges, except that I owe my staff the courtesy of discussing this with them first, since they've given the case so much of their time. But I quite agree. This is a nuisance matter, a routine matter, and we can treat it routinely. So let's give ourselves until tomorrow, Mr. Barrett. Let me smooth any ruffled feathers, and when that is done you can enter your guilty plea, and I can promise you that I'll speak to the judge and the result will be no more than the fine and a suspended jail sentence. Fair enough?"

Barrett stood up. "Fair enough."

The District Attorney came rapidly around the desk to shake Barrett's hand and see him to the door. "You be sure to call me around this time tomorrow."

"Don't worry. I won't forget."

As he opened the door, Duncan seemed to remember something. "And, by the way, if you're seeing Willard Osborn soon . . ."

"I'm having dinner with him tomorrow night."

"Well, don't forget to say that you saw me, and that I wanted you to give him my regards and to tell him how pleased I am about the time and attention his network has given me lately. You can tell him I'm most appreciative."

This, thought Barrett, is what it's like in the marketplace, everywhere.

"I'll certainly tell him," said Barrett.

Duncan was looking up at the wall clock. "Now I'd better get cracking. I've got a busy afternoon and an even busier evening."

ALTHOUGH THE SUMMER'S DAY had been mild and warm, with the coming of darkness the winds had begun to whip up from the west and by late evening it was chilly. Especially was it cold on this drive along the ocean.

Shivering slightly from the unseasonable weather, Elmo Duncan huddled deeper in a corner of the rear seat of the Cadillac limousine that Luther Yerkes had sent for him after dinner. Duncan glanced at the windows to see whether they were completely rolled up; they were. He considered asking the chauffeur to turn on the heat, then realized from the landmarks that they were no more than five minutes or so from the Malibu colony and soon enough he would be insulated from the wind and the cold.

After a long, exhausting day, with hardly time enough for him to exchange gossip with his wife or give the children attention or eat a relaxed meal, this ride from his new house in the Los Feliz district to Yerkes' beach place was doubly tiresome. He wished that Yerkes would use his more accessible dwelling, the vast French country-style habitat in Bel-Air, for these conferences. Or, at least, hold the conferences at his desert residence in Palm Springs—on weekends, when the distance did not matter—because the atmosphere was more relaxing. Yet, despite his chafing, he understood the wisdom of using the beach place. It was secluded. Yerkes put much importance on his right to personal privacy, and more so when he did not wish his behind-the-scenes activities subjected to public knowledge and speculation.

These regular meetings between the District Attorney of Los Angeles and California's wealthiest industrialist, which might be regarded with suspicion by many persons, had begun some months ago as weekly conferences, but now that Harvey Underwood and Irwin Blair had been retained and brought into them they had become two- and three-times-a-week conferences. Later the alliance between Duncan and Yerkes would have to come out. As yet it was too early, and a vital tactic was to keep the opposition, Senator Nickels' political organization, unsuspecting and therefore off guard. Tonight, aside from those with whom Duncan was meeting, only two persons knew of his destination. One was his wife, and the other his chief of police.

As he idly watched the beach cottages that ran along flush with the Pacific Coast Highway pass by his view, the thought came to Duncan—as it often did at this stage in the drive—that he was extremely lucky to have been tapped for bigger things by a king-maker. Many of those beach houses out there were the second homes, the summer homes, of the affluent. It would be nice to have one for the family. It would be nice to have much more than that. Even better, it would be wonderful to have power.

Elmo Duncan had been raised in Glendale, strictly lower middle class, no poverty or real deprivations, but no extras or advantages either. His elders in the caste system of his youth had warned: Never exceed the budget, and know your place. Well, perhaps living with that had been an advantage in itself. He had seethed to rebel against a life that revolved around economy (you thought of money before anything else, because you had to) and against a life that demanded humbleness (you had to listen to other people who were your economic superiors, while they never had to listen to you). All things considered, he had come a long way. The night that he had learned he had been elected district attorney by an amazing majority, he had thought that he had achieved the absolute pinnacle of success. Only after two dramatic court cases, which he had prosecuted with great intensity and skill and which had made his name a household word in Los Angeles, had he heard the first whisperings of what was possible. Even after he became aware that there were summits beyond what he had already achieved, he had not believed himself capable of attaining one of those loftier positions. That is, he had not believed it until the fabulous Luther Yerkes had reached out and knighted him. And even Elmo Duncan knew that Yerkes never picked losers.

Recollecting the golden weekend—last winter, it had been, in Luther Yerkes' desert hideaway in Palm Springs—Duncan was once again warmed and his weariness was shed. When he had arrived on a Friday evening for that weekend, Duncan had tried to speculate on the purpose behind the invitation. Yerkes needed no favor from a mere District Attorney. Yerkes had no interest in collecting Names. So there could be only one motive behind his invitation, and it could not be social. Yet, as the Friday gave way to Saturday, and Saturday passed, and most of Sunday also, without his making any overture, Duncan's hopes had deflated completely.

He remembered that before dinner of that final day in the desert—he was to drive back to Los Angeles immediately afterward—he hated himself for having been unrealistically ambitious, and he hated Yerkes for having made a fool of him in his own eyes. He remembered his first impression of Yerkes. It had been one of distaste, a heresy toward a kingmaker that he would not admit to himself until the beginning of the final evening, when his disenchantment had gradually set in.

Luther Yerkes was a scant five feet five, yet he weighed 180 pounds. He had a round head crowned by a disconcerting auburn hairpiece. His fat face was bland, imperturbable, almost benign at first sight. It was the chubbiness and the layers of chin, plus the external trappings of power, Duncan had guessed, that deceived the court visitor. But as you came to know Yerkes, watch him at the ticker tapes, overhear him on the telephone, talk to him, the blue-tinted glasses he always wore indoors no longer hid the small marble eyes, and the bland fleshy face no longer masked the cunning, conceited, arrogant man behind it. The feminine bejeweled hands and mincing walk were lies also, because the hands figuratively disguised brass knuckles and could sign a death sentence, and the walk enabled him to keep his balance even when he walked over other people's heads.

The last evening of that winter weekend in the desert, they had dined alone. The moment after the entrée had been served, Luther Yerkes had begun to speak in that clipped, faintly hoarse voice, and, except to gulp a mouthful of food, he had not ceased speaking to Duncan for almost a half hour. He had invited Duncan here because he had heard many favorable things about him. Before inviting him, he had investigated Duncan's past and present life and career, and even his family and distant relatives and friends. So he had heard about Duncan. He had learned about him. But he had not seen him in person or in action or listened to him. That was what Friday night and Saturday and most of this day had been all about. To size Duncan up.

Now he wanted to tell Duncan that he had sized him up, and Duncan fit. Fit what? Why, the boots of the next United States Senator from California. Senator Nickels? Certainly he would run for re-election. But he no longer fit. He'd got too big for his boots. He could be defeated. Yet only by the right man. Yerkes had decided that Elmo Duncan was the right man. If he was big enough to take guidance, he would be big enough for the United States Senate. Duncan had always been a quick study, and he understood "guidance" to mean that if he went along, if he were to achieve one of the highest seats in the land, he would be expected to remember who had put him there.

Duncan had always had high regard for, and pride in, his own integrity. He had also learned along the way that one remembers friends and one compromises on small matters to achieve greater

66

ends if one is to be a politician. And somehow one's integrity remains intact, at least most of it, enough of it. And he sensed that Luther Yerkes understood and respected to what degree he might be willing to be Yerkes' man. In Duncan's eyes, Yerkes had undergone one more metamorphosis. Yerkes was kind and intelligent and handsome and fatherly. And by the time Yerkes had walked him to his car, Duncan had agreed to take guidance. Yerkes would be his mentor and his patron.

Elmo Duncan had hummed aloud and happily all the three-hour drive back to Los Angeles.

Only later, a few days later, had he decided to investigate his patron just as his patron had investigated him. Duncan had always known that Yerkes was rich and powerful. Now, because he was curious and his wife was curious, he determined to learn the extent of Yerkes' riches and power. Duncan's wife, Thelma, had done the research. Luther Yerkes' aerospace and electronics holdings were too vast and intricate for a layman to grasp. He owned the fifty-million-dollar Space Parts Center, employing seven thousand workmen and technicians, near San Diego. His Flight Propulsion Division at the edge of Pasadena had grossed one billion dollars last year. His Recomm Company in Dallas had outbid Lockheed Aircraft, Boeing, and Douglas with its air-frame proposal for a new 290-ton supersonic transport plane, and this resulted in a contract that might eventually earn him twenty-seven billion dollars of potential sales. Somewhere he had control of a Data Systems Division that turned out process-control computers. He had joined foreign firms to finance projects in the Middle East and in Latin America.

Yerkes was sixty years old and had not married again after a divorce almost forty years ago. His sports were marlin fishing and a big-league baseball team he owned. His hobbies were collecting French Impressionist art and vintage Rolls-Royces and Bentleys. His interest in politics had never been made public. Yet there was evidence that he had financially supported four presidential candidates, six senatorial candidates, and three candidates for governor, and always against opponents whose campaign promises threatened his holdings. Every candidate Yerkes had supported, as far as Duncan had been able to learn, had been elected to office. Yerkes' obsession was money. His politics backed no one party, only his obsession, and its sole platform appeared to be: Defeat anyone who has obstructed or wishes to obstruct the progress of free enterprise.

It gave Elmo Duncan a heady sensation to know that Luther Yerkes was taking not just a financial interest but a personal interest in building Duncan as a candidate for the Senate.

"Here we are, sir," the chauffeur announced.

Duncan realized that they had turned off the Pacific Coast Highway and entered the gate beside the guardhouse of the Malibu colony, and were now drawing up before Yerkes' sprawling beach place.

As the limousine stopped, Duncan, without waiting for the chauffeur, opened the car door and stepped down on the flagstone walk. The gusty wind tore at his smooth blond hair and curled his trench coat against his legs. He pressed the doorbell, and a few seconds later the Scottish butler admitted him and took his coat.

"They're waiting in the billiard room, Mr. Duncan."

"Thank you."

He strode quickly through the grilled breezeway, a heated kidney-shaped indoor swimming pool on one side of him, a brace of dressing rooms and sauna baths on the other side. Once in the house, he crossed past the grand piano in the parlor and descended the three steps into the comfortable billiard room, which was dominated not by a billiard table but by a huge ornate antique pool table.

Harvey Underwood, who resembled a thoughtful heron, wearing his usual meditative look and inevitable English tweeds, was arranging three balls on the table, as Irwin Blair, rumpled wavy hair and baggy beige Dacron suit, chalked his cue stick and announced that he couldn't make this trick shot more than once out of three times. Luther Yerkes, popping a mint into his mouth (he had given up smoking recently), watched them with disinterest. Yerkes was attired in a checked sport shirt, clay-colored slacks, and ridiculous ankle-high suede Indian boots. To the critical eye, he looked like Hetty Green's twin brother, had she had a twin brother. To Duncan, still, he looked superb.

Duncan ran his comb through his disheveled hair, put it away, and then gave a stage cough. Yerkes looked up, peered through his bluish glasses, and came to him immediately.

"Elmo, glad you made it at last."

"We were delayed by the traffic on Sunset," said Duncan. "I hated to hold you up." The other two were greeting him, and he raised a friendly hand. "Hello Harvey—Irwin."

"Let's go into the living room and get right down to business," said Yerkes. "It's five after ten. We don't want to be all night."

Blair's acne-pocked mobile face registered dismay. "Hey, don't you want to see this trick shot?"

"Yes," said Yerkes with a tinge of sarcasm, "but I want to see you pull one off in your work, not in here. Come on, now."

A cakewalking Punchinello, Yerkes led the procession up the steps and into the huge living room, its airiness stifled by expensive antique furniture of baroque design, gilded mirrors and tables, carved chairs, an aged desk with dazzling mother-of-pearl marquetry. The muffled sounds from the waves rolling up the sand outside were incongruous in this room filled with such furnishings.

There were two deep armchairs facing a ten-foot sofa across a coffee table that looked like a stunted Sendai chest. Yerkes headed toward one armchair, gesturing for Duncan to take the other, and Underwood and Blair automatically found places on the sofa. It was then that Duncan realized that Underwood had been carrying an almost wafer-thin leather portfolio and was now removing some yellow pages from it.

The Scottish butler entered silently with a tray of drinks. The drinking habits of each were already known to him. The butler dispensed the drinks: a brandy snifter of armagnac for Yerkes; another snifter of the same for Duncan, who had ordered armagnac on his very first visit only because Yerkes had ordered it, except that his own had a glass of water on the side; a J and B Scotch on the rocks for Underwood; a Coca-Cola for Blair.

The ritual was one sip and swallow each, and the meeting would be under way. Yerkes took up his armagnac, and the others reached for their drinks.

Duncan enjoyed the warming brandy and watched the pair on the sofa. No two men were more different. Underwood was a quiet, factual man, the perfect mathematical product of an age of communications. Blair was a raucous extrovert, full of exaggerated fancies, the perfect image-maker for this same age. Facts and figures provided precise weekly information on what people out there were concerned with and interested in, and this information could then be catalyzed by fancies and inventions into giving the people out there an approximation of what they wanted. The pair were partners. They represented the brains of Underwood Associates. Underwood was one of America's most respected directors of private public-opinion polls taken for politicians and industrialists. He had established Underwood Associates. Later, realizing that he required an adjunct to his business that would implement his findings, thus giving his wealthy clients a complete service, he had taken Irwin Blair into partnership.

Blair had started out as a Hollywood publicity man, but he had been too talented and creative to confine himself to show business. When an actor he handled had determined to run for the United States House of Representatives despite the gibes of his colleagues, Blair had risen to the challenge. Because the actor had been charming and attractive, an *actor*, Blair had exposed him to endless rounds of handshaking and personal appearances, and because the actor had been slow-witted and superficially informed, an *actor*, Blair had made him keep his mouth shut and permitted him to open it only to smile. Blair had invented a half-dozen simplified slogans and credited them to the actor in advertisements, in pamphlets, on billboards. Then Blair had gone to work destroying his client's opponent, and in this he had adopted the brilliant earlier techniques used by a firm known as Campaigns, Incorporated, while it had been headed by the ingenious man-and-wife team of Clem Whitaker and Leone Baxter, whom Blair worshiped. Whitaker and Baxter had been retained to defeat Upton Sinclair when he ran for governor of California. They had sought to divert attention from Sinclair's attractive program and instead focus attention on what were made to seem apparent threats in his earlier writings. They had hired a cartoonist to draw thirty cartoons showing the more desirable aspects of California life; then they had him smear a blob of black paint over part of each sweet American scene, and within each blob had been implanted a truncated quotation from Upton Sinclair that made him appear a monster and an anarchist. Upton Sinclair had been defeated. Imitating Whitaker and Baxter, Irwin Blair had demolished his actor client's opponent. The actor had become a congressman by a total vote of three to one. Thereafter Blair had promoted himself from his job as publicity man for entertainment personalities to public-relations consultant for politicians. Soon enough he had joined up with Harvey Underwood.

Three months ago, at an astronomical fee, Luther Yerkes had retained the services of Underwood and Blair on behalf of the candidacy of Elmo Duncan.

Watching them now, Duncan was once more uneasy, as he had been since the day Yerkes had hired them. He hated manipulation, of other people, of himself. These men were in the business of sampling the feelings and desires of the public and playing on those feelings and desires, and in this conspiracy Duncan felt himself merely an instrument. It wasn't dishonest, but it felt dishonest. He hated it, but he went along because even his wife said that he was being too square as usual, and because he wanted to be more than a mere county district attorney.

Underwood was rattling his yellow pages, a prelude to reading off the results of the tabulated findings of his trained interviewers throughout the state who had questioned a thousand persons—a stratified random sampling, scientifically based on the sex, age, religion, race, occupation of each person questioned. Out of these pollings the four of them had tried to find issues with which the public was concerned and to which Duncan might devote himself both in his present office and in his increasing public-speaking engagements. When they had agreed on an issue, they tried to decide how Duncan could make use of it. After that it was Blair's task to make the public aware that Duncan's interests coincided with their own, and that he was ready to champion them and solve their problems.

The first goal, Yerkes had pointed out three months ago, was to make Elmo Duncan's name known to the entire voting population of the state. He must become as well known as was his opponent, Senator Nickels. Once this had been accomplished, work would proceed on making his image more attractive and the incumbent's image less attractive. But the wider exposure of Duncan's name was still the primary problem. Duncan was fairly prominent in Southern California, largely because of that last murder case he had prosecuted so brilliantly. But he still remained

71

a local figure, "a provincial hero," as Yerkes put it. He must become a statewide hero, as well known and worshiped in Fresno, San Francisco, Sacramento, in Salinas, Sonora, Eureka, as he was in Los Angeles.

"Elmo needs one big, big court case, one headliner," he now heard Yerkes say to Underwood, repeating what Yerkes had been saying for weeks. "You've got to come up with something, Harvey, something that is real and that can work."

Duncan found himself nodding in agreement.

A big case involving a vital issue. That was the crux of it.

Underwood rattled his yellow sheets once more. "I can't alter facts, Mr. Yerkes. I have here our latest sampling. We are not questioning the public on international issues yet. We are still confining ourselves to what the registered voters in this state are concerned about domestically. And I must report again that by far the biggest concern our public has—by more than thirty percentage points over taxation and education—is their concern about violence in the streets. That is to say, the worry is about lawlessness, danger, unrest, not just racial, not just organized crime, but the violence engendered by the uncontrolled younger generation. I am not generalizing. You know that I never generalize. Our secondary questions about this concern over violence try to uncover reasons why our subjects feel this condition exists. The same reasons are still being given. We had worked on two of the reasons and couldn't develop an issue, a meaningful issue, for Mr. Duncan. Two weeks ago we went to work on the third one, the feeling that much of this youthful violence and threat stems from or is provoked by the overt salacity in reading matter and films in theaters and on television. Well, we agreed that such a threat came within Elmo's province, that it was something he could work on, and our discussion coincided with the appearance of that book that had been brought to Elmo's attention. Then we agreed he was to try to implement the California Criminal Code on censorship, use the book as an issue to build a statewide case in which he was going to fight the . . . the . . ."

"The publishing Mafia subverting morals," volunteered Irwin Blair.

"Yes," said Underwood, "and by this act and the trial that might follow it, he would become known as a protector of the young and

72

the old, and an enemy of violence-inciting literature. We agreed to try that—"

"We did *not* agree," Duncan interrupted. "The three of you agreed. I was against it from the start."

"You went along with us," Yerkes reminded Duncan mildly. "In the end, you agreed to try it."

"Well, of course, but—" Duncan began.

"And now I am given to understand that you *have* tried it," resumed Underwood. "Mr. Yerkes tells me that you finally made an arrest this morning. Don't you think, before we discuss any new steps, that we should wait to—"

"No," said Duncan flatly. "I came here to talk about that very censorship angle, and I want to talk about it right now. I repeat, I didn't like the angle from the start, and I still don't like it. Now I've been proved right by the press reaction. It should be plain to all of us that the whole thing is a flop. So let's forget it and go on to something with more promise."

Irwin Blair wagged his hand. "Hold it, Elmo. Aren't you being a little impatient? Maybe this Section 311 gimmick will catch on gradually. I admit it didn't go off like a rocket, but—"

"It fizzled, it flopped, and it's a dud," said Duncan with emphasis. He got up automatically, because he was always more effective on his feet. "You're a great one for facts, Harvey. Well, so am I. We charge a book with being obscene, and we arrest a bookseller under Section 311 for purveying an obscene work. Of the four newspapers I've seen since this morning, three barely mentioned the arrest, while one didn't bother to do even that. Of the three that mentioned it, one ran two paragraphs on page six, and the other two gave it a paragraph somewhere near either the want ads or the obituaries."

Irwin Blair came forward so fast he almost tumbled off the sofa. "Look, if you're blaming me," he said defensively, "I've got to point out that I've tried. I alerted the press. They promised to give it space. I can't control what finally goes on in the city room. It must've been cut down or crowded out by hotter news. But at least two news commentators mentioned it on television."

"Calm down, Irwin." It was Yerkes. "No one is blaming you for the lack of attention this received. Elmo isn't blaming you, and neither am I. Let's not waste our valuable time and energies on

73

personal bickering. Elmo is right. We must confine ourselves to facts."

Blair sat back disgruntled, as Elmo Duncan moved behind his chair and then turned to the others. "Yes, fact, gentlemen. The harsh fact is that censorship is not a dramatic issue, because the average man, even though he will grumble about the dangers of provocative smut, finds it difficult to relate a book to all the crimes in the streets. A book is inanimate. To begin with, not enough people know books or read them. And when they do, it is difficult for them to realize that printed pages can in any way threaten their security or their personal lives. In fact, some of them may resent us for interfering with their right to read what they wish or to be titillated by what they read. By interfering in this way, we've satisfied only a handful of bluenoses and Grundys who couldn't swing an election one way or another. Look, I sincerely believe some of the salacious stuff found today in books passing as literature is evil and corruptive, and my office tries to clamp down on the worst of it. But what I believe about this has nothing to do with the possibility of turning censorship, censoring a book, into a major problem of passionate concern to the general public. Moreover, initiating this kind of indictment is hardly image-building. What does it do at best? It pits the District Attorney of a great city against some little two-bit bookseller and against some obscure printed words that not one person in a thousand will ever read or maybe even hear about. Gentlemen, that's a wild mismatch, and it makes me look like a bully. Fortunately, not many people out there are going to know about it, because it was too dull an issue to get space. I say we've got a dead issue, and I suggest we bury it as fast as possible. In fact, I half promised this bookseller's counsel I'd let the case expire quickly and quietly. Gentlemen, believe me, you're not going to excite millions of voters with the proposition that a book can do them grave harm."

"But a book can do grave harm." It was Harvey Underwood speaking from the far end of the sofa. Duncan looked at him sharply, and the other two gave him their attention. Underwood pawed at one bushy eyebrow. "I was thinking," he went on. "As you were speaking, Elmo, I was thinking of books that have been earthquakes, have moved masses of men and whole civilizations to do evil, to create change, to become good. How many millions

74

of human beings died because of a book called *Mein Kampf,* by Adolf Hitler? How many people died or were enslaved because of a book called *Das Kapital,* by Karl Marx? How much violence was instigated, for better or for worse, by a pamphlet or book called *Common Sense,* by Thomas Paine; by an essay in a book called *Civil Disobedience,* by Henry Thoreau; by a book called *Uncle Tom's Cabin,* by Harriet Beecher Stowe?" He paused. "Elmo, don't underestimate the incendiary power of a book."

Duncan frowned, knuckles tightening on the back of the chair. "I won't argue with you about those books, about some books. However, you've left out one factor. Those books you mentioned —they were effective in creating or helping create violence, revolutions, wars, protest, because each was linked directly to an immediate need among masses of people. Those books fulfilled or agitated or inflamed because they were aimed at live issues. Hitler's book told the Germans why they were in trouble and showed them how to get out of it. Marx's book gave a hungry Russia, ripe for revolution, a recipe for eating again. Thoreau's writings gave Gandhi a new weapon stronger than British arms, and it freed his country, and this same Thoreau essay gave American youth the same weapon to use in resisting the military clique in the United States. Certainly a book that is explosive can be used as a piece of dynamite. But what are we working with? What have we got? An obscene sex novel written by an author long dead. A nation filled with people frightened for their lives because of lawlessness and violence. Can we say to those people—We're going to convict this book and those like it, and once we've put it away all of your fears will vanish, or most of them will vanish, because you'll be safer? We can say that, certainly, and it would probably be partially true, but I assure you no one is going to believe it. If you haven't got believers, you haven't got a crusade. Without a crusade, you can't make a hero." Duncan came slowly back to the coffee table, where he halted. "That's why we're here, isn't it?" he said, in a half-mocking tone to alleviate his embarrassment. "To make Elmo Duncan a hero?"

"Elmo, sit down," said Luther Yerkes. "You've spoken your piece, now sit down and finish your drink and let me speak my piece." He slowly took off his bluish glasses and squinted at the others. "I've heard your side, Harvey and Irwin. I've listened to your side, Elmo. Let me be the judge." He addressed himself directly to the pair on the sofa. "Elmo Duncan has done everything we've asked of him. He has cooperated. We suggested he initiate the censorship issue as a trial balloon, to see if it would take hold. As District Attorney, Elmo acted. But he was seriously hampered, in a public-relations sense, by our Criminal Code. He was firing at a pornographic book, and a big one, but the law forced him to aim at the vendor of the book, smaller game. The newspapers were not impressed. Even those two television mentions of the arrest—to be truthful, I arranged one of them, I left a personal message with Willard Osborn's secretary saying that I would appreciate it if one of his stations covered it. Nothing much else, especially nothing spontaneous, happened. In my considered judgment, our District Attorney is right about the whole matter. A weak campaign issue is like a weak stock. Don't ride it. Get rid of it. Take a brief setback and find yourself a new stock."

"If you say so, Mr. Yerkes," said Underwood.

"I say so," said Yerkes. "I say let's trust Elmo's instinct. He's a born politician, and every born politician has an instinct about what's good for him or bad for him, and that instinct is more useful in understanding the electorate than any computer on earth. Elmo says drop this, find something that will make millions of people sit up, and I agree. What will make them sit up? Not a book, we know. Then what? I'm reminded of something that some writer once said or wrote somewhere. Maybe that's the answer. This writer said that murder mysteries are popular, and everyone is fascinated by them, because murder is the one irrevocable crime. Murder is final. You can get back the jewels, but never a human being's life. In a way, that's it for us too. Elmo here is a politician and our District Attorney. He needs a public issue that can be dramatized in a public prosecution. He needs a big, irrevocable crime, one that by its very nature affects and disturbs the man in the street and the woman in the kitchen. A crime akin to murder. In the light of that, censorship of a book is a small and iffy crime, like the theft of some jewels, affecting a few people but not touching the masses at all. Our job tonight is to find the big issue. Do you go along with me?"

Duncan and Underwood nodded.

Irwin Blair said, "Let's get to work again."

"All right," said Yerkes. He took up his brandy snifter and gently rolled the liquid around the bottom of the glass. Finally he resumed. "Harvey's latest poll reminds us again that the high-priority concern is violence in the streets, the activities as well as the plight of the young, and the uneasiness this is creating among their elders. Very well. Here we have a huge city, and there are all kinds and types of people seething inside it, and, as Elmo will confirm, no minute passes without some kind of disturbance or conflict or crime of violence. What were the last FBI figures? One forcible rape every thirty minutes in these United States. That's one crime. God knows how many others every minute, let alone every thirty minutes. They are going on, these crimes, and they are happening this very instant, and then over and over again. We have to zero in on the right happening and the right moment, and seize the incident, and hand it to Elmo and say, Make your case with this and we will make you known from one end of the state to the other. Now, Harvey, we want to hear every detail of the results of your latest poll. Then we've got to be imaginative and practical at one and the same time, and we've got to determine what single act going on out there in the far-flung city tonight, or any night, is worth grabbing hold of and converting into a case for our Los Angeles District Attorney and a showcase for the next United States Senator from California. One violent act, in the category of murder, not jewel theft, that's all we need. . . ."

JE-SUS, HE THOUGHT, if anyone ever learned the truth, if anyone ever found out, he'd kill himself.

He wanted to kill himself right now, this second.

It was three hours since it had happened, and George was wrong about his feeling better soon, because nothing had helped. The passage of time hadn't helped. The pot hadn't helped. The being with others, that hadn't helped. Nothing. Except maybe now he was less trembling and shaking all over. Now he was numb all over, and sick and crying in his gut and balls, and he wanted blank oblivion, nothingness, goodbye and no memory.

His eyes went from the road ahead to his white hands welded like white hooks to the wheel of his Rover sedan.

He heard George Perkins speak from the seat beside him. "Hey, you sure you're okay?"

77

"I guess so," said Jerry Griffith. "I guess I'm okay now."

"You don't look it. You look like a zombie."

"I'm okay," Jerry Griffith insisted.

He turned the car into the east block of Kelton Avenue, just off the UCLA campus, where his friend George shared his apartment with two other guys.

"There's nothing to worry about," said George, scratching inside his beard. "Forget it. Make like it never happened. If it never happened, then it didn't happen. Put your mind on another plane, like you were in yoga or something. Know what I mean?"

"I'm okay," said Jerry Griffith.

"Hey, cool it, feller, you're driving right past my pad."

Jerry slammed down on the brake with what felt like a stump, not a foot, and the suddenness of stopping made his chest hit the wheel, but it didn't hurt. "Sorry," he said as George pushed himself back from the dashboard.

He waited for George to get out, but George was still there. He realized George was staring at him. George was smoothing his long sandy sideburns and his beard and still staring at him.

"Jerry, feller, just one thing—" George was saying.

He waited to hear the one thing.

"Like I been telling you all night, you're in the clear, you're free. Nobody knows you were there."

"She knows."

"She doesn't know your name."

"I forgot."

"So you're free," said George. "But one thing. If anything went wrong—"

"You said nothing could go wrong."

"It can't, if you won't let it," said George meaningfully. "Like I sometimes tell you, you're your own worst enemy. Like living at home."

"You know, George—"

"Sure, I know all about your old man and you. That's the only thing that worries me. You go in looking unhinged, and he'll pound the shit out of you until he finds out what's eating you. And that gorgeous piece you call your cousin—that Maggie—"

"Cut it out, George."

78

"I got to say what's on my mind. You're bugged by this, but if you confide in her you'll be digging a hole for yourself."

"I told you this is strictly between us."

"Just be sure it is," said George. "Because if it isn't, and something goes wrong, you remember one thing—you were in this solo. I wasn't there. Only you were there. Because if you ever said I was there, I'd consider that an act of betrayal, and I'd have to tell them it was you who hurt her. If you meant to or not, it was you. So that's our agreement. I wasn't there. So I could never say you were there. Do you understand?"

"Okay, George."

George Perkins opened the door, then he hesitated, and his manner was friendly again. "But like I told you, there's nothing to worry about. It didn't happen."

"Okay."

"Just keep a good thought like I'm keeping. You got to admit, she was one helluva lay."

"Yes."

"You can thank me for opening her up. She was tight as a clam when I shoved it in there. But once I got in there, it was like going down a greased slide, and all her squealing and biting and hitting, I almost popped right off. It was great."

"It was great," said Jerry, "if only—"

"Forget the rest of it," said George. "You know my philosophy. Keep the good thoughts and jettison the garbage. Remember that, feller."

"Okay."

"You going straight home?"

"Straight home."

"See you tomorrow, then. See you when you get out of Knight's Lit class."

"See you."

George Perkins left the car, and went up the apartment-building steps two at a time, and disappeared inside.

Jerry Griffith dropped his numb foot off the brake and pressed on the gas pedal. He pointed the Rover toward Veteran Avenue to take Sunset Boulevard to his home in the Pacific Palisades.

It was the shortest way to get home, and he wanted to get home the shortest way, because he was alone and he couldn't take being alone too long a time, not tonight, not the way he felt, which was sicker than before and still suicidal.

But by the time he had reached Sunset Boulevard, and waited for the light to change, and spun the car left toward the Palisades, he knew something else.

He wasn't alone.

The girl was with him, that squealing girl, that Sheri Moore who was eighteen.

Except she wasn't squealing now, no, she was as still as a cadaver, and not uttering a sound and not moving at all.

Jerry considered himself a visual person, because in his head whatever he thought of or remembered was mainly visual, in graphic pictures, not in a lot of wordy dialogue like other people said they had it. He wished he was alone now, but he wasn't. He wished he wasn't visual, but he was.

It was there, that one picture that kept projecting itself inside his skull.

The one picture that he took with his brain before he left, before George dragged him out of there.

The girl lying flat on her back, stark naked on the rug beside the bed. She was lying spread-eagled, loose, the fleshy creamy thighs loose and apart so that what you saw most was that mound with the crease in between visible through the pubic hairs and looking like the slash of a woman's lips turned sideways. And one hand up against the night table and the other limp across her navel, and the little cream breasts flattened down, as if deflated, and the mouth hung open and the eyes shut and the red blood still trickling down from the scalp and tangled hair.

That was the picture.

He tried to turn it off, and did for a while, except that other pictures kept sliding into its place because he was visual.

He could see them, George and himself with their Cokes, inside The Underground Railroad, their dance hangout on Melrose Avenue, and George hearing the girl saying to someone else she wished she had a ride to her place, and George striking up a conversation and saying that his friend had a car and where did she live because if it wasn't too far out of the way they'd be glad to drop her off. Her name was Sheri and she had an apartment with a roommate, Darlene, and it was just above Santa Monica Boulevard on Doheny Drive, so that wasn't out of the way.

Another picture. They were parked in front, she was in the back seat with George, and George kidded around, and her thigh was partially showing where her cotton dress had climbed up, and Jerry kept wanting to rip her clothes off and make love all night, imagining it, all visual, when suddenly George was getting out and she was getting out and George was signaling him and saying they'd prove to her they were gentlemen and see her to her place upstairs.

Another picture, upstairs, inside. She'd got up to go to the bathroom that was off the bedroom. George winking, patting his crotch, saying no question she wanted it, whether she knew it or not, she was ripe for it, so maybe he'd better wait for her in the bedroom, and when he was done Jerry could have her.

Another picture, this of the bedroom door closing behind George. And of himself drinking from one of the cans of beer she'd brought out. Then in a short while the door opening partially, and George standing there without a stitch of clothes on, big and hairy with that big wang hanging down the middle, and George grinning and saying, "Just wanted you to know I'm still waiting to give her a little surprise." That moment her voice, and George ducking back into the room, and her voice protesting, and something about Darlene, the roommate, and what sounded like scuffling. And then he himself jumping up and shutting the bedroom door tightly so's not to hear them.

Another picture, blurred. Except there was she naked on the bed now, and himself naked, and the moistness between her thighs and his hand clamping over her mouth.

And then the picture of his getting up, getting his shorts and trousers, and her going after him, and his dropping his clothes and trying to bat her, and her jumping back, the rug going out from under her, and her falling, smashing her head against the sharp corner of the night table, then crumpling, sliding down to the floor, trying to rise, and rolling on her back.

And then a montage of many pictures, this time with dialogue. George running in, his saying what in the hell did you do that for, and his own stuttering and stammering it was an accident.

George's saying for him to get dressed fast. George's bending over her and saying what a mess and she's out cold and thank God she's alive and breathing. His dressing and wanting to telephone a doctor. George's snatching the telephone from him, and saying is he crazy, taking a chance of getting themselves caught. His insisting on an anonymous call to a doctor, and George's insisting no, making him finish dressing, telling him her roommate would be back any minute and would get the doctor and the girl's all right and let's get out of here while we can.

The first picture again. Looking down once more at the nude, spread-eagled body.

The rest of the pictures underexposed, no longer clear. Mostly with fragments of dialogue, with some bits and pieces of visual. In his car, George's driving, and George's saying you're in no shape to go home yet, let's go to The Garage, which was a real garage that George and some of the guys had rented and decorated as a kind of clubhouse for getting together and pot parties, and his saying whatever George wanted to do was okay with him. Walking to The Garage and George's saying he had it figured out whatever happened it was going to be all right, because if Sheri was patched up and none the worse for it, she wouldn't talk, because then she'd have to explain how she let herself be picked up, because after all there was no evidence anyone busted into her place to rape her, and if she was in serious shape or worse then she wouldn't be able to talk so that was that. Inside The Garage there were three of the guys, and two of the girls, regulars, and plenty of grass, and despite the incense you could smell it, but nobody cared, and he had himself a joint and inhaled it deeply and held the smoke and it settled him down a little, just a little, but not enough. After that he and George went for another long walk, until he could take the wheel himself and he took it to show he was better and then he drove George to his apartment.

One last picture, again, again, the first one. The girl lying flat on her back, stark naked on the rug beside the bed, with the damp vaginal mound and the blood-clotted hair on her head.

He had to pull himself together or he'd be asking for trouble. He looked at the dashboard clock. It was almost midnight. His mother and father would be asleep. Probably Maggie too. He was safe.

He twisted the wheel at the service station on the corner and left Sunset Boulevard, accelerating the car up the incline until he arrived at their driveway. Entering between the hedges, he turned off the car lights and drove slowly onto the broad concrete parking area before the carport. His father's Bentley S3 was already in its accustomed slot, and he eased his own car in beside it.

Only when he had left the carport and started for the house entrance did he become aware that behind the drapes the living room was illuminated. His mother, an invalid, would be asleep, but his father might be having some friends in. More likely it was Maggie up late reading. He would have to be prepared for anyone. He would have to be controlled and normal.

The pictures had left his mind, and he felt safer, more assured. Reaching the front door, he dropped his car keys into his coat pocket and dug down into his trouser pocket for the key ring, the fancy silver one with the shiny disk engraved with his name that Maggie had given him on his last birthday. He kept his car and house keys separate because Maggie and he shared the Rover and she was always misplacing her car keys and borrowing his.

Standing at the door, Jerry fumbled about inside his pocket for the key ring. It wasn't there. He tried the other pocket. Not there. Worriedly, he went through the pockets of his sport jacket. No key ring. A chill of apprehension swept his chest, and in that moment he felt panic.

He heard a rustle from the hedgerow to his left, and suddenly the bright beam of a flashlight hit his face, and a rangy uniformed police officer loomed over him.

In his free hand, the officer was holding up a gleaming silver disk from which dangled a chain, a metal ring, and a set of keys.

"You looking for these, son?" the officer asked. The beam of his flashlight dropped down to the disk and the ring, now lying in the palm of his hand. Jerry blinked at his name etched in scroll on the disk. "You're Jerry Griffith, aren't you, young man?"

"Yes." He began to shake uncontrollably, and he reached for the keys, but the police officer's fist closed over them. Jerry looked up. "Where—where'd you get them?"

"We found them, Jerry. We found them a couple hours ago. We found them on the floor of the bedroom on Doheny, right

83

near the body of the young girl you're suspected of having raped tonight. That was a rough one, Jerry."

"I didn't rape anyone!"

"No? Well, her roommate, she found Miss Moore, and after she phoned for an ambulance, Miss Moore recovered consciousness for a half minute and she told her roommate that she'd been raped, forcibly violated. She was in a coma when they took her to the hospital. Fractured skull. She's in bad shape, Jerry."

"It was an accident," Jerry blurted. "She slipped, and fell, and hit her head—"

"Or maybe somebody hit her head when she was resisting, eh, Jerry? That's not a question. You don't have to say a word until your attorney gets here." The police officer looked past Jerry, and then Jerry heard the tread of someone else on the cement nearby. "Nat," the officer called out, "this is the kid. Better frisk him."

He heard someone directly behind him, and then a pair of hands was expertly going through his pockets.

The beam of the flashlight was again full on his face. "You alone in this?" the police officer asked.

"I . . . I . . . Yes, I was alone. Listen, let me—"

The police officer was looking past him once more. "What did you find, Nat?"

"Wallet. Small change. Another set of keys. Jackknife."

The police officer with the flashlight nodded. "Knife. Yeah, I expected something like that. They've always got to have something like that when they try to rape a woman alone."

Jerry felt flushed and weak. "Listen—no—that knife's a souvenir from Switzerland, when I was—It's got gadgets—scissors and—"

"And blades?" finished the officer. "What's the other set of keys for?"

"For the . . . for—for the car, my car."

"Hear that, Nat? You better go through his vehicle with a fine-tooth comb. I'll take him in the house now. Nat, meet us inside when you've finished with his car." He took Jerry by the arm. "We're going inside, Jerry."

"No!"

"Don't make any more trouble, young man. You're in enough trouble for a lifetime already. Your family's together in there waiting for you and waiting for the family attorney. You come along. When the charge is forcible rape, with injuries inflicted, you're going to need all the help you can get. So let's get moving, Jerry. In you go."

LUTHER YERKES UNSNAPPED the catch on the heavy gold Rolex watch on his wrist, pulled the watch over his dainty hand, and held it up before his tinted glasses.

"Twelve-thirty," he said. "I had no idea it was this late. I think we've done as much as we can do in one meeting."

Elmo Duncan stood up, stretching, yawning. "I'm bushed."

Underwood had returned his papers to his leather portfolio. "Well, I hope we accomplished something."

"Why don't we meet again in a few days?" said Irwin Blair, rising briskly. "We've got a long enough list of new ideas we can kick around."

"I'm too foggy to know whether we came up with anything constructive," said Duncan. "But I appreciate it, the way you're all pitching in."

Yerkes downed the last of his third armagnac. "We're not going to give up, Elmo." He suddenly cocked his head. "Is that the telephone at this hour?"

There was a faint ringing from the billiard room, and then the muffled sound of the butler's voice.

"Probably my wife," said Duncan with a short laugh. "Well, gentlemen, I'd better be—"

The Scottish butler had materialized in the archway.

"It is a telephone call for you, Mr. Duncan."

"See? I told you," said Duncan.

"Chief of Police Patterson wishes to speak to you, Mr. Duncan," the butler added.

Duncan groaned. "That's worse. That's business."

"If you want to save yourself a walk, Elmo, you can take the call in here. Unless it might be private. We've installed a microphone and loudspeaker—it's called a Speakerphone—for conference calls here." Yerkes pointed to two small green boxes, with the usual perforations over microphone and amplifier, that rested on the table between the armchairs.

85

"It shouldn't be anything private. Turn it on and we'll see, Luther."

Yerkes leaned over and depressed the push button on the microphone.

Duncan nodded his thanks and then called out to the telephone microphone, "Hi, Tim. This is Elmo. What's up?"

The reply crackled through the speaker. "Hate to bother you, Elmo. Nothing unusual, actually. Forcible rape on Doheny in West Hollywood. Victim sustained a head injury, is in a coma, got her over to Mount Sinai. Mostly routine, except some big game involved, so when the officers reported it I thought you might want to be notified."

"Who's the big game, Tim?"

"Well, this twenty-one-year-old kid who did it—he's confessed to the whole thing, that's sewed up—but he's the son of— His father is Frank Griffith."

"The Griffith who has the advertising agencies?" Duncan asked.

"That's the one."

Luther Yerkes had sprung to his feet, waving a hand at Duncan. "Elmo, ask the Chief if he's absolutely positive. Griffith Advertising does a lot of billing for me. I know Frank Griffith. I'm sure it can't be the same—"

Duncan turned back to the microphone. "That was Mr. Yerkes, Tim. Did you hear him?"

The loudspeaker crackled. "I heard. Yes, it's *the* Frank Griffith whose son—"

"I can't believe it," said Yerkes. "Do you know who Frank Griffith is? He's up there with Benton and Bowles, Young and Rubicam, Doyle Dane Bernbach. He's got one of the best reputations in the world. You remember, he was an Olympic hero—decathlon —years ago. Today he's one of the most respected men in the community. How could his son—it can't be his son."

Duncan bent toward the microphone. "You heard that, Tim. Are you positive this is Griffith's boy?"

The Chief's voice came on again. "My men apprehended the boy as he was returning home. Frank Griffith was there and he brought in Ralph Polk, his attorney. And, as I said, the boy confessed to forcible rape."

Duncan glanced at Yerkes, then at the amplifier. "He confessed, fine. Any corroborating evidence?"

"The victim was a Miss Sheri Moore, eighteen. Her roommate was out and returned and found her semiconscious, and she said she'd been raped, and the roommate called the police. Jerry Griffith—that's the boy's name—his keys, with a name disk, were found near the victim. He said he did it alone. We found a knife on him, so that's probably true. We've had a report from the hospital. The tests show she was entered, no question. The boy's car was searched after he was apprehended. There was a cigarette butt with a trace of lipstick—the lab will test it in the morning—and, let me see—oh, yes, four books in the rear trunk, three of them college texts and the fourth one was found under the spare tire— a dirty book—believe it or not, the book that made us haul in that bookseller in Oakwood this morning—what the devil was the title? —yes, *The Seven Minutes*—that was there, and then there was—"

"Tim, you mean you found that book in the Griffith boy's car?"

"Yup. Hidden away under the spare. Anyway, I thought—"

Darting forward, Yerkes reached up and grabbed Duncan's shoulder. "Elmo, tell him goodbye, tell him you'll speak to him later," he whispered urgently. "Let me shut that damn machine off."

Obeying, Duncan called out, "That covers it, Tim. Thanks for checking in. I'll be in touch. Thanks a lot." He freed himself from Yerkes' grasp and pushed down the OFF button on the microphone. Yerkes, who was behaving as if he had St. Vitus' dance, was pulling Underwood and Blair forward, one on either side of him. Now he looked at Duncan with a strange excitement.

"Elmo, Elmo, don't you see it?" Yerkes demanded.

"I think so. The book—the boy—but I'm not sure if we can—"

"I'm sure! I'm positive!" Yerkes shouted. "Griffith's son, that poor kid, he didn't commit forcible rape and grave injury. He didn't do it and he's not responsible for it. You know who is responsible? You know the real criminal out there? It's that filthy, slimy book, *The Seven Minutes*. There's your true criminal, the one that incited a decent boy from a good family to commit rape. There's your clear-cut evidence of what sort of thing is driving youngsters berserk, sending them out into the streets like hordes

87

of beasts to perpetrate the worst kind of criminal attacks. That vicious book, Elmo—there is your rapist!"

Underwood and Blair were bobbing their heads in hypnotized agreement, and Duncan found himself nodding his own assent with fervor.

"Bv God, Luther, you're right, you're right," gasped Duncan. "I think it's possible to—"

Yerkes had whipped off his tinted glasses, and his eyes were fanatical dots.

"Elmo," he said, dropping his voice, "that little censorship arrest of yours this morning—it's no longer the jewel theft—you know what it is?—it's the irrevocable murder—the very act that can arouse millions in this state and country. Elmo, forget sleep and forget caution. You take yourself over to Frank Griffith's place as fast as you can get there, and you take command personally. Because you know what—we've finally got hold of the winner we've been looking for—the big case, the big issue, the big image-maker, the biggest one possible. Pounce on it. Rip those rapemakers limb from limb. Protect the public from those lust-provoking books that lead to terror. Do that, and you've got it made—we've all got it made, Senator Elmo Duncan!"

II

He had been dreaming that he was basking in the Riviera sun on the deck of his white yacht anchored off Cannes, when a sudden explosion shredded the dream, dissolved it, and flung him back on his bed in West Los Angeles.

Eyes closed, he could still hear the reverberations of the explosion, nearby but diminished in volume.

His head cleared, and so the sound became clearer, and he realized that it was the ringing of his telephone.

He opened his eyes, turned his head on the pillow, and saw that it was seven o'clock in the morning. He lifted himself on an elbow, and more to shut up the damn persistence of the telephone than to take a call, he reached for the receiver and brought it to his ear. If it was the wrong number, he would perform mayhem on someone.

It was the right number.

"Mr. Michael Barrett?" The voice was feminine, secretarial, and distant.

"Yes," he croaked in his before-breakfast guttural.

"Mr. Philip Sanford calling you from New York. One moment, please."

Clutching the receiver, he threw aside the blanket, sat up, and swung his legs off the bed.

Philip Sanford came on. "Mike, sorry to wake you. I held off as long as I could."

He sounded agitated, and Barrett dimly wondered. "Never mind, Phil. Is anything—?"

"Have you heard what happened last night out your way? Have you seen this morning's front pages?"

"No, not yet."

"Let me read you one of the headlines. It's not the banner head, but it's on the front page, which is bad enough. Here it is." Sanford seemed to catch his breath, and then he read aloud, " 'Son of Prominent Ad Man Confesses to Rape; Blames Allegedly Porno Book.' Did you hear that? It's our book he blames!"

Barrett was wide awake now. "What's this all about?"

"Every newspaper is carrying it at length. And I've had the television on. All the top news commentators are reporting it. You'd think this is the first time rape had ever been committed."

"Phil, will you please tell me—?"

"Sorry. I thought I was upset yesterday, but after *this* lousy break! Some kid picked up an eighteen-year-old girl and gave her a ride to her apartment, and then he followed her in, and he held a knife over her and raped her. Apparently she tried to resist and he banged her head against something and she suffered a concussion and she's in the hospital now, in a coma. Something dropped out of the boy's pocket when he was trying to dress, and the police traced him and arrested him. Guess what was found hidden in the kid's car? You guessed. A copy of our edition of *The Seven Minutes*. Then the boy admitted rape, and he put the entire blame on the book. In one of the wire stories—where is it?—anyway, he was quoted as saying, 'I read it and it got me all worked up. Then something sort of snapped in my head and I guess I went crazy.' And later on he said, 'Yes, that novel, that's what incited me to do what I did.' "

"Those last words, I'm sure they're not his own," said Barrett. "The word 'incited,' that's not a boy's word. That's a police word or press agent's language. It sounds to me like the boy is being coached."

"But he did it, he plainly did it, and there was our book in his car."

"I'm not questioning that. I meant something else. I meant how the facts are being handled. Never mind. Anyway—"

"Mike, I think we're in the soup. I'm worried. I don't mind publicity for the book. Hell, I want it. But not this kind. It'll turn everyone against us. Wesley R. has been trying to get me on the phone all morning. One of the few times my . . . my . . . my father has ever acknowledged I'm alive. I won't answer. I make them say I'm out."

"The boy, the one who violated the girl, what's his background?"

"Ideal background, the best kind of upbringing. Do you want me to read you the stories?"

"I think you'd better. At least the wire stories."

For the next five minutes, in an unsteady voice, Sanford read the newspaper stories to Barrett. When he had finished he said, "There you have it. I don't know why it's getting such a play, except maybe because the boy is Frank Griffith's son—prominent family."

"No," said Barrett, "that's not it. It's the coincidence of a rape following the arrest of a bookseller for purveying an obscene book. Each act, separate, isolated, would not be news. In juxtaposition, tied together, they appear to make real news and they appear to refute the well-known pronouncement once made by Mayor James J. Walker."

"What do you mean?"

"Jimmy Walker was supposed to have said, 'I never knew of a girl who was made pregnant by a book.' Actually, I think the verbatim version is 'I never knew a girl who was ruined by a book.'"

"Yes, I've heard that."

"Well, here there seems to be an actual situation that refutes that statement. The press has put a case together. Very neat. The cause—a book inciting a boy to attack a girl. The effect—a girl ruined by a book. That *is* news."

Sanford had become increasingly agitated. "All I care about is how this affects us. What does it do to that arrest of Ben Fremont you were going to settle? You did see your District Attorney, didn't you?"

"I did, but one question at a time," Barrett said calmly. He was trying to think it out. "First, as to how this affects our efforts on behalf of Ben Fremont and your book. I stated that the press was trying to couple two separate events and make them one. I stated that that is what made it news. True. It is news, but it is not evidence. One crime has nothing to do with the other, in a strictly legal sense. Forget the press. Let's concern ourselves with the law. Ben Fremont was arrested for purveying obscene reading matter.

That's one thing. Jerry Griffith was arrested for forcibly violating and injuring a girl. That's another thing. Under the law, Jerry Griffith's reading habits have nothing to do with the charges against Fremont. The fact of Griffith's reading *The Seven Minutes* is not relevant and is immaterial to the charge that *The Seven Minutes* is of prurient interest only and therefore violates Section 311 of the California Criminal Code. The Fremont case will be determined on its own merits, as far as the law is concerned."

"But we're not up against the law alone," protested Sanford. "What about public opinion?"

There was the big question, Barrett knew, and he had considered it and anticipated it. But it was too early to answer that one. Perhaps he would have the answer later, even later this day, but he did not have it yet.

"We'll cross that bridge when we get to it," he said. "Right now let's confine ourselves to the law, which is what we have to contend with. This brings me to your second question. Did I see District Attorney Elmo Duncan about the Fremont case? I did, Phil. He was friendly and cooperative. He agreed that the whole censorship business and the arrest were a nuisance, and he made it clear he was no more interested in a costly, time-consuming trial than we were. He wanted to know what would satisfy us, and I told him. He found our request acceptable. We were to have Ben Fremont plead guilty, and then it would be arranged that Fremont be fined the twenty-four hundred dollars and be given a year's sentence which would be suspended. Your book would not be sold in Oakwood, which is an unincorporated area in Los Angeles County, but you'd be free to place the book on sale elsewhere in Los Angeles County."

"Was it settled, then?"

"No, not quite. That's why I postponed calling you back. I wanted it all wrapped up. It's virtually settled. When I left the District Attorney, he asked simply for time to discuss our compromise with his staff, as a gesture of courtesy. He told me to call him today and he'd make his acceptance official. That is where we stand."

"Past tense, Mike," said Sanford. "That is where we *stood*—yesterday. Maybe today's another day."

"Phil, I can only repeat, under the law nothing has changed since yesterday. Duncan's certainly as smart an attorney as I am, and maybe smarter. He knows that a case of forcible rape is utterly immaterial to the 311 charge against Fremont. He will deal with the Fremont affair on its own merits. And if he does so, as I believe he will, he'll stand by our agreement of yesterday. I'm fairly confident about that."

There was a woosh of air in the telephone receiver. Sanford had obviously sighed with his relief. "Thanks, Mike. I feel much better . . . Only one thing. My secretary keeps sticking memos under my nose. Our sales department is starting to get a steady stream of inquiries from booksellers around the country wanting to know what we're going to do about this prosecution of the book. I'd like to be able to tell them that there's nothing to worry about, that we got Fremont off without trouble, and now everyone can go ahead with the book. The sooner we can say that, the better. Can you settle this whole business today?"

"I intend to," said Barrett. "I was supposed to phone the District Attorney. I think it would be better if I drove downtown and saw him in person for a few minutes. Besides, it's to my advantage, too, to get this out of the way as soon as possible. I told you yesterday that I left Thayer and Turner, and that I had something much bigger coming up. Well, it's a vice-presidency with Osborn Enterprises."

"Why, that's great, Mike! Congratulations."

"Thanks. Anyway, I'm settling that tonight, and part of the deal is that I start right in on the new job. So I want to get this censorship nuisance out of the way as quickly as you do. And I expect to. I'll call you later today, the second it's settled."

EVER SINCE SHE had come to California to make her home with the Griffiths, it had seemed to Maggie Russell that the world had somehow ceased revolving on its axis. It was as if all life had come to a standstill. One day succeeded another so quickly, smoothly, without change, each new day as uniform as the last, that one hardly felt the passage of a month or of a season. While it was not truly living, she suspected, it was a peaceful way of existence that she welcomed in this period of her youth. After the frenzy and insecurity of her earlier years, losing first her father and being uprooted from Minnesota, then losing her mother and being uprooted from Ohio, and then living with relatives in Alabama, and then trying to find jobs that would support her and still give her time for a college education in North Carolina and Massachusetts, it was wonderful to have one haven where there were routine and regularity and the days came and went in a soft blur and you could wake and sleep mindless and safe.

That was what made the shock greater, Maggie reflected, as she sat unobtrusively on the bench in the bay window of the Griffith living room, observing all the activity and tension going on before her eyes.

The sudden, unexpected change in the routine and life of the household was what had jolted her so. Not that it had always been so easy to adjust to others, even relatives, especially one as highly regarded and demanding as her Uncle Frank (although her Aunt Ethel and cousin Jerry were paragons of kindness and for them she had an unshakable affection), but as households went, as far as she knew or had known, this one had been a comfortable cocoon with each bright day as predictable as the next. Yet overnight this world had been turned upside down and set spinning uncontrollably.

Yesterday, at this hour, this room had been quiet and restful. Today it was a small madhouse overcharged with emotion and danger.

Or, she wondered, had it always been this way, at least in its potential, and had she shut her eyes and mind to it because she had wanted something perfect?

Besides herself, there were five of them in the living room, seated in a ragged circle, chattering incessantly. Beyond them, at the foot of the staircase and near the home elevator, which had been installed several years ago for Aunt Ethel after she was no longer ambulatory, was the empty wheelchair. Maggie was grateful that it was empty, and that her aunt had been put to bed by the doctor and heavily sedated. Her aunt would have been made more distraught by this scene—last night, with the police, later with the District Attorney, had been bad enough—as Maggie herself had been made distraught seeing Jerry, so troubled and frightened, amidst all those men, returning from the first arraignment fifteen minutes ago.

94

Carefully Maggie Russell studied the men in the room.

Two were strangers to her, although one bore a name that she had often seen in print and had heard her uncle mention. She had been introduced to them both upon their entrance, but this was the first time she had seen either one in this house. One stranger, the one whose name she had known, was Luther Yerkes. She was fascinated by his weird physique and dress, and by his legend. She sensed, also, his importance to her uncle from the way Frank Griffith, usually brusque and authoritative and overwhelming, now showed deference to the industrialist. She tried to gauge the motives behind Griffith's deference. Was it because Yerkes was one of Griffith Advertising's major accounts? Or was it because a man of such wealth and influence had come forward to assist a business friend in an hour of distress?

To Maggie, no Pollyanna, Luther Yerkes appeared a philanthropist with his money, but not the type who was also a philanthropist with his time. Yet she had heard him say, not ten minutes ago, that he was determined to do everything he could for Frank Griffith's son and everything he could to prosecute the real criminal—namely, that polluted book.

Seated beside Yerkes, speaking not at all but steadily making jottings in a black-covered notebook, was the one who had been introduced as Yerkes' public-relations adviser. She hadn't caught his first name—she thought it was Irving or Irvin or maybe Irwin —but she remembered that the last name was Blair. His hair looked like a rummage sale. His voice was a trombone. He was the other stranger, and she could not discern his exact role here.

In the center was one she had seen before from time to time, the family attorney, Ralph Polk, who always came with a Homburg (in California!) and wore bow ties and starched collars and was restrained and archconservative.

Then there was her Uncle Frank, usually a dynamo, now unnaturally quiet, steadily chewing the end of an unlighted cigar. Frank Griffith had cowed her from the first day of her arrival here. It was not merely his success. In the Russell family—her Aunt Ethel was a Russell, and was Maggie's mother's sister—it was known that Frank Griffith had been started on the road to success by his bride's well-invested savings. Her own mother's savings, Maggie had long ago guessed, had been largely squandered by her father, and what remained had been unsuccessfully invested, and when Maggie had been orphaned the Griffith family had had to contribute to the cost of her mother's funeral. But Frank Griffith had used his wife's money well, parlaying that, and his athlete's fame as an Olympic hero, to rise and to establish the advertising agency that now had headquarters on Madison Avenue and growing branch offices in Chicago and Los Angeles. Although Maggie's job was mainly to serve as her aunt's social secretary and companion, she occasionally did some late-night typing at home for her uncle, and she knew that his agency had billings of over eighty million dollars a year, of which seven million dollars came from the Yerkes account.

It was not this part of Frank Griffith that had cowed Maggie from the start. It was his Herculean energy and his incredible self-assurance (he could convince you that he was right even after you knew that he was wrong). In his personal gym, among the framed photographs and trophies attesting to his physical prowess, were sets of barbells, and to these he devoted himself religiously every morning. Then there was his golf and his tennis and his horses at the ranch near Victorville and his private Lear jet plane. And his constant movement: clubs and banquets and social dinners in Los Angeles, as well as constant commuting to Chicago, to New York, to London.

It was enough to make any mere mortal, reflected Maggie, feel as small and inadequate as Toulouse-Lautrec. Physically, anyway.

She watched him now, the freshly trimmed pompadour, the beefy florid yet firm face, the husky body in a lightweight charcoal flannel suit, the big hands with the gold signet ring dominating one. There he was, the stern, driving taskmaster in his business, the outgoing community-minded citizen in his city, Everyman's vision of the perfect self-made success, perfect husband, perfect father.

And there he was, humbled, restrained, brought down by an heir who had been aberrant and weak and had jeopardized not only himself but the entire family's standing. Now Frank Griffith was all concern, and Maggie posed for herself some Socratic questions: Was his concern the result of a paternal confusion about what had gone wrong with an only son so well brought up? Was his concern pragmatic and concentrated on what this scandal would do to his business and his position in the country? Or was it, finally, a concern that was fatherly and protective over the fate of his heir?

Maggie knew him well, but not intimately, and never had known him in crisis, so she could not know the answer for sure.

And, finally, there was the one about whom she asked herself no questions.

The heir.

It was Jerry, the Griffith whom she knew the best and cared for the most, who held her attention now. He was seated on a ladder-back side chair, anxious and nervous, crossing and uncrossing his legs. Looking so pitifully young and lost. She knew the numbers, but numbers lied. Jerry was twenty-one, and she was twenty-four, but to her he was always ten years younger and she was ten years older. To her he was a boy and she was a woman. He was bright but shy and withdrawn. He was a maze of uncertainties and problems (like most of his contemporaries, she had always assumed). His mother was too devoted to her own illness and suffering, his father was too busy, his friends were too fickle, to provide him with the confidant he needed. Because Maggie was quiet, understanding, tolerant, sometimes wise, and always appreciative of his self-deprecating style and dry sense of humor, she had become his confidant and closest friend. Actually, not friend merely, but sort of mother-father and counselor and sounding board.

She had thought that she knew Jerry inside out, better than anyone on earth knew him, yet she had been totally unprepared for his behavior last night. While she knew his problems, she still could not imagine his violently forcing himself upon a girl. It was not as if he were a freak or psychotic or unattractive to girls. He was five feet nine and on the skinny side—which made him seem smaller than he truly was when compared to the bronzed Brobdingnagian Southern California boys who were his college companions—but still he could be appealing.

She continued to study him. His chestnut-brown hair was as neatly parted as ever. His pensive ascetic face now looked more sallow and consumptive than usual because anxiety had eaten into it. But he could be attractive, and he did date, usually double-dated, so it was not that. What evil spirit had possessed him to attack that nobody of a girl? It was the book, his father had bellowed last night. It was the book, the District Attorney had agreed last night. And Jerry had admitted, finally, the lewd fantasies that the book had provoked.

It was difficult for her to believe that a book, any book, but especially this one, could be a Frankenstein creating such malevolence. But there was the fact of his having read the book and having admitted how it had overstimulated him, and only he could know the truth about that, and so she believed him. Furthermore, at some point in the night it had developed that because of the book's influence upon him there might be more sympathy for Jerry and this would mitigate his punishment. For Maggie, this pushed all other possible motivations aside and suspended any disbelief. She was sorry for Jerry. Yet she was also sorry for the book that had betrayed them both.

She stared at Jerry, and it was still impossible. Rapists looked like rapists, she had always believed from the newspaper accounts and grainy pictures. A rapist was supposed to look—what?—mean, deprived, sick, warped. Yet Jerry still resembled Jerry, the same boy with whom she had enjoyed so many secret jokes and with whom she had read and discussed *Alice in Wonderland* and Hermann Hesse and Vivekananda. One night they had discussed Thoreau and nonconformity, and from memory Jerry had quoted, " 'If a man does not keep pace with his companions, perhaps it is because he hears a different drummer.' " Yet, if not in their private talks, at least in his public behavior Jerry had never given indication of hearing a different drummer. Then what drummer had Jerry heard last night? A drummer named J J Jadway, Jerry had said. That was the drummer.

Poor Sheri whateverhername was, poor Sheri in the hospital. And poor Jerry, poor Jerry.

This was a case without criminals. Only victims.

She wondered what would happen to him, and then she realized she had wondered because she was hearing someone in the room speculate on that with a rhetorical question.

It was Ralph Polk, the family lawyer, speaking. Maggie gave him her full attention.

"Let me summarize the procedure once more," Polk was saying. "Last night, when we went to the station, Jerry was booked, and I arranged the bail. Now, despite everything that Jerry has said to this moment under circumstances of extreme emotion, he is still innocent until proved guilty. What I am trying to say is that the law still gives us options, choices, and I intend to take advantage of these choices and go through all the necessary steps, until we are certain that Jerry really wants to plead guilty."

"You are saying he can still plead *not* guilty?" asked Frank Griffith.

"Absolutely. Let me explain. In a case like this there is a first arraignment. Thanks to the accommodation of our cooperative District Attorney, we were able to have that this morning. You saw what happened. The Deputy District Attorney read the charges against Jerry, and a date was set for the preliminary hearing. Now, the purpose of this next step, the preliminary hearing, is for the court to determine whether the prosecution has a sufficient case against the defendant to warrant bringing him to trial. Should we take this step, the District Attorney would present a portion of his evidence against Jerry through submission of certain facts, exhibits, witnesses, and so forth. I would have the right to question these witnesses if I decided to do so. Now, at this hearing, if the judge is satisfied with the prosecution's evidence, he would order Jerry bound over for trial. Step three would be a second arraignment. Jerry would be asked whether he pleads guilty or not guilty. If he pleaded guilty, he would be sentenced several weeks later. If he pleaded not guilty, the case would be placed on the court's calendar for trial. As you know, if he pleads guilty, his sentence can be anywhere from three years to life in prison, in a state prison. The judge has considerable leeway here. Under certain circumstances, the sentence might be a minimum one. Under others, let us say if the young lady, Miss Moore, sustained permanent injuries, the sentence, the penalty, might be the maximum. Now, then—"

"I won't do it!" Jerry Griffith shouted. "What good's it all going to do? I already said I did what I did to her!"

Frank Griffith turned on his son angrily. "Be quiet, will you? Don't interrupt."

Maggie had leaped to her feet, an instinctive need to come between them, to protect Jerry, but then she saw Jerry looking breathlessly at his father, the others, and finally controlling himself.

Polk half turned in his chair, and began to address himself to Jerry, but also seemed to include the frowning Luther Yerkes.

"I was about to explain, and I shall now, why I had suggested we take advantage of every step that is open to us. I know the procedure is trying, Jerry, but there are reasons for doing this. I am your father's attorney, and now I am your attorney, and I want to do the best I can for you. Allow me to elaborate on my strategy. First, as an attorney, I have been involved in too many cases not to know that a client in the period of stress immediately following a seemingly criminal act, behaving out of confusion and remorse, may confess to anything and insist he is guilty. After the cooling-off period, the client will frequently be less sure, or even come to realize he was not guilty. Then we have a chance—"

"I am guilty and I said I'm guilty," Jerry persisted.

"Jerry, I'm warning you, if you don't shut up—" Frank Griffith began.

"It's all right, Frank," said Polk patiently. "Let me try to make him understand." He spoke directly to Jerry now. "Yes, much of this may seem foolish to you, like playing out a losing game. Jerry, I'm not saying we are going to plead you not guilty and put you on trial. I was only trying to point out that the option exists and it is worth considering. The District Attorney doesn't want a trial, either. He's overloaded with work, and a trial would mean lost time for him and expense for the taxpayers. But we can play on this, make him believe we might welcome a trial, and it would put us in a better position to make a deal for a lighter sentence. Yes, I agree with you that, as things stand, a not-guilty plea not only would be dishonest but would be futile. A trial would be a wasted effort, and I wouldn't put you through such an ordeal if you didn't have a chance of winning. The truth is—and this is between us—I intend to plead you guilty at the second arraignment. Because my real reason for stretching this out, putting you through a hearing, is based on quite another strategy, one that developed out of a brief private conversation I had with District Attorney Duncan last night and one I had with Mr. Yerkes this morning. And this —this is important."

Yerkes nodded. "This is for your benefit, Jerry. I suggest you listen."

"Let's be frank," said Polk. "Behind closed doors, the District Attorney can have great influence upon the judge who will pass sentence after a guilty plea for rape. Now, District Attorney Duncan and Mr. Yerkes are of one mind—that you were victimized by the salacity of *The Seven Minutes*. They feel the true criminal is the book, its influence on young impressionable readers. They are prosecuting that book under California state law. They feel that the public will be able to see that if such books were not available to young people like yourself, many acts of violence, such as this rape, might never be committed. In short, you were temporarily inflamed, incited, by that book. Now, we need time to let this sink into the public mind. If it does, it will create an atmosphere much more favorable to you, and we can have hopes that this would influence the judge to pass a more moderate sentence in your case. That is why I want you to suffer through the preliminary hearing and the secondary arraignment—to help us buy time."

Jerry sat up and shook his head, and kept shaking it. "Mr. Polk—Mr. Polk, I don't care about the sentence or what happens to me. I don't care any more."

Polk smiled sympathetically. "I understand, Jerry. You've been through a good deal, and I would expect that to be your mood at the moment." He turned to Frank Griffith. "Which brings up another point, Frank. Considering Jerry's condition, I would recommend—oh, we can let Jerry help us decide about this, but I would recommend that we add one more aspect to the case, to mitigate any future sentence. I would like to claim that this criminal act was totally opposed to your son's nature. Therefore, I would like to offer as a defense that Jerry was not legally sane when he allegedly committed the crime. This will require the services of a top psychiatrist—one like Dr. Roger Trimble."

"We'll do anything if it'll help my son," said Frank Griffith. "Do you think you can get Dr. Trimble to see him?"

"Dr. Trimble is a friend of mine and of Mr. Yerkes'. I think—"

"No!" It was Jerry, and this time he was on his feet, trembling. "Maybe I'll do the other things, but I won't let any headshrinker—"

Griffith stood up, towering over his son.

Seeing this, Maggie felt herself recoil. But then, to her surprise, Griffith's tone was conciliatory for the first time.

"Jerry, we're here to help you in every way humanly possible," said Frank Griffith. "I'm determined to take advantage of anything that can improve your position."

"Yes, I know, Father, but I can't—"

"Ralph Polk knows the law. If he says your seeing a psychiatrist can help you with the judge . . ."

Polk had also come to his feet. "It can, Jerry," he said quickly. "The judge will take into consideration the fact that you've never before been involved in any crime whatsoever. So he'll assign a probation officer to look into your background, obtain whatever information he can about you from your family, friends, teachers. When the probation officer reports that Dr. Trimble is treating you—an analyst of his reputation—that could cut a great many corners and influence recommendations of the probation officer."

Jerry was shaking his head once more. "Mr. Polk, no—I can't—I don't want any psychoanalyst. No matter what you think, I'm not crazy. It was just a—a temporary thing. Even the District Attorney said so last night. He agreed it was that book, that's all."

Polk shrugged. "Of course, nobody can force you to see an analyst, Jerry. But I think it would be a smart move."

Frank Griffith stepped forward and placed an arm around his son while addressing Polk. "Don't worry, Ralph. I feel sure Jerry can be made to realize what's best for him. You go ahead and contact Dr. Trimble and make any arrangements you can. Now, Jerry, I think you've taken about enough. Why don't you go upstairs and lie down a while? Take one of those sedatives, and rest. We can handle what's left to be done without putting you through any more."

Jerry stared up at his father, suddenly broke away, and without another word to anyone he went hastily out of the room and toward the staircase.

Maggie's eyes followed him. As the men in the room began to settle down in their places again and light their cigarettes and cigars, Maggie started to drift toward the hallway. Once out of their sight, she went as fast as she could up the stairs.

She caught Jerry on the second-floor landing.

"Jerry—"

He waited, tried to smile, failed.

"—I'm sorry they had to put you through that."

He remained silent.

"I'm sure they were only trying to be helpful in their way," she said.

Jerry's hands worked nervously at his sweater. "I don't care about anyone being helpful. I did something wrong, crazy, and I deserve to be punished, so let them punish me. But I don't want to go through extra torture besides. I don't want to go in any courtrooms—this morning was enough, the last time—and have lawyers and judges picking my brains in front of the whole world, and I don't want any psychiatrists picking the rest of my brains. I just want them all to leave me alone."

"All right, Jerry."

"Those things—it's like making me open my fly in public."

"I know."

"I did wrong, so let them punish me and leave me alone. I just want to be left alone. I don't mean you, Maggie, but all the rest of them. I just want to be left alone and take what I deserve." He searched her face, and then he said, "You understand. Can you make them understand, Maggie?"

"I—I can try. I will try. Maybe not today. But at the right time."

"Thanks. . . . I guess I am feeling lousy. Maybe I'd better lie down."

"Rest, if you can. You need it."

"Okay."

He turned away and started for his bedroom. When he was inside it, Maggie returned to the staircase. Slowly, thoughtfully, she descended.

At the bottom, she could hear the conversation which was continuing in the living room. She was drawn toward the voices. She walked softly to the entrance of the room and stood watching and listening. They were too engrossed to note her presence.

Ralph Polk was nodding agreement to something Luther Yerkes had said, and then Polk was saying, "Yes, Mr. Yerkes, there is no question about that, no question at all. That pornographic book is our most eloquent argument on Jerry's behalf. It is, as you say, the key factor in our case. For that reason alone, if there were not another, I would want the boy in therapy with Dr. Trimble.

In a few sessions, I am almost certain, Dr. Trimble could learn about and evaluate the trauma that Jerry suffered during and after his reading of *The Seven Minutes*. This would be invaluable for us." He offered Yerkes a brief smile. "And I am sure it would be invaluable for our District Attorney, should he prosecute the book."

Yerkes' eyes were masked behind the tinted spectacles, and his rotund face remained bland. "I suppose that might be so, but I have no idea what Elmo Duncan plans to do. However—" he rose to his feet, and immediately Blair stood up beside him— "I can tell you what *I* plan to do," said Yerkes. "Being here in this house, seeing firsthand what havoc and destruction can be wreaked upon an adolescent, upon a decent family, upon a community, by a piece of slime disguised as literature, has convinced me more than ever to dedicate myself to the proposition that unless we have censorship in this country we will have chaos and increasing violence. I have your pledge that you will join in this fight, not merely because it is beneficial to your own case, but because it is beneficial to the future of our society and to the cause of justice."

"You have my pledge, Mr. Yerkes," said Griffith fervently.

"And *you* have *mine*," said Yerkes. "From this moment on, I am going to devote every energy and resource at my command to rid this community and our country of those mind-corrupting, soul-destroying smut peddlers. Do you know what we're going to do together? We are going to throw the book at them—*their* book at them—and drive the avaricious moneychangers and rapemakers out of the temple forever!"

SOMEHOW, MIKE BARRETT was not surprised that the District Attorney was almost too busy to see him, and that their meeting would be short and simple.

Elmo Duncan had clearly set the time limits a few seconds ago when he had buzzed his secretary and told her to hold off all calls for three or four minutes and to tell persons waiting for their appointments that he would be only a few minutes late.

Driving to the Hall of Justice, Barrett had felt a small hope rekindle, justifying his optimism to Sanford on the long-distance telephone earlier. He had been confident that Duncan would deliver on yesterday's promise, and that the new development concerning *The Seven Minutes* would not influence the prosecutor's original soft attitude toward prosecution of the bookseller.

Barrett had been led from the receptionist's office, past the District Attorney's private kitchen, to the room where Duncan's personal secretary waited. She had shown him into Duncan's spacious, light, modernistic office. Barrett had noted that the doorway to the District Attorney's comfortable lounge was open, and wondered briefly whether Duncan would escort him into it. Instead, Duncan had gestured him toward one of the two leather armchairs facing the broad, handsome Swedish desk. This meant business. No civilities. Barrett's hope began to flicker and fade.

Now Barrett could see plainly that this was not the same man who had received him so amiably yesterday. Duncan's features were taut, as if repressing impatience. The American flag draped from a pole behind his high-backed swivel chair seemed to be growing straight out of his head.

Nervously the District Attorney fiddled with some papers on his desk, glanced at the telephone and the water carafe at his elbow, then at the impressively bound books lining the shelves beyond, and finally, reluctantly, he gave his attention to Barrett. "I didn't expect you to drop by in person," he said. "I understood you were going to phone me. I—I'm afraid I've got a rather crowded calendar."

Duncan offered nothing further. He waited.

"I thought it would be easier this way," said Barrett. "I'll be brief. We were to settle the Ben Fremont matter."

"Yes."

The District Attorney was giving him nothing, and Barrett realized he would have to recognize the new development and tackle it without subterfuge.

"I've seen the newspapers, of course. About the Griffith boy. And about the Jadway book. Are the stories accurate? Is that what happened?"

"They are accurate."

"I see. From the tone taken by the press, one might conclude that the shade of J J Jadway had committed the rape."

Duncan found a Spanish-made letter opener on his desk and picked it up. He contemplated the opener. It was designed in the shape of a sword. Without looking up, Duncan said, "In this office we are handling the Fremont case as one case and the Griffith case as another and separate crime. The press is not trying these cases, Mr. Barrett. My office is trying them."

Barrett remained cautious. "Are you telling me, then, that in your mind one has no bearing on the other, and you are as objective about the Fremont matter as you were yesterday?"

The Toledo blade of the letter opener glittered as it turned slowly in the District Attorney's hand. "I'm telling you no such thing," said Duncan. "I am telling you that under the law we are treating each case separately and judging each on its own evidence. We are perfectly aware that these are two cases. Conversely, we are also aware that in the court of public opinion they may become one case."

"Are you suggesting that public opinion can prejudice your handling of these cases as separate cases?"

Duncan leaned forward, resting his elbows on his desk blotter. His eyes narrowed. "Mr. Barrett, here we have charges against the seller of an obscene book. Here, also, we have charges against a youth who has committed forcible rape and inflicted grave injury and whose criminal act was incited by a reading of the very same book. The public response to this, not only locally but nationally, has been instantaneous and passionate. While a law-enforcement agency need not be responsive to every public whim, it can be responsive when the public's demands coincide with its own activities. You must never forget, Mr. Barrett, the law is an instrument of the public, created by the public to protect itself. And whatever else I am, Mr. Barrett, I *am* a public servant."

Barrett sat very still. The lecture, delivered to him as if he were a schoolboy, had been pretentious and even condescending. It camouflaged any possible motivation of politics. It was double-talk.

Barrett was no longer in a mood to be winning. "Yesterday, Mr. Duncan, performing as a public servant, you were prepared to serve the law and the public by treating the charge against Ben Fremont as a minor, an even debatable, infraction of the law. You practically assured me that if I would enter a plea of guilty for Fremont you would see to it that he was let off with a fine and a suspended sentence, and you'd let it go at that. You wanted only the time to explain this to your staff, as a matter of courtesy. Now

I am here for your official decision. A fine and a suspended sentence. Is that still your intention?"

The District Attorney threw down the sword-shaped opener. "I'm afraid not," he said. "I have consulted my staff. Since yesterday, we have acquired new evidence against *The Seven Minutes.* I've looked into the book a little more closely, and into the specific charge, illuminated as it is by this new evidence, and I have become convinced that we are dealing not with a mere felony but with a crime that could have widespread effects in endangering public safety."

"Are you referring to a widespread rash of rape?" said Barrett dryly.

Duncan was not amused. "I am referring to the distribution of a menacing work of obscenity entitled *The Seven Minutes.*" He stared coldly across the desk. "You can inform your client that if you plead Ben Fremont not guilty we will prosecute the defendant to the very limit of our ability. We will go to trial and employ every resource at our command to prove the defendant, and the book, if you will, guilty as charged. However, if you prefer to enter a plea of guilty, then the defendant will receive the maximum punishment possible for his offense—the fine as well as twelve months in jail. No deals, no compromises, Mr. Barrett."

And no longer any fear of Barrett's friendship with Willard Osborn II, thought Barrett. The District Attorney spoke from strength. Obviously, he had a richer, more influential, more powerful patron than Osborn.

"And the two cases," said Barrett, "you still intend to treat them separately?"

"They are separate cases," said Duncan with a show of ingenuous innocence. "Of course," he added, "if we go to trial over the book, we may be forced to call in Jerry Griffith as a material witness."

"*Material* witness, Mr. Duncan?"

"When a young man in his impressionable years is, by his own admission, inspired to commit a heinous crime because of the contents of a book he has just read, I would suggest that this is relevant to our contention that the book is evil and should be banned and that purveying such a book is a criminal act. Oh, yes, I believe anything Jerry Griffith might tell us about this book, about what it has done to him, is very material to our case."

Involuntarily Barrett shook his head. He wanted to voice his objection. But this was not a court of law. And the District Attorney had, by a circuitous route, arrived before him with two separate cases that now resembled one case. A public servant, Barrett thought bitterly, responding to the public's command. Or, possibly, to Luther Yerkes' command. No, Barrett thought, he would not give the District Attorney such an opportunity to distort the law in any courtroom.

"I gather, then, that this is your last word?" said Barrett.

"Yes," said Duncan. But he made no move to rise. "And now I'd like *your* last word, Mr. Barrett. What plea do you intend to enter—guilty or not guilty?"

"If the decision were mine alone, I could make it now." Barrett stood up. "I'll have to consult with my client in New York."

Rising, Duncan said evenly, "I am sure you'll make it clear to him that there can be no compromise. If the plea is guilty, Fremont lands in jail for a year, and the book is guilty and will not be sold in Oakwood—as a starter. If the plea is not guilty, then that gives you the only chance to see that the seller and—" he gave the last careful emphasis "—the book—could possibly go free. But you'll have to take your gamble in court for that."

"I'll make it clear," said Barrett. You bet your ass I'll make it clear, he thought, I'll make it damn clear to Phil Sanford that we're not giving those bastards a chance for a Roman holiday and a publicity circus at our expense. He went to the door and opened it. "You'll hear from me this afternoon."

Standing behind his desk, more relaxed now, Elmo Duncan smiled for the first time. "I'll be waiting," he said.

Because there was no time to waste, and because Phil Sanford was standing by to hear from him, Mike Barrett had decided to telephone New York at once. Not willing to trust the telephones in the Hall of Justice building, he had gone swiftly up Temple Street to the magnificent Hall of Records and located an empty telephone booth inside.

While there had been no delay in placing his long-distance call, and Sanford had been informed of it at once, it had taken the publisher an uncommonly long period of time to come on the line. Sanford's dilatory treatment of a call he had earlier deemed so important at first confused and then irked Barrett. When at last Sanford had picked up the receiver at his end, absently apologizing for making his friend wait and explaining that his office had become busier than Grand Central Station, Barrett had cut him short and plunged into the business at hand.

Hardly permitting Sanford to interrupt him with a question or comment, Barrett had launched into a monologue reporting the details of the exchange between the District Attorney and himself and the perfidy of Duncan's complete turnabout. More explicitly than even Duncan might have hoped, Barrett had articulated the alternatives and then the legal consequences of both a guilty and a not-guilty plea.

In the claustrophobic confines of the telephone booth, Barrett had been speaking nonstop to Sanford for several minutes now, and he was not yet through.

"So what does this add up to?" Barrett asked, posing the question almost as if to seek clarification for himself. "Let me tell you what it adds up to, Phil, and let me give you my firm advice. Duncan was practically drooling to have me tell him we'd plead not guilty and go to trial. He wants the courtroom as a stage from which he can dramatize the issue and impress his crusading image on the public. And he's got the script for it. One with great mass appeal. I'm not saying he's a phony and nothing more. I want to be fair about him. Evidently he is sincere in his feeling that a novel like *The Seven Minutes* can do incalculable harm. True, he didn't feel that strongly yesterday. But he feels the Griffith rape is a practical demonstration of the antisocial behavior that can be generated by a mere book. I'm certain that he believes this. God knows, he's righteous enough. At the same time, you know my cynicism about righteousness. Poke any saint deeply enough, and you touch self-interest. The fact remains that with the Griffith boy as his star witness, Duncan has himself a trial that transcends the literary and the intellectual and becomes an emotional carnival with wide public appeal. He can make his name nationally famous from that courtroom, if he can pull it off. And he is positive he can pull it off. And, quite frankly, I'm inclined to agree with him."

"What are you saying, Mike? You mean you think he can win?"

Barrett moved closer to the mouthpiece. "I'll be blunt with you. Yes, based on the little we know now, the odds would heavily favor the prosecution. I know that I told you this morning we were dealing with one case, a censorship case, and the Griffith rape has nothing to do with it legally. That's still correct. Duncan admits it. But this session I just had with him made me realize to what extent other forces are at work—public opinion and public pressure—the determination to introduce the Griffith boy into the case by the side door, as a witness—the political ambitions of the District Attorney or his backers. In that climate, they could probably succeed in making both cases seem one case. If they did, it would be almost impossible to obtain a not-guilty verdict from a judge or a jury. How in heaven's name do you defend a case like this? You say this book is a work of art and you invoke the Constitution and freedom of the press for a work of art. For their part, they merely point to that pathetic girl in a coma in the hospital who has just been raped by someone who says he was driven to it by your work of art. How would you judge those arguments? Take my advice. You absolutely cannot plead not guilty and risk a trial. The unfavorable publicity and the almost inevitable loss of the case will get your book banned in every major city in America. You'll be through, Phil—"

"Hold it, Mike, listen, I—"

"Let me finish," said Barrett sharply. "You do as I tell you. Explain the situation to Ben Fremont. He'll understand. He won't want to go through all the pretrial preparations with the accompanying agitation and notoriety. He's ten times better off if he pleads guilty. His fine will be paid for him. And the year in jail, well, it's not fun, but it's not the guillotine either, and you can compensate him for it in some way. Once you've had him plead guilty, you've pulled the tent down on Duncan's circus and you've guaranteed some future to the book. The Fremont sentence will be kicked around for a while in the press, but with nothing new to keep it in the public eye it'll sink out of sight forever. If there are other prosecutions elsewhere, at least they won't be linked to rape. When you've dispensed with them, you can resume selling the book everywhere but in Oakwood. I'm sure you agree with me. It's got to be a guilty plea. Will you let me call Duncan right now and notify him of our decision?"

"Mike . . ."

"Will you?"

There was what seemed an interminable silence. Barrett listened. He could hear only Sanford's labored breathing three thousand miles away.

Sanford spoke at last. "It . . . it's too late, Mike. That's what I've been trying to tell you. It's too late."

"What are you talking about?"

"I've made a public announcement of what we are going to do. I announced we are pleading *not* guilty. I announced we are going to court to defend Ben Fremont and—and *The Seven Minutes*. That's it. It's done."

In an involuntary gesture of disbelief at what he had heard, Barrett took the receiver from his ear, glanced at it, and brought it back to his ear. "Did I hear you right? You're not kidding me, are you? This isn't exactly a laughing matter."

"I made a public announcement less than an hour ago. We're going to court, Mike, and we need all the—"

"If you're leveling with me, what you need is a strait jacket and a dozen psychoanalysts."

"Mike, you haven't given me a chance to talk. You don't know what's been happening here, or you'd understand," Sanford complained. "After I hung up on you this morning, I was deluged by wires and phone calls from every corner of the country. It's been snowing telegrams. From everyone. From most of our major bookstore accounts. From some of the biggest wholesalers—Baker and Taylor, A. C. McClurg, American News, Raymar, Dimondstein, Bookazine, you name them—and every one adding up to the same question. What are we going to do about Ben Fremont? Nobody pulled punches. If we backed down on Ben, then it meant we were backing down on *The Seven Minutes*. If we admitted that Ben was guilty and deserved to be jailed without a fight, then it would look like we were admitting the book was obscene and did not deserve to be put on sale. In fact, our backing down on Ben Fremont meant we were exposing every bookseller, every bookman, to further arrests and yet offering nothing to support them. It was like the American Booksellers Association speaking to me in a single voice. Fight the censors here, and stop the censorship from spreading farther, or forget about the book. Because if Sanford House wouldn't fight here, no one would dare handle the book.

"Look, we know what's happened in a similar situation before, Mike. I've been told that when Grove Press published Henry Miller's *Tropic of Cancer* there were over sixty criminal and civil suits mounted against booksellers. And even though the publisher agreed to defend or assist in defending those booksellers, other booksellers were still sufficiently frightened to return—return, send back, you hear me?—three quarters of a million of the two million copies that had been published. When Putnam published *Fanny Hill*, they made no guarantee of protection to booksellers. But once they saw the tidal wave of bannings and injunctions in the offing, they realized that few booksellers would handle the novel unless it was defended. So they selected three key cities where the book had been attacked—Hackensack, Boston, New York— and they fought the censors. As a result, their book, and the freedom to sell it and read it, survived. In a sense, we're luckier, Mike. We have one instant censorship case mounted against our book, only one, to date, perhaps more difficult and sensational than the others, but one case which, if we fought and won it, would discourage any further criminal and civil actions. But not to try to fight it? Why, wholesalers and bookstores would immediately dump thousands and thousands of copies back into my lap. Our book would be dead before it was born. That was made clear to me today.

"What choice did I have, Mike? I was desperate. I was so desperate that I finally returned Wesley R.'s calls. You know what I got from him? You know why he'd called me after reading the headlines? It was just to tell me he'd always known I was a fool, but now it was confirmed by others—I was not only a fool but a dunderhead for publishing the Jadway. And as for giving me any help, any paternal advice, you know what he gave me? A recipe. 'Stew in your own juice,' he said. And after I was cooked, he said, he hoped there would be enough left of the firm to sell off to someone who'd know how to run it. So there I was, alone, in the pressure cooker, and with the entire book trade waiting for my answer. Well, I stalled and stalled, hoping you'd make that compromise deal with the D.A., but knowing that even if you had, it was too late for that, too late to plead our book guilty of rape. So finally I called in everybody, and we drafted a statement to be wired to our major book accounts and wholesalers and also be released to the press. We reaffirmed our belief in the honesty and literary value of *The Seven Minutes*. We pledged ourselves to defend the book against the forces of comstockery. We announced that we were supporting Ben Fremont and Jadway's book, and we were pleading not guilty, and we were going to court to prove our contention to the people of Los Angeles, of the country, of the entire world. I gave my word—we will fight this with every resource at our command."

"That's what the District Attorney just told me, the exact words he used."

"What?"

"He'd fight *you* with every resource at his command."

"I—I expected that," said Sanford haltingly. "You didn't mean that, before, about our not having a chance in court, did you, Mike?"

Barrett was suddenly sorry for his friend. "Perhaps I was exaggerating to make a point. What I should have said was, I hate to see anyone go to trial. Court trials are messy, costly, and they can become vicious. Sometimes, when they're over, it's hard to tell who won or who lost, because everyone looks like a loser. And this case is a particularly difficult one. The prosecution has got some big guns. Of course, between now and the trial date you may get some impressive weaponry, too." Weariness was beginning to overtake Barrett. "Well, I'd better phone the D.A. and let him know you want Fremont to plead not guilty. I hate to do it, but I guess you've left us no choice in the matter."

"*I* had no choice." Sanford persisted. "If I'd turned my back on this case, that would have opened the floodgate. That would have been the end of freedom of speech in this country."

"That was your principal concern, Phil—freedom of speech?"

"All right, you bastard. And my own neck. That was also my concern."

Barrett could not help smiling. "That's more like it. Well, if it is your neck you are concerned about, let me give you one more piece of advice, and this time follow it. You're on the firing line. You need the best shot there is. Meaning you need the best defense attorney in these United States. You see that you get him."

"I've already got him."

"You have? Good. Who?"

"You, Mike. I retained you yesterday. Remember?"

"Oh, no, no you don't, Phil," Barrett said levelly. "I was just a temporary fill-in for a publisher-in-distress. It was going to be a quick guilty plea and then run. A trial is another matter. It can take weeks or months and I'm tied up."

"You said you quit Thayer and Turner. I wouldn't insist on this if you weren't free."

"Phil, I'm not free," Barrett insisted with exasperation. "Didn't you hear me tell you, not once but twice, that I quit them to take a new job with Osborn Enterprises? The chance of a lifetime. And a condition of the new job is that I start on it immediately. I told you that this morning."

But then he saw that he would have to tell his friend about it again, and in greater, more convincing detail. Trying to hide his weariness, he recounted his entire adventure with Osborn and the opportunity that had been offered to him.

"Now you know why I can't be your legal counsel," he concluded.

Sanford remained adamant. "You can go to Osborn and say you'll take his position after you've finished with the trial."

"I can't see myself making any demands on Osborn. I'm fortunate to have any position with him at all. Look, Phil, there are three hundred thousand lawyers in the United States, and there are at least two hundred thousand of them who'd love to take on your case and who'd be better at it than I would. Hell, Phil, I've never handled a censorship case."

"You handled plenty of cases supporting the guarantees of the First Amendment when you were with the Good Government Institute. Well, this is a First Amendment case, no more, no less. What's the difference if the issue is political or literary? What is still being defended is the right of freedom . . ."

He *did* know what was to be defended. He knew what was at stake. Fleetingly, the placard that had hung in his old office at the Institute, quoting a credo of the American Civil Liberties Union, passed before his eyes. It was a reminder that, in a living society, principles often come into conflict. About some things there could be no conflict. A man could not have the freedom to

injure other people, to slander, to incite mob action, to create the
danger of illegal sexual conduct or revolution or sabotage. But,
and now he remembered exactly, "Within those limits, people
should be able to say what they please, however unpopular, however irresponsible. Otherwise there's no telling when the majority
may decide that your ideas, too, are offensive." This had been his
standard when defending those voicing political opinions, and
Sanford was right. It was also the standard to be applied to the
freedom to write and speak as one pleased, and to read what one
wished. He had taken the wrong tack with Sanford and had made
himself vulnerable.

"Admitted, Phil," he said. "Let's say I am qualified. The fact
remains that I am not available. I repeat, I can find you an attorney, a battery of barristers, not only qualified but also available
and eager to help. So be reasonable. Let me find you someone."

"No," said Sanford flatly. "You are the only one I'd gamble my
whole future on. You alone know me. You know my stake in this.
You'd care. You'd defend me as you'd defend your own life.
You'd devote yourself to me as a friend, not as a mere client. You
know New York publishing as well as California law. And you
know books. You're the only attorney I've ever met who loves
literature as much as law." There was a meaningful pause, and
then Sanford added, "Mike, you owe this to yourself—and to me."

Barrett hesitated. His friend had injected the word "owe."
Barrett knew too well the definitions of the word "owe." "To be
indebted . . . To have an obligation to someone . . ." He had
always been burdened by his unpaid debt to Sanford. The years
had passed, but the memory and the obligation had not faded
with time. When he had been desperate to save his mother, only
one person had volunteered to help. He had long ago repaid Sanford the money owed him. But he had never repaid the interest,
which was payable only in the currency of friendship, a favor for
a favor. No one on earth aided another out of pure altruism.
Everyone on earth expected something back, be it love or loyalty
—or legal counsel.

Still, Barrett could not bring himself to capitulate. Sanford had
said he owed it to himself as well as to their friendship to take on
the case. Meaning, perhaps, that he owed it to himself to fight
a good fight. Or meaning, more likely, he owed it to himself to

support a friend who was cornered, a linguistic effort to soften a harsh demand. But Barrett also knew what he owed himself. He owed himself the right to be his own man, once and forever, to shed all guilts and disown the gouging interest levied on repaid debts. He owed it to himself to reject Sanford, as he had yesterday rejected Zelkin, and to go along with Willard Osborn II. He dared not jeopardize the position offered by Osborn. At the same time, he could not, at least not at this moment, break with a friend.

He realized that Sanford had been speaking to him, asking, "Are you still there, Mike?"

"I'm here. I was trying to think."

The New York voice had become hurt and wheedling. "Mike, you can't let me down in a crisis like this. I need you."

"You're putting me on the spot, Phil," he said. "But let me see what I can do. Let it stand this way. I'll try what you suggested. I'm seeing Osborn tonight. I intend to tell him I'm taking him up on his offer of a vice-presidency. At the same time, I'll ask him for a delay. I'll explain about you and our friendship and the necessity for a trial, and then, well, then I'll hope for the best. But, Phil, one thing. If he refuses to give me a delay, I'll still accept his job. I'll try to find you a top attorney out here. If it has to be someone else, I know you'll understand."

"I'll understand only one thing," said Sanford, invoking the tyranny of the weak. "That friendship comes ahead of anything else. If you were going under, and needed my helping hand, I wouldn't think twice. I'd make any sacrifice to give you a hand."

This got under Barrett's skin. He tried to contain the resentment that he felt. "You know perfectly well I'd do anything to help you, within reason. I said I'll try, and I shall, tonight. The only thing I can't do, if it comes down to it, is blow my whole future. If you don't understand that, Phil, I'm sorry."

"I'll be waiting to hear from you," said Sanford, and he hung up.

Angrily Barrett returned the receiver to the hook. He wanted to flee this booth, the scene of entrapment. But he had one duty left.

Depositing another coin, he dialed the District Attorney's office. Apparently his call was expected. He was put through to Elmo Duncan almost immediately.

He told Duncan that he had discussed the matter with his

116

client in New York, and they had reached a decision on the plea, and he was about to drive over to Oakwood and inform the defendant.

"We're entering a plea of not guilty," said Barrett.

"Not guilty? Good, very good," said Duncan, singing it out as if it were a joyful Christmas carol. "See you in court."

Barrett wanted to reply that the District Attorney would see someone in court, but that it was not likely to be he. "In court," he echoed.

Leaving the booth, he almost hoped that Willard Osborn would not grant him a postponement to undertake the defense.

For the defense, in a trial like this, the court was an exposed battlefield, an indefensible graveyard.

He had spent his life barely escaping from ambushes.

He could not afford a Little Big Horn.

BARRETT HAD BEEN invited to an early dinner at the Osborns', since he was taking Faye to the Music Center in downtown Los Angeles to see a visiting Bolshoi Ballet troupe perform Tchaikovsky's *Sleeping Beauty*.

The meal in the charming, almost rustic dining room, with its roughhewn wood beams above and its hexagonal floor tiles below, had been delicious. Now the last of the serving pieces was being removed from the hand-woven maroon Mexican tablecloth, until only the ancient wrought-iron candelabrum remained as the centerpiece. A servant entered with an open box of cigars. Willard Osborn accepted one, but Barrett declined, indicating his pipe, which he began to fill from his leather pouch.

Across the table, Faye was inserting a fresh cigarette into her gold holder. Her blond hair was swept up high, accenting the strands of pearls around her milky neck. She met Barrett's eyes and winked, inclining her head slightly toward her father, as if to assure Barrett that the moment had come. Barrett turned his gaze toward Willard Osborn, at the head of the table. Osborn had clipped his cigar and was waiting for the servant to light it.

At last the three of them were alone. Throughout dinner the conversation, guided by Faye, had been largely concerned with social gossip and the arts. No business. Barrett had rather expected the subject of his position to be brought up during dinner. But it had been studiously avoided by Willard Osborn. Barrett finally understood that, by Osborn's code, dinner and business did not mix, such mixture being definitely bad manners.

Now dinner was done, and in twenty minutes he and Faye would have to be off to the ballet.

Willard Osborn had straightened his lank frame, and from beneath his heavy lids he was considering Barrett. "Well, now," he said, "we've covered ships and shoes and sealing wax, cabbages and kings, and now I should say there is nothing left to discuss except the most important subject of all—vice-presidencies. I assume you are prepared to tell me tonight, Michael, whether you've made up your mind, and, should your decision be favorable, whether you've been able to work the change out. Are you prepared to discuss it?"

Barrett smiled. "I've only been waiting for you to ask. Of course my decision is favorable. It was favorable the moment you made me the offer. The problem was Thayer and Turner. I'm happy to say that's worked out. I resigned yesterday."

"Wonderful, Mike!" exclaimed Faye jubilantly.

"The only thing—"

"I'm perfectly delighted," Willard Osborn interrupted. "I knew you'd find a means of arranging everything. Very good. Now we can move ahead as I'd planned. There will be offices for you on Monday. I want you to come in, familiarize yourself with the files, become acquainted with your colleagues, and in a week you can lead our small army into Chicago to open negotiations for that television network."

Unable to check Osborn's enthusiasm, Barrett had heard him out with a sinking feeling. He had to speak up before Osborn went further. "There's just one obstacle standing in my way, Willard."

"Standing in your way to what?"

"To going right to work for you. You see, a friend of mine, one of my closest friends, wants me to represent him in a trial soon to be held in Los Angeles. I can't persuade him to retain another attorney. He feels, in this kind of case, he needs someone who knows him, someone he can trust. I wouldn't consider undertaking this, except that the man is my friend, has always been loyal to me, and I owe him a good deal."

Osborn had set down his cigar and pulled himself closer to the table. "I'm afraid you are confusing me, Michael. I can't see what could be important enough to warrant the kind of delay you're speaking about. What is so special about this case that it requires you and only you?"

"Well . . ." Barrett wriggled uncomfortably. "It's the kind of case—well, my friend's entire future career hangs on its outcome. Before I go into it, well, if you don't mind, I think first I had better explain something of my relationship with my friend."

Fixing his eyes on the cold pipe in his hand, not once looking up, Barrett began to speak in hurried, brief sentences of when he had first known Philip Sanford, of their college years together, of Sanford's assistance when Barrett's mother had been gravely ill, of Sanford's difficulties with his famous father, of his opportunity to take over Sanford House on a trial basis to prove his capabilities. Then, even more quickly, Barrett interjected *The Seven Minutes* into his account, describing Ben Fremont's arrest and Phil Sanford's determination to defend both the bookseller and the novel itself in court.

"Today I did as I was instructed and what was perhaps necessary," said Barrett. "I informed the District Attorney we were pleading not guilty. I told Phil that I would try, if it was humanly possible, to represent the defense."

He glanced up as he finished talking, and directed his eyes toward Faye, across from him. But he could see only her profile. Her worried face was pointed toward her father. Barrett forced his eyes to shift to her father.

If a man's countenance could be a synonym for a word, then Willard Osborn's features were a synonym for "appalled." The usually bloodless patrician countenance was amazed, dismayed, distressed, and faintly flushed.

"That book," said Osborn, mouthing "book" as if it were a scatological four-letter word. "You intend to defend that foul book? Surely you're not serious?"

Barrett felt himself bristle. "I have no idea whether the book is or is not foul. Only our District Attorney has said it's foul. The other side hasn't been heard from yet. I haven't read the book, but nevertheless it deserves—"

"It deserves nothing," snapped Osborn. "It deserves to be ripped to shreds and stuffed into the garbage disposal. You have no idea whether the book is foul? I am really surprised at a man of your intelligence making a remark like that, Michael. One doesn't have to read a book to know that it is foul. One can smell it. I, for one, know what it is. There is sufficient evidence to make judgment. I am acquainted with our District Attorney. You yourself have met him in this house. He is an honest man and a decent man, and certainly no prude. If he's seen fit to charge *The Seven Minutes* as obscenity, I would trust his judgment. If that were not enough, consider that book's history. It was all over the newspapers this morning. With the exception of that one ratty underground press in Paris, no publisher in any nation in over three decades has felt that this book should be brought to light. And when your so-called friend, whose morality has plainly been warped by his psychotic resentment of his father—when your friend opportunistically determined to publish the book, what was the first thing to happen? The book found its way into the hands of Frank Griffith's young son, and it unleashed his normal inhibitions and provoked him into an act of violence."

"We only have the boy's word for that," said Barrett, shaken by Osborn's vehemence.

"His word is good enough for me," said Osborn. "Michael, you must realize this. I am no stranger to the Griffith family. Certainly, I've known Frank Griffith well for many years. He has bought endless hours of television time from me for his numerous clients. His clients are drawn from the top business executives in America, and he has them because he has earned their respect. He is an outstanding public citizen, and he has brought up his son in his own image. Nothing could have corrupted the mind of a young man like that except a criminally pornographic work. You've come to know me a little, Michael. You could hardly call me a puritan. You must know I am against those who would restrict our freedoms. I oppose their efforts daily in the never-ending battle in our world of television. But even freedom must have boundaries. Otherwise, the greedy, the vicious, will use our freedom against us and destroy that freedom, as well as destroy our young and innocent. I say open the door to the new candor and realism when it is honest and broadening, but I say shut the door in the ugly face of a monster like *The Seven Minutes*. For your own sake, Michael, let alone our future together, but mainly for your own sake, I trust you are not serious about defending that book."

Listening, Barrett had become frightened. His fear was not a fear of Willard Osborn, but a fear of the reckless anger that had been growing inside himself and a fear that this anger would overcome his rational self, dominate him, and make him give voice to long-forgotten feelings that would destroy his wondrous future. He did not know what to say, but, fortunately, in those seconds he needed to say nothing, for Faye was addressing her father.

"Dad, I'm not disagreeing with what you've said, but I do think you are entirely missing the point that Mike is trying to make. Mike may or may not be serious about defending this book, but the point is that he has said from the start that if he defended it at all, it would be because of his loyalty to an old friend. He's tried to tell you he is considering handling this case because of Mr. Sanford, not because of *The Seven Minutes*."

"Well, that may be, but the very thought of Michael here becoming involved . . ." Osborn had turned to Barrett once more. "As to friends, I understand loyalty to friends. That is admirable. Yet, from long experience, I also know one must not permit friendship to become devouring. Most of us pay our dues to friendship. But we must never do so to the point where we bankrupt ourselves. Remember that, Michael." He took up his cigar and brought a table lighter to it. "Now, then, your place in Osborn Enterprises. I said we must have you at once. Possibly we can reach a compromise. How much time would you have to give this —this trial of yours?"

"It's too early to tell," said Barrett. "I'd say maybe a month. Maybe a little longer."

Osborn shook his head. "Impossible. I'm afraid that is asking too much. I couldn't afford to keep the position unmanned for such a period of time. I'd have to find someone else. Also, to be perfectly frank, there is another aspect of your involvement with Sanford that would be distasteful. This has the makings of a sensational and dirty trial. Some of that dirt would automatically rub off on you, and if you were to become one of our vice-presidents it would in turn rub off on Osborn Enterprises. It would place you and the company in a bad light with the more finicky conservatives who advertise on our stations. I would find it extremely difficult to justify your role in such a trial and, indeed, my having given you so responsible a position in a company involved with communications that influence young and old alike." He suddenly ground out his cigar. "What the devil. You know what I'm driving at. You're smart enough. That's why I want you with us."

Osborn came out of the chair and shoved it aside. He appeared at ease and benign once more. He offered his daughter a slight smile, and then he gave Barrett a broader one.

"I know I can depend on your sense of values, Michael," he said. "All things considered, that trial should have no place in your résumé of achievements. There are more vital, and more attractive, affairs to concern you. My advice is that you forget that courtroom diversion. You can tell your friend Sanford that you made a try on his behalf, but that I was absolutely immovable. You can say that I could not find any way of sparing you, and that you had to honor your earlier commitment to Osborn Enterprises. Once you've told him that, and he realizes you mean it, he'll make no further effort to use you. He'll do what he should have done in the first place. He'll find himself the kind of back-room attorney who specializes in defending the licentious and the lewd, he'll find someone with less integrity than you have. As for you, Michael, I want you on our team, among men of stature, where you belong. I want you among men who are going places. I'll expect to see you bright and early Monday morning. So, off you go, both of you, and enjoy yourselves. After all, you've a lot to celebrate."

THE RUSSIAN BALLET had ended to a dozen curtain calls twenty minutes before eleven o'clock. There had been the usual wait trying to leave the parking area, and the usual jam on the freeway, but once Barrett had made the off ramp he was able to make better time. Now, as his convertible moved along the Sunset Strip, it was a quarter after eleven.

Once again Faye Osborn was chattering about *Sleeping Beauty* and extolling the marvels of the Bolshoi troupe. He realized that he could recall little of what she was describing. Throughout the ballet, he had been inattentive. While the *corps de ballet* lightly soared and pirouetted on the stage, Barrett's mind had been filled with heavier, more disquieting, images that had pranced and skipped through his head.

"That new ballerina," Faye was saying, "the one who was Princess Aurora—I can never remember those ghastly Russian names—do you remember her name, Mike?"

"No."

"Anyway, I don't believe I've ever seen a more beautiful performance. The program said that's the part that made Ulanova famous overnight. Well, I think this girl is going to be even more famous, don't you, Mike?"

"Yes."

"It's positively inspiring. It makes one want to float, or at least swing. . . . There's Whisky a Go Go. Do you feel up to it, Mike?"

"What? Up to what?"

"Dancing. You weren't even listening. I guess you're not in the mood."

"No, not tonight, darling. We'll do it next time."

They had entered Beverly Hills, and he lapsed into silence.

Her hand had reached out, and he felt it touch his arm. "Mike, dear . . ."

He glanced at her. Faye's flawless brow was marked with concern, strange, like a delicate porcelain plate with a crack in it.

"Mike, what is it? You've been locked inside yourself the entire evening. What's troubling you? Is it Dad? Did he upset you?"

She was her father's daughter, and he was always careful about Dad. Not that he'd had much reason to be critical of her father before. Willard Osborn had always treated him graciously. But, on a personal level, he had known Osborn only as father of the fiancée, as host, as career patron. The rest of Osborn, the human Osborn, he had divined only through the conductor that was Faye. Sometimes—rarely, but sometimes—he wondered. For maybe that wasn't Osborn, but Faye alone. It was difficult to strain a bloodline and separate it into two identities. That was why, on the few occasions when Faye had made remarks or shown prejudices that annoyed him, providing no evidence as to whether the biases were her own or parentally derived, he had always been careful.

But tonight he had lived with Osborn throughout the evening, and his resentment had not lessened. He wanted to speak his mind, to rid it of Osborn, and he determined to do so now. He would not be careless. He would simply be forthright. After all, there was an intimacy between Faye and himself, even if they were not yet close. Intimacy counted for something.

"Well, did he?" Faye asked. "Is that what's on your mind?"

"Yes, I guess it is," he said. "I guess I've been thinking of what he said after dinner. And that made me think of other things. So it's not just your father."

"Well, what about my father?"

"I don't think I expected an ultimatum from him. Either or else. When I spilled out my whole dilemma, my friendship and debt to Phil Sanford, I thought he would understand my position. But he didn't. Or at least he chose not to."

"Be fair, Mike. I was there. Despite his feelings about that book, the trial, his own sorrow for Frank Griffith, Dad was sympathetic to your own problem. He was ready to relax his terms, give in a little. That's because he does like you and wants to see you achieve the success you deserve. Mike, he did ask you how much time you wanted for the trial."

"Exactly the point," said Barrett. "He was ready to give me only the time that *he* thought I required. Had the trial been over some other matter, I'm sure he would have been more flexible. Because it was this trial, about this book, he placed a limit on his magnanimity. He made the gesture. Yet he made the terms as impossible as they had been from the start. He knew very well one can't prepare for a trial and go to court and get it over with in a few days or a week. He knew I'd need a month or more. When I said so, he pulled back and said no. Why? If he really needed me on Monday, and in Chicago a week later, he wouldn't have been prepared to release me from the negotiation at all. But he knew, and I know, that you don't make a man a vice-president simply because of one immediate project. If a man is really valuable, then he is valuable to you for years, for a lifetime, and you take the longer view. That's why I say, if I'd asked him for time off to help a friend over some civil matter, a tax case, a corporation suit, some clean, businesslike, red-blooded, Waspish American litigation, he'd have been considerate and given me a break. What he disliked was the issue I wanted to become involved in. So he made it impossible for me to contest that issue—unless I was prepared to give up the position he's offered me."

Faye had heard him out, biting her lower lip, and when he was through she spoke immediately. "Mike, you're torn, and therefore angry, and that's making you distort the whole thing. No one knows Dad the way I know him. You can believe me, he wasn't trying to bludgeon you into standing for what he stands for. He was looking out for you, for your future. He knows how people use people, and he could be more objective than you can and see more clearly how Sanford was manipulating you. He didn't want your reputation hurt by his allowing you to associate yourself with a dirty book."

"Well, I'm not—" Careful, Barrett, careful, he told himself, you've spoken your piece. Now easy does it. "Well, maybe you're right, Faye. It's not fair to guess at someone else's motives. Let's say what disturbed me was his strong prejudgment of a book he's never read, knows nothing about, except what a publicity-minded District Attorney sees fit to release in the press."

"Mike, what about you? You admitted you hadn't read the book, yet you're also making a prejudgment of it, aren't you? You're making a prejudgment in its favor."

He doffed an imaginary hat to her. "Right you are, my dear. I eat my words, although only some of them. Anyway, your father knows nothing about the book, and through Phil Sanford I'm at least familiar with—"

"Mike, reading it or not reading it shouldn't be the issue. I'm surprised at you. We're warned off certain things by the reputation that precedes them, or because people we trust tell us they're bad. If people who know label a bottle 'Poison,' isn't that enough? Does everyone have to sample the poison to be convinced he should stay away from it?"

"Not the same thing," said Barrett. "Poison can be scientifically tested and classified as dangerous beforehand. A work of literature cannot, at least not so simply."

"Oh, please, Mike. This polluted book has been scientifically tested right under our very noses. A human guinea pig was used in the experiment. Jerry Griffith. And he was poisoned."

"You say Jerry Griffith. Let's look at Jerry Griffith more closely. I'm an attorney, Faye. I've been taught not to take people and their actions at face value. You probe, you question, and more often than not you find motives that are quite different from those that

125

first appeared on the surface. Maybe *The Seven Minutes* was solely responsible for Jerry's crime. Again, maybe there were other reasons for his behavior, and the book was only the final thing that tripped the trigger. If it hadn't come along, there would have been something else to trip the trigger. How do we know, how does even Jerry know, unless we look deeper? I'm not prepared to judge the book, condemn it, because of this one piece of evidence. And what surprises me, and upsets me, is how many educated people, like your father, yourself, thousands of others around town, are ready to curb freedom of speech without conclusive evidence."

Faye took her gold holder and a cigarette from her purse. "Well, you're surprised at us, and frankly, Mike, I'm surprised at you. I thought your main motive in wanting to defend that dirty little book was to do a favor for an old friend. That was something I could comprehend. Now, all at once, it's not friendship but freedom of speech."

"I guess I was turned on tonight. I'd long since forgotten I was once an idealist. I didn't believe I had those feelings any more."

"Well, I wish you'd have them over something more deserving, something worthwhile. Not over a piece of incendiary trash." She held up her cigarette holder. "I know, I know, I'm not supposed to say that until I taste the poison."

He tried to contain his pique. "Or at least until you're sure, Faye dear, that the bottle hasn't been mislabeled." An acid tone was creeping into his voice, and he hastened to sweeten it with reasonableness. "Faye, one thing for sure, as you've pointed out, none of us has read the book. You haven't. Your father hasn't. I haven't. So none of us knows first hand whether it is a work of hard-core pornography or a work of erotic art. So how can we discuss it further?"

"A work of art. Ha. You can read it, not me. You read it and tell me. Subject closed. The ballet was more fun." She sat back low, smoking. Then, as Barrett turned the car off Sunset Boulevard, she suddenly craned her neck and sat upright. "Hey, where are you taking me, Mike?"

"Home."

She swung around. "Isn't this something new? Weren't we going to your place? Don't tell me you're peeved with me because I disagreed with you?"

"Of course not. You know me better than that, Faye."

"Then why aren't we going to be together longer?"

"Because tonight I'm going to have other company. Tonight I'm going to bed—with a book." He guided the car into the Osborn driveway. "I'm going to practice what I've been preaching. I'm going to find out whether the poison was mislabeled or not."

"Well, if that's all." She seemed relieved, and suddenly cheerful. "Just remember, if it overstimulates you, you don't have to go galloping out to waylay and rape some poor child. I'm ready, willing and available."

"I'll keep that in mind." He drew up before the impressive Spanish structure, set the shift in "Park," stepped on the emergency brake, but allowed the engine to idle. He was starting to get out, to see her to the door, when she stopped him with a question.

"Mike, are you even considering turning down Dad's position to take on Sanford's case?"

"I don't know what I'm considering. No, the odds are I won't sacrifice your father's job. I probably wouldn't have the guts any more. Besides, I wouldn't want to lose the chance to keep you in the manner to which you're accustomed."

"But you haven't turned down Sanford yet, either. And you *are* going to read the book."

"That's right, darling," he admitted. "Because I don't want to grow rich and fat and old always carrying the niggling and perhaps romantic regret that I once didn't do something important that I should have done. A sage long ago said—there is nothing as futile as regret. Another sage, namely me, said—there is no burden heavier than regret. I want to anticipate and put down that albatross and join the team Monday morning, guiltless and vigorous."

"Silly," she laughed, and then she sobered. "No, seriously, Mike—"

"Very well, seriously. I'm afraid I don't have much choice about what I can do. Still, there's a little bit of my conscience, frightened at an early age by Clarence Darrow, that demands explanations of me for certain moves I make. It's not vociferous, that little bit, but it is there, and it niggles. Before I turn down Phil Sanford tomor-

127

row, before I close the book on *that* book, I feel it deserves one hearing, one chance to speak for itself, one opportunity to be fairly judged. Then my bit of conscience will be satisfied that I've awarded the defendant due process. When I've read *The Seven Minutes* tonight, and convinced myself that it is indeed pornographic, written merely for the purpose of exploiting obscenity, and for no other reason—when I've decided that, then there'll be no difficulty about turning down Phil Sanford."

"What if you read it and believe it to be something more than pornography?"

"I won't let that happen." He smiled. "If it does happen, I'll have to wrestle with my bit of conscience and try to see if I can make it shut up."

He left the car, briskly went around to the other side, and helped Faye out. She took his hand, and they walked silently to the imposing oak door. She sought her key, opened the door partially, and then let go of it and turned back to him.

"Mike, I'm sure you won't do anything foolish about that book. But if . . . if for some irrational reason—if you can't overcome your guilt about not helping Sanford, if you find yourself wrestling your bit of conscience and losing—well, I thought I'd better tell you, I'll stick with you." Her arms had gone around him, and her head lay against his chest. "I can always force Dad to do anything I want. If I have to, I can force him to hold that vice-presidency open for you—until you've had your day in court."

He kissed her, and heard her heart, and felt his own desire rising. Quickly he disengaged himself, whispering, "Thanks, darling." Then he pointed her toward the doorway and started her inside.

After her door had closed, and he was alone, he lingered, peering up at the night's blue sky, illuminated by an infinity of stars, shining gemlike, as dazzling as the pure crystal prisms of a priceless chandelier. Up there, somewhere, was where all bits of conscience were born. Their journey downward to this habitat of man made them fragile, and the protective armor they assumed was so fleshly weak and frail, and they were so susceptible to extinction, that it was a miracle any bit of human conscience survived on earth.

It had shocked him this night to discover that the still small voice of his surviving conscience could demand equal time alongside his lustier, more dominating ambition. And it had shocked him that he had given in to the demands of that squeaky fragment of conscience.

He had promised it a hearing, and now the hearing must be held.

Barrett started for his car.

He would read the goddam book and get that over with, once and for all.

THE ELECTRIC CLOCK on the lamp table beside his bed showed the time to be four o'clock in the morning, and Mike Barrett was almost done.

In his pajamas and flannel robe, propped up by the two large pillows behind him, Barrett turned the last page of *The Seven Minutes*, read the final paragraph, and slowly closed the book. He stared down at it incredulously for a few moments and then reluctantly placed it on the blanket.

He was shaken to the very core of his being.

Only once before could he remember having been affected in this way by a book, and then it had been a work of nonfiction. As a youngster in high school, he had read *A General Introduction to Psychoanalysis*, by Sigmund Freud. While he had not comprehended every word in the Freud book, he had understood enough to know that he had experienced a revelation. Until the Freud book, Barrett had accepted the attitude of Freud's more conservative contemporaries that there was something faintly shameful and indecent about sex. In a single stroke, by giving him a new understanding, Freud had almost succeeded in liberating him from neurotic feelings about sex. At the time, he had been unable to define precisely what he had learned. Only later, in a study of social anthropologists by H. R. Hays, had his youthful revelation been clarified: "A society that modestly draped the legs of pianos was to learn from Freud that the innocence of childhood and the purity of women, two of its favorite illusions, were pure myth. This concept was as shocking as Darwin's assault upon the Garden of Eden."

Now, in these morning hours, for the second time in his life, a book had created an upheaval in Mike Barrett's feelings about sex.

He remained unmoving against his pillows, trying to assess his emotions. One emotion predominated. He was bursting with desire. His desire was to rush into the streets of the city and to search out the first female he could find. His need for her was not carnal, not to satisfy lust, but to confess and expiate the sinful insensitivity most men carried into their relationships with all women. He wanted to cry out to her that he had read a book and seen a light that illuminated completely the true minds and hearts of women, a light that might give him, and other men, a new perception of the opposite sex. In the glare of this pitiless cleansing light, the maggots of shame and fear, guilt and unawareness, would scurry back into primeval darkness, no longer able to gnaw away at the exposed roots of human relationships.

Oh, his thoughts, his hopes were grand tonight.

And all of this desire to spread the news of his find had grown out of these last hours with this remarkable book. It was not the book's style, its characters, its story that had moved him to a reaction of evangelistic fervor. It was the book's insight into the deepest womb where human behavior is born, and the book's naked honesty in exposing every aspect in the evolution of human behavior.

He tried to contain himself, bring his critical faculties to bear on what had moved him so. It was, to be sure, only a novel that he had read. It was no deep study, philosophical or psychological, of humankind. It was simply a brief work of fiction written by a heart, not a head. And if it was considered not as a whole, but piece by piece, if it could be picked apart, it was not without numerous flaws. Certainly, for the brave white hunters, the hunters of the obscene, there was abundant game—the four-letter words, the coarse phrases, the passages of abnormal and sacrilegious sex. But taken in its entirety, the book was not pornography. It was beauty, the beauty of truth that makes possible self-discovery and self-knowledge.

In total, *The Seven Minutes* was—and please forgive me, Faye —a work of art.

With respect and affection, Mike Barrett picked up the book once more. To the hand, it felt more substantial than its size would suggest. It consisted of only 171 printed pages.

He opened the book and studied the end papers. The inside of the hardcover board and the page opposite were illustrated with a photographic reproduction of the title page of the original Paris edition. He had not read this before, but he read it now:

THE SEVEN MINUTES

BY

J J JADWAY

The Étoile Press   18, rue de Berri   Paris

Copyright by The Étolie Press
Paris 1935

Printed in France
All Rights Reserved

Turning to the more attractive title page of the American edition, Barrett saw that only the typeface and the publishing information were different. Same title, same author, except now the imprint was that of Sanford House, Publishers, New York, and the year of publication was the present year.

The card page listed no previous published writings by J J Jadway. Then Barrett remembered that the back of the book jacket had explained that this remarkable tour de force had been the author's first and last novel, and that a potentially great career had been brought to an abrupt end by the author's untimely death in an accident outside Paris. Jadway had died at the age of twenty-seven. There were no further clues to the novelist's life.

The dedication page proved even more enigmatic. It contained only two words:

For
Cassie

The epigraph on the next page, Barrett knew, had provided the author with his structure for the novel. He reread the epigraph:

While there was a great variety in response, the majority
of females who had orgasms, whether brought on manu-

131

ally, orally, or through intercourse, reached the climactic
state in seven minutes.

—*The Collingwood Study of 100 Women,*
Ages 18 to 45 (London, 1931)

Those seven minutes, Barrett now knew, had been represented
by seven chapters in Jadway's book, each chapter in turn representing one minute in the mind of one woman who was lying on
a bed having sexual intercourse with an unnamed, unseen man.
The entire novel was told through the thoughts in this woman's
head, her feelings, her memories, her dreams, during the seven
minutes of copulation.

That was the framework and method of *The Seven Minutes*.

Suddenly Barrett wondered whether Jadway had known or had
at least met James Joyce during Joyce's last years in Paris. And
whether Jadway had read the Odyssey Press edition of *Ulysses*
that had been circulating in Paris in those years. Surely Jadway
had read Joyce's novel, or at least the last 25,000-word section of it,
the sad and happy and so-called salacious section which was Molly
Bloom's brilliant interior monologue.

The descriptions in the seven sensuous and revealing minutes
in the mind of Jadway's Cathleen bore some resemblance to the
stream-of-consciousness reverie in the mind of Joyce's Molly
Bloom. Had Jadway derived the idea for his book from Joyce? Immediately Barrett was curious.

He swung off the bed and padded on bare feet to his bookshelves, scanned the titles, and in seconds he held *Ulysses* in his
hands. He flipped the pages until he found Joyce's Molly in bed,
lying there "fulfilled, recumbent, big with seed."

He read on, joined Molly as she lay in her bed thinking of
Blazes Boylan, of young Stephen Dedalus, of her husband, Leo-
pold Bloom, of lovers possessed and lovers desired, of past and
future.

Molly's mind:

Ill put on my best shift and drawers let him have a good
eyeful out of that to make his micky stand for him Ill let
him know if thats what he wanted that his wife is fucked
yes and damn well fucked too up to my neck nearly not
by him 5 or 6 times handrunning theres the mark of his

spunk on the clean sheet I wouldnt bother to even iron it
out that ought to satisfy him if you dont believe me feel
my belly unless I made him stand there and put him into
me Ive a mind to tell him every scrap and make him do it
in front of me serve him rights its all his own fault if Im
an adultress . . .

But in the end, Molly's joyous mind:

when I put the rose in my hair like the Andalusian girls
used or shall I wear a red yes and how he kissed me under
the Moorish wall and I thought well as well him as another
and then I asked him with my eyes to ask again yes and
then he asked me would I say yes to say yes my mountain
flower and first I put my arms around him yes and drew
him down to me so he could feel my breasts all perfume
yes and his heart was going like mad and yes I said yes I
will Yes.

Absently, Barrett returned Molly Bloom to the bookshelf and
started back to his bed. He was less certain now that Jadway's
heroine, Cathleen, had been derived in any way from Joyce's
Molly. Possibly, possibly, but no matter. What he was absolutely
certain about was that Jadway had derived next to nothing from
Joyce's actual writing. This refresher had reminded Barrett of
Joyce's "stream of consciousness with its ever-shifting kaleidoscopic impressions," as the jurist Woolsey had put it, of Joyce's
loaded if unpunctuated sentences, of Joyce's compound words and
opaque use of English, of Joyce's poetry and parody and ear for
the comic. Jadway's *The Seven Minutes* reflected little of these innovations and flairs. Yet, in a sense, Jadway had undertaken a task
as difficult. For, while his entire novel was an inner monologue,
while occasionally there were effective passages of free word association, for the most the book was controlled and formal in its use
of conventional sentence structure, word order, punctuation, and
it built chronologically to a dramatic story revelation. Where Joyce
had sought the point of view of the character and sought to reproduce the formless meanderings of a person's mind, Jadway had
sought the point of view of the reader who was probing the character's mind and translating the occasional word acrobatics of the

character's mind into the more understandable language of conventional speech.

Barrett sat down on the bed, and reaching over to the table, he took up the bottle of cognac and poured himself a nightcap. Sipping the brandy, Barrett tried to sort out his reason for troubling to compare J J Jadway to James Joyce. At once he knew his reason. It had not been a literary exercise after all. It had been a legal exercise. Joyce's work had been published in Paris in 1922, and had been consistently banned thereafter in the United States as an obscene book until it was brought to trial in the District Court in New York before Judge John Woolsey. In 1933 Woolsey announced that, in spite of the book's "unusual frankness, I do not detect anywhere the leer of the sensualist. I hold, therefore, that it is not pornographic." And in 1934 Judge Augustus Hand of the Circuit Court of Appeals concurred in this opinion.

Now *The Seven Minutes* must undergo a similar, and perhaps more difficult, trial.

Would a judge or a jury hold that it was not pornographic?

Or would it be condemned as an utter obscenity?

He tried to capsulize the story for himself, posing in the role of "the average person, applying contemporary community standards." He reviewed its outlines quickly.

It began inside the mind of this young woman, Cathleen, who was lying on her back, naked, on a bed in a place unknown. It began with her thoughts and feelings as her male bed partner, also naked, made his entry into her and slowly started making love to her. As the sex act progressed, Cathleen's mind reacted to the coupling on two levels. On the first, she recorded her immediate physical sensations. On the second, inspired by her gradually mounting passion, she recollected fragments of sensual experiences from her youthful past and then she projected these memories into wildly erotic fancies of loves that she had not experienced but tried to imagine. Her imagination acted out scenes of physical lovemaking with Jesus, with Julius Caesar, with Shakespeare, with Chopin, with Galileo, with Byron, with Washington, with Parnell. Mixed through these fancies she imagined fornicating with a black African, an Asiatic, an American Indian.

Conjuring up these vivid mental pictures, she also relived moments of carnality with three actual men in her life who had been her lovers. The three men varied widely in their physical endowments and prowess, as well as in their attitudes toward women and love. Each of the three had offered her something, taught her something, and the experiences with all three had fused into making her an entire woman. And such story as there was in the novel was drawn out of Cathleen's decision to accept one of these men as her lifetime mate, the one she had taken to her bed this night, the very one who was inside her these seven minutes. Not until the last page, while gasping her love for him in the final paroxysms of her orgasm, would she call out and reveal the name of the one she had chosen.

This was the barest outline of the book that Barrett had read.

Still in the role of "the average reader," and "applying contemporary community standards," Barrett felt assured that the outline in itself would not be considered legally obscene, since the sex act by itself was not legally obscene.

But then Barrett realized that he had not reviewed the book with an entirely honest eye. He had substituted euphemisms for the realistic bed language that Jadway had employed. In outlining the essential story line of *The Seven Minutes*, he had been dishonest to Jadway's spirit of truth.

In his mind, Cathleen had been indulging in sexual intercourse, copulation, coupling, fornication, lovemaking.

In the mind of Jadway's Cathleen, she had simply been fucking.

The old Saxon word, on its own, might no longer prejudice a judge or a jury against a work of art. Its appearance in modern literature had been frequent and constant. The word no longer automatically made a literary work pornographic. It had won its natural place during an historic exchange that had enlivened the *Ulysses* trial.

Barrett remembered.

The language of James Joyce's novel had been under discussion. And part of the discussion was Joyce's use of the word "fucking."

Joyce's attorney had said to Judge Woolsey, "Judge, as to the word 'fuck,' one etymological dictionary gives its derivation as from *facere*—to make—the farmer fucked the seed into the soil. This, Your Honor, has more integrity than a euphemism used every day in every modern novel to describe precisely the same event."

135

"For example?" Judge Woolsey had asked.

"Oh—'They slept together,'" said Joyce's attorney. "It means the same thing."

Judge Woolsey had smiled. "But, Counselor, that isn't even usually the truth!"

In that exchange, "fucking" had been admitted to the printed page.

No, it was not the language of *The Seven Minutes* that might cause difficulty before a jury of average citizens. It was the context within which the language was used. For Molly Bloom to be fucked by a man named Boylan was one thing. For Jadway's Cathleen to imagine being fucked by the Father of His Country or the Son of God—that might be something else again.

Then there was another problem: the problem of explicit sex, of scenes which went "substantially beyond customary limits of candor in description or representation of such matters . . . matter which is utterly without redeeming social importance."

He had placed a copy of *Lady Chatterley's Lover* and the English edition of *The Trial of Lady Chatterley* on his bedside table earlier, hoping to skim them again after he had finished reading the Jadway novel. It was late now, but he could not resist picking up *Lady Chatterley's Lover* and leafing through it. He sought certain passages, until his eyes held on one. Mellors was making love to the lady. Forgive me, Mr. Joyce. Mellors was fucking the lady. He read the passage:

> . . . and the butting of his haunches seemed ridiculous to her, and the sort of anxiety of his penis to come to its little evacuating crisis seemed farcical. Yes, this was love, this ridiculous bouncing of the buttocks, and the wilting of the poor insignificant, moist little penis. This was the divine love!

Barrett went on through the novel, and here "softly he stroked the silky slope of her loins, down, down between her soft warm buttocks," and there "Tenderness, really—cunt tenderness," and again, "she held the penis soft in her hand."

Barrett closed the novel, set it on the night table, and took up the report of the London trial. Opening it, he came upon a Cambridge lecturer and biographer of D. H. Lawrence who was telling the court, "The sexual passages to which objection is taken I think cannot occupy more than thirty pages of the whole book. The book is some three hundred pages in length. . . . No man in his senses is going to write a book of three hundred pages as mere padding for thirty pages of sexual matter."

Only thirty pages of sexual matter, and 270-odd pages of other matter, and yet Lawrence's Lady had caused years of furor. Had the other matter been of enough social importance to redeem the explicit sexual scenes? Barrett turned back the pages to the opening statement of the defense:

"The author has again, it is clear from the book, had in mind certain things in our society—that is to say, our society as it was then in the twenties, in the years of the depression—of which he wholly disapproved. . . . He thought . . . that the ills from which society was suffering were not going to be cured by political action; and that the remedy lay in the restoration of right relations between human beings, and particularly in unions between men and women. One of the greatest things in life, he thought, was the relationship of a man and a woman in love, and their physical union formed an essential part of a relationship that was normal and wholesome and not something to be ashamed of, something to be discussed openly and frankly."

Redeeming social importance. And only one page in ten devoted to explicit sex.

Yet here was Jadway's *The Seven Minutes*, a book in which not merely one page in ten, but, rather, every single page, 171 out of 171 printed pages, was given over to sexual intercourse. But, dammit, that wasn't what it was all about, just animal fucking, or else why had he felt so purified as a person, and so enlightened about women, when he had finished the book? The protracted sexual intercourse had been beautiful, and a device through which to speak of understanding between the sexes, and of love and pity and tenderness and dreams and the meaning of life and death. Cathleen's behavior needed no redemption, but if the law demanded that Jadway's portrait of her passion required redeeming social importance, why, it was there, it was there in page after page.

Still, Barrett could see, there were other problems, many problems, including the author's motive and intent. How he wished

137

that Jadway had lived, to explain not only why he had written the book, but to solve many mysteries in its pages. But there was only Jadway's legacy, the book, to speak for him at its trial. Yes, there were serious problems, but whether the novel was obscenity or literature was not one of them, at least not to Barrett.

If the book was not obscene, there should be someone to stand up and protect it. Just as there should be someone to stand up and protect the Constitution and the Bill of Rights against those who would make a mockery of its guarantees.

He remembered Zelkin's obsession and Chief Justice Warren's concern that the Bill of Rights—including the portion of the First Amendment, "Congress shall make no law abridging the freedom of speech, or of the press"—might not be passed as a law today. Then he remembered that another lawyer, Edward Bennett Williams, a great trial attorney, had once written about this. Williams had felt that not only would the Bill of Rights fail to be passed as a law today, but that it would not even get out of committee and onto the floor of Congress for a vote.

"We have allowed an erosion of individual liberty and freedom to take place in the last three decades," Williams had stated, "not as the result of the overreaching of big government, nor as the result of the calculated assaults made upon liberties and freedom in the last decade, but rather because of collective lethargy and a cavalier attitude of unconcern. I think we have made a substitution in our national ranking of values—an evolutionary substitution that is only now reaching its culmination. We have placed security in a position of primacy and subordinated individual liberty to it."

If a man could not speak out on sex today, then one day he might not be able to speak out on religion, on politics, on public institutions, on poverty, on racial equality, on representation, on justice. One day that man, who embodied all men, would be mute. The Bill of Rights would be suppressed, banned, held seditious.

It could begin with a book.

Shaken, Barrett stared down at *The Seven Minutes*.

His mind was made up.

He looked at his bedside clock. It was three hours later in New York. It was seven-thirty in the Philip Sanford household.

Phil Sanford would be awake, and he might be waiting.

Barrett took the receiver off the telephone, then dialed Sanford's area code number and then his home number.

Sanford was wide awake, but his voice had been made almost inaudible by his anxiety.

"I don't know how I'll make out with Osborn," Barrett said, "but I do know how I feel about *The Seven Minutes*. I've just read it, Phil, and it deserves to be defended. I have no idea what'll happen to it or to us, but we've got to stand up and be counted. If we buckle under here, show the white flag to the censors, then freedom of speech has no future. They'll overrun us. We'll be silenced forever. This is the moment, and whatever the consequences, I'm ready to go all the way."

"Mike, I love you!"

"From here on in, we hang together, or we hang separately— so pack your bags. I expect you out here in a week. From now on, it's war."

Hanging up, he had no regrets. Perhaps it had cost him his big opportunity with Osborn. Most likely not, since Faye was on his side and had promised to take care of her father. So probably this wasn't much of a sacrifice and he wasn't much of a courageous advocate. But he was doing what he wanted to do. And it felt good for a change.

He took up the clock and set the alarm. He would sleep fast tonight, he knew, and he would awaken rested and strong, even after only four hours. He would rise early, because he must make another call. He would call Abe Zelkin to tell him that he had himself a partner, even if only for one landmark case.

Figuratively, briefly, there would be a shingle: Barrett and Zelkin, Counselors-at-Law and Do-Gooding.

III

When Mike Barrett returned to the Beverly Hills Hotel with Abe Zelkin in tow, Philip Sanford was waiting for them in the cool lobby. Since Zelkin and Sanford had spoken to each other many times on the long-distance telephone in the past ten days, Barrett had no need to introduce them formally. They had shaken hands warmly, and were immediately on a first-name basis.

"Leo Kimura called from Westwood," Barrett explained to the publisher. "He'll be a few minutes late. I told him he'd find us at the pool." Then, as the three of them started for the hotel's swimming pool, Barrett added, "Abe and I feel more secure when Leo is late. It means he's onto something. We couldn't possibly have managed the pretrial preparation in so short a time without a man like Leo Kimura."

"Having him on our side is like having a bevy of bloodhounds, only they still wouldn't add up to one Leo Kimura," said Zelkin with satisfaction.

"And I thought most Japanese in California were gardeners or restaurant proprietors," said Sanford.

"Their fathers were," said Zelkin. "Their fathers were also among the one hundred and ten thousand American citizens interned behind barbed wire after Pearl Harbor. Our own little experiment with concentration camps. Kimura's father was stuck in the Tule Lake Relocation Center. Speak of justice, eh? Well, our generation of Nisei hasn't forgotten it. Anyway, Leo Kimura never forgot it, and he wanted to see that no injustice like that ever happened again, so he worked his way through college and the University of Southern California Law School. The minute I began to interview him, just after I opened my office, I saw he was for me. You know, half of the law cases that come to trial are won or lost in a law library or out in the city where legwork is being done. For you, I'm taking care of the library, and Kimura is taking care of the legwork. And Mike here does something of everything, including saving his vocal cords for the trial."

They filed down to the hotel swimming pool. It was a balmy, windless day, and many of the obviously prosperous guests were seated around the pool in lounge wear or swim suits, and of the half-dozen people in the water three were pretty girls in bikinis. Although Barrett was wearing his summer seersucker, he felt overdressed. But then, he reminded himself, he would not be here long. This day, like every one in the past week and a half, would be a crowded business day.

He realized that Sanford and Zelkin were being led to their reserved table, which was set back from the pool and protected by a yellow sun umbrella. Side by side, Sanford and Zelkin presented an incongruous sight. Zelkin was Zelkin—the animated pumpkin head, below which was draped an oversized greenish sport jacket and uncreased slacks. Philip Sanford was a tailor's delight, and even the resort clothes he had changed into since arriving from the airport—a canvas beach jacket, Bermuda shorts, woven Italian moccasins—were sartorially impeccable. Sanford was Barrett's height, but trimmer, strictly athletic club, yet all this seeming strength was reduced to weakness by his slicked-down rust hair and a chalky complexion which seemed to wash away the individuality of his features, except for his permanent expression of anxiety.

Barrett caught up with his companions and joined them at the table in time to order his drink. The captain was told that they would wait to order lunch until the fourth member of their party had arrived. This reference to the tardy Kimura again provoked a series of nervous questions from Sanford about the progress that had been made in the ten days since Ben Fremont had entered a not-guilty plea and Barrett, together with Zelkin, had taken on the case and got the trial date set. With enthusiasm, Zelkin began outlining some of the preparations for the defense.

Barrett slipped on his sunglasses and stared moodily out at the swimming pool. Briefly his attention was attracted to a slim, ribby

141

California-type girl, maybe twenty, who was pulling herself up out of the water. A strip of bikini bra only partially contained her abundant breasts, and Barrett was sure they would pop free any minute. But they did not, and, dripping as she stood above the pool, triumphantly adjusting the bra, she grinned at Barrett, and he smiled somewhat sheepishly and pretended to give his attention to the conversation at the table.

"So you see, Phil, the first problem is time," Zelkin was saying earnestly. "You've shortchanged us on time. I understand the necessity for this, but—"

The gin and tonics were being served. Barrett took his glass, moving his chair slightly so that he could enjoy some of the sun. Then, sipping the drink, he dropped his head back, letting the sun bathe it, and he closed his eyes.

The problem *was* time, he knew, or the lack of it in this critical pretrial stage. He had brought it up earlier with Sanford at the airport, but he had not pressed his argument for his own selfish reasons.

He had reached International Airport a half hour before Phil Sanford's scheduled morning arrival from New York City. This had been fortunate, since Sanford's jet liner landed fourteen minutes early. Barrett had wasted not a minute posing the problem, actually posing it because Abe Zelkin had implored him to do so.

The skycap had deposited Sanford's luggage next to them on the cement walk before the terminal, and they were waiting for the airport's valet parking service to deliver Barrett's automobile, when Barrett had brought the subject up.

"Phil, we're going into this big trial, and Duncan or someone is making it a big trial—it's becoming a carnival like the Scopes trial or the Bruno Hauptmann trial," Barrett had begun.

"Incredible the way this has caught on," said Sanford with unconcealed pleasure. "Not only in the East, not only with every newspaper in America, but abroad, in England, France, Germany, Italy, everywhere. We retain a clipping service, and—"

"I know what's happening, and that's another thing that bothers me," said Barrett. "It's bad enough to have a complicated case, but it's infinitely worse when most of the newspapers, television, and radio media turn it into a spectacular. So, what I started to say is that we're going into this with little more than two weeks of preparation. The only thing that makes a defense possible is that we've been working double time. So maybe we'll have the equivalent of four weeks' preparation before we go into court. Considering what's at stake, we could easily use twelve to sixteen weeks."

"Your District Attorney won't have any more time than you've had," protested Sanford, "and he seems eager to get into court."

"The prosecution is almost always more eager to get into court than the defense. The state is the aggressor. In this case, the D.A.'s Office was at work, preparing an attack on the book, before we knew there would be an arrest. And they already have a star witness. It is to their advantage to stage their show now, while public opinion is on their side, while hysteria keeps mounting about the rape and that book. Every morning we're greeted by a bedside bulletin from Mount Sinai telling us of Sheri Moore's critical condition, her prolonged coma, and every bulletin is accompanied by a reiteration of what put her in the hospital—not Jerry Griffith but J J Jadway. But as Zelkin keeps reminding me, it is the defense that traditionally fights for more time, stalls, not only to allow any climate of hysteria to change, but to gain time for a thorough preparation. As the defense, we're a step behind. We're counterpunching, and we need time to catch up and then take the initiative. If there were less internal pressure, we could ask for one continuance after another, throw up a screen of pretrial motions and writs, delay the confrontation by as much as six months to a year. Abe begged me to bring it up with you once more. Can't we convince you to let us try to delay the trial?"

"Impossible," said Sanford. "Any long delay would be as disastrous for me as losing the trial itself. All those copies of the book are out. What could the stores do with them? They'd be afraid to display them. They wouldn't have room to stock them if the outcome of the trial were long in doubt and made that necessary. Most of the store owners would probably panic and return their shipments to us. A year from now, it is unlikely that we'd be able to revive a corpse. No, in spite of the risk, we've got to plunge right into it."

Barrett's car had arrived then, and as Sanford's bags were placed in the trunk, Barrett had wondered how truthful were the reasons Sanford had given for wanting a speedy trial. It occurred to him that Sanford, as much as Elmo Duncan, wanted to take advantage of the publicity that the book and the case were receiving.

Then, as he had settled into the driver's seat, Barrett had realized that part of the fault was his own. He had been paying lip service to Zelkin's wish for a postponement. He had not been more persuasive about a delay because of private and selfish reasons. Faye had indeed succeeded in cajoling her father to hold the vice-presidency open for him another month. Barrett had one more option on a successful future. He dared not let it expire.

Yet, as he drove toward the freeway, he had found himself troubled by his conscience. He had committed himself to defending a book in which he believed. At the same time, he was as responsible as his client, Phil Sanford, for not giving his side the days and weeks necessary to build an impregnable and well-armed defense. Their position was not merely risky, but downright perilous.

It was as if Phil Sanford had read his mind. Sanford had been silently brooding, and when they were on the San Diego Freeway he had given voice to his concern. "Mike, you made me a little nervous back there with your talk. You almost sounded defeatist."

"I'm anything but defeatist," Barrett had replied. "I'm determined to win this one. We all are. It just worries me going into battle with a rifle when, if there'd been time, I might have had a rocket launcher."

"Whenever I called you or Abe, you sounded busy enough, like you were getting some big guns on our side."

"We are, we are, but I just want to be sure they're big enough and the very best. In fact, before we sit down to lunch, I'd better bring you up to date."

As they careened over the freeway, Barrett had recited the names of the defense witnesses that had already been lined up. They had Sir Esmond Ingram, the elderly, cranky, and celebrated onetime Oxford don, who had years ago hailed *The Seven Minutes* as being "one of the most honest, sensitive, and distinguished works of art created in modern Western literature," a blurb which Sanford House had used extensively in promoting the novel.

In his retirement, Sir Esmond had devoted himself to three marriages and divorces, to English girls half his age. He had given his energies to foundations supporting a world calendar, a universal language, and a crusade for vegetarianism. He had been twice jailed, briefly, for lying down before No. 10 Downing Street in protest against nuclear armament. Because of Sir Esmond's growing reputation for eccentricity, Barrett had worried that the value of Sir Esmond's championship of the Jadway book might be weakened. But Zelkin had pointed out that elderly Englishmen were understood by Americans to be consistently eccentric, and that an English accent from the witness stand always carried authority and was effective and tended to intimidate a jury, and, besides, who in the hell else was there of such a reputation who had ever praised the book?

Sir Esmond had been reached by transatlantic telephone in his Sussex cottage, and his enthusiasm for the book (although Barrett had a vague suspicion that the English don thought they were talking about *Lady Chatterley's Lover*) had been as great as ever. Yes, he would be delighted to cooperate against "the book burners," provided his sponsors could convince the United States immigration people that he was not an anarchist. Zelkin had been able to so convince immigration, and Sir Esmond Ingram would be one of their chief witnesses.

And, Barrett had reassured Sanford, there were others being assembled for different purposes. Guy Collins, the popular exponent of the naturalistic novel who had often written about how much he had been favorably influenced by Jadway's book, had agreed to be a defense witness. Efforts were being made to obtain the support of two or three other literary experts who admired *The Seven Minutes*. Then, anticipating the District Attorney's effort to prove, through Jerry Griffith and additional witnesses, that the book's prurient appeal endangered the youth of America and general community security, both Barrett and Zelkin had sought witnesses to counteract such a contention. For the defense, they had acquired the services of Dr. Yale Finegood, a psychiatric authority on juvenile violence and delinquency, and of Dr. Rolf Lagergren, a Swedish specialist in sex surveys whose findings had earned him international renown and a visiting professorship at Reardon College in Wisconsin. Both Finegood and Lagergren attributed juvenile crime to causes other than obscene literature and motion pictures, and their enlistment on the side of the defense had been a reason for some optimism.

"But make no mistake about one thing," Barrett had said, guiding the car into the Sunset Boulevard off ramp. "The real defendant in this trial will not be Ben Fremont, but J J Jadway. In every major case of this kind, a central issue has always been the author's motivation and purpose in writing the book, because this would help to establish that his work had some social importance. Now, this is thin ice, and we have to determine whether we dare face crossing it or should detour. We have a choice. So has the District Attorney. Each side has to determine how it intends to proceed before the fireworks begin."

"Exactly what do you mean, Mike?"

"If we don't have sufficient proof that Jadway's intent was beyond reproach in his writing *The Seven Minutes*, we'd be better off asserting that an author's intent has nothing to do with obscenity, which has been done successfully before. We have Justice Douglas' dissent in the Ginzburg case to hide behind. Douglas argued, 'A book should stand on its own, irrespective of the reasons why it was written or the wiles used in selling it.' Even if we hold to this, we still might be pushed out on that thin ice by the prosecution. If that happened, we could always fall back on the argument Charles Rembar used in one *Fanny Hill* appeal. You see, when Rembar defended *Lady Chatterley* earlier, he had had no trouble proving that Lawrence's intentions in writing the book were of the best. But in defending *Fanny Hill* there was rough sledding, because the only evidence about the author's motives showed that he had written the book cynically, for crassly commercial reasons. Remember? John Cleland was in debtor's prison. He needed money to get out. A publisher approached him and offered him twenty guineas, enough to get him out of jail, if he wrote a salacious novel to order, one that might sell. So, presumably, Cleland wrote *Fanny Hill* for that reason, for the money to be freed, and he was released, and the publisher made ten thousand pounds in profit on subsequent sales."

"That's right," said Sanford. "How did the defense lawyer explain that?"

"Rembar explained it sensibly. Cleland's motives, he insisted, were a question of literary history, not of law. As Rembar put it, 'The courts simply could not decide, two and a quarter centuries later, what had gone on inside Cleland's head.' What mattered was the end result, the book, its ideas, its view of life, not the personal reasons that had made an author write his book. Besides, argued Rembar, 'It would be both futile and unbecoming . . . for courts to inquire into the diverse springs of artistic endeavor. The miserable record made by artists as critics of their own work—the ludicrous verbalizations that we sometimes hear from talented people in the nonverbal arts—shows that their stated plans are of little consequence; what they create is of the greatest consequence.' "

"What was the final verdict of the judges?"

"They said nay. Impressive, but not impressive enough," said Barrett sourly. "The judges voted three to two for suppression, because they didn't accept Rembar's arguments generally."

"But you indicated that we have another choice?"

"We do. The other choice is to face up to what is ahead of us. The preponderance of legal opinion holds that an author's motivation and intent is one of the important issues in holding a book to be obscene or not. Take Judge Woolsey in the *Ulysses* trial. He observed, 'In any case where a book is claimed to be obscene it must first be determined whether the intent with which it was written was what is called, according to the usual phrase, pornographic—that is, written for the purpose of exploiting obscenity.' Later, Judge van Pelt Bryan, in one of the *Lady Chatterley* cases, added, 'The sincerity and honesty of purpose of an author as expressed in a manner in which a book is written and in which his theme and ideas are developed has a great deal to do with whether it is of literary and intellectual merit. Here, as in the *Ulysses* case, there is no question about Lawrence's honesty and sincerity of purposes, artistic integrity and lack of intention to appeal to prurient interest.' "

Barrett had paused and glanced at Sanford's troubled profile. "That's our issue, Phil. Did Jadway write his book honestly, sincerely, with artistic integrity? That's the question we have to answer affirmatively and without reservation. It is a question that will be in every juror's mind. Either we pussyfoot and back away or we set out to prove, beyond a shadow of a doubt, that Jadway did not write this book for commercial reasons but wrote it for artistic and moral reasons, so that it has that necessary social importance. Anyway, Abe and I have made our choice. We've decided to attempt to prove Jadway's good intentions."

Sanford had groaned. "How are you ever going to prove that? Jadway's been dead a million years. He was young, he was nobody, he was practically unknown when he died. Nothing remains to prove his good intentions. You know how hard I've dug on my end. I couldn't turn up a thing. He left nothing, and he can tell us nothing. Dead men tell no tales, to coin an expression."

"But ghosts can be very impressive," Barrett had said calmly. He had pointed off to his right. "By the way, there's the UCLA campus. Jerry Griffith's school. I think we may be doing a little research there."

Sanford had showed no interest in the Los Angeles campus of the University of California. "What do you mean about Jadway's ghost?"

"Few people die without leaving some heritage behind. Maybe it's only something of themselves they revealed or bequeathed to friends or acquaintances. We've been making use of the budget you gave us for European investigators. We have several scurrying around Paris, and now other points as well. We're trying to invoke the ghost of Jadway. We've learned there was an Italian artist, da Vecchi by name, who used to frequent the cafés in Paris where Jadway hung out in the thirties. We've learned that da Vecchi is alive, and that he once painted a portrait of Jadway. If so, that'll be the first pictorial representation of him to come to light. Anyway, we're trying to locate the painter. Then we're on the trail of a Contessa Daphne Orsoni. She's a Dallas woman who married a rich Italian count. Shortly after Jadway published his book, he was vacationing in Venice, and the Contessa had heard of Jadway's 'naughty' novel and she invited him to a masked ball at her palazzo. We've traced her to Spain. Apparently she has a place on the Costa Brava. But to invoke the good ghost, our main hope is still centered on the Frenchman who published the underground version of *The Seven Minutes*—"

"Christian Leroux," interrupted Sanford. "Have you heard anything more?"

"Just the same news I gave you a few days ago. Étoile Press has expired, but Leroux is very much among the living. As long as Leroux is alive, we can resurrect Jadway's shade. If we can get our hands on the French publisher, we'll have our own star witness, the one we need to offset the Griffith boy's testimony. After all, Leroux *did* bring out *The Seven Minutes*. He must have believed in it, and he must have known a good deal about the book's author. He's our man. We're on his trail and getting warm. Kimura hoped to have some word on this today."

"We've absolutely got to get Leroux," said Sanford.

Barrett snorted. "You're telling me?"

A few minutes later he had dropped Phil Sanford off at the Beverly Hills Hotel, where Sanford had reserved a bungalow, and then Barrett had gone on to the office on Wilshire Boulevard. He had spent two hours conferring with Zelkin, making telephone calls, and dictating to Donna Novik, the secretary he shared with Zelkin. He enjoyed working with Donna. She was an eyesore, henna hair, narrow eyes, overly powdered bloated face, frumpy clothes on a shapeless body, but she was a delight because she was as trustworthy as a madonna, fiercely devoted and loyal, and had such astonishing skills at the stenotyper, the electric typewriter, and the calculator that Barrett sometimes thought she was plugged into an electrical outlet herself.

After Kimura had telephoned that he would be late, Barrett had buzzed Zelkin, and together they had gone to meet Philip Sanford for lunch.

And here they were now. Barrett realized that his forehead was ablaze from the sun and that the glass in his hand was empty and that Zelkin was introducing Sanford to Leo Kimura. Pulling his chair in under the umbrella, Barrett gave Kimura a mock bow, and Kimura bowed back seriously, then settled down in the place left for him. Balancing his bulging briefcase on his knees, he was already unlocking it.

"You want a drink or are you famished?" asked Barrett.

"Famished," said Kimura. "I feel like the whole Donner Party in one." But then he was at once apologetic, like a servant who had considered his own comfort before his employer's. "I can wait, if you prefer to talk first."

Barrett had great affection for the Nisei attorney. Kimura had a crew cut, a saffron-complected face with features that seemed impassive, and the steely, springy appearance of the kind of person they shoot out of cannons.

149

"We prefer to eat *and* talk," said Barrett.

Zelkin was already signaling for menus, and after the menus came they ordered sparingly.

The moment that the captain had gone, they all concentrated on Kimura. "Well," Zelkin inquired, "what's the latest, Leo?"

Kimura had finished extracting papers from his briefcase. Closing the briefcase, propping it against his chair, he laid his papers on the table before him and looked up. "Some progress, I believe. I will save the best for the last. First, Norman C. Quandt." He addressed himself to their new client. "Mr. Sanford, I have here the information you dictated on how you purchased the rights to *The Seven Minutes* from Mr. Quandt. Now that you are here in person before me, I would like the opportunity to learn whether anything was omitted. Could you review the facts of the acquisition once more?"

Sanford shrugged. "I doubt if there's anything I can add. However, I'll be glad to run through it again. Two years ago my father sent me to represent him at the Frankfurt Book Fair. I was taken to dinner one night by an old friend of my father's, Herr Karl Graeber, who owns a solid and well-known publishing house in Munich. We got to discussing the new freedom in writing and publishing, and Graeber said it was a good thing, because soon many works that had long deserved publication might find their way to the public. He mentioned several such works, but the one he admired first and foremost was something called *The Seven Minutes*. He had hoped to publish it himself, in the period just as Hitler was coming to power, but that had been impossible and he'd been lucky to flee with his life. Since he was re-established in Germany, I asked him why he didn't undertake it once more. He said that by now he was too old to begin a fight against the Bonn conservatives, and, besides, he was now specializing in textbooks and religious books, and a book such as Jadway's in his catalogue might harm the rest of his list. Graeber felt that there was far more freedom in America, and hence the book was more likely to have its first accepted public appearance in our country. He felt also that my father's imprint might give the book a certain protection. I asked who owned the rights to *The Seven Minutes*. Graeber said he had heard that Leroux had sold the rights to some small borderline publisher in New York named Norman C. Quandt.

Graeber located a copy of the Étoile edition and asked me to show it to Wesley R., my father. I was already bringing a number of new books back from the Frankfurt Fair, and so I added the Jadway book to the rest of them. I took a ship home, and since there was plenty of time to read, and what Graeber had told me about the Jadway novel titillated me, I read it. Before I even finished it, I knew that it was nothing I could show my father. It just wasn't his type of literature. So I showed him the other books I'd found, but not this one. Then last year, as you know, my father fell ill, and I was temporarily put in charge of Sanford House. I was eager to find something unusual and provocative, and I remembered the Jadway book. I thought the timing was right. So I looked up Norman C. Quandt."

"He was in New York?" asked Kimura, brandishing a ballpoint pen.

"He had offices right on Forty-fourth Street. I saw him there. Quandt was nothing more than a mail-order publisher of hard-core pornography, original paperbacks that specialized in sadism and masochism. And he was in trouble. He had just been tried in a United States district court on charges brought by the Postmaster General that he was mailing obscene matter. He had been found guilty. He was appealing the lower-court decision and hoping to bring the matter before the United States Supreme Court. He was pressed for money to fight his case, and he was more than happy to sell off his rights to *The Seven Minutes*. Within three days the contracts were drawn and signed, and I had the Jadway book for five thousand dollars. That's all I can tell you, Leo. I'm afraid I've given you nothing new."

Kimura had been checking Sanford's recital with the pages before him. "And after that you never saw Quandt again?"

"Never," said Sanford. "I followed his appeal to the Supreme Court, of course. As we know, the Supreme Court, purely on a technicality, reversed the decision of the lower court by a five-to-four vote. Quandt was acquitted. Of course, he took an awful beating in the appeals. It was clear he'd been running a shoddy operation, pandering to the most perverted tastes, and I suppose he knew better than to tangle with the postal authorities again. Anyway, when I was getting ready to publish *The Seven Minutes*, and we needed more jacket copy on Jadway, I thought Quandt might be able to help. You know, I figured he might have heard something from Leroux. So I did call Quandt. He was no longer at the old stand. That's when I learned he'd given up publishing and moved to Pittsburgh—"

"It says Philadelphia here," said Kimura.

"I'm sorry. Yes, Philadelphia. I couldn't locate him there either, and I had no idea what business he was in by then."

"He is in the motion-picture business and he is in Southern California now," said Kimura.

Barrett sat up. "No kidding, Leo? When did you find that out?"

"Today. But unfortunately there is no Quandt listed in our telephone directories."

"If he's in the movie business, he shouldn't be hard to find," said Zelkin.

For the first time, Kimura smiled faintly. "Mr. Zelkin, there are movies and there are movies. Anyway, I have some leads, and I expect one should eventually bring us to Mr. Quandt."

Sanford had turned worriedly to Barrett. "Mike, you're not thinking of putting that Quandt on the witness stand if you find him, are you?"

"Heaven forbid," said Barrett. "No. But he might provide us with some vital information on Jadway's life. In fact, the very information you'd hoped to get from him before, something he might have heard from Leroux." Barrett directed himself to Kimura once more. "Which brings us to our most important witness. What's the word on Leroux?"

"Christian Leroux," said Kimura, savoring the name. "I was keeping him for last." He shuffled his notes, until he had found what he wanted. "Christian Leroux. Most hopeful. I have just heard from our man in Paris. He tracked Leroux to an apartment on the Left Bank. A hundred-franc tip to the concierge produced the information that Leroux had just gone off to the Riviera and had made a reservation at the Hotel Balmoral in Monte Carlo. He should be there any—well, he should have arrived already. Our Paris man hired a private detective in Nice, a Monsieur Dubois, and fully instructed him. This Dubois drove up to Monte Carlo. He will be in the Hotel Balmoral waiting for Leroux to check in."

"Very thorough," said Barrett. "And most hopeful, Leo, as you put it."

"Wonderful, wonderful," said Sanford, plucking a cigarette from a patch pocket of his canvas jacket.

Kimura had separated a clipped sheaf of notes from the other papers. "As to the Griffith family, I have not been able to add substantially to the dossier we have assembled. A few more facts on the backgrounds of Frank Griffith, his wife, Ethel Griffith. No further data on the niece who lives with them, Margaret or Maggie Russell. No chinks in the family armor—yet."

"What about the boy?" inquired Zelkin.

"I was coming to him," said Kimura, flipping the pages. "I am afraid we will have to press our investigation harder. I have a start—"

"A start?" wailed Zelkin. "We'll be selecting a jury in a couple of days. The minute the jury is impaneled, sworn in, the trial begins."

"Unless one has a start, there can never be a finish," said Kimura. "Forgive me, but there is a difficulty in researching one who is still of college age. With a short life, there is no long history. We are acquainted with certain facts. Jerry Griffith was an honor student in prep school. He is now in his third year of college, and he is not doing so well academically. I visited UCLA today. I remembered there are counselors for the students. I was able to find Jerry Griffith's counselor. She said she couldn't discuss Jerry—there's a rule against giving out information on any student unless there's clearance from on high. So I went through the required procedure and finally got this clearance from the Dean of the College of Letters and Science. The counselor was notified that she could discuss Jerry with any person from our office. That was a start."

Kimura's painstaking, detailed account was making Barrett restless. "What did the counselor have to say, Leo?"

"Once the clearance came, she was eager to be entirely cooperative. It turned out she has had several meetings with Jerry and is most disturbed by what he has done. Because there are so few sources to give us information on Jerry, I felt that she was too important for me to interrogate. I felt it would be better if you or Mr. Zelkin saw her. She is a Mrs. Henrietta Lott. I have arranged an appointment for either one of you this afternoon. Mrs. Lott will be extremely busy later in the week, so I thought I must take advantage of her readiness to discuss Jerry today." He pulled free a slip of paper and held it out tentatively. "Her name, office number—the academic counselors' offices are in the Administration Building—and the time of the appointment. I hope one of you—"

Barrett reached for the slip. "I'll take it," he said to Zelkin. "I intended to drop by UCLA later in the afternoon, anyway. They've got a sharp English department, and I want to learn whether any member of the faculty understands the book well enough to talk about it sympathetically in court. Before that, I'm going to look in on Ben Fremont."

"And I'll be out pounding the pavements, too," said Zelkin.

"Leo," said Barrett to Kimura, "you'd better stick close to the office, or let Donna know where she can find you if you go out, so we don't miss that call from Monte Carlo. Once we've got that French publisher, we've got a real chance. Here comes the food now. . . . Well, Phil, old boy, how does it feel to be where the action is?"

Sanford stretched and beamed. "It's beginning to feel good, now that I can see what's being done. I tell you, if that District Attorney—Duncan—if Duncan knew half of what we're doing, he'd throw in the towel."

Barrett removed his sunglasses and made a wry face. "Don't be too sure of that. If *we* knew half of what *he* is doing, we might want to kill ourselves. One thing you can bet on. Elmo Duncan isn't sitting on his hands."

For Elmo Duncan, the telephone call and the summons early this morning had been unexpected, and his presence here this early afternoon, in this renowned prelate's office, had about it an air of the strange and the mysterious.

Waiting now in the Chancery office for the appearance of His Eminence, Cardinal MacManus, the District Attorney was again conscious of the empty velour armchair facing the portrait of the Pope that hung on an otherwise barren wall. When the Cardinal's secretary had escorted him into this room, Duncan had been told that every prince of the Church had such a chair facing a portrait of the Pope, a chair kept ready should His Holiness ever pay an unexpected visit in person. Tradition.

Elmo Duncan continued his survey of the Chancery office. Every decoration gave the impression of venerable age and continuity. Again, tradition. Rich damask draperies framed the windows. The fireplace hearth was charred, blackened by years of providing warmth. On the old desk, atop a pedestal, stood a driftwood cross bearing a drooping carved figure of the Saviour, a crucifix which might have been carried by Junípero Serra in his trampings through California.

Only one inharmonious object intruded. This on the prince's desk also. A flashy late-model dictating machine. The same model that Duncan had in his very own office.

Although somewhat reassured that he and the prince of the Church might have more in common than he had feared, Duncan still felt uneasy. He yearned for a cigarette. But as a Protestant in the inner headquarters of the Los Angeles diocese of the Catholic Church, he had no idea of the restrictions or, indeed, of the Cardinal's personal quirks. Duncan decided not to smoke.

Once more Duncan speculated on the early-morning summons.

The telephone call had come from the Very Reverend Monsignor Voorhes.

"District Attorney Duncan?" Monsignor Voorhes had introduced himself briskly. "I am secretary to His Eminence, Cardinal MacManus, Archbishop of Los Angeles. I am telephoning at the personal request of Cardinal MacManus. It concerns a matter in which His Eminence has taken a considerable interest."

"Yes?"

"I refer to the forthcoming legal trial regarding the book *The Seven Minutes*, and your prosecution of this work. The Cardinal feels that your civic office and his church office may have a common goal in this affair and may benefit by mutually cooperating."

"Well, I—I'd certainly welcome cooperation from any source. But it's not clear to me what you, or rather His Eminence has in mind."

"It would gratify the Church to have this work obliterated. The Cardinal feels he can achieve this end by being useful to your cause."

"Do you have anything specific in mind?"

"Yes. That is the purpose of my call, Mr. Duncan. His Eminence would like to meet with you at your earliest convenience to explain."

"I'd be glad to see him today."

"Excellent. Perhaps it would be wisest if the meeting were to take place in Cardinal MacManus' Chancery office. We are located at 1519 West Ninth Street, near downtown Los Angeles. Would two o'clock this afternoon be satisfactory?"

"I'll see that it is. You can tell His Eminence that I'll be there at two. And be sure to let him know how much I appreciate his—his interest in this case."

Later, when he had joined Luther Yerkes, Harvey Underwood, and Irwin Blair for a business lunch on the patio of Yerkes' Bel-Air palace, Duncan had brought up the curious call and wondered what it could mean.

Yerkes had warned Duncan immediately not to expect any concrete evidence from Cardinal MacManus. "The Church has a continuing stake in censorship," Yerkes had said, "so he'll probably assure you that you'll have the Lord in your corner. Don't expect more than that." Then the subject of Duncan's appointment with Cardinal MacManus had been dismissed, because there was important work to be done. This very evening a fund-raising affair sponsored by the Strength Through Decency League was being held in the Grand Ballroom of the Beverly Hilton Hotel. The principal speaker, as arranged by Irwin Blair, would be District Attorney Elmo Duncan. The title of his speech would be "The Freedom to Corrupt." It was to the revising and strengthening of this prepared speech that the four of them had devoted the rest of the lunch hour.

And now Elmo Duncan stood in the Chancery office of the Los Angeles diocese, waiting to learn what the Cardinal would offer that might be "useful" to his case. Would the offer be, as Yerkes had so cynically suggested, the blessings of the Lord? Or would it be something more substantial?

"Mr. Duncan, I am sorry to have kept you. How very kind of you to come."

The voice had issued from the far corner of the office, and Duncan whirled around to see Cardinal MacManus shutting a door behind him as he lifted a welcoming hand. Duncan had seen the Cardinal's picture in the newspapers frequently, and in these photographs he had always looked his age, which was seventy-eight. Now, though he wore a Roman collar and a black suit instead of his elaborate ceremonial vestments, he resembled the face and cleric in the photographs—the same cottony white hair, baggy eyes, wrinkled skin, hunched back. What was not the same, what was evident when seen in person, was the Cardinal's alertness. Although limping, he advanced across the room rapidly, his sunken eyes lively, one bony hand vigorously brushing lint off his black jacket and the other hand extended.

Duncan took the prelate's hand. "Cardinal MacManus, this is a pleasure."

"My pleasure, sir, and your kindness to accommodate me by coming such a distance. It was not my age or infirmities that kept me from going to you. It was, in fact, my knowledge that it would serve neither of us—might, indeed, be misrepresented in certain circles—if church and state were not kept separate in the public view, despite the truism that the religious and the secular may have a single goal."

"I quite understand, Your Eminence," said Duncan.

"Make yourself comfortable," said the Cardinal, steering Duncan toward the long brown sofa.

Courteously Duncan waited for the prelate to settle himself on the sofa, and then Duncan sat down a few feet from him.

"I shall not mince words," the Cardinal said. His voice was dry and brittle, and sounded like wrapping paper being crumpled and balled in a fist. "When one is as old as I am, or as young as you are, one has learned not to waste words or time with interminable social amenities. My secretary informed you of my interest in the trial you are about to undertake and the Church's desire to assist you as best it can."

"He did tell me that, and nothing more. So I am not quite certain what . . ."

"What to expect, eh? You may be doubtful of what aid I can give you, and if so, that is understandable. You may think that I have you here merely to bless your crusade and to promise you my prayers. Well, indeed, I do bless your enterprise and I do pledge you my prayers. We have a rather good one on behalf of decent literature, one which received the imprimatur of the Archbishop of Cincinnati." At once, eyes cast upward, jowls shaking, he began to recite in a deep, crackling voice. " 'O God, Who hast said, "Suffer the Little Children to come unto Me," assist and bless us in our efforts to arouse public opinion, so that we may

157

eliminate obscene and indecent literature from bookracks and newsstands. With Your Divine Guidance, may the laws be enforced so that this type of literature may no longer exist in our country and throughout the world.'" He caught his breath, wheezed asthmatically, then resumed, "'Virgin Mary, whose life is an inspiration to all, watch over us and intercede for us so that our efforts may be successful, through Jesus Christ, Our Lord. Amen.'"

Awed, Duncan whispered, "Thank you, Your Eminence."

Cardinal MacManus' hairy nostrils sniffed. "If that were all I had to offer you, you would have no reason to thank me. It is not all that I have to offer you. I have much, much more to offer." He scratched inside his stiff Roman collar, and the great jewel set in the heavy ring on one finger glittered, as he sat lost in thought for several moments. Then he crossed his arms, stared at the ceiling, and began to speak quietly.

"I have said we have a common cause. And we do. Our enemies would like to believe that the Church's only interest is in morality and religion at the sacrifice of freedom of speech. This is not true. We dwell in an ordered society. To keep it ordered and civilized, we must have authority and we must have certain restrictions. Without restrictions, we would have no democratic freedoms left after a time. We would have a godless, pagan society where anarchy reigned and only might made right. The Church wants freedom of speech. We wish to restrict only those who would abuse this freedom. As a Catholic editor has remarked, we do not ask for prudery, we ask only for prudence. We are not, as this editor went on, attempting to be arbiters of the national taste where an adult's freedom of choice is concerned. We are interested only in curbing obvious obscenity and preventing its corruption of youth. We are defenders of real literature, even vulgar literature if it has social value and is sincere. We are the opponents only of pornography, of pornography that disguises itself as literature but has no purpose other than to drive the young into lives of sin. This the Church stands against. I cannot believe that your law-enforcement office of the state thinks differently from us. It was not a priest delivering a church sermon, but a spokesman of the Chicago Police Department, who made the statement, 'Obscene literature is wanton, depraved, nauseating, despicable, demoralizing, destructive and capable of poisoning any mind at any age. Obscene publications mock the marriage vow, scorn chastity and fidelity, and glorify adultery, fornication, prostitution and unnatural sex relations.' I assume, then, Mr. Duncan, we are of one mind about books like *The Seven Minutes?*"

"We are of the same mind," said Duncan with conviction. "We don't want to weaken freedom, but rather reinforce it by eliminating those who would corrupt it."

"Very well. Now, in 1938 the Catholic bishops of the United States, also enlisting the leaders of many other faiths, established NODL—the National Organization for Decent Literature—and they did this, as they stated, 'to set in motion the moral forces of the entire country . . . against the lascivious type of literature which threatens moral, social and national life.' Normally, in a local community action, it would be from NODL's successor, CDL—Citizens for Decent Literature—that you might expect to receive the Church's cooperation. However, because the Church views *The Seven Minutes* as an extraordinarily destructive force, because your case against it exceeds national boundaries and takes on international importance, and because the Church is uniquely equipped to give you special support in this trial, the Church has seen fit to extend cooperation from its very highest level."

"The very highest—?" Duncan repeated, bewildered.

"From the Vatican itself. I have received instructions from the Cardinal in charge of the Sacred Congregation for the Doctrine of the Faith in the Vatican. Mr. Duncan, it is at the personal request of His Holiness the Pope that the Sacred Congregation is volunteering its entire resources to be used on behalf of your case."

Duncan's confusion was complete. "You mean the Pope—His Holiness—he knows about our trial? I'm surprised—delighted, that he is interested, of course—but I can't understand why he . . ."

"I will enlighten you," said Cardinal MacManus. "And then I will help you."

"Please do," said Duncan.

"To enlighten you, to explain when the seed of our interest in a case such as yours was planted, I must start at the very beginning. Soon after Gutenberg made it possible for books to appear in great quantities in Western Europe—that is to say, after 1454— the Vatican realized that it must adjust itself to this new phenomenon. Until then the pulpit had been the primary means by which the priest disseminated knowledge and faith. Now books offered to become a greater transmission agent for good. At the same time, the Vatican became aware of the power of books to spread evil, to subvert men's minds and hearts and cause them to behave in ways harmful to society and religion. In 1557, under the guidance of Pope Paul IV, the Church acted. It drew up a list of books condemned for reasons of sensuality, mysticism, or heretical ideas and it published this condemned list as the first *Index Librorum Expurgatorius.* During the four centuries since its initial publication, the *Index* has been brought up to date and reissued from time to time. Have you ever seen a copy?"

"No," said Duncan.

"Let me show you a recent edition." The Cardinal rose, hobbled to his desk, picked up a small gray paperbound volume, and returned to the sofa with it. "Here it is, five hundred and ten pages, listing approximately five thousand condemned books, each title listed in the language in which it was originally written." He opened the *Index.* "Allow me to translate a few remarks from a preface prepared for the 1929 edition, a preface included in this more recent edition which appeared in 1946. It begins," the Cardinal translated slowly, " 'Throughout its life the Church had always to endure tremendous persecutions of all kinds while the number of its heroes and martyrs grew steadily. But today there is a much more dangerous threat coming from hell: the immoral press. There is no worse danger than that and therefore the Church never ceases to caution the faithful against it.' "

Cardinal MacManus halted, read silently to himself, and then he resumed. "Three or four paragraphs later, the preface clarifies the Church's position. 'It would be wrong to say that condemnation of bad books is a violation of human freedom, for it is clear above everything that the Church teaches that Man is endowed with freedom by his Creator and that the Church has always upheld this doctrine against whoever dared to deny it. Only those suffering from that plague called liberalism can say that these restrictions put by a legitimate power to libertinism are limitations of Man's free will: as if Man, being free of his will, were therefore authorized always to do what he wants.' Then the next paragraph. 'It is clear, therefore, that Church authorities, by preventing through laws the diffusion of errors, by trying to take out of circulation those books apt to corrupt morals and Faith, do nothing but save frail human nature from those sins that by its very weakness it can easily incur.' "

He lifted his head. "Until 1917, the authority for handling the prohibition of books belonged to the Congregation of the Index. After that, the functions of the *Index* were taken over by the Curia office known as the Section for the Censure of Books, under the authority of the Supreme Congregation of the Holy Office. But because the Holy Office was long associated in the minds of many with the Inquisition, and to appease our Protestant brethren, the Holy Office was abolished in 1965 by Pope Paul VI. The work of the *Index* was then taken over by the less conservative Sacred Congregation for the Doctrine of the Faith, and it is this office with which we are concerned. Is what I have explained perfectly clear to you?"

"Absolutely, Your Eminence."

"Mr. Duncan, there are two principal reasons why a book may be condemned by the Church and thus listed in the *Index*. As far back as 1399, a manuscript was forbidden if it taught or told stories 'sensual or related to matters of flesh,' or if it 'aimed at destroying the fundamentals of religion' or 'attacked or ridiculed Catholic dogma or the Catholic hierarchy.' In short, to this very day, a book may be condemned on the grounds of immorality on the one hand or heresy on the other hand. Because of immorality, you will find in the pages of the *Index* such authors as Casanova for his *Memoirs* and Gustave Flaubert for *Madame Bovary*, as well as Balzac, D'Annunzio, Dumas *père* and *fils* for their sensual novels, and as recently as 1952, Alberto Moravia for his obscene books. Because of their anticlericalism, unsound theology, outright heresy, you will find in the *Index* such authors as Laurence Sterne for *A Sentimental Journey Through France and Italy*, Edward Gibbon for *The Decline and Fall of the Roman Empire*, Bergson, Croce, Spinoza, Kant, Zola, and more lately, Jean-Paul Sartre, for their irreligious commentaries, histories, philosophies. But very few authors have been condemned for both immorality *and* heresy. One of the few thus doubly condemned was André Gide."

The Cardinal had begun leafing through his copy of the *Index*.

"And one of the others doubly condemned in the *Index* was a novelist whose work was originally published in the English language. He was the second English-speaking novelist to appear in the *Index*—the first, incidentally, was Samuel Richardson for *Pamela*, proscribed by the Vatican in 1744—but the second English-speaking novelist to be condemned by inclusion in the *Index*, and he was condemned for both immorality and heresy, was—well, here, have a look for yourself."

Duncan accepted the *Index* and followed the Cardinal's finger down page 239, and there, between "Ittigius, Thomas," and "Juénin, Gaspar," stood the name "Jadway, J J," and after his name the following: "The Seven Minutes. Decr. S. Off. 19 apr. 1937."

Duncan looked up with surprise. "Jadway's actually in here."

Cardinal MacManus nodded. "Yes indeed. Had you not known that he was in the *Index*?"

"I'd seen something—in our brief about the author there was some mention, I'm sure—but I didn't give it too much attention at the time. I had little knowledge of the *Index*, although I did assign my assistant to research it further, and I wasn't sure this would have much relevancy in a courtroom. I thought I'd make a passing reference to it, once I was certain that the *Index* still existed."

"Now you know it does," said the Cardinal. "And let me emphasize why *The Seven Minutes* is condemned in these pages. I have said it was a forbidden book because of its immorality and its heretical attitude toward the Christian faith. True. But by the 1930s obscenity alone would not have made the Church condemn *The Seven Minutes*, especially since its obscure imprint, its appearance in a country not the author's own, and its immediate banning gave it only a limited circulation. If you look through those pages you will find no mention of the Obelisk Press edition of John Cleland's *Fanny Hill* or the books written by James Joyce, Henry Miller, William Burroughs. No, it has taken more than a charge of obscenity to earn the condemnation of the *Index* in recent times. Just as Boccaccio's *Decameron* was not placed in the *Index* for its indecency, its immorality, alone. On those grounds, *The Decameron* might have escaped censorship. It was Boccaccio's blasphemy, his attack on the clergy, this coupled with obscenity, that earned him a place in the *Index*. Indeed, when *The De-cameron* was reissued with the sinning monks and nuns replaced by sinning noblemen and ladies, the Council of Trent was satisfied that the blasphemy had been expurgated. His Holiness then saw fit to remove Boccaccio's work from the *Index*. So, you see, Mr. Duncan, it is not immorality alone, but a compounding of immorality with blasphemy, that most surely brings the Church's condemnation. It is this compounding of salacity with heresy that forced the Holy Office to proscribe *The Seven Minutes*. Yes, I have read the Jadway novel, and I cannot bring myself to repeat my feelings about the passage where the author has his sinful heroine—heroine! atheistic prostitute, I would call her—dream of Our Lord and martyred saints of the Church and take His name and their names in vain. A work inspired by the Devil, no less."

Breathing nasally, the Cardinal tried to regain his composure. "But, foul though it was, *The Seven Minutes* might have remained a relic in the lists of the *Index*, out of print and forgotten, and of no further concern to the Church. In its time, as a result of the *Index*, it was banned in all Catholic countries, and, because of its obscene content, in other nations as well. It had enjoyed its one moment of evil and it was no more. However, when a heretofore reputable New York publishing house determined to revive it, the Church hierarchy was alarmed. I cannot say whether the Church would have acted against it alone. Perhaps we might not have done so, for fear of provoking old resentments in many quarters about our alleged repressiveness in earlier centuries. Fortunately, one man, an instrument of the state, and outside our faith, had the courage to rise above fear and strike at the horrendous beast loosed by the New York commercialists. You were and are that man, Mr. Duncan, and we are proud to support your brave crusade."

Duncan glowed. "Thank you, Your Eminence. I am moved by your words."

"I promised you more than words," said Cardinal MacManus. "I promised you help."

"Anything you can offer I shall appreciate."

"The Holy Father has authorized me to offer you the services of Father Sarfatti—one of the two priests in the Vatican directly in charge of the *Index*—as a leading witness for your prosecution. Before proscribing *The Seven Minutes*, the members of the Holy Order carefully investigated the author, J J Jadway, while he was still alive. The findings of three and a half decades ago are at Father Sarfatti's fingertips. I am authorized to inform you that Father Sarfatti is prepared to make public, for the benefit of your prosecution, not only his own experience with Jadway, but all of the classified information the Church has on the infamous book and its equally infamous author."

"About this information," said Duncan eagerly, "I'm curious to learn if you can give me any idea of its—"

"Did you know that the author, J J Jadway, was a Catholic when he wrote the book? Did you know that he was excommunicated before his death for producing this work? Did you know that his death, following his excommunication, was not accidental, as the newspaper reports have been saying, but that he died by his own hand, as a suicide?"

Duncan's jaw fell open, and he sat dazed on the sofa. "Jadway killed himself?"

"After his book appeared he committed suicide, and his remains were cremated."

Duncan was on his feet, his features twitching, as his fingers absently fumbled for a cigarette. "No—I didn't know any of that. Outside of this room, no one in the United States knows that. But they should know. Everyone should know."

With a grunt, Cardinal MacManus rose from the sofa. "It is the truth. There is more. Do you wish Father Sarfatti as a witness for the prosecution?"

"Do I wish him? Yes, a thousand times yes, I *must* have him."

"When do you want him in Los Angeles?"

"Within three days, four at the most, if possible."

"It is possible. I will notify the Vatican. Father Sarfatti will be here. And the Lord will bless our cause. We are ever mindful of St. Augustine's instruction, 'He who created us without our help will not save us without our consent.' We want America to be saved, and you will help us get the consent of our citizens. Thank you, Mr. Duncan."

"Thank *you*, Your Eminence."

LEAVING BEN FREMONT's Book Emporium, Mike Barrett decided to walk the three blocks to the Oakwood Branch Library.

After depositing another dime in the parking meter, he left his car and set out on foot. Since Oakwood was nearer the beach than Beverly Hills, where he had finished lunch less than an hour ago, the air was cleaner, less muggy, more invigorating, and he inhaled deeply as he strode through the shopping district.

Barrett reviewed the conversation he had just concluded with Ben Fremont. It amused Barrett that the thin, nearsighted bookseller was now less unprepossessing than when they had first met on the afternoon of Fremont's arrest. On that afternoon, Fremont had been shriveled by fright and his speech reduced to a gurgle. But the subsequent attention he had received had inflated his ego. He enjoyed receiving the sympathies of that minority of customers, friends, fellow bookmen, who considered him a heroic martyr. He reveled even more in his sudden role as notorious pawn of Satan ascribed to him by the STDL and the sensationalists of the press and television. In his tone of voice Barrett had detected the faintest resentment that J J Jadway and *The Seven Minutes* were getting more recognition than he himself. At one point, Fremont had shyly admitted that his wife was keeping a scrapbook. Further, his bearing was straighter, his speech more authoritative, and the old whining and cringing had all but disappeared. Barrett understood, and liked him. Most men, the very ones who live lives of quiet desperation, receive public recognition only twice in their lives, with their birth notice and their obituary, neither of which can they read. Life had given this obscure bookseller an unexpected bonus. He was, incredibly, fleetingly, a public figure.

But whenever Barrett talked to him, Fremont would eventually become realistic about his status. He was the defendant, under criminal indictment. Incarceration in a jail was a possibility. And so, when Barrett appeared, Fremont was cooperative and before long realistic, as he had been for the last half hour.

Barrett had arrived armed with questions. The police had confiscated eighty copies of *The Seven Minutes,* and Sanford House's sales-department accounts showed that an advance order of one hundred copies had been shipped to Fremont's Book Emporium. Were those figures correct? "Yes, sir, Mr. Barrett." Did that mean that Fremont had sold twenty copies before his arrest? "Yes, sir, except, wait, no, I had one copy at home which my wife was reading. So that means I sold nineteen, two of them to the police officers who arrested me." Did Fremont have any record of the other seventeen customers who had purchased the book? "Only those who charged it, and that would take some looking up. Most of my customers pay cash." Would Fremont mind going through his charge-account records covering the short period between his receiving the shipment and his arrest, and keep an eye open for Jerry Griffith's name? "I can answer that right off, Mr. Barrett. None of the Griffiths carries a charge in this store." Then perhaps Jerry had come in and paid cash for the book? "I doubt it. I've got a good memory for names and faces. The boy's picture has been in all the papers, and I don't remember ever seeing him in this store. Of course, there's a hundred bookstores around L.A. where he might have got a copy." Barrett realized that, and he already had Kimura and several aides canvassing other stores with photographs of Jerry Griffith in hand. "I sure envy those other stores, Mr. Barrett. They must be selling copies like hotcakes, and all because of me." Barrett had doubted that many stores outside Oakwood dared to display the book. Most were awaiting the outcome of the trial. "Not all of them, Mr. Barrett," Fremont had said knowingly.

This had given Barrett pause. He had eyed the bookseller closely. Did Fremont mean that some of his colleagues were selling the book from under the counter? "A few, a few." Did Fremont recollect Barrett's earlier advice? "What was that? Oh, yeah, I remember, you mean about me not trying to sell from under the counter? Don't worry. No chance. Besides, where would I get the copies? God knows, I wish I could sell the book. You have no idea how many phone calls I get every day asking if I have it for sale. Why, you know who called this morning? Rachel Hoyt. Great gal. You don't know her? You should. She's the head branch librarian for the Oakwood Library. Speak of guts. She's stood up against Mrs. St. Clair and the STDL for two years. She's absolutely indignant about my arrest and this attempt to ban *The Seven Minutes*. She thinks that's the real crime. She's so sore that she's not even waiting to order the book through the county acquisitions department. She wants to buy one herself and put it right out on the open shelves and have a showdown with the STDL. That's why she phoned me, trying to get a copy. I was afraid to let her have the one my wife is reading. But that Rachel, she'll find a copy somewhere."

And now Mike Barrett had reached the modern one-story structure that was the Oakwood Branch Library, and was entering it, determined to speak to Rachel Hoyt, librarian.

It had been a long time since Barrett had been inside a public library, and the physical appearance of the interior of the building, as well as the atmosphere there, took him by surprise. His youthful memories of libraries were associated with words like "darkened," "musty," "staid," "hushed." The Oakwood Branch Library was bright, light, airy, and the scene was one of restrained liveliness. Several college-age boys and girls were gathered along the table of Periodical Guides, talking in lowered but animated voices and trying to repress their laughter. Other visitors were comfortably seated at long tables, leisurely reading or studiously note-taking. A romantic couple emerged from the well-illuminated stacks, his free arm around her, and her arms loaded with books. Near the entrance, there was a rack bearing a sign, NEW ARRIVALS, as well as a cork board carrying dust jackets of the latest acquisitions. Barrett hastily examined the fiction titles. *The Seven Minutes* was not yet among them.

At the checkout counter, Barrett asked for Miss Rachel Hoyt and gave his name and his business, and the tiny clerk stared at him with wide eyes and then darted through a doorway behind her.

When she returned, Rachel Hoyt was right at her heels, and Barrett enjoyed his second surprise since his arrival. Like most adults, Barrett's remembrance of librarians who had populated his school years had merged with time into one stereotyped librarian. This stereotype had bunned hair, rimless spectacles, a pointed disapproving nose, and invisible compressed lips. The stereotype was a loveless priss, efficient, mousy, humorless, juiceless.

And here was Rachel Hoyt, branch librarian, as pretty as a Marie Laurencin picture, yet as colorful as a psychedelic poster. Her hair was pulled back softly and held at the nape of her neck by an enameled barrette. There was bright lipstick on her moist lips, and a pink blouse was joined by a wide belt to a short gray wool dirndl.

She was smallish, compact, neat, with an impudent expression and a kind of bursting vitality. She was probably nearer forty than thirty, but she looked thirty. Barrett had no doubt that she had one hell of an intellect. He also had no doubt that she did not allow it to interfere with her social life.

"You *are* the head librarian?" he asked.

"None other," said Rachel Hoyt, shoving a collection of bangle bracelets high on her slender forearm. She cocked an amused eye at him. "What were you expecting—Minnie Mouse or a Bloomer Girl? They threw away that cookie cutter years ago. But then, Mr. Barrett, you don't look like those criminal attorneys we read about or see portrayed on television. You don't look like a shrewd gallus-snapper or a wonderful drunken mumbler defending underdogs. You don't look like Darrow or Rogers—or Howe or Hummel, for that matter."

"I don't?" Barrett complained with mock hurt. "Why not?"

"Too clean-cut and too much jaw. Your eyes aren't even slightly bloodshot. Your tie is expensive. Charles Darnay, maybe. Sydney Carton, no."

"If you knew what I was sacrificing to take on this case, you'd say Sydney Carton, and how."

Rachel Hoyt laughed. "Okay, Sydney, come on in."

He went around the checkout counter and followed her into an office as neat and open as her own person, except for the table in the center that served her as a desk. It was piled high with new books, and stacks of the *Library Journal*, the *Top of the News*, and the *Wilson Library Bulletin*. There were also on the table clutches of three-by-five slips of paper held together by rubber bands, a cup of pencils, an electric percolator bubbling, a paper plate containing part of a sandwich.

"Mind if I finish my ham and cheese and have coffee?" she asked, going behind the table and pouring coffee into a paper cup. "Will you have some?"

"No, thanks."

"Then pull up and make yourself at home."

He started for a chair, but was distracted by a large framed placard on the wall. It bore the heading: LIBRARY BILL OF RIGHTS. It had been prepared by the Council of the American Library Association.

"Our six commandments," called out Rachel Hoyt. "Look at number three and number four."

He looked at number three. It read: "Censorship of books, urged or practiced by volunteer arbiters of morals or political opinion or by organizations that would establish a coercive concept of Americanism, must be challenged by libraries in maintenance of their responsibility to provide public information and enlightenment through the printed word."

His eyes moved down to number four. It read: "Libraries should enlist the cooperation of allied groups in the fields of science, of education, and of book publishing in resisting all abridgment of the free access to ideas and full freedom of expression that are the tradition and heritage of Americans."

He turned back and brought the chair to a position across the table from her. "I guess that about says it all," he said.

She finished the last bite of her sandwich. "Not quite," she said. "I'd say almost every librarian subscribes to those two policies, in fact to all six. Where we come apart is on interpretation of what is or is not 'enlightenment through the printed word.' Whether he knew it or not, President Eisenhower once underlined our problem in a fine speech he gave at Dartmouth College many years ago. 'Don't join the book burners,' he told his audience. He felt that you can't conceal faults by concealing the evidence that they exist. We shouldn't be afraid to go into a library and read every book there as long as our own ideas of decency are not offended. 'That should be the only censorship,' said Eisenhower."

She gulped down her coffee. "Three cheers for Ike. But, indeed, what should be the only censorship? Why, that which offends our ideas of decency, of course. Still, whose ideas exactly? Take a given book. Maybe an Eisenhower says it's indecent, a Justice Warren says it is decent. Take another book. An American Communist says that politically it's decent, a member of the John Birch Society says indecent. Take *The Seven Minutes*. You and I say decent, but Elmo Duncan and Frank Griffith shout indecent. Yes, take this same Jadway book. I say it has social value and literary merit, and I intend to buy it and display it on the shelves of the Oakwood Branch Library. At the same time, the librarians at the book-selection meeting of the Free Library of Philadelphia, Pennsylvania, may decide that the book has a prurient appeal as well as an inferior writing style, and they may refuse to buy and circulate it. The head of some Alabama public library may feel the book has social importance, but, because of fear of some organization like the DAR, he will precensor the novel and not allow his librarians to buy it. Which brings us back to the same question—*whose* idea of decency should we follow? Being a librarian today is about as noncontroversial a job as being a politician. It's one of the most hazardous occupations on earth. No more room for mice. Oh, there are plenty of mice in the profession. But there are more tigers in these hallowed reading rooms, far more, believe me. And yours truly is one of them. I'll growl and stalk and fight to the death to protect my brood, my book collection, my free and open shelves. And now, Mr. Barrett, what in the devil are you doing here?"

"Miss Hoyt, I'm here to ask a favor. Don't buy and display *The Seven Minutes*."

Her eyebrows shot up. "This—from you? You're kidding?"

"I'm serious as can be."

"I want this book made available for people who wish to read it."

"No, not yet."

"Why not?"

Barrett fiddled with his pipe. "I'll tell you why not. We've already got one person who's challenging the law over his freedom to display *The Seven Minutes*. We have our one martyr. Two martyrs would be a crowd. It's as if, well, say two different Christs had been tried by Pilate, and there had been two Messiahs crucified that day on the Hill of Golgotha. Could Christians have been inspired by two martyrdoms? Would Christianity have sprung from that?"

"An improper analogy," said Rachel Hoyt. "When you are defending a beleaguered bastion of freedom, you want all the volunteers you can get. I should think the more the merrier."

"An equally bad analogy," said Barrett. "Look, one Jew is persecuted and sent to Devil's Island, and you can cry out '*J'accuse!*' and rouse the entire world over a single injustice. The world can identify with one helpless martyr. But six million Jews were persecuted and murdered in Germany and the world is intellectually disturbed but emotionally unmoved and tries to go about its own

170

business, because who in the hell can identify with six million dead?"

Miss Hoyt toyed with her paper cup. Then she crushed it. "Yes, I see," she said. "Exactly what am I supposed to do?"

"You're supposed to tell me you are willing to be an expert literary witness for the defense. Will you?"

"You couldn't keep me off the stand with a machine gun."

"Okay, you're enlisted. I gather you have read the Jadway book?"

"Three times. Would you believe it? The first time a half-dozen years ago. I was on one of those chartered bargain flights. I think the plane was made to go by rubber bands—we librarians don't have jet-set salaries, you know. It was a kind of art-museum tour, and after three days in the Louvre I had a free day. I went browsing among the bookstalls along the Seine, and there was this worn old copy of the Étoile edition of *The Seven Minutes*. I'd often heard about it, and I was curious. I sat in a café and spent the morning reading it. For the first time I realized how beautiful it was to be a female. Then, when I learned in *Publishers' Weekly* that Sanford House was publishing the book here, I was thrilled. I thought, My God, this ol' corn-pone country has come of age. When I got home, I reread my old Paris edition. The story was as beautiful as the first time. Then, when Ben Fremont was arrested, I knew I had to make a decision as a responsible librarian. So I read it a third time with a careful, objective librarian's eye."

"And what did your objective librarian's eye tell you?"

"Unblinkingly, it told me my first two reactions had been right. The book belonged on the open shelves, but immediately, if only to show the witch hunters that Ben Fremont was not alone. Now you've persuaded me to defer that gesture. But at least I'll have an opportunity to tell the world where an intelligent librarian stands."

"Have you thought of the consequences?"

"Mr. Barrett, if I worried about consequences, I wouldn't have taken this damn job in the first place. When I look at myself in the mirror each night, I don't want to be ashamed of what I see. So to hell with the consequences. Do you have any idea of what the average librarian is up against every day, not once a month or once a year—not the big whooping issues, but the petty problems

171

she contends with every day of every year? I'm not speaking about the youngsters. They're fine. They're our only hope for saving this old mudball we live on from total extinction. It's their parents and relatives. The wise ones, the elders, who claim they have the answer to what's right and what's wrong and they call it 'common sense.' And what is common sense? A conglomeration of folklore and fables and prejudices handed down from their parents and grandparents, and a pack of half-digested limited experiences and observations and thoughts. The parents are the ones who come into libraries—public libraries and school libraries—to protest how we're destroying their young with this book or that, little realizing that they're the ones who are subverting their offspring because they've gone through parenthood with crusts around their brains. Those people are simply afraid of anything new."

"I'm very well acquainted with them," said Barrett.

"Of course you are. Yet we must live with them, deal with them, and you and I know the stifling limitation that results when society expects every book to meet contemporary community standards. Most of the truly great books became great because they once defied or exceeded formula, banality, community tradition. These were the books that dared say something new or say it in a new way. These were the writings by Copernicus, Newton, Paine, Freud, Darwin, Boas, Spengler, in nonfiction, and by Aristophanes, Rabelais, Voltaire, Heine, Whitman, Shaw, Joyce, in fiction. These were the writings filled with fresh, sometimes shocking, ideas. And we absolutely must support similar writings today. But how? One library dean thought we should stand for selection as opposed to censorship—selection of the best books, based mainly on the presumed intent of the author and his sincerity of purpose. Selection, he said, begins with a presumption in favor of liberty of thought; censorship, with a presumption in favor of thought control."

Rachel Hoyt paused, as if to restrain her indignation, and then she resumed more levelly. "Do you think any of those don't-rock-the-boat people out there understand this? No sirree. We fight for selection, and they fight for censorship. You should hear the day-in, day-out complaints. They come from shame mongers and bigots of every stripe."

"Like what kind of complaints?"

172

"Like I've been asked to remove Hawthorne's *Scarlet Letter* from circulation because it showed licentious behavior, and Pearl Buck's *The Good Earth* because it described childbirth, and Dostoevski's *Crime and Punishment* because it contained profanity, and even Mitchell's *Gone with the Wind* because Scarlett behaved immorally. I've read somewhere that one parent-teacher association wanted *Classic Myths* barred from the shelves because it dealt with incest—incest among the gods. Ye gods! In Cleveland they objected to Apuleius' *The Golden Ass* because of the depraved title, and somewhere else they objected to Henry James's *Turn of the Screw* because you know why. But the height of absurdity was about reached in Downey, California, when some literary vigilantes attempted to have Edgar Rice Burroughs' *Tarzan* series removed from library shelves because they thought Tarzan and Jane had never been married and were living in sin. Can you imagine anything like that?"

Barrett shook his head. "Oh, no."

"Oh, *yes*. And don't think for a minute it's only the illiterates and eccentrics and bigots who give us trouble. Most people—supposedly normal people, I mean—instinctively want everybody else to conform to their own ideas of right and wrong. And since more people—how did Freud put it?—are upset by anything that reminds them unequivocally of their animal nature, they are upset by candor in literature and try to impose their upset upon the rest of us. So we get our share of certified normal people in here giving us trouble. Some perfectly respectable people get involved. Take our community leaders—a man like Frank Griffith, who's now telling the press it was J J Jadway and not Jerry who raped that poor girl. It was neither Jadway nor Jerry who was responsible for the crime. It was a man like Griffith who was responsible."

Barrett sat up. "Griffith? What makes you say that? Do you know him?"

"No, thank you," said Rachel Hoyt. "I had one encounter with him and that was enough. His son, Jerry, used to come in here to check out books or use our reference section. I got to know the boy slightly. A bright, quiet, lovely boy, but reduced to a kind of walking stutter by his overwhelming and know-it-all father. The last time I ever saw Jerry, maybe a year or more ago, he'd come in to do some reference work on a paper he was preparing for an

American Lit class. He was having trouble finding what he wanted, and he approached me, and I knew just the book that might help him. It was the *Dictionary of American Slang*, the one published by Crowell, and since it was late and Jerry didn't have time to look up what he needed, I permitted him to take the reference book home for twenty-four hours. The next thing I knew, it was the following morning, and there was Frank Griffith on the phone giving me hell."

"Frank Griffith called you?"

"You bet he did."

"What did he say?"

"He was apoplectic. How dare I recommend such a book to his son? I said there was nothing wrong with the book—it was a standard reference dictionary that had been used for years. Well, not for Frank Griffith, no sirree. Griffith said he recognized the dirty book. It was one that, in 1963, a San Diego Assemblyman had called 'filthy' and our State Superintendent of Public Instruction had labeled 'a practicing handbook of sexual perversion,' probably because it contained definitions of several lusty Anglo-Saxon words. Griffith wanted that dictionary removed from the shelves, and I refused, saying I couldn't deprive students of a reputable and scholarly reference tool. Griffith told me that if he had the time he'd go to the mat with me over that book, but since he didn't have the time, he was just warning me not to recommend anything questionable to his son again. If I did, he promised he'd have my job. Unfortunately, I never had an opportunity to recommend anything to Jerry again, because he never showed up again. He sent his boy friend over to return the book for him with thanks and apologies for any trouble he'd caused me. I suppose he was too embarrassed to return the dictionary himself, or to come in here again. No doubt he's used the library facilities at UCLA ever since. How do you like that?"

"Jerry's boy friend," said Barrett, suddenly alerted. "Do you remember his name?"

"His boy friend? I'm not sure. You see, Jerry was pretty much of a loner, perhaps a few casual friends, but this bearded boy was the only one I saw him with more than once." She paused. "Is this important, Mr. Barrett?"

"I don't know. It could be."

She leaped to her feet. "Let me see what I can find out." She hastened out the door, calling, "Mary . . ."

Barrett rose, and had barely filled his pipe with tobacco before Rachel Hoyt returned. "Any luck?" he asked.

"Yes, one of my clerks remembered Jerry's friend. His name is George Perkins. He's also a student at UCLA."

Barrett made a note of this and returned his memorandum pad to his pocket. "Thanks. This may be useful. And thanks for enlisting as a defense witness. I'll speak to you before it's your turn to go on the stand. You won't mind repeating that little anecdote about Frank Griffith in court, will you?"

"Nothing would please me more."

"Miss Hoyt, on behalf of Sydney Carton—"

"Let's not be formal. Me Jane. You Tarzan."

He grinned. "Okay. Me Tarzan thanks You Jane."

THE COUNSELING ROOM that they were using was in the Administration Building on the UCLA campus. It was no more than a cubicle, barren except for a swivel chair, a neat steel desk holding a file folder, a telephone, and a green plant, and two straight chairs for visitors. For Mike Barrett it was as cheerless as a doctor's examination room. He had been interviewing Mrs. Henrietta Lott for fifteen minutes, and his surroundings were becoming increasingly claustrophobic and oppressive. He supposed this was so because the session with Mrs. Lott had been, until now, unprofitable.

Henrietta Lott was a kind, dumpy, overworked middle-aged woman, who seemed easiest when she was rattling off information about the curriculum in the College of Letters and Science. Her perception about her students, as best Barrett could make out, was shallow. Her major virtue was probably a lack of any sense of vice. That or her earnestness. She was assigned to advise undergraduates with family names classified in the letter group from G to J. Griffith was G, so she was Jerry Griffith's counselor. She had met with him four times. Except for what was on the college card in her hand, she had no in-depth knowledge of Jerry nor any immediate clear picture of him (in itself a commentary, Barrett realized). She was apologetic about this, but there were so many, so very many students, fifteen thousand in the College of Letters and Science alone.

She had seen Jerry on this date, on that day, then again, and once more. These interviews had been devoted entirely to academic discussions, about a change in classes, about instructors, about grades, about ROTC. Once, when Jerry had wanted to discuss his units in relation to the draft, she had referred him to the Office of Special Services.

"I wish there was more I could tell you," said Mrs. Lott unhappily, "but I'm afraid I can't think of anything else."

Barrett decided to reframe a question he had posed twice before. "Do you have any impression at all of Jerry Griffith's personality?"

"Well, only that he was very serious and rather withdrawn." She stared vaguely at the college card in her hand, and then at the open student's folder on the desk. "And . . . I suppose I can say he seemed to me rather unmotivated, like most of the youngsters today. Compared to the many students I see daily, I might say Jerry was more square or straight, to use the campus vernacular, than his peer group."

"Did you ever hear him speak of his family, Mrs. Lott?"

"No, not really. Well, wait, there was one occasion." She seemed happier now. "Once he inquired about the intramural sports program. Yes, I recall. His father had been some kind of Olympic star—or maybe I just read about that in the papers?—anyway, his father wanted him to go in for sports, felt it would be good for him to get fresh air and exercise and not be just a grind and a bookworm. So Jerry felt he should make some inquiries. He said he wasn't much good at sports, but I think he said he'd had tennis lessons in prep school. As for clubs, he belonged to some kind of bridge—or was it chess?—no, I'm sure it was bridge—some kind of bridge club in Westwood."

"I was told that Jerry took an American Literature course about a year ago. Can you provide me with any details?"

Mrs. Lott bent to her folder. "As a matter of fact," she said, "I have a note here that he has taken seven literature courses—rather, had taken five and is taking two now, or was, before he . . . when he dropped out of the university. Would you like the names of the classes and the instructors?"

She read them off slowly, as Barrett jotted down the details in his notebook. When she was done, Barrett looked up. "That last course," he said, "American Expatriate Literature, being taught by Dr. Hugo Knight. That sounds promising. What's it about?"

Mrs. Lott was in her element now, and suddenly more self-assured. "It's a popular course, and Dr. Knight teaches it with great enthusiasm. Yes, Jerry had signed up for it, was taking it, until his trouble. It's a shame he couldn't see it through to the final exam and get credit for the course."

"What does Dr. Knight cover in this course?"

"The approach is clever. In his lectures Dr. Knight tries to show how the expatriate experience, the feeling of alienation as well as the absorption of foreign mores and backgrounds, the experience of living and creating abroad, has affected the mainstream of American literature, from Nathaniel Hawthorne to Henry James to Ernest Hemingway. The youngsters seem to like it, I gather from my meetings with them, because Dr. Knight rather fearlessly touches on the history and influences of those authors who were avant-garde and too realistic to be published in their native America. Instead they were published in Paris by Jack Kahane's Obelisk Press, between 1931 and 1939, and by the Olympia Press which his son, Maurice Girodias, established in 1953. Between them, they published Frank Harris, Radclyffe Hall, Henry Miller, Lawrence Durrell, James Hanley, Jean Genêt, William Burroughs, all at a time when no one else dared publish such authors. Of course, Dr. Knight stresses the American authors."

"Do you happen to know whether the professor includes Éditions Étoile, founded by Christian Leroux, and the book I represent, *The Seven Minutes*, by J J Jadway, in his lectures?"

"I don't see how he could have helped but refer to Jadway, at least in passing. You really should ask Dr. Knight that question personally. I'm sure you'd find him cooperative. I could set up an appointment for you during his office hours."

"Like maybe today, Mrs. Lott, this afternoon while I'm on the campus? Dr. Knight sounds as if he has the makings of an excellent witness."

Almost with relief, Mrs. Lott started to reach for her telephone, then thought better of it. "I should keep my line open for a call

I'm expecting." She left her executive chair and hastened to the door. "I'll be only a minute. Let me call Dr. Knight's office."

Barrett stood up and massaged his back, and waited.

In less than a minute, Mrs. Lott had returned. "You're in luck, Mr. Barrett. His next office period is a half hour from now. I told him who you were and what it is you wanted to know, and he said he'd be happy to make time for you. Here, let me jot down his location on the campus, and I'll diagram the shortest way you can get there."

As she wrote and drew her diagram, something else occurred to Barrett. He waited until she had handed him the piece of paper.

"Just one more thing, Mrs. Lott," he said. "There is someone else I'd like to see, if possible—an undergraduate, a close friend of Jerry Griffith's. If he's on campus, and if I could find out where, I'd like to talk to him in the half hour before seeing Dr. Knight or right afterward. The young man's name is George Perkins. I hate to bother you further, but—"

"No bother at all," said Henrietta Lott. "Let me see what I can find out."

What she found out was that George Perkins, like Jerry, was a junior, a geology major, and he had a class at this very time. If he was attending his lecture, he could be reached. Mrs. Lott wrote a note to the class instructor, requesting that he ask George Perkins to remain behind after the class was dismissed, and she suggested sending the note with an office secretary, who would bring him to meet Barrett.

Fifteen minutes later, Barrett stood at the edge of Dickson Plaza, the quad west of the old UCLA library building, overlooking the seemingly endless pitch of brick steps leading down toward the gymnasiums, and he tried to remain undistracted by the scrubbed, healthy girls swinging by as he watched for the return of his guide and hopefully the sight of George Perkins.

Suddenly he made out the secretary coming up the patterned walk before Royce Hall, and slouching along beside her was a big ungainly young man with tangled sandy hair and a shrub of beard, dressed in a turtleneck sweater, corduroy trousers, army fatigue boots. The girl halted, and Barrett realized that she was pointing him out to the young man, and the young man nodded, and then she waved at Barrett and he waved back as she hurried away.

The young man was clumping across the quad, making his way toward Barrett. He shifted his textbooks from one arm to the other, and as he came nearer, Barrett could see that his beefy face was puzzled.

"Hiya," he said. "I'm George Perkins. They said somebody wanted to see me. They didn't tell me what about."

"I'm Michael Barrett. I'll be glad to tell you what about." At the mention of Barrett's name, George's brow puckered, as if trying to place it. "You may have read my name in the papers," Barrett went on. "I'm the attorney for Ben Fremont, the bookseller who was arrested for selling *The Seven Minutes.*"

"That's right," muttered George Perkins. "Well, well—" But something had crossed his mind, and his expression became wary. "What do you want with me?"

"Answers to a few questions, nothing more. I thought you might be able to help me out on something. I'm trying to get a fill-in on Jerry Griffith's background. I was told you're a friend of Jerry's."

"No more than lots of others," said George, his manner guarded and suspicious. "I know him a little, see him around here once in a while. A couple of times he gave me a lift to my apartment. And that's it."

"I was told you were close friends."

"Mister, you were told wrong. Naw, nothing like that. Sorry." He squinted off. "Look, mister, if you'll excuse me now, I've got a chance to get a ride to my place. I better get down there."

George Perkins started for the brick steps that brought one to the private street along the athletic fields, but Barrett caught up with him and then kept in stride with him. "Mind if I keep you company to your ride?" said Barrett. "Maybe you can give me some leads."

"You're wasting your time."

"Well, it's my time, so let me waste it," said Barrett cheerfully, as he began descending the stairway alongside George Perkins. "So at least you know Jerry a little. Ever meet any members of his family?"

"Naw."

"Did you ever hear Jerry discuss his father?"

"Nope."

"What did you hear Jerry talk about? Any favorite topic or subject?"

"Nothing special. He's a listener. We're all listeners. Haven't you heard, mister? We're the generation that's soaking it all in, so's we know what not to do." He cast a mocking sidelong glance at Barrett. "We let others do the yakking."

Barrett nodded good-naturedly. "Bully for you. Maybe listeners are also readers. I was told Jerry Griffith read a lot."

"Everybody reads a lot if they want to stick in school."

"Did you ever see Jerry reading or hear him discuss *The Seven Minutes?*"

"Maybe. I don't remember. He was big on Hesse the Hermann. But that Jadway thing, that just came out, didn't it? I probably haven't seen Jerry since that came out, so how would I know if he discussed it? The paper says he read it, so you know as much as I know."

"When did you last see Jerry Griffith?"

George Perkins went down the remaining flight of stairs silently. Then he said, "Maybe about a week before he hopped that broad."

"Have you seen him since, George?"

"No, and I wouldn't want to very much, either."

"Why not?"

"Because he's given sex a bad name. What kind of guy is it—with all the pussy around—who tries to get it that way? Imagine getting it that way *today?*"

"That's what mystifies many of us."

"Well, I gotta go along with Jerry on what he says. He says that book of yours sent him off into orbit. Well, they're always yakking about the power of the press, so here we see the power. Sounds like that book of yours can give a guy a better trip than LSD."

They had reached the bottom of the stairs. Barrett saw that any further talk would be useless. "I guess that does it, George. I appreciate your help."

"You're putting me on. What help?"

"At least I've learned Jerry hasn't got any friends—now."

"Oh, yeah."

"Maybe one of his professors can tell me a little more. I understand he had a class with Dr. Hugo Knight. Know anything about Knight?"

"Fagsville. And a horse's ass besides."

"How do I get to his office from here?"

George Perkins jerked a thumb over his shoulder. "The same way you came down. Only this time up. I hope you had a cardiogram lately."

"Don't worry. Thanks for your time, George."

"Mister, one second . . ."

Barrett hesitated. "Yes?"

"You've been asking questions. Maybe I ought to ask one or two. Like who told you that me and Jerry Griffith were buddy-buddy? Did Jerry himself tell you that?"

"No. I've never met or seen Jerry. I got it from an employee of the Oakwood Library who saw you with Jerry several times."

George seemed at once relieved and for the first time amiable. "Oh, that's who. Well, that explains it. But she was wrong. Well, sorry I couldn't make your day, but good luck anyway."

Barrett watched him go slouching off past the men's gym, and he decided he would not be learning much about Jerry Griffith from his contemporaries. For one like himself, the Union of the Young would remain a closed shop. Ruefully he peered up at the Everest of stairs soaring skyward before him. Was a fag named Dr. Hugo Knight worth it? Well, he had come to UCLA in search of higher education, so it was worth at least one more college try. Laboring, he started to ascend the steep brick staircase.

It was an hour and a half before Mike Barrett returned to his temporary office in the suite Abe Zelkin had leased. Their rooms were on the fifth floor of a recently constructed high-rise building, which was located between Robertson Boulevard and La Cienega Boulevard just before Wilshire Boulevard's Miracle Mile.

Barrett's deeply carpeted corner office had an enlivening, unused feel—one could still smell the fresh pale-green paint on the walls—and Barrett liked its oversized oak desk placed near the large scenic window, the new leather-covered occasional chairs, and, somewhat apart, the cushioned sofa and the two classic lounge chairs surrounding the huge disk of a coffee table. There were not yet any framed college diplomas, civic citations, Impressionist reproductions, or celebrity photographs on the walls. But, hanging on the wall near his desk, he had four small framed quotations which he had paid an art student to reproduce in cursive script. These were among his long-time favorites. The first was to remind him of the enemy without: "The dispensing of injustice is always in the right hands.—STANISLAUS LEC." The next two were amulets against vanity. One read: "Forbear to judge, for we are sinners all.—SHAKESPEARE." The other read: "Perhaps in time the so-called Dark Ages will be thought of as including our own.— GEORG C. LICHTENBERG." The last, recently penned, was to remind him of the unsolvable problem basic to all censorship: "Who shall stand guard to the guards themselves?—JUVENAL."

Three doors broke the monochrome green of the walls. One door opened onto the corridor that brought visitors to him from Donna Novik's spacious reception room. Another door led to a communal area that included a bathroom and shower, a small dining area, and a kitchenette. The third door led to the conference room, which also opened into Zelkin's office, beyond which were Kimura's quarters, Zelkin's law library, and a spare office used as a storeroom.

In Barrett's office only his desk gave evidence of the activity that had been generated in this suite these last days. It was piled high with file folders filled with the typed notes and findings concerning the Ben Fremont case, representing the defense's paper arsenal against the assault being prepared by the prosecution. But what also gave Barrett's desk the appearance of a craggy mountain landscape were the bound court reporters' transcripts of previous English and American censorship cases. Among these, all filled with a forest of paper markers, were Regina v. Hicklin, London, 1868; the Crown's prosecution of *The Well of Loneliness*, London, 1928; the United States government's trial of One Book Entitled *Ulysses*, 1934; the trial of the Grove Press against Postmaster General Christenberry over *Lady Chatterley's Lover*, 1959; the trial of the State of California against bookseller Bradley Reed Smith over *Tropic of Cancer*, 1962; the Massachusetts trial of *Fanny Hill*, 1964. Then there were full decisions and opinions of the United States Supreme Court: Roth v. U.S., 1957; Jacobellis v. Ohio, 1964; Ginzburg v. U.S., 1966, and numerous others. Lost somewhere in the desk landscape was the record of *Hearings on Control of Obscene Material* garnered by a Senate subcommittee investigating juvenile delinquency in 1960.

Upon his return from UCLA, Barrett found added to this mass of material on his desk several memorandums from Leo Kimura, and one was important.

A cable had arrived from Monte Carlo requesting Kimura to telephone the private detective, Dubois, at the Hotel Gardiole in Antibes at five o'clock. This was enigmatic, since Dubois was supposed to have intercepted Jadway's French publisher, Leroux, at the Hotel Balmoral in Monte Carlo much earlier. In his memorandum Kimura did not attempt to speculate on the meaning of the cable. He stated only that he was on his way to Philip Sanford's suite to interrogate Sanford further, but he would be making the overseas call from there and the moment that he had any word, good or bad, he would be in touch with Barrett.

Now it was five o'clock, and Barrett determined to ignore the clock and his suspense about the results of Kimura's call to the Riviera in order to finish his verbal report to Abe Zelkin. For the last fifteen minutes, seated behind his desk, puffing his pipe, Barrett had been summarizing his afternoon interviews for Zelkin, who had been pacing back and forth before him. Barrett had reviewed his meetings with Ben Fremont, Rachel Hoyt, Henrietta Lott, George Perkins, and now he was giving an account of his interview with Dr. Hugo Knight, of the UCLA English department.

"Then I was a little surprised when Dr. Knight told me that Rodriguez, of the District Attorney's Office, had already been by to see him. I think it was some time yesterday."

"No kidding?" said Zelkin. "Well, those boys aren't missing a thing. I suppose Duncan wanted the professor for a witness?"

"Well, they wanted to find out his attitude toward the book," said Barrett. "Rodriguez wanted to know whether the professor had read the novel, what he thought of it, if he encouraged his students to read it. Dr. Knight had read it, had read the copy kept in the UCLA library's department of special collections. He'd never encouraged students to read it, because, until Sanford decided to publish, there were no circulating copies available. As for the book itself, Dr. Knight loved it. So that ended any interest Rodriguez had in the professor as a witness. There was one more thing. Dr. Knight said that Rodriguez kept bugging him to find out whether Jerry Griffith had shown special interest in *The Seven Minutes*. Dr. Knight explained that his classes were so large

—a hundred or more in a lecture room—that he often didn't know an individual student by name. Only after Jerry's picture appeared in the newspapers did he half remember him as one of his students. Also, as far as he could recall, Jerry had never expressed any special interest in that book or any other book mentioned in the lectures. At least, he'd never raised a hand or come forward to discuss one. Anyway, Rodriguez made it clear that the District Attorney's Office had no further interest in him."

Abe Zelkin, hands in his hip pockets, stood over Barrett. "What about us? Do we have any interest in Dr. Knight? He sounds like he can be helpful."

Barrett grimaced. "I don't know. That kid, George Perkins, was right. Dr. Hugo Knight is a bit of a horse's ass. I wanted to find out what he says about *The Seven Minutes* in his lectures. Apparently he says very little. He just touches upon it as one more example of the great writings produced by American expatriate authors. Still, he seemed to be personally well informed about Jadway and the novel. So I asked him, 'Do you know anything about Jadway that has not been in the newspapers lately?' He answered, 'Very few people know Jadway as I know him. I know everything about him.' Well, I tell you, Abe, my hopes rocketed. But in a few seconds they fizzled. It turned out he knew everything about Jadway simply from interpreting the novel. Our professor saw the book as a masterpiece of allegory. Maybe it is, although I find it hard to believe that the characters in that book were really allegorical portrayals of the Seven Deadly Sins."

"He said that?"

"That and more. I think Leda and the Swan got into it somewhere, too."

Zelkin laughed. "I can see twelve good men and true on a jury buying that."

"That wasn't the worst of it. When I challenged the symbolism, tried to make the professor consider the book as a piece of realism, he regarded me as if I were an absolute cretin. He got very supercilious and condescending about the inability of unlettered laymen to comprehend symbology, to comprehend the artistic inventions used to reveal intangible truths. Well, I stopped being contentious, because I realized that so many of those academic double-domes require their little private preserve of superiority and that there was nothing to gain by challenging it."

"What did you decide to do about him?"

"Abe, beggars don't choose. We need witnesses who think *The Seven Minutes* is a literary marvel. I decided that, whatever Dr. Hugo Knight's shortcomings—a manner that might prove offensive, a predilection for speaking a gobbledygook—he was one man with proper credentials who had enthusiasm for *The Seven Minutes*. I asked him whether he would appear as a defense witness. He was thrilled."

"I'm not surprised," said Zelkin. "At the universities it used to be publish or perish—now it's appear as a witness or wither."

"My hope is we can have a few sessions with him pretrial and persuade him that the symbolism angle won't pay off in a public—"

The telephone buzzer sounded, and Barrett shrugged at Zelkin and picked up the receiver. It was Donna on the intercom. She announced that Philip Sanford was on line one.

Barrett pressed down on the lighted button. "Hi, Phil."

"Good news, Mike, the best! We've got our star witness, Jadway's old publisher, got him locked up! Isn't that great?"

"We've got Christian Leroux for a witness?" repeated Barrett, beaming at Zelkin. "That's wonderful. Now what did he—"

"Here, let me put Leo on. He'll give you the details. I just had to let you know first. Here's our genius investigator."

Kimura's voice came on. "Mr. Barrett—"

"I'm here with Abe. He's picking up the extension across the room. Okay, don't skip anything, give us every detail."

"There is not much detail," said Kimura in his precise enunciation. "What there is to tell is highly favorable. I have just finished speaking to Dubois in Antibes. He was waiting in the lobby of the Hotel Balmoral in Monte Carlo when Christian Leroux arrived from Paris to check in. Our man immediately accosted Monsieur Leroux and explained why he was there—the exact nature of his business. Monsieur Leroux indicated at once that it might be possible for him to cooperate if he had even more information. But it fast became apparent to Dubois that what our French publisher desired was not information about our case but information about what we were prepared to pay him as a witness. Leroux was put out of business several years ago when pornographic or banned books, his speciality, began to be published openly by the bigger and more legitimate houses throughout the world. Ever since then Leroux has been trying to make a comeback, raise sufficient money to start a new publishing firm in Paris, one featuring a line of annotated bawdy classics. Dubois presented him our initial offer, as agreed—transportation plus living expenses to and from Los Angeles plus three thousand dollars. Leroux balked at this, mumbling about his time's being worth more than that. Immediately Dubois upped the offer to our top price, transportation and expenses plus five thousand dollars. That was more like it, and Leroux agreed to become our witness."

"You landed a big one," said Zelkin.

"One thing," said Barrett. "Did Leroux indicate what he might say that would be favorable to us?"

"Not exactly. However, he left no doubt in Dubois's mind that he understood what he was being paid for. He wanted to know what was expected of him. After all, he told Dubois, there are facts and there are facts, and truth has many sides. His implication was that he could put in or leave out facts to suit our case. So Dubois told him, from his own limited knowledge, what we were after. He told Leroux that we hoped to prove that J J Jadway had not written *The Seven Minutes* merely as a commercial enterprise, as a pornographer out after quick money, but, rather, as an artist writing with honesty and integrity. To this Leroux replied, 'Voilà, then I can give you what you require, for I was his only publisher, was I not? I was the only one besides himself to believe in the book, was I not? I will provide your defense with whatever it needs.'"

"Jadway," said Barrett, "did he speak of Jadway at all?"

"Only that he had been close to Jadway—"

"Great!" exclaimed Zelkin.

"—and that he will tell us everything once he arrives in Los Angeles and has been paid," said Kimura. "Dubois said that our witness was as shrewd as a French fishwife."

"What's next?" asked Barrett.

"Being a detective, Dubois is most cautious, perhaps more than necessary. Anyway, since some people, friends, knew that Leroux would be staying in Monte Carlo, Dubois decided to remove him from there and secrete him elsewhere, in some place not known to anyone. So Dubois talked Leroux into moving to a small hotel, the Gardiole, in Antibes, and had him register overnight under the name of Sabroux. There Leroux agreed to confine himself to his room until Dubois picks him up tomorrow, gives him his round-trip tickets and a down payment, and puts him on the Caravelle at Nice for Paris and the changeover to Los Angeles. Dubois will cable the exact time we are to meet him at International Airport. So we shall have our star witness the day after tomorrow. I should say that we are fortunate."

After hanging up, Barrett jumped to his feet and pummeled Zelkin jubilantly.

"Easy, easy, there," Zelkin protested, smiling broadly, "or you won't have a partner to help you win the case."

"By God, Abe," said Barrett, "this is absolutely the first time that I've really felt we had a chance."

"Yes, now we have a chance. We also have our first excuse to celebrate something. Why don't I call Sarah and tell her to toss two extra steaks on the broiler and chill some California champagne for two guests tonight—Phil and yourself?"

"That would be—" Barrett began, then remembered, and stopped. "Dammit, no can do. I've got a date with Faye. She agreed to join me tonight. I want to look in on the fund-raising bash the STDL is giving at the Hilton. Main speaker of the evening, our esteemed foe, Elmo Duncan. His subject, 'The Freedom to Corrupt.' I thought I'd try to get in and out without being conspicuous. I thought it might be a good idea to scout the enemy. This could give us a preview of the tenor of his opening statement at the trial and an idea of his oratorical style."

"Okay, the steaks stay in the freezer until Leroux arrives."

"Meanwhile," said Barrett, returning to his desk, "I'm going to devote the next hour to some creative composition."

"Namely?"

"We've got our star," said Barrett. "Now I'd better write him an unforgettable part."

THEY WERE LATE, and Mike Barrett was dismayed.

The fund-raising rally sponsored by the Strength Through Decency League had been scheduled for eight-thirty that evening, and it was ten minutes to nine when they arrived at the Beverly

Hilton Hotel. Barrett had been on time at the Osborns', but Faye, as usual, was still dressing.

At the Beverly Hilton, leaving his car with the parking attendants, Barrett had propelled Faye hastily through the automatic doors into the huge lobby. His hurrying had made her stumble, and now, as he caught hold of her, she was momentarily cross.

"Why this damn rush?" she demanded. "It's not exactly as if you're the guest of honor or anything. Must you always be so prompt?"

"It's not that—" he started to say, but did not finish, because she wouldn't understand, and, besides, it wasn't important. Being on time tonight had nothing to do with ordinary promptness. He had wanted to arrive when everyone else arrived, so that he might be lost in the crowd and his entrance and presence would be less noticeable. After all, this was hostile territory, and to the STDL he was the loathsome adversary. His one hope now was that the members of the audience would be too absorbed in the speechmaking to pay any attention to latecomers.

They resumed their journey through the lobby, walking rapidly, with Faye a half step ahead and leading the way, as if to let him know that she did understand and now regretted her outburst. They went through the wide corridor, past the lower-level pharmacy, and finally reached the foyer and barroom that stood before the Grand Ballroom.

"We're not the last," said Faye.

With relief, he saw that she was right. At least a half-dozen persons were filing slowly by the two card tables behind which several portly women were seated. When it was Barrett's turn, he quickly explained that he'd had no time to send in his check for tickets, and said he hoped there was still seating available. There was indeed, and his ten-dollar bill was accepted.

As he and Faye followed the others toward the ballroom entrance, a number of other guests converged upon the doorway from the direction of the bar. Faye waved to one of these. "There's someone I know." She pulled away from Barrett. "Hello, Maggie. It's so nice to see you again." She was speaking to a strikingly attractive brunette, who was carrying a drink the color of a sloe-gin flip.

"Good to see you, Faye," said the brunette. Self-consciously she held up her glass. "I'm really not a lone drinker. It's just that I need something at lectures. Lectures tend to dehydrate me."

"I meant to phone you," said Faye. "I wanted to tell you how sorry we were about the trouble over Jerry. I think Dad called your uncle. Anyway, we are sorry. Oh, forgive me—" She groped for Barrett's arm and drew him forward. "I don't know if you've met my fiancé. . . . Maggie Russell . . . Michael Barrett."

"I'm pleased to meet you, Miss Russell," said Barrett.

"How do you do," said Maggie Russell, coolly appraising him. "I thought I recognized you."

"You mean those terrible newspaper pictures do me justice?" said Barrett.

"I mean there have been a lot of them," she said without a smile. "And I happen to have a special interest in your case." Before he could reply, she turned to Faye. "You're looking wonderful, Faye."

"Every reason to," said Faye gaily, reaching over to take Barrett's hand. Somehow he did not want a flag planted on him at this moment. He accepted Faye's hand, squeezed it quickly, and dropped it.

Faye and Maggie Russell were moving slowly ahead, conversing in undertones, but Barrett remained where he was, keeping his eyes on the attractive brunette. Inexplicably, he wanted to be alone with her, to try to make her understand—and at once he was confused. Make her understand what? Understand why he was defending a book that had helped destroy her relatives? Or was it—understand why he was with Faye Osborn?

He continued to stare at Maggie Russell. She was Faye's diametric opposite. Faye was taller, thinner, perhaps more classically beautiful, very blond and angular and cool perfection. But Maggie Russell was somehow, indefinably, more appealing.

His eyes held on her head, then moved down her body, trying to discover the source of her attraction. As she turned her head, he noticed that she had a tousled, casual look, perhaps because her shining dark hair was coiffured with the ends—how did the ladies' fashion magazines put it? Yes—with the ends puckishly curling along her cheeks. Her wide-set eyes were gray-green and direct, her nose was small and broad, her mouth moist and partially open, and there was a full lower lip. The contours of both face and figure were soft and sensuous, and what accentuated the rise of her breasts and the fullness of her thighs were her slender waist and slim legs. With Faye, she had now turned sideways in the doorway, and he became aware of the short silk jersey dress that seemed molded to her body so that the lines of her pantie briefs beneath were faintly visible.

He realized that she had suddenly glanced over her shoulder and caught him staring, and now she quickly looked away and straight ahead.

Embarrassed, he guiltily diverted his gaze to Faye, who had just twisted around to beckon him. "Mike, I thought you were in a hurry?"

Striding forward, he caught up with Faye and took her arm, and together they entered the Grand Ballroom behind Maggie Russell. The vast hall had been darkened, he was pleased to see, and it was filled with an audience that probably added up to one thousand persons. There were a number of vacant folding chairs at the rear, and as he and Faye trailed after Maggie Russell he wondered whether they would sit together. But, reaching a make-shift aisle, Maggie found one empty chair at the end of a filled row. Disappointed, Barrett led Faye across the aisle to where a number of unoccupied chairs were clustered, and firmly he directed her to the second seat in from the aisle, while he took the outside place for himself.

Faye leaned toward him, cupping her mouth to his ear. "I apologize," she whispered. "I shouldn't have introduced you to her, but I wasn't thinking. It didn't embarrass you, did it?"

"Why should it embarrass me?" he said.

"She *is* Frank Griffith's niece and very close to the boy."

"So much the better," he whispered. "It might be useful to know someone close to the boy."

Faye removed her gloves. "Forget it," she said. "You're lucky she didn't spit in your eye."

With that, Faye settled back and concentrated on the stage, and for the first time Barrett became aware that all eyes were fixed on the speaker.

The speaker was the evening's main attraction, District Attorney Elmo Duncan, straight and imposing on the platform as his hands held the sides of the lectern and he bent toward the microphone to emphasize a point. Barrett sat fully upright in his chair and listened.

"So let us make no mistake about the word 'pornography' itself," Elmo Duncan was saying. "Let us not forget the derivation of the word. It came from the Greek word *pornographos*, which meant 'the writing of harlots.' It meant any writing or description of the sexual lives of harlots or prostitutes, a special kind of writing that was meant to be aphrodisiac in content. Or, as a modern-day commentator put it, the original pornography was 'the writing of and about whores with the intention of arousing a man's lust so that he would go to a whore.' Centuries have passed, but the word 'pornography' has not changed its meaning. This I affirm although our higher courts have asked those of us devoted to enforcing the law to believe that all pornographic books are not equally criminal. We have been told that a pornographic book that possesses some nonerotic narrative, some passages with so-called social value, must be treated with more tolerance and favor than another book in which the erotic content is unrelieved by any moral digressions. From my personal point of view, this is legal nonsense, this is nit-picking, and this is precisely what has slowed down enforcement of obscenity laws. The diluting of the definition of pornography is what has had law enforcers, to quote Justice Black, hopelessly struggling in a quagmire.

"But, my friends and neighbors, I assure you that I am trapped in no quagmire. To me, a filthy book, even though it pretends to express a social idea or a message, is no less disgusting than a book of total hard-core obscenity. In fact, many jurists contend that literary quality in a written work makes an obscene book all the more destructive. To me, dirt is dirt, no matter how you try to camouflage it. Yes, the Greeks had a word for it, the right word for it, the word that meant writings that excited lascivious thoughts and lustful actions. As a special deputy district attorney and expert in the field of obscenity once stated it, 'The sole purpose of pornographic books is to stimulate erotic response. Pornography encourages people to luxuriate in morbid, sexual-sadist fantasies . . .' And we possess evidence, real evidence, that pornographic books stimulate more than fantasies. We know now that they stimulate crimes of violence.

"The men who are closest to the problem know the truth. Let

me quote to you from Dr. Fredric Wertham, formerly senior psychiatrist at Bellevue Hospital in New York and psychiatric consultant to a Senate subcommittee for the study of organized crime. According to Dr. Wertham, 'Children's attitudes and consequent actions are definitely affected by the reading of literature suggestive of a combination of sex and violence. I am convinced that this combination is creating in the minds of children the ego ideal of the brute who by physical strength takes the law into his own hands, makes his own rules, and solves all his problems by force.' To support this statement, we have the statistics of our Federal Bureau of Investigation covering a recent ten-year period in our history, a period of the greatest production of pornographic books, a period during which forcible rape increased thirty-seven per cent in the United States, and the age bracket of rapists that increased the most was that of late-teen-agers.

"Yet there is more to fear. From the time of that great English jurist of the eighteenth century, Sir William Blackstone, to the present day, we have been on notice that our society may suffer a death of the soul if pornographers are given unlimited license. Blackstone told us that to punish dangerous or offensive writings 'is necessary for the preservation of peace and good order, of government and religion, the only solid foundations of civil liberty.' Now, after two hundred years, we continue to be reminded of our duty. The anthropologist Margaret Mead has told us that every human society on earth exercises some kind of explicit censorship over behavior, especially over sexual behavior. From England, Sir Patrick Devlin has admonished us that we dare not tolerate complete openness about sexual freedom. 'No society,' he said, 'can do without intolerance, indignation, and disgust; they are the forces behind the moral law.' Our own Judge Thurman Arnold has concurred. He has gone so far as to state, 'The fact that laws against obscenity do not have a rational or scientific basis, but rather symbolize a moral taboo, does not make them any the less necessary. They are important because men feel that without them the state would be lacking in moral standards.' In short, whether there is a scientific basis for our obscenity laws or not—and I happen to believe there is such a basis—the laws must be observed and enforced if our society is to survive the eroding effects of immorality.

"My friends, let us not be afraid of being branded censors, and let us not be afraid of justified censorship. The truth is that censorship, which is as old as history itself, has long been known to be a necessity for the common good and civilized man's survival. Far back before Christ's birth, the philosopher Plato asked the question, 'Shall we just carelessly allow children to hear any casual tales which may be devised by casual persons, and to receive into their minds ideas for the most part the very opposite of those which we should wish them to have when they are grown up?' And to this Plato gave civilization's answer, 'Then the first thing will be to establish a censorship of the writers of fiction, and let the censors receive any tale of fiction which is good, and reject the bad; and we will desire mothers and nurses to tell their children the authorized ones only.'

"My friends, the time has come when each and every one of us must face the fact that pornography, no matter what disguise it wears, still remains outright obscenity and a threat to our families, to our future, and to the health of this great nation. We must say to ourselves, to each other, to the entire country, that the time has come to resist and stop the black plague of pornography. The time has come, the time is now, and, as a fellow citizen as well as your district attorney, I pledge every energy and resource at my command to lead this crusade!"

Elmo Duncan had paused, awaiting the expected response, and it came in a thunderclap of applause. As the applause continued, Barrett looked at Faye beside him. Her eyes were bright, fixed upon the figure on the stage, and she was clapping her hands. Troubled, Barrett turned his head and looked across the aisle. Maggie Russell, her face pensive and pale, sat unmoving. Her hands lay still in her lap. Curious, Barrett thought, but then the speaker's deep voice intruded, and Barrett returned his attention to the stage.

"Since the year 1821," Duncan was saying, "when the United States had its first obscenity trial, a year when one Peter Holmes was found guilty of publishing *Memoirs of a Woman of Pleasure*—none other than *Fanny Hill*—various publishers, in recent years a legion of them, have taken advantage of our liberties and freedoms, and made a mockery of our Constitution and instruments of justice. As a result, today the publishing of smut has become a two-billion-dollar-a-year business.

"I blame these publishers for supporting, sometimes encouraging, the production of filth, and I blame them for promoting its sale throughout the land in the name of literature when their only fidelity is to their profit ledgers. I blame the booksellers equally, for lacking the moral fiber to reject this trash, for thinking of private gain rather than public welfare. And I blame the writers of this filth, too. Let no one escape, least of all the creators, those debasers of freedom of expression who hide behind the skirt of the very Muse whom they would soil and defile."

On the platform, Elmo Duncan had paused, shaking his head. "Writers—writers," he said sadly, "who betray not only themselves but one another for Mammon, their true god. Let me quote you the words of a celebrated writer. 'But even I would censor genuine pornography, rigorously,' he wrote. 'Pornography is the attempt to insult sex, to do dirt on it. This is unpardonable.' Unpardonable indeed. And who spoke those glorious words? Let me tell you. D. H. Lawrence, the author of that paean to purity, *Lady Chatterley's Lover!*"

There was laughter and applause, and Elmo Duncan acknowledged it with a smile and held up his hand.

"I'm not through," he said. "Listen to this. When James Joyce published *Ulysses* in Paris, who was among the first to call it obscene and demand that it be suppressed? You guessed it. D. H. Lawrence, author of *Lady Chatterley's Lover* and would-be protector of public morals—protecting them from other people's pornography, that is!"

A raucous burst of laughter greeted the District Attorney's sally.

Duncan was serious again. "I have mentioned Joyce's *Ulysses*, which brings to mind something I've long wanted to say. For years we have had dinned in our ears the bravery of Judge John M. Woolsey for admitting that pornographic work into our land, and for years we have had dinned in our ears the courage of Circuit Judges Augustus and Learned Hand, who sustained Woolsey's lower-court verdict in their appeal court against one dissenting judge. But, friends, and forgive me for this, no Woolseys have been pulled over my eyes, no Hands have ever covered my ears, to prevent my recognizing and listening to the one person who deserved to be heard before all others—for the real bravery and courage in the *Ulysses* case was that of the one arbiter who dissented with the Hands' verdict in that appeal case. I refer to the long-forgotten Circuit Judge Martin Manton, and to his dissent which each of us should carry writ on our banners in this crusade against the corrupters of freedom. 'Congress passed this statute against obscenity for the great mass of our people,' wrote Judge Manton, adding that it is only the unusual person who thinks he can protect himself. Then Judge Manton went on, 'The people do not exist for the sake of literature, to give the author fame, the publisher wealth, and the book a market. On the contrary, literature exists for the sake of the people, to refresh the weary, to console the sad, to hearten the dull and downcast, to increase man's interest in the world, his joy of living, and his sympathy in all sorts and conditions of men. Art for art's sake is heartless and soon grows artless; art for the public market is not art at all, but commerce; art for the people's service is a noble, vital and permanent element of human life . . . Masterpieces have never been produced by men given to obscenity or lustful thoughts—men who have no Master . . . Good work in literature has its permanent mark; it is like all good work, noble and lasting. It requires a human aim—to cheer, console, purify, or ennoble the life of people. With this aim, literature had never sent an arrow close to the mark. It is by good work only that men of letters can justify their right to a place in the world.' These are the words I pray the STDL will continue to support, and the community will begin to heed—"

These words by Circuit Judge Manton. Hearing them, Barrett's gray cells had begun groping, and at last they snared Judge Manton in memory and impaled him. The moral Judge Manton, short years after airing his noble words, had been arrested for his part in a conspiracy to block justice and had wound up in a federal prison for nineteen months. Barrett wondered whether he should offer this postscript to the enthralled Faye. He decided against it. She was too engrossed in the District Attorney's forensics. Barrett settled back to listen further.

"—yes, give heed to these sentiments by Judge Manton," the District Attorney was saying, "for had they been the standard by which a book publisher and seller had made their judgment in recent weeks, I assure you that our city would have known less violence and our neighbors would have suffered less grief."

Elmo Duncan halted, and the swelling of applause was instantaneous in response to his first oblique reference to *The Seven Minutes* and the Jerry Griffith rape case.

Once more Barrett could see that Faye was fervently clapping her hands, and once more he turned to observe Maggie Russell. As before, and like himself, she had not joined in the applause. Instead, picking up the empty glass and her purse, she abruptly rose, met his eyes, then started up the aisle and toward the exit.

Her sudden departure bewildered Barrett. Obviously she had come to this rally because her sympathies were for the STDL and Elmo Duncan, who were trying to punish the book that had, in their view, driven Jerry Griffith to crime. And Jerry was Maggie Russell's close relative. Then why had she, abruptly and with seeming finality, decided to leave before the District Attorney's speech had ended?

A remote possibility passed through Barrett's mind. Unaccountably, this girl had turned her back on the prosecution. Perhaps, given a chance, she might not turn her back on the defense. It was worth finding out.

On the stage, Duncan had resumed speaking, and, beside Barrett, Faye was listening intently. Barrett leaned toward her. "Excuse me a minute, darling. I'll be right back."

"Mike, where are you—?"

"Men's room," he whispered. "Remember to tell me what I missed."

Sliding off his chair, he went up the aisle, around the back row of chairs, and out the exit.

In the foyer, he saw Maggie Russell place her empty glass on the bar. As she was starting for the lobby corridor Barrett hastened to intercept her.

"Miss Russell—" he called out.

She stopped and waited, without surprise.

He caught up with her. "While I had the chance, I wanted a few words with you."

She remained silent, still waiting.

"It's about your relatives, the Griffiths. I understand you live with them."

"I'm Mrs. Griffith's secretary and companion."

"Faye mentioned your relationship with Jerry."

"What did she say?"

"She said you were very close to the boy."

"We're not only relatives, we're friends." She stared up at Barrett, and then she added pointedly, "And I'm prepared to defend him against anyone who wishes to hurt him."

Barrett frowned. "If that was meant for me, you've picked the wrong target. I have no reason to try to hurt Jerry Griffith. Quite the contrary. I'm sorry for him and I sympathize with all of you. My only interest in Jerry is professional. I'm charged with defending a man who sold a book that Jerry claims incited him to a crime. From the little I know of juvenile delinquency, I am not convinced that reading matter alone—if in any way—can be held responsible for antisocial acts. There are many other factors that might be more seriously considered, among them a young man's upbringing and family. I was hoping we could talk about this."

Her gray-green eyes were unblinking. She considered him without emotion. "I'm surprised at myself for listening to you. What made you think even for a moment that I'd talk to you about my family's private affairs?"

"For one thing, your behavior in the ballroom," said Barrett. "Your attending this event seemed perfectly natural. But when you were the only person beside myself not to applaud Duncan's pack of nonsense, and when you got up and walked out on him, it occurred to me that you might not be fully sympathetic with his point of view. Perhaps I misread your actions, but that's what occurred to me. For a second thing, just watching you, I've— Well, you look honest and forthright and intelligent, the kind of person who might see that cooperating with me could not harm Jerry at all, might in some ways be useful to him."

Calmly she folded both hands over her purse before her, and she replied, "Mr. Barrett, to take the last first, I am honest and forthright, and so I can tell you I am intelligent enough to know any further discussion with you would be an act of disloyalty to those who have given me so much. As for Mr. Duncan, I have no interest in his views on censorship in general. My sole interest in life right now is to protect Jerry. I came here tonight to see and hear how the District Attorney performed in public, since by attacking your book in court he will be attacking the source of Jerry's problem. In that sense, Mr. Duncan will be supporting and explaining Jerry, and helping mitigate my cousin's guilt. I walked out because I had seen and heard enough." She paused, and then went on, her tone more earnest than ever. "Mr. Barrett, I have no idea to what degree pornography alone contributes to juvenile delinquency. I only know that someone dear to me has confessed it did him harm. Beyond that, I abhor censorship of any kind, especially as it was being advocated this evening. Nor do I care for the kind of people censorship attracts or the atmosphere it creates. But I am in favor of limited restrictions on what young people may be permitted to read, especially restrictions on prurient books written and manufactured to sell or titillate. I deplore any censorship of honest works, enlightening works, no matter how many four-letter words they contain, no matter how explicit they may be about sex. Those books can't harm young people. Perhaps the other books can. There you have it."

Barrett was sufficiently impressed by her, and encouraged, to ask his next question. "Okay, Miss Russell, reasonable enough. Then can you tell me—assuming you've read the book—do you regard *The Seven Minutes* as an honest book or a prurient one?"

About to reply, she hesitated, and then she said, "I have no desire to discuss my reading tastes with you right now."

"But I am sure you will allow that even if Jerry feels the book influenced his behavior, there may have been other, stronger influences, ones he was unaware of, that disturbed him. Will you allow for that?"

"Mr. Barrett, I'm not a psychoanalyst. I don't know. I do know I've already told you I have no intention of discussing my relatives with you or with anyone."

"Well, perhaps there are some people close to Jerry who would feel that uncovering the whole truth about him, for his sake, for all of us, could be a service to him in the end. I suppose it would be foolish to ask whether Frank Griffith would see me?"

"I think Mr. Griffith would consider you like something that came out from under a rock. If he could, I'm sure he'd stamp you out."

"I've heard Mrs. Griffith is more pacific."

"Obviously she is. But in this matter it seems that way only because she's invalided. You are being foolish, Mr. Barrett. We aren't a house divided. We're together in this. I don't know what you're after."

"I'm after Jerry. I'd like to see him, because I think he can help me, and in so doing help himself."

"You're wasting your time and my time. Jerry wouldn't see you in a million years, and even if he would, none of us would permit it. I must say, Mr. Barrett, your persistence is becoming annoying."

Barrett smiled apologetically. "I'm sorry, I truly am. But you could have snubbed me, you know. Yet you didn't. You suffered my interrogation. Why? Good manners, Miss Russell?"

She was not amused. "Not good manners, Mr. Barrett. I wanted to see if you were really the kind of son of a bitch everyone said you were."

"And—am I?"

"I'm not sure what you are, but from what I've seen tonight I suspect you're heartless and ambitious, with less concern for human feelings than for winning a trial for yourself. Well, I want no part of you or your trial, Mr. Barrett. I don't give a damn about your case, except as it pertains to Jerry. So if you're not what people say you are, you can prove it by not bothering me again. End of interrogation, Mr. Barrett. Good night."

With that, she turned on her heel and went rapidly toward the lobby.

He watched her leave, and when he started back to the ballroom he felt only one emotion toward her. Not anger. Not hurt. Only regret. He felt regret that she was so lovely—he had never met anyone lovelier, except for Faye, who was lovely but not in exactly the same sense—and that life had cast them in opposite camps.

Unhappily he returned to the ballroom and his seat beside Faye. He began an apology to Faye, but she held her forefinger to her lips and then poked it toward the stage. He looked toward the stage, and realized that Elmo Duncan was concluding his address.

"And so, my friends," said the District Attorney, removing the pages of his speech from the lectern, "we know what we must fight, and why we must fight, and we know that we can succeed only by working hand in hand together. As we strive toward our common goal, let us remember the words de Tocqueville spoke long ago of our beloved country. 'America is great,' he said, 'because she is good and when America ceases to be good she will cease to be great.' Let us rededicate ourselves to America's goodness, so that her greatness never, ever diminishes. I thank you."

The thousand members of the audience seemed to rise to their feet in unison, like some giant eruption, beating their palms together, cheering, shouting their enthusiasm.

It disturbed Barrett to observe the numbers, the solidity, the passion of the opposition. He thought, If a like number of people, multiplied by every community in America, were as united and determined to eradicate cancer or poverty or racial inequality or even war, instead of to prevent open discussions about sex, the land of the free would be truly free and good. But fighting other causes is less warped fun, and less therapeutic to the old Calvinistic sickness, than fighting sex. Crazy people. Damn them.

The hurrahing and applause were continuing, and Barrett realized that he alone had remained seated. Lest he be conspicuous, and wind up lynched, he hastily stood up with Faye and the others.

Seeing him watching her, Faye ceased applauding. "I'm afraid I get carried away by oratory," she apologized. "You must agree, whatever else he is, our friend Elmo is effective, even if he is a rabble-rouser. But most politicians have to be, don't they? Don't look so upset, Mike. You're twice as smart as he is, and you'll make mincemeat of him in court. I just meant that he surprised me, the way he handled himself before an audience."

"It was his audience before he opened his mouth," said Barrett. "Even if he were tongue-tied they'd have hailed him as Demosthenes. Come on, let's get out of here."

Faye pointed to the stage. "Wait a second, I think there's going to be something more."

Elmo Duncan had not left the platform. Standing to one side of the lectern, he was listening to a swarthy man who had materialized from somewhere and whom Barrett recognized to be Victor Rodriguez, the Assistant District Attorney. With them also was a tall, horsy woman in an expensive but unbecoming mauve-colored suit who Barrett supposed was Mrs. Olivia St. Clair, president of the STDL. Rodriguez had handed Duncan a sheet of paper, and seemed to be explaining something on it. Then the horsy woman appeared to be asking Duncan a question, to which he responded by nodding vigorously as he handed the paper to her.

The noise had begun to subside, but as Elmo Duncan started to leave the stage, followed by Rodriguez, the applause swelled again, and Duncan beamed gratefully and waved and came down off the stage to be swallowed up in a mass of admirers. Meanwhile, the horsy woman had made her way to the microphone above the lectern. She raised both hands for silence, the piece of paper still clutched in one gloved fist.

To still the audience, the woman screamed shrilly into the microphone, "Your attention, please—your attention for one more minute—because some exciting news has just come to us—something that concerns everyone here!"

Immediately the ballroom was hushed, and some quality of triumph in the piercing voice of the STDL's leader gave Barrett a vague premonition of disaster.

"The most exciting news possible!" the woman shrieked into the microphone, flying the sheet of paper from the one hand that had stayed aloft. "Before announcing it, ladies and gentlemen, fellow members of the Strength Through Decency League, I want to speak as your president, and for all of you—"

This was indeed the formidable Mrs. St. Clair, as Barrett has guessed. She had been the instigator of the events that had led to the indictment of Ben Fremont and *The Seven Minutes,* and Barrett wondered what other woes she was preparing to bring down on him now.

"—in thanking our distinguished and eminent District Attorney for his edifying and inspiring speech here this evening," Mrs. St. Clair continued. "With public servants like Mr. Duncan to implement our work, we know that we shall see victory in the near future. And now—"

She held the sheet of paper up to the microphone.

"—now new evidence has been brought to light, most dramatically, that supports our campaign for increasing vigilance in the control of reading matter and gives our District Attorney the final ammunition he needs to defeat the forces of pornography."

She brought the sheet of paper before her, studied it, then lifted her head.

"Properly this is an announcement that deserves to come from our District Attorney. However, since it directly concerns and affects his prosecution of *The Seven Minutes*, I am advised that it would be unethical for Mr. Duncan to make any public comment on the trial until it is over. While Mr. Duncan has referred, and may continue to refer, to the pending trial itself, he feels he cannot discuss facts that might be considered part of the evidence in that trial. On the other hand, since the STDL has the same concerns as the District Attorney's Office about pornography generally, and *The Seven Minutes* specifically, I have the obligation, as president of the STDL, to keep you informed about the most recent developments related to the prosecution of *The Seven Minutes*."

The audience in the ballroom remained standing, and now it awaited Mrs. St. Clair's announcement with restraint intermingled with curiosity.

Barrett felt his heart begin to pound, and he waited, too.

Mrs. St. Clair looked up from the paper in her hand. "Ladies and gentlemen, fellow members, as many of us know, the original underground publisher of *The Seven Minutes* was a Frenchman, Christian Leroux, who knew the late J J Jadway personally and who was the only man on earth who could possibly shed light on many questions that have continued to stand unanswered concerning this book and its author. All of us have asked ourselves— what manner of a man could write a book such as this? What were his motives in writing the book? What happened to him afterward? What brought about his early death? Tonight we finally have the answers, and we have them directly from the lips of Christian Leroux, Jadway's French publisher."

Barrett's heart was hammering harder, and he exchanged a wordless glance with Faye, then gave his full concentration to the stage.

"Not more than an hour ago, in France, Christian Leroux, after deep soul-searching, emerged from hiding to offer his services to the people of California, America, the world, in the prosecution of *The Seven Minutes*. Christian Leroux confessed his original sin, which was in publishing the vile book. It was, he stated, an error compounded of youth, immaturity, and avarice. But now, rather than see his sin repeated by others who would corrupt mankind with this evil work, he has determined to expiate his sin and work for us in attempting to suppress *The Seven Minutes*."

A spattering of applause had begun, but Olivia St. Clair gestured for it to stop so that she might be heard.

"The unanswered questions are now answered, and they are answered by the only person on earth who can speak for J J Jadway. According to the French publisher, Jadway wrote the book because he was desperate to have money. Jadway lived a dissolute and immoral life on the Left Bank of Paris, dissipating his savings on drink and drugs and his latest mistress. Yes, a mistress he had taken, and whom he was able to keep happy only by lavishing gifts upon her. According to Leroux, the pornographer repaid her for her devotion, repaid her by using her as the model for his lascivious, lewd, shameless heroine in *The Seven Minutes*. This poor creature's real name was Cassie McGraw, and she was made to perform as the Cathleen of that filthy novel. When Jadway had no more money, he dashed off this narrative of unremitting salaciousness for the underground press to get his hands on quick and easy cash. But Jadway had come from a religious background, and after his book had been published he saw the harm that the book was doing to innocent people. At last he realized the depths of his depravity and the extent of his mortal sin. And tonight Christian Leroux has confirmed what our District Attorney had already learned from another reliable source—that in his final moments of sanity J J Jadway understood the horrendous crime he had perpetrated on his fellow men, and he knew that his soul could be saved only if he renounced the disgusting and dangerous book. And so, out of remorse for what he had done, J J Jadway committed suicide!"

There were gaspings and mutterings throughout the ballroom.

Mrs. St. Clair pitched her voice higher. "If the author of the book could kill himself out of shame for having written it, he deserves to have us unite our energies in order to kill this monstrous work for him so that he can know salvation. To help us do this, to help our District Attorney do this, Christian Leroux is on his way to Los Angeles to appear as a witness for the prosecution. His courage and his appearance assure us of a historic victory in a court of law, and we will honor Mr. Leroux as our guest speaker at our very next victory rally. Thank you, friends and members!" The ballroom had become a bedlam of shouts and cheers.

Mike Barrett had heard the announcement in stunned silence. Every word and sentence from the stage had fallen upon him like a meat cleaver. Now, all but beaten, he found his instinct for survival shoring up his resistance to the announcement, suggesting the impossibility of its being true. But he had to know for certain.

He gripped Faye's arm. "Come on," he said harshly.

They broke through the milling crowd into the foyer.

"Where are we going?" Faye wanted to know.

"I can't believe what she was saying," said Barrett, marching Faye with him toward the lobby. "This can't be. Six hours ago we had Christian Leroux locked up as our witness and ready to defend Jadway's motives and his book, and suddenly Duncan claims to have him and to have him vilifying Jadway and the book. I've got to find out the truth."

They had reached the middle of the lobby. "Look, Faye," he said, "you wait here, have a cigarette. I won't be long. I've got to call Abe Zelkin. He should be able to confirm or deny."

Barrett hurried off in search of a phone booth, and when he found one he enclosed himself in it, deposited the necessary coins, and dialed Abe Zelkin.

"I was staying up, waiting for you to get home," said Zelkin in a voice as overwrought as Barrett's own. "I had to speak to you. We just heard from that detective, Dubois, in France. He just rang us. Do you know what? Our star witness, our Christian Leroux, he's disappeared. No one knows where in the devil he is."

Barrett closed his eyes and slumped back against the side of the booth. Then it *was* true. "Abe, I know where that bastard is. He's on his way to Elmo Duncan."

"You're kidding? Oh, no, don't say it."

"Abe, I'm saying it. I'm still at the Hilton. You know what I just heard announced?" Painfully he recounted every detail of Olivia St. Clair's public statement.

When he was through, Barrett added wearily, "I don't know how it could have happened. We had him hidden, and under another name, and he was agreeable to our terms. Only one possibility occurs to me. Our offer made Leroux realize his own value

204

in the marketplace. The minute our man left him alone, Leroux probably got in touch with Duncan and offered to sell out for a higher bid."

"No, Mike. Dubois was clever enough to think of that. Dubois checked with the hotel concierge, telephone operator, manager. From the moment Dubois checked him into that hotel in Antibes, Leroux never left his room, sent no letters, messages, cables, made no outgoing calls and received no calls. All the hotel could report was that a few hours before Dubois went by to pick him up for us a Frenchman asked to see Leroux in his room. Shortly after, Leroux checked out of the hotel, leaving with his visitor, and disappeared."

Barrett had another thought. "There's only one explanation, then. Dubois. Our private detective. He knew he had hot goods. He could have sold us out."

"Absolutely not, Mike," said Zelkin. "I brought that up with Phil Sanford and Leo just before you called. They both said no. Sanford had given us the name of his father's French representative, and it was he who recommended Dubois to us. He vouched for Dubois. A man of long-standing integrity. Incorruptible. No, I doubt if it was Dubois."

"It was someone, something," protested Barrett. "One minute he's here. Presto. The next minute he's melted away. One minute we have him, the next minute they have him. There's got to be an explanation. I don't mind dealing with events I can see and handle—win, lose, or draw—but I'm helpless when I have to deal with the supernatural."

"No use wasting a single erg of energy on speculation. I'm not interested in what happened after the fact. It happened. We lost a round."

"That was round fifteen, Abe."

"No, it wasn't. Let's get some sleep and see what we can salvage tomorrow."

When Barrett wearily returned to the lobby, Faye tamped out her cigarette and got up from the sofa to meet him.

She looked at him worriedly. "Was Mrs. St. Clair's announcement true, Mike?"

"It was true."

"I'm sorry, Mike. Is this real bad for you?"

"Disastrous."

"Does this make your case hopeless?"

"As things stand now—yes—yes—I'm afraid so."

Faye linked her arm in his. "Then, Mike, will you listen to me? I'm the one person who can help you. Please, listen."

"What?"

"Just two little words." She paused. "Get out."

He pulled away and peered down at her. "Get out? You mean quit?"

"I mean get out of it while you can. I can admire a man more for having the sense to abandon a sinking ship than for blindly insisting it isn't sinking and then going down with it. You knew from the start that both Dad and I felt you were on the wrong side, mixed up with all that dirty publicity and all kinds of slimy, unprincipled people. You don't belong in that kind of case. But I wanted you to pay your debt, be satisfied, so I went along. Now I think you've done everything you can do. You've discharged your debt to Sanford. There's a limit to what you owe him. You don't have to commit suicide for him. You've said it's become a hopeless cause. So for my sake, for Dad's, show that you're a man, big enough to know when to reject a lost cause. Promise me you'll do it now, before that horrible trial begins."

He looked at her a moment longer, and then he said, "No, Faye."

"You're being unreasonably stubborn. Weren't you listening to me? I said you've paid your debt to Sanford—"

"It's not Sanford that I give a damn about. It's Jadway. You see, I've read his book. I know Jadway couldn't have been all those things Leroux says he was. I'm convinced Leroux is a fake and a liar. There's only one problem, my dear. How in the hell am I going to prove it?"

IV

MIKE BARRETT steered his convertible into the entrance of the parking lot behind Mount Sinai Hospital, stopped the car to drop a quarter into the meter, waited for the striped gate to creak upward, and then drove into the lot. It was the afternoon visiting hour, and the lot was almost filled to capacity. In the far lane Barrett saw a car backing out, and he sped toward the vacated slot and eased his convertible into it.

The dashboard clock told him that it was ten minutes after three o'clock. He was in no hurry. There would be time enough to learn what more he could of Sheri Moore, the victim of rape, who still lay in a coma on a hospital bed on the fifth floor.

Barrett wanted an interlude in which to gather his wits about him. He sought his shell pipe, packed it, passed a flame over it, and remained seated behind the wheel, smoking, thinking, seeking some degree of optimism. As his mind returned to last night, his feeling of gloom remained unrelieved. The loss of Christian Leroux had been a terrible blow, and he had not yet recovered from it. None of them had.

Usually the morning of a new day held out the promise of some bright and buoyant expectation. But had he been awakened at dawn by Dr. Pangloss and Mr. Micawber together, plying him with pep pills, he knew that his mood could not have been improved. His mood, like the bleak day itself, was overcast and gray. The morning paper had done little to lift his spirits. There had been a front-page story reporting Duncan's speech and Mrs. St. Clair's sensational announcement, as well as later news that Leroux would be arriving from France tomorrow to await his appearance as a witness for the State.

In the office there had been no fresh breaks or leads. Continuing in the effort to turn up something helpful about the author of *The Seven Minutes*, Kimura had reported that he was still on the trail of Norman C. Quandt, the pornography specialist who had acquired publication rights to the novel from Leroux and resold them to Phil Sanford. Despite the knowledge that Quandt had relocated himself in Southern California, Kimura had been unable to find out more about him.

Lunch had been better. For Barrett, it had given the day, if not hope, then direction at least.

He had dined at the bustling, celebrity-filled Bistro restaurant in Beverly Hills with Dr. Yale Finegood, a lively young psychiatrist who had once worked at the Reiss-Davis Child Study Center, but who was now on his own. Finegood, a specialist in the problems of disturbed adolescents, felt that there was no connection between reading a book or viewing a motion picture and committing an act of violence. In fact, he pointed out, many of his colleagues credited pornographic books with keeping down the crime rate, since reading provided an outlet in the form of fantasies of sexual cravings which might otherwise be acted out. Dr. Finegood quoted a study that had been made by a pair of research criminologists, Eleanor and Sheldon Glueck, a study of one thousand delinquent boys in and around Boston. What the Gluecks had learned was that the real factors contributing to their subjects' delinquency were unhappy family relationships, lack of education, conflict with the prevailing culture, inherent psychological problems, and bad social habits such as drug addiction, the use of alcohol, sexual promiscuity. The reading of pornography was no significant factor.

"What specifically might provoke a quiet, shy twenty-one-year-old boy from an upper-class family to become sexually violent?" said Dr. Finegood, echoing Barrett's question. "Every individual case varies, but sexual violence is usually a reflection of sexual incompetence. Rape removes the rapist's feeling of constant inferiority. A boy coming out of a middle- or upper-class environment who commits rape may simply be rebeling against years of repressed resentment toward his mother or father. Most likely the rapist may have had a domineering parent or parents, or, conversely, he may have had an indifferent or inadequate parent or parents. Show me a boy made submissive by a father he fears, and you will be showing me a young man with the potential to assert himself one day by an act of violence in which he can degrade his victim."

When their lunch had ended, and they were leaving the Bistro, Dr. Finegood gave Barrett one last piece of advice. "The importance of information on Jadway to your case I can understand. At the same time, don't overlook the importance of the actors in that rape case. I know you've been frustrated in your efforts to learn more about Jerry Griffith, his family, his friends. Nevertheless, I would suggest you redouble your efforts to obtain more information. If you do, I feel certain you'll unearth other reasons for Jerry's behavior—and then, perhaps, you can convince a jury that Jadway's book was not the motivating force behind the young man's criminal outburst. And if I were you, I would go even further. I'd lose no time in trying to find out something about the victim, that eighteen-year-old girl whom Jerry raped. You'd be surprised what an investigation of both the rapist and the raped can bring to light. I'm not predicting that this will lead to anything. I'm merely advising you to leave no stone unturned. Well, good luck. Do keep me fully informed. I look forward to taking the stand in this trial, even though the prosecution, I hear, will have a psychiatrist no less prominent than Dr. Roger Trimble to contradict me. But I think I can hold my own."

After lunch, Barrett had decided to take Dr. Finegood's advice. He would have a brief look at the life and times of eighteen-year-old Sheri Moore. He doubted whether anything would come of it, but he must turn this stone also.

The newspaper file in the office had supplied only sketchy information on the victim. Sheri Moore was the youngest of five children. Her parents were long divorced. Her father, Howard Moore, was an engineer at North American Rockwell Corporation, and he lived in Santa Monica. Sheri was a freshman at Santa Monica College. She shared an apartment with a girl friend, Darlene Nelson, on Doheny Drive in West Hollywood. The last two facts alone puzzled Barrett. Why would anyone live in West Hollywood if she was attending school in Santa Monica? It was a long commuting trip to make daily, especially for a girl who owned no automobile. The solution to this, as well as more detailed biographical information, might best be found at Sheri's school. And so Barrett had set out to visit Santa Monica College.

There had been only one surprise, and this had come from the records in the administration department. Despite the press stories, Sheri Moore was no longer a student in good standing at the college. After receiving passing grades during the first semester of her freshman year, she had become increasingly erratic about attending classes regularly and handing in papers, and during her second term her tests had consequently been poor. One month before becoming the victim of rape, she had dropped out of Santa Monica College.

Barrett had been introduced to a dozen of Sheri's former classmates, young men and women who were either gathered in raucous conversational groups before the college cafeteria and bookstore or basking in the sun on the grassy slopes of the campus. None of Barrett's questions had elicited an objective or detailed response. One girl, an honor student, recalled that Sheri had become bored with school and had spoken of a career as a model or actress, and that then she had quit school to move to West Hollywood, where she hoped to find a part-time job that would support future acting lessons. A football player had mumbled something about Sheri's being "a fun kid, a swinger." But listening to the other students, any visitor would have thought that they were speaking of Joan of Arc. The fact that one of their own had become the victim of a crime, was seriously injured and still lay in critical condition, seemed to have the effect of making most of them speak of her with reverence, extolling her virtues. Perhaps, Barrett had told himself as he had left the campus, he was being unfairly cynical. Perhaps Sheri Moore had indeed been virtue personified.

Now, on the final lap of his inquiry into the life and times of Sheri Moore, he had arrived at Mount Sinai Hospital.

After locking the door of the convertible, Barrett crossed the parking lot, went up the steps quickly, and entered the rear corridor that led to the downstairs lobby and to the elevators. He caught an elevator to the fifth floor and went directly to the nurses' counter.

A Negro registered nurse greeted him from her desk.

"I'd like to inquire about Sheri Moore," said Barrett. "I'm a friend."

"She's doing just about as well as can be expected," said the nurse. "She's still in a coma." Momentarily she searched for the chart, then gave up. "She had a comfortable night. Do you want to see her? Because if you do, I must tell you visitors are restricted to the names on a list the doctor left. If you want me to check it for your name—"

"No, never mind. I only wanted to find out how she's doing." He hesitated. "Are there many people on that visitors' list?"

Now it was the nurse's turn to be hesitant. "You're not from the press are you?"

"The press? God, no, I'm a friend who—"

"We can't be too careful. The reporters are around here all the time. Well, I suppose there's nothing wrong in telling you that Sheri's relatives and her one closest girl friend are allowed to see her. In fact, her father and her girl friend, the one she was rooming with, Darlene Nelson, they're in her room right now."

"Thanks," said Barrett. "I wonder whether you could let me know when Miss Nelson leaves. I'll be in the waiting room."

"Well, no need your having to wait for that. Darlene's just sitting there. I'd be glad to fetch her for you, Mr. . . ." She drew out the "Mister," turning it into a question.

"Barrett," he said. "Mr. Barrett. Thank you ever so much."

He walked down the hall and turned into the visitors' waiting room, a small alcove furnished with chintz and wicker and a television set. The waiting room was unoccupied. Barrett halted before an ashtray, emptied his pipe, refilled it, and circled the room, smoking, going over Darlene Nelson's connection with the rape case. It was Darlene, he remembered, who had returned to their apartment on Doheny Drive, to discover Sheri Moore sprawled on the bedroom floor, bloodied and only half conscious. It was then that Darlene had heard Sheri murmur that she had been raped, and after that Sheri had lost consciousness. It was Darlene who had summoned the ambulance and the police.

From the recess of the waiting room, Barrett heard two women's voices growing louder. He pivoted around in time to see the nurse and a girl with a boyish haircut and the shirttails of her blouse hanging out over her dungarees come into view. The two were absorbed in conversation.

The nurse was saying, "I sure envy you, Darlene. The Underground Railroad, that's my favorite fun place whenever I can get the time. I'd give anything to be there at that opening."

"It'll be jumping this week and next, so any night'll be as good as tonight. It's just a pity poor Sheri isn't well enough. They're having her favorite group there. She's got all their albums."

"She'll get well."

"Fingers crossed."

The nurse had gone, and Darlene Nelson was approaching Barrett with a quizzical expression.

"I'm Darlene Nelson," she said. "Are you the one who wanted to see me?"

"That's correct. I—"

"Do I know you?" She had a nervous habit, a flick of her hand as if brushing her hair off her shoulder, but she touched nothing, because her hair was cut short. Perhaps the haircut was a recent idea, thought Barrett.

"I'm Michael Barrett," he said. This brought no recognition. "The lawyer representing Ben Fremont, the owner of the bookstore, who—"

Recognition came. "The dirty book," she said. Suspicion followed. "What do you want with me?"

"Just the answers to a couple of questions," said Barrett. "Would you like to sit down?"

She made no move to sit. Her hand brushed past her ear. "What questions?"

"Well, for one thing, had Miss Moore or yourself, either of you, had any acquaintance with Jerry Griffith before the night he—?"

"No," she said.

"All right," Barrett said. "What about any of Jerry's friends? Did you know any of them?"

"How would I know who his friends are? Even if I'd met one by accident, I wouldn't know it."

"Well, Miss Nelson, I'm thinking of one in particular. He's a student at UCLA and lives in Westwood. His name is George Perkins. Did you ever hear Miss Moore—Sheri—mention him?"

"No."

"What about yourself? Do you know George Perkins?"

"No. No, I don't."

"There's another thing I hoped you could tell me. On the night you found Sheri—"

"Mr. Barrett, I don't think I should be talking to you. I can't tell you a thing. Besides, there's nothing to tell. I told it all to the police, and it's been hashed over in the papers. I better go now. Excuse me."

Darlene Nelson had been backing off, and now she rushed out of the room.

Barrett shrugged, emptied and pocketed his pipe, and headed for the elevator.

A few minutes later he descended the rear staircase of the hospital and went out into the parking lot. Starting toward his car, he heard someone running behind him.

He wheeled around to find a stocky, brawny man, older than himself, with a large head and almost no neck, coming toward him. The man was upon him, gasping for breath, face livid, hands knotted into fists.

"Are you the guy named Barrett?" the man demanded. "The lawyer defending that goddam dirty book?"

Recoiling before the other's fury, momentarily stupefied, Barrett nodded. "Yes, I—"

"You listen to me, then!" the man bellowed, shooting both hands forward and clutching the lapels of Barrett's jacket angrily. "You listen to me, you rotten bastard, because I'm going to tell you something—"

He wrenched Barrett toward him, and in self-defense Barrett struck at the man's arms to free himself. For a moment they were apart, and then the wild man lunged at him again. Barrett threw out his hands to fend him off as the man swung a powerful right-hand hook at his face. Barrett tried to duck backward, but the arcing fist grazed his chin, rattling his teeth, and, off balance, he went reeling backward, falling, landing on his haunches.

The suddenness of the assault, more than the force of it, had dazed Barrett, and he sat on the tarred surface of the lot, holding his chin, as powerless to rise as a paraplegic. Above him loomed the distended face of his assailant.

"You listen to me, you bastard," the man panted, hands still

213

clenched. "I'm Sheri's father, see—I'm Howard Moore—and I'm telling you there's more where that came from, see—there's lots more. And I'm warning you to keep your goddam nose out of our private affairs. My poor girl's on the critical list, and all because some little prick was made crazy by your goddam dirty book—and anybody standing up for that kind of book is going to get it from me. So you remember this, mister—you keep your snotty nose out of my affairs—or next time I'll beat you up until you're in worse shape than my poor girl is in now. You just remember that!"

Howard Moore whirled around and went stalking off.

His head clearing, Mike Barrett struggled to his feet. Anger at this attack, at the gross unfairness and injustice of it, began to shake him, and his immediate instinct was to go after Moore and give him back some of the same. But then, watching the pathetic figure slow down at the door of the hospital, watching the older man open the glass door and for an instant hang his head and press it against the door, Barrett's anger gave way to a surge of pity and reason. The man was a father, helpless, and up there five stories was the daughter he had spawned, his little girl, violated, unconscious. And, what the hell, he had to strike out at something, someone.

Barrett reached for his handkerchief and touched it to his mouth. A faint bloodstain showed on the white linen. The inside of his lower lip had been cut. Well, so be it.

Going slowly, dusting himself off, he returned to his car.

Not until an hour later, when he was once more secure in his office and Donna had returned with disinfectant from the pharmacy downstairs, did he ask her the question that he had been waiting to ask. He had remembered hearing Darlene Nelson and the nurse as they talked in the hallway of the hospital, and here was Donna, the office secretary who always read the entertainment pages and gossip columns and who tried to keep young by reading about the young.

"Donna, my pretty, it seems to me I've heard of it, but I just can't remember exactly—forgetting the Civil War, meaning right now, today—what's a place called The Underground Railroad?"

"Boy, are you the straight one. That's the leading hangout for all the youngsters. It's out on Melrose. Strictly rock groups, dancing, near beer and nothing stronger."

"I understand there's a group opening there tonight?"

"Well, now, maybe you're not so straight. Yup. Gregorian Chant."

"Gregorian what? I'm not talking about medieval ecclesiastical music or choirs. I'm—"

"Straight, straight, straight, that's what you are, boss. Gregorian Chant. They used to be called Chauncey and the Snow Shoes until they merged with the L.A. Heat. They're the hottest rock group in the country right now. And they're opening at The Underground Railroad at seven tonight. What have you got in mind?"

"Closing the generation gap. What's the opposite of straight, Donna? Curved?"

"Groovy."

"That'll be me at seven-thirty tonight."

EVEN IN the darkness of the parking area behind the gigantic hardware store that had been converted into a rock haven, Mike Barrett could hear the incessant, cacophonous music blaring through every window and wall of The Underground Railroad.

When he paused under the street light on Melrose Avenue, he could make out the time on his wristwatch. It was twenty minutes after seven in the evening. Across the street there were two other teen-age water holes, one called The Limbo and the other The Raga-Rock, but tonight they were nearly deserted. The real population explosion was occurring thirty feet from him, where two orderly lines of bizarrely costumed youngsters were moving steadily into The Underground Railroad.

Barrett made his way to the end of one line and fell in, and he was relieved that he had followed Donna's advice and not worn a suit and a tie. Actually, his crew-neck cotton pullover and corduroys were still conservative enough to label him, if not exactly an octagon or a rub—oh, he had done some homework—then at least a partial square. But then it wasn't his attire that made him self-conscious, he knew, but his age, and for the first time he believed that half of America's entire population was under the age of twenty-five.

Following the swaying line of youngsters toward the rough-hewn log-cabin entrance, he was satisfied that he had not told

Faye where he was going. She would have wanted to come along, as one goes to the zoo, and, man, that would have been too much. This was one of his standing-date nights with Faye, the special one of the week, the physical one, and he hadn't had the courage to cancel or postpone it. Instead, he had telephoned Faye to explain that they'd have to skip their regular dinner, because a research lead had turned up. He had promised to meet her at his apartment at eleven o'clock.

There was no research lead, of course. There was only his knowledge that this was a happening night at The Underground Railroad, and that Darlene Nelson would be here, and perhaps one of the happenings would be George Perkins. A hunch, no more. If George appeared, he would have friends, and they might also be Jerry Griffith's friends. A fuller roster of Jerry's friends was what Barrett wanted.

"Let's have some green, man," he heard someone say above him, and he realized that the speaker—who resembled Lincoln, assuming Lincoln had been black—was in the doorway collecting the entrance fee. He paid the man the two dollars and proceeded inside.

At once, caught up in a swarm of chattering and singing customers who were seeking tables, he was lost.

He tried to orient himself to the scene and adjust himself to the sound. Before him lay a madhouse of tables around which were packed the music lovers. Then he could see the dance floor, as animated as a bucketful of writhing worms, and, facing the dance floor, the bandstand, over which a giant kaleidoscope kept turning and turning, and, beyond, more tables.

The lighting that came from the rotating stroboscope produced a spinning rainbow of psychedelic colors. On the dance floor, boys and girls of white, black, brown, yellow skin in micro-skirts, capes, hussar uniforms, relating not to one another but to the dissonant music, were going through their highly individual frenetic dance undulations. Yet there was a single movement to the tribal dance: every male native gyrated his pelvis and torso, every female native thrust forward her bust and wiggled her butt, as they paid homage to the howling voices and pinging electric guitars of Gregorian Chant.

Barrett focused upon the group on the bandstand. It consisted of four boys dressed like cotton-picking slaves, and presumably the Gregorian part consisted of the three shaggy-haired whites loosely chained together, strumming away, occasionally joining the Chant, a fat young Negro, in his solo.

Hemmed in on all sides, Barrett began to feel faint. And his ears rang. And his heart yearned for the sweet security of Dave Brubeck and Gerry Mulligan and Davey Pell.

He needed a more isolated lookout post, and then he saw, to his left, past the aisle, the long oak bar. A portion of it was relatively free of humanity. Turning, pushing, excusing himself, pushing, going sideways, he made slow progress toward the bar, and after several minutes he reached it.

"Scotch and water," he gasped.

"Sorry, sir," said the moustached young bartender. "We've got only near beer—and of course any soft drink you can think of."

Barrett had forgotten they had no hard liquor here. "Okay, a near beer."

As the beer foamed into the stein, Barrett scanned the scene. The performing group had segued into a new number. This one was less discordant, less onomatopoeic, less thwacking, less jarring. The number seemed to owe its ancestry to the ethnic music of Bessie Smith, sort of Negro blues and gospel mildly crossed with hillbilly. It was sad and it was message, and it echoed a generation's disillusionment, skepticism, protest, and it called for love of man for Man. And at once Barrett welcomed and enjoyed the sounds and sights and the lost love children on the floor. Somewhere he'd read Bob Dylan's explanation: The only beauty's ugly, man. Yes. But it was beauty nevertheless, its own beauty.

He reached for his near beer, sipped it slowly, looked up at the big posters above the bar—Harriet Beecher Stowe, John Brown and his body, Dred Scott—and he listened to the music.

After a short respite, putting down his beer mug, he faced the entire room once more, determined to search it for his quarry. In a few moments he realized that he had undertaken an impossible assignment. There were simply too many young men, and too many of these who looked like the bearded George Perkins, and not one of them could he distinguish as being George himself.

He decided to scan the club a final time, from the entrance doorway to the farthest reach of the room. His eyes shifted to the entrance, and, to his surprise, standing there inside it was a newcomer whom he recognized instantly.

The newcomer was a slim, haggard boy, neatly combed hair, sallow complexion and pinched features, sport jacket and sport shirt and pressed slacks. He was the one Barrett had never met, yet he was as familiar now as the countless pictures of him that had appeared in the press. Filled with amazement, overlaid by confusion, Barrett stared at the newcomer. Here, within distance of his voice, was Jerry Griffith, searching the club as he himself had been searching it. Barrett wondered, What in the devil was this boy, even though free on bail, doing in this public place? He couldn't imagine Maggie Russell, let alone Frank Griffith, permitting Jerry to leave the house and come to this place. Or didn't they know? Had Jerry slipped out?

This was a perfect opportunity to confront him, to speak sympathetically to him, question him, yet Barrett did not move. As a person he was kept in his place by some sense of decency, and as an attorney he was kept back by some instinct that detected possible good fortune. He maintained his watch over Jerry Griffith and he waited with undefined expectancy.

Barrett tried to read Jerry's eyes. At first they were furtive and afraid, like those of a wanted man on the run who was fearful of being recognized. Then, as if he had realized that the very numbers gave him safety, melted him into the mass, Jerry's eyes lost their fear and became those of the hunter rather than the hunted. Plainly the boy was looking for someone, some specific person.

He was on tiptoes, examining the occupants of each table, when his head gave a short jerk of recognition and he started to wave and then apparently thought better of it. At once his entire expression had become purposeful. He had found the one he wanted.

Jerry Griffith started toward Barrett, abruptly veered between two tables, and then nimbly threaded his way between more of the seated patrons toward his objective. Picking his way forward, he slowed, and at a table of three young men and two girls he halted. He reached out toward the broad-shouldered young man who had his back to him, and he tapped the boy on the shoulder. The young man's head swiveled around, and the bearded profile revealed itself to be George Perkins.

Squinting in the ever-changing light, Barrett tried to catch George's reaction. In all, there were three reactions, one following the other with amazing rapidity. First, surprise. Second, worry. Third, annoyance.

From the distance of the bar, Barrett continued to follow the silent drama.

Jerry was trying to speak to George Perkins. And George wanted nothing to do with him. Jerry gripped George's shoulder several times, whispering to him, and each time George shrugged him off. At last Jerry's persistence appeared to win, for George came heatedly to his feet and, hulking over his friend, shook his head, refusing to listen to him further. Still, Jerry continued speaking against the din. Finally, as if in exasperated agreement, George nodded, and looked around. Just as the music stopped and a member of the performing group announced an intermission, George pointed off, and his finger was directed at a couple who had left the dance floor and were making their way to a table set on an aisle.

Automatically Barrett's attention shifted to the couple. For a moment, the boy blocked the view of his female partner. The boy was clean-shaven except for his long sideburns, and he was husky. Then the girl was in the open. She was Darlene Nelson, none other, still wearing the dungarees and loose shirttails she had worn earlier, during her hospital visit.

Now a third figure crossed swiftly into view. It was that of Jerry Griffith again, almost bowling over customers as he fought his way through the returning dancers to catch Darlene Nelson. Just as Darlene approached her empty chair, Jerry Griffith intercepted her.

Once more, for Barrett, dumb show.

Jerry was blocking the girl from her seat, seeming to introduce himself, trying to address her. Darlene's displeasure was even more clearly visible than George Perkins' had been moments before. She tried to ignore Jerry, push past him to reach her chair, but still he tried to impede her progress long enough to get her to listen to him. With a final effort, she slipped past him. He had begun to follow her, still speaking, when she stopped and did an about-face. She appeared to be speaking sharply, curtly, in an undertone, her face close to his. Whatever she said to Jerry had the effect of a slap in the face. Jerry recoiled, looking stricken, then he tried to say something to her as she sat down, but no words seemed to come. Instead, there was only a kind of breathless mouthing and gesturing in place of the missing words.

Suddenly Jerry seemed to petrify, features livid, and he stared down at her as she gaily resumed conversation with her companions. For a second, Barrett wondered whether Jerry might strike her or attempt to strangle her, but he did neither. His arms went slowly down to his sides. His face went slack. His body appeared to wilt. Dazed, he backed away, turned away, wandered into the passage between the tables, until he seemed to remember where he was and who he was. Then, as if galvanized, in a spurt, he charged past new arrivals and dashed to the entrance and was gone.

Observing Jerry's frantic exit, Barrett remained rooted to his spot at the bar. One thing was evident. Jerry's friend George knew Darlene, or at least knew what she looked like. Jerry, on the other hand, plainly had not known Sheri's friend Darlene before. But what had he said to her, and what had she said to him, that had so infuriated him, finally crushed him and made him flee? That instant, Barrett decided that he must find out. A confrontation with Jerry was not only in order but essential.

Barrett pushed himself from the bar, but before taking three steps he was brought to a standstill by a noisy bevy of teen-age girls who had just entered the club. Trapped in their midst, he found it difficult to escape. And now one little Kewpie-doll blonde in sweat shirt and shorts had discovered him.

She reached up to bring him closer. "Girls," she shrieked, "look what I found—the genuine thousand-year-old man, the missing link! Ain't he the cutest?" She planted a kiss on Barrett's chin, imploring him, "Dance with me, link, come on, let's dance."

Her arms were wrapped tightly around him and she shimmied in semblance of a dance.

"Honey, I was just on my way to the men's room," Barrett protested. "Give a guy a break."

She grinned up at him. "That's more fun than girls?" She released him. "At your age, I guess it is."

Barrett broke away. By the time he had reached the sidewalk, breathless, he knew that he had lost five minutes. He looked up and down Melrose, but no one resembling Jerry Griffith was in sight. There were more youngsters in line, waiting to get inside the club. Barrett approached them. He explained to the ones at the head of the line that he was searching for someone who'd left the club a few minutes earlier. He tried to describe Jerry Griffith. He found he could not do so effectively. The only outstanding describable feature that Jerry had might well be his neatly combed hair. Even that brought no recognition.

"Well, he came out of the club on the run," added Barrett. "Does that ring a bell?"

"He was running?" chirped a long-tressed girl. "Yeah, there was one kid who came out fast, 'cause I remember saying, 'Maybe the Chant scared him.'" The others in line laughed, and then the girl said to Barrett, "I think he went thataway." She pointed west, and there was more laughter. Barrett thanked her and started up Melrose toward La Cienega Boulevard.

He walked and walked, poking into open stores, crossing and recrossing the street, but nowhere was Jerry Griffith to be seen. After fifteen minutes, he was back where he had started.

Disconsolately, Barrett acknowledged defeat. He headed into the darkened dirt parking area. Nearing his convertible, he realized that in his frustration and haste he had overlooked the most obvious lead to Jerry's whereabouts. This parking lot. If Jerry had not left the neighborhood in a rush, his car would have still been parked here when Barrett had come out. He could have waited by the lot entrance until Jerry came by to get the car and drive home. By now he had probably long since taken his car and left.

Yet, small hope, maybe the boy's car was still here. Barrett tried to recall the make of the vehicle. He had seen it noted in his office file folder on the Griffith boy. It was a British automobile. Definitely. At once it came back to him. A recent-model white Rover sedan.

He halted, and glanced about. There was a gray Thunderbird, and there was an old dirty white Jaguar, and there was a recent-model white Rover sedan. His hope quickened. Probably dozens of newish white Rover sedans were out tonight in Los Angeles. Nevertheless, this might be Jerry's own.

Barrett moved toward the Rover. As he came up behind it, even in this poorly lit corner of the parking area, he could see that there was someone in the front seat. He circled the car cautiously, in case the person were two persons and they were making out.

Arriving at the rolled-up window of the front door, he could see that it was one person. It was a young man, and he was slumped over the steering wheel, very still, as if in sleep. The hair, the side of the face—enough to tell him that it was Jerry Griffith.

Barrett hesitated, then a terrible thought entered his head, and he hesitated no longer. He rapped on the glass. The figure draped over the wheel did not move.

Hastily Barrett tried the front door. It opened, and as it opened, Jerry Griffith's limp form slid off the wheel and began to fall sideways. Barrett caught him and with an effort shoved him upright. The boy was unconscious, his eyes closed, his face as ashen as a mask of death.

"Jerry," Barrett whispered to him, "Jerry, can you hear me?"

There was no answer.

The inert form remained lifeless.

Barrett bent into the car, trying to determine whether the boy was breathing and whether any pulse beat could be detected in the wrist. Doing so, he realized that the open door had lighted the car's interior, and for the first time he could see what lay on the front seat beside Jerry. There was an empty pill container. On the car floor, an empty soda bottle, the chaser.

Jerry Griffith had attempted suicide.

Had he succeeded?

Still not sure, Barrett pressed his ear against Jerry's chest and listened for a heartbeat. He could hear none over the sounds of Dylan's "Mr. Tambourine Man" seeping out of the rear of The Underground Railroad. Barrett concentrated on the pulse again. At first his fingers felt nothing, but then there was a tiny jump, and he couldn't be certain whether it was from the boy's pulse or was due to his own fingers' nerve ends.

Instantly Barrett's brain received and sorted the alternatives for his next act. He could summon the Fire Department's emergency squad or he could try to resuscitate the boy himself by getting him on his feet and inducing him to vomit or he could speed him to a private doctor.

Each possibility provided a risk. The Fire Department offered the most expeditious help—and the guarantee of a second scandal visited upon the boy, a second death without dying, presuming he was still alive. An attempt to resuscitate the boy by himself was the fastest kind of first aid, but it was also the most amateurish and inadequate. A private doctor was the slowest but the safest course—and immediately Barrett's mind was made up, for he had thought of a physician who was near and would help. Doc Quigley, his own physician ever since he had made his home in Los Angeles, had his residence on North Arden Drive, in Beverly Hills, just a quick, short drive away. He had called Doc Quigley only last week and set up a dinner date, because he had wanted to ask the Doc some questions about the pathology of rape. Quigley had made the date, busy though he was, working long evenings at home on a professional paper he was soon to deliver. More likely than not, he would be at home. And, no matter what happened, he would be discreet.

Quickly Barrett went through the inert boy's jacket pockets, until at last he located the ignition key. With haste he forced Jerry's body away from the wheel toward the passenger side of the front seat. Once the body lay slumped against the opposite door, Barrett settled himself behind the wheel and started the Rover.

Only when he had swung the car out of the dirt parking area, and onto Melrose, did Barrett wonder whether he was bringing a corpse to Dr. Quigley—or a resurrected star witness to District Attorney Duncan.

FORTY MINUTES had passed since Barrett and Dr. Quigley had carried the body of Jerry Griffith into the physician's house on North Arden Drive. Barrett had explained how he had found Jerry, and the physician had made no comment.

After leaving the boy on the daybed in the physician's study, Barrett had handed the doctor the empty prescription bottle.

Dr. Quigley had glanced at it. "Nembutals," he'd murmured. He had taken up his black bag from beside his desk and pulled a chair up beside the boy.

"Is he alive, Doc?" Barrett had asked.

Dr. Quigley had not looked up. "We'll see. You can wait in the living room, Mike."

That had been forty minutes ago, and Barrett, tensely seated on the sofa, leafing through the same magazine he had unsuccessfully been trying to read all this time, reasoned that the length of time was a good sign. Had Jerry been dead on arrival, Barrett felt, he would have been so informed before now. The length of time meant that the doctor was working to save his patient.

Barrett had again tried to concentrate on the magazine, when he heard Dr. Quigley's cough. He stood up as the physician, still in his blue bathrobe, came tiredly into the room, removing his spectacles and rubbing his eyes.

"He's all right, Mike," Dr. Quigley announced.

"Thank God—and you."

"He took enough sleeping tablets to kill an army. You must have caught him just as he lost consciousness. Lucky you brought him right over. Another five minutes and he'd have been gone. I administered some strong antidotes. He responded, and he's cleaned out now."

"Is he conscious?"

"Fully. But weak, very weak. However, hospitalization won't be necessary. Especially considering his general situation. I think he can be taken home in about an hour. A sound night's sleep, and some rest tomorrow, and he'll be fully recovered. These youngsters have remarkable recuperative powers." Dr. Quigley felt inside his robe pocket and extracted a prescription slip. "Here's a number you're to call. He says that the only person he wants to know about this is a cousin named—it's on here—Maggie Russell." Dr. Quigley gave the slip to Barrett, adding, "That's her telephone number, the private number of a phone she has in her bedroom. Jerry says keep trying it until you get her. He says she'll come by for him."

"I'll take care of it."

"Very well. I'd better get back to my patient." He hesitated. "Frank Griffith owes you a lot, Mike. You should have his gratitude."

"He'll never know," said Barrett. "Anyway, my only interest is in the boy."

"Have it your way." The physician coughed into the palm of his hand. "There's an extension phone in the dining room."

Dr. Quigley left. Barrett went into the dining room, flipped on the overhead light, took the telephone off the marble-topped sideboard and brought it to the dining table. He placed the prescription slip beside the telephone, considered it, and then dialed Maggie Russell's private number.

The telephone rang and rang, without answer. He would give it a few more seconds, he decided, and then try again in a little while. Sooner or later she would return to her room. As he listened to the continuing ring, it suddenly ceased and a breathless feminine voice came on.

"Hello?"

"Miss Russell?"

"This is she."

"Mike Barrett. Sorry to disturb you, but—"

"I thought I told you I didn't want to hear from you again."

"Hold on. I'm not calling for myself. I'm calling for Jerry."

"Jerry?"

"Your cousin. I'm with him now. I—"

"I don't understand. You can't be. He's not allowed to leave the house."

"He left it early this evening, no matter what his orders were. Without wasting words, let me tell you what happened. But first you'd better let me know, can anyone else listen in on this line?"

"No—no, it's my own." Her voice had become anxious. "What happened? Is anything wrong?"

"Jerry's fine now, but it was nip and tuck for a while. Let me make it brief. Sometime after seven, I had reason to drop in on a teen-age hangout on Melrose Avenue . . ." He quickly described Jerry's arrival at The Underground Railroad, what he had witnessed of Jerry's confrontations with George Perkins and Darlene Nelson, and his discovery of Jerry's unconscious body in the Rover. Then he gave her Dr. Quigley's good news. "Jerry wanted someone to get in touch with you. He didn't want anyone else to know."

"No one must know," she said urgently. "But he *is* all right? The doctor said that, didn't he?"

"Absolutely. By the time you get here, Jerry will be able to go home with you."

"I'll be right over."

"Let me give you the address."

He gave it to her, and then she hung up.

Returning the telephone to the sideboard, Barrett wondered

whether he should stay until Maggie Russell arrived. There was no reason to remain, except to see her once more and to ingratiate himself with her. He didn't like that. He also didn't wish to embarrass her with his presence. Despite what he had done for the Griffiths tonight, he was still the enemy.

This brought his mind back to the impending trial. There was so much to do, and there was so little time left. Faye Osborn would not be at his apartment until eleven o'clock. There remained a stretch of several useful hours during which he could research the legal precedents in previous censorship trials.

He would tell Dr. Quigley that Maggie Russell would be along shortly, and let him know that he could be reached at the office should he be needed further, and then, after summoning a taxi to take him back to his own car, he would be on his way.

In the night quiet of his office, Mike Barrett had devoted himself not to a study of legal precedents in earlier censorship trials but to a folder that contained both popular and scholarly writings on censorship that had appeared in American and British magazines during the last dozen years. These were largely articles by authors, critics, publishers, scholars, clipped by Leo Kimura, to give Zelkin and himself an up-to-date background on censorship arguments in the literary field.

He had read nine or ten of these articles and was skimming one written by Maurice Girodias for the London publication *Encounter*, when a single paragraph arrested his attention. Girodias had been saying that most human beings were born from an act of unromantic lust, and that the species was still being propagated through lust, and that most human beings were as preoccupied with sex as they were with food and sleep; yet, even though sex was basic to each person's life, its practice had been complicated and its image distorted by conventional hypocrisy. As a matter of fact, Girodias went on, every man and every woman were involved daily in acts of rape. It was this paragraph that Barrett reread carefully.

"Rape," Girodias had written, "is held to be the most uncivilised form of assault on anyone's privacy. And yet the colourless family man, the sedate and faithful husband whose only memorable feminine conquest was performed through marriage, usually

226

rapes dozens of girls a day. The possession, of course, is only visual; a quick appreciative glance is all there is to that micro-rape, which is always furtive and often even unconscious. But the action is there and it does yield a tiny dose of sexual satisfaction. . . . As to the faithful wife of the same man, does she resort to fashion, jewels, perfumes in order to seduce her own husband? Not at all: she uses all those classical artifacts because she wants to offer herself to the whole race of males, to seduce and be raped by all—visually, of course. The vestigial impulses of prehistoric man are still at work."

How true, Barrett thought.

His own feelings testified to it. He possessed one woman all but legally. He had Faye. Yet yesterday the inner barbarian hiding beneath the civilized veneer had forced him to commit rape at least twice—first the rape of a young girl in a bikini emerging from the Beverly Hills Hotel swimming pool, later the rape of an attractive young woman named Maggie Russell whom he had followed into the bar of the Beverly Hilton Hotel. The only difference between Jerry Griffith and himself, between Jerry and most other men, was that Jerry had forcibly violated another with his penis, while Barrett and most men violated women with their eyes. Jerry's act was criminal, and his own was harmless, true enough. But both kinds of rape were inspired by the same savage and natural drive. The difference was merely that Jerry had been too ill to control his impulse, whereas the vast majority of men were rational enough to channel this impulse in one socially acceptable way or another. The point was, no man should hold himself as being better than his fellow men in his attitude toward sex, or believe he was wholly without blame.

How many visual rapes did Elmo Duncan, protector of public morals, commit every day of every week?

Shaking his head, Barrett resumed his reading. Having finished the article, he was about to pick up the next one, when the telephone at his elbow rang out. He snatched at the receiver.

The voice he heard belonged to Maggie Russell.

"I had expected you to be at Dr. Quigley's when I got there," she said. "He told me you went on to your office."

"Is everything taken care of?"

"Jerry's fine now. I got him into the house unnoticed. He's

asleep. I . . . I wondered if I might see you for just a moment?"

"Of course," said Barrett with genuine enthusiasm. "But there's no need for you to come all the way out to this stuffy place. As a matter of fact, I was going back to my apartment in a little while, and I thought I'd stop off in Westwood for a sandwich and a cup of coffee. Think you could join me?"

"Anywhere you say. I won't take much of your time."

"Let me see. I know—just off Westwood Boulevard there's a little coffee shop, sandwich place called Ell's. It's—"

"I know it."

"Let's say fifteen minutes."

Exactly sixteen minutes later, Mike Barrett drove into the filling station next to Ell's, left instructions for a tank of gas and a quart of oil if required, and hastened to the restaurant.

Entering, he saw that she had arrived before him. She was seated at a table in the rear, thoughtfully smoking, unaware of his entrance.

He moved past the counter and the stools toward her, keeping his eyes on her. Her shining dark hair, seductive wide-set gray-green eyes, full lower lip were as attractive as he had remembered. All that he could make out of her attire above the table top was the diaphanous white silk blouse she was wearing, which clung provocatively to her pointed breasts, and the outline of the lace half-bra beneath was visible.

Another rape, he thought, and could not help but smile.

But then, nearing the table, he could see how serious she was, and, remembering what had occurred earlier in the evening, and how it must have affected her, he became serious, too. Coming here, he had not speculated at length on her motive for wishing to meet him, although he had guessed that motive. And seconds after he had greeted her, taken the chair across from her, and ordered melted-cheese sandwiches and coffee for each of them, she confirmed his guess.

"I had to see you, to apologize for being so rude on the phone," she was saying, "and to thank you, which I neglected to do on the phone, to thank you for what you did for Jerry and . . . and for me. I don't know how we can ever repay you."

"Miss Russell, I did what any other person in my place would have done."

"Not any other person, and certainly not every lawyer," she insisted. "I'm sure there are plenty of shyster lawyers who would look in another direction and let an opposition witness die in a similar situation, just because it would strengthen their position in court. There are plenty of those, I'd wager."

"Miss Russell, you're speaking of subhumans. I was speaking of people."

"Yes," she said. She waited for the waitress to pour the coffee, then she went on. "Anyway, forgive my behavior on the telephone. I took a cab to Dr. Quigley's, and on the way I realized how cold I'd been to you, but then I expected you to be there so I could ask your forgiveness and tell you of my gratefulness in person. Dr. Quigley told me you'd gone to your office. So, once I'd sneaked Jerry up to bed, I got up the courage, and it took some, to phone you."

"I'm glad you did. I've already told you what I saw at The Underground Railroad. I still don't know what sent him rushing out of there the way he did. I wonder if he spoke of that?"

"No. He was too ill and exhausted to speak of anything much. I doubt if he'll tell me about that. I know I won't ask him."

"I didn't mean that you should. But this is a very serious matter. When a boy tries to kill himself, I think it's a good thing to know why. I suppose he said nothing about that either?"

"Nothing. Nor would he explain why he had those pills on him."

"It could have been that his troubles and problems had come to a boil and were ready to explode. I just wondered what set it off. The way George Perkins treated him? Something Darlene Nelson said to him? Or something that happened during the day, this morning, this afternoon?"

"I don't know," she said. Her eyes met his briefly, and then she looked down at the table. "Or maybe I know one thing, something that happened today. Perhaps I should tell you. You've involved yourself enough with Jerry to—to save him, so I suppose you've earned the right to know something. But before I do tell you, I—I have one question, one thing I wanted to ask you."

"Go ahead."

"I wondered what you were doing at that club, of all places, while Jerry was there. Were you following—shadowing him, as they say? I suppose that's one of the things lawyers have to do to get evidence."

"Don't believe everything you see on television, Miss Russell."

"I don't, but—"

"No, as a matter of fact, I was not following Jerry. I didn't think there was one chance in a million that Jerry would dare leave his home while out on bail. I was following someone else. Or, rather, trying to find someone else. I knew Jerry had a friend named George Perkins. I've even met Perkins. I hoped to see him with some of his friends, who I hoped would also be some of Jerry's friends. I learned that The Underground Railroad was the favorite hangout for many of the kids. Tonight was a big opening. I thought it might attract George Perkins. It did. I didn't for one moment imagine it would also attract Jerry Griffith. When he appeared, I—I never went near Jerry—decided not to bother him —until that crazy little scene with Darlene, when he seemed to come apart, before he ran out. Then I decided I'd better find him and find out what was going on. Well, I certainly found him."

"Thank the Lord," she whispered.

"Satisfactory explanation, Miss Russell?"

"I'm sorry. I didn't mean to put you on like that. You must think I suspect every move you make. I did last night. Believe me, Mr. Barrett, I don't tonight, not any more."

"I appreciate that."

The sandwiches were served, and once the waitress had left, Barrett began to eat. Looking up, he realized that Maggie Russell had not touched anything in front of her.

She stared at him worriedly. "I promised to tell you something that happened today that might have—well, might have unduly agitated Jerry."

"It's not necessary that you tell me anything, Miss Russell."

"I don't feel disloyal telling you this. It will all come out, anyway, and it may offer some explanation of what led to Jerry's behavior this evening. Mr. Yerkes, Luther Yerkes—I don't know how he became involved in our affairs, except he is one of my uncle's major accounts, and I suspect he has some political interest in backing the District Attorney for a higher office, so he wants Mr. Duncan to make a great showing against you, and he feels that Jerry can be an important witness against *The Seven Minutes*—

well, he's been over several times, and early this afternoon he came over and brought with him the psychoanalyst that my uncle's lawyer, Mr. Polk, had suggested. He brought with him Dr. Roger Trimble."

"Luther Yerkes at the Griffiths'." Barrett clucked his tongue. "Well, I shouldn't be surprised. It fits. Until now I'd heard only unconfirmed rumors about Yerkes' backing Duncan for the Senate. This would seem to confirm it. It also explains the rash of trial publicity Duncan has been getting. Sorry to interrupt. Please go on."

"Jerry was to go into therapy with Dr. Trimble, against his will. The first session was today, upstairs in Jerry's bedroom, Dr. Trimble and Jerry alone. After about an hour, Dr. Trimble came down and gave a kind of assessment of Jerry's condition. Without going into detail, I don't mind repeating this much. He told us that Jerry was extremely disturbed. He said Jerry was completely ambivalent about the rape. On the one hand, he hated to discuss it. On the other, when he did discuss it, he revealed a certain amount of pride in the act. He said Jerry had a wish for self-destruction, possibly real, more likely fantasy. He felt that Jerry should be subjected to as few pressures as possible. Then Mr. Yerkes wanted to know how Jerry might stand up if he were called as a prosecution witness against the book. Dr. Trimble hedged his answer. He said it was too early to tell. It was true that Jerry felt he had been a victim of the book, and if he maintained this attitude he might be a forceful and articulate witness. At the same time, Jerry was frightened and apprehensive about speaking out publicly, and if he withdrew more deeply into himself he might be useless as a witness. Then Dr. Trimble promised Mr. Yerkes and Uncle Frank that he would try to visit Jerry an hour daily up to and during the trial. None of them seemed to understand, as I do, how upset Jerry is about being made to talk to an analyst. Jerry wants only to be left alone—despite his crazy foray into public tonight—and he resents any doctor's poking into the privacy of his psyche. I'm objective enough to recognize that he does need therapy. This just seems to be the wrong time for it."

"I'm sure Dr. Trimble realizes that," said Barrett. "I think his help will be mainly supportive, to prop Jerry up and see him through the trial."

Maggie Russell nibbled at her sandwich, then put it down and shoved the plate aside. "Yes, I suppose that's it. If it were Dr. Trimble alone, I wouldn't be worried. What bothers me is all the pressure Mr. Yerkes and Uncle Frank are exerting on Jerry. You should have seen what happened after Dr. Trimble left. No sooner was he gone than Mr. Yerkes announced that we were fortunate enough to have the press and television people so interested in Jerry. Mr. Yerkes felt they should be accommodated, because it would give the public a chance to see and hear first hand and read about how a pornographic book had damaged an adolescent, and this would create sympathy for Jerry. Mr. Yerkes said he'd taken the liberty of inviting Merle Reid to interview Jerry. In fact, Merle Reid was waiting outside."

"Reid?" said Barrett. He had been drinking his coffee. Now he set down his cup. "You mean that television commentator?"

"The one who goes on every night coast to coast."

"He's sickening. A one-man soap opera. I saw him interview a prisoner in Death Row one night. You'd have thought he was chatting with someone at a college prom."

"I'm glad to hear that from you. Because that insensitive idiot sickened me. Mr. Yerkes brought him in, along with two technicians, one carrying a hand camera and the other carrying lights. Uncle Frank asked me to bring Jerry down. I refused. And Aunt Ethel was on my side. But Uncle Frank insisted it was all for Jerry's sake, and he went and brought him down. Do I have to tell you more? Jerry was like some poor scared cornered puppy. And when Merle Reid, with that television camera whirring, asked Jerry exactly what section of *The Seven Minutes* drove him to run out and violate a girl—God, it was horrible. Jerry just broke down, began sobbing, and I didn't care what anyone would say to me afterward, I just took him out of that room. No one tried to stop me. But Luther Yerkes was celebrating what had happened as if it were a triumph. He kept saying to Reid, 'You see? You see what a dirty book can do to a youngster?' And that stupid Reid was saying, 'That footage on his cracking up was great, simply marvelous.' Going on like that as if they were dealing with an automaton. Anyway, Mr. Barrett, that gives you an idea of Jerry's emotional condition before he slipped out of the house."

232

She seemed relieved to have unburdened herself of this, and now she finished her coffee with more composure.

Barrett eyed her thoughtfully for several seconds. Finally he spoke. "You know, Miss Russell, I do get the impression that everyone in that household is afraid of Frank Griffith. Am I correct?"

She knitted her brow, and contemplated her coffee cup. "I—I really can't say. Even if I could, I wouldn't. Perhaps I've told you more than I should have already. But anything less would have been unfair."

"Very well. It just surprises me that Mr. Griffith, knowing his son's precarious condition, makes so many demands upon him."

"He means no harm, I'm sure of that. I think he's really trying to help Jerry—but strictly in his own way."

Barrett nodded. "Perhaps you're right. And I promise you, no more questions about the Griffiths. However, I do have one more question, a personal one, about you yourself, if you don't mind."

"It all depends."

"You're attractive, young, intelligent, the kind of person who could accomplish anything she might wish to attempt. Yet you've confined yourself to the Griffith household, and to a job that can't be very demanding. It seems rather self-limiting for a girl of your endowments, I've asked myself why. Now I've gotten up the nerve to ask you. Why, Miss Russell?"

"No mysteries. It's very simple. I'm doing what I want to do."

"I can't believe it's that simple."

She offered him a tentative smile. "Now you're the one who is being suspicious." Then she was serious again. "Yes, I suppose it is more complicated than that. Let me see. To begin with, I've always needed family, someone close. My parents died when I was quite young. There were plenty of relatives, and I was passed around among them, but I was always rather a stranger. When I was old enough, I escaped and tried to make a life of my own. First I went to the University of North Carolina for a year. Then three years at Boston University. I graduated from there."

"What was your major?"

"My major was psychology, my minor English literature. That's inconsequential. All girls have the same major—they major in getting married."

"Have you been married?"

"No. I've been too busy finding myself to worry about finding someone else."

"Does that still hold true?"

"More or less. You *are* getting personal, Mr. Barrett. Anyway, to get back to the odyssey that landed me in Los Angeles. My mother had always been closest to her older sister, Ethel—Ethel Griffith —and Aunt Ethel loved my mother and consequently felt a certain responsibility toward me. She used to send me money, to help me through school. Without her I'd probably never have made it."

Barrett's mind went back to his own relationship with Phil Sanford, and his theorem that had evolved from it: Everyone owes somebody something. Everyone is indebted. Everyone must pay back his debt sooner or later. No free men exist anywhere. The line of everyone's life was not infinite, but a circle, a full caging circle.

He looked at Maggie Russell. "So you felt you had to repay her?"

"It wasn't that alone. It was still my need to experience a sense of family. I wanted to know Aunt Ethel and find out what it would be like to be part of her family. So when she offered me a job as her social secretary and companion, I took her up on it eagerly. Also, I was excited about seeing Los Angeles. Actually, I never meant to stay with my uncle and aunt more than a year. That was understood. But I did become part of the family, and when I saw how much Aunt Ethel needed me and how much Jerry depended upon me, well, I just stayed on. Which brings me to the second and main reason why I'm with the Griffiths. It's Jerry, as I told you yesterday. I'm fond of him. He's devoted to me. He admires my shaky independence. And in his transitional growing-up period I think I've meant a lot to him. And now, of course, now he trusts me more than anyone. Does this make sense to you?"

"Yes, I can understand why you're there. And let me reiterate one thing. Yerkes, Duncan, Frank Griffith, they've all cast me in the role of Jerry's enemy for defending the book they suppose ruined him. But I want to tell you again, I've been miscast. I'm sorry for Jerry. I can't tell you how deeply I felt for him a few hours ago. It was as if he were my own son or younger brother.

I wouldn't do a thing in the world to harm him. You can believe me when I say I wouldn't be defending *The Seven Minutes* if I felt it had been responsible for Jerry's disintegration. I don't believe that for a minute. I believe it's a good and beautiful book."

She met his eyes, and then she said quietly, "I believe it's a good and beautiful book, too."

"You mean you've read it?"

"Yes."

"And you like it?"

"I loved it. Every word moved me. Don't look so bewildered. There's no inconsistency. Individuals have different neurotic structures. We can be faced by a specific object, and some of us will find it beautiful and others will find it ugly. I found the novel beautiful. Jerry found it ugly, and, because he is what he is, it moved him in a terrible way. But that doesn't influence my literary judgment of the book. It just tells me people are different and react to the same thing in different ways. I want to believe that what you've been saying is true, that *The Seven Minutes* was not responsible for Jerry's crime. Because I feel as you do about the book and about censorship in general. At the same time, what you say has not been proved. And the only evidence I have is Jerry's word that the book upset him. If that's true, then what I feel about the book becomes unimportant. If it hurt Jerry, and, through him, Sheri Moore, if it can hurt others, someone, anyone else, then it should be condemned and suppressed. I know this is confusing, Mr. Barrett, but how else can I explain my feelings? Let me put it another way. I'm for the book, but I'm against anything or anyone who can harm Jerry. If the book harmed him, then I must suspend my aesthetic belief in it. Then I want it suppressed, at once."

Leaning forward, Barrett said earnestly, "Miss Russell, if a book can lead an individual to violence, I want it suppressed, too. This was the one criterion for censorship that Judge Curtis Bok set forth in the Roth case. 'A book might constitutionally be condemned as obscene only where there is a reasonable and demonstrable cause to believe that a crime . . . has been committed . . . as the perceptible result of the publication and distribution of the writing in question.' The American Civil Liberties Union set the same standard. 'Any governmental restriction or punishment of any form of expression on the ground of obscenity must require proof beyond a reasonable doubt that such an expression would directly cause in a normal adult behavior which has validly been made criminal by statute.' We both agree to that. The question is, can a pornographic book drive a person to commit a sex crime? Most psychiatrists say no. They say sex offenders are sick from other causes before they ever pick up a pornographic book. Dr. Wardell Pomeroy, Kinsey's heir at the Institute for Sex Research, made a study of sex offenders, and he concluded, 'There is not any evidence that pornography instigates antisocial activities.'

"Forgive me for sounding like a lawyer, but I am one. And I must point out that Mrs. St. Clair, of the STDL, read *The Seven Minutes*. It didn't corrupt her. Elmo Duncan read the book. It didn't deprave him. You read it, Miss Russell, and I don't see you committing any antisocial acts. So why must it be true that Jerry alone was affected? No, Miss Russell, nothing can persuade me, not even Jerry himself, that this book incited him to commit a criminal act. And understand this—I'm not after Jerry or his credibility as a witness. I'm after the truth about Jerry, after the true causes of his behavior. I want to know the other factors in his life that contributed to sending this quiet, decent boy raging into the streets to violate the first girl he could find. I want the truth about the deeper motivations that drive young people to violence. We know there are countless causes. One of them is family, the family relationship, or lack of relationship. Those are the facts I'm after. If I can find them, I'll not only prove the book innocent of this crime, but I'll perform a service to Jerry and every kid like him by exposing the real culprits responsible for their outbursts of violence."

She was silent a moment. Then she said, "Have you found anything yet?"

"In Jerry's background? Maybe a few clues. No evidence. Nothing that would be useful in a court of law."

"But if you did find something—I mean, other than the book —that would explain Jerry's behavior, wouldn't that hurt Jerry's own case?"

"Miss Russell, it would help his case. When he comes up for sentencing, it can provide mitigating circumstances more human

236

and understandable than the evil influence of the printed page. I think it would then behoove the judge to mete out a lighter sentence."

"You really believe that?"

"I honestly do."

"Well . . ." she said, and paused, studying his face. "Maybe I'm beginning to believe what you say. Or maybe I'm a fool and being taken in. But . . ." She hesitated. "While I feel that I can't give you any personal information directly, there might be others who would be willing to speak more freely. You want to know about Jerry's background?"

"Yes."

"You know, before I came here my Aunt Ethel had another companion who was with her for a year or two. She was just a companion and sort of practical nurse, not involved in any secretarial work the way I am. After she quit or was fired or whatever happened, that's when my aunt offered me the job. Maybe that woman could give you a little help."

"What's her name?"

"Mrs. Isabel Vogler. I think she lived out in Van Nuys. That's the most I can offer by way of appreciation for what you did tonight."

"Thank you."

She took up her purse. "You've been asking me questions, Mr. Barrett. You know, I have some personal ones to ask of you, also."

"I wish you would. I enjoy talking about myself."

"No, on second thought, I think not. Besides, it's too late now. I'd better get some sleep, if I expect to cope with Jerry."

"Not even one question?"

"I was going to ask you about Faye Osborn. I know her casually. Now I know you a little. I was just curious."

"About what she sees in me, or vice versa?"

"That was your question, Mr. Barrett, not mine. About the vice versa, I'm curious, not catty. No, I was just curious about how you met and all that. But that can wait." She stood up. "Now I've got to run."

Barrett came to his feet. "You said your question or questions can wait. I take that to mean you would be willing to see me again?"

"Oh, I didn't mean—"

"Then I mean what I'm saying. I would like to see you again. No prying, I promise you. Strictly social."

"It's tempting, Mr. Barrett. But I'm afraid not. If I were seen with you in public, and the family learned I was seeing you, they'd misunderstand. No, let's leave things the way they are. But if . . . if I can ever help you in any way, I mean in a way that doesn't jeopardize my relationship with the family, well, you have my private number."

"I'll remember that."

She started to leave the table, and when he stood up to accompany her she held up her hand. "No, I think it would be wiser if I left alone. Good night, and thanks for the treat."

"Good night, Miss Russell."

He watched her until she had left, and then as he picked up the check he saw beside it the napkin on which he had scrawled the name of the former Griffith employee, Mrs. Isabel Vogler, of Van Nuys.

A possible peephole into the Griffith past.

Maggie Russell's gift out of gratitude.

It was a real lead, and despite the lateness of the hour he determined to pursue it at once. Leaving a tip, he went to the cash register, paid his bill, and then went back to the gas station. He gave the attendant his credit card and asked where there was a telephone booth. The attendant pointed off.

Once inside the booth, Barrett dialed information, and was relieved to learn there was still a Mrs. Isabel Vogler listed in Van Nuys. Immediately he sorted out his change, deposited the required coins, and dialed the number he had been given.

The receiver bumped noisily off the phone cradle in Van Nuys. A little boy's sleepy voice piped, "Hello?"

"Does Mrs. Isabel Vogler live there?"

"Yes. But Mom isn't home. She went next door. She said for me to take any messages. She said to take names and anything else. Are you calling about a job for Mom?"

What he was calling Mrs. Vogler about would be too complicated to explain to a child. He decided to make the message an easy one. "Yes, it's about a job. Do you have a pencil and paper?

Tell her a gentleman by the name of Mike Barrett called." He spelled out his last name slowly. "Got that? Barrett."

"Yes, sir."

"Tell your Mom I'd like to interview her for a job tomorrow morning at ten o'clock. I'll give you my address, and in case she can't make it at that time I'll give you my telephone number." He dictated his address, apartment number, and telephone number with care. "Tell your Mom I hope she can be there. And tell her I'll pay her for her bus fare."

"I'll tell her, Mr. Barridd."

"Barrett. Two *t*'s." He spelled his name again. "Got it now?"

"Yes, sir, I'll tell her."

Leaving the booth, Barrett stopped to sign the charge slip and pick up his credit card. Continuing to the convertible, he found Maggie Russell reclining in his mind. He savored the sight of what his mind's eye focused upon: the parting of her moist lips when she listened, the movement of her breasts beneath her blouse when she was animated, the motion of her supple thighs when she walked. Yes, visual rape. It left him weakened.

Standing beside his car, he wondered what questions she had really meant to ask him about Faye.

Faye.

Christ, he'd almost forgotten. He brought up his wristwatch. It was eighteen minutes after eleven o'clock. Faye would have been waiting a half hour before he got to the apartment. She was not used to being kept waiting, and she would be difficult. He would have to make up a plausible story to explain his tardiness. Scratch Maggie Russell for sure. A witness, a *male* witness, that he'd chased down and interviewed. That might do it.

But perhaps no story would be needed immediately. For, in her irritation, Faye might have slammed out of his apartment and gone home. Then he knew this was not likely. This was the night of the week she called her geisha night. She would never let it pass unconsummated. She loved it. And he usually looked forward to it, too, except tonight he was worn out. He'd already had one woman. He was in no mood for two. Yet two it must be.

He got into the car. Coming, Faye. He sped away to join in geisha night.

SHE HAD ACCEPTED his story, and not been difficult after all. During their first half hour together she had made him two drinks, and two for herself, and she had lain back in his arm on the sofa, gossiping lazily and teasing him with kisses and wanting him to be happy. And soon she had become impatient to go to bed.

Now, a little after midnight, he stood barefoot next to his bed, removing his shirt and his trousers. He was down to his jock shorts when he heard her emerge from the bathroom.

Faye Osborn went to the portable record player, found her favorite bedroom music, Mañuel de Falla's "Ritual Fire Dance." She placed the platter on the turntable, started the player, turning the volume to low. Observing her as she listened, undulating, then gliding toward the opposite side of the bed, Barrett was conscious once more of how much softer and more appealing was her person when divested of outer garments. As usual, she wore only a transparent negligee, pink this time, tied loosely at the neck. Her blond hair was loose, making her angular facial features seem rounder, and the filmy negligee revealed the brown nipples of her moon breasts and her deep navel set in the flat stomach and the triangular pelvic bone that pointed downward to the narrow vaginal area.

His desire mounted, and he began to pull off his jock shorts before he sat down on the edge of the bed.

"Mike, do you always keep this next to your bed like the Bible?" she asked lightly.

He glanced over his shoulder. "What?"

She held up a copy of *The Seven Minutes*. "This. It was right here by your lamp."

"I keep it handy. I continually refer to it. Part of the pretrial preparation. And, as a matter of fact, I never get tired of it." He tossed his shorts on a chair, and swung around onto the bed. "Darling, I still say you ought to read the copy I gave you."

She dropped the book on the table, then lowered herself on the bed, pulling the negligee around her as she settled back against the pillow. She turned her head on the pillow, and said sweetly, "I have read it, Mike. I finished reading it last night."

"Well, why didn't you say so?" He rolled over beside her and propped himself up on one elbow. "Well, now that you've read it, don't you agree I'm right?"

She reached out and touched his naked chest. "Mike, lying here like this, it's one time we should be perfectly honest with each other, isn't it?"

"Honest about what? Are you referring to the book?"

"Yes, because—"

"Sweetie, can't that wait? We can talk afterward. Right now . . ."

With one arm he started to embrace her, but she raised a hand to stop him.

"No, please, Mike. Right now, just for a little bit, I want to talk. Because the book, it's tied up with—with everything else about us. Do you mind?"

His desire had fled. Pique had begun to replace passion. "Mind? Why should I mind?" He tried to keep the irritation out of his tone of voice. "You want to talk first, so let's talk. The chair recognizes Faye Osborn, the gorgeous, irresistible—"

"Mike, what I have to say is serious."

He nodded solemnly. "I'll listen serious."

"And you agree we can be absolutely honest."

"Absolutely honest."

"Very well, then, Mike, I'm going to tell you about your precious book. No, I don't think you are right about it. I think you are wrong." She took his shoulder. "Mike, let's level, let's be truthful. I read the book. I hated it. It's a vulgar, dirty little piece of trash, indescribably filthy and thoroughly dishonest. And I know in your heart of hearts you agree with me. Now nobody's listening. Forget your involvement in the case. That's the truth, isn't it, Mike?"

He sat up, flushing. "No, dammit, it's not the truth. It's the beauty of the book that made me take on the case, and not the other way around, as you'd have it. What are you talking about, Faye? I can't believe my ears. I really can't. What did you call it?"

"I read it, and afterward I wanted to soap and wash myself all over. I called it vulgar, dirty, filthy, dishonest. Had I known what was in it, I would never have permitted you to make a public spectacle of yourself by defending such obscenity. You agreed we could be honest, Mike. I'm being honest."

"Okay, you're being honest. But I'm trying to figure you out. How's what you read about in *The Seven Minutes* any different from what we've been doing every week and were about to do tonight? Is what we're doing vulgar and dirty?"

She sat straight up. "Mike, how dare you compare the two! What we do is decent. Our language is decent. Our love is honest. But, even then, I don't think what we do in privacy should be paraded in public. Sex should be a private matter."

"Maybe it's been kept too private for too many years, and that's what's ailing so many people," he said. "And as for our love being honest, yes—but why is the love in the book any less honest?"

"Because it's false love," Faye persisted. "The heroine, Cathleen —all those thoughts she has during intercourse, they're contrived only to titillate. They have nothing to do with reality. When a real woman is being made love to, that's not how she thinks and feels. That's only the way the author, a man, thought a woman feels or should feel. Even Dr. Kinsey would support me in what I say. You're always throwing experts at me. Let me throw Dr. Kinsey at you. He says that females in those pornographic books always extoll the male's genital size and copulatory capacity, and those books always exaggerate the female's response and her insatiability for sex. Yet that kind of heroine portrays only the kind of female which most males wish all women to be. But in real life—and now I'm quoting me, Mike—women don't think and feel that way ever. Only the Jadways do. It's ridiculous and degrading. Mike, believe me, I know. I'm a woman."

His mind had gone to Maggie, a woman who also knew. He said, "You're one kind of woman, Faye, and you know how you feel when you're being made love to, but many women may feel differently, far differently."

"Like that whore in the book?"

"Like that decent woman in the book who has memories, wishes, thoughts, feelings which probably come close to representing what the majority of women think and feel inside themselves, but they are afraid to admit it."

"No respectable woman on earth ever let that kind of garbage fill her head. And no woman on earth, except maybe a streetwalker, would imagine or express herself in such language."

"What language? What language are you talking about?"

"Language is words. All those words. Like the word she uses for feeling sexy or bitchy or whatever, the word she uses for that and for her—her private parts."

"What word?" he demanded. "What word was so repulsive?"

"Please, Mike, you know I can't use a word like that. I hate it —it's filthy."

"Do you mean when Cathleen says she feels like a cunt all over?"

"Mike!"

"That's it, isn't it? The word 'cunt'?"

"Mike, stop it."

"Honey, listen to me. That word has been in use since the Middle Ages. It's a Teutonic word that corresponds with the Latin word *cuneus*, which means wedge. Jadway wasn't the first to use it. Geoffrey Chaucer used its Middle English equivalent. Laurence Sterne used it. John Fletcher used it. D. H. Lawrence used it. Certainly it's a vulgarism, but it's a word countless men use in their speech and plenty of women have in their heads. What's wrong with a writer's having the courage to describe what really goes on inside a woman's mind?" He tried to calm down, maintain the argument on a plane of reason. "Faye, that word is in *Canterbury Tales*. The Wife of Bath says, 'For certainly, old dotard, by your leave,/You shall have cunt all right enough at eve.' Except that Chaucer used 'queynte,' which is thought to have the same connotation as 'cunt.' Would you ban Chaucer from schools and libraries because he used it?"

Faye's indignation had not abated. "Mike, I'm not a child. Don't lecture me, or try to put me off with pedagoguery. I'm simply telling you I'm a woman, and I'm like most women, and I know what offends me. I don't care who's used the word—Chaucer, Lawrence, any of them—it's still a vomitous word. It's dishonest, and any writer who uses it knows nothing about women, is hostile toward women, wants to degrade them, and is preaching disrespect of women to every male reader, young or old. Don't look down your nose at me, Mike. I know when I'm right and you're wrong. I abhor language like that, and I don't want you having any part of that filth. More and more I see how right Dad was in wanting to keep you away from this kind of case. He knew it could corrupt and warp anyone involved in it. And it's already making you say things and do things that I know are contrary to your real nature."

Her mention of her father had unnerved him again. The last remnants of his wrath were in retreat, and only a small part of resentment remained. "Well, I'm in the case, and I'm staying in," he said, his voice strained. "As for Jadway's judgment, or my own, of what takes place secretly in women's minds, perhaps we are both mistaken. Maybe we can never know. And maybe women themselves don't know. But at the very least, whether we're accurate or inaccurate, the use of certain language as a literary device to point up the mysteries of stream of consciousness may be sufficient defense of such vulgarisms."

All through the last, her head had been cocked sideways as she listened and observed him—trying to assess his annoyance, he guessed—and now she was smiling, softening, ready to reach out for a compromise. Her hand had touched and then covered his hand. "I'm glad you see my side of it a little, and I'll try to understand yours. I only know I'm a woman, and I'm against anything that degrades me. I'm a woman and I want respect and love. You know that, Mike."

"Certainly."

Her hand had gone up his arm, and as she slowly sank back against the pillow she gently pulled him down until he lay beside her. She ran her fingers through his hair. "I'm sorry, Mike," she said softly. "I don't want to fight about all that silliness. I want to love you."

She went closer to him, her head against his chest. "And I know what's been inside my head these last minutes, and there wasn't one dirty word, there was only one word, and that's 'love.' I kept thinking how I want you and need you, and how I want only what's best for you and for us."

"Yes," he said. Corneille was offering him his next line: "O heaven, what a lot of virtues you make me hate." He kept it to himself.

"Don't be cold, Mike, don't punish me," she said in a muffled voice, "not when I want you so much."

His arm tightened around her body and his hand reached toward her breast and caressed it beneath the gown. "I want you, too."

"Then forget books and make-believe," she whispered, "and let's love each other."

244

But while he continued to caress her, he made no other move. Lingering resentment of her attitude, her righteousness, hung between them like a thin curtain, separating her from him, and he could not bring himself to push aside the curtain and find desire.

He felt her cool long fingers trace their way across his ribs and move down his hip and he felt them move between his legs and touch what still lay flaccid, and her fingers curled around it and massaged it and her breath and throaty words penetrated the thin curtain. "I love you down there, Mike, I love him—make him love me—don't hold him back—let him get big, I like to feel him get big."

He meant to resist, but resistance weakened and faded as he grew large in her hand. "All right," he groaned, "all right."

And the curtain was gone.

She had pulled loose the ribbon that held her negligee together, and now the garment fell away, and her breasts trembled and her torso wriggled as he came over her and he kissed her breasts and his lips circled her hardening nipples and then his mouth kissed one nipple and then the other.

He could feel her left leg slipping under him, and one cool hand pushing his head away from the breasts, and he could hear her saying, "Come on, darling, now, right now."

For the brief moment that they were apart, he rising to his knees, she bending her long legs and holding them wide apart, he remembered how she always resisted the heat of prolonged foreplay and always led him to enter her the moment that she saw he was ready. For an instant, he determined to change that, to extend the prelude to love, to bring her to a passion matching his own, to make her commitment and animal-want rise to his own, but the instant eluded him and once more he was subject to her will.

Her firm hands were behind his back, her fingers pressing into his flesh, forcing him down toward her, bringing him down between her legs. He came down to his elbows, until his chest felt her nipples, and his hips were enclosed by the inner part of her thighs, and his rigid hardness, guided by her hand again, slowly sank into the folds of the soft, warm, moist wedge—the warmest part of her, the thought came and went, the warmest, warmest. And he was deeper in her now, and almost out, and deeper again, and back and forth and around and around. And he felt her lips

245

on his ear, and her quickening breath, and he wanted her to moan and give, and open wider and shake, but she remained still and unmoving except below, where her buttocks responded to the rhythm of his motions, not wildly, not totally, but nicely and properly as in a dance on a dance floor, that much, that answering motion that was part of a form and no more.

If she couldn't, then maybe he could, maybe he finally could bring her passion to his pitch. He thrust harder and faster into her, as if trying to weld them into one, and her pelvis lifted and fell with him, and rotated with him, and no more.

Gradually he began to moderate his movement, and he heard her whispering, "Darling, what is it?"

"I want it to go longer. I want to give you a chance to—"

She clutched him. "No . . . no . . . don't hold back. Come now, come right now."

And she dug her fingers into his shoulders and closed her thighs more tightly around him and pressed herself against him, and instantly he was restimulated and no longer in control.

He heard her faintly once more. "That's better, darling, better." And then, "Does it make you happy, darling, are you happy, do you like it?"

And then he heard no more, because he was telling her inside how it was, he was bursting inside her, shuddering, bursting, letting go and suffocating her in his nakedness.

It was over, and he was still inside her, but sanity was returning and soon he would be ready for reality.

He opened his eyes and looked at her. She was unmussed and poised and smiling coolly at him, as if pleased at his pleasure and pleased with herself for what she had done for him. The curl of her mouth told him that she was proud to have been able to serve and yet humble him by still maintaining an attitude above and beyond all this mean coupling, above this necessary act that could be described in books only by using dirty words.

And suddenly the curtain he had put down, tried to put aside earlier, was there once more. Through it he saw her more clearly, more honestly. And what he saw was what she held on to with unwavering self-pride, in a secret recess of her mind: that for her, lovemaking was a thing you did because it was a biological measuring stick of your health and normality, and lovemaking was a thing

246

you offered because in the end it gave you an advantage. They had made love, and behind the invisible curtain she had emerged from the fornication as untouched and unsullied as if she had been a spectator at a sex circus, the bystander, the observer, someone superior to the ridiculous, helpless, uncontrolled, panting male member who required indulgence in this function. As ever, she had survived the filth and the beast to retain on her brow the tiara of civilized decency and ladyship.

And that was not all that Barrett perceived of her secret mind in these fleeting moments. There was not only the moral side of her triumph, but the business side as well. She had invested little in their performance, and yet she had profited so much. There had been no thought of fair trading. It was the way her father did business. You learned where others were weak or susceptible, and you took them over, absorbed them, offering little, only enough to hold them through their need, and then you came out of the partnership as the one in control and in power. You were, in short, Father's daughter. And he, he would become Father's daughter's necessary mate.

He had never read her secret mind so clearly. But he read it now, with a new insight, because he had read *The Seven Minutes*, and she had read it, and that had become the litmus paper that showed truth in its real color. Yet, despite this discovery of her, he felt helpless. He became conscious of his exposed flesh and her own, and it was unbeautiful and unromantic this night. He had played stud for royalty. His reward would be a tiny slice of empire. And this reward was the most intriguing and satisfying seduction of all.

"How was it, Mike?" she was saying. "Did you really enjoy it?"

"You know I did."

"I always like it when you love me. Do you love me?"

"I showed you what I felt, didn't I? That wasn't push-ups I was doing."

"Really, Mike. . . . Are you through? My legs are beginning to ache. Do you mind?"

He withdrew from her, and in the moment of disengagement her legs were wide apart and what could be seen was all of her that was soft and warm and honest and natural. Quickly her lowered legs closed the best of her from view, and quickly the blanket was drawn over it and up to her breasts. The best was hidden, stored from sight for another week, and what was left was the detached genteel head and the smiling glacial outsider's face.

The lips set in the face of the detached head were moving. "There, you see, Mike, love can be decent and clean. You see that, don't you?"

He saw that, yes, he did. He saw her in sharpest focus. His memory evoked pictures projected by J J Jadway and Geoffrey Chaucer, and the pictures revealed Faye Osborn, the simple essence of her, plain and unretouched.

Cunt, they showed.

Inside and all over, cunt, no more, no less.

The clarity of the pictures, their precise exposure, frightened him. This was royalty, and his thoughts were seditious. He fell back on his pillow. Banish sedition. Yet Faye's whore, Cathleen, Jadway's Cathleen, was there also, appreciating him, and her face was strangely the face of a girl named Maggie. Banish sedition, banish it.

And he did. He managed by force to conjure up different pictures, pictures of the safe good years ahead, glimpses of the imposing house in Bel-Air, the staff of servants, the chauffeured Bentley, the private Lear jet, the villa on Cap Ferrat, the celebrities, the social seasons, Faye so stately, so beautiful, so complementary beside him. The life cauterized of meanness and devoid of commonness. The good life. The best.

What more could a man want?

He turned his head on the pillow and smiled back at Faye. "I love you, darling," he said.

V

The following morning, promptly at ten o'clock, the doorbell rang, and Mike Barrett answered it and ushered Mrs. Isabel Vogler into his apartment.

She proved to be a corpulent woman, probably in her middle forties, and on her graying head she wore a Sunday hat braided with limp artificial flowers. Her eyes were creased above two puffs of cheeks, and there was down on her upper lip, and a massive double chin or goiter, but her dark dress was fresh and neat and she moved with remarkable agility for one so obese.

She planted herself in the center of Barrett's living room, surveyed it briefly, and said, "Well, this isn't much of a job to take care of. Looks no problem to me. Like I said in the ad I put in the paper, I'm a real experienced housekeeper. How many rooms have you got?"

"Besides this, there's the bedroom, a bathroom, the kitchenette," said Barrett.

"Can you show me?"

"Later," said Barrett, gesturing her to a chair.

Mrs. Vogler settled down with a grunt. "Don't mind sitting whenever I can," she said. "When you're in my line of work, and on your feet all day, sitting is a real vacation."

Barrett found a place on the sofa across from her, took his pipe from the ashtray, and held it up. "Do you mind?"

"Not at all. Mr. Vogler, rest his soul, was a pipe smoker, but even his awful-smelling corncob was better than those men smoking cigars. You go ahead and smoke your pipe, Mr. Barrett, and take no mind of me. It becomes a man, a pipe, even though it's sure to mean plenty of holes in the furniture."

Barrett lit his pipe. Through the partially open bedroom door he could see the still unmade bed that Faye had left at two in the morning, after extracting the promise from him that they would dine together tonight. He returned his attention to Isabel Vogler. He was not sure how it was best to proceed with this possible witness whom Maggie Russell had suggested, since he had lured Mrs. Vogler to this meeting under false pretenses.

"Was it difficult to make connections from Van Nuys to West Los Angeles?" he inquired.

"No problem at all. I have my own jalopy—didn't my boy tell you? Kids, once they got their heads in the television set, they don't remember anything."

"Well, your youngster did very well with my call. Now, about the ad you placed, Mrs. Vogler. Can you elaborate upon it a little more?"

"You mean—?"

"I mean can you let me know a little more about what you're after and about your background?"

"Like I told you, I have plenty of experience and I'm dependable, if that's what you mean," said Isabel Vogler. "Since Mr. Vogler left me widowed and penniless eight years ago, and with a child to rear, I've been working more or less steady. As a housekeeper, but I can cook too, if nothing fancy is required. When the child was younger, I took live-in positions and boarded him out, but since my last live-in employment, what with the child growing up, I figured he should at least know he's got his own home, so I've been doing only day work. But that's not so good, because it's not regular enough. I want a position where I know I can come in three, four days a week, or, even better, all week, nine to five, and have some income I can depend upon. I'm doing everything I can to save up some money."

"You need money, then?"

"I have a small savings account, but I want a bit more to make the future easier. Because maybe next year, or the year after, I want to have enough to go back to my home town where I came from and where I have friends and some relatives and can be better situated for my boy and me. That's Topeka—Topeka,

Kansas—I'm talking about going back to, and if I'm ever going to do it properly I'll need the money for clothes and transportation and the time it takes getting settled. So that's what I'm wanting, Mr. Barrett, regular employment."

"What I have in mind might offer you a fair sum of money for that savings account," said Barrett. "Tell me, you spoke of your last steady live-in job. When was that?"

"A year and a half ago, I'd say."

"Who was your employer at that time?"

Her face seemed to sink into her double chin or goiter. "He was Mr. Griffith—Mr. Frank Griffith."

"The name's familiar," said Barrett.

"He's pretty well known. He has these advertising agencies, and—"

"Yes, of course, it's that Frank Griffith. How long were you in his employment, Mrs. Vogler?"

"Near on two years."

"That speaks well for you. Do you have a reference from him, or do you think he'd give you one?"

Mrs. Vogler's countenance had become a sorrowful pudding. She kneaded one fat hand with the other. "No, I've got no reference from him and I can't get one. That's been my trouble ever since, and that's what's so unfair. Whenever I tell my prospective employers that—well, they look at me like I'm a liar, like how can anyone take a poor domestic's word over the word of an important man like Mr. Griffith. But believe me, swearing on my only child's head, I'm not lying at all, Mr. Barrett."

"Lying about what?"

"About Mr. Griffith being unfair in firing me and refusing to give me a reference or any good word. It's not fair. And it's been hard on me ever since."

Barrett lit his pipe again. He was coming closer now, and nearer the end of his subterfuge. "I assure you, Mrs. Vogler, your being fired and refused a reference does not prejudice me. However, it does make me curious to know what happened. I'm certainly prepared to hear your side of it." He paused. "Sa-ay, the name just struck a chord. Frank Griffith. Is that the same one whose son's been talked about on television and mentioned in all the newspapers?"

Mrs. Vogler's porker features shook like jelly as she confirmed Barrett's identification. "They're one and the same," she said, "and the boy, that's Jerry Griffith. It's something I'll never understand in a hundred years. Never. Because I know this boy like he's my own. Or I knew him then, but that wasn't so long ago, and nothing can tell me human nature changes in a year and a half. He was a good boy, the nicest person in the whole house, more like his mother, although she was a little creepy. It was his old man that was impossible. That's what never comes out. If people only knew . . ."

"Knew what, Mrs. Vogler?"

"Mr. Barrett, don't get no idea I'm the type that goes around gossiping and saying ill things about my former employers, but that Mr. Griffith, that man, he was almost the death of me. The way he went lording it around the house, not that he was home all that much, but lording it over his wife when he *was* there until you like wanted to crawl into the wallpaper, and lording it over his son, and over me, treating me like I was some kind of alley cat or something. But it was the way he squashed down the boy that riled me more than the way he treated me. I kept it stewing up inside myself all the time, remembering my place and not mixing in, but one day I couldn't stand it no more and I just spoke my piece like any person has to, and you can bet Mr. Griffith wasn't used to that kind of backtalk, and so then he spoke his piece and in an hour I was out of there and gone like I'd never been there so long. And reference, well, how was I supposed to get a reference?"

"Couldn't you get one from Mrs. Griffith?"

"She wouldn't dare. She's agreeable to whatever her husband does, like it or not."

Barrett sat silently a moment, puffing on his pipe. What came next would be crucial. He had to cue her properly. "Uh, Mrs. Vogler, up to this point I'll be glad to take your word that you may have been unfairly treated. Yet, to be perfectly frank with you, it does come down to Frank Griffith's public reputation—which is of the best, absolutely impeccable—against your own complaint against him, which may have no real basis in fact. Don't misunderstand me. I'm prepared to accept your word against his, but I'm afraid I'll have to know a trifle more." He paused, then

252

resumed with emphasis. "Here, on the one hand, we have a famous Olympic hero, a nationally known advertising man, a leading civic figure. On the other hand, we have you with your statement that this man is not all he's supposed to be. Now, which—?"

"He isn't what he looks to be!" Mrs. Vogler exclaimed, almost overturning her chair as she agitatedly shifted her weight. "Mr. Barrett, if you want to know what somebody is really like, you should work intimately inside their house for them. That's where you find out what nobody on the outside ever sees. That Frank Griffith, he isn't what you might think. He drinks, he drinks a lot at night, and there's no man nastier than a mean drunk. And his son, mostly Frank Griffith ignores him, but I've seen him cuff the boy, too, cuff a grown boy. And I've seen him pretty severe with his wife, too, considering she's a permanently suffering invalid from rheumatoid arthritis, and him rough and mistreating of her, and worse—always humiliating her in the most shameful way. If you want to know the truth, he's got no relationship with his wife, didn't have one even before she was sick, because he had some chippy secretary in his office, if you know what I mean. I could tell you more, plenty, but you get the idea, and I'm not making these things up, I could prove them to you if I had to." She was out of breath, and she sat back, adjusting her floral hat on her head. "I'm no gossip, Mr. Barrett, but you wanted to know about taking my word against his, so that wound me up. I don't talk this much ordinarily. But that man cost me plenty, and I have a right to speak up for me. I hope you don't think I was wrong doing that, and I hope I haven't spoiled my chance for your job?"

Barrett stared at her. She was pure gold. She was what the impoverished defense needed. She was a winner, an underdog a jury could sympathize with. He must take care to handle her right. He could not afford to lose her. Yet the truth must come out.

"The job," he said. "Mrs. Vogler, there is no job I can offer you, in the sense you had expected. But there is something else I can offer you. I can offer you money." He stood up. "I know. You're perplexed. You think I've gone off my rocker. But I can explain. I can tell you how you can be of help to me, and how I can be of help to you. First off, I'm the attorney defending that so-called dirty book that both Jerry and Frank Griffith blame for Jerry's trouble. Now, then . . ."

For five minutes, standing over her, Barrett related to the at first bewildered, then fascinated Mrs. Vogler the background of the pending court battle and the means by which the District Attorney hoped to use the Jerry Griffith crime as an indictment of *The Seven Minutes*. Simplifying the patter of psychiatry and sociology as much as possible, trying to translate it into Voglerese, Barrett attempted to explain how Jerry's life in the Griffith household, as well as other outside factors, might have been what influenced Jerry and drove him to an antisocial act rather than any reading he had done. Barrett tried hard, because unless this idea was understood by Mrs. Vogler she would have no comprehension of what he was after and the use she could be to him in the trial.

When he was done, he searched her porcine face for some sign of understanding.

Suddenly she smiled broadly and bobbed her head.

He knew then. She understood.

Now the last step. "Mrs. Vogler, you know what I'm after. I want your cooperation. I want you on the witness stand for the defense. I want nothing from you, at any time, but the truth about what you saw and heard first hand during your employment by the Griffiths. I want you in court not to seek revenge for yourself, but to help me seek justice by exposing the true facts. We'll pay you for your time and information, of course. While not a fortune, certainly it will be as much as you could earn in three or four months of day work. Enough to get you a little closer to Topeka. What do you think? Will you help me?"

"First, I better ask—will my appearing for you get me into any kind of trouble?"

"Not if you confine yourself to the truth. No, Mrs. Vogler, the worst I can see happening to you is that maybe Frank Griffith won't ever hire you again."

She burst into gurgling laughter, and her cheeks and chins shook. "That's a good one, that is!" She climbed to her feet, and her face was pink with excitement. "I like doing this, Mr. Barrett. I'm sure on your side as a witness. I'd almost be ready to do it for nothing, except that I need the money so. I can't wait to make my speech to the public about what that holier-than-thou Griffith has done to his son. That'll be a great day for me."

"Excellent, Mrs. Vogler. You'll never regret this." He took her plump arm. "I'll show you to the elevator. Meanwhile, as I told you, the trial is about to begin. So we'd better have a meeting, plan on conferring for an hour or two, either tomorrow or the day after. I'll call you first to be sure you're home. You will be home, Mrs. Vogler?"

"I'll be out only once, Mr. Barrett. I'm getting me a new hat for my first personal appearance in public. I'm taking me to Ohrbach's store and getting me the sincerest hat that's ever been made."

IMMEDIATELY AFTER Isabel Vogler's departure, Mike Barrett hastened back to his apartment and the living-room telephone. He felt like singing. For the first time in days, he had cause for optimism. Now he was eager to transmit the news of Mrs. Vogler's enlistment to Abe Zelkin, whose own morale was sorely in need of a booster.

He put through the call to the office, and when he asked urgently for Zelkin he could hear Donna's astonishment.

"Mr. Barrett, where's your memory?" she said. "Did you forget? Mr. Zelkin is over at the Hall of Justice—Department 101 of the Superior Court—Judge Nathaniel Upshaw's courtroom. They've been making the selection of the jury out of the pool of veniremen. Mr. Zelkin checked with the office during the last recess, and he said to be sure to tell you it's going very smoothly. He thinks they'll have a jury impaneled and sworn in by late tomorrow, and that means the trial will start Monday morning."

Barrett had forgotten, of course. He and Zelkin had spent a long session together debating the advantages of waiving a jury and letting their entire case ride on a hearing by and the decision of a judge. In the end, they had agreed that their chances were better if they argued their case before twelve dissimilar men and women rather than before a single individual, because this way an extra verdict was possible. From a judge there would be the possibility of only one of two verdicts, guilty or not guilty. From a jury of twelve citizens there was not only the possibility of those two verdicts, but an additional one, disagreement—a hung jury, which in a sense would be a victory for the defense.

Attentive to Donna once more as she ticked off the telephone calls and mail and visitors of the morning, Barrett realized that his work load had increased nearly twofold. In these next few days he would have to fulfill his own duties and Abe Zelkin's as well. Perhaps some of the work could be diverted to Kimura, but not much, since Kimura had enough to worry about already.

Then Barrett heard Donna mention Kimura's name. "He phoned to tell me to remind you that if you're out of the office today, even for lunch, he wants to know where you'll be so he can reach you if he has to."

"Is he on to something?"

"Sounded like it. He didn't say what."

"Well, I'll be over pronto. I'll have lunch in the office."

"One more thing, Mr. Barrett. Your lady friend called about fifteen minutes ago. Miss Osborn asked if you could phone her the moment you were free."

"All right. I'll call her now. Then I'll be in."

Hanging up, he wondered why Faye had telephoned him. He had intended to call her to postpone their dinner date. With Zelkin occupied challenging potential jurors, with the trial looming immediately ahead, he'd have to burn midnight oil tonight, tomorrow night, and over the weekend.

He dialed the Osborn residence, and it was Faye who answered the phone.

"I knew you were busy, but I just wanted to hear your voice, Mike."

"My voice? Are you auditioning me for something?"

"No, truly, darling, I just wanted to know if you sounded angry. I mean, about those things I said last night about that book."

"Everyone has a right to say anything they want about any book."

"This is special, and this is us. Maybe my timing was bad and I came on too strong. Especially when you're so emotionally involved in the damn thing. I was afraid I'd upset you. But I made it up to you, didn't I, darling?"

"I wasn't upset," he lied.

"But I showed you I loved you, didn't I? You can see that how I feel about the book has nothing to do with how I feel about making love." She lowered her voice. "Perhaps tonight I can prove it again."

He remembered why he had been going to phone her. "You're

sweet, Faye, but it'll have to be a rain check, I'm afraid. Abe is tied up in court picking a jury, and I feel like I've been buried under a landslide. Paper work, interviews, phone calls. My libido's going to be wholly diverted to Things Legal tonight and the next few nights. Will you forgive me? I'll try to catch up with you after the weekend."

The other end of the line was silent. Then Faye spoke. "I was just trying to make up my mind whether you're ducking me tonight because of your work or because you're still peeved about my critical judgment of Jadway."

"Honey, I've forgotten our discussion. Believe me, it's the work. I'm happy to say everything's looking up. This morning we got ourselves a devastating witness, a real dilly, someone who may be of real help in blunting Duncan's contention that the book alone was responsible for the Griffith boy's act of violence."

"I'm pleased for you, Mike, but I don't understand. What more can be said about why Jerry Griffith committed that rape? He's said it all himself. It was the book."

"That doesn't necessarily make it true, Faye. Most men don't fully understand the influences that drive them in one direction or another. They may think they know, but that's merely surface causes. The real influences may be buried deep in the subconscious. Look, honey, I'm too busy for Freuding in depth right now. Suffice it to say that someone came out of the woodwork—the Griffiths' own woodwork, mind you—with firsthand evidence that Frank Griffith is anything but a paragon of virtue at home. The old man may have unwittingly done more harm to Jerry than a dozen pornographic books. I know Griffith is a friend of your father's, but I guarantee you that neither your father nor anyone else has the faintest idea what Frank Griffith is like in private."

"It sounds dreadful. Who would have such thoughts and have the nerve to tattle about it? It could only be that Maggie Russell. Is she your turncoat witness? It must be. No one else lives full time in the house."

He was annoyed with her again. "What are you dragging Miss Russell into this for? Of course it's not Maggie Russell. Other women have lived in the house before she did. Like for instance Isabel Vogler."

"The fat one? I remember seeing her there a couple of years ago. Now, isn't that finky of her?"

"Anyone who, for a change, has some truths to tell isn't a fink in my book. Believe me, our witnesses won't be cornering the market on finkiness. Wait until you see the characters our upright Elmo Duncan parades before the public next week."

"Can you trust someone like that?"

"You mean Mrs. Vogler? Why not? As much as any witness. She knows she'll be under oath. One lie and they'd slap her with perjury."

"Not lies, but . . ."

"Exaggerations? Don't worry, Faye, our District Attorney is as much a seeker of truth, when it benefits him, as I am. And as you are right now, for that matter. Why this sudden concern about my witness, Faye? Are you afraid the exposure of the real Frank Griffith will upset your father or rock the establishment?"

"Don't be disagreeable, Mike. That's not it at all, and you know it. It's you, the kind of nasty people you're becoming more and more involved with over an unworthy piece of trash. There I go again, and I'm sorry, but I'm just worrying about you—and about us. I can't stand seeing you, of all people, immersed in that muck and surrounded by those ratty dregs of humanity."

He contained his temper. "Faye, there's nothing to contaminate me. But I do appreciate your concern."

"There you go. I could feel the freeze. Oh, darling, please, let's stop this bickering. Why can't it be like it used to be before that damn book came into our lives? Mike, I do want to see you tonight. I know we'll both feel better after being together."

"Faye, I really can't. I've got to get to the office now. I'll try to call you later. Tomorrow for sure."

His growing irritation with Faye tagged along with him throughout his drive to the office. It amazed him how the appearance of a single object in their lives—in this instance a mere book —had so vividly laid bare the differences in their natures. Until this happened, he had regarded Faye and himself as compatible and their relationship as harmonious. They had both paid lip service to the cliché that they were meant for each other. Recently, most definitely last night and this morning, he was less than certain.

Driving, he continued to ruminate on the matter of Faye and himself. She loved him, or thought she did. More likely, she could love no man beyond her father, and after much trial and error, while experimenting among many men, she had settled upon Barrett as the one to whom she could offer affection (the boiling point of her passion never exceeded affection) and the one best qualified to join (as husband) the other necessities that decorated her life. As for Barrett, he loved her, or thought he did. More likely, since his past relationships with women had been shallow and unstable, he was capable of liking her more than he had liked other women and of loving those things Faye represented, which were status, culture, wealth, and all the other crummy golden calves that he had genuflected before in his rise from rags toward riches.

It was odd, he thought, how the Jadway book, to most at best only a bit of glimmering erotica, had become for him so powerful a searchlight aiding self-examination and self-revelation. Under its merciless glare no inner deception could hide truth. To Faye it must have exposed, for the first time, her inability to give love. Unable to face this truth, she had turned on the instrument of exposure and rejected it as defective and warped. For Barrett, it had exposed to him the ugly truth that in Faye he sought not love but success, and the uglier truth that his goals in life were empty and that by achieving them he would find nothing that could sustain a lifetime of remaining years. Unlike Faye, he had been able to face his truths, but he had not been able to act upon them.

Damn that sonofabitching book, he thought, it *can* be destructive. At least, destructive of peace of mind. Unless a man has license to ignore some truths, and live some lies, he cannot have peace of mind. And most of all what Mike Barrett wanted this day was peace of mind.

It was at least an hour after he had reached his office and settled behind his desk before he was finally absorbed enough in his work to exorcise the unsettling specters of Faye-love and self-hate.

He was deep in a legal brief when Donna's insistent buzzer brought him out of it and back into the workaday world of communication.

The caller was Leo Kimura. The lack of precision in Kimura's speech betrayed his unnatural excitement.

"Good news, very good news, Mr. Barrett," Kimura was saying. "I found him, I tracked down Norman C. Quandt."

"Quandt?" repeated Barrett, his head still stuffed with the legal brief he had been studying. Then he remembered. Quandt had been the mail-order publisher of hard-core pornography, the one who had originally acquired the rights to *The Seven Minutes* from Christian Leroux and had later resold them to Phil Sanford. After being tried and found guilty of mailing obscene matter, Quandt had escaped a jail sentence when the Supreme Court reversed the decision of the lower court. He had disappeared completely, until Kimura learned that he was now in the motion-picture business in Southern California. Their hope had been that Quandt might produce some valuable information about Jadway's character and his writing of the novel. And now Quandt had been found.

"Leo," said Barrett, "you mean you know where he is?"

"I've just come from seeing him," said Kimura triumphantly. "I hurried over to the nearest gas station to call you. He operates an organization called the Arts and Sciences Cinema Company. Impressive?"

"I'll say."

"Do not be fooled," Kimura went on. "That grand euphemism disguises a factory that grinds out low-budget girlie—I should say nudie—films. Quandt's name isn't publicly associated with it. I just happened to find his name on the recorded deed for the building where the cinema company is located. He is, in fact, the company's proprietor. I called on him, and I cannot say my reception was warm. When I began to state my business, Quandt was decidedly uncooperative. It was obvious he wanted as little publicity for or public knowledge of his business, and his own connection with it, as possible. He admitted quite candidly that, should we bring up his name in court, the District Attorney would have men watching his every move from that day on. He wanted nothing to do with our trial. Nevertheless I kept right on talking, and suddenly Quandt became more interested."

"What were you saying to him, Leo?"

"I told him we did not intend to involve him in any way, neither through reference to him nor by asking him to appear in person. When Quandt realized that we did not want him for a witness, and that we had no intention of bandying his name about, he was at once more friendly. It turned out he hated that St. Clair woman and the whole STDL, as well as Elmo Duncan and his office, and he was willing to assist anyone who was ready to take them on. He agreed to meet with you, Mr. Barrett, but briefly and in complete secrecy. He kept protesting to me that he was conducting a legitimate operation, his nudie films were proper enough to be exhibited in two hundred public theaters located throughout the country, and yet he had to be wary because the law and the Grundys liked to persecute men like himself who had once gone to the Supreme Court to overcome his censors. Between us, I have a hunch he's a fanatic about maintaining his secrecy for another reason. Those nudie films of his are legitimate, even if borderline, but I do not think they are what afford him his real profits. I have a hunch they camouflage another operation he may have going on behind closed doors."

"Meaning what?"

"Like maybe stag films. I do not know. I said hunch."

"Savory our Mr. Quandt ain't," said Barrett.

"Still, savior our Mr. Quandt may be," said Kimura, who enjoyed these semantic games with Barrett. "Because he is ready to inform you of all that he knows about Leroux and about the Jadway book. I have no idea how useful his information will be. I only know he is one person you have wanted to see, and now you can see him."

"When?"

"Did I not tell you, Mr. Barrett? Now, right now. You must leave this instant if you want to catch him. After today he will be outside the country for five weeks. So it must be now. Mr. Quandt is expecting you, and he is waiting."

Barrett shoved aside his work and took up a pencil and pad. "Okay, Leo, give me his address. If nothing else comes of it, at least I'll have a chance to see where nudies are born."

THE ADDRESS of the Arts and Sciences Cinema Company proved to be a weather-beaten two-story apartment building located on Vermont Avenue between Olympic and Pico Boulevards.

Puzzled, Barrett stood beside the peeling "No Vacancy" sign near the entrance and examined the stucco front. The name of the firm was nowhere in evidence, nor was there any clue to Quandt's cinema-business headquarters. Barrett wondered whether he had taken the correct address from Kimura.

He stepped back to find out whether the business could be located to one side of the building. To the right was a cottage that housed a dancing school, and to the left was a driveway that apparently led to a garage in the rear where the apartment building's tenants kept their cars. On the far side of the driveway was a vacant store that had recently been a realtor's office.

Barrett decided that he had better telephone Kimura and check out the address once more, but then it occurred to him that one of the tenants in the building might know of the Arts and Sciences Cinema Company.

Entering the central hall, he was confronted by a cardboard sign nailed to the railing of the stairway leading to the second floor. The cardboard sign had lettered on it MAKE INQUIRIES HERE, with an arrow pointing to a plain door next to the stairs.

He crossed to the door and rapped.

A man's voice called out, "Come on in!"

Barrett opened the door and found himself in a cubbyhole of an office, windowless and dark except for a small lamp that threw a beam upon a young man with a pallid face who was busily typing a letter, using the hunt-and-peck system, on an ancient manual typewriter. The table near the typewriter stand was covered with what appeared to be mail-order catalogues. The young man did not look up until he had finished the last line of the letter he was typing. As he withdrew the letter from the machine, he acknowledged his visitor with a display of serrated teeth.

"Sorry," he said. Rising, dropping the letter on the table, he inspected Barrett carefully. "What can I do for you?"

"I'm looking for a firm called the Arts and Sciences Cinema Company. A friend gave me this address, but I'm afraid it's the wrong one. I thought maybe someone in here could help me."

"All depends. Can you state your business?"

"I have an appointment with the head of the company I mentioned—a Mr. Norman C. Quandt. My name is Michael Barrett."

The serrated teeth were in evidence again. "Maybe I can help. Got any identification?"

Curiouser and curiouser, Barrett thought. "Sure." He brought out his wallet and opened it to his driver's license.

The young man peered down at it, rubbing his jaw, and then he nodded. "Guess you're cleared. Can't be too careful." He went to the telephone. "I'll tell Mr. Quandt you're here."

And then Barrett understood completely. There are movies and movies, Kimura had once said. There are legitimate movies and there are—Barrett's mind italicized the word—*art* movies. For certain movies, made on a shoestring, sexually erotic, the contents verging on the borderline of the law, no studio or advertisement was wanted. The stucco apartment building was Norman C. Quandt's Potemkin façade.

"Yeah, that's right. Right," the young man was saying into the telephone. "I'll bring him." He hung up and started for the door. "Mr. Quandt'll see you now. He's on the set. He said he'll see you there. Want to follow me?"

They went into the hall, then bypassed the stairs and walked the length of a poorly illuminated corridor. At the rear of the building the back hall door stood open, and the young man pushed the screen and pointed down. "Watch yourself."

There were three wooden steps, and the middle one was cracked. Barrett descended carefully. There was a patch of a back yard, with two orange trees, circled by a high ivy-covered fence that insured privacy. Barrett's guide had brushed past him and was heading toward what seemed to be a long four-car garage, but no cars were visible because the garage doors were all down. The young man held open a padded side door. "I'll leave you here. Go right in. Mr. Quandt's the one with the cigar."

"Thanks."

Barrett entered, and the padded door shut behind him. At first the sudden change from sunlight to darkness made him blink, and he tried to accustom his eyes to the change. In a moment he got his bearings and saw that the interior of the garage had been remodeled into a cheap semblance of a motion-picture sound stage. The windows and walls were draped with canvas-covered padding and sheets of perforated soundproofing materials. Almost lost in the shadows were domestic props and stacks of stage scenery. Diagonally across from him, in the most distant corner, there was a bright square of light.

Advancing toward the luminous area, Barrett could make out the klieg lights and a surprisingly small motion-picture camera poised high on rollers which were placed on tracks. Near the camera, three men were conferring—one pulling at an eyeshade, another knotting his bathrobe, the third bringing a lighter to his cigar. Beyond them, within the square of klieg lights, was a set furnished as a carpeted master bedroom.

"Zo, we got it straight now?" the stubby man with the cigar said. "Let's stop wasting time and get going. Harry, don't forget to lather your face again. Where in the hell are those goddam dames? Still in the can? Go in there and drag them out if you have to. Why in the name of Christ can't they have diarrhea on their own time? Come on, now—move!"

Hands on hips, he turned away in disgust, and then he became aware of his visitor.

He came forward. "Barrett?"

"Yes, I—"

He stuck out a hand. "I'm Norman Quandt."

They shook hands. Quandt was just under middle height, squat and muscular, garbed in a checkered sport shirt and doeskin slacks. Behind the receding hairline the remaining hair had been heavily greased in an unsuccessful effort to keep it straight and flat. His general aspect was lumpy-tuberous. His forehead was broad, his eyes were close together above a short pug of a nose. His lips were thick, and there was a slight dribble from the cigar corner of his mouth. His jutting chin needed shaving. He appeared to be in his early forties.

When Quandt spoke again, Barrett noted that the man had the habit of not looking at the person he was addressing and that his voice was a rasp that grated on the nerves like a fingernail run down a blackboard.

"Don't have much time for anyone today," he was saying, "but that Jap of yours conned me into seeing you, and I said yes because anyone who's trying to kick that smart-ass Duncan in the balls deserves at least ten minutes of my time."

"I appreciate it, Mr. Quandt."

"Yeah. Well, soon's this take is over, we can talk." He surveyed the set. "Ever see one of these girlie shorts being made before?"

"I'm afraid not."

264

"You'd be surprised what a market there is. There's maybe two hundred public theaters we get them released in. Nothing dirty, if that's what you think. Strictly sexploitation stuff for an audience that likes to see good-looking dames in the buff. We're also making those beaver pictures—you know, mostly closeups of a wriggling dame's snatch—the ones that are so popular in bars and night-clubs all over the country. There's a big audience ready and waiting, respectable people, so why not give the public what it wants. Nothing wrong with that, eh?"

"Nothing at all."

"I always try to make my pictures a little classier than the competition. I don't cut corners. Those twenty-minute shorts take maybe five days to shoot, and they budget in at around twenty thousand dollars each. We shoot them in sixteen-millimeter, which is good enough, and we try to get a high-quality canned sound track. Most of the competition, they don't do any editing and the stories don't have any plot. But we use a moviola, and I always write out some kind of story plot ahead of time. It pays off better at the box office."

"I imagine it does."

"It does." Quandt wiped away the spittle from his mouth and searched off. "Where in the devil are those goddam dames? Oh, yeah, here they come. You'll see what I mean about not cutting corners, Barrett. Some of my competitors, they use beat-up hags with faces that'd stop a clock, with drooping tits and splayed asses and varicose veins, just so's they don't have to pay much. Not me, not Norman C. Quandt. I go by my own feelings about women. I like lookers, head to toe. I cast strictly by my crotch. If a babe walks in, and she's stacked, and I feel a stirring in my crotch, then I know that's how everybody in the audience is going to feel. That's for me. Most of my girls have aspirations to be class models or starlets. Lots of them are teen-agers or in their early twenties, either just out of high school or working their way through college, and they're clean enough to eat." He gave a gross cackle. "And sometimes I do, sometimes I do."

Barrett made no comment. His initial reaction to the producer had hardened. He definitely did not like Norman C. Quandt.

"See those two dames," said Quandt. "Pay them each a hundred twenty-five a day. Name any other dames who get that for just taking off their clothes for six hours." He made a megaphone of one hand. "Nancy! Linda!" he bellowed. "Your places are chalked. Take it up just where you come in, Linda! Okay, Sims, roll it!"

Barrett's attention was fixed on the set. A tall, mature girl with tousled black hair and haughty features, wearing a short frilly nightgown, strolled onto the scene, halted in front of a dressing-table mirror, and lazily stretched before it. A moment later a short buxom blond girl, younger and more voluptuous, garbed as a traditional French maid, in a brief ballet-type black skirt, appeared behind the brunette carrying a department-store box that had apparently just been delivered. The lady of the house, still facing the mirror, told the blond maid to put the delivery on the bed and then help her dress. The blond maid dropped the box on the bed, scurried off the set out of camera range, and returned carrying her mistress's tennis racket and tennis outfit. Languidly the lady of the house reached down and lifted her nightgown, and slowly, ever so slowly, she drew it over her head.

Beside him Barrett heard the camera move in closer on the scene as the nude star half turned toward the camera, cupping her tiny firm breasts in her hands. After a moment she spoke to the maid, who handed her the tennis shorts. She drew on the shorts, and then, taking the tennis racket from the maid, she weighed it, stepped even closer to the camera, and, bare-breasted, began to practice her serve and her forehand. At last she exchanged the racket for her halter, pulled it on, ordered the maid to lay out her new purchases, and hurriedly exited.

The voluptuous young maid watched her go, then quickly went to the bed and opened the newly delivered box. She held up three pairs of bikini panties and admired them. Reluctantly she laid them out on the bed, then went and found the vacuum cleaner. She turned on the vacuum, working it over the carpet toward the camera, then pushed it away, her back to the camera, and bent over to remove the vacuum bag. As she bent over, her brief skirt flipped up, and her bare pink buttocks were revealed.

Barrett realized that Quandt had glanced over his shoulder to wink. Barrett tried to offer a weak smile of approval.

The scene was continuing. The blond maid had been drawn back to the bed by Madame's recent purchases. She was holding a pair of bikini panties against her own torso. Suddenly she decided

266

to try them on. With quick fingers she unzipped her maid's uniform, slipping out of the sleeves of the garment and pushing it down her hips until the uniform fell to the floor. After she stepped out of it, she stood for a few seconds without a stitch on, adroitly hiding her shaved vagina with one hand. Then, turning sideways to the camera, she took up the bikini panties and stepped into them. Now, imitating her mistress, she posed before the mirror and promenaded about the set as the camera moved in closer and closer. The black wisp of bikini briefs seemed to accentuate the whiteness of her globular breasts, which were huge and bobbing. While she was doing her pantomiming about the bedroom, the master of the house appeared, face freshly lathered, shaving brush in one hand, expecting his wife and seeing this happy spectacle instead. He fell back slightly and watched, leering. As the maid danced around, she suddenly came face to face with the master. Her hands went to her open mouth, then down to her panties, and the breasts quivered steadily. In fright, she ran back to her vacuum sweeper, pushing it with one hand as she first tugged to pull off the panties and then retrieved her maid's costume with the other.

"Cut!" bellowed Quandt. "Good work! That'll give us a four-crotch rating from every critic in the country. Okay, take five, and then carry on. I'll be tied up for a few minutes, but I'll be back." He grasped Barrett's arm. "Come on, let's get some sunshine."

They left the garage and emerged into the daylight. Quandt pointed to the rusting white enamel patio table, with several canvas chairs around it, which was set between the orange trees.

"Not bad, was it?" said Quandt, as they sat.

"If you like girls, which I do," said Barrett, putting on his sunglasses and finding his pipe.

"Now, what do you want to know?" asked Quandt, throwing away his cigar stub and unwrapping a fresh cigar. "You want to know how I first got my hands on *The Seven Minutes,* is that it?"

"For the most, yes. I've heard Philip Sanford's version."

"Who in the hell is Philip Sanford?"

"The publisher you finally resold the novel to, the one I'm defending in—"

"Oh, yeah, yeah, I remember. The fancy college kid with the fidgets."

"He's now the head of Sanford House."

"Big deal," said Quandt, chewing on his cigar. "Let me see. Yeah. It was a number of years ago, when I was having a pretty good success with my paperback line. I'd never been to the old country, and I made up my mind to take off a month and gander the sights, and I don't mean the Eiffel Tower and that crap, my friend. I mean I wanted to have a firsthand look at some of that highly touted French and Italian snatch." He grinned, removed his cigar, wiped the corner of his mouth. "I tell you, you don't know what the weather is until you get blown by some broad in Paris. Those French chicks are something. Anyway, anyway, where was I?"

"You were discoursing on fellatio," said Barrett dryly.

Quandt looked at him sharply, then said, "That book, yeah. I figured if I'm going to write the trip off with IRS, I'd better prove it was business. So I started asking around if there was anything available in my line. And some hotel concierge said there was a once-famous French publisher of spicy books who'd recently gone out of business. That was this Christian Leroux. So I looked him up. Most of his line was junk, worthless, full of big words, long sentences, no good. But one of the books was *The Seven Minutes*, and that one I dug pretty good. So I made Leroux an offer. Maybe like seven hundred fifty bucks for the whole world copyright, and he grabbed. He was down at the heels, pretending to be a gentleman, but the holes and ragged edges were showing and he was hungry. While he made a stab at bargaining, I knew he'd take my offer, and he did. The next time I saw him was for the contract signing, which we did at the American Embassy in order to have it notarized right then. That was the whole caper."

"What was this Leroux like?"

"Just another frog. Well, maybe a little more impressive. He looked like a guy who once wore monocle and spats. You know, tight-assed. Big thatch of grayish hair. Bugle of a nose. Pretty good English. Kind of wheezy and asthmatic. I only saw him twice."

"Did he speak at all of the author of *The Seven Minutes*—you know, J J Jadway?"

Quandt tried to think. He held up his cigar. "Once. Yeah, once. It was when he turned over the original contract to me. It wasn't signed by Jadway, but by some woman named Cassie McGraw, and I said who in the hell is that. Leroux said, well, he said, matter of fact, he'd never had personal dealings with the author, Jadway, because Jadway was shy and didn't like to meet people—you know those writer nuts—especially not on business, and so he had delegated all his dealings to this broad he lived with, this Cassie McGraw, an American girl, and she signed the contract and got the money and everything, because she had his power of attorney in this deal. So when I was satisfied the old contract was legit, I accepted the new one."

"But Leroux admitted to you he'd never personally met Jadway?"

"Well, now, I'm not positive. Maybe he did talk to him once or twice, but that's all."

"What about this Cassie? Are you sure Leroux told you Cassie McGraw was Jadway's mistress?"

"Yeah, I remember that. He said—not in these words—that Jadway had found this American broad in Paris and been humping her a year or more than that. Because I remember Leroux saying what a beautiful kid this McGraw girl had been, and how lucky Jadway was. And I guess Jadway used his dame for the model of the horny dame in his book, because I remember in one of Jadway's letters something about how he owed his heroine to the only woman he had ever loved."

"Letters," said Barrett, suddenly sitting up. "You said Jadway's letters. You mean you've read letters actually written by Jadway?"

"Yeah, sure, didn't I mention it? Tell you how that was. About a year or so after I got *The Seven Minutes*, I decided that if I cut the dull passages, left in only the sex, it might be a hot seller. So I began to think of publishing it as a paperback. Then I realized I wanted to put something on the back cover about Jadway, and I didn't have a damn thing. I needed some info for exploitation, you know. So I dropped Leroux a note asking for more info. You know what that frog prick did? He wrote me back and said he had a small file containing some clippings about Jadway's book when it came out, and he had three or four letters from Jadway in which Jadway told a little about his life in Paris as a writer— how he wrote the novel, what he'd had in mind, stuff he'd set down at Leroux's request which had been delivered by hand by this Cassie McGraw. Leroux said I could have the whole caboodle, but

I'd have to pay for it. Pay for it? That mudderfucker. How do you like that? I wanted to say, Up yours, Jack—but I needed the stuff. So what could I do? So I offered him twenty bucks, and he accepted, and I sent him a check, and he sent me the file of Jadway's clips and letters."

A thrill of expectation shot through Barrett. Suddenly Quandt's face resembled a map of the Promised Land. "Mr. Quandt, those letters, can I see those letters?"

Quandt squirmed, and he seemed embarrassed. "Well, I'll tell you about those letters," he said. "When I sold the book to Sanford, I forgot to give him the letters. And when I moved West, after my court trouble, I took my files out of storage and had them sent to me here from Philadelphia. And there in one of the files was a folder with those letters. Well, I just let them sit. I had other things in my mind. Then, a few weeks ago, whenever it was, when our crummy fuck beggar of a District Attorney arrested that schnook bookseller for trying to make a living off the book, and that crazy kid raped that girl, and overnight the book and Jadway was spread all over the papers and on television, and there was all that publicity about Jadway and the mystery of Jadway, I remembered those letters. Then I remembered something else—some autograph dealer in New York who was always advertising in the *New York Times* saying if anyone had authentic letters by historical figures or celebrities to sell, that he was in the market to buy them at good prices. So I thought of that, and thought, By Christ, this Jadway must be a celebrity, so why not see if the letters are worth anything? I mean, I'm not a rich man. I can always use an extra buck. So I went hunting for the letters, had a helluva job finding them, but I did. Then I wrote this autograph dealer what I had, and back comes a telegram saying he'll buy the lot and saying what they're worth. They weren't worth much, but it was a few bucks, so I shipped them on and back came his check."

Barrett's face fell. "You haven't got them? Not even photocopies?"

"Naw, what would I do with copies? I just sent them off, took the dough and ran."

"When was that?"

"Maybe a week—no, closer to ten days ago. Yeah."

"What was in those letters?" Barrett asked anxiously. "Can you recall anything of what was in them?"

"Mister, I'm ashamed to say I never even bothered to read them, except to make sure they were signed 'Sincerely yours, J J Jadway,' which they were. You see, when I got them from Leroux I was already starting to get in trouble with the law. So I never put Jadway's book out. I was in enough hot water as is. All my mind was on was my own trial before the federal judicial officer and later the Supreme Court appeal and after that trying to make a living some new way. So when I got the letters, they didn't interest me and I just put them away. When I dug them out a few weeks ago, before writing that autograph dealer, I was busy as hell, so I just checked to see if Jadway's name was on them and how many pages and that was enough to write the dealer. So I don't know nothing. Why you looking like the whole world died? Those letters important to you?"

"Mr. Quandt, I can't tell you how important. Leroux is here to appear on the witness stand and tell the court that *The Seven Minutes* is hard-core pornography written by a deliberate pornographer. In other words, dirt for dirt's sake. Those letters could contradict his evidence. I'm positive they would. They could spearhead our defense against the State's case, Mr. Quandt."

"You mean, against that bastard Elmo Duncan?"

"That's right."

Quandt made a fist. "Dammit. Why did I give them up? I probably could've got twice as much for them from you."

"You certainly could have," said Barrett. "But now—" He halted. "Sa-ay, you said you sold those letters to a well-known autograph dealer in New York City, didn't you? Well, what does that dealer want with those letters, except to put them on the market, resell them at a profit? Of course. If he hasn't sold them to some customer by now—and he's only had them ten days, you said—then I can still lay my hands on them. What's his name?"

"The autograph dealer?"

"Right."

Quandt rapped his knuckles against his brow. "His name, his name? Christ, I'll be damned if I can remember. . . . One sec. There's got to be something upstairs. Either the advertisement I clipped or the carbon of my letter when I wrote him offering the Jadway letters. I got my correspondence file cabinet upstairs in the mail-order room. You come on up with me and let's see if I can find it."

They left the back yard, and Barrett followed Quandt through the back door of the apartment building and down the hall to the front staircase, which they ascended to the second floor.

Slowing before a door at the rear, Quandt said over his shoulder, "The mail room's in here."

He opened the door and stepped inside, with Barrett right behind him. The first sight that met Barrett's eyes stopped him dead in his tracks. His eyes widened. He was incredulous.

Lying supine on a beige daybed against the opposite wall of the office was a stark-naked nymph, no more than twenty years old, titian-haired, large breasts with protruding crimson nipples, long sinuous body and legs, and she was writhing in ecstasy. One hand was moving between her legs, obviously stimulating her clitoris, and her eyes were closed and her face contorted in self-induced passion.

At once another girl, this one fully clothed in a crisp white blouse and short pleated skirt, appeared in view and walked between Barrett and the writhing naked one masturbating on the daybed. The second girl had straight bangs, severely bunned hair, and horn-rimmed spectacles, and she was carrying a pencil and shorthand pad. As she passed, she suddenly became aware of the activity on the daybed. She halted, and so astounded was she that she dropped her pad and pencil. She knelt to retrieve them, her eyes holding with fascination on the girl beside her. Ignoring her pad and pencil on the floor, she slowly removed her spectacles, crawled closer to the daybed, and bent, placing her open lips on one of the titian-haired beauty's crimson nipples. The supine one opened her eyes, ceased her activity, and fervently embraced the fully clothed secretary.

"Dammit," Quandt muttered, "I forgot we're using the office for a set today."

For the first time Barrett pulled his eyes from the scene before him, and for the first time, to the right, he saw the motion-picture camera on a tripod with a paunchy middle-aged man behind it, one eye glued to the viewer as he concentrated on the shot. Next to him, a single powerful klieg light joined the overhead light bulbs in the office to brighten the scene.

Quandt cast Barrett a sidelong glance. "You guessed it," he rasped defensively. "It's a stag film, a subsidiary part of my operation I don't advertise."

Barrett nodded dumbly.

"We shoot these four-hundred-foot reelers silent and we can do one in a day and they're damn good," he said, still defensive. "We got the classiest clientele—patriotic organizations, veterans' groups, even universities, you name it—and they want the stuff in good taste, and we supply it." He scowled at Barrett, ready to read any signs of disapproval, but Barrett knew that an impassive expression had remained frozen on his face. "They're using my office for this one, and that's my file cabinet back there behind the secretary's desk, but I better not try to get to it until the scene's finished." He edged forward. "Let me see how long it's got to go."

Barrett's attention had gone back to the scene in the making.

The naked girl on the daybed had already unbuttoned the secretary's crisp blouse, and now the kneeling secretary wriggled out of her blouse, cast it aside, stood up, unbuttoned and unzipped her skirt, and stepped out of it. Swiftly she unhooked her brassiere, kicked off her high-heeled pumps, divested herself of garter belt and stockings and flimsy underpants. Now she pirouetted seductively for the girl on the sofa and for the camera, and, doing so, she undid her bunned hair and let it fall to her shoulders in a gesture of liberation and abandonment. Her pear-shaped breasts heaved, her broad buttock with its strawberry mark trembled, and as she came around once more her hand slipped down below the appendix scar to circle her darkly matted vaginal mound teasingly.

Completing her second circle, she looked off at the cameraman, and his hand lifted, directing her to the sofa. Imperceptibly she nodded. In a second she was in the titian-haired girl's arms, and then free of the other's embrace, and then kissing the other's heaving breasts and squirming belly and continuing the amorous foreplay at great length.

The recipient of this lovemaking was now using her hands to direct her partner's head, and as she did this her eyes were shut tightly and she was gasping. Barrett wondered if she was acting or actually becoming sexually aroused. He decided that girls like this couldn't act at all, and that this was for real. And what kind of girls were these, anyway?

He looked at Quandt, and the pornographer's broad forehead glistened, and his close-set eyes shone, and he chewed steadily on the cold cigar as he dribbled from the corner of his mouth. His concentration was intense and total. By God, Barrett thought, he enjoys it. He's in it for love *and* money, the professional Peeping Tom, the true scopophiliac who derives pleasure from watching the sex organs and acts of others. What a field day the American Psychiatric Association might have with a subject like Quandt. According to some psychoanalysts, men's chosen careers were guided by dark and hidden desires. The publicly healing surgeon was subconsciously the sadist finding an outlet in the carving scalpel. The devoted social worker and the charitable clubwoman and the church saint were subconsciously shoring up their neurotic feelings of inferiority by earning the dependence of others, thus providing themselves with feelings of superiority. The analyst himself, sagely listening beside the mentally ill patient on the couch, was in some deep recess of his own ego a voyeur and nothing more. So what were the unknown drives that had brought Quandt to this sick and strange clandestine business of providing sexual excitation by means of a strip of celluloid? And, indeed, thought Barrett, why in the devil had he himself stayed in this room to continue observing what should be a private act being staged under the glare of klieg lights for commercial reasons?

He could not help but see, once more, what was taking place on the daybed. The titian-haired girl on her back, fingers clutching her breasts, torso tautly arched high, was waiting hungrily for fulfillment as the other nude female, between her legs and above her, was fondling a ten-inch hard rubber dildo, the manufactured version of the fantasy penis in millions of minds. As the girl on her knees was about to tie on the dildo, Barrett became aware of a third actor in the room. A sinewy, strapping man in his thirties, who appeared uncomfortable in his conservative business suit, was removing his bowler hat as he viewed the scene with visible annoyance. The girls had seen him now and had ceased their performance, and they cowered before his outrage. He was pointing to the time clock.

Barrett heard Quandt chuckle beside him. Quandt leaned over, grinning, and whispered, "A little touch I put in. The boss arrives at work, finds his two secretaries bare-assed and doing their shtick on his sofa, and all he objects to is that they're wasting office time and not working. Not bad, eh? Watch this."

Barrett watched. Angrily the boss had thrown his hat on a chair, advanced upon his recoiling girls, and snatched the dildo away. He gestured at it with contempt and then held it against his trousers, indicating that it was nothing compared to the real thing, and suddenly he was inviting his girls to make their choice. The histrionic fright of both girls turned to joy, and as the boss dropped the dildo and then his suit coat to the floor, the kneeling girl reached out to help him off with his trousers.

Quandt burst into open laughter and then tried to stifle it, and at once the entire scene came to a standstill. The male actor, stripped down to his shorts, had whirled around at the laughter, and now he eyed Quandt with exasperation.

"Je-sus, Norman, how do you expect me—?" the actor began to complain.

"Sorry, Gil, sorry, I only meant it for a compliment. You go right on. We'll be outside. Go on, go on, don't break the scene, we can't waste time."

Quandt had Barrett by the arm and hustled him out of the office and into the corridor, closing the door softly behind him, shaking his head. "Gil's one of those guys who can't make it if he's reminded that he's being watched. Very temperamental. He's used to the cameraman by now, and that doesn't bother him. But if there's anyone besides the cast in the room, he droops. But I like to use him. I've used him in ten pictures already. If talent could be measured by displacement, Gil would be an Academy Award winner ten times over. When those chippies get through going over him, well, his acting apparatus will make that dildo look like a midget stand-in. What a wang—makes ours look like warts." He eyed Barrett. "First time you've ever seen anything like this?"

"Well, the first time I've ever seen one being made. When I was younger, in college, I saw a few stag films in the frat houses, but that's about it," said Barrett.

"But you never saw one made? Well, what do you think?"

"Every man to his own," said Barrett. "It's just not my type of thing."

"You mean you think it's abnormal," said Quandt with a hint of nastiness in his tone.

"I didn't say that," said Barrett quickly.

"Let me tell you something, maybe teach you a few facts of life from my experience in this business. And from my reading, too. I read plenty. I've even read those Kinsey books. Maybe you didn't, but I did. You know what? In those interviews it was proved that seventy-seven per cent of the males they tested got aroused, got sexy, when they watched portrayals of sexual activity. And as for females, there were even thirty-three per cent of *them* that admitted that stag films and still photographs gave them the hots. What I'm saying is there's a healthy need for this kind of stimulant, see. Did you ever look at pictures of those sculptured carvings on those holy temples in India made nine centuries ago? Those were stag sculptures, and they were there because there was a need for them. That movie I'm making inside my mail-order room, *The Perfect Secretary*, who do you think it's for? For me, to get kicks? Naw. It's for parties in the best college fraternities, and American Legion smokers, and Rotary and Kiwanis meetings where respectable businessmen get together for an evening of relaxation. It's better they get their charges second hand instead of going out and picking up some gash on the street and getting the clap. But that's not all. I'm not just making these pictures to entertain. I'm making them also for scientific reasons, for big universities that keep collections of erotica in order to show all sides of life in our time. You heard that the Kinsey Sex Research Institute at the University of Indiana has a collection of stag reels going back over a half century? Well, you ought to see the list of universities I sell my product to. Our biggest customer is a professor at Reardon College in Wisconsin, Dr. Rolf Lagergren, the sex-survey man—"

"Yes," Barrett interrupted. "I've talked to him on the phone. He's coming here to be one of our witnesses."

"That so? Well, you can bet he'll drop by to see our plant. He and the other profs lay out anywhere from fifty to a hundred bucks to buy prints of each of these four-hundred-foot stags, and they're happy to get them at that price, because it's for science.

How they going to get them for science if somebody doesn't make them? Now, you tell me what's wrong with that."

Although he was an advocate of freedom in all the arts, Barrett was capable of telling Quandt plenty about what was wrong with that, but he knew it would be disastrous to do so. He must not offend Quandt in any way, and he knew it. He evaded Quandt's aggressive question and tried to divert him with a simulated show of interest.

"The girlie or nudie pictures you're making downstairs, those I can readily understand," Barrett said. "That's legal and easy—"

"And the way to the poorhouse," snapped Quandt. "Not enough profit, considering the investment. The stags are easier and sure-fire, and, besides, they're safe. Limited audience. Sold and shown in secrecy. So no civic outcry. And dependable income. If you want to stay in business, idiot laws or no idiot laws, you got to have stags for a sideline."

"But how do you get the—the actors for stag films?"

"That's the easiest part. There are so many young broads giving it out for nothing these days that, comes a day, and some of them get smart and see they can make money doing what comes naturally. We use some prosties, sure, but only the beginners who still got their looks. Mostly we get the girls who can't make it in the major studios, even on the casting couches, and some fashion models who are underpaid, and some neighborhood girls who just get kicks showing it off before thousands of men around the country. Those two broads in there, I'm paying them each a hundred fifty bucks for today's episode. And Gil, he's kept his amateur standing, he plays without pay. He likes to ball it. And why not? His only defect is his pecker. Too big. It's a put-down to many male stag audiences. I like to keep my actors down to six inches or so—for audience identification. But Gil's a great cocksman, puts on a real performance, so I use him. Anyway, someday I'd like to get my hands on someone who becomes a big name in show biz. Then you can replay the same film, especially as rentals, for years. Like some producer in the Southwest, he latched onto that famous stripteaser, the one with the huge bust, you know, Candy Barr. Caught her on the way up about twenty years ago and put her in a stag reel called *Smart Alec*, shot it in a Texas motel on a shoe-string, and later Candy hit the big time and that reel has been an annuity." Quandt paused, studied his watch. "Je-sus, I haven't got much time. Let's see if they're done in there. If they aren't, well, I'll find that autograph dealer's name later and mail it to you."

"Mr. Quandt, I'd give anything to have it right now. The trial's about to start, and any ammunition we have against Duncan . . ."

"Duncan, yeah. Well, let's see."

They went inside, and to Barrett's relief the scene had just been completed. The two girls were seated on the daybed, one lighting a cigarette, the other toweling herself. The male actor was pulling on his trousers. The cameraman had come forward, saying, "Soon's you're ready I'll tell you what we shoot next. It's the one where Gil tries to make a sale to the big buyer from Texas."

Barrett hung back as Quandt proceeded across the room, exchanging a quip with the titian-haired girl, patting a brown teat of the girl with bangs, who giggled. Nervously Barrett waited while Quandt opened a file-cabinet drawer and began to finger through the manila folders. At last he pulled one folder out and began to examine its contents. He returned the folder to the file.

Suddenly, frighteningly, there was an eerie high-pitched buzzing in the room, and a red light above the wall clock began to flash on and off, and Quandt smashed the file drawer shut and shouted, "The alarm, goddammit! You know what to do!"

Barrett was startled not only by the alarm, but by the maelstrom of action in the office. The door behind him had been flung open, and two short swarthy men ran in. A sliding wall beside the daybed had also opened, and the naked girls rushed through it, followed by the cameraman and his equipment, while the two swarthy men took up the klieg light and the other evidences of film-making. In the middle of all this Quandt stood, directing the movements, surveying the room to see if it was in order. In a matter of short seconds the motion-picture set had become transformed into a mail-order office once more.

Barrett saw that Quandt was starting toward him, his features and fists knotted with rage.

"You son of a bitch," he snarled at Barrett, "this is your doing—!"

"I don't know what you're talking about. What's going on?"

"That's a warning from downstairs. The coppers are down there asking for me. Probably the D.A.'s plainclothes goons. And you tipped them—"

"Are you crazy, Quandt? You've read the papers. I'm on the other side."

"Well, it's the first time they've tumbled to this location, and, goddammit, your being here is a pretty damn big coincidence. Until now, they didn't even know I was in business—"

Something had hit Barrett. "Listen, Quandt, listen to me and believe me. That bastard Duncan must have had a tail on me, and they tailed me here. But it's not *you* they're after. It's me! I'm the enemy now. And if they could trap me in your studio—with the stag films—the nudes—me, the big defender of art consorting with illegal pornographers—can't you see the carnival they'd make of it on television and in the newspapers—discrediting me before I got into court—"

Quandt looked off frantically. "I don't know. Maybe you're leveling with me, maybe not. But I guess you're against Duncan, and I got to go with you. Okay, follow me. There's a way out through the back and down under the garage. One of the girls will show you. You'll get out safe and clean."

He had reached the wall beside the sofa, touched the paneling, and the wall slid open again to reveal a narrow passageway.

"Get your ass out of here," ordered Quandt, "and don't let me ever see you near this place again."

"Don't worry," said Barrett. He ducked into the tunnel. He saw Quandt reach to close off the wall. "Mr. Quandt—"

"I don't have any time. I got to meet those coppers downstairs."

"Mr. Quandt," Barrett called out again, "the autograph dealer, the one you sold the Jadway letters to—"

The wall was sliding shut.

And then Barrett heard Quandt's voice. "Olin Adams Autographs —Olin Adams—Fifty-fifth Street—New York."

The wall closed, and Barrett turned away, and in the distance, he could see the light, at last.

IN THE COZY security of his law office an hour and a half later, Mike Barrett had just finished relating his adventure with Norman C. Quandt to Abe Zelkin, who was pacing back and forth in front of Barrett's desk.

"And that Quandt smoked a cigar just like the one you're smoking," Barrett added. "Only you don't dribble and drool the way he does."

Zelkin considered his cigar. "I've got nothing to drool about. He has."

"What a creep." Barrett shook his head. "That stinking business. Close-ups of fellatio, cunnilingus, coitus, sodomy, orgasms, let alone dildos, and all done in the name of sexual liberation and the elevation of science. Maybe those stag films harm no one any more than honestly conceived and executed movies or books harm anyone, yet there is something about the men who create them, the Quandts of the world, that makes me ill. Maybe this sounds inconsistent, Abe, but a man like Norman C. Quandt shouldn't be allowed to stay in business."

"If they ever nab him, he'll get five years."

"Nobody'll catch him. He's too slimy and slippery. Those are the guys who make sex a four-letter word, and make it tough for people like us. It bugs the hell out of me—this is the sad part, Abe —that when we defend freedom of speech and freedom of the press, we're also defending the rights of a whole subterranean reptile community consisting of people like Quandt. They're evil, because they're dishonest. Yet we're forced to have them in our battalion. If you're against censorship, you're made out to be against all censorship. I only wish there were a way to draw the line, select those who deserve defending and those who don't deserve it. But who does the selecting, who separates those with merit from the meretricious? Where is that wisest judge and umpire?"

Zelkin had stopped pacing. His pumpkin face was grave. "Forget it, Mike. We're not defending Quandt. We're defending Jadway. Unwittingly, Quandt may have served freedom, grand as that sounds. He gave you the name of that autograph dealer—Olin Adams, wasn't it?—okay, that may be our biggest gain against Duncan yet. And just in time. Before court adjourned today, we agreed on eight jurors. That leaves four more to decide on tomorrow. If we make it, we'll be ready to go on Monday. I'm grateful for this new break, that's one thing. And I'm grateful that the police didn't find you with Quandt and those naked girls."

"You can say that again. Imagine the headlines. 'Defense Attorney Trapped in Sex Orgy with Topless—and Bottomless—Beauties.' That would have really been curtains for us."

The telephone buzzer sounded, and Barrett picked up the receiver.

It was Donna. "I've got New York, Mr. Barrett. Lucky, we caught Olin Adams just as he was closing shop for the day. He's on the line. Take it on one."

"Thanks, Donna. In case our luck holds, check the earliest flights to New York." He glanced up at Zelkin. "We've got Olin Adams on the other end, Abe. Cross your fingers." Barrett punched the lighted key. "Mr. Olin Adams?"

The voice was distant and gentle. "Yes, sir. What can I do for you, Mr. Barrett?"

"I understand that you acquired a packet of holograph letters about ten days ago—literary letters written in the 1930s by J J Jadway, the author of *The Seven Minutes*. I learned this today from the gentleman who sold them to you."

"The Jadway letters. Yes, I remember. You are quite right."

"Do you still have them on hand, Mr. Adams?" Barrett asked, and then waited anxiously.

"Do I have them? Oh, yes, certainly. I've hardly had time to unpack them, let alone collate them in order to include them in my next catalogue. We've been very busy here going through two large collections, one of Walt Whitman manuscripts and the other of Martin Luther King correspondence, that arrived prior to the Jadway material."

Making a hasty victory sign with his fingers for Zelkin, Barrett concentrated again on the conversation. "Mr. Adams, I'm delighted you still have the Jadway material, because I'm interested in acquiring it. Can you tell me what it consists of?"

"Not exactly, at this moment, Mr. Barrett. The letters are locked up for the night. I was just leaving for home. Perhaps tomorrow—"

"Well, if you could only give me an idea, in general, from memory."

"As I said, I unwrapped the folder they came in a week or two ago and only had time to authenticate the letters. If I recall correctly, there were four pieces, three holograph letters signed by Jadway, and one typescript page with Jadway's signature typed, but on the verso it has the holograph signature of a Miss McGraw, Jadway's inamorata, I understand. In all, about nine pages of material."

"And the contents, Mr. Adams?"

"I hardly remember at this minute. I barely skimmed the material. It's mostly literary—discussions of his writing of the novel and some autobiographical information intended for a book jacket. It is difficult for me to remember more, what with Walt Whitman and—"

"Mr. Adams, I'd like to purchase the Jadway material sight unseen."

"I wouldn't want you to do that. It would be most unwise."

"I don't mind. I must have the letters at once. Can you give me a price?"

"Well, I haven't had time to evaluate—"

"Set a figure, and if you've overpriced the letters I promise you I won't complain."

"Umm. This is difficult, Mr. Barrett. These are the first Jadway letters that have come on the market, to my knowledge, and there's been no auction standard set."

"But you must have some notion, Mr. Adams," persisted Barrett, containing his impatience. "Name a price that you know you'd be happy with."

There was a silence, then the dealer's voice again. "Well, we get fifty dollars for a Sinclair Lewis letter and sometimes two hundred and fifty dollars for a Whitman letter, and while Jadway is neither of these, still he is a rarity, and his recent notoriety may one day lend him a special appeal for certain collectors. It is remotely possible our Jadway packet might one day be worth, umm, let us say perhaps, perhaps as much as eight hundred dollars."

"It's a deal," said Barrett crisply.

The other end of the line was silent again, and when Olin Adams found his voice he sounded confused. "I . . . do you . . . are you saying—?"

"I'm saying I've purchased your Jadway letters for eight hundred dollars. Are you satisfied with the deal?"

"Why—why, yes, sir, if you feel that you are."

"I am, I am."

"Very well, Mr. Barrett, excellent. You have them. If you will mail me your check for the sum and allow time for it to be cleared, I will then send the letters to you by air mail."

"No, I need them more quickly than that, Mr. Adams. I'm flying to New York tonight. What time do you open in the morning?"

"At nine o'clock."

"I'll be in your shop between nine and ten. There'll be no check to clear. I'll pay you in cash. Be sure to have them ready."

"They'll be ready for you, Mr. Barrett. Yes, thank you, thank you very much."

"See you in the morning then."

Barrett dropped the receiver into the telephone cradle and beamed up at Zelkin.

"Good work," said Zelkin, rubbing his hands together. "Now we've got something. Jadway speaking from the grave, hopefully to refute Leroux's contention that he was a commercialist and pornographer. Isabel Vogler to refute Jerry Griffith's testimony that the book alone was what unhinged him. Things are looking up."

"That reminds me. Abe, will you call Mrs. Vogler and tell her I'm off to New York, but I'll phone her when I get back later tomorrow? I definitely want to see her tomorrow. Tell her to sit tight."

"Will do."

The buzzer sounded again, and it was Donna.

"Two things, Mr. Barrett. Your airplane reservations for New York. I've got a hold on flights going out of International at eight tonight and another at nine. That'll get you into Kennedy pretty late."

"I'm taking no chances. Make it the eight-o'clock flight. And get on long distance again and call The Plaza. I'll need a single for late tonight."

"The other thing, Mr. Barrett. While you were on the phone with Mr. Adams, there was a call from Miss Osborn. She said it was urgent and she wants you to call her right back."

"Urgent? Okay, get her for me before you do the rest." He looked up at Zelkin. "I've got to talk to Faye. Something urgent, whatever that means."

"I'll leave you," said Zelkin. "I'll be in my office, calling Mrs. Vogler. Look in on me before you punch out."

Moments after Zelkin left, Barrett was on the phone with Faye Osborn.

The tension in her voice was immediately apparent. "Mike, I know you canceled out on me tonight because you're loaded with work, but I've got to see you. It's terribly important."

"Faye, I'm sorry, it's not only work now—it's work in New York. I'm flying out of here at eight o'clock. But I'll be back tomorrow."

"Mike, it simply can't wait. I've got to speak to you tonight."

"But I told you . . ." He hesitated. "Can't you speak to me now? What's it all about?"

"No, I can't speak to you now."

"Then on the way to the airport. You can drive me."

"No, Mike. This needs a quiet place, and I don't know how long it'll take. We may need a couple of hours." Then, with emphasis, she added, "Mike, this involves your whole future, yours and ours."

This sounded urgent, and it troubled him. "Well, since you put it that way, I'll tell you what. Donna can change my reservation, try to get me the midnight flight out of International, and I can grab some sleep on the plane. I'll have my overnighter with me in the car, and maybe I should allow an hour to get to the airport from town. Want to make it at eight-thirty or nine?"

"I need some time with Dad before seeing you. Make it nine. Where?"

"Let's say the Century Plaza. There's a convivial room downstairs. The Granada Bar. Want to meet me there?"

"At nine sharp," Faye agreed. "I'll be there."

She hung up.

Barrett sat thinking.

Faye had said, *This involves your whole future, yours and ours.* Faye had also said, *I need some time with Dad before seeing you.*

Completely enigmatic, yet vaguely threatening.

After a while, still troubled, he buzzed Donna to tell her to change his airplane reservation.

HE HAD a table in the rear of the Granada Bar. Before him was the Scotch on the rocks which as yet he had not touched. The hotel barroom was half filled, but he was hardly conscious of the constant jabbering of the tourists and transient drummers. He was ready for Olin Adams in New York. His overnighter was in his car and the eight hundred dollars in bills was in an envelope in his inside jacket pocket, along with his wallet. He was not ready for Faye Osborn. He had finally concluded that she had delayed his departure over some frivolous personal matter, and he felt faintly resentful.

Also, she was late, and he was restless.

He had been waiting fifteen minutes, and had begun to drink his Scotch, when he saw her arrive. She was wearing the pale-beige silk coat. As she tried to locate him among the customers at the long bar counter, he half rose, waving, trying to catch her eye, and then he did. Faye came toward him rapidly, and he stood up fully to receive her.

"Darling," she said. She offered her cheek, and he kissed it, and then she slid in behind the table, and he settled down next to her.

"Shall I check your coat?" he asked.

"No, I'll keep it around my shoulders."

He helped her out of it and draped it across her shoulders. Her silk shantung cocktail dress was new.

"That's a nice dress," he said.

"Thank you, Mike," she said, but gave him no appreciative smile. Her face was thin and drawn, almost tight. "What are you having? Scotch? No, thanks. I'll have a crème-de-menthe frappé."

The uniformed waitress was cheerful and cute, and he ordered the crème de menthe and another Scotch.

"Sorry to keep you," she said. "I had to speak to Dad again, and he was late coming from wherever he was, and we talked our way through dinner and kept talking after, and I simply couldn't leave as soon as I had intended."

More enigma, Mike thought. "We have plenty of time," he said.

"Why are you going to New York so suddenly?"

"I'm still on the trail of Jadway's past. There may be some vital information there that will be useful in court."

"I thought maybe you'd found another witness."

"No, not this time. Unless something else turns up, I think we have all the witnesses we'll need."

She started to say something, but held back until the waitress had served them the drinks and laid down the plate of cashews.

"Mike—" she said.

Barrett had already hoisted his fresh drink. "Cheers."

"Yes, cheers," she said, taking up her green drink and sipping briefly at the two short straws set in the shaved ice. Setting down the glass, she added, "Anyway, I hope it is."

"Hope what is?"

"Cheers—cheery, cheerier—after we've talked."

"Faye, I wish you'd tell me what this is about."

She came around to face him. "It's about your witnesses," she said. "At least, one of them."

"Meaning?"

"When we spoke at noon today, or whenever it was—remember?—you told me you'd just found a new witness for the defense. That woman, Isabel Vogler, who used to work for the Griffith family."

"That's right."

"And you were so enthusiastic because that horrible woman was going to take the stand and prove—how did you put it?—that Mr. Griffith was 'anything but a paragon of virtue' and that he'd done more harm to his son than a dozen books. I believe that's what you said."

"Right again."

"And you said something to the effect that not Dad nor any of his friends had the slightest idea of what Frank Griffith was like in private."

"And you thought Isabel Vogler was finky to expose the facts about her former employer on the witness stand."

"More than finky. It's downright immoral and rotten."

"Whereas it's not immoral or rotten for District Attorney Duncan to parade witnesses who will malign a dead author who can no longer defend himself," he said caustically, "and it's not wrong to provide public entertainment by propping up in the witness box an emotionally disturbed young man who has no place in this trial, but is being used the same way Hitler used that poor demented Dutch boy, van der Lubbe, to achieve personal political power?" He made an effort to control himself. "You consider that moral and decent?"

"Mike, please stop it," Faye said with exasperation. "Why do you always do that? I can't stand that habit of yours, of forever reducing what anyone says to lawyer's arguments, of constantly obscuring truth with double-talk smoke screens. Can't you, this one time, leave your law diploma in the office and speak to me like a human being? It is after hours, you know. If you want me to stoop to your argument, I could. That author of yours, Jadway, he's dead and buried, and nothing Elmo Duncan says will do him harm. And as for Jerry, he is a confessed rapist, and he is ruined and he is going to jail, and anything Duncan does with him won't hurt him any further. But your use of someone like Isabel Vogler—that can be damaging to someone who is living and whose reputation is impeccable. Like anyone in public life, Frank Griffith is vulnerable to an attack of lies. His reputation and business could be damaged beyond repair by some common domestic whom he had been forced to fire and who now sees a chance to get even. She's vicious. It appalls me that you'd condone, let alone support and encourage, her spouting these falsehoods. And for what? I know, I know, to make some minor point in court, that maybe it wasn't that filthy book alone that was to blame for Jerry's act, maybe instead it was his father. Really, Mike, knowing you as I do, caring for you as I have, I can't believe this is you who is doing such a thing."

"Can't you?" he said angrily.

"No. Because you are better than that. Oh, dammit, let's not go on with this. It seems we're always fighting lately, and I don't want any more arguments." She bent her head and took a sip of the crème de menthe. "How did we get sidetracked like this?"

"Did we get sidetracked, Faye?" he said more evenly.

Slowly she met his gaze, and then she frowned. "No, maybe we didn't. All right. I'll tell you why I had to see you. You had called me back at noon, and you had mentioned Isabel Vogler. Well, Dad was still home, and maybe he overheard some of my conversation with you, before I told him about your latest witness. I thought I should tell him, because I wanted to know how he would feel about it. You know very well that Dad and Frank Griffith have had a long and rewarding business relationship. They respect one another and they're fond of one another, and Mr. Griffith is responsible for placing a large amount of his clients' advertising in prime time slots on Dad's television stations. So, naturally, you can understand how Dad felt when he heard that you were going to use a witness to malign Frank Griffith."

"And how *did* Dad feel?" he said, mimicking her.

Her features had become rigid. "Are you being sarcastic?"

Dad's daughter, wow, he thought. He had stepped in where angels fear to tread. He changed his tone. "I just want to know how your father felt about that."

"That's better. I'll tell you how he felt. He felt concerned enough to pay a visit to Mr. Griffith and to reveal to him what you were up to—to forewarn a friend, to prepare him for any libel Mrs. Vogler might be spouting forth. Then Dad called me from Griffith's office, and he made it clear to me that Griffith was furious with Mrs. Vogler and just as furious with you for even considering using that harridan publicly in court. Dad was convinced, after his talk with Frank Griffith, that Mrs. Vogler is a psychopathic liar, a really dangerous person to have around—unreliable, fishwifey, a troublemaker, resentful of every employer who's ever fired her for having those faults, and, like all those domestics who are forever brooding about their lot in life, a paranoiac who just wants to have revenge on her betters."

"I see," said Barrett. He was beginning to see a good deal, and he was beginning to see that this was an important meeting between Faye and himself. "So your father believes Frank Griffith, and you do, too?"

"Don't you, now that you've heard this? If it's that wretched woman's word against the word of someone with Mr. Griffith's integrity, can there be any choice?"

"Because he's one of her betters?"

"What did you say, Mike? I didn't hear you."

"Nothing, it was nothing."

"Anyway, after Dad saw Mr. Griffith and called me, he asked me to call you. He wanted me to speak to you about the whole thing. Then, when I phoned Dad back to say you'd agree to delay your trip to see me, Dad said he wanted to talk to me first before I met you. So that was at dinner and after, and that was why I was late."

"So now you've told me," said Barrett.

"Not quite, Mike, not all of it. I haven't told you yet what Dad discussed with me at dinner."

Barrett took up his drink, almost drained the glass of Scotch, and now he was ready. "Okay, tell me."

She sat perfectly erect, and she looked businesslike, as businesslike as Willard Osborn II had ever been. "Mike, we're too close to beat around the bush. I've always been forthright with you, and I assume you've always been the same way with me. So I'll simply say what I've come here to say, and I know you'll take it the way it's meant, because I know you are inherently responsible and have a strong sense of decency. And I know I can speak out frankly because Dad likes you and I care for you, and we believe you feel the same way about us."

Us. He heard the us. All right, us, let's have it. "What do you want to say to me, Faye?"

She moved the straws around the melting shaved ice in her drink.

"It comes to this," she said. "Dad wants me to tell you that any thought you have of using Isabel Vogler on the witness stand is out of the question. He simply cannot let you go ahead with it, not only for Mr. Griffith's sake but for your own. He was positive you'd understand, and I promised him that I'd see that you did. Dad felt that in going along with him you'd be making only the smallest compromise, the kind people in big business are used to making all the time, every day. When you're in the driver's seat, you get someone else to compromise. Then when you're not, you compromise. It's part of getting along, and getting things done smoothly, and getting ahead. It is part of his business, he said, and soon you'll be an important man in his business, and so it is also to your advantage not to antagonize, let alone crucify, a friend upon whose goodwill you and Dad will often be dependent. Dad was certain you'd be reasonable about this, and I assured Dad that once I spoke to you there would be no problem."

There it was.

And where was he?

Memory had carted him back to his sophomore year in college, the year he had collected epigrams, aphorisms, quotations, snatches of sagacity to counsel and direct him and to make him the wiser. There had been intimations of reality when he had

289

noted, courtesy of Juvenal, that integrity is praised, and starves. There had been a final understanding of self when he had realized that, even as Coleridge's Ancient Mariner, he was

> *Like one, that on a lonesome road*
> *Doth walk in fear and dread,*
> *And having once turned round walks on,*
> *And turns no more his head;*
> *Because he knows, a frightful fiend*
> *Doth close behind him tread.*

At last he had seen the fiend. Once more, as so long ago, he walked in fear and dread. Dare he walk on, sure that never, never again would he turn his head?

He stared at her. The composed and confident face of the betters. He revived her command, daughter's Dad's command, that to use Isabel Vogler on the witness stand was out of the question. Dad was certain he'd be reasonable. Daughter had assured Dad that there would be no problem.

"But there is a problem, Faye," he said, and then like the Ancient Mariner he walked on and did not turn his head. "Because, you see, I am going to put Isabel Vogler on the witness stand."

The moving fault beneath, the small quake, and her surface composure cracked. "Mike, you can't mean it, not after what I've just told you. Dad said doing it is out of the question. He won't have her on the stand."

"But I will."

The seismographs of the betters shook, and the crack in Faye's composure widened into open disbelief. "You're teasing me, aren't you? If you are, it's cruel, but if you'll just say it's a joke, I'll forgive you. This is serious, Mike, I can't tell you how serious."

"That's why I'm treating it seriously."

"Mike, you've got a dozen witnesses for that trial—all you need, you said. Why is it so important to you to try to oppose Dad and destroy Mr. Griffith? That witch of a charwoman isn't worth it."

"But truth is, truth is worth it, especially in this trial."

"This trial," she repeated with impotent rage. "I'm bloody sick of this trial, that book, what they've done to you. I'm sick of it, do you hear?" She grabbed hold of his sleeve. "Mike, you listen to me, because it's the last time I'll say this. From the start, Dad was dead set against your becoming involved in the case. He simply wouldn't have it. And I knew he was right. He is always right about matters of that kind. Yet I was caught in between the two of you, and even though I knew it was wrong I wanted to help you. That's why I talked Dad into holding the vice-presidency open and letting you fulfill your commitment to defend your publishing friend's book. Now I regret it, I regret what I did. By going along with you, I've simply allowed you to sink deeper and deeper into muck. I should have put my foot down at the beginning, agreed with Dad, and we'd have prevented all this abrasion, and we'd have all been happier. But there's still time. I couldn't live with myself if I didn't act on your behalf. Mike, please do as I say. Don't allow that character assassination on Frank Griffith. Drop the Vogler woman from your case, and I promise you everything will be as it was between you and Dad."

He continued to stare at her. When he spoke, his words were measured. "I appreciate what you want to do for me, Faye. I appreciate why your father wants you to make me back down about Griffith. But I'm afraid he's wrong—I know he's wrong—and I believe you're wrong. I'm not going to subvert the truth to give aid and comfort to two business cronies, and I'm not joining any cabal to undermine a defense of free speech."

Her cheeks had reddened. "I hate it when you sound like a boy scout flaunting his merit badges. I don't like the snide way you referred to my father and Mr. Griffith."

"That's your problem, Faye, the way you feel about your father."

"And your problem is the way Dad feels about you, once I step aside and stop protecting you. I'm stepping aside right now, Mike. You've just graduated from boy scout, and you'd better be ready for what's out there in the grown-up world. If you don't know, I'll tell you, because you've forced me to be blunt. I'm going to tell you what I've refrained from telling you up to now. I mean, the rest of what Dad told me tonight."

"You can spare me that."

"I'll spare you nothing," said Faye. "Dad told me if you refused to be sensible and cooperative about the Vogler matter, then you just weren't the kind of person who could possibly fit into Osborn Enterprises." She paused meaningfully. "This time, Mike, I'm agreeing with Dad."

Fear had passed. He had left the fiend far behind. "Perhaps I'm not the sort of person who should ever have become involved with Osborn Enterprises," he said calmly.

"Mike, do you know what you're saying, doing? If you are bullheaded enough to reject Dad's request, to throw away the position he's held for you, then you are plainly rejecting me also. You are making our relationship, and any future we might have had, impossible. If you are going to be stubborn and turn down Dad and Mr. Griffith, then I'd better tell you that I am part of that package. I simply couldn't go on with you."

"I'd always hoped I was going with a girl, not a girl and her father."

"I meant what I said. I couldn't go on with you."

"I'd be sorry about that, Faye."

"Then you refuse to change your mind?"

"I refuse to be coerced. If I surrender my independence, my privilege to think and perform as I believe I should right now, if I compromise to please Faye and father right now, I'll be doing just that for the rest of my life with both of you. That wouldn't be much of a life for any man, would it?"

Faye had become livid. "Any man? You call yourself a man? Why, you're behaving like a fool, a child and a fool, and you're diminished in my eyes. But I still won't accept it. I can't believe you'd give up everything to defend your little house of filth and slime. I won't accept it."

"You'd better, because that's the way it's going to be. I can't meet your terms, Faye."

"You *are* a fool." She gathered up her purse and gloves. "If you're through with my father, I'm through with you. And you won't win that trial, you know. You'll be left with nothing. You'll just be a shabby frayed-cuff ambulance chaser because once, when you had the chance, you didn't have the guts to think big and be big. I never saw it before, but I see it now. You're second-rate, Mike, and I have time for only what's first-rate." She stood up, but she did not leave. She looked down at him. "I'm going, Mike. Once I'm gone, I'm never coming back. If you want one last chance to come along, I might give it to you. I'm not sure I would, but I might. Do you have anything more you want to say?"

He half rose, and offered her a mock bow. "Darling, the defense rests."

"You can go to hell."

Later, after he'd had one more drink for the road, and paid his bill, he realized for the first time how utterly liberated he felt, liberated and relieved. He was glad to be done with Faye. About Osborn Enterprises, and his aborted future, he was less certain. But of one thing he was absolutely certain. He was no longer afraid.

He had turned his head.

The fiend was gone.

He was ready for New York and whatever lay before him.

VI

THEN, AS HE CONTINUED walking up Fifth Avenue, caught in the shadows of the mammoth skyscrapers, jostled and stopped and hurried and slowed by the frenetic movement of foot and vehicle traffic, Mike Barrett realized what was happening to him.

It had been defined by Emerson, who had not even seen the towering General Motors Building or the Seagram Building or Rockefeller Center or the careening taxicabs or the fuming buses or the lumbering trucks or the crush of hastening pedestrians. Emerson describing it. Great cities give us collision, and a city like New York takes the nonsense out of man. It was in that moment that New York took the nonsense out of Mike Barrett.

And it was then that the impact of Manhattan hit him fully, as if from behind, catapulting him toward his destination on Fifty-fifth Street, driving him to quicken his pace and alert his senses, revitalizing him with an awareness of the significance of his immediate mission.

Since the moment, last night, when Faye Osborn had left him for good, he had found himself liberated, yet liberated only to float in an inner vacuum.

Throughout most of the long, dark night, reclining in his seat in the jet airliner that was hurtling him from Los Angeles, late village of hope, to New York, old city of failure, he had reconsidered his behavior with Faye and Willard Osborn II and wondered whether he had been rash. Of course, there could always be the shingle reading "Zelkin and Barrett, Counselors at Law," but the promise of that career flickered low and offered too little light for a brighter tomorrow.

Faye had not been right for him, he had subconsciously known, at least not perfectly right, but she had been someone exciting, glamorous, amusing, her very presence in his life a flattery, and he had become accustomed to her and the rosy paradise she symbolized, and now she was gone, too. And he possessed no antidote against loneliness. In those hours on the plane, he had thought of Maggie Russell, of course, and he had enjoyed envisioning her, yet he had not been able to grasp and hold her fully. She had been evasive, elusive, refusing to join him, always returning to the camp of the enemy, where he was forbidden to follow. He supposed that he must have dozed on the plane to have evoked all those confused and uncertain imaginings.

But the point was, during the entire flight, he had not once given a thought to the purpose of his mission or to the courtroom trial in which he was to be a leading player.

In the taxi from Kennedy Airport to The Plaza hotel he had been unable to think of the trial. Of course, he had been sleepy, but even the early-morning daylight in New York and the vitality of the city arousing around him had not awakened him. He had ridden up in the elevator of The Plaza to the seventh floor, gone to his room, undressed, set his alarm, and fallen on the bed like a log. Perhaps the alarm had rung, or perhaps he had forgotten to wind it. But he had not heard it and he had overslept. He had meant to nap for an hour and be at Olin Adams Autographs by nine o'clock, but then he had slept until a few minutes after ten.

Showering, he had told himself that there was no real reason for haste. He had purchased the Jadway letters, and he could read them at his leisure on the return trip to Los Angeles this day. Except he had wanted to get back to the battleground early, to have plenty of time with Isabel Vogler, and enough time for final pretrial preparation with Abe Zelkin over the weekend, before Judge Nathaniel Upshaw and the bailiff opened the trial on Monday morning. Still, going west, he would have the advantage of regaining three lost hours. And so, more relaxed, after showering, shaving, dressing, he had gone down into the lobby, bought *The New York Times* at the tobacco stand, and continued into the Edwardian Room for a breakfast of orange juice, buttered toast, and coffee. His only concession to haste had been to skip his usual bacon and eggs.

He had skimmed the newspaper, read carefully only the prominent story on page three which reported the selection of the jury in the case of the People of California versus Ben Fremont, and which summarized the issues at stake in the case and misspelled his own name twice. What dismayed him most was not the quotation from Christian Leroux on Jadway's commercialism or the one from Frank Griffith on the necessity for the impressionable young like his son to be shielded from vicious literature, but the fact that there was not a single quotation from Zelkin or himself. This omission, which reflected their lack of powerful defense witnesses, was glaringly evident in the news stories. Yet Barrett remembered that they had a strength which had remained unannounced and secret. There was now Isabel Vogler to offset the Griffith boy—and there was Jadway speaking for himself in the packet of letters five blocks away. Despite these thoughts, by the time he had turned to the sports page the trial had no more reality than a dream. Between the box scores of yesterday's baseball games he saw only the ruin he had made of his Main Chance, and he saw only a future of time payments and loans and being forever the fourth at bridge.

At a quarter to eleven, he had emerged from The Plaza into the peculiarly stifling humidity of this antagonistic city and headed toward Fifth Avenue, and along it to wherever he was going.

And then it was that the impact of the city had hit him. For it was that very quality of the place, which at first, as always, he had found oppressive—the too muchness of it, the not caring of it, the inhumanity of it—that had suddenly regenerated and stimulated him. This was New York's other peculiarity, and its wonder, finally. That here, in the superday, there was no time for nonsense or trivia or introspection. To survive its cold bigness, you had to move, to go, to achieve. If you did not come alive and fight the city, and overcome it, grow as large as it was and larger, you would be buried under it and lost. Once it had buried him under. Now he knew its trick. Suddenly he had reacted to its challenge, and there was no more nonsense in him. He was a man with identity, with purpose, with a cause, and he had someplace to go.

Soon he was turning off Fifth Avenue and going energetically toward the shop that housed Olin Adams Autographs. After that, armed with his treasure, he would be going home to join in a fray, a battle that would be watched by the earth's millions, to joust with the black knights of suppression. It was a future, and a commitment. Faye and her roseate paradise and his brief mourning had vanished.

He was alive and excited.

Striding down Fifty-fifth Street, counting off the store and office-building numbers, he realized that his destination was one block farther along. He dashed across Madison Avenue to beat the changing light and went on until, several doors before Park Avenue, he came upon the display window which bore the elongated block lettering: OLIN ADAMS AUTOGRAPHS, FOUNDED 1921, WE BUY AND SELL. The window was filled with attractively framed holograph letters and manuscripts and ephemera of the famous, but he did not bother with them. He was too eager for Jadway now.

He opened the door, and a bell rang overhead, and he took in the wide room that resembled a miniature reproduction of a manuscript room in the British Museum. There were glass-topped showcases scattered everywhere, and behind them the walls were hung with original autographed letters and photographs or portraits of the writers of these letters. Each letter was coupled with its author's portrait and hung in a double frame. A blue sign said "Items on display are for sale. Please inquire for price." At a rectangular antique table, a chunky young woman, who looked like she had attended Vassar and excelled in lacrosse, was concentrating on sorting out a pile of rare letters and enclosing each in an individual transparent acetate folder.

Barrett went directly to her. "Pardon me, but is Mr. Olin Adams around? He's expecting me."

"I believe he's still on the phone. Let me see."

She hurried through a doorway that revealed a portion of a sizable office, although Olin Adams himself was not visible. Barrett waited, and then she was back. "He'll be finished in a minute," she said. She indicated a cane-backed chair. "Make yourself comfortable."

"Thanks." But Barrett was too restless to sit. Instead, he wandered through the showroom and was soon absorbed by the framed materials hung on the walls. To the bottom of each frame there was taped a typewritten description of the item for sale.

Here was a "Kennedy, John F., T.L.s, 1 p., 4to; Congress of the United States, House of Representatives, Washington, 12. Dec. 1951. To American Consular Administrative Officer, Hong Kong." Next to it a "Douglass, Frederick, A.M.s, 1 p., 8vo; American Negro writer and lecturer. Washington, Oct. 20, 1883." Then, "Toulouse-Lautrec, Henri de, A.L.S. in French, pencil, 2 p., 8vo; French artist. Paris, Nov. 11, 1899." Then there was an original signed check for fifty pounds made out to Leigh Hunt by Percy Bysshe Shelley in 1817, and a prescription written out in German in Vienna during 1909 and signed "Dr. Sigmund Freud," and a blue manuscript penned by Alexandre Dumas *père* in 1858, and an undecipherable undated letter scrawled by Sir Walter Scott, and a document signed "A. Lincoln" and a poem signed by F. Scott Fitzgerald and the fragment of a manuscript by Jean-Jacques Rousseau and a part of a composition unsigned but known to be by Ludwig van Beethoven.

To Mike Barrett, this was an experience new and thrilling. He had known that manuscripts, documents, letters written or signed by renowned men and women through all of civilized time had been collected and preserved in the remote recesses of awesome libraries and museums. And, while he had heard of private collectors, and autograph dealers, he had never considered the possibility that precious papers of presidents and kings, authors and artists, scientists and sages were being marketed like Kleenex or cigarettes or a can of peas. Yet here they were for Everyman in a public shop on Fifty-fifth Street, and they could be acquired and actually taken home for the smallest payment. If you wanted the company of Paul Gauguin or Johann Wolfgang von Goethe or Henry VIII, you could have it, that intimacy of long ago, for your own and in your own home. It was incredible, and what was more incredible was that here, in this shop, he could touch history, and know it had been true.

There was something about the heroes and rulers and creators and martyrs of other centuries that was unbelievable. It was as if they were inventions from folklore, myths without human attributes of their own; and though their stories were known and told, it was as if textbooks and biographies and museums had merely mummified them and solidified them as legend. But here on these walls, they were flesh—the misspelled word, the blotted page, the last-minute insertion, the cry of anguish—and, were they from Lord Byron's hand or Sarah Bernhardt's hand, you believed, at last, and finally saw that history was not monuments and statues, but people as frail as your very own self.

And this moment, in this marketplace pantheon, the person of J J Jadway was real to Barrett for the first time in all these weeks. Soon he would see what Jadway's own hand had committed to sheets of paper, and Barrett would hold these sheets, and hear Jadway's own voice, and touch him through the paper he had touched, and Jadway would be transformed into a living witness prepared to defend *The Seven Minutes* before a skeptical world.

He turned around, more eager than ever to know Jadway, and as he did so he saw a gangling New Englander emerge from the rear office and approach him. The proprietor's gray hair stood up like a rooster's comb, and his eyes were watery gray, and his nose was long. He wore a vest and a watch chain and an air of diffident courtesy.

The proprietor smiled tentatively. "I am Olin Adams," he said in a voice attuned to hushed alcoves. "My assistant said you wished to see me. Is there anything here—?"

"Yes, I called you from the West Coast yesterday. We discussed the J J Jadway letters you recently acquired. You agreed to sell them to me for eight hundred dollars and I promised I'd be by to pick them up this morning. I'm Michael Barrett, remember?"

Olin Adams' watery eyes swam with confusion, and his mouth had opened and remained open, so that he looked like a banked perch. "Who did you say—?" he asked.

"I'm Michael Barrett and I've just flown in from Los Angeles. I'm sure you remember our discussion about the Jadway letters."

"Yes, certainly, but . . ."

Barrett threw open his hands cheerfully and smiled. "Well, I'm here to pick them up."

The autograph dealer tried to focus through the mist. "But, sir, a Mr. Barrett has already picked them up."

"Mr. Barrett has already—?" Now it was Mike Barrett's turn to be confused. "I'm sure I don't understand you."

"Sir, a gentleman came by a minute or two after we opened at nine o'clock, and he picked up the letters."

"You must be mistaken. Let me explain. I telephoned you yesterday—"

"I recall every detail, sir. A Mr. Barrett telephoned from Los Angeles stating that he had heard from Mr. Quandt that I possessed the Jadway letters. I offered them for eight hundred dollars, and Mr. Barrett said he would be in New York and drop by to pick them up between nine and ten this morning. When I came in this morning, I got the letters ready. Then, before going out for breakfast, I told Mildred—my assistant here—that a Mr. Michael Barrett was expected, and to give him the letters when he arrived in exchange for eight hundred dollars in cash. I stepped out for my coffee, and twenty minutes later, when I returned, Mildred said that Mr. Barrett had come by and had paid and departed."

All through the last, Barrett had been shaking his head like one afflicted by a seizure. "But that can't be!" he exclaimed. "I can prove who I am! Look!" He pulled out his wallet and showed the puzzled autograph dealer his identification cards, and then he opened the envelope he had carried with the wallet and revealed eight crisp one-hundred-dollar bills. "Now do you believe me, Mr. Adams?"

The dealer appeared dazed. "I believe you, sir, Mr. Barrett, but —but, hell's fire, then who was it that came by and took away your purchase this morning?"

"That's what I want you to tell me. Who was it?"

"I—I haven't the faintest notion. No idea, no more than you have. It was just a natural thing, the way it happened. We expected a Mr. Barrett to come for the Jadway material. A man came, said he was Mr. Barrett, asked for the Jadway material, paid for it, took it, and left. There was no reason to suspect that he was an impostor."

"What did he look like?" Barrett demanded. "Did he look like me?"

Olin Adams turned. "Mildred, you saw the customer—"

The girl with the lacrosse legs had joined them. "Nothing like you," she said. "He was much taller, and formal, very dignified. I didn't pay much attention. So many people come and go who aren't regulars. He wore a brown—sort of gabardine—suit, that I remember. It all took no more than a minute, I guess. He came in and said something like 'I believe you had some autographed letters for me. They are by J J Jadway. I'd like to pick them up now. I'm Mr. Barrett.' Well, I had the letters ready in a box, and he didn't even bother to examine them. He said he was in a hurry. He paid, took the box, and rushed out. I'm not sure, but I think there was a car waiting for him, double-parked, not a taxi but a private car. There was nothing more to it. How was I to know he wasn't the real buyer?"

"Of course, you're not to blame," said Barrett.

Olin Adams had waved the girl off, and he addressed himself to Barrett once more. "This has never before happened in all my years in this business."

"How did he pay for the letters, Mr. Adams? Could he possibly have paid by check?"

"No, it was cash. When I returned from coffee, Mildred showed me the cash in the drawer."

Barrett nodded grimly. "I'm not surprised. Anyone knowing enough to know that I'd bargained for the Jadway letters, that I intended to come here early this morning ready to pay eight hundred dollars for them, would have known that I expected to pay in cash. Besides, someone impersonating me obviously wouldn't be able to give his personal check."

"I wish I could do something for you, Mr. Barrett," said Adams. He shrugged. "I'm afraid it is hopeless. I can only promise you, sir, if more Jadway material shows up I'll know who to notify and offer it to."

"No more Jadway material will show up, Mr. Adams."

"I appreciate your feelings, Mr. Barrett. I understand how keenly collectors feel about each acquisition. But I must say, if you'll permit me, I shouldn't take this loss too much to heart. I don't question my customers' tastes, but in this case let me say Jadway as a literary figure still remains a question mark, and it is quite possible he will never exceed the status of a one-book author who wrote a work that was merely a curiosity and reaped passing notoriety. You might spend the same sum you had earmarked for Jadway more profitably on—well, if your interest is in American authors of the 1930s I would recommend letters and memorabilia of Faulkner, Hemingway, possibly Fitzgerald. I think you will find, as a collector—"

"Mr. Adams, I am not a collector. I'm not interested in collecting Jadway. I'm only interested in defending him. I am the attorney representing Sanford House and Ben Fremont—"

Olin Adams' mouth was open and perchlike again. "My God," he said.

"Exactly. So the loss is irreparable. We know almost nothing about Jadway, and these letters might have—" He paused. "Mr. Adams, yesterday I asked you about the contents of the letters. You didn't know their contents, because you hadn't had time to read them. Had you by chance this morning . . . ?"

The autograph dealer shook his head sadly. "I'm sorry, but no. I opened the shop, and took out the packet in case you called on us before I returned from coffee. If you hadn't called by the time I returned, I meant to peruse them."

"But you're sure the letters were genuine, even though you've never seen Jadway's handwriting before?"

"I had seen it before, Mr. Barrett. Before I received the letters from Mr. Quandt, I had obtained photostats of the flyleaves of several copies of the first edition of *The Seven Minutes*, which Jadway had inscribed in Paris. The inscriptions bore nothing significant, a mere salutation or a signature, but they were sufficient to enable me to authenticate the letters fully. Yes, those letters were in Jadway's hand." Olin Adams' countenance was a study in sorrow. "Too bad, especially since I am sympathetic toward your legal case. I've been less than helpful. And my apologies for not recognizing your name yesterday or today."

"Far too many people seem to know my name—and about my activities," said Barrett wryly. "And someone or some of them seem bent on blocking every effort of the defense. How this job was pulled off baffles me completely."

"You are positive you spoke to no one of your attempt to acquire these Jadway letters?"

"Except for Quandt, who put me onto you, and my associates and secretary, no one knew of this, as far as I can remember." Then another thought had come to Barrett. His brain was functioning more clearly now that the initial shock of his loss had begun to recede. He was once more filled with desperate purpose. "What about you, Mr. Adams? Think carefully. Did you speak to anyone else, besides me, about these Jadway letters?"

"Yes, of course. We keep a record of our regular customers,

and their specialties and interests. When I acquired the Jadway letters—don't forget, that was ten, eleven days ago—Mildred reviewed the list. There was one gentleman, a poet of sorts, who used to drop by here once in a while, to browse, to chat, in fact to try to raise money by disposing of some of his own original manuscripts, which were of no value to us since he had no reputation whatsoever. But Mildred reminded me that on one occasion, reminiscing about his younger days, this gentleman spoke of having been a literary expatriate in Paris and of having been acquainted with J J Jadway. That had made no impression on me, because, at the time, Jadway's name was practically unknown except among collectors of erotica. When was that occasion, Mildred?"

"More than a year ago," she answered. "Maybe closer to two years ago, when I first came to work here."

"Yes," said Olin Adams. "In any event, when I acquired the Jadway letters, the author's name had become better known, and Mildred recalled this poet who had been acquainted with Jadway. On the outside chance that this poet's lot might have improved, and that he might be interested in owning the Jadway material, I contacted him. I received a curt postcard back saying only, 'Can't afford.' Then—By Jupiter, it had almost slipped my mind—yesterday, after you had telephoned me, Mr. Barrett, this same gentleman called on the telephone. I was half out of the shop door, but I returned to take the call. He said that he had got his hands on a few dollars and he would be interested in the letters so that they might form part of his collection at some university. I told him I was sorry, but that he was too late by five minutes. I told him that I had just sold them to another Jadway collector, a Mr. Michael Barrett, of Los Angeles, and that in fact Mr. Barrett was going to be in New York in the morning to pick them up. Our poet was disappointed, but he made me promise that if you failed to pick up the letters or changed your mind, I would notify him."

"This poet," said Barrett, finding his notebook and pencil, "what was his name?"

"Uh, let me see. . . . Irish . . . ah, yes—Mr. Sean O'Flanagan. That's it."

Barrett had jotted down the name. "His phone number?"

"He has no phone."

303

"His address, then. I'd like to pay him a visit."

"No address either, except General Delivery, Queens main post office. That's how I contacted him. If he is any use to you, you might drop him a note there."

"I might," said Barrett, putting away his notebook. He peered past Adams at the girl named Mildred. He said, "Mildred, the man who came by for the letters this morning, using my name, you're sure he wasn't this Sean O'Flanagan?"

She shook her head vigorously. "Not in a million years. I know our Sean. He's seedy, looks as disreputable as a Bowery bum, and he stinks of whiskey. The one who came by this morning—one never knows, but he looked like a gentleman."

"Then there was the other call," said Adams suddenly. "I'm beginning to think my mind is failing. This morning when I opened the shop the phone was ringing—it was just before I went to breakfast. It was someone who said he had heard from Mr. Quandt that I had some Jadway letters for sale. And I said no, they had already been sold. He swore at his bad luck, because he had been notified of the letters yesterday and had been unable to get to me until this morning. Then he hung up. No name, nothing."

"Did he call long-distance?"

"I don't think so. I believe it was a local call. Of course, one never knows in these days of direct dialing."

"Well, all we know is that there was a flurry of interest in those letters *after* I thought I had purchased them. Maybe Quandt did pass the word around, once he'd told me. Although I can't see any motive for his having done that." Barrett reached out and shook the autograph dealer's hand. "Anyway, thanks for your trouble. You too, Mildred."

Olin Adams saw him to the door. "I am deeply sorry, Mr. Barrett. Good luck to you."

On Fifty-fifth Street again, Barrett looked at his watch. He still had two hours to plane time, and he was too depressed to go back to the hotel. He decided to take a walk and see whether the life of the city could once again bolster his sagging spirits.

He had meant to head in the direction of the Museum of Modern Art, but he was in no mood for mobiles and abstracts when his own affairs were so muddled. Aimlessly he started in the opposite direction, crossing Park Avenue, continuing to Lexington Avenue, and then turning right toward the lower Fifties.

Absently he window-shopped, and walked and walked, and tried to resolve the mystery of this morning's defeat. To have Faye, the impossible, out of his life was one thing. To have Maggie, the untouchable, no part of his life was another thing. But to have Jadway, the witness from the grave, removed from his life by a body snatcher was the worst and most stunning thing of all, almost the last straw, for it was as if hope itself had been stolen.

He tried to rid his mind of despair, and he glanced at the shop windows once more. There was a window display of children's wear. There was a display of Dresden china. There was a display of radios and electronic gadgets and a large advertising poster. His eyes had passed over the poster, and then returned to it, and then read it once, twice, three times. There was something about the poster. He moved slowly back to the store window.

The poster read:

> THE SHERLOCK ELECTRONIC EAVESDROPPER!
> FOR BUSINESSMEN, INVESTIGATORS, ATTORNEYS!
> A PRIVATE MONITOR THAT CAN BE FITTED INTO *any* TELEPHONE!
> Install this transmitting bug, smaller than a thimble, in any telephone. It draws its power from the telephone itself. It is hidden from view. Placed inside the telephone, it will broadcast every word spoken into the phone, every two-way conversation, and it will send these conversations to an FM receiver in another building across the city, where every word can be taped. Retail at $350.

As if in a hypnotic trance, Barrett stared up at the poster.

Slowly he pivoted away from the window. His mind felt like a Ferris wheel, spinning round and round, carrying his thoughts round and round, and abruptly the wheel stopped and disgorged a single thought. He had the truth all at once. He was certain. The mysteries of the past weeks, the frustrations and disappointments, were finally explained.

In his mind's eye, the powerful inner Cyclops eye, he could envision the black telephone on his office desk in Los Angeles. On this telephone he had listened to Kimura confide to him Christian Leroux's hideout in Antibes. And then, by coincidence, someone had got to Leroux and spirited him away. On this telephone he had been informed where Norman C. Quandt was secretly located and waiting. And then, by coincidence, someone had alerted the police to raid the place while Barrett was there. On this telephone he had purchased the precious Jadway letters from Olin Adams and told Adams when he would be by to pick them up. And, by coincidence, someone had visited Adams first and deprived the defense of the letters.

By coincidence—crap!

By electronic eavesdropper—you bet!

Why hadn't he thought of that obvious Listening Tom earlier? He was anything but stupid. Yet he *had* thought of it, at least had known of the possibility earlier, only it had been too much earlier, and this was what had made him overlook the danger later. He recalled now the exact moment when a bugging device had first been mentioned. It had been the morning he had checked into Zelkin's suite, and Abe had been taking him on a tour of the premises, and they had arrived in the grand room that was to be Barrett's own office. Zelkin, as pleased as Keats's Cortez on a peak in Darien, had announced, "Here it is, Mike, all yours—spanking new, freshly painted, fully gadgeted, everything in order. Why, we even had a counterbugging outfit in to sweep the room—in fact, kept them half a day to check our entire suite for any possible hidden transmitting equipment. Can't play it too safe, you know. The best offense is a good defense."

That early precaution was what had disarmed Barrett. He had thought that once they were protected, their privacy was certified as safe from that day onward. It had made him forget that bugs could secretly invade at a later time.

Yes, he'd bet on an electronic eavesdropper. But used by whom, exactly?

This had not been authorized by Elmo Duncan personally, of that he was sure. Duncan was not only the District Attorney, but the square of squares. A fancier of Motherhood, Apple Pie, and My Country Right or Wrong does not indulge in illegal wire-tapping. Even if Duncan had wished to do it, he would not have risked it. He wasn't merely a law-enforcement officer. He was a politician on the make. He would not dare exposure.

No, not Duncan, but someone who knew what was best for

Duncan, and who might feel free to act on his behalf without Duncan's knowledge. Someone who knew about industrial espionage and sophisticated electronic devices. Someone with a huge stake in making Duncan a winner. Someone who was above ordinary law and morality. Someone who was behind the scenes.

Duncan's Richelieu and Rasputin.

Namely, Luther Yerkes.

Barrett cast about him, and his eyes held on the street sign. He was standing at the corner of Lexington Avenue and Fifty-second Street. He knew his New York and he knew where there would be a familiar telephone booth.

Turning into Fifty-second Street and moving in the direction of Park Avenue, Mike Barrett walked rapidly to the middle of the block and entered the Four Seasons restaurant.

Along the right wall of the vast foyer was a line of telephone booths. Barrett shut himself into the first booth, and he put through a collect call to Los Angeles.

On the other end of the line, Donna, who was going to work through the weekend, welcomed him and was eager to learn of the contents of the Jadway letters.

"There are no Jadway letters," said Barrett, "and I don't want to go into it now. You let Abe and Leo know, and tell them I'll explain when I get back six hours from now."

"Reminder, boss. You were going to look in on Isabel Vogler after you got off the plane."

"I'll do that. Here's why I'm calling, Donna. I've got a question. Please listen carefully. Since I checked in to work with Abe on this Fremont case—anyway, since my own office telephone was installed—have there been any repairmen working on your phone or mine?"

"On my phone, none. On yours—if you'll hold on a minute, I'll skim back through my appointment book." Donna left the line, but less than a minute later she was back. "As a matter of fact, yes, boss. It says here that the same day you went to International to pick up Philip Sanford, two telephone repairmen came in to check your phone. I remember them. They said some client had complained that he wasn't getting through, and so they wanted to look your phone over."

"Were you with them, Donna, when they checked it?"

"No, I couldn't spare the time, boss. I had to mind my own desk. I did look in once to ask if everything was all right. They had the top plastic cover off the phone base, and they said they'd found what was wrong and had fixed it. So I left them to finish up their job."

"How long were they in there working on it?"

"Hard to remember. Not long. Maybe ten minutes. Maybe not that much. Why? Is something wrong?"

"There has been, and not only with the telephone. Okay. You've told me what I wanted to know. Now let me tell you something, and no questions, please, until I get back. I'll fill you in on everything then. For the next few hours just do as I say, Donna. It's an order. No one, but no one, is to make an outgoing call or accept an incoming one on my office telephone until I return. Get it? If you or Abe or Leo happen to be in my office when my phone rings, don't touch it. Take it on another phone. If Phil Sanford comes by and wants to use my office—"

"He's in Washington, D.C., for the American Booksellers Association convention at the Shoreham."

"That's right. Okay. Hands off my phone today, and that includes any telephone repairmen who might show up again."

"Wilco, boss. Your office is off limits this afternoon."

"I'll see you later in the day, Donna."

"You mean you want me to stay here until you return? I don't mind."

"I forgot. I'm seeing Mrs. Vogler. No, you don't have to hang around tonight. I'll be getting in too late. Bad enough keeping you chained to the desk all day Saturday and Sunday, without making it worse. No, when you're through, go. Leave any messages on my desk. I'll look in before returning to the apartment. One last thing. Give me Mrs. Vogler's address again."

He wrote it down, and then he hung up.

Leaving the booth, he was tempted to forgo food on the plane and to proceed into the dining section of the Four Seasons and lunch beside the spectacular indoor fountain. That was always a lift—an expensive one, but it made you feel like somebody. And he needed to feel like somebody. But he could see that his time was running out. He still had to get to The Plaza, repack his bag, check out, and take the long ride to Kennedy Airport. He would just about make his plane back to Los Angeles. Lunch could wait. He had enough else to digest.

Mike Barrett was in Los Angeles again, but it was later than he had intended it to be, and most of the day had been wasted.

There had been a delay at Kennedy Airport when one engine of the jet airliner had caused some concern and had had to be inspected once more, and the scheduled takeoff had been held up nearly an hour. The cross-country flight itself had been accomplished in the allotted five hours and a half. Then Barrett's convertible, which he had left overnight in the parking lot at International Airport, was heeling over to one side when he found it. The flat tire had taken a half hour to repair.

After that, the going-home traffic had clogged the San Diego Freeway all the way north to the valley, and only after he took the off ramp into Van Nuys did he make time.

Now, as he parked before the modest gray bungalow that Mrs. Vogler rented, it was five-fifty in the afternoon. Shutting off the ignition, he stepped into the street and started for her front door. He prayed that she was home. There had been no time to contact her and explain his tardiness. She would likely be home, he decided, for it was almost dinnertime and she did have a ten-year-old son to feed.

At the stoop, he pressed the doorbell. There was someone running inside, and then the door was thrown open, and a little boy wearing a toy astronaut's space helmet pressed against the porch screen.

"Hey, now," Barrett greeted him, "when you heading for the moon? That's a mighty fine space helmet you've got on."

"It ain't nothing compared to the rest," piped the boy ecstatically. "You should see all the things Mom bought me today. Even an air gun and three games to play."

"Wonderful," said Barrett. "Is your mother in?"

"Not in the house. In the back."

"How do I—?" He looked off. "Is that your driveway?"

"You go that way *zoom* to Cape Kennedy. Yah. That way."

"Thank you, Astronaut Vogler."

Barrett bounded down from the porch, cut across the brownish patch of lawn, and strode up the cracked cement surface toward the old Ford parked in the driveway before the dilapidated garage. He squeezed between the side of the Ford and the hedges along the driveway, ducked under the clothesline, and came upon Isabel Vogler.

She could not see him at first. Her face was hidden behind a large carton—clothes spilled out of the top of it—which she had removed from the garage and was carrying toward several cartons of dishware and furnishings already piled next to her back screen door. He watched her waddle across the yard, lower the carton, and balance it on top of another, and only when she turned to retrace her steps did she see him.

She shaded her eyes and squinted at him.

Quickly he closed the distance between them. Her brow and downy upper lip were beaded with perspiration. She was wiping her plump hands on her already soiled apron. Her eyes offered no sign of recognition.

"Remember me?" he said. "Mike Barrett. I said I'd see you today. Sorry I'm late. Barrett, remember?"

"Oh, yeah, hiya. Somebody left a message with my boy yesterday afternoon you were coming over. There was no return number or I'd of called back."

"Called back?" Barrett echoed. "What did you want to call back about, Mrs. Volger?"

"About if you wanted to see me because you were reconsidering hiring me. Because I couldn't do it no more. I'm all through with day work and live-in work. I'm finished being a domestic, thank the Lord."

More perplexed than ever, Barrett said, "You're confused, Mrs. Vogler. I never intended to hire you as a domestic. Have you—"

"Oh, I know you didn't," she said belligerently, hands on her hips. "No references, no job, I'm not forgetting. But I thought maybe you changed your mind, that's what. If you haven't, what are you doing here, anyway?"

Had this woman suffered amnesia? Or was she plain crazy? "Mrs. Vogler, apparently you've forgotten, but after you came to see me on that interview— Wait, you do agree we met in my apartment yesterday morning, don't you?"

"I just said I saw you. But it was no references, no job, and so that was that."

He decided that she was utterly insane. That, or this was a bad dream. "Mrs. Vogler, surely you remember. We discussed Frank Griffith, your last full-time employer. You said you had a run-in with him, and he fired you and wouldn't give you a reference after that. I told you I wasn't interested in hiring you as a domestic, reference or no reference. I wanted to employ you as a defense witness in our trial, and I was going to recompense you for that. You were to testify how rotten Frank Griffith really is, and how the kind of environment he provided may have hurt his son more than the book I'm representing. Now do you remember?"

She stood solid as the Rock of Gibraltar. "I remember telling you I worked for Griffith, yes, and he never believed in no written references, but I don't remember one other word you're saying, because none of it is true. Where did you get such a story? Lord in Heaven, why would I ever testify against a fine, upstanding man like Frank Griffith? He was always good to me, and we only had a parting because Mrs. Griffith wanted her niece to move out here to be her companion, and that's the whole of it. He hated to let me go. I've always held him up in the highest consideration, as the kindest man to his wife and his boy and the whole world. I never had any employer who was more kind or so *generous*."

He gaped at Isabel Vogler, dumbfounded. He felt as though he had gone down the rabbit hole and found himself face to face with the Mad Hatter. "Mrs. Vogler, listen—"

"You listen, young man. You have your nerve coming here and trying to involve me in your lawyer shenanigans, trying to turn Frank Griffith's friends against him. I have a mind to call the police about you, that's what. You stay away from Frank Griffith, that's my warning to you. He's a good man, and even when he had his odd side, like not giving references to former employees, he was always ready to help any of them if they were in need. Like me. He found out I was having a struggle on my own and trying to raise my young one. So you know what that good man did? He didn't call or send someone around, but he came here to see me himself this morning, right this morning. And you know the first thing he said to me? 'Isabel,' he said to me, 'I hear you're having a little trouble. Now, what's this all about? I'm here to lend a hand to an old friend.' And when he heard out my troubles, he did help me the way he offered. You can see for yourself, I'm packing right now. Mr. Griffith, he said I was always deserving of a bonus, and now he's given it to me so's I can go back to Topeka with my youngster where I always belonged. We're leaving on Monday."

Barrett continued to gape at her, but no longer was he dumbfounded, only struck with wonderment.

Life was imitating art. For his mind had gone back to a baffling and chilling folk tale familiar to him in his youth. It was about the elderly lady en route with her daughter from Bombay, via Paris, to her native village in England. The original vanishing lady. Now you see her, now you don't. The lady and her daughter had stopped overnight at the Hotel Crillon in Paris. The lady had been feeling ill, and her daughter had gone off to a distant sector of Paris to obtain a special medicine from a pharmacist. This had been Paris in 1890, at the time of the Exposition, and the streets had been teeming with people, and the daughter in her quest had been repeatedly delayed. Finally, after a lapse of four of five hours, she had returned with the medicine. At the lobby desk, the clerk had not recognized her. No lady such as the girl's mother had been registered, he said. There was no room that fitted the daughter's description of the one she and her mother had occupied. No one in the hotel, in the British Embassy, in the Sûreté, could help. The lady had no existence. Now you see her, now you don't.

Yesterday morning there had been Isabel Vogler, foe of Frank Griffith, friend of the defense. This afternoon that Isabel Vogler had vanished, and in her place stood Isabel Vogler, supporter of Frank Griffith, enemy of the defense.

Barrett remembered that there had eventually been a solution to the mystery of the English lady who had vanished from the Crillon in 1890. The lady had died of the black plague, and if the cause of her death had been made known, even to the daughter, if it had become public knowledge, not only would the hotel have been ruined, but the mighty Exposition would have been ended and Paris might have become a ghost town. So the truth could not be known, the room had to be repapered and redecorated in hours, and the lady could not be admitted to have existed.

There had been an answer then, and Barrett knew that there must be an answer now. The disappearance of the Isabel Vogler he had met and known might be an act of magic to those in the audience. It could not be an act of magic for those backstage who were aware of the wizard's arsenal of tricks.

Frank Griffith had first tried to make the lady vanish the easy way. He had requested that Willard Osborn II have Faye pressure Barrett into dropping this hostile witness. Barrett had refused. Frank Griffith had then proceeded to eliminate the hostile witness in a more hazardous way. He had gone to her directly, exposed his need to her. He had then diagnosed her need and offered to remedy it. This morning he had performed a financial lobotomy. The prefrontal lobes had been severed. Under the skilled hand of the surgeon, hostility had been excised, and what remained was sweetness and light. Toward Frank Griffith, that is. By Monday, the day of the trial, the operation would have been completed. The witness would have disappeared entirely from the Los Angeles scene. A room to the past had been repapered and redecorated.

"Mrs. Vogler," Barrett said desperately, "I know what you promised me yesterday and I know what you're saying now. It is clear to me what has happened in between. But even though Frank Griffith has tried to buy you off—"

Her porcine features seemed to swell. "Don't you talk to me like that! No matter what you make up, I've told you everything I've got to tell."

"Mrs. Vogler, I could subpoena you," he said feebly.

"What's that?"

"That's getting a court order served on you, and that would force you to appear in court and take the witness stand and tell what you know about Frank Griffith."

"You just do that," she said. Then she added shrewdly, "Because all I'd tell about Mr. Griffith and the way he brought up his boy would be favorable, mightily favorable to him."

Barrett sighed and nodded. "You win, Mrs. Vogler. I know when I'm licked."

"I'm glad you have some sense, young man."

"And I hope you'll have a good trip," he said. He started to go, and then he said, "Where can I find a telephone in this neighborhood?"

"If you mean mine, I just as soon not have you use it. There's a drugstore on the corner. They got a phone. And, Mr. Barrett,

313

about Frank Griffith, I wouldn't bother with him any more if I were you, because you won't find anything against him."

A word from the wise, he thought, and he left for the corner drugstore.

In the drugstore, near the soda fountain, there was an open public telephone on the wall.

In moments, he had Maggie Russell on her private line. She recognized his voice, and she was mildly surprised.

"Maggie," he said urgently, and then realized that in his new Fayeless world he had addressed her by her given name for the first time, "I must discuss a few things with you. Maybe you can clear them up for me."

"Can you give me a clue?"

"Frank Griffith, for one thing."

"I see. Certain subjects are difficult to discuss on the phone."

"Then would you mind doing it in person?"

"I—I'm not sure."

"Maggie, I know the rules. But I have to see you. I have some questions. Maybe you can provide the answers, maybe not. Just speaking to you would be of some help to me. I don't want to put you on the spot. Still, if we could have a quiet dinner tonight . . ."

"Tonight? Well . . ." Her last word hung in the air, then she went on. "Possibly. Is this strictly business—or business and pleasure?"

"Some business, but just seeing you would be a pleasure."

"Won't Faye Osborn mind?"

"Who's Faye Osborn? No, that's over with."

"I see. . . . Where are you now?"

"I'm in Van Nuys, but I'm on my way to the office. I have to check on something there. That's part of it."

"I'll meet you at your office," she said. "Is eight o'clock all right?"

"I'll be waiting, Maggie."

IT WAS evening now, twenty-five minutes before eight o'clock, as Mike Barrett entered the towering high-rise building from Wilshire Boulevard. Going to the elevators, he listened to the echoing clack of his footsteps in this futuristic cavern.

This was Friday night, and the building had been abandoned by

314

all save the scattered janitors lost somewhere well above the ground floor. The marble walls were bleak and indifferent. The elevators were on self-service.

Presently, he consoled himself, Maggie Russell would arrive and there would be humanity and warmth.

Inside an elevator, he pressed the button for the fifth floor, and slowly he was carried aloft. The loss of the Jadway letters, followed so quickly by the loss of Isabel Vogler, had been a shattering blow. He wondered why he had instinctively turned to Maggie Russell. Speaking to her, he had made it sound as if he had a specific problem she might help him solve. Yet, actually, he was not sure what he really wanted of her. Perhaps it was that the real enemy was invisible to him, but known to her, and she might offer him some insight without betraying her allegiance. That was the business. Perhaps it was only that she was she. And that was the pleasure.

The elevator had glided to a halt, the doors quietly parted, and Barrett emerged into the corridor.

The next step was the first in his counterattack against the hidden opposition. The constant frustrations, followed by the chance reminder of electronic eavesdroppers, followed by the information that "repairmen" had dismantled his telephone while he was out of the office, had led him now to seek final confirmation of the enemy's devastating espionage. He must examine his telephone. If, indeed, it had been bugged, then he would reveal this sensational discovery to the press and public. The exposure would indict no one by name. Yet the implications would be comprehended by one and all. It would be the beginning of a bid for public awareness of the ruthless nature of the prosecution forces, perhaps even a bid for public sympathy toward the defense, and the start of the defense's counterattack in the critical arena outside the courtroom. Even though, he knew, his revelation might come about too late.

Barrett inserted his key into the lock, opened the door to Donna's dark office, and turned on the overhead light. Leaving the reception-room door open for Maggie, he went to Donna's desk. No messages. The electric IBM typewriter wore its gray hood. The Dictaphone rested in silence.

He was eager now for a look at the telephone in his office.

He crossed the inner corridor to his door, opened it into the shadowy room, stepped inside, fumbling with his left hand for the light switch. Unexpectedly, he heard a creak, a movement, an inhalation behind him, and the chill that instantly enveloped him froze his fingers above the light switch.

There was Someone.

He had started to turn, when suddenly an arm hooked in front of him, closing in on his neck. Choking, he raised his hands to clutch at the strangling arm, to tear it free. There was a vise clamped on his throat, as he clawed at the arm, and the black room was filling with crazy dots of meteors and stars.

Savagely, panting like a cornered animal, he had freed himself from the muscular noose, and was trying to twist around to get at his unseen assailant, when a fist clubbed against the side of his skull, and his knees buckled. His outstretched hand found his desk and kept him from falling completely, and then wildly, gasping, he staggered upright and forward, plunging at the giant silhouette before him. He had hold of the other now, trying to pin down the flailing arms and hammering fists, trying to wrestle the monster to the floor. But the attacker's arms rammed upward, breaking Barrett's hold, and sent him reeling against the desk.

The black form closed in, and Barrett lashed out, missing, and tried to slide away along the desk. The black form followed relentlessly, and suddenly it had speech.

"Get him," it growled.

Instinctively, Barrett tried to wheel around to protect himself from what was behind him and unknown. In that split second of turning, he saw there was another hulk, arm rising and slashing down toward him. Desperately he tried to duck, as the butt of a pistol drove past his face and smashed into his chest.

Pain opened like an umbrella through his body, and then it spiked upward into his head. His head rolled and his knees were rubber, and as he saw the shape of the arm rise and fall again, he tried to cover his head, but a weight crashed against his skull, and the floor flew up to meet his face.

He felt the rough nap of the carpet on one cheek, and a sticky rivulet roll down past a cheekbone, and brilliant colors swirled behind his eyelids, and faintly, distantly, he heard a reedy voice sing let's go, let's go, let's go.

Colors dissolved. Life died.

Blackness. Nothingness.

INSIDE HIS HEAD, he awakened to a world of inky hue, and he sought freedom from this bottom of the Cimmerian lake, and gradually, ever so gradually, he floated to the surface.

He felt a damp coolness across his forehead and cheeks, and at last the refreshing air and the scent of perfume.

Inhaling deeply, he tentatively opened his eyes.

There was a face above his own, fuzzy, shimmering, and then it became defined. Soft black hair and green eyes and crimson lips.

"Maggie," he whispered.

"Yes, Mike."

"What are you—?" To make sure it was not a dream, his gaze strayed past her to the ceiling fixture, then to the office couch and chairs and open door. Once more he returned to her. His head was in her lap. His coat and shirt had been removed, and he was stretched on the floor, and she was sitting on the carpet, legs tucked beneath her, holding his head on her lap while one hand caressed his brow and the other held a wet handkerchief spotted with blood.

"Are you all right, Mike?" she asked with anxiety. "How do you feel?"

"I'm not sure. Okay, I guess." His hand came up to his temple. "Feels a little like someone is using a pile driver up here, and against my chest."

"I'm not surprised. You've got a lump almost the size of an egg on the back of your head. And you were bleeding along your neck when I found you. I cleaned it. The skin was scraped, torn a little. I took off your shirt. The only other thing I could find was a nasty bruise on your ribs. Do you want me to call your doctor?"

"No . . . no . . . I don't think so. Wait, let me sit up."

He made the effort, and she assisted him. As he came upright his brain felt scrambled and his vision blurred again, but then, quickly, his head felt better and clarity of thought and sight returned.

"What happened, Mike? I got here five minutes ago. The door to the suite was wide open, and the light was on in the reception room. All the other lights were out. I didn't know what was going on. I called for you. No answer. And then I heard what sounded like a moan. It was from this room. So I came in and turned on the lights, and there you were. It was frightening. I was going to phone for an ambulance, but then I thought I'd see how you were first. Are you sure you're better?"

"I'll live. One codeine should do it."

"Do you have some?"

"In the bathroom. I'll get the—"

"Let me." She leaped to her feet, looked around, and, following his pointing finger, disappeared into the bathroom.

After a moment, Mike Barrett struggled to his feet. When Maggie Russell returned with the white pill and a glass of water, he quickly downed the pill.

"Thanks, Maggie."

"Now can you remember what happened?"

He remembered vividly. "After phoning you, I drove back from the Valley. I came up here, and the second I entered my office, before I could turn on the light, some big fellow jumped me from behind. I got free from him, but then he called out to someone else, so there were two of them. The other one started to pistol-whip me. I went down, and I think I heard them saying they'd better get out of here. Then I guess I passed out."

"But who was it? And why?"

"I don't know who. It was dark. I'd just walked in, and my eyes didn't have time to adjust. But I have an idea who was behind it and maybe why."

The telephone.

He turned around. His desk looked like it had been swept by a small typhoon, and the carpet was strewn with papers and a chair was overturned. On the desk his telephone stood in its accustomed place, but the base was dismantled, its casing removed so that the inner mechanism lay exposed.

Head still aching, chest throbbing, he walked stiffly to the telephone and studied the instrument.

"They got away with it," he said at last.

"With what?"

"I came back to the office wanting to make sure, and now I am sure, unless the telephone company is offering a new judo service for subscribers. Someone planted a monitor in my phone, and then they must have found out I knew—that means my secretary's phone had been bugged, also, because I hinted at it pretty broadly when I called her from New York—so they came back after hours to remove the evidence. I happened to stumble in on them." He poked at the telephone. "They took this apart, removed the device, but I came in before they could put Humpty Dumpty together again."

"But who would—? You should call the police."

"The *police?*"

She seemed puzzled by his tone, and then some vague comprehension crossed her features. "Oh," she said.

"I'll enlighten you in a little while," said Barrett. "First I'd better call my partner."

He went into the reception room, and before dialing he examined Donna's telephone. He pried at the casing with a thumbnail. It was loose. Yes, they had come here shortly after Donna had left—they must have waited for her to leave, and she had apparently left late—and then they had removed the electronic bug from her telephone before getting to work on his own.

He lifted up the receiver and dialed Abe Zelkin at home.

He had hardly finished saying hello when Zelkin asked worriedly, "Mike, what's this Donna told me? About our missing out on those Jadway letters?"

"Abe, it's a long story, but I'll make it short and save details for tomorrow."

Recounting what had happened at Olin Adams Autographs, he hurried on to tell how they had all overlooked the obvious from the time that they had lost Christian Leroux to the opposition. Then Barrett related the assault upon him in his office, and the condition of his telephone.

"To heck with that," Zelkin was saying. "The thing is—your condition. Are you sure you're okay?"

The codeine had begun to take effect. "I'm feeling fine, Abe. I'll see how I am in the morning. Maybe I'll look in on Doc Quigley. What's tomorrow? Saturday. I'll drop in on him at home."

"I want you in shape for the trial Monday morning."

"I'll be in shape," said Barrett grimly. "Maybe our case won't be, but I will. As to our case, that brings me to one more piece of bad news. I went straight from the airport to Van Nuys. Abe, I hate to tell you, but we've lost Mrs. Vogler."

He could hear the sharp intake of Zelkin's breath. "No kidding. How did it happen? The telephone bug again?"

"No, this time it was another device. It's called the Osborn Gambit. To fill you in briefly . . ."

In passing, he had mentioned Mrs. Vogler to Faye, he said. Hell, when you're going steady with a girl, you should be able to feel your secrets are safe with her. Not so with Faye. He had underestimated the bonds of Faye's father fixation. She had been the device by which his intention to use Mrs. Vogler had been transmitted to her father, and from her father this information had been passed on to Frank Griffith. And then, simply, Barrett spoke of the scene with Faye last night, his refusal to play the Osborn game. As a result, he had lost Faye and, because money usually undermined principles, he had failed to hold on to Isabel Vogler.

"So on Monday morning, Abe, I'm afraid we're going up against a howitzer with a bow, just a bow, not even arrows."

"Never mind about that. We'll do our best." Zelkin hesitated on the phone. "I'm sorry about you and Faye."

"Faye's the least of it. That one wasn't made in heaven. It would never have worked. As for the vice-presidency—let's be honest—I'd look lousy in a yachting costume. I once suffered *mal de mer* just reading *Twenty Thousand Leagues under the Sea*. Besides, I had an offer of a permanent partnership from a friend named Abe Zelkin. I'm going to write and ask him whether it's still open."

"Cut it out. If I wasn't so worried about you, this would be one of the happy moments of my life."

"Then we're partners, Abe. From here on in, rise or fall, it's Zelkin and Barrett."

"Barrett and Zelkin. The sign goes up tomorrow."

"We'll flip for top billing. Then the first order of business is this. Those specialists in counterbugging you originally had in, that outfit that detects eavesdropping equipment. Can you get hold of them again?"

"I certainly can—and will."

"Are you sure they're really good?"

"Mike, they're the best. When they're through, we'll be foolproof once more, every bug exterminated. They come in with two things. Something called the Sentry 101. They plug it into every phone, and the dial tells if there's a tap on. Then they use a thing called the Sweep. It's a box with antenna and dials, and it shows up any hidden transmitting equipment. And this time we'll have them put a jammer next to each phone. They're around two hundred fifty dollars each, but we can rent them, and they are guaranteed to garble any wireless tap put on in the future."

"Great. I think my phone and Donna's are clean now. But we'd better have our offices looked over, anyway. Including your office, Leo's room, even Phil Sanford's hotel suite. Everything should be checked and debugged. Can you get that outfit in on Monday?"

"I'll have them in Saturday."

"Not that we'll have any more secrets. I've just about run out of leads. Still, you never can tell what'll turn up. If we do get another break, I want them to hear about it first in court."

"Mike, have you given a thought to who is behind this?"

"I could make a good guess. Let's discuss the louse after we've been debugged."

Having finished his phone conversation with Zelkin, Mike Barrett returned to his office.

Maggie Russell had restored order to the room and was gathering up the last of the papers. Silently he observed her as she rose and walked to his desk. Her hair was attractively tousled and her hips moved nicely beneath the short, swinging chiffon dress.

She caught him staring at her, and she flushed.

"Thanks, Maggie," he said. "Well, I'm all set now. I promised you dinner. What are you in the mood for?"

She did not reply at once. Finally she said, "Mike, I didn't mean to listen, but I couldn't help overhearing part of your conversation on the phone."

"There was nothing private."

"The part about Faye Osborn."

"I told you about that earlier, didn't I?"

"I thought it was only part of the lure. To get me to meet you and make me feel more comfortable."

"I wouldn't do that, Maggie."

"Not that Faye has anything to do with our—our business meeting. It's just that, well, if things were the way they were, and

I were seen dining with you, it might have been misunderstood. I mean, women are very possessive—I'm no different—and I wouldn't want to be caught up in anything nasty or bitchy."

"When you speak of Faye, use past tense."

"Well . . . if you say so."

"In fact, let's not speak of her at all. Let's talk about us. I'm hungry, which means I'm feeling better. What about you?"

"Hungry."

"I don't know your tastes yet, Maggie. French, Italian, Mexican, Chinese, Vegetarian?"

"Italian."

"Perfect. What about a really good place? Ever been to La Scala in Beverly Hills?"

"I don't think so. Is it dress-up?"

"You'll do fine."

"I don't mean me. I mean you. Even without a shirt, shouldn't you wear a necktie?"

He looked down at his bare chest, and they both laughed. "I've got a clean shirt in the closet," he said. "I'll just be a jiffy."

ALTHOUGH the two dining areas in La Scala Restaurant were confined, and the booths and tables seemed crowded together, the diners forming couples and groups at the various places did not intrude upon each other's privacy. Such was the atmosphere and ambiance of the restaurant that a man and a woman dining together, although surrounded by other diners, could enjoy a feeling of intimacy and at the same time feel separate from these others.

Seated close to Maggie Russell at a wall table in the rear, Mike Barrett appreciated this intimacy that did not depend on isolation. The codeine had done its work, and the two drinks before dinner had helped. The demi-sized bottle of chianti wine that had come after the minestrone soup and with the fettuccine had been all but emptied. He felt no pain.

During the meal, in response to Maggie's questioning, Barrett had repeated, at greater length, what he had already told Abe Zelkin an hour ago. A wide-eyed Maggie Russell had listened attentively to his recital of Leroux's being whisked away from Antibes, of the plainclothesmen appearing by coincidence at

Quandt's filth factory, of the Jadway letters being spirited off by an impostor, of Isabel Vogler's curious amnesia and change of heart in Van Nuys.

Now, having completed his recital, Barrett caught the last of the buttered flat noodles on his fork and devoured them.

Maggie set down her wine glass. "It's unbelievable," she said. "It's the kind of thing you see or read about in mysteries, but you know they are make-believe. Even when you learn about those electronic devices in the news, it's hard to accept the reality of human beings like us stealing into someone else's office or home and secreting those instruments, and some person somewhere overhearing conversations that are supposed to be private. It's hard to believe that it really happens."

"Well, it happened."

"It's not only immoral, but dirty, just as dirty as some voyeur sneaking up to a private bedroom window at night to watch a couple making love on their bed."

"Your voyeur does it for his own sexual gratification. Yerkes is a member of the Anything Goes Club, and he does it for power."

"Power can be sexual gratification, too," said Maggie. "If you ever saw Luther Yerkes, you'd believe that's the only kind of sexual gratification he is capable of enjoying. He gives me goose pimples. And he's most obvious when he thinks he's being subtle. You should see the way he twists Uncle Frank around his finger. You wouldn't believe it, the way Uncle Frank accepts everything Yerkes says, even thinking he's initiated things Yerkes has suggested to him."

"Frank Griffith has to believe everything that Yerkes advises. After all, in your uncle's world the values and standards he lives by have reached their fullest flowering in the person of a Yerkes. To the merely rich, Luther Yerkes is a maharajah."

"But you don't think it was Yerkes who bought off Isabel Vogler?"

"No," said Barrett. "The highest power wasn't needed for that operation. It was strictly Frank Griffith, I'm almost certain."

"And you don't think the District Attorney was a part of this?"

"I really don't think so. Maybe I tend to be a boy scout, as my ex told me last night when our parting was such unsweet sorrow. No, I don't think Elmo Duncan is the instigator of what's happened. He may know it is happening and with silence give consent, and thus be an accessory after the fact. Yet I'm sure he's not the instigator, only the beneficiary. When Elmo Duncan unloads his big guns come Monday, most of the world will credit him with pounding us to smithereens. Nobody'll know that it is Yerkes who's running the supply line, with assists from Willard Osborn and Frank Griffith and God knows whom else. I'll confess our defenses are damn weak—especially after all the sabotage—to stand up against a formidable lineup like that one."

Impulsively, Maggie reached out and covered Barrett's hand with her own. "Mike, don't include me in that lineup, even if I am a relative of Frank Griffith's."

"You're not a blood relative. You're not anything remotely like Griffith."

He wanted to take her soft hand, hold it, but she had already removed it. She said, "I'm not, and blood or no, neither is his own son like him. I've told you before that I felt I shouldn't see you, because I can't be disloyal to people I'm living with or with whom I'm associated. I've thought about that, and now I can give you a fuller picture of what I honestly feel. It's not the Griffith family as a whole I'm protective about. It's only Jerry, Jerry alone. He's the one I'm loyal to. Aunt Ethel—well, she's helpless and I'm sorry for her. Nothing I do or don't do can hurt her any more. As for Uncle Frank—after the way he has behaved, the way he is still behaving, I care for him less and less. That's not quite true, either. To care for a person less means you've had to care for them somewhat at some time. I've never cared for him in any way. I've tolerated him, survived him, and in my feline way I've protected Jerry from him. I don't give a damn about Frank Griffith. I'm sure he's a self-righteous bastard, everything Isabel Vogler first said he was, doubled and redoubled in spades."

"Maggie, there's no need for you—"

"Let me get it off my chest while I can. Just take one thing. Yerkes wants Duncan to use Jerry as a witness against your book. That's become a big thing. And, while Jerry won't discuss the night he tried to kill himself, he is constantly telling me he'll try it again before he'll go on the witness stand. He's petrified by the very thought of it. Jerry isn't capable of resisting his father any longer, so he speaks only to me and to the psychoanalyst about

324

his fear. But it's not as if Uncle Frank doesn't know what he's doing to the boy. He's heard from Dr. Trimble what an ordeal public exposure in a courtroom would be for Jerry. Nevertheless, Uncle Frank remains adamant. Goddammit, he keeps saying, his son is going to be a man, stand up there like a man and speak out to the world about what your book did to him. Uncle Frank's pretense is that he is demanding this of Jerry to help the boy save himself from the rape charge. But I think all Uncle Frank is doing this for, consciously or unconsciously, is to save his own face and image by diverting everyone's mind from his personal responsibility for Jerry's behavior. I think it's a selfish act, not a fatherly act. He's sacrificing his son to save himself. And I simply can't let it happen."

"What can you do about it, Maggie?"

"Maybe not much. Maybe a lot. Jerry doesn't have to appear as a witness if he doesn't want to, does he?"

Barrett shook his head. "No. Oh, Duncan could subpoena him. But he wouldn't risk it if Jerry promised to be an uncooperative witness. No, it is up to Jerry whether he appears or not."

"It's not up to Jerry. It's up to his father. And it's up to me to see that his father doesn't push him into this—and over the brink of sanity. I've been tempted to take Jerry's part a dozen times in these past days. I've been afraid, I admit. Afraid maybe of endangering my own security. But what you've told me about Uncle Frank's manipulation of Isabel Vogler makes me furious. I'm almost ready to speak up come what may. I hope I can get drunk enough one night to do it. How much time have I got?"

"Probably until the middle of next week."

"I'll do it yet."

"Do you think anything you say can possibly make Frank Griffith change his mind?"

"Yes." She paused. "Telling him that Jerry has tried to commit suicide might."

"You think you could tell your uncle that?" Barrett did not conceal his doubt.

"I—I think so. I'm not sure. I'm only sure that if Uncle Frank is told about it, and knows his pressure may drive Jerry to another attempt, that might make him stop. The possibilities of a scandal like that might outweigh whatever is driving him to put his son on the stand."

"Maggie, even though you'd be doing this for Jerry—and I'd profit from it as well by not having Jerry as a witness against us—I would think it over carefully before having it out with Frank Griffith."

"Why?"

"Because, win or lose, you'd make your own position in the Griffith household untenable. And I'm not sure you're ready to leave there. You yourself told me you needed them. That's why you're there."

"Well, I'm not so sure I need that kind of horrible incubator any longer. I may be ready to risk flying on my own. I'm here in public with you, am I not? That's a step. A small defiance. A shred of courage."

"I wondered."

"About what?"

"Why you took the risk."

"You asked me," she said simply. She brushed a strand of hair away from her eyes. "I like you, that's why mostly."

"And I care for you, Maggie. That must be very apparent to you."

"Oh, that. You're on the rebound."

"I was attracted to you before the rebound."

"The polygamous male," she said. But she had smiled. "I won't hide this. I'm glad you're through with that other female. Or are you?"

"Am I glad or through? Both. Yes, especially glad that I'm through. It's finished and done."

She toyed with a ring on her index finger. "There's another reason I'm here. Despite what it may have done to Jerry—and, as you say, we can't be sure that's all of it—I'm for Jadway and I'm for *The Seven Minutes*. I've told you so before. I wanted to stand up with you in public and be counted."

That instant he wanted to say, Maggie, I love you. He said, "That's wonderful of you."

"Now that you've lost Mrs. Vogler, I wish I could find someone else to help you prove the book alone shouldn't be blamed for Jerry's deed. But there is no one else who can tell the truth—

except . . . myself. And—and I could go far, but not that far, not as far as the witness stand. You understand."

"I wouldn't allow you to be a defense witness even if you wanted to be one."

"I find it unbearable, the crude things I hear and read against Jadway's book. I keep thinking of the heroine, Cathleen, and the real woman, Jadway's mistress, the one they say inspired Cathleen—"

"Cassie McGraw."

"How I envy her having been so liberated about loving, her having been so freed as to experience total love. Most women go their entire lives, to the very grave, without knowing even a small bit of love or being able to accept or appreciate what little love they do get."

"What about you, Maggie?" Barrett asked quietly. "Could you feel toward a man the way Cassie did—or let's say the way Cathleen did in the story?"

Maggie looked away. "I—I don't know. When I think of Cathleen in that book, I sometimes think maybe I could be like that. I mean, that I have it all locked inside me, and I could find myself opening up and giving someone, the right partner, all of me, everything of me, and, in turn, being able to accept and embrace the love given to me. I hope one day I can have my own seven minutes."

"If you want such love enough, you'll have it one day," he said seriously.

She gave an embarrassed shrug. "We'll see. . . . And do you see what time it is? If you're going to be in shape for Monday, you should have been in bed an hour ago, especially considering what's happened to you. I hope you'll be sensible and rest tomorrow."

"I'm afraid not tomorrow, or any day until the trial's done. We've got an Italian painter, da Vecchi, who claims to have known Jadway and done a portrait of him, coming in from Florence tomorrow. And a half-dozen other witnesses to interrogate further."

"Well, try to get some rest."

Barrett stood up and pulled back the table to make room for

her to rise. "And you think twice before tangling with Frank Griffith," he said.

"Only if he sees the light before," she said. "Maybe I'll work on Dr. Trimble first. God, I am a coward. But something will be done."

Barrett scooped up his change and then caught up with Maggie as she reached the aisle between the bar and the exit. There he took her arm, and as he did so he saw that she had recognized someone at the bar.

From the middle of the crowded bar, a young man with curly rumpled hair that was badly in need of a barber, but wearing an expensive silk suit, was waving to Maggie energetically. "Hiya, Miss Russell!" he called out.

She raised her gloved hand tentatively. "Hi," she said without enthusiasm.

Then she pivoted quickly and hastened down the steps and outside. Once again Barrett had to catch up with her.

On the sidewalk in front of La Scala, Barrett inspected her. She was gnawing her lower lip, and her face had gone pale.

"Who was that?" he wanted to know.

"Irwin Blair," she said. "He's a public-relations man. He's in the Luther Yerkes stable, doing some of the publicity on Duncan." She smiled weakly. "Wherever Yerkes is, you can be sure Frank Griffith is not far away."

"I'm damn sorry about that, Maggie. I shouldn't have brought you here." He frowned. "Is this going to mean trouble for you?"

"I don't know and I don't care." This time her smile was full and it was real. She took his hand. "Whatever happens, it was worth it."

IT WAS LATE, and Elmo Duncan had begun to think that this was a helluva way to spend a Friday night.

Worse, tomorrow would be busier, and Sunday would be no day of rest. All weekend, from dawn to late at night, Duncan would be meeting in the Hall of Justice with his staff, his investigators, Leroux, and other prosecution witnesses. Finally, with the coming of Monday morning, the roulette wheel would spin and he would be laying his career and his future on the table.

Yet, even though he was now weary to the very marrow of his

328

bones, Elmo Duncan knew that when the gavel fell on Monday morning and the trial opened he would be refreshed and strong. It had always been thus in his past experience. Time and again he had come into the courtroom suffering fatigue of mind and body, but, once the trial began, it seemed that some hidden reservoir began to feed him from its store of energy, and he was revitalized and revived. One part of this came, he supposed, from having an audience. Spectators, the press, the faceless audience beyond the boundaries of the courtroom always stimulated him, and he might never possess a larger audience than on Monday morning and in the days to follow. Another part of the rejuvenation process sprang from the excitement of challenge, to which he always responded as if his self-preservation, the lives of himself and his family, were at stake. He liked an opponent he could see and hate, and he would cast this enemy as a murderer who was out to destroy him, so that he was forced to kill to prevent being killed. Lately he had begun to regard Michael Barrett, the defense attorney, as such an enemy. A third part of Duncan's renewed vigor derived from a dedication to his cause. He had to believe that his prosecution was just, that his fight was holy, and that if he did not succeed then the great mass of people who depended upon him would be swept away by the barbarians. Rarely before had he believed so absolutely in a cause he represented. He *knew* that the fiendish hordes of lust and decadence had to be stopped (it was as if he were the guardian to the gates of Rome as the ravaging Numidian cavalry of the Carthaginian army approached) if civilization, meaning law and order and morality, were to be preserved.

Yet, most of all, what set Duncan's adrenal glands secreting, what sparked him to life in a courtroom, was the confidence that he was better prepared and better armed than his enemy. And never in his life had he been as confident as he was tonight. Key skirmishes had been won before the final battle had even begun, and the enemy's ranks had been seriously weakened, if not decimated. Conversely, his own ranks had been powerfully strengthened. There had been serious defections from the other side. By what means he did not know or wish to know. He could guess, but he would not seek confirmation. Luther Yerkes was the keeper of the magic. All was fair in love and war, and this was war, this was war for survival. In the ledger that he posted in his head, the enemy had no star witness. While he, Elmo Duncan, had not one but two. He had Christian Leroux and he had Jerry Griffith, and this was an excess of riches.

Yet, despite these reassurances that he would be ready and effective on Monday, this was still late Friday night and he was exhausted.

His mind had wandered, but hearing Jerry Griffith mentioned once more across the coffee table, Elmo Duncan tried to give the other two in the deep armchairs his undivided attention. There was Luther Yerkes, resplendent as ever in his blue-tinted glasses and his ascot and smoking jacket, patting his hairpiece, then gesticulating with one tiny feminine hand at Frank Griffith. There was Griffith, in the other armchair, his beefy countenance absorbed and his athlete's body straining against the side of the chair to catch every word his superior was addressing to him. To Duncan's knowledge, this was the first time that Griffith had been invited to attend a conference in Yerkes' beach house in Malibu colony.

Earlier, the other two regulars had been present. The jumpy publicity man, Irwin Blair, had been here, but only briefly. He had already done the hardest of his work, developing citywide, statewide, nationwide, and, finally, worldwide interest in the forthcoming trial. Once the trial was under way, the publicity would be self-perpetuating. Blair had made only a token appearance this evening and then had skipped out for a dinner date in Beverly Hills with several reporters who had just arrived from New York and London to cover the trial. Harvey Underwood had been on hand earlier and remained for several hours to discuss his testimony and the surprise witnesses he would supply. He had left only thirty minutes ago. Now there were Yerkes, Griffith, and himself, and Duncan speculated on how long the conference would go on.

Duncan could feel a twinge in his back, in the area of his sacroiliac, and he prayed it wouldn't lead to a muscular spasm before the trial. He tensed as the pain shot up his spine, and then he remembered that (as his wife often reminded him) it was a recurring pretrial symptom. Once he was in court, once on his feet in court, his back would not betray him.

Yerkes and Griffith were still engrossed in conversation, and Duncan took the opportunity to leave the center of the ten-foot sofa and seek support for his aching back. Rising, he could hear a telephone ringing in another room. He stretched carefully, kneaded the lower muscles of his back, and sought a straight chair. Then he became aware that Yerkes' Scottish butler had materialized.

"Mr. Yerkes, sir, excuse me—" the butler began.

Yerkes lifted his head with faint annoyance. "What is it?"

"Telephone for you, sir. Mr. Irwin Blair wishes to speak to you."

"Blair? Can't it wait until— Oh, very well, I'll take it. Forgive me, Frank. Let's find out what Irwin thinks is so important."

Yerkes pushed himself out of the chair, planted himself before the green boxes on the table, and pressed the Speakerphone's on button.

"That you, Irwin?" he called down into the machine.

Irwin Blair's voice came honking through the amplifier. "Mr. Yerkes, sorry to interrupt, but I just saw something that I thought you and Mr. Griffith, if he's still there, would want to know about."

"Mr. Griffith is here. So is Elmo Duncan. Go ahead. We're listening."

"I'm calling from La Scala Restaurant in Beverly Hills." Blair's voice assumed the conspiratorial tone of someone about to transmit a choice piece of destructive gossip. "Guess who I saw here a few minutes ago? I was sitting at the bar, waiting for those reporter guests, just watching the door for them, when who comes out of the dining room but Maggie Russell, Mr. Griffith's niece. Only what I figured you should know is that she wasn't alone, no, sir. Miss Russell had a date. You ready? None other than our esteemed member of the opposition, the attorney for the defense, Michael Barrett himself, in person."

Hearing this, Elmo Duncan crossed quickly to Yerkes' side. Yerkes bent closer to the microphone. "Miss Russell and Michael Barrett?" he said. "Are you sure they were together?"

"Positive," chortled Irwin Blair. "They'd been eating together, I guess, then she came out of the dining room first, and he joined her. I called out to Miss Russell to say hello, and she recognized me and said hello back. She didn't look too happy seeing me. And

331

that was Michael Barrett with her. I don't know him, but I've seen him around before. To be sure I'd made no mistake, I went up to the captain after they left and asked if that had been Michael Barrett, the lawyer, and he said yes it was. Anyway, Miss Russell and Barrett, they left La Scala together, just like they were old friends."

Listening, Duncan became aware of Frank Griffith, who was flushed and who had clamped his large hands on his knees. "I can't believe it!" Griffith exclaimed.

"That was Mr. Griffith you just heard," said Yerkes into the amplifier. "He finds it hard to believe."

"It's true, that's all I can say," Blair responded.

Yerkes nodded. "Very well, Irwin. Thanks for staying on your toes. We'll be in touch. Good night." He turned off his Speaker-phone.

"God damn her, what's this all about, now?" growled Griffith, coming out of the chair.

Yerkes eyed the advertising man carefully. "You don't know anything about this, Frank? You're sure this hasn't been going on before?"

"It's absolutely news to me. I couldn't be more shocked." He made a fist. "Maggie. Blast her, how in God's name did she ever get hooked up with Barrett? Of all people—Barrett! Has she gone out of her mind?"

"Just let me get this straight," said Yerkes calmly. "How well do you know this girl? How long has she been living with you?"

"Maybe a year and a half. About that long. When I fired the Vogler woman, my wife felt it would be easier if she could bring her niece in from the East as a companion and secretary. I can't say I was too keen about having a relative underfoot. They're more difficult to give orders to than hired help. But Ethel felt that since Maggie was a member of the family, at least she could be trusted. So I gave in."

"And can Maggie be trusted?" Yerkes wanted to know.

"I always thought so, until right now. She's been good for Ethel. Maybe she's spoiled Jerry a little too much. But she's never gotten in the way. She's efficient, unobtrusive, decorative."

"Quite decorative, I'd say," said Yerkes. He turned to Duncan. "Don't you think so, Elmo?"

"I've noticed her," said Duncan. "Yes, she is attractive."

"And an attractive girl is likely to have plenty of dates, right?" said Yerkes. He turned back to Griffith. "What about that, Frank? What do you know of her personal life?"

"I can't say I've paid much attention," admitted Griffith. "She has her own key to the house, and she comes and goes as she pleases in her free time. She's made a few girl friends, and I've heard her speak of lectures, concerts, the movies. I think she dates men now and then. She's had a few in when they've brought her home. But not many, and not very often."

"And now Michael Barrett," said Yerkes reflectively. "Elmo, what do you make of it?"

Duncan had been giving it some thought. "The explanation is obvious, I'm afraid. The defense has been getting more and more desperate. They've probably been seeking a pipeline into our camp. They hit upon Maggie Russell as one possibility. I suppose Barrett made a point of becoming acquainted with her. He's a good-looking bachelor, and there was this single girl, maybe hoping to have a little fun. So that was the chemistry. Apparently it worked. I'm not sure how much Maggie can give away to him. She's seen us all at the house, probably overheard us talking, and I suppose she may have repeated some things. Not that I'm suggesting she'd be deliberately disloyal. But she may have given away, or may yet give away, some of our plans and tactics. She might do so unwittingly. Barrett's clever. I'm not underestimating him for one minute. What does it add up to? A potential danger, I'd say."

Griffith, reddening, had thrust himself between Yerkes and the District Attorney. "I'll tell you what it adds up to for me. It adds up to having a Trojan horse in my own house. That's one thing I won't stand for. I'm going home tonight, and I'm going to put that girl on the carpet and demand a full confession. If I'm satisfied Blair's story is true, I'm going to tell her that either she stops seeing that shyster or she's fired. In fact, I have a good mind to fire her anyway."

"Hold it, hold it a minute, Frank, not so fast." Yerkes reached down and picked up his brandy. "Not so fast." He sipped the armagnac thoughtfully. "Let's be levelheaded, project the consequences of such an action. Let's suppose you fire her for playing

333

footsie with the opposition. I don't suppose such a parting would be exactly amicable."

"You're darn right it wouldn't be."

"So you tell Maggie off, throw her out, and what have you done? You've thrown a new antagonist into the lap of the opposition, an antagonist toward you and our cause, that is. She'd be furious with you, and here she is friends with Barrett. What do you suppose would happen next? Any inhibitions she might have about keeping her mouth shut would be gone. More than that, she'd want to revenge herself on you. What would be more natural than for her to sign on with those defense pirates? To become a witness for them against us? To make public the—well, any intimate details about your life and about life in your household."

"I've got no secrets, nothing to hide," said Griffith righteously.

"Of course not, Frank, of course not, but you have a personal life, a private one, like the rest of us have, like any man has. This girl has observed it from the inside. Numerous innocent acts you've performed, innocent remarks you've made, taken out of context, could be twisted, exaggerated, misconstrued, and could be damaging to you and to us when heard from the witness stand." He paused, and his small eyes were beady behind the bluish glasses. "After all, Frank, we've just been through that with the Vogler woman. Look at the lies about you that she was prepared to spout from the witness stand. Merely for revenge. Hell hath no fury like a woman fired. That Mrs. Vogler was ready to help Barrett, ruin you, until you were—uh—able to reason with her. Luckily, we got Mrs. Vogler out of the way. We don't want to create a second Mrs. Vogler in the person of Miss Russell. See what I'm driving at?" He turned. "Elmo, you see that, don't you?"

Duncan's respect for Yerkes' shrewdness was again reinforced. "You're absolutely right, Luther. We're sitting pretty now, on the eve of the trial. We don't want to help arm the opposition."

Griffith snorted. "Okay, maybe you're both right about this. But that doesn't solve it. We still can't stand by and let my wife's niece, a girl who's part of my household, go on seeing an attorney who is trying to libel and ruin us."

"Why not?" said Yerkes, suddenly. "Why not let Maggie go on seeing Michael Barrett? It's the lesser of two evils. It might even be turned to our advantage. Hear me out. Suppose they go on seeing one another? Suppose he *is* using her, which we are not certain he is doing. How much can he honestly learn from her? There's little of importance that she's seen or overheard up to this moment. If you watch your step in her presence, if you are cautious, guarded, she'll have less than nothing to spill to Barrett. At the same time, Frank, if you pay no attention, just allow her to go on dating Barrett, or even admit knowing of it and show your trust in her and your generosity by not interfering—in fact, subtly encourage it—it might definitely be to our advantage."

"Our advantage?" echoed Griffith with disbelief.

Even Duncan found himself skeptical, but he knew Yerkes' mind, and he waited for more.

"To our advantage, yes," said Yerkes. "Consider this. For the cost of a puny pipeline into our camp, we've got our hands on a better pipeline into the defense camp. We need one, you know. We don't have any at all. I think it would be valuable for Elmo to know what Barrett and Zelkin are up to, behind the scenes, while the trial is progressing. Like Elmo, I never underestimate the opposition. This young Barrett doesn't have great experience, but he's out to make a reputation, and he's shown himself to be fairly resourceful, original, persistent. He's liable to come up with some new surprise in the trial, and I don't think any of us wants to be surprised. With a pipeline into the defense, there'd be no surprises. Now, this attractive niece of yours, she's a perfect pipeline, but only if she's handled with care. You're in the business of handling products, Frank. From now on treat Maggie as a product."

Frank Griffith's conversion had begun. He was quieter now, interested, yet still confused. "What are you proposing I do with her?"

Yerkes finished his drink and put the snifter down. He was enjoying himself, Duncan could see. "Here is what I suggest," said Yerkes. "Tomorrow—maybe the next day—quite casually—tell Maggie you've learned that she's been seen out in public with Barrett. She'll expect an explosion. Instead, she'll get a purr of understanding. You're going to be sweet reasonableness. That'll disarm her completely, have her eating out of your hand. Let her explain herself. Accept her explanation. Let her know that you don't mean to interfere in her private life, that you really don't mind whom she sees, as long as she is discreet while the family

335

is in the spotlight—point out that she must be especially discreet during the trial in order to protect Jerry's future."

Griffith nodded. "Jerry. Yes, she'll buy that."

"Then, from time to time next week, at the end of the day, discuss the trial with her, what happened and so forth. That would be natural. If you get lucky, she might let slip some of the things Barrett has confided to her or certain activities of the opposition she's discerned. On the other hand, if it turns out that she hasn't learned much from Barrett or won't reveal what she does know, then we're left with another option, which we can pick up if we need to. We can always arrange to have you plant some false or misleading information with Maggie—like letting her overhear you on the phone—or having you leave a memorandum around concerning some mythical strategy Elmo is planning, or a nonexistent new witness who's going to appear—and she can pass this information on to Barrett, to make him believe we're going to do something we're really not doing. That could serve to throw them off balance. Furthermore, after receiving such information, Barrett might trust Maggie enough to confide some of the opposition's real plans. I do believe this is worth trying, Frank. Do you think you can manage it?"

Nervously Frank Griffith fingered the cigar in his breast pocket. "I don't know. I suppose I can try. I still don't like the idea of someone in our house spending nights with an attorney who's trying to defame me—and not just me, you understand, but my son, my son, also. Still, if you and Elmo . . ."

"Try it," said Yerkes firmly. "Don't intervene in Maggie's love life. Let her help dig Barrett's grave. Do it our way."

Duncan offered his patron a nod of admiration and turned to Griffith. "I approve, Frank. It's the best approach for you, your son, our common cause."

Frank Griffith had recovered his old fraternal-club assurance. "Okay, gentlemen, I'm sold. I'm buying air time for Romeo and Miss Judas."

VII

It was Monday morning, finally, June 22 in this year of Our Lord, finally, and Mike Barrett sat in his end seat at the defense counsel's table, every nerve in his system chafing as he waited anxiously for the trial to begin.

Looking over his shoulder at the round wall clock high above the entrance to Courtroom 803 of the Superior Court of the County of Los Angeles, Mike Barrett could make out that the hour hand was past the nine and the minute hand just past the four. It was twenty-two minutes after nine o'clock in the morning.

In eight minutes, the bailiff would make his ceremonial announcement, and then, at last, the battle would be joined.

Barrett's eyes moved from the clock to the jam-packed spectators' seating area below it. Not only was every one of the brown flip-down seats filled, but rows of wooden folding chairs had been brought in from the outside hallway and placed against the walls and in front of the cocoa-colored curtains covering the windows on either side of the air conditioners, and these chairs were filled with part of the overflow. Except for a familiar face that he spotted here and there—Philip Sanford, Irwin Blair, Maggie Russell (whose eye he failed to catch)—these were strangers, these members of the audience, the curious, the concerned, the involved, the species Homo sapiens, whom their District Attorney must protect from depravity, whom he himself must save from a sentence that promised muteness, deafness, blindness.

For a moment, he wondered about all the others who had wanted to get into the courtroom.

When he, with Zelkin, Kimura, Sanford, Fremont, and Donna, had reached the eighth floor of the Hall of Justice forty-five minutes ago—Kimura and Donna had come along to help carry the oversized briefcases and the carton containing the defense's law brief, exhibits, reference books, research notes—Barrett had been astounded by the unruly mob pushing and shoving and crowding the entire length of the corridor that led around the corner to the Superior Court. He had estimated that at least three hundred persons were struggling to get inside. Only one third of them had succeeded.

He remembered striding into the bank of bright lights that accompanied the television cameras in the hall outside the courtroom entrance. One commentator had recognized Ben Fremont and tried to drag him before a camera for an interview, but Fremont had not forgotten yesterday's instructions and had refused. Several newspaper reporters had tried to corner Zelkin and himself, peppering them with impossible questions, but Zelkin had bluntly replied that everything the defense would have to say would be said for the record in the courtroom.

Halted briefly while police officers tried to make a path for them into the courtroom, Barrett had observed and listened to the renowned commentator Merle Reid, whom he had met several times at the Osborns'. Reid was standing before a camera holding a sheaf of notes and describing the scene.

"It is incredible, this scene on the eighth floor of the Hall of Justice," Reid was saying into the microphone dangling from his neck, as he faced the camera, "a scene the authorities were totally unprepared to handle. Some trials attract international attention because they center upon great names and celebrity, and such trials have ranged from the two-day trial of Mary Queen of Scots in Fotheringay Castle, in 1586, to the trial of Bruno Hauptmann in Flemington, New Jersey, for the kidnapping and murder of Charles A. Lindbergh, Jr., in 1935. Some trials attract international attention because they have featured scandal. Such a one was the adultery trial of the Reverend Henry Ward Beecher in Brooklyn City Court in 1875 on a charge of alienation of affections. And such a one was the trial of Oscar Wilde at the Old Bailey in 1895 on a charge of homosexuality. Other trials attract worldwide attention because they are politically controversial.

There have been such trials in America—Mary Surratt and her fellow conspirators being tried in the old Penitentiary Building in Washington for the assassination of President Lincoln, and Nicola Sacco and Bartolomeo Vanzetti being tried in the Dedham Courthouse in Massachusetts as anarchists who had committed murder. There have been such trials in Europe—Émile Zola being tried in Paris for libeling the Ministry of War in his defense of Captain Alfred Dreyfus, and Cardinal Joseph Mindszenty being tried in the Budapest People's Court for attempting to overthrow the Hungarian Communist government.

"And then there are trials that attract international attention because they concern the human right to freedom of speech and freedom of the press. Such a one was the trial of John Peter Zenger, publisher of the *New-York Weekly Journal*, who was accused of libeling the tyrannical royal governor in his writings and who stood trial in New York's city hall in 1735. Zenger had written, 'The loss of liberty in general would soon follow the suppression of the liberty of the press . . . no nation, ancient or modern, ever lost the liberty of freely speaking, writing, or publishing their sentiments, but forthwith lost their liberty in general and became slaves.' Yet only the heroic advocacy of his aged attorney, Andrew Hamilton, won Zenger an acquittal—and won for American free speech a momentous but temporary victory.

"Not since that milestone trial of John Peter Zenger has any trial involving freedom of speech or press been considered as important as this criminal trial involving the state of California against an unknown bookseller named Ben Fremont, who is charged with purveying obscenity in the form of a slender underground novel, *The Seven Minutes*, which was written by an American expatriate author dead over three decades.

"Why has this particular trial, which might have been relegated to the obscurity of a provincial debate over just one more pornographic book, with the authorities threatening the defendant with no more than a felony charge—why has this trial caught the fancy of people everywhere, not only in the United States, but in Great Britain, Scandinavia, France, Germany, Italy, Spain, Mexico, South America, Japan, and elsewhere?

"This reporter can give no single answer. No one I have spoken to of this phenomenon can explain it. At best, we can only conjecture many answers. The trial opens at a decisive moment in the history of civilized man, a moment when the future of human morality hangs in balance. Through books, periodicals, television, stage, motion pictures, freedom of speech has pushed beyond all the old frontiers of acceptable decency, in an attempt to find the farthest reaches of art or in an attempt to assault and destroy the fiber of home and family and society as people in every civilized land have chosen to know it. At the very same time, the authority of religion in nations throughout the world has been challenged and weakened by those testing the outer limits of freedom and black-and-white definitions of right and wrong, of moral and immoral.

"Perhaps it is that at this moment state and church foresee their possible doom unless they rally to stop the destroyers of established moralities, and unless they punish those who have gone too far, and unless they set up new limits to contain the misuses and excesses of anarchistic freedom.

"And for the final battlefield they have selected this court of law in this sprawling southern city of the state of California. The object provoking this showdown is one with unique international appeal and incitement alike. Although written by a male, the novel about which the storm rages is entirely a woman's novel, concerned with a single fictional female's attitudes and feelings toward her psyche and her sex life. Since women of all countries are women first and citizens second, their interest in the fate of Cathleen in this book overcomes national boundaries. Moreover, its explicit sexuality, which the book insists is dominant in the minds of all women, appears to concern and trouble women everywhere, and to concern and worry men everywhere. Above all, because of certain passages that leaders of Western religions consider threatening—not only Catholic leaders in France, Italy, Spain, but Protestant leaders in the United States, Great Britain, Germany —passages that show sacred figures from every religion in the sexual act—the world's churches have quietly joined with temporal authorities in an attempt to suppress *The Seven Minutes* and by this example set new limitations on freedom of speech and working morality.

"Beyond these reasons, there may be other less practical, more romantic reasons for the glamour that has surrounded . . ."

But Mike Barrett, although fascinated, had heard no more. Zelkin had beckoned him, and he had hurried after the others into the courtroom to help unpack the briefcases and the carton and ready himself for the looming battle.

Now, scanning the audience in the courtroom behind him once again, he finally caught Maggie Russell's eye. He nodded to her. She nodded back in grave acknowledgment of his greeting.

Next Barrett quickly reviewed the members of the press. They were seated in folding chairs—no room for tables—the breadth of the courtroom, behind the rail at his back that separated the gallery from the actual court itself. The faces and attire of the journalists confirmed what the television commentator had been saying outside the entrance, that this had become a trial not merely of local interest or national interest, but one with international attraction. There were the obviously American newsmen, chatting, doodling on their pads, reviewing background material, and then there were journalists whose newspapers or syndicates were located in London, Paris, Milan, Munich, Geneva, Mexico City, Barcelona, Tokyo.

From the press row Barrett's attention wandered to the rectangular mahogany double council table that belonged to the prosecution, and that in this cramped space seemed almost an extension of his own table. Peering over Zelkin's head, he could observe District Attorney Duncan, now running his fingers through his smooth blond hair, now scratching his thin nose, now rubbing his cleft chin, as he listened to something said by his assistants, swarthy Victor Rodriguez and suntanned Pete Lucas.

His own mahogany table, Barrett noted, also held three participants, but only two of these were advocates for the defense. There was Barrett himself, in the end chair nearest the jury box, wearing a button-down white shirt and a blue tie and a navy-blue Dacron suit. Beside him, still emptying a briefcase, was pudgy Abe Zelkin. At the far end was the defendant, Ben Fremont, in his best Sunday suit, squinting up through his metal-rimmed spectacles at the six grilled fluorescent lights suspended from the ornate ceiling.

One last time, Barrett inspected the battlefield that lay immediately before him. Off to his extreme right, somewhat beyond the prosecution table, was the graying, broad-shouldered bailiff, a one-man riot squad who maintained decorum in the courtroom and served as a male baby sitter for the twelve jurors. He had been standing, listening to several members of the press, but now he took his station behind his small desk.

From the bailiff Barrett directed his attention across the heads of the opposition to the larger rolltop desk, which partially hid the skinny, giraffish court clerk, who was hunched over his minutes. Late Friday, in the presence of judge and spectators, he had sworn in the jurors with the reminder that they must "well and truly try the cause," and soon, as the judge's secretary in matters of the court, he would develop his minutes of the proceedings as well as accept and tag all exhibits.

In the center of the room, most imposing and formidable, rose the judge's bench, austere despite its desk microphone, pencils, notepad, water carafe, gavel, and an eight-volume set of the *California Criminal Code.* Behind the bench, the high-backed leather seat of justice, and behind the seat a drape-covered door flanked by the American flag and the California state flag.

Below the judge's bench, between Barrett and the witness box affixed to the bench, was the swivel chair, the stenotyper set on a tripod, and the desk belonging to Alvin Cohen, the court reporter assigned to record the proceedings and testimony of the impending trial. At the moment, Cohen was on one knee adjusting the tripod for the stenotyper, and he looked like a youthful associate professor trying to find a cuff link.

Above the court reporter was the witness box, its open side forming a step-up entrance leading to a padded chair and a raised microphone. Barrett stared gloomily at the witness box, for which he and Zelkin were so ill-prepared, and then he swung himself on his own swivel chair to consider the low wall of the elongated jury box only a few feet from his elbow.

The jurors' chairs were still empty.

Barrett's mind traveled back to yesterday morning when Abe Zelkin had tried to fill those chairs for him by reciting the biographies and sketching the personalities of the twelve jurors who had been selected.

Zelkin had been shrewd in his selection of jurors from among those who had survived the peremptory challenges and dismissals for cause by the District Attorney. It was not merely each juror's occupation and way of life, nor even his opinions and prejudices, that had influenced Zelkin's selections; it was the juror's mannerisms, his use of language and inflections of speech when replying to questions, even the newspaper or magazine he carried under his arm. For this was a censorship case, and knowledge of a juror's sophistication, education, literary interests was all-important.

Zelkin had felt that out of the twelve jurors there were at least five who showed definite promise of being in empathy with their cause, and he had only hoped that the other seven were honestly impartial about the issue at stake. Zelkin had felt that they had a good jury. But then, thought Barrett, he was sure Duncan felt equally confident of his own approval of these jurors.

Thinking of yesterday's last-minute preparations, Barrett's attention strayed back to the witness stand, and he recalled that all of Sunday afternoon they had brought their witnesses into the office and privately discussed their testimony with them and made suggestions and taken notes. He thought of the one added disaster that had occurred. Kimura had delivered to them Saturday, directly from International Airport, a witness in whom they had invested considerable hope. This was da Vecchi, the Florentine artist who had met Jadway in Paris in 1935 and who claimed to have painted him once in Montparnasse. Da Vecchi had proved to be a stunted, elderly Italian with the shifty eyes of a Roman pickpocket. For appearance on the witness stand, Barrett had prayed for a Titian or a Carpaccio, but instead he had someone reminiscent of a garrulous Old World shoemaker who always forgot to make the right change.

Da Vecchi, it turned out, had met Jadway only three times —but, although the artist's memory had clouded, he did remember several of Jadway's remarks made while the author had been writing his novel, and these attested to Jadway's integrity—and in one of the three meetings, da Vecchi had done a painting of Jadway. In Zelkin's office, da Vecchi had prepared to unveil the portrait. For Barrett it had been a suspenseful moment, the moment before seeing the real defendant in the case for the first time. Da Vecchi had thrown aside the burlap to reveal his oil, and Barrett's heart had sunk. For the painting was a cubist abstract, a ridiculous crossword puzzle of cones, squares, and perpendicular and horizontal lines dabbed in blue and yellow and crimson and brown.

343

If the canvas depicted a countenance at all, it was that of a dominating centaur's head constructed of nursery-school blocks. The painting was valueless, and da Vecchi not much better, and Barrett sighed once again—beggars cannot be choosers. Da Vecchi would take the stand for the defense in due time.

Brooding, Barrett cast one more sidelong glance at his opponent. The District Attorney was surveying the audience and waving to someone. Barrett wondered how Duncan had spent his Sunday. With Christian Leroux, defamer of Jadway, no, doubt, and possibly with Jerry Griffith. And then he wondered whether Jerry Griffith had seen Duncan. Of course, Maggie would know, but he would not ask her. He stared at his rival, envying him his witness wealth, and then he turned around again to see the time.

The wall clock read half past nine.

Two buzzes sounded through the room, and Barrett saw the hefty bailiff jump to his feet and hasten to the doorway leading upstairs to the jury room. Immediately Barrett sensed that both the press and the spectators understood, for their chatter had begun to subside and everyone was alert.

Suddenly the twelve jurors, eight men, four women, were filing into the courtroom, and they were finding their places in the jury box. As they did so, Abe Selkin tugged Barrett's sleeve and cupped a hand to his ear. "Take a look at the five I told you about, the ones I have hopes for," he whispered. Zelkin had once taken a memory course, in an attempt to match Barrett's natural gift, and now he played one of its games in order to fix the five in Barrett's mind. "Juror number two, the woman who looks like Mao Tse-tung, very good. Number three, the banker who looks like Uncle Sam, pretty good bet. Number seven, the girl who looks like Greta Garbo, real cool. Number ten. The Joe Louis type. He's a teacher. Twelve. The foreman. Twin for Albert Schweitzer. Name's Richardson. Big architect. Got them?"

"Okay," said Barrett.

His eyes followed the jury, and they silently asked Shakespeare's old question, *Are* you good men and true?

The jurors had assumed their places, and from his desk the bailiff was addressing the spectators assembled in the courtroom.

"Please rise," the bailiff commanded, "and face the flag of our

344

country, recognizing the premises for which it stands—liberty and justice for all."

Barrett had risen with everyone else, and now he remained standing as the drapes behind the elevated bench parted and Judge Nathaniel Upshaw entered the court. Gathering part of his black judicial robes in one hand, the judge came around to his presiding chair. He was an imposing figure, Barrett could see, stiff white hair, vigilant eyes cushioned by bags, long gaunt face that was wrinkled, strong, composed. Somehow like the representation of an English lord chief justice on a Toby mug. Slouching, knuckles pressed to the bench, he stood, waiting for the bailiff to finish.

"Division 101 of the Superior Court of the State of California, County of Los Angeles, is now in session," the bailiff intoned. "The Honorable Nathaniel Upshaw, judge, presiding. Please be seated."

There was a shuffling throughout the courtroom, and the audience, the press, the counsels were in their places, and Barrett locked his fingers together as he felt a nervous clutch in his chest and throat.

Judge Upshaw had settled into his chair, taken up the gavel, rapped it once.

He peered down at the court reporter, whose fingers hung poised over the stenotyper. Through the desk microphone he addressed the reporter.

"Case of the People of the State of California versus Ben Fremont is ready for trial." Judge Upshaw's voice was resonant, deep, and it boomed into every corner of the room. "May the record reflect that the People are represented by Mr. Elmo Duncan, and defendant is present with his counsel, Mr. Michael Barrett, and the jury is in the box."

Judge Upshaw spun toward the prosecution table and studied it. At last he spoke again.

"Do you wish to make an opening statement, Mr. Duncan?"

The District Attorney came promptly to his feet.

"Yes, Your Honor, I would like to make such a statement at this time."

"You may proceed."

Elmo Duncan strode briskly across the room. Passing the defense table, he continued to look straight ahead. Reaching the jury box, he gripped the low wall, offered the collective jurors one nod of welcome and a tight smile. Then, releasing the barrier, he stepped back and crossed his arms in front of him, and as he began to speak his voice was forced and strained.

"Ladies and gentlemen of the jury," said Elmo Duncan, "as you may know, in setting the stage for the trial of a criminal case, both the attorney for the People and the attorney for the defendant are permitted to make an opening statement. The purpose of these statements is merely to outline for you what each of us intends to prove in our presentation of our cases. What we can say is limited by one rule. Our opening statements must be confined to the facts we intend to elicit in evidence. At no time are we permitted to plead the case. In short, as one magistrate put it, an opening statement might be compared to the 'table of contents in a book, so that you can follow the chapter and know what the chapter is about.'

"So, in this brief opening, I will not present evidence. Later today, and for the duration of the trial, the evidence will come from there—"

Duncan pointed to the witness stand.

"—from the box where witnesses, under solemn oath to observe complete fidelity to truth, in full knowledge that they may suffer the criminal charge of perjury if they deviate from the truth, will testify to facts and facts only. Generally, the testimony of witnesses in a criminal trial must be limited to what they saw with their own eyes, heard with their own ears, or smelled, touched, felt through use of their physical senses. Only rarely are they permitted to present hearsay evidence—that is, rumors or secondhand accounts relating to the parties to the action. Normally, in a criminal case, witnesses are not encouraged to give their opinions or to draw conclusions. However, in an obscenity case such as this one, I am sure the court will agree that we can make an exception to the rule. In judging whether or not a literary work is obscene, expert opinions from persons qualified to so give such opinions are, because of precedent, usually admissible in evidence as actual facts.

"Keeping this in mind, ladies and gentlemen of the jury, bear with me while I outline the so-called table of contents of the People's case."

District Attorney Duncan's voice had begun to free itself from the initial strangulating effects of tension. It was as if he had employed these preliminary moments not so much to instruct the jurors in the basic procedures as to convince himself that the jurors would be receptive to the prosecution and that all was going to be well from now on.

When he resumed, he was at ease, assured, confident.

"We are gathered here because we, the advocates for the People, have charged the defendant, Ben Fremont, bookseller, with violation of Section 311.2 of the Penal Code of the State of California. This section provides the following, which you will hear repeated many times during the course of this trial—it provides that— 'Every person who knowingly: sends or causes to be sent, or brings or causes to be brought, into this State for sale or distribution, or in this State prepares, publishes, prints, exhibits, distributes, or offers to distribute, or has in his possession with intent to distribute or to exhibit or offer to distribute, any obscene matter is guilty of a misdemeanor.'

"Any may I add, if a person is found guilty of purveying obscene matter—and 'matter' is defined in our Penal Code as being a 'book, magazine, newspaper, or other printed or written material'—if such a person is found guilty of purveying obscene matter a second time, he is guilty not of a misdemeanor but of the graver crime of felony."

As Duncan drove home the last, Barrett saw Ben Fremont wriggling uncomfortably, and this underlined his own instinctive reaction to Duncan's unwarranted mention of second offenses.

Barrett came to his feet. "Objection, Your Honor. Object on the ground that prosecution counsel is not confining himself to stating what he intends to prove, but is arguing his case against the defendant."

Judge Upshaw moved his head in assent. "Objection sustained." He addressed the District Attorney. "Mr. Duncan, I do believe you are exceeding the scope of an opening statement."

Duncan smiled up at the judge apologetically. "Thank you, Your Honor. I am sorry." He turned his smile upon the jurors. "I'm afraid I was carried away."

347

Seated once more, Barrett heard Zelkin whisper, "But charm boy really zinged it in there—two-time loser, felony. I hope you give him some of the same."

"Don't worry," said Barrett quietly, eyes still holding on the District Attorney.

Duncan had resumed his opening statement. "The crux of the section of the Penal Code which we have charged the defendant with violating comes down to a single word in that section—the word 'obscene.' And about this word the Penal Code is very specific. Under Section 311 we find this definition: 'Obscene means that to the average person, applying contemporary standards, the predominant appeal of the matter, taken as a whole, is to prurient interest, i.e., a shameful or morbid interest in nudity, sex, or excretion, which goes substantially beyond customary limits of candor in description or representation of such matters and is matter which is utterly without redeeming social importance.'

"Now, the words 'obscene' and 'prurient' will be heard frequently during the course of this trial. You have just heard their legal definitions. It is useful to be aware, also, of their dictionary definitions. In *The Oxford English Dictionary*, and in others, 'obscene' is found to mean something that is disgusting, filthy, indecent. And matter of 'prurient' interest is matter containing lewd or lascivious or evil ideas, matter that gives readers an impure itch for what is vile.

"The State has charged that a work of fiction known as *The Seven Minutes*, written by one J J Jadway, is a work appealing to a predominantly prurient interest and therefore is criminally obscene, and that because the defendant, Ben Fremont, knowingly distributed such an obscene work, he is guilty of a crime under the law.

"In this case, we shall prove beyond a reasonable doubt three essential aspects of the defendant's violation of the law.

"First, we shall prove that Ben Fremont, as a bookseller in this county, did exhibit and distribute the book called *The Seven Minutes*.

"Second, we shall prove *scienter*. That is, that the defendant, Ben Fremont, distributed this obscene book although he had full knowledge of the book's contents. To establish this, we will introduce the testimony of the sheriff's deputies attached to the Vice Bureau of the county of Los Angeles who, as undercover men, purchased *The Seven Minutes* from the defendant. We shall further support this testimony by introducing tape recordings of the voices of the investigating and arresting police officers' conversation with the defendant, Ben Fremont, and this will further demonstrate that the defendant had full knowledge of what was inside the book and that he agreed its contents were obscene.

"Third, we shall prove beyond a shadow of doubt that, to the average man or woman, applying contemporary community standards, *The Seven Minutes* is obscene within the legal definition of the word and that it is a work without any redeeming social importance whatsoever. To establish these facts, we will produce witnesses in a number of categories. One category of witness, consisting of literary experts or persons who were acquainted with the author of the book, will testify that the work in question is obscenity written for its own sake and devoid of either literary merit or social value. These experts will also reveal that the author created the work for no other purpose than to exploit prurient interest in susceptible readers for the sake of his personal profit. Another category of witness, consisting of respected members of the municipalities of the county of Los Angeles, will testify that the average person in our community would agree that the book shamefully exploits the reader's morbid interest in nudity, sex, or excretion. A final category of witness will testify, on the basis of personal knowledge, that the book is obscene and that its encouragement of prurient interests among the immature has caused emotional disturbance that has led to violence.

"Let me add, I cannot be too emphatic about the importance of the cause-and-effect relationship of pornography to violence. Our highest judicial authorities in the land have told us, time and again, that if proof can be offered that a sex-filled book has incited antisocial conduct, that book no more deserves to circulate freely in a civilized society than a madman or a murderer. The State plans to offer such proof. We will introduce psychiatric experts—"

Barrett was instantly on his feet. "Objection, Your Honor. Counsel for the People is exceeding the scope of his opening statement."

"Objection sustained," said Judge Upshaw. He addressed himself to the District Attorney. "Mr. Duncan, you will confine yourself to facts intended to be elicited in evidence, and refrain from comments that properly belong in your closing argument."

Duncan appeared agreeably chastened. "Thank you, Your Honor." He gave his attention to the jurors once more. "Let me say that our expert witnesses will include psychiatrists who are familiar with the effects of pornographic materials on young minds. Our witnesses will also include, perhaps for the first time in an American courtroom, an actual victim of this gutter literature.

"By proving this point—in fact, all three points that I have presented to you—we shall not only prove that the defendant violated the law and deserves to be found guilty as charged, but in so doing we will also prove, as we must, that the obscene work of fiction that the defendant distributed was equally guilty and should therefore be censored from public view.

"Yes, ladies and gentlemen, censored! To win our case, we are committed to prove, and shall prove, that invoking censorship upon works of obscenity no more abridges human rights and freedoms than invoking arrest and confinement upon individuals who have done harm to our communities by acts of violence. We shall show why, in condemning a work of obscenity, we are not contravening or abridging individual rights as set forth in the First Amendment to the Constitution, which promises that Congress shall make no law 'abridging the freedom of speech or of the Press.'

"Ladies and gentlemen of the jury, in the days to come we shall attempt to show that this book, *The Seven Minutes*, is totally obscene, utterly without redeeming social importance, and therefore is outside the protection guaranteed by the First Amendment of our Constitution. We shall prove that this book deserves to be censored. We shall attempt to prove the premise stated with such clarity by Norman Thomas, a Socialist candidate for President of the United States—yes, Norman Thomas, a radical in the continuing fight to preserve our freedoms—who told a United States Senate subcommittee in 1955, 'I am not at all impressed by the degree to which defenders of . . . pornography, pure and simple, want to press the First Amendment. I do not think the First

Amendment gives any guaranty to men to seduce the innocent and to exploit the kind of unformed mind and unformed emotions of children and adolescents. . . . I do not believe that in order to protect the fundamental liberties of the press we have to turn our children, who are, in a sense, the ward of all our society, over to the kind of visual exploitation of base emotion, and the arousal of base emotion to which, of course, this literature, this pornographic literature . . . and all the rest are directed.' "

Listening, Mike Barrett felt Zelkin nudging him.

"For Chrissakes, Mike," Zelkin whispered fiercely, "he's anticipating and debating you. Aren't you . . . ?"

During Elmo Duncan's last remarks, Barrett had instinctively prepared to interrupt with an objection. The District Attorney was indeed introducing evidence that was out of place in an opening statement. What had deterred Barrett from intervention had been a desire to limit his objections to absolutely prejudicial material. Excessive objections, he knew, often antagonized jurors. Yet Zelkin was right. Duncan had gone too far.

Barrett's arm shot upward, and he followed it. "Objection, Your Honor. People's counsel is being argumentative. He is introducing evidence in his opening statement."

"Objection sustained," Judge Upshaw said immediately. He glowered at the District Attorney. "Mr. Duncan, you are perfectly aware of the limitations of an opening statement. I again admonish you to contain yourself within the bounds of those limitations."

"Thank you, Your Honor," said Duncan. "I am sorry."

But to Barrett, eying his rival from the defense table, Elmo Duncan seemed anything but sorry. Instead, his manner was satisfied and relaxed. It was as if he knew that, despite the scolding from the bench, he had scored with the jurors and was now ready for his closing remarks.

"Ladies and gentlemen of the jury," Duncan said, "in the presentation of our testimony and our evidence, we will prove that it is the average man and his community who are offended and damaged by the ingredients in this book. We will contend that it is the average man, not the special man, the scholar, the liberal, the intellectual, who should interpret our censorship laws. For, as a judge in New York's highest court, in finding *Tropic of Cancer*, by Henry Miller, an obscene work, explained it—it simply does not follow 'that because an alleged work of literature does not appeal to the prurient interest of a small group of intellectuals that it is not obscene under the prurient interest, or for that matter any other legal test of obscenity. This would permit the substitution of the opinions of authors and critics for those of the average person in the contemporary community.' No, it is the average—"

Barrett had suffered enough of this. It was harmful to the defense. He half rose, hoisting an arm toward Judge Upshaw. "I must object, Your Honor. Not only has Mr. Duncan argued his point, rather than outlined it, but he is now arguing with the defense witnesses before they've had an opportunity to appear. Objection on the grounds that People's counsel is giving his closing argument rather than his opening statement."

"Objection sustained!" said Judge Upshaw emphatically. He directed himself to the District Attorney. "Mr. Duncan, you have gone beyond the scope of the opening statement not once but several times. You have entered evidence, you have argued issues, you have been out of order. I caution you most strongly to refrain from using facts at the outset that properly belong in your summation."

Duncan appeared genuinely contrite. "I apologize, Your Honor. I hope you will pardon my overenthusiasm. I was eager to expand, as much as possible, on the points of law we shall attempt to prove."

Judge Upshaw was not appeased. "Mr. Duncan, in regard to the objection I have just sustained, you were not trying to prove a point of law—you were trying to plead your own case. This I will not permit. Please proceed."

Momentarily unnerved, Duncan made a visible effort to recover his poise as he turned back to the jury.

"Ladies and gentlemen of the jury, I will simply say that we shall try to substantiate, through the presentation of testimony and evidence, the fact that the contents of *The Seven Minutes* would be considered to cater to prurient interest by the average person in the community.

"It shall be our contention that the bookseller and defendant on trial, Ben Fremont, distributed this unwholesome novel perfectly aware that many readers would buy it, not because it is a literary work, but principally because it is a work of hard-core pornography—a work manufactured, as we shall also give evidence, by an author with the leer of the professional pornographer and commercialist, an author who possessed no thought of investing his work with any social importance whatsoever.

"If I may conclude on a note of levity, I am reminded of the occasion when *Lady Chatterley's Lover* was defended as a work of pure art and without any appeal to prurient interest, which provoked a judge on the appellate bench, Judge Leonard P. Moore, to remark rather drily, 'As to prurient interest, one can scarcely be so naïve as to believe the avalanche of sales came about as the result of a sudden desire on the part of the American public to become acquainted with the problems of a professional gamekeeper in the management of an English estate.'"

The jurors showed their amusement, and Duncan surveyed them, beaming his appreciation, and then he smoothed his hair and massaged the back of his neck, preparing to resume.

From the defense table, Barrett had intended to protest this irrelevancy, but, law or no law, the jurors were pleased, and an objection to what had given them pleasure might antagonize them and close their ears to the defense. Any legal gain here, Barrett decided, might be an actual loss. With difficulty, he maintained his silence.

Duncan had resumed. "As the People's advocate," he was saying, "I intend to dedicate myself, in this trial, to the proposition that *The Seven Minutes*, by J J Jadway, was not written, was not published, was not sold, and was not bought because the American reading public wanted to know how a young woman could lie in bed for seven minutes without her nightgown and not catch her death of a cold—or wondered to what her mind was given for seven long minutes, if she didn't count sheep, that enabled her to overcome insomnia. No, I don't think that was it."

Several jurors chuckled audibly, but Duncan did not acknowledge them. The smile had fallen from his face. He was intensely serious.

"The People contend that this book was written, was published, was sold, and was intended to be bought solely as an obscene work appealing to a shameful or morbid interest in nudity, sex, excretion. This is what I, what we, contend, and this, ladies and gentlemen of the jury, is what we shall prove in this court of justice. Thank you very much."

Elmo Duncan wheeled away from the jury box, and for an instant his eyes met Barrett's, and his lips turned upward slightly—in pity, Barrett thought—and then he walked to his table at the far side of the room.

"Mr. Barrett—" Barrett's head came up, and he realized Judge Upshaw was addressing him— "are you ready to make your opening statement now or do you wish to reserve it?"

Barrett scrambled to his feet. "I would like to proceed at this time, Your Honor."

"You may proceed."

With a quick glance at Zelkin and Ben Fremont, Barrett pushed aside his chair, left the security of the defense table, and crossed in front of the jury box. He could observe several of the jurors inspecting him or appraising him with curiosity, and he guessed what might be in their minds. Still under the influence of Duncan's opening statement—argument, really—they were telling themselves that everything that could be said had been said, and were wondering what was left for this stranger to say to them.

Barrett consoled himself that it is always thus in a debate when your opponent has spoken first and you have to follow, and it becomes doubly difficult when the first and preceding speaker has been an effective one. Your listeners, then, have been brainwashed, sated, won over, and they are resistant or skeptical or inattentive to anything new or anything more. As number two, you have to climb uphill to reach them. You have to fight and sweat for their interest, and, once gaining it, you have to unwash their brains and then paint their minds full of fresh pictures, and hope that they have the capacity to accept these new images.

Casually brushing his lapel with one hand, Barrett reminded himself that there was one way to capture their instant attention. Startle them. Surprise them, without outraging or antagonizing them. Not easy. Because he was not yet locked into debate, the give and take that goes on between prosecution and defense during examination and cross-examination over specific testimony. As yet he could not jar the minds of the jurors by opposing or refuting something Duncan or his witnesses had drilled into their

354

heads. He could not argue against the prosecution's claims in order to demolish them to make way for his own. He could only state that there was a second side to this censorship matter, a vital and compelling side. This would not be as effective as debate, and therefore it would not be easy to unsettle the jury's already implanted prejudices or uproot these feelings.

There they were, the twelve of them, awaiting the first words. Their fat, thin, open, closed, fleshy, bony countenances offered no friendship, beyond routine courtesy, offered nothing except mild curiosity and dares to his ability. But he would try.

All right. Opening statement. No argument.

"Ladies and gentlemen of the jury," Mike Barrett began, "my colleague seated beside me at the nearest table, Mr. Abraham Zelkin, and I represent the defense in this complex censorship case. Since Mr. Duncan, counsel for the State, has so ably presented the California Penal Code law on criminal obscenity, as well as the law's definitions of the words 'obscene' and 'prurient,' I see no reason to burden you by repeating what he has said.

"However, in defining this law, in understanding it, in measuring it to learn whether it fits the defendant, Mr. Ben Fremont, or Mr. Jadway, the author of the book on trial, or the book itself, we come up against a problem. Mr. Duncan has made it clear that he seeks only the truth in this case. I believe him. I am sure you believe him. I can promise you that my colleague and I, too, seek only the truth in this case. I am certain Mr. Duncan believes me, and I trust that you will believe me. In short, both sides seek the truth, and both sides believe that they have found the truth. But, oddly enough, these truths are different truths. They are two truths, and yet you and I have been raised to believe there is only one truth. To evaluate the two truths, not decide which is real and which the impostor, for both truths are real, that is the problem, your problem—to find out which is the truth that is more applicable to this case involving Mr. Fremont's sale of copies of J J Jadway's *The Seven Minutes*.

"I sympathize with your problem. After all, that most American of American essayists and philosophers, Ralph Waldo Emerson, warned us early in the last century that truth is such a fly-away, such a slyboots, truth is so untransportable and so unbarrelable a commodity that it is as difficult to catch as light itself. Yet, in laying before you the plan and certain particulars of our case for the defense, let me try to catch light and shed some of it on our own image of what is the final truth in this affair.

"You have heard the law of the state as it concerns obscenity. You have heard Mr. Duncan claim that it supports his truth and the prosecution's case. Now permit me to define our truth on behalf of the defense.

"The paramount point that the defense will make, throughout this trial, is that the word 'obscene' and the word 'sex' are not synonymous, are not one and the same."

Barrett heard the scraping of a chair on the other side of the courtroom, and he turned as Elmo Duncan came to his feet.

"I must object, Your Honor," said Duncan. "Counsel for the defense is certainly being argumentative."

Barrett looked toward the bench. Judge Upshaw had knitted his brow. "I don't believe he is arguing, Mr. Duncan. He is defining. A definition can make its way from a negative premise. I am going to overrule the objection, and allow defense counsel to develop his definition. . . . Mr. Barrett, you may continue along this line, but with prudence. Take care not to exceed the limitations of an opening statement."

For a moment, Barrett's hopes had been suspended, threatened, had begun to slip out of reach. Now he almost sagged with relief, grasped hope once again, and turned optimistically to the jury.

"Ladies and gentlemen," he said with quiet insistence, "during the course of this trial the defense will try to prove that because the book *The Seven Minutes* unfolds its human drama within the framework of the sex act, that does not automatically make it a work of obscenity. A student of censorship, Robert W. Haney, has written: 'Law, as conceived in the Declaration of Independence, is not a social device to advance the cause of virtue. It is a protective device to insure the freedom and the opportunities that men need for their happiness and their development. Freedom is not the right to be virtuous; it is the right to do as one pleases . . . limited only when one person's exercise of it endangers the freedom of others, or when it results in overt actions that society deems destructive of its own purposes.'

"Ladies and gentlemen of the jury, I cannot emphasize this interpretation of our law too strongly. Neither federal nor Califor-

356

nia state law was established to promote virtue, but, rather, to protect freedom. The obscenity law that instigated this trial was not placed in the Penal Code in order to inhibit writing and reading about sex or to advance puritanism. It is in the Penal Code only to protect the citizenry against unscrupulous distortion and misrepresentation of pure and healthy sexual acts.

"The procedure of the defense in this case will be guided by the wisdom of some of the most eminent legal minds in our time. It was Judge Jerome Frank who once included the following in a decision: 'I think that no sane man thinks socially dangerous the arousing of normal sex desires. Consequently, if reading obscene books has merely that consequence, Congress, it would seem, can constitutionally no more suppress books than it can prevent the mailing of many other objects, such as perfumes, for example, which notoriously produce that result.'

"Yes, indeed, if a book is to be censored for arousing desire, when shall we bring Arpège to trial?"

Even as many of the jurors smiled, and a few of them laughed, Barrett could hear the District Attorney's stentorian objection behind him.

Barrett turned around in time to hear Judge Upshaw concur with Duncan. "Objection sustained . . . Mr. Barrett, you have gone too far. I must warn you—you are exceeding the limits of the opening statement."

Barrett bowed his head slightly. "Forgive me, Your Honor." He remembered Duncan's earlier words and repeated them. "I hope you will pardon my overenthusiasm."

He could see Duncan's scowl, then Zelkin's broad grin, and he confronted the jury once more. His opponent had opened the door to argument. He had taken advantage of this opening to enter into the minds of the jury. At last, he could see, they had accepted him on equal terms with the prosecutor. Fair enough.

"Ladies and gentlemen of the jury," said Barrett. "The counsel for the People has told us that in a censorship case, centering upon the social merit or lack of that merit in a work of literature, the testimony cannot consist entirely of facts, but must of necessity also include the opinion of experts. With this we concur. Whenever we can, we shall present to you facts in defense of *The Seven Minutes* and of Mr. Fremont's right to sell it. More often,

357

since the social importance of the book—since the story of the book and the sex in the book—since the value of the book—depend upon human judgment of it, we shall present as evidence of its worth representative experts who will offer testimony about the motivations of the author and the meaning of his creative work, and we shall also present the so-called average person in whose contemporary society the book is being sold.

"The first precedent for allowing expert opinion in a trial occurred as far back as 1917, during a censorship trial in New York which concerned the French classic *Mademoiselle de Maupin*, by Gautier. In that trial the judges accepted, in support of the classic, literary testimony quoted from Henry James and other knowledgeable literary figures. Then, in 1938, when *Life* magazine was brought into court for publishing a picture story entitled 'The Birth of a Baby,' which a religious organization condemned and which the New York servants of the law charged with being obscene, lewd, filthy, disgusting—the birth of a baby filthy and disgusting—then and only then was the opinion of expert witnesses who appeared on the stand in person a decisive factor in deciding a criminal obscenity trial. Said the court when rendering its verdict of acquittal, the defense had 'produced as witnesses responsible public health authorities, welfare workers and educators who testified to the sincerity, honesty and educational value of the picture story complained of.' While the prosecution objected to the testimony of such witnesses, and while the court agreed that the prosecution was correct in its protest, the court added, 'Such evidence is, however, rationally helpful and in recent years Courts have considered the opinions of qualified persons.'

"And so the defense shall lean heavily on the opinions of qualified persons. Through these persons we shall prove that *The Seven Minutes* was created with artistic integrity, was accepted in many quarters as a literary masterpiece, and has survived to become a milestone of enlightenment in our understanding of the relationship between the sexes and of sex itself. Through these qualified persons we shall prove that contemporary community standards are not static, are not today what they were a decade or a half century or a century ago, and that J J Jadway was a prophet when he produced a work more than three decades ago that is in keeping with the shift and progress of contemporary standards as they have come to be today. And we shall prove that even if some of the book is still in advance of our times, it nevertheless deserves to be heard."

He was sorely tempted to elaborate.

Seeking time to determine whether he dared risk going beyond the restrictions of his opening statement, Barrett stepped back from the jury box and took a long sip of water from the glass on the defense table.

He considered trying to enter a quotation from Justice Douglas: "Government should be concerned with anti-social conduct, not with utterances. Thus, if the First Amendment guarantee of freedom of speech and press is to mean anything in this field, it must allow protests even against the moral code that the standard of the day sets for the community. In other words, literature should not be suppressed merely because it offends the moral code of the censor."

This was improper evidence, of course, but he might slip it through before an objection stopped him, even as Duncan had succeeded in doing in his own exhortation.

He weighed what might possibly follow this. He might then say, "It will be our argument also, supported by the testimony of witnesses, that *The Seven Minutes* must be judged by the author's utterances alone. Any evidence alleging that antisocial conduct has been provoked by a reading of this book, we shall contend, is legally inadmissible, and if it should be found admissible we shall prove that it has no basis in fact. According to a definition in the California Penal Code, based on Roth versus the United States, 1957, 'Punishment for obscenity is not dependent upon showing that obscene material creates clear and present danger of antisocial conduct or probability that it will induce its recipients to such conduct.' We shall contend, until directed to do otherwise, that conduct resulting from reading a book has no legal bearing on this censorship trial. If we are advised from the bench that it does have bearing, then we shall prove, through the introduction of expert authority, that—in the words of a Supreme Court Justice—written matter is not a significant factor, as balanced against other factors, in influencing an individual's deviation from community standards."

Should this statement stand up, Barrett felt that he might try to clarify it further: "If called upon to do so, we shall prove that the reading of erotica does not beget violence. Dr. Wardell B. Pomeroy, when associated with the Kinsey Institute for Sex Research, participated in team interviews involving more than eighteen thousand subjects. He found that pornographic writings were insignificant sexual stimuli. In this trial, we are prepared to substantiate this finding with the testimony of our own witnesses. And where pornographic writings do produce, in the reader, sexual fantasies, we are prepared to prove not only that this is harmless but that often it has a salutary effect. According to Dr. Sol Gordon, of New York, 'In thirteen years of practice as a clinical psychologist, I have not encountered a single adolescent who was harmed in any way by reading pornography. My own conviction, based on experience, is that the people who organize crusades against pornography are, by and large, the same persons who oppose sex education and who spread the neurosis-breeding notion that it is possible for a thought to be evil. If such people could only realize that thoughts, daydreams, fantasies and desires are not in themselves reprehensible, a large victory would be scored for mental health.' Indeed, years ago, it was Havelock Ellis who suggested that just as youngsters find relief in an escape into fairy tales, adults find similar relief in perusing sex fiction. More recently, two eminent psychoanalysts, Drs. Phyllis and Eberhard Kronhausen, have concluded that the reading of both erotic realism and obscenity is a desirable practice because it provides a safety valve for antisocial feelings by diverting them into acts of mere fantasy."

To elaborate or not to elaborate, this at the moment was Barrett's inner dilemma. What might be attempted had passed through his mind in a matter of seconds. Now his mind tried to resolve the dilemma. Judge Upshaw had suffered Duncan's endeavor, and his own, to encompass closing arguments into opening statements, and at this point the jurist would probably endure no more. A severe or caustic reprimand from the bench would negate all Barrett had achieved for the defense. It was no use. He must abide by the rules.

Barrett's gaze dropped to Zelkin, and it seemed his partner had read his mind, for Zelkin gave him an almost imperceptible nod.

Reassured, Barrett set down his glass and turned back to the jury box.

"The counsel for the People," said Barrett, "sees this case as involving itself with three issues. As counsel for the defense, I see this case as involving only one issue—not three, not two, but one single issue. The State's first issue, whether Ben Fremont did or did not distribute a book called *The Seven Minutes*, will not be an issue for the defense. We concede that Mr. Fremont displayed and sold the book. He is in the business of selling books. He is not an arbiter of literature. He is the proprietor of a bookstore in the community of Oakwood, and his activity and livelihood are the selling of books the year around. He is a member of that noble profession which Thomas Jefferson defended in 1814 when he wrote to a persecuted Philadelphia bookseller: 'I am really mortified to be told that in the United States of America . . . a question about a book can be carried before the civil magistrate.'

"As to the State's second issue, that Mr. Fremont knowingly sold an obscene book, we feel that this so-called issue is not an issue in itself but only a part of the larger issue that we recognize as central to this trial. Because, for the defense, the sole issue that remains is whether *The Seven Minutes*, by J J Jadway, is legally obscene. The entire case, as we see it, centers on what is obscene and what is not."

Once again Barrett was tempted to tread on quicksand, in an effort to underline his point.

He ached to relate what might be an effective anecdote. He wanted to say, "Can anyone dictate tastes, when tastes and taboos differ so? They differ from state to state of this Union, and in every country of this world. One is reminded of Sir Richard Burton's story about a group of Englishmen who went to visit a Moslem sultan in the desert. As the party of Englishmen watched, the Moslem's wife tumbled off her camel. In doing so, her dress slipped up and her private parts were revealed to all. Was the Sultan embarrassed? On the contrary, he was pleased—because his wife had kept her face covered during her accident."

Barrett felt certain that the jurors would enjoy this, and his point would be made. Yet he knew that he would never get that wife off the camel. Duncan's objection would stay her before her fall. There was no point in wasting the Sultan's wife now. He would save her for his summation on some future day.

With an inward sigh, Barrett decided on taking the straight and narrow forensic path.

"Ladies and gentlemen of the jury, if we can prove, as we shall attempt to do, that this book was written honestly, that its contents do not go beyond the limits of candor when judged by contemporary community standards, that the tale it tells is artistic and of vast social importance, then we shall have proved that this work has not violated Section 311.2 of the California Penal Code. And thus, if it is not obscene, it falls naturally into place that Mr. Fremont cannot be charged with knowingly having distributed an obscene work. To state this another way, if we can prove to your satisfaction, ladies and gentlemen of the jury, that *The Seven Minutes* is not obscene, then it holds that we will have proved Ben Fremont innocent of any crime."

Mike Barrett hesitated. Earlier he had planned to conclude on another note. With a flourish, really. In fact, he had rehearsed it before coming to court this morning:

"Once, from the highest bench in the land, Justice Felix Frankfurter laid down the following dictum in voting against an appeal urging censorship. 'The State,' said Justice Frankfurter, 'insists that, by thus quarantining the general reading public against books not too rugged for grown men and women in order to shield juvenile innocence, it is exercising its power to promote general welfare. Surely, this is to burn the house to roast the pig.'

"Ladies and gentlemen of the jury, in this homily the defense has found the legend to place on the banner it will carry aloft throughout this trial, and it is our banner that shall lead us where we must go.

"We refuse to burn down our house—our house and yours—merely to roast a pig."

Beautiful. Effective. And, now, in this growingly nonpermissive atmosphere, totally inadmissible.

Damn.

What had he just said to the jury? Yes. If we can prove *The Seven Minutes* is not obscene, we will have proved Ben Fremont not guilty of any crime.

Better to leave on that pure note than on the discordance of an objection from Duncan.

Barrett fixed his gaze on the jurors.

"You have heard our promise," he said. "Soon you will hear our evidence." He paused. "Ladies and gentlemen of the jury, thank you very much."

Returning to his chair behind the defense table, Barrett felt that he had worn away every muscle and nerve fiber and tissue of his body. He felt that he had reduced himself to the bare bones of a skeleton. But, observing the expression on Abe Zelkin's face, on Ben Fremont's, he realized that it had been worth the effort.

Ben Fremont, excitedly wiping his glasses, was leaning toward him. "You've made me feel much better, Mr. Barrett."

"Good, good." Barrett looked at Zelkin. "How'd I really do, Abe?"

"Excellently. You finally got them to listen. I think you caught up to Duncan. I'd say the first round was a standoff. Which is more than okay by me."

"By me too," Barrett agreed. He shook his head. "From now on, unless some manna drops from heaven, I'm afraid we're in trouble and headed straight downhill."

"Let's play them one at a time," said Zelkin.

Barrett became aware that a hush of silence had blanketed the room.

Judge Upshaw had finished jotting some notes, and from the bench he was addressing District Attorney Duncan.

"Please call your first witness," the Judge ordered.

"Thank you, Your Honor," said Duncan, already on his feet. Briefly he searched the audience. "The People will call Officer Otto Kellog, please."

In short seconds, Kellog, a heavyset plainclothesman in a dark suit, had hastened through the railing gate, traversed the court, and planted himself at attention before the witness chair. The giraffe of a court clerk had loped across the room to meet him.

Quickly the clerk extended a black leatherbound Bible. "Please place your left hand on the Bible, then raise your right hand."

Officer Kellog laid his paw of a hand on the Bible.

The clerk's peppery voice rattled like a machine gun. "Do you swear that the testimony you are about to give in the cause now before the court will be the truth, the whole truth, and nothing but the truth, so help you God?"

"I do."

"State your name, please."

"Otto C. Kellog. K-e-l-l-o-g."

"Please sit down."

Kellog sat down easily and waited expectantly, as one who had played this part before. The court clerk with his Bible had silently vanished, and in his stead stood District Attorney Elmo Duncan.

"Officer Kellog, can you tell us your occupation, please?" asked Duncan.

"I am a police officer, a sergeant, sir, assigned to the vice detail of the Los Angeles County Sheriff's Office."

"Officer, in your work for the vice detail, is it standard procedure for you to wear plainclothes?"

"It is, sir."

"Now, tell me, on the date of the nineteenth of May of this year, did you have reason to visit the premises which are located at 1301 North Third Street in Oakwood, in the county of Los Angeles, California?"

"Yes, sir."

"And did you wear your usual attire of plainclothes on that occasion?"

"Yes, sir, I did, sir."

"Can you tell me exactly what structure stands at 1301 North Third Street in Oakwood?"

"There's a store, sir. It's rented to Ben Fremont, who runs the Book Emporium."

"And you visited these premises. Did you arrive at the premises alone?"

"No, sir, I arrived with my partners, Officer Izaac Iverson and Officer Anthony Eubank. Or do you mean did I go inside the bookstore alone?"

"No, you replied to my question. Now I want to know if your partners accompanied you into the bookstore?"

"I went in alone, sir, the first time."

"You were alone the first time. What was your purpose in entering alone?"

"To look like an ordinary customer who wanted to buy a book for his wife."

"And did you buy a book?"

"I did. Mr. Ben Fremont, the proprietor, he sold me a copy of a book called *The Seven Minutes*, by J J Jadway."

"But that was the first time. Was there a second time you went into the bookstore?"

"Yes, right after I bought the book, I went outside and consulted with my partner, Officer Iverson, for a few minutes, and then we went back into the bookstore together."

"And what was the purpose of your second visit?"

"To arrest Mr. Fremont, sir, for violation of Section 311.2 of the California Penal Code."

At the defense table, Mike Barrett had been listening dutifully to the testimony of the first witness, but now his interest began to wane. This was familiar ground, and he had heard it and read it all before. He only half listened as he sketched caricatures of the jurors on a pad, saving his concentration for the bigger game that lay ahead.

Only once, twenty minutes later, did Barrett become fully alert.

Duncan had been asking the witness whether Ben Fremont had conceded that the Jadway book he was selling was obscene. Officer Kellog, referring to his tape recording of the conversation, insisted that the bookseller had agreed that this novel was obscene.

"He told me it was the most banned book ever," said Officer Kellog. "He said, 'It was banned in every country in the world because it was considered obscene.' Those were Mr. Fremont's own words."

This had scored with the jury, Barrett observed, and immediately he began scribbling on a fresh sheet of notepaper, even as Zelkin began looking for their copy of the transcript which had been made from the police taping recorded on the portable Fargo F-600 that Officer Kellog had worn under his armpit.

Then, closing his ears to the continuing interrogation of the witness, Barrett concentrated on the only key point that he must refute in his cross-examination. He followed Zelkin's forefinger as it moved across the transcript of the tape and revealed in full every word of Ben Fremont's conversation with Officer Kellog before the arrest.

Hastily, Barrett made his notes. Fremont had actually said to the officer that May morning, "It's literature." Later Fremont had said, "Whatever it's been called, obscene or whatever, it is still a masterpiece." And when the officer had baited Fremont, asking the bookseller whether *he* thought *The Seven Minutes* to be obscene, Fremont had refused—thank God—to so label the book. "Who am I to say? That's only another word. There's a four-letter word some people think is dirty and other people think is beautiful. So there we are. Some people, maybe most people, will say this is dirty—but there'll be plenty of people who'll say it's worthwhile." And again, "They don't give a damn about obscenity if in the end they have some great reading that gives them new insights and understanding into human nature."

Smiling to himself, Barrett laid down his pencil at last.

He looked up. Under Duncan's guidance, Officer Kellog was still going through his paces, addressing the microphone and the court with growing assurance.

We'll take care of you, Officer Kellog, we'll take care of you, in due time, Barrett thought.

Due time turned out to be a half hour later.

There was really little for Barrett to question the witness about in the cross-examination. He made much of the policeman's pretense of being a customer. He made much of the policeman's hidden tape recorder. He made much of the policeman's attempts to trap a poor bookseller with leading questions.

But he made the most of the fact that Ben Fremont's conversation, when heard in its entirety, revealed the evidence that the bookseller had believed the novel to be a literary masterpiece and that never once had Fremont himself called the book obscene.

Small victory. A mere balancing of the scales of justice. And of the second truth. A tidying up, no more.

These were bit players, a Greek chorus, setting the stage. The leading players, the luminous stars, would make their entrance soon enough. Then no victories would be small. And no defeats either. Then each witness would be, for the defense, for the prosecution, life or death.

Mike Barrett had finished with Officer Kellog. Duncan was up again for a redirect examination, in an effort to bolster testimony weakened by Barrett's cross-examination. The bolstering attempt was brief and repetitious. Barrett decided to waive his recross. He would save himself for when it counted. Besides, he was hungry now, a good sign.

District Attorney Duncan had completed his redirect.

Judge Upshaw wheeled his chair toward the witness stand. "You may step down now, Officer. You may pass in front of the jury."

As the first witness left the stand, Judge Upshaw carefully enunciated his instructions to the twelve jurors. "We are about to take our noon recess, ladies and gentlemen. I admonish you that during this recess you shall not converse among yourselves, nor with anyone else, on any matter pertaining to this case. Nor shall you express or form an opinion thereon until the matter is finally submitted to you." He rapped his gavel lightly. "Recess until two o'clock."

IT WAS AFTER LUNCH, Judge Upshaw, the jurors, the officers of the court were in their places, and once again the press and the spectators crowded every available inch of the room.

Standing, the bailiff was announcing, "Please remain seated. Court is now again in session."

Judge Upshaw sorted some papers before him and spoke into his desk microphone. "The jury is present. Mr. Duncan, you may call your next witness."

The next witness was Officer Izaac "Ike" Iverson, who had been present in Ben Fremont's Book Emporium when Kellog arrested the bookseller, and the District Attorney quickly guided him through his testimony. Iverson's testimony did little more than corroborate what his colleague had already mentioned of the arrest itself and the dialogue exchanged with Fremont.

In the cross-examination, realizing there had been almost nothing in Iverson's testimony that the defense could make use of, Mike Barrett kept his questions limited. He touched on Officer Iverson's background as a policeman and the kind of assignments he had previously undertaken for the vice detail. Barrett's tactic was an attempt to show the jury how unfair the law was in submitting a respectable book dealer to the same treatment given pimps and prostitutes.

With the appearance of the People's third witness, Barrett saw more possibilities.

The third witness was Officer Anthony Eubank, who had remained in the unmarked police car outside the bookstore throughout the period of Kellog's purchase of the book and during the arrest that followed it. Officer Eubank's task had been to operate the Fargo F-600 unit that received and taped the conversations going on inside the shop. Examining him, Duncan merely tried to have the witness confirm that the use of tape in such arrests was routine, and that the receiver and the tape machine had recorded everything spoken by Ben Fremont and the two police officers accurately and correctly.

In cross-examination, Barrett displayed persistent curiosity about certain aspects of the Fargo F-600 unit: the means by which it was concealed, the way it picked up dialogue, the operation of the receiver by Kellog in the shop and the operation of the recorder by Eubank in the back seat. At one point, Barrett suggested that the equipment be brought into the courtroom and its use be demonstrated for the enlightenment of the jury. And, despite Duncan's mild objection that this acting out was immaterial, Judge Upshaw decided that such a demonstration was a good idea.

When his cross-examination had been completed, Barrett saw that he had gained no ground. He had tried to give the jurors the impression that a naïve and helpless citizen had been the victim of a police conspiracy. He had tried to imply, without ever stating it, that Ben Fremont, a guileless merchant and an ordinary family man like so many members of the jury, had been beset by sinister forces—police officers disguised as book buyers, concealed sending and recording equipment, an electronics expert hidden in an automobile that looked like anything but a squad car. He had failed to sway the jurors because the witness had been miscast for Barrett's role. Officer Eubank was filled with enthusiasm for anything electronic. He was as proud of his Fargo F-600 unit as a child might be of a new Erector set on Christmas morning. He was open, eager, winning. He was the last person on earth one would connect with sinister conspiracy. For the defense, Barrett concluded, he was impossible.

Ah, well, Barrett thought when he returned to the defense table, nothing had been lost or gained as yet. Officer Eubank, like Kellog and Iverson before him, was unimportant. These officers were only the preliminary card. The main event lay in the offing.

Or did it? Would Elmo Duncan come to grips with the central issue, start the big fight, immediately? Barrett sought the time. It was a few minutes after four o'clock. Barrett decided that it was unlikely the prosecution would unveil a big punch at this hour. The effectiveness of a key witness might be weakened by the impending recess. Still, one never knew.

"Mr. Duncan," the Judge was saying, "you may call your next witness."

Elmo Duncan had risen, and he was holding a copy of the Sanford House edition of *The Seven Minutes*. "Your Honor, if you please, may we approach the bench at this time?"

Judge Upshaw nodded. "Yes, of course . . . Mr. Barrett . . . Mr. Reporter."

Barrett quickly joined Duncan and the court reporter, Alvin Cohen, at the bench. Barrett and Duncan were elbow to elbow, and Judge Upshaw had come forward as far as he could, so that the intimate conference would be out of earshot of the jurors.

"Your Honor," Duncan began quietly, "out of the presence of the jury, I would like to move that the People's Exhibit Three— the People's Three—which is this copy of *The Seven Minutes* that was purchased by Officer Kellog be received in evidence, but with one modification. We object to the book jacket's going into evidence with the book."

"One moment, Your Honor—" Barrett started to protest.

Judge Upshaw raised one gnarled hand. "Mr. Barrett, you will permit counsel for the People to finish. Or, Mr. Duncan, have you finished?"

"Not quite," said Duncan. "We feel that the book should be entered into evidence without the jacket because we are concerned here with the contents of the book itself and not with the publicity copy on the jacket, which does not represent what Jadway has written." He turned the book over to reveal the back of

369

the white book jacket. "As you can see, Your Honor, the rear of the jacket contains, above the brief biography of the author, a number of extracted quotations concerning the contents of the book which have been taken from various international periodicals. It is our contention that since these quotations represent, in fact, hearsay statements of various writers, critics, editors, and since we don't have the opportunity to subpoena these people and bring them into court for cross-examination, their alleged remarks on the book jacket are not admissible to a trial that will determine whether or not *The Seven Minutes* is obscene."

"You are finished?" asked Judge Upshaw. "Very well. Now, let me see if I have this clearly, Mr. Duncan. Your motion is that the court receive in evidence as People's Exhibit Three a copy of the book, *The Seven Minutes*, without the book jacket, as I believe those covers are called. Is that correct?"

"It is correct, Your Honor."

Judge Upshaw's gaze moved to Barrett. "Now you may have your turn, Mr. Barrett. Do you have any objection to this motion?"

"I have a strong objection to Mr. Duncan's motion, the strongest," said Barrett. "Mr. Duncan's prosecution is based on the purchase of an allegedly obscene novel. We agree that Mr. Fremont sold this book to Officer Kellog. We agree that Officer Kellog purchased and paid for the book in legal tender. We agree that the book, just as Mr. Duncan has it in his hand right now, the jacketed book, is the purchase in contention in this case. *The Seven Minutes* came out of the book bindery in the East with this jacket on it. The book and jacket were and are a single unit. The book was shipped from warehouse to wholesalers and stores like Mr. Fremont's as a package, as a jacket and book, and Mr. Fremont had it for sale in that form. Officer Kellog acquired it in that form. I firmly believe that the court and the jury have every right to consider as evidence every part of the purchase. I don't believe that because some portion of the purchase does not suit the prosecutor, he should be permitted to remove it, any more than I believe he should have the right to remove those passages inside the book that are of no interest to him because they don't support his charge of obscenity. Would the court allow him to snip out pages—?"

"That's ridiculous," Duncan interrupted huffily. "Counsel knows better than—"

"Hold it, Mr. Duncan," said Judge Upshaw. "You will permit Mr. Barrett to complete his argument. Go ahead, Mr. Barrett."

"As to whether the quotations on the jacket are immaterial," said Barrett. "There are five quotations written by five persons in the nineteen-thirties. Three are credited to the periodicals in which the quotations first appeared, but the writers were obviously anonymous staff members of these publications. I wish we had both the time and the money to discover and subpoena these writers, but we don't. However, we do possess photostatic records of the original publications, to prove that the book jacket quotations are accurate. Regarding the two quotations attributed to critics, one critic is long dead, but the other is alive, namely Sir Esmond Ingram, of England, and in due course he shall appear in this court to submit himself to cross-examination. As to the prejudicial nature of the quotations, if you will examine them, Your Honor, you will see that they are not mere puffs, that some are favorable to the book, some are qualified, and some should not make the prosecution entirely unhappy. I refer to the Vatican newspaper's calling this book the most widely banned in history. Also to the French newspaper's saying that while the book is brilliant, it is also the most obscene work in history. In short, both pro and con. If the defense doesn't mind the con, why should the prosecution mind the pro? We contend that at Mr. Duncan's instigation a police officer purchased an object that was on sale, an object that his superior considered obscene, and if this object is entered into evidence, we insist it should be entered in its entirety, not in parts, but as a whole."

Judge Upshaw looked at Duncan. "Very well. Mr. Duncan, do you have anything more?"

"Yes, Your Honor. I would liken the book's being entered into evidence with its jacket as analogous to the Fargo F-600 unit's being entered into evidence with its price tag still on it, with its guarantee Scotch-taped to it, with its advertising brochure included, the brochure perhaps reading, 'The most widely used transmitting and receiving set in the world, according to one hundred leading businessmen.' Mr. Barrett was concerned with the Fargo F-600 itself, not the extraneous trimming and window dressing. I repeat, Your Honor, that these statements by five writers, three of them anonymous, on the back of the jacket represent hearsay evidence, are inadmissible and prejudicial to the prosecution case, and bear no objective relevancy to the central issue, which is, in short, whether or not the Jadway book is obscene."

Judge Upshaw placed his hands flat on the desk before him. "All right, gentlemen, let me rule on this matter. Now, I confess it is somewhat unusual for People's counsel to offer an exhibit of which he wishes only one part entered into evidence. At the same time, there is no immutable law that demands that materials acquired in a single purchase must be received in evidence as a unit. We are in this court to judge whether or not the contents of an entire book—in this instance with pages numbering from one to one hundred seventy-one—are or are not obscene when the narrative is considered as a whole. In this light, in considering what J J Jadway wrote, it would appear that the drawing on the front of the jacket, the quotations and copy on the rear of the jacket, none of which are by Jadway and none of which form a part of the narrative of the novel, need not be considered when judging whether the book is or is not obscene. Therefore, I will rule that the request of the People that the jacket be removed from this copy of *The Seven Minutes* is a proper one, and I will order that the jacket now be removed from People's Exhibit Three and the book devoid of covering be received in evidence by the court."

"Your Honor, I would like my objection noted for the record," Barrett demanded.

"It has been so noted," said Judge Upshaw calmly. His attention shifted to the District Attorney. "Now, Mr. Duncan, are you ready with your next witness?"

Removing the book jacket from the novel, Duncan said, "Thank you, Your Honor. As a matter of fact, in a manner of speaking, my next witness on the book will be the book itself. We are now prepared to have the book read aloud to the members of the jury, so that, for the first time, they may become acquainted with its contents in its entirety. I have a reader available, a neutral, impartial young man, a Mr. Charles Wynter, who was recommended to us. I have no personal knowledge of him—he was recommended by a friend of my wife's. He is a substitute secondary teacher locally, and in his spare time he has taped recordings for the blind, so he is used to reading aloud without overdramatizing or unduly emphasizing passages, which a professional actor might do. While I already have this young man available, I would willingly agree to let anyone of Mr. Barrett's choosing read the book to the jury. But this is our next witness, Your Honor, a reader who will read the book aloud."

"Very well, Mr. Duncan," said the Judge. "Now let us hear from Mr. Barrett. Do you have any comment on this procedure, Mr. Barrett?"

"I do, Your Honor," said Barrett. "As strenuously as I objected to the book's being entered into evidence in part, just as strenuously do I object to its being submitted to a jury orally. The Penal Code is specific in defining printed matter as one thing and public performances as another. *The Seven Minutes* is printed matter. It was written by J J Jadway not as a play to be spoken or read aloud, but as a novel put down on paper to be read silently and privately by a single reader. Jadway wrote this work in order to communicate directly with a reader's mind and to stir his emotions. Undoubtedly the author's intention was that the reader be allowed to add or subtract mentally from the narrative, to skip or linger over whatever the reader wished, to let the reader emphasize in his own mind certain words or sentences and slide over others. In short, as someone once put it, reading is essentially like marriage, an act involving two persons, the reader and the writer, and not three persons, involving also an actor. Three people involved in a reading, like in a marriage, is a crowd, one too many. Inevitably, the amateur who will play actor will direct the audience's attention to certain passages through conscious or unconscious inflections of speech, through phrasing, timing, pauses, pronunciations and whatnot.

"Your Honor, the moment that *The Seven Minutes* is read aloud, in mixed company, the very candor and language of the narrative, which is enjoyable and acceptable in the privacy of one's own room, may become an embarrassment. What will be judged, in this tiresome, cumbersome, time-consuming process, will be not the book alone, the book itself, but also the person reading it and directing it to his audience. Your Honor, I have twelve copies of *The Seven Minutes,* made available to me by the publisher, and I would suggest that it would be more just to our case if I were permitted to have these copies passed out to the jurors and let each read his own copy to himself or herself. From the point of view of the defense, that would be the only fair procedure."

Judge Upshaw stared past the two attorneys, lost in thought. At last he looked at them and spoke.

"Gentlemen, the book has been received in evidence and is an exhibit. It is within the court's province to decide how this exhibit should be presented to the jury. In my past experience on the bench, I have sat in judgment on several trials where books were read aloud, always in a careful monotone, and I have sat in judgment on one trial where the jurors read individual copies silently and to themselves in a vacated courtroom. I have found that usually a jury listens better than it reads. The act of listening and comprehending is simpler and more common than the act of reading. The members of this jury have been listening all this day. They are conditioned to listen. Reading to themselves might be more difficult. Some are fast readers. Some are slow readers. Some are used to reading books. Others are not. Gentlemen, I am convinced that the simplest and fairest way to present People's Exhibit Three, the most expeditious method of conveying the contents of the book to the jury, would be to do as Mr. Duncan has suggested. I am, therefore, granting the District Attorney's request. As to the person assigned to read the book aloud, does defense counsel have any objection to this Mr. Wynter's reading from the book?"

Barrett was distressed by the judge's rebuff, by this second decision against him, and he had to struggle to keep resentment out of his voice. "Your Honor, I don't care who reads the book aloud. What I care about is that it is being read aloud when a novel is not meant to be presented to readers in such a fashion." He paused. "That is my only objection."

"Well, Mr. Barrett, your objection has already been ruled upon," said Judge Upshaw. "*The Seven Minutes* will be read in the manner that I have indicated . . . Mr. Duncan, if you will produce Mr. Wynter, we will proceed with this case. We will seat Mr. Wynter in the witness box and order him to read this book aloud in its entirety, instructing him to read it clearly, distinctly, in a monotone that will preclude inflections or dramatics. Now let us resume."

THE REMAINDER of this first day in court, and all the morning of the second day and afternoon of the second day, Mr. Charles Wynter, substitute teacher, a rather dour, phlegmatic slender man in his early thirties with an engaging bass voice, sat on the chair in the witness box and read aloud to the jurors the words written in *The Seven Minutes* by J J Jadway.

For Mike Barrett, it was a small calvary, an excruciating and painful experience, hearing the beautiful story torn away from the privacy of the printed page and broadcast by an alien voice in a public place. It was as if Cathleen, the heroine, whose nakedness and love and emotions, so poignant in the bedroom of two hardcovers, had been brutally dragged out into the open, before leering eyes at a sex circus, to be humiliated and cheapened and made to seem indecent.

Throughout the recital, Barrett had found himself squirming. And he knew Abe Zelkin was squirming beside him. But even though he heard words skipped or mispronounced, he restrained himself from objecting. He wanted this done and over with as fast as possible.

Only once, on Tuesday afternoon, the second day of the trial, just after the noon recess, did Mike Barrett voice any objection, and then he did it at the bench and out of the hearing of the jury.

"Your Honor," he said, "I want to record my concern about one mannerism that the reader, Mr. Wynter, possesses, which may be prejudicial to the defense."

"What is that, Mr. Barrett?"

"As he reads, he concentrates his attention fully on the pages before him. But whenever he reaches a passage that might be termed sexually realistic, or that employs words or language that are frank, he has the habit of raising his head, glancing at the jury, before continuing, as if to tell them, 'Wait'll you hear what's coming next,' or 'Hey, I've got something hot for you, but don't blame me, I'm only reading it, I didn't write it.' Then, after that little visual gesture, that warning to the jury, he goes back to the page again. Now, I've observed him do that a dozen times. I'm sure it is unconscious on his part. Still, it serves as a sort of snicker, an adverse commentary on certain portions of the narrative. It would make me happier if Your Honor would point this out to Mr. Wynter and caution him to cease looking up, or at least cease looking up as his prelude to the more realistic sections."

Judge Upshaw turned his head. "Mr. Duncan?"

"Your Honor, I too have been observing the reader, and I have seen him look up at the jury from time to time, but that is normal for a person reading aloud, and he does not seem to look up merely when undertaking obscene—or let us say, risqué—risqué passages, but he looks up when he is reading other passages as well. I'm afraid I cannot agree with Mr. Barrett. I think he is being unduly concerned."

Judge Upshaw nodded and addressed Barrett. "Mr. Barrett, I concur with the prosecution counsel. I am seated right next to the reader. I have watched him closely. I am satisfied that he is performing in a manner as mechanical and objective as possible for a human being. I am sympathetic with your desire to protect the interests of the defendant, and to see justice in this case, and I will listen to any further objections you see fit to make. In this instance, I can find nothing wrong with the performance of the reader. As a consequence, I must deny your request."

"Thank you, Your Honor."

After that, Barrett protested no more.

It was late Tuesday afternoon when Mr. Wynter finished reading aloud the final paragraph of the book, paused, intoned, "The end," and looked up, as if expecting applause.

Immediately the reader was dismissed, the court recessed until nine-thirty Wednesday morning, and Mike Barrett, like someone who has finally escaped the Iron Maiden, felt restored after the grim ordeal.

As he and Zelkin began to stuff their briefcases he said, "Well, now we've got to pick up the pieces. At least we've got a chance to fight back tomorrow. Whom do you think Duncan'll open with?"

"A big one, one of his two biggest guns," said Zelkin. "Today was the lull before the storm. Tomorrow he'll shoot the works, try to demolish Jadway and wipe out the book and the defense in one thunderous shot."

"You mean Leroux?"

"None other."

"Do you know for sure or is that a guess?"

"Mike, when it's going to rain, I get cramps in my legs. When there's going to be an earthquake, I get an ache in my bones. And when the roof's about to fall in, I get a pain in my ass." He snapped his briefcase shut. "Right now, friend, I got a pain in my ass."

How PEOPLE find out when something important is going to happen you never know, Barrett thought. It must be in the air. Psychic waves in the air. A kind of mass ESP. Or some damn thing. Because if the courtroom of the Superior Court of the County of Los Angeles had been filled to capacity the first two days of the trial, this Wednesday morning it appeared to be bursting at the seams.

And now, two minutes after Judge Nathaniel Upshaw had settled behind the bench, the room was silent except for the court clerk's rat-a-tat recital of the oath to the prosecution's first witness of the morning.

". . . the whole truth, and nothing but the truth, so help you God?"

"I do," said the witness.

"State your name, please."

"Christian Leroux."

"Spell the last name."

"L-e-r-o-u-x."

From the bench, Judge Upshaw called down, "You may be seated now, Mr. Leroux."

During the swearing in, Mike Barrett had been studying Elmo Duncan's co-star in the prosecution's elaborate production. Still influenced by Quandt's description of the French publisher, Barrett had expected a person seedy and run-down, yet clinging to some shred of dignity from better days, like an exiled Czarist nobleman who had become a waiter or a doorman. However, there was no air of defeat, no visible signs of poverty, in the publisher's bearing and dress. He was as much a dandy as any aristocratic peacock who had stepped out of the pages of Proust. His recent return to affluence showed.

Except for something furtive and cunning in his manner, battle scars common to many men who have known hard times and survived to their mid-sixties, Christian Leroux was impressive. He must have been taller once, Barrett thought, but his bearing was still grand, which gave an illusion of height. His hair had been dyed and was wavy, with not a strand out of place. The eyes were small, faded blue, darting. The aquiline nose had with age become a veiny bill. The weak chin showed a razor cut. He wore an ultramarine chalk-striped suit with flap pockets, and the jacket was short and tight in the French fashion. There was a neat bow tie and there were jade cuff links and tasseled shoes. In replying to the court clerk, his English had a Mayfair slur punctuated by a sibilant French accent, slight but enough to remind one this was a visitor from Paris.

Observing him take his seat in the witness box, Barrett detected a quality at once unctuous and pretentious, something canting, perhaps a Parisian Pecksniff. If this quality existed, it might not be revealed in the People's examination. Perhaps, Barrett thought, he could find it and expose it in his cross-examination. If it was there. As matters stood, he distrusted Leroux's honesty, oath or no oath. The Frenchman had been ready to say one thing for the defense, and now he had agreed to say another thing for the prosecution. He had been for sale to the highest bidder. That might make him twice as difficult to dissect, Barrett suspected. There is no morality as high-purposed, nor any integrity as staunch, as that possessed by a reformed whore. Well, Barrett decided, he would watch for the signs of cracks, and if possible he would pry them open to reveal the real Christian Leroux.

"Okay," he heard Zelkin whisper, "the assassination of J J Jadway beginneth."

Elmo Duncan, arriving at the witness stand, had greeted his distinguished Gallic visitor with a respectful bow.

"Mr. Leroux, sir, where is your present residence or home?"

"I am a citizen of France, and I have always made Paris my home. I have an apartment in an old and quiet section of the Left Bank in Paris."

"What is your present occupation?"

"I am a publisher of books."

"In Paris?"

"Yes."

"Do you have a place of business?"

"I do. I have my offices in the Rue Sébastien Bottin. This is nearby the distinguished house of the Éditions Gallimard."

At his table, Barrett was amused. The old pornographer was shoring up his own respectability by association. Barrett wondered whether he was this clever or whether this had been Duncan's doing.

"Mr. Leroux, briefly, what is your educational background? Are you a college graduate?"

"I graduated from the Sorbonne in Paris. My specialty was in seventeenth-century French literature, the period of Racine, La Fontaine, La Rochefoucauld, Jean Poquelin—known to most as Molière."

Not only pretentious, Barrett thought, but a small snob as well. Good, very good.

Apparently Duncan had been worried about this condescension, too, for he quickly asked, "But you also studied more popular writers—I mean, like—"

Barrett was on his feet instantly. "Objection, Your Honor. Counsel is leading the witness."

"Objection sustained," said Judge Upshaw.

Duncan cast Barrett an irritated glance. He turned to the witness once more. "Mr. Leroux, have you kept abreast of the writings of more popular writers?"

"Definitely. I have always read everything. As Valéry has said, one reads well only when one reads with some quite personal goal in mind. As a publisher, I have read well, because it has been my goal to learn about writing, so that I might be able to recognize new authors who deserved to be heard and thus enlighten the reading public."

"Mr. Leroux, you have told us your present occupation is that of publisher. Have you had any other occupations?"

"No. I have always been in this field, either employed by others or self-employed, that is to say a proprietor."

"When did you first become a publisher on your own?"

"In 1933. I was very young. I was still in my early thirties. My father had died, and I had a modest inheritance. So I established my own publishing house."

"What was the name of this firm?"

"The Étoile Press. It was so called because my location was at 18 Rue de Berri, which is off the Champs Elysées, only a short distance from the Étoile and the Arc de Triomphe."

"The Étoile Press," repeated Duncan. "Is this the same press, the same imprint, that brought out a work of fiction in 1935 entitled *The Seven Minutes*, by J J Jadway?"

"The same," said Christian Leroux.

At last, Barrett told himself. He leaned forward on the table and listened intently.

"Mr. Leroux, I have seen your original edition of this book. I noted that it was printed in English. Since it was published in Paris, why was it not in the French language?"

"The French government would not permit its publication in French."

"Why not?"

"The French censorship bureau determined it was obscene."

"Obscene? I see, yes. Well, now, was *The Seven Minutes* ever published in any other country, in any other language?"

"No. Absolutely no nation on earth would pass on it or accept it. Everywhere it was considered too obscene. Many critics, of many countries, have regarded it as the most obscene and depraved book every published in the history of literature."

"Then how were you able to bring out an edition in English, in Paris?"

"Ah, precisely because it *was* in English, and the average French reader could not read English and be disturbed by it. At the same time, the French government has, until recent years, always been liberal in its regard of books, especially books in a language foreign to France. I need only point out that it was in Paris that James Joyce's *Ulysses* was first published in English, though it could not be printed in Great Britain or America. It was in Paris that Radclyffe Hall found her publisher for *The Well of Loneliness* and Wallace Smith found his publisher for *Bessie Cotter*. The French authorities did not mind. They looked the other way, since those books were in English and could not corrupt the French. They could only corrupt the tourists, and that did not matter, that was amusing."

"So under those circumstances," said Duncan, "you were able to circumvent the censors and undertake publishing the book that has been called the filthiest book in the history of publishing?"

"Objection, Your Honor," Barrett protested, "on the grounds of hearsay evidence."

Judge Upshaw cleared his throat and addressed the District Attorney. "Mr. Duncan, no proper foundation has been laid. The objection is sustained."

Duncan was apologetic. "Very well, Your Honor." He returned to the witness. "Mr. Leroux, did you always publish mainly pornography?"

Christian Leroux appeared mildly offended. "No, that is not so. In the first few years, my list consisted mainly of very acceptable and scholarly literature. There were histories, biographies, art books, classical fiction."

"But soon your list was comprised, for the most part, of books that were obscene or pornographic in content?"

"Yes, I regret to say."

"Why did you turn largely to this sort of publishing?"

Leroux gave the court a Gallic shrug. "Because we are often victims of life and the world. Let me put it another way. *Sans argent l'honneur n'est qu'une maladie.* You understand? It is from Jean-Baptiste Racine. Honor, without money, is a mere malady. True, a malady. And I wished to be well and healthy. Yet there is more. Permit me to elaborate—"

"Please go ahead."

"I was inspired to change the character and product of the Étoile Press by the overnight success of another publisher, the publisher of the Obelisk Press in Paris. It was this way. The owner of the Obelisk Press was a gentleman named Jack Kahane, a businessman from Manchester, England, a most colorful and tasteful gentleman. Mr. Kahane had served in the Bengal Lancers. Also in the French Foreign Legion. In business, he was not successful. He was a failure. So he emigrated to France and in 1931 he founded the Obelisk Press to publish books that were not allowed to be published in England. He did so not only to rehabilitate his fortune, but to combat censorship and prudery. Mr. Kahane, prior to his death in 1939, had dared to be the first to publish *My Life and Loves*, by Frank Harris, and *Tropic of Cancer*, by Henry Miller, of which Ezra Pound said, 'At last an unprintable book that is fit to read.' It was Mr. Kahane's success, I repeat, that encouraged me to concentrate fully on pornography and obscenity. My motives were the same as Mr. Kahane's. To make a livelihood, for one thing. But perhaps more important, to see that the best literature that suffered suppression would see the light of day."

"Let me be sure that I understand you fully, Mr. Leroux. Are you saying that all of the books you published were worthwhile literature and deserved to be published?"

"No, no, not all. I brought out perhaps a dozen new titles every year, and at least half of these were not worthy to be called literature. I must confess, many were commissioned by me, were written to order by hack authors. I had learned that Petronius had written his *Satyricon* to titillate the Emperor Nero. I reasoned I could arrange for other writers to titillate the tourists. Of course, some of these, the filthier books, the ones totally without merit, they were not commissioned. They just came to me, to my desk. But *voilà*, the dirty ones without literary merit, they were necessary to support the better ones and to support me."

"Can you name some of these dirty ones that had no literary merit?"

"Let me remember. There was one called *The Hundred Whips*. There was another called *The Sex Life of Anna Karenina*. Then —of course, it is only my opinion that it belongs in the same category—there was *The Seven Minutes*."

"*The Seven Minutes*," repeated Duncan, half facing the jury. "This is the same book, *The Seven Minutes*, by J J Jadway, that is being charged as obscene in this court?"

"It is the same one."

"This was not one of your pornographic books that you would classify as among the best of the literature that was being suppressed?"

"No, never."

"It was—and this is offered only as your personal opinion—one

382

of your dirty books without literary merit, published merely to make money?"

"Yes, exactly, that is true. I knew from the first it was a low-grade book, the most vile, but there is every kind of taste and I thought it might sell. For me it was business. Besides, the author needed money, and I was always sympathetic toward authors. So I published this filth in order to earn enough to allow me to publish Aubrey Beardsley's *Under the Hill*, which was pornography but not obscenity."

"Mr. Leroux, you've just said you wished to publish something that was pornography but not obscenity. Most dictionaries consider the two words as synonymous. Pornography is often defined as obscene literature. In this trial we are using the words synonymously, interchangeably. Yet are you saying that, in your opinion, there is a difference?"

"Definitely. Even though I may have employed the words as synonyms, there is a fine shade of difference between them, I believe. A pornographic book most often will depict sex naturally, healthily, realistically, and while it may arouse lustful thoughts and desires, its main purpose is to show a full picture of man's nature and life. An obscene book, on the other hand, is an aphrodisiac and nothing else. It depicts only sex, no other side of life, just sex and more sex, with its entire purpose being to inflame a reader's morbid interest through fantasized sex."

"Well, then, by your literary standards, *The Seven Minutes* was —wait, let me rephrase—Did you consider the Jadway book to be a work of honest pornography?"

"I did not. Casanova's memoirs, Frank Harris' autobiography, even one work by Mark Twain, were honest pornography. Jadway's book was not of that class. It was obscene and no more."

"Then you believe the Jadway book to be a totally obscene work, and nothing more?"

"Yes. Obscene. Nothing more. A prose aphrodisiac. Nothing else. I have no doubt about that. The author knew it. His mistress, who was his agent, knew it. I knew it. It was a commercial enterprise for all of us, with no redeeming purpose. Today, looking back, I am ashamed of what I helped perpetuate. Today, by this confession of truth, perhaps I can make reparation and cleanse my soul."

"We understand and appreciate that, Mr. Leroux."

At the defense table, Zelkin had Barrett's ear. "Our witness is a sanctimonious prick," he whispered, "and so is our D.A."

Surprised at his partner's blunt language, which revealed the depth of his anger, Barrett nodded his agreement, and unhappily turned his attention back to the witness box.

"Mr. Leroux," said Duncan, "can you now tell us, in your own words, sparing us nothing, how you came to publish *The Seven Minutes* and of your relationship with the author and his agent?"

"Yes. I will relate only what I can recollect clearly and what is true." Leroux rubbed his veiny nose, squinted up at the ceiling, and then resumed speaking. "Late in the year 1934, an attractive young lady appeared in my office in the Rue de Berri and identified herself as Miss Cassie McGraw. She was an American girl of Irish descent. She had come to Paris several years earlier from the American Middle West, to be an artist, and she had lived in the St.-Germain-des-Prés section of the Left Bank ever since. There she had met another American expatriate, and they had become friends. Later she admitted to me they were lovers. This other expatriate, her lover, was J J Jadway. He had rebelled against his father, who was an important Catholic, and against his New England strictness of upbringing, and, leaving his parents and two younger sisters behind, he had fled to Paris. He was determined to live as a bohemian, and to write, and as a writer to liberate not only himself but all of literature. Unfortunately, he was one of those writers so familiar to publishers who talk writing but do not write. Because he was weak and frustrated, he drank and took to drugs—"

"Pardon me, Mr. Leroux. What you are speaking of now is not hearsay, not knowledge acquired second hand?"

"This I heard first hand, directly from the lips of J J Jadway himself, in times when he was in despair, and I heard it again from Miss McGraw herself when I saw her after Jadway's death."

"Mr. Leroux, since anything you may have heard from Cassie McGraw, who was Jadway's mistress as well as his agent, would be regarded as hearsay evidence, and therefore not admissible in this courtroom, let us confine ourselves strictly to what you heard from J J Jadway first hand. How many times did you speak with him?"

"Four times."

"You spoke to Jadway four times? Were these lengthy conversations? By that I mean, did the conversations go on for more than—well, let's say for more than a few minutes?"

"Always longer. Once, when he was very drunk—by his own admission—he told me the whole story about Cassie and himself and how the book came to be written. He told me that after he took Cassie in and she became his mistress, she tried to rehabilitate him. She thought he had great creative gifts. And she wanted him to write. But he would not or could not. Then, he confessed, when they were having an impoverished winter, hungry, starving, cold, soon to be evicted from their dwelling, Cassie McGraw told Jadway that if he would not write to earn them some bread, then let him earn money some other way or she would have no choice but to leave him. So Jadway said to her, as he reported it to me, 'All right, I'll make us some money, plenty of money. I'll do what Cleland did. I'll write the dirtiest book that's ever been written, dirtier than his, and that should make it sell.' Then, according to Jadway, he sat down, driven by his need for money, supported by absinthe, and he wrote *The Seven Minutes* in three weeks."

Duncan held up his hand. "One moment, Mr. Leroux. I'd like you to explain one thing. You referred to the name Cleland. You quoted Jadway as remarking that he'd do what Cleland did, he'd write the dirtiest book ever written, one even dirtier than Cleland's. Can you tell us who this Cleland was?"

"John Cleland?" Leroux said with surprise. "Why, he was the foremost writer of obscenity in history, until Jadway came along. Cleland was—"

Barrett came to his feet. "Your Honor, objection! The question is completely irrelevant."

"Your Honor—" Duncan protested.

"Mr. Duncan," said Judge Upshaw, "do you wish to be heard on this objection?"

"Yes, Your Honor, I do."

"Approach the bench."

Immediately, in an undertone, the District Attorney tried to outline the relevancy of his question about John Cleland. The witness Leroux, he pointed out, had personally been acquainted with the author of the book on trial. Since the motivations of an author were relevant to learning whether a book had any redeeming social importance, it would be valuable to know that the author had once admitted he had undertaken the writing of the book only for money, and that he had intended to make the book dirtier than anything Cleland had ever written. Since many jurors might not have heard of Cleland, it was vital to elicit information about Cleland in order to reveal exactly what Jadway had in mind while preparing *The Seven Minutes*.

Judge Upshaw had a question. Just what kind of information did the District Attorney expect to bring out about Cleland? Duncan replied that the witness, who was learned about this genre of literature, no doubt would explain John Cleland's background. Cleland had come from a good English family and had been well educated. After leaving school, he had first served as British consul in Smyrna. He had then been employed by the East India Company in Bombay, but after a quarrel with his employers, he had returned to England. Bankrupt at the age of forty, Cleland had been thrown into debtor's prison. In order to get out of jail, he had written *Memoirs of a Woman of Pleasure* —the book popularly known as *Fanny Hill*—for a publisher who had paid him twenty guineas for this obscene work. When the book had become a best seller in 1749, Cleland had been brought before the Privy Council in London to receive his sentence, his punishment. Fortunately for Cleland, a relative of his, the Earl of Granville, had been president of the Privy Council. Granville had suspended punishment and awarded Cleland a pension of one hundred pounds a year with the provision that he turn his talents to more respectable writings. Cleland later penned two more mildly erotic books, and some scholarly studies on the English language before his death in France at the age of eighty-two. All through history, Cleland's name had been synonymous with obscenity. Since he had produced *Fanny Hill* only to get out of debtor's prison, with no motive other than to save his neck, it would be useful to learn that Jadway had once confessed to Christian Leroux that he intended to manufacture an obscene novel exactly as Cleland had done.

Barrett's own plea, defending his objection, was curt and to the point. This trial concerned one issue and one issue alone, he said

—whether an Oakwood bookseller had or had not sold an obscene book. Admittedly, Jadway's motives in preparing that book were a factor in judging obscenity under the law. But any discussion of another author's motives amounted to no more than gossip. Such information was absolutely irrelevant to the central issue of the trial.

Without hesitation, Judge Upshaw sustained Barrett's objection. Testimony concerning John Cleland was not relevant to the case being tried.

"You may proceed with your examination, confining yourself to what is material to this case, Mr. Duncan," the judge concluded.

With the bench conference ended, the court reporter returned to his desk, Barrett went back to his table, and a chastened Elmo Duncan once more confronted Christian Leroux, who had been waiting in the witness box.

"Mr. Leroux," said the District Attorney, "let us dwell a bit longer on J J Jadway's motive for writing *The Seven Minutes*. He told you that he would write the dirtiest book that's ever been written. But did the author, Jadway, ever speak of any other reason for writing this book—any reason or motive beyond the commercial one?"

"No, never. Jadway's Muse was a cash register."

There was laughter throughout the court. Several jurors smiled understandingly. Leroux appeared pleased. Judge Upshaw was less amused, and he rapped his gavel sharply.

"Mr. Leroux," said Duncan, as soon as order was restored, "what kind of commercial success did *The Seven Minutes* have after you published it in 1935?"

"Not as much success as we had hoped," replied Leroux. "Cleland's publisher was said to have profited to the amount of ten thousand pounds. I am afraid I made less than one twentieth of that sum. At first there was some optimism. My initial printing was five thousand copies. This sold out in a year. I ordered another press run of five thousand copies. But the sales slowed down and eventually stopped. I think that was after the Vatican placed the book on the *Index*. I never did sell the last copies of that second printing."

"*The Seven Minutes* was officially condemned by the Catholic Church?"

"The year after publication. And not by the Catholic Church alone. It was also condemned by the Protestant clergy throughout Europe and to a lesser extent in America, where the title was not as well known."

"Mr. Leroux, didn't Jadway's death coincide with the condemnation of the Church?"

"Not precisely. The book was condemned in 1936. Jadway died early in 1937."

"Do you know what led to Jadway's death?"

"I know what I was told by Cassie McGraw, who witnessed his death. You wish to know what led to it? I will—"

Vigorously, Barrett voiced his objection on the grounds that the question was irrelevant and involved a response based on hearsay.

Briskly Judge Upshaw sustained the objection.

With a frown, the District Attorney accepted the rebuff, and turned away from the witness briefly, to stare over the heads of the spectators.

Wondering whether his opponent was lost in thought or searching for someone in the court, Barrett glanced over his shoulder. As he did so, he saw a formidable woman rise from her aisle seat in the last row and start for the exit. Instantly Barrett recognized the woman. She was Olivia St. Clair, president of the Strength Through Decency League. Observing her, Barrett became curious. Had her departure been a coincidence? Or had she received some kind of signal from Duncan? Then Barrett entertained a dark suspicion. Moments ago, the circumstances of Jadway's death had been refused admission in this court of law. Were Duncan and Mrs. St. Clair preparing to enter these facts in the more permissive court of public opinion?

On hearing the District Attorney address the witness again, Barrett returned his attention to the examination.

"Mr. Leroux," Duncan was saying, "do you still own any rights to *The Seven Minutes?*"

"No. From the day of Jadway's suicide, I wanted to be rid of the book. I could find no buyer. Then, a few years ago, an American came to me in Paris. He had heard of *The Seven Minutes*. He was a publisher of obscene material in New York. He wished to buy my rights to the book. I sold them to him at once, gladly. I practically gave it away. I was relieved to have it out of my life. I have been relieved ever since. Such books destroy all whom they touch, and I want no part of them again."

"Thank you very much, Mr. Leroux," said Duncan. He looked up at the bench. "I have no further questions, Your Honor."

As the District Attorney, his expression reflecting self-satisfaction, returned to the prosecution table, Judge Upshaw addressed the defense.

"You may cross-examine, Mr. Barrett."

"Thank you, Your Honor," said Barrett. Gathering together the notes that he and Zelkin had made, he said in an undertone, "Abe, it's not going to be easy. I don't know whether I can pull this one out."

Zelkin uttered one word. "Try."

Rising with his handful of papers, Barrett made his way past the jury to the witness box. The French publisher, arms crossed complacently on his chest, jade cuff links shining in the light of the overhead fluorescent lights, waited with equanimity.

"Mr. Leroux," Barrett began casually, "let me take you back to the time when you first received the J J Jadway manuscript from Cassie McGraw." He consulted his notes. "You told People's counsel that the time was 'late in the year 1934.' Correct?"

"Yes, correct."

"Can you be more exact? Do you recall the exact date, or at least the week, when Miss McGraw appeared with the manuscript?"

"Why, certainly. It was the last week in November of 1934. A Friday, a Friday morning."

"Very good. Do you recall Cassie McGraw's appearance? Can you tell us what she looked like?"

Leroux smiled. "I remember precisely. She was about five feet two. She wore a yellow raincoat of the kind Americans called slickers. She had brunet hair, bobbed, shingled. Gray eyes. Small upturned nose, some freckles, pretty. Most generous lips, a cute pout. In all, a gamin, clever, bright, witty, amusing. But she could be very serious when discussing Jadway."

Barrett nodded appreciatively. "Good. And you received her at your office in—where was it again? I know it's printed in the book—"

"My office was 18 Rue de Berri."

"That's right. Thank you, Mr. Leroux. It had slipped my mind. Uh—where were you living at the time?"

Leroux hesitated. "I am trying to remember. There was so much moving from place to place, so much dislocation during the war and after."

"But this was the last week of November in 1934. That was well before the war had even begun."

"Yes, of course," said Leroux, "but I still am not certain. I think it was an apartment in Neuilly, or possibly—"

"Well, if you can't remember exactly—"

Leroux shrugged. "I am afraid not."

"—perhaps it would help you if you tried to remember your landlord's name or the name of your concierge. Can you recollect the name of either one?"

"No."

"Well, perhaps you remember your apartment telephone number?"

"Hardly. No, I am sorry."

"Then certainly your office telephone. You must have used it constantly. Can you tell me the office number?"

Leroux had become mildly exasperated. "Of course not, not after almost forty years. To be reasonable, that was far back in 1934, and one cannot be expected to remember every . . ." His voice drifted off.

"I agree with you, one cannot be expected to remember everything that happened so long ago," said Barrett softly. He paused. Suddenly his tone hardened. "Yet, Mr. Leroux, I have heard you state from this witness box that you *do* remember every single word that J J Jadway and Cassie McGraw said to you in 1934, almost forty years ago. Is that not—?"

"Objection!" bellowed Duncan from across the courtroom. "I object, Your Honor. Defense counsel is being argumentative."

"Sustained," announced Judge Upshaw.

"Yes, Your Honor," Barrett murmured. He was satisfied. He had struck a blow at the veracity of the witness's testimony by stressing the frailty of memory. Objection or no, the jury had heard the exchange. Now he determined to make certain that no member of the jury had missed the point. "Mr. Leroux, in your testimony you have claimed that you heard first hand that J J

Jadway drank heavily, was addicted to drugs, dashed off his book for money and only money, and more of the same. A question. After giving it a second thought, are you absolutely positive that you remember every word and every alleged fact told to you almost forty years ago?"

"Your Honor, again I must object!" Duncan protested. "Witness has already testified to these conversations and facts under oath. This is repetitious."

"Objection is sustained on that ground," said Judge Upshaw. He fixed his unsmiling visage upon Barrett. "Court also admonishes defense counsel not to persist in argument with the witness."

Barrett's expression was contrite. "I am sorry, Your Honor. It was unintentional." He turned back to Christian Leroux, who was sitting erect, arms no longer complacently crossed, hands now planted firmly on his knees. "Mr. Leroux, let us return to the years 1934 and 1935. You have stated—you have recollected—that you spoke to J J Jadway exactly four times. Is that correct?"

"It is correct."

"Where did you have your conversations with Jadway? By that I mean, did you visit his apartment or receive him in your office or see him in a restaurant? Where did you meet with him?"

Leroux hesitated. "I—I never said that I met with him. I said I spoke with him."

Barrett was surprised, and he showed it. "You never met J J Jadway in person?"

"No. I spoke with him four times on the telephone."

"On the telephone? I see. You were positive it was Jadway on the other end?"

"Of course. Cassie McGraw would telephone and then put him on the line."

"Isn't that unusual, Mr. Leroux—a publisher who lives in the same city as his author confining their relationship to telephone calls? Did you ever make an effort to meet him in person?"

"No."

"You made no effort to meet him face to face?"

"I did not, because there was no reason to," said Leroux testily. "Cassie McGraw had told me he was a recluse, withdrawn, and

391

often under the influence of drink or drugs, and so I felt I would not be warmly received. Therefore, I made no effort—"

"Did you know for a fact, let us say had you been told by Jadway himself, that you would not be warmly received?"

"I just felt it. There could have been no mistake about my not being welcome."

"Did you have any other reasons for not attempting to meet your author in person?"

"No other reasons. I might add that it is not a common practice for publishers to go calling upon their authors. Especially upon authors with unsavory reputations. Furthermore, I had other new authors to contend with every year, and Jadway was just one more and not a particularly promising one."

"I see. You were too busy to give any one author your full attention, especially a lesser author. Well—"

"Objection, Your Honor!" It was Duncan flagging the bench. "Counsel is calling for a conclusion the witness has not made."

"Objection is sustained."

"All right," said Barrett. He considered the witness once more. "Then your contact with J J Jadway was entirely by telephone or through Cassie McGraw. Is that correct?"

"Correct."

"And except for what Miss McGraw told you, your knowledge of Jadway's habits, his feelings about writing, motivations for writing the book, these came to you over the telephone, never from personal meetings. Is that correct?"

"No, it is not. I just remembered something else."

"Oh—?"

"There was another source. I required biographical information from the author to include in the book. I requested that he fill in a questionnaire. It is a routine procedure. Jadway did not fill in the questionnaire. Instead, he wrote me several letters about himself—first one, then another with afterthoughts, and eventually a few more about the editing. So in this way there was more information that came from Jadway himself."

"Precisely what information came from Jadway in this correspondence?"

"Information about his background, his family background, couched in generalities, his desire to write."

"His motives for writing *The Seven Minutes?*"

"I don't remember," said Leroux.

"Those letters might be very useful to us and perhaps provide information relevant to this case. Do you have those letters in your possession?"

"No."

"Do you know what happened to them?"

"I can't say. They were probably thrown out with thousands of others when I ceased publishing under the Étoile Press imprint."

"Might you have sold these letters when you sold the rights to *The Seven Minutes* to another publisher?"

"I—" Leroux faltered, and he was suddenly wary. "I might have. I can't say."

"I merely wondered," said Barrett, "because some Jadway letters, remarkably like the ones you've described, were recently put on sale by an autograph dealer in New York. The dealer obtained them from a former publisher. He sold them to an unidentified party. I wondered whether they might be the same letters you received. Do you believe that they may have been?"

Leroux seemed relieved, almost jaunty. "I have no idea. But I doubt it."

"Did Jadway have Cassie McGraw bring his letters to you?"

"I believe he mailed one or two. The others she brought to me in person."

"You appear to have seen a good deal of Cassie McGraw. Can you remember how many times you saw her?"

Before Leroux could reply, the District Attorney sounded his objection. The question was irrelevant, he stated. What Duncan did not state, Barrett now perceived, was that Duncan himself had not been allowed to bring Cassie McGraw into the case, and now he was against the defense counsel's attempting to do so. Barrett heard Judge Upshaw's prompt agreement with the objection.

Since Barrett had expected this, he was ready with another line of questioning. "Mr. Leroux, let's devote ourselves once more to the book, to *The Seven Minutes.* You have told the court that you eventually sold your rights in it to another publisher. Do you remember this other publisher's name?"

The District Attorney's objection forestalled any reply. Barrett requested a bench conference with Judge Upshaw. It was of brief

393

duration. Barrett explained that his question was intended to lay a foundation to explore the integrity and honesty of this key witness. After hearing out both counsels, the judge overruled Duncan's objection and advised Barrett to proceed.

Confronting the witness once more, Barrett repeated his question. "You sold your rights to *The Seven Minutes* to another publisher. Do you remember this other publisher's name?"

"I do not remember his name," said Leroux.

"Perhaps I can refresh your memory. Was the publisher to whom you sold the rights a man named Norman C. Quandt, who was indicted in New York for peddling hard-core pornography?"

"Quandt? Yes, I believe that was his name. Thank you."

"Why did you sell Mr. Quandt all rights to *The Seven Minutes?*"

"I have already testified to my reason. I feared the book had a destructive influence. I wanted to be rid of it. I was relieved to be rid of it."

"Yet, Mr. Leroux, you were not concerned that by selling the book to another publisher you were keeping alive its so-called destructive influence?"

"No, I was not concerned—because I did not think Quandt would ever be allowed to publish the book. In the end I thought it would serve him as no more than a tax loss. I sold the book to kill it—and to save myself."

"And you had absolutely no other motive for selling it?"

"None whatsoever."

"I see. And when did you give up the Étoile Press?"

"Four years ago."

"For what reason did you give it up?"

"For the same reason I gave up *The Seven Minutes*. I had finally come to see the evil of publishing obscenity, and I wanted to sever my connection with it and start my life afresh."

"This was your only purpose?"

"Yes."

"Well, now . . ." Barrett strode to the desk of the court clerk, found the exhibit folder that he wanted, and returned to the witness box with it. "I have here before me an interview, marked Exhibit H, a press interview you gave to a journalist from *L'Express* at the time. I have two copies. You may have one to follow me as I translate from the other. If I translate incorrectly, please stop me and correct me." He handed Leroux one clipping, and then he held the other before him. "In this interview, the reporter asks why you have given up publishing pornography. You answer as follows: 'For the same reason there are fewer prostitutes today. Sex is too easily available everywhere for everyone in these new times. If it is free, why should one pay?' Then, Mr. Leroux, you go on and you are quoted as saying, 'In the years past, there was so much censorship, so much banned material, that we had the market for this material almost to ourselves. But since recognized publishing houses in every country are now allowed to publish freely what used to be banned, they are taking away our readers and the market that once belonged exclusively to the Obelisk Press, the Olympia Press, the Étoile Press. I have given up because I have lost my audience.'" Barrett raised his head. "Will you acknowledge that you made those remarks?"

Leroux's lips were pursed. At last he spoke. "I will acknowledge that I gave this interview and that it appeared in print. I will not acknowledge that I was quoted with exactitude."

"Do you disown this article completely?"

"I do not disown it completely. I object to its lack of precision, its omissions, its overemphasis on one point. Yes, I may have made the remark that one minor factor that made me close the Étoile Press was the new sexual permissiveness in society today. But it was a secondary factor. The primary reason for my quitting was that I saw the dangers in unrelieved and obscene pornography, and as I had grown older and had more understanding of this, I wanted to do no more harm to my fellow human beings."

"Fine, and laudable," said Barrett. "Now, if you will look down at the last two paragraphs of that article, you will see a quotation from Maurice Girodias, who is identified there as the son of Jack Kahane, founder of the Obelisk Press. Girodias is further identified as the proprietor of the Olympia Press, another of your competitors. You see that?"

"Yes."

"The reporter is quoting Girodias to you. He quotes Girodias as saying, in defense of his own publishing career, the following. 'Obscenity and pornography are ugly phantoms which will disappear in the morning light when we rehabilitate sex and eroticism. We must accept love and lust as complementary movements, and not as incompatible elements. We must discover desire as the source of all the positive actions in our life, and stop opposing every natural instinct and every pleasure-giving activity. That result cannot be achieved without a series of mental shocks.'" Barrett paused. "The reporter says he read you Girodias' remarks and asked for your reaction to them. And here you reply, 'I concur. I agree wholeheartedly with Mr. Girodias. Those of us who've published obscenity and pornography should be honored. We destroyed taboos. We taught people that love and lust were one. We made sex healthy.'" Barrett looked up. "Well, Mr. Leroux, did you make those remarks that have been attributed to you? Yes or no?"

"What was printed here is misleading."

"Can you give me a yes or no answer? Did you make those remarks?"

"Yes, but—"

"Thank you, Mr. Leroux."

"—but in support of decent pornography that is literary, not for filth like *The Seven Minutes!*"

About to appeal to the bench to have Leroux's outburst stricken, Barrett thought better of it. To some of the jurors, any protest about the behavior of the witness might seem like bullying. Barrett considered going on with the cross-examination. He had scored a few points, perhaps too few. Possibly Leroux had scored more for the prosecution. Still, in the minds of three or four jurors there might have been planted the first seeds of reasonable doubt. To go on, with a witness now so hostile, so aggressive, might lead to disaster.

From the exhibit and the notes in his hand, Barrett lifted his eyes to glance at his partner. Zelkin looked worried.

Red light.

Stop.

He faced the witness. "Thank you, Mr. Leroux." He looked at the Judge. "I believe I have nothing further, Your Honor."

He returned to the table and slumped wearily into his chair. "I did my best, Abe," he said. "I tried. They've got Jadway's life all tied up and they've put out the sign that says 'No Trespassing.' What in the hell have we got?"

Zelkin was looking off. "We've got a short recess, that's what we've got."

DURING THE RECESS, the dark suspicion Mike Barrett had entertained earlier that Duncan and Mrs. St. Clair might arrange to have the French publisher continue his testimony in a more public place was confirmed.

In a private office on the sixth floor of the Hall of Justice, Barrett, followed by Zelkin and Fremont, joined Philip Sanford, who had his mini-sized portable television set going full blast. The screen was filled with a close-up of Christian Leroux.

"It's a press conference somewhere in this building," explained Sanford hastily. "Mrs. St. Clair of the STDL arranged it. She's got reporters from all over the world throwing questions at Leroux. She introduced him. She started by saying that since Leroux had completed his testimony in court, he was free to answer questions outside court, although he can't discuss what he said in the courtroom until the verdict is in. Now he's—"

"Let's see for ourselves," said Barrett, pulling up a chair.

The four of them closed in on the tiny television set, as a voluble Christian Leroux, basking in the limelight, replied to the next reporter's question.

"No, I was not permitted to discuss J J Jadway's death in the court," the French publisher was saying, "but I am willing to make the truth, every detail, known now. I heard the facts from Jadway's mistress, Cassie McGraw. You want to know what led to Jadway's death? I will tell you. It was *The Seven Minutes* that killed him in the end. His family in New England did not know he had written this book. The first to learn of its existence was the elder of Jadway's two younger sisters. Foolishly, he had sent her a copy. According to Miss McGraw, he did not wish his sister to wither on the vine, become a dried-up spinster, so he decided to give her an example of his new freedom and inspire her to rebel also. He inspired her, I must say. The book so shook her that she took to drink and to having affairs with men, until she became a hopeless alcoholic tramp. I cannot say what happened to the other sister. I know only of how the older one was affected. At the same time, Jadway's father learned about the book because his Church had been circularized to condemn it. His father—especially

397

after Jadway was excommunicated—his father suffered from the disgrace, and suffered an illness from which he never recovered. Also, according to Miss McGraw, the daughter of one of Jadway's closest friends got her hands on *The Seven Minutes* while she was still an impressionable adolescent, and she was warped sufficiently by it to emulate the heroine of the book and she fell into evil ways."

"Fell into evil ways?" The voice was plainly that of a German-accented correspondent. "Can you be more specific, Mr. Leroux?"

"She became the mistress of a series of men. Soon she was reduced to little better than a streetwalker."

"Did J J Jadway know what his book had done to his family, to his friend's daughter?" the same correspondent inquired.

"Certainly. He discussed it with Cassie—with Miss McGraw. He was filled with remorse. He drank more and more. He brooded. He sank into a deep depression. At last, in February of 1937, in a little house he and his mistress had rented outside Paris—in the village of Vaucresson—he went into the bathroom one night and shot himself through the head. He committed suicide, and he left a note for Miss McGraw. 'This is what I must do to expiate my sin in having fostered that monstrous book,' he wrote her."

"Did you see this suicide note, Mr. Leroux?" a British-accented voice called out.

"See it? No, no, of course not. At the memorial service, Miss McGraw, in her grief, told me of it."

"Do you know if this suicide note still exists?"

"If Miss McGraw still exists, perhaps the note exists."

"I'm from Associated Press, Mr. Leroux," a new voice chimed in. "I have a few more questions about Cassie McGraw, if you don't mind. You've said she represented J J Jadway in the handling of *The Seven Minutes?*"

"She submitted the manuscript on his behalf, negotiated with me for him, served as his literary agent, in fact, and as a go-between in the editing."

"And after his death, did you see her more than once?"

"After Jadway's death I saw Cassie McGraw twice. At the services and then several months later, when she came to my office and showed me that she had inherited the ownership of the book, and she wanted to sell me her interest in the book outright for a flat sum. This was because she was through with Paris by then and needed money to return to America with her daughter."

"Daughter?" The television screen showed a close shot of a renowned United Press International columnist, and the surprised reaction on his face. "You mean Cassie McGraw had a child?"

"Jadway's child. Had I forgotten to speak of her? Yes, of course. She had a child by him, born two months after his death."

"A daughter? Do you know her name?"

"Judith."

Barrett's attention was diverted from the television screen by Zelkin, who was furiously scribbling notes. A new lead. Jadway's daughter. Elsewhere in the building, he guessed, Duncan or one of his aides would also be hastily writing—that is, presuming the prosecution did not already possess this information. A new hunt, and race, for a promising new witness was in the making.

"Mr. Leroux, did Cassie McGraw come to see you only because she needed money to take her daughter back to America?" an Italian correspondent inquired.

"Yes. She offered me her interest in *The Seven Minutes* for the price of the passage home. From a business point of view, it was senseless for me to buy her interest. The book was no longer selling well. Nevertheless, because I had great affection and great pity for this lovely young girl, I paid her a sum of money for her interest and sent her off."

"Did you ever see Cassie McGraw or her daughter Judith again?" someone in the room wanted to know.

"Never."

"Or hear from either of them or about them again?"

"Never a word. Nothing. Only silence in the decades since."

"Did you ever hear from Jadway's family or his friends after his death?"

"No."

There were several voices shouting questions simultaneously, and the camera pulled back to reveal not only Leroux but Mrs. St. Clair beside him.

"One at a time, please," Mrs. St. Clair called to the press off camera. She pointed to someone. "The gentleman with his hand up. Will you identify yourself, sir?"

"Yes. I'm from the *New York Times*. I have several questions for Mr. Leroux."

The screen displayed a benign Leroux. "Ask as many as you wish," he said.

"I'd like to go back to your relationship with Cassie McGraw. In the court, as I recall, the counsel for the defense wondered how many times you had seen Miss McGraw during the entire period you knew her. The question was stricken at that time. Can you reply to it now?"

"I am pleased to. How many times I saw her? I cannot calculate precisely. I first saw her in 1934. I last saw her in 1937, after Jadway's death."

"Would you say that you saw her more than a dozen times?" the man from the *New York Times* persisted.

"Possibly. But not much more. Very little after the book was published. They were not in Paris all the time. They were away for one trip, to Italy, I think. She was trying to change his environment to rehabilitate him. Then, when they returned, they moved to that village outside Paris."

"Would you describe your relationship with Cassie McGraw as a close one?"

"Close one? I am afraid I do not understand."

"Let me clarify my question, Mr. Leroux. You've spoken of Jadway as being weak, frustrated, commercially minded, unsavory, which can best be interpreted to mean you had only contempt for him. At the same time, you have spoken of Cassie McGraw with affection. You have repeated intimate details of Jadway's life which Cassie McGraw confided to you. That she would divulge such intimate details to you makes me wonder about your own relationship with her. Was it confined to business? Or was it also social?"

"It was strictly business."

Listening, watching, Barrett smiled. The dogged *Times* reporter, Barrett mused, would have made an excellent trial attorney. The reporter was still engaging Leroux.

"Yet your conversations with her also elicited her innermost feelings and emotions, did they not?"

"She had no other person to speak to in a foreign country, to tell of her unhappy love or troubles or problems. Her family and friends were not in Paris. She was a stranger, an alien. She needed someone trustworthy and sympathetic with whom she might— how do you say?—get things off her chest. Because I was sympathetic, she confided in me, yes, and because I was sorry for her, I listened."

"Did you ever go to a café with her?"

Leroux smiled thinly. "We Frenchmen do our business in cafés. Yes, I suppose we discussed business at Fouquet's or the Select, which existed in that time. Yes, I think so."

"Did you ever entertain Cassie McGraw in the privacy of your apartment?"

Leroux's eyes twinkled. "Certainly, sir, you have heard that the French never invite Americans to their homes or their apartments."

There was a tittering throughout the press gathering, and Leroux smiled and displayed the same satisfaction as an actor taking a curtain call.

Still the New York inquisitor persisted. "Mr. Leroux, you haven't replied to my question. Did you ever entertain Miss McGraw in your apartment?"

Leroux's smile disappeared. "No, I did not," he answered with a flare of anger. "If you are saying that I was hostile to Jadway because I was competing with him for Miss McGraw's affection, it is an unfounded imputation. To keep the record straight, my relationship with Miss McGraw was strictly business, literary business between a publisher and an agent, and no more." He blinked into the camera. "Any other questions?"

Zelkin snapped off the television set. "Frenchy's a slick one. He isn't doing us much good in or out of court. Well, we're due back now. Duncan should be ready with his next witness. I wonder who in the devil it's going to be?"

THE NEXT WITNESS for the People, it turned out, proved to be another visitor from afar and, for Barrett and Zelkin, a complete surprise.

The next witness was an awesome figure wearing the black robes of the Catholic clergy. He reminded Barrett of the bas-relief of a Jesuit martyr carved out of stone adorning one of the caskets among the tombs in St. Peter's, one that had been raised to a vertical position and restored to life. His frosted Savonarola features, the piercing eyes, the high arched nose, the jutting jaw, were an instant rebuke to the frivolous, the licentious, the blasphemous. He moved with the assurance of a messenger of the Almighty. It was evident that he would brook no nonsense, entertain no pettiness. He was on a mission. Our Lord's work. When he perfunctorily took the oath, you felt that he had invented it.

This next witness was Father Sarfatti, member of the Sacred Congregation for the Doctrine of the Faith and servant of the Apostolic See of Rome.

Once he was on the witness stand, once District Attorney Duncan had begun to guide him through the early phase of the examination, establishing his background and authority, Barrett and Zelkin undertook a hurried whispered conference.

The appearance of a witness attached to the Vatican had caught them off guard. Zelkin had always complained about the procedure in criminal cases which, unlike civil cases, did not require pretrial knowledge or interrogation of the witnesses. Despite this secrecy, neither Barrett nor Zelkin had expected to be surprised in the Fremont case. The State's major witnesses—Christian Leroux for one, Jerry Griffith for another—had been widely publicized. The supporting witnesses in a censorship case most often followed a stock pattern. There would be psychiatrists, educators, literary experts, community leaders, and the like. The fact that the District Attorney might draw upon the resources of the Vatican for a specialist on the *Index Librorum Expurgatorius* was a move that neither Barrett nor Zelkin anticipated.

Yet, instinctively, Barrett had been constantly mindful of one commandment of his profession: A good attorney must always be ready for the worst.

Fortunately, in reviewing his notes less than a week ago, and while preparing for the worst, Barrett had been reminded that a year after the publication of *The Seven Minutes* its author had been condemned by the Catholic Church and his book sentenced to inclusion in the *Index*. Because the *Index* invoked images of the ancient past, of a harsher, more implacable Church, because its existence and activity were so remote from the lives of the people of Oakwood and Los Angeles and America, Barrett guessed that the District Attorney might refer to it during the trial only

402

in passing. Nevertheless, because Barrett was thorough and because he knew that more criminal cases were won in the preparatory stages than in the trials themselves, he had initiated a superficial research project on the Vatican's historic censorship apparatus and on the *Index* itself. Barrett had done some reading, and he had assigned Kimura to interview several theologians. Their results had barely filled a single manila folder.

But now that Duncan had trained a big gun from the Vatican upon the already weakened defense emplacements, Barrett knew that desperate reinforcements were wanted. Even as he tried to listen to Father Sarfatti's testimony, Barrett was consulting his partner on what must be done. Within a few minutes, they had agreed on countermeasures. Zelkin would telephone Donna at the office and have her send along, by the office messenger, their "Jadway—Catholic *Index*" file. Zelkin would also locate Kimura and send him scurrying back to his scholarly theologians for more information that might be of use to the defense. If Barrett's cross-examination came up shortly, he would make every effort to drag it out until the lunch hour, so that if Kimura phoned in any information they could take advantage of the noon recess to digest it before he resumed cross-examination in the afternoon.

After Zelkin had left the defense table and slipped out of the courtroom for the few moments it would take him to call Donna and Kimura, Barrett had tried to concentrate on the new testimony. It was difficult to be attentive. His power of concentration had been heavily taxed by Leroux's examination and cross-examination, and it took an effort to follow closely every question and answer being exchanged before him. Yet he trusted his instinct to tune in automatically on what was vital, and then to tune out.

In the fifty-five minutes that followed, there were a half-dozen times when an exchange both relevant and important was caught by Barrett's antenna and then he tuned in full blast.

The procedure of the Sacred Congregation for the Doctrine of the Faith in proscribing a book.

Barrett tuned in full blast.

"Father Sarfatti, so that we may better understand why the Church condemned *The Seven Minutes*, and to help us in our judgment of the book's obscenity and in our case against the bookseller who sold it, can you explain the procedure of the Church in a matter like this?"

"Certainly, Mr. Duncan. Since various Curia offices have been revamped or streamlined in recent years, we must discuss these offices as they existed in 1935, the year that *The Seven Minutes* was published in Paris. At that time, any objectionable writings fell under the surveillance of the Section for the Censure of Books, which was that Curia department directed by the Supreme Congregation of the Holy Office. When a bishop or a priest in one of our dioceses in any land found a book that contained a doctrine contrary to the morals and faith of the Church, he submitted it to the Section for the Censure of Books in the Holy See."

"Contrary to the morals—?"

"Morals and faith, Mr. Duncan. I will be specific. Books which treat *ex professo* those subjects which are lascivious or obscene have always been prohibited. Also, all books which expound either heresies or schisms have been proscribed. In the past, when a suspected book was submitted to the Holy Office, it was turned over to a religious order in Rome whose members spoke and read the language in which the book had been printed. Experts would then examine it and submit their verdict, written in Latin, to the Holy Office. At the same time, a priest representing the Section for the Censure of Books might conduct an investigation into the life of the author of the denounced book and into the circumstances surrounding the book's creation. The sum of this material would then be presented to a meeting of the counselors of the Holy Office, and the work would be debated, and a vote taken. If the vote was still for condemnation, a report on the book was then turned over to a plenary session of the College of Cardinals. Finally, the Cardinal Prefect passed on the verdict of the College, as well as the previous reports, to the Supreme Pontiff. If the Pope confirmed the findings and recommendations, His Holiness then ordered the book added to the *Index of Prohibited Books*."

"And this was the procedure followed in condemning *The Seven Minutes*, Father Sarfatti?"

"Precisely."

"I have here Exhibit E, a copy of the *Index* published in 1940—"

"May I commend you for your acumen and thoroughness."

"Thank you, Father. Now, this is the earliest edition that I could locate in which J J Jadway and *The Seven Minutes* were listed. Yet, as I understand it, the book was prohibited in 1937, three years earlier. Can you clarify this?"

"It is quite simple, Mr. Duncan. New editions of the *Index* are published at irregular intervals. When J J Jadway's book was condemned in 1937, the decree of prohibition was first published in the *Acta Apostolicae Sedis*, the official bulletin of the Holy See, and this bulletin was sent to bishops throughout the world to inform them of the official condemnation. Subsequently, all bishops and parish priests, to protect the souls entrusted to their guidance, announced the ban to their parishioners. After that, the book was listed as prohibited in the very next edition of the *Index* to appear, which was three years later. I am pleased to add that our Protestant brothers, especially those in Europe, on their own initiative, also spoke out against the dangers from this particular book."

"Father, to understand better the gravity of this condemnation, I should like to ask you a number of questions about the *Index* itself and . . ."

Mike Barrett had tuned out, and was devoting himself to his notes.

Ten minutes later, his antenna caught something else. *Curious about the investigation of J J Jadway himself.*

Quickly Barrett tuned in, volume high.

"Father Sarfatti, were you personally entrusted with this investigation of the author of *The Seven Minutes?*"

"Yes, or rather I participated. I was a young priest at the time. In the years that followed, I assumed other duties in the Holy See. But recently I was reassigned to the Curia, to work in their new office known as the Sacred Congregation for the Doctrine of the Faith, which now has authority over the *Index*. When the Supreme Pontiff took an interest in your case, Mr. Duncan, I was selected to offer what help I could, because of my early familiarity with the Jadway case and with our records of this case in the archives of the Vatican. Before coming to America, I extracted and examined those documents in our files that pertained to the prohibition of *The Seven Minutes*. The actual informal investigation of the author Jadway was conducted by the Arch-

405

bishop of Paris in 1935 and 1936. I served as one of his assistants in the investigation."

"And your findings, Father Sarfatti, were they based on second-hand information or actual personal contact with J J Jadway?"

"Everything I have submitted to be used in court was obtained first hand. You have the records."

Duncan held up three sheets of paper, one of them affixed with a wax seal and ribbon. "I have these three records which I received from you. Do you recognize them as the documents from the Vatican file?"

"I do."

Duncan stepped away and moved toward the bench. "Your Honor, I would like to introduce into the trial new material that has not heretofore been marked. I would now like to have these documents marked as evidence."

At the defense table, Barrett met Zelkin's eyes. "Dammit," he muttered, and then he rose to join Duncan, the court clerk, and the Judge at the bench. During the next minutes, Judge Upshaw scanned the exhibits, then Barrett read them hastily, and then they were approved. The documents were given numbers by the clerk, and now they would be part of the evidence in the case against Ben Fremont and *The Seven Minutes*.

As Barrett returned to the defense table and sank into his chair, Zelkin looked anxious. "Well?" he demanded.

"We're in trouble," said Barrett.

The District Attorney was again stationed before the witness box. "Father Sarfatti, in your own words, can you summarize the contents of these exhibits?"

"Yes. The first is a transcript of a telephone conversation I had in Paris with J J Jadway. I had written to him from Rome that I would like to interview him, but I had received no reply. Once in Paris, I telephoned him several times and missed him. Finally he called me back, and I transcribed our discussion. The second document is a letter that Jadway wrote me—a rather defiant one, I might say—and this was sent me after our telephone conversation. The last document is a transcript prepared by a member of the Curia, since deceased, reporting on a statement Jadway made to him during a meeting in Italy. This statement was signed by Jadway and notarized."

"Does this information from Jadway confirm the testimony of his French publisher, Mr. Leroux, about Jadway's attitudes and motives relevant to his writing of *The Seven Minutes?*"

"To that question I would reply in the affirmative. Yes, the sum total of the Church's findings, including these documents, tends to confirm what Mr. Leroux has already revealed. I will say that, aside from these documents, our records of the investigation are somewhat circumscribed and formal. We possess no information about the author Jadway's family or his life in America. But from these documents we know that the author Jadway was a Catholic, one who had fallen away from the faith. We know his tastes in literature were for the immoral and the atheistic. As he told me, his library contained Casanova's *Memoirs*, as well as works by Henri Bergson, Benedetto Croce, and Karl Pelz, all of which were prohibited to Catholics. He had once participated in an anticlerical demonstration before Notre-Dame. His circle consisted of dissolute freethinkers who frequented the cafés of the Left Bank. He had consorted with prostitutes before living a life of sin with the young woman known as Cassie McGraw. I doubt that the Church's condemnation played any part in his suicide. His suicide was a consequence of his having no moral standards, which is reflected in his single published work. After his death he was cremated, and it was said that Miss McGraw carried out his last wish. His ashes were scattered from a balloon over Montparnasse. It is a sad story."

Throughout Father Sarfatti's recital, especially during the last of it, Barrett felt the urge to voice legal objection. He had grounds —much of the clergyman's testimony was irrelevant, and the last of it was hearsay—yet Barrett resisted speaking up. The material, in a different context, had previously been made known inside and outside the court by Leroux. Any objection, under these circumstances, might make it appear to some jurors that the defense was trying to gag a minion of the Lord. Right or wrong, Barrett kept his peace and continued to listen closely.

"Father Sarfatti, do your records give any evidence as to J J Jadway's motives for writing *The Seven Minutes?*"

"Only in his remark, contained in the letter to me, that all religions and institutions of learning were trying to pretend the world was one huge candy box, whereas in his book he had set out to prove that it was—it was a dunghill—a dunghill that could ultimately fertilize truth and produce beauty if one ceased to pretend. Beyond that, I might suggest that his printed words, as well as his manner of life in Paris, bespeak his motives. He had no legitimate ties in Paris at any time. You may draw what inference you wish from that."

"Do your records give evidence of Cassie McGraw's influence on Jadway during his writing of *The Seven Minutes* or, in fact, anything about Cassie McGraw's—?"

"Your Honor, I object!" interrupted Barrett. He could not let this go through or be stricken only after it had been answered. But Duncan, apparently, was going to make an effort to bring Cassie McGraw into the trial, for he was requesting a bench conference.

At the conference, Duncan tried to bend the information he knew Father Sarfatti was ready to offer by trying to relate it to obscene material in the novel. After all, Duncan argued, Cassie McGraw had been the prototype for the heroine. In his eagerness, Duncan not only bent testimony yet to come, but finally snapped it in two. "The Church has a copy of the birth certificate of Cassie McGraw's child by Jadway," Duncan was saying. "The child was christened Judith Jan Jadway. Father Sarfatti is prepared to tell us that the last and most recent note in the Vatican file reveals that Miss McGraw was married in the city of Detroit in 1940 and that her husband was killed in Salerno during the Second World War. While neither his full name nor her married name were recorded, and while there is no indication of Miss McGraw's eventual fate or her daughter's fate, still I believe what is known about her will help tell the jury . . ." He went on, and when he was done, Judge Upshaw impatiently chastised him for trying to introduce material entirely irrelevant to the case. "On this matter, your witness can tell the jury nothing of value," concluded Judge Upshaw. "I am sustaining defense counsel's objection."

Back at his table, Barrett could hear the District Attorney resuming his interrogation.

"Now, Father, if we can return briefly to the procedure of . . ."

Mike Barrett tuned out.

Fifteen minutes later, his antenna trapped a sound. *Offered the chance to recant while he was in Italy.*

Swiftly Barrett tuned in.

"You mean, Father Sarfatti, a member of the Church met with Jadway personally and offered him the opportunity to recant his errors?"

"Exactly. It is not unusual, Mr. Duncan. The Church moves slowly, and with considerable tolerance, against the author of a denounced work. Often an author will appeal to the Vatican, saying that he had written in good faith and had not realized fully the error of his doctrine. On such occasions the Congregation of the Holy Office, after making public the decree of condemnation, might then make public a notice reading, 'The author has recanted and has repudiated his work.' The first condemnation will stand, but his name and work may be kept from the *Index* itself. I can give you one example. Henry Lasserre, an orthodox Catholic who wrote an excellent book on the miracle at Lourdes, decided to translate the Gospels into French. He was not satisfied to follow the original. He invested his translation with some of his own imaginings. This translation was soon condemned and prohibited. But, fortunately, Lasserre saw the error of his ways. Quickly he took his book out of circulation. He recanted. As a consequence, the Holy Office withdrew its prohibition and expunged the author's name from subsequent editions of the *Index*."

"And J J Jadway—now, let me understand, did he wish to recant on his own initiative or was he offered the chance?"

"He was offered one last chance. He had arrived with his mistress in Italy, and was visiting Venice, when a Church emissary was dispatched to meet with him. He was tendered the opportunity—a generous one, I must say—to repudiate *The Seven Minutes* and to take it out of circulation. He refused. You have the document signed by Jadway to that effect. The Church then had no choice but to condemn the work for its obscenity and sacrilege."

Barrett tuned out.

With the end of Duncan's effective examination, Judge Upshaw declared a two-hour lunch recess. Abe Zelkin already had the *Index* file from Donna and several pages of scrawled notes taken during a telephone conversation with Kimura minutes earlier. Sending an errand boy down to the lobby of the Hall of Justice for sandwiches and soft drinks, Barrett and Zelkin retired to a vacant office in the municipal building and spent the better part of the two hours reviewing the research and mapping out the strategy of the cross-examination.

Preparing to return to the courtroom, Barrett was briefly tempted to take the offensive in his cross-examination. The Church that Father Sarfatti represented must be held sacrosanct. Yet Barrett was aware that some of its history, like that of every other faith in the world, was highly vulnerable to attack. In the Middle Ages, and at the very time when the *Index* was being prepared, the Church and its flock were obsessed with sex. St. Augustine had confessed that, before embracing Christianity, he had possessed "an insatiable appetite" for sex and had "boiled over in . . . fornication." Whereas Augustine had overcome his weakness of the flesh, his successors to the cloth had often been less resolute. The Bishop of Liège had been known to have had sixty-five illegitimate children. A Spanish abbot at St. Pelayo was said to have kept, in his lifetime, seventy mistresses. In Switzerland, married men had been forced to protect their wives from seduction in the confessional by petitioning authorities to permit their priests to keep one mistress apiece. In the Holy See itself, Marozia, daughter of a papal official, had had Pope Sergius III for her lover and her pawn; and in 931 A.D. she had conspired to have her illegitimate son named Pope John XI. Pope Leo VIII had expired of a stroke suffered while engaging in sexual intercourse. And Pope Alexander VI, admitted father of the Borgias, had possessed two mistresses while in the Vatican, one of them the seventeen-year-old Giulia Farnese. And this little more than fifty years before the Holy See had begun to condemn authors for immorality in the first *Index*.

What would Jesus have made of this? Might he not have said what he had said to the Pharisees on the occasion when they had brought before him an adulteress who they thought should be stoned to death? Might not Jesus have said, "He that is without sin among you, let him first cast a stone at her"?

Now, in open court, Barrett must contest a Church representative who was a protector of morals. Dare Barrett say, " 'He that is without sin among you . . .'?"

He was sorely tempted. Then, finally, he knew that such an attack was impossible. It would be misconstrued. And if he did attempt it, he could predict Elmo Duncan's protest: Irrelevant!

He would have to play it the hard way.

At two o'clock, confronting the formidable Father Sarfatti, Mike Barrett knew that he was not the match of the witness. In his knowledge of Church history in the matter of condemned literature, the prelate stood on a solid foundation, while Barrett realized his own footing was on quicksand. But still, he was charged to offer for the defense, and so now he did.

First, the procedure of the censuring apparatus.

"Father Sarfatti, I heard you remark—correct me if I heard wrongly—I believe you stated that the Curia offices have been revamped and streamlined since J J Jadway's book was published in 1935. Can you expand upon this as it would relate to book censorship?"

"To be brief—"

"Forgive me, Father, but there is no need to be brief. It would be useful to hear every detail you feel to be relevant to this trial."

"I thank you for your courtesy, sir. Let me say that in 1966, in keeping with the new Ecumenical Council spirit that pervaded the Church and all Christendom, Pope Paul VI abolished the title of the Supreme Congregation of the Holy Office, because it had long been held offensive by Protestants who associated it with what they regarded as persecutions in early Church history. By the elimination of the Holy Office, the Section for the Censure of Books was also eliminated."

"Why was this done?"

"As I have said, sir, it was in keeping with the new spirit of unity among the various Christian faiths."

"I see. I'm interested to know whether there were other motives. Is it not true, Father, that at the convening of the Ecumenical Council in Rome there were numerous Roman Catholic clerics who protested against the old Holy Office, the very office that had condemned Jadway, because it did not hold fair hearings for authors, and these clerics felt that the *Index of Prohibited Books* should be permanently abolished?"

"Well, there was a minority of clerics who felt that way. That is true."

"And, Father, is it not also true, as our Associated Press reported from the Vatican City, that 'by wiping out the Section for the Censure of Books, the Pope made a dramatic gesture signifying a major de-emphasis of the *Index* mentality of the past'?"

"Of course, we must accept the fact that news services often employ sweeping generalizations and tend to exaggerate. In essence, I would say that there was this effort to de-emphasize any function of the Holy Office that had once antagonized non-Catholics."

"Wouldn't it hold then, Father, in view of this new liberality on the part of the Church, that what the Church condemned and prohibited in 1935 it might not condemn and prohibit today?"

"Sir, that is a hypothetical question which I have neither the qualifications nor the authority to answer. I can submit certain facts that might point to a conclusion. For one thing, the new Congregation for the Doctrine of the Faith, of which I am a member, is continuing to review and examine published writings denounced as contrary to the doctrines of the Church. For another, the *Index* has not been abolished. It still exists. His Holiness may assign any written work to the *Index* that he wishes. Finally, sir, I am here before you as a representative of the Vatican because the Church is just as concerned today as it was in 1935 about the publication and circulation of an immoral and sacrilegious work of fiction entitled *The Seven Minutes*."

Barrett went no further on the procedure of the Church's censuring apparatus. He had fumbled that one. Another tack.

Second, the infallibility of the *Index*.

"Father, like the learned counsel for the People, I too have been examining a copy of the *Index*—in fact, the edition in which J J Jadway's name was first listed—as well as some writings about the *Index*. I would like to ask you a number of questions about this censorship calendar or encyclopedia. I was surprised to find Gibbon's *Decline and Fall of the Roman Empire*, and Pascal's *Pensées*, and J. S. Mill's *Principles of Political Economy*, and Sterne's *A Sentimental Journey through France and Italy*, and all of Zola's works still listed in the *Index* and hence still prohibited.

Why were they condemned—because they were obscene or because they were anticlerical?"

"Because they were anticlerical."

"Not because they were harmful to morals?"

"Because they were harmful to the faith."

"And *The Seven Minutes*, Father Sarfatti? I remind you, this is a trial concerned only with the question of whether or not the book is obscene. Whether Jadway's writings were contrary to the faith or anticlerical does not enter into the discussion in this courtroom. With this in mind, will you tell me officially, was *The Seven Minutes* condemned to the *Index* because it is obscene or because it is heretical?"

"It was condemned because it is *both*—both obscene *and* heretical."

"Very well, Father. As to the burning question of what is obscene and what is not obscene, this is, of course, a value judgment. Do you feel you can recognize an obscene work when you read it or hear it read aloud?"

"Speaking for myself, yes. I cannot speak for the Church."

"Suppose I read you a brief passage from a novel. Do you think that you could tell me whether it is immoral or obscene or neither?"

"I could try, but I would be speaking for myself alone."

"But speaking as an expert on obscene literature?"

"Very well. As an expert."

"I will read to you two excerpts from a popular novel. I would appreciate your judgment of them. The first excerpt: 'I found his hand in my bosom; and when my fright let me know it, I was ready to die; and I sighed and screamed, and fainted away.' The second excerpt: 'But he kissed me with frightful vehemence; and then his voice broke upon me like a clap of thunder. Now . . . said he, is the dreadful time of reckoning come, that I have threatened—I screamed out in such a manner, as never anybody heard the like. But there was nobody to help me: and both my hands were secured, as I said. Sure never poor soul was in such agonies as I. Wicked man! said I. . . . O God! my God! this *time!* this *one time!* deliver me from this distress!' "

"Did God deliver her, Mr. Barrett?"

413

"He did . . . Father Sarfatti, do you judge these two excerpts to be obscene?"

"I regard them as immature, suggestive, but I do not regard them, by today's lights, as obscene. However, the Holy Office did consider them obscene in 1755 when it placed those passages, along with the rest of Samuel Richardson's *Pamela*, in the *Index*. I am sorry to spoil your sport, Mr. Barrett, but I will not question the wisdom of the Church in condemning *Pamela* in 1755 even as it condemned *The Seven Minutes* in 1937. The modern trend toward permissive immorality may mock those old judgments, but if they had been heeded, all society and moral standards might be the better for it today."

"Are you saying, Father, that the censors on the *Index* are without human fallibility, have never committed errors of judgment?"

From across the courtroom, Duncan voiced his objection. Defense counsel was being argumentative. Objection sustained.

Barrett sought to rephrase his question. "Father Sarfatti, does any factual evidence exist that the censors assigned to the *Index* have ever, at any time, admitted to errors in judgment?"

"Of course errors have been made," said Father Sarfatti calmly. "When members of the Holy Office, after further consideration, have found that they have been mistaken about any writings, they have never failed to see justice done, to admit their errors and rectify them. The works of Galileo were placed on the *Index*. When this was later proved unjustified, our censors removed the prohibition against Galileo's writings. But I cannot persuade myself that the Church will ever remove its prohibition from J J Jadway's book."

Bloodied, Barrett considered releasing the witness. Yet, one more try.

Third, the meeting with J J Jadway in Venice.

"Father, you stated earlier that a Vatican emissary had personally met with Jadway in Venice to ask him to repudiate the book. Do your records tell exactly where this meeting was held?"

"In the ducal palace, the Doge's Palace—in the Sala del Consiglio dei Dieci, the Hall of the Council of Ten."

"How long did the meeting last?"

"Fifteen minutes."

414

"Did Jadway, in the affidavit he signed, give his reasons for refusing to repudiate *The Seven Minutes?*"

"There is no record of his reasons."

"According to Mr. Leroux, this was a low point in Jadway's life, a period when he was alleged to have been remorseful about having written the book and was only months away from taking his life because of it. If this were so, wouldn't it have been natural for Jadway to repudiate the book and recant?"

"I possess no information about what would have been natural or unnatural for him at that time. I can only repeat that he was obstinate and refused to recant."

"Did the report of the meeting contain any description of Jadway?"

"It did not."

Barrett hesitated. He was inclined to end on this note. Yet he could not resist one more question.

"Father Sarfatti, did the Vatican archives report whether Jadway was drunk at that meeting?"

"It did not report that he was drunk. . . . On the other hand, sir, it did not say that he was sober either."

Barrett smiled. *"Touché."* He had deserved it. He had asked for it, and he had got it. He had broken a golden rule of the cross-examiner's art: Never, never pose an important question unless you know what the witness will answer. You get to where you are going, and then you stop. You never ask that extra question, take that added step which leads into the unknown. Barrett surrendered his witness with a bow of his head. "Thank you, Father. . . . I have no further questions, Your Honor."

FOLLOWING the Italian priest, District Attorney Duncan had brought a renowned British literary agent, just arrived from London, to the witness stand. He was appearing as a qualified authority to testify on the obscene nature of Jadway's book. The agent, Ian Ashcroft, who reeked of Zizanie de Fragonard, was fey, amusing, charming. He was one of those people who always topped you, whose last lines always carried the quick lash and sting of a scorpion's tail. He was the kind of person Mike Barrett always did poorly with in the living room. Ashcroft would be more danger-

415

ous in a court. Barrett determined to limit his cross-examination to a few minutes, no more.

As a young agent employed by a large literary agency in London in 1935, Ashcroft had been in charge of what is known in the publishing trade as permissions, the licensing of excerpts as well as the dispensing of foreign rights, and he had been given the opportunity to try to sell the foreign rights to *The Seven Minutes*. Duncan wondered how he had fared. He had fared poorly, dreadfully, Ashcroft confessed. He had submitted copies of the Jadway novel to cooperating agents or publishers in Great Britain, the Netherlands, Scandinavia, Germany, France, Italy, Spain, Portugal. Except for brief interest shown by one publisher in Germany ("morals had broken down there, anyway, more brothels than homes in Hamburg and Frankfurt")—and finally even this publisher had declined—there had been no interest in the book anywhere. It had been rejected by every foreign publisher to whom it had been submitted.

Duncan wanted to know why *The Seven Minutes* had been unanimously rejected.

"I think that's fairly obvious," Ashcroft had said. "It was a frightful book, unfailingly indecent, total trash. Publishers in the Netherlands, Italy, Spain used nearly identical sentences in rejecting it. They wrote, in effect: 'Mr. Jadway has the dubious distinction of having written the most depraved and obscene book in the history of literature.'"

In cross-examination, Barrett handled the London agent gingerly. If Mr. Ashcroft had held such a low opinion of *The Seven Minutes*, why had he sullied himself by representing it at all?

"Mr. Barrett, I was a pink-faced, cheeky young chap, ambitious, eager to make my mark, and at that time I should have been delighted to represent *Mein Kampf* if it had been handed to me."

Would Mr. Ashcroft agree that few American novels of that period, or even the present, were widely translated and published in Europe?

"I've had some American novels that I've sold to as many as a dozen foreign publishers."

But a first novel by an unknown American author? Was it to be expected that it would be published in Sweden, Germany, France, Italy, Spain?

"No, Mr. Barrett, I should not expect it to be translated and

416

published in those countries. However, it would be published in Great Britain. I would expect at least one sale in Great Britain or elsewhere."

Then what did Mr. Ashcroft find so unusual about not being able to sell Jadway's first little-known novel to foreign publishers?

"Well, Mr. Barrett, what was unusual about the experience was that *The Seven Minutes* was the only published novel I have ever handled or heard about that no secondary publisher—not one—in Great Britain, on the Continent, in the entire world, would agree to bring out. A remarkable nonachievement, you must concede, and worthy of inclusion in the *Guinness Book of World Records* alongside the notice that the crossword puzzle was invented by an Englishman named Arthur Wynne for a New York newspaper in 1913. I think we have something better here, don't you?"

The next half hour had sped by, and now yet another witness was about to finish his testimony for the People under the guidance of Elmo Duncan.

This witness, smooth as velvet, exact as a computer, was Harvey Underwood, dean of America's pollsters.

His appearance had been, for both Barrett and Zelkin, as unexpected as had Father Sarfatti's, and at first they had been unable to discern what use the prosecution intended to make of this witness. Soon it had become clear, and even Barrett had muttered his admiration for the cleverness of the District Attorney.

Harvey Underwood was in the witness box to lay the foundation for the prosecution's argument that *The Seven Minutes* appealed to prurient interest, according to the judgment of the average person. Usually, in censorship cases, the prosecution made this point by presenting community leaders—a Parent-Teacher Association president, a college dean, a church pastor—people who presumably had regular contact with the average person in their community and who could speak authoritatively for the community on the corrupting possibilities of a given book. But Duncan had not been satisfied to reflect the feelings of the average person in the traditional way. In this electronic age of the computer, in this age of the scientific sampling poll for determining public opinion, Duncan had gone to the nation's foremost authority to learn who that average person was, so that such a plastic-wrapped, perfectly-marketed person might be delivered before the court. It was madness, it was dehumanizing, it was ridiculous. It was reflective of the sorry state of a consumer culture that lived by numbers and surveys and committees and averages.

And the jury was enchanted.

For a half hour, with the devotion of a mathematical Luther, the articulate Harvey Underwood described the methods of selective sampling—how the public was divided into subpublics, how stratified random interviews were conducted, how answers to questions were fed into IBM equipment and the results assessed. And for his appearance in court Underwood had readied himself to supply his findings from a massive poll that had been devoted to questions dealing with the personal habits, statistics, and possessions of the persons interviewed.

"It is very intricate," Harvey Underwood was telling the jurors. "Along with our own poll, we have integrated the polls taken by the American Booksellers Association and United Press International, as well as the statistical information provided by the United States Census Bureau through the year 1966. All of this data we have fed into our computers, and what has come out with mathematical certainty is a profile of the average person in the United States. Thus, for the first time, we have obtained a complete portrait of the average person in the average American community —and for the first time, Mr. Duncan, you may have witnesses, or a witness, to reflect that section of the California Penal Code which states, 'Obscene means that to the average person, applying contemporary standards, the predominant appeal of the matter, taken as a whole, is to prurient interest.'"

"Mr. Underwood, can you offer us this scientific profile of the average person?"

At this point, Mike Barrett, having pulled himself together, and acting before the jury succumbed completely, rose to voice his objection.

"If it please the court, I am objecting on the grounds that the question calls for speculation on the part of the witness."

Judge Upshaw lifted both hands to beckon Barrett and Duncan, and then he summoned the stenotypist. "Will you please approach the bench, gentlemen."

The Judge requested Barrett to elaborate on the grounds for his objection.

Barrett explained that there could be no profile of an average person, scientific or otherwise. "The word 'average' usually refers to the arithmetical mean. It can be applied accurately to figures only. At best, an average man could only be an ordinary or common or conforming man, not a living 'mean' derived from adding up disparate sums. As Richard Scammon, former director of the United States Bureau of the Census, and Ben Wattenberg stated it in *This U.S.A.*, 'Mississippi sharecroppers and Marin County, California, commuters do not "average" out to Toledo factory workers. A Ph.D. in physics and a high-school dropout don't average out to a college education for two. Similarly, one man making a hundred thousand dollars a year and five men making four thousand a year does not mean that six men are earning twenty thousand a year . . . the concept of the average man, while convenient, is usually nonsensical.' "

The Judge waited for the District Attorney's response.

"Your Honor, allow me to quote further from the very same source that counsel for the defense has used," said Duncan. "Scammon and Wattenberg say, 'We can legitimately talk of the "average" man . . . because all of the facts given about him are true for the *majority* of American households. . . . For example, over ninety per cent of American households have at least one radio set. It is accurate then, to attribute a radio set to a "typical" or "average" household.' Moreover, Your Honor, gathering such statistics has become a scientific endeavor. Statistics do exist, and they do reveal to us an average person, and my witness is an expert in such fact-finding."

Judge Upshaw had been ruminating upon the matter, and at last he turned to Barrett. "Mr. Barrett, the term 'average man' is a part of the criminal code in this instance. The problem is simply one of definition. I have earlier done some homework on this matter, and I have one definition that gave some sense to the term." He had brought a file folder before him, opened it, and was poring over his notes. He found what he wanted. "Presiding Judge Vincent A. Carroll, of Philadelphia County's Court of Common Pleas, gave the following definition in a similar case: 'Material is now to be judged by its effect on the average person in the community. To relate this term to the specific, we consider that the average person might well be a composite of the jurors whom we have observed during our forty-five years at the bar and on the bench. Such a person is neither saint nor volitional sinner.

He is not a literary critic nor a book burner. He is in fact an average person with average enthusiasms, average prejudices, and with normal propensity for sexual activity (which happily, for the most part, is exercised in procreating the race), but who, if given sufficient erotic stimulus, may be distorted to engaging in sexually abnormal or illegal behavior. This, then, is the average person to whom we apply the contemporary community standard.' Now, much of this, I feel, is applicable here. And if counsel for the State can further define 'average man' through scientific evidence, I believe that he should be permitted to do so. Your objection, Mr. Barrett, is overruled. Mr. Duncan may continue his examination, and as for you, Mr. Barrett, if you wish to probe further the validity of there being an 'average man,' I would suggest you do so in your cross-examination of the witness. . . . You may proceed, Mr. Duncan."

"Thank you, Your Honor."

Exulting in his breakthrough, Elmo Duncan returned to the witness box. Disappointed, Barrett went back to the defense table, and as he sat down he heard the District Attorney resume.

"Mr. Underwood, to repeat my question, can you offer us, based on your scientific researches, an accurate profile of the average person?"

"I can."

Without consulting a note, with his teeth clicking like an adding machine, Harvey Underwood revealed the results of his findings.

"Since we are concerned in this trial with a book, we have tested and found that the average reader of books among the average citizens in our communities is a female. So I shall discuss the average female in this country at this time. She is Caucasian, she is Protestant, she has had at least twelve years of formal education—a decade ago the average woman had had only ten years of education. She is twenty-four years old. She is five feet four inches tall and weighs one hundred thirty pounds. She was married at the age of twenty to a man two years older than herself. She has two children. She and her husband share one car and the same religious faith. She attends church twice a month. Her husband has a manual or a service job, and he earns $7,114 a year. Our average woman resides in an urban area, a city under one hundred thousand in population, which qualifies Oakwood to supply this woman. She has a five-room home worth $11,900. Half of the house is mortgaged. The house has a bathtub or shower, a flush toilet, electricity, one telephone, one television set, a washing machine, no air conditioning, no clothes dryer, no food freezer. The average woman spends seven hours a day performing her household chores, three of these hours in the kitchen. There you have her, sir. That is an accurate profile."

"Mr. Underwood, do you know any actual persons who fit this average even approximately?"

"I know many such persons, and I have chosen one Oakwood woman who matches these statistics exactly. She has volunteered to give testimony in this case."

"Thank you, Mr. Underwood. Now, to return to your statistics a moment . . ."

Barrett had ceased being attentive. He was writing several reminders to himself.

Ten minutes later, Mike Barrett came to his feet to cross-examine Harvey Underwood.

"Mr. Underwood, let's go back to the legal phrasing of the censorship section in the California Penal Code. That refers to 'the average *person*,' does it not?"

"It does."

"And you feel that the average person can be approximated statistically?"

"I do."

"Well, now, Mr. Underwood, you are going to have to enlighten me a little more about the average person. When I use your statistics, I come up with a strange result. As I understand it, fifty-one per cent of the population of the United States is female, while forty-nine per cent is male. According to what you've said, that means the average American is only female. Now, is that true?"

Underwood's scowl deepened. "Of course not. One can't average two absolutes."

"Oh, you can't?"

"I was referring to concepts that can be converted into statistics, such as age or income—a concept where a total can be divided by the number of persons tested to obtain an average or mean."

"Well, I appreciate your wanting to talk about numbers, Mr. Underwood, but I want to talk about persons—specifically, the average person mentioned in the criminal code. Let me ask you this. Supposing fifty per cent of all Americans were male and fifty per cent were female. Wouldn't the average American be a queer?"

"Objection, Your Honor!"

"The question is withdrawn, Your Honor," said Barrett with mock gravity. "All right, Mr. Underwood, let's go on. . . ."

AT THREE FORTY-FIVE in the afternoon, District Attorney Duncan produced the average woman as his next witness.

She was Anne Lou White, and she lived in a five-room house with a husband two years her senior and with their two children in the community of Oakwood, California, Los Angeles County.

She had the dead prettiness of a vapid face in an eye-drop advertisement, and her voice was a sweet soprano whine. She was wide-eyed, smiling, and determined to be very real.

Nimbly, winningly, Elmo Duncan elicited her rehearsed answers. The performance was all straight, and short, and perfect.

After twenty minutes of tête-à-tête, having established and dramatized Mrs. White's averageness, Duncan posed his climactic questions.

"Mrs. White, have you read a novel called *The Seven Minutes*, by J J Jadway?"

"I have. It wasn't easy. It was nauseating. But I forced myself to read it cover to cover."

"As an average person in your community, applying contemporary standards, what was your reaction to this book?"

"I found it sickeningly obscene."

"Did you feel that it went beyond the customary limits of candor in its descriptions of nudity, sex, excretion?"

"Far beyond any acceptable limits of candor. I'm used to frank and realistic writings. But *The Seven Minutes* belongs in the garbage disposal."

"Ha, ha—but does the average woman have a garbage disposal?"

"No, and I don't, but if I had one that is where the book would belong."

"Mrs. White, did you find anything in the novel that could be considered as having 'redeeming social importance'?"

"It was sex and more sex and nothing else. After I put it down, I wanted to wash my hands. I've never laid eyes on any reading matter more obscene."

"Thank you, Mrs. White."

At the defense table, Mike Barrett was seething. For some reason, this product of Underwood's polls and computers angered him more than any witness he had heard this entire day. Perhaps it was because she reminded him of Faye Osborn. They were unlike in every way, this computer-created creature and Faye. Yet not in every way. Like Faye, this Anne Lou White preserved a holier-than-thou attitude, an antiseptic attitude, toward the book. Even more irritating was her righteous self-assurance.

Zelkin was shaking his arm. "Your turn, Mike."

"I'm going to muss her up," Barrett growled.

"Not too much," Zelkin warned. "The jury is identifying with her. She's one of them. Don't antagonize them."

Rising, hands thrust in his trouser pockets, Mike Barrett strode to the witness box where Mrs. Anne Lou White sat exuding self-satisfaction.

"Mrs. White," said Barrett, "since you are the first average woman I've ever had the pleasure to meet, I am going to be eager to know more about your tastes. Not as to food or furniture, but as to books. I'm curious to know if your reading habits are average."

"They are," said Mrs. White.

"How do you know they are?"

"Because—why, because I read a lot, all the popular things that come into the library and in paperback, just the run-of-the-mill things, none of the deep ones I'd never understand. I'm sure my reading tastes are average."

"Have you read *Peyton Place*, by Grace Metalious?"

"Of course not!"

"Have you read *God's Little Acre*, by Erskine Caldwell?"

"No, I haven't."

"Have you read *Lady Chatterley's Lover*, by D. H. Lawrence?"

"I wouldn't be seen with it. No, I have not."

"Have you read *In His Steps*, by Charles Sheldon?"

"No. I've never even heard of it."

"Very well, Mrs. White. Then, by Mr. Underwood's standards, your reading habits are far from average. Those four novels I spoke of have sold, in hardbound and paperback editions, over thirty million copies in this country. Those are four of the five all-time leading best sellers in American history."

Anne Lou White's smile had evaporated. "Well, I think that's shocking. I'm sure the average American hasn't read those four books."

"Mrs. White, in your opinion, would the average American read *The Seven Minutes?*"

"Absolutely not."

"But you are average, and you read it, didn't you?"

"I—I was requested to read it for this trial."

"Otherwise you would not have read it?"

"Most certainly not. I don't waste my time with obscene reading."

"But, Mrs. White, how would you know whether this is obscene reading if you didn't read it?"

"I don't have to drink poison to know it's poison."

Her taunt reminded him that Faye Osborn had used almost the same analogy with him before he had undertaken the case. If this woman proved as much a zealot of purity as Faye, he might be in for trouble. He decided to find out.

"Well, I'd like to test your judgment of what is obscene and not obscene, if I may."

"Go right ahead."

He went back to the table and took the four photostats that Zelkin handed him. Examining them, he returned slowly to stand before the witness.

"Mrs. White, allow me to read you some excerpts from recent translations or renderings of four popular books, all written by famous authors. Please tell me, as I finish reading each of my four excerpts, whether in your opinion it is or is not obscene. Ready?"

"Go ahead," she said uncertainly.

He began to read excerpt one to her. " 'There was but one point forgot in this treaty, and that was the manner in which the lady and myself should be obliged to undress and get to bed . . .' "

When he had finished, he looked up. "Mrs. White, was that obscene or not obscene?"

"Not obscene," she said with obvious relief.

"Very well. Now excerpt two."

He began to read to her from excerpt two. " 'She undressed brutally, ripping off the thin laces of her corset so violently that they would whistle round her hips like a gliding snake. She went on tiptoe, barefooted, to see once more that the door was locked, then with one movement, she would let her clothes fall at once to the ground;—then, pale and serious, without a word, she would throw herself against his breast with a long shudder.'"

He read on for another paragraph, and then he looked at the witness. "Obscene or not obscene?" he asked.

"Not obscene."

"Thank you, Mrs. White. Next, excerpt three."

Carefully he read excerpt three to her. "'The manager looked at his lovely prize, so beautiful, so winsome, so difficult to be won, and made strange resolutions. His passion had gotten to that stage now where it was no longer colored with reason. He did not trouble over little barriers of this sort in the face of so much loveliness. He would accept the situation with all its difficulties; he would not try to answer the objections which cold truth thrust upon him. He would promise anything, everything, and trust to fortune to disentangle him. He would make a try for Paradise . . .'"

Barrett raised his head. "Mrs. White, tell us, obscene or not obscene?"

She wore an adenoidal smile. "Not obscene, not at all."

"Finally, the fourth and last excerpt. Actually, these passages are too lengthy to quote from in detail. If you don't mind, I'll take the liberty of synopsizing some of the passages—I'll show you the original passages marked in the book when I've finished—and I'll also read you some of the words and phrases in this work."

He glanced down at the sheet in his hand. "We have here a young man who is married to a young woman, but he has been unable to consummate their marriage. The young man dies and his wife is widowed. Now the brother of the dead young man appears before the widow, determined to impregnate her. Either before or during copulation with her, he has second thoughts about what he is doing. He refrains from giving her his semen, and he masturbates instead. Later we have another adventure in this young widow's life. She is angry at her father-in-law. She wants to expose his own lechery. One day she disguises herself as a prostitute and allows her father-in-law to pick her up and copulate with her. When the father-in-law learns that his widowed daughter-in-law has become pregnant, he wants to punish her, but then he is exposed as the one who made her pregnant."

Next Barrett began to read phrases and words from the book.

Here "everyone neighed after his neighbor's wife." Here there was "whoring" and "whoremongers" and the description of a gang rape. Here there were "breasts" and "tits" and "buttocks uncovered" and "dung" and "piss" and "fornicators" and "lewdness."

He stopped. "So much for the fourth extract. Now, tell me, Mrs. White, is this book obscene or not obscene?"

"Obscene," she said. "Utterly and definitely obscene."

"Perhaps, Mrs. White, you might like to see the photocopies of all four books in question, each marked numerically in the order that I read it." He set the photostats on the edge of the witness box, but she did not touch them. She waited.

Barrett half turned toward the jury, then he swung back to confront the average woman. "Mrs. White, the first extract that I read you was the most suggestive passage I could find in Sterne's *A Sentimental Journey through France and Italy*. You said that passage was *not* obscene. But in 1819 the book was declared obscene by the Vatican and banned throughout the world. The second extract was one of the more controversial ones from Flaubert's *Madame Bovary*. You said this passage was *not* obscene. But in 1856, when Flaubert's book was published in France, it was taken into court on charges of obscenity, and as recently as 1954 it was blacklisted by certain purity groups in the United States. The third extract was one of the more suggestive ones from Dreiser's *Sister Carrie*. You said this passage was *not* obscene. But in 1900, when the book appeared, it was banned in Boston, and to avoid further charges of obscenity it was withdrawn from circulation and suppressed. As for the fourth and last book from which I quoted, the only extract you said *was* obscene, utterly obscene, that extract was taken from a modern translation of the Old Testament of the Holy Bible!"

Momentarily Mrs. White was in shock. With a struggle, she began to recover. "Tha—that's a cheap trick," she stammered, still shaken.

Barrett ignored her distress. "Mrs. White, do you still feel as certain about your ability to recognize what is obscene and what is not obscene?"

Mrs. White was becoming mussed. "It's not the same—you pulled out that Bible material—all those words—from lots of different chapters of the Bible—"

Judge Upshaw interrupted. "Mrs. White, you must reply to defense counsel's question. . . . Mr. Reporter, the answer will be stricken as not being responsive. Read the question again, please."

The question was read again.

"Of course I know what is obscene and what isn't!" she exclaimed. "I'm trying to say the Bible isn't obscene. Anyone knows that. Everybody knows it is the *Good* Book. If you don't read it completely, spiritually, if you pick out words or modernize certain customs, put them in modern language, of course you can make it sound awful. As I said, it's a trick you—"

Barrett looked up at the bench. "Your Honor, I do not wish to be argumentative in any sense. But since the witness impugns my motives, may I respond and clarify this aspect of the cross-examination?"

"Proceed," said Judge Upshaw curtly.

Barrett considered the witness again. "Mrs. White, in 1895 a gentleman in Clay Center, Kansas, was arrested and found guilty of purveying obscene writing through the mails—obscene quotations—and it was with much embarrassment that the prosecution later learned that these quotations had merely been extracts from the Holy Bible. As you suggest, anything may be found obscene if portions of it are read out of context. In 1928, Radclyffe Hall published a sad and tender story about two lesbians. This novel was called *The Well of Loneliness.* The book contained no coarse language, no overt sexual descriptions. It was a dignified appeal to the public to treat female homosexuality with tolerance. Yet, under an antiquated definition of obscenity laid down by Chief Justice Cockburn in 1868, a phrase taken out of context did indeed condemn this book. The phrase found in *The Well of Loneliness* read, 'And that night they were not divided.' Seven words were enough to condemn the entire book. But when Judge Woolsey, in his opinion on *Ulysses,* announced that a book must be judged 'in its entirety,' a new and better standard was established for guiding obscenity rulings.

"No, Mrs. White, you and I do not differ on this point. No work should be judged by passages taken out of context. All works, including the Bible, should be examined as a whole. In employing extracts, I was merely trying to show how difficult it is for any person, even the justifiably concerned average person, to know what really is or is not obscene for someone else. Of course I am in complete agreement with you about the Bible. I do not for one moment believe that the Bible is obscene. Yet there are others who disagree with the two of us. Havelock Ellis has said, 'There appears to be no definition of obscenity which will not condemn the Bible.' In fact, in studies Ellis made of children, he learned that many youngsters were sexually confused, possibly aroused, by portions of the Bible. For example, the story I synopsized for you of the brother who goes to copulate with his sister-in-law, and then masturbates—that, of course, was from Chapter Thirty-eight of Genesis, where Onan spills his seed upon the ground, thereby adding the word 'onanism,' a synonym for 'masturbation,' to our vocabulary. Yet we agree that, when taken as a whole, the Bible is worthwhile literature because it reflects not only the reality of life, with all its ugliness and violence and perversions, but the wonder and beauty of life as well. When the Bible dwells on sex, even though this portrayal of sex may evoke lustful images and sexual desire in the reader, it is not considered harmful, because it is true. It was Judge Jerome Frank who remarked that no sane person could believe it to be socially harmful if sexual desires led to normal sexual behavior, since without such behavior the human race would soon disappear. This is why, Mrs. White—"

Mrs. White was getting angrier. "But you made the Bible sound dirty, just to confuse me."

"I couldn't make it sound dirty, because, I repeat, it is *not* dirty. They made love in those days too. They procreated and—"

Elmo Duncan was on his feet. "Objection, Your Honor! I do believe counsel for the defense is going too far. I object on the grounds that he is continuing to be argumentative."

"Objection sustained."

"Sorry, Your Honor," said Barrett.

But Mrs. White was not through. She waved aloft the photostats and began to upbraid Barrett. "And the other three extracts from Flaubert and Dreiser and—and Sterne. I don't care what once happened to their books, that they were once called obscene. I still say they are not obscene right now, because we're talking about today, community standards today—"

"Exactly, and how they continue to change. Now, then—"

"—and we're talking about *The Seven Minutes*, that's the subject," said Mrs. White. "That doesn't reflect life like the Bible. That only reflects the sick mind of a pornographer."

Barrett could see that Judge Upshaw was about to admonish

the witness to cease debating, but then the Judge realized that Barrett was ready to resume. The Judge nodded to him, and Barrett resumed.

"Mrs. White, let's get back to *The Seven Minutes*."

He turned and formally requested People's Exhibit Three, and once he had received the court copy of the Jadway book from the clerk, he turned to an early section in the book, marked it with a paper clip, and then turned to another section near the back and marked it with another paper clip. He handed the novel to Mrs. White.

"You will note, Mrs. White," said Barrett, "that I have marked two scenes in *The Seven Minutes*—each is no longer than a page—and now I would like you to read them aloud to the court."

Mrs. White had the book open on her lap. She skimmed the first scene, turned to the second, then slapped the book shut and handed it back to Barrett. "I refuse to read this aloud. Why should I read it?"

"Merely to clarify the subject matter for the jury," said Barrett, "before we discuss these passages."

Judge Upshaw bent toward the witness. "Mrs. White, the defense counsel's request is not unreasonable. Of course, you don't have to read the passages aloud, if that is your wish."

"It is my wish. Let the defense counsel read them aloud."

Barrett shrugged. "I'll waive the reading, Your Honor. The jury may be sufficiently acquainted with the scenes in question already. I should like to interrogate the witness about these two scenes, if I may."

"Proceed," said Judge Upshaw.

Barrett turned to the witness once more. The apple-pie face was no longer pretty. "Mrs. White, as an average person, what are your objections to these passages?"

"The language, for one thing, the filthy words."

Barrett hesitated. Through his head there passed the warning from two psychoanalysts, Drs. Eberhard and Phyllis Kronhausen: If we encourage a patient who does not dare to pronounce a taboo word to use it, without removing simultaneously from his conscience the gnawing sense of wrongdoing, we are doing him more harm than good. Such attempts would be just as ill-advised as telling a sexually inhibited person to go ahead and indulge himself while he is still plagued by feelings of remorse and shame. Yet once the patient was made guilt-free, then the expression of otherwise unacceptable ideas and words would be far preferable to their suppression. But now how to overcome the average person's feelings of shame? The language in *The Seven Minutes* had to be discussed openly, but he must bring the witness to this slowly.

Mrs. White had objected to Jadway's language, the filthy words.

"Mrs. White, the great Chinese philosopher Confucius once wrote, 'If language is not used rightly, then what is said is not what is meant. If what is said is not what is meant, then that which ought to be done is left undone; if it remains undone, morals and art will be corrupted; if morals and art are corrupted, justice will go awry, and if justice goes awry, the people will stand about in helpless confusion.' Do you agree to that?"

She was cautious. "I agree people should say what they mean."

"Do you feel writers should say what they mean when writing about sex?"

"Yes. But they can do that without using indecent words—like the words in that book."

"Can you be specific, Mrs. White, about the words in *The Seven Minutes* that offend you?"

"Well, I'm certainly not going to use them."

"Then point them out. Let me see what you object to." He held the book open for her, and she leaned forward, scanned the pages and pointed to the words. "Fine, Mrs. White," said Barrett. "I appreciate your cooperation. Now, one word we have here is the word 'fuck,' and the other word is 'fucking,' and you object to them?"

"They're absolutely dirty."

"Would you have been happier, Mrs. White, if the author had used such euphemisms or circumlocutions as 'they slept together,' or 'they were intimate,' or 'they made love'?"

"It would have been better. I'd have understood just as well what he was trying to say."

"But you might have been wrong. If Cathleen and her man slept together, were intimate, made love, they might have been doing many things other than simply fucking." He paused. "Mrs. White, the word 'fuck' is the only exact word for this particular act. It cannot be mistaken. Since the euphemisms give you the same mental image, why do you consider the precise word to be obscene?"

"Because no clean person uses it." Then she added triumphantly, "It's not even in the dictionaries."

He wanted the jury with him, so Barrett decided to concede the last. "You are quite right about the dictionaries, Mrs. White. From Dr. Johnson's A *Dictionary of the English Language* to *The Oxford English Dictionary* and *The Random House Dictionary* the word 'fuck' has been held taboo and omitted. *Webster's New International Dictionary* also has left the word out, because, as the editors frankly admitted, it might trouble some readers and provoke controversy and harm the reference work commercially. Yet, as men become more educated, as the pace of life quickens and communications need to become more precise, this word is gaining acceptance in print, as are many other similar words. Eric Partridge, in his *Dictionary of Slang and Unconventional English,* used it and defined it. Do you know the derivation of the word 'fuck,' Mrs. White?"

"I do not."

"The word has an honorable history. According to Partridge, the word 'fuck' derives from a German word meaning to strike, to bang someone, to knock them up, and therefore is used as a slang expression for 'to copulate with.' According to Lord Kennet, writing as Wayland Young, the word derives in turn from Greek, Latin, and French words dealing with bearing fruit and with fetus and with felicity. Therefore, 'We enjoy one another and bear fruit . . . we build a fetus in felicity and become fecund.' To do this, we fuck. Indeed, Mrs. White, had you been familiar with Shakespeare or Burns, Joyce or D. H. Lawrence, you would have been familiar with that word long before you came upon it in *The Seven Minutes.* In fact, when D. H. Lawrence's *Lady Chatterley's Lover* went on trial in England in 1960, the public prosecutor, Mr. Griffith-Jones, discovered, and so informed the court, that 'the word fuck or fucking occurs no less than thirty times.' Yet the court found this acceptable and the book was acquitted. Moreover, in reporting that trial, *The Guardian* of London and *The Observer* of London both candidly and honestly used the word 'fuck' in print. Nor did they ever have to report later that any of their readers were corrupted by their having done so."

"They were trying to sell newspapers, just like Jadway was trying to sell books," said Mrs. White firmly. "I still say it's wrong and immoral."

"Suppose, Mrs. White, that we return to *The Seven Minutes* and some of the other language that has offended you. The next word that troubled you is the word 'prick.' You regard that as dirty?"

"Dirt for dirt's sake."

"Our etymological dictionaries indicate 'prick' has had many meanings over the years, and one meaning that goes as far back as 1592, says *The Oxford English Dictionary*, is that 'prick' is slang for 'penis.' The word means anything that pricks or pierces, anything sharply pointed like spurs or with a tapering point like a thorn or a goad or, indeed, the male phallus. Now, William Shakespeare used that word exactly as J J Jadway used it. And you still feel it is obscene?"

"I do."

"Another word that appears to have offended you is 'cock,' which means a bird, a faucet, or a male penis. The great playwrights Beaumont and Fletcher used this word in their play *The Custom of the Country*. I would agree with you if you called it a vulgarism, but I doubt if it could be called obscene."

"I'm calling it obscene."

"And you object to the word 'condom,' is that right?"

"I think so. Yes, I do."

" 'Condom' is defined as a thin safety sheath, usually made of rubber, worn over the penis during sexual intercourse or coitus to prevent conception or the contracting of a venereal infection. I can't imagine what is objectionable about such a word. It has had a long and honorable history. As far back as 1560, Dr. Fallopia devised a condom, but in a most primitive form. He introduced a crude sheath of linen, which was rarely used. Then, in the eighteenth century, an English physician named Dr. Conton created a less discomforting contraceptive made of fish bladder and lambskin. From Dr. Conton's name came the modern word 'condom.' Of course Jadway had to use a condom in his book, because in 1934 they didn't have a birth-control pill or shots."

Mrs. White's lips had become a singular lip, and Barrett momentarily wondered if he should go on to the last word that had offended the witness. He decided that he must continue.

"Finally, Mrs. White, we come to the last word you pointed out, the word 'cunt.' Jadway used that vulgarism honestly, too. It dates from Middle English times. It derives from the Latin *cuneus*, meaning a wedge. In 1387 Chaucer used it when he wrote, 'He caught her by the cunt.' In *Twelfth Night*, Shakespeare spelled it out. In one of his plays Fletcher used it, saying, 'They write sunt with a C, which is abominable.' Well, Jadway wrote it with a C, just as Pietro Aretino, the Italian satirist who was a protégé of the popes of Rome, wrote it with a C in the early 1500s, and added with exasperation, 'If you want to be understood by anyone outside the University of Rome, speak clearly and say fuck, prick, cunt and ass. You and your thread in the eye . . . key in the lock . . . why don't you say yes when you mean yes and no when you mean no . . . ?' Mrs. White, can you not see the value to literature when the writer of sexual realism says yes when he means yes?"

"I'm saying no when I mean no," she snapped.

A burst of laughter swept the courtroom, and Barrett considered the witness with more respect. The pudding was not quite as bland as he had come to believe.

"Mrs. White, understand the context of my line of questioning. I am not advocating that coarse or vulgar words should be used by everyone everywhere. I don't say you have to use them or listen to them. I personally am certainly too inhibited to use them in mixed company frequently. Not because the words are wrong, but because I was raised in a culture that generally disapproves of them. I am only saying that writers, from Chaucer to Jadway, should be permitted the freedom to use honest words, precise words when they are writing realistically, dramatically, and attempting to be faithful to their characters and times. And all this in the privacy of a book you may pick up or put down, read or reject as you wish. Jadway sought that freedom. Great authors before him possessed it. I hope to get you to agree, Mrs. White, that J J Jadway, in his effort to be faithful to his talent, craft, and story, in his attempt to write truly and without shame, had behind him sound historical precedent for using the direct language found in *The Seven Minutes*."

"I'm not interested in the past, Mr. Barrett. I'm interested in protecting our morality in the present, especially the morality of the young, so we don't decay and decline the way other nations have done."

"Mrs. White, as a representative of what is average, do you believe that the average student in our high schools, on our college campuses, is being harmed, even ruined, by reading this sort of language?"

"I certainly do. It's terrible, what's happening to our young. They use foul words in ordinary speech, they use those words openly, and they scrawl them on walls in public places, and use them in those horrible little weekly newspapers they write and circulate, and because of this the next generation will have no respect for decency and laugh at good morals. And why are they doing it? Who's to blame? I can tell you. They're doing it because they've read those words in books like *The Seven Minutes* and they've been hypnotized by evil prophets like J J Jadway." She halted, triumphantly, and then dared Barrett. "What else could cause them to use such foul language?"

"Mrs. White, even though I am supposed to be doing the questioning, and you the answering, I'll be only too pleased to answer your question if I am permitted to do so." He glanced up at Judge Upshaw, who remained impassive. He waited for Duncan's objection. There was none. He resumed. "Mrs. White, there are many scholarly authorities who do not believe that our young people today use vulgarisms in their speech because they have been corrupted or hypnotized by realistic books. Rather, these authorities believe that vulgarisms are more frequently used in the language of the young because it is their means of shocking and rebelling against the establishment, their elders, those who have imposed upon them standards and a way of life, often repressive and cynical and hypocritical, that they don't like. This language is a sort of rallying cry for those who want to sweep out the old way, with its guilts, fears, shames, inhibitions, to make room for what they hope will be a better and healthier society. The words are merely a small symptom of a great and growing revolution in feelings and attitudes about how mature people might live together more happily. I would suggest it might be this desire for improvement rather than realistic books that has made the usage of vulgarisms more common today than at any time since the bawdy Elizabethan Age. Does that answer your question, Mrs. White?"

"No, it does not. Most of them wouldn't even know those words, except for dirty books."

"Wouldn't even know those words? Why, long before the first printed books were circulated, many of those old Anglo-Saxon words were in common usage. No matter. Perhaps we'd best proceed." Barrett held the book up. "Mrs. White, besides the time-tested, unconventional English words in these pages, words used by every class of people in America, what else in these two scenes offended you?"

"What they're about. What that woman is doing. The author—he doesn't have to write about that."

"Let's see what Cathleen was doing in this first scene. She's remembering when she was eighteen, desiring a man and afraid to have one. Yet she needs sexual release. Let's read it aloud. 'Finally she was naked, and now she knew that it had not been the clothes that had made her hot—but her skin, her blazing skin—and, most excruciating of all, the relentless burning between her thighs. It must be stopped or she would die. She rocked back and forth on the edge of the bed, pressing her thighs together to suffocate the burning, then releasing her thighs, then bringing them together tighter, rubbing them together until the pain was unbearable. She went on like this for minutes, eyes shut, shaking her head, moaning, until finally she fell back on the bed, wriggling until she was all on the bed, then lying rigid while her hand found her belly, and massaged it, and moved downward until her trembling fingers touched the silky pubic hair and finally reached the tiny protruding bud, and now at first gently she caressed and massaged it, and then faster and faster and faster . . .'" Barrett looked up at the witness. "She's simply masturbating, Mrs. White, and the way it's written—"

"It's obscene! It could serve no purpose except to excite sick people."

"But in the context of the whole book, this scene had an important purpose, Mrs. White, as defense literary experts will testify. And this second scene. Simple precoital petting, and coitus with the female atop the male. Do you consider that obscene?"

"Utterly obscene."

"You consider those passages as going beyond the contemporary standards of behavior in your community?"

"Yes, I do."

"As the average woman from Oakwood, Mrs. White, can you tell me what the average single girl does to achieve sexual release if she doesn't have premarital intercourse with a man—and what the average young married woman does in bed with her husband?"

435

"Objection, Your Honor!" Duncan roared out. "Witness has no firsthand knowledge of the behavior of other average single or married women."

"The objection is sustained."

Barrett nodded. "All right, Mrs. White, then let's take you. You are an average young woman, we are told. Perhaps you would be willing to tell us from your own sexual experience—"

"Objection, Your Honor, as being immaterial."

"Sustained."

"Mrs. White, did you know that the average girl in the United States does masturbate and that the average married woman does frequently assume a coital position astride her mate? According to Dr. Alfred C. Kinsey's survey on the human female, six out of ten women masturbated sometime during their lives, and forty-five per cent of these reached orgasms in three minutes or less, and in precoital petting, ninety-one per cent of all women manually stimulated the male genitalia and fifty-four per cent of the women permitted men to stimulate their genitalia orally, and fifty-two per cent of the females reported coitus while they lay on top of their male partner, and—"

"Your Honor," Duncan shouted, "objection as being argumentative and immaterial!"

"Objection sustained on the ground of being immaterial."

Barrett stared at Mrs. White, then at Duncan, and then he looked up at the Judge. "I'm finished with our average witness, Your Honor."

AFTER RESUMING his seat beside Zelkin at the defense table, Barrett knew that while he had satisfied himself in his cross-examination of Mrs. White, he had not endeared himself to the jurors. Ignoring what had been drummed into his head way back in law school, that when you are questioning a witness you are really speaking to the jury, he had become emotionally engaged with the witness, instead of concentrating on the impression he was making on the twelve jurors. He had indulged himself, his personal indignation at middle-class self-righteousness and prudery, and probably had offended those jurors who were middle-class themselves. He had spoken of certain subjects that needed airing, forgetting in his passion that this was not a classroom but a courtroom, and now afterward, recalling his obligation to his client, he regretted his outbursts and his badgering and harassment of the witness. His commitment to a cause was beginning to cloud his objectivity. It was that, he told himself, that and this long abrasive day. His nerves were strained and beginning to unravel.

Now, discouraged, emotionally spent, Barrett tried to be attentive to District Attorney Duncan's smooth, swiftly paced examination of the day's final witness.

With this witness, Paul Van Fleet, the prosecution had entered upon the traditional last phase of its case—offering "expert opinions from persons qualified to so give such opinions"—opinions from persons who would support the prosecution's contention that *The Seven Minutes* was an obscene work without redeeming social importance.

Duncan's questions, the witness's answers, established the fact that few American literary critics were better qualified to discuss the merit or lack of merit of a book than Paul Van Fleet. While the sleepy-eyed, nasal young critic might be too devoted to hyperbole and erudition to be fully understood by the jury, Barrett had to admit to himself that the witness was proving effective.

The fact that Van Fleet was obviously a homosexual—there was a long-standing rumor that he had once wedded a widow with a second-rate mind so that he might more conveniently possess her beautiful adolescent son—did not seem to be prejudicing the jurors. Nor, Barrett decided, did the jurors understand that Van Fleet would be automatically hostile to a novel that was, if nothing else, an ode to healthy, lusty heterosexuality, with all its subheters. Barrett guessed that the jurors would, instead, interpret Van Fleet's deviate characteristics—as they had probably interpreted the idiosyncrasies of so many well-known homosexuals who had been successful in the arts—as evidence of a special mystique that guaranteed his superior wisdom and aesthetical judgment. Moreover, Van Fleet's literary credentials were irrefutable: three published collections of learned essays devoted to such subjects as Ellen Glasgow, Lytton Strachey, the death of the Freudian novel, Hart Crane, Ronald Firbank, polemics and the artist; a series of critical articles in *Partisan Review*, the *New York Review of Books*, *Encounter*, *Commentary*, with an occasional popularized, better-paying piece in *The New Yorker*; a frequent judge for the National Book Awards.

His opinion of *The Seven Minutes?*

"It is not uncommon, Mr. Duncan, for the arm of literature to be occasionally marred by blemishes—tiny boils or papulae of books that fester briefly, burst, and disappear. *The Seven Minutes* is such a boil swollen to dangerous proportions by the publicity of this trial. It is my duty, as one of the protectors of literature's fine arm, to lance this boil at this time, so that the pus of its pruriency be drained, the blemish eradicated, and the good health of literature be restored. In response to your inquiry, it is not only my pleasure but my duty, as a guardian of American taste, to reassure you that the late Mr. Jadway's novel, *The Seven Minutes*, is utterly devoid of literary or social excellence. It is to literature what a filthy French postcard is to art. It is obscene in the rankest sense of the word."

Later. Did Mr. Van Fleet feel that J J Jadway tried to give the reader some understanding or vision of love?

"Surely, Mr. Duncan, you are twitting me. Love? Mr. Jadway knew nothing of love. There exists a telling anecdote about the author's attitude toward love. Apparently, the story was obtained first hand by the scholar who originally reported it. If I may, I shall quote from the source directly. In an admirable study entitled *Outside the Mainstream*, the highly respected Columbia University professor Dr. Hiram Eberhart writes, 'One night, after listening to a prize fight on the radio, a contest in which Joe Louis wrested the heavyweight championship from one James Braddock, Jadway told friends who had been listening to it with him that love between a man and a woman was most often performed like a prize fight, the dancing, the feinting, the blow and counterblow, the anger, the savagery, the struggle for ascendancy and physical domination. But rare true love, Jadway went on, had nothing of pugilism in it. When Jadway was asked to give examples of books that depicted the more common hostile love, Jadway cited Henry Miller's *Tropic of Capricorn*, which he had just read, as a book that reflected perfectly the brutality of love. Yet, curiously, although Jadway appeared to recognize various aspects of love, and the treatments of it in the writing of others, he was blind to any understanding of what he had committed to paper in his only published novel. For in *The Seven Minutes*, despite a handful of misguided cultists who believed otherwise, the handling of love throughout is an act of hatred against womanhood. With the action, imagery, language he has used in developing a portrait of his heroine, action, imagery, and language that is unremittingly pornographic and coarse, Jadway has unconsciously taken on the role of a pugilist attempting to down and humiliate the opposite sex.' I find myself in total agreement with Dr. Eberhart."

During this testimony, an oddity, an incongruity actually, had caught Barrett's attention, dominating his thoughts, at once encouraging him to record all of what he had just heard.

Presently, Elmo Duncan's examination of Paul Van Fleet was concluded, and it was the defense's turn.

Rising to cross-examine the witness, Barrett was tempted to bring out the strange incongruity, to delve into this unusual evidence of time out of joint. Yet, after his questioning began, when the moment came to bring up what was foremost on his mind, he refrained from mentioning it. For one thing, he was not absolutely certain that he was right about the oddity that he had detected. If he was wrong, the waspish Van Fleet would make a fool of him. If he was right, he might have an ace in the hole, one too important to the defense to reveal to the opposition at this stage.

Barrett filed his question in a far corner of his mind. Tonight he would take it out and try to find the answer to it himself. If he was right, the defense would have a new lead, a fresh possibility, a kindled hope.

By NINE O'CLOCK that night, the corned-beef sandwich and coffee beside him still untouched, Mike Barrett suddenly closed the international almanac he had been poring over, dropped it on his office desk, and gleefully shouted through the open door for Abe Zelkin to join him.

Zelkin came in hurriedly, holding a half-finished kosher pickle and a paper cup of coffee.

"What is it, Mike?"

"Abe, can you define 'anachronism' for me?"

"Anachronism? Sure. It's when you refer to the wrong time."

"Or, as Webster's has it, 'An error in chronology by which events are misplaced in regard to each other,' like 'the antedating of an event,' like 'anything incongruous in point of time with its surroundings.' Well, Abe, I've discovered not one but two striking anachronisms in Van Fleet's testimony. I suspected it when I heard them in court, but I couldn't be positive until I checked them out." He tapped the almanac. "I've just checked them out."

"Anachronisms. What's there to get so excited—?"

Barrett jumped up. "Listen, Abe, I'm not nit-picking. There may be something to get mighty excited about." He waited for Zelkin to sit down, and then, as Zelkin nibbled at the pickle, Barrett began to pace before him. "Remember that part of Van Fleet's testimony where he quoted from some literary work called *Outside the Mainstream*, by Dr. Hiram Eberhart of Columbia University?"

"I remember."

"And remember the Eberhart quote where he tells the anecdote of the night Jadway was listening to Louis win the heavyweight title by knocking out Braddock, and then, afterward, the way Jadway spoke about how so much lovemaking of the garden variety was like that prize fight, and then going on to say that Henry Miller's *Tropic of Capricorn* depicted lovemaking in that manner?"

"Yes, I recall—"

"Okay, Abe. The first anachronism, the one that struck me while we were in court. To lay the foundation, when did J J Jadway die?"

"February, 1937."

"Exactly. Jadway killed himself and was promptly cremated in February, 1937. But here we have Dr. Eberhart telling us how Jadway read and discussed Miller's *Tropic of Capricorn*. Yet *Capricorn* was not published by the Obelisk Press until 1939. In short, Jadway was reading and discussing a book published two years after his death. How do you like that?"

Zelkin finished his pickle. "Flimsy," he said. "Van Fleet may have misquoted Dr. Eberhart."

"Nope. I had my favorite librarian, Rachel Hoyt, at the Oakwood Branch Library, look it up. The quote was correct word for word."

"Still flimsy," persisted Zelkin. "Dr. Eberhart made an understandable mistake in his writing. He mixed up *Tropic of Capricorn*, published in 1939, with Miller's *Tropic of Cancer*, which was published in 1934, when Jadway was still very much alive."

"I'm a step ahead of you, Abe. I, too, saw that such an error would be an easy one to make. As a matter of fact, the error must

440

have been made, because of the second discrepancy. Hear this one. We have Jadway dead and gone in February, 1937. We also have—according to the highly esteemed Dr. Eberhart—Jadway listening to Joe Louis beat Braddock for the boxing title. Know when Louis beat Braddock? Joe Louis knocked out Jim Braddock in the eighth round in Chicago in June, 1937. Get it? *June*, 1937. That means Jadway was listening to the fight four months after he was supposed to be dead. How do you like that?"

Zelkin set down his coffee. "I like that better."

"Now, I know the distinguished Dr. Eberhart may have been in error a second time. But twice in one paragraph, from a renowned scholar, with all that proofreading? Maybe. Yet unlikely. So supposing our Dr. Eberhart was accurate about this second oddity? What does that give us? It gives us a new and revived Jadway who did not die in February, 1937, as Cassie McGraw, Christian Leroux, and Father Sarfatti have reported. It gives us a Jadway very much alive four months later. And perhaps discussing Miller's book two years later. It upends all the testimony on Jadway so far. It puts us back in business."

"It sure does—*if* Dr. Eberhart's anecdote is at least half true. Is Dr. Eberhart still around?"

"Very much so. Still at Columbia. Has an apartment in Morningside Heights. All that's left is to phone him, try to wake him up, and, presuming he's in New York and not off on a sabbatical or something, tell him it is urgent that I see him on a matter involving the integrity of his scholarship."

"You can be sure that'll wake him up."

"And it should get me to him and nearer the final truth. I know the dice are loaded against us. But I'm willing to roll them again. What do you say, Abe?"

"What can I say? I got a partner who likes to travel. I say take a trip. When you're going under, even a straw is worth a grab. Okay, I'll stand in for you in court tomorrow. Only see that you get back before they put Jerry Griffith on the stand. He's your baby."

"Don't worry. Thanks, Abe." Barrett was momentarily reflective. "Jadway not dead in 1937. My God, wouldn't that be something?"

VIII

WHEN HE first sat down across from Dr. Hiram Eberhart at the lunch table, Mike Barrett had been as stoical about his duty and the probable result as an eighteenth-century executioner in France preparing to decapitate the aristocrat bowing beneath the guillotine.

Barrett had had no worry about suffering from hemophobia. His mind was on truth, truth and justice.

But now that the coup de grace had been delivered, now that Dr. Eberhart's head had rolled, now that he looked as if he had been severed from his senses, Barrett was sorry and felt a twinge of remorse.

They had been sitting at a small table on the second floor of the exclusive Century Club on Forty-third Street, a few doors off Fifth Avenue, in New York City. Barrett's midnight call last night had not awakened Dr. Eberhart—he always read late, it turned out —and Barrett's enigmatic challenge to his proud scholarship had quickly provoked curiosity and an appointment. Dr. Eberhart had said that he was a member of the Century Club and suggested that Barrett meet him there in the lobby near the first-floor entrance at one o'clock. Barrett had come straight from the airport and had arrived before the appointed time, but Dr. Eberhart was already there, and by one o'clock they had been shown to their table upstairs.

Barrett had not wasted a minute, and Dr. Eberhart also had no interest in cordiality. Unlocking his briefcase, Barrett had explained to his host who he was and what was the reason for his interest in J J Jadway and therefore in Dr. Eberhart, and then he had read to Dr. Eberhart the professor's own anecdote about

Jadway. He had then related how Van Fleet had quoted the passage in court late yesterday afternoon. Then, mercilessly, Barrett had turned the knob and let the guillotine's blade flash downward.

Two unexpected anachronisms, Dr. Eberhart. Did the professor know when Jadway had died? No, it had not been relevant to what he had been writing. Well, Dr. Eberhart, now it would seem to be relevant. Jadway died in February, 1937. Here you write of his discussing the Louis–Braddock fight, which in fact was staged four months later in 1937, and here you have him discussing *Tropic of Capricorn*, which in fact was not published until two years after his death. There you have it, Dr. Eberhart.

Barrett had once heard that it took the guillotine ten seconds to behead its victim. After the careful preparation, it had taken Barrett no longer than that to separate Dr. Eberhart from his senses.

Dr. Hiram Eberhart was a neat gnome of a scholar, perfectly fitted into an academic box, with no world beyond his literary scholarship. He knew very little about many things, but very much, perhaps all there was to know, about his one thing. He was not a snob, not mean, but merely an authority. He was musty, fussy, tidy, complacent. An elderly bachelor on the verge of becoming a professor emeritus. Strands of dull gray hair, myopia, a shiny red button of a nose (decades of medicinal sherry), chicken-breasted, an old-fashioned dull charcoal suit. What he knew he knew best of all, and he was never contradicted. Quoted, yes, but contradicted never.

Now he was undone.

The weak eyes tried to focus. "Are you sure, are you sure, Mr. Barrett? Let me see what you have there, let me see for myself. It can't be."

He had taken Barrett's notes, and it was there.

"Mr. Barrett, this has never happened to me before. In a long lifetime dedicated purely to scholarship, I have never been confronted with such a contradiction in my facts. I do not mean to imply that there can exist a man who is without fallibility and error, but I have always been meticulous about my research and my accuracy. I have four textbooks in regular use in university literature courses. This volume, my most recently published work, appeared only the year before last. It was ten years in the making. Despite the imprecations of my publisher, I postponed releasing it for publication three times, in order to check and double-check my facts. Now, this dreadful error. I blame myself only for overlooking Jadway's date of death. Had I not done that, this gruesome mistake would have been averted. But Jadway's death date seemed so unnecessary. I had the information first hand—about Jadway's comment on *Tropic of Capricorn*, and his analogy about the prize fight and love. I was accurate about tape-recording what I had learned. The mistake could have been made only by my source. He must be given the blame."

"Your source?" said Barrett. "It was not evident to me there was any source other than yourself. You credited no one in a footnote for the anecdote. I assumed you were present when Jadway—"

"No, I was not. I recall it fully now. I received this material on the condition that I not publicly credit my source. My source was Jadway's—one of Jadway's closest friends in Paris in the nineteen-thirties. Entirely trustworthy. He had been with Jadway when the events in the anecdote transpired."

"Who was your source?"

"Well, considering how I was misled, I see no reason not to reveal his name. I acquired the information from Sean O'Flanagan, a poet who had known Jadway in Paris."

"Sean O'Flanagan," Barrett murmured. "I've heard the name." He tried to recollect where or from whom, and then he remembered. From Olin Adams, the autograph dealer. "Yes," Barrett went on, "I'd hoped to see O'Flanagan myself recently, but he had no phone, no address, received his mail in care of General Delivery. How did you get to him, Dr. Eberhart, and when?"

"It was three years ago, while I was still rewriting *Outside the Mainstream*. By an accident of good luck—it seemed good luck then—I came across an obscure poetry quarterly being published in Greenwich Village. It contained an anonymously written verse about Jadway. The publisher of the poetry magazine was Sean O'Flanagan—publisher and editor, according to the masthead. I traveled to Greenwich Village to find him. At the publication's address I learned that, weeks before, the magazine had been foreclosed on by creditors such as the printer and the landlord. I was directed to a neighborhood pub which, I was told, was O'Flanagan's hangout, as it had been for many years."

"And you found him there?"

444

"Not on my first visit, but I did on my third. There was a round corner table and a padded chair on which O'Flanagan had staked a claim, and from which he had held forth for almost a decade. The proprietor tolerated him as a character, a part of the decor, and he was regarded rather as the Ezra Pound of the pub. He had the reputation, I learned, of being a heavy drinker, an alcoholic, living off some meager private income, while occupying himself with reminiscing of his days as an expatriate in Paris and Rapallo and dispensing advice to the younger poets who gathered around."

"His drinking," said Barrett. "Perhaps that accounts for his misinforming you."

"I think not," said Dr. Eberhart. "The late afternoon that he received me, he was stone cold sober, at least in my view, and meticulous about the information that he gave me. He had agreed to speak to me providing I would not ask him any personal questions about Jadway. I promised to confine my interview to literary matters and did. It was O'Flanagan who, near the end of the interview, volunteered the personal anecdote in which you have discovered two horrifying anachronisms."

"What was O'Flanagan like?"

"I have only a dim impression of him now. A somewhat rheumy, bucolic, ill-clad old man—in years perhaps younger than myself, but in appearance seemingly much my senior. I imagine he could be a nuisance and tiresome when tippling from the bottle. However, he determinedly avoided drink in my presence. One beer, I believe, and no more. I perceived he wanted his wits about him and was eager to put his best foot forward. A rather egotistical old man who felt that the world was remiss for not having crowned his own genius. In his failure he took refuge in self-deception. But I fear the world is right and O'Flanagan wrong. I have read his poetry. Now, presuming he is still alive—"

"He is," said Barrett. "Or at least he was a week ago."

"Well, then, no doubt you will want to see him and probe for the truth behind this unfortunate anecdote. If you do, I am sure he is still entering that pub in Greenwich Village every cocktail hour, which is around five in the afternoon, assuming his place of honor at the corner table below the frosted window, and there nodding over memories of happier times. Should you find him, and straighten out the dates of Jadway mort and Jadway redivivus, I would be grateful if you would keep me informed. I must correct the unhappy error in the next edition of my book, or else excise the anecdote completely."

"I owe you a good deal, Dr. Eberhart, and I promise to keep you informed. That club in Greenwich Village where Sean O'Flanagan hangs out. Can you tell me its name?"

"O'Flanagan's pub? It is called—forgive me—The Appropoet. No orchestra or dancing or floor show in the usual sense. The only entertainment consists of a poetry-reading session during every cocktail hour. Aspiring amateurs are invited to declaim their verse to the intoxicated clientele. The readings are accompanied by much hooting and catcalling. Deserved. The new poetry, the formlessness of it, the wretched corruption of the language, is enough to drive one to drink. I imagine that's the point of it. What happened to Sara Teasdale? Now, that's rather a good title, isn't it? At any rate, I wish you luck with the Keeper of the Anachronisms."

THE CLUB had not been listed in the New York telephone directory. A new thing. Anticonformity, anticommercialism, antiestablishment. Barrett had supposed that to Charles Dodgson this might have made sense. After all, did Wonderland have an address? Did Eden? Does an oasis?

By late afternoon, carrying his briefcase, Barrett had caught a taxi and directed the driver to take him to Greenwich Village. After leaving the cab near Washington Square, he had bought a copy of *The Village Voice*. It contained no listing or advertisement of the club. At last he had approached a boy and a girl—they both turned out to be girls, one in pea jacket and dungarees, the other in a colorful short shift and sandals—and they pointed the way.

Now, after walking four blocks through the Village, Mike Barrett had arrived at his destination.

There was a sign over a striped canopy that stretched above the sidewalk. The sign read: THE APPROPOET. BAR—SNACKS. OPEN 10 A.M. TO 3 A.M. Along the border of the fringed canopy, in Irish half-uncials, was the lettering "A Book of Verses underneath the Bough . . . A Jug of Wine, a Loaf of Bread—and Thou . . . Beside me singing in the Wilderness . . . Oh, Wilderness were Paradise enow!"

There were two worn steps between wrought-iron rails leading

446

down to the entrance. Barrett descended and went inside. The room was crowded and cramped, with clouds of smoke curling beneath the ceiling. The professor had been wrong about the absence of music. Today there was the mournful strumming of a single guitar above the low-keyed chatter. Leaning against the far brick wall, a long-haired, bearded young man, holding a yellow sheet of paper, was reading a poem. "Paint me by number / And perforate me for a machine." One more voice singing in the Wilderness, Barrett thought, and he headed for the nearest side of the bar just ahead.

The bartender, a black patch over one eye, was rinsing glasses. Barrett coughed to get attention. "I wonder if you can help me. I'm supposed to meet Sean O'Flanagan here."

"He's at his regular table."

Barrett looked about, confused, and the bartender pointed over Barrett's shoulder.

"Next to the window," the bartender added, "the fellow with the beret."

"Thanks," said Barrett. He turned around, waited for some new arrivals to pass, and then moved between the tables toward the fellow with the beret, who sat hunched over a drink beneath the oblong frosted window.

As he neared Sean O'Flanagan, the face of the poet took on definition. The beret was a soiled faded blue and was worn like a skullcap. The eyes were rheumy, the wrinkles above and below gouged deeply like seams stitched to hold the flesh together. There was a grayish stubble on the protruding chin. A rubbed corduroy jacket was draped over thin coat-hanger shoulders, and a string of love beads hung from the scrawny neck. All in all, he gave the impression of a failed André Gide.

"Mr. Sean O'Flanagan?"

The poet had been staring off into space. Now he lifted his gaze in the manner of one who was used to having strangers introduce themselves to him. "Yes, young man?" he said.

"I'm Mike Barrett. I'm in from Los Angeles. A mutual acquaintance suggested I look you up. There's something I wanted to talk to you about. Mind if I sit down?"

O'Flanagan's voice was whisky-hoarse, and doubtful. "Depends. What you want to talk to me about?"

"Mainly about your period in Paris."

"You're not a poet?"

"No, I—"

"You can't tell any more, these days. Now poets wear ties and crew cuts and some of them work as dentists."

"Well, I did want to ask you a few questions about writing and writers. Can I treat you to a drink?"

O'Flanagan considered his almost empty glass, and then his head came up and the mouth cracked at the corners and wrinkled into a smile of brotherhood. "That last was poetry, Mr. Banner. You are a qualified versifier. Grab a chair."

Barrett found a free one nearby and dragged it to a spot across the circular table from O'Flanagan. No sooner was he seated than the poet had caught the attention of a waiter. "Chuck, I'll be having another brandy and water. Make it a double—the brandy, not the water."

"Scotch on the rocks," Barrett called out.

O'Flanagan launched into a long, humorous anecdote about a St. Bernard dog and its keg of brandy, and at its conclusion he cackled with glee, and Barrett laughed and felt better. The drinks appeared, and O'Flanagan's hand trembled as he brought the glass to his mouth. He gulped, smacked his lips, gulped again. Half of the brandy and water had disappeared.

He winked at Barrett. "Needed that fueling up, Mr. . . ." He looked blank. "Lost my memory for names."

"Mike Barrett."

"Barrett, Barrett. Okay. Now, what's it you wanted to ask me about Paris?"

"Exactly when were you there?"

"When was I? Let me see. Got there as a puling kid in 1929. Stayed on until 1938, I guess. About ten years. Never been years like those years. 'Paris rawly waking, crude sunlight on her lemon streets.' That's Joyce. Knew him. First met him at La Maison des Amis des Livres. Knew Sylvia Beach too. And Gert Stein. But the main watering place was the Dôme. You know Paris? The café in Montparnasse? It's still there on the corner, I guess. That was real Bohemia. This—" he waved his hand to take in the room—"this is dross, fake, synthetic Bohemia."

"Have you ever been back to Paris?" asked Barrett.

"Back? No. I wouldn't want to spoil the dream. Every man has his own annuity for his later years. Mine is the old dream. It was incredible, everybody writing way out ahead of the world, or painting, or getting laid. God, what a Mohammedan heaven for a kid with a questing cock. You know what? One night I banged some old frump. Turned out she had been one of Modigliani's models once. And one night, Christ, I must've been loaded, I let some old buzzard bugger me. Know why? Because I was told he used to bugger Rimbaud or Verlaine, forget which. Ah, well, here's mud in your eye, Barrett."

He finished his drink.

"Have another," said Barrett.

O'Flanagan signaled the waiter for a refill and nodded his thanks to Barrett. "My old pal Wilson Mizner used to say, 'As a writer I am a stylist, and the most beautiful sentence I have ever heard is "Have one on the house."' Ha!" He broke into a fit of cackling and coughing, and at last he wiped his mouth with his sleeve. "Now, where were we?"

"In Paris."

"Paris, that's right."

Barrett waited for the refill to be served and watched O'Flanagan go at it. "Mr. O'Flanagan, when did you meet J J Jadway in Paris?"

With the mention of Jadway's name, the poet stopped drinking. "What makes you think I knew Jadway?"

"Several people told me you did. In fact, this morning, a man who once spent time with you, Dr. Hiram Eberhart—"

"Who?"

"He's a professor at Columbia. He wrote a book called *Outside the Mainstream* and he mentions Jadway in it. He said you gave him an interview once, right here."

"A little runt of a guy? Yes, I remember him. Why are you interested in Jadway? Are you writing a paper or book or something?"

"I'll be truthful. I'm an attorney. I'm the lawyer who's defending Jadway's book, *The Seven Minutes*, in the trial in Los Angeles."

O'Flanagan looked troubled. "That trial. Been reading about it. You're the lawyer, eh? Well, from where I sit, they're making mincemeat out of you—and poor Jad."

"That's why I'm here. To try to improve our case. I was told you were one of Jadway's closest friends."

449

"And that's why I'm not going to talk about him, Barrett. I made a vow after he was gone. He was—he was driven to his death. Now he deserves to rest in peace. He deserves that much."

"Well, the censors aren't letting him rest in peace. I want to defend him, not only to save his book, liberate it, but to see that his memory and name are honored. I'm afraid I've just about reached dead end. I need your help." Barrett stared at O'Flanagan, who was drinking silently. "Mr. O'Flanagan, you were his friend, weren't you?"

"The only friend he ever had and trusted, besides Cassie Mc-Graw. I'll tell you this much, and with great pride in it. I knew him. I knew Jad and Cassie, and I was their friend. Met them the first time in Sylvia Beach's bookshop, Shakespeare and Company, in the Rue de l'Odéon, number 12 Rue de l'Odéon. Hemingway, Pound, Fitzgerald, they all browsed and bought and gabbed there, along with Joyce. And I came in there one day, and there was Jadway and there was Cassie."

"When was that?"

"Summer of 1934, when he was writing his book."

"Christian Leroux testified that he wrote the book in three weeks."

"Leroux's a turd. He'd say anything for a buck."

Barrett's heart leaped. "You mean he lied in his testimony?"

O'Flanagan drank. "I'm not saying he lied. I'm saying he has not always been a devotee of the truth. I don't like him, never did, and I don't want to talk about him."

"But was most of his testimony accurate?"

"Most of it."

"The part about Jadway's death?"

"Generally true. The book came out. The daughter of another one of Jadway's friends got in trouble, and the friend blamed it on Jadway because of the book. Then there was some other trouble Jadway had with his parents. He was very sensitive. He fell into a depression. He killed himself. It's already in the record."

"When did he kill himself?"

"In February, the year of Our Lord 1937 A.D. Amen."

"It was in February of 1937? All right, that's what I really came here to speak to you about."

Barrett felt the poet's suspicious eyes upon him as he unlatched his briefcase and brought out a copy of Dr. Eberhart's book. He opened it at the bookmark and showed O'Flanagan the under-lined passage.

When he had finished reading it, O'Flanagan looked up. "What about it?"

"Dr. Eberhart says you gave him that material about Jadway's discussing the Louis–Braddock fight and commenting on the 1939 publication of *Tropic of Capricorn.*"

"Maybe I did."

"Can you explain this, then. Jadway died in February, 1937. How could he have heard the heavyweight fight four months after his death and read the Miller book two years later?"

O'Flanagan did not reply. He stared blankly at Barrett, groped beside him for the glass, and slowly drank. He set the glass down. "Maybe that Eberhart took it down wrong, didn't hear me right."

"Mr. O'Flanagan, even if he heard you wrong, his tape recorder heard you right. He taped the interview with you. He played it back for me over the phone two hours ago."

"Then maybe I made the mistake. I must've been boozing that night."

"Eberhart said you were cold sober."

"How in the hell would he know?"

"You sounded sober to me on the tape."

O'Flanagan grunted. "Maybe the sober are the drunks of the world, and vice versa." He straightened. "I guess I got screwed up on my dates and time. My memory's been going. That's the only explanation. I'll have another drink."

Barrett caught a waiter by the arm and ordered a third double brandy for O'Flanagan and a second Scotch for himself. "Mr. O'Flanagan, couldn't you be mistaken about the date of Jadway's death as well? Maybe he died later, say in 1939 or 1940, instead of 1937."

"No, I remember the time exactly. I remember the services. I was with Cassie all through that period after."

The drinks came. O'Flanagan took up his glass. Barrett ignored his own drink. He decided to pursue a new line of inquiry. "You were with Cassie," he repeated. "Whatever happened to her?"

"She left Paris. There was nothing more for her there." O'Flan-agan was speaking between gulps, and his words had begun to slur. "She went back to America. To the Midwest, I think."

"Whatever happened to her child?"

"Judith? I had a postcard from her once, maybe ten years ago. She was moving to California to get married. That's the last I heard from her."

"Any idea where in California?"

"How would I know?"

"There was testimony that Cassie McGraw herself finally married some other man and lived in Detroit. Do you know anything about that?"

"I know she married someone and was widowed not long after. I know that. But I never heard from her again after. I don't know what happened to her. Probably dead and gone for years. There was no life for her after Jadway." He shook his head drunkenly. "They were great ones, those two. He was tall and consumptive-looking, like Robert Louis Stevenson. She was a beauty, a lot of woman. She's all in his book. We used to have great times together, arms linked, strolling along the Seine, reciting poetry. They had favorites. There was one I remember most." Laying his head back against the wall, eyes closed, O'Flanagan said, "By Pietro Aretino, the Renaissance man." He paused, then recited softly, " 'Could man but *fotter* post mortem, I would cry: / Let's *fotter* ourselves to death, and wake to *fotter* / With Eve and Adam, who were doomed to die / By that *fotteren* apple and their rotten luck.' " He opened his eyes. "For *fotter*, and all its correct forms in Italian that I don't remember, you can substitute 'fuck,' which is less elegant. That was Aretino's poem, and it was like four hundred years ago when he wrote it and we recited it. That was the favorite."

"Whose favorite? Jadway's?"

"No. Cassie's."

Barrett could see that O'Flanagan would not be articulate much longer. He must make haste.

"Mr. O'Flanagan, would you consider appearing for the defense —as a defense witness for Jadway—in the trial? We would pay you handsomely for your time and trouble."

"You couldn't pay me enough, Barrett. There's not enough money minted on earth to make me talk about Jadway any more."

"You could be subpoenaed, you know."

"I could suffer amnesia, you know. Don't threaten me, Barrett.

Jadway and Cassie, they're the best part of my private past. I'm not robbing their graves and my dreams for pay."

"I'm sorry," said Barrett. "I won't bother you about this again. Just one last point. A short time ago, an autograph dealer in this city, Olin Adams, got his hands on several Jadway letters. He told me that he offered them to you. You didn't have the money to buy them, and so you declined. Right after that, you called Adams and said you had got money and wanted to buy them. Why?"

O'Flanagan grunted. "Why? Tell you why. I wanted them as part of the O'Flanagan Manuscript Collection in the Special Collections Department at the library of Parktown College. That's a small school just before you get to Boston. They once gave me an honorary degree when I was editing my magazine. In return I donated to them all my personal memorabilia and papers. Always wanted something of Jadway's in my collection. I had nothing. Cassie had what little Jadway left behind. Don't know if she destroyed his papers and letters or kept them. But when these few letters came up for sale, I wanted them. Couldn't afford them. Then had a chance to borrow some money. So tried to get them. Too late." He sighed. "Too bad. Would have looked good in my collection at Parktown. Too bad."

"This collection of yours," said Barrett thoughtfully, "do you think I might be allowed to see it?"

"It's public. Anyone who rides up to Parktown College can see it. If you do, you'll probably be the first person who's ever asked to have a look at it. That young curator up there, Virgil Crawford, I think he'd faint dead away if someone asked to see the Sean O'Flanagan Collection."

"Well, I'd like to go to Parktown and have a look. Virgil Crawford? May I use your name with him?"

As O'Flanagan tried to place his elbows on the table, one elbow missed and he started to fall. Barrett reached out and rescued him. "Thanks," the poet mumbled.

"May I use your name when I see Crawford?" Barrett asked again.

"Use whatever the hell name you want to use."

Barrett took the bill, and his briefcase, and stood up. "I appreciate your talking to me. I'd better leave now."

"An' order me another drink on the way out, will you?"

"Sure thing."

"An' Barrett, listen to me—you're wasting your time. You're not going to find any more about Jad anywheres. Least nothing that'll help defend him against those witch burners. Jad—Jadway—he was ahead of his time, in his time, and he's still ahead, and nothing's going to help his book or reputation until another time comes when the world's ready for the resurrection. Until then, don't bother his poor bones, poor bastard, let him sleep in peace until the new day of the new world."

Barrett had listened, and now he replied quietly. "For me, there is only this old world, the today world. In the future maybe there will be a better world. Mr. O'Flanagan, I can't afford to wait for it."

THE NEXT had gone better than he had expected.

From Greenwich Village, Barrett had caught a taxi back to midtown Manhattan. Once in his room at The Plaza, he had put in a long-distance call for the library at Parktown College in Parktown, Massachusetts. Knowing that it was the dinner hour, he had not been optimistic about locating Virgil Crawford, the head of Special Collections. A female clerk had taken his call and told him Mr. Crawford had already gone home and would not be available until Monday. When Barrett had insisted that he must speak to Mr. Crawford at once on an important business matter, the clerk (one of those women who believed that it had to be important if the call was long distance) had given him the number without hesitation.

Within short minutes, Barrett had made connection with the amiable Virgil Crawford. The instant that Barrett had mentioned his role in the censorship trial on the West Coast, Crawford was intrigued. Then, after Barrett had spoken of his interview with Sean O'Flanagan, and his desire to examine the O'Flanagan Collection at Parktown for possible evidence, Crawford was flattered, engaged, and cooperative. They had agreed to meet in the library's ground-floor rotunda at ten o'clock in the morning.

After a leisurely dinner in the Oak Room, and a brief call to Mrs. Zelkin (Abe was out somewhere working) in order to leave word of his whereabouts, Barrett had checked out of The Plaza. He had taken the first flight he could get to Boston, and there had obtained a room for the night in the Ritz-Carlton Hotel.

454

The following morning, a sunny Friday morning, he had rented a Mustang and started for Parktown College, which was fifty miles outside Boston on the road to Worcester. He had been tempted to cover the distance in as little time as possible. He was curious to see the O'Flanagan Collection. Yet, tempted as he had been to speed, to get his hands on the poet's papers, he knew that he was early enough to take his time. Moreover, the balmy Massachusetts morning was one of Nature's infrequent caresses. There were meadows and lakes and brooks, birch and willow and pine, and every so often the clean white spires of a Congregational meetinghouse or the moss-covered burial stones in a Pilgrim graveyard, and all of this made time timeless, and so he drove at a reasonable speed.

Parktown College proved more modern and more sprawling than he had expected. Leaving his car in the lot next to the student union, he asked directions of a campus guard, and then he walked to the gushing fountain and beyond it he saw the two-story college library.

Now, at two minutes before ten o'clock, he was shaking hands with Virgil Crawford.

To Barrett's surprise, Crawford turned out to be lively and boyish. He was slight, trim, bouncy, enthusiastic, and eager to please.

As he led Barrett up a flight of stairs to the second floor, he explained, "Most small schools don't have a Department of Special Collections. It takes money, not so much for the floor space or staffing, but to buy meaningful acquisitions. We've been fortunate enough to have an interested and aggressive Friends of Parktown Library group, and they've been tireless in their efforts to raise funds to support us. We're quite proud of our holdings of New England writers and poets. Last month we purchased two lots of John Greenleaf Whittier's papers—a treasure trove, drafts of poems, correspondence, journals—and I don't mind telling you we're close to getting a priceless collection of papers by various New England abolitionists. You know, Wendell Phillips, Charles Sumner, other antislavery people."

"Where does Sean O'Flanagan fit into that?" Barrett wanted to know.

"Oh, he was born in Provincetown. I don't suppose he spent more than a year or two of his life in New England, not that that matters, either. He's a poet, and that matters. I'm trying to build up our avant-garde holdings. Oh, we go pretty far afield. We've got some Burns and Swinburne letters, and several manuscripts by Apollinaire."

They were passing through an upstairs corridor, and Crawford pointed out his office to the right and a room containing microfilm readers to the left.

They entered a spacious room furnished with oversized tables and glass-fronted bookcases.

"Here we are," said Crawford. He gestured toward a doorway beside the library counter. "The holdings of the Department of Special Collections are in wire cages behind there. I don't suppose you have time to see some of our prizes?"

"I'm afraid not," said Barrett.

"Now, as to the Sean O'Flanagan Collection you're interested in seeing, we have it catalogued item by item. Is there anything specific I can show you?"

"Well, actually, it's not O'Flanagan himself I'm curious about. It's his friendship, while in Paris, with J J Jadway that brought me here. It is Jadway I'm after."

"Jadway," said Crawford with surprise. "You're only looking into Jadway?"

"That's right."

"I guess I misunderstood you on the phone, Mr. Barrett. I thought you were using O'Flanagan in your trial, and you wanted . . ." He shook his head unhappily. "But if it's just Jadway, I'm afraid we're not going to be as useful to you as I had hoped. Jadway died too young to have left any meaningful corpus of work. Also, I understand that his original papers relating to *The Seven Minutes* were not saved. It is the bane of our profession, this destruction of working materials of a promising author. I doubt that you'll find anything by Jadway in O'Flanagan's collection. If you'll wait a moment, I'll make doubly sure. Let me check our catalogue."

"Fingers crossed," said Barrett.

Crawford hastened to the drawers of catalogue cards, while Barrett wandered aimlessly around the reading room, pausing only to study the contents of the bookcases.

"Mr. Barrett." Crawford was advancing toward him. "I'm terribly sorry. It's just as I suspected. Not a single item by Jadway."

"Might there be any material *about* Jadway? After all, O'Flanagan claims to have been his closest friend."

"Oh, there might possibly be that, perhaps a reference or two to Jadway in O'Flanagan's notes or correspondence. But you'd have to comb through the entire collection to find out. Actually, it wouldn't take you much time. Aside from the poetry quarterly that O'Flanagan published and edited, and the inscribed books he's donated to us, there are only three manuscript boxes of his papers. Would you like to see them?"

"Absolutely."

"You make yourself comfortable at one of those tables. I'll fetch the manuscript boxes."

Five minutes later, Barrett was seated at a long table with one gray box resembling a file case before him and two others at his elbow. Crawford had left him to go about his work, but promised he would be nearby if he was wanted.

Opening the first box, Barrett found it filled with numbered manila folders containing various drafts of O'Flanagan's poems. Carefully at first, then more impatiently, he examined these manuscripts for annotations that might include Jadway's name, or references to Paris or to the period between 1934 and 1937. The manuscripts offered nothing, except incredibly pedestrian and incomprehensible verse.

Returning the folders to the first box and shoving it aside, Barrett opened the second box. For the most part, this held more of the same. Draft upon draft of handwritten and typewritten poems, and last, three folders of correspondence. Hope flickered again, but was quickly smothered. All of the letters were post-Paris, and almost all were correspondence between O'Flanagan and contributors to the quarterly. None of them carried even the most oblique reference to Jadway.

Discouraged, Barrett opened the third and final box. It was only half filled with folders. There were folders stuffed with clippings and advertisements in which either O'Flanagan or his periodical were mentioned. There was a folder of loose scratch sheets or pages torn from memorandum pads on which O'Flanagan had, over many years, jotted down ideas for poems, stray stanzas, and favorite phrases or quotations.

Although two folders remained, Barrett's depression was growing.

He opened one. Inside it were photographs—photographs of O'Flanagan's parents, of O'Flanagan himself as a boy, of himself as a publisher and editor in Greenwich Village, of T. S. Eliot and e e cummings, autographed—and one last picture, mutilated, and Barrett gripped it and his heart almost stood still.

It was a snapshot, slightly yellowed, and it had been taken at the base of the Eiffel Tower. There were three persons in the snapshot. From left to right: a younger—by more than three decades younger—clear-eyed, rakish Sean O'Flanagan; a small, amply endowed, pretty and smiling colleen, squinting into the sun; a lanky male figure in baggy slacks and sweater and headless. The corner of the snapshot had been ripped off, leaving the third figure headless—and faceless.

Quickly, Barrett turned the snapshot over. On the back, in a slanting, delicate feminine hand, was written the caption "Dear Sean. Thought you'd like this remembrance of the three of us for your scrapbook. Jad says you look the novelist, and he the poet. What think you? Affectionately, Cassie."

Cassie McGraw, at last! And Jadway—dammit, Jadway, almost.

Barrett turned back to the photograph again. The Cathleen of the snapshot appeared anything but the naked, sensual female in the novel. She looked—but what can looks tell, especially in a discolored snapshot? As for Jadway, what there remained to see of him from the shoulders down hardly appeared the unkempt and dissolute rebel and pornographer that Leroux and Father Sarfatti had described. But then, perhaps this photograph had been taken before his book and his downfall.

The discovery excited Barrett, and question marks followed his thoughts. Exactly when had this photograph been taken? When had Cassie given it to O'Flanagan? Who had torn off Jadway's face? Had it been O'Flanagan? Cassie? Jadway himself? And—why had it been done?

Barrett had no idea what value the snapshot might have, but he discerned the reasons for its exciting him. For weeks Cassie McGraw and J J Jadway had eluded him, had become increasingly unbelievable, less real than characters invented for a work of fiction. They had become myths. Now, blessedly, their reality was reaffirmed by this find. They had hearts that beat and blood that flowed, and somehow, at once, they had become human beings of this earth with more substance than shadow and were persons worthy to defend.

He was no longer counsel for an apparition. Yet, beyond this, what did he truly have? A likeness of Cassie McGraw in her twenties. A likeness of the body of Jadway in his Paris years. A sample of Cassie's calligraphy. Would this excite the less romantic Abe Zelkin? Or blunt Elmo Duncan's attacks? Barrett knew the answers. Nevertheless, he did not return the snapshot to his folder. Gently he laid it aside.

A single folder concealed what remained of the Sean O'Flanagan Collection in Parktown College.

Barrett parted the folder. The tab was marked "Ephemera." The contents were ephemera: calling cards, citations, address books, postcards. He went through it all hastily, item by item. No Jadway, no Cassie, no Paris, no 1930s. A half-dozen postcards, one, two, three, four, five, six—and then back to five. Not Jadway, not Cassie, but another name had rung a bell.

It was not a pictorial postcard. It was a plain prestamped one, a light-brown one that had been purchased at the post office, with one side imprinted "This side of the card is for address," and the other side blank and for a message.

The other side was not blank. It carried a brief message, written in purple ink, and it read: "Dear Uncle Sean. Tomorrow I marry. My address will be—215 E. Alhambra Road, Alhambra, Calif. I am happy. Hope you are, too. Love—Judith."

Judith!

He had found the illegitimate wraith borne by Cassie McGraw as the result of accepting J J Jadway's love. Judith Jadway, or Judith McGraw, or Judith whatever-name-given-to-her if Cassie's later husband had adopted her. Judith would be the instrument to open the door to Jadway's past and to tell what had happened to Cassie McGraw.

Barrett examined the front of the card once more. The postmark and cancellation lines were blurred, but the stamped date of the mailing could be made out. It said 1956. Barrett did some rapid calculations in his head. Jadway's daughter had been nineteen years old, and about to be married, when she had mailed this card. Today she would be thirty-three years old. Fourteen years had passed since she had given her address as 215 East Alhambra Road, Alhambra, California. Suddenly she seemed wraithlike again.

459

Most Southern Californians do not live at one address for fourteen years. Especially young married ones. Still, it was possible. And, at worst, Alhambra Road might be the beginning of a trail that would lead him to an informant and witness who could be the match of any that the prosecution had produced or would yet produce.

Placing the precious postcard atop the mutilated photograph, he restored the loose folders to their box. He knew what must be done.

He would have Virgil Crawford order photocopies of both sides of the snapshot and both sides of the postcard. Toward what end, these photocopies, he was not certain. But he was an attorney, and he was thorough.

His next move was foreordained. He must return to Los Angeles immediately, and drive directly to 215 East Alhambra Road, where his quest for a confrontation with Jadway's daughter might be resolved.

Rising, he glanced at his wristwatch. He could be in Los Angeles by late afternoon.

He took up the postcard and the photograph. His eyes held on the three boxes, and silently he gave his thanks and blessing to the Sean O'Flanagan Collection. Then, almost gaily, he went in search of Virgil Crawford. He was filled with optimism once more.

HE WAS back in Los Angeles.

Following his automobile-club map of Los Angeles County, Mike Barrett had spent three quarters of an hour driving his convertible from the airport to his destination. He had lost his way once, been delayed by a detour another time, but now he was on East Alhambra Road.

And now he was puzzled.

This was a quiet old residential street, shaded by hoary oak trees and palms, and the address he sought was the only number on the opposite side of the street from where he had parked.

Peering through the window on the driver's side, he read the metal sign a second time. It stood between a row of bushes and a step leading to a walk. It read:

215

CARMEL OF ST. THERESA

Behind the sign and the walk stood a chapel with high stained-glass windows. To the left of the chapel and adjoining it was a red brick building with shuttered cell-like windows on the second floor and an ornate Victorian-type bell tower rising above the rooftop.

Barrett's bewilderment intensified. Fourteen years ago, Jadway's daughter had given 215 East Alhambra Road as the address of her honeymoon home. Now the address had become a church and a—well, whatever that adjoining red brick building was called.

Barrett had enough of the mystery. He wanted the solution. Quickly easing out of his car, he crossed the street and hastened up the walk. Off to his right was a solid wood gate overlaid with black iron grillwork, and the gate was set in a five-foot wall. Ahead of him was the chapel door. To his left was another cement walk leading to the red brick building. Barrett veered left and followed the cement walk around the chapel toward porch steps that led up to an entrance between arched pillars.

He rang the bell. A moment later the door opened to reveal a young nun in a floor-length brown habit.

"Yes?" she inquired softly.

Utterly disconcerted, Barrett stammered, "Uh—I—I was—was given this address to look up someone. But it doesn't seem to be a private residence."

"This is a Carmelite monastery of cloistered nuns. You must have the wrong address."

"No. I believe that I have the right address. I may have the wrong year. Do you have any idea whether this was a private residence fourteen years ago?"

"Nothing has changed since then. Fourteen years ago it was as it is now."

"You're sure?" But Barrett knew that she was not mistaken, and a suspicion of the truth had entered his head. "I must trace someone who once gave this as her address. Is there any person here who might help me?"

"Perhaps the Mother Prioress."

"Could I see her?"

"If you will wait." She indicated a stone bench on the covered porch. "I will try to find her."

Barrett strolled over to the bench, took out his pipe, then put it away, and sat down on the edge of the bench. He gazed past the pillar to his right and saw the wire fence and the hedge which ran along the side street until they met the low retaining wall fronting Alhambra Road, and then together the two walls encompassed the green lawn before him.

He heard a door squeak, and saw a plump woman, veiled, attired in white choir mantle, white guimpe, and thick brown habit, briskly coming toward him. Barrett leaped to his feet.

"I am Sister Arilda," she announced. "May I be of assistance to you?"

Barrett saw inside the veil a full, round authoritarian face, as agelessly waxen and contented as the countenances of all nuns he had ever observed. These faces always made him feel inexplicably uncomfortable. Perhaps it was that their devotion to God's work, their communion with the final mystery, made his own knowledge and purpose seem pointless and petty. Or perhaps it was something else: that their way was unnatural and anti-life, a permanent prolongation of childhood. They were probably saints or maybe some were sinners, but, regardless, their presence had always embarrassed him into awkwardness.

Here was the Mother Prioress, and she waited placidly for an explanation of his visit.

After introducing himself, Barrett went on. "I—I'm an attorney in Los Angeles. I'm trying to locate a young lady, someone I must see about a rather critical matter. The last address I have for her is fourteen years old. It is this address. The sister I spoke to first said that this was a monastery fourteen years ago. Could she be mistaken?"

"She was not mistaken," said the Mother Prioress. "The sisters of Our Lady of Mount Carmel, as well as the Carmelite monastery itself, were here fourteen years ago." She paused, and then she said, "The young lady who gave this address—can you tell me more about her?"

"Very little, I'm afraid." Barrett reached into his inside breast pocket and extracted the photostats of the postcard that Jadway's daughter had sent to Sean O'Flanagan fourteen years earlier. Unfolding the two sheets, Barrett handed them to the Mother Prioress. "Here are copies of both sides of a postcard she sent to a family friend. You can see that she gave this address."

Taking the pages, the Mother Prioress sat down on the porch

bench. "Do sit down, Mr. Barrett," she said. As he lowered himself to the bench beside her, the Mother Prioress studied the photocopies.

Watching her read, Barrett said, "All I can add are a few fragmentary facts. You can see, she signs her name simply Judith. I have no idea what last name she used fourteen years ago. She was born out of wedlock in Paris to a woman named Cassie McGraw and a man named J J Jadway. So she may have been called either Judith Jan Jadway or Judith Jan McGraw. And then later, in the United States, her mother married and Judith's stepfather may have adopted her, although we have found no legal record of that in Detroit. She may or may not have taken his name, whatever it was. Shortly after Cassie McGraw's marriage, Judith's stepfather was killed in the Second World War. After that, we don't know what happened, until Judith mailed this card fourteen years ago. Of course, she may have been mistaken about the address she gave. Because if this was a convent—or, rather, a monastery—at that time, it certainly doesn't jibe with the fact that Judith was getting married the following day."

The Mother Prioress had finished studying the photostats, and she handed them back to Barrett. Now she folded her smooth hands in her lap and considered Barrett levelly from the security of her veil.

"She was married the following day, and she did give the right address," said the Mother Prioress. "She and five other sisters were wedded to Our Lord Jesus Christ in that year."

Despite his earlier suspicion, Barrett sat stunned and speechless.

"After formal training and experiencing the contemplative life according to the primitive rule given to the hermits of Mount Carmel by Albert of Jerusalem in the year 1207 and according to Saint Theresa's Constitutions, she completed her novitiate and then took her temporary vows. Finally, in 1956, she took her final vows, and she was consecrated to God forever."

Trying to recover his poise, Barrett asked, "You mean Judith is here in this monastery right now?"

"There is no Judith, Mr. Barrett. There is a Sister Francesca."

"Whatever her name, it's urgent that I speak with her. Could I see her, even briefly?"

The Mother Prioress's hand had gone to the scapular hanging

over her brown habit. She looked off beyond the porch at a cluster of sparrows on the lawn. Finally she spoke. "A sister who takes the solemn vows of this order, who becomes a Carmelite nun, has offered her person in total dedication to God. In the spirit of Saint Theresa, she thereafter pursues the contemplative life, pursues an intimacy with the divine, embraces the entire world through her apostolate of prayer and penance. It is this intimacy with God that makes her self-sacrifice effective and lends power to her prayer. To become a true collaborator in the redeeming work of Christ, the discalced Carmelite nun must renounce all that is on the outside. In her habit, and barefooted, she spends each day in fasting, in manual labor, in mental prayer, in spiritual reading, in chanting the Divine Office in Latin. One so consecrated, Mr. Barrett, would not be personally tempted or officially permitted to concern herself with the secular matters you consider so urgent. I am sorry."

"But I only wish to know from her anything that she can relate about her father and perhaps the whereabouts of her mother, assuming her mother is still alive. Aren't exceptions ever made in special cases?"

"There may be exceptions. It is not for me to say. You would have to apply to the office of Cardinal MacManus, who is the Archbishop of the Archdiocese of Los Angeles. However, I doubt that you would have any success in persuading His Eminence."

"May I ask why you doubt it?"

He thought he saw a cool smile within the frame of the veil. Then the Mother Prioress spoke. "Mr. Barrett, this is a cloistered order, but in my role as head of the monastery my contacts are frequently more worldly than those of the other sisters. It is necessary for me to be as informed as the sisters of our Third Order, who dwell and toil in the Little Flower Missionary House and go out among people as social workers. I have followed recent events. I have had reason to refer to the *Index Librorum Prohibitorum*. I have been apprised of Father Sarfatti's testimony in court. I have become familiar with the name of Jadway and, indeed, with your own name, Mr. Barrett. Knowing the circumstances, I strongly doubt that an exception would be made because of your application. I doubt it very much, Mr. Barrett."

Barrett smiled. "I doubt it, too." He stood up. "Thank you for your time."

464

She rose. "I cannot wish you luck. I can only hope you will find God's path."

He started to go, then hesitated. "Does Judith—Sister Francesca—does she know of the trial?"

"She has her own trial," the Mother Prioress said cryptically. "Her sole interest is to achieve divine intimacy. Good day, Mr. Barrett."

He left the porch and walked slowly to the corner. Glancing back, he saw that the Mother Prioress had disappeared inside the monastery. Then, on the side street, he could see three nuns picking up cartons at what appeared to be a delivery gate. He halted to watch them, their robes flowing as they moved silently back through the gate toward the cloistered building.

He wondered, could one of them be the daughter of Jadway and Cassie McGraw?

Then, swiftly, he walked away from this place of God and its sisters who collaborated with Christ. He was ready to re-enter the ruder world beyond, where most men had no time for heaven in their unremitting struggle to survive hell on earth.

AFTER PICKING UP a pastrami sandwich and coleslaw at the delicatessen in the Vicente Food Market, Mike Barrett had gone on to his apartment. Munching the sandwich, and drinking root beer, he had propped the telephone receiver between his ear and shoulder and tried to locate Abe Zelkin.

There was no response at the office, and he left word with the answering service for Zelkin to call him when he checked in with the service. Then he tried Zelkin's residence, and the baby-sitter explained that Mr. Zelkin had driven his wife and son somewhere. Again Barrett left word to be called.

After that, Barrett stayed in the apartment, concentrating on the transcripts that Donna had made of Zelkin's and his own pretrial taped interviews with their own witnesses. He lost himself in this, and time flew by, and it was nine-fifteen in the evening when the telephone finally rang.

The caller was Abe Zelkin, at last.

"Where have you been, Abe?" Barrett demanded. "I've been anxious to know what really happened at the trial yesterday. The newspapers seemed to shy away from a lot of the testimony."

"Because it wasn't for family audiences. More important, Mike,

I've been waiting to hear how you made out. Not very well, I gather, or I'd have heard from you."

"Not very well."

"If you're free now, we can catch up. I had to drive my wife and boy and leave them at the Griffith Observatory earlier. Leo was with us, and then he and I went out to dinner and we started reviewing some new stuff that's come in and I guess we forgot the time. But I finally checked with the message service, and here I am. Look, I've got to pick up my wife and kid in a half hour—it'll take that long to get there—so why don't I pick you up first and we can gab on the way? Leo's still with me and we're in your neighborhood. We can bring each other up to date on everything."

"I'll be waiting downstairs."

Now, twenty-five minutes later, with Zelkin at the wheel of his station wagon and Barrett sitting beside him, and Kimura in the rear, they were spiraling up toward the summit of Mount Wilson. Through the windshield, Barrett could make out the domes of the observatory and the planetarium a short distance above them.

Barrett had been recounting his adventures with Dr. Hiram Eberhart and Sean O'Flanagan in New York, with Virgil Crawford at Parktown College, and with the Mother Prioress of the Carmelite Monastery in Alhambra. Concluding his recital, he said, "So all that heavy traveling and high hopes and what have I got to show for it? These lousy photostats of a photograph and a postcard and not a damn thing more. Ask me about poetry, special collections, Carmelite nuns, and I'm an expert. Ask me about Jadway and Cassie and Judith and anachronisms, and I'm a bum. Gentlemen, I've just run out of leads. The bottom of the barrel. The only one I can think of who could help us now would be Cassie McGraw, and the odds are she's six feet deep in some plot of ground, and if she isn't, where in God's name is she? I hate to be the voice of doom, but I don't see any ray of light. Until late this afternoon, I always had some hope, but not tonight."

He heard Kimura stir behind him. "Hope is not everything," he said. "Maybe we should heed the old English proverb—he who lives on hope will die fasting. Maybe we have enough without needing to hope for more."

"Sure," said Zelkin. "We'll just go with what we have. Well, here we are. The Griffith Observatory. No relation to their Attila, Frank Griffith." He parked the station wagon. "I guess the planetarium show isn't over yet. Ever been in that theater? Crazy. The ceiling of the dome is the screen. The night I went they projected the Star of Bethlehem in the sky as it was supposed to have been the night the Three Wise Men followed it."

"What about the Three Wise Guys in this car?" asked Barrett. "What star have we got to follow?"

"It does look like Elmo Duncan has cornered the market on stars," said Zelkin. "He spent most of yesterday clearing the way for his second big star."

"I've been waiting to hear what happened while I was gone," said Barrett.

"I've been waiting to tell you," said Zelkin, "only you wouldn't stop talking."

Suddenly Barrett grinned. "You're right, Abe. Go ahead."

"Let me find my notes," said Zelkin. He found them and reviewed them. "Like the newspapers reported—no top performers. Most of it was a buildup for what's coming. Duncan brought out two more literary experts, a professor from Colorado, Dr. Dean Woodcourt, and some syndicated book reviewer, Ted Taylor, and they pronounced the book obscene and damned it for its prurient appeal. There wasn't much I could do. It was their opinion. I took a few stabs at their authority and prejudices, but I don't think that made much impression on the jury. Where Duncan really scored was when he elicited from his witness, Taylor, things the newspapers didn't print, concrete examples of instances where specific books supposedly have led individuals to acts of violence. All groundwork for—"

"What instances did the witness cite?" interrupted Barrett.

Zelkin squinted at his notes below the dashboard light. "Two instances based on two pornographers, so-called. The first pornographer was that old Roman gossip, the historian Suetonius, and his book was *The Lives of the Twelve Caesars*. Choice example from the book. The Empress Valeria Messalina challenging the union of prostitutes in Rome to find one woman who could satisfy as many lovers as she could in one night. The challenge was accepted. The contest was held. The bedweight championship. No match. Messalina won lying down. She had sexual intercourse with twenty-five men in twenty-four hours. So what about the evil influence of Suetonius' history book?"

"What about it?" Barrett wanted to know.

467

"The witness claimed that Suetonius' book perverted Gilles de Rais. You know of him?"

"The original Bluebeard."

"Right. The best of credentials, to start with. A wealthy marshal of France. A man who fought alongside Joan of Arc. So Gilles de Rais was tried in 1440 on the charge of committing sodomy with fifty or so boys and girls before murdering them. During the trial Gilles pleaded that he had read Suetonius and become corrupted by the historian. All very impressive. What could I bring out in the cross-examination? That Gilles de Rais very likely hadn't committed sodomy or murdered anyone, but instead, according to many modern historians, had simply been framed by the clergy so the Church could confiscate his real-estate holdings? I'm afraid that wasn't good enough for the jury. Then Duncan got the witness to tell us about another author of obscene books, namely the Marquis de Sade."

Barrett groaned. "I wondered how long it would take for them to drag him in."

"Duncan had the witness recite some high spots of de Sade's life. Distinguished family. Cavalry officer. Married man. The incident where de Sade tricked a thirty-six-year-old woman into coming to his home, tied her to his bed, whipped her, cut her up with a knife, poured hot wax into her wounds. And then his downfall, in Marseilles, when he met with four prostitutes in the apartment of one, passed around a box of chocolates which were really filled with overdoses of aphrodisiacs, and the girls went crazy, an orgy of profane love. The Marquis de Sade was tried and condemned in 1772. He eventually spent twelve years in prison and died in a lunatic asylum. But meanwhile he wrote his encyclopedia of sexual perversions—*Justine, The 120 Days of Sodom, The Crimes of Love,* and the rest—based on his firsthand experiences. Well, insisted the witness, those writings and their author were responsible for inspiring countless readers to perform criminal acts in emulation of this author. Example. Those young monsters in England who so savagely killed at least two innocent children and possibly one teen-ager in the Moors murder case. During the Moors trial, in 1966, the defendants claimed they had been under the influence of the writings of the Marquis de Sade. In my cross-examination, I tried to get Taylor to admit that influences other than de Sade might have inspired the Moors murders, and that if there had been no de Sade those monsters would have committed the Moors killings anyway, because they were sick through and through. But the witness wouldn't have it, and I'm afraid the jury wouldn't, either."

"Too bad."

Zelkin laid aside his notes. "Then, after the lunch recess, Duncan really started setting the stage for his next star. As you probably read, he put on the two cops, one after the other, who were summoned by Darlene Nelson after Sheri Moore was raped. They testified as to Sheri's condition, her being unconscious, and how Darlene had repeated to them what Sheri had told her, that she'd been forcibly raped. Then the police physician came on to testify about his examination of Sheri shortly after. Details of her head injury. Details of his internal examination of her vagina. He'd found definite evidence of live spermatozoa, indicating she'd been entered not long before. That always shakes up a jury."

"What about you, Abe? Did you go after Duncan's introduction of that whole rape bit?"

"First thing. Duncan and I had our angry exchange before Judge Upshaw. I said immaterial. I pleaded that the violation of the Moore girl had nothing to do with our obscenity case. Duncan argued that the police witnesses were foundation for Jerry Griffith's appearance, and this was relevant and material because he would show that the obscene passages in the Jadway book had created the wish to commit rape in Jerry and had driven him to act out this wish. I argued until I was blue in the face. Overruled. But it's on the record if we appeal later. For now, well, they're going to get their chance to try the book for rape, Mike, and there isn't anything we can do to stop it. Anyway, there was one more hostile witness."

"Mr. Howard Moore," said Kimura. "Sheri's father."

"That's material?" said Barrett.

"Objection overruled," said Zelkin. "Moore was more foundation. So he was material. His daughter was Miss Purity herself. The soul of virtue. A vestal virgin. Until the goddam book, via Jerry, sullied and ruined and crippled her. I handled him tenderly in the cross-examination, believe me. First off, I was afraid he'd belt me one, the way he did you at the hospital. Second place, this is the father of a daughter, a daughter in a coma yet, so if I got smart with him, I knew the jury would lynch me. So I handled him sympathetically and tried to separate his daughter's sufferings from Jadway's book, all this while being machine-gunned with objections. After ten minutes, I put my tail between my legs—the devil has a tail, hasn't he?—and I beat it back to the slit trench behind our table. I'm sure glad you're back, Mike. You can be the devil again on Monday. Hey, I just remembered, I promised to meet the family inside by the Foucault pendulum. Come on, join us, Mike. Leo and I have more to tell you."

They got out of the station wagon and walked together toward the entrance to the Griffith Observatory.

"How come you let your boy stay up this late?" asked Barrett.

"What the heck, it's Friday night," said Zelkin. "Besides, he's an astronomy nut, and Sarah is becoming one, too. They've been up here a dozen times. She complains she never sees me any more, so at least this gives her a change from being alone with our youngsters all the time."

They were inside the observatory, and presently they arrived at a huge well over which a pendulum swung back and forth, above a replica of the earth that slowly rotated beneath it. From the rim of the well, the three of them tried to discern the movement of the earth under the pendulum ball. Hypnotized, Barrett watched below, until he felt Zelkin tugging at his sleeve.

"Before the frau and heir turn up," said Zelkin, "I want you to lend an ear to what Leo and I were discussing through dinner. We know definitely what Duncan is going to do Monday morning. He had intended to lead off with Darlene Nelson, but now Darlene is in the same hospital as Sheri. Ruptured appendix. She's okay, but can't testify right now, thank God. So our D.A. is leading off with Dr. Roger Trimble, former president of the American Psychiatric Association. Leo's read some of this Trimble's papers. Like Dr. Fredric Wertham, he's of the school that believes books, comics, magazines, movies create a climate of violence and contribute to juvenile delinquency. So that'll be Duncan's curtain raiser. Dr. Trimble has had Jerry in therapy since the rape, and he will state that the major contributing factor to the rape was *The Seven Minutes*. Then, and only then, after the buildup, will the curtain go up on Jerry Griffith himself. Duncan's placing Jerry on the stand Monday morning."

"For sure?"

"Positively. Leo and I were putting our heads together on Jerry's appearance before we picked you up. This may be our last big chance to save our case. We've absolutely got to wipe out Duncan's second star witness. We failed with Leroux. We don't dare fail with Jerry Griffith. It'll be in your hands, Mike. You've got to take the boy apart and put him away and separate him from the book forever."

Barrett frowned. "Take him apart with what? With a meat ax? I certainly don't have any evidence to bash him with."

"You don't. But we have. While you've been away in the East, we got hold of a hunk of tremendous evidence you can use, got it this afternoon. Remember that detective agency we retained to look into the Griffith family?"

"I'd given up on them. You mean they finally found something?"

"They're slow but they're sure." Zelkin reached behind him and took an envelope from Kimura. He handed it to Barrett. "Here's a copy of the private detective's investigation report. Bits and pieces. But one eye-opener. Enough to reduce a star to dust. And this we have to do, Mike. We've got to be ruthless. I repeat, it's our last chance to make a showing." Barrett had started to open the envelope, when Zelkin stopped him. "Not now, Mike. You have the rest of tonight and all of tomorrow to read and reread what's there and figure out how to use it."

"Well, what's there, Abe?"

"In essence, it comes down to this, and it's explosive. A half year before Jerry had ever even heard of *The Seven Minutes*, he was taken out of town secretly to spend time with a doctor in San Francisco. What kind of doctor? A psychoanalyst. Why? Because he'd tried to commit suicide just before. You hear that? Tried to kill himself. How'd the agency get on to it? They discovered that Jerry had a protracted absence from his classes at UCLA. Illness. What was the illness? A nervous breakdown, says a source who prefers to remain anonymous, and that breakdown led Jerry to take an overdose of sleeping pills, which in turn led to his being taken to the psychoanalyst up north."

"Who took him up north?"

"His cousin. Your recent dinner companion, Maggie Russell. You mean she never even hinted anything of the sort to you?"

"I wouldn't expect her to, Abe."

"No, you're right. Anyway, how's that for openers? The boy was unstable long before he read Jadway's book. So there must be other factors that contributed to the rape."

"There must be."

"Jerry's got suicidal tendencies. That's quite a find, isn't it?"

"Not exactly," said Barrett. "I didn't know about his first try. But I was fully aware of his desire for self-destruction."

"You were aware?" said Zelkin with surprise. "What made you aware?"

"Maggie Russell made me aware of it. The boy talks to her constantly about doing away with himself. And before I heard about this from her, I saw evidence of it myself. I was present after Jerry made his second attempt to kill himself. In fact, I helped save him. It was this act that brought Maggie and me together."

Both Zelkin and Kimura were dumbfounded. "He tried to kill himself a second time? And you were there?" asked Zelkin. He was becoming angry. "What does that mean?"

Quickly Barrett related the entire episode that had occurred in The Underground Railroad and in the parking lot later.

When he finished, he could see that Zelkin was still upset.

"Mike," said Zelkin slowly, "why didn't you tell us about this before?"

"Why didn't I?" Barrett considered the question carefully. "I guess I felt it was a personal thing, unrelated to the trial, and that telling you or Leo about it would further discredit the boy. But putting that reasoning aside, suppose I had told you, and you then thought we should make use of it. I felt any revelation of that sort would have done us, our case, a disservice. After all, this second suicide attempt, the one I stumbled upon, was an attempt made after Jerry had read Jadway's book. Duncan could have claimed that the book had led Jerry to this, and I suspect the jury would have believed him."

Zelkin accepted his partner's conclusions. "Fair enough for the kid's second attempt." He tapped the envelope in Barrett's hand. "But that first attempt, that was *before* he read the book. That's why it is dynamite. It'll undermine the testimony of the witness and rock the prosecution's case. Agreed?"

"I'm not so sure." Barrett bit his lip, and tried to formulate his thoughts. "Yes, I suppose it would finally divorce the boy from the book. But at an awful cost, Abe. We might be destroying the boy."

"Look, Mike, I'm as sorry for this kid as you are, and I'm as sensitive as you about youngsters and their feelings. But we're in a shooting war, Mike. People have to get hurt. Figuratively, our witnesses may lose their limbs, and you and I may wind up losing our lives. We've got to cut down a few of Duncan's people before we're massacred ourselves. Jerry Griffith's testimony on Monday can demolish our case and drive the last nail in the coffin. You know what's in that coffin, Mike? Not only you and me. Not only Fremont and Sanford. But freedom, Mike—and I'm not being pretentious, you've got to believe me—freedom's in that coffin, too. We can't let the boy drive that last nail into the lid. We've got to nail him first. We're attorneys, Mike. We have an obligation to our client. And to truth."

Barrett sighed. "I guess you're right."

"I know I'm right," Zelkin persisted. "If we were loaded, if we had an army of powerful witnesses, if Jadway and Cassie McGraw were alive and here to help us, if their Judith could climb over the wall to help us, if Leroux hadn't finked out and Mrs. Vogler hadn't backed out and Sean O'Flanagan had joined in and all of them were here to help us, then, Mike, I'd say to heck with tearing that boy apart under cross-examination—he's a poor little rich kid who needs tender loving care—I'd say go easy, live and let live. But that's not the way it is. Duncan's the one who's loaded and we're the ones who are helpless. So now we've got a little something, I say use it, go for broke."

Barrett gave Zelkin an uncomfortable smile of reassurance. "Okay, partner. I'll study this poison tomorrow. I'll administer it on Monday. We'll go for broke. Here comes your missus, and the young man. Maybe they can tell us more about the life—and death—of a star."

LATER, leaving Mount Wilson, and on the drive back to West Los Angeles, Barrett's mind kept returning to Maggie Russell.

But it was not until much later, long after midnight, as he sleepily read in bed, that he actually heard Maggie Russell's voice.

The ringing of the telephone, at this hour, startled him.

"Mike, did I wake you?" Maggie's voice was hushed.

"No."

"I tried to get hold of you last night. There was no answer."

"I was out of town. I had a couple of hot leads." He paused. "Why are you calling? Is there anything wrong?"

"Nothing especially wrong. I just wanted to— oh, it can wait. First I'm dying to know about your sudden trip. Did you find something new?"

"I thought I might. I went out like Napoleon going against Russia. And I came back the same way he did. Hassled, busted, and empty-handed. Maggie, I was everywhere. And you wouldn't believe where I wound up. Would you believe a nunnery?"

"A nunnery?"

"I'll tell you all about it someday. Now you tell me—"

"Mike, don't be a tease. Please tell me right now. I can't stand unfinished stories."

"Well, you asked for it." Briefly he recounted how Dr. Eberhart had led him to O'Flanagan, who had led him to the Department of Special Collections at Parktown College, where a clue had led him to Judith, Cassie McGraw's daughter by Jadway. And Judith, he concluded, was now a member of a cloistered order of nuns, and beyond his reach.

"A nun, Mike? You mean she's really a nun?" There was awe in Maggie's tone.

"Absolutely. God's work only. The salary's low, but the side benefits are great. And how are you? In fact, now can we get back to you? Why did you want to get hold of me yesterday? And what's with all the whispering now?"

"I don't want to be overheard. Mike, I can't speak right now, but I've got to see you. That's why I called."

"Whenever you say."

"I can't get out until tomorrow night. Can you make it tomorrow night?"

"Sure. Let's make it dinner."

"Good. I'll tell you what, Mike. Is eight-thirty in front of the Westwood Village Theatre convenient for you?"

"I'll pick you up there. Eight-thirty sharp. Then we'll have a bite."

Her voice went lower. "Let's go on to someplace out of the way. Maybe toward the beach."

"The beach it is." Curiosity consumed him. "Maggie, you're sure there's nothing you can discuss now?"

"Tomorrow, Mike, tomorrow night."

474

"I'll look forward to it."

But then, hanging up, he knew that he did not look forward to it at all, not this time, not since talking to Zelkin. He remembered what he must do Monday, and then, more than ever, he felt like Judas Iscariot before that last supper. This would be his last supper with Maggie, before he killed the thing she loved. After that, there would be no more Maggie.

And then, to his surprise, he realized that he would be killing one that he loved, also. He allowed himself to see it now. He was in love. And whom did it have to be with? His next victim.

Life was a bitch.

SATURDAY night.

Chez Jay was the out-of-the-way restaurant near the beach. It was on Ocean Avenue in Santa Monica. If you passed it and didn't look twice, you missed it. Although you might hear it.

Chez Jay was this kind of place: small as a hollowed-out child's building block, it seemed; confined; darkish; crowded; with piped-in music, loud; people standing two deep at the bar; tables and booths and waxy candles; sawdust; peanuts you shucked, and a floor strewn with shells; magnificent food; some celebrities; girls in shifts on the make; privacy and relative quiet only if you got the large booth in the rear.

Mike Barrett and Maggie Russell had the large booth in the rear.

When they first came in and were being led to their table, Barrett said, "You wanted something off the beaten track. I doubt if any of Griffith's crowd or Yerkes' gang will see you here."

Maggie said, "That wasn't why I wanted an out-of-the-way place." After they had been seated and drinks had been ordered, she explained. "I just wanted to be someplace where I could be more alone with you."

She was beautiful, and he wanted to touch the lids of those gray-green eyes with his lips, and the red mouth too, and the deep cleft between the breasts, and etcetera.

"I'm glad," he said.

"Besides, Uncle Frank knows I've been seeing you. After that toad Irwin Blair saw us at La Scala, he must have reported right back to Luther Yerkes, and Yerkes gave the word to Uncle Frank.

The next morning, Uncle Frank mentioned it casually. He wondered how we'd first met. Of course I couldn't tell him what Jerry had tried to do, and how you saved him, and all that. I simply told him Faye Osborn had introduced us at a lecture, which was true. His only worry was that you might be using me. I assured him you weren't. I said you'd fallen for me because I was so sexy." She smiled shyly. "I'm only kidding."

"Well, I'm not," said Barrett. "I did fall for you. And you are sexy. And you're also a lot of other attractive things."

"Mike, I wasn't begging for that. Although someday I'd like to hear about those other attractive things."

Thinking of what lay ahead Monday, he said without conviction, "All right. Someday very soon."

"But back to Frank Griffith, Uncle. Anyway, he went on in a friendly tone and said he never wanted to interfere with my private life, and whatever I did was my business, as long as I was discreet. It was so out of character, and so transparent. I could just see him conferring with Duncan and Yerkes, and the three of them trying to decide how this Maggie-Mike thing might best be handled. Should they break it up. And then Underwood computerizing similar pairings in history—like look what happened when the Montagues and the Capulets interfered with Romeo and Juliet, or look at the Cohens and the Kellys—and then a decision. Why not use Maggie by having her use Mike Barrett? That must have been it, because in the last few days Uncle Frank has asked me several times if I've been seeing you, and once he asked what we talked about and how you felt the trial was going. Anyway, Mike, be on your guard. I may be using you—"

"I want you to use me."

"—on behalf of the forces of evil. And they are evil, every one of them, and Uncle Frank most of all, I'm convinced of that now." She stopped abruptly. "I don't want to talk about that right away. I want to enjoy the drinks."

She took up her Gibson, and he his Scotch, and they toasted each other and they drank.

During this, the proprietor, a friend of Barrett's, had decided to have some sport with him by putting a Tom Lehrer record on the player, and one of Lehrer's songs that came blasting across the din of the room was "Smut":

I thrill
To any book like "Fanny Hill."
And I suppose I always will,
If it is swill,
And really fil-thy.
Who needs a hobby like tennis or philately?
I've got a hobby: rereading "Lady Chatterley."
But now they're trying to take it all away from us
Unless we take a stand,
And hand in hand
We fight for freedom of the press.
In other words, Smut!
Like the adventures of a slut.
Oh, I'm a market they can't glut.
I don't know what compares with Smut.
Hip, hip hooray!
Let's hear it for the Supreme Court!
Don't let them take it away!

Maggie and Barrett laughed, and they continued to drink.

That had been more than two hours ago, and now, three drinks later, a salad, a bottle of wine, a serving of beef Stroganoff, a slice of cheesecake later, an intimate autobiography later, they were closer than they had ever been before. They sat side by side in the flickering candlelight, their thighs touching, her hand rubbing his, both of them silent and reflective.

Suddenly she sighed, released his hand, and moved away from him. He looked at her, and she was sitting straight now, and she appeared intent and disturbed.

"Mike, before I become completely sober, there's something— as I told you on the phone last night, there's something I want to discuss with you."

"You have the floor."

"Earlier, I spoke of the forces of evil, and I said my uncle was the most evil one of all. He is. He's a monster. Whatever residue of goodwill I may have had for him has evaporated completely by now. You have no idea of the conflict going on in that house."

"Over Jerry?"

"That's right. Over Jerry. Over Jerry's testifying as a witness on Monday."

"Is the boy still resisting it?"

"More than ever. And Uncle Frank is more adamant than ever that Jerry must stand up there in court and condemn Jadway's book for what it did to him. Uncle Frank continues to shout that he's thinking only of his son and his son's future. Like hell he is. He's thinking only of himself and what people will say about him. If he thought of Jerry the least bit, he wouldn't give a damn about public opinion. He wouldn't let his son undergo that ordeal. He's had Yerkes in to wheedle and soft-soap Jerry. He's had Elmo Duncan in to reassure Jerry and demonstrate how easy it's going to be. And yesterday—it was terrible—there was a terrible scene between Uncle Frank and Aunt Ethel. It was one of the rare occasions when I ever heard her speak her mind. Jerry's her son, too, she said, she'd borne him, raised him, and she had every right to speak. And she wasn't going to sit there and see her husband and the rest of those men bully her son into doing what was against his nature. She felt the decision should be left to Jerry himself. Well, Uncle Frank just about blew his top. He said Jerry had better start doing plenty of things that were against his nature, if screwing—his word—girls against their will was part of his true nature. And furthermore, he shouted, she'd had no part in raising Jerry, because she was too damn preoccupied with herself and her illness, and that was a large part of what was wrong with the boy, and she had no equal claim on him, because she'd been too self-centered and permissive and had let him go his way, and now it was time somebody stepped in and started thinking for the boy and brought him back into line. I thought Aunt Ethel would pass out right in her wheelchair, and when she got a fit of choking, I stepped in and rescued her. She's still confined to bed. Dreadful, isn't it?"

"Yes, it is."

"Life in a not too atypical upper-class American home. Nor am I entirely blameless. The last time I saw you, I said I was going to try to prevent this by intervening with Uncle Frank or Dr. Trimble, the analyst. I had the courage to speak only to Dr. Trimble. I told him exactly what Jerry had been telling me every day. That if he was forced to testify in public, he would commit suicide—if not before, then after appearing on the stand. I pleaded with Dr. Trimble to take it up with Uncle Frank. But Dr. Trimble said no, there was no necessity to bother Frank

Griffith with that. He said that Jerry, like most youngsters, had more resilience than people imagined, and that Jerry would endure and survive the questioning in court very well. In fact, Dr. Trimble thought it might even be a healthy experience for him —sort of a public expiation and cleansing. As for suicide, no, that was just so much talk. Most people who talk suicide don't try it, and Jerry was just using it as a threat to have his way and punish those around him. I was furious. I wanted to take that dumbhead of a doctor and shake him and tell him what Jerry had not told him, or admitted to anyone but me—that Jerry *had* tried to kill himself a few days ago—that he meant it and would do it again, and next time he would succeed. But I couldn't—I just couldn't give our secret away and betray Jerry. After that, I knew it was useless to speak to Uncle Frank. Except for his recent clumsy cozying around me to find out what I know about you, he doesn't know I exist. I have no more meaning to him or identity or influence than a piece of statuary. So the only person I could think of speaking to about this, the only person that I knew would understand, was you, Mike. You do believe me, Mike, when I say Jerry will kill himself? After all, you know he did try it once."

She waited, watching him, and his gaze met hers evenly. He said, "Not once, Maggie. He's tried it twice."

Her eyes widened, and a hand went to her mouth. She murmured something that he could not hear. Then she lowered her hand from her mouth and said, "How do you know?"

"The District Attorney's Office and the defense are both in the business of knowing, of continually trying to find out everything there is to know. My partner retained a private detective agency—we don't have the resources of the police department, which are at Duncan's command, so we have to resort to private investigators. They traced Jerry's absence from school, his movements during that time, and so forth. And they learned he had tried to kill himself months ago—long before he'd read the book —and that you'd taken him up to San Francisco right afterward to see an analyst."

She looked tortured, and he wanted to take her in his arms and soothe her pain and promise her that none of this would be made public. But he could not do it, for it would be a lie. So now this was in the open, and it was there between them.

She was speaking. "What else do they know?" she asked.

479

"Just that."

"And you're going to bring it up in court?"

"I have to."

"Mike, don't, please don't."

"Maggie, I have no choice. But I do want to know one thing. I understand Jerry's condition, that he's on the borderline of becoming psychotic. Still, why is he so scared about appearing as a witness? I realize it is a horrible thing for him to undergo, but everyone is already familiar with his crime and sickness, so why is his appearance in court a matter of life or death to him? To me that's the issue."

She knitted her brow and was silent for many seconds, as if trying to decide what to answer. At last she met Barrett's eyes. "Maybe it all has to do with why I felt that I had to see you tonight, Mike. Because I know you have humanity, an understanding of others, and you have a deep sense of decency. I will tell you this. Jerry isn't really afraid of going to court and sitting in the witness box in public and being questioned by Elmo Duncan. He knows that he is Duncan's witness and Duncan will be gentle with him and won't do him any deliberate harm. It is you he's afraid of, Mike. It is the cross-examination that he's in deathly fear of. He senses you must discredit, even destroy him, if you are to have a chance to win your case. That's the whole truth. He's afraid of what the defense will do to him."

"You still haven't told me *why*. Except for making him admit to that first suicide attempt, what other information can I get out of him that isn't already known by everybody? As for making him admit the first suicide attempt, what is so ghastly about that after everything else—after the rape and its consequences—has been brought out? It may even gain him sympathy. Exactly why this wild fear of being in court, and of the cross-examination?"

She was hesitant. "I—I can't explain, Mike. It's part of his whole neurotic illness. When you've been overwhelmed, put down, your whole life by a dominating parent, you're not sure any more of what you are, what your value is, if you're a whole person even. You've always been made to feel inadequate. You arrive at a breaking point. Then to be stripped and lashed further and in public by a cross-examiner, to have your worst weaknesses made naked, to be humiliated further, I guess that's too much.

That can break you." She paused. "Your questions—they would humiliate him, wouldn't they?"

"Maggie, a cross-examination is never easy for any witness to handle. Despite that, most people, no matter how frail, manage to weather it and survive intact. For someone like Jerry, I can't say. I can only say this—knowing him, through you—I won't be vicious or cruel, not the Grand Inquisitor, not Torquemada. But I will question him, and he will have to answer, since he will be under oath."

She was silent again, and something was forming behind her eyes. "Mike, must you question him? Must you cross-examine him?"

"If Duncan didn't bring him into court, I wouldn't have to. But Duncan is bringing him into court. Duncan is going to examine him. So there Jerry is, and I must cross-examine him."

"But you don't *have* to do it, do you? Legally, you can waive the cross-examination, can't you?"

"Certainly, counsel can always pass, waive the cross-examination, but—"

She grasped Barrett's arm with both hands. "Then do that, Mike. That's what I wanted to—to ask of you tonight. Not to cross-examine Jerry. I couldn't keep him from being forced into court. But he can still be saved, if your side doesn't go after him. I won't say do it for me, Mike. I have no right to ask that. But for the boy's sake, thinking of him, please waive your cross-examination."

She took her hands from his arm and clenched them tightly, waiting.

It was hard, it was painful, this next gesture, but Barrett shook his head slowly. "No, Maggie, I can't do that. I can't betray the people who have retained me and are depending on me. I can't betray Jadway or his book and the freedoms I believe in. Darling, listen to me, and be as reasonable as possible. The District Attorney has had it all his way so far. He's made a powerful case against Jadway and the book. We've been thwarted in our every effort to refute or counteract the case against Jadway. Now he's going to prove the dangerous influence of Jadway's work by bludgeoning us with Jerry Griffith. This is our first opportunity to stop him. If we don't defend ourselves here, then we go under, and the censors win control. If Duncan examines Jerry, I absolutely have to cross-examine him. It's our last, last hope. If things had gone differently before, or were a little different now, I would certainly consider doing what you asked—waive the cross-examination—because then it might be less crucial."

She had drawn nearer to him. "What—what do you mean, if things had gone differently or were different now? What things?"

He remembered Zelkin's argument to him last night, and he used it for Maggie now. "Well, if we'd had Leroux on our side earlier, and the Vogler woman, even that little, I would certainly consider skipping my cross-examination of Jerry, because, as I say, it would be less important. Or even now, if I had one really star witness who could refute Leroux and build up our case for Jadway and the book, I might not have to bother with Jerry. But I don't have that one witness. I don't have anyone remotely like that, and so—"

"Mike."

He looked up sharply, because the tone of her voice had been so firm.

"That one witness you need," she said. "Who could that be— who'd be so important to you?"

"Who? Well, I'd say there'd only be one left who would mean anything. And she'd mean everything. I'm speaking of Cassie McGraw. Now, if I had her—"

"You can have her, Mike."

It was so sudden that he almost failed to understand it or to react. He stared dumbly at Maggie Russell.

She was cool and composed, and when she spoke again it was with quiet assurance.

"I'll make you a fair trade, Mike. You promise not to cross-examine Jerry Griffith, and I promise to get you to Cassie McGraw—to Cassie McGraw herself, in person."

IX

"PLEASE PLACE your left hand on the Bible and raise your right hand. You do swear that the testimony you are about to give in the cause now before the court will be the truth, the whole truth and nothing but the truth, so help you God?"

"I do."

"State your name, please."

"Jerry—Jerome Griffith."

"Spell the last name, please."

"Grif—Griffith . . . uh . . . G . . . uh . . . G-r-i-f-f-i-t-h."

"Please be seated in the witness box, Mr. Griffith."

From his corner of the defense table, Mike Barrett watched the slender young man go to the witness box and nervously sit down in the witness chair. His chestnut-brown hair was freshly trimmed, his eyes (a persistent tic in the left one) darted here and there across the courtroom and avoided the silver microphone before him, his face was pale, and his shoulders were hunched—like a frightened tortoise ready to pull its head inside its protective shell. The tip of Jerry's tongue constantly licked at his dry lips as he waited for his Charon to start him on the journey across his private River Styx.

Now Barrett's gaze left the prosecution's star to take in the overflowing courtroom behind him. He knew that Maggie Russell was present somewhere in that sea of faces, and that her attention was focused not only on Jerry but on Barrett himself. He was conscious also of the presence of Philip Sanford among the spectators directly behind him, and of a grim and determined Abe Zelkin and a worried and anxious Ben Fremont sitting beside him.

He remembered yesterday, a day not of rest but of unremitting restlessness.

He had reviewed everything that Maggie had told him. Every detail of it. He had reviewed and weighed it over and over again.

Incredibly, or perhaps not so incredibly, the legendary Cassie McGraw, mistress of J J Jadway—Cassie McGraw, prototype of the heroine in *The Seven Minutes*—was alive, very much alive, in the Midwest. She had read of the trial. She had written to Frank Griffith in defense of Jadway. As part-time social secretary, Maggie always saw the family's mail first, and she had intercepted Cassie McGraw's communiqué, had hidden it from Griffith and had kept it hidden for two weeks. Since it was favorable to the defense, Maggie had saved it for its bargaining power. Not to use on Barrett, originally, but on Frank Griffith. Then, fearing that Frank Griffith had become too fanatic and obsessed to bargain with—too dogmatic to agree to keep Jerry off the stand in return for the destruction of Cassie's communiqué—fearing, also, that Griffith might learn about the missive and wrest it from her, she had decided to offer it to Barrett as a last resort, in a last effort to save Jerry.

Barrett had given Maggie no decision on Saturday night.

Throughout Sunday, from waking to sleeping, he had weighed the pros and cons of the proposed trade.

Pro: a living Cassie McGraw as a defense witness would be a sensation. Pro: Cassie's communiqué had defended Jadway's motives and integrity in writing *The Seven Minutes* and would wipe out the testimony of Leroux and Father Sarfatti and the rest, for Cassie had been Jadway's alter ego, had known his mind and words first hand, and she alone could be the final voice of truth. Pro: Cassie could wash away the calumnies that had been mounted against Jadway's way of life and at the same time soften the impression left by his way of death. Pro: Cassie McGraw, now an older woman, by her very appearance in the flesh, the admitted model for the heroine of the book, would be a living exhibit to challenge the charge that her performance in the novel was pornographic and obscene. (After all, who could imagine Whistler's Mother fucking?)

But there were cons, perhaps few strong ones, but in some ways these were the more compelling.

Con: if Cassie McGraw had defended the book in a communiqué meant for Frank Griffith, why had she not come forward at a subsequent time to volunteer as a defense witness? Con: perhaps because she did not look with entire favor upon Jadway's book or his life? Con: and what if she were to be forced, under oath, not only to confirm but to substantiate the damaging testimony already given by the French publisher and the Vatican priest? Con: and what if this aging woman's appearance and speech, instead of giving the lie to Duncan's picture of a wayward, loose woman, only supported the prosecution's version of her? Con: in short, what if she had become one of those winking, drinking, foul-mouthed, unkempt, cackling old harridans with dyed hair that one sees not only on mean streets but also at exclusive charity balls? Con: what if the whole trade was a con in itself, the biggest of cons, and was being perpetrated by Maggie on behalf of the Griffith family? Maggie had joked about Griffith's clumsy attempt to get her to use Barrett, but what if that really were a cover-up? And why hadn't she at least shown him Cassie's communiqué and divulged her exact whereabouts? Was it, as she had said, because she could not get to the evidence on Sunday because Frank Griffith was home that day? Or was it that she was as suspicious—well, as wary—of Barrett's using her as he now was of her using him (meaning she knew that once he learned of Cassie's whereabouts, he would not have to honor his part of the trade)? Or was it that evidence of Cassie McGraw alive simply did not exist?

The cons, the pros. The pros and cons.

The decision had to be made on Maggie Russell's terms. First Barrett must deliver on his part of the bargain. No cross-examination of Jerry Griffith. Then, within a few hours, Maggie would deliver on her part of the bargain. She would deliver, in effect, Cassie McGraw.

If he delivered, and Maggie delivered, the defense would have more than hope. It would have potential victory. But if he delivered, and Maggie did not, Barrett would have betrayed the trust placed in him by his clients. And not only the defense, but he personally would suffer the bitterest of defeats.

He had not been able to come to a decision yesterday.

And he had not come to a decision this morning.

Once, an hour ago, before the court was called to order, before the prosecution had put Dr. Roger Trimble on the stand to testify to the grave trauma Jerry had sustained from his reading of the Jadway book, Barrett had been tempted to disclose Maggie's offer to Abe Zelkin. Yet he had not been able to bring himself to do this, for he had instinctively known what Zelkin's decision would be. It would be for a bird in the hand, because Zelkin did not know Maggie, and the whole thing came down to a question of Maggie's honesty and trustworthiness. Zelkin did not know her and would flatly distrust any ally from the house of Griffith. So the decision was Barrett's to make alone. He knew Maggie. The decision must be based on his personal judgment of Maggie, and this made it doubly difficult. His past judgments of women had been consistently poor, so the question, dear counsel, came to this: Was Maggie Russell all the women he had known in the past, or was she *his* woman, the first real woman he had ever known?

He could not answer. He could not decide.

And then he realized that he would have to decide and answer very soon. For minutes earlier he had made a last gesture at preventing Jerry Griffith's appearance. He had objected to the calling up of this witness on the grounds of irrelevancy. The jury had filed out, and he had argued the point with Duncan before the bench. Judge Upshaw had based his decision on Judicial Canon 36, that it was the judge's function to make sure that proceedings in court should be so conducted as to reflect the importance and seriousness of the inquiry to ascertain the truth. Since the prosecution was arguing that a bookseller had sold a book injurious to the public, and a member of the public had confessed that he had been driven to crime by that book, then it was indeed in the interests of truth to hear the witness out.

Defense's objection overruled. Witness would be sworn and permitted to speak.

Thus, the last loophole that would have saved Barrett from making a decision about Maggie's integrity had been ruled out. He was still left with his terrible choice. He would still have to answer those nagging questions and make his decision quickly, too quickly. Before him already, directly in front of him, exuding the warmest and most ingratiating of manners and wearing his quietest and most friendly suit, stood blond Elmo Duncan, District Attorney of Los Angeles and United States Senator to-be.

Duncan was facing the witness box, smiling sympathetically

at Jerry Griffith, and softly, nicely, winningly undertaking the People's direct examination of its leading star.

"Jerry Griffith, may I ask, what is your present or most recent occupation?"

"Student."

"Would you mind speaking up? You said—?"

"I'm a student."

"Attending school. Can you tell us where?"

"The University of California at Los Angeles."

"In Westwood?"

"Yes."

"How long have you been at the university?"

"Almost three years."

"Before that, did you attend a city high school?"

"Palisades High School. Except the first semester. I was at Webb. But I transferred."

"You transferred? Why?"

"My father wanted me to go to a coeducational school."

"And Palisades is coeducational? Is UCLA coeducational?"

"Yes, sir."

"Did you go out on dates with girls while you were in high school and college?"

"Yes, sir."

"Before this year, let's say during your last year in high school and your first two years at UCLA, how frequently did you go out on dates with girls?"

"It—it's hard to remember. I can't remember how frequently. I—"

"Can you give us an approximation of how frequently?"

From the defense table, Barrett half rose. "Objection, Your Honor. The witness has stated that he does not remember. I am going to object on the grounds that the question has been asked and answered. Also, it is speculative."

Judge Upshaw nodded. "Objection sustained."

Lowering himself into his chair, Barrett had a glimpse of Jerry Griffith, and he became aware that for the first time the boy was looking at him. Jerry's eyes were afraid, and he seemed to have wilted in the witness chair. Barrett had once seen that look in the eyes of a dog whose master had threatened to beat him, and Barrett regretted that it had been necessary to voice an objection. He determined to be more lenient about his rival's examination, before the witness was entirely overcome by fear.

Apparently Elmo Duncan was also concerned about the stability and endurance of his witness, for he abandoned his leisurely questioning and moved more swiftly to the core of his star's testimony.

"Mr. Griffith, what is your major at UCLA?"

"English literature."

"Do your courses demand considerable reading—say at least three books a week?"

"Yes, sir."

"Do you also read many books on your own, so to speak, that is, books not on the required reading lists for your English courses?"

"Yes, sir."

"How many of these so-called outside books would you say you read each week on the average?"

"About two or three."

"Are these outside books predominantly fiction?"

"Yes, sir."

"Can you recall the titles of any of the books you've read in the last six months? The titles and authors?"

"I read . . . I read *Steppenwolf*, by Hesse. Also, his *Siddhartha*. And *Of Human Bondage*. That's by Maugham. And F. Scott Fitzgerald's *Tender Is the Night*. Also, *The Red and the Black*, by Stendhal. Then . . . it—it's hard to remember—well, *Point Counter Point*, by Aldous Huxley. And *A Passage to India*, by E. M. Forster. All of Kafka, and Camus. I—I'd have to think—"

"That's a fair enough sampling. Tell me, do you regard any of those books as being pornographic or obscene?"

"No, sir."

"Is there any reason why you read those particular books?"

"To . . . I guess to find out more about myself—how I should think and feel about things."

"Are you saying you are responsive to what you read—that is, react strongly to what you read?"

"Yes, sir."

"Have you ever read *Justine*, by the Marquis de Sade?"

"No, sir."

"Have you read a translation of the pornographic Oriental work the *Kama-Sutra?*"

"No, sir."

Barrett stirred and then spoke up. "I would like to object, Your Honor, on the grounds that the question is immaterial."

Judge Upshaw brought himself nearer his desk microphone. "Objection overruled. Proceed, Mr. Duncan."

Elmo Duncan turned back to his witness. "Mr. Griffith, have you ever read *My Life and Loves,* by Frank Harris?"

"No, sir."

"Or *Lady Chatterley's Lover?*"

"No, sir."

"Or *Sexus,* by Henry Miller?"

"No, sir."

"Have you read *Fanny Hill,* in all or in part?"

"No, sir."

Duncan gave Jerry an approving smile, glanced at the jurors, then turned back to his witness.

"Recently an attempt was made to publish—well, actually it *was* published, published openly for the first time—a book of the same genre, one similar to those I have been asking you about. I want to know whether you've read it. Did you read *The Seven Minutes,* by J J Jadway?"

"Yes, sir, I did."

"Had you ever heard of the book or known of it before its publication in the United States by Sanford House?"

"Not . . . Well, only in passing—I heard it mentioned vaguely in one of my English lectures at UCLA."

"Did the lecture stimulate you to read it?"

"No, sir. Even if it—it had—there were no copies anywhere. The lecture was some months ago."

"But if there had been copies available at the time, would the lecture have encouraged you to obtain one?"

Barrett rose. "Objection, Your Honor. People's counsel has asked a speculative question."

"Objection sustained."

Duncan was facing his witness once more. "Did the professor's mention of *The Seven Minutes* make you feel you wanted to read the book?"

"No, sir."

"Can you tell us what finally made you decide to read *The Seven Minutes?*"

"I—I saw something about it in one of those bookstores that sell those—those protest and avant-garde weekly newspapers and magazines. I was looking through one of the magazines—"

"Do you recall the name of the magazine?"

"No. But it was from New York. There were about a hundred different ones on the racks, and I looked at this one, and there was this article about the book coming out."

"Was the article a review or a preview or a news story about the Jadway book?"

"I guess a preview. It sort of summarized certain sections of the book."

"And these summaries stimulated you to read the book?"

"They made me curious."

"Why?"

"I—I don't know—not for—because—I think because I never knew women were so interested in sex."

"Well, Mr. Griffith, up to that time what had you thought was the reason that women participated in sexual intercourse and other sexual acts?"

"I—I guess I thought they—they did it because everyone did . . . or was supposed to . . . to keep in the swing. I mean, to keep their boy friends happy."

"And reading about the Jadway book gave you an entirely different view of this?"

"Yes. After that I thought they actually wanted to—to—do it."

"I see. And when you finally read the book itself, did you get this same impression?"

"Yes."

"Even though you knew the book was fiction?"

"I forgot it was fiction. I believed it."

"You believed all women, or most women, were as hungry for sex, and every perversion of sex, as Cathleen, the heroine of *The Seven Minutes?*"

"Yes, sir."

"Do you believe that today?"

"No, sir."

"Do you feel the book misled you?"

"Objection, Your Honor. Mr. Duncan is leading the witness."

"Objection sustained."

"Now, then, Mr. Griffith, in your opinion is Jadway's portrait of Cathleen in the novel a realistic and true picture of a young girl or is it an unusual and warped one?"

"Unusual and warped."

"So after reading that article about *The Seven Minutes*, you read the book?"

"Not right away. It wasn't out yet. I kept thinking about what the article said, then I forgot about it for a little while until I saw a big ad in a newspaper here saying the book was for sale. Then I got a copy and read it."

"When was that? When did you read it?"

"The night of May eighteenth."

Barrett had been concentrating on the testimony, but he was distracted by Zelkin's shaking his arm. He had started to turn, when he saw that Zelkin was passing him a note. It read: "Slick boy, our Elmo. Didn't ask where or how kid got book. Don't forget to ask in cross." Barrett nodded absently and gave his attention to the witness box.

"You read *The Seven Minutes* from cover to cover, every word of it?"

"Yes, sir."

"What was your reaction to it?"

"I was upset."

"What do you mean, upset?"

"I—I was mixed up inside, all mixed up. I couldn't sleep."

"Did you go to school the next day?"

"Yes, but I cut some of my late-afternoon classes."

"Why?"

"I had my mind on that book. I went to my car—I kept it in my car—"

"Why in your car?"

"I didn't want my father to know I had it."

"Were you afraid your father would object to that kind of reading?"

"Yes, sir."

"Had your father always disapproved of pornographic books?"

"Yes, sir. He would not allow them in the house. He said they were not healthy."

"Do you agree with him?"

"I do now, yes, sir."

"So you went out to your car, and then what did you do?"

"I drove it out of the UCLA parking lot, and I drove around a while, and then I found a lonely road up in the hills above Hollywood and I reread parts of the book."

"Can you recall what sections you reread?"

"I don't remember exactly. Some of the first chapter, the first of the seven minutes in the story. I read that several times."

"What was in those pages?"

"She's lying waiting for him . . . and she thinks how much he looks like those Greek statues, I believe that was in the beginning—"

"If I may refresh your memory of that part, Mr. Griffith. She's lying naked, and she thinks of the statues of Priapus that stood on some of the streets of ancient Greece—the statues consisting of the bust of a bearded man set on a stone base or block, and out of the center of this plinth there projected a male penis in a condition of erection. And then Cathleen's mind goes from those statues to a Grecian vase she had once seen in some museum, and engraved on the vase there was an abandoned young woman holding an *olisbos*, an artificial penis made out of hard leather, and Cathleen remembers how Lysistrata complained that there were none of these dildos around for her and her sisters to console themselves with. And then Cathleen thinks how lucky she is, and she stares at the unnamed hero of the book, not at him but at his—what were Jadway's words?—at 'his fat brown stubby swollen cock.' She thinks, 'my own *olisbos*,' and then she is moved to perform, or starts to perform, fellatio, and then she falls back and spreads her legs—and the first of her seven minutes begins. Now, Mr. Griffith, do you recognize that as the part you reread several times?"

"Yes, sir."

"Did you feel that was artistic writing at the time?"

"I didn't think about the writing."

"Well, did you feel at the time that the author was trying to do any more than excite the reader?"

"No."

"Did this passage and the other excite you?"

"Yes, sir."

"In what way did this excitement manifest itself?"

"Physically. I wanted to have a girl."

"Do you mean that you wanted to have sexual intercourse with a girl?"

"Yes, sir."

"With some particular girl or just any girl?"

"Any girl."

"What did you do next?"

"I wanted to find a girl. So I drove down to Melrose . . . it was nighttime . . . I drove to the club where I sometimes went —The Underground Railroad—and I looked for some girls . . . and drank a couple of Cokes. And there was this girl who was leaving to go to her apartment—she looked just like I'd imagined Cathleen—"

"You mean like the heroine of *The Seven Minutes?*"

"Yes. I offered her a lift—"

"By 'her' do you mean Sheri Moore?"

"I didn't know her name then. She said sure. So I drove her to her apartment. I said I'd see her upstairs. So I did. And when she opened her door, I pushed her inside, and made her go to the bedroom and undress."

"You made her do this? How?"

"I had a knife."

"Did she undress?"

"She was scared. Yes."

"Did you undress?"

"Yes."

"What happened next?"

"I don't remember. I went kind of crazy. It was like it wasn't my own mind any more—"

"It was Jadway's mind—"

Barrett came to his feet angrily. "Objection, Your Honor! The counsel—"

Duncan was all apologies. "I withdraw the remark, Your Honor. Forgive me."

Judge Upshaw's displeasure showed as he brusquely gave the court reporter his command. "Remark by People's counsel will be stricken." He turned to the District Attorney, and his voice was a whiplash. "Mr. Duncan, your remark was unbecoming a

493

counsel in a court of law and does nothing to improve your cause. I am certain you regret it, so I will not reprimand you further."

Swallowing hard, Duncan murmured his second apology, and, with an air that was self-reproachful and humble, he returned to his witness and with grave deliberation resumed his questioning. "You have testified, Mr. Griffith, that the girl, Miss Moore, had undressed and you had done the same, and that you had then become irresponsible—kind of crazy, as you put it. You went out of your mind, you said. Now, can you tell us, what did you do next, Mr. Griffith?"

"I forced myself on her."

"Did she resist?"

"Yes."

"But you violated her anyway?"

"I didn't know what I was doing."

"Did you think of *The Seven Minutes* at all?"

"When she was naked, yes—then I don't remember, after that—except that I did it—I couldn't help doing it."

"And during the course of this sex act, Miss Moore was injured?"

"It was after, when I was trying to dress. She tried to hit me or get my knife, I don't remember which, and I think . . . somehow she slipped and fell—it was an accident—"

"Did you know Miss Moore was unconscious?"

"I don't remember if I knew it or not. I only knew she had a roommate who might be coming back soon. So I just left. I felt miserable. I—I wanted to kill myself . . . because this wasn't me . . . what I'd done . . . it wasn't my fault, I didn't know what I was doing."

"Jerry Griffith, do you hold *The Seven Minutes*, by J J Jadway, responsible for your violent behavior?"

"I—I do."

"Have you ever in your life behaved this way before?"

"No, sir."

"You definitely feel the obscene passages in the book inflamed you until you were impelled to commit a criminal act?"

"Yes, sir. I—I can't explain any other reason for it."

"You know that Dr. Roger Trimble preceded you on the witness stand. Did you follow his testimony?"

"Yes, sir."

"Dr. Trimble quoted Ernest van den Haag as stating that pornog-

494

raphy is seductive to a part of the human personality, that 'it severs sex from its human context (the Id from the Ego and the Super-ego), reduces the world to orifices and organs, the action to their combinations.' Do you agree with this?"

"I guess so—yes, I do."

"Dr. Trimble spoke of the relationship between pornography and violent crime. He elaborated upon the horrible Moors Case in England which concerned the torture and killing of a ten-year-old girl and a twelve-year-old boy by Ian Brady and Myra Hindley, and it was found that Ian Brady had been influenced by those writings of the Marquis de Sade which dealt with sadistic sex. Do you feel, from your own experience, there is such a cause-and-effect relationship between pornographic books and acts of crime?"

"I—I only know . . . only know . . . what—what happened—happened to me."

Suddenly Jerry's hands had gone to his eyes, covering them, as if to hide the impending tears.

Elmo Duncan averted his face from this show of emotion. He looked up at the bench. "I have no further questions, Your Honor."

Mike Barrett stared at Jerry. The District Attorney had passed out of his vision. The boy was left. Through wet eyes the boy stared back at Barrett, like one of the tortured Moors Case kids waiting for death.

This was it, now.

Destroy this boy. Destroy him now, along with his evidence that Jadway's book was as lethal to the human psyche as a murder weapon.

Or use Cassie McGraw to destroy Leroux and all the rest who had sought to prove that Jadway's book was a deliberately obscene work written by a self-confessed pornographer.

Jerry Griffith?

Or Cassie McGraw?

Which?

Distantly he heard Judge Upshaw intoning, "You may cross-examine the witness, Mr. Barrett."

He heard Abe Zelkin beside him whispering urgently, "This is it, Mike. Give them hell."

Decision.

495

He came slowly to his feet. With difficulty, he found his voice. "Your Honor, the defense has no questions."

He could see that the Judge could not believe the evidence of his ears. "Mr. Barrett, do you mean that you wish to reserve your cross-examination until later?"

"No, Your Honor, I do not mean that. As far as the defense is concerned, the witness may be permanently dismissed."

He heard the unified gasp of the spectators behind him, and the rising hubbub that followed it. Ignoring Zelkin, who was tearing at his arm, and the Judge's stern gavel and voice, demanding order in the courtroom, he half turned.

Maggie, dabbing at her eyes, had just risen and moved into the center aisle. Now her eyes sought him. Her face was suffused with relief and gratefulness. Then she gave a short nod, and then she was gone.

He heard Judge Upshaw announcing, "Ladies and gentlemen of the jury, we will now take our noon recess. I again admonish you that during this recess you shall not converse among yourselves nor with anyone else on any matter pertaining to this case, nor shall you express or form an opinion thereon until the matter is finally submitted to you. Recess until two o'clock!"

He heard Abe Zelkin's bewilderment and anger. "You've blown the case, goddammit! What in the hell happened? Are you out of your mind or crazy or what?"

Was he out of his mind or crazy or what?

He had not been able to answer his partner's compound question at once, nor had he answered it in the twenty minutes that followed. For, with the announcement of the noon recess, there had been no privacy. Pushing their way out of the courtroom, they had been surrounded by reporters who had demanded to know the defense's motive in not cross-examining Jerry Griffith. In the corridor of the Hall of Justice, in the elevator, in the downstairs lobby, the newspapermen around them had been joined by radio and television reporters.

No comment, no comment, no comment.

Even on Broadway, where a panting Philip Sanford had caught up with them, they were not alone, but still were chased by at least a half-dozen members of the press.

No comment, no comment.

Even as the three of them strode grimly south on Broadway toward First Street, past the Hall of Records and then the Law Library, toward the Redwood Restaurant, where they had agreed to meet Leo Kimura for lunch, two stalwarts of the communications media, one a wire-service man, the other the television broadcaster Merle Reid, had stayed doggedly at their heels.

As they turned into First Street, the wire-service man had abandoned them, but Reid had remained as adhesive as a leech. He had continued to pepper them with inquiries until they reached the brick exterior of the Redwood Restaurant, that luncheon refuge for attorneys and judges working in the Hall of Justice and the County Law Library, and there Merle Reid had partially blocked their way, insisting upon some explanation.

No comment.

"Well, maybe *I've* got a comment!" Reid had blurted out, eying Barrett unpleasantly. "It looks to all of us like Luther Yerkes has made a new acquisition. He already owns the prosecution. Maybe now he's bought the defense. Now do *you* want to comment?"

Barrett's first impulse had been to slug him, but the defense had enough troubles without adding an assault-and-battery charge. He'd given himself a second to simmer down. At last reason had prevailed. "I have one comment," he had said. "Beat it, you phony."

And with that he had shoved past Reid and gone through the restaurant entrance, followed closely by Zelkin and Sanford. Inside, the affable manager had been expecting them, and he had quickly led them beyond the lunch-counter area to a white-covered table in the rear dining room, where Kimura was already seated in a red-upholstered chair, thumbing through his portable file. Not until they had settled in their places, and the dark-eyed waitress in the white blouse and black skirt had left them their menus and gone off to fill their beer orders, had they been able to consider exchanging their first words since leaving the courtroom.

Now, trying to maintain calm in the eye of the storm, Mike Barrett was packing his pipe as he watched Phil Sanford lean toward Kimura and whisper something, and he was aware that a flushed and still furious Abe Zelkin was continuing to glower at him.

"Goddammit, Mike, you still haven't answered," Zelkin began harshly. "What in the hell happened to you back there, letting

Duncan and that kid cream us, letting them go unscathed? What happened—did you flip your lid or what?"

Barrett lit his pipe, then put it down. "I was waiting to tell you and Phil, and you, Leo, in private. That's why I told Ben Fremont to eat someplace else. Now I'll explain."

"It better be damn good," said Zelkin.

"I made a deal," said Barrett tersely. "I traded off the cross-examination of Jerry Griffith for an examination of Cassie McGraw."

"Cassie McGraw?" said Sanford with astonishment. "You mean she's alive?"

"That's right. She's alive, and she's on our side, and we've got an opportunity to use her. We'll have our star witness at last."

"Wow!" exclaimed Sanford. "Jadway's mistress, Cathleen's prototype, with us, in the flesh. Well, now, I'd say that puts a new light—"

"Never mind that, Phil," interrupted Zelkin curtly, his narrowed eyes holding on Barrett from behind his thick glasses. "Okay, Mike, you made a deal." He paused. "Who'd you make the deal with?"

Barrett shifted uncomfortably. This was the moment that he had anticipated and dreaded. "With Maggie Russell."

"I thought as much," said Zelkin, unrelenting.

Barrett was annoyed. "Now, wait a minute—"

"You wait," said Zelkin, his voice rising. "If you won't cross-examine in court, at least let me have the chance to do it here. So it's that Russell dame, and it's a deal. Well, first off, this business of your doing things on your own is beginning to be a habit with you. What is this, a one-man show? Because if it is, then I'm—"

"Cut it out, Abe, will you? You know me better than that. We're partners and we're in this together. Only—"

"Then why didn't you consult me or inform me about it before making any goddam deals?"

"Because looking at it on paper, based on cold one-dimensional facts, I knew you'd turn it down. There would have been no possible way for me to convey to you what cold facts can't convey—the feeling you get from knowing someone as well as I know Maggie Russell—the feeling that is built not only on facts but on an emotional understanding which gives support to instinct, to hunch. And my knowledge of Maggie told me to consider her offer and finally convinced me to accept it. There are some decisions a person has to make on his own."

Zelkin would not have it. "You're not defending yourself in that courtroom, Mike. We're all in this together, and we're in there defending not ourselves but Ben Fremont and every book vendor in America, and Phil Sanford and every book publisher in the world, and a piece of our Bill of Rights as well. Not one of us here has the right to act unilaterally, or go off half-cocked on his own because of some emotional—"

Sanford cast aside the spoon he had been toying with. "Hold it a minute, Abe. I think we should at least allow Mike to explain."

"Okay," said Zelkin. "Let's have your facts, Mike. You tell us the deal you were offered and decided to make on your own. Go ahead."

Before Barrett could reply, the waitress had reappeared with a tray of beers. She asked for their orders. None of them had looked at their menus, but now they did so hastily. Two Reuben sandwiches and one hot turkey sandwich. Barrett had no appetite, but to prove he was not upset he ordered a Smokey Joe's barbecued beef on a French roll.

The waitress had gone. Determinedly, Barrett met Zelkin's challenge. "All right. If you'll listen, I'll tell you what happened and on what I based my decision. First, as you know, I've been seeing Maggie socially. Through her, I've got a better picture of Jerry's condition."

"We knew enough about Jerry's condition before," said Zelkin, "and I had the apparently mistaken impression that we were honest attorneys out to expose his condition in court, not physicians who were expected to treat it in private."

Barrett kept his temper, because there was a logical reason for his partner's anger, hurt, and skepticism. "Okay, Abe, you know the boy's condition. Self-destructive, and absolutely paranoid about facing a hostile interrogation. Now, that's not the issue, and certainly not the one that influenced me. But I'd better fill you in on Maggie's relationship with the boy and with Frank Griffith, so you can know why she was driven to offer me a deal that might save the boy and ruin the Duncan-Yerkes-Osborn-Griffith axis. And then I'll tell you exactly what happened the night before last."

He told them. Without any interruption, except when the waitress delivered their sandwiches, he related the essence of what

499

he had learned of Maggie and Jerry, of Maggie and Frank Griffith. He began with his first meetings with her at the STDL lecture and at Ell's coffee shop after Jerry's attempted suicide, and ended with his last meeting with her Saturday night at Chez Jay in Santa Monica. Then he recounted the details of Maggie's offer, and now he told them what she had to trade.

"Frank Griffith has his own secretaries to handle his business mail at his advertising agency," Barrett went on, "but the personal mail that comes to Frank Griffith or Ethel Griffith, that comes to their house, is opened and screened by Maggie. She's not only a relative and her aunt's companion, but she's also a sort of social secretary for the Griffith family. Well, because of all the publicity our case has been getting, with Griffith and his boy receiving a fair share of the attention, there's been a steady stream of mail to the Griffith house, mostly supportive of or favorable to Griffith and his fight against the book. Maggie has been going through this mail daily. Well, two weeks ago, a little more now, the usual morning mail arrived, and Maggie was seated at her uncle's desk going through it, when suddenly there it was—a postcard for Frank Griffith signed 'Cassie McGraw.' "

"Just a postcard?" said Sanford.

"Just a postcard," repeated Barrett. "Hell, you can put the Ten Commandments, or the Golden Rule, or 'Eureka! Eureka! I have found it!' on a simple postcard, also. Maggie couldn't believe her eyes, but there it was, mailed from Chicago, with a return address. On the card written to Frank Griffith, Cassie said she had read about the trial in the newspapers. Apparently she had seen some kind of strong statement to the press by Mr. Griffith attacking *The Seven Minutes* and accusing Jadway of ruining his son. Anyway, Cassie had seen something like that and she was moved to reply, to tell Griffith who she was, that no one knew Jadway as intimately as she had known him, and that she would swear on her daughter's life that he had created the novel with the purest motives in mind, with the hope of liberating new generations, and that Leroux's testimony had been a pack of lies."

"All of that on a postcard," said Zelkin with sarcasm.

"Why not? Look what people have written on the head of a pin. Somewhere at home I've got the Lord's Prayer—I picked it up in Mainz, Germany—published in a book less than half a square inch in size."

"What made her think it was from the real Cassie McGraw?" said Zelkin. "It could have been sent by a crank."

"I was coming to that. Maggie wasn't sure, at first. It just read like it was for real. She allowed that it might not be. But on the chance that it just might be genuine, she separated it from the rest of the mail and hid it from Frank Griffith. She figured that if it was authentic, it could lead us—the defense, that is—to Cassie, and this would give us a powerful weapon and do irreparable harm to Duncan's case as well as help Jerry in the long run. So she chose to hold it back to bargain with Griffith, to make him go easy on Jerry, to keep him from forcing Jerry to face us on the stand. But finally she decided her uncle was beyond reasoning with, and so she decided to approach me. Actually, what made her approach me was something I had told her that confirmed the authenticity and value of the card."

"What was that?" Sanford wanted to know.

"During a phone call, I mentioned to Maggie that I had located the daughter of Jadway and Cassie McGraw—this Judith Jan—and our luck—that she had turned out to be a cloistered Carmelite nun. Now, everyone knows about the daughter, but how many people know that the daughter became a nun? Maggie knew, because I had mentioned it, and all of us here know. Sean O'Flanagan knows. Some people in the Church know. But who else? Only someone very close to Jadway—and Cassie McGraw herself. Well, Maggie told me it's in the message on that card from Chicago. Cassie wrote to the effect that Jadway's own daughter, Judith, was a nun—not doing penance for Jadway's sins, but to serve God, as her father had served humanity. When Maggie told me the writer of the postcard had mentioned the word 'nun,' I knew that it had been sent by Cassie McGraw—that Cassie was alive."

He looked at the others, but their facial expressions showed neither belief nor disbelief. They were waiting to hear whether there was anything more.

Barrett resumed. "Well, that was the offer, then. We could have Cassie McGraw if we kept our hands off Jerry in public. It was an awful decision to make. In the end, I guess what determined my decision was a purely legal consideration. Jerry Griffith came on strong and affirmative for Duncan. If I gave up Cassie to cross-examine him, I would at best achieve a small gain, a negative gain.

I might cast doubt on Jerry's testimony, negate some of it. Achieving even that is debatable, however, because disclosing the new material I had, Jerry's attempt at suicide before he ever read the book, might have the added effect of appearing as harassment of a sick, cornered boy. It would be unsympathetic matter, in the eyes of most jurors. Intellectually they might have been persuaded to believe that it was not our book alone that had ruined Jerry, but emotionally they might be made to feel sorry for him and hostile toward us. On the other hand, I argued with myself, if I permitted Jerry to get away with it, I would in return have the most sensational witness yet presented in the court, an unimpeachable headline witness, one who would build up the affirmative side for the defense. It would be dramatic, irrefutable, firsthand testimony, and it would in one stroke eliminate Leroux and his ilk and give the lie to what Dr. Trimble and Jerry believed the book had done to Jerry. It would impart to the book honesty, decency, social redemption. And the book is what this censorship trial is really all about. So I decided to sacrifice Jerry for Cassie— for Cassie and Jadway's book. Gentlemen, those are the facts plus, and there's nothing more I can add."

Zelkin was polishing his spectacles with a napkin. He seemed less angry now. Only sour. "Okay, Mike, except you haven't told us one thing."

"What's that?"

"Did you see that postcard that Cassie McGraw allegedly sent?"

"See it? You mean look at it myself? No. Maggie couldn't get to Griffith's desk yesterday. It's the desk in his study that she ordinarily uses for her work. She'd hidden the postcard under the lining of a bottom drawer where he'd have no reason to look—safer, she felt, than keeping it in her room. Lately she's suspected that he snoops around in her room, especially since he learned she's been seeing me. So there it was hidden in that desk, but Griffith was in his study the entire day. It was Sunday, you know. And early this morning, when she learned that I hadn't made up my mind, she said she'd wait and see what I decided. If I waived Jerry's cross-examination, she'd hand over the postcard to me this afternoon."

"If the postcard exists," said Zelkin quietly.

"What do you mean?"

"I mean there's every likelihood it exists only in your girl friend's imagination. You did say she'd do almost anything for the boy. Well, okay, this is almost anything."

"Abe, much of what we accomplish in life is based on trusting another person."

"Is that so?" said Zelkin. "If it is, you've just put the American Bar Association out of business. Maybe I trust my mother, my wife, my children a little, my best friends a little. But what I trust completely is a contract. Let's not be romantic. That's what most of law is all about. What I trust is what is enforceable and legal. What I trust is what is tangible. What I trust is what I have in my hand in return for what I pay. Okay, Mike, what's done is done, and we've been too close to each other for me to be angry with you any more. Maybe my neck is tight and my stomach is churning, and maybe I'm a little sore, but I'll have to go along and sink or swim—and I think it's sink—with you."

Philip Sanford pulled his chair closer. His chalky complexion appeared totally bloodless. "Well, I'm not sure I'm quite that forgiving, Mike. Maybe Abe doesn't mind sinking with you, but I tell you, I'm not ready to go under. Mike, my whole career, my family, my life are riding on your performance and judgment. I think you've committed a big fat boner. I won't pull punches, either. Let's be truthful, lay truth right on this table. I hope you can take it in that spirit."

"You can say whatever is on your mind," said Barrett, surprised by the bluntness of Sanford's uncharacteristic outburst.

"I believe that the one truth you can't or won't face is that Luther Yerkes and Frank Griffith have used that girl to talk you into doing this. She's dependent on them, on Griffith anyway, and they know you've fallen for her, and so they made her take advantage of you. I think they made a fool of you, Mike, and I'm just damn sorry so many other people will have to suffer the consequences of your mistake. I'm with Abe. I'm not sure that the postcard from Cassie McGraw exists, or if it does, that you'll ever see it until the trial's over and they've won and we've wound up in the poorhouse or some booby hatch. Now you've heard. For better or worse, I've spoken my mind."

Barrett refused to become ruffled. He relit his pipe, and then he nodded agreeably. "Yes, Phil, those possibilities have crossed my mind, too. I considered them. While I can't account for my unconscious, I do believe I acted with cold objectivity. Maybe I'll be proved a fool. Or maybe I'll be proved a prophet. The stakes are big. I laid all our chips on Maggie because I sense and believe she is honest. As I said, there are times when you have to trust others."

"Like we trusted Christian Leroux?" said Sanford. "Like we trusted Isabel Vogler? Like we trusted the privacy of our telephones and the decency of the opposition these past weeks?"

Barrett shrugged and turned to Kimura, who was fingering a fork across the table. "Leo, you've not been heard from," said Barrett. "What's your opinion? Have I been a fool?"

Kimura continued to play with his fork. His sallow face remained impassive. "I can give no opinion on right or wrong, Mr. Barrett. I could, however, give an opinion, based on researched facts, as to the probable outcome of your decision. I work only from data. I know the fact that Miss Russell has lived in the Griffith house X-number of years and never had reason to leave. I know the fact that in those X-number of years Miss Russell never made a move or act contrary to the interests of Frank and Ethel Griffith. I know the fact that an enormous amount of money and time has been spent on the investigation of Cassie McGraw and there is not one shred of evidence that she is alive. I know the fact that tigresses come forward to protect their mates when their mates are attacked. Even aged ones like Cassie, they come forward. They do not protest from afar. At the same time, I know that a research project is never complete, all the facts are never known, and also data can often be misinterpreted. So I prefer not to offer an opinion on the outcome, Mr. Barrett. I could instead give odds, although I shall not do that either in this matter."

"I'll give you the odds, Mike," said Sanford. "When is Maggie supposed to turn over that postcard with Cassie McGraw's address?"

"Five o'clock this afternoon. She's coming to my office."

"Then I'm posting odds," said Sanford. "One gets you twenty that she doesn't show or call. One gets you ten that she calls with some excuse about the postcard being lost or having disappeared. One gets you five that if she does show or call and produces the postcard, it turns out to be a phony or from a crank. Any bets?"

Barrett shook his head. "Nope. Because if you're right, we'll both be broke."

Zelkin had been studying his watch. "No use going on with this," he said. "Mike will know for sure one way or the other in three and a half hours. Let's eat up and get back to the courtroom. I think Duncan is finished with his witnesses, and we'll be on with ours after two o'clock. We'd better have a few minutes with Ben Fremont before we trot him out." He looked at Barrett. "Who's kicking off for the defense today, Mike, you or me?"

"You'd better take over this afternoon," said Barrett. "I'll have to leave by four-fifteen to get back to the office to meet Maggie."

"You still believe?" asked Zelkin.

"I believe," said Barrett.

IT WAS exactly two o'clock and the courtroom was again filled and the bailiff was standing.

The drapes behind the judge's seat on the bench parted, and black-robed Judge Nathaniel Upshaw entered, briefly surveyed his domain, and started for his chair.

"Please remain seated," the bailiff commanded the spectators and the trial participants. "Court is now again in session."

Judge Upshaw cleared his throat. "The jury is present. Mr. Duncan, you may call your next witness."

The District Attorney came to his feet. "Your Honor, I have no additional witnesses. Mr. Jerry Griffith was the People's final witness. The People rest."

As Duncan sat down, Judge Upshaw swiveled toward the defense table. "If the defense is ready, may I inquire which counsel will represent the defense?"

Zelkin sprang to his feet. "Abraham Zelkin, Your Honor."

"Very well, Mr. Zelkin. You may proceed with your first witness."

"Thank you, Your Honor," said Abe Zelkin. "At this time we would like to introduce as our first witness the defendant, Ben Fremont."

"Fine," said Judge Upshaw. "Mr. Fremont, will you come forward now and raise your right hand and be sworn?"

As the bookseller, baldish, myopic, defiant, left the defense table and walked toward the witness stand in his oddly pecking gait, Mike Barrett watched him briefly. He wished that he had forced Fremont to go to a barbershop before his appearance. Fremont's sideburns and the growth of hair at the back of his head were too long and bushy. Some older jurors might equate this with unorthodoxy and rebellion and be prejudiced against the defendant. But almost instantly Barrett was ashamed of his thoughts, these leftovers of his old preoccupation with getting-ahead, keeping-in-step, conforming, of his old Osborn-oriented self, and he told himself wryly that what really needed trimming were some of his thoughts.

Fremont had met the court clerk, and Barrett observed that when the Bible was held up for him he refused to place his left hand on it. Barrett could not hear the court clerk's question, but he did hear Fremont's answer, "I'm an atheist." Barrett winced and wondered whether any jurors had overheard this. He glanced at the jury box. Several jurors were frowning.

Keeping the Bible at his side, the court clerk reeled off the atheist's affirmation, "You do affirm that the testimony that you are about to give in the cause now before the court will be the truth, the whole truth, and nothing but the truth."

Without God's help, Fremont said, too loudly, "I do!"

As Fremont mounted the witness stand, Abe Zelkin, who had been standing beside Barrett, muttered in an undertone, "Here I come, Peter Zenger." Then, like an oversized beach ball being rolled toward the box, Abe Zelkin went bouncing toward the first witness for the defense.

Distressed, Barrett drew a pad of legal-sized lined yellow paper in front of him. His distress, he discerned, stemmed less from any apprehensions he was having about how his client, or any of the other defense witnesses, would be received than from the consensus of opinion accorded his deal with Maggie when they had discussed it during the recent lunch period. He had faith in Maggie, but it was difficult to be a lone believer. Zelkin, Sanford, even Kimura, had been so doubtful of the wisdom of his act, so suspicious of Maggie's motives, so unconvinced that the postcard existed, that Barrett was plagued by misgivings.

He had no patience for the defense's witnesses. His mind was only on the clock, whose hands were moving as if coated with molasses, the clock that was bringing him closer and closer to the truth about Maggie Russell and perhaps to the reality of Cassie McGraw. Knowing it would be this way, he had set the yellow pad before him to record the highlights of the afternoon. While the court reporter's official transcript of what was being enacted could be made available to him by tomorrow—for a price—Barrett preferred an immediate record. He wanted some diary, some reminder, of what was happening, because he knew that once he left the courtroom his mind would be entirely enlisted in the search for Cassie McGraw.

Behind him, the hands of the court clock made their maddeningly slow orbits of the waning afternoon. Ahead of him, as unreal as mannequins in a department-store window, the familiar and carefully coached witnesses displayed their wares to the receptive Zelkin, the critical Duncan. The witnesses came and went. The time passed. And suddenly he realized it was after four o'clock, and in fifteen minutes he must leave the courtroom to face what might be another trial.

He stared down at the yellow pad before him. He did not know how those blank pages had become filled with his loose scrawl. Before taking his leave, he decided to review his personal record and evaluation of the skirmishes of the past two hours. His eyes fixed on the name of the first witness, which he had printed in block letters, and then went on to the writing that followed the name. He read swiftly.

BEN FREMONT:

Zelkin's exam—Fremont's good education, worked way through school—twenty years in book business, always paid bills, solvent, best of relations with publishers, customers—are 30,000 new titles a year, can stock only 5,000 old and new—time to read only relative handful —always ordered all Sanford House titles, because firm of high repute— ordered Jadway book not only because Sanford House, but because had read it in Leroux edition—was astounded when arrested—yes, officer fooled him by pretending to be ordinary customer—Abe doing well here—some jurors may be resentful of police trickery, bullying, because they've been so ill-used and fooled themselves—Fremont acknowledges his part of verbal exchange on police reel of tape—now adds to it— thinks *Minutes* in no way obscene—thinks book magnificent "X-ray of female mind" and its social importance is that it will teach women of selves, and men about opposite sex—Fremont says knows local community standards and interests because his business caters to community, average person who reads—yes, has heard people use four-letter words such as in Jadway book—yes, women also—says his customers, mostly women, have bought heavily other books with same words and describing acts similar to Jadway's book—cites how many times he reordered *Fanny Hill, My Secret Life, Chatterley, Life and Loves* by

507

Frank Harris—believes *Minutes* more artful, has more redeeming social importance than others—no, not many of his customers offended by such a book, few ever bring books back for a refund—oh, yes, are a few rare exceptions because after all, a work of art can't please everyone—as someone said, even the Venus de Milo might be found offensive by every flat-chested woman in the world—so someone might find Jadway's book offensive, but most readers will consider it pure art, as he, Fremont, does.

Duncan's cross—oh geez—bastard has Fremont on the ropes right off—Was defendant ever arrested before for violating obscene section of California Penal Code?—but Fremont's "yes" not enough for prosecution, dammit—should have known that if Duncan mentioned it in opening statement, he'd hit it again—should have forestalled him by introducing details ourselves, but now the bastard's bringing out the whole thing—Fremont arrested dozen years ago, not in Oakwood, small shop on Hill Street, downtown LA—it was not for books but magazines—not his kind of magazines, but stuff wholesaler dumped on him—just sold, paid no attention to contents—DA roughs him up—Did he plead not guilty?—no—He pleaded guilty of purveying obscene material?—yes, but only on advice of attorney to get lighter sentence—But admitted guilt?—yes—Since first offense, guilty of misdemeanor, did he pay a fine?—yes—Go to jail?—no, sentence suspended—Aware that second offense is not misdemeanor but felony?—yes—Aware second time can go to jail for year, be fined up to $25,000—yes—Did he know publisher advertised Jadway book as dirtiest book in history of literature?—well, it was a quote on posters, so yes, but also on posters that it was a distinguished work of art—Did witness know that until now, excepting original underground publication, no publisher in any nation dared bring it out?—yes, but—Nevertheless, Fremont ordered book and sold it?—yes—And ten minutes more of the same.

Score—Duncan on points. Made mincemeat of Fremont.

PHIL SANFORD:

Zelkin's exam—Elicits details Sanford's background, good family, Harvard, always in publishing—When contracted for *Minutes*, was he worried about obscenity? No, not really, because book beautiful, touching, truthful, too honest and well-done to appeal to prurient interest—Beyond customary limits of candor by contemporary community standards?—certainly not—Sanford discourses on how times

508

change. Funny story. Once, in the pages of *Godey's Lady's Book*, the eager-to-be-correct hostess was admonished to see that "the works of male and female authors be properly separated on her bookshelves." Also, at one time neither piano nor chicken mentioned as having legs, only limbs. Sanford says in 1929 U.S. Customs barred Rousseau's *Confessions* as immoral, and same year banned de Sade's *Justine* as smut, and in 1927 Sinclair Lewis' *Elmer Gantry* banned in Boston as obscene, and two years later Remarque's *All Quiet on the Western Front* banned for same reason, but now everyone considers those works mild, accepts them, because times change—today perfume ads, in magazines, on television, lingerie and soap ads, brassiere ads, show females nude or semi-nude and sell seduction—today movies and stage plays parade nudity, copulation, oral-genital love, masturbation, homosexuality, lesbianism—today the age of the Pill, unmarried youngsters live together openly—community standards changed. Sanford says *Minutes* not beyond such standards. Starts to cite several good reviews—Duncan objects. Reviews hearsay, besides reviews can't be cross-examined. Objection overruled, reviews discussed. Abe helps witness develop point that Sanford House has highest literary repute—Sanford recounts older and modern classics they've published, also works by Nobel Prize winners—would never put imprint on anything lacking literary merit, as past record proves—and *Minutes* meets this standard. Etc.

Duncan's cross—How did Sanford acquire *Minutes*? From whom? —dammit, expected this—Quandt's name comes up. Also, Quandt's unsavory record as pornographer—So Sanford had to go to professional pornographer to acquire book?—Sanford valiant here. Says Quandt felt book too tame and literary for him to publish, and so Quandt never published it—Duncan discusses reputation of Sanford House, reels off a selection of firm's best titles—Were you the head and publisher of Sanford House when those books were brought out?—no, but I was working in the firm then—Were you responsible for buying, publishing them?—no—Who was?—my father, Wesley R. Sanford—But today you are the head of firm?—yes—Since when?—two years ago, almost—Your Honor, prosecution wishes to introduce exhibits—Introduces clippings *NY Times, Wall Street Journal*, showing shaky financial position of Sanford House in last two years, Wesley R. Sanford considering selling off to big industrial bidders who seek diversification—Are these news accounts substantially true?—yes—In short, since you took over, Sanford House has not fared as well as in past?—Sanford hems, haws, says depends what you mean by doing well, admits firm's book sales have gone down—Then Duncan, bastard, slips it to him—Perhaps, Mr. Sanford, you were desperate, desperate enough to ignore your father's previous good taste, and try to save your position in firm by undertaking publication of an obscene work?—Zelkin objects. Upshaw sustains. But it got over to jurors.

Score—maybe a draw.

DR. HUGO KNIGHT:

Zelkin's exam—Witness's credentials impressive, teaching and UCLA professorial background, but manner unfortunate—supercilious, know-it-all, talked over jurors' heads, literary jargon incomprehensible as Sanskrit—says Jadway's gifts limited, but used them well—book excellent example of interior monologue—used Cathleen as oracle for own feelings—book realistically pornographic but not obscene—pornography only a device—Can you be more explicit, Professor?—*The Seven Minutes* not about sex at all—Poor Abe. Not only jury but he, himself, appears astounded. Knight never used that answer in briefings. Abe resumes, tries—Not about sex?—No, because the sex is merely symbolism, the means by which the author inveighs against The Seven Deadly Sins, or The Seven Mortal Sins, namely pride, wrath, envy, lust, gluttony, avarice, sloth—each of Cathleen's seven minutes is symbol of a mortal sin—Zelkin attempts divert witness from symbolism kick, but idiot keeps labeling everything symbolism—and sure enough, enter Leda and the Swan.

Duncan's cross—Dr. Knight, if you will enlighten us further about J J Jadway's hidden meanings, pray tell, is "cunt" symbolism?— Laughter.

Score—disaster. The witness is our eighth deadly sin. Duncan's round easily.

DA VECCHI:

Zelkin's exam—da Vecchi a cheerful little Italian singing out answers like a gondolier—an art student in Paris in the 1930s—met J J Jadway in Montparnasse, in the Dôme, used to see him at Brasserie Lipp, got to know Jadway quite well in period he was working on *Minutes*—Did you ever hear him speak of his work then in progress? —ah, yes, yes—Did he speak of it as a commercial undertaking?—no, never never, only as an artist, he said, "It is my opus, the work of my life," always proud—Did you feel that Jadway was a man of esthetic sensibilities?—you mean what?—I'm sorry, I mean did he have an understanding of art?—ah, yes, yes, of writing, of painting, of what is in the Louvre, of what is in my studio when I paint him—Do you believe Jadway's book is obscene?—never, never, it is from the soul of an artist. Effective witness, so far.

Duncan's cross—The cookie crumbles fast—So you knew Jadway quite well. Were you friends?—yes, friends—How many times did you see him in Paris?—many times—By "see him," Mr. da Vecchi, I do not mean see him pass in the street or sitting in a café, but rather, how much time did you spend with him alone?—alone together? oh, now and then—Were you alone with him more than three or four times?—I cannot remember—Perhaps you can remember where you were after Jadway's death, when the Second World War began?—I was in France still, in the maquis underground near Marseilles—Doing what? What was your occupation in the underground?—I was an artist—Painting pictures?—no, no, I make forged passports to help refugees—Did you pursue this same occupation after the war was over?—forge passports, never, no, I am a painter—Yes, you are a painter. I'd like to explore some of your more creative activities. I have evidence from Italy that you have painted under several names. One name you used was Vermeer, another was Raphael, another was Tintoretto. There is an old quip to the effect that, "Of the 2,500 paintings done by Corot in his lifetime, 7,800 are to be found in America." According to the police dossier in Rome, you painted at least eight Corots and sold them as authentic Corots. Now, of course, having once served a prison sentence for committing forgeries and perpetrating hoaxes need not necessarily impugn your honesty as a witness, but considering this record— Damn Duncan and that son-of-a-bitching witness. Why couldn't he have told us? He wanted a free trip, publicity. Now look at him. Smile gone. Shifty, cunning, scared. Goddammit.

Score—Duncan has it by a knockout.

SIR ESMOND INGRAM:
Zelkin's exam—Better, much better right away—celebrated Oxford don—celebrated literary critic—cranky, but pixie-charm, witty, an impressive sage—jury very attentive—Sir Esmond, you once wrote in *The Times* of London that *The Seven Minutes* was "one of the most honest, sensitive, and distinguished works of art created in modern Western literature." Do you still hold that view?—I do—Then you do not hold it to be an obscene book?—there are no obscene books, only

obscene men with obscene minds—Later: Then you feel it was honest and valid for Jadway to tell his story as he did?—it was the honest approach, the courageous one—many authors can denude the human body, but few have the nerve or genius to denude the human spirit—a French publisher once wrote that the most interesting thing about eroticism was not that there were thirty-two coital positions, but rather "what goes on inside people's heads, the way in which lovers react to each other," and this mystery Jadway penetrated and exposed completely—Do you believe that Jadway's book has redeeming social value? —It is a work of considerable social value. Jadway attempted to give sex its natural and proper place in the spectrum of human behavior. The editor of *Les Lettres Nouvelles*, Maurice Nadeau, once asked, "Why should love—which forms the principal or subsidiary subject of eight novels out of ten—stop at the edge of the bed, around which the curtains are then drawn?" After all, the function of literature, he said, was to explore the human heart, to explore every manifestation of being. And then he added, "The way in which people make love may tell us more about them than any searching analysis could. It, too, reveals a form of truth which is interesting because it is usually concealed." With this book, Ingram says, Jadway did humankind a service.

Mike Barrett had finished reviewing his notes of the afternoon's testimony. When he looked up, he saw that Sir Esmond Ingram was still in the witness box and was now submitting to Elmo Duncan's pressing cross-examination.

". . . and because of this background, Sir Esmond, you consider yourself an arbiter of what is good literature or bad?"

"It is not I who consider myself an arbiter of art, but my readers who regard me as such and who depend upon me to help them form their own judgments."

"But you do consider yourself qualified to advise readers what is of literary value and what is simply scatological?"

"I believe that I am highly qualified."

"Because of your erudition alone, Sir Esmond?"

"Heavens, no. Because of my experience of life, my empathy for and understanding of my public."

"Then you feel, Sir Esmond, your life has much in common with that of your average reader?"

"I would say so, yes."

"Sir Esmond, how many times have you been married?"

"Three times, sir."

"Have you ever been in jail?"

"Two times, sir."

"Do you eat meat, like the average reader?"

"I am a vegetarian, sir. May I add, counselor, the line you are taking is quite clever, and altogether naughty, yes, extremely naughty."

Goodbye, Sir Esmond, Barrett thought.

Barrett looked over his shoulder. He would just make it back to the office in time to meet Maggie Russell.

He folded his notes and shoved them into his pocket. He glanced at Abe Zelkin. "I'm leaving now, Abe."

Zelkin closed his eyes and shook his head mournfully. "Bring back Cassie McGraw," he said. "We need her, Mike. We're dead and buried without her."

"I'll find her," said Barrett. "I won't come back without her."

Then, quietly slipping out of his chair, he left behind him the scene of carnage—determined to return with the only ally alive who might save them and their cause.

FOR MAGGIE RUSSELL, it had been a wonderful afternoon.

Her relief over Jerry's escape from the cross-examination, her affection for Mike Barrett in making this possible, had been so great that she had been in a maniacally festive mood throughout her drive from downtown Los Angeles.

Wanting some kind of celebration, she had stopped in Beverly Hills, and at a table in Leon's restaurant she had indulged in a martini and a high-caloric lunch and her fantasies of the future. After that she had driven to Saks and shopped for a new dress there and at I. Magnin's down the block. The dress had been less a celebration than an investment. Intuition had warned her that by now, certainly by five o'clock, Mike Barrett would have had second thoughts about having bypassed his questioning of Jerry no matter what he expected in return. The best way to soften a man's regrets over what he had given up was to remind him that he may have gained something more. The dress, a short sheath, low-cut, soft, supple, silky, might help a little. Maggie hated women's games. By nature she was direct. But the situation warranted an extra effort. When she saw him, she wanted her appearance to remind him that if he had lost something important he had also gained something more lasting. That is, if he was still interested in her.

It was after four o'clock when she had returned to Pacific Palisades, and to her surprise Frank Griffith was home. He was at the telephone in his study, and his voice was booming cheerfully and Luthering all over the place, so she knew that he was speaking to that horrible Yerkes. Upstairs, Aunt Ethel was napping, and the door to Jerry's room was locked from the inside, but she could hear his record player. She had changed quickly into the new sheath, a smasher, and then she had brushed her hair and freshened her make-up.

Now she was hastening down the stairs, just as Frank Griffith, his beefy sunburned face aglow with some kind of self-satisfaction, emerged from his study.

Seeing her, he waited at the foot of the staircase.

"Hiya, Maggie girl. I heard you were in court this morning."

She reached the bottom of the staircase. "How did you know?"

"That was Luther Yerkes on the phone. Some of his lieutenants were in the courtroom, and they spotted you. I had no idea how we made out this morning until just now. I wanted to be on hand there, give Jerry some support, see for myself what was going on, but Dr. Trimble vetoed it. He felt my presence would make Jerry too self-conscious. So I agreed to pass. Doctor's orders. Anyway, I had some important business in San Diego. I was in conference down there all morning. But the second I was through, I thought I'd come straight back and find out what happened. I got home just after Jerry did, but that little snot son of mine wouldn't tell me a thing. Just clammed up and locked himself in. How do you like that for gratitude—with all we've done for him? Once this trial is over, and his own case is settled, I'll attend to him, straighten him out, teach him to show some respect."

"What does that mean?"

"It means we've been too lax with him, coddling him, and you can see what results that brings. Never mind. He'll be made to toe the mark in due time."

His big country-club face had become ugly during the last, but the transformation was brief, for he was still reveling in his triumph. His exhilaration over the public victory quickly restored his good humor. Oh, Lord, Maggie thought, how I hate that man.

"Anyway, first things first," he boomed. "We won, and that's

514

what counts. Luther Yerkes just gave me a complete rundown on what happened this morning. I knew we'd make those shysters on the defense fold up, and sure enough, they did." Jubilantly he put an arm around Maggie's waist and began to steer her into the living room. "Come on, Maggie, you were there. Now I want to hear what you think of it. I can't hear enough of it."

Maggie resented his grip, but not until they reached the middle of the living room was she able to free herself from him.

"What do you want to hear?" she asked.

"How Elmo made them cry Uncle, and how Jerry handled himself. Was my name mentioned?"

"I don't recall. As for Jerry, he stood up wonderfully. I was proud of him."

"I told you he would. From now on you'll listen to me. All these weeks, you and Ethel fluttering around him, whining about keeping him off the stand, treating him like some invalid, when from the start I knew there was more in him, plenty of gumption like his old man. Now you've got to admit I was right in the end, don't you?"

"I'll admit nothing of the sort, Uncle Frank. It was a terrible ordeal for Jerry. You should have seen him. He only survived it because—because Mr. Barrett didn't cross-examine him."

"Hogwash. He'd have put down your friend Barrett too. Why do you think Barrett closed shop and ran? Why do you think he quit? He quit because he knew Elmo Duncan and our side had him whipped, and we'd prepared Jerry for him, and he couldn't get anywhere. So he waived the cross-examination—trying to make a bid for public sympathy, as Luther put it—but the fact is, and I'm sorry if this offends you, Maggie girl, but you'll find out for yourself sooner or later, the fact is your friend Barrett was gutless and afraid. That's why he backed away from the cross-examination."

She had listened to Griffith with incredulity. For a person in his position, the degree of his stupidity and insensitivity was beyond belief. Hatred of his dumb arrogance almost gagged her. All these weeks of pent-up, repressed resentments pounded inside her, demanding to be heard. What was it he had said? That Mike was gutless, afraid?

She found her voice. "It wasn't because Mr. Barrett was afraid that he didn't cross-examine. It was because he was—he was decent and kind, among other reasons."

"Decent and kind?" Griffith threw back his head and gave a roar of laughter. "That's the best one I've heard yet. A shyster attorney, working for a fee, refusing to try to score a point because he's—what was it?—ho!—*decent and kind.*" He wagged his head. "Maggie girl, you know as little about human nature as your mother did. Less, maybe. Listen to me, young lady, and grow up. I'm in the business of knowing about people. And you'll thank me one day for warning you in time. That shyster friend of yours hasn't got an ounce of guts in his whole body."

"He's got as much guts as you have," she flared. It was all too much. She'd had enough. It was time to let go. "If you want the truth, the reason Mike Barrett didn't cross-examine Jerry was that *I* asked him not to, and there were other reasons, and one of these was that Mike understands your own son better than you do. He was ready to sacrifice a part of his case, his trial, because he agreed with me that Jerry's future was at stake, and that's more than you were ready to do or understand."

Frank Griffith's face grew ugly again. "Look, young lady, you're getting a little out of line there. Don't you go comparing me to that stud of yours. He didn't cross-examine Jerry because *you* asked him not to? You expect me to believe that? Why should he listen to you when his whole career's riding on this trial? Or maybe—no, I got it—maybe you have a way of making men listen to you, eh Maggie? Maybe some men will do anything for a little piece of nooky?"

The last had been spoken viciously, and Maggie wanted to strike him. Had she been a man, she would have had him by the throat. But it was precisely because she was a woman that he had tried to degrade her.

"That's rotten of you," she said, "really rotten."

He was not through. "Even if I can see what's in it for Barrett, what I want to know is what's in it for you, Maggie girl? What would you be after?"

"How can I speak to you?" Her voice was quavering. "You won't try to understand. Both Mike and I are essentially out to win one thing. A chance to live at peace with our consciences. No matter what else I might have offered Mike Barrett, his final decision had to be based on the one thing I haven't seen around here lately—a sense of decency." Oh, she wanted to destroy that big, smug, smirking, filthy-minded goon. "You want to know how it happened? I'll be glad to let you in on it. I went to Mike Barrett and I told him that you and your upper-bracket-Mafia friends were going to force Jerry to stand in the witness box, even though Jerry begged you not to force him. But you were determined to make him do it, to put the blame for Jerry's condition on the book. And I told Mike Barrett what he already was aware of, that Jerry was sick and suicidal, and that if he managed to survive Duncan's examination he'd never be able to come through Mike's cross-examination. I reminded Mike that he had seen Jerry try to kill himself once, and now the defense investigators had learned Jerry's secret, that he had tried to kill himself another time, before that book came out, and now, in his condition, if the ordeal in the court was too much, he'd try to kill himself again—and this time he might succeed."

Frank Griffith had turned livid. "What kind of bullshit is that?" he bellowed. "Where did you pick up that line of crap? From your pornographer friends?"

"Can't you face the truth once in your life? We're not talking about the fairy tales you deal with in your advertising world. We're talking about your son's life, and the truth about it. The defense investigators found out that Jerry had suffered a breakdown and tried to do away with himself last year. And a couple of weeks ago Jerry took an overdose of sleeping pills in his car, and Mike Barrett happened to find him in time to save him."

"So that's it! Your source for all that bullshit is your shyster friend Barrett, eh? I should have known it. I should have known he'd try anything. Even to making up that suicide bit, and planting it in your head to brainwash you, and telling you he saved Jerry—*he* saved Jerry? ha!—so you'd be beholden to him. What a crummy, scurvy trick to get you to work on Ethel to work on me to keep Jerry off the stand as a witness, so that your Barrett could win the trial. And you fell for it, you actually fell for it."

It was the moment for the entire truth. It was the moment to say that this had not come from Barrett alone. That it was she herself who had saved Jerry after his first suicide attempt, and she who had taken him up to San Francisco for therapy. That it was she herself who had brought Jerry home from the doctor's house, after Barrett had called her about the second attempt. Yet she could not bear to speak of this last truth. Griffith would

517

not believe her, anyway. He could not afford to believe her. Worse, he would immediately fall upon his son either to repudiate what she'd said or to confess to it—one way or another he'd bedevil Jerry further—and in the end Frank Griffith would still believe only what he wanted to believe, and the one loser would be Jerry.

"I've told you the whole truth," she said finally. "If you can't accept it, that's too bad, for you and for Jerry."

Frank Griffith glared at her. "If I had any sense, I'd kick you out of here right now, this second. But now I can see that your misbehavior and your foul tongue are not really you, and since you're not yourself you're not responsible for what you say. You've been influenced by that clip artist Barrett, used and manipulated by him, so that you no longer know what you're saying and what is true or not true. So maybe I'll give you another chance, young lady. Just maybe. Because it's not my son's condition I'm worried about. It's your condition and the trouble you might get into, being as unbalanced as you are, and that might involve all of us, because you are our responsibility."

The hell you're worried about me, buster, Maggie thought. What you're worried about, if you kick me out of here, is having another antagonist on the outside who might go around telling people what Frank Griffith is really like.

But she did not speak her mind. She waited.

"At the same time, I'm not letting you off so easy, young lady, not after your performance in this room just now," Griffith went on, still trying to control his fury. "I think I should tell you that you'd better make up your mind damn fast whose camp you are in, which side you are on, where your loyalties belong. I think you better remember damn fast that I'm the one who's been supporting you, paying you, keeping you in clover, and putting up with more than any other relative ever would, and you'd better decide if you appreciate this and are on my side or their side."

"I'm on neither side," she said. "I'm not on your side, and I'm not on Mike Barrett's. I'm on Jerry's side. I'm for whoever and whatever is good for him."

"So, it's only for him now, for Jerry, eh? Well, I'm not buying that either, young lady. I can see it all coming into focus now. Jerry isn't, and never was, the real issue in your mind. You tell me you're for the boy, just so you can hold on to your cushiony life in this house, but at the same time you got the hots for that shyster stud, that big bold sex crusader who's been humping you and keeping you tranquilized below while he's brainwashing you on top and sending you back here every night to play his little Trojan horse in this house. Well, let me tell you something, young lady. I've had enough of that, and I'll have no more. You're not playing both sides of the street, not from here on in, not when the stakes are this high. There's only one side, my side, see, and either you're on it or out you go. I'm giving you no choice, and I think I'm being damn sporting and fair about it. I'll put it another way. You want a place to eat and live—and you'll never find a better one—you want to stay among your relatives, and, as you say, you want to be near Jerry? you want that? Okay, then from now on you do as I tell you. And what I'm telling you is—no more Mike Barrett. If you see that shyster again, even once, you're kaput, fired, out on your ass. Right now, from this moment on, I'm ordering you not to see him. If you go out to see him, sister, you just stay out and don't bother to come back. Now, there you have it."

Maggie felt herself trembling. "You've no right to tell me what I can or can't do socially. I'm not in bondage. And I'm not a charity case. I work, I work hard for my pay, and I deserve time off and the freedom to spend that time as I wish. I'm not a chattel of yours, like your wife and son are. I'm me and I'm my own person. I can see any man I choose to see. If the man's name happens to be Mike Barrett, I'll see him. As a matter of fact, I intend to see him today."

"I don't give a damn what you intend. I've laid down the law that's going to be observed in my house. If you've got a date with Barrett, you'd better cancel it damn quick, and cancel him out of your life just as quick—if you want to stay on here. But if you're going out there to see Barrett today, you better pack your bags first. Now, Maggie girl, it's up to you. I want your answer right now. Are you going or are you staying?"

She wanted to spit in his face. She wanted to run from him. She wanted to be liberated from his oppression forever.

And she wanted Mike Barrett—if he still wanted her, after today.

But then her mind traveled upstairs, and on its way to her room and the packing, it paused outside Jerry's room.

The worst days for Jerry might be those immediately ahead. How could she abandon the boy to this monster right now? She teetered on the dilemma.

What was that old story that ended with the question mark?

"The Lady or the Tiger"?

Yes.

Now—which? And—what would happen then?

Nor until five-fifteen did Mike Barrett seriously begin to worry.

He had reached his office before five o'clock, but had expected no messages from Maggie Russell, and Donna had confirmed that there had been none. Nor had he expected Maggie to appear promptly at five, as they had agreed, because many women (especially the most feminine of them) are rarely on time, and he suspected Maggie was one of these.

He had tried to busy himself at his desk with the files on the remaining witnesses he and Abe had enlisted, but he knew they were a weak army, almost useless to the cause, and he gave them short shrift. He had then sought the file on Cassie McGraw, the savior, the miracle woman, the goddess Athena of the defense, and had tried to absorb himself in rereading what was known of her, in preparation for seeing her. Because now, with no more than two or three days of the trial left, it all came down to Cassie. Their final victory or defeat rode on Cassie. Yet he found himself unable to concentrate on her past either, because what interested him was Cassie in the present. He had kept looking up at his open door and toward the reception room, alerted by every footstep, every creak, waiting for a door that would open and bring Cassie McGraw, alive, to him in the person of Maggie Russell.

Five minutes, ten minutes, fifteen minutes. Lifetimes, eternities.

No Maggie.

And it was after she was fifteen minutes late, on the sixteenth minute, that he cast aside the folder containing Cassie past, and heaved himself to his feet to be ready for Cassie present.

Now he wandered about the room, emptying ashtrays, straightening pillows, picking up lint, bumping into furniture, listening to the hum of his electric desk clock. Twenty minutes, twenty-five, thirty minutes after the appointed time.

No Maggie.

He determined to calm himself with his pipe. He found his pipe in his jacket, and then the tobacco pouch, and filled the bowl and lit it. He was irritated to find the bowl heating up quickly because of the rate at which he was smoking. Nor was he just wandering about his office any more. By now he was pacing.

He was afraid to look at the time, but he did.

It was five minutes before six o'clock.

He stood at his high window and glumly watched the traffic, the beetle automobiles coming and going, the tiny figurines in the streets coming and going, but nowhere Maggie Russell.

He tried to conjure up reasons for her delay. There were so many possibilities. A misunderstanding about the time of their meeting. He was sure that she had said five o'clock. But maybe she had said six and in his head he had erroneously moved it up to five.

Or an accident. There were always car accidents in Los Angeles. There had been fifty-two thousand persons killed or injured in motor-vehicle accidents in this city during the last twelve months. She could have been in a smashup while driving the hellish freeway from downtown Los Angeles to the Pacific Palisades.

Or illness. She had looked fine in court this morning. But the flesh was heir to a million sicknesses, and she was run-down, and maybe she was in bed with a racking fever.

Or work. After all, she had a job, and there may have been some work that her Aunt Ethel had insisted she finish.

Or Jerry. He had been spared in court, but the mere fact of his forced appearance might have been too much for his palsied nervous system. Maybe he had fallen completely apart and Maggie, devoting herself to helping him, was heedless of the time.

Yet if it were any of these she would have called or have had someone call on her behalf. That is, unless she were unconscious or dead, which she surely wasn't. Yet the telephone had not rung once in the past hour.

He turned from the window and looked across the room in the direction of Abe Zelkin's office, and he wondered when Zelkin would be back, and what Zelkin would say if he found him still waiting this way.

This way. What way?

Their way. He had to face it now, at twenty minutes past six. They, meaning Zelkin, Sanford, Kimura, had as much as predicted it would be this way—which meant their way. They had called the shot at noon. And here it was the last of daylight, when reality still remained and one could not yet escape into dreams.

Zelkin had said, "If the postcard exists." He had said, "What I trust is what is tangible." He had said, "You still believe?"

And now the cruel voice in his skull for the first time said, Abe, I don't know.

Someone had appeared in the doorway. He looked up quickly, and sagged with disappointment. It was Donna Novik, her coat on one arm.

"If there's nothing else, boss, I think I'll be getting home."

"Thanks, Donna. There's nothing—" But there was something, one last thing he must do. He must let Maggie know what she had done to him and what he thought of her. "I'll tell you what you can do for me before you go, if you don't mind."

"Anything, boss."

"You have Miss Russell's private number on your Rolodex, haven't you? I want you to call her, get her on the line, and then I'll take it and you can leave. One sec. If someone else answers— they won't, but if it should happen—don't mention our office or my name. Okay?"

"Got it."

Donna disappeared, and he took himself back to the window, staring absently into the darkening street. He prayed that Maggie had been in a minor accident or was mildly ill and that it was not the other, not the betrayal of the promise of what they might yet mean to each other.

He could hear Donna's muffled voice on the telephone in the reception room.

He moved to his own desk phone, waiting to pick up the receiver. His hand hovered over the lighted key as he waited for the buzz, but suddenly the light blinked out and there had been no buzz.

Confused, he started for his open door, but Donna was already coming in with a message written on a sheet from her memo pad.

"What happened?" he demanded.

"Well, I dialed Miss Russell's number, and the phone rang and rang and rang, and I was about to give up when some man answered."

"An older man or a kid?"

"It was Frank Griffith."

"Dammit."

"I said that I'd like to speak to Miss Russell. He said—" she consulted her memo page—"just this, 'Miss Russell is not with us any more. She left this afternoon for New York. She'll be making her home there.' I started to ask for her forwarding address, but he just hung up. Should I try again and ask him if she—?"

"No," he said, almost inaudibly. "No, that won't be necessary. Thanks, Donna. You'd better go now."

"See you tomorrow, boss."

"Yeah, tomorrow."

He was alone and he felt empty and cold.

He stood there, unmoving, unable to move. There was no place to go now.

After a while, he gave a little shudder and dragged the hollow man that was all that was left of him into the lounge, and absently he filled a glass with ice and poured two jiggers of Scotch over the ice. He drank slowly, bitterly, toasting the Cassie McGraw who-never-was and Maggie Russell who had restored his faith in the faithlessness of women.

He put down the glass of cubes, worked his suit coat off the hanger and pulled it on, and left his office to find some dark place where all failures huddle to anesthetize their brains with booze against their yesterdays and tomorrows.

Pausing at the door as he left the reception room, he reached to turn off the lights. That instant, the telephone on Donna's desk rang out, and the light stayed on. The telephone rang again, and his heart leaped for it, and he followed in two quick strides.

He snatched up the receiver. "Hello?"

"Mike, it's I."

It was Maggie.

"What the hell, Maggie—where are you?"

"I'm in a telephone booth at the Texaco station a block down from the house. I couldn't call you before."

"Your uncle said you'd left his—"

"You talked to him?"

"My secretary did."

"Yes, I left. We had it out, and I left."

"The evidence—the postcard from Cassie McGraw—have you got it?" He heard his heart, and he waited.

"Mike, let me—"

"Have you got it?" he demanded.

"No."

"No?"

"Listen, I'll explain later. Please come here. I need your help. I can't stay in this booth any longer. I'll tell you everything when you get here. I'll be outside the gas station. Will you come, Mike?"

"I don't know," he said.

And then he hung up.

BUT A half hour later he was on Sunset Boulevard, and in Pacific Palisades, and he could see her out on the sidewalk beside the Texaco station. Her back was to him and she was shading her eyes from the glare of the overhead lights as she looked up the street toward the slope on which the Griffith house perched.

He had not known what was impelling him to come to her when he left the office.

Seeing her now, under the street light, her hair and slight sheath dress whipped by the wind, he knew. He was here because he was in love, and he had to know why she had betrayed that love. He was here because anyone in love is a fool, and he was the biggest fool of all. He was here because there was nowhere else for him to go, as an attorney or as a man. This was the end of the line.

He swung into the gas station, rolled up alongside the pumps, stepped out and told the service-station attendant to fill the tank.

He started for Maggie, and he was almost upon her when she saw him.

She stood there, lips trembling, and then her fist went to her mouth, and he thought that she was going to cry.

"Oh, Mike," she gasped, "I didn't think you were going to come." Then she was against him, arms around him, her head on his chest. "You don't know how much I wanted you here. Thank God you've come."

He pushed her from him and clutched her shoulders so tightly that she winced. "What's going on with you?" he demanded. "Why did you stand me up?"

"Don't be angry with me, Mike. It's not my fault. I didn't want to stand you up. It's just that everything went wrong. You have no idea what's gone on in that horrible house the last couple of hours, between Frank Griffith and me. I couldn't take the time to explain on the phone, because I didn't want to take my eyes off the house, and I couldn't see the driveway from the phone booth. I could see it only from here, and I had to watch so I'd know if there's a chance."

"Maggie, for Chrissakes, you're speaking gibberish. Now, once and for all, will you tell me what happened? Where's Cassie's address?"

"I haven't got it," she said with despair. "Let me explain—"

"Explain, then."

She looked past him, up the hill, and then she said quickly, "I didn't double-cross you, if that's what you're thinking. I made some stops after leaving the courtroom—I was so proud of what you did, Mike—but when I got home Uncle Frank was there. He's usually not through with work that early. But he'd been out of town, and when he got back he decided to come directly home. He was in his study, on the phone, and I couldn't get to his desk. That's where the postcard is—I told you, didn't I?—in the bottom drawer of his desk, hidden beneath the drawer lining and a batch of correspondence I was supposed to answer. So I changed clothes, stalling until he left the room, and when I came down to see if he'd gone he was just coming out of the study. Well, he was high over the way it had gone in court this morning, about your waiving the defense's cross-examination of Jerry—"

"I'll bet he was," said Barrett bitterly.

"But then I still couldn't get into his study, because he wanted to talk to me, to hear my version of what had gone on in court. Anyway, one thing led to another, and the way he started to speak of Jerry and—and of you—I just couldn't hold myself in any more, and I guess I exploded, let him have the whole truth. Well, not all, not about our trade, the deal we made, but the truth about how you had acted as you did at least partially for me, and how he didn't understand his son's condition, and how Jerry had twice attempted suicide—"

525

"What did he say?"

"He didn't believe it. He said it was stuff you were inventing to brainwash me so I'd work to keep Jerry from appearing in court as a witness against you. We had an awful fight, Mike, absolutely dreadful. Then he gave me an ultimatum. If I wanted to stay in his house, work for him, be around Jerry, then I had to vow never to see you again. He was adamant. I must never see you again, not even once, not even today. If I insisted on seeing you, he said, then I had to pack up right then and get out. I didn't know what to do. It was either leave Jerry to his father's mercy or—or give you up. I wasn't concerned about Cassie's postcard at that moment, Mike. If I chose to stay on there, on Uncle Frank's terms, I could have got to the postcard and dropped it off for you somewhere—at least I think I could have done that before the trial ends. But—but that wasn't it finally. I couldn't—I don't know how to say this, Mike—I couldn't bear not seeing you again."

He was deeply moved. It was that rare moment when feelings transcend words. He reached for her and brought her close to him, loving her warmness and softness, and returning her love. "I'm glad," he whispered. "I feel the same way, Maggie."

For seconds she remained blissfully in his embrace, but suddenly her eyes opened and she said, "I almost forgot, Mike. About Cassie McGraw, I mean. Your whole case depends on that, doesn't it?"

"Yes."

She came out of his arms. "Mike, I'm afraid I've made a real mess of everything. Because when I made my decision, when I told Uncle Frank I was going to see you tonight, then he got more vicious than ever. He told me to get out of the house as fast as possible and never show my face there again. He told me to pack what I needed for now and he'd send the rest when I had an address. Pack and get out, that was the order. But the worst thing was, he wouldn't leave me alone for even a minute. I tried to stall, said I wanted to get some personal things from the desk, but he wouldn't allow me to touch it. He told me to pack and beat it. And then he followed me upstairs, and stood in my doorway while I took some things out of the closet and emptied my bureau and threw everything into a couple of suitcases. And then he followed me downstairs, made me give him my key, and waited until I was outside in the front drive before he slammed the door. So I lugged my things down here—they're over there by the water cooler—"

"And Cassie McGraw's postcard is still in Griffith's desk?"

"I'm sorry—yes. I'm really miserable about that. And when I got down here, I didn't call you right away because from the sidewalk I could just see Uncle Frank's driveway, and I figured I'd watch, on the chance that he'd be going out. The moment he left, I planned to rush back and steal the postcard."

"Maggie, you've got to get back in that house this evening. Do you have a way? You said you had to give up your key, didn't you?"

She had opened her purse. "The front-door key, yes." She rummaged inside her purse and then held up a dull-finished metal key. "But not the one to the rear service porch. He overlooked that. This would get me inside. But how can I use it as long as Uncle Frank is in there?"

"You can't. So our job is to get him out of there."

"How?"

Barrett was thinking. Suddenly he smiled. "I've got it. Maybe it'll work. It's worth a try. Anything goes now. Is Luther Yerkes in town?"

"Yes. He phoned Uncle Frank earlier, just before our fight."

"Where does Yerkes live?"

"Everywhere. Recently he's been staying at his Bel-Air house."

"Does he have a personal secretary living there?"

"Yes. I've often taken calls. She comes on first—"

"A she? Good, we'll try it." He had taken Maggie's arm and started her toward the gas-station office.

"Try what, Mike?"

He pointed ahead. "See that redheaded girl sitting inside reading a magazine? You're looking at Yerkes' secretary."

They entered the gas-station office, and the freckled redhead, chewing bubble gum as she flipped the pages of a movie fan magazine, greeted them with a bubble.

"Do you work here?" inquired Barrett.

The girl looked startled. "No, I'm waiting for Mac—my boy friend. He's the mechanic."

Barrett had reached into his pocket for his wallet. "How'd you like to make an easy fiver?"

The redhead's eyes went from Barrett to Maggie and back to Barrett. "For doing what?" she asked warily.

"For making a phone call. We'll give you a number. When someone answers, you simply say you'd like to speak to Mr. Griffith, Mr. Frank Griffith, and if he's the one who answers, or when he gets on the line, you say, 'This is Mr. Luther Yerkes' secretary. He's asked me to call you and tell you something urgent has just come up. He wants you to meet him at his Bel-Air home immediately.' Don't answer any questions. Just see that he's understood the message and then hang up."

The girl stopped chewing her gum. "That's all—for five dollars?"

"That's all."

He held out the five-dollar bill, and she started to reach for it, then hesitated. "This is nothing illegal, is it?"

"Perfectly aboveboard," Barrett assured her winningly. "We're merely playing a joke on a friend."

She took the bill. "Okay. Let me get a pencil and paper, and tell me again what I have to say so I get it right."

She searched through the office desk until she found a scratch pad and a pencil stub, and then Barrett dictated the message to her. When he was through, he asked Maggie to give her Griffith's telephone number. Maggie took the pencil and wrote the number down.

"Should I do it now?" the girl asked.

"Right now."

"Do you mind waiting outside? Otherwise I'll be self-conscious."

"We'll be outside," said Barrett.

When they had gone outside, he walked Maggie over to the gas pumps and then said, "You stay here, Maggie, and keep an eye on her. Make sure she puts through the call. I'll be loading your things into my car."

Leaving Maggie, he went to the water cooler, threw Maggie's garment bag across one arm, gripped a suitcase in each hand, and carried the load around to the back of his convertible. After he'd placed her luggage in the trunk and closed the lid, he saw Maggie beckoning him as the redhead emerged from the station office. He hastened toward them.

"How'd it go?" he asked.

"Just like you told me," she said. "I called. The man who answered said he was Mr. Griffith. I read off what you told me to say. He sounded worried, and he said, 'Thanks, tell Mr. Yerkes I'm on my way.'"

Barrett grinned. "Good girl—and good Samaritan."

Pleased, she smiled back at him, and then she blew a bubble and turned toward the station office and her magazine.

Maggie had taken Barrett's arm. "Mike, if this really works, he'll be coming down this street in a minute to take Sunset. We don't want him to see us."

"Right." He started her for his car.

At the door, she pulled back. "He might recognize me if he sees me sitting here in the light."

"Okay. Go to the washroom until I honk you twice. I'll sit in the car and keep my eye on the rear-view mirror." She was leaving him, when he called out, "Hey, Maggie, what does he drive?"

"A Bentley. A blue S3 sports model. You can't miss it."

As Barrett settled into the front seat, he watched Maggie disappear into the ladies' room, and then he fixed his sight on his rear-view mirror. Briefly an old Buick filled the mirror, and then was gone. After that, for perhaps a full minute, there was nothing to be seen at the street intersection behind him except the traffic light changing again. Then, all at once, the gleaming grill and the majestic B of the sleek blue Bentley slid across his rear-view mirror. As it slowed to turn left on Sunset, Barrett came quickly around in his seat, in time to catch a glimpse of Frank Griffith's grim profile. Then there was the back of Griffith's head, and then the Bentley continued away, going east on Sunset Boulevard, until it had receded from view.

Barrett hit his horn twice. Maggie and the service-station attendant appeared almost simultaneously. While Barrett signed the charge slip, Maggie clambered into the seat beside him.

She looked at him inquiringly.

He felt triumphant and showed his elation. "Scratch one blue Bentley," he said. "We're home free. Now let's rescue Cassie McGraw."

Some new concern crossed Maggie's face. "Mike, I think we'd better hurry. We told Uncle Frank to go to Luther Yerkes' Bel-Air house, didn't we?"

"Yes. Why?"

"Darn it, we should have made it his Malibu house. Bel-Air's practically around the corner from here. Yerkes has his place on Stone Canyon Road. That's the nearest part of Bel-Air, just past UCLA. Uncle Frank will be there in ten or twelve minutes at the most. The second he gets there, he'll know he's been had. I'll bet he makes it back here in eight minutes flat. That gives us less than twenty minutes."

Barrett had already started his car. "Okay, you get in there and out of there in ten minutes. Think you can do it?"

"Unless something goes wrong. Please hurry, Mike."

Barrett made a right-hand circle around the station lot and then drove out of it and swung north up the long block leading to the Griffith residence. The entrance lights were on, but only a side section of the house was visible from the driveway. The rest of the residence was hidden behind hedges and trees.

As he neared the driveway Barrett said, "You've got the key to the back service porch?"

"Yes."

"Then you get out here." He had slowed the convertible in front of the driveway and applied the brakes. "I'll back up along the hedge. That way I'll be able to spot you when you come out from the side yard, and at the same time I'll be able to keep an eye on the street we just took up here. I'll watch for Griffith when he comes up from Sunset."

She opened the door and stepped out. "How much time have we got left, Mike?"

He peered at the dial of his wristwatch. "To play it safe, give yourself nine minutes, ten at the most. Now move. Good luck."

He saw her hasten up the driveway and cut left across the lawn to the walk leading around the house toward the service porch. When he could no longer see her, he shifted into reverse and backed slowly away from the driveway and against the curbing beneath the hedges. He switched off the ignition and turned off his lights.

It should be easy, he thought. In short minutes he would have what he wanted and could restore to Zelkin and Sanford their faith in the word "trust" and in his own judgment, and he would have his lead to the witness who might save the crumbling defense and *The Seven Minutes.*

With his left arm propped up on the steering wheel so he could constantly check the time, Barrett took his eyes at short intervals from the watch in order to look down the street toward Sunset, then he looked at the watch again, then the street again.

Maggie had been gone six minutes.

Soon, eight minutes.

Now, surprisingly, a full ten minutes had passed, and still there was no sign of her, and now each fleeting minute seemed to be composed of only six seconds, not sixty seconds.

Around and around his dial the second hand raced.

Now thirteen minutes . . . fourteen . . . fifteen.

Mike Barrett blinked and he realized that a set of powerful headlights was rising up the street from Sunset Boulevard far below. He could feel the perspiration on his brow. God, if it was Griffith . . .

It *was* Griffith.

In its ascent the car traveling up from Sunset Boulevard had passed beneath a bright street lamp, and the silver of its grill and the rich blueness of its bonnet announced it as the Bentley. It was coming up faster now, faster and faster.

He acted instinctively. No conscious thought sparked his act. On with the ignition. Foot pumping the starter. Hand releasing the emergency brake. Foot clamping down on the gas pedal.

Just as the blue Bentley loomed in full view, heading for the driveway, Barrett's convertible plunged straight into its path, blocking its access to the driveway.

Barrett clutched the steering wheel, waiting for the impact of steel against steel, but instead there was the rubbery screeching of tires, then brakes, as Griffith wrenched his Bentley aside to avoid the crash. The squalling and slithering of tires on pavement, the other car's, Barrett's own car's, and then, finally, came the grazing of metal upon metal.

Both cars had shuddered to a rest in the street in front of the driveway. Griffith's car was almost parallel to Barrett's, but ahead of his own, its right side against his left fender.

The driver's door of the Bentley was flung open, and a large, husky man was bulling out of the car and charging toward him. It was Frank Griffith, and his face was red with rage.

"What kind of idiot driving is that?" he bellowed, as he advanced. "You could have killed us both! What in the hell kind of driving is that? Don't you look to your left at a cross street?"

"I'm sorry," said Barrett, summoning up his most contrite expression. "I guess I had my mind on something else. It's entirely my fault. I really am sorry. Are you all right?"

"Guys like you ought to be put away," growled Griffith. "Sure I'm all right. Lucky for you. But I don't know what in the hell you've done to my car. Back up, will you, and let me see. And don't you take off."

Good, thought Barrett. Eat up time. Stall. Don't let him trap Maggie inside the house.

He fumbled with the ignition key, starting the car several times, deliberately letting it choke each time.

"Goddammit!" roared Griffith. "Will you back up or won't you?"

At last Barrett had the motor going. He set the gear in reverse and backed up a few yards. At last he got out of the car, and strolled toward Griffith, who was standing wide-legged, belligerent, his meaty fists on his hips, waiting for him. Barrett noticed the dent in his own fender.

"Look what you did to my car," said Griffith.

What he had done, Barrett could see, was scrape a strip of blue paint off the Bentley's passenger door and a portion of its fender.

"This is going to take a whole new paint job to make it match," grumbled Griffith. "This is going to cost your insurance people at least eight hundred bucks. You've got insurance, haven't you?"

"Yes, I have."

Griffith had taken a pen and a small address book out of his jacket pocket. "You'd better find your insurance card while I'm taking down your license."

As Griffith went to make a note of the license number, Barrett sought the insurance company's card in his wallet, and he wondered about Maggie and silently prayed for her.

He found the card as Frank Griffith returned to him. Just as Griffith snatched the card from him, Barrett remembered that his name, address, and telephone number had been typed on the card.

He held his breath.

Griffith was copying down the name of the insurance company and its address. Now his eyes had come to the name of the policy holder. For a moment, he stood motionless, and then he lifted his massive head and stared at Barrett. His hands stuffed address book, pen, insurance card into his pockets, and when they came out again they were knotted. He stepped closer, and automatically Barrett retreated, until he was pinned against the Bentley. Never in Barrett's life had he seen such hatred in another's face.

"I should have recognized you, you sonofabitch," Griffith was saying. "What in the hell are you doing here?"

"It's a free country," Barrett said inanely.

"A free country, eh? Not for the likes of you, it isn't. What were you hanging around here for—to spy on me and my son?"

"I have no further interest in you or your son."

"I'm not so sure. You showed you had no balls this morning in court. Now maybe you're trying to find something to make up for it."

Barrett had raised his left arm slightly. He waited for Griffith to swing at him.

Griffith emitted a snarl. "I'd like to clobber you, but I'm not giving you any more publicity. You're not suckering me into that. But I'll tell you what I am doing. I'm putting you on warning. You beat it, see. You get your ass out of here as fast as you can. Me, I'm going inside. But I'm coming out in five minutes. If you're still here snooping around, I'll beat you up, and then I'll turn you over to the cops for prowling. You hear me?"

With that, he spun away from Barrett, stomped around his car, and got behind the wheel. Barrett flashed a glance at the house. No Maggie. He stepped into his convertible and backed off farther and waited, engine idling. Griffith's Bentley shot into the driveway. Barrett closed his eyes, offered another prayer for Maggie, then opened them and eased his car forward for a better view.

He could see Griffith striding out of the carport. He could see Griffith opening the front door. Then he could see Griffith no more.

Poor Maggie.

There was nothing to do. It was too late.

And then, beyond the driveway lights, he saw a movement. Someone was hurrying along the side of the house, and suddenly the figure of a woman broke into the open, darted across the lawn and onto the driveway, and it was Maggie.

She was beside the car door, and she was breathless. "Oh, God, I was scared."

"Get in," he ordered her.

She was in the car, beside him. "I got into the house okay, Mike, but then I had to hide from some practical nurse they've just hired to replace me. She was bringing Aunt Ethel downstairs. Then finally I was able to sneak into the study. But as I was coming out, Aunt Ethel spotted me. She knew I'd been fired, and I had to tell her I'd come back to get some personal belongings I'd forgotten. Then she wanted to talk—she went on and on about how I shouldn't have fought with her husband, and how sorry she was that she couldn't make him change his mind about me. Time was going, and I was dying. Then I heard the noise outside, your cars colliding, and I told her I'd better see what had happened. I rushed out the back way and circled the house, and there you were with Uncle Frank. So I ducked behind the house again. When I heard him drive in, I crept along the side yard, and when I heard the front door close I made my dash. Whew. And here I am."

Barrett had wheeled his convertible and was speeding down the hill. When they neared the gasoline station, he pulled up beside the curb and parked.

He held out one hand. "Have you got it, Maggie?"

She smiled, and pulled a postcard out of her purse, and laid it daintily in his outstretched palm. "Here it is. The keys to the kingdom."

He studied the glossy color reproduction of the Sunnyside Convalescent Sanitarium on the front. He turned it over. To the right was Frank Griffith's name and address. To the left, the space for a message was filled to the last millimeter with crowded sentence after sentence of antlike words written painstakingly in a pinched hand. Only the signature was easily legible. The signature read "Cassie McGraw."

"The message and the signature are in different hands," said Barrett. "Let's see if the signature is for real."

From his inside pocket he removed the photostats he had had made at Parktown College. He unfolded them. He took the one that bore Cassie's signature as it appeared on the back of the old photograph of O'Flanagan, Jadway, and Cassie in Paris, and he set it alongside Cassie's alleged recent signature on the postcard.

"Well?" Maggie asked him.

"The early one is firm, and this one is as wavering as a cardiogram, but both have the same heavy flat-topped r's, the same sort of arrow-like dotting of the *i*'s, the same distinctive downstroke, the same—" He looked up and smiled. "Yes, the signatures are by the same person. We've found Cassie McGraw."

"Thank God."

"And thank you." He started the car once more. "Where should I take you?"

"I was hoping you'd take me home."

"Home?"

"With you."

He was about to release the brakes. "I've got only one bed, Maggie, one double bed."

"Double means for two, doesn't it?"

He covered her hands resting in her lap with his own hand. "Did I tell you I love you?"

"Why don't you tell me later tonight?"

"I should leave for Chicago later tonight."

Maggie was close to him now, and her lips were parted, and they kissed, tongues touching. Then she whispered, "Can't Cassie wait until tomorrow?"

Barrett released her. "She'll wait until tomorrow." And then he released the brakes, and they were free and they were moving.

X

CHICAGO was not what came between Los Angeles and New York, he decided. It was distinctive.

So many unfriendly eyes had seen it as unbeautiful. Chicago was Carl Sandburg's "Hog-butcher for the world" and Arnold Bennett's "suburb of Warsaw" and Rudyard Kipling's place of "dirt" and "savages." To others who knew it better, Chicago was also the Chicago *Tribune* and Vachel Lindsay, the Everleigh Sisters and Jane Addams, Al Capone and Edgar Lee Masters, Samuel Insull and Marshall Field. To others, Chicago was the Loop, the El, the University, the Illinois Central, and it was Sears, Roebuck, and Lincoln Park, and Lake Shore Drive, and Cook County, the Windy City, squalid, attractive, dreary, invigorating, the city you always left when you were very young and that somehow remained in your bones.

Yes, it was all things good and bad, like many cities and most men, but one thing it was not, Mike Barrett decided as he observed it from his taxicab window. It was not where you would expect to find Miss Cassie McGraw, onetime resident of Montparnasse and Paris, France.

But here she was and here he was, and in minutes they would be confronting each other. And this city of his birth, known to him only as a dim nostalgia for his youth, was suddenly beautiful to his eyes.

It had been daybreak when he had gone from his apartment and Maggie, and taken off from Los Angeles, and now it was early Tuesday afternoon in Chicago. In the sky, the uncertain sun had argued briefly with a horde of bellicose clouds and lost, and the day was gray and gusty and challenging. He had already traveled most of the distance between the Ambassador East Hotel and the Sunnyside Convalescent Sanitarium, which was located on the edge of Chicago's North Side, and he felt alive and expectant.

Rolling up the taxicab window, he shut the city from his mind, with somewhat more difficulty asked Maggie to wait for any further mental attentiveness (knowing she'd understand), tried not to think of Abe Zelkin's fruitless task in court today, and finally offered all of his concentration to the impending meeting with Cassie McGraw.

Almost automatically, as if it were a permanent habit by now, he brought the postcard out of his pocket and reread the ant-words addressed to Frank Griffith:

> Saw in paper here where I live & read about yr son & trial & yr attack on The Seven Minutes & blaming the author. I was Mr. Jadway's friend. I inspired book. I swear on life of our daughter Judith—who now serves Lord as nun, as her father once served human freedom—that Mr. Jadway wrote book as artist, out of love & desire to liberate young of tomorrow. Book could not harm yr son, could improve & save him in future. Leroux & others don't know truth. Believe me. Be charitable.
>
> Yrs truly,
> CASSIE McGRAW

I believe you, Cassie, he wanted to say and would say, whatever your truth. But will you believe me that the dead past must no longer continue dead and buried? Will you have the courage to shed anonymity, risk scandal, and come forth to save the living?

Will you help us, Cassie?

They had halted, and the cabbie had stopped the meter and twisted around to announce the fare.

While groping for his wallet, Mike Barrett bent his head and peered through the window. Convalescent hospitals were not unfamiliar to him. His mother, in her last years, had vegetated in three different ones in the East. What he saw now merely confirmed what he had known, that they all possessed the same façade, a one-storied, low-slung, whitewashed, locked-in look—except that this one was more stylish and expensive than the average, and there were brilliant potted geraniums on either side of the high glass doors.

Barrett paid the cabbie and tipped him, then stepped quickly out of the taxi, strode up the short cement walk, and entered the Sunnyside Convalescent Sanitarium.

Summoning up memories of the sanitariums of his past, he had prepared himself for the inevitable faint odor that was a combination of urine and detergents. To his surprise and pleasure, what assailed him instead was the smell of lilacs. He had come up a carpeted ramp to the broad main corridor, and ahead of him the glass doors to the enclosed patio showed that the patio was rimmed with boxes of flowers in full bloom, and in the middle of this profusion was a cluster of metal tables sprouting brightly colored umbrellas. Except for one elderly gentleman wearing a hat, a bulky sweater, and baggy slacks and nodding in a chair, the patio was unoccupied.

From a reception desk to the left of the patio doors, a well-groomed, well-bloused, chubby female receptionist was watching him curiously.

Mike Barrett went over to her, introduced himself, and explained that he had just flown in from Los Angeles and was here to see the manager of the sanitarium. Minutes later, after inquiries on the public-address system, after being guided past the physiotherapy room, the vast recreation room with its droning television sets, the hanging cork bulletin board, he was inside the the manager's claustrophobic office and seated across from a Mr. Holliday.

The manager resembled a clean-shaven Christ had the Saviour once been an accountant. His set smile was gracious but harried, a smile reserved for those callers who had not made appointments yet might be relatives of potential patients. He fingered his Rotary Club button as he spoke.

"All the way from Los Angeles," he was saying, "to see me? Or do I misunderstand? Do you have someone here with us?"

"I wanted to see you as well as someone you have living here."

"Los Angeles. I was there once about five years ago for a convention," said Mr. Holliday, reminiscing fondly, and Barrett knew that he had been there without his wife. "Didn't have time to see much, except Disneyland and Knott's Berry Farm. Great sanitarium city. SRO all over the place."

"I guess I never thought of it that way," said Barrett with a smile.

"Well, now—" Mr. Holliday moved the adding machine slightly

538

on his desk and emptied an ashtray into the wastebasket. "Well, Mr. Barrett, what can I do for you?"

"I want to see one of your patients—or, for that matter, one of your employees. I don't know which she is."

Mr. Holliday had taken up a pencil. "Her name?"

"Cassie McGraw."

The manager wrinkled his forehead. "Caucasian?"

"Yes."

"Except for two head nurses, all of our help is colored. So that would rule them out. So that means a patient, except the name doesn't ring a bell." He reached up and unhooked a clip of papers from the wall beside his desk. "McGraw, you said? Let me see." He flipped over the first pages, then with his pencil went down the pages of *M*'s. "We've got more than one hundred patients in the san right now, but I'm sorry, no McGraw's, no one with a name remotely resembling McGraw. Perhaps the person you are referring to was someone who was here previously and isn't with us any longer. There's a constant turnover in these sanitariums, you know. The result of paranoia and guilts. Old people are brought in, and they resent it and resist what they feel is abandonment and confinement, and they fancy every kind of persecution. When visitors, usually relatives, come once or twice a week, they hear continual grievances and complaints against the administration. The relatives have built-in guilts to start with, so they are conditioned to believe what they hear. Sooner or later they move their mothers or fathers to another sanitarium, and when the same complaints occur again and then again, two or three times, they finally get the message. It's not us. It's the old-age syndrome. So likely your Cassie McGraw was here once—"

"Mr. Holliday, she was here two and a half weeks ago."

"Really? Well, let's see our checkouts in the last month." He opened one desk drawer, then another, until he found the right batch of papers. He went down the top page slowly, frowned, and returned the papers to the drawer. "No one by that name was here two and a half weeks ago or at any time in the past month. I'm sorry, Mr. Barrett. Perhaps you have the wrong sanitarium."

Barrett took the postcard, as well as the photostats from Parktown College, out of his pocket. He handed the postcard to the manager. "Is that yours?"

Mr. Holliday glanced at the photograph on the front of the

card. "That's us. We supply these to our patients as a convenience, and also hand them out to visitors as advertisements."

"Turn it over." As the manager did so, Barrett added, "Cassie McGraw signed one of your postcards—it is definitely her signature—and she clearly states that she's living here in your sanitarium."

"This isn't easy to read," muttered Mr. Holliday as he read. "Yes, it appears she is a patient—"

"Of course, the message is written in someone else's hand, but the signature is her own. Can you explain that?"

The manager glanced up. "Yes. That's not the least bit unusual. Most of our elderly patients are arthritic or have unsteady hands, so they'll ask a visitor to write. Actually, different organizations send volunteers around every few weeks, also, to assist our senior citizens in this sort of thing, writing for them, reading aloud to them, entertaining, so this was probably dictated to some visitor and then signed by the patient herself."

"Are most of the volunteers from one particular organization, so that I might—?"

"No hope of tracing the person who did this. There are dozens of philanthropic organizations, hundreds of volunteers."

"But on the date that was written?"

"Well, I see your point. Yes, I'll check the head nurse on that." He resumed reading the postcard message, and at the end he sought some elusive recollection, and all at once his head came up fast. "Jadway," he said. "It struck a chord, but now I remember. It's in the papers all the time. That censorship trial."

"I'm the attorney for the defendant," said Barrett.

Mr. Holliday was suddenly respectful and eager. "We-ll," said Mr. Holliday, "why didn't you say so in the first place? We don't get celebrities here every day. Of course I'll do anything in my power to help you." He waved the postcard. "Has this got anything to do with your trial?"

"Everything," said Barrett.

Immediately he launched into an explanation of Cassie McGraw's background, her relationship with J J Jadway, and her importance to the defense's case.

Mr. Holliday was as deeply attentive to Barrett's words as he might have been to a legal drama being enacted on television.

540

When Barrett was through, the manager said, "She was something, wasn't she? But I'm afraid we've never had anyone that colorful in a place like this."

"Why not? Elderly people who are alone, no matter how colorful or famous or infamous they were in their early years, have to wind up somewhere. Cassie must be in her sixties by now. She may be infirm. There is evidence that she has no one to take care of her. So why shouldn't she be here?"

"Now, wouldn't that be something?" said Mr. Holliday with a note of reverence in his voice. "Let me recheck our lists of current patients and recent patients. I'll go through them like I'm after the Mother Lode."

Five minutes later he had again failed to find Cassie's name or any name resembling McGraw in his lists.

"Nothing?" said Barrett.

"Nothing. The only remaining possibility would be that she is registered here under her maiden name."

"McGraw is her maiden name," said Barrett. "But she was married once, briefly, after Jadway's death."

"Well, that may be it, then. What was her married name?"

"I don't know," said Barrett wretchedly. "What about her first name, Mr. Holliday? Do you have any Cassies among your female patients, no matter what their family names?"

"I'll look again." The manager's eyes followed his finger down the given names, and at the last they registered disappointment. "No Cassies either," he said.

"Let's try another approach," said Barrett. He handed the manager one of the photostats. "Here is a sample of Cassie's handwriting and signature in the 1930s. And you have the postcard with her signature as it is today. You can see they are not exactly alike, but similar enough. Do you have any means of comparing these two signatures with the signatures of your patients? After all, in a way, a signature is like a fingerprint."

Mr. Holliday made a negative gesture. "Not here it isn't. Few patients sign their own names any more, and if they did, their writing might vary completely from one day to the next. We have no file of patients' signatures. The relatives who put them in here usually do the signing. As for going around this afternoon trying to collect every old lady's autograph, I couldn't. It would be an

541

embarrassment to those of our patients who have trouble writing, and some would resist. Oh, maybe if you gave me a few weeks . . ."

"I haven't got a few weeks, Mr. Holliday, only a few days. Okay, so much for that idea. Could you have a nurse go around and show these signatures to each female patient? I don't want to disrupt your operation, but this is so—"

"I'll tell you what," said Mr. Holliday. "I'll do it myself." He stood up. "I'll do more—I'll show each patient these signatures and ask if she recognizes them, and I'll ask each one if she is familiar with the name Cassie McGraw. A few may be napping, but I'll wake them. I'll cover them individually, if you don't mind waiting maybe a half hour or so."

"Mind? I can't tell you how much I appreciate this. I wish there was some way to repay you."

Mr. Holliday had gone to the door. "There is. If I find Cassie McGraw for you, you just send me a copy of *The Seven Minutes* with your autograph in it."

Barrett rose. "If you find her, I'll be able to send you ten copies. Otherwise I'm afraid there'll be no copies at all, anywhere."

"You can keep yourself busy with television in the recreation room, if you like."

"I think I'll take a walk. I'll be back here in a half hour."

"Make it closer to three quarters of an hour."

After the manager had departed, Barrett sat himself down, smoked his pipe, and brooded. Frustration had become an almost physical ache. Considering all that Maggie and he had gone through to bring him here, realizing how much Zelkin and he had at stake in this quest, it was maddening to be this close to Cassie and still be as far away as he had been a week or a month ago.

The door behind him opened, and he jumped to his feet.

It was Mr. Holliday, poking his head into the office. "Wondered if you were still here. Just checked with my head R.N. about the volunteer organization that was here two and a half weeks ago. Worse luck. It was a band of senior citizens, hale and hearty ones, taking a bus vacation across the country and stopping off at sanitariums along the route to cheer up and lend encouragement to their less fortunate fellows and then going on their way again. They were here about three or four hours that afternoon. No record of the name of their group or where they're from. Sorry. Now I'll get going on questioning my patients."

542

Discouraged, but clinging to some invisible long-shot ticket, Barrett finally left the manager's office. The sanitarium corridor was busier now. Several old ladies were inching along with the support of rolling walkers. Two were in wheelchairs. One was making slow progress along the wall by grasping the railing there. In the patio, blurred sunlight could be seen at last, as well as a half-dozen women in shawls and bathrobes, and a scattering of elderly men with canes.

Once more Barrett was overwhelmed by a feeling of frustration. One of these women, or one woman lying in one of the bedrooms or wards beyond, must be Cassie McGraw.

But which?

Unless she had determined to hide herself from the world, surely she would admit her identity to the manager when he spoke her name and exhibited her autographs. This was a hope. He carried it out the exit with him and into the Chicago afternoon.

He walked and walked—how many blocks he did not know—until he reached a shopping district and saw the time, and then he did an about-face and started to retrace his steps to the Sunnyside Convalescent Sanitarium on the double.

When he returned, he had been away fifty-five minutes, and Mr. Holliday was waiting for him outside his office.

"It's pretty much as I had expected it would be, Mr. Barrett," he said. "No recognition of the name Cassie McGraw whatsoever. Not even the slightest hint of recognition. Either because none of them is Miss McGraw or because the real Miss McGraw doesn't want to acknowledge it. I'm afraid that's it, Mr. Barrett. I don't know what else I can suggest. I guess we've got to add her name to the roll call of the vanished. Charlie Ross, Ambrose Bierce, Judge Crater, now Cassie McGraw."

"I'm afraid you're right, only I hate to admit it," said Barrett.

As he retrieved the postcard and the photostat and began to shove them into his pocket, he felt the other photostats. He extracted them, considered one, then handed it to Mr. Holliday. "I didn't show you this, did I? That's taken from an old photograph, Cassie in Paris in the 1930s. Would there be any point in circulating that among the patients?"

"Hardly. If they wouldn't admit to the name or identify the autograph, they'd hardly respond to this."

"What about your personnel here? Maybe one of the staff might see something in that face that would remind them of one of the patients?"

"Most unlikely, Mr. Barrett. This is a picture of a girl in her twenties. I doubt if anyone would find the remotest resemblance between this girl and a patient who is in her sixties or seventies."

There was nothing left to say, except one thing, the forever final act of desperation. "I'd like to offer a reward, Mr. Holliday." He still had the postcard, and he pushed it into the manager's hand. "Would you mind showing the postcard and photograph to your nurses, and telling them that if either exhibit sparks something it's worth a hundred dollars to anyone if they'll call me at the Ambassador East by early evening."

"We-ll, I don't know. Most of the nurses on this shift have already seen the postcard, and the old photo won't mean a thing. I think it's useless—"

"Just on the off chance, Mr. Holliday."

"I assure you, I want to be of assistance. It wouldn't be bad publicity for us if you did find Cassie McGraw here. But I don't think these two exhibits can produce anything further. Still, if it'll make you happy—well, we have another shift coming on at four o'clock. So I'll tell you what I'll do. I'll pin the postcard and the photo up on the bulletin board along with a notice instructing any employee who knows anything about the card, or who recognizes the girl in the photo, to get in touch with me, or if I'm not in, with you at the Ambassador East, and I'll make it clear that you're offering a hundred-dollar reward. How's that?"

"It's all I can ask."

"I won't be here when the new shift comes on at four. But I'll be looking in again around eight in the evening. So if I learn anything then that you haven't already heard, I'll get in touch with you myself. Though, frankly, Mr. Barrett, I think you'd better consider this a lost cause."

"I know." Barrett allowed the manager to accompany him down the ramp to the street door. At the door he paused. "I'll be at the hotel until eight, Mr. Holliday. If I don't hear from you by then, I'll go back to where I came from."

"Can't you win your case without Cassie McGraw?"

"No," said Barrett flatly, and with that he went out the door.

By FIVE-THIRTY in the afternoon, he had needed a drink, and he was having one at the darkened plush bar in the elevated alcove of the Pump Room of the Ambassador East.

He had spent a mean and wasted afternoon in his single room upstairs, the Chicago telephone directory in his lap, calling every major sanitarium and rest home in Cook County, monotonously inquiring over and over whether there was a patient on the premises named Cassie McGraw.

There was not, any place, anywhere.

It had been an illogical effort, based on no reason, and it had provided him with what he had expected—no information at all.

After that he had telephoned Donna in Los Angeles, so that she might report his failure to Abe Zelkin later, and to ask how Zelkin was faring with the day's defense witnesses. Zelkin had checked in once, briefly, during the noon recess, to inquire whether there had been any word from Barrett and to bemoan the fact that the defense witnesses were continuing to prove unimpressive and inept and were sitting ducks for Duncan's cannonading in the cross- and re-cross-examinations.

Hanging up, Barrett had felt so low that he was tempted to telephone his apartment, just to hear Maggie's voice, just for some kind of lift. But then the time was already well after four o'clock, and if he was going to bother to wait on here he should keep his phone open for any possible calls.

He had smoked a half pouch of tobacco, and throughout, the telephone remained mute.

And so, after leaving notice of his whereabouts with the switchboard, he had come down to the lobby to make reservations for the flight back to Los Angeles and then had moved on to the Pump Room bar to see whether it worked and whether there would be no pain.

He was drinking, and it wasn't working, and he was wondering whether a defeated and impoverished and unpromising middle-aged attorney had the right to ask a girl like Maggie Russell to spend her life with him. She was magnificent, he remembered, and he revived the pleasure of her company in his head, and the sweetness of her in his heart, and the heat of her in his loins, and he realized that last night had been the first time in all his years that he had ever experienced a complete and honest relationship with a woman who was totally female.

The period with Faye had not been a relationship. It had been one-sided. He had not been a man with a woman, but a stud who filled her with intimations of normality. The others before Faye had been little better, like two people dancing to no music.

For years he had felt a misfit, as if there wasn't anyone on earth with whom to connect. Constantly he had read of fantastically satisfying relationships in novels, and these had depressed him, because they had told him that he could not measure up to any woman, could not find a relationship that would be comparable to the love scenes he read about in books. Most of the novels had led him to believe that any relationship with a woman was largely dependent upon sex.

But now he knew those books were fakes and he had been deceived.

He had divined the truth of what was a genuine and what was a counterfeit man-woman relationship during his studies before the trial. Last night, in fact, he had experienced what was truth and what was real.

This trial had taught him exactly what was lying, deceptive, delusive about most written pornographic fiction, even the best of it. Silently he sipped his drink and thanked his mentors.

Thank you, Professor Ernest van den Haag, mentor one, for exposing the fiction of pornography: "Sex rages in an empty world as people use each other as its anonymous bearers or vessels, bereaved of love and hate, thought and feeling, reduced to bare sensations of pain and pleasure, existing only in (and for) incessant copulations without apprehension, conflict, or relationship."

Thank you, Jacques Barzun, mentor two: "The standardized sexual act for literary use" starts with a brief conversation, moves to a couch or bed, has a man undress a woman or the woman disrobe herself, gives attention to some physical detail of her body, and then devotes itself to copulation at military speed. "In most cases, the enterprise is successful, despite the lack of preliminaries, such as the works of theory deem imperative; in most cases no thought is given to consequences," and "in most cases there is no repetition of the act, or indeed any sort of artistic conclusion, unless the orgasm itself and a sketchy resumption of clothes are to be taken as such. . . . The modern sex act in print is only a fable, a device to correct this or that deficiency of our upbringing and culture."

546

Thank you, Professor Steven Marcus, mentor three: In "Porno-topia," which describes the pornographic utopia of books, the landscape world consists of "two immense snowy white hil-locks . . . Farther down, the scene narrows and changes in perspec-tive. Off to the right and left jut two smooth snowy ridges. Between them, at their point of juncture, is a dark wood . . . This dark wood—sometimes it is called a thicket—is triangular in shape. It is also like a cedarn cover, and in its midst is a dark ro-mantic chasm. In this chasm the wonders of nature abound . . . This is the center of the earth and the home of man." The nature of pornotopia "is this immense, supine, female form . . . As for the man in this setting, he is really not part of nature. In the first place, he is actually not man. He is an enormous erect penis, to which there happens to be attached a human figure."

This was the fairy tale about man and woman, the fairy tale exposed. It must necessarily be defended. But it must never be believed in.

Reality, in life, in literature, honest literature, was something else. It was, as Professor Marcus pointed out, how people lived with one another, what their changing feelings and emotions were, what their complex motives, and what their conflicts were with one another and within themselves. Reality was, as Barzun saw it, all the tenderness and hesitancies, the sensations and fan-tasies of love. Reality was precisely as Jadway's Cathleen remem-bered it.

Last night, with Maggie Russell, Barrett had enjoyed and suffered reality in a reciprocal relationship with a woman for the first time.

It had been more than her pointed hillocks and wide chasm, and more than his erect penis, and more than the wonders inside the chasm. It had been the hours of talk before, the discovering things held in common, the laughter, sorrow, indignation, and a secret knowledge that they were united and special and above the world and appreciative of their secret uniqueness. It had been their desire to be closer, touching, loving, merging into one. It had been their simultaneous decision, and their wordless going into the bedroom, and her use of a contraceptive before, and their initial embarrassment at their nakedness, and her appendix scar, and his wishing he had lost weight before he'd ever met her, and their awkwardness, and his difficulty entering, and her initial out-cry not of ecstasy but of discomfort, and their victory in joining, and the sound of a gas burble in her stomach, and the fleeting thought of Cassie McGraw and Chicago in his mind before his early orgasm, and his apologies, and her kisses, and their whisperings afterward, and their tea and crackers together, and more sleepy talk, and her rhythmic breathing in her sleep, and his catching himself snoring.

It was this, and so very much more.

Still, even though he was sure of his feelings for her, positive about the rightness of the two of them, he was uncertain and worried about her feelings for him, feelings that must wear for a lifetime. She had endured too much insecurity, he suspected, to invest the rest of her love, her vitality, her childbearing, her chances for safety, her years on earth, in a man who would be a failure. In this society, a failure was only half a man, and Maggie needed an entire man. If he failed to win this case, he knew that he would never be able to ask her to join him in partnership, and even if he did ask her it was unlikely that she would be imprudent enough to say yes.

He turned on his bar stool to order a third drink.

"Mr. Michael Barrett!"

He spun the rest of the way around to face the maître d' approaching him. He raised an arm to acknowledge his name.

"Mr. Barrett, there is a telephone call for you."

He paid his bar bill quickly, and chased after the maître d', asking, "Is it long distance or local?"

"I do not know, sir. Please accept it in the booth in the lobby."

He hastened into the booth, took up the receiver, and identified himself.

The call was local.

It was a feminine voice that he heard. "Oh, Mr. Barrett—I am phoning about the reward—"

He was instantly alert. "Yes? Who is this?"

"My name is Avis Jefferson. I am one of the practical nurses on the late shift at the Sunnyside Sanitarium. I was busy earlier, so I just now saw what was on the bulletin board. Mr. Holliday is out, so I thought I'd call you direct. It says there you'll pay anyone a hundred dollars who can help you about the postal card or picture on the board."

"Th—that's right," he stammered.

548

"I can help you. About the picture, I mean."

"You recognize the woman in the photograph, Miss Jefferson? That photograph was taken almost forty years ago."

"I've seen the picture before, Mr. Barrett."

"Where?"

"In the sanitarium here. I can even show it to you. If that's what you want."

He was sky high, beyond gravity now. "Honey, that's exactly what I want! I'll be over immediately. Don't go away. I'll be there in twenty minutes flat. Meet me at the reception desk."

Avis Jefferson was waiting at the reception desk of the Sunny-side Convalescent Sanitarium when he arrived. She towered over him by three or four inches when they shook hands. The inky blackness of her skin was broken by the whiteness of her buck teeth and accented by the clean white nurse's uniform. She was friendly, effervescent, and Mike Barrett liked and trusted her at once.

"Follow me," she said to Barrett, and she led him up the corridor. Feeling as clumsy as a schoolboy going to his first prom, he carried the bouquet of long-stemmed roses with which he hoped to woo Cassie McGraw, *if* there was finally and actually a Cassie McGraw.

As they turned the corner, Miss Jefferson said, "The minute I saw that photograph on the bulletin board, I said to myself, I've seen that before. And I remembered right off when and where. It was a year ago when we were doing some spring housecleaning in the patients' rooms, and it was in 34A. I was going through her suitcases, inventorying and straightening her personal effects, and seeing if there was anything wearable that wasn't being used, when I came across one of those old paste-in photo albums. So just out of natural curiosity—because you always think of the patients as old people only, forgetting they were once young like yourself—I looked to see what she was like when she was young. There were pages of snapshots inside, and some were taken in Paris—she'd told me she'd traveled and lived abroad, but I was never sure if it was true—and there was this one of her between the two young gentlemen in front of that Eiffel Tower, and it stuck in my mind because she had the devil in her eyes and looked so

549

full of nature, if you know what I mean. So when I saw that photo again, on the bulletin board, where you had Mr. Holliday put it, I remembered the same one in her album, and another thing made me remember it especially. The one in her album had a corner torn off just like yours. That made me positive."

"Jadway's face was torn off?"

"I don't know whose face."

"You never heard her mention Jadway?"

"Not so's I can recall. For that matter, I never heard Katie mention the name Cassie McGraw either."

"What is her name here?"

"Katie's? Well, formally I've always known her to be Mrs. Katherine Sullivan."

"Sullivan." Barrett savored the sound of the family name that had so long eluded him. "That must have been the name of the man she married after Jadway died, her husband who was killed in the Second World War. Did she ever speak of him?"

"Not by using the name Sullivan. Only a couple times saying as to how she'd been widowed and that's what made her girl turn to the Lord."

"I see. So it is Katherine Sullivan. Okay, the Sullivan part is solved. But I wonder where she got that given name of Katherine." No sooner had he asked himself the question than he had the answer. Early in the case, when he had been browsing about Ben Fremont's Book Emporium, he had come across a book called *Naming the New Arrival*, which gave the derivation of female and male Christian names, and he had looked up his first name and Zelkin's. He had learned that the name Michael was not Irish, as he had always thought, but of Hebrew origin, meaning "who is like God," and one diminutive was Mike, and that Abraham was also from the Hebrew, meaning "father of the multitude," and one diminutive was Abe. Then, fascinated, he had looked up other names that had become familiar to him in the pretrial preparation, and one of these had been Cassie, and he had read that Cassie was derived from the Greek and meant "pure" and was one of the diminutives of Katherine. And just now he realized that one variant of Katherine was Cathleen, the name of the fictional heroine of *The Seven Minutes*.

He had forgotten this archeological dig into appellations until this very moment. Now it was clear. With her marriage Cassie had shed the past and even taken on a new given name, yet she had paid homage to her immortality in Jadway's book and to her fictionalized self in its pages, and from Cathleen she had also held on to a single strand of a more wondrous time by calling herself Katherine.

Miss Jefferson had halted before an open doorway. On the wall next to it was painted "34A-34B." The nurse crooked her finger. "Right in here."

He followed her inside. There were two single beds, neatly made up with maroon covers, and separated by a hospital curtain. Beyond the beds there were sliding glass doors and screens that opened into the inner patio.

Miss Jefferson touched the headboard of the first bed. "This one here is Katie's," she said. "We let her stay up a while after dinner, before bringing her back to tuck her in."

Barrett surveyed Cassie's nook, so removed from Montparnasse's Dôme and the Brasserie Lipp. There was a movable tray, perched on rollers, across the foot of the bed, and it held a half-filled glass of orange juice and a paper cup of pink pills. Beside the head of the bed was a metal night table holding a carafe of water, a drinking glass, a transistor radio, and a pair of spectacles.

Barrett turned back to find Miss Jefferson kneeling before a built-in wardrobe from which she had removed a scuffed brown suitcase. She opened the suitcase—her back blocked him from a view of the contents—and then with a gurgle of triumph she held up a rectangular photograph album with navy-blue imitation-leather binding.

"Here it is, just like I remembered," chortled Miss Jefferson, rising to her feet.

A veteran of so many disappointments, Barrett entertained one last doubt. "Miss Jefferson, I was wondering, does this Katherine Sullivan who is here, who owns that album, does she in any way resemble the Cassie McGraw in that old photograph taken in front of the Eiffel Tower?"

"Of course not. Who would, after so much time? Even me. Do I look like I used to look when I was going to school? No, not a bit."

"Then how do we know the photograph in Mrs. Sullivan's album is of her? Maybe it's a keepsake sent by the real Cassie McGraw, who might have been a friend of Mrs. Sullivan's."

Avis Jefferson's buck teeth showed in a broad grin. "You are the worryingest man. You don't need to question this. There's other pictures in this book of hers and under some she wrote long ago such things as 'Me in Paris in '35'—and they're the same, I mean the woman in the other pictures is the same one that's in the Eiffel Tower picture with the two men. You'll see."

Miss Jefferson was flipping the loose pages, and abruptly she stopped and handed the album to Barrett.

There were four snapshots on the facing pages, two of them discolored and brittle, and the one at the extreme left was the one he had discovered in the Sean O'Flanagan Collection. It was the exact photograph: O'Flanagan, Cassie, the headless Jadway. The snapshot next to it showed Cassie in front of a medieval building, and beneath it she had written, "At the Musée de Cluny, Oct., 1936." The handwriting was as familiar as that on the photostat of the back of the picture, which was in his pocket. The snapshots on the right-hand page showed Cassie alone, one posing on what Barrett guessed to be the Pont-Neuf, with the Seine behind her, and the other showing her saluting into the camera while standing smartly at attention beneath a street plaque that read "Boulevard St.-Michel."

Oblivious of the gangling nurse who was peering down over his shoulder, Barrett leafed hastily through the entire album, from the first page to the last. Most of the pages were empty. There were only about a dozen more photographs. Two stiff portraits that Barrett presumed to be of Cassie's parents. Some mementos of her childhood—Cassie between the ages of six and twelve, in a wagon, on a sled, in a tree. A photograph of the young Sean O'Flanagan in Paris. A few snapshots of Cassie in Zurich, and one of her feeding pigeons in St. Mark's Square in Venice. A lone snapshot of a curly-headed, plain-faced, unsmiling girl of perhaps fourteen, with the single name "Judith" printed beneath it. Then there was a shot, streaked with light from overexposure, that appeared to be of a youngish soldier, with crew cut, crooked smile, blocky build, in the uniform of an enlisted man in the United States Army. No doubt this was Sullivan after the marriage and before being shipped out to become a casualty. And one final picture. No human figure in it. Simply a doorway above which was clearly visible the lettering: "The Étoile Press—18 rue de Berri."

Barrett stared down at that final photograph, and the album was unsteady in his hands.

That clinched it. He closed the album. Cassie McGraw, at last.

He waited for Avis Jefferson to return the album to the suitcase and lift the suitcase back into the wardrobe.

The nurse shut the wardrobe and came around to face him once more.

"Where is she?" Barrett asked nervously.

"In the recreation room," said Miss Jefferson. "I always leave her there, in her wheelchair, after dinner. I like her to have some company before bedtime."

Barrett picked up the bouquet of roses from the bed. "Let's go," he said.

They were in the corridor again, on their way to the recreation room. Miss Jefferson looked at him approvingly. "That's nice of you, bringing those roses. When I first saw the notice on the board, I thought you were a distant relative or something. I sure hoped so. Because no one ever comes to see her."

Barrett shook his head. "She has no one left, except a daughter in a convent."

"But then that postcard that you had posted on the bulletin board puzzled me, and I asked about you, and our R.N. reminded me you were a lawyer mixed up with that sexy book and the trial out in California, and that our Katie Sullivan had something to do with that book."

"She was the mistress of the man who wrote that book."

"You're kidding! Our Katie? That nice little old lady? Lordy, the things you don't know about people. It's hard to believe that, when you see her sitting like anybody's grandma in that wheelchair."

Something new niggled at him. The wheelchair. He would uphold his reputation as the worryingest man. "Why is she in a wheelchair, Miss Jefferson? She's ambulatory, isn't she?"

"Not no more. When I first came here a few years back, she was recovering from a broken hip, and getting therapy and using a walker. Then, right after that, she had another fall, shattered the same hip, nearly died of pneumonia after the surgery. But she's a sturdy one. She came through. But no more walking for her. Too

553

bad, you know, because sitting like that all the time makes you get sort of frail and wasting away."

"Yes, it's pitiful," he agreed. Even as he spoke, Barrett was considering the difficulties of transporting Cassie McGraw to Los Angeles and delivering her into the courtroom, but it could be done. Perhaps, if the price was right, Mr. Holliday would loan him the services of Avis Jefferson to look after their star witness. With every step he took, every word he heard, Cassie McGraw was closer to being a real person for him. He thought about her sentenced to that wheelchair. "What does she do with herself all day?" he inquired. "What's she doing now—watching television?"

"No, she hardly ever watches for long. She just likes to sit and dream and think, the way most of them do. I sometimes wonder what she's thinking. I asked her one time, but she just smiled at me sweetly like she always does and said nothing. I sure wish I knew."

"Oh, she's probably thinking of her youth and the past. That's the only game for old folks."

"Maybe, but probably not," said Miss Jefferson. "Thinking much about the past would be pretty hard for her." They had reached the swinging doors that led into the recreation room. "So sad, the way it has to happen, but Katie or Cassie or whatever you call her, she's lost most of her memory by now."

"Lost her memory?" Barrett stood stock-still, aghast. This had never occurred to him. This was the only obstacle that he had not anticipated, and it was a shock. "You mean—do you mean she can't remember anything any more?"

"She's senile," Miss Jefferson said. Then, seeing the expression on Barrett's face, she let go of the door she had pushed half open. "What's the matter?"

"It was her memory that I was counting on for the trial."

"Aw, that's too bad. You mean finding her won't help you now?"

"Not if she can't recall the past."

"That's real bad luck. Well, I shouldn't take any reward from you, then."

"No, you found her. You deserve the money. But senile? Nobody mentioned it earlier. Yet I should have suspected it when Mr. Holliday took that postcard and photograph around to every female patient today and none of them recognized either item.

554

Cassie must have looked right at the postcard and the photograph without remembering them. Still—" Another related thought had come to him. "Miss Jefferson, tell me one thing. The postcard signed by her and sent to Los Angeles. In it she recalls and defends Jadway and *The Seven Minutes*, and speaks of herself as Jadway's friend. That memory goes back almost forty years. So she *did* remember when she dictated her message on the card. How can you explain that?"

"You just don't know about senility cases, Mr. Barrett. They're most of them like your Cassie. She's got hardening of the arteries to the brain. It's gradual-like, but it keeps getting more and more so. At first it makes the patient confused and she loses her sense of time. Little by little her memory fades away, until one day it's gone and maybe she won't even know who I am. Of course, it's not to that point with Katie yet, but it's getting close. There's just one crazy thing about those senile cases when they're in the stage she's in. Sometimes, on certain days, they can remember what happened to them maybe forty or fifty years ago, yet not remember what they ate or who they met five minutes ago. Other times they can remember what's just happened, but not another fact about where they were years ago or the people in their lives or anything. But most of the time their brains are like a horse's, I heard one doctor say, meaning if a horse does something wrong and you punish him ten minutes later, he won't know why you're punishing him, won't remember at all what it was he done wrong. No memory except for what's happened this second. That's it usually for our Katie."

"But the postcard, Miss Jefferson?"

"Well, like I said, that must've been one of her sharp days. She has maybe an hour or two when she makes sense a couple days a month. I can pretty nearly tell you what probably happened with that postal card. When me or one of the other nurses sees she's suddenly having one of her good alert spells, no confusion, alert and understanding everything, we take advantage of it by maybe reading to her from some newspaper or magazine that's handy, just so she sort of should know there's a world out there and know what's been going on. So that postal card— When was it written?"

"About two and a half weeks ago."

"So she was probably pretty alert on that day, the fogginess gone, real sharp for a short time, so then me or one of the others read to her from the front page of the newspaper, this and that, maybe a little politics, a murder, or something lively like that sexy trial. One of us probably read to her from the trial story, and it stuck in her head for an hour or two and she remembered Jadway and that book. And when whoever was reading to her stopped to go on with their other work, just then some of those volunteer helpers must have come around asking each patient if they could do anything, and one probably asked Katie. And since she had this trial on her mind until it slipped away again, she said, Yes, get me one of the picture postal cards and write down something I'll tell you and send it for me, and address it to the home of that man with the son who was involved in that censorship case that was in the paper—and the volunteer did it and sent it off, and that's how it happened."

That was the way it had happened, and now Barrett understood. His hopes, like Cassie's mind, had faded. Still, there was a mind that had a few good hours one or two days a month, and if there was that, then there was also hope.

"How is she today?" he asked.

"Don't know. Haven't had a chance to talk to her since I came on. Let's find out right now. I can see her from here, over there by herself in the wheelchair at the far table next to the patio door. Come on in and let me introduce you."

Avis Jefferson wended her way through the recreation room, and Barrett stayed at her heels. Once they had passed the group around the droning color-television set and arrived at the center of the room, Barrett had his first full view of the legendary Cassie McGraw.

He had been prepared, yet he knew one could never be entirely prepared. He understood that the pert and lovely gamin of the Left Bank and the 1930s was no more, just as Zelda Fitzgerald was no more, yet he had expected some recognizable relic of the heyday past. Perhaps a lovely old lady with traces still of a lost beauty and her bohemian heritage.

What he saw now was the concave shaving of what had once been a woman. An old lady, aged beyond her years, with flour-white mussed hair, dull eyes, sunken cheeks, a few sprouts of stiff gray hair on her chin, wrinkled thin neck and wrinkled blue-veined hands and swollen feet, draped all around with an oversized pale-blue bathrobe. She sat at the circular wooden table, staring not at the wax fruit centerpiece, not at the patio beyond, not at anyone or anything, not even inward.

Jadway's mistress, the lusty, love-giving heroine of the most suppressed novel ever written.

This was Cassie McGraw.

Barrett dropped his senseless red roses on a nearby chair as Miss Jefferson brought him past the table and into Cassie McGraw's line of vision.

"Hi, Katie, how are you?" Miss Jefferson asked. She tugged at Barrett. "Katie, look at the nice man I've brought to see you. This is Mr. Barrett, all the way from Los Angeles, California, come here all this way to Chicago just to see you. Isn't that nice?"

Barrett took a hesitant step forward. "I'm pleased to meet you, Miss McGraw."

Cassie's head came up slowly, ever so slowly, and her dim eyes gradually seemed to fix her visitor in their focus. She held her eyes on him a number of seconds, and then as her head nodded slightly, ever so slightly, her chapped lips formed into a sweet smile. The effort of the smile had been her acknowledgment of a presence, and her welcome, and then her attention was given back to an object that lay in her lap. It was a shredded ball of Kleenex. Her weak bony fingers began to play with it, shredding it further.

"You saw her smile," said Miss Jefferson with the overenthusiasm of a USO hostess. "That means she's pleased to have you here. Do sit down, Mr. Barrett. You go right on and talk to her. Ask her anything you like."

Barrett accepted the chair, drew it up closer to Cassie McGraw, and sat down. Avis Jefferson took the remaining chair across the table for herself.

"Miss McGraw," said Barrett earnestly, "do you remember a man who was a very close friend of yours years ago, a man named J J Jadway, or Jad, as you may have called him?"

Her eyes seemed to watch his lips as he spoke, but there was no recognition or understanding in them, and her fingers continued to pick at the Kleenex tissues.

She said nothing.

"Perhaps, Miss McGraw, you remember a book that Jadway wrote. You helped get it published in Paris. It was called *The Seven Minutes*. Do you remember?"

557

She was attentive to his voice, and her brow contracted. She appeared interested but mildly confused.

"Miss McGraw, do the names Christian Leroux and Sean O'Flanagan mean anything to you?"

She did not answer, but she seemed to be chewing something in her mouth.

"She's got a loose denture," Miss Jefferson explained, "and now she's rocking it." The nurse wagged a finger at Cassie McGraw. "Now, Katie, don't be stubborn and play possum like that. I know you can do better. This man, he's here to ask you to help him with his trial over that book in Los Angeles. I seen with my own eyes that postal card you dictated a few weeks ago and signed. You were sensible enough to sign it by your own hand then, and now I think you should tell this fine man why you wrote that postal card."

The old lady offered a sweet smile to her nurse, as if commending a singer for a virtuoso performance. But still she said nothing.

"Katie, you remember your daughter, don't you?" Miss Jefferson asked.

Cassie's eyes flickered, and the same smile remained, but so did the silence.

Avis Jefferson looked mournfully at Barrett and shrugged. "I guess you're out of luck, Mr. Barrett. Like I warned you, this is most usually the way she is, this is normal for such patients. It's no use."

Barrett sighed. "I'm afraid you're right, Miss Jefferson. What disappoints me so is to have finally got to her and to know how much is locked up inside her about J J Jadway—oh, well, I'm sorry not only for myself, but for her. Dammit, that's life, I guess."

He pushed back his chair to rise, and then he heard an odd sound, almost a croak, and then a thick voice said, "How is Mr. Jadway?"

He came down hard in his chair, facing Cassie McGraw, murmuring the Lord's name in vain, watching as her lips continued to try to form words.

"How is Mr. Jadway?" Cassie McGraw repeated.

"Well, he was fine, he was fine, the last I heard," said Barrett quickly. He glanced over his shoulder at Miss Jefferson, who was excitedly waving her hand at him as if imploring him to continue. He turned back to the old lady. "Mr. Jadway was fine. How was he when you last saw him?"

"He was unhappy to leave Paris," said Cassie McGraw thickly. "We were both unhappy, but he had to go home."

"He went home? You mean he left Paris and went home to the United States?"

"To his family in Conn . . . Conn . . ."

"Connecticut?"

"He went back because of his father. I was with Judy in New York. I thought maybe . . ." Her voice trailed off. She chewed silently, trying to remember. She shook her head slowly. "No. I couldn't stay. I had to leave him. I had to." Her eyes blinked, and her fingers found the tissues in her lap again, and she picked at them.

Trying to contain himself, Barrett reached out and touched her thin hand, which had the texture of old parchment, as he sought to regain her attention. "Miss McGraw—"

Cassie McGraw lifted her head, but the eyes had dulled.

"What were you telling me?" Barrett urged. "Were you telling me that you and Jadway left Paris together and returned to the United States for good? That he didn't kill himself? That he came back here to live with his family in Connecticut and kept you in New York? And you didn't like it, being kept or being in America or having him go back to his family again? Is that what you were trying to say?"

Cassie McGraw's expression was one of bewilderment. Her fingers worked at the Kleenex, but her lips did not move.

"Cassie, Cassie," he implored her, "we were so close to it, almost there. Please try, try to remember, try to finish or at least explain what you started to say. Tell me, please, did Jadway commit suicide in Paris, or is that a lie? Did he return to live in this country healthy and well? Please remember!"

She had become fascinated by Barrett's intentness, as if it were an offer of devotion and love, but her sweet smile was like a non sequitur.

"Cassie—Katie—try, try," he pleaded. "Just tell me this. Was Jadway alive after he was supposed to be dead? Is he—is he alive today?"

Her eyes had become vacant, and her mind, what was left of it, had returned to limbo.

There would be no more, he knew. The promise of lightning and thunder, and then only the silence of the senile which was like the silence of the dead, only worse.

He pushed the chair away from the table and stood up as Avis Jefferson came to her feet.

"She was trying to tell you something," said the nurse, "but I suppose she couldn't. It flew away. She just got lost. Or did she tell you something?"

"Not enough, really, nothing I could count on, considering her condition."

"Well, I was going to suggest, maybe if you could stay around here a week or two, you just might catch her on one of those good remembering days, like when she dictated that postal card."

Barrett smiled wanly. "If I were writing history, I'd stay. But I'm conducting a trial, and I've run out of time. The trial may end the day after tomorrow. I guess we're just cooked." He looked down at the old lady. "She was nice. She tried. She tried very hard. She's a fine lady. She must have been a remarkable young woman."

He saw his wilting bouquet of red roses. He went to get them and brought them back. "She deserves this, at least."

He bent, and gently he placed the bouquet in Cassie's lap. She looked up with a flicker of surprise, then looked down, touching the rose petals, then raised her head once more, and for the first time her smile had another characteristic. It was impish.

"Flowers," Cassie McGraw said. "Is it my birthday?"

Miss Jefferson laughed gleefully, and Barrett chuckled, and finally Cassie McGraw began picking the petals off the roses and was lost to human contact again.

Miss Jefferson was still laughing, shaking her head, as they walked away. "She's a card, that one. Did you hear her? 'Is it my birthday?' she says. You see, she can remember, she can remember some things. Once a year she gets flowers on her birthday, that's the only time, just on her birthday, and I guess that's what flowers mean to her now, and so she thought it was her birthday."

Barrett's inner ear heard his inner voice. He repeated its question aloud. "I thought she was alone? You say she gets a bouquet of flowers on every birthday? From whom? Who sends them?"

And another question. "And by the way, who's footing the bill for her in this sanitarium?"

"I asked Mr. Holliday about that once. He says the money comes from her estate, what was left when she was confined."

"And the flowers on her birthday? From her daughter? From Sean O'Flanagan? Any name to the card?"

"Mr. Barrett, they come with no card, no card at all."

They had left the recreation room and were in the corridor once more.

Barrett was not satisfied. "If there are flowers, *someone* has to send them."

"I don't know who, Mr. Barrett. All I know is they're delivered every birthday morning, each year, from Milton's Florists."

"Where is Milton's Florists?"

"Here in Chicago, on State Street."

"You're sure that's where they come from?"

"Sure I'm sure, and I'll tell you why. The delivery boy for that florist, he's in and out of here, and he's a cute one. Him and me, we're always kidding around. And whenever he brings in the once-a-year bouquet for Katie—your Miss Cassie—he always insists on going along when I give her the flowers, so he can sing Happy Birthday. What a kook."

Barrett had his wallet out. He extracted five twenty-dollar bills. He pushed them into Miss Jefferson's palm. "Your reward," he said.

"That's mighty nice, but you didn't have to, considering—"

He held up one more twenty-dollar bill. "How'd you like to earn this? What I want you to do is call your friend, that delivery boy at Milton's Florists, and find out where Cassie's—Mrs. Sullivan, I should say—where her birthday flowers come from every year. Want to do that?"

Miss Jefferson plucked the bill from his fingers. "You wait right here, Mr. Barrett."

She hurried around the corner, and he waited, too overwrought to smoke his pipe.

In less than five minutes, Avis Jefferson was back and breathless. "I still got my friend on the phone, because I wasn't sure I got the right kind of answer you wanted."

"What answer did he give you?"

"He looked it up and he said the flowers for Katie Sullivan are a standing order from the Capitol Hill Florists in Washington, D.C. That doesn't tell you *who* they come from, and that's what you want to know, isn't it?"

"That's what I want to know. Who pays for the standing order in Washington, D.C.?"

"Just what I thought. That's what I asked him, and he said he doesn't know. But seeing as how I think you're so nice and generous, I suggested you'd pay for the long-distance call—you can leave the money for him with me—if he'll phone the Capitol Hill Florists in Washington, D.C., and since he's alone in the shop now he can say he's the boss and he can try to find out for you. Do you want him to try?"

Quickly Barrett drew a ten-dollar bill out of his wallet and pressed it into Miss Jefferson's hand. "Tell your friend to call Washington, D.C."

"It might take like ten or fifteen minutes."

"I'll be here."

Once again she was gone. And once again he was waiting. He would not allow himself to think. He remained standing, numbed.

Less than ten minutes had passed when he saw the ungainly figure of Avis Jefferson loping down the hall toward him. Her countenance was wreathed with joy.

"He got it for you, Mr. Barrett. That smart black boy got it. He went on like he was the boss and made up some fib about their being in the exchange business together and this being so important—and they looked it up there in that Washington florist's—and they said all they had was to where they should send their bill so's to be paid once a year, a woman's name with a recent changed address and phone number, because she's the one who pays the bill every year with her check. Here it is. I wrote it down."

She handed him a slip of paper.

Barrett looked at it. On the slip was written: "Miss Xavier, United States Senate, Old Building, Washington, D.C. To reach by phone, call Capitol exchange Area Code 180, number 224-3121, then ask for Miss Xavier's number, 4989."

He folded it and put it in his pocket.

"Miss Jefferson, I could kiss you for this."

"Don't you dare."

562

"Where can I get a cab?"

And then he was off.

Twenty-five minutes later, at the telephone in his room in the Ambassador East, he had dialed the Capitol exchange operator.

He knew all that was to be known now, all that he had sought from Cassie McGraw. She had told him part of it. And then she had said, *Is it my birthday?*, and with that she had told him the rest.

He had the Senate operator in Washington, and he asked to speak to Miss Xavier and gave the special number 4989, in the Senate's Old Building.

"One moment, please. I'll try to put you through."

There was an interminable buzzing, but no answer.

At last the operator was on the line again. "Sorry, sir. Miss Xavier must have gone home. There seems to be no one in Senator Bainbridge's office—"

Senator Bainbridge, was it?

"—but if it is of any urgency, I can try to contact Miss Xavier or the Senator at home for you."

"It's the Senator I really want to speak to. It is urgent, very urgent."

"I'll try to contact him, then. Who shall I tell him is calling?"

He thought quickly, and then he said as businesslike as possible, "Advise him that Mr. Michael Barrett is on the line. Tell him Mr. Barrett, a friend of Miss Cassie McGraw's, is phoning him from Chicago."

"Michael Barrett. Friend of Cassie McGraw's. Very well. If you'll hold on, please, I'll see what I can do."

The receiver went dumb, except for darts of static, and Barrett held the receiver to his ear and hoped his last hope.

The operator was on again. "Mr. Barrett?"

"I'm here."

"I have Senator Bainbridge for you. He'll speak to you now. Go ahead, please."

There was a beat of silence, and then a gruff voice at the other end. "Hello, there."

"Senator Bainbridge? This is Michael Barrett. I am the attorney defending the Jadway book in that Los Angeles trial."

There was a long pause.

When the voice on the other end was heard again, the gruffness had gone out of it.

The voice was weary. "Yes, Mr. Barrett, we've been wondering how long it would take you. Jadway and I—we've been expecting to hear from you . . . for a long time."

MISS XAVIER proved to be a small, compact, reserved woman in her thirties, with shining black hair hanging to her shoulders, a bronze complexion suggesting American Indian ancestry, and unrouged lips, and she was waiting for him beside the escalator inside the Capitol.

The moment the Senator's chauffeur had left to return to his car, she said, "Senator Bainbridge was not sure last night if he would see you here or in his office in the Old Senate Building. He had to rearrange two appointments first. But I am to bring you to his office, where he can give you twenty minutes."

"Thank you," said Mike Barrett.

"We'll take the motor stairs down to the Senate subway."

"After you, Miss Xavier."

She stepped on the escalator, and Barrett stepped on behind her.

Remembering his brief conversation with Senator Bainbridge last night, he realized that he had learned nothing from it except that a chauffeur would pick him up before the Mayflower Hotel at a quarter to eleven in the morning. Still, what he had learned before his call to the Senator had been enough. All of his mounting suspicions—beginning with Dr. Hiram Eberhart's anachronism of dates, and Sean O'Flanagan's quoting from a discussion with an author after the author's supposed death—had finally been confirmed.

Darkness had given way to blinding light.

J J Jadway was alive.

After that, from Chicago, he had arranged a conference call with his associates in Los Angeles, and he had announced his astounding discovery to Zelkin, Sanford, and Kimura simultaneously. Hearing him, they had been speechless, and then uncontrollably excited and wildly enthusiastic.

"Golly, golly," Zelkin had kept chanting, "you pulled off Operation Lazarus!" He had sung out as if it were an incantation,

"You cried, 'Jadway, come forth!' and he that was dead came forth! Mike, you've raised Jadway from the dead!"

And the other three, like maniacs on the transcontinental wire, had bellowed in chorus, "Amen!"

For thirty minutes, reviewing every step of Barrett's hunt, weighing every word concerning his find, they had speculated upon the celebrated Jadway's resurrection and their new life. At last Barrett had succeeded in restoring some semblance of calm to his colleagues. He had begged Zelkin to bring him up to date on the trial, so that he would know exactly where he stood when he came face to face with Bainbridge and Jadway short hours from now.

Zelkin had reported that the defense witnesses had been more effective during the afternoon. They had got off to a shaky start when the Contessa Daphne Orsoni, who had been imported from the Costa Brava in Spain to attest to Jadway's good character and motives, had been forced to confess under the fire of Duncan's cross-examination that she had met Jadway only at the masked ball she had given in Venice, and Jadway had never once removed his mask, and no, she could not swear under oath that her guest had been Jadway or that she had "seen" him. Then the Swedish sex-survey expert, Dr. Rolf Lagergren, had given a brilliant discourse on modern community standards and the average man's attitude toward the sex act, but the doctor had been manhandled during Duncan's cross-examination.

After eliciting a statement from Dr. Lagergren that *The Seven Minutes* was an accurate representation in fictional form of the feelings and behavior of the majority of women in real life, Duncan had quoted the report of the sexologist's most recent survey to challenge his statement. In this survey of one thousand married and unmarried females, Dr. Lagergren had discovered that three out of four women, a solid majority of women, reached orgasm not in seven minutes, but in from one to six minutes, and that only one out of four women took seven minutes or longer—from seven minutes to as much as twenty minutes—to attain orgasm. Realizing that his statements about female orgasm were in conflict, Dr. Lagergren had lost his cool briefly, and quickly stated that Jadway had structured his novel on an earlier and less comprehensive sex survey, and yes, perhaps the author had taken some literary license. Recovering his poise, Dr. Lagergren had insisted that even if Jadway's heroine did not qualify as average, using the recent survey's orgasm timetable, still Jadway's portrait of a woman's sexual feelings reflected that of most women. Following the Swedish expert's appearance, the librarian, Rachel Hoyt, had taken the stand and had been magnificent in her eloquent proclamation about the book's essential purity and worth.

Tomorrow there would be more witnesses, articulate ones like the novelist Guy Collins, to speak on behalf of the merits of *The Seven Minutes*. And the next day there would remain only Dr. Yale Finegood to attempt to prove that it was not reading that provoked violence in young people like Jerry Griffith.

"And after that, we're through," Zelkin had said on the long-distance telephone. "After that we have to rest our case, and what we're leaving with the jury just isn't enough, Mike. We've gained some ground, but we haven't caught up. As it stands, Ben Fremont is going to wind up in jail and *The Seven Minutes* is going to end up in a bonfire. We need one—just one—smashing witness to put us over. And if that witness is Jadway himself, we're in—we've made it. You've pulled off a miracle, Mike. You've proved he's alive. But can you bring him here to testify for us?"

"I don't know," he had said, "but now that he's been found out, I can't see why he would refuse to come forward."

"Was there any indication that Jadway would be there when you meet the Senator tomorrow?"

"None whatsoever. Jadway may very well be there. I'll have to wait and see. As for Bainbridge, I don't know his role, but he apparently handles, or has handled, some of Jadway's affairs. It's strange, considering the fact that he is a senator, that I don't know a damn thing about him. I'd like to know *something* before talking to him."

They had agreed that Kimura would drive immediately to the Los Angeles Public Library and then visit the newspaper morgue of the *Los Angeles Times*, and whatever he dug up would be reported to Barrett later in the evening.

After the conference call, Barrett had telephoned his apartment and spoken at length to Maggie Russell. She had been thrilled that her lead to Cassie McGraw had in turn led to the discovery of J J Jadway resurrected. And she had been proud of

Barrett, and had spoken affectionately, and promised to be waiting for him when he returned.

Two hours later, Zelkin had telephoned back to read him Kimura's hastily garnered notes, and the information had been scanty.

"The reason you haven't heard much about Senator Thomas Bainbridge is that he's been in public life only a short time," Zelkin had reported. "One of the Senators from Connecticut died —I remember that now, it was only four months ago—and the Governor appointed Thomas Bainbridge for the unfulfilled term of office. Bainbridge was Dean of the Yale School of Law at the time, and he had some kind of connection with a law firm in Washington, and a second home there. Before that, let me see, he was a judge for the State Court of Appeals. And before that, president of a big manufacturing firm—doesn't say here what they manufactured. No matter. As for his educational background, he graduated from Yale, and then in 1932 got his LL.B. from their law school."

That had been it last night, and before midnight Barrett had boarded a flight from Chicago to Washington, and then he had taken a taxi from National Airport to the Mayflower Hotel.

This morning, promptly at a quarter to eleven, a liveried chauffeur had picked him up and driven him along Pennsylvania Avenue to Capitol Hill and then turned him over to Miss Xavier.

Miss Xavier's voice now brought him back to the present. They were beneath the Capitol, in the private congressional subway, and Miss Xavier was indicating a miniature train. "The Toonerville Trolley," she said without smiling. "It'll take us six hundred feet to the Old Senate Building."

A half minute later they had got off the pygmy train, and seconds after that they were riding up in an elevator. It was a short walk to Senator Bainbridge's suite.

In the reception room there were two secretarial desks, and the walls were decorated with scenic photographs and a huge relief map of Connecticut. To his right Barrett could see two more rooms filled with desks and files and members of the staff, male and female, Negro and white. Barrett loitered before the relief map, wondering whether it would be the Senator alone

567

or the Senator and Jadway, and he listened to Miss Xavier, at her telephone, announcing his arrival. He tried to hide his anxiety.

"Yes, Senator, I'll send him right in," she said. She nodded to Barrett. "This way, sir."

She had reached the polished oak door and had begun to open it.

In those seconds, Barrett hesitated. It had been such a long and despairing hunt, so many peaks and valleys, so many bright dreams and black nightmares, so much that was tangible and so much more that was mirage. And throughout this odyssey, going forward into the past, he had always felt that he had been drawing nearer and nearer to that shade of Jadway that was hidden around every next turning. And though Jadway had taken form in his mind, a substance, a person, a companion finally, who deserved to be saved and in turn might save them all, Barrett had always accepted, until recently, that Jadway was no more, was ashes to ashes and dust to dust literally, and not a substance in fact, or a person or a companion or a savior. But now, as Abe had put it, J J Jadway was real, a Lazarus brought forth from those ashes scattered over the Seine. A few steps, and lo, Jadway, to be touched, to be heard, to be spoken to—that strange and mysterious author of one book, the most condemned book, the most suppressed book ever to come from the pen of a man. There he would be, that lover of Cassie, that conceiver of Judith, that creator of Cathleen, that poet of a panegyric to love who had made "fuck" a word that could be printed without shame and the symbol of an act of beauty. Jadway, that magical name which Duncan and Yerkes had evoked as their Sesame to power, that basilisk name which fanatic thousands, millions, had used to put flames to books and to freedom of speech.

Barrett held back. He was gripped by an emotion that he struggled to understand. It was an emotion that he supposed the reporter Henry Morton Stanley had felt on that day—after a two-month search through Central Africa for a missing Scottish explorer-missionary—when he came to the village of Ujiji and found alive the one who had so long eluded him. "I would have run to him, only I was a coward in the presence of such a mob —would have embraced him, but that I did not know how he would receive me; so I did what moral cowardice and false pride suggested was the best thing—walked deliberately to him, took off my hat, and said: 'Dr. Livingstone, I presume?'"

Stanley had concluded: *"Finis coronat opus."* Barrett understood: The end crowns the work.

He wanted to run to Jadway now, to embrace him, but instead he walked deliberately toward the polished oak door that Miss Xavier held open.

He went inside.

There was one man, alone. There was Senator Thomas Bainbridge. There was no J J Jadway. Only Bainbridge, Friend and Go-between.

Senator Bainbridge was standing as straight as if his spine were made of steel—standing beside his desk, rigid, bloodless, aloof, immaculate, resembling more a portrait by Gilbert Stuart or Thomas Sully than a living and breathing twentieth-century man. He was, Barrett perceived in his disappointment, like one of those early American portraits of a Federalist judge, one such as Chief Justice John Marshall. His features were even more chiseled than Marshall's, Barrett decided. They were Caesarean, the personification of instant authority. His smooth iron-gray hair was parted on one side. His brow was large, his eyes penetrating, his nose Roman, his lips tight. He had height, no excess weight, and the carefully tailored, conservative gray suit bore not a wrinkle. Here, the austere Connecticut Yankee.

It surprised Barrett when Bainbridge moved. He was extending a hand. "Mr. Barrett, I presume?"

Momentarily, Barrett was startled, remembering Stanley to Livingstone, and knowing that his host had appropriated the one line that he himself should have spoken. Was it offered with irony or humor? Or with neither? Barrett could not tell. He shook the outstretched hand, and the grip was firm.

As he released the hand, Barrett's eyes left Bainbridge's and automatically strayed about the room, just to be certain.

"No," said Bainbridge dryly. "I thought it best to receive you by myself. Do have a seat, Mr. Barrett."

There was a dark-green upholstered chair before the carved desk, and Barrett took it. Waiting for the Senator to fortify himself behind the massive desk, Barrett now examined—instead of searched—the office briefly. There was a conference table, a luxurious leather sofa, a low-slung leather chair and ottoman, several bookcases, a craggy Giacometti sculpture on a lamp table, and numerous diplomas and citations hanging on the walls, and through the window behind the Senator's high-backed swivel chair Barrett could see the Carroll Arms Hotel across the way.

The Senator was in his chair, and the patrician countenance offered no verbal amenity.

Barrett determined to offer one. "I understand you've recently been appointed to the Senate. My congratulations."

"Thank you. It was nothing I sought or desired. It was a duty. Have you read de Tocqueville? A little spot, he called our Connecticut, a little spot, one that gives America the clock peddler, the schoolmaster, the senator. 'The first gives you time; the second tells you what to do with it; the third makes your law and your civilization.' Someone must make our law. Perhaps I am as qualified as most."

"From your background, I'm sure you are more than qualified." But Barrett was concerned with the time allotted him and what he must do with it. "Based on the little I do know of your background, Senator, I must say I'm surprised to find J J Jadway figuring in it."

Bainbridge's eyes were unwavering. "Life makes strange bedfellows, Mr. Barrett. I grew up with Jadway. We were in the same fraternity at Yale."

"Have you remained in touch with him all these years?"

"More or less."

"The fact that you have maintained contact with Cassie McGraw—but he has not—strikes me as odd."

"Does it? You are the counsel for *The Seven Minutes*. You have heard the calumnies heaped upon the book and its author. Do you find it surprising that in his later years he does not wish to be burdened by a past that might make his present position in life untenable?"

"If you are acquainted with our trial—"

"I am, sir."

"—then you know that my colleagues and I regard the work we are defending as a work of art, of genius, and as one that its author, we had hoped, would have as much pride in defending as we have."

"I am afraid you are a romantic, Mr. Barrett," said the Senator. "Life is less so. Jadway learned that soon enough."

570

"So he did not want to keep in personal contact with Miss Mc-Graw for fear of being exposed?"

"That is correct. In matters concerning his long-buried past, I have, out of consideration for his wish for anonymity, represented him in those matters. In the trifling business of an annual birthday memento for Miss McGraw, for one thing. And a few others, very few."

It was going to be difficult, Barrett could see, and he wished that he had Cassie McGraw beside him, and Abe Zelkin, and Maggie, to help, to soften this Yankee. But the seconds were ticking away, and the minutes, and he had better use them well and use them fast.

"Senator, J J Jadway *is* alive, isn't he?"

"You knew that before you telephoned me last night. I saw no reason to deny it."

"I merely wanted to hear you affirm it again. You made a curious remark last night. You said that you and Jadway were wondering how long it would take me to learn he was alive, and you implied that you had both been expecting I'd get to you sooner or later. Jadway thought I'd find him? What gave him reason to think so?"

Bainbridge leaned forward, resting his elbows on his desk, interlocking his fingers. "From the moment that you bid on the Jadway letters in the possession of the autograph dealer, Olin Adams, we suspected that you might find us."

"You knew about those letters?"

"Certainly, Mr. Barrett. How else could I have acquired them? It was I who recovered them for Jadway."

Barrett sat up, astonished. "You were the buyer? I would have sworn it was the Los Angeles District Attorney who beat me to them. My phone was bugged at the time, by Luther Yerkes, an industrialist who's supporting District Attorney Duncan politically."

"Yerkes may have more power than I. But perhaps I have better connections."

"Better connections, Senator?"

"Sean O'Flanagan, for instance. He'd been told the letters were for sale. He thought he had better inform Jadway of them. So he called me. I authorized him to buy them at once. But when he tried, it was too late. A Mr. Michael Barrett had purchased them and was flying in from Los Angeles the next morning to pick them up. So I flew into New York, also, and I picked them up in Mr. Barrett's name. Forgive me, Mr. Barrett. Again, remember I am pledged to help Jadway preserve his anonymity."

"Even at the cost of allowing Jadway's name to be traduced and maligned?"

"You forget. Jadway is dead. He is buried with the past. Only history is interested in the past. Jadway has built a new and better present."

Barrett took hold of the edge of the desk. "Senator, as long as Cassie McGraw and Sean O'Flanagan live and *The Seven Minutes* exists, Jadway can never turn his back on the past."

Bainbridge unlocked his fingers and drew himself up. "Cassie McGraw—O'Flanagan—Jadway has taken care of them—I have taken care of them for him. I saw that O'Flanagan was provided for. First with his poetry quarterly, and then, when it went under, he was given a yearly stipend, sufficient to keep him with a roof over his head and in food and drink."

"And in silence."

"Yes, of course, that too. As for Cassie, we had O'Flanagan keep an eye on her. When she was no longer self-sufficient, physically or financially, O'Flanagan was empowered to see that she received convalescent care. We've managed this through him until lately, when excessive drinking has made him less reliable. More recently, Miss Xavier has been writing the checks sent to Mr. Holliday and the florist. So, you see, Jadway has provided for these two friends from the past. And soon enough, being merely mortal, they and he will be cremated or entombed as Jadway's own name was in Paris. This would leave only *The Seven Minutes*. But it will die, too, when your jury in Los Angeles returns its verdict."

"And Jadway would let it die?"

"Yes."

"Why? Because he's ashamed of it?"

"No, Mr. Barrett, he is not ashamed of it. I often sense that he is very proud of it. He feels it was honest, true, perhaps even of value to some readers. Certainly, I can say to you, it was created out of love. But in the end, the law of survival pertains to books as well as species. If the world will not let it live, it must die."

"It is not just a book that will die, Senator. I don't want to sound pompous, but I believe this with all my heart. If that book dies because of legal suppression, then a human freedom dies in our society."

For the first time, Bainbridge gave an indication of human emotion. He frowned. "What are you saying, Mr. Barrett?"

"I am saying there is more at stake in our trial than a mere book," said Barrett passionately. "I am saying freedom of speech is on trial. It has often been on trial, but it has never had so many enemies gathered together before. Recent years of permissiveness in the arts have made freedom's advocates complacent, made them blind. They have not seen the massive gathering of the forces of censorship. We've reached a crossroads. If Jadway's book goes under, I foresee the beginning of a new Dark Age."

"You need not lecture me about freedom, Mr. Barrett. All I have asked you to tell me is—what are you trying to say?"

"I am trying to say that now that we have learned Jadway is alive, now that he can reveal the facts about himself and about his book, we implore him to do so. We feel it is imperative that he do so, no matter what the cost to his privacy. The impact of his appearance in court, the sensation of his testimony, the exposure of truth for the first time, these can overturn the case that the prosecution has built, and win us a verdict of not guilty, and defeat the censors and free *The Seven Minutes*. Senator, I want Jadway to know what I am saying—"

"I promise you that he shall know."

"—and I want you to ask him to appear in person as a witness for the defense in Los Angeles tomorrow."

"I can ask him. I can also give you his answer. His answer will be no."

"You are sure of that?"

"I am positive."

Barrett came to his feet, agitated. "I can't understand it, I simply don't understand it, how a man who has accomplished such a miracle of liberation in his past can now disown the miracle and the past. How is that possible? What kind of cowardice or selfishness is that? What kind of man is Jadway, anyway?"

He was aware that Bainbridge had been watching him, listening to his every word, and now he saw that Bainbridge wanted to answer. Barrett waited, and the Senator spoke, choosing his own words with care. "I will tell you what kind of man Jadway is, and then you will understand his reason for not coming forward. If, in his youth, Jadway was an idealist, he is now, in his advanced years, a pragmatist. He knows that what is best for the many, for the common weal, is in the end best for Jadway himself, since he is a part of the whole. Anything less would be self-indulgence. Do I sound enigmatic? Then I will resolve the riddle for you. Jadway graduated from law school when I did. He had no taste for the law. He felt his greater talent lay in writing. He went to Paris. He tried to write, and under the influence of Miss McGraw, he wrote. He was satisfied that he could do more for the cause of freedom, do more to liberate the human soul, through writing than through practicing law. But other circumstances intervened—do not inquire what circumstances, for I cannot divulge them—but as a result, Jadway had to forfeit his writing career, and law as well. Some years later, when there was the possibility of a choice, he had lost his interest in writing, but there was still the law. So he returned to it, to serve it as best he could. He has risen high. Now he will rise higher. In short weeks, I can tell you in confidence, there will be a vacancy on the bench of the Supreme Court of the United States, and the President has privately asked Jadway whether he would accept an appointment to the Supreme Court."

"The Supreme Court?" Barrett gasped. He was truly taken aback. "I—I keep picturing Jadway today as a bohemian, just as he was in his Paris days, since that's the way he's been described to the world in court. Do you mean he's become a man of such stature and respectability that he is eligible for appointment to the Supreme Court?"

"He is eligible and he will be nominated."

The full meaning of this information now took hold of Barrett and brought him closer to Bainbridge.

"Senator, do you know what that means?" Barrett beseeched him. "It means Jadway—or whatever he's called today—is a hundredfold more valuable a witness than I had ever imagined he could be. And it is a hundred times more imperative that he now come forward for us, for himself."

Bainbridge began to protest, but Barrett overrode him and continued his peroration with growing conviction. "Imagine the appearance in court of such a man on behalf of his book, how it would contradict the charges against him," said Barrett. "I'll tell you what it would be—at least from a defense counsel's point of view—it would be one of those incredible naturals just like—like, well, the high spot in the Lizzie Borden trial. You remember, I'm sure. Lizzie's father and stepmother had been found horribly, brutally bludgeoned to death. Everything, all circumstantial evidence, was against Lizzie Borden. Nevertheless, her defense counsel put her on the witness stand. It was a daring move, and proved to be a brilliant one. There Lizzie sat, the well-bred, well-groomed, delicate, ladylike spinster. And her counsel merely pointed to her as he addressed the jurors. 'To find her guilty, you must believe she is a fiend. Gentlemen, does she look it?' Did she look it? She did not look it. She would never look it, this prim lady. It was unthinkable. All other evidence went out the window. Lizzie was declared not guilty."

Barrett caught his breath, then resumed. "Senator Bainbridge, if fitting Lizzie Borden to such a crime was unthinkable, then I suggest to you that judging a candidate for the Supreme Court, a gentleman who has won high esteem, who is a scholar, judging this man to be a pornographer and purveyor of filth is impossible. Let Jadway take the stand as my final witness, my star witness, and it will be enough. The jury will know, from the very moment I point to him, that such a man could not have written a dirty book that might deprave and corrupt the young. They will know, before he answers a single question, that his motives must have been of the best. They will trust his moral values and his testimony. Senator, we'd get an acquittal for Ben Fremont, for *The Seven Minutes*, for Jadway himself, just as Lizzie Borden got—"

"Mr. Barrett," the Senator interrupted. "You need not burden me further with the legal tactics in the Borden case." Then he added caustically, "After all, I *was* Dean of the Law School at Yale."

Barrett was instantly contrite. "Forgive me, sir. It's just that such a perfect witness rarely comes—"

"Mr. Barrett, if you will, permit me to finish what I had begun to say."

"Please."

"I have no doubt Jadway would be your perfect defense witness. However, there is considerably more at stake in this matter than your trial. There is a Supreme Court appointment in the balance. The announcement will be made soon enough, and you shall know Jadway's identity, though no one else beyond this room, save dear senile Cassie and our befuddled friend O'Flanagan, will know that the new Justice of the Supreme Court was once the author of *The Seven Minutes*. Now, Mr. Barrett, in all good sense, were you Jadway, would you sacrifice this opportunity of a lifetime in order to go out to California simply to defend, in a mere felony trial, a book that you had written in your youth? That, I suggest, would be self-indulgence. For, I assure you, should Jadway reveal his past in the witness box, should he go out there to save your censorship case, it would mean the destruction of his reputation. The offer to become a justice of the Supreme Court would be instantly withdrawn. Yes, your call to me last night was brought to Jadway's attention swiftly enough. It gave him considerable anguish and invited much soul-searching. It was not the damage to his reputation or ambition or social standing or family that prompted his decision. It was this—that he might do far more for the cause of freedom from his seat on the highest bench in the land, over the years to come, than if he sacrificed that opportunity in order to speak out in one court case on behalf of his own past. It was the opportunity to defend many freedoms, rather than only one, that motivated his decision. I say to you that this is not the choice of a selfish but of a public-spirited man, not of a man of cowardice but of a man of courage. That is the kind of man J J Jadway is. And—that is why he will not appear at your trial."

Barrett was very still. He walked slowly to the window, gazed absently into the street, and finally returned to the desk.

"Senator Bainbridge," he said with control, "I think Mr. Jadway is wrong. I know I can't persuade you, or him through you, but I must tell you what I feel. I think he is wrong. I believe that there are other great men in law who might fill the Supreme Court vacancy as capably as Mr. Jadway might, and who might dispense wisdom and justice as well as he might. However, there is only one man, one man on earth, who can save this particular book, and all it represents, and all it means to the future. I think that this is where Mr. Jadway should fight his fight, in the here and now, down among the people, where he, and he alone, can save us, and save himself by refusing to repudiate his past. I do believe his past means more to the present, his present and ours, than does his future. That's what I feel. And there is something more. If this case is lost, it will establish as a legal precedent that the courts believe men can be driven to violence—as the prosecution has contended with its example of Jerry Griffith—by a work of literature. Should this go unchallenged, should this fallacy be upheld and become legally accepted in our time, then all words spoken or written hereafter will be under the sentence of death, and the real evils in our society that nourish and breed violence will be acquitted to grow on and on until all of us, and our heirs, and everything we cherish will be destroyed. Thank you for the hearing, Senator Bainbridge. Tell Mr. Jadway I hope he sleeps well tonight."

He was at the door when Bainbridge's voice caught him.

"Mr. Barrett—"

He waited.

Bainbridge was standing behind his desk. "I'll see that Mr. Jadway considers everything you have said. Should he change his mind, he'll know where to reach you."

Barrett tried to smile. "But you know he won't change his mind, don't you?"

The Senator did not reply. He appeared bemused. He said, "You might like to hear that in the matter of Jadway's writing the book, his life, his suicide, the reasons for his suicide, Christian Leroux did not knowingly lie. He simply did not tell the truth. Because he did not know the truth. He knew only the lie. Just as Father Sarfatti knew only the lie. Jadway's and Cassie's lie. Perhaps that is of importance now. I cannot say. One thing I am sorry about. I am sorry that it will be believed that a book could drive a boy to commit rape, to act violently. Rape was an avocation of men long before they learned to read. This aspect of the result of your case will be unfortunate. But perhaps Mr. Jadway will be able to rectify that one day—in another way, one day."

"Senator, there is no one day. There is only tomorrow. Goodbye."

Going down to the street level, he knew that he had reached rock bottom at last. How many times had he thought he had reached the floor of the pit of despair? He could scarcely count the number. But this time it was the bottom. There was no place else he could go. The last light of hope had been extinguished.

He emerged into the sunlight and went dejectedly down the flight of stairs to the street, and then he started toward a taxi.

A newsboy who was hawking papers on the corner was calling out to passersby, "Read it, just in—latest sensation in Los Angeles sex-book trial!"

The latest? What in the devil could that be?

Barrett hastened to the corner, handed the boy a coin, and unfolded the front page of the newspaper.

The bold black banner headline lashed at him like a whip:

SHERI MOORE IS DEAD!
RAPE VICTIM IN JADWAY "MINUTES" CASE
DIES UNEXPECTEDLY; DEBATED PORNOGRAPHIC BOOK
GOES TO JURY TOMORROW.

He recoiled.

His first thought was of that poor kid in the hospital, gone, ended, and then his thoughts were of her father, Howard Moore, of Jerry Griffith, of Maggie, and finally, of Abe and himself.

Minutes ago he had thought that he had reached bottom, but it had been a false bottom, for now the last trapdoor had been sprung from under him, and he found that it was possible to sink even lower, and it was black down there, the blackest day he had ever known.

IT WAS late morning in Los Angeles, and in the bedroom of Barrett's apartment Maggie Russell had finished drying after her shower, and was just fastening her brassiere, when the telephone rang for the second time in the past hour. Still clad in only her half slip and brassiere, she hurried into the living room to catch the call.

To her relief, it was Mike Barrett calling from Washington.

"Mike, I was praying it would be you," she said into the telephone. "I wanted to call you, but I knew you wouldn't be in. Have you heard? I mean, about Sheri—Sheri Moore. She died in the night."

"Yes, I saw the headlines a half hour ago."

"Isn't it pitiful? She was so young. I feel awful. And Jerry is desperate. And you—I can hear it in your voice—you sound so low."

"I am low. That poor kid, Sheri—I never knew her, but still, when something like that occurs, it makes everything else seem unimportant."

"Yes, it does. I can't get her out of my mind—and, selfishly, I keep worrying about Jerry also, how it'll all affect him." She paused. "And I'm worried about you, Mike."

"Forget about me. Sure, I'm low. It's been a rotten morning all around, but at least I'm alive, sort of."

"What does that mean? I thought you'd—well, aside from everything else that's taken place, I thought you'd have *some* good news. You were seeing Senator Bainbridge and Jadway this morning, weren't you?"

"I saw Bainbridge. Period. I just came from him."

"What happened, Mike? Don't tell me he wouldn't—?"

"He wouldn't. It's no go."

"Oh, Mike, I'm so sorry. I was sure once they realized you knew Jadway was alive, they'd—"

"It's not that simple. Bainbridge's main sideline seems to be perpetuating the myth that Jadway is dead. He threw me one crumb. He'll see that Jadway considers everything I said, my whole plea. But that won't come to anything."

"Can't you subpoena Jadway?"

"Where? How? How do you subpoena a ghost?"

"I guess that was a stupid suggestion, but I'm so upset for you, I—I'm trying to think of something." She thought of something else. "Mike, what happened between you and Bainbridge? What did he say? Do you want to talk about it?"

His voice sounded so dispirited that her heart ached for him, but she coaxed him to talk, and before long he had told her everything that had transpired from the moment he had met Miss Xavier in the Capitol until he had left the Senator's office.

Then he went on. After this failure to reach Jadway, he had learned about Sheri's death. He had returned to his hotel, and because of the time difference he had been able to catch Zelkin before he had gone into court. Zelkin too had been rocked by Sheri's death, and crushed by the refusal of Bainbridge and Jadway to cooperate.

579

"As Abe put it, if the author wouldn't defend his own book and his own life, how could we hope to defend it successfully for him?" said Barrett. "And Sheri Moore's dying, that certainly upset Abe—he feels as we do about the poor kid. But quite apart from that, there is the question of how Sheri's death will influence the result of the trial. Abe had to admit that even though her death has nothing to do with the legal aspects of the case, the emotional effect it will have on the jurors—and you can be sure one of them, somehow, will hear about it—the effect it will have on everyone connected with the trial, today and tomorrow, will be tremendous. It puts the final exclamation mark to Duncan's argument that Jadway's book drove Jerry to do what he did to Sheri and was the real cause of her death. Jadway is no longer a rapist. He is now a murderer, he and anyone else who ever wants to express himself freely."

"And there's nothing more you can do about it?" she asked slowly.

"Nothing anyone can do about it, Maggie, except Jadway himself. Had he agreed to come forward, even the emotionalism surrounding Sheri's death might have been overcome. His appearance might have put the whole focus of the trial back on the book itself. He could have succeeded in getting it a clean bill of goods. In that way, we would have had a chance to prove, with living evidence, that such an author and such a book could have done Jerry no harm and therefore was in no way responsible for Sheri's death. But what's the use of speculating? It's over. To all intents and purposes, Jadway is as dead today as he was the day the trial started. And those who feel as we do are going to suffer for it. The censors are in the saddle. The witch hunters ride again. Freedom to speak, to dissent, to protest, they'll all be cut down along with freedom to read. Well, why go on? I might as well come back to Sheri's funeral—"

"Mike—"

"Yes?"

She had been listening carefully, and thinking a lot, and she had to know one last thing.

"Besides what happens to your case now, Mike, this latest development is going to make it much harder on Jerry, isn't it?"

He seemed reluctant to reply. Finally he did. "Yes, I'm afraid so, Maggie."

"How much harder?"

"We can talk about that when I get back."

"I want to know now, Mike. I'm a grown girl. Tell me straight."

"All right. Up to now, with the victim alive, Jerry could have got anywhere from three years to life in the state prison, but inasmuch as he cooperated with the D.A.'s Office, and what with the psychiatric evidence and so forth, he might have come off with one to three years at the most. However, with Sheri's death, the forcible-rape charge has been compounded by homicide, and the probability is he'll get—well, he could be sentenced to prison for life."

"*Life?*" Maggie shuddered. "That's not possible. It's not fair. They don't know Jerry."

"Maggie, the law knows only what it has seen and heard."

Only what it has seen and heard, she thought.

"Mike, Jerry found out where I was staying through Donna at your office. I heard from him this morning."

Barrett sounded disbelieving. "You did? Isn't he in jail yet?"

"Jail? What do you mean, Mike?"

"I thought you understood. As long as Sheri was alive, he could remain free on bail. Now that she's dead, it's murder, and Jerry has to be confined to the county prison."

She nodded at the telephone. "Then that explains it. He called just to talk to me. He has no one to talk to. So we discussed what had happened, and I tried to calm him down, and finally I asked him if he could get out and come over here, and he said he'd try to sneak past his father and see me, but he'd have to get right back. He said the District Attorney was coming over during the noon recess, at one o'clock, to see him and Uncle Frank. Mike, is Duncan going to arrest him?"

"Yes. Normally, Jerry would be in jail already. But since his father and Duncan are chummy—well, I guess that's why the arrest was delayed a few hours. But I'm afraid he'll be in jail this afternoon."

"Then I'm glad he's on his way here. I just wanted to calm him down, but now— Well, never mind. I better finish dressing. Are you coming back today?"

"They should have my reservation by now. I'll go straight to the courtroom, if that trial's still on. If not, I'd better stop off at the office. I'll see you tonight."

"Tonight," she said uncertainly. Then she said, "Mike, don't give up. Maybe something will happen."

"Darling, I think the guy up there has a certain quota of miracles for each of his children, and I'm afraid mine has been used up."

Maybe yours, she wanted to say, but maybe not mine. Instead, she said goodbye.

After she had hung up, she stood beside the telephone and tried to remember what Mike had said to her.

He had said, *Maggie, the law knows only what it has seen and heard.* But, Mike, what if it has not seen and heard everything?

He had said, *How do you subpoena a ghost?* But, Mike, why not try?

He had said, *The guy up there has a certain quota of miracles for each of his children.* That's right, Mike, but maybe I'm not overdrawn yet.

What was it that the clerk always said in court? The truth, the whole truth, and nothing but the truth, so help you God.

All right, help me God. The time had come for the whole truth, and nothing but the truth.

She tried to think it out. When she had done so, when each step fell into place, she was ready to begin.

First, the long-distance call to Washington.

In less than a minute she had her connection.

"Miss Xavier? Senator Bainbridge's secretary?"

"Yes."

"This is Miss Maggie Russell in Los Angeles." Now a white lie. "I'm associated with the Griffith Advertising Agency. It's quite important that I see Senator Bainbridge tomorrow, on Mr. Griffith's behalf, on a business matter. I wonder if it would be possible to arrange an appointment."

"I'm afraid tomorrow is impossible, Miss Russell. The Senator will be out of the city tomorrow."

"Will he be away long?"

"I can't say, Miss Russell. I do know for certain that he will be leaving in the morning. Of course, there is a possibility that he'll be back from Chicago later in the day. If you want to state the nature of your business, maybe I can arrange—"

"No, never mind. Thanks. I'll get back to you next week."

She dropped the receiver in the cradle.

So it *was* Chicago. Senator Bainbridge would be in Chicago. Somehow, she was not at all surprised.

That was the first step. So far, so good.

Now the second step. Jerry Griffith. He would be over shortly, and she would be dressed and waiting. He would be over expecting to use her shoulder to cry on, and expecting the usual placebo pill. But not this time, Jerry. No placebos, no faking it. And no shoulder either, because she needed it for something else, for giving it to him straight from the shoulder.

Then the third step. Howard Moore. Even in his bereavement over his daughter's death, especially in his bereavement, he would see her, she knew.

Finally the last step. She would call International Airport. A jet-liner reservation to Chicago for tonight.

That was it—if you believed in miracles.

She started for the bedroom, the refrain singing in her head. California, here I go . . . California, here I go . . .

XI

THE FOLLOWING MORNING, Thursday, the second day of July, a hired chauffeur and limousine, recently arrived from O'Hare International Airport, stood waiting outside the Sunnyside Convalescent Sanitarium in Chicago.

Inside the nursing home, beyond the bustle of employees removing breakfast dishes from the patients' rooms to the kitchen, and two handymen swabbing the corridor floor with some antiseptic solution, the door of the administrator's office was opening.

It was Senator Thomas Bainbridge who emerged from the office first, and right behind him, pleased and bobbing with deference, came Mr. Holliday.

"No, no, no, Senator," Mr. Holliday was repeating once more, "I assure you, you haven't disturbed the routine one mite. Our visiting hours are always flexible."

"Thank you, Mr. Holliday. I shan't be long."

"This is an honor, our pleasure, Senator Bainbridge. I know Miss McGraw—Mrs. Sullivan, I should say—I know she'll be pleased. This is the second—uh—prominent visitor she will have had in two days. Yesterday, from Los Angeles—"

"I know, Mr. Holliday."

They had come to the recreation-room entrance. "Now, of course, as I've cautioned you, Senator Bainbridge, she is not always communicative. She can be lucid, she can make good sense, but frequently these patients tend to be somewhat, well, a trifle —confused. But if she is having one of her better days, you understand . . ."

"I understand perfectly, Mr. Holliday."

"She's just finished her breakfast, and at this hour you can have a fair amount of privacy."

Bainbridge had entered the recreation room, and Mr. Holliday was beside him again.

"Which one is she?" asked Bainbridge.

"At the table, alone, next to the patio window," said Mr. Holliday. "In the wheelchair, wearing the pink model coat. Her nurse is tidying her up. . . . Oh, Miss Jefferson! Can I see you?"

The lanky nurse came rapidly across the hall. "I got her all prettied, Mr. Holliday."

"Excellent, excellent. Now, Miss Jefferson, I've promised the Senator some privacy. See that nobody interrupts."

"I'll watch for that, Mr. Holliday."

"Well, Senator—" the manager began.

"If you don't mind," Bainbridge interrupted, "I'd like to be alone with her now."

"Of course, of course," Mr. Holliday apologized, and he retreated through the door, taking Miss Jefferson with him.

Bainbridge remained where he had been standing.

He steeled himself. There were some things one had to do. Now he must proceed, he told himself. Right now.

He advanced quickly with his one-pound box of candy.

When almost upon her, he slowed, going around the wheelchair, so as not to startle her.

She had been staring at the centerpiece on the table, but then she was conscious of someone, and she turned the sunken face toward him, looked at him up and down, without reaction.

"Cassie McGraw," he said.

She did not acknowledge her name or his presence.

"Do you mind if I sit down?"

Without waiting for her answer, Bainbridge placed the box of candy on the table, threw his light raincoat across the back of the chair, and sat across from her.

"I am Thomas Bainbridge," he said. "You don't remember my name, do you?"

She was interested in the yellow ribbon on the gift wrap of the candy box. She tried to touch it. He took up the box and offered it to her. She patted the bow, but did not accept the box.

"It is for you," he said. "Would you like me to open it?"

She smiled sweetly.

585

He tore off the ribbon and the wrapping, and opened the box, and held it before her. "Will you have one?"

She looked down at the candies, but made no move to choose one.

"What will it be?" he said. "Would you like a soft one?"

She nodded.

He found a chocolate with a cream center, and he placed it in her hand. She brought her hand to her mouth, then put the candy in her mouth and chewed it absently as she continued to smile at him.

Now, he told himself, now.

"Cassie," he said, "I am here on a special errand, a mission, one might say, for a man you once knew and loved, and who loved you and has not ceased loving you to this day. I'm here on behalf of J J Jadway."

He waited for her response to the name, but she did not appear to have heard him. She was fascinated by his gold tie clip. She chewed her candy and fixed her eyes on the glittering tie clip.

"Cassie," he resumed urgently, "I know that newspapers are sometimes read to you, and that occasionally you watch and hear the news on television. I'm sure you've been informed of that trial in Los Angeles over Jadway's book—that book he wrote, you must remember, *The Seven Minutes*. Well, Jadway—I'm sure you know that he is alive—"

But then he was not sure, and he waited for some recognition of the fact from her. There was none, but her gaze had finally gone from the tie clip to his face, and he thought perhaps she might be ready to listen.

"You remember how you stayed behind in Paris, and did what he told you to do," he was saying, "and how he came back to get you at Cherbourg, and you both returned to New York together? You and he had arranged it. He was to be declared dead. But you and I—and Sean—we knew he was not dead. It was our secret. But now this Los Angeles attorney who saw you yesterday, he's found out Jadway is alive, and he wants Jadway to stand as a witness at the trial. It was a terrible decision for Jadway to make. But he made it. He could not appear at that trial, Cassie. Because the Jadway you and I once knew, he is no more, and he saw no value in destroying the present in order to save something of the past.

He had only one concern after making his decision, and it was for you. One day you might learn that the trial had been lost, and that he had not been there to defend his past and yours and all that both of you had stood for. He wanted you to know that that past could not be revived—that a part of it would always live inside each of you, but it could not be made all of you, consuming all of the present. He wanted you to know, Cassie, and he wanted you to understand." Bainbridge paused. "I only want to tell you, for him, so that you do understand and can forgive Jadway."

She had swallowed the last of the candy, and now her lips moved.

"Who is Jadway?" she asked.

He sat straight and unmoving, and then he sagged slightly. He thought, Now cracks a noble heart. He thought, Good night, sweet princess . . .

Who is Jadway?

His head went up and down. "That's right, Cassie. Who is Jadway? He is dead, isn't he? He died in Paris long ago. You are right, and he is right, to let the past stay buried."

She nodded blankly and smiled.

Bainbridge rose and lifted his raincoat off the chair.

"Goodbye, Cassie," he said gently.

He could not be sure that she had heard him. Her wasted hand had already reached for the ribbon on the candy box.

Quietly he turned away.

When he came into the corridor again, he was grateful that Mr. Holliday was not to be seen. He walked to the reception desk, pulled out the long envelope, and gave it to the receptionist.

"It is a check," he said. "Please apply it to Mrs. Sullivan's account for the balance of the year."

He went outside. The limousine was waiting, and the chauffeur had leaped from his seat to open the rear door.

Then he noticed that another car door was opening—the passenger door of a taxicab parked immediately behind his limousine. A pretty young girl, dark bouffant hair and gray-green eyes, vivacious and alive and eager as Cassie had once been, had stepped down to the sidewalk and seemed to be hurrying toward him.

A few yards from the limousine, she intercepted him.

"Senator Thomas Bainbridge," she said, with no question in her voice.

Bewildered, he nodded. "Yes, I'm Senator Bainbridge."

"I've been waiting for you out here for the last fifteen minutes," she said. "My name is Margaret Russell. I flew in from Los Angeles to see you. It is about the censorship trial that is ending in Los Angeles this afternoon. No, Mike Barrett did not send me. It was Jerry Griffith who sent me."

"Jerry—?"

"The boy who testified that it was Jadway's book that drove him to—to violate the girl, the girl who died yesterday. You know about that?"

"Yes, of course I know."

"Well, I'm here for Jerry, because you're the only one left who can help him."

"Young lady, how can I possibly help him?"

"By making J J Jadway come to Los Angeles today, this very day, to meet with Jerry, and then—"

"Young lady, I have no idea who you are. And I can see no possible reason for trying to persuade Mr. Jadway—"

"If you'll listen to reason, my reason—not only for Jerry's sake, but for Cassie's as well— Please, Senator, won't you even listen?"

He stared at her, and he saw the same face and dedication that Jadway must have seen in the Cassie of so long ago.

"All right," he said gruffly, "you can ride with me to the airport. But, whatever you may have to say, I think I can promise you that you're on a fool's errand. Now get in. I have to catch a plane."

In Los Angeles, the trial had been temporarily adjourned and the lunch recess had just begun.

On the sixth floor of the Hall of Justice, inside the District Attorney's personal lounge adjacent to his office, the four of them had cheerfully gathered to enjoy a noonday meal that an expansive Luther Yerkes had had catered by Scandia Restaurant.

Yerkes had arrived early, before the recess and before the press and the spectators had emptied out of the courtroom. Now, sporting a new auburn hairpiece, blue-tinted glasses, a capacious light-blue sport jacket with medallion buttons, and navy summer slacks, Luther Yerkes squatted like a festive Buddha on the gray linen-covered sofa and devoted himself to the dish of Kalvfilet Oskar

—veal cutlets with crab legs—set on the marble-topped coffee table in front of him. Reclining in armchairs on either side of Yerkes, their plates in their laps, were Harvey Underwood and Irwin Blair. Only Elmo Duncan was not seated. He had consumed but a small portion of the Kalvfilet Oskar and had then restlessly returned to his stapled notes lying atop the walnut radio console.

Chewing steadily, Yerkes watched the District Attorney concentrating on his notes. "Elmo, you ought to finish eating—" Yerkes began.

Duncan looked up from the notes. "Too much food slows me down," he said. "I think we've got a big afternoon ahead."

"Well, you've got nothing to worry about," said Yerkes. "You've been magnificent. It's in the bag."

Duncan sauntered to the center of the lounge. "It's in the bag when the foreman says Guilty." Then he smiled. "But I think we're in good shape. They've about run out of witnesses. I'm sure Barrett will rest the defense's case this afternoon. I'd better be ready for my summation to the jury." He tapped his notes. "I know you've already heard me rehearse this two or three times—"

"Four times," agreed Irwin Blair with a grin.

Duncan ignored him. "There are a few more points I'd like to work in. Mind if I try them out on you?"

"Love to hear them," said Yerkes, patting his mouth with his napkin. "Every syllable is pure gold to me. Speak on, Demosthenes."

"First, the part where I review Dr. Trimble's testimony on the relationship of pornography to antisocial conduct. I'd like to shore up this part by citing at least one other authority. Something like this." Duncan cleared his throat and automatically assumed an orator's stance. "The findings of numerous other psychiatric specialists support the opinion of Dr. Roger Trimble. Among the most respected of these is Dr. Nicholas G. Frignito, head psychiatrist of the Philadelphia Municipal Court. It was Dr. Frignito who told a congressional committee that fifty per cent of all juvenile delinquents have access to salacious literature or similar materials. It was Dr. Frignito who told the committee, 'Antisocial, delinquent, and criminal activity frequently results from sexual stimulation by pornography. This abnormal sexual stimulation creates such a demand for expression that gratification by vicarious means follows. Girls run away from their homes and become entangled in prostitution. Boys and young men . . . become sexually aggressive and generally incorrigible.' In this very court, you have seen and heard a young man, a decent young man, who was transformed into a sexually aggressive and incorrigible animal by a book, by a book called *The Seven Minutes.*" Duncan paused, and his tone became informal. "Then I'll go on with what you heard when I rehearsed it before, and I'll dramatize what the book did to Jerry Griffith."

"Good," said Yerkes.

"Also, I'd like to anticipate Barrett and cut the ground from under him before he begins prattling, as he's sure to do, about the guaranties of the First Amendment, and how we're trying to suppress freedom of speech. Like this." Duncan resumed his orator's pose. "In our condemnation of *The Seven Minutes,* we are not seeking to curb those freedoms spelled out in the First Amendment. For I want to make it clear, this foul book does not fall within the protection of the First Amendment. The fact remains that in the majority opinion on behalf of the Supreme Court in the celebrated Samuel Roth case in 1957, Mr. Justice Brennan firmly stated that the First Amendment does not guaranty freedom of speech to the purveyors of obscene material. 'The protection given speech and press was fashioned to assure unfettered interchange of ideas for the bringing about of political and social changes desired by the people. . . . All ideas having even the slightest redeeming social importance—unorthodox ideas, controversial ideas, even ideas hateful to the prevailing climate of opinion—have the full protection of the guaranties. . . . But—' "

Duncan paused dramatically, and his last word dangled over his listeners like a swaying figure in a cliff-hanger, and then he caught the word, rescued it, and went on. " 'But implicit in the history of the First Amendment,' stated Mr. Justice Brennan, still giving the majority opinion of the Court, 'is the rejection of obscenity as utterly without redeeming social importance. This rejection for that reason is mirrored in the universal judgment that obscenity should be restrained, reflected in the international agreement of over fifty nations, in the obscenity laws of all of the . . . states, and in the twenty obscenity laws enacted by the Congress from 1842 to 1956. . . . We hold that obscenity is not within the area of constitutionally protected speech or press.'

"Ladies and gentlemen of the jury, during the days of this trial we have attempted to show you that this book, *The Seven Minutes*, is totally obscene, utterly without redeeming social importance, and therefore is outside the protection guarantied by the First Amendment to our Constitution. We trust that we have proved that this book deserves to be censored—indeed, to be banished from civilized society forever." He looked at the others. "How's that?"

"Smackeroo, the Kayo punch, the flattener," Blair chortled. "Count ten thousand over Barrett and he still won't get up."

"It's excellent," said Underwood.

Yerkes cupped a hand over his gold toothpick. "I'm more interested in the tag of your closing argument. You were going to make it meatier."

"I have," said Duncan. He walked to the console, dropped his notes on it, and returned to the center of the lounge, rubbing his dry hands together. "You ready? Here goes." He drew himself up and began to address the unseen jurors. "Ladies and gentlemen of the jury, it is the State's belief that this book was manufactured by an author with the leer of the professional pornographer and commercialist. To support this contention, we have laid bare the cynical and sick mind, the sadistic mind, of this pornographer and of all other depraved ghouls like him. We have escorted you on a journey through a subterranean world where dwells, as Senator Smoot once said of the author of *Ulysses*, 'a man with a diseased mind and soul so black that he would even obscure the darkness of hell.' This man is the pornographer whose sole vocation is to survive, even become rich, even derive pleasure, by degrading love, by extolling sin, by infecting the innocent with lust—and who, with every filthy word, continues to rape the Muse. This is the mentality that would pervert the young, mocking the warning of Jesus Christ that 'if anyone hurts the conscience of one of these little ones that believe in me, he had better have been drowned in the depths of the sea, with a millstone hung about his neck.' This is the pornographer who, if indulged, we have been told by the most respected authorities, will turn our society into a world that is 'even more coarse, brutal, anxious, indifferent, de-individualized, hedonistic.'

"We know, for a fact, from the testimony of our illustrious witness from France, Christian Leroux, and our honorable witness from the Vatican, Father Sarfatti, that J J Jadway was just such a pornographer, was an admitted pornographer who set out to turn our society into a world both coarse and brutal. That he was one of the first victims of his own disreputable work is not our concern here today. What *is* our concern is that the obscenity that Jadway created not be let loose to seek more victims. We know, to our sorrow, that this book has only recently claimed two new victims, turning Jerry Griffith into a sex criminal against his will, destroying an innocent girl, Sheri Moore. How many more victims will you allow this monster of obscenity, this vile book, this book by J J Jadway, to claim? I implore you to save your children, your homes, your society, your very world, your world and ours, by shackling this monster while you can.

"Ladies and gentlemen of the jury, unto your hands I commend the doing of justice in this case, in the knowledge that by your so doing, by your performing this act of justice, you will sleep all the better, because the world will sleep more safely for your verdict. Ladies and gentlemen, thank you."

Yerkes jumped to his feet, and Underwood and Blair followed him, each of them applauding vigorously.

Duncan, still flushed, offered a sheepish smile. Then, meeting their eyes, he said, "I mean it, you know. I mean every word . . . Well, any suggestions?"

"Just one," said Yerkes. "I think we're ready for our dessert."

ELSEWHERE on the sixth floor of the Hall of Justice, within the private quarters of the conference room that the defense had used frequently for the two-hour noon recess, the five of them sat slumped around the table in various attitudes of despondency.

It was supposed to be lunch, but to Mike Barrett it was a wake.

Gloomily Barrett, his own sandwich untouched on the plate before him, contemplated first Zelkin and Kimura, then Sanford and Fremont, who were munching their sandwiches and sipping the last of their tepid coffee or flat soft drinks.

Zelkin pushed aside his plate. "Well," he said, "this isn't exactly the most optimistic victory rally I've ever attended."

"What's to cheer about?" asked Sanford.

Zelkin brought the black portable cassette tape recorder nearer to him. "There's the closing argument Mike dictated in the wee hours this morning. I think it's a dilly." He addressed his partner.

"Mind if I pick it up where we left off? It might give us a shot in the arm."

"What good's a shot in the arm," said Barrett, "when the patient's already expired?"

"Let's listen anyway," persisted Zelkin. "Maybe we'll get some ideas."

He punched the play key, and immediately the tape began unwinding, and Barrett's recorded summation came metallically through the miniature speaker.

"The procedure of the defense in this case has been guided by the wisdom of the most eminent legal minds of our time," announced Barrett's voice from the tape. "It was Supreme Court Justice Douglas who wrote, 'The idea of using censors to bar thoughts of sex is dangerous. A person without sex thoughts is abnormal. Sex thoughts may induce sex practices that make for better marital relations. Sex thoughts that make love attractive certainly should not be outlawed. If the illicit is included, that should make no constitutional difference. For education concerning the illicit may well stimulate people to seek their experiences in wedlock rather than out of it.'

"So spoke a Justice of the United States Supreme Court. Not to have sex thoughts is abnormal. To have them is normal. To use laws of obscenity to bar thoughts of sex is dangerous. To ban a work of art because it encourages thinking about sex is menacing to the health of our society. That has been the contention of the defense during the days of this trial.

"Nor did Justice Douglas alone define our case. In 1957, as a consequence of the celebrated Roth case, another Justice of the Supreme Court, Justice Brennan, told us the following: 'Sex and obscenity are not synonymous. Obscene material is material which deals with sex in a manner appealing to prurient interest. The portrayal of sex—in art, literature, and scientific works, is not itself sufficient reason to deny material the constitutional protection of freedom of speech and press. Sex, a great and mysterious motive force in human life, has indisputably been a subject of absorbing interest to mankind through the ages; it is one of the vital problems of human interest and public concern.'"

Barrett winced, hearing his own dictated rehearsal matter, but Zelkin remained fascinated. He fiddled with the tape machine,

593

moving the tape forward, stopping it, starting it again. "There are a couple of passages I'm trying to— Wait, I have it. I want to hear this part again, Mike. Where you discuss the fantasies that pornographic books inspire. Listen, everyone."

Barrett's taped speech filled the room.

"Ladies and gentlemen of the jury, from the witness stand you have heard the renowned psychiatrist Dr. Yale Finegood speak of the harmless effects of pornography. The most sinister effect of such reading, you have heard the witness state, is that it conjures up fantasies in the mind of the reader. Concerning this point, two English psychologists have asked the question, What is so terribly wrong about erotic fantasy and the dissemination of material, even shocking material, that feeds the sexually immature person's craving for such fantasy? It is an important question, this one. Before answering it, we might try to learn to what kind of behavior such hallucinations lead the reader. It is on record that the great diarist Samuel Pepys read a pornographic book in 1668 and was mightily stimulated by it. The book, published three years earlier, was *L'Escole des filles*, by Michel Millilot. The story consisted of a dialogue between two women, one a virgin and the other a woman well experienced in sexual intercourse. Pepys called it 'a mighty lewd book,' but he read it through and later recorded that it gave him an erection and excited him enough to make him masturbate. This occasional effect of reading a lewd book was understood by another literary figure, the Comte de Mirabeau, a statesman who played a role in the French Revolution and became president of the National Assembly in 1791. When Mirabeau was imprisoned for running off with the nineteen-year-old wife of a seventy-year-old husband, he tried to alleviate the boredom of incarceration by writing both social tracts and books that were pornographic in content. One of the latter was a work entitled *Ma Conversion*, and with healthy candor Mirabeau prefaced the erotic work with this forthright invitation to his public, 'And now, read, devour, masturbate.' "

Zelkin chuckled. "Great, Mike. The jury will be hanging on every word. Let's have the rest."

Barrett's voice continued to emerge from the tape machine's speaker. " 'Masturbate.' Perhaps the word makes one uneasy. Certainly it is not an act that the defense is advocating—although

Mark Twain, tongue in cheek, advocated it in his privately printed treatise *Some Thoughts on the Science of Onanism.* What the defense is saying is that the worst result of reading an erotic book might be masturbation, an act harmful to no one, whereas the reader of a book dealing with criminal homicide would have no such harmless outlet to satisfy his overstimulated hostilities— only possibly a harmful outlet like rushing out to beat someone up or murder him.

"Which brings me to another point that the defense has sought to develop through its witnesses. There is a certain paradox that was stated succinctly by that student of censorship Gershon Legman, who put it this way: 'Murder is a crime. Describing murder is not. Sex is not a crime. Describing sex is.' This point may be developed in another direction. The well-known British anthropologist Geoffrey Gorer has wondered why censors believe that reading a book about sex will deprave and corrupt and lead a person to sexual violence, but that reading a book about murder, a detective story, a mystery, will neither deprave and corrupt nor lead a person to commit homicide. There are psychological answers, and you have heard them propounded in this courtroom.

"As this trial has unfolded, the defense has presented evidence to support two statements, one made by a psychiatrist and the other by a newspaper columnist. The psychiatrist Dr. Robert Lindner once wrote the following: 'I am convinced that were all so-called objectionable books and like material to disappear from the face of the earth tomorrow this would in no way affect the statistics of crime, delinquency, amoral and anti-social behavior, or personal illness and distress. The same frustrating and denying society would still exist, and both children and adults would express themselves mutinously against it. These problems will be solved only when we have the courage to face the fundamental social issues and personal perplexities that cause such behavior.'

"As to the newspaper columnist Sydney J. Harris, he put it this way: 'I don't happen to believe that obscenity, of any sort, is as harmful as some people seem to think. The profound immoralities of our time are cruelty, indifference, injustice, and the use of others as means rather than as ends in themselves. If everything deemed indecent or obscene were wiped out overnight, it would not make for a conspicuously better world, or for a more "moral" citizenry.' "

Zelkin pressed the stop key on the tape machine and then punched the forward key.

Barrett protested the resumption of the tape. "I think we've heard about enough, Abe."

"Just one more passage, Mike. Where you start with Plato." He tried to locate it on the machine. As he did so he asked, "Hey, how do you know he'll bring up that Plato quote in his summation?"

"I heard him use it once in a speech to the STDL," said Barrett. "He won't be able to resist using it again. He'll want to give classical authority to his argument."

"Here, I've found it," said Zelkin. "Quiet, everyone. Attention. Our master's voice."

Barrett heard his voice spin off the tape once more, and he shut his eyes if not his ears. With the others, he listened to himself.

"The honorable counsel for the State has told you that the philosopher Plato favored censorship of reading. Indeed, he did. In fact, he wanted to censor Homer's *Odyssey* for the young. But what opposition counsel has not told you is that Plato also wanted to censor music—particularly flute players. Now, this would not make me too happy if I lived in Plato's Republic. Because I like the flute. But Plato didn't. Therefore, I would not be able to buy a flute or play one privately or even listen to the sweet sounds of the flute in his utopia, because a censor had told me that the flute would deprave and corrupt me. In short, who knows what should be banned for everyone? Indeed, who knows what is obscene for anyone else?

"The counsel for the State is confident that he knows what is obscene. With this confidence, he feels that you must know not only the activities but the motives of two persons—the pornographer and the bookseller. However, learned counsel has omitted one key person with this duo. He has omitted—the censor himself. And I am suggesting that if knowledge of the pornographer has been relevant to this trial, then knowledge of the psyche of the censor, the one who can tell us what is obscene and what is not, is equally relevant and important in judging *The Seven Minutes*.

"One common trait seems to distinguish censors from ordinary people. Members of this breed alone are self-assured, positive, even righteous in their belief that they know what is good and what is bad for the rest of us. A book like *The Seven Minutes* can harm us, the censors say, can even drive us to commit crimes of violence. But why is it 'us' who have to be protected, and never 'them?' Why is it that the censor, who is exposed to the same dangerous writing that we are, never becomes corrupted by it, is never infected by it, never turns rapist after reading it? Why does the censor have this immunity, and no one else? Why will others be harmed, but never the censor himself?

"And this leads to a correlated question. What of the thousands of respectable people throughout history who have read and collected pornographic books, yet have not been destroyed or driven to violence by these books? What of Richard Monckton Milnes, the first Baron Houghton, a cultured man who collected pornography? What of Coventry Patmore, the Catholic poet who collected pornography? What about J. Pierpont Morgan and Henry E. Huntington, our American success symbols, who collected pornography for their libraries, and Dr. Alfred Kinsey, our sex liberator, who collected it for science? What of the librarians at the British Museum in London, who look after twenty thousand so-called obscene books, and the prelates of the Vatican Library in Rome, who oversee twenty-five thousand volumes of erotica? Where is the evidence that sex books have debased any of these men?

"Briefly, let us probe further. The two best-known censors in the English-speaking world were Thomas Bowdler, who died in England in 1825, and Anthony Comstock, who died in the United States in 1915. Each of these men lived seventy-one years, devoting many of those years to censoring literature, and neither one was incited by pornography to commit rape or murder.

"Thomas Bowdler, a physician, a clergyman, read the plays of Shakespeare and was appalled. There was *Twelfth Night*, which abounded in salacious lines such as 'By my life, this is my lady's hand! these be her very C's, her U's 'n her T's, and thus makes she her great P's.' There was *Much Ado about Nothing*, in which Hercules' 'cod-piece seems as massie as his club.' There were plays like *Romeo and Juliet*, *Hamlet*, *Macbeth*, with their coarse jests and words like 'bitch' and 'whore.' Bowdler knew what must be done to save the young from corruption by Shakespeare, and he did it. In 1818 Bowdler published his expurgated ten-volume set, which he called *The Family Shakespeare*, and he explained, 'Many words and expressions occur which are of so indecent a nature as to render it highly desirable that they should be erased.' To indignant reviewers who were infuriated by the censor's prudery and excisions Bowdler replied, 'If any word or expression is of such a nature that the first impression it excites is an impression of obscenity, that word ought not to be spoken or written or printed; and, if printed, it ought to be erased.' Thus did one man, a censor, move Shakespeare's bones. And in the year of his death Bowdler published his own version of Gibbon's *History of the Decline and Fall of the Roman Empire*, also censored, purified, made aseptic for the backward public out there who he believed must be told what it could read.

"In New York, our own Anthony Comstock—a Civil War veteran, a stalwart of the YMCA, with his muttonchop whiskers and red flannel underwear that peeked out from below the cuffs of his black frock coat—set out with his trusted Bible on a life-long crusade against all that was 'lewd and lascivious' in literature and art. In 1913, as a veteran United States Post Office inspector and long-time head of the New York Society for the Suppression of Vice, he boasted that he had sent enough publishers and writers to jail to fill sixty-one railroad coaches, and that he had destroyed one hundred and sixty tons of obscene literature. He had also, he admitted, destroyed sixteen lives, the lives of persons who had in most cases been hounded to suicide and death by his fanatical puritanism. Along the way, Comstock got Walt Whitman fired from his job with the Department of the Interior for having written *Leaves of Grass*. He got Margaret Sanger's books on birth control banned and sent her husband to jail for selling these obscene publications. He attacked George Bernard Shaw's play *Mrs. Warren's Profession* and Paul Chabas' innocuous nude painting 'September Morn.' After Comstock's death, Heywood Broun wrote his epitaph: 'Anthony Comstock may have been entirely correct in his assumption that the division of living creatures into male and female was a vulgar mistake, but a conspiracy of silence about the matter will hardly alter the facts.'

"Thomas Bowdler and Anthony Comstock live on in our language. In 1836, Perronet Thompson coined the verb 'bowdlerize,' meaning 'to expurgate.' In 1905 George Bernard Shaw coined the noun 'comstockery' as a synonym for meddling, bluenosed censorship. Today the shades of Bowdler and Comstock live on in our lives, yours and mine, whenever an individual, or a group, insists he or it knows what we should read or think about sex. We are here in this courtroom because we have been told that we should not read *The Seven Minutes*, whether we want to read it or not. We have been told, by a consensus of a few minds, that this book is obscene, dangerous, and beyond redemption. My colleague and I are here to say that what is obscene in the eye of one beholder may be moral and valuable in the eye of another beholder."

Barrett had had enough of listening to himself on the tape recorder. "For Chrissake, Abe, shut the damn thing off!"

Startled, Zelkin hit the stop key, and the machine was stilled.

"I'm sorry, Abe," said Barrett, "but hearing myself say just then that what is obscene in the eye of one beholder may be moral and valuable in the eye of another—it made me realize our predicament all over again. I can read the jurors' minds, as they ask themselves—*The Seven Minutes* moral and valuable to whom? To that dead girl, Sheri Moore—presuming they've heard what happened to her—or to that poor boy, Jerry Griffith? No good, Abe."

"It's a powerful closing argument, Mike," said Zelkin seriously.

"Not enough," said Barrett.

Zelkin had lapsed into silence with the others, and Barrett, to be alone, had turned his eyes inward, rummaging through what lay behind him in the past days of the trial, and then trying to envision the death in the afternoon that lay immediately ahead.

The defense had presented and examined its final witness this morning, and the prosecution would complete its cross-examination of that witness shortly after lunch. With that, the string and time had run out. They had come to the end, Barrett knew, without denting Duncan's case. The People's evidence remained as strong and unbreakable as it had been in the first week of the trial: Jadway was a dissolute and commercially minded pornographer who had committed suicide in his remorse for having written *The Seven Minutes*, and the book had incited violence (and was capable of continuing to corrupt readers), as proved by Jerry Griffith's crime, which had since led to the death of an innocent victim.

All of this morning, Barrett had seen it in the faces of the twelve jurors. Most of them had avoided his eyes, because of what they already knew they must do to him and to the defendant. The few remaining jurors, whom he caught observing him surreptitiously from time to time, also seemed to regard him as Satan's counsel for advocating and promoting what was evil.

At this point, Barrett guessed, the twelve jurors were about as objective and unbiased as would be the mourners tomorrow at Sheri Moore's graveside.

Sitting there, Barrett closed his smarting eyes and tried to picture those jurors' reactions, their faces, if they knew as much of the truth as he now knew but could not prove. How astounded they would be, how shocked, how suddenly they would see him and Jadway and *The Seven Minutes* in a different light.

His mind went to Cassie McGraw, wondering whether she would ever have another good day, and if she did, what she would make of this repudiation of her healthy love and her past and the interred book that might have been her monument and a beacon for all inhibited and fearful women.

His mind jumped to Washington, and from there to some nebulous and unknown place where the aging J J Jadway dwelt with his safe secret. Barrett speculated on Jadway's mingled misgivings and relief, and then he wondered how much Jadway would enjoy his seat on the highest bench of the land.

Yet the jurors did not know, and would not know, that they had not heard the main actors in the case or witnessed the real performance of truth. Soon they would listen to Duncan's closing arguments, then to his own, and then they would hear Judge Upshaw's instructions. They would be led upstairs to their room by the bailiff to pretend to deliberate upon a verdict that was already predetermined. After a respectable lapse of time (this to underline their integrity), they would reappear to render their final judgment. And they would go home again, to their familiar kitchens and dining rooms and bedrooms, positive that they had served justice and democracy and the Constitution and had upheld the cause of truth and freedom.

Barrett's mind sought and found a passage from Eggleston that he had read when he had been in law school: "I do not think I am exaggerating when I say that the evidence contains only kaleidoscopic fragments of the facts. It is as if a checker of light and dark patches were held over all reality. All that gets down in the record is that seen through the light patches."

Those dutiful and complacent dismissed jurors would never know, as Barrett knew, what reality lay behind the dark patches.

And there were still dark patches that hid reality from him too. He knew more than the jurors, more than the People's counsel, but he did not know it all, and he did not know enough. Then, unaccountably, his mind went to Maggie Russell, who had not been in the apartment when he had returned last night. There had been a cryptic note propped against the telephone: "Had to go away on important business. See you tomorrow." Tomorrow was now today, and where had she gone, and on what business?

And Faye, Faye Osborn, damn her for having predicted this outcome of the case. She had been wrong about the wrongness of their cause, but she had been right about the hopelessness of their winning and about the disastrous effects the case would have on his morale and reputation.

He wished it were over. He could not bring himself to return to the court and the scene of carnage.

An old, old boyhood refrain that had come into his head last night and not gone away, but had continued to hector him in the night and throughout the morning, was monotonously replaying in his head. He was not a baseball fan, except at World Series time, but he was acquainted with the literature and the lore of baseball, and once in his high-school auditorium he had heard E. L. Thayer's poem recited from the stage, and at moments of impending defeat the last stanza always mocked him. The stuck needle replayed the last stanza once more.

> Oh! somewhere in this favored land
> the sun is shining bright.
> The band is playing somewhere, and
> somewhere hearts are light,
> And somewhere men are laughing, and
> somewhere children shout;
> But there is no joy in Mudville—
> mighty Casey has struck out.

And there is no joy in free men—poor Barrett has struck out. He opened his eyes to rejoin the others.

Zelkin was addressing Phil Sanford. "Well, Phil, when the court reconvenes in a half hour, Duncan will go back to completing his cross-examination of our Dr. Finegood. Then we'll be asked to present our next witness. We have no next witness. So I'll simply rest our case. Then Duncan will offer his closing argument, and Mike will offer the final sum-up for us. As you know, it's even better than the excerpts you just heard on tape. Then Upshaw will instruct the jury, and away they go, and back they come. Yes, I think we'll have our verdict by midafternoon."

Ben Fremont ceased polishing his glasses. "I can't wait," he said bitterly.

"You're not the only one who's in trouble," said Sanford to the bookseller. "Think what's going to happen to me."

Zelkin squinted across the table at Barrett. "You ready to wind it up, Mike?"

"No," said Barrett dully. "But I will."

"Maybe you can still put a small fire under that jury," said Ben Fremont.

"Without a light?" said Barrett.

By word association, an old aphorism surfaced in his mind. Burning stakes do not lighten the darkness. No, they don't, he thought. Listlessly he tore off a corner of his sandwich and chewed it. He had never realized before that bread could taste like ashes.

There were three distinct raps on the door behind him, and he called over his shoulder, "Come in."

The door opened partially as Barrett swung around. A police officer stuck his head into the room. "There's a lady here asking for Mr. Barrett."

"A lady? Who—well, who is it?"

The officer stepped aside, and Maggie Russell came hastily into the room, her eyes luminous and her features reflecting some secret excitement.

"Maggie—" Barrett said, half rising. "Where have you—?"

"Chicago," she said quickly. "I went alone. But I've come back with someone. You've met him, Mike, but I'll introduce him to the rest of you." She opened the door wide. "They're all here," she called into the corridor.

A dignified, stately figure filled the doorway, surveyed them, came forward, and closed the door behind him.

"Gentlemen," Maggie said, "may I introduce Senator Thomas Bainbridge!"

Barrett, who had scrambled awkwardly to his feet, righted his toppling chair as he stared at Bainbridge, dumbfounded.

"Senator," he gasped, and he heard the others stand up behind him.

Thomas Bainbridge moved across the room in a measured tread, and when he reached Barrett he halted, and then he did what Barrett had not seen him do before. He smiled. Not easily. But he smiled.

"Mr. Barrett," he said, "yesterday you were persuasive. But in the end, it was your young lady who was convincing. This young lady, and—and another once-young lady in Chicago, I should say, were the ones who were convincing. I was made to remember by one—man's responsibility to the past—by another—man's responsibility to the future." Then he said unexpectedly, "Are you a reader of poetry, Mr. Barrett?"

The old Thayer stanza lingered in Barrett's head, but now he was ashamed of it, and he banished it.

Senator Bainbridge had not waited for his answer. "Well, Mr. Jadway has always been interested in poetry, and there is one particular verse from James Russell Lowell that speaks most eloquently for Mr. Jadway's own feelings. In effect, Lowell says he honors the man who is willing to sink—half his present repute for the freedom to think—and then there's more to the effect that be this man's cause strong or weak, he'll risk the other half for the freedom to speak."

He stopped, without embarrassment, as Barrett and the others waited in confused silence.

He cleared his throat. "A wretched rhyme," he said, "but a perfect sentiment." His gaze went past Barrett to the others and then returned and held on Barrett. "There is your answer, sir. Yes, you shall have your star witness. I personally will lay the foundation. And then, if it is still your wish, I shall produce J J Jadway on the witness stand, before the world, today."

"You may call your next witness, Mr. Barrett."

"Thank you, Your Honor."

He announced the next witness, heard the rustle in the courtroom, then summoned the witness.

As the clerk hastened to the box with his Bible, and the witness came forward to meet him, Mike Barrett stood beside the court reporter and stared down at the softly clacking stenotyper and the phonograms speeding across the spindle of moving paper. Watching the symbols, mesmerized by their portent, he could visualize them in the final typed transcript of *The People of the State of California v. Ben Fremont:*

SENATOR THOMAS BAINBRIDGE

called as a witness by and on behalf of the defendant, having been first duly sworn, was examined and testified as follows:

THE CLERK: State your name, please.
THE WITNESS: Senator Thomas Bainbridge.
THE CLERK: Spell the last name, please.
THE WITNESS: B-a-i-n-b-r-i-d-g-e.
THE COURT: Be seated, Senator.

Barrett turned to the witness box.

He knew that he had the jury's attention, the Judge's, the concentrated attention of everyone in the packed courtroom, because he had before him the most puzzling and most distinguished witness yet to appear in the trial.

"Senator Bainbridge, what is your present occupation?"

"I am a member of the United States Senate, in Washington, D.C., recently appointed by the Governor of Connecticut to finish the term of the late Senator Mawson."

"What was your immediate occupation preceding your present one?"

"I served as Dean of the School of Law at Yale University, in New Haven, Connecticut."

"And before that?"

"I was a judge for the Court of Appeals in Connecticut."

"Have you ever held any position that was not connected with the law?"

"Yes. When I was younger, for a period of ten years, I was president of a manufacturing company inherited from my father, who had inherited it from his father before him."

"It was after that, after those ten years, that you became a judge?"

"Yes."

"May I ask why you left private business for the law?"

"Because the family firm no longer required my services. I thought that what abilities I did possess might be put to better use in the service of my state and my country."

"During the time when you were an officer and teacher of the law, and now as a senator, did you ever write and publish any books?"

"I did."

"Were they works of fiction?"

"Hardly. They were nonfiction. I wrote and published two legal textbooks."

"Are you acquainted with fiction, classical or modern?"

"As a reader, yes, I am. Classical *and* modern. I find reading novels a prime way to relax."

"Have you ever read a novel entitled *The Seven Minutes*, by J J Jadway?"

"I have, sir."

"Have you read it more than once?"

"I have read it many times."

"How recently have you read the book in its entirety?"

"As recently as last night."

"Are you familiar with Section 311.2 of the California Penal Code?"

"I am."

"Do you know that *The Seven Minutes* is being charged as obscene matter under that section of the Penal Code?"

"I do know that."

"Senator Bainbridge, do you consider *The Seven Minutes* to be an obscene book?"

"I do not. I consider it to be a highly moral book."

"Do you believe that the author of this work was pandering to prurient interest, to shameful or morbid interest in nudity, sex, excretion, in writing this book?"

"I not only believe that he was not pandering to the prurient interest of the reader in writing that book, but I know for a fact that he was not pandering to prurient interest."

"You *know* the book was not written to appeal to prurient interest. May I inquire, Senator, how do you know?"

"Because I am intimately acquainted with the circumstances surrounding the creation and publication of *The Seven Minutes*."

There was a low buzz of perplexity from the press corps and the spectators. Before Judge Upshaw could find his gavel, Barrett's resumption of questioning had stilled the room.

"Will you explain to the jurors and the court how you came by this intimate knowledge?"

"Gladly, Counsel. No person alive, not even the estimable Miss Cassie McGraw, was closer or better acquainted with the author J J Jadway than I."

Barrett could see the curious jurors leaning forward intently in their chairs, and again he could hear, from the rear, the whisperings among the spectators. Then the court was hushed, eager for more.

"Senator, are you saying that you were present in Paris when J J Jadway wrote *The Seven Minutes*?"

"I am saying that I was in Paris when he wrote the book."

"Do you know his motivations for writing it?"

"I do."

"Do you know his mode of living when he wrote the book?"

"I do."

"Are you acquainted with the events of his life that followed the underground publication of his book?"

"I am."

"Does this firsthand knowledge which you possess about J J Jadway and *The Seven Minutes* confirm or contradict the testimony given in this courtroom by the People's witnesses?"

"My information about the real Jadway and his real purpose in writing and publishing this book completely and entirely contradicts the evidence so far presented to this court."

Listening to the rising murmur of excited voices behind him, Barrett waited for the Judge's gavel, and when he heard it he swiftly took advantage of the silence it brought.

"Senator Bainbridge, you do understand that the previous witnesses were sworn, gave their testimony under oath, and risked facing a charge of perjury if they lied—that they were under oath just as you are this moment?"

"They did not lie. They simply did not tell the truth. Because they did not know the truth. Everything heard in this courtroom until now about J J Jadway, everything concerning his writing of the book, concerning his feelings about it, concerning his intent and purpose, concerning his character and habits and condition and his end has been the purest fiction, and this fiction was planned and perpetrated by Jadway himself for reasons involving his private life."

"Senator, are you prepared to give us your version of Jadway's life and the circumstances that surrounded the publication of *The Seven Minutes?*"

"I am."

"Senator Bainbridge, before you begin, I believe the court would be interested in knowing why you have come forward now to give this testimony."

"Why I have come forward? It was John Milton who gave my answer three centuries ago. 'As good almost kill a man as kill a good book; who kills a man kills a reasonable creature, God's Image; but he who destroys a good book, kills reason itself, kills the Image of God.' That, Counsel, tells why I am here."

"To save *The Seven Minutes?*"

"To save all books, the pleasure and wisdom and experience in all books, and to save those who would profit by reading them."

"Senator Bainbridge, will you now tell us what you personally know of J J Jadway and his book that contradicts the testimony so far presented to the court?"

"I will."

"Senator Bainbridge, please tell us what you consider to be the true story, as opposed to what you have labeled the false story invented by Jadway about himself which has been given currency to this day by those who did not know better. Please proceed under the oath of truth, Senator."

"The truth, then, as I am qualified to speak it. J J Jadway did not write *The Seven Minutes* for money. He had money. He had a fortune. He came from a wealthy family. Jadway was not addicted to drink or drugs, nor was he in any way dissolute. He had been brought up strictly, but belonged to no religious faith. He had been well disciplined and well educated in his youth. His rebellion was the rebellion that all youth must finally make against parental authority, if youth is to stand alone one day, with the strength to develop its own individuality and authority. Jadway had left his family and his home in New England and gone to

Paris to find his own freedom, his own identity, to become a man instead of merely a father's son. He had gone to Paris with a problem, the result of his upbringing and environment, and there he met Cassie McGraw and freed himself from the bondage that had restrained and crippled him. He had wanted to know love, and Miss McGraw taught him the meaning of love. He had wanted to be well after being sexually ill, and she made him well. He had wanted to be a creative writer, in defiance of the traditions of his background, and she encouraged him to express himself and to write. He wrote *The Seven Minutes* as a memorial to Cassie McGraw and their love, for it was the only personal experience entirely his own that he had ever known. He wrote this book to celebrate his own salvation from sexual fear and sexual shame, to celebrate the riddance of an infirmity that had grown out of this fear and shame, and out of his feelings of guilt about sex—"

"If I may interrupt you, Senator Bainbridge, are you speaking literally of an infirmity?"

"Yes, I am speaking of a real infirmity, not physical but psychic, that is inflicted upon half of civilized man. It takes many forms. In Jadway's case, it took a sexual form, and it was Cassie McGraw's love that gave Jadway back his manhood and his normalcy. It is a condition that Jadway wrote about in *The Seven Minutes*. He burdened one of his three male characters with it, the male character who in the end was the one whom Cathleen had taken to her bed to love, and who was able to love her in those seven mystical minutes. The framework for Jadway's book grew out of a passage he had read in the Old Testament of the Holy Bible. But the content of the book was his effort to record the story of the freedom that Cassie knew, and that she had taught him so that he himself could be free. J J Jadway wrote the book so that it could liberate others from fear and shame and guilt. And Jadway succeeded, for his words have freed others."

"One moment, Senator Bainbridge. Are you saying that *The Seven Minutes* has liberated certain readers from sexual fear, shame, guilt?"

"I am saying that Jadway's words freed a young man only today and enabled him to confide to me the truth about himself, a truth he has told no other person until now. Jerry Griffith was not driven to commit rape by reading this book. He was not driven to commit rape, because Jerry Griffith was incapable of attaining an erection. Jerry Griffith did not try to enter Sheri Moore against her will. He tried to enter her at her invitation. But he failed then, as he had always failed before, and would fail today, because Jerry Griffith was then, was before, and is today sexually impotent."

The courtroom seemed to explode, and Judge Upshaw's gavel crashed hard, time and again, on the bench, and not until the noise began to subside could Elmo Duncan's voice be heard crying out from the prosecution table.

"Objection, Your Honor, objection!" the District Attorney was shouting.

"Yes, Mr. Duncan, on what grounds?"

"Objection on the grounds that the counsel for the defense is eliciting absolute hearsay evidence from the witness, evidence that falls beyond the ken of the witness's knowledge, and which, moreover, bears no relevancy—"

"Is the People's counsel objecting on the grounds of irrelevancy or hearsay evidence?"

"Hearsay evidence, Your Honor."

"Objection is sustained. . . . Mr. Barrett, I must caution you that throughout your examination of the witness your questions have come perilously close to calling for an answer or an opinion that might be regarded as being based on hearsay. I refer specifically to the questions and answers concerning J J Jadway. The question and answer concerning Jerry Griffith are definitely hearsay, unless you are preparing to lay foundation and intend to prove."

"Thank you, Your Honor," said Barrett respectfully. "I shall attempt to lay proper foundation, if I may, for what has already come before the court and for what shall soon follow."

"Proceed with the witness."

Barrett moved closer to Senator Bainbridge, who sat somberly in the witness box waiting for him.

"Senator, you have already stated that, during your years as a judge, dean of a law school, senator, you wrote and published two books, and that these were textbooks on law. Under what name were these two books published?"

"Under my given and family names. Under the name Thomas Bainbridge."

"Had you at any time before you became a judge, in an earlier period, written or published any other books?"

"Yes, I had."

"How many other books?"

"One book."

"Was that book published under the name of Thomas Bainbridge?"

"It was not. It was published under a pseudonym."

"Can you tell us the title of that book and the pseudonym under which you wrote it?"

"The book was *The Seven Minutes*, by J J Jadway. I am J J Jadway."

Pandemonium swept the room, and in seconds the court had become a bedlam. Several jurors had come out of their seats. The press was on the run. The District Attorney's face was a death mask. And the Judge, thunderstruck and slack-jawed, had forgotten to wield his gavel.

Only J J Jadway, Barrett could see, was calm. For he had suffered and survived his crisis of conscience, and now he too, like his book, might be free at last.

THE REST had gone quickly.

Bainbridge's confession of his double life had unfolded, and Duncan's cross-examination had been perfunctory, as if wishing the witness off the stand and out of sight as soon as possible. When the witness was dismissed, Barrett was certain that Leroux and almost every prosecution witness had been repudiated, and Jerry Griffith's testimony had been relegated to fantasy and lie, and the integrity and truth of *The Seven Minutes* had been restored.

What remained debatable, and to this Elmo Duncan devoted his desperate closing argument, was a single question.

Was the book obscene as charged?

But when the jury had been instructed by the Judge and had disappeared from the court to deliberate, Barrett knew that they took with them other questions. Had Senator Bainbridge, this pillar of New England who had sacrificed his privacy to appear here this day—had this man writing as J J Jadway been a pornographer? Had Jerry Griffith, the pitiful sick boy who preferred to be convicted of rape and murder rather than be mocked for impotency, been hurt or finally helped by the book? Had the book itself, written by an author to rhapsodize the glory of a free woman who had liberated her man, been a work designed to excite prurient interest?

When the jurors asked themselves whether *The Seven Minutes* was obscene, Barrett knew that they must ask themselves these questions also.

Now the court had been reconvened, and the jurors were filing back into the room and taking their places in the jury box.

Judge Upshaw peered at the foreman of the jury. "Have you reached a verdict?"

"We have, Your Honor."

"Please hand your verdict to the bailiff."

The bailiff had received the piece of paper, and now he took it to the bench and handed it to the magistrate. Judge Upshaw glanced at it, then handed it back to the bailiff.

The bailiff marched to center stage, drew himself up to his full height, and then, in a great stentorian roar, he announced the verdict:

"We, the jury, in the People versus Ben Fremont, do hereby find the defendant *not guilty* of distributing or purveying obscene matter!"

"Is that your unanimous verdict?" Judge Upshaw called down from the bench.

In unison, the twelve jurors chorused back, "Yes, Your Honor."

But by now they could not be heard above the thunder in the room.

A HALF HOUR LATER, after the tumult and shouting had ceased, and the jury had been thanked and discharged, and Zelkin and Sanford and Kimura and Fremont had embraced Barrett, and reporters with notepads had swarmed around Barrett, Courtroom 803 of the Superior Court of Los Angeles was finally empty of all but two persons.

Mike Barrett was alone at the defense table, slowly gathering up his papers and putting them into his briefcase. The milling crowd had moved out into the corridor of the Hall of Justice, where Jadway—Bainbridge—had agreed to hold a press conference before television cameras, which had not been admitted into the courtroom. Barrett could barely hear the din and chaos outside the courtroom doors, and he was unable yet to exult in his triumph. The sudden turn of events, the electrifying appearance of Bainbridge, the smashing victory that had replaced certain defeat, had been too much for his mind and body to assimilate.

It was as if he were still on the quest, taut and hunting. For, now closing his briefcase, he realized that there remained small mysteries. Bainbridge's sensational testimony had solved much, and the reappearance in court of Jerry Griffith, followed by the appearances of the convalescing Darlene Nelson and the bereaved Howard Moore, had solved more, enough to gain a verdict of complete acquittal for Ben Fremont and total freedom for *The Seven Minutes*. But for Mike Barrett there were still "dark patches" that continued to be "held over all reality."

He heard his name spoken, and he wheeled around. He had thought that he was alone, but he was not, and he was grateful. Maggie Russell was hurrying down the aisle toward him.

She was in his arms. "Mike, you were magnificent. It's over and you won. I'm so proud of you, and so happy."

"Thanks to you, darling."

"I was in there at the end, but it was you all the way. These last weeks the world seemed to be standing still. Now it's turning again, sunrises, sunsets, life, hope."

He released her. "Maggie, what happened?"

"You know what happened. You heard it in this room."

"But how did it get to this room? I want the answers, before we go ahead. Tell me."

He drew her down to a chair at the defense table and sat next to her, and he waited.

"Well, I'm not sure where to—to—" she said.

"To begin? Begin with the one thing most of us didn't know about—Jerry's impotence."

"Yes." She was lost in thought a moment. "Jerry had so many problems. Too many to go into now. But one of his major problems was with girls. With them he was shy, afraid, uncertain. I used to talk to him about this. There were months of heart-to-heart talks. I did my best to instill in him some sense of his own value and identity. To make him feel as attractive as he really was.

Well, finally, gradually, he began dating. He was surprised at how easy it was, how easily girls were attracted not merely by his car and money, but by his own person."

Pouring a glass of water for Maggie, and one for himself, Barrett asked, "Did Jerry go to bed with any of those girls? Or even before, had he ever—?"

"No, never," she said flatly. "He was a virgin. I didn't know it at first. That came out later. Right after he began dating, he found out that the kiss at the door was not the end of an evening but the beginning. Poor kid. Because he was afraid. Yet, afraid or not, he had to go through with it. From the kiss at the door to the thing in the bed. Yes, he joined his dates in their beds. One girl, a second girl, a third girl, and each time he failed to consummate the sexual act. It wasn't merely premature ejaculation. It was— well, you know—flaccid impotence. Yet somehow Jerry survived those failures because, I gather, the girls had been kind. But then there was another date, another type of girl, and she was less kind. In fact, she was cruel. And Jerry—he returned home frenzied, ill with despair, determined that he couldn't live on any longer as a virtual eunuch."

Maggie had halted, absently sipping at her glass of water.

Barrett quietly prompted her. "And that led to his first suicide attempt?"

"That led to the first," she said. "Luckily, I discovered him in time and saved him. That was when I learned the truth. While he was still hung over from the drugs and his shame—in his room, morose and babbling, he spilled out his secret to me. From that time on, except for the girls he had dated, I was the only person in the world who shared his secret—until today."

"Was it then that you thought of San Francisco?"

"Well, I saw something had to be done, Mike. There was no one to consult. Certainly not Uncle Frank or Aunt Ethel, God forbid. It *was* a secret, and Jerry was dependent upon me. So I took matters into my own hands. I did some investigating and learned the names of two reliable doctors up north, one a physician, the other a psychoanalyst, and I made appointments for Jerry with them. Then, on some pretext or other—I forget what, and anyway, Uncle Frank was on a business trip, and that made it easier—I got Jerry out of the house for a week and accompanied him to San Francisco. First the physician. Thorough examination.

Absolute assurance that the impotence was not physical but psychic. Next, two long sessions with the psychoanalyst, who confirmed the physician's diagnosis. Jerry's condition was psychic —and curable with time and therapy. The facts were made clear to Jerry. Neither hormone shots nor medicine would help. Only treatment by a dependable analyst could assist him in overcoming his feelings of inferiority and guilt, could make him understand his hostilities and somehow guide him to finding his own identity."

"Then back to Los Angeles," said Barrett. "One point I've wondered about. Did you try to get long-range help for Jerry from some analyst down here?"

"Mike, it isn't a question of whether or not I tried. Jerry was on his feet again, and it was up to him. I encouraged him, of course, but I could only go so far without alienating him. So the next move was his. He had had good advice, the best. What he didn't have was the will, the courage and confidence to act on it. He knew perfectly well what his first step should be, but he simply wasn't able to bring himself to move out of his parents' house and go off on his own. Oh, in a roundabout way he broached the subject of analysis to his father—and what did he get back? A long tirade, a denunciation of Freud and other head-shrinkers, so that was that, and Jerry never brought up the subject again. For Jerry, there was only one logical thing left to do—try to *be* normal."

Barrett shook his head. "Christ. Try to be an Olympic hero when you've got no legs. Okay, Maggie. Go on. There we have Jerry about to walk in front of a truck, so to speak. What happened on the way?"

"On the way?" she repeated vaguely. "Well, for one thing, trying to be normal means attempting to have normal friends. Jerry latched onto an acquaintance, George Perkins, tried to make him into a friend, because George was natural, no obvious hang-ups, and he had an easy way with women. I suppose Jerry hoped to become normal by osmosis. One night, with George taking the lead, they picked up—well, it was Sheri Moore, and they took her to her apartment."

"And she turned out to be a little swinger," said Barrett. "You know, I suspected it when I first started asking about her. I had a hunch she was permissive, liked to make the boys happy. I don't know why I didn't follow through on the hunch. I guess I allowed myself to be propagandized by everyone."

"You propagandized yourself," Maggie said with a slight smile. "You come from a generation that was taught to believe that all girls are—or should be—innocents. You wanted to believe little Sheri was sweetness and light, like your own mother had been, and your mother's mother had been. I'm not speaking of the intellectual you. I mean, the son you."

"Maybe," said Barrett with an answering smile. "We'll explore that when we're on a couch together. Okay, Sheri's bed a welcome mat. George went first. Token resistance. But no problem. He and Sheri made out. Then Jerry's turn. We didn't get it all from the stand, Maggie. What actually took place?"

Maggie resumed slowly. Listening, Barrett closed his eyes, and her recital was transformed into a series of vivid stereopticon slides inside his head.

Well, Mike . . .

Maggie's low voice, and the colorful slides.

Jerry had gone into Sheri's bedroom after George had left it, and he had undressed and crawled into bed with her. But it had not been Jerry who entered her. He had been incapable, impotent. And Sheri, brainless child of hedonism, at first amused, was soon challenged. She'd had her boys and men, and this had never happened to her before. When they got on Sheri, they got it big. They always made it big with Sheri, because Sheri was a *femme fatale*. Jerry wasn't making it at all, and this was a rebuke to her own ego and talents. She worked on Jerry, a circus of foreplay, with no result. And soon there was no longer challenge for the girl, only impatience, irritation, annoyance, and finally anger. This was a put-down to her sexuality. This was the ultimate insult. Perhaps she thought the failure was primarily her own, not his, and she would not have it. She had begun to tease him, to mock him, to ridicule him.

Blinded by rage and tears, Jerry had tried to escape, to dress and escape. She would not let him off so easily. She had followed him from the bed, and he had tried to push her away, be rid of her, until her taunts had become filthy and vicious. When he'd tried to answer back, she had struck at him, and missed, and slipped on the throw rug, and fallen, and her head had gone down against the knifing corner of the table and it had cracked her skull like an eggshell, and she was unconscious. Jerry had wanted to summon help, but George Perkins had wanted them to have no part of that mess.

Shortly afterward, Darlene Nelson had come back to the apartment, to find her roommate struggling briefly to hold on to consciousness. Darlene had kneeled over Sheri, trying to discover what had happened. Sheri had whispered the truth, but begged for only one thing. Her father must not know of her behavior, how she was with the boys. Tell them anything, Darlene, anything, she had pleaded, tell them rape. And when the police came and the ambulance came and Howard Moore came, Darlene had told them rape.

Then there was Jerry, caught and arrested. There was the code. No squealing on friends, especially a friend like George who had balls. And rape, yes, rape was a way to hide the ultimate shame of exposure and disgrace, and escape the laughter of all you knew. Forcible entry had a manly ring to it. It was one way to prove you could get an erection, make it big. There was even black humor in it, the sick joke: rape is assault with a friendly weapon. At least a weapon, a potent weapon. With rape you were a criminal, but you were a man. With the truth, you were sentenced to impotence and ridicule forever.

Mike Barrett had opened his eyes, and the slides had disappeared, and there was Maggie speaking.

"So it was rape," she was saying.

"And suddenly it was the book that made him do it," Barrett interrupted. "Overnight, *The Seven Minutes* was the criminal. But one fact never came out in court, Maggie. Where did Jerry get the book?"

She did not reply. She looked down at her fingers.

"Well, Maggie?"

"Is it important now?"

"I want to know," he said firmly. "Where did he get the book?"

"From me."

His eyes widened. *From me.* Zap. Had he heard her right? "From you, Maggie?"

She held her head high. "Yes. I bought it for myself, because I wanted to read it, and I bought it for Aunt Ethel also, because I knew she'd wanted to read it."

He listened incredulously, then less so as Maggie went on.

616

Maggie had learned that Aunt Ethel liked those novels, actually craved them, found a world in them that she had never been permitted to know. So the game was always that Maggie acquired the books for her own reading, and then, when Uncle Frank was not home, she passed them on to Aunt Ethel to read.

But Aunt Ethel had never got to read *The Seven Minutes*, because once Maggie had read it she had passed it on to Jerry instead. He had said that he had no interest in the book, but Maggie had insisted that he read it. She knew Jerry's problem, since she had been to San Francisco with him, and she had wanted him to know that others who had suffered the same problem had been helped and had even been able to write about it openly and frankly. For, in the fiction, as Cathleen lay on her bed enjoying the man inside her, she thought of many men, but mostly of three men in her life.

"Remember how it was in the book, Mike?" Maggie asked. "If you remember, you'll understand why I gave it to Jerry."

He took a moment to remember, and then he did.

There was Jadway's Cathleen, lying there, recollecting her adventures with the three men who wanted her, and trying to imagine what it would be like to belong to each one. The first man, she knew, was spoiled and self-centered, yet a great lover, a Casanova, skilled and experienced, promising a memorable life of the flesh. The second man was, she knew, a conservative lover, Everyman, who would devote more time to achieving success in his work than to his woman, but who promised a comfortable material life. The third man was, she knew, a temporarily impotent lover, but he was a man of much sensitivity, creative, understanding, promising intellectual and spiritual fascination. And to one of these she had finally given herself completely, but which one it was Jadway did not disclose until the last page of the book. And in the end the reader learned that it was the third man with whom she had been living these seven memorable minutes. Through her own warmth and tenderness, she had made him a man, and in making him a man she had found her greatest fulfillment as a woman. Of course the third man was Jadway himself. It had been so obviously autobiographical. And that was what Maggie had wanted Jerry to read.

"Then you actually got Jerry to read it?" Barrett asked.

"I did. He read it not once but twice. And while a good deal of the novel made him uneasy, it shook him and gave him some understanding of women and some hope for himself. Yet that wasn't enough. Without the guidance of an analyst, or the author himself, there was no way Jerry could translate Jadway's experience in the book to serve his own purposes. Jadway could do little for him. Jadway gave him some words, helpful ones, but Jerry needed more from the author, and the author was dead. So what was left? To emulate someone living, someone successful with women. Namely, his friend George Perkins. So he lamely followed George to Sheri Moore on her bed. But Jerry wasn't George. Jerry was Jadway's impotent hero, only Sheri wasn't Jadway's Cathleen."

"I see," said Barrett. "Jerry took credit for George's semen in the victim, and he opted for rape. And then he was caught, and then the book . . ."

It was becoming clearer now.

The book—Maggie's copy—had been found where she'd hidden it from Frank Griffith in the trunk of the car that she and Jerry shared. And, believing the book to be the real culprit (or wanting to believe it), and prodded by Elmo Duncan and Luther Yerkes, Frank Griffith had immediately railed against the book for corrupting his son. Yes, it was becoming clearer. And Jerry, not daring to contradict his father, afraid to contradict the law, perhaps wanting to believe it was the book so he could plead extenuating circumstances to his supposed crime, went along, picked up the chant, made his confession, appeared in court.

"Maggie, what about Jerry's second suicide attempt?" Barrett wanted to know. "What was behind it?"

"He'd been depressed about Sheri's condition in the hospital. That really bothered him. And he wanted a few kind words from George and a chance to meet Sheri's roommate, not to reveal the whole truth but simply a chance to explain to her that Sheri's head injury had honestly been an accident. And so he got out of the house and went hunting for George in that club on Melrose, but as you saw for yourself, George wanted nothing to do with him, wanted no part of the trouble. So in order to get rid of Jerry, friend George pointed out Darlene Nelson. You saw Jerry try to speak to her. He just wanted to plead accident, beg forgiveness, derive some relief through expiation, but instead, well, she stunned him by lashing out at him with her knowledge of his impotence. It was callous, unfeeling, but—" Maggie shrugged—

"I guess all of us can be vicious sometimes. Darlene—she taunted Jerry with that old Irish goodbye, 'God stiffen you.' Jerry just came apart, unraveled. He was sure that the whole world now knew or soon would know his condition. He couldn't face that. So he tried to kill himself. You can see how he would want to, can't you?"

"Yes," said Barrett.

"It was this same fear, Mike, that made him continually threaten to commit suicide to avoid testifying in court. It was not Duncan that he was afraid of. Nor even you personally. It was the weapon you possessed—the meanness of the cross-examination, the chilling panic that he would crack under hostile questioning and that the truth of his impotence would be divulged to everyone on earth."

Another unanswered question nagged Barrett, and now he posed it. "Maggie, if you knew all along about Jerry's sexual problem, why didn't you come forward right away to save him from the charge of rape?" He posed the question again, more forcefully. "If you knew he was incapable of rape, why in the devil didn't you say so?"

"Because I wasn't that certain that Jerry had been impotent the night of the so-called rape. I only knew for certain what his condition had been before that night. But then I thought—I don't know—maybe out of some kind of ill desperation he had attempted rape, and the stimulation of trying to violate a girl, the way many men are supposed to become potent only if their victim resists— well, I thought maybe that kind of excitement had given Jerry his first erection and a kind of dreadful success."

Barrett nodded. "Yes, it makes sense."

"But yesterday, Mike, after Sheri Moore died, the truth suddenly seemed to dawn on me. I guess there were certain things that happened, or rather, didn't happen. Like Howard Moore. In such grief, he should have been in a murderous rage against Jerry yet, in the radio and television interviews he gave right after his daughter died, there was not one word spoken by him against Jerry or against *The Seven Minutes*. So, knowing what I knew of Jerry, I began to suspect that something else had happened on the night Jerry was with Sheri Moore. Then I recalled another thing. When I gave *The Seven Minutes* to Jerry, and after he read it, he had said he wished the author, Jadway, were still alive so that he could talk to him. Why? Because Jadway might be the only man on earth who would understand Jerry's problem and be sympathetic. Jerry wouldn't tell me more at the time, wouldn't tell me what he wished he could say to Jadway. I guess he felt that he had already told me too much, and that I secretly did not respect him because of his problem. I even suspect that he believed the prowess his rape had proved had regained him some of the respect he'd lost in my eyes—warped, but anyway—anyway, he wouldn't tell me more about how he felt. It was only to another human being who had been through what he had, one like Jadway, that Jerry felt he might be able to pour out the whole story of his failure that night with Sheri Moore. And then—"

She paused, thinking, and finally Barrett prompted her. "Then what, Maggie?"

"Then there was the news from you that Jadway was alive, actually alive. And after you phoned from Washington that you'd seen Senator Bainbridge, and he'd told you Jadway would not cooperate, well, that's when I determined to see Senator Bainbridge and plead with him to bring the living Jadway and the dying Jerry together. Right after, when I phoned Washington myself and learned that Bainbridge was on his way to Chicago—to Chicago, where you'd found Cassie McGraw—that was when the niggling thought in the back of my head came forward as a certainty. I was sure—deduction, intuition, dumb guesswork—that Bainbridge was going to Chicago to see Cassie McGraw, and that he was going to see Cassie because he himself was J J Jadway. Mike, did you suspect the possibility?"

"It crossed my mind. But I couldn't accept it, because Bainbridge didn't fit my image of Jadway. And as to Jerry, of course, I had no idea of his—his problem."

"You couldn't have, because you didn't know what I knew about Jerry. Now let me tell you what happened when Jerry came to your apartment yesterday morning."

Barrett listened intently, as Maggie went on.

Jerry had come to see her yesterday before submitting to imprisonment. After his arrival, she had taken the reckless chance of pretending to Jerry that she knew the truth about his night with Sheri Moore. She pretended that she had learned it from Sheri's father. With this she had finally harpooned the truth. Jerry had broken down and confessed his lie. She had pleaded with him to make the truth public, to save himself from jail, from jail immediately and perhaps for the rest of his life. Jerry had refused to do this. Jail for rape he might endure, but public knowledge of his final fiasco he could never survive. Then it was that Maggie had told him that J J Jadway was alive. The news had seemed to have a remarkable effect on Jerry. If only he could speak to Jadway. And Maggie had told him she would try to arrange it.

She had meant to see Howard Moore originally, to learn whether he knew as truth what she had only suspected. But when she did see Moore, she told him the truth that she had tricked Jerry into confessing. Sadly he had confirmed it. Immediately after his daughter's death, her roommate, Darlene Nelson, had broken down and he had heard from her of his daughter's last words. Yes, he knew it had been his girl's fault. His poor lost baby. Yes, her fault and not Jerry's. No, he would not make the truth public if the boy didn't want to make it public. But if Jerry was ready to change his testimony, he would back up the boy in court.

And so, for Maggie, the resolution hinged on one person.

She had flown to Chicago to find Bainbridge. As she had expected (or at least hoped), she had found J J Jadway instead. On the way to the airport, she had related to the great man the story of Jerry Griffith. At the airport, he had finally come to his decision. He had said that if he could give Jerry the courage to stand up and confess the truth, then perhaps he himself would find the courage to do the same.

They had flown to Los Angeles together. They had gone to the county jail, where she had left Bainbridge with Jerry for an hour. When Bainbridge emerged from the jail to meet her, he was no longer Bainbridge. He was J J Jadway. He had said simply, "Jerry is ready to have the truth known, and so is Thomas Bainbridge, to save the book and all who may be freed by it and by other books like it in the years to come. We are ready for the truth, so that we may both be free."

Maggie had finished her story. "That's about all I can tell you, Mike. Do you have any more questions?"

"No," he said quietly. Across the room, through the high-set windows, he could see that the day was coming to an end. "Let's go, Maggie." They stood up. He said, "What would you like to do to celebrate tonight?"

"Be with you."

He said, "We'll go out to dinner. We'll start with that."

As they went up the aisle she said, "I may be a little late for our dinner. After Jerry was released, I told him to meet me at the Beverly Wilshire Hotel bar. Senator Bainbridge is going to join us there after he gets rid of the television people. You know what we're going to tell Jerry? To get out of that house. To do it on his own. To get supportive treatment from your Dr. Finegood. I'll pay his bills until he can make his own way."

"Do you think he'll do it?"

"What?"

"Make his own way?"

She considered this at the courtroom doors. "I don't know, Mike. Maybe not right off. Freedom's a hard thing to get used to. But once you get used to it, it's a glorious thing. I know. I've learned. And I hope that one day Jerry will learn."

They were in the corridor.

"Well, if you're going to be busy for a while," said Barrett, "then I just might hang around here a little longer. There are a few questions that have to do with Jadway. I'd like to hear Bainbridge's answers, if he's still in the building."

"You are determined to know it all, aren't you?"

He smiled. "There are seven minutes. I can't settle for six."

She started to leave. "See you soon."

"Make it sooner," he called out.

After she had gone, he wondered where Senator Bainbridge could be found. A police guard was passing, and Barrett asked him.

"They just moved from here to the sixth floor," said the officer. "Another network's set up there in Room 603, and they're just starting to interview the Senator again."

Room 603 was the press room of the Hall of Justice.

There were three mahogany desks, and the *Los Angeles Times* man had vacated the center desk and given Senator Thomas Bainbridge his place.

Except for the circle of free space around this desk, bathed in a white glare of lights, and the two boxy television cameras directing their glass eyes on the desk within this circle, and their bustling crews, every other inch of the press room was filled with curious spectators.

Mike Barrett crowded in at the far fringe of this mob and tried to find out how the Senator was faring.

Senator Bainbridge sat at the desk, cool and imperturbable, waiting.

Somewhere, from behind a camera, someone called out, "Okay, Senator, we're rolling. You're on camera. You can begin your statement."

Senator Thomas Bainbridge gave a short nod and looked squarely into the nearest television camera.

One hand folded across the other on the desk blotter before him, he spoke intimately and directly in a flat, unhurried monotone.

"I have already testified in the courtroom, little more than an hour ago, that in 1934 I wrote the book known as *The Seven Minutes* under the name of J J Jadway," began Senator Bainbridge. "Now, since you are interested, I will summarize the essential facts of my testimony, and perhaps add a few autobiographical details more pertinent to this kind of informal statement than they might have been to legal testimony. You want the full story, and you are entitled to have it. You see, friends, I not only support freedom of speech but take advantage of it, now that I have a book to sell."

Barrett joined in the laughter, and he was pleased that the Senator could smile, too.

Bainbridge's patrician face was again serious. "I was brought up in a strict and formal New England household," he resumed. "There were five of us. There was my father, self-made, strong-willed, well-intentioned but dogmatic and domineering. There was my mother, a timid servant. There were my two younger sisters, frightened of our father, obedient to his every wish, repressed and hopelessly unworldly. And there was I, the heir, considered by my father as merely an extension of himself, born only to help him in his business and to succeed him in it.

"My attendance at law school was only window dressing, to make me a more attractive commodity in the family business and socially. I had no real identity, and before being swallowed up by my father and his business, I made one last effort to find out who I was or could be. It required all my courage to demand a year

623

abroad, one year, and because I pleaded that this was a cultural necessity and promised to behave, this leave and the money for it were granted me. In 1934 I set off on my voyage of discovery—self-discovery. My destination was Paris, where such explorations must inevitably begin.

"I had to learn not only that I was a man, but that I was a person. Until then I had not been a man, in either the broadest sense of the word or the narrowest sense of the word. I was as fearful of independence as I was of sex. In truth, as I wrote in my book and told the court, I was impotent, both creatively and sexually. I wanted to write, and could not. I wanted to love, and was incapable of doing so. I wanted to be a person who was an individual, with his own history, and not a footnote to his father's history.

"During my first months in Paris, I was helpless, inert, lost. I did nothing, gained nothing, won nothing. This was my condition, and my despair, when I met a young American girl in Paris, an artist, who had come abroad seeking the same personal identity and freedom that I sought. She had found what, until then, I had failed to find. This was Cassie McGraw. We fell in love. What she saw in me I shall never know. Perhaps she saw that there was a more attractive hidden person imprisoned inside me, imprisoned and hammering and bursting to get out, and this was the person she loved and made an effort to liberate. This is the person she did liberate, the one known as J J Jadway.

"Cassie and I lived together. She inspired me not only to do what I wanted to do most of all on earth, to write out of myself and my perceptions, truly and honestly, but she gave me an awareness of pleasures no money on earth could buy—the enjoyment of birds on the wing, the comforting greenness of grassy fields, the understanding of stone monuments as living history, the invigorating discovery of the art of conversation, the toleration of alien viewpoints, and, above everything, the knowledge of love that transcended sex.

"I celebrated Cassie and our love in *The Seven Minutes*. While I was writing it, my leave abroad expired. I kept making excuses to my father, extending my stay. In exasperation, he cut off my funds, and then my mother and sisters secretly supported me out of their allowances. Christian Leroux was incorrect in telling the court that I had written the novel in three weeks. I wrote a first draft in three months and spent three added months rewriting it. I did not write it, as Cleland wrote *Fanny Hill*, to stay out of debtors' prison. I had sufficient money from my family.

"As for the book itself, it was drawn upon my experience with and of Cassie McGraw. There was no conscious allegory. This was meant to be a naturalistic novel, perhaps influenced ever so slightly by one writer who moved and another who shook literature, namely D. H. Lawrence and James Joyce. It was not only my new feeling about sex, or even Cassie's encouragement, that enabled me to write the book honestly. It was the counseling I received from an essay once written by Lawrence, 'A propos of Lady Chatterley's Lover,' that gave me the strength to create the book without inhibition.

"There was, for one thing, the problem of language. And Lawrence advised me, 'The words that shock so much at first don't shock at all after a while. Is this because the mind is depraved by habit? Not a bit. It is that the words merely shocked the eye, they never shocked the mind at all. People without minds may go on being shocked, but they don't matter. People with minds realize that they aren't shocked, and never really were: and they experience a sense of relief. And that is the whole point. We are today, as human beings, evolved and cultured far beyond the taboos which are inherent in our culture.'

"Then there was the hesitation about honestly describing various acts of sex in narrative. And once again Lawrence collaborated with Cassie to show me the way, telling me, 'I want men and women to be able to think sex, fully, completely, honestly, and cleanly. Even if we can't act sexually to our complete satisfaction, let us at least think sexually, complete and clear. All this talk of young girls and virginity, like a blank white sheet on which nothing is written, is pure nonsense. A young girl and a young boy is a tormented tangle, a seething confusion of sexual feelings and sexual thoughts which only the years will disentangle. Years of honest thoughts of sex and years of struggling action in sex will bring us at last where we want to get, to our real and accomplished chastity, our completeness, when our sexual act and our sexual thought are in harmony, and the one does not interfere with the other.'

"Thus encouraged, I swept aside the dishonest innuendo, the suggestion, the leer, I brushed away the last asterisk, and I wrote my truth. To guide my pen, I derived my outline from Chapter Seven of the Song of Solomon in the Old Testament. You may remember— 'The joints of thy thighs are like jewels, the work of the hands of a cunning workman. Thy navel is like a round goblet, which wanteth not liquor: thy belly is like an heap of wheat set about with lilies. Thy two breasts are like two young roes that are twins.' And then you may remember 'I am my beloved's, and his desire is toward me,' and then 'Let us get up early to the vineyards; let us see if the vine flourish, whether the tender grape appear, and the pomegranates bud forth: there will I give thee my loves.'

"Thus *The Seven Minutes* was written, and then it was published. I kept my anonymity, refusing to see even my publisher, because it was too early to dare let my father or my family know what I was doing. I waited to see whether the book would be a success and enable me to embark fully on the one career I wanted. Because of its limited publication, and general censorship, the book made me little money. However, it did give me the encouragement to go on, from the talk I heard about it in the cafés, from the letters I received from foreign students and tourists. Initially, I did not repudiate the book. It was only later that I wanted Monsieur Leroux and others to believe that I had repudiated it, out of compelling necessity, and so this fable was given out and gained circulation.

"At last my time for decision came. Cassie was pregnant. I had more books waiting to be born. I was ready to be my own man. I returned alone to Connecticut to have the final scene with my father. I could not have it. He was gravely ill. My mother was near a nervous breakdown, and my sisters were living in terror, so entire was their dependency on him. What sustained my father, gave the entire family at home hope for his survival, was his return to the Church. He had embraced Catholicism again, devoutly, and it sustained him. It was then that I learned that the Church was investigating J J Jadway, and that Jadway's book—my secret book —would be listed in the *Index*. This, I knew, would be a fatal blow to my father—indeed, to my mother and sisters as well. Out of fear for his life, I determined to obliterate J J Jadway forever, so that Jadway could never be traced to me and destroy my parents.

"I wrote to Paris at once. I wrote to Cassie and to Sean O'Flanagan. I gave them explicit instructions and sent money for them to carry out these instructions. They believed in my good intentions—that while I was obliterating a pseudonym, I would yet be Jadway under another name. I arranged for Jadway's bad character, his remorse, his suicide, all the worst I could conceive, so that the curious, the investigators, Leroux, the Archbishop of Paris, Father Sarfatti, others, would be satisfied and never again come around questioning. When Father Sarfatti tried to reach me, it was Sean O'Flanagan who telephoned him, using my name, and who played the role of Jadway. It was Cassie McGraw who forwarded to Father Sarfatti the letter that I had carefully prepared. It was Sean O'Flanagan who accompanied Cassie to Venice, representing himself as Jadway at the masked ball and at the Curia interrogation in the ducal palace. As for those telephone conversations I was supposed to have had with my publisher, Christian Leroux, it was Sean who made the calls as Jadway, acting out a script I had prepared for him. These conversations were held by Sean and Leroux while I was in the United States, and long after my book had been published, and Leroux reported them accurately as to content, but placed them wrongly in time. From the witness stand, Leroux indicated that his conversations with Jadway had taken place earlier. Either he forgot when they had actually taken place or he deliberately misrepresented the year they had occurred in order to strengthen his importance to the prosecution as a witness.

"Arranging my fictitious death proved to be the simplest task of all. Sean O'Flanagan was doing part-time work for the Paris edition of the New York *Herald Tribune* early in 1937. It was easy enough for him to write and plant the obituary of J J Jadway. It was just as easy to buy the venal French press of the period and get them to run an obituary and a few short feature articles. It was easy for Sean to fan the gossip in the cafés. But it had to be more than this. It had to be real. It was Cassie who arranged a private memorial service for Jadway, which she and some admirers of the book and Leroux attended.

"It was done. Jadway was no more. I was safe, my father's life and faith preserved, my family insulated from disgrace. Then I learned that Cassie had been delivered of my child, my daughter, Judith. I left my father's bedside and returned to France, and had Cassie, with Judith, meet me in Cherbourg. From there we sailed back to New York. I wanted to set a date for our marriage. Cassie would not have it yet. She would marry me once my father was well and I had broken with him and I could again be the man she loved. She waited in New York, and I kept the family and the family business propped up, and waited in New England.

"My father did not recover. My father died terribly. My father died without my having broken from him. I remained as his extension, his proxy, in life. My mother collapsed. My sisters were helpless and afraid. The business my father had built now floundered, waiting for a strong hand. These responsibilities came pressing down on me. Could I abandon my family? Cassie had done much toward making me independent, but she had not had time to do enough. I was still the victim of my past.

"I went to Cassie, pleaded with her to become my wife, to stand beside me until I had straightened out my family and the business on which the women depended. I said I would become Jadway again one day and we could resume our old life. Cassie said simply, 'But Jadway is dead, and I loved Jadway.' The next time I went to see her, she was gone. Cassie had disappeared. Only Sean knew where she was, and he kept the promise of silence he had made her. I supported our daughter through Sean until I learned Cassie had married. Later, when I heard that Cassie was ill and destitute, I supported her in a convalescent home.

"As the years passed, I realized that Cassie was right. Jadway was gone and would never return. The years passed, and I had a wife, more children, enough wealth finally to leave the business. Without Cassie, I lacked the courage to write again. Yes, Jadway was dead. So I revived my interest in the law, where I could serve to keep the word free, and I have been a part of the world of the law ever since.

"Not until yesterday, when the counsel for the defense, Mr. Michael Barrett, found me, was I forced to face the fact that J J Jadway was not dead after all. This morning I made my decision. But before doing so, I telephoned my wife and my children. My wife had suspected the truth; my children had not. They wholeheartedly stood behind my decision. Then I telephoned the President of the United States and asked him not to offer my name to Congress for the Supreme Court vacancy, and I told him why. He was sorry, he was gracious, and he said, in his amusing way, that at least the First Lady would now find me even more fascinating.

Finally I telephoned one more person. I called Cassie McGraw. I could not speak to her, so I spoke to her nurse. 'Give her this message when she has a good day,' I said. 'Tell her simply, "Jadway lives." She will understand.'"

Listening, Mike Barrett exhaled softly.

Then he turned and left the press room—and Jadway.

OUTSIDE, night had fallen, and the air was clean and crisp.

Entering the Temple Street Auto Park, where his convertible was waiting, he became aware of someone coming up behind him.

He halted, uncertain who the blond man was, and then he recognized him. He stood there wondering, until District Attorney Elmo Duncan reached him.

"I don't know if you heard me during all that noise after the verdict," Elmo Duncan said, "but I did congratulate you, Mike."

"I appreciate that, Elmo."

"Come on, I'll walk you to your car." They strode in silence for several seconds, and then Duncan spoke again, not bitterly, but wryly, and almost to himself. "When I was a kid in Glendale, there was one sports hero I had. That was Babe Ruth. And he once said something that has always stuck in my head, something wiser than anything I ever read by Socrates or Spinoza or Kant. The Babe said, 'One day you're a hero and the next you're a bum, so what the hell.'" Duncan gave Barrett a boyish grin. "So, Mike, I say, what the hell."

This moment Barrett liked him more than he had at any time before or during the trial. And he knew why. It was because the other Duncan had not been this Duncan, but merely part of a cabal controlled by Luther Yerkes, a cabal that had been joined by Frank Griffith and Willard Osborn II and promoted by Harvey Underwood and Irwin Blair. This was Duncan, plain.

"You almost had us there, Elmo," said Barrett. "You did a great job. Until today, you had us on the ropes. We got lucky with one big punch."

"You didn't get lucky," said Duncan. "You deserved winning and I deserved losing. I tried, but you tried harder. You never quit. At some point, I became too confident. I depended on—on others, and I began looking beyond the trial while the trial was still going on. If I'd been on my own, fighting for my life, depending on no one, I might have kept going, got to Cassie and Jadway

629

ahead of you, even learned the truth about Jerry Griffith and done something about that. Well, it was a lesson. I won't forget it."

"I'd still bet on your becoming senator one day."

Duncan snorted. "I'd be satisfied if it was safe to bet on my being district attorney again."

They had come to Barrett's car.

"Well, again, thanks, Elmo," Barrett said.

"There's just one more thing," said Duncan. "Believe me, I'm not saying it because I'm a sorehead."

"What's that?"

"I still believe *The Seven Minutes* is obscene. I hadn't read it the first day you came to my office, so I wasn't sure then. But right now, Jadway or no Jadway, Jerry or no Jerry, I believe that book is obscene and harmful and should have been found guilty. You freed it because you proved that one of my witnesses perjured himself and another of my witnesses unwittingly lied. But, Mike, you did not prove—at least not to me—that this book belongs in a decent household. Maybe it's me and my upbringing and my standards, and my overprotective concern about my family, but I still contend that such books are dangerous and should not be published. I believe they can hurt immature or disturbed adults. Even worse, I think they can overstimulate a child in his latency period, before he's come to accept his sex thoughts as natural. These books can drive him into sex fantasies, divert him from normal growth and from seeking real experiences on his own level, until his fantasies become a preoccupation that cripples his chance for normality."

"In other words, Elmo, you feel that all literature, all ideas, should be aimed at satisfying the twelve-year-old reader? If we did so, we would eventually wind up with an adult nation of twelve-year-olds, wouldn't we? No, I can't buy that. The very young aren't keenly interested in grown-up sex, and by the time they are they're usually old enough to cope with reading about it. Anyway, it's been argued that books represent only a small part of a youngster's sexual environment, perhaps the least part. Remember that survey they took among four hundred college girls many years ago? The girls were asked what stimulated them sexually the most—a play? a movie? a photograph? a book? The overwhelming majority answered—a man. As for the influence of books on the young, well, if there has to be censorship, then it shouldn't come from you or the state—it should come from parents, from the mother and father, in the home. Let each family decide for itself how its own offspring should be raised and what they can or cannot read."

Duncan stared at the ground. Then he shook his head. "No, Mike. Too uncertain. I believe in censorship as it is now constituted by the law, not only because it is the law but because it safeguards freedom and protects it from vigilantes. There have simply got to be rules. I remember a censorship case we had down here some years ago concerning *Tropic of Cancer*. One of the prosecution witnesses, a professor of English named Baxter, was particularly eloquent about this necessity, and I still recall what he said—well, most of it—and I still go along with him. He admitted that censorship troubled him because he hated the idea of censors imposing their opinions and wills upon the conflicting opinions and wills of other people. Nevertheless, he said, in a complex society like ours we've got to live by some rules. There's got to be a rule about automobiles driving on the right-hand side of the road. Now, this may impair the freedom of the driver, infringe on his individual rights, but the rule must be imposed. Then he said, 'We know that we can't sell with impunity cancer cures by mail, which are fraudulent quackeries. We know you can't sell pornographic postcards in the school yard. There is a level, in short, that is the great concern and the difficulty in the twilight zone of all censorship. . . . Our American society grants a great deal of leeway . . . but down here there is a level beyond which it is not socially desirable, safe, or healthy for people to be allowed to go.' "

Barrett nodded. "Agreed, Elmo. Now we've about made the full circle. Rules. Who sets them? You? Me? Frank Griffith? Senator Bainbridge? I'll go with the answer given by Supreme Court Justice Stewart. He argued that those who charted our First Amendment believed a society could be truly strong only when it was truly free. 'The Constitution protects coarse expression as well as refined, and vulgarity no less than elegance. A book worthless to me may convey something of value to my neighbor. In the free society to which our Constitution has committed us, it is for each to choose for himself.' Elmo, there can be no arbiter for everyone, not in the matter of taste. There's an old joke that tells it best. A patient went in to see a psychiatrist. The patient agreed to take the word-association test, a kind of oral Rorschach inkblot. The psychiatrist was to read aloud a series of words, and the patient was to respond immediately to each word with the first word that came into his mind. So the psychiatrist started with the word 'House,' and the patient answered, 'Sex.' The psychiatrist said, 'Chair,' and the patient answered, 'Sex.' The psychiatrist said, 'Table,' and the patient answered, 'Sex.' After twenty more routine words—like 'Kitchen' and 'Garden'—each of which brought the response 'Sex,' the psychiatrist became annoyed. 'Look here,' he said to the patient, 'I must say you've got an unusually one-track mind.' The patient appeared surprised. 'But, Doctor,' he protested, 'you're the one who's bringing up all those sexy words!' " Barrett grinned and shrugged. "There you are."

The District Attorney smiled briefly. But only briefly. He was not amused. "Mike, most of us know what is sexy and what is not. We also know what is dirty and what is not. And I believe most of us feel that *The Seven Minutes* and books like it are dirty, they're obscene, and they don't deserve to be circulated. No matter what, Mike, but as long as that sort of thing keeps coming out, I'll keep fighting it."

Barrett nodded. "Okay, Elmo. As long as you keep fighting it, I'll be fighting you." He paused, and then he added, "And I'll also be fighting those things I consider to be really obscene today."

"Meaning what?"

"Meaning the real fight to be fought is not against writings about sexual intercourse or the use of four-letter words, but against obscenities like calling a black man 'nigger' or labeling a person you disagree with 'Commie.' What is truly obscene is clubbing or persecuting a man because he is different from you or has different ideas, or forcing young boys to murder other young boys in distant countries in the name of self-defense, or as one preacher stated it, seeing 'a fully clothed man twitching and writhing as the shock of electricity applied by our state prison officials burns through his body.' What is really obscene is teaching students lies, promoting hypocrisy and dishonesty with a wink, making material goals a way of life, ignoring poverty in a land of plenty, condoning injustice and inequality while paying lip service to the

Flag, the Founding Fathers, and the Constitution. Those are the obscenities that concern me."

"They concern me just as much," said Duncan. "And when I can, I'll be battling them side by side with you. But where we part company is over the matter of freedom of speech and the rights of those who take advantage of it for sick or selfish reasons and to the detriment of our families and our nation." He stopped and stared at Barrett. "Okay, we're still at odds over the subject of pornography. But leveling now, Mike, you do believe in a little censorship, don't you?"

"If you can make me believe in a little pregnant, you can make me believe in a little censorship. And even a little censorship, I suspect, were such a thing possible, might be too much, far too much, because of what it could lead to. George Bernard Shaw spelled it out. Assassination, he said, is the extreme form of censorship. And it is, and I'm not forgetting that. But I'll tell you what, Elmo. When scientists can prove by tests that obscenity in books is harmful, when the courts can truly distinguish between what is obscene and what is not, and when we can find umpires wiser than any men on earth right now to rule on what should be censored and what should not, without invading and endangering other human freedoms, then and only then will I stop fighting you. How's that?"

"Maybe that day will come, Mike."

"We can both pray for it." He was about to take his leave when something came to mind, from where he did not know, for it was irrelevant to what had passed between them—or perhaps, after all, it was more relevant than anything that they had discussed. "Elmo," he said, "have you ever heard of the best last will and testament ever written? It was written by a Chicago attorney, Williston Fish, in 1897, in collaboration with and for his client Charles Lounsbury. Do you know it?"

"I don't believe I do."

"I think those of us in the legal profession might read it and reread it from time to time. I'll try to remember to send you a copy."

"What's in it?"

"Well, just to give you an idea. The will starts off: 'I, Charles Lounsbury, being of sound and disposing mind and memory, do now make and publish this my last will and testament, in order,

633

as justly as I may, to distribute my interests in the world among succeeding men . . . First, I give to good fathers and mothers, but in trust for their children, nevertheless, all good little words of praise and all quaint pet names, and I charge said parents to use them justly but generously as the needs of their children shall require.

" 'I leave to children exclusively, but only for the life of their childhood, all and every the dandelions of the fields and the daisies thereof, with the right to play among them freely, according to the custom of children, warning them at the same time against the thistles. And I devise to children the yellow shores of creeks and the golden sands beneath the waters thereof, with the dragon-flies that skim the surface of said waters, and the odors of the willows that dip into said waters, and the white clouds that float high over the giant trees.

" 'And I leave to children the long, long days to be merry in, in a thousand ways, and the Night and the Moon and the train of the Milky Way to wonder at, but subject, nevertheless, to the rights hereinafter given to lovers; and I give to each child the right to choose a star that shall be his. . . .

" 'To lovers I devise their imaginary world, with whatever they may need, as the stars of the sky, the red, red roses by the wall, the snow of the hawthorn, the sweet strains of music, or aught else they may desire to figure to each other the lastingness and beauty of their love.

" 'And to those who are no longer children or youths or lovers I leave Memory . . .' "

Barrett paused, and he offered Duncan a warm smile.

"Elmo, whichever side we may be on," he said, "I think we agree that that's what it's all about, don't we?"

Duncan was smiling easily at last. "Yes," he said. "Yes, that's what it's all about. Good night, Mike."

"Good night, Elmo, and good luck—to both of us."

Three quarters of an hour later, when Mike Barrett arrived at his apartment, he found a huge magnum of G. H. Mumm's champagne, beribboned and gaudily gift-wrapped, standing in splendor before his door.

As he unlocked the door and went inside, he tried to find the donor's card. But the room inside was dark, meaning Maggie was not yet here, and he had to turn up the lamps and search for the card again. At last he had it. He extracted the white card from the envelope and he read the message:

> To Michael Barrett:
>
> I salute you on your deserved victory. I also recommend to you the wisdom of Charles Lamb, to wit: "He is no lawyer who cannot take two sides." When you have the time, I would like to interest you in my side. You might not find it disagreeable, and you could find it profitable.
>
> Best,
Luther Yerkes

Barrett tore the card in two and dropped the pieces into the wastebasket.

He considered the magnum of champagne.

The spoils of the victor.

He would keep it.

The telephone rang, and he hastened to pick it up. The voice he heard was the one he had least expected.

"Hello, champion," said Faye Osborn. "I've just finished eating a great big dinner of five courses—all of them crow. I thought I'd tell you, Mike."

"Well, that's nice of you, Faye."

"You've turned out to be one helluva barrister. Even Dad says so. Anyone who could make that dirty little book look as pure as driven snow deserves the Osborn Admiration Award as well as the Nobel Prize. In fact, Dad was so impressed, I believe he's almost ready to reverse his decision about you."

"That would be generous of him."

"Mike, I'll tell you why I'm calling. I think we're both big enough to forget what we said to each other in anger. I thought I'd give a little party for you, but then I thought, Why wait for anything so formal? Why not tonight? You must be in a celebrating mood. Anyway, I rather hoped you'd be free for dinner tonight."

Barrett heard the key in the lock and saw the front door open, to show him Maggie's shining face.

He looked down at the telephone mouthpiece and then brought it closer. "I'm sorry, Faye. I have another engagement. I'm afraid I'm going to be pretty well occupied from now on."

8 N

"I see. It's like that. Well, I just thought I'd take a chance and find out. Au revoir, Mike, and maybe we'll run into each other one day."

"Maybe," he said. "Goodbye, Faye."

He looked up.

"Hello, Maggie," he said.

THERE HAD BEEN the champagne, and they had both been too tired and happy for more than a simple early dinner out, and now they were driving back through Oakwood toward West Los Angeles.

Mike Barrett slowed his car on Center Boulevard, then turned it into Third Street and guided it into the first empty parking space.

Opening the passenger door and helping Maggie out, he said, "Let's take a little walk before turning in."

He led her toward a furniture display in the nearest store, and then they strolled hand in hand past the other stores, window-shopping.

At Ben Fremont's Book Emporium, they stopped. The main display window was piled high again with copies of *The Seven Minutes*, each pile appearing like nothing less than a massive bouquet of flowers. Inside, the store was brightly lit, and Ben Fremont was at his old stand behind the cash register, and there were customers and readers.

From the entrance two young men in leather jackets emerged, and one was pulling a book out of a bag, and Barrett could see that it was *The Seven Minutes*. As they passed behind him, Barrett could hear the one with the book saying to his companion, "Yeah, and besides that I heard there's even a scene where he goes down on her. No kidding."

No kidding.

Another couple had come up beside them, halting to study the window display, a middle-aged, respectably dressed couple. "There it is," she said. "That's the one that's been in all the papers. They say it's really something. And don't go making that face. Your daughter could already tell this writer a thing or two. Kids nowadays, it's changing, and you know it. Come on, be a sport, let's get a copy just for kicks."

For kicks.

Barrett watched them enter the store. He felt the tiniest ping of

636

concern. It would be read, as other books would be read, for the wrong reasons. There were decent books, and there were indecent readers. But then his concern evaporated. No one, in an open society, following the rules of that society, had the right to come between an idea and its audience.

He remembered a brief of the Authors' League of America: The contents of a book—obscene or unobscene—only becomes known to those who choose to read it, or to continue reading it when they come upon objectionable portions. That choice is not legitimately the concern of other citizens, who are not compelled to read objectionable work, nor should it be the concern of the state.

He remembered a brief by Charles Rembar, another attorney who had fought censorship to preserve the word: Books provide a vehicle for the transmission of thought that is not matched by other forms of expression. . . . Other forms of expression may be as good or better for entertainment, excitement, or provoking emotional response, but the printed word remains the most important medium for the communication between mind and mind on which our civilization rests. Any exercise of governmental power that hampers the free circulation of books therefore threatens our society.

A book was not a wad of paper. A book was a mind, a person, many persons, our society, civilization itself.

He told himself, In the end, it is not art that must be changed and improved, but people.

It was always people. To have educated people was to have air, free air.

He glanced at the books in the window one last time.

Not guilty.

He felt Maggie's hand on his arm.

"Would you like to go inside?" she asked.

"Not tonight," he said. "I think I can leave Cathleen and her bed at last. I think I'd prefer to spend my time from here on in with Maggie." He felt her arm slip gently inside his, and they began to walk back to the car.

He said, "You know, Maggie, we've had our seven minutes. I was wondering about what came after."

"The eighth minute?"

"And the ninth and tenth and all the millions of minutes of a person's life that follow. They count, too. As much. Maybe more."

"Yes, they do."

"Wouldn't you care to know what they'd be like for you and someone who loved you?"

"I would. But it would have to be someone who loved me as much as I loved him, as much as Cassie and Jadway loved each other. Except, in my case, no more minutes, only infinity, forever."

"Well, your case is a tough one, Maggie, but you know what? I'd like to try it."

"Would you really?"

He smiled down at her. "Maggie," he said, "for better or for worse, you've got yourself a lawyer."

THE DEVELOPING CANADIAN COMMUNITY

The Developing Canadian Community

Second Edition

S. D. Clark

UNIVERSITY OF TORONTO PRESS

© University of Toronto Press 1962

Second Edition, 1968

Reprinted, 1970

ISBN 0-8020-1537-9

Printed in Canada

To the Memory of

GEORGE E. BRITNELL

Preface

THE ESSAYS brought together in this volume are intended to serve as an introduction to the study of the Canadian community. Though *The Developing Canadian Community* is not in any strict sense a textbook, much that is contained in it has developed out of the effort of instruction over the years and it can be hoped it will do something to meet the need of the Canadian student of sociology anxious to learn more about his own society. A social science is made meaningful only when the boxes it constructs out of its theory and method come to have something in them; what is offered here can be thought of as an effort directed towards the filling of some of the emptier of sociology's boxes.

I am indebted to Mr. Jeanneret, Miss Harman, Miss Halpenny and the editorial staff of the University of Toronto Press for their encouragement and assistance in the preparation of this volume for publication. Special thanks are owing Miss Jamieson in seeing the book through the press. There is much as well for which I owe thanks to Dean Bladen, Professor Easterbrook, and Professor Burnet. The dedication of the book to the memory of the late Professor Britnell offers itself as a small way of acknowledging a debt of friendship acquired over many years.

The University of Toronto   S.D.C.
May 15, 1962

Preface to the Second Edition

WHEN a new edition of *The Developing Canadian Community* became necessary, it was decided to include six essays written after the first edition was published. Four of these essays appear in Part III, as Chapters XIV–XVII, and two in Part IV, as Chapters XX–XXI. Though written with no thought that they would be made a part of this volume, they further develop ideas contained in the essays which appeared in the original edition. Apart from the addition of these six essays, no changes have been made in the volume as published in 1962. I decided to let the Introduction stand as it was written, introducing only three footnotes to take account of the essays added. The Introduction was a piece with the rest of the volume, and should be read as reflecting the state of my thought as of that time.

In the Preface to the first edition I had good reason to thank certain members of the staff of the University of Toronto Press. I wish now to add the name of Mr. R. M. Schoeffel, who has been of very great assistance to me in the preparation of this second edition.

February 3, 1968
University of Toronto   S.D.C.

Contents

Preface   vii
Preface to the Second Edition   viii
Introduction   xi

PART I: THE FRONTIER IN THE SOCIAL DEVELOPMENT OF CANADA

I   Social Organization and the Changing Structure of the Community   3
II   The Farming–Fur-Trade Society of New France   20
III   The Rural Village Society of the Maritimes   41
IV   The Backwoods Society of Upper Canada   63
V   The Gold-Rush Society of British Columbia and the Yukon   81
VI   The Prairie Wheat-Farming Frontier and the New Industrial City   99

PART II: RELIGIOUS ORGANIZATION IN THE DEVELOPMENT OF THE CANADIAN COMMUNITY

VII   Religious Organization and the Rise of the Canadian Nation, 1850–85   115
VIII   The Religious Sect in Canadian Politics   131
IX   The Religious Sect in Canadian Economic Development   147
X   The Religious Influence in Canadian Society   167

PART III: FORMATIVE INFLUENCES
IN THE DEVELOPMENT OF THE CANADIAN SOCIETY

XI   The Canadian Community and the American
            Continental System   185
XII   Education and Social Change in Canada   199
XIII   The Frontier in the Development of the
            Canadian Political Community   207
XIV   Canada and Her Great Neighbour   221
XV   Canada and the American Value System   233
       The Limitations of Capitalist Enterprise in
            Canadian Society   243
XVII   Higher Education and the New Men of Power in
            Society   253

PART IV: SOCIOLOGY AND HISTORY

XVIII Sociology, History, and the Problem of Social
            Change   269
XIX   History and the Sociological Method   284
XX   Social Change and the Community   295
IXX   Comparative Sociological Analysis and the
            Problem of Social Change   306

Introduction

THIS VOLUME BRINGS together papers and essays written as far apart in time as twenty or more years. Yet, what is contained herein is very much a piece. It was in 1938 that I determined to undertake a study of the development of the Canadian community. Behind this determination was the conviction that sociology had much to gain from the study of the society of the past and that the sensible place for the Canadian sociologist to begin was with the study of his own society. Thus was begun in 1938 a task which in 1962 must yet be considered far from complete.

The task might have been made easier, and more immediately rewarding, had I been able to bring to bear upon the problem of analysing the development of the Canadian community a clearly formulated theory of historical development. But I had no such theory and I have none yet. It has been my belief that any effort on the part of the sociologist to fit history into a tight, preconceived, theoretical scheme could only result in the producing of poor history—and poor sociology. If the sociologist was to turn to history it was essential that he bring to the work he undertook a spirit of free historical inquiry.

This is not to say that in turning to history he should forget about his theory. In the end, whatever the sociologist does must be judged in terms of its theoretical significance. What this means is looking at history sociologically, seeking always the sociological meaning of what is found. But this can be done without commitment to any particular theory and it certainly can be done without commitment to a theory of historical development. The sociologist can turn sociological historian without becoming a philosopher of history.

It is perhaps a crude sociological theory which got written into much that follows in this volume. Work on the development of the Canadian community was begun by concentrating on those areas of development where the sociological significance of what was happening could be seen most clearly. In the winter of 1938–9 my fourth-year honour students in sociology joined with me in the task of analysing the kind of developments which had taken place in the Klondike during the period of the gold rush. Here there was available a massive body of data and an example of a full-fledged society springing into being almost overnight. For a study of social change the Klondike during the period of the gold rush offered itself as an almost ideal sociological laboratory.

From the Klondike, the study of other areas was undertaken. The next was the backwoods society of Upper Canada. As inquiry was pushed back to the period of the old régime and forward to the period of industrialization and urban growth the complexity of the development of the Canadian community became increasingly apparent. No simple conception of development could account for all which had taken place.

In the preparation of *The Social Development of Canada* for publication, however, it seemed essential that the analysis be in terms of as simple a conception of development as possible. Otherwise, in the effort to cover such an extended period, the danger was very great that what was sociological would become lost in the presentation of a mass of facts. Thus attention was centred upon developments occurring in new frontier areas and analysis was largely concerned with the process of the breaking down of established forms of social organization and the emergence of new forms. *The Social Development of Canada* might have been described as a study of the role of the frontier in the development of Canadian society.

However it might be described, this book was intended to do nothing more than break the ground. It might have led on my part to a very much more detailed study of particular areas of development. Instead, it led to an effort to examine the development of particular forms of social organization. Religious developments attracted attention first not only because of the wealth of material available but because such developments lent themselves readily to sociological analysis. *Church and Sect in Canada* grew very directly out of *The Social Development of Canada*. In turn, the study of religious developments gave emphasis to the importance of political developments. Canadian society in important respects was a political creation. Thus resulted the study *Movements of Political Protest in Canada.*

In this shift from the study of the Canadian community in general to a study of particular forms of social organization there had come a growing realization of the complexity of the forces shaping the character of the Canadian society. The role of the frontier had given emphasis to the importance of forces developing out of the position of the Canadian community within the American continental system. The role of empire and nation gave emphasis to the importance of forces developing out of Canada's peculiar position as a society occupying the northern half of the continent.

The reader of *The Developing Canadian Community* will be made aware of this changing emphasis. The first six chapters of this volume are taken from *The Social Development of Canada.* Separated here from the documentary material which was incorporated in that volume, these six chapters assume the character of essays introductory to a study of the development of the Canadian community. The next four chapters, in Part II, grew out of work on *Church and Sect in Canada* and the first three in Part III out of work on *Movements of Political Protest in Canada.** Some of the ideas contained in these papers find fuller expression in the studies to which they are related. Many, however, might be described as in the nature of afterthought. One can make bold to develop ideas in a paper which might have no proper place in a book.

The reader may well feel that the final two essays of this volume should have been placed at the beginning.† But they were written after the others and represent in a very real sense an effort to pull together ideas growing out of work on the development of the Canadian community. They are perhaps something in the nature of a swan song.

In preparing the essays for publication in this volume only the slightest of editorial revision was attempted. In some of the essays statements made in the present tense have had to be changed to the past where the references were to developments occurring at the time of writing. Other references of a more general sort to the present have been let stand even though made fifteen or more years ago. The reader should bear in mind the time the different essays were written. Many of the ideas in the early essays I would today express differently. A heavy emphasis on the economic factor is

*In turn, the four essays which have now been added to Part III in the second edition grew out of work on the *The Suburban Society* and an as yet unpublished study on the position of the French-speaking population in the northern industrial community. †Now, in the second edition, four essays.

particularly apparent in the essays taken from *The Social Development of Canada*. Here also there is a very considerable reliance upon the W. I. Thomas theory of social disorganization and reorganization though at no time was there an acceptance of the notion that these processes had any meaning except in terms of the particular forms of organization being analysed. The second-last essay appearing in the volume better presents the theoretical framework which was employed in the analysis of the problem of change throughout all the essays.

To give everything included in the volume the character of essays, all footnote references have been omitted with the exception of three illustrative quotations. For the sources of the data on which the essays rest the reader is referred to *The Social Development of Canada, Church and Sect in Canada,* and *Movements of Political Protest in Canada.**No attempt can be made to indicate the titles of the large number of books and articles on the economic, political, and social history of Canada upon which the essays rely. The sociologist in whatever he may attempt to do in the study of the Canadian community must place himself under a heavy obligation to the historian. To the economic historian as well the obligation cannot be a small one. Only the mention of the name of the late H. A. Innis is sufficient to give some indication of it. In Canada there is not yet a significant body of sociological literature relating to the development of the Canadian society of the past. But a beginning has been made in the building up of such a literature, particularly having to do with the early development of French Canada, and in the study of the present-day Canadian community the pioneer work done by C. A. Dawson and E. C. Hughes has been carried forward by a great number of younger sociologists.

It has never been my view that in the development of sociology all sociologists must become historians. There is much sociological work to be done in Canada of a non-historical character. Indeed, it is to the study of the contemporary scene that the major effort must be directed. But it is not unbecoming perhaps on the part of a Canadian sociologist to plead the cause of a sociology directed primarily to the understanding of Canadian problems. We have yet too few resources to dissipate them by riding off in all directions. It is to be hoped that the present volume will strengthen sociological interest in the study of our own Canadian society. There is much certainly about this society that we have yet to learn.

*And to *The Suburban Society* and the study to be published, now in multilith, "The Position of the French-Speaking Population in the Northern Industrial Community."

PART I

The Frontier in the
Social Development of Canada

CHAPTER I

Social Organization
and the Changing Structure of
the Community*

THE IMPORTANCE of the opening up of new areas of economic exploitation in the economic history of Canada serves to justify
concern with the effects of such developments upon the development
of social organization. If some of the older settled areas in Canada
early reached a state of economic maturity, and if at times economic recession halted the pushing out into new areas, these developments did little more than punctuate the sweep of frontier
economic expansion. The drying up of resources or the loss of
markets resulted in a shift to new economic activities rather than in
a prolonged economic regression; the succession of export staples
provides evidence of the importance in the economy of Canada of
new techniques of production rather than of techniques of conservation. The establishment of the fishing industry in the Gulf of St. Lawrence led to the traffic in furs with the Indians and to the settlement
of the Annapolis and St. Lawrence valleys. To fish and fur was later
added the important staple of timber, opening up for agricultural
exploitation the interior of New Brunswick and the new Province
of Upper Canada. Expansion of the fur trade to the West brought
about the sudden rush for gold in British Columbia, and eventually
in the Yukon, and the settlement of the wheat lands of the prairies,

*From *The Social Development of Canada* (Toronto, 1942), pp. 1–20.

and these developments hastened the growth of industrial capitalism in the East. The pushing out of the frontiers of manufacturing, and the exploitation of the mining and pulp and paper resources of the North, mark the final phases of the frontier expansion of economic life in Canada.

Social problems in Canada, accordingly, have been largely associated with frontier economic developments. The opening up of new areas or fields of economic exploitation made certain special kinds of demands upon social organization, and the failure to meet fully these demands resulted in disturbances in social relationships which may be described as social problems. Centres of new economic activity became the points of origin of forces of disturbance, and these forces extended to the peripheries of such activity. The areas of greatest social disturbance were to be found where the impacts of the new techniques of production were most felt, and the intensity of the disturbance reached its peak during the interval in which the new economic developments were most rapidly taking place. As the economy became more mature, the social organization adjusted itself to the conditions of production, and an approximate state of equilibrium was attained by the time the economy passed beyond the frontier stage.

Frontier economic expansion involved the recruitment of capital and labour from outside, and this growth of population made necessary the extension of institutional controls and often their establishment beyond customary boundaries. Since institutions are essentially a body of trained functionaries performing specialized services, organization had to be widened and personnel enlarged if the needs of growing populations were to be adequately served. The considerable distance which often separated new areas of development from centres of control and supply made difficult the maintenance of effective supervision from the homeland in establishing institutional agencies and also imposed severe limitations upon the recruitment of personnel. In addition, conditions within such areas discouraged the financial support of institutions which did not directly promote economic exploitation and the immigration of professionally trained workers. The drain of capital into economic enterprise left little for community services while the demand for labour meant that even those who possessed specialized training of some sort were attracted into economic vocations. The failure of churches or educational institutions to secure adequate financial support, problems of public finance, and the lack of sufficient school-teachers, clergymen, and medical practitioners were characteristic features of Canadian frontier communities. The stronger pull of economic enterprise meant that capital and labour flowed beyond the boundaries of institutional systems. Where economic development took place rapidly and considerable additions to the labour force could be immediately absorbed, as in mining frontiers, the lag of such systems was most conspicuous, but even when development took place slowly and the exploitative process did not require great numbers of workers there was a considerable interval before social organization could catch up with the movement of population.

When the economic exploitation was carried on by monopolies, controls of a political (and to some extent of a cultural) character were secured through the economic organization. Administrative obligations ordinarily accompanied the rights of monopoly, and, even when such obligations were not imposed, the monopolistic enterprise recognized the advantage of assuming considerable responsibility for at least the maintenance of law and order. The early trading companies of New France, and the Hudson's Bay Company, received extensive prerogatives of government, and even such semi-monopolistic enterprises as land colonization companies were endowed with a measure of political sovereignty. Though cultural obligations were less clearly defined, monopolistic organizations were expected to support the basic services of the community, and usually this support took the form of favours and financial assistance to an established church which in turn accepted the responsibility of such social services as education, relief, hospitalization, and recreation as well as religious teaching. For the most part, however, the economic development of frontier areas took place in terms of free enterprise rather than monopoly with the result that this agency for the transfer of social institutions was lacking. Monopoly tended to accompany the exploratory rather than expansionist phase of frontier development, or emerged later as a means of securing a greater conservation of resources. The development of new forms of economic exploitation implied the application of new techniques and skills, and this factor favoured individual enterprise. The very nature of monopoly discouraged efforts to expand the volume of production beyond an amount which the market would profitably absorb in terms of existing cost schedules, and, when abundant resources were available for exploitation as in frontiers, the restrictive policy of monopolistic enterprise led to the eventual triumph of free enterprise. As the expansion of the fur trade into the interior of the continent led to the collapse of trading companies in New France, the development of mining in British Columbia and of agriculture on the prairies marked the end of the western monopoly of the Hudson's Bay Company; land colonization companies as a means of controlling agricultural settlement were generally even more short-lived.

To some extent, the failure of economic enterprise to provide an agency for the transfer of social institutions to frontier areas was offset by efforts put forth by the state. Imperial, or later, national forces promoted the extension of political agencies into new areas of development in Canada. Frontiers have always assumed considerable strategical importance in the political organization of the northern half of the continent, and, for this reason, never became unrestricted areas of economic exploitation. The presence to the south of a rapidly expanding nation served to emphasize the need of maintaining close political contacts with the frontier. The police force and courts of law, or at any rate the army, pushed out with the frontiersmen. The maintenance of military garrisons in New France and later in the British American colonies, the construction of roads and canals to serve as military routes, the dispatch of a force of Royal Engineers to Victoria in 1859, and the organization of the North West Mounted Police in 1874 were instances of efforts to promote imperial or national interests in outlying areas of economic development. To some extent the political controls imposed by the state were paralleled by controls of a social or cultural character. Land grants to favoured individuals or organizations, financial subsidies, preferments in political appointments, or measures restricting the operation of competitive interests were means employed to build up privileged social institutions such as an aristocratic class or established church. The object was to assure the loyalty of frontier populations to the mother country, and such aids therefore served the same purpose as military garrisons or police forces. However, even when such supports of the state were extensive, there remained in new areas of development many needs not immediately taken care of by institutions. The coercive controls of the state, or of privileged social institutions, tended to be of a negative rather than positive character. The instruments of law provided no direction to behaviour outside of prohibitions, while institutions such as established churches supplied leadership only to those who were their adherents. For the large number of people who committed no infractions of the law or who did not owe allegiance to the formally constituted social institutions, authority was for the most part morally indifferent. The extension of social organization into all areas of social behaviour required the active participation of the population itself, and this involved more than simply the transfer of formal machinery.

The lack of institutional agencies securing the active participation of frontier populations increased the reliance upon individual resources, and the greater the lack the greater was this reliance. As frontier populations were left without leadership, they tended to become less dependent upon traditional institutions even after they were established. The weakened state of social organization thereby tended to perpetuate itself. Habits of independence were converted into attitudes of nonconformity, and what was first perhaps missed came later to be resented. New patterns of behaviour inevitably developed which did not fit into traditional systems of institutional control, and efforts of institutions to secure greater conformity led to a conflict of social values and to a condition which might be described as one of social disorganization. The difficulty faced by churches in reviving habits of worship after a considerable interval during which religious services were not provided and other ways of occupying the time on the sabbath day had developed illustrate the kind of problems resulting from the extension of social organization into new areas of development.

The character of the population which moved to frontier areas tended to strengthen nonconformist attitudes and to make more difficult the establishment of institutional systems. If the very fact of movement resulted in a considerable dislocation in habits and beliefs, this dislocation was greater when the population was recruited from a number of different cultural milieus. Conflicts emerged between opposing systems of control; the folkways, mores, and social codes of the various groups strove for supremacy. The efforts of some institutions to strengthen their position by privileges secured from the state were offset by the vigorous propaganda of less favoured organizations. The disturbances resulting from associations with strange people, in weakening traditional habits and beliefs, increased the area of cultural indifference and intensified as a result institutional competition. To the extent that segregation could not be achieved and long-established attachments preserved, frontier populations tended to be indifferent as to the particular institutions to which they gave their support. The effects were evident in a large, culturally detached population in new areas of development which floated from one institution or group to another, their momentary attachments depending largely upon circumstances of convenience and waves of enthusiasm.

This tendency was accentuated when the population contained elements which had joined the movement to new areas as means of escape from restraining influences at home. In some respects, this was characteristic of all frontier populations in Canada. Those people migrated who were most exposed to economic, political, or cultural pressures. New areas of economic development provided greater opportunities to realize potentialities of certain kinds. The worker, peasant, entrepreneur, and the religious or political heretic found there an outlet for their particular aptitudes or beliefs. These types of people made more difficult the establishment of certain forms of social organization. The extension of institutions is facilitated by the presence of a body of receptive attitudes and a favourable set of social customs, and, where these were lacking, dependence had to be placed upon the exercise of powers of coercion or upon propaganda. The weaknesses of economic monopolies, colonial class systems, established churches, or authoritarian systems of government, and the steady drain of the United States upon the population of Canada, were directly related to these characteristics of the settlers in Canadian frontier communities. When the nonconformist elements included those who sought escape from moral codes or agencies of law enforcement, the strains upon social organization in the newly settled areas were even greater. Habits of resistance of such groups to authority were carried over from the old to the new society and increased the general tendency of frontier populations to become independent of traditional institutions. The emigration of social misfits resulted partly from the social pressures applied to get them out of the way and partly from the opportunities of escape or freedom from restraint provided within rapidly growing and largely inaccessible communities. Though the nature of the frontier economy determined to a considerable extent the particular character of these people, in all of the newly developing Canadian communities there were outcasts of some sort from older societies.

Similarly, the presence in frontier areas of people who had emigrated because they were failures at home, whether because of economic adversity, ill health, or some other reason, made more difficult the establishment of community organization. It is true that the rehabilitation of the individual's economic, physical, or mental condition often accompanied settlement in new areas, but this did not relieve the strain upon social organization in the interval before such rehabilitation was accomplished. The inability of such persons to provide for their needs meant that they could not fully participate in community life but were rather a burden upon frontier society. Numbers of such socially dependent persons have invariably accompanied the movement of population into Canadian frontier communities; if some found their way to such communities in the hope of bettering their state, others were sent there as a means of reducing the burdens of relief faced by local and national agencies in the home community. Efforts of France and later of Britain to secure through overseas colonization a solution to the problem of mounting poor-rates were paralleled by attempts on the part of Canadian cities to reduce burdens of relief by the promotion of settlement in the West and in recent years a back-to-the-land movement.

Other characteristics of the population served to make more difficult the establishment of orderly social relationships. Movements of people into new areas almost invariably involved disturbances in the equilibrium of age and sex groups. Though the nature of the economy largely determined the extent of these disturbances, migration ordinarily cut through the population structure to eliminate the very young and the very old and to secure a considerable predominance of men. Hazards of travel discouraged the migration of women, children, and old people, while the frontier society placed an emphasis upon productive as distinguished from service occupations and favoured as a result adult males who could take part directly in the process of economic exploitation. The age and sex composition of the population had considerable significance with respect to the stability of social organization. The absence of the older age groups in frontier areas relieved the pressure upon health and welfare institutions but removed the steadying influence of tradition and deprived the communities of the leadership of those who were not strenuously engaged in making a living. Since there were relatively few children among the early settlers, recreational and educational facilities were not required in the first years of development, but, where settlement of young persons of both sexes took place, problems of maternity and infant welfare quickly assumed considerable importance, and, in later years, an abnormally high proportion of school-age children imposed a heavy burden upon elementary educational institutions; it was not until after the passing of the first generation of settlers in frontier communities that a stable balance was secured between the school-age and total population. A predominance of men in the population raised problems of institutional adjustment of an even more critical character. Social organizations which depended upon the family unit, or which chiefly served the needs of women or children, failed to become established or remained largely ineffective. The result was that a large proportion of the normal controls of society were absent or greatly weakened. Apart from the mores of the family, religious and neighbourhood institutions were most affected. Devoutness tended to disappear when female influences were absent, while most of the niceties and refinements of social relationships depending upon companionship within the family group were disregarded or coarsened when such companionship was lacking. Where conditions were favourable, prostitution developed as a substitute for familial relationships, and the prevalence of drinking, gambling, and certain forms of crime in many frontier areas was indicative of general weaknesses of social organization resulting largely from the disproportionate number of men. In brief, the age and sex composition, like other characteristics, of the population intensified problems of institutional adjustment which resulted from the opening up and peopling of new frontier areas.

Such problems were still further accentuated by the contact of frontier populations with strange environmental influences, since adjustments to these influences were made much more quickly on the individual than on the institutional level. More strictly, adjustments took place most rapidly among that section of the population most exposed to strange environmental influences and were most resisted by that section least exposed, and it was those people least exposed who had chief voice in the direction of traditional institutional policies and activities. The dignitaries, priests, or official classes of the community were very largely sheltered from disturbing influences; the very nature of their roles meant that their employments were not directly related to frontier economic enterprise. It was the new occupational groups who faced the full force of new economic developments, and these groups had few claims upon the offices or emoluments of established social institutions. Individuals participating in frontier economic enterprise came in contact with new problems of life for which new solutions were necessary; the application of new techniques of production, and the development of new ways of living, involved a rational appraisal of the relation of means to desired ends and required the formulation of new habits of behaviour and thought. In a sense, such people moved out to the margins of society, and, while they carried with them some of the habits of thought and behaviour which had been implanted by previous forms of control, they had to leave behind, or cast off on the way, the great body of habits not fitted to the new conditions of life. Habits, like tools, were abandoned through non-usage because they failed to work. Whether this represented a failure to maintain conditions of life which had been considered desirable, or a release from social obligations which had been felt as irksome, the effect was to emancipate the individual from controls to which he had been accustomed. He was left to work out by himself a code of conduct and philosophy of life which more nearly satisfied his present needs. The immediate reaction was one of uneasiness, relieved partly by a feeling of exhilaration. The ultimate result, if new group attachments failed to be forged, was complete personal disorganization. Problems of mental health and suicide, and to some extent of intemperance, in periods of rapid social development, were an indication of the failure of individuals to resolve the personal crisis in face of radically new conditions of living.

Usually, however, some sort of adjustment was brought about. New habits developed to take the place of those discarded. But such habits were not co-ordinated within any institutional system of social control. They represented individual responses to the new conditions of life. Since social institutions, by their very nature, were established ways of doing things, cultural conflict emerged at the point of divergence between the new and old ways of life. The controls imposed by institutions had the object of making behaviour conform to socially approved standards, while adjustments to new conditions implied the emergence of kinds of behaviour which had not yet secured such approval. Thus until new social standards were incorporated within institutional systems, there existed a condition of *anomie* which was characterized by a considerable reliance upon individual effort and upon individual solutions to pressing problems. It is true that problems shared by large numbers of people called forth identical or at least similar solutions, but behind these there was little sense of obligation. Certain ways proved better than others; their approval rested upon individual experience or at most upon the immediate experiences of the group as a whole.

There was lacking any attempt to justify them within a traditional philosophy of the social good. Behaviour was in terms of a rational interpretation of the relation of means to ends lying within the range of experiences of the individual members of the group rather than in terms of past loyalties and sentimental attachments. Reliance upon such criteria meant a relaxation of previously accepted standards and a freer expression of immediately felt wants; social considerations acted only slightly as forces inhibiting behaviour.

The emergence of deviate forms of behaviour in periods of rapid social development demonstrated the failure of large sections of the population to erect successfully group codes of conduct when freed from the controls of social institutions. The breakdown of the traditional institutional structure resulted in the emergence of random types of social action which, when proceeding along certain lines, came to be defined as social problems. Such definitions of social problems, however, were necessarily subjective in that unrestrained behaviour represented nothing more than deviations from generally prevalent social norms; the mores disintegrated, but the behaviour which took place through release from their control could be termed undesirable only when assessed in terms of some set of social standards. The existence of social institutions depended upon conformity, and that behaviour was condemned which did not conform. In a sense, therefore, the emergence of social problems in periods of rapid development was a condition of the successful adjustment of individuals to the new environment. It indicated that while social institutions failed to meet new needs, solutions had been attained or at least were being sought on the individual level or within nonconformist groups.

To some extent, even though resisting or failing to make adjustments, established institutions were able to maintain their controls among certain sections of the population. This was particularly the case if they had at their disposal powerful means of imposing their sanctions. By taboos and moral restraints which carried with them punitive means of securing conformity, deviations from established norms were held in check. The criminal law of the state was the most effective instrument in securing such conformity. It was the expression of the established institutional set-up, and, supported by authoritarian sanctions, it served to check the development of behaviour patterns damaging to prevailing mores. A number of other institutions possessed some power of coercion. The compulsive attributes of religious denominations, the family, and more general communal institutions, tended to assume considerable importance when behaviour became particularly refractory. Resort to coercive measures, however, was an indication of institutional weakness; the imposition of sanctions implied that the habitual behaviour of large numbers of the population was no longer in conformity with established norms. It is true that where the deviations were not too extensive, or the forces of disturbance not too compelling, institutions were to some extent successful in re-establishing normative behaviour. The taboo preserved certain habits which, once fully accepted, converted the taboo into a moral attitude. Generally, however, the forces of adjustment could not be checked by restraints imposed by external sanctions; even the controls of the state tended to break down when faced with conditions of far-reaching social disturbance.

With the failure to maintain traditional controls, adjustments were made within the social organization, and those adjustments went furthest and proceeded most rapidly along lines which did not involve vested interests of some sort. Certain changes were readily permissible; for instance, in the case of churches, the building of places of worship with logs instead of with stones; that which proved of advantage to all the participants within an institution was ordinarily accepted without any prolonged delay. Rigidities entered at that point where certain groups, or officials, had something to lose by change. Opposition was greatest among those people furthest removed from new social conditions, while the dissatisfaction gathered greatest force among those most exposed to these conditions. Where flexibility was provided within the organization of the institution, successful accommodations often could be secured between these conflicting interests. Adjustments entered at the points of greatest disturbance even though disapproved of by those farther removed. Where such flexibility was lacking, however (and in all institutions it was lacking to some extent), attempts on the part of subordinate officials and dissatisfied members to bring about changes were promptly checked from above, and reform depended upon leadership from outside rather than within the organization.

This leadership came both from the ranks of specially trained persons dissatisfied with prevailing methods and from those who lacked any particular qualification to perform the services which they undertook to improve. The physician or judge who attempted to introduce changes at the risk of his professional reputation or employment by a public board was an example of the reformer

drawn from the ranks of the technicians. Though reforms having
to do with such matters as the practice of medicine or the administration of justice ordinarily were undertaken by those familiar
with the techniques of these highly specialized services, in those
situations where the need for improved methods was very pressing,
leadership sometimes came from outside professional circles; the
"quack" became a familiar figure during the cholera plagues in
Upper Canada, and vigilante committees emerged (though not for
long) in British Columbia and the Yukon when regularly constituted authorities of law enforcement were no longer able to
maintain order. In other more legitimate ways people of non-
professional status were able to make their influence felt in the
advocacy of social reforms in fields where specialized training was
required in the actual performance of the services. The royal commission emerged in Canada towards the middle of the nineteenth
century and provided a means for the expression of opinion,
although it was some time before its possibilities as an instrument of
investigation and propaganda were fully appreciated. About the
same time the newspaper developed as a recognized channel for the
dissemination of opinions, and reform editors came to assume an
increasingly important role as critics of social services. In the case
of problems of a less technical nature, not only proposals for reform
but participation could come from those who lacked any sort of
specialized training, and, for this reason, there was a significant
difference in the character of reform movements in, for instance,
health and law on the one side, and morality and religion on the
other. The guardians of public morals or the ministers of the gospel
did not possess a body of skills which could not be quickly acquired
by the layman. The temperance advocate needed to rely upon few
of the findings of science to demonstrate to the satisfaction of many
the evils of alcohol, while, if church bodies made efforts to
establish standards of entrance to the ministry, few qualifications to
preach could be insisted upon when the authority of the churches
was called into question. The appointment and theological principles of the religious prophet depended upon no institutional
intermediary since the truth of his version of the gospel and his
charge to expound it came through special revelation; he answered
an inner call, and God and his conscience were judges of the worth
of his efforts. If perhaps unusual in some respects, the unlicensed
religious preacher was typical in many ways of the reform leader
who emerged at a time when traditional leadership was proving
unacceptable.

By the very nature of their role reform leaders tended to be people devoid of "respectable" attributes. The professional person who practised unorthodox methods or advocated revolutionary changes was as likely to be denied "official" recognition as the person who lacked the qualifications required to serve within regularly constituted social institutions. Similarly, if the one type of reformer usually belonged to, the other was closely identified with, that class in the community which was without any acceptable social status. Reformers were social revolutionists in the sense that what they advocated involved an upsetting of traditional standards and very often traditional social distinctions. Thus they brought down upon themselves the full force of vested interests. In championing the cause of the unprivileged or unpopular, they challenged the privileges and accepted beliefs of the "respectable" leaders of the community. The influences which prompted people to break from established institutions and to take up the cause of reform often increased opposition against them. Desire to escape from the boredom of routine tasks, inability to secure a living or recognition in any other way, love of power which was experienced in swaying large audiences or large reading publics, and personal "grudges" against persons in authority, may have mingled, along with other motives, with the sincere conviction of doing good. But if their ideas caught on, it was because the underlying social consciousness provided a sympathetic response. The reformer differed from the "crank" in that he gave expression to genuine and persistent social needs and dissatisfactions; within programmes of reform, the vague and inarticulate feelings of large numbers of people were crystallized and identified with a clearly defined goal. It was this need for social expression rather than the character or motives of reformers which gave rise to reform movements.

If the motives of reform leaders provide no explanation of the rise of reform movements, neither do the motives of the followers. Nothing inherent within a particular reform idea determined its success in meeting the personal needs of frontier populations. The enthusiasm aroused by inspiring leadership offered to the frontier settler, perplexed by strange surroundings, a means of escape from the task of determining by himself standards of thought and behaviour. In other words, from the point of view of the individual, the movement served as a means of reorganizing the personality in terms of a particular focus of group attention. Joining or supporting the movement, particularly one of a moral or religious evangelical character but even one of health or prison reform, involved some sort of conversion which brought about a reformation of attitudes and established a set of standards depending upon group sanctions. Conversion involved the organization of habits in terms of a definite purpose and in this way it secured a stable personality. But any one of many movements would have been equally effective in meeting such individual needs. Different kinds of personal "crises," such as financial reverses, the death of a dearly loved one, or the loss of good health, caused people to endorse the cause of reform, but life histories which revealed the nature of these would throw little light upon the forces giving rise to particular reform movements. Movements developed because they provided machinery for the rationalization of individual wants on the basis of the common good. They provided an interpretation of new phenomena, and in so doing developed habits in the individual which conformed to a general pattern of social behaviour. The solution of individual "crises" was directed along channels securing the solution of social "crises"; in this way, movements became instruments of social as distinct from individual reorganization.

Similarly, cultural diffusion or environmental determinism provide no adequate explanation of the rise of reform movements. The reform movements which sprang up in Canadian frontier areas did not, of course, develop independently of outside influences. The close connection with Britain and the United States, or earlier with France, and the fact that economic developments in Canada were similar to those taking place in these other countries, meant that new ideas usually were derived from British, American, or in some cases French sources. Often local reform leaders identified their programmes with those of reform movements in outside countries; occasionally, the leaders actually came in from outside. That does not mean, however, that the development of these movements in Canada can be explained in terms of the relation with outside movements since the fact that such a relation became established (or, indeed, in many cases did not become established) requires explanation. Though related to movements outside, reform movements in Canadian frontier communities were products of forces generated from within. On the other hand, the assumption of environmental determinism that the population within these new areas of development individually readjusted their habits of thought and behaviour, and that such random adjustments explain the character of new social developments, disregards the fact that environmental forces did not act equally and in the same way upon

all the individuals of an area. These forces made adjustments necessary, but it was only through group leadership that general patterns
of social adjustment were brought about. It does not matter whether
that leadership was provided, as Walter Bagehot would have supposed, by the intellectually élite, or, as Veblen would have argued,
by the members of that class most exposed to the full force of
changing conditions; the point is that the adjustment in the first
instance was peculiar to a few, and only became generally accepted
through the unifying influence of reform movements. It is true that
where needs were fairly well defined, the nature of acceptable
beliefs was reasonably predictable. The range of choice was confined to a limited number of solutions. In most cases, however,
possible solutions were numerous and highly unpredictable as needs
were ill defined and variable in character, and here the process of
reorganization, through the establishment of dominant and generally
accepted patterns of behaviour, was more halting and painful as
competition between alternative solutions was more strenuous and
drawn-out. The ultimate form of social reorganization depended, in
the final analysis, upon the strength of appeal of rival movements or
institutions.

It was in those areas undergoing rapid change that competition
in social appeals was most apparent and keen. The weakness of
old-established forms of control meant that converts were easily
won and the field was relatively open to a great variety of social
doctrines. The "floating" character of frontier populations was
indicative of the weaknesses of social organization and the tendency
of individual grievances to find outlet in sporadic popular movements. Schisms within social institutions gave rise to new social
movements, and schisms within these, in turn, intensified still
further the disunities in the social structure. The break with old
loyalties tended to create a disposition which discouraged stable
loyalties of any sort. Sectarian religious groups, rebel trade-union
organizations, and new political parties constantly faced disaffec-
tions within their own ranks. Offsetting these schismatic tendencies,
however, there developed new stabilizing forces within reform
movements. With institutionalization, the role of reformers was
taken by that of officials, and programmes of reform became
translated into group philosophies and sets of doctrines. Vested
interests were accumulated which sought to perpetuate the organization of the reform movement by widening its area of control. In a
sense, the organization became a repository of the attitudes and

beliefs of the followers. That is to say, attitudes and beliefs, resulting from conversion, secured justification and a degree of security when officially accepted. In another sense, the organization became a repository of offices. The leaders, officials, and even the lay members were dependent upon it for their own welfare, whether it was a matter of making a living, obtaining prestige, or simply securing status in the local community. Denied leading roles in established or "respectable" institutions, nonconformists sought prestige through leadership or membership within reform organizations.

The increasing institutionalization of reform movements brought about significant changes in their role and personnel. Points of prestige tended to develop within such movements, and efforts were made to secure accommodations with older-established or traditional institutions. The nonconformists came to accept, and consequently to be accepted by, the society in which they lived, and, in return for recognition, ceased warring upon the whole social front. Greater attention was given to the qualification of officials, and even the recruitment of new followers tended to be much more selective. While these changes may have indicated an abandonment of the more advanced claims of the earlier reformers, they meant on the other hand the attainment of many of their chief objectives. With at least partial acceptance of their programmes, reform movements became incorporated within the social structure, and their controls became accepted as normative rather than revolutionary. Such changes may be described as the final phase of social reorganization, when ordered and generally recognized controls replaced those imposed, on the one hand, by authoritarian and unadjusted social institutions, or, on the other hand, by aggressive and non-accommodated social movements. The establishment of stable institutional systems, providing for such needs as those of law enforcement, health, destitution, education, recreation, cultural expression, and religion, marks the stage when the social organization had become fully adjusted to new social conditions, and mores had grown up to sustain its controls. The cycle, it is true, was never completed, as new disturbances threw up problems of social organization and adjustment, but if attention is focused upon the broad stream of development in Canada, it is possible with respect to such frontier areas as those of the fur trade in the valley of the St. Lawrence, the fisheries in Nova Scotia, the timber trade and agriculture in New Brunswick, Prince Edward Island, and Upper Canada, mining in British Columbia, the Yukon, and northern

Ontario, wheat growing in the prairies, and industrial manufacturing in the central Canadian cities to describe the process by which controls became accommodated if not thoroughly integrated.

This process may be considered as a general *movement* bringing about the establishment of a new social equilibrium. Thus with respect to social developments in Canada, the large number of different efforts to secure reform, with respect to matters of crime, intemperance, education, the class system, and religion, together with the less conspicuous changes taking place in the nature of services of medical, social welfare, and other institutions, was closely related within a general movement of social reorganization. Further, this complex of reform efforts extended beyond the purely social to include the economic and political since problems within these fields as within the social grew out of conditions of disturbance which extended throughout the society. Demands for changes in the system of government or in economic policy were indicative ordinarily of states of unrest which found expression in a wide variety of social movements. An emphasis, consequently, upon the purely social or cultural, as distinguished from the economic or political, involves a limitation to but one aspect of a much more general social phenomenon. This limitation affords a means of distinguishing sociology from economics or political science; at the same time, however, it emphasizes the close connection between these social science disciplines.

The Farming–Fur-Trade Society of New France*

THE MOST STRIKING FEATURE in the social development of New France was the conflict of two sets of frontier social values, the one promoting stability and the other expansion. The rich resources of the St. Lawrence Valley favoured the development of agriculture while the extensive continental system of waterways favoured that of the fur trade, and the uneasy accommodation between these two forms of economic enterprise threatened the stability of the society of the colony until the fur-trade frontier pushed so far west as to be almost completely divorced from the agrarian community. If the effects of the clash of the opposing interests of agriculture and the fur trade were evident in the instability of economic and political organization and were in some measure responsible for the eventual fall of New France, they were no less pronounced in social organization. Most of the social problems of the community were the direct product of the pull of these two antagonistic sets of cultural values.

The character of settlement favoured the easy transition of the agricultural society from a frontier to a mature state. The establishment of monopoly control of the fur trade meant that early colonization was wholly in terms of agriculture and tended to take place slowly. Lack of interest if not hostility on the part of the trading companies, the ban upon the immigration of Huguenots, the policy of making large grants of land to individuals who made no effort to

*From *The Social Development of Canada*, pp. 21–44.

develop them, and the constant danger of attacks from the Indians checked rapid settlement. The state itself showed little interest in colonization. The revocation of the charters of successive trading companies when they failed to fulfil their engagements in bringing out colonists indicated the concern of the French government with matters of defence more than with problems of economic welfare. In 1663, only about two thousand people were to be found in the colony. After this date, it is true, far-reaching changes in the economic organization of the colony and in the colonial relation brought about more rapid settlement. So long as the bonds of loyalty established with the Indians through commercial ties could be maintained, reliance upon trading companies and a small number of settlers had incurred no great risk to the state, but, with the alliance of the Dutch and the Iroquois, the balance of power among the Indian tribes collapsed, and the French were exposed to English competition and hostile attack. At the same time, the depletion of the fur-bearing animals in the area immediately adjacent to the colony, and the loss of the Huron Indians as middlemen in the western trade, cut the French off from any secure supply of furs; if a supply was to be obtained, it was necessary to penetrate into the distant hunting grounds of the Indians, and this western extension of the fur-trade organization and reliance upon individual traders not only imposed new strains upon defence forces but made impossible the maintenance of monopoly conditions in local trade. Changes in defence needs, and in the character of the fur trade, brought company rule to an end in 1661 and resulted in the establishment of New France as a royal colony, and the direct intervention of the state led to the institution of a vigorous policy of colonization. The dispatch of the Carignan-Salières Regiment to make war upon the Iroquois, and the settlement of the soldiers of the disbanded regiment along the Richelieu River, were means of closing up the western line of defence left exposed by the Huron defeat. The sending out of girls to marry the disbanded soldier settlers, and the encouragement of the birth rate by gifts to the heads of large families and of marriage by gifts to married couples, were designed to further the combined objects of settlement and defence. Subsidies to local industries, the introduction of an apprenticeship system, and the importation of skilled workers from France did something to widen economic opportunities in the colony. Yet agricultural settlement did not grow rapidly. Limitations in the very nature of the agricultural industry were reinforced by limitations in geography and in political and cultural controls. The western extension of agricultural settlement was halted by the closing in of the St. Lawrence Valley, while the seigneurial tenure checked agricultural expansion. By 1673, 6,705 people had settled in the colony, and by the end of the century (1706), the number had increased to only 16,417. If the increase in population represented a gain upon the rate of settlement before 1660, it could scarcely be considered sufficiently great to impose serious strains upon social organization.

Moreover, the character of the colonists made for the development of stable social organization in the rural frontier. Before 1660, the Jesuits carefully passed upon those intending to settle in the colony, and an effort was made to prevent any persons of immoral habits from embarking or to deport them if they arrived. What colonization took place during this period consisted chiefly of families rather than of detached individuals, and this meant that no serious break occurred in family attachments. Settlement involved very largely the transfer of a peasant population, and peasant social institutions, to a new environment not strikingly different from the old. After 1660, many of less desirable character did find their way to the colony in America. The disbanded soldiers were not as likely to adapt themselves to farming conditions as peasant settlers; some of the destitute of relief-burdened French parishes were dumped down in the colony; absconded debtors and criminals escaping the restraints of justice were not entirely absent among incoming settlers; and young women of undesirable moral reputation were occasionally sent, or came out of their own accord, to marry unattached men in the colony. But the numbers of those who might have been described as disreputable were not considerable, while those who had little inclination to farm would readily have adjusted themselves if the fur trade had not discouraged such adjustment. The agricultural industry, in itself, imposed severe demands upon the inhabitants and offered few opportunities to maintain habits of dissipation which the individual may have brought in with him.

Finally, conditions within the rural frontier served to favour the establishment of traditional institutional controls. The danger of Indian attacks, the difficulties of carrying on agricultural operations, and the lack of available markets, made for a considerable dependence upon the state. The organization of the rural districts under militia captains, the development of an extensive system

of economic controls, and the widening of the criminal law to cover
almost all forms of undesirable behaviour were indicative of the
part played by the state in the rural society of New France. The
establishment of the seigneurial system extended formal controls
into the cultural realm, and the limited amount of good agricultural
land secured the stability of this system in the rural society. The
dues and acts of respect which the habitant owed to his seigneur,
and the political and social prerogatives of the seigneurs, such as
that of holding court, made for a hierarchical social order in which
the leadership of the privileged class was accepted by the rural
population. Family attachments were also strengthened by the
character of settlement in the colony. The extension of settlement
along the river, and the failure, as a result, of vigorous village groups
to emerge, enhanced the dependence of the individual upon the
family unit. The low illegitimacy rate, before the development of
the western fur trade, indicated the strength of the pioneer rural
family. Only one of 674 children baptized between 1621 and 1661
was illegitimate. More important still, conditions within the rural
frontier of New France favoured the establishment of religious
controls upon a firm basis. Within the organization of the Catholic
Church, and particularly of the Jesuit Order, there had developed
techniques highly adapted to the needs of a rural frontier. The
Jesuit missionaries, fired with the evangelical zeal of their first
leader, Ignatius Loyola, and devoted to service in distant parts from
the time their order was founded, quickly secured a strong position
within rural New France. The other religious orders established in
later years likewise readily fitted into the community structure; the
Sulpician Order of the seigneury of Montreal, the Hôtel-Dieu, the
Ursuline Order, and the Congrégation de Notre-Dame restricted
themselves to fields of labour in which they were specially qualified.
The episcopacy, itself, particularly during the incumbency of
Bishop Laval, was well adapted to serve the needs of a frontier
society; Laval had been trained in one of the schools of the Jesuits
and his appointment was largely the result of their influence. The
geography of New France reinforced the position of the Catholic
Church. The parish organization was unsuited to the needs of the
extremely scattered rural population, and, until 1679, itinerant missionaries closely controlled by the Jesuit Superior, or later the
Bishop, took the place of settled parish priests. Their preaching
assignments required the missionaries to travel over large areas,
holding mass in each place about once in six weeks, and this lack

of any regular relationship between the priests and particular groups of inhabitants, and the absence of any strong feeling of local community solidarity, made for the dependence of the population upon the central authority of the church. The unifying influence of the river highway favoured centralization in the church as in the community generally. The payment of all tithes into the Seminary in Quebec, and the retention by the Superior or Bishop of full control over the appointment and pay of the missionaries were forms of centralization within the organization of the church; the influence of the church in the choice of early governors, and the right of the Bishop to appoint members of the Sovereign Council, were indicative of the extension of such centralizing tendencies into the wider organization of the community.

If the slow growth of settlement, the character of the colonists, and the nature of geographical conditions within the rural community made for the ready transition of New France from a frontier to a mature agricultural society, that is not to say that problems of social organization did not emerge as a result of frontier agrarian development. The distance of the colony from the homeland, the isolation of the settlers, the difficulty of establishing any sort of primary group life apart from the family because of the centralizing influences of geography, the dependence of the agricultural community upon military protection, the failure of the French government to adapt its restrictive economic policies to the needs of a frontier agricultural economy, and the generally paternalistic attitude of both the state and the church had effects which were evident in the inertia, extreme poverty, economic dependence, and cultural indifference of many of the inhabitants. Society in New France inevitably felt the disorganizing influence of the agrarian frontier. But it was an influence not sufficiently great to lead to any general breakdown of social organization. Rigid limitations of geography and also culture were imposed upon the expansion of frontier agricultural enterprise; the agricultural community became a closed rather than an open frontier. Forces of social reorganization, as a result, quickly asserted themselves in establishing a considerable degree of equilibrium within the rural community and in bringing about the transition from a frontier to a mature society. In terms, therefore, of the agrarian frontier in itself, problems of social organization in New France were neither extensive nor of long duration.

The opening up of a new frontier of individual economic enterprise associated with the fur trade, however, introduced far-reaching problems of social organization which extended back into the rural community and seriously disturbed society in New France throughout the latter half of the seventeenth and early part of the eighteenth century. The collapse of economic monopoly in the trade with the Indians, and the necessity of extending trading operations further inland to tap supplies of beaver, led to the increasing participation of the colonists in the fur trade, and such participation resulted in weakening the restraints of the rural society. Those engaged in the trade came to constitute a large proportion of the young men in the colony. It is possible at the peak that close to one thousand were fully employed in this occupation; Du Chesneau estimated the number as between five and six hundred in 1679, not including those who made daily excursions into nearby woods. Though there was in the life of the bush ranger much which was squalid and mean, and little which was as colourful as fireside stories suggested, it made an irresistible appeal to the youth in the colony. Traders who returned from the hazardous journey into the interior played freely upon their imaginations—like most travellers from distant lands—in recounting their experiences, and there developed as a result a romantic picture of the *coureurs de bois* which stirred the imaginations of the sons of every habitant and seigneur in the colony. It is true, on the other hand, that the drabness and bleak poverty of rural life in New France provided little inducement to young men to remain at home. The hard work in clearing and cultivating the land, the lack of interesting diversions, and the puritanical restrictions of Jesuit priests, contrasted unfavourably with the fur trader's freedom from monotonous toil, his opportunities to experience new and exciting adventures, and his seclusion from the watchful eye of the cleric. Though bush ranging involved the sacrifice of modest comforts and of a degree of security, there were few youths who did not feel that the many compensations offset the sacrifices.

By providing an outlet for the young men in the rural communities, the fur trade broke down the isolation of the scattered settlements, and quickened the tempo of social life. In this way, it probably exerted an invigorating influence in the colony. But it carried in its train social problems which seriously disturbed the rural frontier society. Those engaged in the trade came to lead a highly nomadic existence. Fur-trading parties setting out from the settlements journeyed into the upper reaches of the St. Lawrence waterways system, and were absent for as long as from one to three years. Among such groups the controls of the community broke down through the sheer impossibility of applying the sanctions upon which they rested. Always on the move, and returning to their homes for only short periods of time, the youthful traders could readily avoid the scrutiny or coercive controls of responsible community leaders. The emancipation secured through mobility was furthered by the adjustments made necessary by new conditions of life. The freedom of the woods developed in those engaged in the trade an irresponsibility which made it difficult for them to accept the discipline of rural life. The *coureurs de bois* lived recklessly, heedless of what the future held in store for them. Danger was cheerfully faced, and privation grimly accepted. Few undertakings were too fatiguing or too perilous if they offered lucrative returns from trade with the Indians. These qualities were essential in the bush ranger as such; as early a governor as Champlain had recognized the contribution which could be made by enterprising and courageous traders who found their way into the territory of the Indian hunters. But these same qualities unfitted this group of young men to settle down in and accept the controls of the rural society. A distaste for routine and steady labour and an impatience of restraints of any sort became characteristic traits of the hardened bush rangers. These traits were the product of the conditions under which they lived. Their way of life required adjustments which involved the abandonment of many old habits and the forming of many new. The chief selective agency in this process was the geographical environment of the interior of the North American Continent.

But in addition to a new geographical environment, the *coureurs de bois* came in contact with a new culture, that of the North American Indian, and the habits they formed resulted to some extent from the accommodation of the values of this new culture with those of an old. Sharing with the Indians many experiences and problems, the *coureurs de bois* readily adopted many of their ways of behaviour and with these much of their philosophy of life. Many of these acquisitions, such as techniques of travel and manner of dressing, were essential for survival under conditions faced by the traders. Even the adoption of the attitude of mind of the native, of not worrying about the future, was necessary as a means of avoiding the nervous strain of the trader's precarious way of life. But as many of the worse features of western civilization were acquired by the Indians, so many of their most dissolute habits were copied by the white inhabitants. The presence within the neighbourhood of the colony of Indian tribes, who as a result of the depletion of furs had lost their economic security, intensified the disorganizing effects of the contact with Europeans. The demands made by the French fur-trading organization upon the native culture resulted in changes in the Indians' mode of life and increased their dependence upon their European neighbours. The disorganization resulting from this loss of independence, in turn, contributed to the disorganization of the white culture through contact with these Indians. Even those habits of the Indian, however, which were not of a dissolute character took on that character when borrowed by the whites. Customs and attitudes which conformed to the Indian culture became forms of social disorganization when introduced into a different culture. Thus simple recreational and ceremonial activities indulged in by the natives tended to assume an immoral character when taken over by the *coureurs de bois*.

Through their contacts with the Indians, and because of their extreme mobility, the *coureurs de bois* came to constitute a distinct social group in which conformity to collective ways of behaviour and collective ways of thought was maintained by group loyalties. This emergence of new cultural patterns carried no threat to the traditional rural culture to the extent that the *coureurs de bois* were completely separated from the settled agricultural community. In such places as Michilimackinac, Green Bay, and Detroit, with populations consisting of western traders and transient Indians, social disorganization was wholly confined to the Indian society. But the influence of the fur traders inevitably reached back into the settled community because it was from this community that they were recruited and it was there that they made their headquarters.

Montreal became the chief centre of conflict between the settled rural and the mobile trading groups. Situated near the junction of the Ottawa and St. Lawrence rivers, it constituted the natural geographical centre for the western trade; on the other hand, situated at the point where the Laurentian and Appalachian ranges close together, it marked the western extremity of the settlements extending up the rich lowlands of the St. Lawrence Valley. In Montreal consequently trader and habitant met. Here the traders returned with their furs and secured the necessary goods to outfit another voyage. Although the importance of the fair in the town declined with the western extension of the trade, many Indians continued to frequent the place to sell their furs or for other purposes, and their presence was a further disorganizing influence in the community. The effects reached inevitably beyond the town to the rural society. Montreal provided an active labour market for farm youth. Young boys from the rural settlements, seeking an entry into the fur trade, found their way to the town; in the interval between western excursions, they often returned to their farm homes. The drift of this occupational group was the chief channel by which the values of the trading culture were transmitted to the rural. Although the truly floating population was largely confined to Montreal, the towns of Three Rivers and Quebec, and even the old-established rural settlements between, did not escape the pull of the fur-trade frontier upon their populations. The colony came increasingly to be made up of a body of traders continually on the move; the fur-trade party, in contrast to the rural neighbourhood group, exemplified the unsettled character of community life. Problems of social organization in the rural society were largely the result of the unsettlement which occurred.

Much of the destitution in the colony was indirectly if not directly related to the disturbing influence of the fur trade. The manner in which the *coureurs de bois* were paid when they returned to Montreal, and the example set them by the Indians of living from day to day, encouraged habits of extravagance which left numbers of those, too old to continue as traders, without means of livelihood. The periodic crop failures which occurred partly because of the neglect of farming through participation in the fur trade contributed further to problems of destitution. The practice of begging spread and assumed serious proportions in the town of Quebec, and, if many of the beggars were social dependants who had been shipped out by parishes in the homeland, their numbers were probably increased by the addition of persons demoralized by the fur trade. Within the Catholic Church there existed agencies adequate to deal with the wants resulting from genuine poverty as such, but the association of destitution with begging or vagrancy raised problems which required the exercise of powers of police. The establishment of poor-boards by the state, and state support of poor-houses or hospitals, were prompted by the urgency of the problem of vagabondage attributed by the sponsors of these measures to the influence of the fur trade. More extensive controls involved the intervention of the formal authority of the criminal law.

Efforts were made by the French government or the local governmental authorities to suppress some of the worst evils emerging in the rural communities as a result of the fur trade. Trading in the woods was prohibited by law or subjected to regulation. Heavy penalties were provided for those selling brandy to the Indians. Taverns were licensed, drunkenness on occasion treated as a criminal offence, and prostitution rigorously suppressed. But such coercive measures of the state were largely ineffective in securing conformity of the fur traders to the norms of the rural society. Constant violations of the law occurred among the inveterate rangers of the woods, and the ease with which they could hide in the forests, and the inclination of the inhabitants to assist them in escape, made it almost impossible to effect arrests. The influence of the traders resulted in an increasing problem of crime in the settled community as well as on the fur-trade frontier. Acts of violence, armed robberies, and murders were not infrequently committed, while sex crimes were sufficiently widespread to attract attention and call forth measures of suppression. A number of taverns along the river front became hangouts of robber gangs, and the existence of the open frontier to the West made difficult effective policing. Criminals could readily escape into the interior, and, like the *coureurs de bois*, were often aided by local inhabitants, such as the tavern keepers, in making such escapes. The lack of respect for authority which the conditions of the fur trade encouraged gave rise to some extent to attitudes of indifference on the part of the public to general problems of order and crime. The *coureurs de bois* who disregarded regulations of the fur trade became popular heroes in the eyes of many of the inhabitants, and this partiality for the outlaw traders asserted itself in a tendency to take the side of violators of the law in general. The fact that most forms of crime in the colony, apart from unlawful participation in the fur trade, involved little threat to the rights of private property but were rather acts of personal violence contributed further to the unconcern of many of the colonists with matters of law enforcement.

The fur trade not only encouraged attitudes of disrespect for the authority of the law, but introduced discordant interests into the councils of the state itself. There developed a set of problems respecting which there were serious conflicts between governmental and ecclesiastical officials, and even between the various governmental officials; and the divided jurisdiction, and the failure of the government to follow a consistent policy, weakened efforts to enforce the law. Some of the governors, and a number of the local councillors, under the influence of the ecclesiastical party, were prepared to go to considerable lengths in carrying out a policy of rigorous control of the fur trade, but their restrictions usually met with a cool reception from the Minister of Colonies in Versailles. The vacillation of official attitudes led to a policy wavering from stern oppression to mild tolerance.

The failure of governmental controls, however, reflected more fundamental weaknesses of the colonial organization than simply that of the conflict between secular and ecclesiastical authorities. Efforts to suppress the evils of the fur trade by confining it to Quebec, Three Rivers, and Montreal failed in face of economic forces pushing it westward. Competition from the English in the south and north could be met by the French only through the extension of the fur-trade organization into the interior. The *coureurs de bois* played a vitally necessary role in the maintenance of French control over the western trade. The disorganizing effects of their activities were an inevitable result of the con-tradictions within the economic organization of the colony. The weakness of the state in controlling the *coureurs de bois* or checking the brandy trade lay in its dependence upon the fur trade as its chief source of revenue. Expansion westward, in response to English competition, involved increasing governmental outlays, and the heavy fixed costs of the trade made necessary a policy of pro-moting still further expansion. In the long run, expansion was economically as well as socially disastrous to the colony, but the burdens of overhead costs made impossible a policy of curtailment. Problems of social disorganization were the immediate effects of economic contradictions which led evenutally to political collapse.

Expansion of the fur trade involved the weakening of the moral and cultural controls of the local community and primary groups. The effects upon the family were the most immediate, and, in the eyes of those concerned with the welfare of the colony, the most readily discernible. The opportunity of joining at a very early age fur-trading parties going west gave to young boys a feeling of independence of their parents. Sex mores as well suffered from the participation of so many young men in the fur trade. The domestic requirements of the fur traders encouraged the legitimate employ-ment of Indian squaws; but demoralization of the natives, and their impoverishment with the decline in returns from hunting and increasing dependence upon European goods, led to a reliance upon such employment as a means of subsistence. Such contacts with the

Indians resulted in sexual irregularities. Cohabitation with Indian squaws was common among the single young men, and even those who were married often had native mistresses. Illegitimacy, encouraged by the Indians as a means of establishing ties with the whites, increased in the Indian villages, and prostitution developed in the chief centres of trade. The fact that the economic relationships of the French with the Indians were of a bargaining character favoured the commercialization of sexual relationships. The traders possessed commodities readily available to the natives, and the desire for these commodities resulted in a willingness on the part of Indian women to engage in prostitution. The small number of white prostitutes in the colony increased the dependence of the traders upon the natives, and there developed a regularized if not extensive trade of prostitution in Montreal and Michilimackinac in which Indian women were employed. The effects of the fur trade extended back to weaken the family organization of the rural communities. Relationships with the Indians, and the free and easy life, made the *coureurs de bois* reluctant to accept the responsibilities of marriage. To acquire a wife meant settling down in the colony or at any rate making some provision for her maintenance. Efforts of the colonial governors to encourage marriage largely failed with respect to this group, and many of the daughters of the habitants were left without husbands. The prolonged absence of married men on excursions to the West further served to weaken the family and to give rise to problems such as adultery. Family disorganization, to the extent that it emerged, reflected the wider disorganization in the rural mores of New France. The pull of the fur trade made more difficult the establishment of a stable community life, and the family suffered from the general unsettlement which obtained.

The weakening of family controls in the colony was not offset by the strengthening of other primary group attachments. Inherited cultural values associated with the ethnic background of the population had quickly weakened in face of forces of geography, and the fur trade checked the development of new cultural attachments to take the place of those transmitted from the homeland. As a result of the influence of the traders, no group emerged with a strong sense of collective interest in, and a consciousness of, its obligations to the rural community. The attractions of the fur trade led to the neglect of agriculture and prevented the development of distinctions of social worth resting upon successes achieved in husbandry or rural public life. The enterprising but reckless *coureur de bois* tended to command, particularly among rural youth, more respect than the hard-working and patient habitant, while the swashbuckling leader of fur-trading parties won a position of prestige denied the public-spirited leader in the rural community. The agricultural class lacked definite social status so long as farming remained subordinate to the occupation of fur trading. Other social classes in the community were little more able to provide cultural leadership. The centralized character of the overseas trade in furs checked the growth of a well-to-do merchant class within the colony. The large merchants who reaped the really substantial profits from the fur trade by providing the necessary provisions for carrying on the trade with the Indians and by marketing the furs brought down to Montreal did not become settled inhabitants. Often they were represented in the colony by agents, and, if they personally transacted their business, they returned to France when their affairs were wound up. This outside control of the fur trade resulted in a heavy cultural loss to New France. In effect, the only group which secured large material benefits from the fur trade made no contribution to the cultural life of the colony. The local bourgeoisie, petty traders, innkeepers, and others, did not acquire wealth and consequently failed to acquire attributes of social worth which would have separated them off from the great bulk of the inhabitants. Instead of providing leadership within the colony, they were subject with the rest of the population to the demoralizing influences of the western trade. The official class, likewise, failed to develop any strong sense of being a distinctive social élite. Though the members of this group were least exposed to the influence of the fur trade, their occupation was not sufficiently attractive to offset the prestige of the *coureurs de bois*. Salaries of the councillors were extremely small and did not induce the immigration of persons trained in jurisprudence; most of the local officials found it necessary to engage in petty trade to supplement their meagre incomes.

If, of all classes in the colony, the seigneurs were the most securely established, a number of factors limited the effectiveness of their leadership in resisting the disorganizing influences of the fur trade. The Crown, jealous of the royal prerogative, took care not to endow them with powers which would have made possible the erection of a genuine feudal order on the American frontier. They were deprived of privileges of a military character, and were not endowed with any real political power. Limitations imposed by the Crown were reinforced by the forces of geography. Defence from Indian attacks required the centralization of the control of the army in the hands of the Governor, the building up of a mobile military force to wage war upon the Indians, and the appointment of militia captains throughout the rural districts who were directly responsible to the chief executive. As a result, the patriotism which was aroused by the fear of the Indian enemy was directed towards the Governor rather than towards the local seigneurs, while the militia captain in many respects became the most important person in the local community. Furthermore, expansion of the fur trade westward resulted in the emergence of a distant frontier in which problems of criminal and civil jurisdiction could not be handled by the seigneurial courts. The heavy burden imposed upon the Sovereign Council with the increasing number of cases relating to trading matters or to the activities of western traders led to the erection of a system of royal courts throughout the colony and this development brought about a steady decline in the influence and prestige of the seigneurial courts. The result of this combination of pressures of a political and geographical character was to divest the seigneurial system of New France of many of the attributes of feudalism.

The direct influence of the fur trade led to a further loss of such attributes. The interest of the seigneurs was wholly identified with the land since their economic welfare depended upon returns from agriculture, and the diversion of much of the resources and energies of the colony into the fur trade and the small returns from agriculture left them in a state often bordering on penury. At the same time, the little interest taken in rural problems, and lack of prestige attached to rural leadership, lowered their status in many cases to little more than that of debt-ridden farmers. The attempt to lead the life of gentlemen on incomes derived from feudal dues which from the circumstances of a new country could scarcely ever be profitable inevitably rendered the economic position of this class insecure. To reduce their standard of living to conform to their meagre incomes was as objectionable to their tastes as to increase their incomes by engaging in trade was disastrous to their social position. Some accepted the inevitable, and became little more than substantial farmers, working side by side with the habitants in the field; by such an adjustment the seigneurial institution was to survive and become an established feature of rural life in French Canada. Commercial vocations in the colony provided a more happy means of adjusting to economic demands, but petty trade offered little in the way of remuneration or prestige, and the seigneurs were ill qualified to engage in the more lucrative exploits of commerce. They lacked the capacity and financial resources to compete successfully with merchants who came out from France; the bourgeoisie which attained a position of supremacy after the British conquest recruited few from the ranks of the seigneurial class. The participation of many of the sons of seigneurs, and even of seigneurs themselves, in the fur trade, to the extent of becoming *coureurs de bois*, was indicative of the disintegration of the class rather than of its adjustment to the conditions of a fur-trade–agrarian society. Some of the more adventurous of the seigneurs, it is true, were able to place themselves in charge of fur-trading parties made up of their own habitants, and thus achieved a position of leadership as fur lords which they failed to achieve as lords of the land. For the most part, however, the conditions of the fur trade favoured more rugged qualities of leadership than those possessed by the seigneurs. The fur trade gave rise to a type of hierarchical organization which made no provision for such attributes of worth as those to which the *gentilhommes* could lay claim. It was *coureurs de bois* like Du Lhut who were able to assume charge of trading parties or military expeditions. The result was that the entry of seigneurs into the fur trade meant the loss of those distinguishing marks of superiority derived from the system of landholding.

Intendants and priests, in denouncing the *coureurs de bois*, made little distinction between the sons of seigneurs and other followers of this vocation. The social background of the former made them if anything more difficult to control. They shared with the common bush rangers a dislike for discipline of any sort, while their aristocratic ties gave them an exalted opinion of their own worth. For this reason, the more spectacular forms of disorder and dissipation of the *coureurs de bois* were likely to be indulged in by these scions of the colonial nobility. The demoralization of a large number of the sons of seigneurs, in combination with the abject poverty of many of the seigneurs themselves, destroyed the vestiges of aristocracy which the feudal system in the colony was intended to create. A few of the seigneurs, it is true, with more favourable holdings or other means of subsistence achieved a position of influence and prestige in the community. A very great number, however, fell hopelessly into debt, and were constantly facing difficulties in relations with their creditors. Appearances were often kept up though it meant doing without the decencies of life. In many cases the condition of their families was so critical as to make them objects of charity from the government. Appeals of the governors or intendants seeking assistance from the King for distressed seigneurs became increasingly frequent, and such appeals were usually accompanied by urgent pleas to bring to an end the creation of new seigneuries, or at any rate to give grants only to those who would not become a burden to the government. A variety of aids was designed to relieve the situation of hard-pressed seigneurs. Some secured political appointments, while others were granted the privilege of selling licences for the fur trade. Such expedients, however, offered little in the way of a solution to a problem, the existence of which was inherent in a social system torn between farming and fur trading. As the prestige of the class declined, a less desirable type of persons sought seigneurial grants. Originally intended to attract the lesser nobles of France, the seigneuries tended increasingly to be occupied by adventurers who had made money following other pursuits or by retired officers of the army who lacked other means of support. The seigneurial grants became for a certain class of persons a speculative venture and, for another class, a government sinecure. This disintegration of the colonial class structure would have been no great loss if conditions in the colony had given rise to a genuine rural social élite. But the attractions of the fur trade rendered this impossible until after the turn of the seventeenth century. The *coureurs de bois* came to constitute in the period 1660–1700 the aristocracy of the colonial society, and it was this class which set to some considerable extent the standards for the community as a whole.

The absence of any group able to assume a position of cultural leadership increased reliance upon the church. Vigorous efforts were made by the local bishops to check evils emerging in the colony as a result of the fur trade, and these efforts were ably supported by the Jesuit missionaries and by the Sulpicians in Montreal. Every opportunity was seized by the missionaries to denounce the trade in brandy, and *mandements* promulgated by the Bishop carried the penalty of excommunication for this offence. Religious and moral prohibitions were widened to embrace a great variety of evils associated with the fur trade. But these efforts were largely ineffective so far as the *coureurs de bois* were concerned. Though Jesuit missionaries were stationed at the various trading posts, and very often went along with the traders to and from the settlements, this intercourse seldom led to the establishment of relationships such as ordinarily exist between priests and their parishioners. The *coureurs de bois* could readily escape from the watchful eye of the missionaries, and on occasion successfully contrived to leave them behind when setting off on trading excursions. Once in the woods, the traders were too far removed from the influence of the church to observe their religious duties seriously, and tended to develop attitudes of careless indifference to things sacred which were mitigated only by a fund of superstitious beliefs made up of a mixture of Indian mythological and Catholic theological tenets. The irreverence of the sceptic and the superstition of the pagan became combined in the outlook of the bush rangers.

Consequently the Jesuits and the higher ecclesiastical authorities recognized that the secure establishment of the church in the colony and of successful missionary enterprises among the Indians depended upon checking the development of the western fur trade. In their eyes, most of the evils in New France lay in the practice of young men going off to the woods to engage in trade with the Indians. The *coureurs de bois* sensed this threat to their economic welfare; encroachments of the missionaries, and controls of the church, as a result were met with suspicion and no little hostility. This conflict between the church and the traders turned mostly about the brandy trade. While the traders may have had no strong religious feelings, they viewed with alarm the possibility of excommunication; few of even the boldest *coureurs de bois* were prepared to accept with equanimity the prospect of being turned adrift from the church. Accordingly, many of them developed a conscience which permitted their engaging in the brandy trade without feeling the necessity of confession, and to meet this threat to its control the church undertook to determine guilt outside the confessional, and upon such external evidence to apply its sanction of excommunication. Exercise of virtual police powers involved the ecclesiastical authorities in conflict with the secular, and gave rise to violent protests against any exercise of the power of excommunication in relation to the brandy trade. Early governors such as Argenson and Avaugour, though under the influence of the ecclesiastical party, found themselves opposed to the clergy in their treatment of the brandy trade as a crime, and Mésy, likewise, broke with the Bishop over this question. But it was under the vigorous leadership of Talon and later Frontenac that the controversy was finally brought to a head. The Recollets, absent from the colony from the rural attained a greater degree of maturity. There developed a distinct agricultural group with its distinctive set of social mores. It was this development within the agrarian society which paved the way for the moral solidarity which became pronounced after the British conquest.

Immediately, however, after the turn of the century, new disturbing influences made themselves felt within the colony. As the organization of the fur trade became more complex and far flung, government came to play an increasingly important role and a greater dependence came to be placed upon military forces to defend the lines of trade and to resist the rapidly growing colonies to the south. A powerful bureaucracy emerged in Quebec, and the colony tended to be converted into something of an armed camp. The growth of a "smart set" in the capital, engaged in a round of dinners, balls, and theatrical entertainments (and in political corruption), carried threats to the simple virtues of a pioneer rural society. Scepticism found its way into the colony through the contacts of officials with liberal elements in Europe, and society in New France after 1750 felt to some extent the effects of the *philosophes* emerging in old France. These influences were confined to small circles in the towns, but the increase in military forces had much more general effects upon moral standards; the growth of problems of adultery and illegitimacy in the colony was closely related to the new demands being made by defence and war. In the end, some sort of satisfactory accommodation would probably have been made between interests identified with the rural society and official and military interests; even before 1760 the seigneurial class was becoming more closely identified with bureaucracy, and the church was beginning to lose much of its evangelical pioneer attitude—the Jesuits were coming into disrepute—and was tending to adopt a more tolerant outlook. But other developments after the turn of the century carried much more serious threats to the rural way of life. The western extension of the fur trade served to promote the growth of a group of local merchants, and the challenge of this class to the leadership of the seigneurial class and of the church was beginning to make itself evident before 1760. Ultimately, the strengthening of commercial interests would have meant a dominance of pecuniary values through the society of New France. Such developments, however, were sharply arrested by the British conquest. Both the tightening grip of colonial officialdom and the growing power of local French commercial interests were destroyed by the Treaty of Paris which transferred the administration and defence of the colony to British officials and military forces and made possible the dominance in commerce of American and Scottish merchants. With political and commercial control in the hands of a "foreign" group, the seigneurial class and more particularly the church emerged as the dominant institutions of the new social order of French Canada.

In some ways the conquest and the assertion of supremacy of the rural way of life were the inevitable consequences of developments which had taken place throughout the French colonial period. If the growth of commercial interests before 1760 involved a threat to traditional authority, these interests did not become sufficiently powerful to bring about a modification of colonial policy and avert the disaster of military conquest. The dominance of the fur trade, and the highly centralized character of its organization, had led to the failure to develop a diversified economy, and this dependence upon a single staple made necessary increasing support from the state. The inevitable concentration of control checked the development of a powerful and independent commercial class as a support of the colonial system, and, involved in the contradictions of the economic order, the state collapsed with the decline of the fur trade upon which it depended. Traditional cultural institutions, such as the church, on the other hand, weakened during the long period when the fur trade was supreme, benefited when it declined and eventually passed under foreign control. Whereas the state, in the end, broke down because it lacked supports outside the interests of the fur trade, the church obtained a dominant position largely because of the lack of other strong interests in the colony.

CHAPTER III

The Rural Village Society
of the Maritimes*

IF THE DISORGANIZING FORCES in the early social development of the Maritime region were less far-reaching than those evident in New France during the period of rapid expansion of the fur trade, they were considerably more diversified in character. The kind of socio-economic unity secured in New France by the St. Lawrence Valley was conspicuously lacking. Flexibility in economic organization resulted from the variety of resources and from the number of points of entry by which they could be exploited. Early development took place in terms of the fisheries, and the large number of different bases in the region and of centres of supply in Europe emphasized the diversity of economic interests. The result was the emergence of several widely separated settlements each of which gave rise to its own kinds of social problems. The different social heritages of the population and economic and technological conditions of life led to different sorts of social adjustments and different forms of cultural development. Only slowly did there emerge integrated social organizations for larger areas which became organized as provinces. The persistence of diversity made impossible any real cultural unity for the whole Maritime region.

Although the colonization of the Maritimes began about the same time as that of the St. Lawrence Valley, the character of economic development checked any considerable settlement. Exploitation of the Gulf fisheries by the French led to trade with the Indians and

*From *The Social Development of Canada*, pp. 95–119.

to the establishment of a settlement about the Bay of Fundy as well as along the banks of the St. Lawrence, but the hunting hinterland of the Maritime Indians was not sufficiently extensive to support any profitable trade in furs. The rapid destruction of the fur-bearing animals within the region, and the absence of any approaches to the interior of the continent, reduced the fur trade to a secondary interest of the inhabitants. Both the Indians and the whites found it necessary to depend very largely upon other means of livelihood. The raising of cattle became the chief industry of the French colonists about the Minas Basin. The Bank and Newfoundland fisheries developed as the dominant interest of French and English trading-capitalist organization.

The nature of the fishing industry discouraged the promotion of settlement. Unlike the fur trade which came increasingly to depend upon the participation of local colonists, the fisheries were exploited by interests operating from a large number of European bases from which the necessary labour and supplies were secured. Attempts to promote colonization met with the vigorous opposition of these interests which feared the competition of local capitalists and labour. The long struggle to prevent the establishment of fishing settlements in Newfoundland was indicative of efforts to preserve the ship fisheries carried on from European bases. The policy of carrying on the fisheries from home bases was favoured particularly by the British who looked upon the development of this industry as a means of strengthening the navy. In the French Empire, emphasis upon land garrisons led to a greater interest in permanent colonization. Settlement on the mainland, accordingly, took place slowly, and was more in relation to the overseas-controlled fishing industry than in response to a genuine desire for the development of colonies. The retreat of France from most of Newfoundland and from Acadia with the Treaty of Utrecht in 1713 led to the establishment of a fishing base in Cape Breton and of an agricultural settlement in what later became known as Prince Edward Island. The British, in turn, established a military garrison at Annapolis to police the rural Acadian settlements and to check the considerable smuggling trade growing up in Louisbourg. Encroachments of the French upon the English base near the Strait of Canso and upon the New England fisheries led to the capture of Louisbourg by a party of New Englanders in 1745, and, when the post was returned to France in 1748 and heavily fortified, Halifax was founded to offset its military importance. Growing concern on the part of the British government with respect to the French settlements in the Minas Basin gave rise to the project of establishing a number of German protestant communities among them, and, when this failed through the danger of Indian attacks, and the Germans were settled at Lunenburg, the evacuation of the Acadians was undertaken.

The subordination of the interest of these scattered communities to that of the fishing industry weakened their social organization. The rich marshlands of the Minas Basin favoured the development of an agricultural industry in Acadia, and settlement spread down the Annapolis Valley and around the Bay of Fundy to the head of Cobequid Bay, but, though an uncertain market for livestock was early secured in New England and a smuggling trade with Cape Breton later developed, the Acadians remained largely isolated and became increasingly dependent upon their own resources. The lack of economic opportunities, and the ease with which agricultural operations could be carried on, destroyed any spirit of enterprise and made them content with their drab existence. To some extent this indolence was a protective device in resisting the demands of an aggressive commercialism. Security could be gained only through exerting a stubborn independence in face of governmental pressures. The hostile attitude of French and English officials was the price paid for the refusal to serve the needs of the fishing industry of either France or Britain. The reluctance of the settlers to move to French-controlled areas rendered their production of less value to the French fishing base of Cape Breton, while their opposition to taking the oath of allegiance made them a threat to the English fishing interests. If heavy cultural losses, and eventual evacuation, were the prices paid, the Acadians were able to secure, by clinging to isolation, a degree of economic self-sufficiency and thus to avoid the immediate disaster of commercial exploitation.

Problems of social organization of the French settlement in Prince Edward Island, in contrast, reflected very clearly the effects of commercial exploitation and displayed the weaknesses of the precarious relation between agricultural and fishing interests. The colonization of Prince Edward Island, in the end, contributed little to the economic organization of the French colonial Empire. Frequent and disastrous raids by field mice, and other misfortunes, rendered the colony of little value as a supply base for the fisheries of Cape Breton, while the prohibition by the French government of the right to fish prevented the inhabitants from seeking other means of livelihood. Many of the colonists brought out to found the settlement were of an unenterprising character, while those Acadians induced to move to the island were unwilling to engage in the difficult task of clearing the land. The result was that the settlement remained largely dependent upon assistance from the home government. Supplying Cape Breton with such products as beef, this provisioning trade deprived the colony of sufficient livestock to establish the agricultural industry on a firm basis. The problems of the settlement were indicative of the failure to establish healthy relations between agricultural and overseas-controlled fishing communities. The burden of military support for the fisheries imposed increasing strains upon the agricultural community, while the influence of military garrisons checked the development of stable social organization in the fishing community.

In the case of the British colonization ventures there was a similar failure to relate settlement to the dominant economic interest of the fisheries. Promotion came for the purpose of securing the strategic lines of empire and thereby removing any naval menace to the fishing industry. The choice of the site of Halifax emphasized considerations of strategy rather than of economic resources. Situated in an area of poor soil, a profitable agricultural industry could not be developed, and, until the province could support a considerable trade, the only source of wealth of the town was in its function as a governmental centre and naval base. Its economically dependent character was enhanced by the type of colonists brought out to found the settlement in 1749. While the influx during the winter of 1749–50 of a number of families from New England served to promote a local fishing industry, the German colonists after 1750 and the Acadian French who drifted into the town were useful only in providing labour in building fortifications. A system of municipal relief early developed to meet problems of destitution, and the presence of large numbers of physically unfit persons, vagrants, disorderly characters, and homeless children gave rise to institutional methods of treatment. A hospital was erected in 1750 to care for the destitute ill, an orphanage established in 1752 to provide for the large number of homeless children among the German settlers, and a workhouse founded in 1759 for the confinement of vagrants and disorderly persons. The drinking of rum assumed major proportions in the habits of the population, while theft, smuggling, usury, and libel were common in the roll of crimes. The presence of naval garrisons gave rise to problems of illegitimacy and desertion. The economic and social dependence of the population upon institutions of the state checked the development of any vigorous cultural life. Governmental and military officials, and the few merchants, constituted something of a local aristocracy, but until the functions of government were broadened, and trade developed, there were lacking the supports of a true social élite. The large number of ethnic-religious groups within the town gave to it a cosmopolitan air, but the cultural effects were evident in the absence of a spirit of community or a pride in local undertakings. Although plans had been made for the recruitment of teachers, no schools were established before 1760. The interests of religion were almost as neglected as those of cultural welfare. Two places of worship, St. Paul's Anglican and Mather's Congregational, were constructed, and a resident Church of England clergyman secured, but neither of these religious denominations exerted much immediate influence in the province. The Society for the Propagation of the Gospel provided missionaries to Annapolis and Lunenburg, but for the most part, with the exception of Catholicism, the formal organization of religion was confined to military and official circles and, in the case of Congregationalism, to the small merchant group in Halifax.

The German settlement in Lunenburg did little to strengthen the social organization of the colony. Though Lunenburg was favourably situated with respect to the fisheries, neither the policy of the colonial administration nor the inclination of the German colonists encouraged their prosecution. Farmers rather than fishermen had been recruited with the intention of forming a number of agricultural settlements interspersed among the French Acadian population. The abandonment of this plan and the final selection of Lunenburg as the site of the German settlement involved the heavy social costs of promoting an agricultural industry in an area more adapted to the fisheries. In addition to the failure to select the occupational types suitable to settlement in such an area, there was a failure to discriminate properly between those able and unable to face the conditions of pioneer life. The activities of the over-zealous colonization agent in Germany resulted in the recruitment of large numbers of persons hopelessly incapable of supporting themselves in the New World. The imperial government as a result found it necessary to make annual grants for the relief of the settlers and efforts to discontinue these allowances were vigorously resisted by the colonial governors on the ground that in no other way could order and harmony be maintained. Riots in Lunenburg, and the desertion of some of the Germans to join the French in the interior, indicated that the fears of the governors had foundation in fact. The German settlement remained on the cultural fringe of the English colony, and yet lacked sufficient means to develop any independent cultural life of its own. Most of the settlers were Lutherans or Calvinists, and the failure to provide them with ministers of their own persuasian while supporting in the community an S.P.G. missionary did little to keep alive religious interests and much to antagonize the population against the Church of England. The weaknesses of the social organization of Lunenburg, like that of the French agricultural settlement in Prince Edward Island, resulted from the tenuous ties between agricultural colonization and the overseas or New England controlled fishing industry. Local industry and trade were alike discouraged, and this check to free economic enterprise not only reduced the agricultural communities to a state of economic self-sufficiency but prevented the rise of any towns except those which were the centres of government and military garrisons. Thus the English like the French settlements in the Maritime region before 1760 failed to develop any secure cultural life. Intended primarily to supply fishing bases or to check foreign encroachments, they remained little more than outposts of empire or temporary bases of New England.

Settlement in terms of free economic enterprise took place only after 1760 with the collapse of the French empire in America and the expansion of New England into Nova Scotia. A close relation between settlement and the fisheries had emerged in New England with changes in the nature of the fishing industry involving the use of smaller units and the employment of local labour, and with the growth of trade which depended upon local bases of supply. Though the decline of French interest in the Maritime region strengthened the hold of the west county interests of England upon the fisheries of eastern Nova Scotia, it made possible the extension of New England's control over the fisheries of western Nova Scotia, and the growth in importance of New England commercial interests resulted in the promotion of schemes of settlement. Anxiety in Britain respecting the danger of depopulation resulted in a policy of discouraging emigration, and settlement after 1760 was largely of people from the Atlantic seaboard. Nova Scotia shared in a general movement of population which greatly extended the frontiers of New England.

The New England migration brought new sources of strength to the social organization of Nova Scotia. The settlements which grew up shared in the economic expansion of New England. The origin of the settlers, the advantages of the direct transportation route to Boston, and the character of economic production favoured the close relationship with the Atlantic seaboard colonies. The New Englanders were pioneers from a pioneer community, and they possessed all the advantages of familiarity with their environment. Fishing, farming, or, later, shipbuilding, was undertaken, and the products of their labour found a sale in the markets opened up by commercial interests in New England from which necessary manufactured goods, largely imported from England, were received in return. The result was the absence of any considerable problem of social dependency, though some of the settlers had to be given provisions during the first year or two in the province. Destitution was associated very largely with the individual hazards involved in fishing or farming, and those people who found themselves without means of support were readily assisted by local agencies of the community. The town meeting inherited from New England provided available machinery for poor relief. The nature of problems of crime and morality likewise reflected the influence of the New England social heritage. Few of the settlers were without their vices, such as the drinking of rum, but these vices represented deviations from, rather than any general breakdown, of the mores. The New Englanders inherited the close village organization developed in the older colonies. The town meeting and the congregational organization of the church moved with the settlers, and the transfer of these institutions did not involve the intervention of secondary and thereby more rigid social agencies. Settlement in villages followed the pattern established in New England, and, to the extent that whole communities emigrated, there was no break in social continuity. Even movement of individual families involved little adjustment, as all the inhabitants were familiar with the form of community organization and readily participated in its erection in the new homeland. The result was that the New Englanders in Nova Scotia were not to any considerable extent emancipated from the moral controls of the communities from which they emigrated. The strict puritanical attitudes of the inhabitants of the older colonies were brought over without any serious impairment, and their preservation was secured through the sanctions imposed by the close village group and religious congregation.

The town meeting provided an effective agency of cultural leadership in the villages settled by New Englanders. Though many of

the privileges claimed by the town proprietors such as the appointment of town officers, the levying of local taxes, and the surveying
of land were assumed by the provincial government to the indignation of people highly jealous of the rights of local autonomy, these
constitutional limitations upon their functions did not render them
wholly unimportant in the pioneer communities. On the one hand,
means of communication were not sufficiently developed to enable
Halifax to maintain effective controls in outlying areas, and, on the
other hand, the feeling of local autonomy on the part of the New
Englanders was too strong to be suppressed by administrative
devices erected in the capital. The result was that many of the
vestiges of the proprietary system persisted in the village organization of these settlements. The proprietors provided the nucleus of
an upper social class. As substantial farmers and tradespeople or
persons of superior education, they gained a position of influence in
the local villages, and, when located in the larger towns such
as Horton, Falmouth, and Cornwallis, their influence extended
throughout the larger community. The "Esquires" and "Gentlemen," such as Simeon Perkins in Liverpool, enjoyed a standard of
life somewhat above that of the ordinary inhabitants, but in return
they provided the leadership so necessary in the pioneer settlements.
These settlements, consequently, were not exposed to levelling
influences which led to a complete disregard of class distinctions,
while at the same time their economic progress was not retarded by
a rigid class system.

Only in the failure to provide education were the cultural limitations of the village organization much in evidence. More extensive
machinery than the town meeting was required for the erection of
educational institutions and the recruitment of teachers. Many of
the effects of inadequate educational institutions, however, were
postponed until the neglected generation reached maturity, and in
the meantime local pride and a consciousness of the worth of the
group's inheritance preserved those cultural values which did not
depend upon such secondary services as those of education. Most of
the demands of the pioneer society could be met within the village
organization. It was only when this primary group relationship
became insufficient, and the support of the tie with New England
was lost, that the need for more effective agencies to preserve
cultural values became acute.

Religious interests during the early period of settlement were
likewise strong among the New Englanders. These settlers inherited

the attitudes of devoutness typical of the population of the older Atlantic colonies, and the persistence of these attitudes was secured through the strong link between the church and the local community. The village settlement and town meeting provided the framework of the congregational organization. The prominent citizens of the community served as elders of the church, and the town meetings assumed the responsibility of erecting meeting houses. The result of this close tie between the church and the village was that devotional services were carried on even when ministers were not available, a situation which obtained in a large number of the early settlements. That is not to say that Congregational clergymen were not eagerly sought and that their ministry was not essential for the ultimate survival of the church, but only that the character of Congregationalism made it possible to keep alive religious interests during the interval when regular services could not be provided. Eventually ministers were secured for the chief settlements of New Englanders with the conspicuous exception of Halifax where Mather's Congregational Church was left unsupplied. If difficulties were still being faced in a number of communities, the church appeared to be firmly established in the province as a whole by 1775.

Though New Englanders comprised the great bulk of the population settling in Nova Scotia during the period 1760–75, a number of other groups found their way into the province. Ulster Irish from New Hampshire, Boston, and from overseas settled in Truro, Onslow, and Londonderry at the head of Cobequid Bay and a few along the banks of La Have River beyond Lunenburg. During the years 1773–5 a large number of Yorkshire English families came out and settled among New Englanders at Amherst, Cumberland, and Sackville in the Chignecto peninsula. The first group of Highland Scots arrived just before the American Revolution and joined a number of Pennsylvania settlers in Pictou. Irish Catholics from Newfoundland and French Acadians from the mainland located along with transient New England fishermen in Cape Breton. Because of their isolation, however, these various settlements contributed little to integrating the social organization of the province.

The Ulster Irish, most of whom were from the older American colonies, brought with them much the same heritage of village organization as the New Englanders, and they tended to accept the leadership of this larger group. The fact that the principles of church government of American Presbyterianism were very similar to those of Congregationalism strengthened the ties. The Yorkshire English, locating in communities containing numbers of New Englanders, were likewise influenced to some considerable extent by the cultural values of this group. Though followers of John Wesley, no missionaries came out before the Revolution, and the form of religious worship followed by the Yorkshiremen within their Methodist societies was not radically different from that followed by the New Englanders within their Congregational organizations. The Highland Scots of Pictou had no time to establish any sort of settled community life before the outbreak of revolution led to their recruitment in Highland military regiments. In the case of the settlements in Cape Breton, what cultural ties existed were mostly with New England, but for the most part the population of the island became detached from outside centres of influence almost entirely. Here Channel Island interests employing bilingual labour dominated in the control of the fisheries, and most of the local fishermen engaged in the industry without licences. In contrast with the South Shore, temporary stations took the place of settled villages, and the New England fishermen returned to their homes in the winter after spending the summer in Cape Breton. The isolation from Halifax made impossible effective policing, and when the British garrison was removed in 1768 the local authorities were left without support in maintaining law. The large number of inlets, and the proximity to Newfoundland, provided means by which the population could evade officers of the law sent to apprehend them, and a condition of almost general disorder prevailed along the coastline.

The New England migration, and the smaller settlements in the interior and in Cape Breton, did little to strengthen the position of Halifax or extend her influence. The capital shared in few of the economic advantages from the extensive *entrepôt* trade being developed with Nova Scotia as an important base. Lacking an immediate hinterland of her own, she did not possess the resources or organization to compete with the powerful commercial interests in New England in providing markets for the fishing and farming settlements along the South Shore, the Annapolis Valley, and in the interior, while the costs of policing Cape Breton were offset by few economic gains. Some industries were established in the town—a brick factory, distillery, and sugar factory—but the government and military base continued as the chief means of support. When the strategy of imperial defence made necessary the stationing of a large military force in the province, the town prospered, but when it was withdrawn local trade declined and there were few alternative occupations to which the population could turn. The lack of economic opportunities, and the attractions of the town as the centre of governmental institutions and military forces, accentuated problems of destitution which had emerged before 1760. Hangers-on of the army fell on the relief roll when the army was withdrawn, while a continual influx of transient workers and indigent persons from outside added to the responsibilities of local authorities. In 1759, and again in 1768, the Nova Scotia legislature attempted to check the immigration of socially dependent persons by means of legislation, but on both occasions the Act was disallowed by the British government. In 1770, chiefly as a means of relieving Halifax of the burden of supporting transient workers from the country districts, an Act of the provincial legislature introduced a residence qualification for relief. Efforts to check the influx of undesirable population elements, however, failed to provide any real solution to a problem which resulted from the weakness of the town's economic and social supports, and the result was a continuance and elaboration of the aids found necessary in the fifties.

Other forms of social life in the town were strengthened little more by the developments which took place in the province after 1760. The army and navy continued to set the moral standards of the community, and the puritanism of the New England settlements exerted no conspicuous influence. Similarly, the leavening effect of the New England migration upon cultural organization was not greatly felt within the capital. The exclusiveness of the colonial aristocracy tended to be maintained, and as a result the economic isolation of the capital found emphasis in its cultural isolation. Intervention by the colonial administration in matters of local government in the out-settlements was indicative of the extension of political controls in the province, but these efforts found little support in the cultural influence of the governing classes. The predominant interests of these classes remained sharply divorced from the interests of the large fishing and farming population in the colony, and there was a failure to develop a social class equipped to provide leadership for the whole province. Ethnic differences increased the cultural particularism of the various settlements, and Halifax failed conspicuously to give a lead in establishing some sort of cultural integration.

This failure was also conspicuous in the field of religion. Apart from the Congregationalists, a number of religious denominations became established in the province—Presbyterians, Methodists, Roman Catholics, and a few Baptists and Quakers—emphasizing the autonomy of the out-settlements, and the established Church of England proved unable to provide leadership to offset their decentralizing influence. With the growth of settlement after 1760, the church, with the support of the government, undertook to win the adherence of the large nonconformist population lacking the services of regular ministers. The promotion of the interests of the church had the important object of securing more firmly the political allegiance of the new settlers in the colony. A corresponding society made up of prominent members of the government as well as of the church in the colony was organized to supervise missionary activities and to seize opportunities of extending Anglican influence, and, paid by the Society for the Propagation of the Gospel and the British government, missionaries were located at the chief centres of settlement, Annapolis, Windsor, Cumberland, Prince Edward Island, and Lunenburg. The record of achievement, however, was not noteworthy. In spite of efforts to make the church a truly provincial denomination, it remained representative of only the official and military interests in the colony, drawing its chief support from within the town of Halifax. The tie with the government proved in the end as much a weakness as a strength of the church. Identity with the ruling minority divorced the church from the great mass of the population. The bulk of the people were of religious persuasions other than that of Anglicanism, and, while the problems of the pioneer society made difficult the maintenance of their denominational connections, they showed little inclination to support a church almost completely lacking in an understanding of their needs. The failure to develop an itinerant missionary organization, and its reliance upon holding services in the chief centres of population, contributed further to its lack of influence in the rural settlements. The weakness of the Church of England in the society of Nova Scotia before 1776 was a measure of the weakness of the economic and cultural interests of Halifax. Efforts to extend the controls of the provincial capital met with the stiff resistance of the out-settlements, and the lack of support of the Church of England was simply one expression of these resistant attitudes.

The effects of the failure of Halifax to provide leadership did not result in any serious breakdown of controls in the provincial society so long as the local village organizations remained strong.

The socially vigorous and community-conscious New England settlements provided an element of strength to the whole social organization of Nova Scotia before 1776. It is true that the failure of Halifax to integrate the out-settlements within the provincial system of government weakened the colonial administration and institutions identified with this administration, but the effects of lack of leadership from the capital were offset by the strength of local organization and by the leadership provided from New England. The town meetings and Congregational churches derived sufficient support from the older colonies to function without the co-operation of the provincial government. But this dependence upon outside aids and detachment from Halifax involved dangers which became conspicuous when the American Revolution cut these settlements off from their established lines of communication. Failure to retain cultural ties with New England was to reveal weaknesses in the organization of the local community while the aggressive feeling of local autonomy was not sufficient to withstand completely the centralizing influence of war and trade after 1776. Largely independent of the provincial capital before the outbreak of revolution, the New England settlements after 1776 were to become to some considerable extent an economic hinterland of the rapidly expanding metropolis.

The shift of trade routes and the growing importance of commercial interests in Nova Scotia resulting from the Revolution led to fundamental reorientations in community organization. Whereas Halifax before 1776 had been divorced from the main stream of development, the Revolutionary War tended to emphasize her strategic position and thereby enhance her economic as well as political importance. She seized the trade with the out-settlements and with the British West Indies which formerly had been controlled by New England. But the activities of American privateers in raiding coastal towns and of American traders in smuggling commodities into and out of the province, during the Revolution, were an indication that economic integration in terms of the dominance of Halifax was not readily brought about; efforts of the provincial authorities to police the waters of Cape Breton were only partially successful in preventing contraband trade in this area, and little more success attended similar efforts to restrict the trade of the rural settlements with the revolutionary colonies. After the Revolution, the aggressive commercialism of New England continued to provide a serious threat to the new *entrepôt* trade being developed by Nova Scotian interests, and the advantages secured in the imperial Navigation System were offset by restrictions upon the trading operations of British vessels in American ports and by smuggling carried on by American ships in the Maritime and West Indian waters. Efforts to meet this competition by a policy of bounties to the fisheries when export took place in British boats led to conflict between Halifax and the outports which secured expression in the secession of Cape Breton from Nova Scotia in 1784 and in the increasing opposition of the Assembly to the Council in provincial politics.

This tendency towards centralization and increasing regional conflict was equally apparent with respect to social organization. Although the relief machinery developed in the early years of settlement continued, apart from Halifax, to meet problems of individual destitution as they occurred in the local communities, the Revolution and movements of population after gave rise to problems of destitution for which local agencies were wholly inadequate. The influx of refugees with the evacuation of Boston in 1776, the large migration of Loyalists at the conclusion of war, the periodic arrival of boatloads of destitute colonists during the eighties and nineties, and the immigration of Highland Scots, many of whom were poverty-stricken, towards the end of the century, taxed the resources of local communities and led to efforts on the part of the provincial government (supported in the case of the war refugees and Loyalists by the imperial Parliament) to provide relief. The intervention of provincial authorities emphasized centralizing tendencies in the colonial society, and the shift of the function of relief brought with it a decline in the importance of local organizations. That is not to say that the colonial administration succeeded in building up any permanent organization of poor-relief. Particular problems of destitution called forth some sort of action, but there was no attempt to regularize such activities within a general system of relief. The nearest approach to the development of institutional methods of action was the establishment of boards to determine among what Loyalists and disbanded soldiers assistance was required. Agencies of relief still remained institutions of the local community, and aids from the provincial authorities were in the way of emergency measures. But the increasing reliance upon such aids emphasized the inadequacies of the local machinery.

With respect to matters of order and morality, the immediate effects of the Revolutionary War and the expansion of trade were felt most fully by Halifax, but the developments of this period unloosed forces which extended throughout the rural society. The close group controls of the village settlements tended to disintegrate in face of the influences of war and trade, and these tendencies were considerably accentuated with the Loyalist migration. The new population elements cut across established community lines and introduced habits of behaviour which had an unsettling effect upon moral standards and social order. The most independent of the Loyalists settled at Shelburne and in the St. John Valley, and the difficulties of administration in the latter area resulting from its remoteness hastened the organization of the province of New Brunswick. Apart from these two settlements, disorganization was greatest in those areas where a large number of the Loyalist settlers were disbanded soldiers. Long association in army camps had developed habits of heavy drinking and dissipation, and intemperance became increasingly prevalent in the rural districts. The importance of molasses and rum in the trade of Nova Scotia fostered the traffic in liquor and discouraged efforts of reform such as stringent licensing laws and temperance movements. Crime increased as pecuniary relationships assumed greater importance, and the change in its character was evident in the shift from a reliance upon primary group controls to a reliance upon controls of a secondary and impersonal nature. Gaols were erected in the various towns, and the formal law came to play a greater part in the maintenance of order in the community.

More far-reaching still were the adjustments which took place in cultural organization. The break with New England, the growth of commerce, and the war led to the disintegration of those ethnic and social bonds which had grown up in the local communities before the Revolution. Some of the more respectable members of the local communities, particularly those communities settled by New Englanders, identified themselves with the revolutionary cause of the American colonies, and, if they did not withdraw from the province, they lost considerably in prestige. The Loyalist migration served to weaken still further rural leadership in Nova Scotia. The Loyalists challenged established status relationships while they failed to achieve, except in New Brunswick, a privileged social position. These tendencies of disintegration of the rural class structure were accentuated by the expansion of trade which resulted to some extent in rural business men being overshadowed by those in large centres. The efforts of the new trading interests to integrate the economic life of the province in terms of the dominance of Halifax were paralleled by efforts to integrate the cultural life. But the resistance of the out-settlements to the controls of the metropolis evident in the economic sphere was even more evident in the cultural sphere. The tenuous commercial ties provided no solid cultural bond between the capital and the rest of the province. As the forces of centralization increased subordination to Halifax, forces of decentralization, together with the incapacity of the governing aristocracy to provide effective leadership, checked the establishment of a stable equilibrium in the relations between Halifax and the hinterland.

The pull between forces of centralization and of local autonomy was even more apparent within religious movements. The developments resulting from the Revolution and expansion of trade had direct and far-reaching effects upon religious interests and attitudes, and led to fundamental adjustments in the organization and appeal of religious denominations. The period, indeed, was one of revolution within the churches which produced an almost completely new institutional structure by the time it had run its course. Old religious forms were swept aside, and new denominations arose and were accepted within the Nova Scotian society. These sweeping changes involved issues of control which extended throughout the organization of the provincial society. Efforts of Halifax to strengthen the controls of political and cultural institutions centred in the capital as a means of securing a position of metropolitan dominance were paralleled by efforts to strengthen the controls of the Church of England. The immediate effect of the Revolution was to weaken seriously religious leadership in the out-settlements.

Before the Revolution, Congregationalism had been undergoing changes which greatly limited its spiritual influence. Schisms in New England resulting from the "Great Awakening" had enhanced the conservatism of the orthodox churches with effects evident in the increasing emphasis upon the form rather than upon the substance of religious services. Though the churches in Nova Scotia before 1776 escaped the direct influence of the evangelical movements, they felt the influence of the reactionary tendencies which had set in. Among the various Congregational organizations in the province at the time the Revolution broke out, there was lacking any vigorous spiritual life. So long as there was no threat to the social influences of the churches, this lack was not seriously felt. What was lost in religious fervour was gained in social respectability; status in the community implied membership in the church. With the outbreak of the American Revolution, however, the social supports of the churches were greatly impaired. Many of the Congregational ministers identified themselves with the revolutionary cause and eventually withdrew to the American colonies, and, although the great body of members remained loyal, the churches became suspect in the eyes of colonial officials. As a result of the stigma of disloyalty, they lost the prestige and claim to respectability which had been the chief forces holding them together. Without a sufficient supply of ministers, many of the regularly constituted Congregational organizations found it increasingly difficult to maintain the controls of church government, and a spirit of acrimony tended to replace one of harmony among the general membership.

The effect of the Revolution upon the Methodist societies of the Yorkshire English was almost as unfavourable. The strength of the Methodist societies depended upon the evangelical fervour of the members, and this led to a reliance upon vigorous evangelical leadership. The Revolution cut off a supply of Wesleyan missionaries and new additions to the population from Yorkshire, and, divorced from outside contacts, the evangelical enthusiasm which had been aroused by Wesley's preaching in England steadily cooled under pioneer conditions of life. The other nonconformist religious denominations were also weakened to some extent by the Revolution. The Presbyterians of Truro were cut off from a supply of ministers from the American colonies. The German Lutherans and French and Swiss Calvinists faced even greater official indifference than before 1776 to the problem of supplying them with clergymen of their own faith. The Quakers, at no time influential, increasingly lost their identity as a religious sect when they became divorced from their fellow brethren in the old colonies. The Roman Catholic Church, though maintaining the attachments of the Micmac Indians, the French Acadians, and the Irish from Newfoundland continued to suffer under constitutional disabilities which the Revolution did not tend to ease.

The Church of England, on the other hand, secured new supports as a result of the war. Advantages which the Congregational churches lost with the increasing emphasis upon loyalty the Anglican Church gained. The colonial government vigorously promoted its interests as a means of strengthening the imperial connection. The greater importance of military interests enhanced its favourable position. Finally, the Loyalist migration brought new additions to membership and a considerable number of ministers to extend its constituency throughout a large section of the province. Yet, in spite of these favourable circumstances, the influence of the Church of England was not greatly increased. The new economic ties being forged by Halifax with its hinterland failed to be reinforced by spiritual ties forged by the church. The reason, on the one side, lay in the lack of vigorous leadership within the church itself, and, on the other side, in the stiff cultural resistance of the out-settlements. Though an episcopacy was erected with a resident bishop in charge, the control of missionary activities remained in the hands of the Society for the Propagation of the Gospel and only slowly was there any improvement in the type of clergymen sent to the colony. Opportunities to extend the influence of the church were lost by the reluctance of missionaries to undertake strenuous preaching assignments and by their lack of a sympathetic understanding of the problems of the colonists. The result was that the church gained few if any new recruits from the ranks of those denominations disorganized by the Revolution, while it eventually was to lose a number of its own followers.

The failure of the Church of England to provide effective leadership was emphasized by the success of new religious movements in the out-settlements. The evangelical preaching of Henry Alline among the New England settlers and of William Black among the Yorkshire English represented an effort to revive the religious feeling cooling within the Congregational churches and Methodist societies. The Newlight movement was a direct product of the disintegration of the Congregational churches, while Black's evangelical labours were undertaken to meet needs left unfilled by the Wesleyan Conference in England. But the implications of these movements extended much further. The spread of religious evangelism emphasized the cultural autonomy of the hinterland, and sharpened the divorce between the colonial aristocracy of Halifax identified with official and trading interests and the great mass of the population identified with fishing and farming interests. The conflict of economic interests, evident in the strained relations between the Legislative Assembly and the Council, found expression in the antagonism between the nonconformist churches and the Church of England, and that antagonism was brought into bold relief by the evangelical movements. The problem presented in the out-settlements in maintaining their economic autonomy with the loss of their markets in New England found its counterpart in the problem of maintaining their cultural autonomy with the loss of New England leadership. The relief secured in the economic sphere through smuggling, privateering, and representation in the Legislative Assembly was secured in the cultural sphere through evangelical religious movements. Eventually there emerged powerful Baptist and Methodist churches out of the ferment aroused by Henry Alline and William Black. With the turn of the century, two other religious denominations gained considerable accessions of strength and served to reinforce autonomous tendencies in the hinterland of the province. The shift to Baptist doctrines in the Newlight churches brought about the defection of the more orthodox Congregationalists and their eventual absorption into the Presbyterian Church, and with the Highland Scot migration to Pictou County and Cape Breton, Presbyterianism became firmly established in eastern Nova Scotia. Roman Catholicism likewise grew rapidly in influence as Antigonish County and Cape Breton became populated largely by Highland Scots of that faith.

The organization of these four denominations upon a provincial basis effectively isolated the Church of England in Halifax and Windsor and paved the way to the abandonment of its claim as the established colonial church. From Sydney to Yarmouth, along a line extending through Pictou, Truro, Cornwallis, and Annapolis, and back through Liverpool and Lunenburg, the Anglican Church had been forced to retreat in face of rival religious denominations. The struggle was far from over at the end of the century, and continued particularly around the controversial issue of denominational colleges, but from it the church steadily emerged with fewer special privileges and with greatly reduced influence.

The migration of Highland Scots closed the last frontier in the settlement of Nova Scotia, and later movements of population largely passed by this province. Developments in the Maritime region after 1800 brought into prominence new forms of economic exploitation which shifted attention to New Brunswick. The rapid expansion of the timber trade was the chief note in the economic development of British North America during the early part of the nineteenth century, and the St. John, Miramichi, and Ottawa valleys became areas of dominant importance. In New Brunswick, entrepreneurship from Maine and capital from overseas combined to set in motion the streams of squared timber destined for the overseas market. A shipbuilding industry developed to support the growing trade in timber, and ships as well as timber usually found a ready sale in Brtiain. The growing industrial structure gave rise to an increasing demand for labour, and waves of Irish immigrants populated the new towns and the frontier areas of settlement. Since the soft-timber lands bordered rich river valleys, the expansion of the timber trade was accompanied by the expansion of agriculture, in eastern Nova Scotia and Prince Edward Island as well as in New Brunswick. The economic and social effects of the timber trade were felt throughout New Brunswick and to some extent also in Prince Edward Island and Nova Scotia. Where the industry was dominant, other economic activities were subordinated to its interests, and there was a consequent failure to build up a diversified economy to meet the shocks of a rapidly shrinking market when British trade policy ceased to provide preferential protection for colonial timber.

The farmers and young men engaged in the trade developed habits which unfitted them for the conditions of rural life. The life of the lumbermen resembled in many ways that of the *coureurs de bois*. Neither completely detached from, nor completely a part of, the rural communities, they exerted a disturbing influence upon established social controls while failing to develop new controls adapted to their particular needs. Where there were regular camps there emerged something of a distinctive group life with its distinctive set of social mores, but the habits developed in this environment rendered more difficult the adjustment when the camps broke up and farm work commenced. Only slowly did there appear any sort of occupational demarcation between the lumbering and farming classes. This development awaited the pushing back of the timber frontier out of the reach of the farm communities, and the shift to industrial techniques requiring a full-time labour force. Until such economic specialization occurred, communities in close proximity to the timber trade felt the full force of its disorganizing effects.

The growth of an irregular labour force in the timber trade, and unemployment in the shipbuilding industry in times of depression, gave rise to problems of destitution particularly in such towns as Saint John. Crime emerged along the highways of trade and in the centres of industry, and intemperance increased throughout the rural society and assumed considerable proportions among those engaged in the timber industry. Growing debts, and a greater emphasis upon money values, weakened the moral as well as economic basis of the agricultural communities.

The growth of commercial organization in the timber trade introduced new economic interests and had an unsettling effect upon the class structure, particularly of New Brunswick. The growing body of American and Scottish merchants assumed an increasingly important role in the economic and social life of the province and steadily challenged the pretensions to social superiority of the old landowning and professional aristocracy established after the Loyalist migration. On the other side, the large Irish immigrant group became sharply marked off from the more substantial elements of the population, and tended to become associated on the cultural fringe with the Acadian French. Religious differences, especially between Protestant and Roman Catholic, hardened the social divisions forming along cultural lines. As industrial techniques became more elaborate and day labour more in demand, a social group approaching in character a proletariat made its appearance. These tendencies were most evident within the St. John Valley where capitalistic developments in the timber trade and shipbuilding industry had progressed furthest, but the hardening lines of class conflict extended out into the fringe settlements of New Brunswick. In Prince Edward Island, the system of absentee ownership introduced a different sort of rigidity in cultural organization. Disturbances in religious organization also accompanied the developments taking place in New Brunswick after 1800. The immigration of Americans, English, and Irish, and the intrusion of evangelical movements from outside, destroyed many of the supports which the Church of England had established in the province after the Loyalist migration. Roman Catholicism gained in strength as the Irish immigration brought in great numbers of adherents, and the evangelical work of Baptist and Methodist missionaries, from Nova Scotia and the United States, won the allegiance of the considerable nonconformist population and gained numbers of recruits from the ranks of the Anglicans. The Baptist Church emerged here, as in Nova Scotia, as the chief religious denomination, and the growing influence of the Methodist, Presbyterian, and Roman Catholic bodies emphasized still further the failure of the Church of England to maintain its position of dominance. In Prince Edward Island the predominant Scottish population secured the supremacy of the Presbyterian Church.

With the development of the timber trade the continental pull upon the economy of the Maritime region became marked and this shift in emphasis introduced striking differences between the development of New Brunswick and that of Nova Scotia. The

tightening bonds of American capital, and the increasing dependence upon the American market with the shrinking of the British
market for timber, were powerful forces pulling New Brunswick
into the American orbit. Railway projects designed to strengthen
the links with the United States were only abandoned when Confederation provided a tie with the continental British colonies.
For this reason, the development of New Brunswick was in many
ways more closely related to that of the Canadas than to that of
Nova Scotia. It constituted something of a watershed between
the development of the purely Maritime colony reaching out into
the Atlantic and that of the St. Lawrence–Great Lakes colony
reaching into the continent. By the early part of the nineteenth
century the chief lines of development in Nova Scotia had become
firmly established. The fishing industry and trade gave to the
province its basic social character and not until those economic
activities were severely dislocated by the industrial revolution in
iron and steel was this character materially changed. In New
Brunswick, the frontier phase of development had no more than
set in by 1800. The developments which took place after were of
a kind which involved expansion into the continent, into the
Ottawa Valley and Great Lakes region as into the St. John and
Miramichi valleys.

CHAPTER IV

The Backwoods Society
of Upper Canada*

WITH THE SETTLEMENT of Upper Canada in the early nineteenth century, there emerged the first distinctively agricultural frontier in British North America. The agricultural industry assumed considerable importance in New France and the Maritime colonies, but other interests—the fur trade, fisheries, or timber trade—constituted the main drive of economic exploitation, and it was not until expansionist forces had been spent that agriculture began to assert itself as a primary industry. In Upper Canada a similar dualism appeared in the frontier economy to the extent that agricultural settlement was related to the development of the timber trade in the Ottawa Valley, but the relation was one which did not extend beyond the recruitment of settlers as such. Once settled in the country, the farm population was considerably removed from the area in which the timber industry was being developed and thereby was sheltered from its disturbing influence. The social problems of Upper Canada were almost entirely those of a purely agrarian frontier, and consequently were in striking contrast to those of New France or the Maritime colonies.

Although the opening up of the agricultural resources of Upper Canada really began in the early years of the nineteenth century, some colonization was under way considerably earlier. The conclusion of the American Revolution released a large body of people who had favoured the British cause, and those in the up-country

*From *The Social Development of Canada*, pp. 204–24.

turned to Canada as a field for settlement. The Loyalist migration hastened the organization of the Province of Upper Canada and led to the adoption of a policy encouraging colonization. Simcoe's vigorous programme of road building had in view the closely related needs of defence and settlement, and these early efforts to open up the country did much to divert to the province a part of the great western migration of American peoples which set in after 1790 with the end of the Indian wars. American frontier farmers poured across the St. Lawrence and Niagara, to join the Loyalists about the Bay of Quinte and in the Niagara district and to extend settlement along the whole north shore of Lake Ontario. Scattered overseas colonization ventures, chiefly of Scottish Highlanders, served to push settlement into less accessible areas within the province.

This influx of population, however, was unrelated to the activities of any dominant set of economic interests within the colony. A large part of it represented a spilling over of the American frontier movement of people. The fur-trade merchants located in Montreal thought in terms of a commercial empire reaching into the Northwest, and agricultural settlement played little part in the erection of such an empire; the problems of Upper Canadian pioneer farmers did not enter into the politics of the Beaver Club. Promotion of agricultural settlement in Upper Canada by the state arose largely from the interest in the strategic military value of the area. Transportation facilities were geared to the needs of defence rather than markets, and the limitations of economic self-sufficiency sharply restricted settlement. So long as the population remained small and hugged the lake and river shores no considerable problem of markets arose. The chief concern of the settlers before 1812 was that of clearing the land and establishing homes, and the simple wants of the household could be met by domestic manufacture or through the sale of the readily transportable commodity of potash. The pioneer economy of Upper Canada during this period, as distinguished from the frontier economy which developed after 1814, was one based upon self-sufficiency, and the independence gained therefrom enabled the colony to escape problems associated with the price system.

A similar self-sufficiency obtained very largely with respect to social and cultural needs. The farm communities of Upper Canada before 1812 inherited the simple, primary social institutions of the American frontier. The Loyalist and American settlers, for the most part, were thoroughly adjusted to the conditions of pioneer life.

That is not to say that they accepted a completely orderly and settled mode of life in their new homes. The frontier was the habitat of the impatient and restless, and its very character implied an emancipation from social controls and a reliance upon individual effort and will. The people found in Upper Canada before 1812 were a product of the frontier heritage. However, though many of their habits and ways of life appeared distasteful to cultured observers from overseas, the early pioneer farmers drawn from the American frontier possessed a resourcefulness which enabled them to surmount the difficulties which they faced. The apparent absence of problems of destitution and mental disease might be taken as indicative of the capacity of these settlers to adjust their habits to new needs. Personal disorganization resulting from the sudden emancipation from all social control was avoided by the flexibility of social organization.

Pioneer social institutions were for the most part closely adapted to the simple needs and wants of the population. The family constituted the basic institution in the economy and social structure, while strict codes of honesty and morality rested upon the sanctions of the neighbourhood group, and forms of mutual assistance and relief provided for the wants arising from misfortune. Distinctions of social class found little recognition in the pioneer communities where the demands of neighbourhood association pressed so heavily upon the inhabitants. Even with respect to religion there was no great failure to meet the needs of the population. Itinerant Methodist preachers, already familiar with the pathways leading into the American frontier communities, found their way across the St. Lawrence River to carry the message of the gospel to the Upper Canadian farmers. Many of the Loyalist and American settlers were Methodists, and the highly centralized missionary organization built up by the Methodist Episcopal Church in the United States made possible a ready supply of clergy. Quakers, Moravians, and members of other religious sects who settled in Upper Canada carried with them the simple organizations of their faith.

What colonization from overseas took place in Upper Canada before 1812 did not introduce disturbing influences into the rural society to any considerable extent. Most of the overseas colonists were Higland Scots, and, if they lacked the experience and resourcefulness of the American settlers, they inherited the traditional close group controls of the clan organization. Their tendency to settle together enabled them to resist many of the disorganizing effects of new social conditions. Adjustments of the individual came about with the support of the group, and too radical deviations from traditional mores were strictly checked. This group or clan authoritarianism was reinforced by the authoritarianism of the Roman Catholic priest or Presbyterian minister. Though few clergy were available, the ecclesiastical system of government was preserved as part of the group organization. The inevitable conservatism of such leadership within the Scottish communities had the effect of arresting economic progress and cultural advancement, but during the early years of settlement the strain upon the individual in adjusting himself was considerably eased and any general breakdown of the social organization avoided.

Only in the small towns growing up along the shore of Lake Ontario did the simplicity of pioneer life give way to the greater complexity of a pecuniary civilization. Here the erection of gaols indicated the approach of problems of social welfare which were to bear more heavily upon the society in a later period. The tavern and retail store emerged as the chief centres of contact between the town and the country. The army, church, and, in the capital, governmental services introduced a hierarchy of social classes which became more pronounced as the towns grew in size. The establishment of schools indicated a growing concern for education, and emphasized more sharply still the distinction between this privileged group in the towns and the mass of pioneer farmers without. The inhabitants of the towns tended to be attached to the Church of England, and the colonial government sought to vest this church with the privileges of establishment. The erection of places of worship and rectories in the chief centres of population indicated the church's anxiety to identify itself with official and military interests in the province and provided something of a forecast of its later incapacity to serve the rural communities. For the most part, the towns exerted little influence beyond their immediate surroundings. They were garrison centres of the Empire in Upper Canada, and, if they provided the rural society with little leadership, their contacts with the country were so few that they introduced no disturbing influences.

The society of Upper Canada before the War of 1812, of course, was far from stable, but the absence of serious problems of social organization stands out in striking contrast to the later period. In 1812, the population of Upper Canada was 80,000 after thirty years of settlement; by 1851 it had grown to 952,000. The contrast between the rate of increase of population in these two periods provides in itself sufficient reason to consider the interval 1812–20 as the watershed between two sharply separated phases of development. After the war, a set of forces were unloosed which brought about far-reaching changes in the character of society in Upper Canada.

If the war appeared to re-emphasize the strategic military position of Upper Canada, the developments after asserted her importance as an economic frontier within the British colonial system. Restrictions upon alien landholdings which stopped up the flow of American settlers coincided with a newly awakened fear in Britain of over-population which gave rise to schemes for encouraging emigration to the colonies. The settlement of disbanded soldiers in strategically if not agriculturally favourable areas of the province served the purpose of defence while at the same time relieving the home exchequer. Government- and parish-assisted emigration was undertaken to lessen the burden of poor-rates and to strengthen the loyalty of the colonial population. The real impetus to settlement, however, came from the development of the timber trade. The shift from a reliance upon furs to timber involved the transportation of a bulky rather than compact cargo to the British market and raised the problem of a return cargo. The desire of shipowners to secure a profitable return load for their timber vessels resulted in unloosing upon Upper Canada a swelling tide of immigration. The port of Quebec developed as the poor man's route to Upper Canada, and the large numbers coming in this way were sharply differentiated from the more fortunate arriving by way of New York. Cheap ocean rates and a more liberal policy of granting land made possible the unassisted movement of population to Upper Canada during the twenties and thirties. Settlers pushed into the interior of the province, and backwoods communities separated by many miles from the lake shore came into being. The growth of settlement about Perth, Peterborough, in the heart of the western peninsula, and on Lake Huron marked the widening belt of population stretching across the province.

Economic expansion and the rapid growth of population imposed heavy strains upon the pioneer social organization which had been established before 1812. The opening up of the Ottawa Valley gave rise to a society of unattached male workers who spent the winters in camp and the summers in floating timber down to the market in Quebec City. But the disorganizing effects of this society were little felt by the rural frontier pushing westward into Upper Canada. The Precambrian Shield sharply separated the soft-timber lands of the Ottawa Valley from the hard-timber lands of the Great Lakes region, and those engaged in the timber industry were chiefly recruited in the cities of Montreal and Quebec from the surplus labour force of the mature French Canadian farming community or, later, from the bodies of Irish immigrants. The timber trade, as a result, did not noticeably increase the mobility of the population of the frontier rural areas. It was a metropolitan industry, involving large capital outlays—the timber merchant—and a regular labour force which increasingly became differentiated from the rural population and came to constitute rather a part of an urban proletariat.

Problems of the rural frontier of Upper Canada derived largely from the character of colonists and of settlement in the period after 1814. The great bulk of overseas settlers came in as single individuals or families, and lacked the group supports enjoyed by the Highland Scots. Complete strangers to the conditions of pioneer life, their adjustments were slowly and painfully made. The large number of failures was evidence of the trials they faced. The disbanded soldiers and commuted pensioners were the least able to adapt themselves to the demands of pioneer farm life, and contributed most heavily to the ranks of habitual drunkards and vagrants, but among the whole body of overseas colonists the incidence of failure was high. The considerable number of pauper immigrants added to the difficulties of social adjustment while it increased the strains upon the inadequate social services of the colony. The lack of agencies to provide assistance and advice to recently arrived immigrants shifted heavy burdens upon the local community; an absence of leadership in the location of settlement involved severe personal hardships when a reckless land policy made the individual selection of location an extremely hazardous undertaking. Though the local communities assumed extensive functions of relief and assistance, such agencies proved less effective when settlement tended to become dispersed and needy families were separated by considerable distances from neighbours. The accumulation of distressed persons in the small towns, the result of failure on the land or the lack of capital to begin farming, gave rise to a growing need for such agencies as houses of refuge, hospitals, and mental homes. The establishment of a house of industry in Toronto was a recognition of the new demands pressing upon the social organization. For the most part, where indiscriminate charity failed to provide for the needs of the unfortunate classes, the gaols served as a means of removing them from the local communities.

The increasing mobility of population, and the growing numbers of those drifting into the towns, added to the tasks of law-enforcement authorities. The rural society as such produced no serious problem of crime. The modest equipment of the pioneer farm homes offered little temptation to commit burglary, and the capital of the backwoodsman could not readily be removed or disposed of. Breaches of the criminal law, however, became more prevalent as the simplicity of early pioneer life tended to disappear. The presence in the country of ne'er-do-weels shipped out from respectable English middle-class homes, the influx of Irish workers and female domestics, and the construction of canals in various parts of the province introduced new disturbing influences in the society of Upper Canada which were reflected in the pressure upon gaol accommodation and in the establishment of a provincial penitentiary. The growing problem of classification of penal inmates, and the lack of institutions to care for juvenile offenders, were indicative of the increasing diversity in the character of crime and criminals.

The increasing strains upon social organization were more evident with respect to the primary and cultural institutions of the local pioneer communities. Though the family retained many important economic and social functions, it proved a far less effective social institution among the overseas colonists than among the early Loyalist and American settlers. The long frontier tradition in America had produced a type of family closely adapted to the needs of rural pioneer conditions. The overseas colonists did not share in this tradition, and the individual, accustomed to look outside for the satisfaction of many of those needs which in a pioneer society could be taken care of only within the family, found himself frustrated and dependent upon his own resources. The considerable nervous strain imposed upon overseas farm women in the country as a result of isolation, and the prevalence of drinking habits among the men, were indications of the failure of the family to satisfy such needs as that of companionship when other social supports were absent. Though limitations of the family were not wholly responsible, the personal disorganization of so many overseas colonists revealed, at least in part, the failure of this primary institution to assume functions ordinarily performed in mature societies by secondary organizations.

If human companionship was the want most keenly felt by recent overseas settlers in Upper Canada, the lack of vigorous cultural leadership left marks more deeply impressed upon the rural communities. The poverty, hard work, and deadening routine of pioneer farming discouraged efforts to maintain social or cultural standards. Superior educational attainments, certainly, were of little advantage in wringing a livelihood from the soil, while the preservation of the refinements or impedimenta of "polite society" served only to divert much needed labour or capital from the farm. This ceaseless pressure of the pioneer economy involved sacrifices which in the end impoverished the cultural life of the community. A disregard for precautions with respect to health and physical welfare imposed eventually heavy costs upon both the individual and the society. If the neglect of such things as the teeth and eyesight of children transmitted physical handicaps to the new generation, the neglect of elementary principles of sanitation imperilled the health of whole communities. The pioneer began unable to afford the decencies of life; he often ended by losing an appreciation of their worth.

This was true of educational institutions. The isolation of farm homes, and the urgent requirements for farm labour, made school attendance difficult in the rural districts. Even where country schools were established, the teaching was so bad that little learning was imparted. The emphasis in the frontier upon economic exploitation discouraged entry into service occupations such as teaching, and the scattered teachers in Upper Canada were largely recruited from the ranks of those who had failed in other occupations. These obstacles to the establishment of an effective educational system were largely unavoidable in the early years of pioneer settlement, but they contributed to the growth of an attitude of indifference to education which provided little preparation to meet the more exacting demands of society when pioneer conditions had disappeared. The social costs of some of this negligence tended to be postponed, but the pioneer society did not escape certain immediate effects. Observations made by British travellers in the country were coloured by their class bias, but they do suggest serious shortcomings in the cultural life of the communities of Upper Canada. The influences of the frontier upon a population unequipped to deal with its demands tended to a general lowering rather than raising of standards, and this tendency became more pronounced when standards became increasingly diversified.

The large overseas immigration introduced new ethnic and cultural distinctions between groups in the rural communities of Upper Canada. The lines forming to mark off the Loyalist from the American settlers, largely as a result of prejudices arising out of the War of 1812, were extended when the English colonists held themselves aloof from the Americans. The Scots, Irish, and other ethnic groups, in turn, tended to form cultural islands in the larger community. This ethnic segregation weakened relationships of co-operation and mutual assistance in the pioneer society. On the other hand, to the extent that assimiliation did occur, it tended to take the form of accepting American habits of thought without acquiring the American's pioneer way of life. The doctrine of equality went to the heads of the overseas immigrants, and they exerted their emancipation from traditional controls before they had fully learned the lessons from their new experiences. Assimilation, or Americanization, consequently, had something of a disorganizing effect in destroying the inherited culture of the overseas colonists before they had become a part of the pioneer culture.

The class distinctions among the overseas immigrants served even further to weaken the social organization of the rural communities of Upper Canada. The two ports of entry, Quebec and New York, symbolized the new social division which was transposed from the homeland to the Canadian backwoods. The attempt to maintain this division made more difficult the task of erecting new social controls in communities which could not afford the luxury of segregation. For the most part, the attempt ended eventually in failure. Only in a few instances, such as in that of the settlement north of Peterborough, were members of the socially superior class able to segregate themselves in some degree from the common folk, and then only at a price which was socially painful. Throughout rural Upper Canada class distinctions tended to disappear. Efforts to erect a colonial aristocracy through making large grants of land to favoured individuals failed to produce more than a class of speculators as greater profits could be made by dealing in, than by working, the land. Apart from a few isolated cases, such as Talbot and MacNab, landholders did not seek to secure social position by establishing themselves on large estates. The economic laws which discouraged the growth of a landed gentry operated equally effectively in reducing the farm class to a common social level. The capital, educational attainments, and refined tastes which some of the overseas colonists brought with them were little if any advantage in achieving success in agriculture, and distinctions arising out of inherited wealth disappeared when those who began with the least worldly goods often ended by acquiring the most. Furthermore, the frontier did not produce a labour group which became distinguished from the body of farm employers, and attempts to maintain traditional master–servant relationships soon had to be abandoned. The social demands of the pioneer society reinforced the economic demands, and select social circles disappeared in face of the need among neighbours for mutual help and sympathy. Only in the towns, where governmental and military officials, Anglican clergymen, and well-to-do merchants congregated, did there emerge anything approaching a socially superior class.

This disintegration of class distinctions served to release the expansionist forces of an agrarian frontier. Economic resources were not diverted into wasteful channels to support the vestiges of aristocracy; nor was the development of new techniques and methods of farming retarded by influences of tradition. Whatever course of action appeared to promise the greatest pecuniary returns was followed regardless of standards of respectability or social worth. But, while the economic gains from the disintegration of class distinctions were immediate and direct, some of the social gains were more remote and were offset by immediate cultural losses. Emancipation of the lower-class overseas immigrants from the obligations imposed upon them by the traditional class structure encouraged the display of vulgar pretensions of equality which had little relation to pioneer standards of social worth. On the other hand, the loss by the socially superior class of their hereditary prerogatives discouraged the preservation of values of social leadership accepted within the traditional class structure. A disregard on the part of both classes for standards of respectability and social worth meant, to some extent at least, a disregard for standards of moral decency. Much of the cultural heritage of the overseas immigrants consisted of rules of conduct governing relationships between the privileged and unprivileged, and the breakdown of these relationships weakened considerably the mores. The effects were evident in a general lowering of standards, among the emancipated "gentry" as well as among the common folk. The latter lacked the cultural and moral leadership of a true social élite, the former felt no obligation to provide such leadership.

The sharp division between town and country meant that the leadership lacking in the rural communities was not supplied by the urban centres. Among a considerable section of the population of the towns the chief concern was that of securing political or military preferments, and those with more ambitious prospects sought gain from the speculation in land. The economic welfare of the farmers was of little consequence. Even the retail merchants, who apparently sought a livelihood by trade with the rural inhabitants, were often more interested in acquiring land in payment for debts than in building up a healthy cash business. The pecuniary and cultural interests of the town inhabitants divorced them from the rural communities. The political organization of the colony reinforced the exclusiveness of these groups and accentuated the isolation of the rural communities. The state was closely identified with urban interests in the colony, and responded slowly to the feelings and demands of the farm population. The irresponsibility of the executive, and the lack of popularly organized parties, deprived the common citizens of an avenue of political expression. The failure of the rural inhabitants to secure cultural status combined with their failure to secure political status. Demands for responsible government were closely related to the social needs of the farm communities. Political unrest was symptomatic of disturbances extending through the entire range of the pioneer society of Upper Canada.

The disturbing effects of overseas settlement in Upper Canada after the War of 1812 were as apparent in religious as in cultural and political organization. A large number of the overseas colonists were members of the Church of England, and it was upon this church as a result that the heaviest strain was placed in meeting the needs of rapidly growing rural communities. Before 1812, the church could fairly adequately serve the colony through its establishments in the chief centres of population; its lack of an effective missionary organization occasioned little loss since it was in the towns that most of its supporters resided and those settled in the country were usually sufficiently near the towns to attend services of worship. But the rapid increase after 1820 of rural adherents of the Church of England in Upper Canada, and the pushing of settlement into the inaccessible backwoods, revealed the inadequacies of the church's policies and methods. Attitudes of religious indifference attributed to the inhabitants of Upper Canada by outside observers probably were confined chiefly to those people belonging to the national church. Certainly, evidence of rural inhabitants failing to support religious services was most pronounced in the case of this religious denomination.

It is true that the very character of pioneer society discouraged acts of religious devotion on the part of the population. The isolation and hard work of pioneer farm life made impossible the observance of many religious practices, and this unsettlement of old habits tended to the neglect of even those practices which could have been observed. Profanity appeared an inevitable ingredient in the habits of pioneer farm work, while Sabbath days provided the only occasions for such recreational activities as hunting or fishing. The lack of opportunities of worshipping collectively discouraged, in the end, private worship among individuals. Pioneer rural conditions, furthermore, tended to weaken those habits of thought which supported devout attitudes. Life in the backwoods of Upper Canada emphasized the ruthlessness of materialistic forces, and the struggle to gain a livelihood forced obedience to them. The atmosphere—and neighbours—were uncongenial to the religious mystic as they were to the poet. Yet the reality of the want felt by large numbers of the inhabitants to join in religious worship was made evident by the success achieved by the evangelical sects.

Where the neglect of religious habits occurred among the population, therefore, the reason would seem to lie largely in the failure of the Church of England to adapt itself to the conditions of the pioneer society. The reluctance of hard-working farmers to drive many miles over bad roads to attend a brief devotional service which offered little in the way of emotional stimulation could rarely be overcome by appeals to the feeling of loyalty to the church. With its dependence upon services in regularly appointed places of worship, and its reliance upon a ritual attractive to a sophisticated population, the church found itself unable to maintain the support of rural parishioners scattered over large areas. Its class and political bias served to divorce it even further from the rural communities. The concern to establish exclusive educational institutions, the partiality shown by many of the clergymen for the company of "polite society," and the anxiety of the ecclesiastical authorities to court the favour of a government upon which it depended for its privileged position, won for the church a claim to respectability but only at the price of losing its title to spiritual leadership. The shift of the allegiance of a large number of the rural inhabitants from the church to the more evangelical denominations provided concrete evidence of its weakening influence in the community. Efforts to bring about reforms within the organization of the church and to build up a competent staff of missionaries suited to the type of work required came too late to arrest its decline in leadership.

The other denominations did not wholly escape the disturbing effects of rapid settlement after the War of 1812. The great advantage of Presbyterianism in the early years of settlement lay in its reliance upon congregational principles of church government. To a very considerable extent, the people made the church, and, wherever the people moved, the organization of the church followed. The fact that most of the early Presbyterians in Upper Canada were Scots had simplified the task of organizing the church. Clan and congregational loyalties combined to favour the preservation of habits of religious worship. With the increase in the number of Presbyterian adherents in Upper Canada in the twenties and thirties, however, the strengths of congregational principles became less apparent and the weaknesses of a lack of strong centralized organization more evident. The strict Presbyterian discipline required trained clergymen, and with increasing population a sufficient supply was not readily available. The jealousy with which congregations preserved the right to appoint and dismiss those who served them discouraged ministers from emigrating from Scotland when they were uncertain of obtaining or retaining a position. The trials incurred by the Rev. William Proudfoot in Upper Canada before he received a call to a charge were illustrative of the weaknesses of congregational principles of church government. The development in Scotland of missionary organizations did something to meet the difficulties. Schisms within the church produced liberal denominations more alive to the possibilities of missionary work than was the Church of Scotland. Nevertheless, the supply of clergy remained for some considerable time insufficient to meet the demand.

Other weaknesses in Presbyterianism in a rural frontier became apparent. The obstinacy with which ministers conformed to the Presbyterian discipline tended to confine their influence to the faithful adherents. So long as Presbyterians were settled in compact communities, the refusal of the minister to dispense the sacraments to non-members of the church occasioned no great hardship, but as population became more scattered, and members of other religious denominations became interspersed among Presbyterians, the rigidity of the church's discipline made itself more felt. In sparsely settled communities, where a minister for each denomination was a luxury which could not be afforded, a degree of co-operation between the churches was highly necessary, and the Presbyterian Church failed to avail itself of the opportunities which such co-operation offered.

A shift in the attachments of a number of Presbyterians to the Methodist or Baptist denominations indicated weaknesses in that church as well as the aggressiveness of the evangelical sects. More striking still was the challenge to the Scottish leadership within the church itself and the growing strength of evangelical Presby-terianism. This movement, it is true, derived its support chiefly from the American-born settlers in the border communities where ministers, thoroughly schooled in the religious evangelism of the American West, introduced such practices as the protracted meeting and temperance pledges, but it had the effect of restricting the influence of the Scottish churches to the immigrants from overseas. The stern and uncompromising theological doctrines and scholarly erudition of the Scottish pastors made little appeal to those who had not been reared in a strictly Calvinist society. Evangelical Presby-terianism spread as the demand for a more sympathetic religion made itself felt in the rural settlements of Upper Canada.

For the most part, the developments in Upper Canada served to emphasize the strengths of Methodism as a frontier religious move-ment, but, even with respect to this denomination, the War of 1812 and its aftermath brought disturbing influences to bear. The cutting off of the supply of Methodist Episcopal preachers during 1812–14, the outburst of ill feeling against the United States, and the immi-gration after 1814 of Methodists from Great Britain encouraged the intrusion of Wesleyan missionaries into Upper Canada, and the internecine struggle for ecclesiastical sovereignty which ensued darkened the pages of the history of Methodism during the next two decades and embittered relationships within the church particu-larly in those areas where the rivalry was most keen. The conflict, however, was not wholly disadvantageous to the Methodist cause as the number of missionaries in Upper Canada was actually increased thereby. Moreover, to the extent that the field was successfully divided between the Wesleyans and the Episcopal Methodists, the one group of missionaries tended to maintain the support of the overseas immigrants and the other group the support of the American-born settlers.

In other respects, the organization and practices of the Methodist

Church proved extremely well adapted to the conditions which developed in Upper Canada with the rapid growth of settlement. The retention by the central Methodist conferences of the right of making appointments saved Methodism from the damaging effects of long-drawn-out negotiations between congregations and ministers such as was evident in the case of Presbyterianism. In a community where the population was extremely scattered, the Methodists did not wait until congregations could be formed, but rather relied upon the itinerant preacher who travelled from one settlement to another, and from one household to another, holding devotional services where people could be got together. The division of the province into a number of circuits, and the shift of preachers to different circuits at the end of each year, not only assured that no section would be overlooked but provided the inhabitants with a wide variety of talent. The local preachers in the more settled communities performed those day-by-day tasks of a regular clergy which could not be taken care of by itinerants.

The enterprising character of both the itinerant and local preachers of the Methodist Church was in striking contrast to the more leisurely manners of the clergy of the Church of England. The fact that many of the former possessed scarcely the rudiments of learning was little disadvantage in a community which set no high value upon knowledge. The fervour and earnestness with which they performed their duty, and the highly emotional content of their preaching, appealed to a population which knew few diversions. No intellectual or social chasm separated the Methodist preachers from their followers, and they were able to meet on a common basis of experience and understanding. The development of such techniques as the protracted and camp meetings enabled the Methodists to overcome even more successfully the obstacles to religious services in the backwoods. While the itinerant preacher sought out the household of the pioneer, the camp meeting, in turn, provided the pioneer with sufficient occasion to search out the religious service. It offered an opportunity, in communities where such opportunities occurred only infrequently, for numbers of people to participate in social gatherings. If the distance travelled was considerable the attractions of the week-long camp meeting afforded ample compensation.

The fanaticism loosed by the Methodist evangelical movement proved something of a disturbing force in the society of Upper

Canada. Work and domestic duties were often neglected to attend religious services, and the highly emotional reaction resulting from conversion occasionally led to personal disorganization. In addition, the aggressiveness of the evangelical sects contributed to a growing intolerance of different religious faiths. There was lacking in Methodism the deeply embedded liberal philosophy evident in the secessionist Presbyterianism of such people as Proudfoot. The mass appeal of the Methodist preachers did much to strengthen the popular will but less perhaps to increase public intelligence. There emerged a type of leadership which, as exemplified in Egerton Ryerson, might be described in some respects as "boss" rule; a not wholly satisfactory substitute for the rule of the Family Compact. But these undesirable features of the Methodist movement were largely the inevitable by-products of a far-reaching social revolution taking place in Upper Canadian society. Evangelical Methodism was an expression of social dissatisfactions with an order of privilege; it provided, at a time when secular means of communication were still largely ineffective, a means of outlet for democratic feelings being generated on the frontier. This political appeal of Methodism was closely related to its religious and moral appeals. The spread of a belief in temperance, a quickening of the cultural life of farm communities, and a strengthening of religious sentiments followed in the wake of revivals, and the group rapport developed through such religious association provided a basis for the erection of the democratic party system.

Other religious sects, particularly the Baptists, tended to support the evangelical movement set under way by the Methodists. As the spirit of revival gained force, an increasing number of churches felt to some degree its influence. On the other hand, the unity of the Protestant body was considerably weakened by denominational schisms which resulted in the emergence of a great variety of religious sects. The bitter conflicts between the different branches of the Protestant churches evident during the thirties and forties were symptomatic of the passing of the simplicity and co-operative spirit of pioneer social conditions. Other influences tended to widen and deepen the roots of such conflicts. The immigration of Irish peoples which began in the 1820's and continued throughout the next two decades considerably increased the Roman Catholic population in the province, and the hostile attitudes to the Irish, derived largely from economic and social sources, found expression in movements directed at the Roman Catholic Church. It is true that the earliest formed lodges of the Orange Order, emerging in those sections of the province where the population was predominantly Protestant, performed chiefly social functions; they provided the one means of social intercourse familiar to the early settlers from overseas. A much more aggressive set of lodges, however, were organized in the 1830's, almost wholly within the triangular area formed by the towns of Kingston, Bytown (Ottawa), and Peterborough, and these arose directly in response to the growing threat of the large Irish Catholic population. The bitterness of religious conflict immediately made itself apparent in the local communities, and its effects upon colonial politics became increasingly felt with the union of Lower and Upper Canada and the extension of the democratic process.

The growth of religious conflict was indicative of the emergence of new disturbances in the society of central Canada. The focal points of Protestant-Catholic antagonism were to be found very largely in areas where public works were undertaken and in towns growing rapidly from the influx of workers, and this was true also of sectarian conflict within Protestantism and of more general forms of social conflict. The increase in the number of people dependent upon wages for a livelihood, and the growth of towns, introduced new kinds of tensions in the society. The large Irish immigration, and seasonal unemployment associated with the construction industry, imposed heavy strains upon the inadequate social services of local communities, and still greater burdens had to be assumed during those intervals when the railway "booms" of the forties and fifties collapsed. The business cycle was essentially a new phenomenon in the economy of Upper Canada, and few supports had been erected to relieve the effects of its downward swing. The apprehension resulting from the increase in the numbers of those people who were not satisfactorily provided for within the economic structure found expression in attitudes of hostility, apparent in the bitter feelings towards the Irish Catholics, and in the development of new economic philosophies some of which, as propounded for instance within one or two religious sects, had definite socialistic tendencies. The increase in the number of Irish inmates in the gaols and penitentiary, and the emergence of a problem of prostitution, indicative of the wider social effects of commercial expansion and the growth of towns, reinforced attitudes of hostility which had their basis in fear or dissatisfaction.

Social alignments emerged in terms of new social divisions. The increase in the numbers of the wealthy class paralleled the growth of an urban proletariat, and the segregation which had proved impossible in the rural communities became conspicuous in the urban centres when the rise of real-estate values produced exclusive residential areas. The extension in the influence of select social and cultural institutions was only partly offset by the establishment of organizations serving the needs of the working population—trade unionism awaited the development of industrial capitalism after 1870—and this cultural disfranchisement of a large section of the urban population was accompanied by an increasing divorce between religious leadership and the unfortunate classes. Such disturbances in social organization, if little more than a warning of the kind of social problems which were to be thrown up by the expansion of industrial capitalism in the latter part of the century, had already become apparent in central Canada in the fifties and sixties.

Actually, however, the problems of social organization which emerged after 1850 had little to do with adjustments which had been set under way with the frontier expansion of agriculture after the turn of the century. The growing trade in wheat, and railway building, increased the importance of commercial interests, and it was commercial expansion which produced the town and the resulting problems of social organization. Within the rural communities, by 1850, cultural stability had become established to a very considerable extent. Social welfare institutions had grown up to meet the simple needs of a farm population; the family had become fully adapted to a rural environment; strains within the class structure had been eased by the growing preponderance of second-generation settlers and by the ceaseless pressure of the rural agricultural economy; a provincial system of education had been established; and rural religious sects and denominations were becoming accommodated to one another and satisfactorily meeting the needs of the population. A complete integration of the culture was not accomplished—the rise of the city and opening of the West resulted in new pulls upon the population of the rural communities—but by 1850 the frontier expansionist phase of agriculture in central Canada had run its course, and social reorganization in terms of a mature agricultural economy had proceeded a considerable distance. Later forces of social disorganization emerged outside of rather than within the rural communities of this region.

CHAPTER V

The Gold-Rush Society
of British Columbia and the Yukon*

D E V E L O P M E N T of placer gold mining on the Pacific Coast
in what was to become the province of British Columbia gave rise
to a type of society very different from any which had grown up in
the eastern regions of Canada. The phenomenal rate of growth,
the character of the population attracted by a gold rush, the high
mobility of those engaged in mining, and the isolation of the area
from the outside world gave to the gold-mining society a distinctive character. The long streams of eager miners reaching into the
interior in search of gold, and the sudden accumulation by the
fortunate few of substantial fortunes, struck the imaginations of
those both within and outside the area in a way that scarcely any
other kind of social phenomenon did. The unsettling effects of the
gold rush reached back into older societies thousands of miles
removed, and forward into a distant interior inhabited by natives
and fur traders.

The development of the Fraser and Cariboo mining regions took
place in terms of "rushes." Placer gold mining made heavy demands
upon labour and provided a field of endeavour in which returns,
occasionally fabulous in size, could be secured without any lengthy
period of outlay or preparation. In spite, therefore, of restrictions
imposed by the Hudson's Bay Company, hostile to the mining
industry, and the lack of adequate transportation facilities, the
movement of population into the two colonies of Vancouver Island

*From *The Social Development of Canada*, pp. 308–26.

and British Columbia from 1858 to 1862 was phenomenal. The influx began in the early spring of 1858. In the four months of April, May, June, and July of that year, something like twenty-five thousand persons arrived in Victoria or found their way overland to the Fraser River. Though the next year the movement abated, and, indeed, many returned to California disappointed with the findings, a steady stream of miners during the years 1860, 1861, and 1862 pushed into the mining areas. In the latter year the influx of population once more assumed the character of a rush, several thousands leaving England, Canada, Australia, and New Zealand to seek their fortunes mining gold.

The extremely rapid growth of population in such a short time imposed strains upon social organization which were intensified by the character of the people who joined in the rush. Before 1860 the lower Fraser constituted a frontier of California and almost the whole of its population was drawn from this older mining area; but as the fame of the Fraser River diggings became more widespread, people poured in from various parts of the world and many of these had had no previous mining experience. If many of the problems of the new society resulted from the undisciplined character of the California miners, others resulted from the inexperience of adventurers from outside. These two layers of population remained sharply distinct during the early years of development, and each set its distinctive imprint upon the society. Other characteristics of the population carried threats to the new social order. The gold rush involved, as scarcely any other movement of population, a complete tearing away from old ties and traditional controls, and this emancipation was more thorough because it extended to such large numbers of people at the same time. Joining the rush to the mining frontier was something in the nature of a "grand spree" for the individual. The engagement in mining was not intended to be of long duration, and this feeling that the return to a settled mode of life was not far off encouraged an attitude of making the most of a brief period of freedom. The seasoned miners looked upon their occupation as of a more permanent character, but even among them the dominant urge was to strike it rich and then get out of the country. The result was that the temptation to enjoy life to the full tended to be overwhelming, and defeated any desire to establish enduring social relationships and institutions for the future.

Finally, the absence of family settlers made for unstable conditions in the mining frontier. The hazards accompanying the journey to the Pacific Coast, and the nature of the mining occupation, discouraged female immigration, and the society became almost wholly made up of men. Only in the towns, more especially Victoria, did anything approaching normal family life appear. Some alliances between the Indians and whites took place within the mining interior, but most of these were between retired Scottish fur traders turned hostel keepers and squaws presumably gifted in the culinary art. The miners had little desire to settle down to home life and particularly in a country in which they intended to stay for only a short time. Little promise of matrimony accordingly was held out to girls immigrating to the colony, and their opportunities for employment were confined to domestic work in Victoria. Some women were sent to the country by charitable organizations in Great Britain, but the movement never assumed more than trifling dimensions.

In addition to the rapid growth and composition of the population, the nature of the mining industry itself made difficult the establishment of stable social organization. A considerable mobility was characteristic of the total population. Exhaustion of the bars on the lower Fraser led to the pushing of miners farther up the river and eventually into the Cariboo country, and this shift of population came about by a series of sudden rushes after the circulation of reports of new findings. New mining camps grew up overnight; old mining towns vanished almost as suddenly. There was little in the mining community which possessed the character of permanency.

The seasonal nature of the mining industry intensified the mobility of the population. Large numbers of miners returned to Victoria to spend the winter, and this influx and exodus of people weakened community organization in the capital as in the mining interior. The summer tended to be a period of feverish activity and the winter a period of complete idleness. The sharp separation of work from leisure meant that when working the miners neglected interests other than the purely economic while during periods of leisure they tended to give themselves up wholly to play. Placer gold mining was fatiguing and was carried on largely in isolation from fellow men, but, when the season came to an end and the miners returned to the city, the rigorous tasks of the summer gave way to the more pleasant pursuits of the winter. Emotional urges long held in restraint through the lack of leisure and human companionship suddenly found release, and, with the proceeds of the year's labour, the miners enjoyed an interval of complete relaxation. It was in the mining towns, accordingly, that some of the most serious problems of the mining society emerged. Here miners returning from the interior joined recent arrivals, and the total population tended to be of a floating character. Problems of destitution, crime, morality, cultural organization, and religion, though extending into the interior, centred very largely in the town of Victoria.

Problems of destitution were associated with the influx of people unsuited to the life of a mining community, the highly speculative character of gold mining, and the long period of idleness during winter months. The familiarity of the Californians with mining techniques, and their willingness to accept the trials and discomforts of mining life, gave them a great advantage over others in making the personal adjustments necessary for success on the new frontier. Failure recorded in terms of destitution or personal disorganization had a much higher incidence among those who lacked experience in mining. They were less prepared to face reverses, hardships, and strenuous toil than those with a disciplined schooling in mining, and consequently their over-optimism when they arrived in the country quickly gave way to despondency and despair when the first efforts to locate gold ended in failure. On the other hand, if they chanced to stumble upon a rich find they seldom considered the possibility of their luck coming to an end. As a result, a large proportion of the destitute and personally disorganized individuals found in Victoria during winter months was made up of those who had entered upon the occupation of mining from other walks of life; even in adversity, many of the panhandlers and casual labourers who frequented the poolrooms and taverns of the town were people who boasted of their family connections and educational attainments. Not all the failures in Victoria, however, were drawn from the ranks of those unsuited to the conditions of mining life. The highly speculative character of mining meant that even some of the most seasoned miners failed to secure returns from their labour and capital. The miner often had to be "staked," and he faced the risk of not being able to pay off his debts or to accumulate sufficient to carry him over the winter months. Even when the season had been a successful one in the way of returns, the miners often spent everything they had during the early part of the winter and were left with nothing to live on for the rest of the year. In gambling, drinking, and other forms of dissipation, men of wealth sometimes became paupers in a single evening.

The mining population, for the most part, treated none too kindly those unprepared to pass the severe tests imposed by the rigours of work and manner of life. Few had time or inclination to show concern for the failure. The claims of friendship operated within small groups, and a helping hand was readily given out to the needy "pal"; but there was no strong sense of community obligation, and collective efforts to provide charity met with the resistance of a stubborn individualism. The lack of alternative occupations accentuated the difficulties of those who had failed in mining. Within Victoria, organizations made up particularly of philanthropic-minded ladies undertook to provide aid to some of those in need; the unfortunate miner, however, was likely to be too proud to accept assistance proffered in this way. A form of begging grew up as a regularized system of taking care of those without means. For those with Oxford degrees or with other attributes which secured the favourable attention of colonial officials, employment by the government provided a welcome shelter from the harsh penalties imposed upon the unsuccessful by the frontier mining society.

The influx, into Victoria and the mining interior, of criminal elements from California, the isolation of the colony from the outside world, and the considerable mobility of the population gave rise to immediate and pressing problems of law and order. The danger of disastrous clashes between the American miners and the Indians was only narrowly averted by decisive action on the part of the authorities, and the gangster rule which such leaders as Ned McGowan sought to establish threatened to remove policing powers entirely out of the hands of the government. Though no complete breakdown occurred in the administration of justice, the limitations of the policing power were evident in the failure to prevent criminals from escaping across the border or evading arrest in the interior. Even after criminals had been arrested it proved difficult to bring them to a place of trial and to keep them under confinement. The frequent escape of prisoners on the way to trial or after they had been sentenced to gaol discouraged arrest on the part of the police, and, if punitive measures could not be immediately applied, the offenders were often permitted to remain at large. Instances of miners taking the law into their own hands were not absent in the distant interior, and these efforts to secure justice probably met with little disapproval from the few police on patrol. Even more difficult in many ways was the task of maintaining order in the rapidly growing town of Victoria. Here, particularly during winter months, large numbers of professional crooks, gamblers, and confidence men mingled with the miners recently returned from the summer's toil and with the local inhabitants. Petty crimes, street and dance-hall brawls and bar-room fights were frequent occurrences in the town.

In addition, the highly lucrative but illegitimate trade in whisky with the Indians constituted a serious threat to order. The proximity to Victoria of the demoralized tribes of Songish Indians increased very considerably the tasks of policing and law enforcement. The apprehension of the whisky traders was extremely difficult because of the lack of reliable witnesses willing to testify and the corruption of police officials, while the sale of liquor to the Indians introduced new problems of order when fights broke out between the intoxicated natives or between them and the white men. The increase in the penalties imposed upon conviction was offset by the high profits from the trade and the comparative immunity from arrest. The trade continued to flourish in spite of efforts to suppress it, and its demoralizing effects upon the white community were as great as upon the native.

To meet the problem of crime, agencies of law enforcement were created and improved. The administrative officials in Victoria profited by their long experience in the service of the Hudson's Bay Company, and to the tradition of law and order secured through the Company was added the prestige and power of the British Empire. A contingent of Royal Engineers was dispatched to the colonies, and it combined policing functions with such other duties as that of building roads. The number of regular police was increased, gaols were established in Victoria and New Westminster, and a system of law courts was erected for the whole area. As a result of such measures, an uncontrolled frontier dependent entirely upon vigilante committees for the maintenance of law and order never emerged in British Columbia. The presence of a large number of Californians in the area constituted a serious threat to the formal institutions of law. With the experiences of the 1849's still fresh in their minds, the Californians placed little reliance upon the police and courts of law to preserve order, and, while this suspicion of state institutions gave to the informal organization of the mining frontier a flexibility which enabled it to withstand the social strains of the early stages of the mining rush, the failure to admit the supremacy of the formal law carried ultimate threats to the whole system of justice. As the society became more complex, direct action in the maintenance of law would have become increasingly ineffectual and would eventually have taken on the character of gangster as opposed to collective rule. But this development was successfully checked by the colonial authorities supported by British elements in the population. That is not to say that problems of crime were not of a serious character within the mining frontier of British Columbia. But the existence of such problems did not lead to a breakdown of the authority of law. The tradition of British justice secured respect for the institutions of judicial administration even when those institutions failed to maintain complete order.

In the wider sphere of morality, the major problems of the mining society were drinking, gambling, and prostitution. These problems were largely confined to the towns and particularly to Victoria. Drinking was prevalent within the mining camps as within the towns, but in the mining camps liquor constituted more an item of diet than a means of dissipation. The same was true, though to a lesser extent, of the liquor served by the hostels along the road reaching into the interior. Here drinking was heavy but it took place among miners who lingered only long enough to secure food and rest before continuing their journey. In the towns, however, drinking became associated with idleness, and during the winter the numerous taverns of Victoria were thronged with miners returned from the interior. The sale of liquor constituted one of the chief business interests of the capital, and heavy drinking in the town contributed to rowdyism, petty crime, and personal demoralization.

Gambling was likewise common in the mining society and particularly in the mining towns. The playing of cards or the participation in other gambling games provided a means of passing the time and satisfied the needs of the miners for human companionship. The very nature of the mining occupation favoured a gambling spirit. Chance played a great part in the finding of gold, and considerable risks were taken with the uncertain prospects of high returns. Broke on one day and rich on the next was a familiar experience of many miners, and there was a tendency as a result to assume a careless and, at the same time, sporting attitude to the making of money. Gambling during the winter in the towns was little more than a continuation of the gambling carried on during the summer in the search for gold. Confined to the miners themselves, the recreation of gambling, though at times involving high stakes, was generally harmless, but professional gamblers quickly took up positions at strategic points and much of the fruits of the miners' toil was drained into these parasitic channels. Almost every poolroom, bar, and barber shop in Victoria combined gambling with its legitimate function, and, wherever any concentration of miners took place, small knots of earnest gamblers were to be found.

Prostitution emerged inevitably out of a situation in which the population was predominantly male and was engaged in an occupation which brought in ready cash. The inaccessibility of the area to prostitutes from outside was offset by the proximity to Victoria of a large demoralized Indian population, and a regular trade grew up between the town and the native encampments. Squaws plied the streets of Victoria, and brothels, under the management of white men, were established in the town and along the road leading to the Indian villages. The survival of practices of slavery among the Indians promoted prostitution as girls were virtually sold to white managers. The traffic in Indian females became closely linked with the liquor traffic, and the trade in the one promoted the trade in the other. Prostitutes served as go-betweens in the sale of whisky to the Indians, and the demoralization resulting from the drinking of whisky increased reliance upon prostitution. At the height of the mining boom, the traffic assumed considerable proportions. As the community became older, and links with the outside world closer, professional prostitutes began to replace those secured from the Indian tribes.

Within the community, movements emerged to raise moral standards. The small but substantial group of respectable heads of families in Victoria became increasingly alarmed as the widespread immorality of the society began to threaten their own security. Efforts to establish healthy recreational facilities and to promote reforms such as temperance were indicative of the growing moral consciousness of the community, and more stringent police regulations were secured to support these informal controls. But such measures of reform were more in the way of guarding against the moral contamination of contacts with the mining masses than in the way of raising the moral standards of the miners themselves. The temperance reformers and youth leaders played heavily upon their claims to respectability, and their usefulness was confined very largely to those who belonged to the exclusive circles of Victoria society. Moral reform among the mining population awaited leadership which relied upon appeals to their distinctive interests, and such leadership developed slowly without the aid of the family group.

Like problems of morality, those of cultural organization revealed in striking fashion the effects of the rapid growth and instability of the mining society. The population was made up of a great number of nationalities suddenly thrown together in a community where no sort of segregation was possible. Canadians, Americans, Australians, New Zealanders, English, Irish, Scots, and various national groups from Europe jostled together along the trails into the mining interior or within the mining towns. To some extent the English, and particularly those who boasted university degrees or aristocratic ancestry, kept themselves apart from the rest of the population, but such distinctions tended to be artificial and aroused no recognition on the part of the general population. The cultural heritages of the various groups were largely lost in the general mixture of nationalities. Social divisions did appear along economic or political lines, but they tended to emphasize the lack of distinctive features within the mining population. The older inhabitants in the colony had been traders in the Hudson's Bay Company, and, identified with government employment, they considered themselves something of an aristocracy apart from the great mass of miners. The struggle for responsible government hardened the lines marking off this privileged group, and the prerogatives of class superiority became caught up in political issues. The acrimonious relations between newspapers in the colony reflected underlying animosities between economic and cultural groups.

Other social divisions quickly developed in the colony along racial lines. The inherited antagonism of the Americans to Negroes came to the fore when large numbers of the dark race, many of them escaped slaves, found their way into Victoria and some of the smaller mining towns. Displays of racial tolerance on the part of the British peoples served only to aggravate the strained relationships by giving the Negroes an undue sense of their importance and thereby irritating even more the American populace. Riots in the theatre of Victoria and bitter controversies over the issue of attendance of Negroes at religious worship were indicative of the intensity of the racial conflict. Besides the Negroes, the Chinese constituted something of a despised race in the mining society, though their general inoffensiveness provided little occasion for acts of vituperation. The Chinese worked the diggings abandoned by the whites, and, so long as apparently inexhaustible supplies of gold were to be found further inland, their presence aroused little resentment by the miners. It was when the supplies began to be exhausted, and opportunities for employment scarce, that feelings of racial antagonism towards the Chinese became widespread among the population. Economic recession and eventual industrialization finally crystallized the extremely bitter issue of Oriental immigration.

Institutions developed to provide cultural leadership, but little support was secured from the great mass of gold-hungry miners. Newspapers played the chief role in arousing opinion about public issues and in developing a community consciousness. The reform editor who boldly challenged the vested privileges of party, class, and church won a position of influence equal to that attained by the evangelical religious leaders in the older Canadian colonies. But the newspapers of the time, and particularly those appealing to a somewhat crude and preoccupied mining population, set no high standards of propriety in manners of expression or questions of discussion, and accordingly took no conspicuous lead in the raising of the cultural level of the mining community. Fraternal societies and clubs made their appearance in Victoria and New Westminster where there was a concentration of persons of wealth and leisure, and libraries were established to serve the needs of the reading public, but few of the large body of miners profited from these cultural agencies. Similarly, education remained an insignificant cultural force, though institutions grew up under the direction largely of the church or private individuals to provide instruction to children found in the larger centres. The absence of the family accounted for much of the weakness of cultural organization, as the effects of its absence extended into every sphere of social life. Cultural values were forgotten in the mad search for gold. The character of the mining society emphasized the present at the expense of the past and future. The community inherited no rich cultural life and it built up no tradition to be passed on to new generations.

Concentration upon the present became still more conspicuous in the weakness of religious organization. If the miners gave little attention to the future, they were likely to prepare even less for life in the hereafter. The nature of their occupation discouraged attitudes of devoutness, and carelessness towards matters of religion was enhanced by the absence of female companionship. There is little evidence that the miners, cut off from any sort of religious service, felt the lack of means of worship as, for instance, did many of the pioneers of Upper Canada. Some of them, it is true, carried with them to the mining frontier habits of devoutness which persisted within the highly materialistic social milieu. But most of them quite cheerfully accepted a state in which the minister of the gospel did not enter to disturb the customary disregard of the Sabbath or the indulgence in playful vices.

Vigorous efforts were made by the various churches to propagate the faith on the mining frontier, and some success was achieved by the more enterprising of the missionaries. Roman Catholic, Church of England, Congregational, Presbyterian, and Wesleyan denominations were represented, and the first two quickly became organized into bishoprics. Proselytization among the native populations gave to the churches a vast constituency in which to work, and, for the most part, the same missionary organization was employed in serving the mining communities. The Roman Catholic Church had become most deeply entrenched in the work with the Indians, but the Church of England secured the advantages of official recognition and enjoyed a privileged position. The bitterly controversial issues in the politics of the colony were closely identified with the issue of Church of England supremacy, and attacks upon the governing clique were indistinguishable from attacks upon the hierarchy of the church. Much of the attention directed towards religious matters in the colony, as a result, was concerned with questions of privilege rather than with those of spiritual leadership. The Church of England, as so often in colonial possessions, sacrificed the goodwill of the great mass of the people in return for the uncertain advantage of securing official favour. The bitter attacks made upon it in the press and on the platform lowered the tone of political life and served to bring religion into discredit.

These controversies, of course, were largely confined to Victoria and New Westminster. Within the mining interior the various missionaries carried on their work with less regard to matters of politics or denominational rivalry. The highly mobile character of the mining population made the task of holding religious services an extremely difficult one. Towns or mining camps suddenly grew up and then as suddenly disappeared, and efforts, particularly of the Church of England, to build places of worship were largely wasted when depopulation left church buildings without congregations. Even itinerant missionary activities proved largely ineffectual as miners were often isolated in groups of two or three and few of them showed any inclination to go long distances to a religious service on the only day in the week in which they could rest and attend to such menial tasks as cooking and mending. In a frontier mining community such as British Columbia there was no great concentration of miners settled in village communities with their wives and families, and opportunities of evangelization like those seized by Wesley among the miners in England did not occur. Religious evangelism made no conspicuous headway among the population. The highly individualistic character of placer gold mining may have been in part responsible, but even more the absence of a female population left religion without its chief support. Social reorganization on any sort of permanent foundation awaited the establishment of the family, and the slowness with which this basic institution was introduced checked reorganizing movements such as religious evangelism.

In a sense, the reorganization of the mining society never became complete. As the community became older, and the rapid influx of population into the area came to an end, the institutional structure was able to embrace a greater number of the needs of the population. The administration of government underwent improvement, systems of police and courts of law were extended and made more effective, charitable organizations and recreational facilities developed, the moral sense of the community became more alive to the dangers of intemperance and vice, the basis of a system of elementary public schools was laid, and churches gained prestige with the erection of permanent and imposing places of worship.

But these gains were being made at the very time when exhaustion of gold was bringing near to collapse the whole economic structure erected upon the foundation of mining. In British Columbia there was no easy transition from a frontier to a diversified economy. In many respects, the mining society was swept aside before a new society could be erected. Other industries, such as farming and lumbering, grew up around mining and eventually came to supplant it in large part, but the labour force and capital structure fostered by the mining boom could not be supported by these secondary economic activities, and adjustment involved the painful processes of depopulation and economic recession. To some extent development after 1870 took place upon the economic wreckage left behind with the passing of the mining period. Eventually the potentialities of the area were sufficiently attractive to promote new economic activities and the erection of a society upon a more secure basis. By the latter part of the century the sweep of industrial-capitalist forces generated in eastern Canada was wide enough to embrace the Pacific region. Economic growth took place in terms of the links forged by the Canadian Pacific Railway, and British Columbia became now a frontier of industrialism.

The opening up and exploitation of the mining resources of the Kootenay were part of the process of industrialization which included the development of the lumbering industry, the fisheries, fruit growing and canning. While industrialism in British Columbia, however, led to an increasing emphasis upon capital in mining as in other activities, a new frontier emerged in the Yukon where individual miners once more took the lead. The Yukon inherited many of the economic techniques of the Fraser River and Cariboo mining areas, and developments during the period 1897–1905 resembled in many respects those which had taken place in British Columbia forty years earlier. The undoubted richness in gold of the Klondike River bed, and the subsidiary streams of the Yukon, quickly attracted a large body of experienced prospectors and miners once the first discoveries had been made. But very soon fabulous stories of enormous wealth spread, and there followed a mad rush into the area of people from all walks of life. Reports of the hardships of the trip, and lurid descriptions of society in the mining camps, served only to fire the imagination of those seeking release from the boredom of life in settled communities. Something like 40,000 people found their way into the area during the period of the rush; the police estimated the population on January 10, 1899, as 28,018.

Of these the great majority were people who lacked any previous experience in mining. The Yukon made an appeal which attracted an overwhelming number of raw recruits who were only painfully organized into a disciplined army of miners. It was this body of gold seekers, composed of men of all ages and of a great variety of occupations and social backgrounds, who proved so difficult to absorb during the period of rapid development from 1898 to 1902. In contrast, the seasoned American and Australian miners, like the Californians in British Columbia, readily adapted themselves to life in the diggings. On the other hand, the Americans and Australians, by the very fact that they had previous experience in mining, carried with them habits of thought which clashed with inherited British cultural values, and this conflict of authority was to prove a seriously disturbing factor in the political and social life of the Yukon. Problems of law enforcement, morality, cultural organization, and religion reflected the pull of these two opposing systems of thought, and, if the stubborn individualism of the seasoned miners checked the establishment of order through constituted authority, the intolerance of the Canadian official class prevented the easy working of the informal controls of the miners' code. These problems were complicated by the influx along with Americans and Australians of numerous other ethnic and racial groups. The diversified cultural heritages of the Yukon population made difficult the establishment of any set of social values either through constituted authority or voluntary association.

The large number of professional criminals, gamblers, whisky runners, and prostitutes who arrived in Dawson during the period of the rush added to the problem of erecting a stable social organization. In many respects, the activities of these parasitical groups were subject to the control of the code of the seasoned miners and suitable sanctions had evolved, but such activities were not recognized, except within the criminal code, in the system of Canadian cultural values which had been imported from without. The formal machinery of the state proved highly effective in dealing with the depradations of the criminal, but efforts to treat the activities of gamblers and prostitutes as crimes resulted in releasing such people from the more effective controls of the informal community. Though unrecognized by authority, the gamblers and prostitutes in Dawson City constituted an unavoidable element within the population. The predominance of men in the mining population enhanced the disorganizing influence of parasitical social groups. Some women came in with, or later joined, their husbands, but the female population for the most part consisted of public entertainers, dance-hall girls, and prostitutes. The free flow of gold

in the community encouraged such occupations, while other occupations were lacking to attract more respectable women. Dawson
with its mining hinterland was a male society, and it was the needs
of the men which determined very largely the kind of services and
social institutions found in the community.

The nature of placer gold mining in the Yukon added to the
difficulty of erecting stable social institutions. Even more speculative in character than that in the Fraser and Cariboo had been,
gold mining in the Yukon led to a population which was kept
continually on the alert, waiting to hear of new finds richer than
anything which had already been discovered. Dawson City was
something of a nerve centre of the whole area, and here newcomers
and returned miners congregated, ready to dash off at the first
whisperings of a strike. Rumour came to play a dominant part in
setting in motion the springs of collective action, and sudden
rushes punctuated the constant milling around of the aimless mass
of gold seekers. The tempo of the society of Dawson as a result was
kept at fever pitch. While one part of the population was anxiously
waiting opportunities to stake profitable claims, another part was
recklessly spending the returns from previous operations. The
seasonal nature of the mining occupation intensified the unsettled
character of society in Dawson. While the long days of the Arctic
summer led to a period of strenuous activity in the diggings, the
long nights of the Arctic winter led to a period of relative inactivity
in Dawson. There was little time during the summer for such menial
tasks as the cooking of proper foods; there was a great deal of time
in winter for loafing and dissipation. Dance halls and saloons
thrived in a climate where warmth and cheerful illumination were
not easy to find.

The geography of the Yukon basin tended to concentrate the
population in and about Dawson. The richest of the creeks were
not far distant, and all the creeks upon which mining took place
were tributaries of the Yukon or Klondike rivers which joined at
the site of the town. Other mining centres—Circle City, Rampart,
Nome, Sunrise, and Fairbanks—grew up in the Alaska territory,
but the Yukon developed largely in isolation from these areas.
There was not, as in British Columbia, a string of mining towns
or camps reaching far into the interior, each serving the more
immediate needs of the population though depending upon larger
centres to supply a number of secondary services. Centralization
within the one town of Dawson intensified very considerably the

problem of community organization. Here the task was faced of converting a huge mining camp into a stable community. A complete lack of sewerage facilities, sidewalks, and zoning restrictions was an inevitable accompaniment of conditions where the first residents simply pitched tents or built rude shacks preparatory to engaging in prospecting and mining operations. The cabins of the mining creeks reached back into the town, and there was virtually no distinction between the mining population and town residents.

Other factors enhanced the dominance of the mining population within the town of Dawson itself. Unlike Victoria, which had grown up as a fur-trading post and which continued to support a local aristocracy of officials sharply divorced from mining interests, Dawson lacked any tradition of past greatness and contained no population identified with rival interests to mining. The erection of the miners' tents or shacks marked the beginnings of the town's history, and the few government officials who later came in never became socially differentiated from the great mass of inhabitants. Business and social services emphasized the absence of needs other than those of a mining population. Dawson was completely exposed to the influences of the frontier which surrounded it on all sides. Within the town as a result the disorganizing features of the mining society were sharply focused.

The disorganization of the society was more complete because of the short time within which the gold rush took place. Though miners had come into the Yukon in the early 1890's and there were many new arrivals after 1900, the mass movement of gold-seekers occupied little more than eighteen months. The influx of population did not occur in terms of a number of waves between which there were periods of adjustment but rather took place in terms of one mighty wave which was only checked through the lack of winter transportation facilities. The whole community was populated by newcomers at the same time, and the result was an almost complete absence of experience within the community upon which to erect stable social institutions. Few societies of comparable population were ever so completely unorganized as that of the Yukon in the early summer of 1898. Orderly social relationships and social controls were almost entirely lacking where all the members of the community had been suddenly brought together for the first time.

Yet the very factors which accentuated the early disorganization of the mining society promoted the establishment of a new social order. The growth of a community consciousness and the erection of a network of social institutions and controls proceeded rapidly in an environment where all the people had equally few ties with the past, experienced much the same kind of problems of livelihood, and were engaged in the same occupation of gold mining. The completeness of the break with the society of the outside world and the concentration upon a single economic interest meant that new adjustments came about readily and tended to proceed at the same rate among all the members of the group. Cultural conflict as a result did not seriously delay the creation of a new social order. It is true that the old miners disliked the newcomers and that bitter controversies raged about issues of government and the regulation of mining, but these conflicts were not a reflection of deeply embedded interests which set up barriers between social groups and made effective collective action difficult. The absence of privilege and vested interest as means of establishing authority in the Yukon allowed freer expression to the natural impulses of the population, and, if those impulses tended immediately to an unrestrained licence, they favoured eventually the establishment of orderly conditions in the community.

Outside aids, of course, were of considerable importance in establishing a stable organization. The chief of such agencies was the North West Mounted Police which quickly took up strategic positions in the Yukon territory and not only succeeded in maintaining a state of law and order but, by means of checking the supplies people had before setting out on the inland journey to Dawson and by constant patrols along the routes of travel and the mining creeks, served as something of a social welfare institution. Behind the Mounted Police rested the authority of the Canadian government, and, although many of the local officials were accused of corruption and the officials in Ottawa were often ignorant of conditions in the mining frontier, the introduction of British traditions and practices of justice arrested the development of popular methods of law enforcement such as those secured within miners' meetings and associations. Fraternal societies and lodges, and even to some extent trade-union organizations, reached out from older communities to assist in establishing institutions within the distant mining frontier. Finally, religious denominations vigorously promoted the spiritual and social interests of the mining population. Among the older denominations, the Roman Catholic, Anglican, Presbyterian, and Methodist churches were most active.

Of evangelical religious organizations, the work of the Salvation
Army was conspicuously successful, and here, as in the rapidly
growing urban communities, the methods employed by the Army
were closely adapted to the needs of the population.

Institutional controls derived from outside, however, were
effective only as a result of the development of an underlying social
consciousness favourable to the establishment of order within the
community. This was true even of the work performed by the
Mounted Police. That is to say that processes of social reorganization were generated from within rather than from outside the
society. Lacking external aids the establishment of social order
would have come about more slowly as the experience of mining
communities in Alaska amply demonstrates, but these aids in
themselves provided no solid basis upon which to erect a stable
society. Collective efforts were canalized and provided a more
permanent goal of achievement; they sprang, however, from the
urge of the people themselves to better their conditions.

New accommodations and the establishment of order did not
proceed unhampered by forces of disturbance within the society.
Institutional rivalries particularly between religious denominations,
increasing racial bitterness with the growth of feelings of self-
consciousness on the part of certain groups, and problems of
capital and labour as the operation of mining passed into the hands
of large corporations and the miners found themselves becoming
day labourers, gave rise to new points of conflict within the community. For the most part, however, these disturbances were
associated with the developments of a society which had already
passed beyond the frontier stage. Like British Columbia, the
Yukon very soon faced problems of economic recession and depopulation when exhaustion of resources began to take place. The
development of secondary economic activities, and the shift to
machine methods of production and large capital organization in
mining, were indicative of the passing of the earlier frontier of
individual enterprise. The Yukon became caught up, if somewhat
remotely, in the wider structure of industrial capitalism in Canada.
But these new adjustments came about very largely after the
boom society of 1898–1902 had disappeared. Within this four-
year period the development of the Yukon passed through the
full cycle of social disorganization and reorganization; for study
of these social processes, few social laboratories could be more
revealing.

The Prairie Wheat-Farming Frontier and the New Industrial City*

THE CONSTRUCTION of the Canadian Pacific Railway, the exploitation of the mineral resources of the Kootenay, and the gold rush to the Yukon paved the way for the rapid economic expansion in Canada after 1900. Manufacturing industries which had survived the long depression of the seventies and eighties by means of protection secured through the National Policy and by combination and price control responded quickly to new developments taking place after the turn of the century. The enormous demands made by gold mining in the Yukon for capital and consumers' goods promoted industrial expansion and the establishment of new manufacturing plants, while the considerable movement of population into the Northwest resulting from the gold rush contributed to the settlement of the prairies, and the expansion of wheat farming in turn led to still greater demands for manufactured commodities. The building of two new transcontinental railways reflected the buoyant prospects of manufacturing and wheat farming, and metal mining in Northern Ontario developed largely as a by-product of these railway undertakings. The emergence of the pulp and paper industry emphasized the importance of the new northern frontier, while the daily newspaper which this industry made possible increased the extent of urban concentration and metropolitan control. Expansion into new frontiers in Canada after 1900 took place through the leadership of dominant industrial

*From *The Social Development of Canada*, pp. 380–94.

and financial centres, particularly Montreal and Toronto. The enlarged scope of financial organizations, improved techniques of transportation and production, and new sources of power made possible a diversity in the nature of economic activities and in the kind of resources brought under exploitation. The great number of new frontiers—manufacturing, agricultural, mining, lumbering, pulp and paper, and fishing—which emerged after the turn of the century was indicative of the wide sweep of industrial-capitalist expansion. Problems of social organization in various Canadian communities were evidence of the disturbing effects of such expansion.

To the extent that these problems were associated with the development of industrial manufacturing and the rise of cities they were not strikingly different from those found in such older industrialized countries as Great Britain, Germany, and the United States. Canada shared in technological improvements in the use of iron and steel which led to far-reaching changes in processes of production and in methods of transportation, and the effects of such developments upon social organization tended to be much the same throughout the western world. The fact that industrial entrepreneurship and organization extended into Canada from Britain and the United States gave her the advantage of the experiences of these countries. A considerable familiarity with the nature of the problems of industrialism was secured even before these problems had appeared in Canadian communities.

But if Canada profited some from the experiences of her neighbours, vested interests operated as an effectual check to the easy diffusion of ideas from outside. The claim, as made for instance by manufacturers with respect to problems of labour, that conditions were different in Canada retarded the acceptance of social policies successful elsewhere. The result was that problems even when not distinctive to Canada required solutions which could only be fashioned out of the raw materials of Canadian experience. However, the most crucial problems were distinctive to Canada in that the particular character they assumed resulted from a great variety of economic developments rather than from the development of industrial manufacturing by itself. The opening of the West and the exploitation of the pulp and mineral resources of the Precambrian Shield accompanied the growth of manufacturing in the central provinces, and it was this combination of economic developments which gave to the industrial-capitalist society of Canada its distinctive character. A purely urban society did not emerge in central Canada; nor did a purely agricultural society grow up in western Canada. Metropolitanism became a dominant feature of Canadian community organization, but it was a metropolitanism in terms not of one economic interest but of a great variety of such interests, and the way in which these interests were related to one another determined the distinctive pattern of social development.

It was this fact, furthermore, which sharply set off developments in Canada after the turn of the century from developments which had taken place before. Urbanization as such was not something which began at any particular time; Montreal, Quebec, Halifax, and Toronto grew into substantial cities during the nineteenth century, and, if Montreal and Toronto (together with Hamilton and Winnipeg) forged ahead more rapidly after 1900, the growth of the twentieth century was a continuation of that of the nineteenth. Similarly manufacturing had grown up throughout the whole of the nineteenth century, and by 1870 many of the towns along the Grand Trunk Railway from Montreal to Sarnia had become important industrial centres. But it was not until the end of the century that urbanization and industrialization joined forces, and industrial concentration—and industrial cities—became a dominant feature of Canadian life. This development was made possible by the sudden opening up of new resources of industrial capitalism—in the West and the North—which called for large-scale organization and mass production in manufacturing. The new industrial-capitalist society was one associated with the extension of metropolitan organization into fields of economic exploitation stretching across the whole of Canada. Thus the problems of Canadian communities after 1900 were not simply the problems of the preceding century on a grander scale. New forces combined to give rise to distinctively new social developments, in urban and rural communities alike; an examination of problems of social welfare, crime, morality, cultural organization, and religion serves to emphasize this fact.

Immigration in large numbers from overseas, expansion of manufacturing enterprises, and the rapid growth of urban communities after 1900 resulted in new problems of social welfare associated with the slum, overcrowding, and poverty. The opening up of new farming, mining, and lumbering frontiers made possible the absorption of that surplus labour which possessed the character of mobility, but within the recesses of the cities there accumulated a growing number of people who possessed neither the desire nor the ability to move. The city selected the failures out of the streams of overseas immigrants and out of the armies of industrial workers recruited by, and often ill paid within, the factory. Even the extractive frontier industries, though absorbing increasing numbers of workers, contributed to social dependency, over-crowding, and the development of slums when seasonal unemployment resulted in the drifting of unattached and homeless men to the city to spend the winter. The rural background of a large section of the urban population, and the exaggerated view of the potentialities of western expansion, led to a failure to appreciate the nature and extent of the social effects of industrialization and urban growth. It is true that the period before 1913 was one of un-bounded prosperity, and the demands made upon social welfare agencies were not overwhelming, but the feeling of security to which these buoyant prospects gave rise accounted for the failure to do anything about those very real problems which emerged inde-pendently of, and in some cases conditiond by, prosperity. Straitened financial resources, a reliance upon obsolete techniques of charity, and an almost complete lack of trained workers were characteristics of institutions of social welfare before the First World War.

Similar factors gave rise to new forms of crime and explain the failure of law enforcement agencies to deal adequately with this problem. Crime inevitably accompanied the process of assimilation of immigrant groups and infractions of the criminal code were particularly evident among second-generation immigrants where social and personal disorganization extended furthest. It was within the community structure, however, that the chief factors determining the extent and nature of crime were to be found. In some respects, Canadian institutions of law and order escaped disorganizing forces evident in the United States. The influence of the West in regard to crime was very different in the two countries. Though an interval of general disorder occurred between the passing of the control of the Hudson's Bay Company in 1871 and the organization of the North West Mounted Police in 1874, and immigration and railway building provided points of disturbance throughout the period of development before 1914, the vigilance of the Mounted Police and the predominantly British background of the population checked the growth of crime in the Canadian

West, and the habit of carrying fire-arms evident in many western American communities never developed; here neither the Indian nor the desperado was a continual threat to the life of the settler.

Again, the larger Canadian cities were more sheltered than were the American cities from any undesirable influence the West might have exerted; the Great Lakes and Precambrian Shield provided an effective barrier to close and constant intercourse. The result was that organized crime in Canada emerged almost wholly out of conditions within local urban communities and from the influence of the larger American cities. If this meant a slower growth of the more elaborate forms of crime, the development of improved techniques of dealing with the criminal was similarly retarded. Though the British heritage, and the dominantly rural background of the population in the cities, had the effect of making law-enforcement agencies highly effective in the apprehension and conviction of criminal offenders, the nature of the problem of urban crime required new tools of reformation and, in the forging of these, judicial agencies in Canada lagged behind those of other countries. The necessity of paying greater attention to the character of the criminal and less attention to the nature of the crime, and of devising improved methods of treating criminal offenders, was only slowly realized by Canadian judicial authorities.

The effects of this lag were evident with respect to crime in general, but they were most seriously felt with respect to the particular problem of juvenile delinquency. Juvenile delinquency was almost wholly peculiar to the city. Conditions of urban life greatly restricted the scope of parental controls while increasing immensely the variety of activities indulged in by children, and only slowly did there arise agencies to meet the needs of the juvenile population and new methods of treatment in dealing with juvenile criminal offenders. To the extent that public recreational facilities failed to be developed to offset the loss of those means of recreation which had been provided within the rural environment, the child was forced to place dependence upon street play-groups and gangs. On the other side, to the extent that there was a failure to distinguish between juvenile delinquents and adult criminals, within the police court and penal institutions, the child was subjected to the demoralizing influence of traditional methods in the treatment of crime. The establishment of reformatory institutions after 1860 was a recognition of the desirability of classifying prisoners, but such institutions did little in the way of improving methods of punishing or reforming juvenile offenders. The distinction between juveniles and adults in methods of determining guilt and of reformation came only with the establishment of juvenile courts and with legislation dealing with juvenile delinquency; the next logical step of abandoning the distinction between socially dependent and delinquent children, though increasingly made within social welfare institutions, was retarded by the constitutional rigidities of a federal system where social dependency was a provincial and crime a Dominion matter. In the field of prevention, reform efforts consisted largely of the public-playground movement and the establishment of juvenile and youth organizations chiefly under church leadership. Distinct advances were made in both directions, but vested interests, particularly of old established institutions, and public indifference checked the introduction of fundamental changes. Ultimately, attacks upon methods of dealing with juvenile delinquency involved an attack upon methods of dealing with crime in general, and here traditional interests offered more determined resistance. Though the work of voluntary associations such as the Salvation Army, and the appointment of royal commissions to inquire into penal methods, were indicative of the growing appreciation of the nature of the problem among certain sections of the community, eventual reform awaited more widespread changes in public attitudes.

Developments in Canada after 1900 provided new points of disturbance to the moral order. As in most rural frontiers, no serious problems of morality emerged in the rapidly expanding wheat-growing communities of western Canada, but in other areas which came into prominence after the turn of the century such problems tended to become widespread. Extractive industries grew up along the Precambrian Shield or within the mountain valleys of British Columbia, and here the predominance of men led to a weakening of mores associated with family life. The disintegration of moral standards which resulted from adjustments of such a large, purely male, population was not confined to these frontier communities. The chief centres of mining, lumbering, or of the pulp and paper industry were to be found in areas which skirted the thickly populated communities of central Canada or which reached back from the urban communities on the Pacific Coast. The presence of these male-populated centres within short railway distance of Montreal, Toronto, Winnipeg, or Vancouver constituted one of the most distinctive features of urban society in Canada and accounted in large part for the particular character of moral problems. Workers engaged in the outlying industries found their way readily into one of the cities, particularly during winter months; professional prostitutes serving the needs of a purely male population passed backwards and forwards between cities and centres in the hinterland. Vice suppression in the cities intensified the moral problems of the hinterland, while suppression in the hinterland intensified the problems of the cities. In addition to such influences, moral standards in Canadian cities were subject to the various disorganizing effects of rapid urban growth. The strains upon family organization, particularly of immigrant groups, resulting from the new conditions of life, the greater opportunities for sexual licence made possible by the breakdown of neighbourhood controls, and the demoralizing effects of starvation wages in marginal industries and service occupations, were evident in the increase of desertion, illegitimacy, and prostitution.

The predominantly rural background of the Canadian urban population checked effective movements of reform. Most of the immigration to Canada after 1900 came from European peasant districts, and, by segregation, the immigrants who settled in the city clung tenaciously to the strict mores which they brought with them. The rural–urban movement of population within Canada resulted in a similar transference of mores from an environment to which they were adapted to one to which they were not. The recruitment by Canadian cities of a peasant or rural population secured strong supports for traditional moral standards, but it retarded the adjustment of those standards to the new conditions of urban life. Puritanical moral controls within the family and community involved the heavy price of failing to meet some of the most crucial social problems of urban society. Prostitution, venereal disease, and illegitimacy taxed the resources of welfare and medical agencies so long as the first was treated as a crime and the other two as just punishments for sin. Reliance upon police controls and social ostracism served only to drive prostitution underground and to shroud the whole subject of sex under a veil of ignorance; commercialized vice, venereal disease, and illegitimacy rapidly increased in situations where even the discussion of sexual problems was strictly tabooed. These particular forms of social disorganization were part of the much larger problem of adjustment of moral standards in the urban community. The law, custom, and formal organization of Canadian cities were only slowly adapted to meet the new demands of urban life upon the individual and family group.

The development of industrial capitalism, urban growth, and the appearance of new outlying frontiers imposed heavy strains upon cultural organization. A Canadian proletariat grew rapidly as manufacturing extended throughout central Canada, and for a considerable interval agencies such as trade-union organizations were lacking to secure the social status of this class in the community. Conflicts of interest between employers and workers were typical of strains in cultural organization resulting from social divisions along economic, regional, ethnic, or religious lines. The increase in value of real-estate property in certain sections of the city, and building restrictions secured by property owners jealous of the advantages of exclusiveness, made possible a segregation of social classes which had been impossible in rural communities. The settlement of immigrant peoples in isolated groups accentuated the tendency for a number of cultural islands to develop in the city sharply separated from one another. Natural areas emerged in terms of processes of urban growth, and the boundaries of these areas coincided with cultural boundaries imposing strict limitations upon social intercourse. Consciousness of community lagged behind the erection of the urban physical structure, and community services rested upon no solid basis of collective sentiment. Efforts of those institutions which sought to develop a realization of common interests were offset by the activities of those institutions which emphasized cultural differences within the population. Even those institutions which presumably existed to serve the total community —churches, fraternal societies, and certain welfare organizations— recognized the reality of social divisions, and, indeed, tended to maintain such divisions, by organizing along class or ethnic lines. Cultural conflicts secured accommodation within the institutional structure, but these conflicts made impossible any sort of real integration in the total social organization of the urban community.

Cultural strains resulting from metropolitan expansion and urban growth extended into the rural hinterland of central and eastern Canada. The movement of population from the country to the city presented rural districts with problems of depopulation and a serious lack of leadership. There was no longer felt the invigorating influence of new population elements, and in some marginal farm communities isolation led to a degree of inbreeding dangerous to the physical and cultural welfare of the inhabitants. To some extent, closer contacts with the city, made possible by improved means of transportation and agencies of communication, served to offset the effects of the drain of the city upon the rural population. Rural organizations developed to capitalize upon the advantages of increased communication with the outside world and, at the same time, to assert the distinctiveness of the rural way of life. There was implied in the rise of such movements a realization of the threat of metropolitan expansion (in the form, for instance, of the tourist trade) to the rural culture. In areas where vigorous leadership was lacking, the rural culture suffered either through isolation or through the dominance of the nearby urban centres.

In the northern and western frontier areas of development, problems of cultural organization were very different. The absence of family life, and a concentration upon a single economic interest, had the effect of weakening cultural interests in the mining, pulp and paper, and lumbering communities of northern Quebec, Ontario, and the interior of British Columbia. Trade-union organizations made little headway, and the most active form of cultural association was to be found in nationalist groups. Fraternal societies, libraries, and educational institutions were erected only with the establishment of family life. In western Canada, the rapid growth of population, the settlement of large blocks of land by immigrants unacquainted with the English language and Canadian customs, and the concentration of people upon the task of making a living from wheat growing made difficult the creation of cultural institutions adequate to serve the needs of the community. The segregation of ethnic groups, in particular, limited social intercourse and weakened organizations depending upon the active participation of the members of the whole community. Social clubs, libraries, and other cultural institutions grew up slowly in the prairie towns and rural districts.

More serious still was the problem of providing elementary education to the large school-age population. The scattered nature of settlement, the lack of trained teachers, and the indifference to education of the foreign and of some of the English-speaking settlers were obstacles to the establishment of educational institutions. The considerable use of cash, however, in an agricultural region where wheat was the chief staple made possible the rapid accumulation of financial resources to support public schools, and an increasing number of trained teachers were recruited from eastern Canada as large salaries made teaching an attractive profession. Problems of education, and of cultural leadership generally, persisted in those areas where poor soil made farming a marginal industry or where foreign groups remained isolated from the English-speaking community. Throughout the prairies, the occurrence of drought seasons or sharp declines in the price of wheat resulted in placing heavy strains upon cultural institutions.

Other cultural problems evident in Canada after the First World War had already become apparent before 1914. The shift of the flow of the surplus labour force of rural Quebec from industrial centres in the United States to industrial centres within the province itself involved far-reaching adjustments in the cultural institutions of French Canada and raised new problems of conflict in the relationship of French and English peoples. The growing importance of the northern mining and pulp and paper frontiers in the economy and politics of central Canada hardened tendencies of regionalism in Canadian national life. The development of manufacturing in western Canadian cities, and rural–urban migration, had effects upon the older settled rural prairie districts, particularly Manitoba, similar to those which had become pronounced in central and eastern Canada. These and other problems were evidence of the continual emergence of new points of disturbance in Canadian cultural life. On the other hand, much had been accomplished by 1914 in the way of adjustment to conditions thrown up by industrial-capitalist expansion after the turn of the century. Trade-union movements in central Canada and farm movements in western Canada were typical of the sort of solutions being attained on the cultural level. More significantly still, the strengthening of national sentiment was indicative of far-reaching adjustments to the metropolitan organization of industrial capitalism. The nation emerged as something of a cultural focus in Canadian community life; national associations with headquarters in one of the larger cities and regional offices across the country provided a type of leadership in keeping with the demands of the new metropolitan economy.

Industrialization and expansion into the West and North widened the field of religious institutions and called for the development of radically new methods of organization and of new sorts of appeals. Churches organized on a national basis had grown up by the turn of the century and were much better equipped as a result than the earlier colonial denominations to meet the needs of rapidly growing and distant communities. The establishment of mission stations in western Canada was evidence of efforts to extend the field of religious ministrations. By 1900 leaders of most of the religious denominations had been thoroughly schooled in the needs of a rural society, and lessons learnt from experiences in older agricultural communities proved useful when the church moved into the western rural frontier. Yet many shortcomings in religious organization and appeal quickly became apparent in efforts to serve the scattered prairie settlements devoted to the raising of wheat. Denominational rivalry prevented effective co-operation, and centres of population were provided with far more churches than they required while isolated areas were left without regular services of any sort. Dominance by eastern interests in the councils of the churches, moreover, checked the development of an aggressive policy of championing the interests of western farmers. Unlike the evangelical sects of earlier Canadian rural frontiers which owed no close allegiance to any outside body and which could therefore crystallize in their religious appeal the political dissatisfactions of the population, the churches in western Canada found it necessary to avoid any close identification with economic or political interests. The failure to associate with powerful farm movements involved an immediate loss of influence in the western prairie communities and, in some instances, ultimately led to the emergence of new religious movements which combined their religious appeal with an appeal to economic and political dissatisfactions.

The failure of the church to align itself with new occupational interests and marginal social groups was even more conspicuous in the growing Canadian cities and their industrial hinterlands. The fact that urban communities in Canada inherited a culture largely agrarian in its origin enabled the churches to maintain an appearance of strength. But many of their most faithful followers were people who had moved from rural areas, and participation in religious activities represented a survival of habits of an older culture. Problems of an essentially urban or industrial-capitalist society lay largely outside the province of interest of the churches. The failure to develop a social philosophy offering any solution to the pressing problems of industrial workers—in the factory or in mining communities—had the effect of lessening the dependence of this section of the population upon religion. Successful business people tended to dominate in church politics, and the middle and upper classes came to form the chief body of church supporters, while skilled workers and the industrial proletariat turned increasingly to other agencies for leadership. When the church took the side of employers on issues such as strikes, as it sometimes did in the early years of the century, the loss of goodwill among the labouring population became still more pronounced, but even efforts to assume a neutral position did not keep the support of workers who felt the need of a positive policy on the part of the church. Among some of the leaders of the church, even before the First World War, there was a realization of the necessity of developing a more sympathetic and understanding approach to the problems of labour, but the defections from the church among working-class people indicated that such adjustments were not sufficiently extensive to maintain unimpaired the influence of religion.

The churches failed even more to meet the needs of that large section of the population upon the cultural fringe of the urban community: slum dwellers, transient workers, petty crooks, prostitutes, and others. These "outcasts" of polite society found no recognition within religious denominations. Respectability was a condition of membership in the church, and respectability was maintained by ignoring undesirable members of the population. Charitable contributions to the poor and sermons denouncing vice were means of preserving the isolation of these contaminating elements within the urban community. The psychological and philosophical assumptions of most of the leaders of the church, and the orthodox techniques of evangelization, made almost impossible the adoption of effective methods of dealing with problems such as the slum, crime, and prostitution. Some of the more enterprising of the churches undertook programmes of an experimental character, but early activities for the most part were confined to pious declarations from the pulpit.

Religious leadership among such marginal groups in the urban community came from new evangelical sects, particularly the Salvation Army. The rapid growth of this movement in Canada, with the immigration from Britain in the 1890's, paralleled the successes of the Methodist and Baptist revivalist sects in the early part of the century. The Army was a product of the industrial revolution, and its organization, techniques of preaching, and appeal were thoroughly adapted to the conditions of the urban environment. By 1900, it had made considerable inroads into the followings of the established denominations, and, if the rate of its growth fell off after 1914, it was because the traditional churches learnt valuable lessons from its experience. The securer establishment of the foundations of religion in urban society came with the recognition of the possibilities of evangelism among the newer sections of the population. In the pushing of religious influences into these frontier urban areas, the Salvation Army played a highly important role.

The First World War marked something of a transition in developments in Canada after the turn of the century. Social problems which had arisen in the period before the war had by no means secured complete solution, and new social problems emerged, but in many respects there was established some sort of equilibrium in social structure. Industrial-urban communities by 1914 had attained some degree of maturity, and most sections of the western prairies and the older established centres of the pulp and paper industry and of mining in the North had passed out of the raw frontier stage. If new areas still were being opened up, as in the Peace River district, and if industrialization was being extended beyond its former limits (into Quebec and the West), these developments did not become the dominant note in Canadian social life. Financial concentration, rather than the concentration of industrial plants, was the most marked economic tendency after the First World War. Social problems associated with industrial urbanism and metropolitan expansion in the 1920's were not essentially different from those social problems which had emerged during the early years of the century, and developments in the early period consequently provided a wealth of experience to meet the needs which arose in the later period. The elaboration of social welfare agencies, the growth of a familiarity with improved techniques in dealing with problems of crime and juvenile delinquency, the rise of a more realistic attitude to questions of morality, the establishment of organizations providing more vigorous cultural and educational leadership, and the broadening of religious programmes were an indication that reorganization had advanced considerably in the chief social institutions of the community. Much remained to be done it is true, but the most critical problems of Canadian communities after 1918 were no longer associated with the development of new economic enterprise and the opening up of new areas of economic exploitation.

War and depression imposed new and heavy strains upon institutions of social life, and adjustment to the conditions which arose from these developments became the chief problem of social organization. The sudden collapse after the inflationary boom in 1919 and the much more prolonged depression which followed the stock-market boom of 1929 were accompanied by widespread unemployment and acute economic dislocations in exposed areas. To some extent the problems of Canada were problems of the western world resulting from the First World War and national policies of economic autarchy. To a very considerable extent, however, the Canadian depressions represented the backwash of forces of frontier economic expansion which had run their course. Depletion of resources and loss of markets for staples were not something new in Canadian experience. Earlier frontier economic enterprises —the fur trade, fisheries, timber trade, wheat growing in central Canada, and gold mining in British Columbia—eventually encountered either or both of these limitations to expansion. But the decline of one frontier economic enterprise led quickly to the promotion of another. Expansion in new directions made possible the avoidance of general economic depression resulting from the economic recession of older industries. After 1920 until the Second World War no conspicuous new development took place to offset the depletion of the resources or the drying up of the markets of those frontier enterprises which had expanded rapidly in the early years of the century. The exhaustion of gold in the Yukon, the emergence of a dry belt in the western prairies, the disappearance of timber stands in northern lumber communities, the increasing overhead costs of and declining returns from the coal industry in Nova Scotia were problems of exposed areas which reached back into the whole Canadian economy. The social maladjustments resulting directly or indirectly from these economic dislocations became the major note in the social development of Canada in the years after 1920. They were an indication of the passing of the frontier stage of economic expansion; on the other hand, they gave emphasis to the importance of such expansion in the building of the Canadian community structure.

PART II

Religious Organization in the Development of the Canadian Community

Religious Organization
and the Rise of the
Canadian Nation, 1850–85*

I N   1824 the Canada Conference of the Methodist Episcopal Church was formed. In 1925 the United Church of Canada came into being. The story of Methodist development in Canada within this hundred-year period appears at first glance to be very largely a story of successful efforts to bring about the independence of the church of outside controls, and the union within one body of the different Methodist groups in the country. That was particularly true of developments within the period from 1850 to 1885. In 1850 there were five distinct Methodist churches in Canada and only a few less in the Maritime Provinces, most of them owing some attachment to outside ecclesiastical bodies. By 1885 these various churches had become united within one self-governing religious denomination—the Methodist Church of Canada.

Developments within the other leading Protestant denominations were not unlike those which took place within Methodism. With them, also, the movement seems to have been one of increasing union within the national community, and, again, this was particularly true of the period from 1850 to 1885. Though the Church of England faced no problem of disunity, except as related to the

*From *The Report of the Annual Meeting of the Canadian Historical Association*, 1944, pp. 86–96. With permission of the publisher.

conflict between high church and evangelical elements, the need of identifying itself more closely with the Canadian national community led first to the organization of synods within the various dioceses, beginning in 1857, then to the organization of provincial synods, beginning in 1861, and eventually to the organization of a general synod for Canada in 1893. By means of these constitutional adjustments, the Church of England in Canada emerged in fact as well as in name. The achievements of Presbyterianism in the same period were even more spectacular. In 1844 there were eleven separate Presbyterian churches in Canada and the Maritime Provinces, many of them closely tied up with mother churches in Scotland. By 1875 these eleven churches had given way to the one self-governing national church—the Presbyterian Church in Canada. The development of the other Protestant denominations followed very much the same pattern. Lutherans, Baptists, and Disciples of Christ, to mention only the more important, moved steadily in the direction of a closer identification with the Canadian national community during the years from 1850 to 1885.

The conclusion, therefore, would seem to be that the period from 1850 to 1885 was one characterized by a growing national consciousness within all the churches in Canada, not excepting, indeed, the Roman Catholic Church. Religious bodies which had grown up in the country without any close relation to the community in which they operated had come increasingly to identify themselves with that community in the form of the Canadian nation. The striking coincidences, within this period, in the development of religious, political, and economic organization appeared particularly to support the thesis that the movement in the direction of unity and national autonomy was a movement characteristic of all forms of association, including churches. Efforts of religious bodies to strengthen denominational organization and means of self-government derived support from, and in turn provided support to, such efforts in the political and economic field.

The history of the larger denominations after 1885 seems to confirm the view that the development of religious organization has been closely related to the development of a united autonomous nation. The union of the Methodist, Presbyterian, and Congregational churches in 1925 might well be considered as simply another step in the direction of a complete uniting of religious forces—or, at least, of Protestant religious forces—within the national community. Strengthening of means of denominational co-operation has been accompanied by a weakening of doctrinal differences. The increasing social consciousness of the churches has led not only to a closer identification with the national community but to an increasing awareness of the fact that the differences within their teachings were of little significance in relation to their common interest in promoting the cause of Christianity. It is not very easy to determine today, from the character of the religious service, the denominational affiliation of the particular Protestant church one may find himself in. War and depression have emphasized the singleness of purpose of religious organization.

These facts have been well recognized, and their significance is not questioned here. The movement towards closer union within the national community has certainly been one of the striking characteristics of recent developments in religious organization in other countries as well as in Canada. It may be questioned, however, whether this movement has proceeded in as unqualified a fashion as many church historians have assumed. The church historian has almost invariably been a historian associated with one of the large denominations; only such denominations can support schools of theology on a sufficiently high academic level to promote research in church history. The result is that a biased view of religious development has tended to prevail. Church history has been written very largely in terms of the history of those denominations which have attained a position of respectability in the community; only passing notice has been given to the role of religious movements operating on the social fringe of the community. This has been particularly true of church history in Canada. Developments of the past have been viewed in relation to the position of the larger denominations of today; an evolutionary conception of growth has been accepted. The result, it is submitted, is a distorted picture. It would be no more unjustifiable to view religious developments in Canada as culminating in the rise of the Jehovah's Witnesses than it is to view such developments as culminating in the formation of the United Church of Canada. When religious developments in Canada are viewed as a whole, rather than as something relating simply to the larger denominations, a very different picture emerges. It becomes evident then that the movement within religious organization in the direction of a closer union within the community has almost invariably been accompanied by a movement in the opposite direction of division and separation from the community.

This was true of religious developments within Nova Scotia after

1760 with the growth of Protestant settlement and the establishment in the country of Protestant churches. Congregationalism, which was carried over from New England as a part of the social structure of the village community, shortly broke up into a number of divided churches in Nova Scotia as a result of the religious revival promoted by Henry Alline. The Newlight movement involved a disintegration of the ties of church and village and the organization of religion free of any entanglements with the community; the worldliness of the church gave way to the other-wordliness of the sect. Similarly, efforts of the Church of England to secure its position as the established church of the province received a sharp check with the rise of the Methodist movement under William Black which, like the Newlight movement, disavowed temporal ties of any sort. Newlightism and Methodism represented a break away from a traditional order of political patronage and social status and a reassertion of the purely religious message of individual salvation. It was no accident that these movements grew up during the period of the American War of Independence and the migration of United Empire Loyalists. Revolution and migration imposed heavy strains upon both the political ties of Empire and the social ties of the local village. To a population cut off from the traditional controls of a secular society, the religious message of the evangelical sect provided a new basis for fellowship and belief.

By the end of the century, the Newlight and Methodist movements had become the dominant forces in the religious life of Nova Scotia and also of New Brunswick. Striking changes, however, by then had become apparent in the character of these movements. With the shift of the Newlights to a Baptist position and the organization of a Baptist Association in 1800, and with the break of the Methodists from American sectarianism and their tie with the English Wesleyan Conference in the same year, there emerged out of the earlier Newlight and Methodist evangelical sects the Baptist and Wesleyan Methodist churches closely associated with the political-social order of the community which they served. These developments are the sort seized upon by the church historian in support of the view that a movement towards union and autonomy has characterized the growth of churches in the country. The important fact is overlooked that the establishment of Baptist and Methodist denominational organization in 1800 was followed by the emergence of new evangelical sects—the Newlights as a religious group separate from the Baptists, the Freewill Baptists, the Scotch

Baptists, Bible Christians, Primitive Methodists, Methodist Protestants, Campbellites, and others.

Efforts of the Baptist and Methodist churches to identify their interests more closely with the interests of the community—evident, for instance, in the support given to the establishment of educational institutions and to temperance reform—led to a strengthening of their social position, but at the price of weakening their position of religious leadership among those masses of the population standing on the social fringe of the community. The growth of the timber trade and of trade with the West Indies, and the rise of the ship-building industry, brought new wealth to the Maritime Provinces and supported tendencies towards a sharpening of class divisions within the colonial society, but these developments also promoted increased mobility of population and the extension of settlement into areas of the country hitherto populated only by Indians and Acadian French. It was within these areas of change of population that the newer evangelical sects gained their chief support. The Freewill Baptist movement grew very rapidly in western Nova Scotia and in New Brunswick, the Scotch Baptists and Bible Christians exerted their greatest influence in Prince Edward Island, while such sects as the Primitive Methodists were most active in the rapidly growing town of Saint John. The principle of the sect, of separation of the religious body from the community, persisted in the religious organization of the Maritime Provinces at least until well past the end of the first half of the nineteenth century. The reason is to be found in the persistence during this period of a condition where the opening up of new areas of social life offered challenges to a traditional order of social status in the community.

If attention is directed to Upper Canada, much the same pattern is evident in the development of religious organization. The spread of Methodist and Baptist movements from the United States into Upper Canada followed the rapid settlement of the country with the conclusion of the American War of Independence in 1783 and the Indian War in the West in 1795. The early Methodist and Baptist preachers, notwithstanding charges by spokesmen of the traditional churches that they were foreign agitators intent on promoting republican ideas of government, were interested in only one thing—the salvation of individual souls. They interpreted their function as one which had nothing to do with the jurisdiction of states or philosophies of political parties. Thus they challenged the political privileges and claims of the Church of England and the Church of

Scotland, not by attacking these churches, but by withdrawing themselves from the community and promoting the establishment of an order of society on a purely spiritual basis. This character of the early Methodist movement needs to be emphasized in particular because of the tendency to associate the name of the political-minded Egerton Ryerson so closely with its development, overlooking the fact that the movement had existed for over a quarter of a century in the country before the Ryerson brothers joined its ranks. During that earlier period of Methodist growth, the movement assumed very much the character of a religious sect.

The pamphlet written by Egerton Ryerson attacking the position taken by the Rev. John Strachan in promoting the cause of the Church of England represented a fundamental shift in the Methodist viewpoint. The Methodist and Baptist movements had grown out of the social situation of the backwoods community. With overseas immigration, particularly of people with wealth, and the growth of towns, strains within the organization of these evangelical sects became evident, and adjustment involved a strengthening of ties with the community. Union of the Canadian Methodists and English Wesleyans in 1832, which gave rise to the Wesleyan Methodist Church of Canada, involved an almost complete abandonment of the sect principle of separation from the secular world. The growing importance of the Methodist religious journal—the *Christian Guardian*—and the increasing participation of Methodist leaders in politics, brought new sources of strength to the Methodist denomination in the political and social order of the colony. Likewise, the tie of the Canadian Baptists with the English Baptists in 1837, and the organization of the Canada Baptist Union in 1843, resulted in a considerable weakening of the sect principle of other-worldliness and in a strengthening of the social supports of the Baptist denomination. It is not insignificant that the work of the Rev. Egerton Ryerson, the most prominent of the leaders within the Wesleyan Methodist Church, was largely associated with the towns of Toronto and Kingston, while the work of the Rev. John Gilmour, equally prominent within the Canada Baptist Union, was largely associated with the towns of Montreal and Peterborough. The Methodist and Baptist churches oriented themselves increasingly about the new centres of social and political influence.

As in the Maritime Provinces, however, such tendencies towards a greater integration within the colonial structure were offset by tendencies towards religious division and withdrawal from the secular world. The union of Canadian Methodism and English Wesleyanism in 1832 was followed almost immediately by a break of a number of local preachers from the Canadian Conference and the organization of the Methodist Episcopal Church of Canada. At the same time, new Methodist sects entered the country—the Primitive Methodists in 1830, the Bible Christians in 1831, and the Methodist New Connexion in 1837. The Baptists were also faced with a problem of religious division and conflict. Organization of the Canada Baptist Union in 1843 led to schisms within a large number of the local churches and in the organization of the Regular Baptist Union of Canada in 1848 with membership confined to strict Baptist churches. The separation of the close communionists from the open communionists represented a break in Baptist ranks which reached much deeper than doctrinal differences; the intolerance of the close communionists was an intolerance of a religious sect which set itself solidly against the more worldly attitude of their open communion brethren. The multiplication in the number of Methodist and Baptist groups after 1830 was accompanied by the spread of new religious movements into the country. The Christian Church, Disciples of Christ, Irvingites, Mormons, Millerites, and Davidites were some of the religious sects which came to exert a considerable influence in Canada in the years from 1830 to 1850. The shift in religious organization back to the principle of the sect indicated very clearly that the conditions which had promoted the rise of the Methodist and Baptist movements in the first place had not disappeared. The extension of backwoods settlement, and the growth of public works, had the effect of throwing up new "social masses" made up of people who lacked status within the established social order of the community. Status was attained by such people within the religious order in the separation of the "elect" from the unsaved of the world, and in the substitution of spiritual for secular standards of social worth. Thus the movement within religious organization in the direction of a closer identification with the values of the outside world could be carried only so far. The sect principle in religious organization continued with the persistence of conditions of social disequilibrium.

After 1850, again, in spite of achievements in the way of church union, tendencies towards religious division were not completely absent. The Plymouth Brethren, Christadelphians, and a number of other sects made their appearance in Canada within the period 1850–85. Nevertheless, the view that the development of religious

organization in this period was characterized by an increasing movement towards unity and autonomy is substantially correct. The
explanation of such a movement, however, was not to be found in
any general principle of evolution but rather in conditions which
were peculiar to the social situation at that time. The kind of
church unity which became established was the kind associated with
a social system which had no further means of expansion. After
1850 Canada was left without any real frontier; population movement was largely into the United States—to the rapidly growing
industrial cities of the East and to the rapidly settling prairies of the
West. What frontier areas Canada possessed—in her pioneer industrial towns along the Grand Trunk Railway and in her government-
sponsored agricultural settlements in Muskoka—had a population
too small to support any significant movement of social or religious
reorganization. Within the new mining towns of British Columbia,
movements growing out of a condition of social unrest were not
lacking, but the population of these mining towns was largely a
male population which sought other than religious means of social
expression. The emphasis in religious organization in Canada, as a
result, was upon consolidation; upon efforts to control the home
market. Church union, like confederation or associations of economic
groups, was a protective device. Religious enterprise could no more
afford the wastes of competition than economic enterprise. Both
found support in the strengthening of ties with the state. Sabbath
observance laws, in the same way as tariffs, were means of enlisting the support of the state in meeting what was considered unfair
competition. This alliance of the churches with the secular community in promoting the interests of a moral order was one which
met with little challenge from religious bodies disavowing any
connection with the secular community because of the absence of
conditions disturbing to an established order of social status.
The sect gave way almost entirely to the church, and the cause
of national solidarity was furthered by the close identification
of religious organization with the organization of the national
community.

That condition came to an abrupt halt about 1885. Almost the
very year which witnessed the union of the Methodist churches in
Canada witnessed also the rise of the Holiness Church and the
Salvation Army. During the thirty years from 1885 to 1914, new
evangelical movements grew very rapidly in the country; abandoned

Salvation Army temples in a great many small towns in Ontario today afford an idea of the strength of this religious body about 1900. In some of the larger cities, evangelical mission churches, without any denominational connection, made their appearance, and the size of their Sunday as well as week-day congregations attested to the declining influence of the traditional religious denominations. Efforts on the part of the older churches to forestall the growth of the new evangelical sects were not lacking, in the establishment, for instance, of city missions, but these efforts for the most part were ineffectual. Among very large sections of the Canadian population after 1885—in the new and isolated prairie settlements and in the transitional areas of the growing cities—the evangelical sect crowded out the traditional church.

The instabilities of religious organization were closely related to the instabilities of the Canadian community structure after 1885. The opening of the West, the discovery of gold in the Yukon, and industrial growth in central Canada led to new movements of population and to the emergence of social conditions unfavourable to an established order of social status. The rise of the Holiness Church and the Salvation Army coincided with the completion of the Canadian Pacific Railway. The organization of mission churches and the spread of the Pentecostal movement into Canada took place during the years which witnessed the promotion of amalgamations in Canadian industry, industrial concentration in strategic urban centres, and the construction of two new transcontinental railways. The evangelical preaching of the Rev. P. W. Philpott in Hamilton in the early years of the present century was a social phenomenon not unrelated to the establishment by American manufacturing enterprises of branch plants in the country. Growth of population and increasing population mobility reflected the expansion of economic life, and, in turn, were reflected in the growth in variety of religious sects. The "closed frontier" of 1850–85 which restricted the development of new religious movements gave way to the "open frontier" of 1885–1914 which promoted the breakdown of the established religious order and the emergence of new religious divisions.

Developments in religious organization since 1914 have taken place too near in time to be clearly discerned, but certain tendencies seem evident. Those evangelical religious movements which took their rise within the period 1885–1914 have moved steadily in the

direction of a greater accommodation with the community in which
they operate. That tendency is very obvious in the case of the Salvation Army. In spite of control from headquarters, the Army in
Canada has become very much a Canadian Army, while, at the
same time, social pressures have led to a shift away from the position of the religious sect; the Army has assumed increasingly the
character of a social service agency. Such a development has not
been unrelated to developments taking place within the older
religious denominations; the increasing emphasis upon social service
activities among them also has been evident in the emergence of the
institutional church with its imposing buildings housing swimming
pools, gymnasia, and facilities for club meetings, and with its elaborate administrative organization. The humble origin of the Salvation Army may still be reflected in the social standing of the majority of its following, but an increasing number of wealthy patrons
indicates a move in the direction of increased respectability. The
other evangelical sects which took their rise before 1914 have been
faced with much the same sort of problems of adjustment though
social accommodation has not gone quite as far as in the case of the
Salvation Army. The organization in 1919 of the Pentecostal Assemblies of Canada is significant as indicating an effort to relate
the Pentecostal movement more closely to the Canadian national
community. Change in the form of organization of the movement
was accompanied by fundamental changes in its social basis.

Yet a glance at developments in religious organization in
Canada after 1919 is sufficient to dispel any notion that there was
an uninterrupted movement towards religious union and closer
identification with the national community. Organization of the
Pentecostal Assemblies of Canada was followed by religious
schisms which gave rise to a number of new Pentecostal sects under
different names. Union of the Methodist, Presbyterian, and Congregational churches not only left in its wake a continuing Presbyterian Church more fundamentalist than the old, but a great
number of unused church buildings which were taken up by various
evangelical sects or by free-lance evangelical preachers. In Alberta,
union was followed by the almost complete breakdown of denominationalism with the rise of the Social Credit movement. It is not
sufficient to answer that these new religious movements were mere
ripples in the religious current which did not affect the direction
of flow of the main stream; the break of Luther from the Church

of Rome or of Wesley from the Church of England might likewise have been viewed by contemporaries as a mere ripple in the religious current. The new evangelical sects in Canada after 1919 grew out of social disturbances related to new developments in the community. The strength of these sects in northern Alberta and Saskatchewan, in the mining towns of northern Ontario, and in the newer industrial communities of central Canada and the West in the 1920's and 1930's suggests the close relation between their rise and the emergence of new "social masses" on the fringe of the social order.

From this it would seem apparent that developments in religious organization in Canada in the years after the First World War were following along lines very similar to those which had been followed earlier. Throughout, a movement towards a strengthening of the ties of church and community was accompanied by a movement in the opposite direction of a separation of the religious from the secular order. Such a development was inevitable in the very nature of the religious institution. The religious sect, the moment it was organized, came to be made up of people holding office, and the prestige attached to such office was determined very largely by the social position of the religious body in the community. Salaries could be paid, and large church edifices constructed, only if financial contributions could be secured from the wealthy or, at least, from the well-to-do. Thus, inevitably, the religious sect came increasingly to accommodate itself to the secular order. Secular values permeated its teachings; the energies of its leaders were directed into channels of community endeavour. The result was, in the end, that the status system of the religious order came to coincide with the status system of the social order. The religious sect passed from being a sect to become a church.

In doing so, it did not cease to perform its religious function, but it did cease to perform the social function of providing leadership to those foot-loose elements of the population which had no recognized place within the established social order. The person, for instance, of rural background who found himself in the rapidly growing city was essentially a person cut adrift from society. His integration into the new society could be brought about only through a redefinition of standards of social worth. Such a redefinition could be secured in the fellowship of the saloon where worth was measured in terms of the tippler's capacity to consume.

It was secured very effectively in the fellowship of the religious sect where worth was associated with the convert's degree of spirituality. The insistence on the part of the sect that it was not of the temporal world derived not from any peculiarity of religious doctrine but simply from its peculiar social function. It separated itself from the traditional social order in erecting a new social order in which status was given a spiritual basis. Thus the other-worldliness of the sect sprang from social pressures which were as insistent as the pressures which determined the worldliness of the church.

The effect of social influences tending towards sectarianism has been strikingly evident in the development of Protestantism in Canada. Whether it has been equally evident in the development of Roman Catholicism is a question not considered in this paper. It may be suggested, however, that the differences in the development of Protestantism and Roman Catholicism are more apparent than real. In French Canada after 1760, the Roman Catholic Church developed within a closed social system, and there were as a result few pressures of a kind which threatened the close tie between church and community. Where those pressures have arisen, the church has sought adjustment through an extension of its system of religious orders; the new religious order assumed very much the character of the new religious sect. Thus within Roman Catholicism, as within Protestantism, there has been a shifting away from, as well as a shifting towards, a worldly position in the community, the only difference being that in the case of Roman Catholicism it has usually taken place within the framework of the Church. That, however, has not invariably been the case. There have not been lacking in Canada reformation movements not greatly different from the Protestant Reformation in Europe in the fifteenth and sixteenth centuries. It is only necessary here to call attention to the recent schism within the Ukrainian Catholic Church in Canada. Other less spectacular, but no less significant, examples could be found. Furthermore, there has probably been a greater shift of Roman Catholics to Protestant religious sects than is generally realized.

One difference has to be recognized between the development of Roman Catholicism and Protestantism. The Roman Catholic Church has been able to a greater degree to check or control movements of its adherents into new areas of development, and in Roman Catholic communities there has been less as a result of that unrestricted type of development associated with frontier movements of population. This fact, however, provides no reason for qualifying the thesis set forth in this paper. To the extent that a closed social system obtained, regardless of the nature of the forces which promoted such a condition, the full identification of religious organization with the community was possible. Consequently, where a church was able to control effectively a social system in the way of preventing any development unfavourable to its position, conditions were established which stifled the free operation of processes of social expansion.

This is simply another way of saying that religious systems are dynamic only so long as social systems are. There is no intention in this paper to suggest that tendencies towards division and sectarianism are at all times characteristic of religious development. Such tendencies obviously are not characteristic of religious development in isolated primitive societies nor were they of religious development under feudalism. In a primitive society the conditions of a closed social system are maintained through the heavy weight of what Bagehot called the "cake of custom," and in feudal society they were maintained through the authoritarian controls of a rigid institutional order. Furthermore, for very much the same reasons, a tendency towards division and sectarianism has been less evident in the religious development of Canada than of the United States. Forces of expansion in American national life have been a great deal stronger than such forces in Canadian national life; the American frontier developed unchecked by political and cultural influences of traditional authority which operated so powerfully within the Canadian frontier. The result has been that established religious systems have found even less support within the social order. Union of churches and their identification with the national community have proceeded much more slowly than in Canada; division and separation of religious organization from the community have assumed a great deal more prominence. Religious sectarianism, indeed, had its principles written into the formal constitution of the Republic!

These considerations suggest that the sectarian religious movements with which we are familiar have been movements closely related to the commercial and industrial expansion of the western world during the past three or four centuries. It is true, of course, that very similar movements emerged much earlier in the development of Christianity and were particularly evident during the eleventh and twelfth centuries, but there was a period in between, associated with the high-water mark in feudal development, when a condition of stability in religious organization tended to prevail. It was with the breakdown of the feudal order that there were unleashed forces of expansion in economic and social life which resulted in an upsetting of established religious systems. The conflict which emerged, centred about the issue of church and state, was very largely a conflict between the church and sect ideas of religious organization, and, as such, it was not essentially different from the conflict in religious organization in more recent times, even though what has been known as the state church has ceased to exist. The long struggle of the Baptists, for instance, to free religion from the control of the state was simply an expression of the sect principle that the spiritual and temporal belonged to separate worlds. The struggle in this instance took the form of challenging vested interests of land and office because the church which was attacked was a church which clung to feudal types of relations within the community. When attention is directed to the efforts of Pentecostal sects in Canada to purify religious teachings, the point of attack is not greatly different; it is the relation of the church to the community which is challenged. That relation, over the years, has changed somewhat in character—financial contributions from wealthy citizens (many of them, in fact, not belonging to the church to which they contribute), and propaganda and lobbying, have taken the place of grants of public land and prerogatives of public office—but it still rests upon a body of vested interests in the community.

With the rise of nationalism in the western world, the identification of the church with the community has come very largely to be an identification with that particular form of community which is known as the nation. One of the fullest expressions of such identification is to be found in one of our own churches, the United Church of Canada, but this tendency has been characteristic of the development of religious organization generally. Even churches which have claimed to be universal have found it necessary to exploit national sentiment in the interests of solidarity. It is not without reason, therefore, that considerable emphasis has been placed by church historians upon the close relation between religious and nationalist movements. What is so often overlooked, however, is the fact that nation building, like empire building, involved a very considerable upsetting of traditional social relations; nationalism was closely associated with rapid economic expansion in terms of metropolitan centres and free enterprise, and the folk cultures of the local community disintegrated in face of the intrusion of the pecuniary conventions of the national community. Thus tendencies in religious organization towards a closer identification with the national community resulting from the rise of nationalism have been offset by tendencies towards religious division growing out of conditions of social disequilibrium produced by economic expansion through free enterprise. National unity in the past has depended upon the operation of forces making for disunity as well as unity in the social structure of the community.

It may be that movements of sectarianism will be much less evident in the future development of religious organization. Nationalism in recent years has come increasingly to depend upon the control of economic enterprise, and the nation state, like the earlier feudal state, may very well succeed as a result in erecting about itself a closed social system. The almost complete identification of religious organization with the nation under such circumstances would be inevitable. Economic forces which check any easy rise in the individual's social position in the community lend support to a movement in the direction of a rigid organization of religious life. Thus, while many Methodists and Baptists in Canada in the nineteenth century became rich and the change in their social status carried with it changes in the social position of the churches to which they belonged, the Jehovah's Witnesses and Four Square Gospellers of today may remain forever poor with the result that the religious sect of today may be the religious sect of tomorrow. If that should be the case the stratifications within the religious structure would assume much more of a feudal character. Present religious divisions would be perpetuated, and the historic role of the religious sect in forcing adjustment within religious organization would be brought to an end.

The very existence, indeed, of the religious sect would be jeopardized in face of the powerful combination of church and state. The legal ban placed upon the Jehovah's Witnesses in Canada during the Second World War could be considered an act justified in terms of the military crisis, but it had a significance which reached far beyond the problem growing out of the situation produced by war. There was much in the character of the Jehovah's Witnesses which was a painful reminder of the Anabaptist sects in Europe at the time of the Protestant Reformation. Religious sects by their very nature are at war with society, but where conditions are such that eventual accommodation is possible, this act of war assumes the form of a withdrawal into a spiritual world. Where, however, eventual accommodation is denied, the sect's reaction may be one of militant aggressiveness in an effort to make over society to its liking. Thus a strengthening of the ties of church and community through the support of the state results almost inevitably in forcing deviant religious movements into a revolutionary position, and the acceptance of such a position brings about in the end their extinction through the action of the state. Out of such a development state and church would emerge as one.

CHAPTER VIII

The Religious Sect in Canadian Politics*

THIS PAPER IS CONCERNED with the part played by evangelistic religious movements in Canadian politics and, more particularly, with their influence upon the development of liberal political thought in the country. It has been assumed by most students of Canadian church history that the evangelistic religious movements, through the support of radical programmes of political reform, have made substantial contributions to liberal thought. This paper contends that such a view has been based upon a superficial examination of the facts. While it is true that the evangelical churches have at times lent support to the cause of political radicalism, it is questionable whether such support has been nearly as significant as supposed in revealing their political thinking. It is argued here that the political activities of the evangelical churches have not grown out of a deeply embedded political philosophy and that the real contribution to the development of liberal principles of government must be sought not in their activities but rather in the peculiar role of the religious sect out of which the evangelical churches had developed. Discussion of the part played by evangelistic religious movements in politics compels consideration of the political influence of the sect as well as the church.

For the purposes of this paper, it seems best to confine the discussion to three evangelical groups which have played an important role in Canadian politics: the Baptists in Nova Scotia, the

*From the *American Journal of Sociology*, LI, no. 3, Nov., 1945, pp. 207–16. With permission of the publisher.

Methodists in Upper Canada, and the followers of William Aberhart in Alberta. The contribution of these groups to the cause of
political radicalism has been well recognized.

In Nova Scotia the Baptists constituted a distinctive revolutionary
force in religious and social life toward the close of the eighteenth
century, and early movements of political reform owed much to
their indirect and direct support. Similarly, in Upper Canada, the
Methodists, in the two decades of political turmoil after the war of
1812–14, strongly supported radical political movements in the
country in opposition to the Family Compact; and the close
working alliance which grew up between Egerton Ryerson, the
acknowledged leader of the Methodist Church, and William Lyon
Mackenzie, the leader of the Reform party, was indicative of the increasing active participation of Methodists in politics. The radical
political implications of the religious movement in Alberta founded
by William Aberhart are obvious: the Social Credit party, with its
sweeping programme of monetary reform, grew directly out of
Aberhart's Prophetic Bible Institute. Here, very definitely, political
revolt was born out of a movement which had grown up on a
religious foundation.

A combination of forces led to this alignment of the evangelical
churches with radical movements in the country. In the first place,
vested interests of denominationalism tended to produce such an
alignment. The evangelical churches found themselves opposed by
the old, traditional churches closely associated with the state or
with ruling parties in the state. The Baptists in Nova Scotia and the
Methodists in Upper Canada were compelled to fight church establishment to secure the rights to which they felt themselves entitled
as religious denominations, and, in fighting church establishment,
they inevitably found themselves fighting all the forces of special
privilege and reaction in the country. Somewhat similarly, William
Aberhart, in attacking the claims of the powerful and wealthy
churches represented in Alberta, many of them with strong creditor
interests in the province, found himself launching out in an attack
upon those business and political interests which largely supported,
and in turn were supported by, these churches. The evangelical
church, the moment it became denominationally conscious, very
naturally championed the cause of religious freedom in one form
or another, and such championship threw it on the side of political
radicalism in the country.

Strong social forces as well, however, tended to an identification of the evangelical churches with the cause of political radicalism. Of these, regional-economic interests were by far the most important. Their effect was to strengthen greatly the tendencies deriving from denominational interests.

The political affiliations of the evangelical churches were determined by the kind of area from which they drew their support. The established or traditional churches were the churches of the metropolis. Their most imposing houses of worship were located in the better residential sections of the larger centres of population; their most successful ministers occupied city pulpits. Within governmental centres, in particular, their influence tended to be dominant. They gave expression to the interests of Empire or nation. The evangelical churches, on the other hand, grew up as religious sects on the social fringes of the community. Their emergence as new sects represented efforts of scattered or downtrodden folk, neglected by the traditional churches, to develop a form of religious fellowship on their own. It was in outlying areas of the country, or within working-class sections of the city, that sectarian activity flourished.

Thus the separatism of the sect, its efforts to separate itself from the worldly society, became, within the evangelical church, closely related to political separatist movements in the hinterland or in marginal urban areas. The political reaction against the control of the metropolis—the struggle to secure a greater measure of local political autonomy—found support in, and in turn supported, the isolationism of the religious sect. Rebellion in the backlands expressed itself usually in religious as well as in political form; few movements of political independence in history have been unrelated to movements of religious schism. The attempt of Brigham Young in Utah to bring into being a theocratic state largely independent of the federal authority provides possibly the best example on this continent of the combination of sectarian religious and frontier political separatism, but similar forces in Canada led to like forms of political and religious expression.

The struggle of the Baptists in Nova Scotia in the late eighteenth century to secure an independent religious life was simply a part of the much larger struggle of the Nova Scotian out-settlements to resist the domination of Halifax and to free themselves from the restrictions of the British colonial system. The collapse of Congregationalism had followed upon the break of Nova Scotia from New England with the American Revolution, and the rise of the New-light Baptist movement represented an effort to strengthen the position of the out-settlements which had lost the support of the tie with New England. The aggressive separatism of the new religious sect was not unrelated to the efforts of the town meeting to control local village affairs, to the refusal of local magistrates to convict for offences against unpopular colonial laws, and, during the Revolution, to smuggling and tax evasion, and, after the Revolution, to the conflict between the Assembly and the Council and the growing demand for responsible government.

Similarly, the struggle of Methodism in Upper Canada became closely tied up with efforts of the backwoods farm communities to free themselves from the controls of centralized land-granting, taxing, and road-building authorities. The chief strength of the traditional churches, and especially of the Church of England and Church of Scotland, was in the larger towns and the provincial capital. These churches represented the official classes of the community—the classes which had a stake in the imperial connection —but made no effective effort to serve the outlying backwoods farm population. Political dissatisfactions of people who, because of their isolation, had little voice in government, found expression in religious separatism. Methodism grew rapidly in outlying sections of the country and supported efforts to secure a greater measure of local independence and colonial autonomy.

The close relation between frontier political and religious sectarian separatism can be seen even more clearly in Alberta in the religious-political movement led by Aberhart. Aberhart's break with the traditional organization of religion forced him into an isolationist position. The dominance of the national churches became closely associated in his eyes, and in the eyes of his followers, with the dominance of the large eastern cities and of the federal authority. On the other hand, the religious separatism of Aberhart's new sect—its attempt to stand apart from the worldly society—became closely associated with the political separatism of such a frontier area as Alberta. It was not difficult for Aberhart to translate the religious exclusiveness of the Prophetic Bible Institute into a political exclusiveness, once he became leader of the Social Credit party. The society of the elect found expression now in political terms. It was not without significance that some of the more prominent members of the Social Credit Government belonged to the Mormon church in southern Alberta. The religious-political experiment in Alberta resembled very closely that tried much earlier in Utah; in both cases, religious separatism sought support in political separatism, and encroachments of the federal authority were viewed as encroachments of the worldly society.

Regional interests which found expression in movements of religious and political separatism were closely related to economic interests. The society of the backlands or of the urban working-class area was a debtor society. The religious sect attracted the support not only of the isolated but of the economically dispossessed. It provided a cheap religion in that it did not make heavy financial demands for the support of elaborate places of worship and highly educated clergymen. Furthermore, it provided, in the way of preaching appointments, occupational opportunities for young men (and, in some cases, young women) who did not have the means of securing the training necessary for a professional career. It was the poor fishermen and farmers of Nova Scotia who largely comprised the early following of the Baptist Church. The debt-ridden farmers of the Upper Canadian backwoods communities rallied about the banner of the Methodist itinerant preachers. Aberhart secured his greatest support, both as a religious evangelist and as a political campaigner, in that area of Alberta stretching northeast from Calgary to the Saskatchewan border, the approximate centre of which is the town of Hanna. It was here that the drought was most fully felt.

The message of the religious evangelist as a result became easily translated into economic panaceas of various sorts. Magical remedies were seized upon to solve problems of the economic system just as patent medicines and the prescriptions of the quack are seized upon to deal with bodily ills. Monetary experiments, in particular, have tended to be closely related to religious experiments in the means of salvation. Resort to the use of scrip or to the establishment of special banks served the purpose of strengthening the isolation of the religious group and, at the same time, of offering a solution to the problem of debt. The close relation between sectarian techniques of religious control and monetary techniques of economic and political control has been most evident, of course, in the Social Credit experiment in Alberta; here the Mormon members of the Government in particular had a perfectly good historic example in the use of scrip and the carrying-on of banking operations by the Mormons in Utah. Awareness of monetary solutions of economic problems was less fully developed among the earlier evangelical religious groups in Canada, but the pressures of a rigid credit system in the hands of the merchant class in Nova

Scotia and Upper Canada, and the shortage of money, led to economic dissatisfactions which found expression among Baptists and Methodists in demands for economic reforms not unlike those of Social Credit.

The denominational, regional, and economic interests of the evangelical churches were probably most responsible for their support of radical political movements in the community. To some extent, as well, the nature of the evangelical religious appeal in itself may have contributed to a fostering of an attitude of political radicalism. Such an appeal involved a sharp break from traditional theological systems; theological trappings, and an elaborate ritualistic system, were cut through to emphasize the elementary problem of man's relation to his God. At the same time, conversion involved an equally sharp break with his past for the individual. The effect of this was to encourage an untraditional approach to problems of life in general. It was for this reason that followers of new religious sects often became the most active in promoting novel types of economic activity. Something of the experimental attitude was carried over into politics as well.

These considerations suggest the nature of some of the more important factors favouring the alignment of the evangelical churches with radical political forces in the community. It would be a mistake to conclude from this, however, that these churches have invariably lent support to the cause of radicalism. If the political activities of the Baptists in Nova Scotia, the Methodists in Upper Canada, and the followers of William Aberhart in Alberta are examined further, it will be found that these groups, while at times supporting radical political movements, have at other times constituted a distinctive conservative influence in the community. Indeed, in the decisive tests of strength between opposing political forces in the country, they have more often thrown their weight on the side of conservatism. This fact has to be recognized before any conclusion can be drawn respecting the relation of the evangelical churches to political thought.

In Nova Scotia, in the second quarter of the nineteenth century, opposition to the non-sectarian educational policy of Joseph Howe, the leader of the Reform party, led the Baptists to shift to the Conservatives in the province. It was a prominent Baptist—J. W. Johnson—who became the leader of the Conservative party, and the votes of the Baptist population were decisive in bringing about the defeat of the Reformers in the election of 1843. Likewise, in

Upper Canada, the early alliance between the Methodists and Reformers was sharply broken in 1833, when Egerton Ryerson came out in opposition to William Lyon Mackenzie; and in the election of 1836, and again in the election of 1844, the Methodist vote was at least in part responsible for the Tory victories. Even moderate reform leaders, like the Baldwins, were unable to rely upon Methodist support. In Alberta similar tendencies were evident within the combination erected by Aberhart out of religious and political materials. Aberhart himself never really ceased to be a conservative in political outlook, and the political party which he founded moved steadily in a conservative direction. The radicalism which persisted within the party came very largely from elements which became a part of the political movement after 1935 but which were quite unrelated to the religious movement led by Aberhart. Frontier agrarianism continued to force the party into a radical position, but radical tendencies were sharply checked by the strength of sectarian religious influences.

Factors which at one time favoured the alignment of the evangelical churches with political reform in the community favoured their alignment with conservative forces at another. Denominational vested interests changed in character as the evangelical church became less concerned about the privileges enjoyed by the older, established churches in the community and more concerned about protecting privileges which it itself had secured. The sect grew into the church and, in doing so, found its interests more closely identified with the interests of the traditional churches. Promotion of such objects as education, temperance, and Sabbath observance forced the evangelical church into opposition to religious movements more evangelistically aggressive, and secular movements which threatened the teachings of religion. Baptist Church leaders in Nova Scotia and Methodist Church leaders in Upper Canada increasingly directed their fire against the new religious sects which sprang up in the community, while by 1935 Aberhart in Alberta was feeling very keenly the competition of rival radio evangelists in Calgary. Subsequently his churches in the country were steadily crowded out by churches organized by the new sects. The threat of the loss of some of its members to other religious bodies weakened in the evangelical church an interest in the cause of religious freedom, and only in those churches, such as the Quakers and some of the smaller Baptist groups, where the spirit of the sect remained strong, have liberal principles been adhered to consistently. Denominationalism tended to make the more prosperous evangelical churches increasingly dependent upon the state and the community at large.

At the same time the evangelical churches, in gradually withdrawing from sectarianism, became much more a part of the metropolitan structure. With the migration of their followers, they established themselves in the larger centres of population, and their leaders became much more sympathetic to the views of city residents. Their houses of worship began to rival in elegance those of the older churches, and most of their leading ministers came to occupy city pulpits. Country stations were increasingly neglected, and methods of organization such as itinerancy and street preaching, which had been developed to make possible the serving of people in the country or in working-class districts of the city who could not be reached within regular places of worship, were abandoned. The evangelical churches came to draw most of their financial support from the cities, and from the better residential sections and, consequently, to identify their interests with the interests of the metropolitan population. They became churches of Empire or nation rather than the churches of the social fringe.

Such a development was clearly evident with respect to the Baptists in Nova Scotia and the Methodists in Upper Canada. The considerable influence exerted within the Baptist denomination by the Granville Street Church in Halifax, after its break in 1827 from the Church of England, and the shift of denominational leadership from preachers and laymen attached to churches in the outsettlements to preachers and laymen attached to the church in the capital, were indicative of fundamental changes in the position of the Baptist group. The leadership of Dr. E. A. Crawley in Baptist educational endeavours reflected the greater dependence upon the resources of the metropolis. Likewise, with the Methodists in Upper Canada, the increasing importance of Toronto as a Methodist centre, and the union in 1832 with the English Wesleyan Conference, reflected the closer identification with the political interests of the capital and with the British imperial system. New Methodist leaders emerged with much stronger urban ties, and new techniques, such as the religious journal, developed which strengthened the influence of churches in the larger centres. The change in the character of the Methodist camp meeting from a religious gathering held in the backwoods to a religious gathering held in summer resorts and attracting city people was suggestive of the new Methodist appeal.

At first glance it might seem that the religious-political movement founded by Aberhart in Alberta escaped developments leading to a closer identification with metropolitan interests, but in actual fact it did not. The increasing competition of radio evangelists led Aberhart and his fellow preachers to place less emphasis upon the appeal to country people and to think more in terms of the work of the large city churches in Calgary and Edmonton, while, at the same time, the political party which grew out of the religious movement steadily ceased to be a frontier party and became more interested in building up a national following or, at least, in securing acceptance within the nation at large. Efforts in various parts of the country to secure the election to Parliament of Social Credit members was an indication of the extent of the shift away from the early position of sectarian and provincial separatism.

The change in the position of the evangelical churches in the cities was accompanied by a change in their relation to the wealthier economic classes. Substantial men of business, though not necessarily changing their religious affiliations, began to make financial contributions to these churches on the theory that their teachings made for good citizens and for well-disciplined workers. At the same time, many of the adherents of the evangelical church became rich themselves. The asceticism cultivated within the religious sect tended to success in business enterprise, and religious nonconformists were likely to find their way into mercantile pursuits in particular. Commercialism favoured the sort of qualities developed within the sect, while, on the other hand, members of the more traditional churches were likely to avoid commerce as something not becoming their social position.

Commercial prosperity thus inevitably resulted in considerable changes in the economic status of the membership of the evangelical churches as over against the membership of the traditional churches. The evangelical churches ceased to be churches of the poor as an increasing number of their members became substantial citizens, and such a shift in social status led to a shift in political attachments. An anxiety to establish a claim to a position of respectability led these churches to repudiate their earlier connections with the socially humble and politically radical. The increasing conservatism of the Baptists in Nova Scotia and the Methodists in Upper Canada can be explained at least in part on these grounds. By the middle of the nineteenth century these churches had many wealthy members. In Alberta the same sort of thing happened, but it was more evident

within the Social Credit party than within the Prophetic Bible
Institute. In the election of 1944 many prominent Alberta business
men—and, there is reason to believe, a number of large business
firms outside—lent their active support to the party which nine
years earlier had advocated a radical programme of monetary
reform.

In the end the evangelistic religious appeal also tended to the
development of attitudes of conservatism among the followers of
the evangelical churches. While such an appeal did promote, on the
one hand, a more rationalist approach to the problems of life, it
promoted, on the other hand, a narrow intolerance which increasingly found expression in anti-liberal forms of behaviour. Religious
sectarianism involved a shift to a more fundamentalist, elementary
conception of religion; it represented a reversion to a simpler form
of Christianity. Its appeal, therefore, was essentially reactionary in
character. New movements within theological thought were strongly
resisted by the religious sect, and it was almost inevitable that
something of this theological illiberalism would be carried over and
become identified with political illiberalism. The feeling developed
by the evangelistic religious sect that it possessed the only true
means of salvation led to a type of bigotry which found expression
in politics as well as in religion. Reliance upon special revelation
ruled out discussion as a way of arriving at decisions, and the
religious evangelist was likely to prove highly impatient when
caught within the checks and balances of democratic political
processes.

Consideration of the influences which tended to force the evangelical churches into a conservative position in politics, as over
against those influences which tended to force them into a radical
position, suggests that the nature of their political alignments at
most can only in part be explained in terms of a fundamental
political philosophy. Evangelical church leaders displayed considerable capacity to change their minds, and the minds of their followers, to suit circumstances; and it was never possible to predict
what political programme they would support at any particular time.
They developed no consistent body of political principles.

The explanation for this would seem to lie in the sectarian origin
of the evangelical church. Religious sectarianism as such tended to
foster an attitude of political indifference. The whole attention of
the individual was directed to the state of his (and of his neighbour's) soul. So long as the sect remained truly evangelical in

character, it avoided any connection whatsoever with secular groups or associations, remaining wholly other-worldly. This was true of the Baptists in Nova Scotia, of the Methodists in Upper Canada, and of the religious movement led by Aberhart in Alberta, as it has been true of all other sects.

Although the preaching career of Henry Alline, the founder of the Newlight Baptist Church in Nova Scotia, coincided almost exactly with the period of the American Revolutionary War, he referred to it only twice in his journal, and then quite incidentally. The Newlight movement grew out of the unrest created by the Revolution, but the Newlights carefully avoided any identification with political interests. Their strength as a religious sect largely derived from such non-involvement in politics. Similarly, the Methodists in Upper Canada made their greatest gains just before and after the War of 1812–14, but few Methodist preachers expressed any interest in the controversies growing out of the war or in the subsequent fierce political conflicts. Methodist preachers and Methodist converts subordinated political allegiances to what they considered the much more important allegiance to their God. Likewise, during the period in which Aberhart gained his greatest influence as a religious leader in Alberta, he had no interest whatsoever in politics, and his followers tended to be people who engaged very little in political activities and who were little informed respecting political issues.

The effect of the sectarian religious appeal thus was virtually to disfranchise a considerable section of the population. The religious sectarian in many cases did not vote; if he did vote, he very often took no other interest in public questions. His political allegiances were of a tenuous sort; he made a poor party member because he was seldom prepared to accept the obligations of party loyalty. His religious conscience too often served to justify an attitude of non-co-operation. This resulted in fostering a state of political illiteracy. For the most part, the membership of religious sects was drawn from the least-educated sections of the population, and no attempt was made, within religious teachings, to correct this initial disadvantage in exercising the privileges of citizenship. Rather, ignorance of political matters was considered a virtue of the evangelical-minded person; it was indicative of his complete break from the fellowship of the ungodly and his full participation in the fellowship of the elect. Thus political illiteracy was deliberately promoted by discouraging contact with people outside the group and by discouraging the reading of non-religious publications. Theological commentaries and religious journals, as well as the evangelical sermon, served to weaken efforts of the secular press to build up party loyalties and a political consciousness.

Political indifference gave way to an interest in public issues only when the position of the religious sect was threatened by public policy. It was the leaders who were most alive to the effects of public policy and who, therefore, were most likely to initiate political action to protect the interests of the sect. Indeed, the followers of the religious sect tended to be little more concerned about its interests as a religious denomination than they were about the interests of any secular institution; sectarianism encouraged an attitude of non-denominationalism. The truly saved were members of the spiritual elect, and the preservation of that connection depended upon no formal institutional organization, a common experience of faith being sufficient bond of attachment. The leaders, however—those whose livelihood or prestige depended upon the continued existence of the sect as a religious denomination—became increasingly jealous of its rights and privileges. They built it into a church because their security depended upon the security of denominational attachments. Efforts to strengthen the social position of the church led to the promotion of activities, such as education and temperance, which brought it more closely into contact with other groups. Challenges to such activities compelled the leaders to mobilize their following for collective political action.

It was such vested interests of office which led to the active political participation of the followers of religious sects. Baptist leaders in Nova Scotia, after the turn of the nineteenth century, could not afford to adhere to the position of political neutrality taken earlier by Henry Alline. Attacks upon denominational enterprises which they promoted, in particular a Baptist college, compelled them to interest themselves in matters of politics. If effective political pressure was to be exerted, they had, in addition, to arouse a strong political interest in their followers. Similarly, Methodist leaders in Upper Canada after 1828, in contrast with the earlier Methodist itinerants, found themselves becoming involved in political controversies in support of their denominational claims. Attacks upon Methodist undertakings were in the nature of attacks upon the vested interests of leadership; a denominational college, Sabbath observance, and the cause of temperance were issues which continued to force Methodist leaders into politics in the provincial and municipal as well as the federal field. Aberhart's sudden break into politics can be explained likewise. Increasing competition from rival radio evangelists led him to search for something new in his appeal, and he seized upon the message of Social Credit. Attacks upon his political teachings forced him into politics in their defence. What he did was to convert a religious crusade into a political crusade; political allegiances were forged to take the place of weakening religious allegiances. None of this, of course, was done with a clear consciousness of the effect. Leadership very seldom appreciated the nature of the forces which drove it into certain lines of action, and in no case, perhaps, was this more evident than in the emergence of the Social Credit movement out of the evangelical preaching of Mr. Aberhart.

It was, indeed, one of the paradoxes in the role of the sectarian leader that his evangelical message should lead him, in the end, into political controversy. To arouse concern in the cause of religious salvation—that is to say, to win converts—the evangelical preacher had to resort to the spectacular, and, as the spectacular in religion ceased to be effective in meeting the competition of more aggressive evangelists or of more highly organized religious institutions, the spectacular in politics was sometimes turned to. It was not in any way remarkable that the Rev. T. T. Shields of Toronto, who broke from the main Baptist body on religious fundamentalist grounds, should have sought to maintain the support of his following by discussing in the pulpit highly controversial political issues. Violent attacks upon public men, like the noise of a brass band, create something of a sensation and provide effective advertising. Such attacks, in the end, can only be sustained by pulling the whole following of the church into politics in support of certain lines of action.

The way in which the evangelical church was drawn into the field of politics explains its failure to develop any consistent programme of political action. Lacking any clearly defined political principles, opportunism was the most natural determinant of political action on the part of leaders and followers alike. The nature of the evangelistic religious appeal placed the leaders in a particularly powerful position in mobilizing the support of the followers for political action.

The religious evangelist escaped the checks upon leadership secured through an elaborate denominational organization and an accepted ritual. His relationship to the convert was a purely personal one; it was he rather than any formal church which offered the means of salvation. The result was that the religious evangelist came to assume a very considerable dominance over those whom he converted. The democratization of the institution of religion made possible the concentration of authority in one who enjoyed the privilege of divine revelation. When the religious evangelist moved into the political field, he lost little of his charismatic influence. His strong personal authority made it possible to carry his followers with him no matter what political line he might take. No Roman Catholic bishop could, in fact, ever hope to exert the personal influence over his following as was exerted by Joseph Smith, the founder of the Mormon Church, or by Brigham Young, his successor.

Although Ryerson in Upper Canada was never able to command the support of the whole membership of the Wesleyan Methodist Church, he nevertheless achieved striking success in swinging the Methodist body behind whatever political party he favoured. The Methodists became a powerful pressure group in Canadian politics about the middle of the nineteenth century simply because expediency determined to a considerable extent their actions; they tended to vote in terms of the interests of their denomination without regard to wider public issues, and political solidarity was maintained by effective leadership, at any rate during the period of ascendancy of Egerton Ryerson. Similarly, Aberhart in Alberta could mobilize his following in support of a personally sponsored political programme because of the peculiar type of influence which he had built up as a religious evangelist. It was his boast that he was completely ignorant of economics before his advocacy of Social Credit ideas, but his economic pronouncements were readily accepted because of the claim to divine revelation which he had established as a religious evangelist.

It would be an exaggeration to conclude from this that the influence of the evangelical churches in Canadian political life has been to produce a citizen body politically illiterate or unprincipled, but such a conclusion would contain an element of truth. An indifference to politics which religious sectarianism engendered has checked the growth of political thought, and the weakness of political thought, in turn, in contributing to a political opportunism on the part of evangelical church leaders, has checked the growth of political statesmanship. It is significant that leadership in politics from the Protestant group in the country has come very largely from people with a Scottish Presbyterian or Scottish Baptist background. Denominationalism and religious fundamentalism have exerted too strong a hold upon members of the evangelical churches for them to go far in a career of politics. Much of their energy has been dissipated in support of programmes of moral reform sponsored by religious groups. They have as a result tended to be more successful in municipal or provincial politics, where party organization has been weak and where voting blocs have exerted a much greater influence, than in federal politics. The repeated failure, in Canada as well as in the United States, to build a national party around the prohibition issue was an indication of the limitations of evangelistic religious thinking in politics.

It is questionable, however, whether the political influence exerted by the evangelical church reveals the real contribution of the religious sect to the development of political thought. That is to say, the contribution of the sect should not be sought in the political activities of the evangelical church, whether those activities were in the way of supporting radical or conservative political movements in the community, but rather it should be sought in the religious influence of the sect as such, before it developed into the evangelical church. Its political contribution lay in its very emphasis upon the separation of the religious from the political. The indifference of the religious sect to politics provided a healthy corrective to tendencies within the church to become greatly occupied with political matters and so entrenched in the political interests of the state. It was in the teachings of religious sectarianism that the threat to liberal principles through the alliance of church and state was most effectively met. The religious sect, by concentrating upon the purely religious message of salvation, escaped the demands of nationalism so evident in times of war. Moreover, by placing the emphasis upon spiritual values in the making of preaching appointments, the sect was freed from social pressures making for the development of a denominational bureaucracy which sought support in the bureaucracy of big business and the state. In Canada the maintenance of a successful federal system in particular has depended upon the strength of forces of decentralization, secured, within religious organization, through the influence of new religious sects.

As the sect has grown into the church, new sects have grown out of the church. Thus the effect of the increasing participation of evangelical church leaders in politics has been offset by secession and the emergence of new sects which have withdrawn completely from political activity. In Nova Scotia the rapid growth of the Free-will Baptist movement after 1820 emphasized the weaknesses of the Baptist Church as a result of its shift away from an evangelical position. The entry of the Methodists in Upper Canada into politics under the leadership of Egerton Ryerson was followed almost immediately by the break of the local preachers and the organiz-ation of the Methodist Episcopal Church. In Alberta, likewise, the participation of Aberhart in politics led very quickly to the weaken-ing of his religious influence and to the shift of evangelical leader-ship to new religious sects. It is this persistence of the sectarian spirit in religious organization which has given religion its dynamic force in society. It has exerted a decisive influence upon determining the relation of the church to the state and thereby upon determining the contribution of religion to political thought.

The Religious Sect in
Canadian Economic Development*

THERE IS PROBABLY NO OTHER FORM of organized group life in the Canadian community which has been more unstable than the organization of religion. The history of Protestantism in the country is very largely a history of church unions and sectarian divisions. If account were taken of the activities of the Jesuit Order in New France, of the defection at various times of many Roman Catholics to Protestant religious sects, and of recent anti-clerical movements in the province of Quebec and among the Roman Catholic immigrant population in western Canada, the same would be found to be true in a general way of Roman Catholic development in the country.

The dream of the universal church, of the church which would unite all nations and all classes, has never been fully realized, in Canada as elsewhere in the western world. Efforts to accomplish such an object by the establishment of a state church, by the union of separate religious bodies, or by the initiation of a new religious movement which would transcend all other religious groups have invariably failed in face of the expression of strong separatist forces in religious organization. Out of every such effort to create an all-embracing religious body in the community have come new movements of religious protest—the religious sects.

On the other hand, the sect form of religious organization has

*From the *Canadian Journal of Economics and Political Science*, vol. XII, no. 4, Nov., 1946, pp. 439–53. With permission of the publisher.

proved equally unstable. The pure sect, the religious group organized exclusively in terms of the other-worldly or spiritual interests of its members, has never been more than an idealistic conception of religious organization finding expression in movements of religious reform at various times. The necessity of existing in a worldly society has led religious sects from the very beginning to accept to some extent a worldly outlook. Where they have not succeeded in developing into churches, or at any rate into types of religious organization accommodated to the secular community, they have perished. Almost from the moment of their inception they have been forced to make such a choice between social accommodation or extinction.

The explanation of these various movements, of church union and sectarian schism, must be sought within the particular situations out of which they developed. A wide variety of different sorts of factors operated to bring about changes in forms of religious organization and in religious thinking. No attempt can be made here to set forth the underlying conditions of religious development. All that can be attempted is to suggest in general terms the way in which religious developments were related to other developments in the community.

The instability of religious organization, characteristic of so much of the religious development of Canada, as of the western world generally during the past nineteen centuries, may be considered in part a reflection of the underlying instability of western economic society. That would appear particularly true of Canada where the economic factor has been so important. Canada grew out of the expansion of western capitalism (the Canadian frontier from the beginning has been an area of capitalistic exploitation) and the demands of capitalism may be expected as a result to have made their effects felt upon the organization of religion as, on the other side, the demands of religion have made their effects felt upon the organization of capitalism. The institutions of religion and the institutions of capitalism have grown out of much the same social situation in the Canadian community. To some extent at least, as a consequence, the instability of religious organization and the instability of capitalism find a similar explanation.

It was out of the social conditions which produced new capitalist enterprise that the religious sect developed, while it was in face of social demands related to the development of large-scale capitalist organization that the religious sect was forced to give way to church forms of religious fellowship. The frontier of capitalism—the area, that is, of new capitalist enterprise—was a breeding ground of the religious sect. The metropolitan society, the society of large-scale capitalist organization, tended to produce the church, or formally organized religious denomination.

Thus, in Canada, the great revivals of religion, the new movements of sectarian religious protest, have been closely related, chronologically and geographically, to the development of new staple or secondary industries in various parts of the country, while the recessions of waves of religious revival, the growth of conditions favourable to the church form of religious organization, have been closely related to the passing of the pioneer stage of capitalist expansion and the emergence of large-scale capitalist organization. The expansion of the fur trade in New France, trade and the fishing industry in Nova Scotia, agriculture and the timber trade in New Brunswick, Prince Edward Island, and Upper Canada, mining on the Pacific Coast and Precambrian Shield, wheat farming on the western prairies and manufacturing in the St. Lawrence–Great Lakes area grew out of conditions which favoured the break from ecclesiastical forms of religious control evident in the rise of the Jesuits, Newlight Baptists, Methodists, Disciples of Christ, Plymouth Brethren, Salvation Army, Pentecostals, Jehovah's Witnesses, and other sects. On the other hand, the development of mature forms of economic organization in the fur trade, fishing industry, timber trade, commerce, agriculture, mining, and manufacturing grew out of conditions which favoured the shift away from religious sectarianism and the strengthening of ecclesiastical forms of organization within the Roman Catholic, Anglican, Presbyterian, Congregational, Baptist, Methodist, and Disciples of Christ churches and within some of the more recently organized religious bodies.

The breakdown of religious denominationalism and the rise of new religious sects on the frontier of capitalism could be accounted for to some extent in terms of elementary economic factors. The primary problem of capitalist growth was the mobilization of capital and labour for economic production. Thus an effort was made to avoid the demands of any elaborate system of social services. It was for this reason that frontier capitalist societies were unfavourable to the strengthening of the organization of the state; extension of state services involved draining off capital and labour into unproductive channels. For the same reason, such societies were unfavourable to the building up of an elaborate ecclesiastical organization.

Church buildings had to be provided and manpower released for the carrying on of religious instruction. Insistence on maintaining certain prescribed standards in the character of places of worship and in the qualifications of the ministry raised costs in the way of building materials, wages, and salaries. The break from religion of frontier populations was a break from a religion which was expensive.[1] Taxation by ecclesiastical authorities was resisted as strongly as taxation by state authorities. The dominant drive of the capitalist frontier was that of economic exploitation.

In contrast, the services of the religious sect were provided virtually free of cost. Few demands were made either in the way of buildings or labour. Much of the preaching of the sectaries was carried on in open fields, barns, private homes, or on the streets, and, where houses of worship were required, they were simply built from local materials and through co-operative labour during slack seasons of the year. The sectarian preachers, likewise, imposed no great economic burden upon the new capitalist society. Many of them were employed on a part-time basis, working during the week and preaching in the evenings and on Sunday, but even when they were employed on a full-time basis they made little demand in the way of salary. They were men without professional training, and, having developed none of the tastes of the social élite, they were prepared to live simply in the manner of the people they served. The contrast in this regard, for instance, between the Methodist saddle-bag preacher and the Church of England clergyman in Upper Canada was striking. No less striking is the contrast today between the Jehovah's Witness worker and the college-trained minister of the United Church of Canada.

It is true that as religious revivalist movements grew, a very great number of men (and, in some cases, women) were drawn into preaching employments with a resulting drain of labour from more productive forms of work, but it is doubtful if this involved any great economic loss to the frontier society. Generally, those people who turned evangelical preachers were the economic misfits of the

---

[1]"All commercial communities," Brooks Adams wrote, "have rebelled against paying for miracles, and it was the spread of a scepticism already well developed in the thirteenth century among the manufacturing towns which caused the Reformation of the sixteenth." *The Law of Civilization and Decay: An Essay on History* (London, 1895), p. 129. Of developments after about 1400, Adams wrote: "Year by year, as society consolidated, the economic type was propagated; and as the pressure of a contracting currency stimulated these men to action, the demand for cheap religion grew fierce." *Ibid.*, p. 157.

community who had no great contribution to make to economic enterprise. Thus Henry Alline, the Newlight preacher of Nova Scotia, dying of tuberculosis, probably would have had to be supported by his family if he had not been supported by the community at large through voluntary contributions. The same was true of at least some of the others who, during the early period of sectarian development, joined the preaching ranks of the Newlights, or of the Baptists, Methodists, Campbellites, Plymouth Brethren, Salvation Army, Pentecostals, and Jehovah's Witnesses. Possessed of few skills and of little education, such people were denied the means of entering other professions, while in temperament or physique they were unsuited to manual labour. If they had not become evangelical preachers, they might well have become pedlars, horse traders, medical quacks, or unemployed village philosophers.

An accounting of the total costs of providing religious services would reveal a very considerable difference between the church and the sect, and in terms of the development of capitalist enterprise this difference has been very important. Shift of support to new sectarian movements resulted in a real economic saving at a time when the community had few reserves in the way of capital or labour. The effect of this saving was evident in the impetus given to the growth of economic enterprise in areas where religious sectarianism developed strongly, as for instance in the Annapolis Valley in Nova Scotia, while the effect of the drain upon economic resources in support of an elaborate ecclesiastical system was equally evident in the weakness of economic enterprise where church forms of religious organization continued strongly, as for instance in Quebec or along the north shore of Cape Breton.

In a more positive way as well, the religious sect contributed to meeting the problem of mobilizing capital and labour in frontier areas and thus in encouraging the development of new economic enterprise. The sect became an important economic group by virtue of the cohesiveness which it developed as a religious group. The economic solidarity of the sect offered a means of offsetting the limitations of individual economic enterprise. Members came to one another's assistance, through co-operative labour, buying and selling, borrowing and lending. Fortunes were kept within the group through restrictions upon marrying outside.[2] The collective

[2]"Religion," H. A. Innis wrote, "has been vitally related to the mysteries of life and death and to the family. The decline of the Church in Europe reflected the impact of birth control on the confessional.... Religious sects have fostered the

feeling of responsibility for the business reputation of the individual member increased the capacity to borrow. In a larger way, the religious sect developed many of the economic strengths of the closely knit family group; it could operate as a collective body in the labour, commercial, and financial market. Where corporate forms of economic organization were lacking, such an informal corporate organization became of considerable economic importance. The strong position of the Scottish and English Baptists in the business life of Toronto about the middle of the nineteenth century affords an illustration of the economic strengths deriving from the close group controls of the religious sect.

The relation of religious sectarian movements to the development of capitalism, however, was more far-reaching than that suggested in any contribution which such movements may have made to meeting the problem of mobilizing capital and labour. The development of capitalist enterprise required more than simply a reserve force of capital and labour. It required in general terms what has been called the spirit of capitalism. More particularly, it required a population disciplined to the economic demands of capitalistic exploitation. It was in providing such a discipline that religious sectarianism made its most distinctive contribution to the development of capitalist enterprise.

Frontier areas, that is, areas of new economic enterprise, tended to attract a socially undisciplined population; it was the restless, adventurous, and, often, the thriftless and irresponsible who sought their fortune in new lands or in new forms of economic activity. Conditions of life in such areas accentuated the break away from a disciplined routine and from accepted principles of conduct. The sudden break from past associations and the experience of many things which were new and unfamiliar had unsettling effects which were economically as well as socially disorganizing. The importance of chance in determining economic fortune encouraged a

accumulation of wealth over long periods by intermarriage of families. Whereas the Church in its fight for sacerdotal celibacy as a means of preventing the dispersion of wealth left itself open to the looting of its monasteries, the Jews and other sects have been persecuted because of the building up of large fortunes. . . .

"In the United States the importance of religion to the growth of trade is shown in the large numbers of denominational periodicals and their promising returns to advertisers in a national market. Significantly, among the first advertisers who were alert to these possibilities were those large-scale dealers in human credulity, the patent-medicine firms." H. A. Innis, "On the Economic Significance of Culture" in *The Tasks of Economic History*, Supplement IV to the *Journal of Economic History*, Dec., 1944, p. 89.

reckless speculative spirit, while disappointment as a result of the failure to achieve immediate riches led to an attitude of irresponsibility and despondency. An unreliability with respect to work, the payment of debts, or the quality of goods offered for sale was an inevitable consequence of the unrestricted exploitation of human and material resources on the frontier of capitalism. To a considerable extent, the most elementary economic virtues such as business honesty, frugality, and industry were lacking among a frontier population.

Indirectly, the social costs of conditions of life in new areas of economic development imposed as well a heavy toll upon economic enterprise. Drinking and gambling, prevalent vices of frontiersmen, cut heavily into savings and greatly reduced the efficiency of labour. Family disorganization weakened one of the important group supports of economic life. Mental breakdowns, suicides, and an increase generally in emotional instability, reduced the number of the steady and reliable among the working population. Economic failure and personal demoralization were closely related in an area which made heavy economic and social demands upon the population. The frontier capitalist society tended to become a society of economic and social misfits.

It was just in its role of converting the economic and social misfits of such a society into useful members that the religious sect gained its enormous importance in the development of new economic enterprise. Religion was made a powerful economic as well as social reorganizing influence by virtue of the very fact that it was made to appeal to those people who were the economically unadjusted within society. It offered a new standard of social conduct, and, in the end, a new economic discipline.

This was true even though the immediate effect of religious sectarianism may actually have accentuated the economic and social disorganization of the community. The difficulties of adjusting to new economic and social demands accounted to some extent for the resort in the first place to a religious interpretation of the problems of life. Religion offered a means of rationalizing failure. The religious convert as a result tended to view with indifference worldly values of economic and social success. The conception of the spiritual elect offered a means of achieving a sense of worth through the experience of religious faith. The saved, though unsuccessful in material terms, could look down with contempt upon those who were successful but were among the unsaved. Thus to some extent worldly standards of industry, frugality, and even, indeed, of moral righteousness were abandoned for standards of spiritual perfection. In extreme cases, complete personal demoralization resulted from participation in religious sectarian activity.

The fanaticism culitvated by the religious sect tended to weaken, in particular, habits of work and saving. All those people who disliked work or who were disinclined to save found a means of escape from such obligations by becoming caught up in religious activities. This was very much true of those people who became preachers, exhorters, or who, in some other capacity, assumed the role of religious teachers, but it was also true in a general way of all those who came to feel that salvation was the only problem of importance to mankind. Attendance, sometimes day after day for weeks at a time, at revivalist, protracted or camp meetings during busy seasons of the year interfered seriously with work, while constant concern with religious matters led to a neglect of family responsibilities in the way of caring for the home and providing some sort of economic security. During 1842, the year of the Millerite craze, for instance, great numbers of farmers and small-town folk in Canada and the Maritime Provinces abandoned work, and not a few of the more ardent sold or gave away their farms or businesses in preparation for the day of the Second Coming. Though in somewhat less spectacular form, the Newlight revivals in Nova Scotia and New Brunswick, the Methodist revivals in Upper Canada, the Salvation Army revivals towards the close of the nineteenth century, and more recent revivals—of Pentecostals, Jehovah's Witnesses, and others—have had similar effects. The economic costs of religious fanatacism at times could be high; there have been instances where whole communities were impoverished through unrestrained participation of the population in religious activity.

There would also seem good reason to believe that fanatical religious movements at times led to a serious weakening of moral standards. The doctrine of salvation by faith when taken literally, as for instance among many of the Newlights in Nova Scotia, gave rise to the view that good works in the way of strict moral conduct or, indeed, of conduct which conformed to accepted standards of decency and honesty were of no account; if a man believed, he was saved regardless of what might be his outward behaviour. An undue emphasis upon spiritual values led almost inevitably to a dulling of people's conceptions of what was right and wrong and, in cases of extreme religious fanaticism, to a complete distortion of moral values. This was particularly true during periods of religious revival when the frenzied religious excitement produced psychological conditions of intimate association favourable to the reckless abandonment of all social taboos and conventions. Sudden increases in illegitimacy rates have been found, on occasion, to have a close relation to outbursts of religious feelings, as for instance in the Onslow Baptist Church in Nova Scotia in 1818. In a general way, those people who were most religious have been found often to be the least reliable with respect to fair dealing and the payment of debts, with consequent economic losses to the community as a whole.

Finally, fanatical religious movements have very often had the effect of increasing personal disorganization in the community, evident in mental breakdown, suicide, and alcoholism. The experience of a sense of sinfulness, as a result of evangelical religious preaching, was intended to be terrifying; the whole complex of reactions to the highly emotional religious appeal was mentally disturbing. When the appeal was made to people who were emotionally unstable to begin with, the results were very often disastrous. Those who were unable to gain the experience of faith in their saviour were driven to the lowest depths of despair, but even those who experienced successful conversion were not always emotionally secure, as the large number of evangelical preachers who suffered mental breakdowns would suggest. The effort to maintain faith involved almost as great a mental strain as the effort to gain faith, and not a few broke under the strain. The view of the Superintendent of the Toronto Lunatic Asylum in 1860 that religious fanaticism was responsible for the mental breakdown of many of the inmates probably had some basis in fact. Outbreaks of religious hysteria were never clearly distinguishable from other manifestations of mass psychic disturbances.

If religious sectarian movements had had no other effect than that of resulting in fanatical expressions of religious feelings, their contribution to the development of economic enterprise would have been limited. The effect of religious fanaticism in weakening habits of work and saving and moral standards and in accentuating the emotional instability of the population certainly was to delay the economic reorganization of frontier society. Among certain sections of the population, religious sectarianism did result in indefinitely retarding economic progress.

Among other sections of the population, however, the disorganizing effects of sectarian religious teachings tended in time to be more than offset by the disciplined effects of sectarian religious controls. The religious sects were compelled to bring the fanaticism resulting from their teachings under control if it were not to develop to the point where it completely discredited religion. Thus the enthusiasm aroused by the religious revival came increasingly to be directed along channels to the advantage of the religious group. The exclusive emphasis upon spiritual values persisted but such values found interpretation within the collective religious body. Authority shifted from the individual to the sect as such, and it was the complete and absolute authority which it came to possess which constituted its distinctive strength as a disciplining social agency.

To develop a body of steady followers out of the sort of people it attracted into its fold, the religious sect was compelled to cultivate an ascetic outlook on life. The sectarian was the kind of person who could not afford to conform to the conventions of polite society; his break from many of the norms of social behaviour, which found expression in forms of fanatical religious activity, was a reflection of his failure to fit into a traditional economic and social order. What, in effect, the religious sect did was to develop, and rigorously enforce, its own distinctive standards of conduct. It was in this way that its influence gained such importance in the growth of new economic enterprise.

In a general way, this shift within the religious sect from a free and unrestrained expression of religious feelings to the exercise of close group controls over religious conduct was closely related to the shift from a state of economic depression to a state of economic prosperity in new areas of development. The pioneer stage of frontier development tended to be characterized by inefficiency in methods of production, shortage of money, and lack of markets, and the consequent discouragement of the population led to a frantic search for means of escape in religion and in economic and political panaceas of various sorts. With improvements in methods of production, the increase in the supply of money, and the opening up of outside markets, economic conditions generally improved, and the growing importance of the economic motive discouraged a too great emphasis upon purely spiritual values. The unrestrained display of emotional feelings of the religious convert gave way to the carefully controlled religious feelings of the sectarian. The ascetic outlook gained importance as a condition of economic success.

Once cultivated as a means of securing the solidarity of the religious group, asceticism inevitably exerted a considerable influence upon economic and social conduct. Its effect in cultivating habits of saving and thus encouraging the accumulation of capital was particularly important, but hardly less important was its effect in promoting temperate drinking habits and checking gambling and thereby contributing to the creation of a disciplined labour force. Religious asceticism was hostile to the conventional dissipations of the gentleman and to the slothful vices of the poor. Industry, frugality, and moral uprightness became the attributes of those belonging to the spiritual elect. It was through the cultivation of such virtues that economic success was determined in new areas of development. If the ascetic outlook on life developed persons who were dull, narrow, and intolerant, such persons were people of great drive and forceful character. It was out of such stuff that capitalist society was built.

The rise of the Baptists and Methodists to positions of importance in the business life of Canada during the latter half of the nineteenth century offers an illustration of the close relation between the development of religious asceticism and the growth of capitalism. On the other hand, the weakness of a spirit of economic enterprise in areas where traditional forms of religious organization persisted strong, as for instance in areas where religious life centred about the Church of England or the Roman Catholic Church, suggests that where religious asceticism did not develop conditions were unfavourable to capitalist growth. The traditional church, the religious denomination made up of people with social status, was not faced like the religious sect with the problem of creating out of the economic and social misfits of society a body of steady religious followers. The traditional church enjoyed the support of people who already had their own standards of conduct and who, like gentlemen of means for instance, could afford to indulge in such conventional forms of dissipation as drinking and gambling or, indeed, of failing to pay their debts. Class controls defined the limits of permissible behaviour, and the threat of disgrace secured conformity to generally accepted standards.[3] Thus, unlike the

[3]"A man of rank and fortune," Adam Smith wrote, "is by his very station the distinguished member of a great society, who attend to every part of his conduct, and who thereby oblige him to attend to every part of it himself. His authority and consideration depend very much upon the respect which this society bears to him. He dare not do anything which would disgrace or discredit him in it, and he is obliged to a very strict observation of that species of morals, whether liberal or austere, which the general consent of this society prescribes to persons of his rank and fortune. A man of low condition, on the contrary, is far from being a distinguished member of any great society. While he remains in a country village his conduct may be attended to, and he may be obliged to attend to it himself. In this situation, and in this situation only, he may have what is called a character to

religious sect, the church had no need of interfering with the private lives of its members; indeed, the condition of continuing to enjoy their support was the refraining from such interference. For this reason, the church was able to exert little moral influence upon those members of society who had broken away from conventional habits of behaviour. The development out of a frontier population of an enterprising business class and a sober, steady, working class could not come through an emphasis upon traditional values of decorum and moral decency. It required the sort of rigid discipline provided by religious asceticism.

That was true so long as the problem of capitalist growth was one of accumulating capital, recruiting labour, and developing new techniques of production. As capitalist enterprise continued to grow, however, conditions increasingly developed which came to weaken the religious sectarian spirit and to favour the more formal type of religious organization characteristic of the church. Indeed, the very influence of the religious sect furthered the development of those conditions which made its survival impossible. With the expansion of capitalism, wealth accumulated and large-scale economic organization developed. Many of those people who began life in new areas of economic development as failures and who became caught up in sectarian religious movements became the successful of the new capitalist society; their participation in sectarian religious activity was an important condition of their success. Thus the religious sect, in the beginning a religious movement of the economically dispossessed of the community, came increasingly to draw its support from the substantial economic classes of capitalist society, and the conflict of the sectarian outlook with the outlook of the economically successful forced a modification in the character of the sect if it were to avoid extinction.

The ascetic way of life favoured the accumulation of wealth,

---

lose. But as soon as he comes into a great city, he is sunk into obscurity and darkness. His conduct is observed and attended to by nobody, and he is therefore very likely to neglect it himself, and to abandon himself to every sort of low profligacy and vice. He never emerges so effectually from this obscurity, his conduct never excites so much the attention of any respectable society, as by his becoming the member of a small religious sect. He from that moment acquires a degree of consideration which he never had before. All his brother sectaries are, for the credit of the sect, interested to observe his conduct, and if he gives occasion to any scandal, if he deviates very much from those austere morals which they almost always require of one another, to punish him by what is always a very severe punishment, even where no civil effects attend it, expulsion or excommunication from the sect." *The Wealth of Nations* (Oxford, 1880), vol. II, p. 380.

but wealth in itself seriously weakened the values of asceticism. The successful man could afford to indulge in the comforts and dissipations of the gentleman, and became impatient of restraints which denied him the means of such conspicuous forms of consumption. More than this, the ascetic way of life came to act as a positive brake upon the development of economic enterprise. Where emphasis shifted from production to salesmanship, economic expansion demanded the continual increase of consumer wants and consequently an abandonment of the austere values cultivated by the religious sect. The luxury trade became of considerable importance in the development of a mature capitalist economy.

At the same time, religious sectarianism as a disciplining force lost its importance with the increasing emphasis upon pecuniary values and the development of various forms of economic association. Profits or wages served as driving influences in maintaining habits of industry and a spirit of enterprise; economic associations, of farmers, workers, or manufacturers, for instance, established standards of economic conduct through the formulation of codes and through the development of a class consciousness. Such secular forms of control grew up almost entirely outside the province of religious controls and were able therefore to exist in complete independence of religious values. Thus they inevitably came in conflict with sectarian controls based on the view that the only values of life were those of a spiritual character.

If the conditions of capitalist expansion became increasingly unfavourable to the survival of religious sectarianism, they became increasingly favourable to the growth of religious denominationalism. The growth of wealth made possible the support of religious institutions making heavy demands in the way of expensive church structures, denominational colleges, religious newspapers, and highly paid ministers, while the economic and social demands of the capitalist society made virtually necessary the development of such religious institutions. The expensive religious service became an important form of conspicuous consumption; distinctions arising from attendance in exclusive places of worship served as a strong support of a system of class stratification. The religious teachings of the church, with their emphasis upon the virtues of the successful, offered a rationalization of forms of economic behaviour leading to the concentration of wealth and power. At the same time, the good works in which the church was engaged served to cultivate among the poor the sort of virtues necessary to successful capitalist

enterprise. The church, in contrast with the sect, recognized
different standards of morality for different classes of society. Thus
the temperance movement, as over against the sect prohibition on
drinking among all its members, tended to represent an effort on
the part of the capitalist middle class to control the drinking habits
of the working lower class. In various other ways as well, the
·church became an important support of large-scale capitalist enterprise. The increasing dependence of capitalism upon collective
social controls and propaganda was evident in the close relation
of big business to the church and to the state. The bureaucracy of
business combined with the bureaucracies of church and state in
maintaining the controls of the new capitalist society.

So long as capitalism continued to expand, however, such tendencies towards the concentration of power and control in society
were checked through the development of new forms of individual
economic enterprise and through the consequent emergence of
conditions unfavourable to the maintenance of centralized
economic and cultural controls. The big business of the metropolis
gave way to the individually owned small business of the frontier,
and religious denominationalism weakened in the face of social
pressures favouring the assertion of the sectarian spirit in religious
organization. It was in this way that the expansion of capitalism
made for a persistent state of instability in religious organization,
in the recurrent conflict between the sect and church form of
religious fellowship. Where capitalist development implied the
growth, at one and the same time, of new economic enterprise and
of large-scale economic organization, there operated in society
forces tending to make impossible the stabilization of forms of
religious organization either in terms of the principles of the sect
or of the church. If sects were no sooner organized than they developed into churches, churches no sooner became denominationally powerful than they lost much of their support to new sects.

Yet the stability of the Roman Catholic Church in the province
of Quebec throughout almost the whole of the nineteenth century,
and of a number of religious sects in various isolated parts of the
country in the past and at the present day, would suggest that
there have been certain areas in the Canadian community, social
pockets so to speak, in which religious organization has stood
largely outside the sphere of influence of capitalist expansion.
Within such areas the controls of the local society have been so
strong that the population has tended to remain completely

divorced from the economic and social order of capitalism. Lack of social mobility has meant little change in the social status of people, and a rigid status system has supported, and in turn been supported by, a sort of ecclesiastical or sectarian theocracy all-embracing in so far as the local society was concerned. Thus in nineteenth-century Quebec religion was organized in terms of a hierarchy of social classes which had little relation to the much more fluid class system of capitalism, and sharp separation from the outside capitalist world was maintained through an emphasis upon ethnic and religious differences and through geographical isolation. Similarly, within the ethnic-religious colony, such as that of the Mennonites, Doukhobors, or Hutterites, the secular influences of capitalism have been resisted with some success, and religious organization has tended to remain stable.

As a result of somewhat similar influences, slum areas whether urban or rural likewise have stood largely outside the range of influence of capitalist expansion, and here also as a result, religion has tended to become organized in terms of a rigid status system. The material and human resources of slum areas are so limited as to make impossible any real participation in capitalist enterprise. People in the slum do not move, either out of the area or upwards in the social scale. Lack of mobility has meant that the status of such people has been fixed, within the slum itself and within the society at large. The result has been an absence of those influences which make for change in forms of religious association. It is not the slum population which affords support to new sectarian movements; the religious sect is a movement of the restless, the insecure, of the people who have lost status and are striving to regain it. The slum population is a population which enjoys social status, accepted by itself and by the outside society; its forms of religious organization, typified by the church mission and "queer" sect, give expression to such a social state.

It is true that to a considerable extent such areas have only succeeded in sheltering themselves from the effects of capitalist expansion on a sort of sufferance. The breaking down of the old French Canadian Roman Catholic society in Quebec in the years since the First World War suggests the failure of efforts to maintain a position of isolation through an emphasis upon ethnic and religious differences in face of irresistible forces of industrialization. Similarly, the increasing secularization of Mennonite society in Manitoba is indicative of the difficulty of maintaining the conditions of a closed social system by a reliance upon religious controls once geographical separation ceases. Where a society stands directly in the path of capitalist expansion it is placed in an extremely insecure position. Even the population of slum areas has been drawn into the productive forces of capitalism when fully exposed to its economic and social demands.

Still, it is easy to exaggerate the strength of capitalist influences in breaking down traditional forms of social and religious control. There is a certain incalculable toughness in society in resisting that which is upsetting or disturbing. Such a toughness is evident within the traditional Roman Catholic society such as that of Quebec and also within such an ethnic-religious society as that of the Hutterites in Alberta and Manitoba. Influences of the capitalist secular society may not be kept out entirely but complete absorption is avoided by some sort of limited accommodation.

In a general way, what is true of such isolated groups in the community has been true to some extent of the Canadian community as a whole in relation to the outside capitalist world. Conditions of Canadian political and cultural development have set sharp limitations upon the uncontrolled expansion of individual capitalist enterprise in the country. The peculiar vulnerability of the Canadian frontier in face of the rapid expansion of the American community to the south has forced a considerable degree of political and cultural control over economic development. The Canadian nation has been produced out of the forces of counter-revolution. Thus the collapse of the old régime in French Canada reflected the growing strength of New England commercialism, but maintenance of the British tie after 1763 compelled the isolation of the Canadian and Maritime colonies from the influence of economic and cultural forces developing strongly within the revolutionary colonies along the Atlantic seaboard. Similarly, the weakening of the British imperial tie evident for instance in the growth of radical political movements in the colonies after 1800 was a reflection of the strength of the new American capitalism with western expansion, but the threat of political encroachment in 1812–14, 1837–40, and again in the early 1860's was met by efforts to isolate the Canadian society from American economic and cultural influences, evident in restrictions after 1814 on Americans settling in the country, the Act of Union in 1840, and Confederation in 1867. Since 1867, the struggle to preserve the political independence of the Canadian community has continued to force a considerable degree of economic and cultural independence. Although the pioneers of new developments in Canada, in mining, wheat farming, and manufacturing for instance, have come very largely from the United States, American economic and cultural dominance has been stiffly resisted by resort to such political weapons of control as tariffs, prohibitions upon the circulation of literature, and imperial preferences. In a sense, because of its political insecurity, the Canadian community has not been able to risk any break with its colonial tradition. Throughout, the state has been forced to intervene, in the opening up of the frontier and in the later development of the more mature economic society. The effects have been evident in the limitations upon individual economic enterprise with consequent limitations upon social experimentation.

With respect to religious organization, the struggle to maintain political independence has meant placing a check upon developments leading to any too great a break from traditional religious authority. Economic and cultural isolation has given support to a sort of ecclesiastical or sectarian theocracy within the Canadian community as a whole. The strength of traditional authority in religious organization has been evident not only in the position of the Roman Catholic Church in the province of Quebec and in the early privileges enjoyed by the Church of England and the Church of Scotland, but in the tendency of such evangelical religious bodies as Wesleyan Methodism and the Salvation Army to identify their interests with the imperial connection and of such present-day denominations as the United Church of Canada to identify their interests with Canadian nationalism. Canada has proved hostile, on the one side, to the influences of extreme forms of religious sectarianism as they developed on the American frontier, and, on the other side, to liberal religious influences as they developed in the larger American centres and in western Europe. The collective influence of the community has been exerted to maintain traditional authority in religion. The strength of religious denominationalism and religious fundamentalism in Canadian society today would suggest that this influence has been exerted with considerable effectiveness.

There would seem some reason to believe that such rigidity in forms of religious organization has become even more characteristic of present-day Canadian society as a result of recent tendencies towards an economic and political collectivism. New technological developments and new techniques of business organization and finance have provided large-scale capitalist enterprise with enormous advantages in production and marketing, while the importance of the economic factor in national prestige and defence has forced the even closer control of the state over economic life. Government soil surveys afford an illustration of more careful planning through state direction of agricultural settlement, while the factory town exemplifies the sort of controlled direction of industrial development secured through large-scale private enterprise. The new frontier of capitalism is to some extent an area of planned economic development. It has become as a consequence an area of planned social development as well. The provision of educational institutions, recreational facilities, health services, and, even housing is a responsibility now often assumed by large-scale capitalist enterprise and the state, and the assumption of responsibility carries with it the exercise of a considerable measure of control. The implications with respect to religious organization are particularly far-reaching.

Where the support of large-scale capitalist enterprise and the state is secured, the church is able to entrench itself so deeply in the community that new religious movements have little opportunity to develop. Thus in recently settled areas of Quebec, the direction and control exercised by the state has secured as one of its objectives the preferred position of the church. Similarly, within the factory town, as for instance in Arvida, the financial support of large-scale capitalist organization has provided those churches which meet with favour with overwhelming advantages in competing with rival religious bodies. Economic and political collectivism makes inevitably for a religious collectivism. The centralization of economic and political life favours the centralization of religious life; the claim of patriotism in itself has come to constitute a powerful force in securing conformity to church establishment. The wartime legal ban on the activities of the Jehovah's Witnesses is suggestive in this regard.

If tendencies towards a centralization of control within the state and business have led to a strengthening of the position of the churches in relation to new religious movements in the community, on the other side, tendencies towards a greater rigidity in the social class structure of capitalism have checked the growth of already established religious sects into churches or formally organized religious denominations. In modern capitalist society it is no longer easy to rise rapidly in the social scale; the wealthy have devised effective means of perpetuating their command of wealth while the working masses face the prospect of becoming permanently proletarianized. As a result, the religious sect has tended to become much more, as for instance in the case of the Salvation Army or Jehovah's Witnesses, a form of religious organization serving people of fixed social status in the community, and as a consequence social pressures forcing it to abandon its sectarian character and to seek a fuller accommodation to the secular community have somewhat weakened.

Where social stratification in religious organization has developed to the point where the religious sect and the church have come to serve two distinctly different population groups in the community, the historic role of the sect as a liberalizing influence in society may be considered to have come to an end. The sect operated as a liberal influence because it was composed of people on the make. The striving of sectarian leaders, and of sectarian members generally, for social position meant that the collective influence of the sect was exerted to break the dominance of privileged institutions and groups in society. Sectarianism served as an effective check upon any too great concentration of religious authority in the community or upon any close alliance of the church, the state, and big business. Where the sect, however, has come to be made up of people who accept their position in society, it no longer seriously challenges the vested interests of the established social system. Instead, it secures the patronage of wealthy business men, politicians, and other well-meaning citizens who feel that its teachings, though unacceptable to them, are beneficial to the sort of people it serves. In its relation to the church, it assumes something of the character of the mission or religious order, appealing to that section of the population which the more respectable religious denominations prefer to have nothing to do with. The real conflict tends to become one with secular movements of a political or social revolutionary character which seek the support of the same sort of people the sect seeks. In time to come it will probably be recognized that, from the point of view of maintaining the political, economic, and social status quo, the legal ban during the Second World War on the activities of the Jehovah's Witnesses was a blunder on the part of the Canadian government.

It would be foolhardy to speculate here as to future developments in religious organization. In terms of present-day tendencies towards totalitarianism, an increasingly close alliance of economic, political, and religious forces would seem likely. We are not so far now from having a state religion; much nearer, perhaps, than from having a state church. It is possible that an identification of religious interests with the interests of the nation and big business will become very much more complete in the not too distant future. On the other hand, it is equally possible that the deeply rooted urge within society for the free expression of religious feelings and beliefs will arrest the trend toward such an identification. It is only necessary to recall, and stress, the importance of the role played by religious sectarian movements in sixteenth-century Germany and England in weakening centralized authority within the church and the state, and in economic organization.

CHAPTER X

The Religious Influence in Canadian Society*

CANADA HAS SUFFERED THROUGHOUT HER HISTORY by the comparison of her rate of progress with that of the United States. Almost every traveller to this continent during the past two or more centuries has found occasion to comment on the apparent difference in the degree of economic prosperity on the two sides of the border. Lord Durham was compelled to recognize this difference as one of the underlying causes of political disaffection in the country. Local observers joined in deploring the failure of Canada to keep pace economically with the United States. Haliburton, expressing his views through his fictitious Yankee clockmaker, was scathing in his denunciation of the lack of industry and business imagination among his fellow Nova Scotians. Canadians today, with a similarly critical insight into the economic state of their country, are but little less inclined to point out the unfavourable comparison it makes with the neighbour to the south. The belief persists that the really enterprising Canadian must cross the border if he is to realize his fullest ambitions.

To some extent this comparison of the rate of economic growth of the two countries to the disadvantage of Canada has been based on a failure to see any of the favourable aspects in the development of the one country and any of the unfavourable aspects in the development of the other. The comparison has seldom, for instance, taken

*From *The Tasks of Economic History*, a supplement of the *Journal of Economic History*, 1947, pp. 89–103. With permission of the publisher. The original title read: "The Religious Factor in Canadian Economic Development."

into account the lack of economic progressiveness of the southern United States. But when due allowance is made for distortions of the facts, it remains true that there has been absent in Canada to some extent that spirit of economic enterprise, that drive to secure the fullest exploitation of natural resources, which has been so characteristic of the development of the United States. The growth of capitalism has come about in a slower and more halting fashion.

As a new country with unexploited natural resources, and no elaborate and costly structure of social services to begin with, Canada has offered almost as strong inducements to the development of new forms of economic enterprise as the United States. In Canada, however, in a way that has not been as true of the United States, various influences of a political, cultural, and religious character have served to check the free play of economic forces and as a result to limit economic growth. Rigidities have entered into the development of the Canadian community which have had the effect of diverting the resources of the country and the energies of the people into channels of advantage to non-economic interests. It would be difficult to say which of such influences, the political, cultural, or religious, has assumed greatest importance in establishing such rigidities; all three have been closely related. The political influence perhaps has been of chief significance in that the building of a Canadian society has been essentially a political problem. But if the cultural and religious influences have derived much of their support from the political, they have served to act, in turn, as powerful forces in its support. This has been especially true of the religious influence.

In few countries in the western world has religion exerted as great an influence upon the development of the community as it has in Canada. There have been areas, the southern states of the United States for instance, where it perhaps has been a more powerful force in local social life, but the influence of such areas in the larger national community has been offset by that of other areas where it has had little strength. The so-called Bible Belt might be thought of as extending not only through the southern but through the northern sections of the North American Continent to include almost the whole of Canada within its range. The peculiar political and cultural insecurity of the country in the face of, first, the rapid expansion of the neighbour to the south and, second, the deeply embedded and often bitter ethnic and regional dissensions among the population has led to a considerable dependence upon religion as a force in maintaining community solidarity. At no time has religion assumed an insignificant role in the life of the Canadian community. On occasion, it has been a force of dominant importance.

New France began almost as an experiment in theocratic-ecclesiastical control. Not only were Huguenots excluded from the colony but an effort was made to restrict immigration to those who in the eyes of the Jesuit priests could be considered good Catholics. The precarious position of the colony within the American continental system led to the maintenance of strong religious controls as a means of preserving the connection with France. When political collapse did come to the French Empire in America, religion assumed even greater importance as a force resisting absorption into the larger American society. In Acadia, it is true, the militant efforts of anti-British missionaries to isolate their Roman Catholic following led to the complete destruction of the French society, but in Quebec conflict between English governmental, military, and trading interests served to strengthen the position of the church and to make its influence more effective as a barrier to communication between the French and Anglo-Saxon populations. The colony escaped the influence of strong anti-religious movements of thought growing up in revolutionary France through severance of the political tie by the British conquest, and it escaped the influence of similar movements of thought gaining strength in English-speaking America through isolation from the English colonies by the Revolution. As re-established by the Quebec Act, the church of French Canada found new support in the close alliance with the state. Its character was shaped and its strong position determined by forces of counter-revolution.

In the Maritime colonies religion was little less important as a force maintaining political control. Although freedom of worship was granted the early New England settlers, the Church of England was established by law, and efforts of the church to minister to the religious wants of the population secured the full support of colonial authorities. Attendance upon religious services took on the character of a civic duty; indeed, in Halifax, it was made a legal obligation. The effect of the American Revolution was to reinforce these strong religious influences in the cultural life of the community. The large New England population offered a natural channel of communication for the spread into the Maritimes of revolutionary influences; most of the New Englanders sympathized with the revolutionary cause and many of them gave to it their active support. The break with the Atlantic seaboard colonies on the outbreak of war, however, effectively isolated the New England group and led to a considerable strengthening of British influences. Organized religion as a result gained a greatly increased importance as a force supporting the British connection. Efforts to establish a powerful ecclesiastical-religious structure and to capture the West India trade were not unrelated phases of the general struggle to build up in the Maritime Provinces after 1800 a political system secure against attack by the United States.

In the St. Lawrence waterways region, the western movement of American population after 1790 breached temporarily the isolation of the British colony which had resulted from the Revolutionary War; people poured across the border to form the new province of Upper Canada and to bring into being the settlements of the Eastern Townships. But barriers to communication provided by language and culture made it possible for the Roman Catholic Church to maintain its strong position of control among the French Canadians in Lower Canada (especially in face of the threat to the political security of the province as a result of the operations of French agents in the United States) while the precarious political situation in Upper Canada where the vast majority of the population was American led to a vigorous effort to build up the influence of an established Protestant ecclesiastical system. The War of 1812 served in Upper Canada, as the Revolutionary War had done in Nova Scotia, to cut off any close contact with the United States. After 1815 a British influence that tended on the whole to be traditionalistic and illiberal became predominant. Anxiety on the part of the growing overseas population to maintain its political attachments intensified the dependence upon religious attachments. Religion operated as a powerful force in checking the spread of liberal influences from the United States and from Britain; in return, it secured the support in the colony of those interests identified with the British connection. Failure of the rebellion in 1837 completed the political and religious isolation of the colony that had its beginnings in the American Revolution and the War of 1812.

Of even more crucial importance in the preservation of the religious influence in Canadian life was the failure of outside liberal movements to gain a hold in the country in the period from 1850 to the close of the century. This was the period in Great Britain and the United States that witnessed the growth of almost literally hundreds of rationalist, free-thinking societies. Scarcely one such society made its appearance in Canada before the closing years of the century. Instead, the period witnessed the emergence of powerful new religious denominations, the Methodist Church (Canada), the Presbyterian Church in Canada, the Church of England in Canada, and the Baptist Conference of Canada, fused out of smaller and less politically effective religious bodies. Nationalism served to emphasize, as colonialism had done earlier, the need of limiting contacts with liberal-revolutionary movements outside the country. The Civil War in the United States was for Canada, in effect, the fourth phase of the revolution that began with the War of Independence in 1776 and continued into the War of 1812 and the Rebellion of 1837. Confederation, as an effort to consolidate politically scattered communities which in themselves had few means of resisting encroachments on the part of the powerful neighbour to the south, grew, like the Constitutional Act and the Act of Union before it, out of forces of counter-revolution in the country. Lacking new frontiers for expansion the Canadian nation in the years after 1867 was able to gather strength through isolation. Within such a community, thus turned in on itself, religion faced no real challenge to its authority.

Developments in Canada since the turn of the century have been too complex to make possible any easy generalization respecting the strength of religious influences. In large areas of Canadian life, especially since the First World War, there has been a steady move away from a religious point of view. Nevertheless, the influence of organized religion in the country has perhaps never been stronger. Union of the Presbyterian, Methodist, and Congregational churches in 1925 has been followed by the development of new forms of interdenominational co-operation which have enormously strengthened the influence of Protestantism. At the same time, there has been a strengthening of the Roman Catholic ecclesiastical structure. Because of the political pressure they are able to exert, both Protestant and Roman Catholic churches have secured a degree of state support which provides them with many of the privileges of establishment. No political party in the country could survive if it openly attacked either of these churches.

International developments of the past quarter-century have had the effect of intensifying some of the conditions of insecurity of the Canadian national community. Preservation of national independence has involved a rejection of such anti-religious ways of thought as those associated not only with the American revolutionary tradition but with the revolutionary tradition of Russia. Canadians have not felt sufficiently secure in their national attachments to cultivate an attitude of tolerance. At the same time, developments within the country have led to a growing provincial or regional isolationism. Threats to the autonomy of French Canada have had the effect of increasing dependence upon the leadership provided by the Roman Catholic Church, while the growing political strength of French Canada in turn, has made English-speaking Canada more conscious of its Protestantism.

As a result of this continuous dependence upon the influence of religion in resisting outside political and cultural pressures, it is almost possible to think of the development of the Canadian community as having taken place within a closed theocratic-ecclesiastical system. The Canadian frontier has never been, like the American frontier, an area of unrestricted economic development. Rather, it has developed under what might be described as conditions of monopoly control. One of the important forces securing such control has been organized religion.

As all monopoly control tends to do, that of religion has placed a sharp brake upon the economic growth of the country. It has done so directly where, for instance, the church has been actually able to direct the movement of population and to prohibit any sort of economic endeavour which has threatened the religious interest. Out of such control there has developed at most a sort of theocratic monopolistic capitalism. But religion also, indirectly, has served to retard economic enterprise. The promotion of the religious interest in itself has involved a weakening of the economic interest because of the fundamental antagonism of the one to the other.

In the first place, the heavy drain upon the material resources of the country in maintaining institutions of religious worship has weakened the economic energies of the population. Church buildings have had to be erected, a body of religious teachers supported, and a decent portion of people's time devoted to performing the necessary rites and ceremonies of religion. The fundamental economic problem of a new country such as Canada has been that of mobilizing a sufficient supply of capital and labour to exploit fully its available resources. Where a large share of the capital and labour of the society has been diverted to the support of religious establishments the problem of securing a sufficient surplus to promote economic growth has been considerably intensified. The economic costs of religion cannot be easily calculated, but there would seem little doubt but that they have borne heavily upon various areas of the country at different times. In French Canada heavy ecclesiastical taxation in one form or another has meant that the capital required for the establishment of industry has come to a considerable extent either from outside capitalist groups, from the state, or from the church itself. In English-speaking Canada the burden of maintaining a religious structure has also made itself felt. In the colonial period, governmental, military, and ecclesiastical establishments made about equally heavy demands on the resources of a poor pioneer population, and, although the growing wealth of the country since the middle of the nineteenth century has made possible the easier financial support of religious institutions, the economic costs of religion in the way of large buildings, denominational colleges, missionary organizations, and salaried ministers have vastly increased. In poorer sections of the country where the resources of the population are limited, as for instance in certain parts of the Maritime Provinces, financial contributions to religious bodies have probably continued to be a factor in retarding economic growth.

In another closely related way, the religious interests of the population have tended to obstruct economic interests. Religion has given support to an attitude of mind, and a governmental policy, which has placed a check upon that kind of economic and social mobility conductive to the development of capitalism. Churches are essentially status institutions, and this has meant that the organization of religion has served to maintain status distinctions that have had no meaning in terms of economic endeavour. The strength of the aristocratic tradition in Canada owes much to the influence of religion. In Roman Catholic Quebec the notion of a socially superior class based upon family connection, education, and, usually, the ownership of land has been rooted deeply in the teachings of the church; there has been an aristocracy of old families that has proved itself on the whole inept in promoting new forms of economic enterprise. In English-speaking Canada, if the relation between religion and the class structure has been less obvious, it has been little less important. Church establishment in colonial times placed a considerable dependence upon a close alliance with a privileged upper class that lacked the imagination or inclination to take any sort of lead in the economic development of the country, and, although the formal disestablishment of the church weakened the religious support of such a class system, the organization of religion has continued to be sufficiently powerful to maintain to some degree the status distinctions of a religiously oriented rather than economically oriented society. By nepotism and other means church bureaucracy has succeeded in securing to the proper people positions of social distinction in the community. To the extent that such has been the case, and economic success as a result has not been the determinant of social worth, the economic ambitions of the population have been weakened.

Again, with respect to the moral results of its teachings, it would appear that the influence of religion has not been wholly favourable to economic development. The other-worldliness of the highly religious has resulted to some extent in an attitude of indifference to such worldly obligations as the payment of debts. If the judgment of various observers is to be trusted, business honesty has not been characteristic of religious populations. Rather, such business honesty has developed when people's positions in the community have become dependent upon social judgments in terms of secular values of worth. The development of capitalist economic enterprise, therefore, has involved the building of an ethical system opposed in many ways to that of religion. This has been successfully done only where the economic interest has gained dominance over the religious.

Finally, the influence of religion has checked the growth of that sort of rationalist attitude of mind favourable to economic activity. Economic success depends upon a clear appraisal of the relation of means to ends. Religion has tended to a confusion of this relation which inevitably has been carried over into the field of economic activity. It is scarcely correct to assume that religious-minded populations have successfully kept separate their religious and their economic attitudes and have been able to act perfectly rational outside the province of religious conduct. That has been possible only where emancipation from religious controls has been secured to some extent. Where religion has operated as a dominant force in people's lives, irrationality has tended to be characteristic of their way of thought and behaviour in general. Thus the effect of the religious influence has been to retard the development of that kind of coldly calculating mentality that has made for economic success. A readiness to place dependence upon divine intervention, as upon luck, is perhaps a necessary quality of the good gambler but not of the good business man.

If the effect of the religious influence generally has been to check economic growth, there would seem no reason to believe that any particular set of religious doctrines has been of importance as a factor in the economic development of the Canadian community. Essentially, the religious influence exerted through Protestantism in Canada has been no more favourable to the promotion of economic enterprise than the religious influence exerted through Roman Catholicism. If Roman Catholicism has appeared to offer a greater obstacle than Protestantism to economic growth, that has been largely because the religious influence has found stronger support in the Roman Catholic than in the Protestant ecclesiastical system. Where the Protestant religious organization has been strong the Protestant population has tended to be as economically unprogressive as the Roman Catholic population.

It has been the character of instability of the Protestant religious organization that has chiefly accounted for what difference there has been in the influence of Protestantism and of Roman Catholicism upon economic development. Where the Protestant organization of religion has faced continuous attack from schismatic sects, the religious influence of Protestantism in general has been weakened. It is true that the growth of new religious movements has tended to a strengthening immediately of the religious interests of the population; such movements have grown out of deep emotional experiences that have served to emphasize the importance of spiritual values of life. Ultimately, however, the effect has been to weaken the influence of religion by weakening its denominational supports; by producing divisions within religious organization the sects have destroyed some of religion's authority. It has been this indirect result of sectarian religious activity that has been so important in relation to economic development. The religious influence as such, exerted by the sects, has been no more favourable to economic growth than that exerted by the old, established, ecclesiastical bodies.

Thus, with respect to the effect upon economic development of the costs of supporting religious services, there has been no fundamental difference between the church and the sect forms of religious organization. It is true that the sects have not made as large financial demands upon the population as the more elaborately organized ecclesiastical bodies, but this has been so mainly because they have operated in areas of society that have not been able to support more expensive forms of religious organization. It has been "good business" in a sense to get along with cheaply constructed church buildings and low-paid religious teachers; a church that made greater demands had little chance to survive. The areas in which religious sects have grown up have been those that have had no surplus of capital and labour to be placed at the disposal either of expensive religious establishments or of new forms of economic enterprise. Only after such a surplus has appeared have the economic costs of sectarian religion become important in relation to economic development. With the increase in the wealth of the community, sectarian religious groups have sought to build about themselves elaborate ecclesiastical structures. But their primary influence as movements of religious separation has tended to the defeat of their ultimate purpose as religious institutions. Resentment of ecclesiastical taxation which they have cultivated among their followings in meeting the competition of more richly endowed religious bodies has persisted even after they themselves have become dependent upon such taxation. The result has been that the economic costs of religion have tended to fall below the level that the community has been able to afford, and the surplus of capital and labour that has accumulated has found an outlet in the development of economic enterprise.

Similarly, new sectarian religious movements, in their effect in weakening the traditional class structure of the community, have only indirectly favoured the growth of new forms of economic enterprise. Such movements have grown up in areas of society where class lines already had broken down; they have been a means of giving people who have had no definite status within the community a feeling of being important. This has meant that, rather than giving rise to a non-religiously oriented class system, they have created a class system in which the spiritually elect stood against the non-elect, and which rested accordingly upon a religious foundation. A social class that bases its claim to superiority on its special piety is not the sort of class that is likely to take a lead in promoting economic growth. Only after the influence of religion has been weakened as a result of division has the class system that sectarianism has created shifted from a religious to a secular basis. The spiritual elect of the sectarian society has very easily transformed itself into a class of economic entrepreneurs when the early enthusiasm of the religious revival has passed; the behaviour of such a class has been free of the controls of an institutionally powerful ecclesiastical system.

Again, with respect to the effect of their teachings upon the moral values of society, new sectarian religious movements only indirectly have favoured the growth of economic enterprise. These movements have grown up on what might be called the moral frontiers of society; they have developed out of conditions of moral breakdown where traditional standards of behaviour have no longer commanded respect. The task performed by them has been that of reawakening the moral sense of the population by bringing the moral problem into close relation with the problem of personal salvation. Thus their moral teachings, concerned almost wholly with the sin of man, have tended to be very largely other-worldly in emphasis. Within the moral system of the religious sectarian society there has been little room for the development of ethical standards associated with such worldly problems of behaviour as business activity. Yet the religious teachings of the sect have not provided a solid basis on which to erect a system of moral values; only when religious teachings have been caught up within a powerful religious organization have they been able to retain their moral force. It has been here, in the effect of weakening the organization of religion, that sectarian activity has contributed to the development of a system of moral values free of the religious influence. Once the extremely rigid controls exercised within the closed sectarian religious group have broken down, moral values have shifted easily from a religious to a secular basis. In this way the business ethics of capitalism have grown out of the moral teachings of religious sectarianism.

Finally, sectarian religious teachings scarcely have promoted that rational attitude of mind so essential for the successful prosecution of economic affairs. Rather the sects, growing up among those sections of the population that have placed little reliance upon reason, have tended to promote a state of general irrationality through their highly emotional appeal. Yet, paradoxical as it may appear, the ultimate effect often has been to encourage such highly rational forms of behaviour as business activity and scientific experiment. If religious fanaticism has resulted in a flight from reason, it also has resulted in a flight from the well-tried teachings of the church. Thus, whereas the irrationality produced through the influence of an ecclesiastically organized religion has rested upon a solid foundation of superstitions, myths, and dogma, the greater irrationality produced by religious sectarianism has tended to be converted into a rationalism the moment the hold of organized religion has weakened. It has been this indirect effect of sectarian religious activity in breaking through the walls of traditional beliefs and freeing the minds of people for more rational ways of thought that has given to it such importance in promoting economic development.

One of the distinctive characteristics of the development of the western world has been the maintenance of a condition of continuous instability in the organization of religion as a result of the rise of new sectarian religious movements. This has been particularly true of the United States where the failure to build up an elaborate ecclesiastical system supported by the state has been largely owing to the strength of the sectarian spirit in American religious life. This characteristic of religious organization has accounted in part for the rapid growth of American capitalism. With a religious organization not sufficiently strong to divert the energies of the population along channels of endeavour of advantage to the religious interest, such energies have found release in capitalistic activity.

A significant difference can be found here in the religious development of Canada and the United States. Canada, it is true, has had its sectarian religious movements as has the United States, but they have operated much less as a force weakening the hold of organized religion. The reason has been that Canada in a sense has not been able to afford the price it has been necessary to pay for religious division. Political pressures have forced the community to come to the support of organized religion and such support has placed a definite limitation upon sectarian activity. With the collective weight of the community brought to bear upon them, the sects have been forced either to retreat behind a wall of isolation or build themselves into an integral part of the community, or else they have been extinguished. Thus they have tended rather quickly to seek denominational supports by aligning themselves with the state and with the traditional institutions of the community. By accommodating themselves to powerful political and cultural interests they have come to secure strong support from such interests.

To some extent this was the case with respect to the development of the church in French Canada. Under Jesuit leadership, Roman Catholicism assumed in the beginning something of the character of a sectarian religion at war with the society about it. The uncompromising opposition to the fur trade led to the growing divorce of the church from politics and trade and to its isolation as the church of the habitant population. The steady decline of the religious influence in the colony after 1700 was indicative of the growing weakness of the social supports of Roman Catholicism with the expansion of commerce. But the precarious military situation forced the state to come to the support of religion even at the expense of trade, and the dissolution of the Jesuit Order paved the way for the accommodation of the church to the secular community. The effect of the British conquest was to accentuate dependence upon religion in maintaining the separate community identity of French Canada and thus to secure even more completely the secular support of religious organization. The narrow, separatist church which developed out of the frontier situation under Jesuit leadership grew into the socially and politically powerful church of nineteenth-century French Canada.

Similarly, in the Maritime Provinces, the rise of new sectarian religious movements, rather than weakening, resulted in the end in actually strengthening the Protestant church as a religious force in the community. The Maritimes shared with New England in the great awakening of the mid-eighteenth century, but, whereas in New England the resulting religious division led to the dissipation of much of the evangelical religious energies of the population and to the growth of strong liberal movements, in the Maritimes religious division was checked through political pressure and much of the religious fundamentalist outlook was preserved within the organized church. In New England, Unitarianism as well as Newlightism grew out of Congregationalism; in the Maritimes, only Newlightism survived the break-up of the Congregational churches. The counter-revolution following the Loyalist migration intensified dependence upon religious organization and forced the Protestant sectarian churches to identify themselves with colonial political interests in the colony. The formal alliance of Methodism with the English Wesleyan Conference was paralleled by the increasing dependence of the Newlight Baptist movement upon English Baptist leadership. Thus the break of the Methodists and Baptists from their American frontier origin, while it involved a shift from their earlier narrow sectarian position, did not involve a weakening of their religious influence. What the establishment of the British connection meant was a considerable strengthening of the denominational supports of religion and, in the end, a consequent strengthening of religion itself. The Protestant sectarian churches came to derive almost as much support from the colonial tie as the established church, and joined with the latter in resisting the spread of liberal influences into the area, either from Britain or the United States.

In Upper Canada, likewise, the religious sects that grew out of the great revival after 1800 were able in a way that they were not in the United States to preserve their original religious influence. In a sense, the effect of the War of 1812 was to perpetuate in Upper Canada the ways of thinking of the American frontier. By 1815 the western movement of American population had pretty well pushed beyond avenues reaching into the Canadian colony, and the later Upper Canadian society might have been expected to be increasingly affected by currents of thought reaching out from the East. It was this line of contact that was broken by the war. Upper Canada inherited the strong religious tradition of the American frontier but shared in little of the equally strong rationalist tradition associated with the great eastern universities and with the political and social thought growing out of the American and French revolutions. Paine was read in the United States but not across the border. Instead, the increasing British influence after 1815 brought to the sectarian churches the support of the whole colonial political system. The break of Canadian Methodism with American Methodism, and its alliance with English Wesleyanism, signified the shift to a position of accommodation to conservative political forces. Upper Canadian radicalism, with its ties with American and British radicalism, gained little support from religious movements that earlier had fought the established political-ecclesiastical order. Egerton Ryerson of the Methodist Church joined with Bishop Strachan of the Church of England in building up a politically powerful Protestant church that could command the support of the state. Isolation of liberal forces with the failure of the Rebellion of 1837 secured the dominant position of ecclesiasticism in the colony.

From 1850 until the opening of the West towards the close of the century the strength of forces of national consolidation was so great as virtually to prevent the growth of any free sectarian religious movements. The armed might of the state was brought to bear to crush the revolt of Louis Riel from the Roman Catholic Church in 1885. Small sects sought survival through isolation, as for instance the Mennonites in Manitoba and the Mormons in Alberta. No important religious denomination emerged out of a sectarian movement which grew up in the country during these years. Only the Salvation Army gathered any real strength as a force of religious separatism and, in its case, developments after the turn of the century, particularly the First World War, had the effect of making it an integral part of the community structure as a sort of social welfare institution.

It is still too early to determine how successful those religious sectarian movements that have grown up since 1900 will be in building themselves into powerful religious organizations with the support of the community behind them. The way in which the religious movement founded by William Aberhart in Alberta became caught up within a provincial political movement suggests that provincial political forces may become as important as are national forces in supporting a theocratic-ecclesiastical system. The Social Credit Government of the province of Alberta became virtually dedicated to the preservation of a religious fundamentalist outlook. The effort of the government of Ontario to introduce religious teachings in the public schools and the very active measures taken by the government of Quebec to oust the Jehovah's Witnesses and other sects from the province offer further examples of the growing support of ecclesiasticism by provincial political interests.

The close alliance between the state and the church in Canada has preserved more fully the influence of religion within an established ecclesiastical system and thus checked the free play of economic forces in the country. In contrast with the United States, the sects have been much less important in breaking down the hold of organized religion and thus in releasing the energies of the population for economic pursuits. Rather, the sects have been drawn into the theocratic-ecclesiastical structure of the community and have served to increase resistance to secular forces. This has been most evident within isolated ethnic-religious communities in the country such as those of the Mennonites, Doukhobors, or Hutterites. Here the conditions established by the simple sectarian organization of religion, the frugality and industry of the population, and the taboo upon expensive luxuries would seem such as to have encouraged economic enterprise, and yet these communities, though they have been agriculturally prosperous, have not produced a class of successful capitalists. Farming has involved no challenge to the religious way of life, but capitalist enterprise has. Thus, while the organized religious community has promoted collectively large-scale capitalist undertakings, as, for instance, the co-operative enterprises established in the Doukhobor communities in British Columbia, it has prevented individual members from acting as free economic agents.

Not all religious bodies in Canada have been as successful as the isolated ethnic-religious groups in building the organization of religion into the total community structure. In large areas of the Canadian society, division, in spite of efforts to check it, has served to weaken the influence of organized religion and to make for the strengthening of economic forces; it has been within such areas that the great capitalist enterprises have grown up in Canada. But even where emancipation from religious controls has extended furthest a sharp limitation has been placed upon activity of a purely secular character. Canada has been, and remains, a fundamentally religious nation. No great political or social upheaval in the country has served to break the close ties with a past which placed a great emphasis upon religious values of life. Insecurity has forced a dependence upon isolation, and in isolation the hold of tradition has been preserved.

PART III

Formative Influences in the Development of the Canadian Society

CHAPTER XI

The Canadian Community and the American Continental System*

RECENT STUDIES of Canadian-American relations, particularly in the social field, have served to give emphasis to the importance of the continental environment in the development of a common way of life on the North American Continent. Indeed, one is almost tempted to begin a paper such as this with the bald assertion that the Canadian community is but a pale reflection of the American community, and that if the reader wishes to learn something about it he need only refer to the extensive body of literature relating to social institutions and social behaviour in the United States. Nothing, it would seem at first glance, could be said about the Canadian community which has not already been said about the American.

Certainly, in many ways the Canadian community has been a northern extension of the American; population movements and the sharing of a common environment have led to a close similarity in social development. Exploitation of their North American resources has been a joint enterprise of the two peoples. There have emerged not two separate cultural systems—an American and a Canadian—but rather a number of distinctive forms of community organization, related more to underlying conditions of economic life than to political developments.

*From *Canada*, edited by George W. Brown (Berkeley and Toronto, 1950), pp. 375–89. With permission of the publisher. The original title read: "The Canadian Community."

On the Atlantic Coast, exploitation of the fisheries early led to the development of a form of community organization—the fishing village—which differed little in New England and Nova Scotia. In the continental interior the trade in furs made much the same social demands whether the traders were operating out of Albany or Montreal. The timber-lumbering industry of New Brunswick and the Ottawa Valley grew up in close relation to that of Maine, Vermont, and, later, Michigan and Wisconsin. The agricultural settlement of New Brunswick, the Eastern Townships, and Upper Canada was part of the great western movement of agricultural peoples which led after 1790 to the occupation of Upper New York State, western Pennsylvania, and the new states of Ohio, Tennessee, and Kentucky. The discovery of gold in the Fraser River Valley in the 1850's followed the discovery of gold in California, and the mining camps in British territory differed little from those which had grown up in the American West. Wheat farming on the plains of Canada gave rise to a society much like that which developed out of wheat farming on the plains of the United States. Out of the Industrial Revolution there grew up in English-speaking 'Canada cities which had little to distinguish them from those which had grown up across the border.

The forms of community organization which developed in Canada represented the adjustments of the population to their North American environment. Like similar forms across the border, they were the products of social experiments forced upon a people faced with new conditions of living. The effort to build societies on a common front brought the populations of the two parts of the continent close together. Though their cultural heritages were different, particularly before 1760, cultural differences tended to disappear upon settlement in America. The move from the Old World to the New, and from one area of the New World to another, often involved an almost complete break with the past. The very character of the settlement of America made for little continuity in the development of forms of social organization.

The settlement of America did not take place gradually. Rather, there were long periods when movements of population came almost to a halt. Wars and political uprisings, lack of transportation, ignorance of resources or failure to develop technological means of exploiting them, speculation in land, and the resistance of large economic organizations such as fur-trading companies to developments which threatened their monopolistic positions were some of the factors which held back the spread of population across the continent. When the barriers to migration did break down, the movement of population tended to be a flood. New means of transportation, technological developments in methods of production, realization of resources hitherto unknown, the up-swing of the business cycle, or sudden climatic changes were sufficient to attract attention to new areas of the continent and to set under way a mass movement of people.

Thus the settlement of America might be thought of as having taken place in a series of great "rushes." The sudden occupation of the Fraser River Valley after 1857 and of the Klondike after 1897 by gold seekers are two of the best examples of such rushes in the settlement of Canada, but other areas—the St. Lawrence Valley after 1660, the Annapolis Valley and the South Shore of Nova Scotia after 1760, the St. John and Miramichi valleys and the Great Lakes region after 1800, the Red River and Assiniboine valleys after 1880, the western prairies and the industrial city after 1900, the Canadian Shield after 1920—were occupied in much the same fashion by mass movements of population. It is true that settlement began long before the mass movement set in, but the simple forms of social organization established by the pioneers were swept aside by later comers. With thousands of bewildered people suddenly thrown together, strangers to one another and to the environment, pressing problems had to be solved hurriedly. New conditions forced an abandonment of traditional ways of thinking and behaving. In many respects the population began anew the task of building up a social system.

It is true that the loss of the Old World social heritage was offset in some degree by borrowings from the culture of the native. In North America, however, the native culture played no such role as in South America, where social continuity was secured through the absorption of the old society by the new. In North America, for the most part, the white man looked upon the Indian as a nuisance to be got out of the way; the Calvinist doctrine of predestination, in particular, offered an easy justification for the ruthless extermination of a race who were not of the elect. Only here and there, chiefly where the Roman Catholic attitude towards the native tended to prevail over the Protestant, were efforts made to draw upon the experience of the aboriginal inhabitants. In Canada there was no such military slaughter of the Indians as in the United States, but deprivation of their means of livelihood and the spread of disease served as effectively to decimate the Indians and to place them in a position of subjection. In much of Canada today Indian placenames are all that is left to remind one that the land was once occupied by the red man.

This sharp break with the past has accounted for much that is distinctive in American life. Out of the new societies growing up in America have come the challenges to Old World ways of doing things and Old World ways of thinking. Such societies have been the chief breeding grounds of the great American economic, political, social, and religious movements. The break with the cultural past has been evident in the development of the Canadian as of the American community. Movements of social reform have spread from one side of the border to the other. Canada has shared with the United States in the frontier revolt against established society.

Geography has drawn the two countries together socially, yet there are many striking differences between them. Powerful forces have operated to bring about a distinctive development of many important aspects of Canadian society. The influence of these forces was most evident in the frontier—the very area where a common way of life showed most signs of developing. In the United States— or in that part of America which later became the United States— few restraints were imposed upon the opening up of new areas of settlement. Population moved in freely, and there was little interference from the outside in the building of the new society. People were left largely to rely on their own resources. In Canada, however, the risk of absorption by the southern neighbour was too great to permit the unrestricted development of new areas of settlement.

The frontier was a great leveller in a political as well as in a social sense; it tended to destroy Old World political loyalties and thus to weaken Old World political attachments. The movement for the political independence of the British colonies in America before 1774 was a reflection to some extent of the separatist political tendencies of the frontier, but the political independence of the colonies, especially after the collapse of the French Empire in America, involved no great danger of the intrusion of a foreign power. For Canada, however, such intrusion was always a real danger. Before 1760 the lines of the French Empire reaching into the interior of the continent lay exposed on the south to attack from the English-speaking colonies. After 1760 British control of the interior through the St. Lawrence was similarly challenged by the independent-minded Atlantic seaboard colonies and, after 1784, by the new Republic of the United States. The Quebec Act of 1774, the American War of Independence, the long struggle after 1784 for control of the western posts, and the War of 1812–14 revealed the intensity of the conflict for lines of communication reaching into the interior. Outlying settlements in British North America, in New Brunswick, Upper Canada, the Eastern Townships, and the Red River Valley, on the Pacific Coast, and even on the western prairies, faced the threat, as had the earlier French settlements, of absorption by their neighbour to the south.

Because of this threat the grip of political authority could not be relaxed within new areas of settlement in Canada as it tended to be south of the border. The Canadian frontier grew up within the protective custody, first, of the French colonial Empire, then of the colonial Empire of Britain, and finally, after 1867, of the Dominion itself. Thus the fur-trading posts of New France, the fishing villages of Nova Scotia, the lumbering camps and agricultural settlements of New Brunswick and Upper Canada, the mining towns of the Pacific Coast and of the Klondike, and the prairie farm communities of the West did not develop merely as economic areas of production and exchange; they were also important outposts of Empire or nation. Defence constituted, along with trade, a determinant of lines of community development and forms of social organization. An army, or at least a special constabulary force, usually followed close upon the heels of the frontiersmen; indeed, many of the earliest settlements, for instance that of the Richelieu Valley in New France and of Perth in Upper Canada, were effected by military organization. Other agencies, particularly the church, played an equally important role in maintaining political control in frontier areas. The result was to make for the more orderly development of the Canadian than of the American frontier. The radical departures from accepted practice which were characteristic of the behaviour and thinking of American frontier populations in political organization, justice, family life, cultural relationships, and religious organization were less evident in the Canadian frontier population. The conservatism of the country as a whole operated as a powerful force in checking innovations.

In political organization the spirit of revolt and experimentation has not been lacking. Support of the revolutionary cause by large numbers of Nova Scotians and French Canadians in 1776, the movement of political disaffection among many Upper Canadians during the War of 1812–14, the Gourlay agitation and the rebellions in Lower and Upper Canada in 1837, the rise of the Clear Grit movement after 1850, the Red River Rebellion of 1870 and the Northwest Rebellion of 1885, the defiance of Canadian political authority by miners' associations in the Klondike in 1900, the rise of farm political movements in western Canada after the First World War, the Winnipeg general strike in 1919, and the growth of the Social Credit movement in Alberta and of the C.C.F. movement in western Canada and industrial Ontario after 1932 are indications of the strength of the challenges to constituted authority. But such movements of revolt, in contrast with similar movements in the United States, were arrested before they could make their influence significantly felt in the political life of the country.

In the United States, support of political reform offered a means of strengthening the political structure of the nation; the Republic was in effect a product of revolution, and movements of political reform after 1784 served to sharpen politically the divorce from the Old World and to make American institutions more distinctive. In Canada, however, reform movements threatened to draw the population more closely to the southern neighbour and to weaken if not destroy the political ties of Empire or, after 1867, of nation. This was true even when such movements drew their inspiration from the Old World, as, for instance, in New France before 1760, in Upper Canada during the 1830's, and in western Canada after 1920. The attack upon political institutions implied a challenge to constituted authority, and the danger was great that a state of confusion would lead to the intervention of the southern neighbour. William Lyon Mackenzie and Louis Riel are obvious examples of reform leaders who, though advocating ideas only partly American in origin, found themselves leading movements which derived much of their support from across the border.

Thus the effort to build up a political system in Canada which would remain independent of the United States involved the imposition of strong checks upon revolutionary tendencies. New France was isolated from revolutionary France through the building up in the colony of a powerfully centralized political and ecclesiastical system. The British colonies and, after 1867, the Canadian nation were similarly isolated from outside revolutionary influences by the maintenance of a strong system of political control, supported by the church, a privileged upper class, and, before 1870, the British army and navy. Whereas the American nation was a product of the revolutionary spirit, the Canadian nation grew mainly out of forces of a counter-revolutionary character.

In the development of institutions of law and order, similar forces of conservatism operated to restrain the influence of the frontier. Areas developing beyond the reach of the law have not been unknown in Canada. In the fur-trading interior of New France, the transient fishing settlements of Cape Breton and the east shore of New Brunswick, the lumbering camps of the St. John, Miramichi, and Ottawa valleys, the shanty towns of Irish canal-workers, the mining camps of the Fraser River Valley and the Klondike, and the congested areas of the growing cities, widespread lawlessness and disorder developed. Crime was an expression of the emancipation of the population from the traditional controls of an Old World society. Efforts to enforce the law assumed the character of interference from outside; the authority of the police and the courts was challenged by that of the gang, the vigilante committee, and the mob. Yet, in contrast with the United States, such challenges to constituted authority were never strong enough to lead to a general breakdown of law and order.The fire-arm was much less important in Canada than it was in the United States in defending the frontiersman from the North American Indian and from his fellow frontiersman. Seldom in the Canadian frontier did force pass out of the hands of the state. The Vigilante Committee organized in San Francisco in 1857 or the gang rule of Soapy Smith in Skagway in 1897 has no true parallel in Canadian experience.

The reason was that frontier settlement in Canada rarely extended far beyond the reach of the military forces of Empire or nation. The United States had no pressing reason for providing military protection to outlying settlements; border warfare, whether with the Indians, the Spanish, the Mexicans, or, before 1760, the French, was left mainly to the settlers. The vulnerability of the Canadian frontier, however, forced early attention to problems of defence, with the result that law-enforcement agencies could usually rely upon the support of military forces. Thus about the fur-trading posts of New France, in the agricultural settlements of New Brunswick and Upper Canada, and in the shanty towns of Irish canal-workers the army played an important role in maintaining order. In the isolated fishing settlements of Nova Scotia, policing was a function of the navy. A force of Royal Engineers put an end to lawlessness in the mining camps of British Columbia. Settlement of the western prairies and the gold rush to the Klondike took place under the close control of the North West Mounted Police. Even in Canadian cities, serious threats to law and order have been met by the decisive use of force.

The result was to establish a tradition of respect for the institutions of law and order. The population generally did not feel the need of taking the law into its own hands through mob action or the organization of vigilantes. There was lacking that intense jealousy of local rights which in the United States made it difficult for federal forces to intervene. The way in which the North West Mounted Police came into being was in striking contrast with that of the Texas Rangers. In the United States the frontier bred a spirit of liberty which often opposed efforts to maintain order. In Canada, order was maintained at the price of weakening that spirit.

The institution of the family similarly has found support from conservative forces in the Canadian community. In the family, as in other forms of social organization, the disturbing influence of the frontier made itself felt. The rapid increase in the Canadian divorce rate in recent years is a reflection of family disorganization which is closely related to urban growth and the weakening of puritan values. Before the turn of the century few divorces were known, but family disorganization as a social phenomenon reaches back to the beginnings of the Canadian community. By its very character the frontier tended to be a society of men: the fur-trading post, the lumbering camp, the agricultural settlement, the mining town, the ranching community, and even the manufacturing city (as distinguished from the more mature urban community with a diversity of economic interests) were made up predominantly of men in the age group from eighteen to forty. In such areas, large sections of the population lived entirely outside the family system, and there developed such substitute forms of social organization as prostitution and the partnership of two men to meet needs ordinarily satisfied within the family. The disorganizing effects of such developments upon the mores of the community were evident, for instance, in the rural society of New France brought into close contact with the fur-trading frontier, the agricultural settlements of New Brunswick which grew up alongside timber and lumbering camps, the old fur-trading and governmental centre of Victoria which served during the gold rush as the disembarking point and supply centre of the mining population, and the urban community developing in relation to manufacturing and the new northern frontier of mining and pulp and paper. The two world wars have

only accentuated the effect upon family life of the disorganizing influences growing out of conditions within the Canadian
community.

The much lower divorce rate in Canada than in the United
States, however, indicates a greater stability in family organization,
which has been as true of the past as of the present. The restraining
influence exerted upon Canadian frontier development had the
effect of limiting the degree of emancipation from moral values.
Controls of social class and the church lent strong support to the
controls of a traditional morality. There was less readiness to
accept unconventional forms of behaviour in matters relating to
the family. Whereas in the United States the frontier spirit of experimentation led to a modification of forms of family life and to
a tolerant attitude towards deviations from traditional moral
standards, in Canada such a spirit was severely checked through
the pressure of strong forces of social conservatism. Frontier patterns of revolt against the controls of a formal family system, as for
instance among the *coureurs de bois* of New France or within the
bohemias of the urban community, tended to be confined to the
peripheral areas of society and to have little effect upon behaviour
generally.

The strength of the puritan tradition in Canadian society has not
been unrelated to the strength of the aristocratic tradition; the spirit
of equalitarianism generated within the frontier situation, like that
of libertarianism, was greatly moderated by the opposing spirit of
conservatism. Canada shared with the United States in the great
democratic movement, with its almost fanatical emphasis upon the
principle that all men are equal. The frontier provided unfavourable
ground on which to build an elaborate structure of social classes,
which broke down under the influence of the common experience
of frontier life. The social worth of the individual was measured in
terms of accomplishment rather than in terms of family background.
Thus, in New France, seigneurs had difficulty in maintaining a social
status which set them apart from the lowly habitants or, indeed,
from the bush rangers. In the new agricultural settlements of the
Maritime colonies, the Eastern Townships, Upper Canada, and,
much later, the western prairies, upper-class families were forced
into close social association with families of lower standing, and
differences in social worth quickly disappeared along with differences in economic worth. Even more, in such highly mobile areas
as mining towns and industrial cities, an inherited class structure

tended to disintegrate in the face of powerful forces of equalitarianism. Yet, in spite of the strength of such forces, the aristocratic principle has persisted as an important organizing influence in Canadian society.

The strength of the military interest in itself served to emphasize the importance of class distinctions. Because the frontier was usually garrisoned by military forces, there was present from the beginning a strong influence operating against democratic tendencies. The military emphasized and lent support to distinctions in status. In the town of Quebec under the French régime, and in the British colonial centres of Halifax, Fredericton, Kingston, York (Toronto), and Victoria, the army or navy, with its officers in smart uniform, gave the local society a colour and dash which were lacking in American frontier communities. Even in the new Canadian frontiers, the Klondike, the western prairies, the industrial city, and the northern mining communities, the military tradition, as represented by the Northwest or later the Royal Canadian Mounted Police, had some influence upon social class relationships.

Efforts to strengthen the political ties of Empire or of nation led to deliberate attempts, through land grants and political preferments, to create and strengthen an aristocracy in the colonies of New France, Nova Scotia, Prince Edward Island, New Brunswick, Upper Canada, and British Columbia, and, later, in a less obvious fashion, in the Canadian nation. The democratic movement, it was felt, was liable to draw Canadian people closer to their neighbours to the south; and a privileged upper class was a bulwark of loyalty and conservatism. Though the economic forces of the frontier tended to the destruction of class differences, as, for instance, in the Upper Canadian backwoods community of the 1830's, the effect was neutralized in some degree within a political and military system of class privilege; many upper-class persons who proved unsuccessful as farmers obtained appointments in the government or the army. The frontier had two things of value to offer—land and offices—and both were reserved to an important degree for a privileged few.

The strength of the aristocratic tradition in Canada, though not easily measured, is revealed in the political attitudes of the population, the educational institutions, the patriarchal organization of the family, and the respect for old and established leaders. Though few Canadians would consciously subscribe to a society based upon class distinctions, the belief in the social superiority of certain groups underlies much of their thinking. There has been lacking in

Canadian experience that explicit rationalization of an equalitarian philosophy which in the United States was a product of revolution. The aristocratic tradition was too deeply rooted in the political philosophy of Empire to be destroyed by the equalitarian forces of the frontier.

In Canada, as in the United States, the frontier acted as a great melting pot of different ethnic cultures whereby the population was forced to conform to a common pattern of thought and behaviour. Though New France after 1660, Upper Canada after 1800, and the western prairies and industrial cities after 1900 were settled by people of diverse cultural backgrounds, a common cultural type soon emerged in these different areas. Assimilation proceeded even more rapidly in such highly mobile areas as the mining frontier. The breakdown of cultural differences on the frontier hastened the development of a single Canadian type.

Yet the persistence of ethnic differences suggests that assimilation did not proceed unchecked. The separation of the two chief cultural groups, the French-speaking and the English-speaking, offers the best example of the preservation of inherited ethnic loyalties within the Canadian cultural system, but ethnic separatism has not been a characteristic of the French Canadians only. Throughout English-speaking Canada there has been a similar tendency towards the preservation of inherited cultural attachments among English, Irish, Scots, Americans, central Europeans, and Asiatics.

Such a tendency has been a reflection of the colonial character of Canadian society. Assimilation in Canada meant an increasing conformity to American values of life and standards of behaviour. Efforts to check American influences in Canadian cultural life thus involved the strengthening of the supports of ethnic group loyalties. British colonial policy offered no real encouragement to the assimilation of the French-Canadian population, particularly after 1774, when assimilation would have meant the more rapid spread of American revolutionary ideas in the colony. Similarly, in Nova Scotia, New Brunswick, and Upper Canada the chief bulwarks against the growth of the American revolutionary movement were the Old World loyalties of the population; state support of an upper-class social system offered one means of keeping such loyalties alive. Since 1867, paradoxically, the security of the Canadian nation has depended upon discouraging a too strong Canadian nationalism. Preservation of English and Scots and Irish group loyalties served to perpetuate the colonial attitude of the Canadian people and thus to check the spread of American influence. In the United States the Briton hastened to become a good American; in Canada he has been encouraged to remain a good Briton. Nor has any vigorous effort been made to assimilate continental European peoples in Canada, except through the public schools; as with the French Canadians, the break of continental Europeans from their cultural past has tended to expose them to American influences. The maintenance of the political attachments of Empire or nation depended upon the cultural isolation of the population within the American continental system, and such isolation has been secured most effectively through the preservation of Old World loyalties.

Finally, the religious development of Canada, in contrast with that of the United States, has reflected the influence of strong conservative or traditionalist forces operating to check the influence of the frontier. In Canada, as in the United States, the frontier was a breeding ground of new churches and sects. The failure of Old World churches to gain leadership in frontier areas, and the weakening of traditional social values and forms of social organization encouraged the population to join whatever religious groups made their appearance. Sects developed naturally out of the frontier situation in response to the need for new and satisfying group loyalties. No Canadian frontier escaped the phenomenon of religious upheaval.

In New France, it is true, restrictions upon the settlement of Huguenots made impossible the development of any religious movement outside the Roman Catholic Church, but much the same sort of spirit as sectarianism found expression within the Jesuit Order. Later religious movements, both within and outside the church, have similarly tended to weaken the Roman Catholic ecclesiastical structure in Canada; schisms among central European Catholics in western Canada are recent examples of sectarian development. Among Protestants, of course, religious division has been much more pronounced. The history of Protestantism in Canada has been characterized by a series of religious upheavals which have precluded the development of unity within the church as a whole. Even to list the names of the sects which have appeared at different times would be impossible. Schisms within churches have been succeeded by new schisms to add to the confusion. The recent growth of movements such as the Pentecostal, Pentecostal Holiness, Nazarene, Apostolic, Church of God, Four Square Gospel, Christian and Missionary Alliance, and Jehovah's Witnesses demonstrates the continuing state of disunity of the Protestant body.

Nevertheless, a considerable degree of stability has been characteristic of the religious organization of the Canadian community. The large denominations have succeeded in maintaining a strongly influential position in spite of the weakening effects of religious division. Soon after Confederation the various branches of Presbyterians and Methodists came together in two great national churches. The Baptists, the Disciples of Christ, and even the Salvation Army and the Pentecostals gradually lost much of their extreme separatist character in accommodating themselves to the secular social structure. The union of the Methodist, Presbyterian, and Congregational churches to form the United Church of Canada in 1925 and the more recent formation of the Canadian Council of Churches mark a culmination of developments reaching back to the beginnings of Protestant religious organization in the country.

Powerful political and cultural forces served to support the denominational organization of religion and to check extreme manifestations of religious division. The church, as distinguished from the sect, closely identified itself with the interests of Empire or nation. By its very nature it depended upon the maintenance of the traditional loyalties. In offering support to established political attachments, it was able to command, in turn, a measure of political support. Thus the Roman Catholic Church in French Canada, the Church of England in the British colonies, and more recently the United Church of Canada enjoyed many of the privileges of a state church, whether or not legally established. Maintenance of the political ties of Empire or nation has depended upon the maintenance of a system of ecclesiastical control in the Canadian community.

Movements of religious division, on the other hand, have been viewed as threats to traditional political attachments. By its otherworldly appeal, the sect tended to deprecate the importance of such secular interests as the state; it sought the full and undivided loyalty of its followers. When the sect was American in origin, the political implications of its teachings were particularly disturbing. Lack of interest in the welfare of the state was assumed to be a disguise for attitudes of political disloyalty. Thus the full weight of the traditional political and social order was brought to bear, directly and indirectly, against the development of sectarian movements. The result was to make for the rapid accommodation of such movements to secular interests. The Newlight Baptists, the Methodists, the Disciples of Christ, and the Salvation Army early broke with the parent churches in the United States and shifted from a separatist position to seek closer ties within the Canadian community. Where such ties were not secured, as in the Jesuit Order in New France and the Riel group in the Northwest Territories, the sect was virtually outlawed by the state.

The effect has been to give a conservative character to religious organization in Canada. The hold of tradition has been strong, and new forms of religious organization and new types of appeal have received little encouragement. Fanaticism has been confined mainly to the fringes of society. On the other hand, Canada has been unfriendly to a too liberal approach to religious teachings; such movements as Unitarianism have made little headway. Religious organization has been built closely into the political and social structure of the community, and change has come slowly in the face of resistance from powerful interests identified with the established order.

The strength of the ties with the Old World is exemplified in the maintenance of the imperial connection. Canada has no revolutionary tradition. At no time in their history have the people turned their back on the past and placed their whole faith in the future. The lack of such an emotional experience has affected the development of all aspects of Canadian society. It is this which accounts for what is most distinctive in the national character.

CHAPTER XII

Education and
Social Change in Canada*

IN A PAPER concerned with the problem of education and social change in the twentieth century it is tempting to turn, as most other Canadian commentators have done, to the case of French Canada where developments of the past half-century have presented a striking example of how a tradition-bound educational system has failed to meet the needs of a rapidly changing society. Here the problem remains largely one of seeking to persuade educators who do not want to change that change is vitally necessary. In English-speaking Canada, in contrast, those who command the important posts of education, with only a few exceptions, have been persons who have clearly identified themselves with the cause of social progress and advancement. Almost every official release, of the various provincial departments of education, urges the importance of new and advanced methods of classroom teaching and school organization, and the boast is constantly made that in the nature of the school curriculum and the style of school architecture education is keeping abreast of the times. Under such circumstances, it might appear that there was little to be said about the problem of education and social change in English-speaking Canada.

Yet in certain respects, perhaps, the educational system of English-speaking Canada has been no more responsive to social change than the educational system of French-speaking Canada. An

*From *Transactions of the Third World Congress of Sociology*, 1956, vol. V, pp. 64–70. With permission of the publisher.

educational system may become a powerful force directed towards maintaining the status quo not only because of its command of the resources of the state or of the church and its elaborate and propaganda-minded bureaucratic organization but because every person in the community whose social position depends upon the education he received is in some way its apologist. The doctor of medicine, the lawyer, the engineer, the druggist, the minister of the gospel, and indeed even the minor civil servant, are possessors of certain special educational qualifications which entitle them to perform certain special services, and the education of which they were recipients can scarcely be repudiated without repudiating the claims which are made on the basis of that education. It is just here that education can operate so powerfully as a force of conservatism in society. Changing social conditions lead to a demand for new kinds of services and thus for new types of training but such changes tend to be strongly resisted by those with vested interests in old established forms of training. The greater freedom of the educator in English-speaking Canada from what might be called parochial influences has made it more possible for him than for his counterpart in French-speaking Canada to overcome the resistance of that powerful class within the community and within educational circles which has a stake in established forms of education, and to introduce change. Yet there is a point beyond which even the most socially conscious educators have not been prepared to go in the effort to adapt an educational system to changing social needs, and in this respect there has been no essential difference between English- and French-speaking Canada.

To the educator who likes to think of himself as socially conscious, whatever is directed towards the object of adapting education more fully to the needs of present-day society is considered desirable, but this may mean little more than making education serve better the interests of dominant cultural groups in society. Educational reform thus becomes a force in support of the established order of things. In a business culture such as ours, extension of the hold of rational forms of thought tends to become the end to which education strives. For the vast majority of the population an education such as this may well serve its best interests, but this may clearly not be true of certain sections of the population whose needs are not being taken care of within the dominant culture, and it is these sections of the population which are the most caught up in social change. Under such circumstances, the traditionalist, intent on cherishing values of the past and acutely aware of the danger of any slavish conforming to the present, may well prove the real radical in education.

In a new country like Canada, the development of which has been characterized by the sudden opening up and settlement of large, hitherto unoccupied land areas and by the equally sudden conversion of peaceful countrysides and small rural towns into great sprawling industrial cities, the problem of building up a social system which would meet all the various needs of the population has been very great, and the rise at different times and in different places of new movements of economic, political, social and religious organization indicates that the effort to establish such a system has not always and everywhere been wholly successful. In what might be called the outer fringes of the society, in the new farming, mining, lumbering and fishing communities and in the new growing areas of the industrial cities, large sections of the population have found themselves in sharp conflict with the dominant interests and social groupings of the established society.

Primarily, the problem of social organization here, as in all situations of social change, is one of the development of kinds of social needs which can be satisfied only by persons possessing a different kind of educational training from that which hitherto has been provided within society, but here the changes required in the form of educational training offered are of a sort which cannot readily be made within the established educational system. What occurs, where new movements of social organization take their rise, is in effect a revolt against the leadership of the established society and consequently, indirectly but in a very real fashion, against the kind of education upon which such a leadership bases its claims.

To persons economically and socially insecure, seeking within a new kind of social order a more satisfactory form of life, there are two things basically wrong with the leadership of the established society: it imposes upon the population for its support too heavy financial demands and it fails to provide the kind of leadership which is wanted. Both failings to some extent can be attributed to the kind of educational training of which it is a product. A long, expensive educational training makes necessary substantial rewards in the way of fees, salaries, or financial returns of other sorts while a training designed to fit persons to serve in the more favoured circles of society may have the effect of making them unfit to serve in less favoured circles. So it seems to those more socially harassed sections of the population which is offered, by the leaders of the old established political parties, by ministers of the gospel in the traditional churches, and by the representatives of such socially protected professions as medicine and law, cures for its political, spiritual, physical and litigious ills which while costly produce no certain results. To get the kind of government, spiritual solace, medical attention, or legal aid wanted, and which is not too costly, may involve breaking outside the social system established for providing such services and turning to persons who lack the kind of educational qualifications demanded within the society at large.

Thus, for instance, the farmers of Alberta in 1920, in seeking a change of government, entered into a political association which stipulated that no one could run for political office who was not a bona fide farmer. Fifteen years of Liberal rule in Alberta had demonstrated the extreme difficulty faced by anyone who had not come up through the usual channels of party preferment, beginning ordinarily with a career in law or small-town business, of getting anywhere in politics. At one stroke, in the election of 1921, all those persons who had what hitherto had been an accepted background of training and experience for politics were swept from office and an entirely new kind of leadership created.

Similarly, in Alberta again, in 1935, when the leaders of the United Farmers' party could now boast of fifteen years of education through political and administrative experience, there occurred, out of the desperation created by the great depression, a new sudden break from an accepted type of leadership. Newspaper interviews held with the members of the Social Credit administration were revealing of the kind of claims made by the new political leaders of Alberta. Almost without exception these new ministers of the Crown boasted that they were men completely lacking in political experience, in many cases previously so uninterested in politics that they had not voted, or subscribed to any newspaper or magazine; that until the truths of Major Douglas and Mr. Aberhart were made known to them they had been wholly ignorant of economic matters; that, indeed, they had none of the preparation usually expected of people entering into public life.

The significant thing about these two political movements in Alberta was that they based their appeal on their freedom from dependence on a leadership made up of men of education and experience. There was no apology that, because they were a new party, they had not yet got their full share of leaders with acceptable qualifications. Their virtue lay in the fact that the men they put forward for public office, being of simple tastes, would not expect the kind of material rewards accorded to persons of more accomplished attainments and, being comparatively uneducated and wholly inexperienced, would neither have been misled by the false teachings of, for instance, economics and political science as offered within the universities nor have been taught the arts of political corruption by service in a party organization. They were thus men who could be expected to serve the people of Alberta honestly and well.

Something of this sort of thing occurs with the rise of any new political movement, such as the C.C.F., the Union Nationale, and, where it seeks to make a popular appeal, Communism. The attack upon the entrenched positions of established political parties and institutions involves, to some degree at least, an attack upon that whole system of training upon which the leadership of these parties and institutions bases its claims. Thus Jacksonian democracy, as represented in Canada by various movements seeking a more direct control by the people of its political affairs, contained within it something of an anti-educational philosophy.

Even clearer was the attitude of hostility to an educational training which found expression in those new movements of religious reform the growth of which has been such a characteristic feature of the religious development of Canada. The new religious sects very deliberately turned to the leadership of men who had little or no academic or theological training. The less education a preacher had the closer to God he was believed to be. Thus, in denying the value of an educational training, the sects demolished virtually all those special claims of the established clergy as ministers of the gospel. The way was opened for the intrusion of the part-time local preacher and the itinerant evangelist who because he "lived off the country" expected no great material reward, and because he had no great education could be expected to have a firmer hold upon the simple truths of Christianity.

With respect to medicine and law there is no way of knowing to what extent certain elements of the population have turned to the services of persons lacking prescribed educational qualifications. Judging from newspaper reports, and from knowledge of conditions in such a city as Calgary, Alberta, in the 1930's the number of what might be called quacks practising medicine in various parts of Canada at different times has not been inconsiderable, but the strength of the reaction against the medical or the legal profession cannot be determined by the incidence of those sorts of acts which involve a breach of public regulations. Thousands of people, it may be suspected, in those areas of the community least economically and socially well off, stay away from doctors and lawyers except in cases of urgent necessity and turn for medical or legal advice to persons who, because they publicly make no claims to possession of the skills of the doctor or lawyer, cannot be apprehended by the authorities of the law. A reluctance to pay the fees exacted by the medical or the legal profession (the size of which is often exaggerated in the minds of such people) has much to do with this tendency to "shop around" and find someone who can provide the same sort of services at much less cost. In addition, however, there is, among such sections of the population, a deeply rooted distrust and suspicion of the kind of learning possessed by medically or legally trained persons. Getting "into the clutches" of the doctor or lawyer is something which strikes terror into the hearts of such people.

It should not be concluded from this that movements directed against the established leadership of society grow out of feelings of unconditional hostility to education. There is, among people caught up in such movements, an ambivalence in their attitude to education as, indeed, there is in their attitude to many institutions of society. Such people may have an overwhelming desire to secure for their sons and daughters that education which will provide them with the kind of opportunities enjoyed by young persons in more favoured social circles and thus may be insistent that nothing is too good— and thereby too modern—in the way of educational institutions. More than that, such people may develop an enormous faith in "education," meaning by education that which offers easy and immediate solutions to the kind of problems they face. Such attitudes to education as these may be combined in a way not entirely contradictory with one of distrust and suspicion. The very same person who wants his son to become a lawyer, or who joins a study group to learn more about the legal problems of, for instance, trade unionism, may be highly distrustful of lawyers or lawyer-politicians, and that on the grounds of the kind of training they had received.

It is easy for the apologist of an established educational system to take comfort in the view that this failure of certain persons to recognize the value of an educational training is a result of ignorance and that all that is necessary is to reveal to them some of the "truths" of which the educated person is a recipient. It was this sort of thinking which, in the Alberta election of 1935, led one of the old parties to bring into the province a professor of economics to expose the falsehoods of Social Credit and another of these parties to arrange for a series of radio broadcasts to be given by its intellectually most able leader on the unconstitutionality of the Social Credit programme. Nothing could have been better calculated than either of these two acts to convince the Alberta electorate that the old party leadership of the province, with all its learning, had nothing to offer it. The truth was that, given the kind of economic and political ills this electorate was suffering at the time, the old party leadership, wedded to certain economic, political and constitutional doctrines currently being taught in the universities, had nothing to offer it. Likewise, it would appear evident that in those areas where the old established churches or such professions as those of medicine and law have come under attack, the reason has been that they were not able to offer cures (given the uncertain definition of what a cure really is) of the kind of spiritual, physical, or legal ills being suffered by certain people.

One might well question thus some of the sociological assumptions underlying discussion of such a movement of educational reform as that in French Canada. Wedded as many of them have become to a functionalist theory of society, sociologists, like psychologists, have been too much inclined to stress the importance of processes of adjustment and integration at the expense of processes of conflict and disorder as forces of change in personality or social organization. To build bigger and better equipped engineering schools, to crowd classics and philosophy out of the school curricula to make room for the social and natural sciences and to introduce programmes of teacher training are thought of as steps in advance in making over the educational system of French Canada. Like all persons in economically and socially insecure positions, the French Canadian is faced with the problem of providing for the future of his son or daughter, and if the young French-speaking Canadian is to compete successfully with the young English-speaking Canadian he must have an educational equipment which is equal to the latter's. Thus the drive to "modernize" the educational system of French Canada, to make it conform to the demands of the dominant Anglo-Saxon culture. But the French Canadian, caught up in the changes taking place in his society, and seeking relief, turns to values of the past and to a reassertion of the simple truths of nationality and religion. It would be foolhardy to suggest that he is mistaken in doing so, considering what the dominant Anglo-Saxon culture has immediately to offer him. Rather the real radical in French Canada may well be that person determined to resist at all costs the values of this dominant culture.

What this means is that an educational system which seeks "to keep astride of the times" may fail to meet the needs of those people most fully exposed to forces of social change. That is not to say that the simple reaction of distrust of education offers any real solution in itself to the kinds of problems such people face. Nor is it to say that those expedients which may be resorted to as alternatives to an educational training represent any real advance in preparing people for positions of leadership in society. The establishment, within new movements of political, social, or religious reform, of various kinds of training schools such as labour or bible colleges, may lead, in certain particulars, to new and improved methods of training within the established educational system, but developments such as these, for the most part, are in the way of compromises forced upon movements if they are to survive in the social world in which they find themselves. The siginfiance of the growth of an attitude of distrust of education lies not in the direct effect of leading to improvements in forms of educational training but in the indirect effect of giving support to movements directed against the established leadership structure of society. Change is forced upon the social system from without, by the repudiation of that form of educational training of which its leadership is a product. It is thus that reactionism may operate, within education as within other areas of social life, as a revolutionary force within society.

CHAPTER XIII

The Frontier
in the Development of the
Canadian Political Community*

IMPLICIT IN MUCH OF THE WRITING on Canadian political history has been the assumption that an entirely different set of forces have shaped the development of democratic institutions in this country than in the United States. Whether because Canada learnt from the political experience of nineteenth- rather than eighteenth-century Britain, or because the tradition of the country has been more British, Canadians have been thought less inclined than their neighbours across the border to experiment with radical political solutions to their problems. Rather, they have sought through an orderly process to adapt their political institutions to changing circumstances. Thus the distinctive Canadian contribution to the development of democratic political organization has been considered the working out of the principles of responsible government within the framework of a system of imperial, and later federal, control. The more radical principle of checks and balances, involving the separation of the executive and legislative functions of government, written into the Constitution of the United States, has been avoided as foreign to the spirit of Canadian political life.

*From *Transactions of the Royal Society of Canada*, vol. XXVIII, Series III, June, 1954, Section Two, pp. 65–75. With permission of the publisher. The original title read: "The Frontier and Democratic Theory."

That Canada has a political tradition more conservative than the United States would seem evident. This country remained within the British Empire, ultimately to secure separation by peaceful means; the people of the United States fought for and won their independence on the field of battle. The contrast today between the political institutions, and the informal processes of government, of the two countries reflects the different background of political development.

Concern to demonstrate the distinctiveness of Canada's political institutions, however, has led to a failure to recognize fully the importance of very similar forces in the political life of the two countries. The assumption that the Constitution of the United States grew out of the political experience of eighteenth-century Europe, while the constitution of Canada (that is, the unwritten part determining the form of parliamentary government) grew out of the political experience of nineteenth-century Europe, overlooks as Turner emphasized a half-century ago the extent to which the principles of American government reflect very directly the political experience of American frontier peoples. What this paper seeks to demonstrate is that Canada shared in the revolutionary tradition of this continent which found its fullest expression in the American War of Independence and the principle of checks and balances written into the American Constitution, that, however, geography favoured the maintenance in this part of the continent of the controls of an Old World imperial, and later of a close federal, system, and that the effort to maintain these controls in face of the continuous threat of the expanding revolutionary community to the south led to the development of a form of government directly opposed to the principles of political organization growing out of the frontier experience of Canadian peoples. Thus what has been thought of in Canada as an orderly process of adapting political institutions to changing circumstances has actually represented an effort to hold in check the kind of democratic forces which were growing up from within the Canadian community. Responsible government developed in reaction rather than in response to the true democratic spirit of the Canadian people.

For the three centuries of its history the North American Continent has been a breeding ground of economic, political, social, and religious experiments of various sorts. Such was particularly the case during the latter half of the eighteenth and the first half of the nineteenth centuries. These one hundred years witnessed not only the Revolutionary War of Independence but most of the great utopian experiments in economic, political, and religious reform. It was not an accident that it was on the North American Continent that the ideas of the English utopian, Robert Owen, and the French utopian, Charles Fourier, were tried out or that on the Euro-Asiatic Continent were tried out almost a century later the ideas of the German utopian, Karl Marx. Great land masses present problems of control. The ineptness of political administration where distances are great breeds political discontent and offers opportunities for the growth of revolutionary movements. On the North American Continent political authority was established only in face of almost continuous resistance on the part of the population in outlying areas. The American people fought not one but many wars of independence. Thrown onto their own resources, the populations of isolated areas or of areas of new economic growth organized their own systems of control and, when central authority sought to establish itself, movements of revolt quickly developed. The committee of safety, the territorial convention, the bill of rights, a locally issued currency, and encouragement of smuggling and tax evasion afforded means of politically organizing the frontier and of securing its autonomy in relation to outside government bodies.

It was this insistence upon local autonomy, this separatist spirit, which was the dominant characteristic of those revolutionary or reform movements which grew up in the interior parts of the continent. Such movements sought to build the new society not by making over the old, but by separating from it. The reason, of course, lay in the economic and political weakness of the frontier community. The thirteen small, scattered, English colonies of 1775 could not hope to reform the British Empire but they could escape its exactions by separating from it. Similarly, the few Mormons settled on the desert wastes of Utah one hundred years later could have little hope of transforming to their liking the society of the United States (though the founder of the Mormon sect, Joseph Smith, did for a time aspire to the American presidency), but they could retreat from that society and secure their isolation by establishing a strong form of local theocratic government, a distinctive and to the outside world morally repugnant family system, and their own banking and currency system.

There was something of this intense localism, an almost sectarian exclusiveness, in all American reform movements of the frontier.

The dominant urge of frontier populations was to be left alone, to escape the exactions and restrictions of outside political authority. This was not because the frontier was poor but because it was rich. As politically virgin territory, it offered almost unlimited opportunities for office seekers from the outside; its virgin natural resources invited economic exploitation. It was in the struggle for the control of these two things of value on the frontier—office and land—that there developed much of the resistance to central government. Reform on the frontier was directed against such social evils of the outside world as political patronage, the payment of excessive salaries to governmental officials, economic monopoly, a stringent money supply, exorbitant interest charges, and burdensome taxation. Remedy for the ills of the frontier was sought in the effort to develop its own means of exploiting its economic and political resources.

It was no easy task for the central authorities to hold in check these separatist movements, to put down what amounted in effect to revolts against the state. Such movements had enormous advantages in geography and in the fanatical zeal of their leaders and followers growing out of strong feelings of righteousness. Where few qualifications for office were insisted on, an unlimited supply of people to fill positions of leadership and trust was available. Frontier conditions made for great mobility of agitators, self-appointed prophets, and organizers. On the other hand, the difficulties of policing, the ineptness of officials unfamiliar with local conditions, and the limitation in the supply of trained personnel handicapped severely governments seeking to impose their authority from the outside. When force was resorted to, a rebelling population, by delaying tactics, by hit-and-run raids, and by scattering when faced with a force more formidable than its own, could make the cost of defeating it so great as to discourage any determined effort directed to such an end.

Yet it would not be correct to say simply that the state was powerless to deal with frontier movements of revolt in America. The fact was that in that part of the continent which became the United States the authority of the central government was seldom employed with any resoluteness of purpose in putting down such movements. The American political society tended to be highly tolerant of the non-conforming elements of its population. The very weakness of the military forces of the country until recent years has been a reflection of such tolerance.

The constituted political authorities in the American society had no reason to be greatly concerned about movements of political separatism except when, as in 1776, they threatened to carry the population out of the British Empire or, as in 1860, they threatened the dismemberment of the Union. Rather, until recent years at any rate, such movements have constituted an important means of extending and strengthening American society. The major task of that society has been the conquering and occupation of a continent. In undertaking that task, it faced no organized political community on the continent as powerful as itself. There were, however, two serious claims to the continent which had to be destroyed if the Manifest Destiny of American peoples was to be realized.

The first, of course, was that of the North American Indian. Experience had demonstrated the costliness of trying to subdue the Indian by open warfare and the use of regular armies. The Indian enjoyed the advantages of all frontier people: great mobility, thorough knowledge of the terrain, and familiarity with the kind of weapons and tactics most suitable for frontier warfare. In challenging the claim of the Indian to the continent, accordingly, reliance was placed upon the resourcefulness (and unscrupulousness) of the white settlers. Treaties with the Indians solemnly entered into by the government were disregarded by these land-hungry settlers, and resistance on the part of the red man was used as an excuse for wars of extermination. The advance of American white society on the continent took place by means of this continuous pushing back and destruction of the native by people who took the law into their own hands. The same result would have been secured in the end, and at much less cost in human life, had the central government maintained a greater degree of order on the frontier, but only by delaying the advance of the white man's civilization. By tolerating the frontier settler's exercise of a large measure of independence, by granting in effect a large degree of autonomy to frontier communities, the American society was able that much more speedily to complete the occupation of the continent.

The second important claim to the North American Continent was that of the overseas empires. In the effort to destroy this claim, the interests of the British governing authorities before 1760, as of the central governing authorities of the united colonies or united states after 1776, were closely identified with the interests of the American frontier population. With no standing army on the continent sufficiently powerful to challenge the French Empire in America before 1760, and no navy sufficiently powerful to challenge the British Empire in America after 1776, the claims of the American political society to the continent were most successfully championed by the advancing frontiersmen fighting on ground on which the advantages were on their side and often through acts of warfare which were formally repudiated by the responsible governing authorities. Frontier armies or border raiding parties played an important part in the French-English wars, the War of Independence, and the War of 1812–14, while the two later invasions of Canadian territory, by the Patriots in 1838 and by the Fenians in the 1860's, were carried out entirely by armed forces of this sort. Spanish and French claims to the southern part of the continent were attacked by military forces of a similar character.

The invasion of territory outside the formal jurisdiction of the American political society was not simply an act of aggression of a land-hungry people. Frontier populations were land-hungry, but land hunger became closely identified with an interest in political reform. To wrest territory away from the control of France, Britain, or Spain was to "liberate" not only the territory but the inhabitants from the control of an Old World empire system. Here was to be found the significance of the revolutionary movement in the strengthening of the continental claims of the American political society. Wars with neighbouring communities assumed something of the character of wars of independence. In terms of the local scene, for instance, there was little essential difference between the border fighting in the Seven Years' War, the Revolutionary War, the War of 1812–14, and that which took place after the Canadian rebellions of 1837. In all these cases, the drive to liberate Canada came largely from what was then the American West, and in all of them, important support was obtained from within the Canadian community. Frontier populations on both sides of the border faced much the same problems and readily joined forces in protesting against the exactions and restrictions of outside political authorities. Within the continental situation, such movements of protest meant inevitably the weakening of the position of the overseas empires and the consequent strengthening of the position of the American political society.

Until at least the present century, thus, American expansionism and American reformism were closely linked to one another. The doctrine of Manifest Destiny found important support in the doctrine of revolutionary republicanism; or, to look at the matter from the other side, the isolationism of the American Republic was born out of the isolationism of the frontier and was a natural response to a situation where the nation felt no real threat to its position within the American continental system and craved no allies. What this meant was a form of government based upon the principle of a separation of powers and a limitation of centralized authority. Though in the writing of the Constitution of the American Republic powerful conservative interests, identified with sound finance and the promotion of overseas trade, did succeed in securing certain safeguards against the development of a system of political irresponsibility, the separatist-isolationist spirit of the American political community was too strong to be effectively checked by particular constitutional expedients such as the method of the election of the president or federal senators. American political theorists may have read Blackstone and Montesquieu, but the form of gevernment they devised was one which reflected very directly the frontier political experience of American peoples.

In Canada there was not lacking among the people a frontier political experience similar to that of American peoples. Developing as the American frontier did through the spread of settlement into the interior of the continent, the Canadian frontier offered an almost equally fertile field for the growth of movements of a reform or revolutionary character. The insurrection of the *coureurs de bois* and the generally unco-operative attitude of the population during the period of the old régime, widespread disaffection in Nova Scotia and Quebec during the American Revolutionary War and in Upper Canada during the War of 1812–14, the rebellions of 1837, the Irish riots and the Clear Grit movement of the 1850's, the Red River and Northwest rebellions of 1870 and 1885, the development of militant miners' associations in the Klondike following the gold rush, the Winnipeg general strike in 1919, and the rise of the western agrarian political movement in the 1920's and of the Social Credit movement in the 1930's afford examples of efforts upon the part of Canadian people to create for themselves a better world in which to live. As across the border, these movements were essentially separatist and anti-authoritarian in character. They grew out of the feelings of isolated people that their problems were peculiar to themselves and could only be solved through their own efforts. Thus the resort to similar forms of political organization and instruments of political expression designed to limit the authority of central governments: the committee of safety, convention, bill of rights, election of executive as well as legislative officers, group representation, referendum, and recall.

But whereas in the United States the development of separatist political movements meant freeing the expansive energies of the frontier and thus strengthening the political society as a whole, in Canada it meant exposing the frontier to forces of American expansion and threatening thereby the separate political existence of the Canadian community. The Canadian frontier lay alongside the line of advance of the American, and, while it could be reached only with great difficulty by armed forces moving out from the established centres of government, it could be swiftly invaded from across the border or from it Canadian rebellious forces could as readily withdraw to American territory. John Allan, William Lyon Mackenzie, Joseph Papineau, and Louis Riel found refuge in the United States when rebellions they had led in Canada failed, and new rebellious uprisings were plotted on the other side of the line with the aid of American sympathizers. What this meant, therefore, was that any assertion of greater independence on the part of the Canadian frontier society drew it closer to the American and paved the way for its ultimate absorption.

Had the advantages of geography been all on one side, of course, no effort to maintain in the northern part of the continent a politically separate community would have been successful. But though American expansionism threatened Canadian lines of communication with the interior, no American liberation movement was sufficiently powerful to completely destroy in this part of the continent the claims of a rival political power. Canada maintained her separate political existence but only by resisting any movement on the part of her population which had the effect of weakening the controls of central political authority. The claims to the interior of the continent were staked not by advancing frontiersmen, acting on their own, but by advancing armies and police forces, large corporate economic enterprises and ecclesiastical organizations, supported by the state. The Canadian political temper, as a result, has run sharply counter to the American. Those creeds of American political life—individual rights, local autonomy, and limitation of executive power—which have contributed so much to the political strength of the American community have found less strong support within the Canadian political system. Canada sought political strength through alliance with the North American Indian and the support of ties which bound her people to the Old World and to a highly centralized federal system. In turn this meant a political system which emphasized the responsibility of governing authorities and tended to concentrate power in the hands of the executive. In this respect, it is easy to exaggerate the change which came with the establishment of responsible government in Canada. The two-party, cabinet system of government grew out of those conditions of rule in Canada which required the maintenance of a highly centralized political community and, as such, it stood sharply opposed to the separatist principles of political organization growing out of the frontier experience of the Canadian people. In the 1830's the Canadian frontier community found its true champions in Joseph Papineau and William Lyon Mackenzie. Responsible government came not as the climax but the anticlimax to the long struggle in Canada to secure the reform of colonial institutions. It represented an accommodative movement in the political organization of the Canadian community.

That is not to say that reform thought has developed no strength in Canada. The American revolutionary movement has made its influence felt in spite of strong forces of resistance which have been built up. Important also has been the influence of overseas reform movements and particularly the great reform movements of nineteenth-century Britain. But if the effect of such influences has been to soften the character of Old World political toryism in the country, the effect of powerful conservative forces has been to convert the harsh and politically irresponsible radicalism of the frontier into more accommodative forms of reform thought. Canadian reform, as a result, has displayed a less uncompromising spirit than American reform; it has sought more to rebuild the old society than to separate from it.

Enough perhaps has been said to indicate the nature of some of the forces which have determined the character of development of the political institutions of this country. It is not the purpose of this paper to examine in any detail recent political developments which have taken place in Canada or the United States. The fact, however, that the United States today appears to be more intolerant of radical political movements than Canada or her other immediate neighbour, Mexico, may seem strange in the light of what has been said above.

If this is so, the reason in part would seem to lie in the changed position of the United States in world affairs. Until about the turn of the present century, as this paper has attempted to demonstrate, the main energies of the American people were directed towards the occupation of the continent and in the carrying out of this task reformism and expansionism were closely linked. Facing no serious threat to its political existence, the American society could tolerate the growth of noncomformist movements and the growth of such movements contributed to the extension of American territorial claims on the continent. Faced now with a threat to its national existence, and that from another continental power which has linked closely together forces of expansion and reform, the United States would appear to have turned its back on its revolutionary tradition and to be seeking strength by consolidation of the forces of the state. Canada, by withdrawing less from the Old World society in the past, is now perhaps more able to infuse into her society something of the reform spirit developing strength outside the country.

To say this, however, is to risk exaggerating the difference between the political temper of the United States of today and of the United States of the past. The American people are perhaps no more intolerant of nonconformity within their midst than they ever were. What they are intolerant of, as they have always been, is any interference in their affairs from the outside. The attack of Joseph McCarthy upon Communist influences in the government of the United States was a clear and genuine expression of the American frontier, isolationist spirit. It was no accident that McCarthy came from the Middle West and represented an ethnic-religious minority population in the United States. His attack was directed not against poor, downtrodden people crying for a voice in the affairs of the state but against powerful political leaders, of unquestioned social respectability, largely of Anglo-Saxon background. Critics outside the country might well pause to consider not the intolerance which found expression in McCarthyism but the tolerance which made it possible for McCarthyism to develop. In Canada it would be hard to conceive of a state of political freedom great enough to permit the kind of attacks upon responsible leaders of the government which have been carried out in the United States. More careful examination of the American community in general, and perhaps of the academic community in particular, would probably reveal that, in spite of the witch hunts in that country, the people of the United States enjoy in fact a much greater degree of freedom than do the people of Canada. We could scarcely have a witch hunt when we have no witches!

Such considerations suggest the need for caution in the use of such terms as radical and reactionary. A student of Social Credit in

Alberta is quickly made aware of the fact that here was a movement which from one point of view could be thought of as radical, from another point of view as reactionary. The same would seem to have been true of the McCarthy movement in the United States. It is not sufficient to say that these were movements which went "bad," because of their unfortunate leadership or for some other reason peculiar to themselves. What appears evident is that all those movements which grew out of the American—or Canadian—frontier were of this character, radical in the sense that they involved a break from established political practice, reactionary in the sense that their efforts were directed towards the creation of a more simple, primitive type of political world.

The farm movements of the western United States or of western Canada, for instance, sought the reform of political institutions not in a strengthening by more subtle means of the responsibility of the governors to the governed but by the development of simple, direct means of popular control over government. Thus the convention, referendum and recall, election of public officials, rotation of offices, and group representation were intended to weaken the executive branch of government and thereby strengthen the voice of the people in the affairs of the state. As instruments of political separatism, such forms of popular government were highly effective. They afforded a means of mobilizing the resistance of a population, often geographically remote and isolated, to a political authority which failed to give adequate expression to its interests. It is in these terms that must be viewed, for instance, the U.F.A. experiment in political democracy—convention rule and group representation. By giving to the convention what was hoped would be the decisive voice in determining, within the provincial sphere, the personnel of the cabinet and the legislative programme of the government, and by giving to the constituency associations control, in the federal sphere, of the voting behaviour of Alberta members of Parliament, a form of government was devised which promised to destroy party discipline and bring to an end cabinet domination over the legislature. The significance of such a development lay in its effect in weakening the influence of Ottawa in Alberta. By breaking from the federal party system, and by undermining the whole system of parliamentary government both in Ottawa and Edmonton, the people of Alberta, at least theoretically, were given a dominant voice in the governing of their own affairs.

What eventually became evident, however, even to some of the U.F.A. leaders themselves, was that a form of political organization devised to strengthen the control of the people of Alberta over their own affairs had the effect of seriously weakening their control over the affairs of the country at large. In Ottawa, the members from Alberta, acting as delegates of the people, were forced into a position of political irresponsibility. They could not be held accountable for any actions of the Government, or for any actions of that party which on defeat of the governing party would succeed it. Even more than this, to the extent that convention rule really operated, the governing authorities in Alberta were placed in a politically irresponsible position. They could not be held accountable for acts dictated by the convention. Examination of the behind-the-scenes role played by Henry Wise Wood in the U.F.A. provincial conventions reveals how readily such an instrument of popular government could have been manipulated by an unscrupulous leadership to serve its own ends. That it was not so manipulated and that convention rule was as little damaging as it was in Alberta were largely owing to the high idealism which characterized the leadership of Mr. Wood and to the good sense, tact, and intellectual strength of the province's second U.F.A. premier, Mr. Brownlee.

The truth is that the forms of political organization which grew out of the frontier experience were not well designed to secure the effective, continuous control of the population over its affairs. Immediately, the revolt from outside authority did lead to an increased control over matters of local concern, but such a result was secured at the price of destroying some of the most important of the safeguards of political organization against the concentration of power in the hands of irresponsible leaders or groups. Such an effect was not intended, of course, but the insensitiveness of frontier democratic theory to the importance of executive responsibility meant inevitably a failure to provide the conditions necessary for effective democratic control.

We have been too much inclined perhaps to exaggerate the political intelligence of frontier populations. It comes hard to one brought up in Alberta to suggest that the people of that province who thought of themselves as in the vanguard of reform actually had only a limited appreciation of the complexities of modern government and no great understanding of the conditions necessary for the preservation of individual rights and a sense of community responsibility. In a cultural sense, the frontier was not a rich and progressive but a poor and retarded society. Its effort to break from the old political and social system of which it had been a part and to create a new system of its liking involved the disowning of a heritage which it had in large measure lost and the building anew of a political and social life with tools fashioned out of its rough and limited experience.

This fact becomes evident when it is recognized that the political reform movement was only one of many forms of frontier protest. Religious sectarianism, vigilantism, medical quackery, mob rioting, tax evasion, smuggling, and political apathy were other means of resistance by a frontier population to the interferences of an outside society in its affairs. What was apparent in all the various kinds of movements which came out of the frontier was an underlying attitude of irresponsibility with respect to the affairs of the larger community. The frontiersman was a difficult person to govern in that he was not prepared to accept the normal obligations of a member of society. One of the primary objects of convention rule, as the U.F.A. sought to establish it in Alberta, was to make the individual a bad party man and thereby in a sense a poor citizen. In the emphasis of Social Credit upon results rather than means, poor citizenship in the form of lack of concern for the actual management of political affairs became almost a condition of membership in the party.

If what is said here is true, one is forced to the conclusion that the development in Canada of parliamentary institutions of government within the framework of the British imperial, and later the Canadian federal, system represented a more enlightened approach to the problem of government in the modern world than did the development of those forms of political organization which found expression in the constitution of the United States. Canada can assume a more responsible and thus more effective role in world affairs than can the United States not because its government is less responsive to the people but because its government's freedom of action is not continuously hampered by the behaviour of irresponsible parties and groups. In this sense, McCarthyism did represent a reactionary force in American political life.

In another sense, however, McCarthyism might be thought to represent a progressive force. By bringing about a break from established practice and forms of organization, the frontier separatist movement had the effect of weakening the hold of tradition upon men's thoughts and actions and thus in making possible a more rational approach to society's problems. There is nothing paradoxical in the fact that religious sectarianism, though in its teachings intensely hostile to science, did much nevertheless to further its growth. The very violence of the sectarian break from traditional forms of thought meant that it was not easy for those caught up in its teachings to fall back into old, accepted ways of thinking once their religious fervour had cooled. Such persons were able as a result to embark upon new and what might be considered socially dangerous lines of thought. Thus did Protestantism contribute to the growth of science and to the development of new forms of economic enterprise. In a similar way, it may be argued that the frontier political protest movement, though reactionary in terms of the ends it sought to accomplish, has been progressive in terms of its ultimate effect upon the organization of society. A native son of Alberta might well take comfort in the view that once the people of that province learn wisdom their inclination to go on trying something new will result in their contributing in a very real way to political advancement. Critics of the United States need to recognize that a country which has so little respect for the past is perhaps the country most able to learn what the past has to teach.

CHAPTER XIV

Canada and Her Great Neighbour*

I HAVE BEEN ASKED TO TALK THIS EVENING about Canada and the United States. I do so with certain misgivings, speaking to an audience that is largely American. If we Canadians are beginning to grow weary of comparing ourselves to Americans, Americans I am sure have long since grown heartily sick of being made the object of such comparisons, more particularly since they usually end up as the unfavoured party. We certainly play hard at pretending that we are superior to you, though the claim to superiority almost invariably becomes confused by an admission that you as a nation are bigger, more powerful and, indeed, more enterprising. It is not my intention to undertake a psycho-analytic probing of the mixed feelings of Canadians. I attempt a much simpler task: that of making a few observations about the reasons for and some of the consequences of the efforts of Canadians to maintain on this continent their separate national identity. We have had to keep comparing ourselves to you because we have had to show that somehow we are different from you. Canadian national identity has depended heavily upon the fostering of a feeling of anti-Americanism.

For Canadians to act in this manner should occasion no surprise.

*Presented at the general session on Canadian Society of the American Sociological Association, Montreal, 1964, published in *The Canadian Review of Sociology and Anthropology,* vol. 1, no. 4, November, 1964, pp. 193–201. Reprinted with permission of the publisher.

The world today provides many examples better than Canada of how a sense of national identity has come to be created by arousing among people feelings of hostility—and superiority—directed to outside powers. No better laboratory than present-day Africa can perhaps be found for an examination of the phenomenon of emergent nationalism. Yet, if there is nothing startlingly new or different about the forces which have produced a Canadian nationalism —or in this part of the country a nationalism that is French Canadian—the example of Canada may still be worth examining for the reason that there is not involved here, in support of national identity, a consciousness of racial difference or a social class ideology. It is not too difficult to understand the appeal of nationalism to the African. One can be left wondering how Canadians were made into a national group.

The truth is that we only became Canadian by being made to remain British or, before 1760, French. The people who settled the part of the continent which became Canada had no reason to make themselves into a separate national community. What was offered them, together with their neighbours to the south, was a whole continent to exploit. The riches of this continent were too great, its avenues of access too easy, to encourage on the part of any large number of people acts of withdrawal or retreat. Here and there, it is true, for example, in the quiet retreat of a valley community in the Kentucky Mountains or a desert community on the Utah plains, people did drop aside and for many years maintain in isolation a separate and distinctive existence as a social group, but over most of the continent the forces of expansionism and growth were too powerful to be held for long in check. It was a large free market in goods and services which the occupation of the North American Continent offered.

Only the claims of old world empires stood seriously in the way of the establishment of such a market. The Seven Years' War came near to ending the claims of the French Empire on the Continent and with the American War of Independence there was the promise of bringing to an end the claims of the British Empire as well. Spanish claims, less threatening, could be left for another century to be fully destroyed. With the union of the thirteen rebelling colonies and the formation of the Republic of the United States the political basis was laid for the creation of one great free market in goods and services on the North American Continent.

But geography, which favoured the American revolutionary

movement in its sweep over a large part of the Continent, favoured the maintenance of old world empire claims on the two extremities. France's hold on the northern half of the Continent had been broken only when the border war between the English and French colonies was turned into a war of empires and it was the British army and navy which had turned back the military forces of the rebelling English colonies and defeated what at the beginning had been the main purpose of the revolution, the liberation of the northern half of the Continent from outside control. Canadians today may like to pretend that as a people they played an important part in saving their country from domination by its southern neighbour but in fact, had the people at the time had their way, in 1760, and again in 1775, 1812 and 1838, and possibly even in 1860, the society growing up on the northern half of the Continent would have joined forces politically with the society growing out from the Atlantic sea-board. It was only a small minority of the population, individuals and groups identified with the vested interests of empire or, later, nation, who had any real desire to remain politically separate from their American neighbours. But the forces of geography were on their side, in promoting the growth and secure establishment on the northern half of the Continent of powerful monopolies of a business, ecclesiastical and other such character. Canada developed from the beginning not as a free but as a protected market, in goods and services, religions and, indeed, to some degree, in ideas. For the maintenance of such a market political separation from the United States or, before 1784, the English colonies, was essential.

Thus, there could be no fostering of a Canadian national identity which involved repudiating the ties of empire upon which such identity depended. Visitors to this country may well be perplexed by the difficulties we have encountered in settling upon a national flag. But the national feeling which is supposed to find expression in such a symbol as a flag develops out of forces so contradictory in their nature that the very existence of the feeling may be questioned. Almost everywhere that nationalism has developed great strength it has been closely associated with the efforts of people to better their lot. The modern nation is very largely a product of the revolutionary liberal-democratic movement. So it was in the United States and in the countries of Western Europe, including England. And so as well it has been in the new countries of Africa, however confused their political objectives may have become. But in Canada the forces of liberal democracy ran counter to the forces seeking the separate political existence of the country on the continent. Efforts of the people to free themselves from monopolistic economic, ecclesiastical and other such controls secured within the French or British colonial system or, later, the Canadian federal system, involved acts directed to the end of making Canada more a part of the North American political community. Reform became political treason where support of a protected market, in goods, services, religion and such, was made a condition of loyalty.

The effect was to cripple the development, on the one side, of a truly Canadian nationalist movement, on the other side, of a movement of liberal-democratic reform. The cause of patriotism, of course, never lacked powerful support. The major institutions of the country, of an economic, political, ecclesiastical, educational, welfare and other such character had strong vested interests in keeping Canada politically separate from the United States, and in times of political crisis their voice could be decisive. The military interest could always be counted upon to come to the support of the political, a condition that distinguished the development of Canada from that of most Latin-American countries. But, however decisive may have been the influence exerted by those interests in the country identified with the cause of maintaining the separate political existence of Canada from the United States, there was lacking any truly popular or mass support for such a cause. The country's most ardent patriots were necessarily its dignitaries—business leaders, ministers of the crown, church bishops, military officers and the like, and, while there was always a sufficient number of office-holders, in a country heavily committed to a bureaucratic structure of economic, political and religious life, to tip the balance in favour of the patriotic cause, it was not the voice of the great mass of people which was heard. Canadian patriotism could not be made into a mass movement where the maintenance of a separate Canadian political community was directed to the end of securing the conditions of a closed market, in the conduct of business, religious and other such affairs.

On the other side, the liberal-democratic movement, directed against the conditions of such a closed market, could find no support by identification with the patriotic cause. In the United States, even the most radical of the reform political movements growing up in the years after the revolution was able to appeal to the patriotic sentiment of the American people; the liberation of the North-

American Continent from old world systems of political, economic and ecclesiastical control was made the end of the American revolutionary movement. In Canada, however, the end to which the liberal-democratic movement was directed was that of opening up to the Canadian population the opportunities for advancement, economically, culturally and intellectually, offered by the large and expanding society of North America. Such an end did not necessarily mean the espousal of political union with the United States, or, before 1784, the English colonies, but it did mean promoting conditions unfavourable to the maintenance of the kind of closed economic-political-ecclesiastical system secured through the political separation of the Canadian community.

The result was an environment hostile to Canadian movements of a liberal-democratic character. It was so easy to accuse the advocate of non-conformist political ideas of disloyalty. The reform spirit in Canada depended heavily upon American sources for support. It was from the United States that most of the ideas came, and there were few Canadian reform leaders who were not schooled in the techniques of the American revolutionary movement. Nor was the direct intervention of the American people an idle threat. In 1759, 1775, 1812, 1838 and in the late 1850's and early 1860's, movements of political disaffection within the country came quickly to assume a guise of insignificance in face of the intrusion of an army of liberation from across the border. If the Fenian raids marked the end of any effort upon the part of the American people to intervene by force in the affairs of Canada, for another quarter of a century at least the threat of war remained, and for still long after that there could be no doubting the liveliness of the American interest in the cause of the political liberation of the Canadian people. Thus war upon disaffected political forces within the country could find justification in the cause of war upon the enemy without. Anti-Americanism served as an exceedingly powerful appeal in massing support behind the vested interests of empire or nation.

This is not to say that Canada is without a liberal-democratic revolutionary tradition. Much of its history had been written in a way to suggest that such is the case. But almost inevitably the people who have written Canada's history have been committed to the cause of Canadian national existence. How could one be a Canadian historian if there were no Canada? Even more, the material upon which the historian relies—the written document—

results in a biased view of events and happenings in the Canadian community. The written document, by and large, represents a record of the world about as seen through the eyes of persons possessed of the capacity to write, very usually functionaries or office-holders, whether of the government, business establishments, churches or other such bureaucratic organizations. It is the interest of the functionary to play down, to minimize, expressions of disaffection towards the established order of which he is a part. Thus a movement like Social Credit could spring up almost full-blown in Alberta in the early 1930's and in Quebec in the early 1960's with scarcely anyone, except for those people involved, knowing of its existence. When the pages of history are turned back and there results a still greater dependence upon written records, it becomes possible for the historian to dismiss what were great mass movements of political disaffection as nothing more than expressions of the discontent of a few disgruntled office-seekers.

There is no way of measuring the true strength of mass social movements, particularly of the past, and how strong were those movements of political disaffection which at different times grew up in Canada must remain a matter of debate. It can only be argued here—as I have argued elsewhere[1]—that there existed throughout the development of the Canadian community a much greater opposition to the conditions of economic-political-ecclesiastical control secured through the separate political existence of this community than has been generally recognized. Canadians have not so much wanted to be Canadians as to be North Americans. Whether in search of the cheapest market in which to buy or the dearest market in which to sell, and whether what was involved were goods produced or services offered, the restrictions upon free movement beyond the limited boundaries of the Canadian political society assumed the character of a hardship. Thus the fur trader, fisherman, farmer, lumberman, miner, unorganized factory worker and tradesman, no part of a large bureaucratic system of monopoly control, could not readily be convinced that it was in their interest to promote the political conditions which made possible the maintenance of such a system of monopoly control. Their interest found truer expression in those movements of a liberal-democratic character directed to the end of making Canada a much more integral part of the larger North American society.

[1]S. D. Clark, *Movements of Political Protest in Canada, 1640–1840* (Toronto, 1959).

But if, in the writing of Canadian history, powerful influences operated to lead to a playing down of the importance of forces of disaffection in Canadian political society, even more, such influences operated, in the end, to weaken or destroy these forces themselves. We have in our history hanged very few rebels. Rather, we have succeeded in turning most of them into patriots. Indeed, some we have hanged have even been so transformed after their hanging. Certainly such was the case with Louis Riel, the leader of the North-West rebellion, when he was made a martyr to the cause of French-Canadian Catholicism and nationalism. Interests identified with the maintenance of a separate Canadian political society were too powerful to be long resisted. Movements which in their beginnings were directed to liberal-democratic ends became in time transformed into movements in support of the economic-political-ecclesiastical establishment, or else they were destroyed or withered away.

The threat of force in the suppression of such movements could in itself be a highly persuasive influence in leading to their shift to a position in support of the established order, but more persuasive still was the influence of the strengthening interests of bureaucracy within these movements themselves. In the United States, an Andrew Jackson could become president of the Republic and still remain faithful to his frontier tradition. The American society grew and prospered in giving expression to the free enterprise interests of the middle class. Patriotism here could make a mass appeal in the close identification of the interests of the masses with the interests of the middle class. But in Canada the very existence of the middle class depended upon the bureaucratic supports of a closed economic-political-ecclesiastical system. The Canadian middle class man was a bureaucratic man. Not all our free enterprisers, of course, have been lowly farmers, fishermen, lumbermen, miners, unorganized factory workers and such; there have been Canadian business men, and, indeed, Canadian politicians and churchmen as well, prepared to seize the opportunities offered by the expanding North American society. But a large number of such Canadians crossed the border to become American citizens. In Canada, the certain line of advancement was the one provided within the hierarchical structure of the governing bureaucracy. Thus it was that the Canadian who prospered, whether by the exploits of business or by attaining a position of political, church or other such form of leadership, became one who sought to protect his position by the strengthened isolation of the Canadian community within the larger North American society. Anti-Americanism developed as an expression of Canadian middle-class interests.

Throughout much of Canada's history it was upon the ties of empire that the maintenance of a closed economic-political-ecclesiastical system depended. The Canadian patriot for a long time was not a nationalist but an imperialist. The result was to give a curious twist to nationalistic forces. The nationalist became the person who was anti-imperialist. He came close to being pro-American. Indeed, in the mid-nineteenth century, there developed a very real confusion between Canadian nationalist movements and movements favouring closer ties between Canada and the United States. But this confusion resulted because Canadian nationalism, in its early development as a force, was much more negative than positive in its appeal. It developed as a movement opposed to the empire connection. Its support thus came not from bureaucratic interests within the Canadian society but from interests identified with the opportunities offered by an expanding society of North America. A nationalism of this sort could make no appeal to people of the middle class, save only to a few intellectuals.

With the weakening of the empire tie, however, the closed economic-political-ecclesiastical system which developed in terms of that tie became increasingly dependent upon the tie of nation. This is not the place to attempt an examination of the process of evolution which followed. The lead was taken, as would be expected, by business interests, but in the end there were few large-scale bureaucratic interests in the country which failed to shift to a nationalist position. The changes occurring in Canadian religious establishments after the mid-nineteenth century reflected very clearly the character of the changes occurring in Canadian society generally; even the Church of England, long an important spokesman of empire, underwent this transformation and became the Church of England in Canada. The effect was evident in the growing national consciousness of the office-holding Canadian middle-class. Canadian nationalism ceased to represent a protest against the imperialist connection and the closed economic-political-ecclesiastical system secured by that connection. It became rather the chief support of this closed system. In doing so, it aligned itself closely with the cause of anti-Americanism.

Nowhere perhaps was the resulting change more apparent than in the society of French Canada. In the early development of this society there was no mistaking the character of the establishment. Protestant commercial interests had early combined with Catholic ecclesiastical interests to secure within the French colonial system a tightly closed economic-political-religious order, and, though the combination was seriously threatened in 1760 and again in 1775, it survived war and revolution to become within the British colonial system more firmly established than ever. Though within the society of French Canada what middle class existed was one closely associated with the Church, it found important support in a powerful English-speaking middle class associated with business, the government and the military. Thus there developed the close dependence of the French-Canadian elite upon the British tie.

Under such circumstances, there could be nothing surprising about the strongly nationalist character of French-Canadian protest movements. In its early development, French-Canadian nationalism was vigorously anti-imperialist. It represented the strivings of the masses of French Canada—of habitants, fishermen, traders in furs, lumbermen, small merchants and others—to break free of the closed system of bureaucratic controls within their society secured through the imperial tie. Though never without an anti-English over-tone, the appeal of French-Canadian nationalism was the appeal very largely of a liberal-democratic movement. This certainly was true of the nationalist appeal of Louis-Joseph Papineau in the 1830's. Though the language employed was different, it was difficult to distinguish the programme of Papineau's political-economic-social reform from that of the Scots reformer in Upper Canada of the same time, William Lyon Mackenzie. Nor was the difference very great between what Papineau stood for in French Canada in the 1830's and what Henry Wise Wood stood for in Western Canada in the 1920's.

There is not wholly lacking today in French-Canadian nationalism the kind of appeal which so clearly distinguished it a century ago. Certainly, Social Credit, in its early development in the Province of Quebec, assumed much of the character of a mass movement of protest directed against the established order. If its overtones were nationalistic and anti-English, it was because its economic doctrines made the financial interests the chief villain, and, of course, the financial interests were English. The dominant appeal of the movement was to those elements of the French-Canadian population strongly anti-bureaucratic in sentiment. Until made over by its leader, Réal Caouette, in face of the changing political situation in the Province, the movement had much more of a populist than of a nationalist character; or, to put it another way, the nationalist character of the movement was subsumed in its populist character.

But the nationalism which has developed as such a force in French Canada today is one which no longer has its roots primarily in populist discontent. It is the nationalism of the new bureaucratically-oriented French-Canadian middle class. This nationalism, it is true, like the old, is anti-establishment in its appeal. Business, controlled by the English-speaking group, is vigorously attacked, and so as well, in many quarters, is the old governing elite of French Canada, including the Church. But what is sought is not an end to a bureaucratically structured society, but the erecting of a new bureaucratic order in the place of an old.

Thus the forces which find expression in present-day French Canadian nationalism are not too different from those which find expression in the present-day nationalism of the Canadian community at large. The nationalism of the Canadian community at large is wholly anti-American in its direction. French-Canadian nationalism is directed against the economic and cultural dominance of English-speaking Canada in the Province of Quebec as well as against the economic and cultural dominance of the United States in the same Province. In the end, however, it is the economic and cultural dominance of the United States which will almost certainly become uppermost in the appeal of French-Canadian nationalism. Apart from a larger share of offices in the federal public service and in a few public corporations, there is not much that English Canada has to offer French Canada. The real gains can come only by severing the close connections of business in the Province of Quebec with American business and by shutting out American cultural influences. What French-Canadian nationalism promises is to carry the isolation of French Canada within the larger North American society to a point well beyond that which could ever possibly be reached by Canada as a whole.

There exist very real limits to the extent to which English Canada can isolate itself from its American neighbour. English Canadians speak the same language as Americans. No Canadian nationalism can develop as a force strong enough to prevent English-speaking Canadians from abandoning their country if the opportunities across the border appear vastly greater. Many distinguished public men—business leaders, scholars, journalists, musicians and the like—in the United States today are persons born and brought up in Canada. On the other side, there are more than a few distinguished men in this country who can claim the United States as their birth-place. Ideas have flowed across the border and with them fashions and fads, right and wrong ways of doing things. Canadian nationalist interests, as earlier interests identified with the imperial connection, have been sufficiently powerful to maintain intact the country's separate political structure and to secure within that structure a large measure of economic protectionism, but intellectual and cultural exchanges between English-speaking Canada and the United States have proceeded largely unhampered. The meeting of the American Sociological Association on this side of the border offers testimony to the closeness of the intellectual contacts between the people of the two countries.

In the Province of Quebec, however, the possibility is very great that the nationalist movement will succeed in carrying the French-Canadian society out of the North American intellectual and cultural as well as economic world. Closer associations with the old world, particularly with France, may bring new sources of strength, but in the end the society of French Canada, like that of English Canada, cannot escape, except at a very heavy price, from its position as a part of the North American Continent. If French Canadians (or English Canadians) have a culture worth preserving, it is one that comes out of their experience of meeting on equal terms the other peoples on this Continent and proving their worth. Some of the great trail-blazers in early North America were Canadian explorers and traders, men who let no political boundaries, or boundaries of an ethnic or cultural character, impede their movements or restrain their ambitions. May I suggest, looking to the future, that our strength as a nation will come not by turning our back upon the larger North American society but by our full and free participation in it.

The truth is that we as a people have been persuaded to settle for too little: an executive position in a Canadian (or French-Canadian) controlled business, the authorship of a book with a sure but limited Canadian sale, the directorship of a Canadian trade union or film society, a professorship in a Canadian university. Recent immigrants to Canada have demonstrated, by their achievements in business, the professions and the arts that enterprise does not wholly lack opportunities in this country. Too many of us have not yet rid ourselves of the outlook and habits of thought which were bred into us as a colonial people, whether of the French

Empire or the British. It was an imperial bureaucracy which tried for long to shape our character in a manner contrary to the North-American spirit of individual enterprise and social equality. It is a question now, with the disintegration of that imperial bureaucracy, whether one that is Canadian (or French-Canadian) based, and even more powerful and far-flung, is going to take over.

Perhaps it could be said that Canada's social-democratic revolution came one century too late. It is only in the very recent past that we have produced a substantial middle class in this country. A century ago what middle class we had could largely be absorbed by the governing bureaucracies (of the state, business, church and such) or else drained off into the United States. The very great increase in the size of the Canadian middle class has come at a time when there has been a vast extension of bureaucratic forms of organization. The flow of talent to the United States may thus still be large enough to make possible the absorption of what middle class remains in Canada by the country's governing bureaucracies. But there are surely great risks involved, not the least of which is that the Canadian society, or here the society of French Canada, will be driven into a more and more isolationist position. I do not believe that a country can remain culturally rich if it is made economically poor. The present is a time of political and social ferment in Canada. If good is to come out of that ferment, the beneficiaries must be the great mass of Canadian people, not a favoured few able to better their position within a strengthened bureaucratic order.

CHAPTER XV

Canada and the
American Value System*

IN AN EARLIER PAPER I argued that Canadians only became Canadians by being made to remain British or, before 1760, French. For the great mass of people settling this northern half of the continent there was no interest in maintaining a separate political existence. What was offered were the resources of a whole vast continent to exploit, in fish, furs, timber, minerals, farm land and, as technological development advanced, coal, oil, water power and pulpwood. The establishment of a separate political community on the northern half of the continent could have no other effect than that of restricting the access of the people of such a community to these resources. The Canadian political community was not the creation of a people seeking a distinctive national identity. It was the creation rather of certain business, political, religious and cultural interests, seeking the establishment of a monopolistic system of control. Geography, which favoured individual enterprise and limited political interference in the conduct of economic, social and religious affairs over a large part of the continent, favoured on this part of the continent large-scale bureaucratic forms of organization and wide-spread intervention by the state. Canada never developed, as did the United States, a mass basis of support of political patriot-

*Presented at the Congrès des Affaires Canadiennes, Laval University, Quebec City, 1964, and published in *La Dualité Canadienne à l'heure des Etats-Unis*, Quebec, Los Presses de l'université Laval, 1965, pp. 93–102. Reprinted with permission of the publisher.

ism. Political patriotism was an expression of those monopolistic or semi-monopolistic economic, religious or cultural interests identified with the imperial tie, or later, with the Canadian federal state.

The consequence has been, or so I argued in this earlier paper, that there has failed to develop in Canada, in contrast to the United States, a large vigorous middle class. The Canadian middle class has grown up, very largely, within a bureaucratic structure of power—economic, political, ecclesiastical. Typically, the Canadian middle class person has been an office-holder, whether in the service of government, a business corporation, church or other such type of bureaucratic organization. Individuals seeking to advance themselves outside the bureaucratic order have tended to a very large extent to cross the border into the United States. It has been there that the J. J. Fullers, the Cyrus Eatons, the Aimee Semple Macphersons have made their fortune or achieved their fame. The Canadian middle class has maintained its middle class position, not by engaging in the competitive struggle which the larger American continental system invited but by building about itself, in this more restricted, and in terms of physical resources poorer, area of the continent, a very largely closed bureaucratic system of control. Such a middle class has inevitably remained small but it has been one which, in control of the strategic institutions of the Canadian society, could wield enormous influence and power. It was upon the support of this middle class, for more than two centuries, that the colonial tie of Canada with the old world depended, and it has been upon its support that has depended very largely, in the years since Confederation, the tie of nation. In a way scarcely true of any other Western nation, the middle class, in Canada, has been the Establishment.

Here I want to pick up where I left off in this earlier paper, and to argue that the concern which is so often expressed about the growing economic, political and cultural influence of the United States in Canada is very largely the concern of a bureaucratically-oriented Canadian middle class anxious to protect its favoured position within the Canadian community. We talk a great deal about the importance of preserving our distinctive Canadian values, ways of life, political and moral principles, but in all this discussion not many of us, it seems to me, stop to enquire what the values, ways of life, political and moral principles really are that we are trying to preserve. For a long time, colonial bureaucrats in Canada could link with American republicanism such values as democracy, equality and individual liberty, and deplore non-shame-facedly the spread of these values across the border into Canada. Today not even the most tory of tories would openly express disapproval of such values, but there has been no lessening of talk about the danger to Canadian national life of the influence of the United States upon Canadian ways of thinking and behaving.

It has not been difficult for Canadians to find much in the United States with which to find fault. But neither was it so for a Barry Goldwater, seeking in election the highest political office his country offered. And one may wonder whether the judgment of those Canadians so ready to condemn the moral behaviour and values of Americans is any less open to question than the judgment of Senator Goldwater. Any society as large and complex as that of the United States is not likely to be found faultless, if judged in terms of a particular set of standards. Canadians for long have been too ready to compare their political and social institutions, ways of doing things, ethical practices and beliefs with the worst examples in American life and to comfort themselves with the thought that if poorer than their American cousins they have been more virtuous or high minded.

There can be no question that there are considerable differences between the institutions, patterns of social relationships, ways of life and values of Canadians and Americans. Those differences show up most markedly when the society of French-speaking Canada is compared with that of the United States, but there are very real differences as well between English-speaking Canadian society and American society. Among others, Professor S. M. Lipset has attempted to spell out these differences: the much greater operation in Canada of the aristocratic principle in government, of the state, business corporation, church, educational institution, trade union organization, and such; the greater readiness to concentrate authority and accept its dictates; the much wider interpretation of what is private and not open to public enquiry.[1] In very broad, general terms, the temper of Canadian society can be described as more conservative, less dedicated to such cherished American values as democracy, equality and liberty. Ours is a society more ready to compromise with the past, to accept without protest the limitations upon individual endeavour, freedom of expression and achievement which our institutional heritage prescribes. We are less concerned

[1]S. M. Lipset, *The First New Nation* (New York, 1963).

about getting on, being successful. We are not to the same extent as Americans a status-seeking people. The Protestant ethic here early became sharply modified by a strong Catholic spirit.

There are many other ways as well that Canadian society differs from American, in the conduct of family affairs, the structure of religious life, the role assigned ethnic minorities, and such. The important question, however, would seem to be not whether there are differences between Canadian and American society but what accounts for these differences and whether they are of a sort which should be preserved. Where environmental forces have led to different manners of behaving, or thinking, on the part of the two peoples there can be no sociological quarrel with the resulting feelings of ethnocentrism. Albertans have no reason to apologize for ways in which they are different from Nova Scotians. There is much that is different as well between Californians and Vermonters. But a good many of the differences between the society of Canada and that of the United States cannot be accounted for in simple environmental terms. The environment to a very large extent made us one people. It was the forces of history which made us two.

As a Canadian of four generations I do not lightly reject the heritage of our historical past, Indeed, I am convinced that when Canadians, English-speaking and French-speaking, come to really know themselves they will find much in that heritage worth cherishing. Certainly, there is no reason for us to seek to turn ourselves into Americans and to forget all that in our past which has made us Canadian.

But much in our past which we have thought of as Canadian has been nothing more than an expression of sentiments or attitudes which have been anti-American. Such sentiments and attitudes may be associated with things British, such as the flag which we claimed, or the honour system of university education of which we have been so proud; or they may be associated with things French. Yet institutions and values in Canadian life, in origin British or French, in reality may be no more truly British or French than they are Canadian. It has often been said that the British-minded Canadian is more British than the British and perhaps it can be said that the French-minded Canadian is more French than the French.

The persons who have spoken for Canada in business, the public service, the church, education, mass communication and, indeed, in literature and the arts as well have been very largely persons depending for their positions of influence, power or wealth upon keeping Canada politically separate and economically and culturally isolated from the United States. Thus political and social ideas developing out of the experience of people living under North American conditions of life have been rejected by Canadian spokesmen as being American. Canadians have been persuaded that their national identity has been threatened by the spread of these ideas from across the border. Yet in fact the ideas have been as much Canadian as American. What Lipset and others tell us are the basic values of American political society—the limitation upon the power of the executive, the election of public officials, the decentralization of financial institutions such as banks, the right of the people by means of referenda to participate directly in the legislative process, the separation of church and state, the right of such agencies as newspapers to enquire into and report fully public proceedings—are values developing out of the experience of Canadian people as well as American.

But whereas in the United States these values have given expression to the interests of the middle classes as well as the masses, in Canada they have represented a threat to the interest of the middle classes. American business men, politicians, churchmen, newspaper, magazine and book publishers, educators, public entertainers, sports promoters and the like have prospered and grown in numbers by furthering in their society opportunities for individual enterprise. The poor boy could become a rich man without the rich man being compelled to give up his riches. Fame and fortune have been there, in the expanding society of America, for all to strive for. The American middle class has derived its strength from the condition of competition fostered and supported by values of democracy, equality and individual freedom.

It has been a condition the very opposite upon which the Canadian middle class has depended. Here the long reach of the St. Lawrence waterways system into the centre of the continent, and the island character of the Maritime region, early made possible the restriction of competition, with the consequence that the maintenance of monopolistic conditions of control through state intervention became a primary end of business, ecclesiastical, educational and other such interests. Individual enterprise from the very beginning represented a threat to the developing structure of Canadian economic, political, cultural and religious life. To a very large extent, as a result, what middle class has grown up in the country has been one developing within a bureaucratic order. Individual enterprise, seeking opportunities for advancement, has turned to the neighbouring republic to the south.

Thus, in ironic and somewhat paradoxical fashion, the very close presence of the United States has made possible the preservation in Canada of the conditions of a closed market, in business, religious and cultural affairs. For large numbers of enterprising persons, generation after generation, there has been no place to go in the country. In the public service, the great railway, banking and insurance companies, churches, publishing houses, universities and so on, the positions at the top or near the top have been quickly filled—there have not been a great number of these large bureaucratic organizations. Under conditions such as these, it might have been expected that new avenues of advancement would have developed, however determined the efforts to resist encroachments upon the preserves of bureaucratic establishments, and, of course, to some small degree, there has been such a development. Enterprises of various sorts established by recent immigrants to the country offer an example of how new lines of advancement may be opened up outside the bureaucratic structure of business. The reform party in politics, the sectarian church in religion, the faith-healer in medicine offer examples in fields other than business. But the resistance to such encroachments upon bureaucratic preserves has been formidable, and for persons seeking advancement through individual enterprise the more inviting opportunities appeared to lie across the border in the United States. Throughout Canada's history, from the days of the fur trade to the present day, there has been a continuous flow of dissident elements of the middle class out of the country, persons unwilling or unable to fit into the cramping structure of Canadian life.

The effect has been to weaken in the Canadian middle class any interest in making over the society of which it has been a part, in ridding that society of the built-in restrictions upon individual enterprise which have closed for Canadians so many lines of advancement. Where in Britain and France, and even more in the United States, commercial and industrial expansion led to the growth of a large, new middle class which could not fit itself into the established order of economic, political and social privilege and thus was compelled to take a lead in the breaking down of this order of privilege (it was the middle class in the English colonies which took the most prominent part in the American War of Independence), in Canada the middle class to a considerable extent has been able to maintain its position within a protected order of privilege by ridding itself, through the exodus of population to the United States, of those middle class elements that could not be fitted in.

There is no suggestion, of course, that in the one hundred years or more since Family Compact days there has not been a considerable making over of Canadian society. Then it was, indeed, an exceedingly small and specially privileged middle class which was in command of Canadian economic, political, cultural and religious affairs. In the years since, with commercial and industrial growth, the opening up of new areas of the country, the advance of science and technological development and rapid urbanization, there has been a release of new, powerful forces in Canadian society. Fortunes have been made or fame achieved by persons who have been no part of the establishment, and no longer do old family names or honorific posts command the respect they once did. Ours has become more an equalitarian type of society. The very considerable growth of public interest in education in recent years is a reflection of the change taking place in Canadian values.

Yet I think it can be argued that fundamentally Canada remains a bureaucratically structured type of society, in the conduct of business, political, religious, cultural and educational affairs, and that the main line of advancement into the middle class is still through the winning of the favour of persons who have command over the staffing of bureaucratic establishments. Too much significance can be attached to developments such as those which have taken place in education. Educational opportunities in the country have been greatly increased but for the reason very largely that there has been an increased demand for trained personnel to man the posts in bureaucratic establishments. We are witnessing today a rapid growth in the size of our middle class. It is a middle class, however, that stands as sharply separated from the mass of the population as did the middle class of one hundred years ago. Indeed, in certain important respects, it stands even more sharply separated. Education can be a great leveller in society but it can also be a divisive force. More and more, the lines of advancement in our society are being determined by educational qualifications. Persons lacking such qualifications are left hopelessly behind. They have nowhere to go.

It is true that what has been happening in Canada has been happening as well in other countries of the Western world, including the United States. Society generally is much more bureaucratic in form than it was a generation ago. But there is still in this respect a great difference between our society and that particularly of the United States. There certainly are in the United States bureaucratic establishments of vast dimensions, such as great, powerful banks and trusts, insurance companies, manufacturing firms, air carriers, mass communication agencies, churches, universities, and trade unions. Yet, although the number of bureaucratic establishments is enormous, beyond their reach there remains a large area in which individual enterprise still is given almost unlimited opportunities for advancement. One can agree with Lipset that the new forms of organization and behaviour patterns emerging in American society have been made to conform to the basic democratic and equalitarian values of American life. The pressure to conform to these values is clearly apparent in the conduct of business, politics, education, religion, industrial relations, and in many other spheres.

In Canada, the strain upon the dominant values of the society has developed out of forces precisely of an opposite character. Here, in face of new technological development, large-scale immigration from Europe, the growth of new media of mass communication, the vast extension of facilities of education, and rapid urbanization, values long dominant in Canadian economic, political, cultural and religious life have been placed under severe attack. Perhaps as much indicative as anything of the strains in Canadian social institutions and values have been the near breakdown of our parliamentary system of government with the rise of new, nonconforming political parties, and the severe weakening of our federal political structure with the growing determination of the provincial governments to play a part in economic development.

But there is no clear and certain sign that the old established values of the Canadian society are going to give way to new values, not even in the Province of Quebec where the attack upon the old values has gathered its greatest strength. In Quebec, certainly, the long established claims of the British minority to a position of economic, political and cultural supremacy can never again be reasserted. French-speaking Canadians have done with symbols which give expression more to Canada's empire ties than to her nationhood. But as well, if not to the same degree, so have English-speaking Canadians. There is being waged within the Canadian society today an intensely severe struggle between English-speaking and French-speaking peoples, but as the struggle is working itself out it is coming less and less to touch upon the area of values. The rapidly growing middle class in French Canada might well have taken a lead in the making over of Canadian society. Certainly, it was a class which could not readily be accommodated within an English-Canadian dominated establishment. A few posts, particularly of an honorific character, could be opened up for French-speaking claimants; there is no bureaucrat who is not alive to the political usefulness of vice-presidential appointments. But the time has long since passed when those French-speaking middle class persons who were not a part of the very narrow political-ecclesiastical establishment of French Canada could be so accommodated. The number of such persons has become too great, their claims too strong. The resulting social ferment, though still with us, is now becoming a matter of history.

It would be highly impertinent on my part to attempt here to assess the significance of recent developments in the province of Quebec. To an outsider like myself there has appeared good reason for applauding. The attack upon the entrenched position of such institutions as the Church within French Canadian society holds out the promise of bringing into being a much more liberal social state. Even more promising has been the attack upon the entrenched position of the English-speaking middle class within the bureaucratic structure of the larger Canadian society. Yet there is reason for lament as well as for applause in the anxious striving of the new middle class of French Canada to entrench itself in a bureaucratic structure even more tightly integrated and sheltered than was the bureaucratic structure it so vigorously brought under attack. Feeling against English-speaking Canada, I am certain, is yet a long way from expiring, but more and more, I suspect, this feeling will give way to an anti-American feeling. It is American influences which will come to constitute the greatest threat to the newly established position of the middle class in the society of French Canada. The two establishments, the English-speaking and the French-speaking, will discover how much they have in common. There can be no quarrel between an Ontario Hydro and a Quebec Hydro, nor between an English and a French television network.

I cannot conclude without some reference to the take-over of Canadian business by American firms, though I could not here go into a detailed discussion of this problem. Canadians perhaps have good reason for concern that such a large part of their resources has fallen under foreign control. But the very conditions which have fostered monopolistic type enterprises under the control of Canadians have led to the intrusion into the country of monopolistic type enterprises under the control of Americans. In the end, where American control of such vital Canadian enterprises as those of banking and mass communication has appeared to threaten national independence, the only possible recourse, given the conditions of Canadian development, has been to move in the direction of state socialism. Canada could become another Cuba, rejecting everything American in the interest of maintaining a state of economic, political and cultural independence, and the consequences, I fear, for the great mass of the people, would be little more fortunate. We are bigger than Cuba, and wealthier, but not that much bigger and wealthier that we can withdraw from the larger economic and cultural world of North America without paying a heavy price.

It may be argued that the price is worth it, and if it is clear that the great mass of Canadians agree on such a view there can be no cause for complaint. But I am not convinced that such is the case, any more today than one hundred or two hundred years ago. The middle class in Canada is still exceedingly small, entrenched very largely within a bureaucratic structure of economic, political, cultural and religious life. For this middle class, isolationism offers very substantial compensations. Sheltered from the competitive struggle of the larger North American society, the members of the middle class can remain secure in their middle class positions within the Canadian society. But for such isolationism, the price paid by the great mass of Canadians can be a heavy one. The fact that there may be widespread popular support for isolationist programmes can be accepted as no argument in their favour. It is the middle class which is in command of the important educational and propagandist agencies in the country with the result, as in the past, that it is those values which give expression to the interests of the middle class which are represented as distinctively Canadian. Where there has been a true expression of mass sentiments and attitudes, in Quebec as elsewhere in Canada, support for isolationist economic, political and cultural programmes has been very much less evident. The opportunities for advancement offered by participation in the larger economic and cultural, if not political, society of North America have been too inviting.

CHAPTER XVI

The Limitations of Capitalist Enterprise in Canadian Society*

IN AN INTERNATIONAL GATHERING OF SOCIOLOGISTS, it would be presumptuous on the part of a Canadian sociologist to suggest that there was much about his society which holds interest for the student engaged in the comparative analysis of economic and social systems. Certainly, the newly developing nations of the world offer examples of societies more exciting from a sociological standpoint than the society of Canada. Ours is a society not greatly different from that of the United States. Yet there are certain characteristics of Canadian society which may not be without interest, since they suggest comparisons with societies ordinarily thought of as much less highly developed in a way that American society does not. It is to a consideration of some of these characteristics that this paper addresses itself.

It is perhaps not surprising that American sociologists, turning to an examination of how over the past their society has developed, should reject Marxist theories of change and development in favour of the theories of change and development of Herbert Spencer and Max Weber. Everything about the development of American society appeared to prove Marx wrong. Here, with capitalist growth, there came no polarisation of the society between a small propertied class and a large working class, but instead a very con-

*Presented at the Sixth World Congress of Sociology, Evian, France, 1966.

siderable diffusion of power and wealth throughout the population. The whole society became caught up in powerful forces of a socially integrating nature—industrialization, urbanization, bureaucratization. If not all parts of the nation have developed at the same rate, and serious divisions within the society of a sectional and racial character remain, divisive interests have been largely subordinated to the dominant interests of capitalist enterprise, political democracy and nationalism. American society is clearly and unambiguously a capitalist society. It is also, no less clearly and unambiguously, an urban and middle class society. Every American, almost, even without the prompting of the advertisements of United States Steel, thinks of himself as a capitalist, and as an urban and a middle class person. The geography of the country, and the nature of its resources, favoured the very wide participation of the population in economic, political and cultural endeavours.

To the casual visitor to Canada, there might appear in this respect little difference between it and the United States. Capitalist forms of economic enterprise operate on both sides of the border, Canada has its big cities as has the United States, and extensive suburban developments outside urban centres reflect here, as do similar developments in the United States, the growing strength of middle class elements of the population. Yet, in a way that distinguishes it from the American, the Canadian society is not truly a capitalist society, nor an urban or middle class society.

In the United States, it was out of a thriving agricultural industry that capitalist enterprise, and the structure of an urban, middle class society, developed. American claims to the continent were staked by the farmer. With the advance of farm settlement, the civilization of the native Indian was destroyed and the new nation of the United States brought into being, extending from the Atlantic to the Pacific. Farming could not be carried on with success everywhere, of course, and much of the riches of the American people very early came to be derived from other sources—the exploitation of the continent's fisheries, minerals, timber supplies and such—but the farm industry played an important part in generating the spirit of enterprise, and in providing the capital and the markets, for industrial and urban growth. Central in the value system of the American society has been the belief that the farm life is the good life. For long it could be the boast of the successful American businessman or politician that he began life as a farm boy.

In Canada, in contrast, claims to the continent were staked not by the farmer but by the army, and the large-scale monopolistic business enterprise. The wealth of Canada was derived from the export of such staples as furs, fish, timber, gold and pulpwood which required for their exploitation large accumulations of capital and a large measure of monopolistic control in production and marketing. It was the military occupation of the northern half of the continent which secured the existence of the Canadian nation. The economic base of monopolistic enterprise, and of the military outpost, extended far beyond the reach of farm settlement.

Yet as an objective of public policy farm settlement assumed even greater importance in Canada than in the United States. In the establishment of the fisheries on the Atlantic seaboard, the extension of the fur trade across the continent, and the development of the timber trade, mining, and the pulp and paper industry, settlements of farmers on the land were considered a vital second line of defence, and an important local source of supply of foodstuffs. Thus, while it was the fisheries and overseas trade that brought wealth to Nova Scotia, not until well on in the nineteenth century was the effort to make Nova Scotians a farm people abandoned. The farm settlement of the St. Lawrence valley offered itself as an important source of support of the fur trade and as a means of securing the claims of the French Catholic Church to the dominion of that part of the continent being staked out by the fur trader and the army. In New Brunswick and Upper Canada, it was people who had been transported across the Atlantic as ballast for timber ships on their way for a return cargo who made up a large part of the population settled on the land. In western Canada farm settlement was a necessary condition for the building of a transcontinental railway to reach the mineral and timber riches of British Columbia. Even northern Quebec and Ontario, rich in minerals, pulpwood and hydro electric power, were made by public policy important areas for the promotion of farm settlement. As late as the nineteen fifties thousands of families were being transported to and settled at public cost on the rocky and isolated farm lands of the Quebec interior.

From the settlement of the western peninsula of Ontario and the prairies of western Canada there developed a prosperous agricultural industry. The production of wheat in these areas contributed substantially to the wealth of Canada. But in Canada, as a whole, from the early seventeenth century to the present day, farming has assumed the character of a marginal economic enterprise.[1] By propaganda in Canada and overseas, government subsidies, church pressure, and other means, people have been persuaded to settle on land from which they could wring little more than a subsistence living. The wealth-producing industries of the country grew up largely apart from agriculture through the development of large-scale capitalist types of economic enterprise. The farm settlement provided the growing industry with a supply of foodstuffs, and, more important still, in the end, with a source of cheap labour, but the capital, entrepreneurship, management, and skilled work force for industrial development were recruited from older established industrial centres, within the country and outside, and it was from outside the country that the chief markets came. Only to a very limited degree did capitalist enterprise develop, even indirectly, out of the farm industry.

The industrial development of northern Quebec offers a striking example. The wealth of northern Quebec lay in its minerals, and, with the extension of railways into this part of the country after the First World War, there grew up an important mining industry. In this development, however, the people of Quebec played no part. It was from outside the Province that was drawn the capital, managerial skill, and trained workers for mining. In promoting the development of the North, the chief energies of the Quebec Government and of the Quebec Catholic Church were directed to the end of securing the settlement of people on the land. Almost everywhere that roads could be built and land cleared, farm settlement was encouraged. There resulted, as a consequence, two parallel but clearly separate developments in northern Quebec: on the one side, of a highly capitalistic and urban centred mining industry, controlled and largely manned by English-speaking people from outside the province, and, on the other side, of a farm industry which could only be kept in existence by government subsidies but upon which the French-speaking population settling in the north was made dependent.

In the end, these two parallel developments became one. The French-Canadian population, unable to make a living on the land, was gradually forced out of farming into industrial employment. But the years spent eking out a livelihood in farming left this population without the skills or the resources necessary for successfully

[1]See V. C. Fowke, *Canadian Agricultural Policy: The Historical Pattern* (Toronto, 1946).

making its way in an urban world of work. Today, in northern Quebec, as throughout the province, the vast majority of French-speaking people live in urban centres. The census classifies them as urban. But, in manner of life and social va!ues, very few of these people are really urban.

In northern Quebec, the urban centre was typified by the company town. The nature of mining was such that there was seldom more than one company operating in any one area. Every company almost had its own town, large or small, and, within the boundaries of this town, all development was under the control of the company. Thus, from its very beginning, the town of northern Quebec had been given a highly urban character. It was not permitted to grow, as most towns have grown, from a rural village to an urban form. Everything about the company town was urban, including its population. The company personnel set the tone of the town, and this was a personnel highly urban in social background. It was from the outside urban world that were recruited by the company the plant managers, engineers, accountants, technicians, and even skilled workers who made up a large part of the population of the company town.

The real industrial community of the north, however, extended far beyond the boundaries of the company town. It was outside the company town limits that the great mass of northern industrial workers came to live. These were industrial workers recruited from northern farm settlements. It was by a number of prolonged and painful stages that the move was made from the farm to industrial employment. Uually the first move was to part-time employment off the farm. Unable to make a living from the land, the farmer sought a means of supplementing his income. The next move, from part-time to full-time employment off the farm, could occur without any shift in place of residence, or simply by a shift of residence from the farmstead to the nearby village. The individual remained a member of the rural society while becoming a full-time worker in the urban society. Ultimately there occurred the shift of residence from the rural farm community to the urban industrial. Even then, however, no significant change in manner of living resulted. It was on the outskirts of the urban industrial community that the population moving in from the farm settlements located. Here the newcomer could build his own crude home out of the raw lumber readily available in the north, seek whatever employment the simple skills brought from the farm suited him for and go on living much as he had done in the farm community. What emerged in the northern industrial community were two sharply separated social worlds: the highly urban—capitalist and middle class— social world of the company town, and outside of it a social world made up of a population vastly larger in numbers that still remained, in structure, manner of life, and social values, highly rural.

Movement from the one social world to the other could be made only with great difficulty. It was a single enterprise type of community that developed in the north. In such a community, opportunities for advancement into middle class types of occupation were few. The personnel that the industrial enterprise valued were brought in from the outside. For this personnel, career lines were determined by the corporate structure of capitalist enterprise, within the northern industrial community and the outside world. Few young people of middle class parents remained in the north. For the great mass of the working population, however, the only move possible was from one nothern industrial community to another where the same type of work was available. Neither the farm industry, nor the form of industrial employment it was compelled to enter on abandoning the farm industry, prepared this population for advancement to positions in the community that made possible an urban, middle class way of life.

It was, of course, upon a very narrow economic base that the northern industrial community was built. Capitalist forms of economic enterprise here could not extend far beyond the major industrial establishment. It was this concentration of the whole structure of economic life about the one major industry that imposed such sharp limits upon the growth in the northern industrial community of an urban, middle class type of society.

Yet there was much about the society of the northern industrial community that was not unlike the society of the Canadian community at large. It was upon a very narrow economic base that the Canadian community was built. Canada has been what the late H. A. Innis called a "hard frontier." The exploitation of her resources has required large accumulations of capital, corporate forms of business enterprise, and state support. In the structure of its economic life, the country as a whole has had much of the character of a single enterprise community.

The effect has been to weaken the development within the Canadian society of capitalist, urban, middle class social values and forms of social structure. Marx was not too wide of the mark as far as the development of capitalism in Canada is concerned. Compared to the United States, the population of Canada has been given no great opportunity to participate in capitalist types of economic endeavour. Capitalism came to Canada much more fully-grown, typified by the large-scale economic organization dependent upon outside capital, and managerial and technical skill. The position occupied by the great mass of the Canadian population has been one largely peripheral to capitalist enterprise.

Thus today, while the population of Canada is predominantly urban in place of residence, and an increasing proportion of it is becoming middle class in type of occupation and range of income, it is questionable whether the Canadian society can be described as a truly urban, middle class society. The Canadian urban centre has had about it something of the character of the company town. Very often, it has grown up about one major industry. Even where economic growth attracted the establishment of several industries, as in the case of the larger Canadian city, there has tended still to be a concentration of economic activity within a few large corporate enterprises. Montreal and Toronto were almost as much single enterprise communities as were Hamilton, Cornwall, Drummondville, Brantford, and other such cities.

Within the inner bounds of the Canadian urban centre, where the industrial-financial establishment dominated, there developed, as in the northern industrial community, a type of society that was highly urban and middle class. Outside these bounds, however, and increasingly as the outskirts of the urban community were reached, the society that became established was one scarcely at all middle class and only in a limited way urban. This has been a society made up very largely of a population forced out of economically depressed rural areas of the country and which, because of its lack of the necessary skills and aptitudes, has not been highly valued by the industrial establishment. For its skilled workers, as well as for its highly trained personnel, Canadian industry has relied heavily upon immigration. It has been in the central areas of the urban community that the immigrant has tended to locate. Here, with urban growth, he has had no choice but to move out, and, with moving out, he has tended to move up. The Canadian working class has been largely built out of its immigrant population, and it has been by recruitment from this population that the Canadian middle class has grown. For that element of the Canadian population forced out of rural areas, however, what resulted was a movement only part way into the urban society. The proximity of the Canadian urban centre to depressed rural areas has made possible such a partial movement. There was no turning back on the part of the European immigrant once he had made the move from the old world to the new and from a society that was rural to one that was urban. But the migrant from poor farm areas in Canada could for a very long time in effect camp on the edge of the urban society without becoming a part of it. Indeed, where the conditions of urban growth tended to perpetuate the isolation of residential areas occupied by a population of rural background, the clinging to rural ways of life and to rural social values could persist through several generations.

It has been scarcely less easy for this rural-reared population, in the Canadian community at large, than in the northern industrial community, to transform itself into an urban, middle-class population. The Canadian middle class, historically, has tended to be a tight little social group. Scarcely more than a century ago it was called the Family Compact. Today, in many quarters, and more especially in French Canada, it goes by the title of the Establishment. Higher Education in Canada has reflected to a considerable extent the exclusiveness of the middle class. Such education has served the function of preparing the new generation of middle-class people for the limited number of positions which the Establishment has to offer. Not the whole of the new generation of middle-class people, it is true, could be accommodated in this manner. The number of positions available for middle class persons in the Canadian society has never kept pace with the number of persons seeking such positions. But opportunities for advancement of the new generation of middle-class persons, if not available in Canada, have been available in the United States. We have in our history avoided a middle-class revolution because of the important safety valve provided by easy migration to the United States. It has been to the United States that Canadians for long have turned in search of opportunities which their own country has denied them.

For the Canadian middle class the presence to the south of the wide-open society of the United States has been important in its being able to maintain its middle-class position. But this has been so only to the extent that this class has not been culture-bound. There have been few obstacles to the migration of English-speaking persons to the United States. The same language is spoken on one side of the border as on the other. For French-speaking Canadians, however, migration to the United States has appeared much less attractive and here, as a consequence, there has developed a much greater concern about opportunities for advancement within the Canadian society. The so-called "quiet revolution" now going forward in French Canada has been very largely directed to the end of opening up to French-speaking middle-class persons a larger share of the positions which the Canadian Establishment has to offer. Even to the extent, however, that the ends of the quiet revolution have been realized, there has resulted no significant broadening of the base of the Canadian urban middle-class society. Although, in certain important sectors of the Canadian Establishment—Quebec Hydro is a conspicuous example—French-speaking middle-class persons have taken the place of English-speaking, outside this Establishment there remains a large section of the Canadian population, French and English, integrated only in a limited way into the Canadian urban, middle-class society.

With the economic and technological advances of recent years, the size of the Canadian population peripheral to the urban, middle-class society has diminished. In both French- and English-speaking Canada, the facilities of higher education in recent years have been vastly extended. But if in this manner there has been a broadening of the base of the Canadian urban middle-class society, the increasing emphasis given to higher education in this society has had the effect, on the other side, of culturally isolating more than ever those elements of the population which do not share its values and way of life. A very large cultural barrier has become erected within the Canadian society between that section of the population which is becoming increasingly urban and middle class and that section of the population which, though now largely situated in urban centres, remains tied to its rural heritage.

Comparative sociological study of the phenomenon of urbanism has given emphasis to the fact that what is urban in the American society may not be urban in some other society even though in superficial appearance the phenomenon may appear the same. A town or a city may be nothing more than a gathering together of a number of rural villages. Though the ecological structure may be urban, the society remains rural. It has been the thesis of this paper that to an extent greater than in the United States this has been the character of the Canadian urban community. The difference has been one of degree. The American society is not as highly urban, nor as fully caught up in middle-class capitalist values, as certain remarks made in this paper would suggest. Certainly, the integration of the Negro population of the United States into a capitalist, urban, middle-class social world is far from complete. Yet, in the over-all view, there are, in this regard, very real differences between the Canadian society and the American. It is almost possible to describe the United States today as one great urban community: urban influences reach out into all parts of the society. Such is clearly not the case in Canada. Here, for reasons touched upon in this paper, the development of an urban, and of a middle-class, capitalist, society has been a great deal more halting. We are, still, in many respects, an undeveloped nation.

CHAPTER XVII

Higher Education and the New Men of Power in Society*

THE DISCUSSION IN THIS PAPER is directed towards an examination of higher education in our society. The concern here, however, is not with the need for extending the benefits of higher education, nor with the problem of securing the necessary financial support for such an extension. That need has been well demonstrated and that problem fully explored by the Commission on the Financing of Higher Education in Canada, established by the Association of Universities and Colleges of Canada.[1] What this paper is concerned with is the problem of the consequences for society when a large part, but by no means the whole, of our body of young people is provided with the benefits of a university education. Its concern is the young people left behind: those young people who, for one reason or another, fail to mount the educational ladder to success and whose position in society, as a consequence of the growing importance of higher education, grows relatively worse rather than better. Nothing that is said in this regard should be taken to suggest that we ought to slacken in any degree our efforts to extend the

*Presented at the University of Calgary and the University of Alberta, Edmonton, 1965. Published in *The Journal of Educational Thought,* vol. 1, no. 2, pp. 77–87. Reprinted, with revisions, with permission of the publisher.
[1]*Financing Higher Education in Canada, being the Report of a Commission to the Association of Universities & Colleges of Canada* (Toronto & Laval, 1965).

benefits of a higher education. If, underlying the discussion in this paper, there is implied an end towards which we should strive it is that the whole of our population should eventually come to enjoy the benefits of such an education, whether secured in a university or in some other type of institution. But the realization of such an end is not yet in sight, and in the meantime it is urgent to take account of the consequences for society of the very considerably increased importance which has been given to higher education.

What has happened in the past fifty years, and particularly in the years since the Second World War, is a development that can truly be described as a revolution in our society. Increasingly, in government, business, philanthropy and in the management of community affairs, there has been a turning to the man with a university education. For many positions where once nothing more at most than a high school education was required, a Bachelor of Arts degree at least is now demanded. The vast extension in our society of the facilities for a higher education, and the greatly increased proportion of the population provided the benefits of such an education, are a reflection of the changed character of the world of work in which we now live.

It is scarcely necessary to detail the beneficial consequences for society at large of the new role which has come to be played in it by higher education. Two of the most obvious, however, should be mentioned since they have relevance to what this paper has to say later.

The increased importance of higher education in our society is directly related to the much higher standard of living we have come to enjoy. The investment in higher education, as the report of the Commission on the Financing of Higher Education in Canada convincingly demonstrates, has proved a good investment. Society reaps the benefits in vastly more efficient forms of management and means of production, and these benefits have been spread over the whole population. The rich may be becoming richer but so are the poor. Large segments of our population which a generation or two ago could not hope to aspire to anything more than a subsistence standard of living now enjoy the kind of amenities which once only the rich could afford. The automobile, the summer cottage, the outboard motor boat, indeed even the winter in Florida, are items of consumption of the carpenter and factory-worker almost as much as of the surgeon or banker. If the chauffeur and butler have survived at all, they have only as an expression of taste of the eccentric rich. In style of life, we have gone a long way towards closing the gaps between social classes.

Still more, the spread of the benefits of higher education in our society has done much to remove the social barriers which once existed to movement from one social class to another. Education is a social leveller. Whatever his social origins, the man educated and highly trained can command the leading positions in our society—in government, business, the church, and the community at large. The advantages are no longer with the man of good family, of aristocratic background; nor with the man who attains his position through wealth or demagogic appeal. The business executive, army general, or politician, in pressing the acceptance of his views, may sputter and fume, but he knows that in the end it is the judgment of the engineer, economist, accountant, scientist or other specialist which must prevail, for only he possesses the knowledge that makes judgment possible.

In the long-run interests of society there can be little reason for deploring the importance now attached to a university education. It is a complex world in which people live and it is becoming more so. The time was when mistakes in the management of society's affairs had no serious consequences. People lived very much to themselves, and what happened in one small part of the world had little effect upon other parts. In the kind of world we live in today, however, mistakes on the part of men in charge of the conduct of affairs can bring disaster to great large areas of the world—indeed, to the world as a whole. Thus, surrounding governments, businesses, armies, churches, social agencies and the like, there must now be staffs of highly trained technical persons alive to the consequences of every action that is taken. Even the most innocent-appearing act of a government or of a business corporation may have repercussions of a sort which only a computer could predict.

Society is the richer by this vast extension of the body of human knowledge and by the development of means by which this knowledge can be preserved and transmitted. But the price paid by society, at least for some time to come, because of its increased dependence upon knowledge cannot be overlooked. Knowledge, in increasingly large areas, has ceased to be something shared in by the whole population, the man with knowledge being distinguished from the man without only by the amount of knowledge he possessed. Once every man could be something of an economist, physicist or military strategist, and self-education offered a means of climbing to the highest rungs of learning. Today, however, the laboratory of the scientist, or even of the economist or psychologist, represents a world of learning which can only be penetrated by those who have undergone the scholastically prescribed form of training. The air of mystery surrounding the ministrations of the medicine man of old was as nothing compared with the air of mystery surrounding the ministrations of the man of scientific training of today.

The consequences of this change in the character of knowledge, and the increased dependence now placed upon the man of knowledge, have been to create new, sharp divisions in society. While education has done much to narrow the gap between social classes, where the privileged social class owed its position to family background or wealth, and to make easier movement from one social class to another, it threatens, on the other side, to create a new set of social class divisions to take the place of the set it destroyed. The college man no longer stands out, as he once did, as one in a small group in society set apart to do only a very special kind of job: to practice medicine or the law, teach in the university, serve in the priesthood or the ministry, or the like. Then he could be accorded respect—but was not feared—because he commanded no great power, and his manner of life did not sharply separate him from the people he served. It was truly an elite, not a social class, to which he belonged.

The man of education is no longer, however, a member of a very small—and politically powerless—social elite. He commands the most important posts in government, industry, finance, mass communication and even entertainment, and because of the great power he wields he can be very much distrusted or even feared. Still more, his manner of life—the self-assurance he displays in mode of dress and speech, the easy informality which characterizes his social relations, his conversational skills—can arouse among persons deprived of his educational and social advantages strong feelings of envy and resentment. The strength of anti-intellectual forces in society today, and the widespread revolt of young persons, in urban areas and in small town and rural communities, against what might be called middle-class social values, are a consequence in very large part of the new social divisions which have been created by giving to education such an important place in society.

It is scarcely possible to exaggerate the strength in our society today of anti-intellectual forces; or the danger of such forces. The Nazi revolution in Germany offers an example only in extreme form of how a whole nation can be caught up in a movement directed against standards of rational judgment in the conduct of government. In 1935 the people of Alberta were persuaded by a bible-prophesying preacher to put into office a political party advancing economic doctrines that were demonstrably false. The appeal made by John Diefenbaker to the Canadian electorate in 1957–58 gained much of its strength from the attack made upon what was called the Liberal Establishment. It was the "smart economists in Ottawa" that people were made to fear. What was wrong with the government was not its mismanagement of affairs but its arrogance. Diefenbaker promised to return government to the people. In 1962, in the province of Quebec, with the upsurge of the movement led by Réal Caouette, and in 1964, in the United States, with the movement to secure the election of Barry Goldwater as president, there were manifested in similar manner strong anti-intellectual forces.

In the end, anti-intellectual forces are bound to blow themselves out. Hitler left his country in ruin. Social Credit in Alberta, with the passing of Aberhart, transformed itself into a party concerned with providing good government. Diefenbaker, once in office, quickly demonstrated the political as well as administrative ineptness of a party scorning the counsel of intellectually alert advisors. Goldwater, as the Republican candidate for president, was lacking in the personal appeal which might have made possible his heading a mass anti-intellectual crusade in the United States. The movement of Caouette in the province of Quebec survived only by converting itself into a small minority party held together by loyalty to the leader.

But the damage done by such anti-intellectual movements in the course of their development can nevertheless be very great. Scarcely more than a century ago Western society faced the problem of attempting to achieve a condition of stability in a situation where a large part of the population was illiterate. Today Western society faces the problem of attempting to achieve a condition of stability in a situation where a large part of the population is denied the advantages which come from a university education. The issues that arise are seldom defined in such a way as to bring into the open such divisions in society. The social and political upheavals of Europe in the eighteenth and nineteenth centuries fastened attention upon very real economic grievances. So, as well, have those social and political upheavals which have occurred in recent years. But, if economic issues appeared to dominate in the political and social upheavals of an earlier time and in the recent past, there was no hiding the people's underlying resentment towards and fear of a leadership which had become separated from it by style of life and way of thinking. From the ivory tower of the social scientist it is possible to describe as a lunatic fringe that section of the population which lets itself become caught up in extremist movements of various sorts. In such a manner was described the following of Hitler in the nineteen twenties. But the Germany of the 1930's had to reckon with this following, and for the disaster which followed, the leaders of the German nation of the 1920's cannot wholly escape responsibility. Nor, to turn to an example closer to home, can the so-called Liberal Establishment in Ottawa in the 1950's avoid being held in some way accountable for the kind of attack made upon it by Mr. Diefenbaker. The man who knows the answers can too easily display an attitude of impatience towards the man who does not, in a way that assumes a character of arrogance. What, indeed, was wrong with the Liberal government in Ottawa in 1957 was that it was too good a government. It was a government that knew the right things to do from the wrong. But, surrounded by a body of highly competent technical advisors, it had after long years in office grown weary of the task of trying to explain to the public in language that it understood what was being done. The arrogance of the Liberal Establishment came close to reflecting the arrogance of the university educated person to the person denied the advantages of a university education.

If it is not possible to exaggerate the strength of anti-intellectual forces in our society today—or the danger of such forces—neither is it possible to exaggerate the extent and seriousness of the revolt of young persons against the values and moral standards of our society. For examples we need not look only to the Negro youth in the United States, or to the youth gangs, white and coloured, of New York City, to find evidence of an increase in forms of delinquent and lawless behavior among large sections of our youthful population. In every city and in every small town, in this country and the United States, there is apparent among large numbers of young people a feeling of resentment and indeed of hostility to persons in authority.

It is not suggested that all young people who are without the advantage of a university education become social delinquents. But it is suggested that delinquency is a manifestation of feelings of insecurity and resentment which develop among young persons who find themselves deprived of the kinds of material and social rewards which other young people enjoy and that it has assumed urgency today because of the wide social gap that has developed between such persons and persons given the advantage of a university education. The swagger of the hoodlum—the type of jacket he wears, the way the cigarette is let droop from his mouth, the language used—is intended to convey an air of bravado, but in reality it conceals a deep feeling of unease and, indeed, even of fear. There are so many doors in our society closed to this kind of young person.

For the great bulk of the young people entering its halls, the chief function of a university is to make gentlemen of them. It has always been so. But a century ago it was a highly select group of young people, chosen largely in terms of wealth and family background, who went to university and were made by it into gentlemen. In the Britain of the nineteenth century, only a very few careers, such as those of the foreign service, the army and the church, required persons who possessed the kind of self-assurance, easy mode of speech and polished manners which a university training provided. Today, however, in almost all branches of the public service, in business, finance, insurance, and in many other areas, there is a demand for the sort of person a university produces. In university, the raw youngster of eighteen years, awkward in his manners of speech and behaviour, is turned into a man with considerable self-assurance, possessed of a facility for relating himself easily to other people, and for persuading them to adopt his views.

The consequence is a widening social gap between forms of employment requiring those personal qualities possessed by the university educated and those forms of employment not requiring them. This gap shows up, as a recent study by two Canadian sociologists clearly demonstrates, in the work world of the male.[2] Our high schools do a fairly successful job of turning awkward fourteen year old girls into poised ladies of eighteen. The high school system is agreeable to the girl, but disagreeable to the boy. In high school, the girl is able to prepare herself for the demands of the adult world without having to rebel against the system, and, without necessarily being academically highly successful, she can move out of the high school at grade ten or eleven, secure training for a vocation such as secretarial work, nursing, or school-teaching and continue to dress, speak and behave in the manner of a young lady. In

[2]Oswald Hall & Bruce McFarlane, *Transition from School to Work* (Ottawa, 1963).

her way of life she is not set off from the girl who proceeds through high school on to university. Nylon stockings have been an important social leveller among the female sex.

The boy, in contrast, can survive the high school system only by gaining distinction in athletics or by becoming academically highly proficient. If he survives, he will, on the average, achieve greater success than the girl; there are few outstanding female lawyers, surgeons, scientists, or business executives. But if he fails to survive, there is no easy route marked out for the boy's entry into the work world. He may, if wisely guided, enter a trade school or undertake some form of apprenticeship. But the temptation is very strong to enter upon a form of employment that makes no demand of training —work in a service station, as a truck driver, factory labourer, and such. There were avenues of occupational advancement once open to boys which required no special training. The bank clerk who could aspire to becoming a bank president was a conspicuous example. But much of this kind of work now at the lower levels of the bureaucratic hierarchy becomes defined as "women's work." "Man's work," for the boy entering employment at a level which demands no special training, tends to be associated with manners of dress, speech and behaviour which sharply differentiate him socially from the boy engaged in employment requiring such training. A consciousness of difference leads to a vigorous assertion of difference. The black leather jacket cannot be mistaken for the college jacket.

There are, of course, in the move of young people out of the school into the adult world and the world of work, casualties among the girls as well as among the boys. Every large city has its quota of female delinquents. But this is no new problem in society, and measured in terms of numbers it is not of large proportions. The problem of delinquency as we know it today is a problem of our male youth. More than that, it is a problem of our male youth in particular sectors of our society. There is a very much higher incidence of juvenile delinquency among children of working-class parents than among children of middle-class parents.[3] If our school system favours girls over boys, among boys it favours those of middle-class upbringing over those of working-class. It is not only economic pressures which force the working-class boy out of the school system into the world of work without adequate preparation. There is much about this school system that is repugnant to him. It is a conveyor of middle-class social values.

[3]Albert K. Cohen, *Delinquent Boys* (Glencoe, 1955).

Forced into revolt against the school system, the working-class boy too often is forced into revolt against society. He finds himself left behind, deprived of the social regard accorded the boy who survived the school system, and, proceeding on to university, becomes successfully established in the adult world. Social class divisions prevailing in one generation thus shift their basis and become reinforced in the next.

The revolt of young people against middle-class social values is a problem which has become much more apparent in the United States than in Canada. On the one side, the advantages of a university education have been extended to a much larger segment of the population. On the other side, with the gathering in the cities of great numbers of Negro youth, the social deprivations of the non-university educated show up in much more stark fashion. The young Negroes who ran wild in Watts County in the spring of 1965 live in a vastly different world from that lived in by university-educated young Americans, yet it is a world separated from the other by only a few city blocks.

We can applaud the achievement of the United States in making more available to its young people the advantages of a university education, but the consequences of such a development in creating new sharp divisions in the society must be recognized. Manifestations of widespread revolt among American youth, paradoxically, are not unrelated to the widening of opportunities in American society for a university education. Negro young people in the United States today are better off than they have ever been, but not only has their social position worsened in relative terms, it has been made very much more visible.

In Canada, on the one hand, we have not created as large a socially advantaged class of university-educated young people as has the United States, and, on the other hand, there has not developed in our cities as large and conspicuous a body of socially deprived young people. But we are moving rapidly in the direction of making a university education more widely available to our young people; and, in our cities, there is being produced a body of young people who, deprived of a university education, are becoming increasingly conscious of their socially disadvantaged position. To a very large extent, it is out of the poor farm areas of Canada that these socially disadvantaged young people are coming. A very great number of them are young people of French Canadian origin.

In the late nineteenth and early twentieth centuries, the cities of

North America grew by the recruiting of a population from overseas. In the literature of Sociology there are a vast number of studies relating to the problems of the assimilation of the immigrant. For a long time, sociologists did not talk about social class divisions in American society. Attention was largely directed to ethnic divisions. There was, of course, a working class, but so closely identified was this class with the European immigrant that it largely became defined in ethnic terms. In studies thus of the problems of young people of the urban community, emphasis tended to be placed upon their immigrant heritage. The problems were rightly viewed as those of the second generation immigrant.

Today, however, sociological literature has shifted away from a concern about ethnic divisions in society to a concern about social class divisions. We talk now a good deal about social class life styles, and, in dealing with the problem of young people in the urban community, tend largely to relate that problem to working class parentage. It can be demonstrated that the rate of juvenile delinquency is much higher among children of working-class than among children of middle-class parents. What tends to get overlooked in the sociological literature, however, is the fact that a great part of the working-class population of the urban community today is as much a migrant population as was the working-class population a generation ago. The only difference is that this is a population that has moved into the urban community from rural areas within America rather than from outside. Thus, so often when we speak of urban young people of working class parents, what we are really taking about are urban young people of parents of farm background.

In the shift from a dependence upon the recruitment of population from overseas to a dependence upon the recruitment of population from rural areas, the Canadian city, in its development, is about two decades behind the American. Canada has experienced a very large post-war immigration. Canadian sociologists thus tend still to think very much in terms of the ethnic problem. We have mounted in recent years a great number of studies of ethnic groups in Canada: Italians, Ukranians, Poles, Germans, and the like. But no study has been undertaken of the Canadian rural migrant. Yet, in fact, in Canada, urban growth in the past twenty years is to be accounted for far more in terms of migration from rural areas than migration from Europe.

Where the migration was one out of prosperous farm areas

no serious problem of adjustment resulted. The boy brought up on the farm who was educated in a way to meet the demands of the urban work world had no great difficulty in fitting himself into the society of which he became a part. In much of North America, differences between rural and urban have largely disappeared. The farmer, equipped with all the amenities of the city, has come to live, and think and behave, like a city man. He has come to have the same aspirations, the same driving ambition, not only to better his lot, but the lot of the offspring that he has reared. What has happened has been an extension of middle-class social values out of the city into the country. Where, under such circumstances, there results a movement of population out of the country into the city the problems of adjustment are little more than those associated with the occupational shift which so often occurs between one generation and the next.

But where farm settlement led to the occupation of land badly suited for farm purposes (whether because of soil, climate or distance from markets), there could occur no great extension of middle-class social values out of the city to the country. The conditions of life in the depressed rural community offered little preparation to that element of the population which was forced out of the rural community into the urban. What resulted was a movement only part way into the urban society. It was the proximity of the urban community to depressed rural communities which made possible such a partial movement. The migrant from poor farm areas in Canada could for a very long time in effect camp on the edge of the urban society without becoming a part of it. It is from such areas that our urban communities have drawn heavily their population in recent years.

For long we have been committed to the view that the rural life is the good life. Until only a few years ago, as a consequence, public policy has been directed to the end of putting people on farms. Where this policy led to the settlement of such fertile areas as the Annapolis Valley, the St. Lawrence Valley, Western Ontario and much of the Western Provinces, there were created thriving agricultural communities. But colonization efforts were not limited to the settlement of people on good farm land. Wherever land was available on which some sort of agriculture could be carried on, settlement was undertaken. In the province of Quebec, farm settlement of this sort assumed very considerable proportions.

Quebec was perhaps no more committed than the rest of Canada to the view that the rural life was the good life, but because of the resources at its command, particularly in the Catholic Church, it was much more successful in achieving the end of putting its people on the land. The contrast between Ontario and Quebec in this respect was striking. In the 1860's, millions of dollars were spent by the Ontario Government in the effort to settle the pre-Cambrian shield, but all that resulted were a few scattered pockets of settlement. Similarly, the efforts to settle the Great Clay Belt of Northern Ontario proved largely a failure; indeed, they would have proved an almost complete failure had there not occurred settlement in this area out of the Province of Quebec. In contrast, within the Province of Quebec, there is scarcely an area where a farm can be carved out and which can be reached by a road that has not been settled. Quebec sought vigorously to maintain its culture by extending ever further out the boundaries of its rural society.

Until 1940, or thereabouts, Quebec was highly successful in achieving the end of putting its people on the land and, indeed, in keeping them there. But even land that would support a subsistence agriculture ran out, and, with rising expectations of an acceptable standard of living, there has been occurring since about 1940 a large-scale migration of people out of rural areas in the province of Quebec into urban areas. The problem of French Canada today is the problem of transforming into an urban population a population that is highly rural.

Here the concern is not with those great masses of people drawn from the depressed rural areas of the Ottawa Valley, Lake St. John, Abitibi and Timiskaming which have come to make up a very large part of the working class population of the new industrial cities of Quebec and, indeed, as well, of Ontario and New Brunswick. The concern is with the new generation of French Canadians growing up in these cities of parents of such rural background.[4] There is a mounting wave of delinquency and crime in the urban centres of the Province of Quebec. Though we need to know more about what is happening, it would seem clear that these manifestations of social disorganization are closely related to the socially disadvantaged position so many young French Canadians find themselves in, growing up in an urban environment without the skills, aptitudes, social values, manners of speech and behaviour which make

---

[4] See Yves De Jocas & Guy Rocher, "Inter-Generation Occupational Mobility in the Province of Quebec," *Canadian Journal of Economics & Political Science* (XXIII, February, 1957), pp. 58–66.

possible a successful adjustment to the urban world of work and social living.

The very rapid extension of the facilities of higher education by the Province of Quebec within the last few years represents an effort to prepare its young people for life in an urban-industrial society. There has, indeed, been a quiet revolution going on in French Canada. A major break-through in education has occurred at all levels.

But if in Canada generally, and in the United States, the effect of the widening of the opportunities for a university education has been to accentuate the division in society between the socially advantaged and disadvantaged, that has been even more the case in French Canada. In political and religious structure, French Canada has always been a highly bureaucratic type of society. Today, with the effort to secure a greater degree of control over its own affairs, it is moving rapidly in the direction of becoming a highly bureaucratic type of society in economic structure as well. The young university-trained French Canadian is taking his rightful place in the economic life of his Province by becoming a part of an economic order over which he has some control; Quebec Hydro offers an obvious example. But far from all young French Canadians are becoming university trained, and, with avenues of advancement increasingly determined within a bureaucratic economic, and political and ecclesiastical, order, the gap between the socially advantaged and the disadvantaged in the rapidly growing urban centres of French Canada is widening. Much has been heard in recent years from the new middle class of French Canada; the university campus, the coffee shop, the political arena provide an effective platform for the airing of grievances. But from those young French Canadians gathered in the cities who are not equipped to make their way in the new industrial-urban society in which they find themselves nothing is heard, unless count is taken of acts of delinquency and crime.

It is not only in French Canada that are to be found great numbers of young people who are not equipped to make their way in the new industrial-urban society in which they find themselves. We might well be alarmed if we knew more about what is happening to those young people in the Canadian city from Northern Ontario, eastern Nova Scotia, Newfoundland, or northern parts of the Western Prairies. We are today paying a heavy price for a public policy which permitted to develop and persist areas of rural settlement in which people could not make a decent living. The result is the gathering in our cities of great masses of young people who are yet far from ready to take advantage of whatever opportunities for a higher education may be offered them. We need, certainly, in this country, to vastly expand the facilities for a higher education. We need more universities, and we need to make these universities better. There can be no compromise in the ends of a university education. Universities are not community colleges, developed to meet the immediate needs of the communities in which they are situated. But if this is so, it only gives emphasis to the importance of developing types of educational institutions which serve very different needs of our society. The high school drop-out is, indeed, a casualty of our educational system whom we cannot afford to ignore.

One, indeed, can be hopeful about the future. But it is not to the problem of the future that this paper addresses itself. The young people of today will be the grown men of tomorrow, and whatever shape the education of the future may take, it will have nothing to offer those who, now reaching manhood, have failed to secure its benefits. We are passing today into a world that can only be manned by highly trained persons. It is a world in which the untrained are coming to fit badly. Power is shifting to new classes in society. There is being created now, as a result, a deep gulf in society between the people who are educated and people who are not, and, if history teaches anything it is the precariousness of the position of any group of people who are privileged if they seek to insulate themselves, whether socially or intellectually, from the non-privileged. The social class system of England survived and was transformed because it provided against making arrogant the privileged class. On the Continent of Europe it was an arrogant upper class which invited its own ruin. The competence to perform the tasks they are called upon to undertake establishes the claim of the university educated in our society to a position of social privilege. But it is only a very narrow line indeed which separates a claim to competence from arrogance.

PART IV

Sociology and History

CHAPTER XVIII

Sociology, History, and the Problem of Social Change[*]

ON THE ANNIVERSARY OF THE PUBLICATION of Darwin's *Origin of Species* it is appropriate to turn at this time to a consideration of the problem of social change. The development of the theory of evolution reflected a growing general awareness one hundred years ago of the fact of change, in the biological, physical, and social world. In the century before Darwin, concern in the social sphere had been largely with the basis of political and social organization and with the relation of the individual to society and, more specifically, to the state. The sociology of Thomas Hobbes was a sociology of social order. In contrast, the sociology of Herbert Spencer was a sociology of social change. Social evolutionary theory, drawing on the data of anthropology, and borrowing its analytical tools from the physical and biological sciences, developed as an explanation of man's social past, of the progress of his society from a primitive to a civilized state.

Though among continental social theorists there was much less readiness to accept the evolutionary thesis, with its strong overtones of individualism, gradualism, and belief in progress, the sociology which they developed was no less challenging to a conception of a static social order. Indeed, with little tendency to distinguish between the social sciences, history, and philosophy, the continental attack on the problem of change could be bold and sweeping in character. Thus emerged that body of work, in general terms

*From the *Canadian Journal of Economics and Political Science*, vol. XXV, no. 4, Nov., 1959, pp. 389–400. With permission of the publisher.

described as philosophy of history, with which have been associated such distinguished names as Hegel, Feuerbach, Marx, and, more lately, Spengler.

Yet today on this continent, one hundred years after Darwin, there appears in the work of sociology little concern with the problem of social change. Indeed, a glance at any one of a great number of introductory textbooks in sociology will reveal that so little is this problem integrated into the general body of sociological theory that it can only be dealt with in a chapter by itself, invariably tacked on at the very end. American sociologists have tended to restrict themselves to the investigation of kinds of problems which have involved the consideration, only within a very narrow range, of the fact of change. Concern has been largely with the way society operates as a functioning system. Thus library shelves have been well laden with studies relating to the family, the community, racial and ethnic relations, social stratification, the professions, labour and other types of occupational association, forms of mass communication, and the like, but few empirical studies will be found that are directed to an analysis of the phenomenon of social change.

To say this is not to suggest that there should be a return to the nineteenth-century search for grand laws of social evolution or social development. Better sociology is being written today largely because sociologists have succeeded in ridding themselves of the false conceptions and illusory ambitions of their nineteenth-century namesakes. By concentrating attention on clearly observable social phenomena, by seeking by painstaking methods of research to determine the nature of the relationships among the different elements which make up society, an enormous advance has been made within the past half-century in the sociological understanding of the world in which we live. Certainly there could be no quarrel here with the view taken by Talcott Parsons that the development of an adequate theory of social change must await the development of a theory of the social system.

Unfortunately, however, or so it would seem, this great advance in the development of the method of sociology has not taken place without the building into it of a bias which has made almost impossible the growth out of an interest in the problem of social order of an interest in the problem of social change. The eyes of sociology are geography and chronology. To view society as an ordered social system, account clearly has to be taken of the spatial dimension, and in the development of sociological method on this continent scrupulous regard has come to be paid to techniques designed to determine the facts of society as they are found in space. But, if social order can only be viewed within the spatial dimension, social change can only be viewed within the dimension of time. Change in society takes place in time. It has a chronology. Yet the use of the chronological method, dealing with facts in any sort of temporal sequence, appears to the sociologist as a task properly belonging to the historian. If historical facts are to be used at all, it is felt, they should be provided by the historian and not by the sociologist.

Where in the grand manner of a Harry Elmer Barnes the sociologist has made of the historian a hewer of wood and drawer of water the result has been to produce poor history and poor sociology; few sociologists would subscribe today to such an unprofitable exploitation of the labours of their historical colleagues. But the repudiation of such an abuse of historical knowledge has not led sociologists to turn to historical research. It has led to an ignoring of almost everything that has to do with history.

Given the kind of environment in which American sociology grew up this perhaps is understandable. To the mid-West sociologist of the 1920's there was nothing terribly exciting about the past of America. It was scarcely necessary to look back to the centuries that had gone before to seek an understanding of the slums and the gangs, the racial riots, the public immorality of the Chicago of W. I. Thomas, Robert E. Park, and Ellsworth Faris. The pressing problems of American society were problems which had their origin in developments of the very recent past. Chicago a hundred years before was nothing but a name on a map. To have turned to an examination of the way in which civilizations are born and develop would have involved a colossal waste of the resources of American sociology.

But the result of this was to get American sociologists into the habit of looking at their society here and now rather than in the past, and the techniques of research they employed became primarily adapted to this task. In the search for leads, in the development of their analytical tools, they turned, not to history, but to anthropology and psychology, and the dependence of sociology on these two sister disciplines has steadily strengthened over the years. Indeed, in Harvard University, the closeness of the tie found recognition in the establishment of the new Department of Social Relations, linking together sociology, social anthropology, and social psychology.

There is no attempt here to belittle the gains to sociology which have come from this association. Only the mention of such names as Malinowski, Radcliffe-Brown, and George Herbert Mead is sufficient to suggest the greatness of sociology's debt to its sister disciplines. But one effect of this close tie of sociology to anthropology and psychology has been to strengthen the bias in sociological method directed towards the investigation of problems of social order rather than social change.

A half-century or more ago anthropology encouraged a sweeping approach to the study of the societies of primitive peoples. It was for long committed to the evolutionary theory, and in seeking support for this theory it had no hesitation in speculating about the origins of primitive forms of social organization or the way in which these forms had evolved or changed over time. Nor did it have any reason for not welcoming forces bringing about the change of primitive society to a more advanced state. The belief in progress was strong, and whatever, therefore, appeared to contribute to the break-up of the old, custom-bound society was viewed as ultimately to the advantage of the peoples concerned. Thus the early anthropologist marched hand in hand with the colonial administrator and church missionary in the effort to civilize primitive man, to reform or rebuild his society.

But that was in the day when few anthropologists did fieldwork and knowledge of the primitive world was based largely on speculation. Once fieldwork was undertaken it quickly became apparent that theories of change which had developed on the basis of speculation could find no support in the facts. Primitive societies have no history in the sense of having a body of written records relating to their past. Thus the anthropologist, once he became concerned about scientific method, had no means of ascertaining the nature of the development of the society under investigation. His study was limited to the society as he saw it before him and, within such a perspective, the spatial dimension assumed enormous significance and the temporal dimension appeared of little account. What seemed to require explanation was not how the society was changing but how it was holding together, operating as a functioning unit. There was much about it which at first glance made little sense in the way of religious practices and beliefs, forms of family organization, taboos, rituals, and ceremonial functions. Such elements took on meaning, however, when they were examined in relation to the whole complex of the culture. What the anthropologist discovered was a social system, an order made up of independent and functionally related elements. Thus was developed the social theory of functionalism.

The personal involvement of the anthropologist in the life of primitive peoples gave to this functional theory thus developed a strong moral force. Fieldwork revealed that the changes that were being forced on primitive society through contact with the white man were exacting a heavy price in the demoralization of primitive peoples. What the colonial administrator or church missionary failed to realize, or so the anthropologist was led to argue, was that to interfere with primitive society at any particular point meant upsetting the whole delicate balance of relationships among its various parts. However repugnant to the outsider certain social practices or beliefs might appear to be, such practices or beliefs were functional to the society in the sense that its survival was dependent on them.

Thus, in his concern to protect primitive peoples from the misguided efforts of reformers and do-gooders, the anthropologist became something of a propagandist for the status quo. Not all anthropologists, of course, so followed through the logic of their functional theory. The old interest in evolution was still sufficiently strong to prompt the development by an anthropologist such as Robert Redfield of a new, and skilful, interpretation of the process of change of primitive society from a folk to a civilized state. But in the application and elaboration of the functional approach, the anthropologist tended to find himself arguing, both out of the logic of his theory and out of his feelings, in support of the view that, since all the elements of primitive society contributed to its survival, to destroy any of them would result in its weakening or disruption. Change thus came almost to assume the character of a nasty word in anthropology.

In psychology, a similar kind of bias has tended to become rooted in functional theory. If the anthropologist, concerned for the welfare of primitive peoples, has reason for viewing with disfavour anything which upsets their society, even more has the psychologist, concerned for the mental health of people generally, for viewing with disfavour anything which upsets individual personality. The psychologist tends to like that which makes for the better adjustment of the individual, for the fuller integration of his personality. A person living in harmony with his environment becomes the end of therapeutic psychology. Conflict is thought of as a destructive force in the development of personality. Organization is set over against disorganization as a measure of psychological well-being.

No psychologist, of course, is so naïve as to suppose that a well-adjusted individual is one who slavishly conforms to his social environment. Yet because his inquiries tend to be carried out within a limited social situation such as that of a clinical laboratory or schoolroom, the term well-adjusted tends to assume this meaning. Investigation is confined to an examination of the adjustment of individuals to an environment which is treated as constant. To seek to examine how the environment itself undergoes change, how indeed it is changed by individuals who have failed to adjust themselves to it, would require the use of very different techniques of research on the part of the psychologist. The psychologist, in a word, would have to become a historian.

To say all this is to imply no criticism of anthropology or psychology as such. Certainly, in the case of psychology, the terms order and disorder have a very real meaning when applied to human personality. When, however, the way of thinking of the anthropologist and psychologist, and their techniques of investigation, have been taken over by the sociologist, the effect has been in sociological thinking to lead to an over-emphasis on such processes as socialization and social integration, to the neglect of processes of social change. The sociologist has been too much inclined to impose on his own material the limitations which are inherent in the material of the anthropologist and psychologist. Non-primitive societies, unlike primitive societies, do have a history, and they are not confined, as is the individual personality under investigation by the psychologist, within the four walls of a clinical laboratory. Yet the sociologist has tended to proceed as if both of these things were characteristic of his society.

Indeed, Talcott Parsons, in urging the importance of the small group approach to the study of social processes, seeks in effect deliberately to impose on his materials the limitations which are inherent in the material of the anthropologist and psychologist. By subjecting the small group, assembled within the laboratory, to investigation, much certainly can be learned about the way people sort themselves out in society, come to accept certain roles, and develop some sort of social hierarchy. But such a microcosmic society is a society without a history, or with a history covering a span of time no greater than the investigation itself. And, by the very nature of the situation created, such a society starts out as indeed not a society at all and ends up (unless the individuals selected for the experiment are stubbornly anti-social in character) as one possessing form and a sense of order. What is being studied is the process of social formation but not of social change. Forces which might operate to arrest or even reverse the process of group formation are effectively excluded by the laboratory's walls.

As the functional theory has been developed within anthropology and sociology since the day of Malinowski and Radcliffe-Brown, it has been given a much more dynamic meaning. It has been made, particularly by such sociologists as Robert K. Merton, a theory of social change as well as of social order. And yet, or so it seems, there persists some sort of blockage or bias in sociological thinking which results, when the theory is put to work, in imputing to society a static quality or a character of order which it does not possess. The twisting of the meaning given to certain terms may be only so little but its cumulative effect can determine much of the character of the work done in sociology. Thus in the use of such terms as survival, integration, and equilibrium there is suggested the idea that, unless certain conditions are fulfilled, society will not survive or will cease to be fully integrated or in a state of equilibrium. In reality, two people cannot interact without there being a society, and all societies, by virtue of the very fact that they are societies, are integrated and in a state of equilibrium. Thus, for instance, it cannot make sense to talk about a society such as that of Toronto in a state of equilibrium or disequilibrium, of integration or disintegration. Something may be happening to this society: it now can boast Sunday baseball and movies, cocktail bars, and people speaking many tongues. But the society is as completely integrated, as fully in a state of equilibrium, today as it was twelve months or ten years ago. It is just a different society.

The trouble would appear to be, in the use of the functional theory, that society has been stripped of the attribute of time and assigned boundaries which in fact it does not possess. Because of the extreme isolation of Radcliffe-Brown's Andaman Islanders, and the slow rate of the change taking place in their social relationships, it was almost possible to think of the various patterns of behaviour and modes of thinking of the people, within the particular area inhabited and at the time these patterns were observed by the anthropological fieldworker, as making up *the* society. Actually, however, the Andaman Islanders were never wholly cut off from contact with other people, and though social relationships were changing slowly they were nevertheless changing. Thus, even in such a simple social situation, no attribute of the culture could be thought of as functional to the society in the sense that it was essential to the society's survival. Certain items of culture secured, obviously, the survival of one kind of society: the society which got recorded in the anthropologist's field notes. But by the time the anthropologist was ready to leave the field, a different kind of society, even if so very slightly different, had come into being; and the items of culture which were clearly functional to the society which had been observed were not necessarily functional to this new society.

If this was true of the society of the Andaman Islanders, it is, of course, even more true of our highly complex and rapidly changing Western society. Here it is impossible to speak with exactness of any one society as over against another. People live and work, and eat and sleep, in a great number of different societies. Where lines must be drawn, as for instance between the country and the city, we are forced in the end to resort to an arbitrary statistical index; that is an urban society which has a certain specified density of population. No man can be certain when he is acting as a member of a family, an ethnic group, a church, or a nation. And affiliations which appear clear today may by tomorrow become confused or radically altered. Every day we awake to participate in what in effect is a different society.

Nowhere perhaps is this more apparent than in the area of social class, and in perhaps no area of sociological analysis has the sociologist been more influenced by the functional anthropologist in treating what is under examination in static terms. There is a mounting body of literature in sociology relating to social class but almost all of it is posited on the naïve Warner assumption that society can be divided up into a number of different classes, three, nine, twenty-seven, or a number still larger, and that these different classes possess a character of fixity. What has been developed is a sociology of social stratification but not of social class relations. Society can be ranked in terms of some sort of hierarchy just as it can be ranked in terms of age. The eleven-year-old boy recognizes himself as an eleven-year-old, and in certain situations this precise age of his will be important in determining the kind of social relations in which he becomes involved. Similarly a man's rank in the hierarchical structure may determine the time he eats his evening meal, and whether he calls it supper or dinner. But in the total complex of social relations in which he is involved, class affiliation may have no social significance whatsoever or the nature of the affiliation may vary widely depending on the particular situation he finds himself in. What Warner does, for example in the case of Newburyport, Massachusetts, is to treat the society he is examining as an entity and an unchanging entity at that. Thus there can be no allowance for the fact that people participate not within one social class system but in a great number, forming and reforming in different and changing situations. Nor can there be any allowance for the fact that the social class relations which do develop in various situations give expression, in no small degree, to feelings of animosity, developing at times, indeed, to the point where, by rebellion or revolution, the existing class lines in society may be destroyed. One can read almost everything that has been written by American sociologists on social class without once coming across the nasty word "conflict." Emphasis is placed on social class as a system of order, not as a force of social division, of social change.

What, therefore, can we mean by such terms as survival, integration, or equilibrium when they are applied to a society such as ours? The swinging door on the old-time saloon clearly had a function or purpose; it made it possible for the lonely passer-by to see what was going on inside before committing himself to enter. It contributed to the survival of the social system of the saloon. But it did the social system of the family no good, or that of the church. Looked at from one vantage point, such an item of culture, therefore, would have to be considered as functional to the society, from another vantage point as dysfunctional, to use the term made current by Merton. Certainly, in a community like Dawson City, in the boom days of the gold rush, the saloon did much to give the population a sense of social belonging, of being part of society. It was clearly a force of social reorganization. But it was also a force of social disorganization in its effect in weakening within the society traditional values of behaviour and forms of organization.

What becomes apparent, the moment we turn to the examination of any item of our culture, is that it is both functional and dysfunctional at the same time, that is, it contributes to the survival of certain forms of social relationship while weakening or destroying other forms. If such is the case, how then can functionalism be made a useful theoretical tool in the analysis of society? The answer lies in seizing on what appear to be, at a particular point of time and within a defined area, the most distinctive features of a society and building these into a theoretical model. It is in these terms that Talcott Parsons conceives of society as a boundary-maintaining social system. Thus, for instance, the society of Dawson City, let us say on January 1, 1900, with boundaries clearly fixed by geography, could be thought of as a boundary-maintaining social system. Defined in this fashion, its distinctive features could be described and the conditions necessary for its survival determined. Now, conceivably, the functional significance of a social institution such as the saloon could be empirically established. Given the nature of the social system thus defined, it was probably more sensible for the population to spend its leisure time fraternizing about the bar and the gambling table than in struggling to maintain some form of religious worship or some kind of family life. Beliefs or habits which placed a heavy emphasis on the importance of religion or family values might well be found on investigation to be dysfunctional to the society, caught up as they were in types of behaviour which assumed the character of being queer or, in extreme cases, pathological.

What must be made clear, however, about such a theoretical model is that it has had imposed on it two important limitations. It has been fixed in terms of its boundaries and it has been fixed in terms of time. For consideration of the problem of social order, it is essential that there be these limitations. There can come no sociological understanding of how man relates himself to man, and builds of these relationships the thing we call society, unless we are prepared for purposes of analysis to impute a quality of permanence to what in reality is highly impermanent and indeterminant.

But if these two limitations on the theoretical model of the social system are not kept clearly in mind, such terms as survival, integration, and equilibrium, as used in the functional theory, can play treacherous tricks. Once attention is shifted from the problem of social order to the problem of social change, what we are searching for are not the forces operating within the society to secure a boundary-maintaining social system but the forces operating within the society to bring about the breakdown of such a system. Change in society is spread over the horizon of time and over the horizon of space. It is of various sorts and takes place at all different levels of social organization: in the ecological ordering of man and his social institutions, in the forms of social interaction in which he becomes involved, in his ideas, ideologies, and values of life. No facet of our society exists whose origin could not be traced back to the beginning of man. And social changes taking place today will not really have run their course until human civilization vanishes from the earth.

What more then can we do than simply chronicle the changes taking place in our society and rely on our descriptive powers to make such a chronicling appear interesting and worth while? Much social history is written in this manner and from it we can learn a good deal about how people lived in the past, how they changed their habits, their manner of dress, their style of housing, their ideas of what constitutes the good life. But clearly there can come in this way no understanding of the process of change in society. There are patterns of social change. Changes in one area of social life are related to changes in another. The task of the student of social change is the searching out and systematic analysis of these relationships.

In doing so, he must obviously have some place to begin and some place to end. Otherwise, every Ph.D. thesis having to do with change would tiresomely trace its way back to Adam and Eve, and, however narrow the original focus of attention, searching for the relationships between the different facts relating to the change under consideration would involve reaching into all four corners of the earth. If there is to be a systematic analysis of the process of change, the sociologist must have some sort of theoretical frame of reference.

Such a theoretical frame of reference is provided by functionalism, and more specifically by Talcott Parsons' conception of the boundary-maintaining social system. To say this may appear strange in the light of the argument thus far advanced in this paper. But if we want to grasp what happens to a thing undergoing motion we must somehow get a look at it when it is still. Though society is never actually in such a state of stillness, it can be conceived to be at certain points in time, the point at which the analysis of change begins and the point at which it ends. Snapshots, in a sense, are taken of the society, but snapshots which are then touched up by the artist to bring out more clearly the distinctive features of the object. What we seek is to get to know as far as possible what the society was like before undergoing the change we are examining. And what it has come to be like after having changed.

In such a context the functional theory takes on dynamic meaning. Analysis begins at that point where the society has been fixed in its boundaries and in time. Such a society is considered as being in a state of equilibrium. Thus the changes taking place in it can be thought of as a movement from a state of equilibrium to a state of disequilibrium and, eventually, at that point where the society has once more been fixed in its boundaries and in time, to a new state of equilibrium. In these terms, we can talk about survival and integration, disorder and disintegration.

Such a fixing of society in its boundaries and in time, at the point of departure and at the terminal point of the analysis of social change, is not so arbitrary as at first glance it might appear. If we are engaged in the examination of a society undergoing change, it requires no great knowledge of it to discern the approximate point at which the change became pronounced and the approximate point at which it had pretty well ceased. Thus, to turn to an actual example—the town of Newmarket some twenty-five miles outside of Toronto—a few casual inquiries made around and about the town will reveal the fact that something began to happen there about ten years ago which in the years since then has been transforming the character of the community. People began to move out to Newmarket from Toronto in great numbers, to build for themselves on the town's outskirts vast subdivisions and new shopping centres. Today Newmarket is in the process of becoming a suburb of Toronto. Eventually, and in years not far distant, it will become an integral part of the Toronto urban community.

Here, obviously, the analysis of the changes that are taking place begins with the town as it once was. For certain purposes, the inquiry could be extended back to the establishment of the town at the beginning of the last century, to the changes wrought upon it with the changing character of the larger community during the nineteenth and early years of the twentieth century. Certainly we would want to know something about the forces that made the community the kind of community it became. But to understand the nature of the changes taking place in the community today, the impact on it of the suburban movement of population, it is scarcely necessary to go back beyond a point in time ten years or so ago. What we want to know is what the community was like before there was any substantial movement out to it of population from the city. We seize on this point in time as our starting point, and seek to discover what, at that time and within the limits of an area that can be fairly clearly defined, were the distinctive features of the society. The society of Newmarket at that point in time is thought of as a boundary-maintaining social system. The analysis of change thus involves the examination of those forces bringing about the disintegration of this social system, its transformation into something different, first partly small town, partly suburban, later almost completely suburban, and, finally, though that time has not yet come, into a social system purely urban.

Implied within such a framework of analysis is the notion that it is possible not only to define in fairly clear terms the nature of the society as it once was and the nature of the society that it became but to identify the main force of change. In the case of Newmarket, the assumption is that the invasion of the community by people from the city has had something to do with the way it has changed. Of all the facts relating to the community, none stands out so clearly and obviously as this one. It would appear only sensible, therefore, to begin with it as the jumping-off point in the analysis and seek to relate all the other facts of change about the community to it. Thus the study of Newmarket becomes a study of suburbanism, of the impact on the society of a small Ontario rural town of the suburban movement of population.

But if the student of social change in his analysis of a situation such as this prefers to start somewhere else, with, for instance, the rise of the birth rate after the Second World War, or the increased concern of urban people with the kind of environment in which their children were to be reared, the results achieved would be equally revealing. It is not the task of the social theorist to seek to discover whether social change is caused by the thoughts men hold, the tools they employ, or the way they order their economic lives. Much too much ink has been wasted in debating what comes before what. It is not what causes what but what is related to what that is the concern of the social scientist. A wheat farmer thinks as a wheat farmer and a South Carolina cotton picker is not likely to develop a religious philosophy as sophisticated as that of an Oxford don. When Turner wrote his classic on the frontier in American history he put his finger on what was a very obvious fact about the development of American society: that there was a relationship between the frontier experience of American people and the forms of social organization they developed and the thoughts they came to hold. Only a very curious reading of Canadian history could lead one to deny that Canada had no frontier or that there was no relationship between the Canadian frontier and the development of the Canadian society. It would be tantamount to arguing that because the sun has no means of compelling me to walk on the shady side of the street there is in fact no relationship between my so walking and the sun's existence. There is nothing deterministic about social science though a good many historians and humanists seem to think there is. Perhaps, indeed, it is not unfair to suggest that no one but a determinist can read into what the social scientist is trying to do a deterministic philosophy. If we believe that princes and kings, or what some are pleased to call the higher values of life, determine man's destiny on earth we cannot but view with dismay any effort of the social scientist to treat these things as only some among many elements within a vast system of interrelationships.

To the philosopher must be left the task of searching out the inner meaning of change in society, of discovering those laws which determine the course of history or the future progress of man. To the social scientist belongs the much more modest task of trying to discover how one thing is related to another, of formulating principles of economic, political, and social organization from the examination of the way in which people behave, think, and feel. Although, as the economic and social theorist have demonstrated, there is a value in seeking out logical relationships within a purely theoretical model, the test of the validity of the social scientist's principles, in the end, is whether they are founded on fact.

Thus the development of a sociology of social change involves the examination of societies in change. To say this seems almost trite. And yet, or so this paper has argued, it is just such an examination of societies in change which the sociologist has not been prepared to undertake, except to a very limited degree. We cannot become students of change without becoming historians. It is only by looking at what has happened to societies of the past, and over time, that the sociologist can derive the data on which to build his principles of social change.

To say this is to raise the question of what are the proper limits of sociological as over against historical investigation. So long as the task of history was conceived of as simply that of discovering and making known the facts of the past, and the task of the social sciences that of discovering immutable laws of human conduct rooted in nature, the distinction between them rested on a logical basis. History had nothing to gain from the social sciences and the social sciences had nothing to gain from history. But we have moved a long way from Darwin and the naïve conceptions of nineteenth-century history and social science, and nothing today would appear to set off these disciplines from one another other than the biases and prejudices inherited from the past. The search for the nature of the relationships among happenings in society, the explanation of what occurs by comparing a particular occurrence with other occurrences, is the task which the historian performs and it is a task which must be performed by the sociologist the moment he turns to examine the process of change in society. All facts relating to man's conduct, of the present or the past, have a character of uniqueness in the sense that acts are performed by individuals at particular times and places. But the moment we recognize these facts as facts they lose their character of uniqueness. We can only talk about a horse if we have seen more than one horse, and similarly when we speak of revolutions and wars, and princes and principalities, it is clear that we have formed in our mind an image of what these things are by looking at more than one of them. In method, sociology must come closer and join forces with history. Would it, however, be impertinent to suggest than in theory it is history which should come closer and join forces with sociology? One might wish that sociologists like Talcott Parsons, in the development of their sociological theory, would take time off to do empirical studies of a historical nature. But one might also wish that more historians would turn for a brief spell from their historical writings to an examination of the work of sociological theorists.

CHAPTER XIX

History and
the Sociological Method[*]

IN A PAPER written twenty-three years ago, entitled "Sociology and Canadian Social History," I argued for a greater use of history by the sociologist. What was said in that paper by way of criticism of sociology was largely directed at what seemed to be certain dominant characteristics of the discipline as it had grown up on this continent. Developing in reaction to the philosophical tradition of nineteenth-century European sociology, American sociology, so it seemed, had moved so far in the direction of being concerned about scientific methods of investigation that it had lost the capacity to deal with the really significant problems of a sociological character. Too much of the research being done was directed simply to the end of testing the methodological tools being employed. The result only too often was the reporting of things already known about society or, if not known, of such a trivial character that they were scarcely worth being made known. Theory as well as research suffered from this concentration upon the study of small, narrowly defined problems of a sort which lent themselves readily to the use of certain approved methods of scientific inquiry. In particular, there was an almost complete failure to grapple with the major problems of historical development.

However justified may have been such criticism of American sociology twenty-three years ago, there would seem to be little basis for similar criticism today. Sociological method, with its vastly im-

[*]Presented at the World Congress of Sociology, Washington, 1962. Published with permission of the International Sociological Association.

proved techniques of investigation, has been made to grapple with problems of almost unlimited scope while theory building, as undertaken by a Talcott Parsons, has become a task which knows no empirical bounds. With this development in theory and method has come a greatly strengthened interest in the use of history. There are few sociologists today who would subscribe to the view that the sociological method limits investigation to the contemporary society. There is nothing in history any longer which would be considered beyond the reach of sociological analysis.

The growing literature in the field of sociological history attests to how effectively history has been made to serve the ends of sociological analysis in the work of a number of American sociologists. To mention the names of Reinhard Bendix and Sigmund Diamond should not be taken to imply that the list could be quickly exhausted.

Yet what was said twenty-three years ago with reference to the anti-historical bias of American sociology may not be wholly inappropriate today. Though there has been much talk in recent years about the importance of history to sociology, it is perhaps not unfair to suggest that a good deal of this talk has come from sociologists who themselves have done little or no history. It is now fashionable to pretend an interest in history and so long as such an interest demands nothing more than making use of work already done by the historian it can be subscribed to at no great cost. The question has to be asked, however, whether a good many American sociologists have not become so unhistorical in their way of thinking, and in their methods of investigation, that, in turning to history, they find themselves unable to become sufficient of historians to make effective use of what history has to offer. In effect, the sociologist too often wants to use history without doing history. However much he may talk about the importance of history, the conviction remains strong that there is a difference between sociology and history, that is, between the method of the sociologist and that of the historian.

Park and Burgess had stated this difference, in their textbook which has now become a classic in sociology, as one between *natural history* and history and, though the difference would not be expressed in this way today, the notion that there is a difference persists. What the historian presumably is interested in are the facts of history; what the sociologist is interested in is in the way these facts are related in some sociologically significant pattern. It is unnecessary to argue here how impossible it is to logically distinguish between these two exercises. If pressed, probably no sociologist could be found who would insist upon such a distinction. Yet implicitly, whenever they turn to history, many sociologists proceed on the assumption that such a distinction in fact exists.

The result only too often is that the sociologist will not let himself do in the study of past society what he is quite prepared to do in the study of society here and now: be guided to his theory by the facts he discovers as well as to the facts by the theory he has formulated. He will not let himself do this because its doing appears to involve turning himself into an historian. He may, in the manner of the grand theorist, so enclose himself in the armour of his theory that only that part of history which fits into his analytical and empirical framework is taken notice of; the theoretical boxes are filled before the task of historical investigation is begun. Or he may, like the functional anthropologist, avoid entirely the tangled problem of motion or movement in history by making a study of a society or institution of the past fixed in time. More usually, however, resort is had to what is called the comparative historical method, where developments in one place or time are compared with developments in another. Here the sociologist appears to be exploiting to the full what history has to offer while still avoiding the awful charge that he has become an historian.

There is no suggestion here that great gains have not come from any of these sociological approaches to history. But involved in all of them is the danger of taking on faith a part of the history used. The result can be a gross distortion of the facts upon which the sociologist bases his generalizations. Indeed, what were some of the worst faults of the nineteenth-century evolutionists, in the methods they employed, appear in the work today of some of those sociologists who in this fashion have turned to investigation of the historical past. It is perhaps in no way surprising that when Talcott Parsons seeks to incorporate within his general theory a theory of change it is upon the sociology of Herbert Spencer that he largely relies. Spencer was no historian, and with the example of biological evolution before him he perhaps can be forgiven for viewing change in society as being one in the direction of increasing structural differentiation. But by building the process of structural differentiation into his model of social change, Parsons from the very beginning seriously limits the range of historical investigation. Among the changes taking place in society can be discerned certainly changes in the direction of increasing structural differentiation. But so also can be discerned changes of the very opposite character. The fact that the model used excludes consideration of changes of this latter sort cannot be taken as sufficient answer to the charge that what is offered is a distorted picture of what is happening to society as it changes over time. Movements in the direction of increasing structural differentiation (and as well social integration) are intimately related to movements in the opposite direction and any theory of change must be able to account for one type of movement as well as the other.

Among those sociologists who make no claim to having a general theory of change there is, of course, no such effort as that represented by the sociology of Talcott Parsons to fit all the facts of history into a tight theoretical framework. The problems of investigation undertaken are of a much more modest character. Here what is sought are theories of social organization or development of what a Merton would call "the middle range." Work of this sort thus appears much more defensible than that undertaken within the framework of a general theory.

What cannot be overlooked, however, is that there is here involved, in the effort to select out of history only that part which is considered sociologically relevant, the same danger of forcing the facts of history into a preconceived theoretical framework. The sociologist, acting on the assumption that the peculiar method of sociology is that of comparative analysis, only too often leaves the important task which must be done before comparative analysis can be undertaken—the task of discovering what are the facts of history —wholly to the historian.

Thus can occur that curious joining together of comparative sociological analysis with the most conventional kind of historical analysis. This is not the place to attempt an assessment of work done by the historian as such but this much certainly can be said, that only a small part of that work has been directed towards the investigation of problems of concern to the sociologist. The result is that the latter, where he limits his investigation by the method of comparative analysis, only too often finds himself relying upon what is far from complete information. Meanings of facts change when viewed within a different kind of context. What to the historian may not have been recognized as a fact, or if recognized considered so trivial that it was not taken notice of, may to the sociologist be a fact of enormous significance. Yet such a fact lies buried, unknown to the sociologist, if reliance is placed upon only those facts which come to be reported by the historian. What this can mean is the building up of a body of sociological generalizations on the basis of comparison when what is being compared is not really comparable.

Efforts to examine over a period of time reaching back into history the relation of social class to voting behaviour afford an example of the hazards involved in this type of comparative sociological analysis. Here the sociologist approaches his task with a fairly good idea of what social class means in his contemporary society and so long as he confines himself to an analysis of the relation of class to voting in this society he can avoid getting into trouble. Not only is his definition of social class based upon a very substantial knowledge of present-day societies but he can be expected to revise it, in the course of his investigations, if new facts come to light. The moment, however, he turns to history his definition no longer is amenable to change for the reason that he now makes himself dependent upon this definition for selecting from the facts of history—as set forward by the historian—those which he considers relevant to the problem at hand. The almost inevitable consequence is the formation of conclusions about the relation of social class to voting behaviour on the basis of facts which have come to be known through the employment of two very different definitions of social class, the definition of the historian and that of the sociologist.

If Canadian history can be taken as representative, it is not hard to see how seriously misled the sociologist can be who proceeds in this fashion to make a comparative sociological analysis of the relation of social class to voting behaviour. Canadian history has tended to be written as if social classes were something almost which did not exist. There are a number of reasons for this. The historian's bias which leads him to place a heavy emphasis upon the role of ideas and leaders may be one. Another is that the techniques of investigation upon which he relies result in a failure to distinguish clearly between the interests of social class and those other much more prominent interests such as regionalism and religion. But whatever may be the reasons, the fact certainly is that what the historian has done offers no clear picture of the part social class may have played in the forming of men's thoughts and actions in the Canadian political society of the past.

On the other hand, the techniques employed by the sociologist in the study of contemporary society tend perhaps to exaggerate the role played by social class. A man's position in the status hierarchy is something which can be measured, and the temptation thus is strong to seize upon such tangible attributes in seeking an explanation of why people behave in the way they do. Be that as it may, certainly few sociologists can be accused of giving insufficient recognition to the fact of class in the organization of society about them. What this can mean, however, the moment the sociologist seeks to draw comparisons between the role of social class in society of the past and its role in present-day society is the forming of generalizations on the basis of very different kinds of facts. Even more treacherous can be the effort to cast the comparative net beyond the society of one country and treat as meaning the same thing what the historians of different countries have written about social class. To compare the role of social class in the political development of two or more countries assumes a knowledge of the history of these countries such as the sociologist is scarcely likely to have if in his investigations he has strictly limited himself to the problem at hand.

This is not to argue, of course, that the sociologist, in the manner of the antiquarian, should allow himself to be guided by no theory in his historical investigations. Nor is it to argue, indeed, that in turning to history he should not attempt to take advantage of work already done by the historian if by chance what the historian has done serves fully the purposes of sociological analysis. In the end, sociological historian and historian may become one, and, where that happens, the division of labour which results would naturally be on the level of generality of analysis. But this clearly is far from the case today. Historians have not become sociologists and as a consequence sociologists, seeking to use history, have no real choice but to become historians.

It is no answer that the sociologist has no time to do the painstaking task of historical research and that in the interests of an economy of effort it is better that this part of the task of historical comparative analysis be left to the historian. It involved a lifetime of work on the part of the late H. A. Innis to rewrite the economic history of Canada, but economic theory, particularly as it relates to problems of economic development, would be vastly poorer today if work such as his had not been done. It is perhaps no exaggeration to say that what is written into the textbooks of sociology comes almost wholly from the study of contemporary societies, literate and non-literate. The consequences are certain serious misjudgments about the character of society and social change.

The effect in developing within sociological theory a static bias, where emphasis tends to be placed upon the phenomenon of social order at the expense of the phenomenon of social change, is a consideration which need not be gone into here. Of greater concern is the nature of the theory of change which has come out of the way many sociologists have approached the task of historical investigation. Parsons is not alone in his use of a kind of nineteenth-century evolutionary theory to account for the character of change over time. There is in the work of a number of sociologists a curious mixture of the sociology of Spencer, Weber, and Durkheim which becomes particularly pronounced the moment there is a turning to consideration of developments taking place in the past. It was a crude kind of Spencerian sociology which got written into the Park and Burgess notion of *natural history*, but even today, if it is not Spencer alone, it is a compounding of his ideas with those of Weber and Durkheim which determine in large part the nature of the theory of change in much American sociology.

Thus comes the emphasis in the study of American society upon the role of values as a conservative force in social development. Values as they find expression in written records and the speeches of public men appear as something which change little over time. If attention is fastened upon such values, what Americans believe today seems not greatly different from what they believed almost two hundred years ago when, having got rid of the British with their aristocratic notions of government, they proceeded to establish the institutions of their society on the basis of principles of liberty and equality. Change as it has taken place since in these institutions can be made thus to appear as involving little more than the giving of fuller expression to the basic values of American life.

It is in terms of such a conception of change in American society that what had been elaborated as a theory of social order with a heavy dependence upon Durkheim has been made into a theory of social development with a heavy dependence upon Spencer. In particular, the sociology of Talcott Parsons would appear to have undergone a transformation of this character. This is not the place to argue whether any useful purpose can be served by the effort to erect a general theory of society in the manner undertaken by Parsons. What must be noted, however, is the fact that the Parsonian theory maintains at best its character of generality only in so far as it has to do with the problem of order in society. The moment it becomes a theory of change rather than order it loses its character of generality and takes on a highly particularistic reference. It is a theory which accounts for certain kinds of changes taking place in society but quite clearly not for other kinds.

Given the high rate of growth and general prosperity which has been characteristic of American society in recent years, it is perhaps not surprising that sociologists such as Parsons should mistake as general patterns of change in society certain developments taking place within their own. Something of the same sort of mistake had been made in their different ways by Marx and Weber, and, of course, even more by Herbert Spencer. Thus in the treatment, for instance, of such social phenomena as bureaucracy or social stratification, there is the implicit assumption that what is being looked at is a reflection of tendencies or patterns of change in the organization of society in general. It is hard not to believe that American society compared with other societies represents in some fashion or other a higher stage of development in forms of economic, political, and social life.

The difficulty in part comes from the failure to look at the society of the United States as an integral part of a larger society. It is easy enough to believe, for instance, that wide differences in income and styles of life between social classes, and class conflict, are disappearing if attention is confined to the example of American society. Nor is this impression little corrected if what consideration is given to societies in other parts of the world is in the way of comparing these societies with the American rather than treating them as part of the same society. It is in this manner that account can be taken, for instance, of the kinds of developments taking place in Latin America or in the newer nations of Africa without any modification of the conception of development occurring in the American society. No attempt is made to examine what is happening outside the United States as a response to what is happening within and to explore the possibility that social class conflict now finds expression less through the existence within American society of social classes with sharply divided interests than through the existence of such classes within the larger society of which American society is a part. To a very considerable extent the United States has become an area of residence of a privileged social class. To find the people living "across the tracks" it is now necessary to look beyond the boundaries of the United States.

Much the same can be said of power and the bureaucratic organization of society. To talk of a power vacuum and to describe society in terms of an impersonal bureaucratic structure operating almost automatically without any manifest exercise of power may appear to make sense to an American looking at the state of politics and the organization of economic life within his own society but to a Canadian residing across the border from the United States conscious of the might of the neighbouring republic and of its large industrial and financial corporations there can be little doubt where power resides. What American sociology perhaps needs more than anything else is a new Frederick Jackson Turner to call attention to the importance of the forces developing within what has become the new frontier of the western world. A greater recognition of these forces would result certainly in a more sceptical treatment of conclusions regarding the nature of bureaucratic organization, social stratification, and such other features of modern society drawn from the study of the society of the United States. There is the very real danger that a whole generation of American sociologists will be misled by Parsons' insistence on treating American society as a boundary-maintaining social system.

It is not ethnocentrism alone, however, which accounts for this failure on the part of a number of American sociologists to recognize that what they are treating as developments of a general character are in fact developments of a highly particularistic kind. The determination to view society as an orderly social system has led to an unwillingness to look beyond those nice comfortable segments of the American society itself where talk about integration and consensus appear to have some meaning and examine within the same theoretical framework those areas of the society that are characterized by disintegration and conflict. A sociology of deviance has been made to account for what it is in the society that is not liked. Thus emerges a conception of change as development in the direction of increasing rationality in human affairs. It is this sort of conception of evolutionary change which has largely determined the way in which a number of American sociologists have approached the study of the development of their society.

It would be beyond the limits of space imposed on this paper to attempt to indicate the kind of things the sociologist can learn from history if prepared to explore all the various avenues of historical investigation without regard to where those avenues may lead. But this much perhaps can be said. What he almost certainly can learn is that what has happened in society in the past was not greatly different from what is happening now. There has always appeared to man something mysterious about his past and from this feeling many sociologists have not escaped. What spreads back behind— the society of the past—seems much more forbidding than what spreads before his eyes—the society of the present. Thus methods of investigation which are used with great confidence in exploring the society today come to be considered inadequate when there is a turning to an exploration of the past. What now seems to be required is not a theory to guide the way but a theory which will determine the precise route to be followed. Even Barrington Moore, Jr., though arguing valiantly the need for the sociologist to make greater use of history, feels nevertheless compelled to advance as a condition of such use a general sociological theory of historical development. Long scorning history, sociology is perhaps now in danger of expecting from history more than it has to offer.

In the end, the chief contribution which can be made by investigation of a sociological-historical character may be that simply of calling into question many of the theories about society now held. But if this is so, it is as it should be. History has not one social theory to offer and the study of present-day society another; which is simply another way of saying that there is no such thing as a theory of social change as such. In studying the past the sociologist must find himself doing nothing different from what he is doing when studying society here and about. And he must expect no more miraculous results from his investigations. There is no theory to be discovered which will unlock the gates of history. The most any theory can do is guide the investigator to certain historical facts. If such a theory is not to be made a dead thing, investigation must be pushed on to other facts and to the development of other theories.

What this means is that there is nothing in history that the sociologist can safely disregard. If he is to use history he must be prepared to do history without fear of being charged that he has become an historian. There are involved, of course, perils of no inconsiderable sort. It is easy to get bogged down in historical facts. But so as well is it easy to get bogged down in facts about society of the present. There can be no abandonment of theory in investigation of a historical or non-historical character. But, on the other hand, there can be no enslavement to it.

This paper began with a reference to American sociology as it was twenty-three years ago. It can well conclude with a similar reference. In their concentration upon the problems of the immediate society about them, sociologists of that time had essentially sound instincts. The whole vast society of the United States was a problem area and particularly that part of it of which Chicago was the centre, and it would have been strange indeed if American sociology had assumed a character very different from what it did. The sociology of Park has led naturally to the sociology of Parsons with the kinds of changes which have taken place within American society over the past quarter-century. There has grown as could be expected an increasing concern with the character of the forces which have shaped this society. Out of micro-sociology has developed a macro-sociology. The new approach has given emphasis to new kinds of limitations not too unlike those that were characteristic of the sociology of the "grand theory" of the nineteenth century. The growing interest in historical investigation has been a welcome consequence of the new macro approach but it is in the type of historical investigation undertaken that the limitations of this approach most clearly show up. This paper has been concerned with these limitations. It can scarcely overlook, however, the importance of the advance which has been made. Whatever the limitations of some of the work now being done, there has come from the new strengthening interest in historical investigation a greatly strengthened sociology. And the move forward is not likely to stop at the point of advance now reached. It is hard to believe that the sociologist who has turned to history will remain for long so little curious about the facts of history that he will be content to leave to others the task of historical research. The sociologist who uses history is almost bound in the end to find himself doing history.

CHAPTER XX

Social Change
and the Community*

THIS PAPER IS CONCERNED WITH some of the theoretical issues involved in efforts in sociology to deal with the problem of social change. What is said here proceeds largely from the conviction that either too little or too much has been made of this problem. On the one side, in much sociological work, so great has been the concern with how society is made into a functioning social system that how it undergoes change and is made into a different society becomes almost completely ignored. On the other side, where attention has been directed to social change, the tendency has been to treat it as a phenomenon subject to laws and principles of its own standing apart from the main body of sociological theory. Only in a very limited way has sociology succeeded in fitting social change into its general framework of theory.

Elsewhere an attempt has been made to indicate why this has been the case. It is not necessary in this paper to develop the argument further. What is attempted here is the formulation in very general terms of a theoretical framework for the analysis of social change. More particularly, there is an effort to demonstrate that in any examination of the problem of how a society undergoes change it is necessary to place the society in its community setting.

As the starting point in the analysis of the process of social change, it would seem apparent, there must be a clear settling upon

*Presented at the meeting of the Canadian Political Science Association, Quebec City, 1963.

the unit or area of change. It is not possible to examine social change as it takes place here, there and everywhere. On the other hand, the effort to limit analysis to a particular and narrowly defined social institution or social group—the family, the organization of labour, the church, for instance—makes impossible the development of any conception of a general process of social change. There is a revealing of how the institution or group adapts to the society of which it is a part but there is no revealing how the society as such changes. If what is sought is an understanding of the process of change of society then the unit of analysis must be as inclusive in its character as society itself. However difficult such a formulation may be, there can be no settling for less than a conception of the complete society.

Where the society can be conceived most nearly complete is within the structural boundaries of the community. For some time now in sociology the study of the community has been in bad odour. The theoretical shortcomings of the human ecological approach may in part be responsible. Sociology on this continent early came to suffer the reputation of an academic discipline which had no other concern than the gathering of facts about the communities in which people lived and the social groups to which they belonged. There can be no quarrel here with the efforts of such sociologists as Talcott Parsons to secure a strengthened basis in theory for sociology. Yet the limitations of such efforts should not be overlooked. A price has been paid for the abandonment by sociology of the community as its main unit of analysis.

The effort to build human ecology into a general theoretical system may have failed, but not much time or energy was devoted to such an effort. For the most part, human ecologists got on with the task of examining the relationship of the changing social structure of the community to its ecological base without too much concern about the broader theoretical implications of their work. It cannot be pretended, of course, that this lack of a theoretical sophistication did not have certain serious consequences. In the conception of process as natural there was a hovering in the background the ghost of Herbert Spencer. But the human ecologists had a very clear appreciation of the way in which the structure of society was related to its community setting, and it was out of this appreciation that their sociology of social change emerged.

It is perhaps not surprising, given the dominant influences in the development of sociology during the past two decades, that the community study which has had the most lasting influence in sociology was one which was modelled on the method of functional anthropology rather than human ecology—the study of *Middletown* by the Lynds. In spite of the effort to compare Middletown at different points in time, the mode of analysis here used was one which gave emphasis to the static quality of the social structure. What was sought were the functional inter-relationships of the different parts of the society. The use in this way of the functional method made this community study sociologically respectable, and in the years since a number of community studies have been carried out on the Middletown model, modified and set into an even tighter functional framework by the Yankee City studies of Warner—*Plainville, Family and Community in Ireland, Elmtown's Youth* and *Urban Villagers,* to mention only four. In none of these studies has there been an effort to carry forward the work of the human ecologists. Ecology has been left largely to the demographers, where it has ceased to be concerned with the changing social structure of the community. With sociological study of the community becoming restricted to the analysis of society as a static social order through reliance on the functional method, and human ecology moving almost completely out of sociology to become attached to a different discipline, there has been a general abandonment of the analysis of the process of change within the general framework of the community.

New theoretical supports for the analysis of how social change comes about have developed, it is true. Even in its most extreme formulation, the structural-functional theory is not without significance for such an analysis. Certainly, if there is to come an advance in the sociology of change, a heavy reliance upon the theoretical work of such sociologists as Talcott Parsons can be expected. It is to Parsons that is largely owing the concept of the boundary-maintaining social system, so essential to the formulation of a theoretical framework for the analysis of social change.

Yet Parsons in his sociology has not fully succeeded in escaping the theoretical straight-jacket he created for himself by starting with the individual act as the unit of analysis. By the use of the concept of social system there has been an attempt to give meaning to society as an order of social relationships but, once the concept is made to apply to the real world about, it takes on a character of vagueness and indeterminateness. It is never too clear to what extent the social system talked about is intended to be thought of as an abstract entity.

This would appear very much the case in Parsons' effort to treat American society as a social system.

There is no reason why American society—that is, the society of the United States—cannot be treated as a social system provided it is recognized that it is no more a social system than, for example, the City of Chicago or the small hamlet of Fishers Ferry in central Pennsylvania. American society has meaning only as a way of identifying that complex of social institutions and values which have developed within the borders of a community called the United States. Identified thus with the community, the term society loses its character of vagueness and indeterminateness. What then comes to be talked about is the structure of a society within a particular geographical area—Western society, North American society, urban society, the society of French Canada, for example.

Here there can be no pretending that the society is more than a theoretical construct. Yet for purposes of analysis its limits can be clearly established, its boundaries defined. Thus, by determining what is the essential character of, for instance, an urban society, this society can be distinguished from a rural society; so, in like manner, can a particular type of urban society be distinguished from another type. What in a sense the sociologist does is to take a picture of the society he wishes to analyze, remove those outer parts of the picture which do not belong and touch up what remains to get rid of extraneous or foreign elements. No urban society, for instance, in reality is purely and unambiguously an urban society, but if what does not belong is disregarded, for purposes of definition and analysis, the boundaries and limits of such a society can be clearly established.

The structure of a society thus defined can be analyzed as a social system or social order. But so as well can it be analyzed as a society undergoing change. As a social system, analysis would reveal the functional inter-relationships within and between the different orders and levels of the social structure: the economic, ecological, social class, social stratification, institutional, primary group and value orders. If there were not such functional inter-relationships the society could not be described as a social system. Thus, for instance, where people make their living under economic conditions of urban life and distribute themselves ecologically in a distinctively urban manner, it would be expected that the social class, social stratification, institutional, primary group and value orders of the society would be of an urban character. Instances can be found in the real world, of course, where a society is partly urban and partly something else, but such a society would be rejected as a model of an urban society.

This is not to suggest that the model of the society as a social system loses its usefulness if there enter in phenomena which disturb and upset the society. Deviance can be considered as "normal" to the society. Thus urban society becomes no less urban because its institutions and values are threatened by the depredations of criminals, corrupt politicians and dishonest citizens. So long as forms of behaviour at variance with the values and institutions of the society do not develop to the point where they destroy the society's basic character, the model of the society as a social order can be maintained. Such developments can be described, following Parsons, as stresses and strains within the system resulting in a move from a state of equilibrium, but controlled and contained by the vested interests of the system in a way that secures a return to equilibrium.

Even, indeed, where the disturbance is such as to bring about a change in the internal structure of the society, the model of the society as a social order can be maintained if the society is considered to have not lost its essential character. Thus, still following Parsons, it is possible to talk of "change within the system" and to analyze such change in terms of the concept of a moving equilibrium. An urban society, for instance, is still an urban society though now a smaller proportion of its population may be of the working class. The emphasis remains upon the character of the society as a social order. From such a perspective, all change comes to be viewed as "change within the system."

However, the moment interest shifts from the analysis of the society as a social order to its analysis as a society changing in character, what comes to be talked about is not "change within the system" but "change of the system." There is no point in actuality where the one type of change gives way to the other. All change can be viewed as change within the system, but so as well can all change be viewed as change of the system. What is important, however, is that these two analytical procedures be kept clearly distinct. If they are not, sociology loses its capacity to distinguish between change as it affects the whole society and change as it takes place in only one part of the society. This it would appear is the logical impasse into which Parsonian sociology has been driven. By making so indeterminate the boundaries of the society being analyzed that there remains nothing that cannot be made a part of the society, the problem of change of the society is effectively excluded from consideration. Thus Smelser's study of the family and industrial development in early nineteenth-century Britain becomes in effect a study of social order rather than social change.[1] By assuming that the basic values of the late eighteenth- and early nineteenth-century society of Britain remained unchanged, Smelser was able to examine change as it took place within the society without having to reckon with the problem of how the society as such was changing. Defined in terms of certain very general values, the society of Britain could be viewed as unchanging, and where the interest was in the way such an institution as the family under changing circumstances adapted to these values there was a usefulness in so viewing it.

The fact remains, however, that the society of Britain of the mid-nineteenth century was a very different society from that of Britain of the mid-eighteenth century, and if the manner by which this change came about is to be analyzed it must be in terms other than of "change within the system." It was truly the society itself which was changing and becoming a different society. What now becomes necessary is more than one model of the society.

It has been the failure of Parsons to see his model of the society within clearly defined physical and temporal boundaries which has made so difficult his relating it to the real world. The conception of American society as a social system has been given a character of physical indeterminateness and timelessness, and yet every school child knows that the society of the United States today is a very different society in shape as well as in character from what it was fifty or one hundred years ago. Indeed, it is a different society from what it was twelve months ago, but given the dimensions of this particular society (as over against, for instance, a newly established mining town) the change occurring in such a short interval of time is too little perceptible to be meaningfully analyzed. Clearly, if any society is to be treated as an analytical unit it must be given temporal as well as spatial boundaries, and how broad or narrow these boundaries are must be determined by the purposes of the analysis. Thus, for instance, if we wished to examine how the society of French Canada had changed over the past half century or so it would be necessary to decide what were the physical limits of this society (whether it was considered co-terminus with the boundaries

---

[1]Neil I. Smelser, *Social Change in the Industrial Revolution* (Chicago, 1959).

of the Province of Quebec or more narrowly or broadly conceived than this) and it would also be necessary to decide at what point in time the old order of this society ceased longer to exist. Historians, of course, would be right to insist that there was no change taking place in French Canada in the past fifty years which had not had its beginnings long before that time, and no sociologist would pretend that there was anything occurring within the society's boundaries which was not unrelated to what was occurring outside; but considerations such as these should not be permitted to obscure the fact that the society of French Canada today is a very different society from that of fifty years or so ago.

If change of this sort is to be analyzed, what is required is a model of the society as it was and a model of the society as it has become or is becoming. Within such a framework of analysis interest shifts from those disturbances within the social order which, while imposing stress and strain upon the structure, are contained and brought under control by forces finding support within the vested interests of the order to those disturbances which result in a change in the basic character of the order. Whether a particular disturbance is considered one producing stress and strain within the order or one bringing about a change of the order depends upon how the society's basic character has been defined. In the example of social change in French Canada there would be general agreement that at no time over the whole course of its development was this society free of disturbances of one sort or another. Yet, in terms of their consequences, there was a vast difference between the kinds of disturbances which characterized the development of French Canada in the two centuries before 1900 and the kinds of disturbances which have characterized her development since. It is scarcely necessary here to detail those disturbances of the past half century which have led, or are leading, to a fundamental change in the character of the society of French Canada. In considering the effect of such disturbances, enquiry necessarily becomes directed to an analysis of the way in which the established forms of the old order of the society broke down and gave place to new forms.

What this means is a conception of change in terms of some sort of sequence of developments (or events). Otherwise the problem of analysis becomes unmanageable. Everything that is happening cannot be focussed upon at once. But there can be no assumption that such a sequence of developments is empirically prescribed. Thus, following Smelser, it may be possible to analyze the changes

occurring in the structure of the English working-class family in
the early nineteenth century in terms of such a sequence as dissatisfaction, symptoms of disturbance, efforts to control, reaffirmation
of basic values and encouragement of new ideas, increasing speci-
ficity of ideas, attempts to reorganize, and routinization, provided
it is made clear that such a sequence does not actually occur in
time. The conception of a sequence becomes only a means of ana-
lytically distinguishing among different aspects of the process of
social change. What in the end is being analyzed is a total process,
indivisible in temporal terms.

Even when viewed as such, however, the sequence elaborated by
Smelser of one in the direction of increasing structural differentiation must be considered theoretically inadequate for the analysis
of the process of social change. Where the basic character of the
society is assumed to remain unchanged, and attention is focussed
upon certain structural changes going on within the society, the
process subject to examination can be analyzed in terms of a
sequence of structural differentiation. Thus, for instance, it is not
difficult to show how the Protestant churches in North American
society moved from being very simple to becoming very complex
social structures. Similarly, from the perspective of the larger North
American continental society, developments occurring in French
Canada may be viewed as a movement in the direction of increasing structural differentiation. Wherever there develop new forms of
social organization the effect is to make more complex, more highly
differentiated, the total structure of social life. Thus civilization
could not come into being, or any change occur in the manner by
which people lived, without increased structural differentiation
being the result.

But while change necessarily involves movement in the direction
of increasing structural differentiation it just as necessarily involves
movement in the opposite direction. The sect grows into the church
but the church disintegrates and gives way to the sect as well. The
history of Protestantism on the North American continent is as
much a history of how simple forms of sectarian religious organization grew out of the more highly differentiated forms of denominational religious organization as it is the reverse. The whole is made
more differentiated by the part becoming less. Social change, viewed
within the perspective of the society that was, clearly has the effect
of making more complex and differentiated the structure of social
life. This cannot help but be the case if as a result of change there

is anything at all that is new and different. But the new society which grows out of the old is clearly not more complex and differentiated. Viewed within the perspective of this society, what social change means is a movement to a social state less complete, less highly structured. There emerges here new forms of social organization but only by the breaking down of other and more highly developed forms. Change involves disintegration as much as it involves integration. Disintegration and integration (or social disorganization and social reorganization) are but the two sides of a single process.

It was the fault of the social evolutionships and particularly of Herbert Spencer that the conception of the society being talked about remained so vague and indeterminate that all change occurring could be described as change in the direction of increasing complexity and differentiation. Spencer took as his model Western industrial society and with such a model it was not difficult to show how primitive society was less complex and differentiated than the society of his day. But Spencer, disdaining history and with no taste for field research, made no effort to enquire into the kinds of developments which had occurred or were occurring within the communuty in which he lived. Had he done so, and without going further than the examination of the social consequences of industrialization and urbanization, he would have discovered that what social change meant was the throwing up at one and the same time of simpler and more complex forms of social structure. There was, indeed, in the new industrial cities of early nineteenth-century England, a return on the part of large sections of the population to an almost primitive state of social life.

Sociology has not yet wholly rid itself of the evolutionary conception of change as movement in the direction of more complex social forms, and for the reason that the model of society it works with is almost as vague and indeterminate in its boundaries as the social evolutionist's model. In the analysis by the human ecologist of the changing social structure of the community there was no falling into the theoretical trap of social evolution. Here the society talked about had very clear physical and temporal boundaries and change could be examined as a process, whether described in terms of invasion and succession or disorganization and reorganization, leading to the development both of simpler and more complex forms of social organization. In the effort to elaborate a model of society independent of its community setting, sociology has been forced back to the search for a general theory of social change. Though disguised by a new terminology, the theory that has been espoused comes perilously close to being a theory of social evolution.

It should not, of course, be condemned outright for this reason. To some extent, there was a falling back rather than a moving forward in the repudiation of the evolutionary theory by the American sociology of the 1920's. The abandonment of a search for a general theory led to the acceptance of a theory so empirically restricted that it could be used for the analysis of only a very narrow range of phenomena. Elaboration of the concept of a boundary-maintaining social system represents a very real theoretical advance. What is required is only a greater readiness to give more precise definition to the boundaries of the social system and to work thus with more than one model of the system. By doing this, emphasis comes to be shifted away from the problem of how the system is maintained as a system to a consideration of how the system disintegrates and gives way to another system.

In the limits of space imposed on this paper it is not possible to do more than outline in very general terms the procedural steps for such an analysis. If Smelser's sequence of structural differentiation be considered a satisfactory framework for the analysis of the process of society formation, all that is required is the elaboration of a sequence of structural breakdown and distintegration. With some modification of the Smelser framework, and the putting back of the sequence to take care of the total process of change, the seven stages or phases of change can be made twelve, thus: disturbance, the breakdown of individual habits of behaviour and thought, disintegration of the traditional value system and of institutional controls, efforts to contain, growth of random forms of behaviour (anomie), social deviance, dissatisfaction, agitation, utopia building, separation, reaffirmation of traditional values and the accommodation of new and old values, routinization and the establishment of a new order of values. In proposing such a sequence for the analysis of the process of change there is no suggestion that it has any empirical basis or that any particular stage of change necessarily follows another. There is no limit to the number of ways the facts relating to change may be ordered. The only important point is that the theoretical framework should be one which takes account of the fact that disintegration is as much a part of any social process as is integration. The sociologist who studies change cannot get along without a model of the fully integrated society, but he cannot get along without a model of a society completely lacking in integration either. Neither the one nor the other society, of course, has any meaning except as a theoretical construct. No society can be more or less integrated. It is only when it is defined as a certain kind of society that it becomes possible to talk about it as being integrated or not integrated. In a very real sense, human society as such is unchanging. It is only societies which change. Thus the task of sociological analysis is the determination of the temporal and spatial boundaries of those societies it is seeking to examine. Societies, like monarchs, never die—the king is dead, long live the king. The social order disintegrates but the new order is already in being. It is this dual character of the social process which can never be lost sight of if social change is to be meaningfully fitted into the general framework of sociological theory.

Comparative Sociological Analysis and the Problem of Social Change*

THIS PAPER MIGHT HAVE BEEN GIVEN THE TITLE "Comparative Sociological Analysis: From Park to Parsons." When I turned, almost thirty years ago, to work on the development of Canadian society, what I attempted could perhaps best be described as an effort to put Robert E. Park to work in the analysis of societies of the past. Park, one would have to say, was no strict methodologist; neither was I.

Park's great virtue as a sociologist was his interest in the intimacies—the revealing details—of the structure of social life. It was this interest that led to his heavy reliance upon field work. He wanted to discover how people really behaved in social groups; what it was that made a society a going concern. Among European sociologists, it was to Georg Simmel rather than Max Weber that he turned for guidance. He had no high regard for the efforts of sociologists to deal with whole civilizations, to discover general patterns of change and development. Much of such work he viewed as nothing more than philosophy of history.

It was this Parkian bias that largely influenced at the beginning

---

*A paper presented at the meeting of the American Sociological Association, Chicago, 1965, under the title "History and the Sociological Method: A New Appraisal."

my sociological-historical research. In terms of an economy of effort, there is much to be said for the sociologist relying upon work already done by the historian. The sociologist can pick up where the historian leaves off, examining in much more general and comparative terms patterns of development which have taken place. The work of Bendix, Lipset and many others in American sociology offers ample testimony to the usefulness of such an approach.

The result is to produce one kind of sociological history. I can only argue that my interest has been in producing another kind. Where the concern is with very broad movements or patterns of change—patterns of industrial growth in the Western world, for example—there is little need to go beyond work already done by the historian, or economic historian. Lipset could write his *The First New Nation* without going back in any great degree to primary sources. What information he required was ready at hand in work done by the historian.

But when interest shifts to a more detailed analysis of the structure of social life and movements of social change in the past, the sociologist has to go searching for a type of information which few historians will make known to him. He must develop the kind of curiosity which led Park out of the library into the field. He must become his own researcher, probing into the character of societies of the past.

Field work methods of research, of course, cannot be employed by the sociological historian. But there is available for his use a body of material not greatly different from that which comes to be accumulated by field work research. Societies of the past had their field workers, and some of them were exceedingly good, whether it was a Simeon Perkins in Liverpool, Nova Scotia, faithfully recording in his diary for more than thirty years the goings-on in his home village, a Mrs. Jamieson, travelling about the backwoods of Upper Canada and making note of all she saw and heard, or an Armin Huber, writing for his German compatriots about his experiences as a Western-Canadian farm labourer and adventure seeker. What was recorded by such observers, it is true, was not always free of bias. And there was much that was happening to the society in which they lived that could not be known to them. But there are offered many means of checking upon the bias of informants and what information they provide can readily be supplemented from other sources. Indeed, for most literate societies, so extensive are the sources of information that it would be impossible to indicate here even in a general way their variety and character. By written or statistical records of one sort or another, in public or private collections, published or unpublished, it is possible for the sociological historian to gain a very thorough and intimate knowledge of those past societies he may seek to investigate. Certainly, the Canadian sociological historian does not suffer from a lack of information about his society of the past.

The problem is not only of obtaining information—the amount of information available can often be overwhelming—but of determining how to use it. Sociological history is not social history. In the end, it is theory which must determine the ordering of facts by the sociologist, whether he is working with materials of the past or present. No sociologist can escape the use of the comparative method.

What is crucial, however, in sociological-historical investigation is the point at which the comparative method is introduced. The village society of Nova Scotia can be compared with the village society of New England, or the suburbs of Toronto with the suburbs of Los Angeles. Or, to move to a very much larger canvas, Canadian society can be compared with American society, as it is today or as it was one hundred years ago.

There can be no quarrel, here, with this sort of comparative sociological analysis. By such analysis it becomes possible to identify types of social structures, the inner-directed society of puritan New England, for example, or the family-centred society of eighteenth-century French Canada. But when comparison intervenes at this point, the emphasis necessarily must be upon the characteristics of order and stability in the phenomenon being examined. The village society of Nova Scotia can be compared with the village society of New England only if attention is not permitted to shift from the stable to the unstable features of this form of community life, as it was found in Nova Scotia or New England. One has to talk about a structure of village society as if such a structure had actually existed. This can be done if account is taken of only a certain order of facts. For purposes of comparative analysis such a procedure is justified.

But what investigation of any phenomenon reveals is a character of instability as well as stability, and, if this character of instability is to be taken into account, the analysis must be one of process rather than of structure. There was a very great difference, for instance, between the village society of Nova Scotia of 1760 and of 1800. What, indeed, upon investigation, becomes clear is that at no time, within this forty year period, or before or after, was there to be found a form of community life in Nova Scotia which fully conformed to the village type. The same would be true of the New England village community, or of any other social form we might choose to examine.

This does not mean that the sociologist cannot talk about structure or undertake comparative analysis. But if the interest is in understanding how societies change as well as how they are formed, the analysis of structure must be linked with the analysis of process. To compare the village society of Nova Scotia with that of New England offers a means of identifying this form of community life, but equally crucial is the comparison of the village society of Nova Scotia at one point in time with another. Things were happening to this society, it was undergoing change, and as a society undergoing change it must be viewed not as a social system of order but as a social state of disorder. Disintegrative forces must be taken into account as fully as integrative.

Yet, if the sociologist permits himself to concentrate attention upon "the things that were happening to a society," without, at any point, introducing a conception of an ordered social system, his analysis takes on a character of simply chronicling events. His history becomes social history, not sociological history. There can be no quarrel here with Talcott Parson's conception of the boundary maintaining social system. Unless we are prepared to talk about structure, we cannot talk about process.

Where the interest, however, is in social change, and this must be the primary interest of the sociological historian, it becomes essential to attempt to identify, at different points in time, what can be described as different boundary-maintaining social systems. For instance, it is possible to describe, and analyze as a structure, the village society of Nova Scotia of 1760. So also can be described and analyzed the village society of Nova Scotia of 1800.

When, now, analysis turns to the processes which brought about the change from the society as it existed in 1760 to the society as it existed in 1800, attention becomes focussed upon the forces of disintegration of the one society and the forces of integration of the other. These are not two different sets of forces. The forces that secure the integration of one social structure secure the disintegration of another. Terms like equilibrium, consensus, organization, conformity must similarly always be used by the student of social change in partnership with their opposites, disequilibrium, dissensus, disorganization, deviance. A state of equilibrium is not possible without there existing also a state of disequilibrium. So also consensus, organization or conformity.

But to use such terms in partnership does not mean using them at the same time. It may be necessary to talk about integration before talking about disintegration even though they are part of the some process. An analysis of change involves the construction of a model or sequence of change. Analysis must begin somewhere and proceed from the examination of one aspect of change to another. Otherwise we would end up with no conception of change whatsoever.

What is important to recognize, however, is that there is nothing historically given about any sequence of change we may construct. If we begin our analysis with a society at a certain point in time, let us say the village society of Nova Scotia in 1760, the first step is a conception of this society as an integrated social structure. Whatever happens to the society, thus, which brings about its change can be viewed, and analyzed, as a process of disintegration. A sequence of disintegration can be constructed: disturbance, a breaking down of established habits of thought and behaviour in individuals, the weakening of controls of established institutions, the development of new social forms unrelated to the structure (and values) of the society as it was, a state of anomie or social disorganization. In terms of the example of the Nova Scotia village society in 1760, such a sequence of disintegration can readily be demonstrated by historical happenings in the years after 1760; for instance, the breakdown of the proprietory system of village government, the shift from Congregational to Newlight religious values, the weakening of the puritan ethic, the increasing intervention of the colonial government in village affairs. By 1800, the village society of Nova Scotia, as it was in 1760, had virtually ceased to exist. Viewed from the perspective of this society of 1760, there had developed what might be described as a general state of social anomie.

Yet, in actual fact, the society that had come into being by 1800 was no more in a state of disequilibrium—no more disintegrated—than the society that was in 1760. It was simply a different society. Thus, if we turn to seek an understanding of how this society came into being, forces that had been viewed as disintegrative come now to be viewed as integrative. A sequence of integration, like that of disintegration, can be constructed: dissatisfaction with the present state, agitation and collective expressions of grievance, utopian movements of reform, organization and separation from established institutional forms, accommodation, routinization. Historical happenings in the years after 1760, in the example we have been using, are now examined from the perspective of the society that was in the process of formation. Thus, in the first context, it was the breakdown of the proprietory system of village government and such that commanded attention; in the second context it was the development of new forms of institutional control.

What we have been talking about here is a problem of change "of the social system" rather than of change "within the social system," to use Parson's phraseology. But this is so only because of the way the problem was stated. It would have been just as possible, in the example given, to have viewed the changes occurring to the village society of Nova Scotia in the years 1760–1800 as change within the system. To have done so, we would simply have had to construct a model of the society in such a way that it would have taken account of what it was like in 1800 as well as what it was like in 1760. We would then have found ourselves talking, as Parsons does, about stresses and strains, efforts to restore, a moving equilibrium, and such. With reference to any particular situation of change, it is simply not possible to make any valid empirical distinction between change of the system and change within the system. The same order of facts can be taken care of within the one framework as the other.

For the sociological historian, however, there are advantages in talking about change of the system, and using more than one model of the system, for the reason that it fastens attention primarily upon the fact of change. There is nothing, it is true, in the theory of the boundary maintaining social system as it has been developed by Parsons which precludes the consideration of change. Indeed, there are few better general statements of the problem of change than one which he has made.[1] But Parsons has not put his theory seriously to work within an historical context and the consequence is that, when he seeks to develop this theory, a bias creeps in directing attention away from the problem of social change. By working with only one model of a social system—American society appears now to be the favoured empirical example of such a system—there develops too great a concern to show how the forces operating within the system contribute to its maintenance as a social system

[1]Talcott Parsons, "Some Considerations on the Theory of Social Change," *Rural Sociology,* vol. XXVI, no. 3, September, 1961, pp. 219–39.

or structure. When change is allowed to intrude there is a tendency, so to speak, to keep it under wraps.

By beginning with a conception of American society, structured in terms of certain basic values, all change can be viewed as in the character of adjustments of social forms to the basic values of the society. This is the thesis expounded by Lipset in his *The First New Nation.* By defining the basic values of American society in exceedingly broad general terms, it became possible for Lipset to show that whatever happened in American society involved an adjustment to these values. A still broader definition of basic values would have made possible the treatment of the society of the Western world in a similar manner.

The sociological historian cannot ignore the fact of continuity in human society, but neither can he ignore the fact of change. We want to know how change comes about, not only on a grand scale, in the manner of a Toynbee or Sorokin, but on a scale that reaches down to the local society and, indeed, the small group. We move from Park to Parsons and back to Park. For the examination of certain processes of social change, the larger society—the society of Canada or the United States, for example—is unsuitable as the unit of analysis. Too much has to be overlooked that happened within such a larger society, in the way in which social groupings formed and re-formed, disintegrated and gave way to new and very different social groupings.

What complexes of the size of the local society permit is an examination of change over a considerable period of time; yet not over a period of time that is impossibly long. Thus one is not tempted, as Parsons occasionally seems to be, to view all change in the past as change culminating in society as it is today. From the perspective of the present-day society, the direction of change in the past is necessarily determined. With the highly differentiated American society of today as his model, Parsons can talk about change in terms of a process leading to differentiation. But not all change, very clearly, is in the direction of increasing structural differentiation. The people who moved from the Atlantic sea-board to the California gold fields, or from the old established urban community to the suburbs, moved from a more to a less structurally differentiated society. So also did the people who moved from the old world to the new. Differentiation is a term, like integration, which can only be safely used in partnership with its opposite. All change can be viewed in terms of a process leading to differentiation as all change can be viewed in terms of a process leading away from differentiation. It all depends upon what model, or models, of the society or social system we are using.

There will be no attempt, in bringing this paper to a conclusion, to set forward a theory of social change. In my view there is no such thing as a theory of social change. There is only a theory of society. How the sociologist proceeds to study society will determine how much account he takes of the fact of change. I have argued in an earlier paper, and can only repeat the argument here, that to look at societies in change the sociologist must look at them over time. He must become a sociological historian. But by so doing, he does not become a different kind of sociologist. Whether the society being examined is one of the past or the present, the theory used is the same and so is the method. Only the techniques of investigation may differ.